O9-BUC-246

"A young Norwegian critic of American literature, Per Seyersted, has now taken a giant step toward restoring one more writer to her true place in the republic of letters, American branch."
—*London Times Literary Supplement*

"The first, authoritative edition of Kate Chopin's total *oeuvre*. . . . Indispensable for anyone wanting to explore the achievement of this enterprising and courageous writer."
—*English Studies*

"The initial lack of understanding of [Chopin's] work and the better part of a century of neglect have now been rectified. . . . It is rewarding to readers now to be able to discover this remarkable woman."
—*Jackson (MS) Clarion-Ledger*

"Seyersted has taken charge of a small Kate Chopin revival."
—*New Yorker*

"The *Works* indicate that she belongs in the mainstream of American Realism."
—*New Orleans Times-Picayune*

"Whether her work influenced any other writers is not clear and not important: she was uniquely her own, and for that she richly deserves this belated recognition."
—Jonathan Yardley, *Greensboro Daily News*

DISCARD

DISCARD

Southern Literary Studies

edited by

Louis D. Rubin, Jr.

THE
COMPLETE WORKS
OF
KATE
CHOPIN

Edited and with an Introduction by
PER SEYERSTED

FOREWORD BY EDMUND WILSON

LOUISIANA STATE UNIVERSITY PRESS
Baton Rouge

Copyright © 1969, 1997 by
LOUISIANA STATE UNIVERSITY PRESS
All rights reserved
Manufactured in the United States of America

LOUISIANA PAPERBACK EDITION, 2006
FIRST PRINTING

Composition by ST. CATHERINE PRESS
Designed by ROBERT L. NANCE

Library of Congress Catalog Card Number: 73-800043
ISBN 0-8071-3151-2 (pbk.)

The paper in this book meets the guidelines
for permanence and durability of the Committee on
Production Guidelines for Book Longevity
of the Council on Library Resources. ∞

ACC Library Services
Austin, Texas

CONTENTS

Essays and Comments

Poems

FOREWORD

THE 1890's and the early 1900's now appear, when we look back upon them, a dim period for American literature. The quality and the content of the fiction were mainly determined by the magazines that catered to a feminine public. There were writers of great reputation that no one except literary historians would think of looking into today. But, outsold and outpublicized by these, there existed a kind of underground of real social critics and artists that were either hardly heard of or only heard of when some book was shocking or brilliant enough to attract attention. Harold Frederic's *The Damnation of Theron Ware*, which dealt with the clergy in a realistic way, was a book that everybody read; Stephen Crane's *The Red Badge of Courage*, though pooh-poohed by people like Barrett Wendell, was so intensely conceived and written that it could not be disregarded, and Crane became a public character, though the conventional attempted to outlaw him by regarding him as a disreputable character; George W. Cable, in the eighties, had had his success with a serious novel, *The Grandissimes*, which dealt with the situations created in the South by the mixture of black and white but was driven back by his editors to the more lucrative exploitation of "local color"; John W. De Forest, in spite of his Balzacian ambitions and the championship of Howells, was scarcely read at all, though his obscurity could not have been, as Howells believed, due entirely to his lack of appeal to the feminine audience but was also, I think, deserved by his too frequent bleakness and dullness; Henry B. Fuller of Chicago was mainly known through his least interesting work, his little comedies, then thought charming, of Americans in a leisured Europe of graceful landscapes and elegant titles. It has been only in quite recent years that this period has been gradually excavated. The first collected edition of Crane appeared in 1925. De Forest's *Miss Ravenel's Conversion* was reprinted only in 1939; *The Grandissimes* only in 1957. *The Damnation of Theron Ware* and Fuller's *With the Procession* have only just been made available; and Harold Frederic's remarkable Civil War stories have for the first time been collected in a single volume.

Perhaps the most curious of all these cases has been that of Kate Chopin. She wrote one well-known short story, *Désirée's Baby*, on a miscegenation theme and later published, in 1899, a novel, *The Awakening*, so sensational in its day that it was withdrawn from circulation by the library of her native St. Louis and brought her into such ill-repute that she is said to have been reluctant to publish anything more. *The Awakening* and her two volumes of short stories have now been reprinted in facsimile, but when, a few years ago, I wanted to read her first novel, *At Fault*, published in St. Louis in a very small edition, I had to get a microfilm from the Library of Congress. The only book about Kate Chopin has been a brief and inadequate one by Father Daniel S. Rankin. It was not until a young Norwegian, studying in the United States, became interested in Kate Chopin that anything of importance was done about her. Mr. Seyersted has followed her career from St. Louis to Louisiana, and, in the course of years of research, has traced her published and unpublished writings. It is now for the first time possible to form some coherent idea of the life and the work of this unusual woman.

Kate Chopin was the child of an Irish immigrant father and a St. Louis French mother. She married a French Creole and went to live in Louisiana among the French-speaking Acadians of Cane River. In the United States of that period, she seems to have been unique. What impresses in this collection is the seriousness of her literary ambition. She admired and translated Maupassant, and she combines in her excellent style French limpidity with Irish grace. She was attempting to put on record the real inner emotions of women in relation to their men and their children, and it was this that made the hair stand on end of those genteel readers of the nineties and that caused her to be blackballed when proposed for membership in the St. Louis Fine Arts Club. It was this that caused her to be reprobated by the so sniffishly moral reviewers of that era. I quote from the introduction by Professor Kenneth Eble to the paperback reprint of *The Awakening:* "The St. Louis *Republic* said the novel was, like most of Mrs. Chopin's work, 'too strong drink for moral babes and should be labeled *poison*.' The *Nation* granted its 'fine workmanship and pellucid style,' but went on, 'We cannot see that literature or the criticism of life is helped by the detailed history of the manifold and contemporary love affairs of a wife and mother.' " "Manifold" for the love affairs of the heroine of *The Awakening* is an outrageous exaggeration. Mr. Seyersted has found a review in the St. Louis *Post-Dispatch* which praises Mrs. Chopin's "searching vision into the recesses of the heart" and the "integrity of [her] art," but declares that, nevertheless, "a fact . . . which we have all agreed shall not be acknowledged is as good as no fact at all. And it is disturbing—even indelicate—to mention it as something which, perhaps, does play an important part in the life behind the mask."

Mr. Seyersted is also preparing a biographical study to follow this collection of Kate Chopin's writings, and we are greatly in his debt for his service to American literature in reconstructing from old volumes and periodicals, from her diaries and family papers, both the work and the personality of this daring and accomplished woman.

Edmund Wilson

PREFACE

W HEN Kate Chopin (the name is pronounced in the French way) published her first collection of Louisiana stories, *Bayou Folk*, 1894, she was welcomed as a charming and distinguished local colorist. Her stories do indeed effectively evoke the atmosphere of her enchanting Southern localities. Yet her interest was not so much idyllic localism as what she termed "human existence in its subtle, complex, true meaning, stripped of the veil with which ethical and conventional standards have draped it." Five years later she thoroughly shocked her unsuspecting readers with *The Awakening*, a novel which in some ways is a New Orleans version of *Madame Bovary*. In St. Louis, the author's own city, the book was banned and she herself ostracized. The debacle silenced her as a writer, and after her death in 1904 she was quickly forgotten.

For decades the few critics who recalled Kate Chopin saw her only as a regional writer. In 1953, however, Cyrille Arnavon demonstrated in an introduction to his French translation of *The Awakening* (published under the title *Edna*) that this work reveals her as an early American realist. Since then, other critics have joined him in comparing her to such novelists as Frank Norris and Theodore Dreiser, and university reading lists indicate that many professors now have included her permanently in the group of important American authors of the 1890's.

The Awakening, Bayou Folk, and *A Night in Acadie*, Kate Chopin's second collection of stories (1897), have recently been republished. Her first novel (*At Fault*, 1890) has been out of print since the turn of the century, however, and only a very few copies of it exist today. Furthermore, about half of her stories have remained either uncollected or unpublished.

An edition of Kate Chopin's complete works therefore seems very much called for, and the growing circle of her admirers will now for the first time be able to fully judge her range and importance.

The present volume comprises everything Kate Chopin wrote, with the exception of three unfinished children's stories and some twenty poems, mostly occasional. Verse was clearly not her medium, but half of her poems—that is, all which can be said to bear on her work—are nevertheless published here. Ten stories, one essay, and ten poems appear for the first time, and a fable written when she was very young has been included because it suggests her later work.

Full particulars about the existing documents containing Kate Chopin's work are given in the Appendix. As will be seen, some forty of her stories appeared in both periodical and book form, while nearly as many were printed only in magazines. About twenty were left as unpublished manuscripts; some of these were printed in 1932, and a few others more recently.

The material we have illustrates how Mrs. Chopin's stories progressed, from an early draft to the final book form. She would make a few changes between the first draft and the one she submitted to editors; then, when going over the clippings of her magazine stories in order to include them in a projected collection, she would make a few further alterations. We know that she revised one essay and two stories ("Confidences," "A No-Account Creole," and "A Night in Acadie") at the suggestion of an editor, but these are the only instances in which we have the slightest indication of editorial influence. The fact that she threw away a manuscript or a clipping once the story was published in a magazine or in a collection would seem to prove that she considered any changed version superior to the earlier one. (The reason we have an early draft for a few printed stories is that they were written in a diary rather than on separate sheets.) There can thus be no doubt that the final version of any Kate Chopin story, the one with her latest changes, is the authoritative one.

While Mrs. Chopin clearly was very much in control of any word changes in her texts, she appears to have been indifferent in such matters as spelling and punctuation and glad to let the publisher edit them for her. (Her changes on the extant clippings are entirely confined to the wording.) She was a poor speller, and even her more finished manuscripts show her as uncertain, or at least inconsistent, in for example capitalization and the use of hyphens and apostrophes. This would make it difficult to establish, should we so desire, a "norm" for this aspect of her work.

In consequence, we here give the final version of Kate Chopin's writings—as we have them in book, magazine, or manuscript form, as the case may be—and with no attempt to unify her punctuation and spelling (except within each story). Obvious mistakes have been silently corrected. For instance, a missing indefinite article in the second line of *At Fault* has been added, and a line which disappeared between the newspaper and the book version of "At Chênière Caminada," making the sentence meaningless, has been restored. The word changes the author made as her stories progressed are recorded in the Appendix.

It is with great pleasure that I express my sincere gratitude to those who have made this edition possible. Mr. Edmund Wilson and Mr. Richard L. Wentworth, director of the Louisiana State University Press, backed the project fully from the start. Mr. Robert C. Hattersley, Kate Chopin's grandson, and the Missouri Historical Society, holder of nearly all her papers, gave me the most complete cooperation, and I am indebted to them for permission to print the unpublished Kate Chopin manuscripts. Grants from the American Council of Learned Societies and the Norwegian Research Council for Science and the Humanities enabled me to prepare the works for publication.

I am particularly grateful to Professor Arlin Turner who gave so generously of his time and his invaluable advice. Mrs. Ernst A. Stadler, Manuscripts Librarian, Missouri Historical Society, expertly aided in the sometimes difficult task of deciphering Kate Chopin's handwriting. Miss Suzy Groden ably helped with the final version of the Appendix.

Many libraries assisted me in obtaining copies of rare versions of Kate Chopin's printed works, and I particularly wish to thank the staffs of the St. Louis Public Library, the Cornell University Library, the Widener Library at Harvard, and the Boston Public Library.

INTRODUCTION

KATHERINE O'Flaherty, later Kate Chopin, was born in St. Louis on February 8, 1851. Her mother, descended from early French pioneers, had the poise and quiet self-confidence of the Creole elite. Her father was a native of Ireland. In St. Louis his ambition, intelligence, and good breeding helped him become a prosperous merchant and a prominent figure. After his death in 1855, Kate's great-grandmother, Mme. Charleville, became the person who influenced her most. Conversing with her in French, this wise old lady taught her to face life without embarrassment or self-consciousness, and not to judge people on appearances. At the Academy of the Sacred Heart, the young girl was exposed to Catholic teachings and a French emphasis on intellectual vigor. Through these influences, she became thoughtful and open-eyed, an omnivorous reader and an inquisitive observer. With her combination of abandon and reticent self-sufficiency, she was an enigma to those around her.

When Kate graduated from the academy in 1868, she became one of the most popular belles of St. Louis, even though she preferred her "dear reading and writing" to parties. She was greatly interested in the careers of writers, particularly in that of Mme. de Staël. The only significant piece of writing we have from the young girl's hands is "Emancipation," a fable dealing with an animal which leaves his cage for the unknown, "seeing, smelling, touching of all things; even . . . the noxious pool, thinking it may be sweet."

When Kate met twenty-five-year-old Oscar Chopin, she seemed ready to leap into the unknown, and in 1870 they were married. Her husband was the son of a French father and a Creole mother. He took his wife to his native Louisiana, where for ten years he was active as a cotton factor in New Orleans. The couple were happy together and enjoyed their growing family; whenever she could, however, Mrs. Chopin, inspired by her insatiable curiosity about human nature, fled the daily routine to roam around in the picturesque city. Evidently she had at the time no thought of using the wealth of material she was gathering. She observed the many different groups in the cosmopolitan city; she lived through such bloody Reconstruction upheavals as the Battle of Liberty Place (her husband was a member of the White League); and she experienced the peaceful atmosphere of Grand Isle, a sensuously beautiful vacation place on the Gulf of Mexico.

In 1879, Oscar Chopin's business failed. He then took his family to live in Cloutierville, a hamlet in Natchitoches (pronounced Nack-uh-tush) Parish, where he managed part of the family plantation. The Chopin plantation, which had previously belonged to Robert McAlpin, said by many to be the original Simon Legree of *Uncle Tom's Cabin*, was later to provide the setting for Kate Chopin's first novel, *At Fault*. During her years in this remote part of Louisiana, she became intimately acquainted with the Cane River Creoles, Cajuns, and Negroes. (The Creoles were pure-blooded descendants of French and Spanish colonists; the more impecunious Cajuns [Acadians] were descendants of French settlers whom the British had expelled from Nova Scotia in the eighteenth century.) The Natchitoches planters admired her for her social gifts, and her poorer neighbors worshiped her as a Lady Bountiful who listened sympathetically to their problems.

In 1883, Oscar Chopin died suddenly, and after managing the plantation for a year, Mrs. Chopin moved, with her six children, to her mother's home in St. Louis. In 1885, however, her mother died, and with no close relatives left, Kate Chopin was alone with her deep sorrow. Frederick Kolbenheyer, her family doctor and very close friend, seems to have been the only one who could help her. He was a learned man, full of charm and wit, mentally alert, and very radical. Under his influence, she stopped being a practising Catholic, and he may also have inspired the vigor with which she took up again her former study of Darwin, Huxley, and Spencer. Later he suggested she try to write fiction, and in 1888 she hesitatingly began two stories. At the same time she studied the works of others. She particularly admired Sarah Orne Jewett and Mary E. Wilkins Freeman—the first for her "technique and nicety of construction," the other probably for her ability to depict frustrated women. Maupassant also affected her deeply. "Here was life, not fiction," she said. "Here was a man who had escaped from tradition and authority, who . . . in a direct and simple way . . . [gave us his] genuine and spontaneous . . . impressions."

We do not know how long Kate Chopin kept up her study of style. To be sure, *At Fault* is not free from the stage trappings which she said Maupassant had taught her should be banned from good fiction. But even if her technique was still rather crude when she started this novel in 1889, her views on literature and life were not. In an essay entitled "Confidences" she speaks of having made her "own acquaintance" during the period immediately following her mother's death. Though we can only guess at what opened her eyes to her real self—a fulfillment of her literary ambitions or possibly a liaison—we know that the thirty-eight-year-old Kate Chopin was a very mature person when she turned to writing in earnest with *At Fault*. Certainly, her attitudes are markedly consistent through practically her whole *œuvre*.

Many of the views which informed Kate Chopin's fiction from the start are suggested in her essays of the middle 1890's. She insisted here that no author can be true to life who refuses to pluck from the Darwinian tree of knowledge and to see human existence in its true meaning. Reflecting the tenet that man is a higher animal, she once told a friend that she would rather be a dog than a nun because the existence of the one was "a little picture of life" and that of the other only a "phantasmagoria." To her, nature was amoral, playing with man, and morality was man-made and relative. That she drifted away from Catholicism did not mean that she became an atheist, however, but only that she sought God in nature rather than through the Church. She could not share Spencer's belief in progress, and she did not believe in idealism or reform. In her view, man is basically the same today as he has ever been, that is, ruled by imperative, immutably selfish drives. At the same time she did not deterministically deprive man of the ability to choose between right and wrong and to exert his will and influence his fate; nor did she ever view man as bestial. She was, she said, a lover of "brightness and gaiety and life and sunshine," and though she was not blind to evil, she was unable to see and paint life in the dark colors so often used by the naturalists.

Even while calling Zola "the great French realist," she complained that he took life "too clumsily and seriously." She objected to the "rampant sentimentality" of his *Lourdes,* and also to the gloom and lack of humor in Hardy's *Jude the Obscure.* She objected to Zola's "mass of prosaic data" and his design to instruct, and she saw Hardy's characters as "so plainly constructed with the intention of illustrating the purposes of the author, that they do not for a moment convey any impression of reality." To her, true art was incompatible with a thesis and with a zeal for reform. She was impatient with Hamlin Garland, who declared in *Crumbling Idols* that he preferred "actualities" to the literary master-works of the past, and "sociological" themes to such a subject as love. "Human impulses do not change," Kate Chopin retorted, and when Aeschylus is true today, one reason is that he does not deal with local color or with "social problems which by their very nature are mutable."

As for herself, Kate Chopin concentrated on the immutable impulses of love and sex, and Whitman and Maupassant were two of the authors who spoke most deeply to her, probably because they acknowledged the existence of Eros and because they had helped to extend the literary limits to the treatment of sex. Though she leaned to the French school, she believed that American writers, with their "wider and more variegated field of observation," might equal, and perhaps even surpass, the French authors, "were it not that the limitations imposed upon their art by their environment hamper a full and spontaneous expression." Mrs. Chopin wanted to express herself freely, but she did not so much aspire to the somewhat external realism of a Zola as to the more inward, psychological realism of a Maupassant. Her ideal was the invisible and impersonal author who wrote with an objectivity coupled with humor and sympathy.

In May, 1889, Kate Chopin offered her first completed story to the *Home Magazine.* The editor thought it well written, but objected to a "not desirable" incident in the story. Her next two tales, the first to survive, both appeared at the end of 1889, one in a newspaper and the other in a magazine. In September, 1890, she brought out the novel *At Fault* in St. Louis at her own expense. Its heroine, who is opposed to divorce, makes the man she loves and who loves her remarry the woman he divorced because she drank. The wife soon falls back into drinking, and the heroine questions what earlier had been absolute moral truths to her and her right to force her views on others.

In reviewing the novel, St. Louis critics paid tribute to the author's style, but objected to her view that man was unimprovable. In a lone eastern review, the *Nation* also praised her artistry while criticizing the book on moral grounds.

Stimulated by her modest success, Kate Chopin soon finished a second novel. All we know about it is that a number of publishers refused it and that she later destroyed it. She had more luck with her stories, which soon appeared locally, then in national children's magazines, and finally—from 1893—in such well-known eastern periodicals as *Vogue*, the *Century*, and the *Atlantic*. She reached the high-point of her public success when Houghton Mifflin Company in March, 1894, published *Bayou Folk*, which included half of the fifty tales and sketches she had then written. She was welcomed in more than a hundred press notices as a distinguished local colorist. The *Atlantic*, meanwhile, suspected that a wider role might be cut out for her when it observed that her occasional "passionate note" was "characteristic of power awaiting opportunity."

The sudden national fame inspired Kate Chopin to write "The Story of an Hour," a most remarkable account of a woman who exclaims: "Free! free! free!" when she hears of her husband's sudden death. A month later Kate Chopin declared in a diary entry that she would now be willing to "forget the past ten years of [her] growth—real growth" and with a new, "perfect acquiescence" join Oscar were it possible for him to come back to earth. The story and the diary entry suggest that Mrs. Chopin may have felt repressed in her marriage, perhaps because of an unfulfilled literary ambition, and that the success with *Bayou Folk* gave her a release from her frustration. What is certain is that her subsequent writings reflect an increasing self-confidence and daring.

"The Story of an Hour" was refused by Richard Watson Gilder of the *Century*, no doubt because he felt it lacked "ethical value," as he expressed it in connection with another tale she submitted. The reason why editors now turned down a number of her stories was very likely that her women became more passionate and emancipated. The heroine of "Two Portraits," for example, insists on giving herself "when and where she chooses." When *A Night in Acadie*, Mrs. Chopin's second collection, was published in Chicago in November, 1897, it received less notice than its predecessor. The critics again praised her art, but they objected to "coarsenesses" in the book and to its sensuous ambiance. While these reviews appeared, the author was completing *The Awakening*, her masterpiece.

By 1897, Kate Chopin had written three novels and nearly a hundred stories and sketches. A large number of her works are set in Natchitoches, which she made her special literary province, and inevitably they have many traits in common with the local color literature of her time. Discreetly, yet forcefully, she evokes her particular locality with the enchanting Cane River atmosphere, the quaint idioms, and the charming idiosyncrasies of the Natchitoches people. But though she concentrated on what was then a distant, exotic community, she never emphasized the strange or remote; and though, like George W. Cable and Grace King, she commanded a wealth of local material, she did not join them in focusing on old Creole days. She was concerned with the living present rather than the past, with universal rather than regional aspects of life, and the fact that she gave only a few early stories to certain Southern issues which necessarily affected her suggests that she wanted to free her mind of them and move on to more timeless or immutable matters.

When Kate Chopin dealt with such problems as slavery, miscegenation, and integration, she concentrated on the psychology of the individual rather than the social issue as such. If she exposes the institution of slavery in "La Belle Zoraïde," she does so only indirectly as she depicts the pride of a woman who forbids her mulatto slave girl to marry a Negro. Likewise, the subject is pride rather than race when Mrs. Chopin treats mixed marriage in her best-known story, "Désirée's Baby," and when she treats segregation in "A Little Free-Mulatto."

Regarding the author's own attitudes, we may perhaps say there are indications that she condemns slavery in "La Belle Zoraïde"; belittles desegregation in the tale "In and Out of Old Natchitoches"; reflects the sentimentality of her time about devoted former slaves in "Nég Créol"; and suggests in "Ma'ame Pélagie" that the legend of the glorious Southern past should be discarded. But even in these stories, she is so much an author interested in human characteristics rather than issues or races, so much a detached observer that her own views never impose themselves upon the reader.

She undoubtedly had her own set of social values, but though they were often at variance with those of the ruthless, money-making Gilded Age, she never preached or advocated any change. Thus we find that her one story which might deserve the term of social criticism, "Miss McEnders," shows the awakening of a moral reformer to the rottenness in her own family.

The literary precepts of the Gilded Age were more of a challenge to her. While the influential Richard Watson Gilder, for example, felt that fiction should be pleasant and avoid the horrifying, the indelicate, or the immoral, Mrs. Chopin wrote in her first novel about murder, drunkenness, and infidelity. Her women particularly were objectionable to the editors. Her very first, Paula Von Stoltz of "WiserThan a God," refuses the "labor of loving" which a man wants to impose upon her, and becomes instead a famous pianist. In thus opposing the traditional female duties and limitations, she has not a little of what Simone de Beauvoir in *Le Deuxième Sexe* terms the "emancipated woman," that is, a female who insists on the active transcendence of a subject rather than the passive immanence of an object, on an existentialist authenticity obtained through exerting a conscious choice, giving her own laws, and making herself her own destiny. Mildred Orme of "A Shameful Affair" is another illustration of this type; she rejects the role of the passive, innocent party who makes no advances in sexual relations and demands instead the responsibility of an active subject.

The new force which was freed in Kate Chopin through the success of *Bayou Folk* is seen particularly in her heroines who live out their strong impulses. She saw and understood all aspects of the female psyche, and her particular interest was woman's awakening to her true nature, whether traditional, emancipated, or a mixture of the two. In "Regret" she describes how the middle-aged Mamzelle Aurélie all of a sudden realizes what she has missed by not having children. The heroine of "Athénaïse" is an example of the young woman who marries before she is ready; she runs away, but Cazeau, her husband, fetches her back. On the way they pass a "solitary oak-tree, with its seemingly immutable outlines, that had been a landmark for ages," and Cazeau suddenly recalls how his father had recaptured Gabe, a runaway slave, near this spot. Athénaïse runs away again, but only to hurry back to her husband when she realizes that she is bearing his child; as the song comes to the bird, she is now awakened to motherhood and passionate wifehood.

In spite of its "happy ending," this tale is on a deeper level a protest against woman's condition. Athénaïse's "realization of the futility of rebellion against a social and sacred institution" is supported by the story's subtle symbolism. Cazeau's name stands for the *casa* or chateau in which woman lives her hemmed-in existence, and his stern manner and jangling spur stand for the authority which forces her to submission. Athénaïse is indirectly compared to a slave; Gabe then represents the Archangel Gabriel, the herald of pregnancy; and the oak tree represents marriage and motherhood, woman's immutable destiny which makes her the tree of life.

Kate Chopin returned to this subject in *The Awakening*, her most profound treatment of the fundamental problem of what it means to be a woman. The novel has much in common with *Madame Bovary* and with Maupassant's "Réveil," a story which relates how Mme. Vasseur, the heroine, is caught in the romantic syndrome of the supposedly great, noble, undivided, transcendent love, and, like the other two heroines, is seduced by a rake after the departure of the more decent young man who has stirred her.

The crucial point is how this event affects the three women. Emma Bovary, of course, continues her self-dramatization, trying to conform to models and gaining little insight into her own nature as she more and more frenetically attempts to escape her dull environment. Mme. Vasseur, on the other hand, perceives that she had never loved the young man except in a dream from which the roué had awakened her, and she returns to a submissive, disappointed respectability with her husband. Edna, meanwhile, has awakened in full to an imperative craving for sex, for independence, and for clarity and self-knowledge; for her, all return to past submission and all continuation of self-delusion is impossible. Instead of blaming the rake as Mme. Vasseur does, she accepts her animalism, feeling neither shame nor remorse. She realizes that sex is largely independent of our volition.

Just as Edna makes no attempt to suppress her sexual desire, she does not hesitate to throw off her traditional duties towards her family. She realizes she is unable to live as the inessential adjunct to man, as the object over which man rules. "I give myself where I choose," she declares when Robert, her young man, suggests he might ask her husband to set her free. What she craves is to be an independent subject, to dictate her own destiny. "I would give up the inessential," she observes. "I would give my money, I would give my life for my children; but I wouldn't give myself." In other words, it is less important for her to live than to have a self, to be able to exert a conscious choice which can bring out her own essence.

Edna thus believes that she can direct her own life. But she comes to acknowledge a responsibility towards her children to spare them the stigma her kind of life would attach to them. Seeing that we are pawns in the hands of procreational nature, and how patriarchal society condemns particularly a freedom-seeking woman who neglects her children, she inevitably finds her power to dictate her own life to be illusory. Wanting her own way at all cost, she chooses the supreme exertion of her freedom: she takes her own life.

Mrs. Pontellier's defeat lies in the fact that she cannot integrate her demands with those of society; her victory is her awakening to consciousness and authenticity. Earlier, she had "wanted to swim far out, where no woman has swum before." Now she swims to her death, thinking of the clanging spurs of an officer who had attracted her, the emblem of male dominance, and of the bees humming among the pinks, the symbol of procreation. Nature and man dictate the life of the woman, and independence is much harder to obtain and much more of a curse for her than for the man, because she is handicapped by biology and because she must justify an untraditional existence against the heaviest possible odds.

The fable "Emancipation" suggests that Kate O'Flaherty may have hoped to live an expansive life not unlike that of some of her later heroines, and a friend of hers observed that she might have developed earlier as a writer, had her environment been different. According to all accounts, she was a perfect wife and mother; under the surface, however—and even unknown to herself, as we see in the poem "The Haunted Chamber"— she identified deeply with Edna Pontellier.

When Kate Chopin's novel about the sensuous, independent Edna was accepted by a publisher in the early summer of 1898, the author must have felt she could do anything. Such a feeling seems to have inspired "The Storm," which is a first-rate short story, and so daring that she never tried to publish it. That she here deals with sex even more unreservedly than Flaubert or Zola is only a minor point compared to the fact that she depicted it as "happy"—not frantic as it is in parts of *Madame Bovary* or destructive as in *Nana*, but as something as natural and beautiful as life itself. There is a cosmic exuberance and a mystic contact with the elements in "The Storm" which, together with its frankness, foreshadow D.H. Lawrence.

Another important aspect of this story is that Kate Chopin is able to treat the most crucial of relationships between man and woman entirely without bias. Even in her emancipationist writings there is no misandry and no suggestion that either sex is superior to the other; and now, with the female protest of *The Awakening* off her mind and fame within her reach, she shows no slightest trace of being a woman "at war with her lot," as Virginia Woolf expressed it in *A Room of One's Own*. "The Storm" is the detached and objective story of a female author who does not write consciously as a woman, who has reached that "freedom" and "peace" which Mrs. Woolf saw as necessary if the genius of an authoress is to be "expressed whole and entire."

The Awakening was published on April 22, 1899. It was immediately condemned all over America. While the critics called the novel a brilliant piece of writing, they violently attacked it on moral grounds. One reviewer considered Edna's love to be so "sensual and devilish" that the book should not have been written. The author was told that she was "at her best as a creator of sweet and lovable characters." The novel was taken out of circulation at the St. Louis libraries, and Mrs. Chopin was shunned by some of her friends and denied membership in a local arts club.

This persecution affected her very deeply; as one who knew her well has said, "it was unbelievable how she was crushed . . . [since her book represented] truth as she saw it and people would not see." In "A Reflection," a short piece dated November, 1899, she appears to say that the critics who refuse to see "the significance of things" had banned her from the procession of writers. When her third collection of stories was turned down by her publisher a few months later, she evidently felt herself a literary outcast, and her writing, which had slowed down after *The Awakening*, was soon to cease altogether. In "Charlie," a story written at this time, she can be seen as taking revenge on the males who had killed her creativity when she—in her only example of emasculation—dismembers the father who forbids his daughter to act the role of a man.

When Kate Chopin died on August 22, 1904, she was already practically forgotten, and since her death, less than twenty critics of any note have commented upon her writings. Father Daniel S. Rankin performed an invaluable service when he saved her manuscripts from possible destruction and interviewed those who had known her, but in his book on her (*Kate Chopin and Her Creole Stories*, Philadelphia, 1932), he joined the other commentators in emphasizing her use of local color and brushing aside *The Awakening* as morbid. In 1953, however, Cyrille Arnavon published his searching analysis of Kate Chopin's courageous realism. Since then, several critics, including Kenneth Eble, Robert B. Bush, Edmund Wilson, Larzer Ziff, and George Arms, have done their part in elevating her from the status of a regional writer to a pioneer realist. Professor Ziff terms her premature silence a loss comparable to the early deaths of Stephen Crane and Frank Norris. In his recent book, *Kate Chopin: A Critical Biography* (Baton Rouge and Oslo, 1969), the present editor attempts a new approach to both her life and her writings.

Mrs. Chopin's significance lies in her artistry, which already in 1894 was compared to that of Maupassant, and in her daring treatment of vital subjects, in which she was decades ahead of her time.

She took her writing seriously. Not depending on it for a living, she wrote as she pleased, jealously guarding her literary integrity in form and subject. She was a spontaneous storyteller, and she insisted that a tale should write itself "without any perceptible effort on . . . [her] part." She put no word on paper until the story had come to her complete. Then she wrote it down very rapidly. Preferring, in her own words, "the integrity of crudities to artificialities," she made only a few, insignificant changes before offering a story for publication. As a result of her refusal to revise, her stories are occasionally marred by awkward language or improbable coincidences, and though the last sentence of such a story as "Désirée's Baby" has a poignancy unsurpassed by Maupassant, it is nevertheless a trick ending.

But what she lost in this way, she gained in freshness of feeling and perception, and she had such an intuitive sense of the artistic that her stories occasionally came to her in a form as finished as that of the French master. Her art is a living thing, as effortless and natural as breathing. Emphasizing character rather than plot, she centers on a small event, takes us right into the story, and develops it logically towards an inevitable conclusion. She achieves her effects through her insight into character, her sense of form, her lucid and precise language, and her light touch. The story "Regret" is a perfect illustration of these qualities and of how she could pack a whole drama into a few, unemphatic last lines. It also shows her Gallic simplicity and economy of means, her unobtrusive humor, and the sympathy and intensity she hid behind her restraint and objectivity.

At Fault, her first novel, was written before she was ready for this longer form of fiction. One reason for her writing it was that she had to get her irritation with moral reformers out of her system. This explains in part the artificiality of the plot, the occasionally stilted language, and the woodenness of the central characters. On the other hand, many of the supporting figures—such as the impetuous Grégoire and the worldly Aunt Belindy—are true to life and fully convincing, and a number of scenes are effectively realized.

When Kate Chopin came to *The Awakening*, she was in complete command of her art. Form and content are organically fused. The book is a grand orchestration of the symphony of imperative Eros, in which the theme of sex and procreation is played off against that of illusions about love and independence. Hardly a word or a picture is accidental; nothing unessential is included. Man and nature form a continuum of union and solitude, with the sea as the central symbol of Eros and self-assertion. The symbolism of the supporting pairs of lovers is a little too heavy, and certain expressions are mannered, but otherwise the book is a great literary achievement. The author's easy, graceful, and clear style is a perfect vehicle for the unsparing and deeply moving emotional truth.

In the *Literary History of the United States*, although Kate Chopin is highly praised as an outstanding local color artist, no mention is made of *The Awakening* or her importance as a realist. Yet she was the first woman writer in America to accept sex with its profound repercussions as a legitimate subject for serious fiction. In her attitude towards passion, she represented a healthy, matter-of-fact acceptance of the whole of man. She was familiar with the newest developments in science and in world literature, and her aim was to describe—unhampered by tradition and authority—man's immutable impulses. Because she was vigorous, intelligent, and eminently sane, and because her background had made her morally tolerant and socially secure, she could write with a balance and maturity, a warmth and humor not often found in her contemporaries.

Mrs. Chopin was influenced by the feminism of Madame de Staël and George Sand and the realism of Flaubert and Maupassant. Yet she is independent and original. She turns to aspects of the feminine condition which were taboo to the two women and of little interest to the two men, even introducing an existentialist philosophy which foreshadows Simone de Beauvoir. Though she describes many women who are perfectly happy in conventional marriage, she has a number of heroines who demand freedom and an authentic existence. But, as certain of her stories show, she saw at the same time the idea of male supremacy and female submission as so ingrained that women may never achieve emancipation in the very deepest sense. Furthermore, she also looked beyond this emancipation, and there she saw the horror of an unsupported freedom. This, and her awareness of how the woman in particular is a toy in the hands of nature's procreational imperative, lend a note of despair to such a work as *The Awakening*.

The basic pessimism and the ruthless honesty of this novel unite Kate Chopin more closely with Theodore Dreiser than with any other of the contemporary American writers. These two authors, who both came from Catholic, non-Anglo-Saxon backgrounds, are alike in taking man as the given, the unimprovable. There is a fundamental seriousness and lack of all moralism in *The Awakening* and *Sister Carrie* which sets them off from such works as *Maggie: A Girl of the Streets*, Stephen Crane's stereotype seduction story, and *Rose of Dutcher's Coolly*, Hamlin Garland's ethical emancipationist novel. Edna's and Carrie's violations of man's arbitrary code of morals are given without shame or apology; the unillusioned, unidealistic authors present no villains—except the chimeras pursued by their heroines.

Carrie's universality lies in her irresistible fight to get ahead in society, and Dreiser affronted America by glorifying his heroine and letting her succeed in spite of her amorality. Edna, too, has a universal quality in her open-eyed choice to defy illusions and to question the sacredness of morals. Though apparently a loser, she wins an inner victory of knowledge and of authenticity which Carrie—who so often mimics those one step above her on the ladder—can never achieve for all her outer success.

Kate Chopin had no noticeable influence on other American writers. It is doubtful that she was read by Dreiser, for example, even though he started *Sister Carrie* just when *The Awakening* was being condemned, or by Ellen Glasgow, who was just beginning to describe unsatisfactory marriages. Had she, like Crane or Norris, been backed by the influential William Dean Howells, or had her novel been put on trial like *Madame Bovary* or *Lady Chatterley's Lover*, she might not only have gained lasting fame, but also have been inspired further to unfold her creative powers.

She was too much of a pioneer to be accepted in her time and place. She had a daring and a vision all her own, a unique combination of realism and pessimism applied to woman's immutable condition. Adverse criticism and early death stopped her from delving as deeply as she could have done into the psychology of her women. But as it is, her best writings are minor masterpieces. They demonstrate an independence and courage, a warm understanding, and more than a touch of artistic genius which entitle them, and their author, to a permanent place in American literature.

SHORT STORIES
AND SKETCHES

Emancipation. A Life Fable

There was once an animal born into this world, and opening his eyes upon Life, he saw above and about him confining walls, and before him were bars of iron through which came air and light from without; this animal was born in a cage.

Here he grew, and throve in strength and beauty under care of an invisible protecting hand. Hungering, food was ever at hand. When he thirsted water was brought, and when he felt the need of rest, there was provided a bed of straw upon which to lie: and here he found it good, licking his handsome flanks, to bask in the sun beam that he thought existed but to lighten his home.

Awaking one day from his slothful rest, lo! the door of his cage stood open: accident had opened it. In the corner he crouched, wondering and fearingly. Then slowly did he approach the door, dreading the un-accustomed, and would have closed it, but for such a task his limbs were purposeless. So out the opening he thrust his head, to see the canopy of the sky grow broader, and the world waxing wider.

Back to his corner but not to rest, for the spell of the Unknown was over him, and again and again he goes to the open door, seeing each time more Light.

Then one time standing in the flood of it; a deep in-drawn breath—a bracing of strong limbs, and with a bound he was gone.

On he rushes, in his mad flight, heedless that he is wounding and tearing his sleek sides—seeing, smelling, touching of all things; even stopping to put his lips to the noxious pool, thinking it may be sweet.

Hungering there is no food but such as he must seek and ofttimes

37

fight for; and his limbs are weighted before he reaches the water that is good to his thirsting throat.

So does he live, seeking, finding, joying and suffering. The door which accident had opened is open still, but the cage remains forever empty!

Wiser Than a God

"To love and be wise is scarcely granted even to a god."—Latin Proverb.

I

"You might at least show some distaste for the task, Paula," said Mrs. Von Stoltz, in her querulous invalid voice, to her daughter who stood before the glass bestowing a few final touches of embellishment upon an otherwise plain toilet.

"And to what purpose, Mutterchen? The task is not entirely to my liking, I'll admit; but there can be no question as to its results, which you even must concede are gratifying."

"Well, it's not the career your poor father had in view for you. How often he has told me when I complained that you were kept too closely at work, 'I want that Paula shall be at the head,' " with appealing look through the window and up into the gray, November sky into that far "somewhere," which might be the abode of her departed husband.

"It isn't a career at all, mamma; it's only a make-shift," answered the girl, noting the happy effect of an amber pin that she had thrust through the coils of her lustrous yellow hair. "The pot must be kept boiling at all hazards, pending the appearance of that hoped for career. And you forget that an occasion like this gives me the very opportunities I want."

"I can't see the advantages of bringing your talent down to such banale servitude. Who are those people, anyway?"

The mother's question ended in a cough which shook her into speechless exhaustion.

"Ah! I have let you sit too long by the window, mother," said Paula, hastening to wheel the invalid's chair nearer the grate fire that was throwing genial light and warmth into the room, turning its plainness to beauty as by a touch of enchantment. "By the way," she added, having arranged her mother as comfortably as might be, "I haven't yet qualified

39

for that 'banale servitude,' as you call it." And approaching the piano which stood in a distant alcove of the room, she took up a roll of music that lay curled up on the instrument, straightened it out before her. Then, seeming to remember the question which her mother had asked, turned on the stool to answer it. "Don't you know? The Brainards, very swell people, and awfully rich. The daughter is that girl whom I once told you about, having gone to the Conservatory to cultivate her voice and old Engfelder told her in his brusque way to go back home, that his system was not equal to overcoming impossibilities."

"Oh, those people."

"Yes; this little party is given in honor of the son's return from Yale or Harvard, or some place or other." And turning to the piano she softly ran over the dances, whilst the mother gazed into the fire with unresigned sadness, which the bright music seemed to deepen.

"Well, there'll be no trouble about *that*," said Paula, with comfortable assurance, having ended the last waltz. "There's nothing here to tempt me into flights of originality; there'll be no difficulty in keeping to the hand-organ effect."

"Don't leave me with those dreadful impressions, Paula; my poor nerves are on edge."

"You are too hard on the dances, mamma. There are certain strains here and there that I thought not bad."

"It's your youth that finds it so; I have outlived such illusions."

"What an inconsistent little mother it is!" the girl exclaimed, laughing. "You told me only yesterday it was my youth that was so impatient with the commonplace happenings of everyday life. That age, needing to seek its delights, finds them often in unsuspected places, wasn't that it?"

"Don't chatter, Paula; some music, some music!"

"What shall it be?" asked Paula, touching a succession of harmonious chords. "It must be short."

"The 'Berceuse,' then; Chopin's. But soft, soft and a little slowly as your dear father used to play it."

Mrs. Von Stoltz leaned her head back amongst the cushions, and with eyes closed, drank in the wonderful strains that came like an ethereal voice out of the past, lulling her spirit into the quiet of sweet memories.

When the last soft notes had melted into silence, Paula approached her mother and looking into the pale face saw that tears stood beneath the closed eyelids. "Ah! mamma, I have made you unhappy," she cried, in distress.

"No, my child; you have given me a joy that you don't dream of. I have no more pain. Your music has done for me what Faranelli's singing did for poor King Philip of Spain; it has cured me."

There was a glow of pleasure on the warm face and the eyes with almost the brightness of health. "Whilst I listened to you, Paula, my soul went out from me and lived again through an evening long ago. We were in our pretty room at Leipsic. The soft air and the moonlight came through the open-curtained window, making a quivering fret-work along the gleaming waxed floor. You lay in my arms and I felt again the pressure of your warm, plump little body against me. Your father was at the piano playing the 'Berceuse,' and all at once you drew my head down and whispered, 'Ist es nicht wonderschen, mama?' When it ended, you were sleeping and your father took you from my arms and laid you gently in bed."

Paula knelt beside her mother, holding the frail hands which she kissed tenderly.

"Now you must go, liebchen. Ring for Berta, she will do all that is needed. I feel very strong to-night. But do not come back too late."

"I shall be home as early as possible; likely in the last car, I couldn't stay longer or I should have to walk. You know the house in case there should be need to send for me?"

"Yes, yes; but there will be no need."

Paula kissed her mother lovingly and went out into the drear November night with the roll of dances under her arm.

II

The door of the stately mansion at which Paula rang, was opened by a footman, who invited her to "kindly walk upstairs."

"Show the young lady into the music room, James," called from some upper region a voice, doubtless the same whose impossibilities had been so summarily dealt with by Herr Engfelder, and Paula was led through a suite of handsome apartments, the warmth and mellow light of which were very grateful, after the chill out-door air.

Once in the music room, she removed her wraps and seated herself comfortably to await developments. Before her stood the magnificent "Steinway," on which her eyes rested with greedy admiration, and her fingers twitched with a desire to awaken its inviting possibilities. The odor of flowers impregnated the air like a subtle intoxicant and over everything hung a quiet smile of expectancy, disturbed by an occasional feminine flutter above stairs, or muffled suggestions of distant household sounds.

Presently, a young man entered the drawing-room,—no doubt, the college student, for he looked critically and with an air of proprietorship at the festive arrangements, venturing the bestowal of a few improving touches. Then, gazing with pardonable complacency at his own handsome, athletic figure in the mirror, he saw reflected Paula looking at him, with a demure smile lighting her blue eyes.

"By Jove!" was his startled exclamation. Then, approaching, "I beg pardon, Miss—Miss—"

"Von Stoltz."

"Miss Von Stoltz," drawing the right conclusion from her simple toilet and the roll of music. "I hadn't seen you when I came in. Have you been here long? and sitting all alone, too? That's certainly rough."

"Oh, I've been here but a few moments, and was very well entertained."

"I dare say," with a glance full of prognostic complimentary utterances, which a further acquaintance might develop.

As he was lighting the gas of a side bracket that she might better see to read her music, Mrs. Brainard and her daughter came into the room, radiantly attired and both approached Paula with sweet and polite greeting.

"George, in mercy!" exclaimed his mother, "put out that gas, you are killing the effect of the candle light."

"But Miss Von Stoltz can't read her music without it, mother."

"I've no doubt Miss Von Stoltz knows her pieces by heart," Mrs. Brainard replied, seeking corroboration from Paula's glance.

"No, madam; I'm not accustomed to playing dance music, and this is quite new to me," the girl rejoined, touching the loose sheets that George had conveniently straightened out and placed on the rack.

"Oh, dear! 'not accustomed'?" said Miss Brainard. "And Mr. Sohmeir told us he knew you would give satisfaction."

Paula hastened to re-assure the thoroughly alarmed young lady on the point of her ability to give perfect satisfaction.

The door bell now began to ring incessantly. Up the stairs, tripped fleeting opera-cloaked figures, followed by their black robed attendants. The rooms commenced to fill with the pretty hub-bub that a bevy of girls can make when inspired by a close masculine proximity; and

Paula, not waiting to be asked, struck the opening bars of an inspiring waltz.

Some hours later, during a lull in the dancing, when the men were making vigorous applications of fans and handkerchiefs; and the girls beginning to throw themselves into attitudes of picturesque exhaustion— save for the always indefatigable few— a proposition was ventured, backed by clamorous entreaties, which induced George to bring forth his banjo. And an agreeable moment followed, in which that young man's skill met with a truly deserving applause. Never had his audience beheld such proficiency as he displayed in the handling of his instrument, which was now behind him, now over-head, and again swinging in mid-air like the pendulum of a clock and sending forth the sounds of stirring melody. Sounds so inspiring that a pretty little black-eyed fairy, an acknowledged votary of Terpsichore, and George's particular admiration, was moved to contribute a few passes of a Virginia break-down, as she had studied it from life on a Southern plantation. The act closing amid a spontaneous babel of hand clapping and admiring bravos.

It must be admitted that this little episode, however graceful, was hardly a fitting prelude to the magnificent "Jewel Song from 'Faust,' " with which Miss Brainard next consented to regale the company. That Miss Brainard possessed a voice, was a fact that had existed as matter of tradition in the family as far back almost as the days of that young lady's baby utterances, in which loving ears had already detected the promise which time had so recklessly fulfilled.

True genius is not to be held in abeyance, though a host of Engfelders would rise to quell it with their mundane protests!

Miss Brainard's rendition was a triumphant achievement of sound, and with the proud flush of success moving her to kind condescension, she asked Miss Von Stoltz to "please play something."

Paula amiably consented, choosing a selection from the Modern Classic. How little did her auditors appreciate in the performance the results of a life study, of a drilling that had made her amongst the knowing an acknowledged mistress of technique. But to her skill she added the touch and interpretation of the artist; and in hearing her, even Ignorance paid to her genius the tribute of a silent emotion.

When she arose there was a moment of quiet, which was broken by the black-eyed fairy, always ready to cast herself into a breach, observing, flippantly, "How pretty!" "Just lovely!" from another; and "What wouldn't I give to play like that." Each inane compliment falling like a dash of cold water on Paula's ardor.

She then became solicitous about the hour, with reference to her car, and George who stood near looked at his watch and informed her that the last car had gone by a full half hour before.

"But," he added, "if you are not expecting any one to call for you, I will gladly see you home."

"I expect no one, for the car that passes here would have set me down at my door," and in this avowal of difficulties, she tacitly accepted George's offer.

The situation was new. It gave her a feeling of elation to be walking through the quiet night with this handsome young fellow. He talked so freely and so pleasantly. She felt such a comfort in his strong protective nearness. In clinging to him against the buffets of the staggering wind she could feel the muscles of his arms, like steel.

He was so unlike any man of her acquaintance. Strictly unlike Poldorf, the pianist, the short rotundity of whose person could have been less objectionable, if she had not known its cause to lie in an inordinate consumption of beer. Old Engfelder, with his long hair, his spectacles and his loose, disjointed figure, was hors de combat in comparison. And of Max Kuntzler, the talented composer, her teacher of harmony, she could at the moment think of no positive point of objection against him, save the vague, general, serious one of his unlikeness to George.

Her new-awakened admiration, though, was not deaf to a little inexplicable wish that he had not been so proficient with the banjo.

On they went chatting gaily, until turning the corner of the street in which she lived, Paula saw that before the door stood Dr. Sinn's buggy.

Brainard could feel the quiver of surprised distress that shook her frame, as she said, hurrying along, "Oh! mamma must be ill—worse; they have called the doctor."

Reaching the house, she threw open wide the door that was unlocked, and he stood hesitatingly back. The gas in the small hall burned at its full, and showed Berta at the top of the stairs, speechless, with terrified eyes, looking down at her. And coming to meet her, was a neighbor, who strove with well-meaning solicitude to keep her back, to hold her yet a moment in ignorance of the cruel blow that fate had dealt her whilst she had in happy unconsciousness played her music for the dance.

III

Several months had passed since the dreadful night when death had deprived Paula for the second time of a loved parent.

After the first shock of grief was over, the girl had thrown all her energies into work, with the view of attaining that position in the musical world which her father and mother had dreamed might be hers.

She had remained in the small home occupying now but the half of it; and here she kept house with the faithful Berta's aid.

Friends were both kind and attentive to the stricken girl. But there had been two, whose constant devotion spoke of an interest deeper than mere friendly solicitude.

Max Kuntzler's love for Paula was something that had taken hold of his sober middle age with an enduring strength which was not to be lessened or shaken, by her rejection of it. He had asked leave to remain her friend, and while holding the tender, watchful privileges which that comprehensive title may imply, had refrained from further thrusting a warmer feeling on her acceptance.

Paula one evening was seated in her small sitting-room, working over some musical transpositions, when a ring at the bell was followed by a footstep in the hall which made her hand and heart tremble.

George Brainard entered the room, and before she could rise to greet him, had seated himself in the vacant chair beside her.

"What an untiring worker you are," he said, glancing down at the scores before her. "I always feel that my presence interrupts you; and yet I don't know that a judicious interruption isn't the wholesomest thing for you sometimes."

"You forget," she said, smiling into his face, "that I was trained to it. I must keep myself fitted to my calling. Rest would mean deterioration."

"Would you not be willing to follow some other calling?" he asked, looking at her with unusual earnestness in his dark, handsome eyes.

"Oh, never!"

"Not if it were a calling that asked only for the labor of loving?"

She made no answer, but kept her eyes fixed on the idle traceries that she drew with her pencil on the sheets before her.

He arose and made a few impatient turns about the room, then coming again to her side, said abruptly:

"Paula, I love you. It isn't telling you something that you don't know, unless you have been without bodily perceptions. To-day there is some-thing driving me to speak it out in words. Since I have known you," he continued, striving to look into her face that bent low over the work before her, "I have been mounting into higher and always higher circles of Paradise, under a blessed illusion that you—cared for me. But to-day, a feeling of dread has been forcing itself upon me—dread that with a word you might throw me back into a gulf that would now be one of everlasting misery. Say if you love me, Paula. I believe you do, and yet I wait with indefinable doubts for your answer."

He took her hand which she did not withdraw from his.

"Why are you speechless? Why don't you say something to me!" he asked desperately.

"I am speechless with joy and misery," she answered. "To know that you love me, gives me happiness enough to brighten a lifetime. And I am miserable, feeling that you have spoken the signal that must part us."

"You love me, and speak of parting. Never! You will be my wife. From this moment we belong to each other. Oh, my Paula," he said, drawing her to his side, "my whole existence will be devoted to your happiness."

"I can't marry you," she said shortly, disengaging his hand from her waist.

"Why?" he asked abruptly. They stood looking into each other's eyes.

"Because it doesn't enter into the purpose of my life."

"I don't ask you to give up anything in your life. I only beg you to let me share it with you."

George had known Paula only as the daughter of the undemonstrative American woman. He had never before seen her with the father's emo-tional nature aroused in her. The color mounted into her cheeks, and her blue eyes were almost black with intensity of feeling.

"Hush," she said; "don't tempt me further." And she cast herself on her knees before the table near which they stood, gathering the music that lay upon it into an armful, and resting her hot cheek upon it.

"What do you know of my life," she exclaimed passionately. "What can you guess of it? Is music anything more to you than the pleasing distraction of an idle moment? Can't you feel that with me, it courses with the blood through my veins? That it's something dearer than life, than riches, even than love?" with a quiver of pain.

"Paula listen to me; don't speak like a mad woman."

She sprang up and held out an arm to ward away his nearer approach.

"Would you go into a convent, and ask to be your wife a nun who has vowed herself to the service of God?"

"Yes, if that nun loved me; she would owe to herself, to me and to God to be my wife."

Paula seated herself on the sofa, all emotion seeming suddenly to have left her; and he came and sat beside her.

"Say only that you love me, Paula," he urged persistently.

"I love you," she answered low and with pale lips.

He took her in his arms, holding her in silent rapture against his heart and kissing the white lips back into red life.

"You will be my wife?"

"You must wait. Come back in a week and I will answer you." He was forced to be content with the delay.

The days of probation being over, George went for his answer, which was given him by the old lady who occupied the upper story.

"Ach Gott! Fräulein Von Stoltz ist schon im Leipsic gegangen!"— All that has not been many years ago. George Brainard is as handsome as ever, though growing a little stout in the quiet routine of domestic life. He has quite lost a pretty taste for music that formerly distinguished him as a skilful banjoist. This loss his little black-eyed wife deplores; though she has herself made concessions to the advancing years, and abandoned Virginia break-downs as incompatible with the serious offices of wifehood and matrimony.

You may have seen in the morning paper, that the renowned pianist, Fräulein Paula Von Stoltz, is resting in Leipsic, after an extended and remunerative concert tour.

Professor Max Kuntzler is also in Leipsic—with the ever persistent will—the dogged patience that so often wins in the end.

A Point at Issue!

MARRIED—On Tuesday, May 11, Eleanor Gail to Charles Faraday.

Nothing bearing the shape of a wedding announcement could have been less obtrusive than the foregoing hidden in a remote corner of the Plymdale *Promulgator*, clothed in the palest and smallest of type, and modestly wedged in between the big, black-lettered offer of the *Promulgator* to mail itself free of extra charge to subscribers leaving home for the summer months, and an equally somber-clad notice (doubtless astray as to place and application) that Hammersmith & Co. were carrying a large and varied assortment of marble and granite monuments!

Yet notwithstanding its sandwiched condition, that little marriage announcement seemed to Eleanor to parade the whole street.

Whichever way she turned her eyes, it glowered at her with scornful reproach.

She felt it to be an indelicate thrusting of herself upon the public notice; and at the sight she was plunged in regret at having made to the proprieties the concession of permitting it.

She hoped now that the period for making concessions was ended. She had endured long and patiently the trials that beset her path when she chose to diverge from the beaten walks of female Plymdaledom. Had stood stoically enough the questionable distinction of being relegated to a place amid that large and ill-assorted family of "cranks," feeling the discomfit and attending opprobrium to be far outbalanced by the satisfying consciousness of roaming the heights of free thought, and tasting the sweets of a spiritual emancipation.

The closing act of Eleanor's young ladyhood, when she chose to be married without pre-announcement, without the paraphernalia of accessories so dear to a curious public—had been in keeping with previous methods distinguishing her career. The disappointed public cheated of its entertainment, was forced to seek such compensation for the loss as was offered in reflections that while condemning her present, were unsparing of her past, and full with damning prognostic of her future.

Charles Faraday, who added to his unembellished title that of Professor of Mathematics of the Plymdale University, had found in Eleanor Gail his ideal woman.

Indeed, she rather surpassed that ideal, which had of necessity been but an adorned picture of woman as he had known her. A mild emphasizing of her merits, a soft toning down of her defects had served to offer to his fancy a prototype of that bequoted creature.

"Not too good for human nature's daily food," yet so good that he had cherished no hope of beholding such a one in the flesh. Until Eleanor had come, supplanting his ideal, and making of that fanciful creation a very simpleton by contrast. In the beginning he had found her extremely good to look at, with her combination of graceful womanly charms, unmarred by self-conscious mannerisms that was as rare as it was engaging. Talking with her, he had caught a look from her eyes into his that he recognized at once as a free masonry of intellect. And the longer he knew her, the greater grew his wonder at the beautiful revelations of her mind that unfurled itself to his, like the curling petals of some hardy blossom that opens to the inviting warmth of the sun. It was not that Eleanor knew many things. According to her own modest estimate of herself, she knew nothing. There were school girls in Plymdale who surpassed her in the amount of their positive knowledge. But she was possessed of a clear intellect: sharp in its reasoning, strong and unprejudiced in its outlook. She was that *rara avis,* a logical woman—something which Faraday had not encountered in his life before. True, he was not hoary with age. At 30 the types of women he had met with were not legion; but he felt safe in doubting that the hedges of the future would grow logical women for him, more than they had borne such prodigies in the past.

He found Eleanor ready to take broad views of life and humanity; able to grasp a question and anticipate conclusions by a quick intuition which he himself reached by the slower, consecutive steps of reason.

During the months that shaped themselves into the cycle of a year these two dwelt together in the harmony of a united purpose.

Together they went looking for the good things of life, knocking at the closed doors of philosophy; venturing into the open fields of science, she, with uncertain steps, made steady by his help.

Whithersoever he led she followed, oftentimes in her eagerness taking the lead into unfamiliar ways in which he, weighted with a lingering conservatism, had hesitated to venture.

So did they grow in their oneness of thought to belong each so absolutely to the other that the idea seemed not to have come to them that this union might be made faster by marriage. Until one day it broke upon Faraday, like a revelation from the unknown, the possibility of making her his wife.

When he spoke, eager with the new awakened impulse, she laughingly replied:

"Why not?" She had thought of it long ago.

In entering upon their new life they decided to be governed by no precedential methods. Marriage was to be a form, that while fixing legally their relation to each other, was in no wise to touch the individuality of either; that was to be preserved intact. Each was to remain a free integral of humanity, responsible to no dominating exactions of so-called marriage laws. And the element that was to make possible such a union was trust in each other's love, honor, courtesy, tempered by the reserving clause of readiness to meet the consequences of reciprocal liberty.

Faraday appreciated the need of offering to his wife advantages for culture which had been of impossible attainment during her girlhood.

Marriage, which marks too often the closing period of a woman's intellectual existence, was to be in her case the open portal through which she might seek the embellishments that her strong, graceful mentality deserved.

An urgent desire with Eleanor was to acquire a thorough speaking knowledge of the French language. They agreed that a lengthy sojourn in Paris could be the only practical and reliable means of accomplishing such an end.

Faraday's three months of vacation were to be spent by them in the idle happiness of a loitering honeymoon through the continent of Europe, then he would leave his wife in the French capital for a stay that might extend indefinitely—two, three years—as long as should be found needful, he returning to join her with the advent of each summer, to renew their love in a fresh and re-strengthened union.

And so, in May, they were married, and in September we find Eleanor established in the pension of the old couple Clairegobeau and comfortably ensconced in her pretty room that opened on to the Rue Rivoli, her heart full of sweet memories that were to cheer her coming solitude.

On the wall, looking always down at her with his quiet, kind glance, hung the portrait of her husband. Beneath it stood the fanciful little desk at which she hoped to spend many happy hours.

Books were everywhere, giving character to the graceful furnishings which their united taste had evolved from the paucity of the Clairegobeau germ, and out of the window was Paris!

Eleanor was supremely satisfied amid her new and attractive surroundings. The pang of parting from her husband seeming to lend sharp zest to a situation that offered the fulfillment of a cherished purpose.

Faraday, with the stronger man-nature, felt more keenly the discomfit of giving up a companionship that in its brief duration had been replete with the duality of accomplished delight and growing promise.

But to him also was the situation made acceptable by its involving a principle which he felt it incumbent upon him to uphold. He returned to Plymdale and to his duties at the university, and resumed his bachelor existence as quietly as though it had been interrupted but by the interval of a day.

The small public with which he had acquaintance, and which had forgotten his existence during the past few months, was fired anew with indignant astonishment at the effrontery of the situation which his singular coming back offered to their contemplation.

That two young people should presume to introduce such innovations into matrimony!

It was uncalled for!

It was improper!

It was indecent!

He must have already tired of her idiosyncrasies, since he had left her in Paris.

And in Paris, of all places, to leave a young woman alone! Why not at once in Hades?

She had been left in Paris forsooth to learn French. And since when was Mme. Belaire's French, as it had been taught to select generations of Plymdalions, considered insufficient for the practical needs of existence as related by that foreign tongue?

But Faraday's life was full with occupation and his brief moments of leisure were too precious to give to heeding the idle gossip that floated to his hearing and away again without holding his thoughts an instant.

He lived uninterruptedly a certain existence with his wife through the medium of letters. True, an inadequate substitute for her actual presence, but there was much satisfaction in this constant communion of thought between them.

They told such details of their daily lives as they thought worth the telling.

Their readings were discussed. Opinions exchanged. Newspaper cuttings sent back and forth, bearing upon questions that interested them. And what did not interest them?

Nothing was so large that they dared not look at it. Happenings, small in themselves, but big in their psychological comprehensiveness, held them with strange fascination. Her earnestness and intensity in such matters were extreme; but happily, Faraday brought to this union humorous instincts, and an optimism that saved it from a too monotonous sombreness.

The young man had his friends in Plymdale. Certainly none that ever remotely approached the position which Eleanor held in that regard. She stood pre-eminent. She was himself.

But his nature was genial. He invited companionship from his fellow beings, who, however short that companionship might be, carried always away a gratifying consciousness of having made their personalities felt.

The society in Plymdale which he most frequented was that of the Beatons.

Beaton père was a fellow professor, many years older than Faraday, but one of those men with whom time, after putting its customary stamp upon his outward being, took no further care.

The spirit of his youth had remained untouched, and formed the nucleus around which the family gathered, drawing the light of their own cheerfulness.

Mrs. Beaton was a woman whose aspirations went not further than the desire for her family's good, and her bearing announced in its every feature, the satisfaction of completed hopes.

Of the daughters, Margaret, the eldest, was looked upon as slightly erratic, owing to a timid leaning in the direction of Woman's Suffrage.

Her activity in that regard, taking the form of a desultory correspondence with members of a certain society of protest; the fashioning and donning of garments of mysterious shape, which, while stamping their wearer with the distinction of a quasi-emancipation, defeated the ulti-mate purpose of their construction by inflicting a personal discomfort that extended beyond the powers of long endurance. Miss Kitty Beaton, the youngest daughter, and just returned from boarding-school, while clamoring for no privileges doubtful of attainment and of remote and questionable benefit, with a Napoleonic grip, possessed herself of such rights as were at hand and exercised them in keeping the household under her capricious command.

She was at that age of blissful illusion when a girl is in love with her own youth and beauty and happiness. That age which heeds no purpose in the scope of creation further than may touch her majesty's enjoyment. Who would not smilingly endure with that charming selfishness of youth, knowing that the rough hand of experience is inevitably descend-ing to disturb the short-lived dream?

They were all clever people, bright and interesting, and in this family circle Faraday found an acceptable relaxation from work and enforced solitude.

If they ever doubted the wisdom or expediency of his domestic relations, courtesy withheld the expression of any such doubts. Their welcome was always complete in its friendliness, and the interest which they evinced in the absent Eleanor proved that she was held in the highest esteem.

With Beaton Faraday enjoyed that pleasant intercourse which may exist between men whose ways, while not too divergent, are yet divided by an appreciable interval.

But it remained for Kitty to touch him with her girlish charms in a way, which, though not too usual with Faraday, meant so little to the man that he did not take the trouble to resent it.

Her laughter and song, the restless motions of her bubbling happiness, he watched with the casual pleasure that one follows the playful gambols of a graceful kitten.

He liked the soft shining light of her eyes. When she was near him the velvet smoothness of her pink cheeks stirred him with a feeling that could have found satisfying expression in a kiss.

It is idle to suppose that even the most exemplary men go through life with their eyes closed to woman's beauty and their senses steeled against its charm.

Faraday thought little of this feeling (and so should we if it were not outspoken).

In writing one day to his wife, with the cold-blooded impartiality

of choosing a subject which he thought of neither more nor less prominence than the next, he descanted at some length upon the interesting
emotions which Miss Kitty's pretty femininity aroused in him.

If he had given serious thought to the expediency of touching upon such
a theme with one's wife, he still would not have been deterred. Was not
Eleanor's large comprehensiveness far above the littleness of ordinary
women?

Did it not enter into the scheme of their lives, to keep free from prejudices that hold their sway over the masses?

But he thought not of that, for, after all, his interest in Kitty and his
interest in his university class bore about an equal reference to Eleanor
and his love for her.

His letter was sent, and he gave no second thought to the matter of
its contents.

The months went by for Faraday with few distinctive features to
mark them outside the enduring desire for his wife's presence.

There had been a visit of sharp disturbance once when her customary
letter failed him, and the tardy missive coming, carried an inexplicable
coldness that dealt him a pain which, however, did not long survive a
little judicious reflection and a very deluge of letters from Paris that
shook him with their unusual ardor.

May had come again, and at its approach Faraday with the impatience
of a hundred lovers hastened across the seas to join his Eleanor.

It was evening and Eleanor paced to and fro in her room, making the
last of a series of efforts that she had been putting forth all day to fight
down a misery of the heart, against which her reason was in armed
rebellion. She had tried the strategy of simply ignoring its presence, but
the attempt had failed utterly. During her daily walk it had embodied
itself in every object that her eyes rested upon. It had enveloped her
like a smoke mist, through which Paris looked more dull than the desolation of Sahara.

She had thought to displace it with work, but, like the disturbing
element in the chemist's crucible, it rose again and again overspreading the
surface of her labor.

Alone in her room, the hour had come when she meant to succeed
by the unaided force of reason—proceeding first to make herself bodily
comfortable in the folds of a majestic flowing gown, in which she looked
a distressed goddess.

Her hair hung heavy and free about her shoulders, for those reasoning powers were to be spurred by a plunging of white fingers into the golden mass.

In this dishevelled state Eleanor's presence seemed too large for the room and its delicate furnishings. The place fitted well an Eleanor in repose but not an Eleanor who swept the narrow confines like an incipient cyclone.

Reason did good work and stood its ground bravely, but against it were the too great odds of a woman's heart, backed by the soft prejudices of a far-reaching heredity.

She finally sank into a chair before her pretty writing desk. The golden head fell upon the outspread arms waiting to receive it, and she burst into a storm of sobs and tears. It was the signal of surrender.

It is a gratifying privilege to be permitted to ignore the reason of such unusual disturbance in a woman of Eleanor's high qualifications. The cause of that abandonment of grief will never be learned unless she chooses to disclose it herself.

When Faraday first folded his wife in his arms he saw but the Eleanor of his constant dreams. But he soon began to perceive how more beautiful she had grown; with a richness of coloring and fullness of health that Plymdale had never been able to bestow. And the object of her stay in Paris was gaining fast to accomplishment, for she had already acquired a knowledge of French that would not require much longer to perfect.

They sat together in her room discussing plans for the summer, when a timid knock at the door caused Eleanor to look up, to see the little housemaid eyeing her with the glance of a fellow conspirator and holding in her hand a card that she suffered to be but partly visible.

Eleanor hastily approached her, and reading the name upon the card thrust it into her pocket, exchanging some whispered words with the girl, among which were audible, "excuse me," "engaged," "another time." She came back to her husband looking a little flustered, to resume the conversation where it had been interrupted and he offered no inquiries about her mysterious caller.

Entering the salon not many days later he found that in doing so he interrupted a conversation between his wife and a very striking looking gentleman who seemed on the point of taking his leave.

They were both disconcerted; she especially, in bowing, almost thrusting him out, had the appearance of wanting to run away; to do any thing but meet her husband's glance.

He asked with assumed indifference who her friend might be.

"Oh, no one special," with a hopeless attempt at brazenness.

He accepted the situation without protest, only indulging the reflection that Eleanor was losing something of her frankness.

But when his wife asked him on another occasion to dispense with her company for a whole afternoon, saying that she had an urgent call upon her time, he began to wonder if there might not be modifications to this marital liberty of which he was so staunch an advocate.

She left him with a hundred little endearments that she seemed to have acquired with her French.

He forced himself to the writing of a few urgent letters, but his restlessness did not permit him to do more.

It drove him to ugly thoughts, then to the means of dispelling them.

He gazed out of the window, wondered why he was remaining indoors, and followed up the reflection by seizing his hat and plunging out into the street.

The Paris boulevards of a day in early summer are calculated to dispel almost any ache but one of that nature, which was making itself incipiently felt with Faraday.

It was at that stage when it moves a man to take exception at the inadequacy of every thing that is offered to his contemplation or entertainment.

The sun was too hot.

The shop windows were vulgar; lacking artistic detail in their make-up.

How could he ever have found the Paris women attractive? They had lost their chic. Most of them were scrawny—not worth looking at.

He thought to go and stroll through the galleries of art. He knew Eleanor would wish to be with him; then he was tempted to go alone.

Finally, more tired from inward than outward restlessness, he took refuge at one of the small tables of a café, called for a "Mazarin," and, so seated for an unheeded time, let the panorama of Paris pass before his indifferent eyes.

When suddenly one of the scenes in this shifting show struck him with stunning effect.

It was the sight of his wife riding in a fiacre with her caller of a few days back, both conversing and in high spirits.

He remained for a moment enervated, then the blood came tingling back into his veins like fire, making his finger ends twitch with a desire (full worthy of any one of the "prejudiced masses") to tear the scoundrel from his seat and paint the boulevard red with his villainous blood.

A rush of wild intentions crowded into his brain.

Should he follow and demand an explanation? Leave Paris without ever looking into her face again? and more not worthy of the man.

It is right to say that his better self and better senses came quickly back to him.

That first revolt was like the unwilling protest of the flesh against the surgeon's knife before a man has steeled himself to its endurance.

Every thing came back to him from their short, common past—their dreams, their large intentions for the shaping of their lives. Here was the first test, and should he be the one to cry out, "I cannot endure it."

When he returned to the pension, Eleanor was impatiently waiting for him in the entry, radiant with gladness at his coming.

She was under a suppressed excitement that prevented her noting his disturbed appearance.

She took his listless hand and led him into the small drawing-room that adjoined their sleeping chamber.

There stood her companion of the fiacre, smiling as was she at the pleasure of introducing him to another Eleanor disposed on the wall in the best possible light to display the gorgeous radiance of her wonderful beauty and the skill of the man who had portrayed it.

The most sanguine hopes of Eleanor and her artist could not have anticipated anything like the rapture with which Faraday received this surprise.

"Monsieur l'Artiste" went away with his belief in the undemonstrative-ness of the American very much shaken; and in his pocket substantial evidence of American appreciation of art.

Then the story was told how the portrait was intended as a surprise for his arrival. How there had been delay in its completion. The artist had required one more sitting, which she gave him that day, and the two had brought the picture home in the fiacre, he to give it the final advantages of a judicious light; to witness its effect upon Mons. Faraday and finally the excusable wish to be presented to the husband of the lady who had captivated his deepest admiration and esteem.

"You shall take it home with you," said Eleanor.

Both were looking at the lovely creation by the soft light of a reckless expenditure of bougie.

"Yes, dearest," he answered, with feeble elation at the prospect of returning home with that exquisite piece of inanimation.

"Have you engaged your return passage?" she asked.

She sat at his knee, arrayed in the gown that had one evening clothed such a goddess in distress.

"Oh, no. There's plenty time for that," was his answer. "Why do you ask?"

"I'm sure I don't know," and after a while:

"Charlie, I think—I mean, don't you think—I have made wonderful progress in French?"

"You've done marvels, Nellie. I find no difference between your French and Mme. Clairegobeau's, except that yours is far prettier."

"Yes?" she rejoined, with a little squeeze of the hand.

"I mayn't be right and I want you to give me your candid opinion. I believe Mme. Belaire—now that I have gone so far—don't you think— hadn't you better engage passage for two?"

His answer took the form of a pantomimic rapture of assenting grate- fulness, during which each gave speechless assurance of a love that could never more take a second place.

"Nellie," he asked, looking into the face that nestled in close reach of his warm kisses, "I have often wanted to know, though you needn't tell it if it doesn't suit you," he added, laughing, "why you once failed to write to me, and then sent a letter whose coldness gave me a week's heart trouble?"

She flushed, and hesitated, but finally answered him bravely, "It was when—when you cared so much for that Kitty Beaton."

Astonishment for a moment deprived him of speech.

"But Eleanor! In the name of reason! It isn't possible!"

"I know all you would say," she replied, "I have been over the whole ground myself, over and over, but it is useless. I have found that there are certain things which a woman can't philosophize about, any more than she can about death when it touches that which is near to her."

"But you don't think—"

"Hush! don't speak of it ever again. I think nothing!" closing her eyes, and with a little shudder drawing closer to him.

As he kissed his wife with passionate fondness, Faraday thought, "I love her none the less for it, but my Nellie is only a woman, after all."

With man's usual inconsistency, he had quite forgotten the episode of the portrait.

Miss Witherwell's Mistake

It was seldom that the Saturday edition, of the Boredomville *Battery* appeared with its pages ungraced by a contribution from Miss Frances Witherwell's lively and prolific pen. If it were not a tale of passion, acted beneath those blue and southern skies—traditionally supposed to foster the growth of soft desire, and whither she loved to cast her lines—it might be an able treatise on "The Wintering of Canaries," or "Security Against the Moth." I recall at the moment, a paper for which the matrons of Boredomville were themselves much beholden to the spinster, Miss Witherwell, entitled, "A Word to Mothers."

Her neat and pretty home standing on the outskirts of the town, proved that she held nothing in common with that oft-cited Mrs. Jelleby, who has served not a little to bring the female litterateur into disrepute. Indeed, many of her most pungent conceptions are known to have come to her, whilst engaged in some such domestic occupation as sprinkling camphor in the folds of the winter curtains, or lining trunks with tar-paper, to prevent moths. And she herself tells of that poetic, enigmatic inspiration "Trust Not!" having flashed upon her, whilst she stood at the pantry-shelf washing with her own safe hands, her cut-glass goblets in warm soap-suds.

Being exact and punctilious in her working methods, and moreover, holding a moneyed interest in the *Battery*, she stood well with the staff of that journal. With promptness and precision that seldom miscarried, her article was handed in on Wednesday; the following Friday found her in the editorial rooms, proof before her. Then, with eagle eye to detect, and bold hand to eliminate, she removed the possibility of those demoniac vagaries, in which the type-setter proverbially delights.

59

One crisp November morning, a letter came to Miss Witherwell. It was from her brother Hiram, a St. Louis merchant, who had removed from Boredomville with his modest capital, when he sagaciously detected signs of commercial paralysis falling upon that otherwise attractive town. The letter threw Miss Witherwell into a singular flutter of contending sensations; announcing as it did, a visit from her niece, Mildred. Naturally to a maiden lady of fixed and lofty intellectual and other habits, there could only be a foretaste of disturbance in such an announcement. That the girl had had a love affair, made the situation none the more inviting to Miss Witherwell, for whom two such divergent cupids, as love in real life, and love in fiction, held themselves at widely distant points of view. It was hoped that a visit to her aunt, would help to turn the fair Mildred's thoughts from a lover, to whom her parents strongly objected. Not on any ground touching his personality, as Hiram Witherwell informed his sister; for the young man possessed the desirable qualifications of gentle birth, exceptional education, and no pronounced bad habits. Yet, was he so ineligible, from the well understood, worldly standpoint, that not for a moment, could he be thought a fitting mate for Mildred. Mr. Witherwell went on to say that his daughter had behaved well, in the somewhat painful matter of submitting to her parents' wishes. The young man had been no less tractable; indeed, he had lately quitted St Louis; and Mr. Witherwell felt hopeful, that time and change of scene would bring Mildred back to them completely reconciled, poor child, to the wordly wisdom of those who know the world so much better than she.

Miss Witherwell's agitation upon the receipt of this letter, resolved itself into a kind of folded and practical resignation, which moved her to the inspection of the cakebox. She remembered her niece as a girl of twelve, afflicted with a morbid craving for sweets, which might have survived her young ladyhood; possibly, too, she had retained the habits of teasing Mouchette, and bothering the cook out of her seven senses. Her astonishment partook therefore of the nature of a shock, at beholding the tall, handsome girl who kissed her effusively, and greeted her with an impressive, "dear aunt Frances" and brought into the quiet household a whiff of ozone that actually waked the slumbering songsters.

So little of the hoyden of twelve remained in this well mannered young lady of nineteen, that it was, with hesitancy, that Miss Witherwell passed her the large cake at tea, and was well pleased to find one recognizable trait enduring in spite of years and thwarted love.

"I very much fear, my dear, that such attractions as Boredomville can offer will prove inadequate in reconciling you to this temporary separation from the more varied enjoyments of your St. Louis life," said Miss Witherwell to her niece, with a dignity vastly impressive, but quite ordinary, with the august spinster.

"You mistake my purpose in coming to you, dear aunt, if you fancy I am seeking vain enjoyment," answered the girl, spreading a generous layer of delicious peach jam on her third slice of buttered bread. "The joys of life, with much of its sorrows, I hope, lie behind me. If I could feel sure that the future held some field of usefulness! Let me trouble you for half a cup of that exquisite tea—thanks, aunt Frances—as I was saying— another lump of sugar, please—some field of usefulness; don't you know, that would serve to draw me out of myself; that would let me forget my own troubles in lightening the misery of others."

"Ah! to have tasted the bitter cup so young," thought Miss Witherwell; "poor girl! poor heart!" But being an undemonstrative woman she said nothing; only coughed behind her hand, and then looked gloomily down whilst she rolled a very large napkin and forced it into the compass of a very small ring.

A few eventful days went by, in which Mildred gathered mild solace from the sympathetic hearing which her aunt lent to the unfolding of her pessimistic views of life. At last there came some very ugly weather, and with it, what Miss Witherwell called one of her "staying colds."

"Mildred, my dear," she said to her niece on a Friday morning, when icy honors held possession of out-doors, "I shall ask you to do me a service to-day. I have observed that however inclement the weather may be, it does not deter you from your daily walk. And you are right. Therein, lies the secret of the canker at your heart, having left the bloom in your cheek untouched." Then laying a finger lightly on the girl's glowing cheek, "You will stop at the office of the *Battery*, will you not, my dear? and say that I sent you. There will be no impropriety, else I should not want you to go. Ask to see the proof of my article which will appear to- morrow, and look it carefully over, correcting all errors. If you should encounter difficulties, Mr. Wilson will gladly assist you in meeting them." "Mr. Wilson?" "Yes, the new assistant editor; a charming young man whom I find much more amenable than Hudson Jones."

The wind and an open umbrella helped to hurry her over the glassy street, and as the driving sleet pricked her glowing face like sharp needles, Mildred clutched tragically at her ulster, muttering, "Wilson, Wilson;

heaven and earth, what memories!'' Her heart sank as she realized how common the name was. Had she ever looked into a newspaper that it had not confronted her with its prefixes of Johns, Toms or Harrys, and usually, heaven save the mark, in the police record. In yielding to her parents' wishes, and shutting Roland Wilson out of her life, Mildred meant and hoped to put him as effectually from out of her heart. Much help that promised to count, was at hand, in her happy and healthful youth with its unbounded resources, but!—

After bewildering the small Cerberus, who mounted guard at the head of the editorial stairs, with the glaringly unbelievable announcement that she was "Miss Witherwell," and then, making known her errand to a person whose province in life seemed the acceptance of any and everything with impartial resignation, she was politely seated at a desk and left to her own devices, and Miss Witherwell's proof.

The situation was certainly new, and she thought extremely interesting, as she flutteringly settled herself and qualified for her unaccustomed task by a generous moistening of her Faber No. 2 between the prettiest of red lips. She was quick enough to detect errors, and at the same time to feel her ignorance of what she knew must be technical methods of correction. She looked about her for the outside assistance which her aunt suggested, but she was quite alone in the small room that was separated from an adjoining one by a light partition. Through the door that stood ajar she could hear that some one was at work. By leaning and peering forward she saw the angle of a shirt-sleeved arm. A further craning of the neck and she caught sight of a shoulder, a leg, and a section of a blonde head that made her heart leap and beat in a most undisciplined manner. Another and more comprehensive look into the adjoining room revealed to her Roland Wilson standing behind a high desk. She trembled lest he should see her; then grew faint at the possibility of his *not* seeing her. When the latter contingency seemed likely to become a certainty, she coughed, an aggressive little cough, and so probably unreal and unlike anything which had ever afflicted her before, that it failed to bring the hoped-for recognition from Roland Wilson. A second and third repetition of that exasperating little cough, finally moved the young man to the consciousness that some female, with a trouble of the larynx, was somewhere in his *too* close vicinity, and turning to close the door and shut out the interruption, he saw Mildred, pale and red—almost crying, but most certainly laughing, looking up at him.

There was a rapturous meeting of outstretched hands, followed by a moment of hesitancy. Uncertainty on his part—indecision on hers. Then a spontaneous pressure of the yet clasped hands, warm and full of assurance from each. If little Cerberus had not been so near, and if there had not been the likelihood of sudden interruption, there is every reason to believe the cordiality of this unlooked-for meeting would have waxed much more emphatic; for surely, youth and red lips are temptations.

"Mildred, child! this passes my understanding," said Miss Witherwell on the following morning to her niece, as she looked over her article in the *Battery*, "The Use and Abuse of the Corset," an unusually strong thing, Hudson Jones had pronounced it—handled in that free, fearless, almost heroic style, permitted to so well established a veteran in journalism as Miss Witherwell. Never before had anything from her pen appeared in so slovenly garb. Instinctively she sent her pencil dashing through it in cabalistic correction. The defects were grievous; the errata appalling!

"Can it be possible you saw Mr. Wilson?" she asked. "A tall, light young man?"

"Oh! yes, aunt, quite certain. Tall as you say, and fair; with dark-blue eyes like two deep wells of thought; a man to remind one of celestial music, and a silky moustache. Oh! I'm quite sure!"

"Humph! that will do; I dare say it was he; but not in his proper mind."

"Well, aunt Frances, I admit that I don't believe he saw it."

"What?" turning upon her in blank surprise.

"Yes; you see, I tried to correct the thing—I mean the article—myself, and didn't know how. Mr. Wilson was willing enough to help me, but I bundled it up and told him it was all right. You know, yourself, aunt Frances, it isn't a theme any girl would like to dwell upon with a young man—highly indelicate. I couldn't have done it."

"False modesty, indeed; perniciously false! This confession implies a serious error in your bringing up, and I wonder at your father for it."

Mildred begged permission to vindicate herself on the following week, and so skilfully did she perform her task; in such trim and pleasing shape did "Some Errors in Modern Elocution" appear, on the following Saturday, that Miss Witherwell was ready to forgive. Thereafter, as the winter was very inclement and Miss Witherwell's cold clung to her with more than the persistency of a lover, besides the lady thought it was well to give her niece something to keep her out of mischief, Mildred was entrusted with the proud task of correcting Miss Witherwell's proof-sheets, once a week, at the *Battery* office.

The days crept into midwinter, and Mildred had yet shown no disposition to return home. This was considered a good omen by all, and no interference was offered to what seemed a whimsical idea of hers, to linger so long in Boredomville.

Mildred sat one day, deep in a comfortable arm-chair on one side the pleasant grate-fire, that was throwing dim and fitful lights into the cosy room. Miss Witherwell occupied the other side, but not in the same lounging attitude as her niece. Miss Witherwell, the elder, sat prim and upright. The canaries were dead asleep under the dark cover that she had thrown over their cage; and Mouchette lay curled on the rug, insensible to any world but that which haunts feline dreams.

"Aunt," said Mildred, moved by a sudden impulse to be communicative, "do you know, I have a little story in my mind: a little love story."

"Ah!" exclaimed Miss Witherwell in pleased surprise; and seizing the poker she drove it into the soft yielding coal with an emphasis that started a burst of joyous, dancing lights. What she *thought* was, that a happy deliverance from love-sickness and a colorless future had come to her niece in the form of this pleasing vocation. What she *said* was: "Have you thought it out fully? I shall be pleased to hear the synopsis."

"No," returned Mildred, dubiously fixing her gaze far in the fire and clasping her hands over her knee. "That's where I want your help, don't you know, to complete it. You see, it's about two lovers—"

"Yes, certainly. It is a very proper number."

"They, poor things, have been separated by a cruel, unjust fate or by a sordid parent. What do you think of the situation?"

"An excellent one," said Miss Witherwell, approvingly. "Not altogether new, yet with capabilities of development. Well?"

"Well, he's just the noblest, the truest of men, with every honorable instinct that a human being could possess."

"Be careful not to overdraw, Mildred."

"Yes, to be sure. That is an important point I had forgotten. In short, however, he has everything in his favor, save wealth. And they love each other—oh, devotedly! But they submit to what seems an inevitable decree and part, thinking never to meet again; then this same capricious fate brings them once more together, under peculiar circumstances."

"That might be made extremely effective," interrupted Miss Witherwell, her bold imagination crowded with situations which offered only the difficulty of a choice.

"This is the point where I need your advice, aunt. Bear in mind that being brought—almost forced together—through outside influences, they grow to love each other to desperation."

"Your hero must now perform some act to ingratiate himself with the obdurate parent," spoke Miss Witherwell, didactically, but warmly. "Let him save the father from some imminent peril—a railroad accident— a shipwreck. Let him, by some clever combination, avert a business catastrophe—let him—"

"No, no, aunt! I can't force situations. You'll find I'm extremely realistic. The only point for consideration is, to marry or not to marry; that is the question."

Miss Witherwell looked at her niece, aghast. "The poison of the realistic school has certainly tainted and withered your fancy in the bud, my dear, if you hesitate a moment. Marry them, most certainly, or let them die."

"Thanks, aunt Frances; I believe your suggestion is worth consideration."

This ended the conversation; but, needless to say, Miss Witherwell took a keen, though unobtrusive interest in the course of her niece's love story, and she could not so far do violence to her journalistic habit that had become second nature, as to withhold points that were always gratefully received.

"I think I shall end it to-day, aunt; you shall know the dénouement this evening," said Mildred, as she started for her accustomed Friday afternoon visit to the *Battery* office.

It was later than her usual hour for returning. The lamps had long been lighted, and Miss Witherwell had grown first a little impatient at her niece's prolonged absence, then disturbed; and was finally becoming alarmed, when she heard the garden gate slam. This was the signal with her to pour boiling water on the tea, which having done, she reseated herself with regained composure.

Mildred entered the room, followed by a tall young man whose handsome, open countenance beamed with happiness.

"Mr. Wilson," said Miss Witherwell, advancing toward him with dignity and extending her hand, "I am pleased to see you, and glad that you should have accompanied my niece home. An unseemly hour for her to have been on the streets alone," with a reproving glance at Mildred. "Pray be seated, and permit me to offer you a cup of tea."

The young man stood erect and unbending before her, not offering to take the hand which she held out to him.

"Miss Witherwell," he said, "before accepting your hospitality, I must make a disclosure!"

Miss Witherwell sank into a chair under pressure of a premonitory suspicion.

"He only wants to tell you the end of my story, aunt Frances," said Mildred, kneeling upon the low cushion which stood beside her aunt's chair, and at the same time taking that lady's hand in both hers. Then she turned toward Roland Wilson, saying : "Come, Roland, I know that aunt Frances will forgive us; for I have only followed her advice in closing my little love story with the happiest of marriages!"

Roland Wilson is now editor in chief of the Boredomville *Battery*, and is in a fair way to realize a handsome competence, if not a large fortune. Hiram Witherwell has grown reconciled to the match, and is secretly very proud of his son-in-law. Miss Witherwell still writes her brilliant articles for the *Battery;* she has grown older in years, but not in reality; indeed, the company and proximity of her niece and nephew has so brightened and cheered her, that she seems to grow younger every day; and is often heard to say, in her decided manner, that no mistake was ever more lucky.

With the Violin

"And he over the mantel-piece with big black eyes, and such long black hair, and a violin; is he your brother too, Papa Konrad? And why do you keep a green branch always hanging over his picture?"

"No, that is not my brother, Sophie; that is an angel whom the good God allowed once, to save a poor desperate human being from sin and death."

"But where are his wings, Papa Konrad? I never saw an angel look like that; and so black too!"

"There *are* some angels without wings, little Grissel. Not many I admit; but I have known a few."

"Tell us how he saved the poor desperate man, Papa Konrad."

"Well, Sophie, if you will brush up the hearth like a good little house-wife; and Ernst throw some coals on the fire; and little Grissel come and sit here on my knee, I will try to tell you the story. It happened a good many years ago—as you little ones count them. As many years, I suppose, as Ernst has been living in the world, How old are you, Ernst?"

"Ten years old, going on eleven."

"Then it was before your time, for it happened just twelve years ago to-night. My! but that was a cold night!"

"Colder than it is to-night, Papa Konrad?"

"Oh, far, far colder. There was no snow on the ground as there is to-night, but the air seemed filtered through ice. People hurried from one shop to another to keep away from the cold. And the coachmen, driving their fine carriages, were wrapped in great furs till only their eyes peeped out. All the shops were ablaze; but there were not many, on such a night, willing to stand and look into their windows. Yet there stood the poor devil I am going to tell you about, looking into a jeweler's big show-case, where the workmen had just laid aside their tools. Those watch-menders, whom you have seen wearing a big round glass in one eye, you know."

"That's what you are—a watch-mender, isn't it, Papa Konrad?"

"To be sure, Sophie. Well, he had been inside, asking for work, and there was none for him. He had said to himself before going in, this shall be my last trial. So now he stood looking absently in at the window; the frozen air penetrating his body; for his clothes were thin and few. He was hungry, and very, very miserable. Only think, he was in a strange city, without friends, and without work, and with no money. He still had a little room, away up in the top story of a very high, rickety old building."

"How high was the building, Papa Konrad? I bet, not so high as the little windows of the Cathedral steeple."

"No, no, Ernst, not so high, but quite high enough, that when he reached the top he was faint and exhausted from mounting the stairs. I believe that little room was colder than out-doors. At any rate, it was more cheerless. Another lump of coal on the fire, Ernst; that's a fine boy, and how strong! Little Grissel is not sleeping? that's well. The broken windows were rattling in their loose casings, and the bitter cold was sweeping in gusts down the bleak chimney, through the empty fire-place and into the room. He went in and sat right down—for he had no great coat to stop and take off, you know. He spread his arms out on the table, and stared blankly before him through the window, into the darkness. But I think he saw nothing save his own heart that was sore and tired, and did not care to beat any longer and keep him alive. It seemed to him as if the world had pushed him aside; as if mankind had shut him out from a share in their common existence, and left him alone with a misery that he could no longer bear. The truth is, he wanted to die, and he was so reckless he never thought if the good God wanted him to go or not, before he was called. He just wanted to die; and he had something in his pocket that was going to help him end his unhappy life."

"I know: it was a pistol, and he was going to shoot himself."

"No, Ernst, it was not a pistol. He had none; nor money to buy one either. It was only a little white deadly powder. On the mantle-shelf there was a cracked tea cup, and an end of candle which he lighted. He wiped out the cup—for it was dusty, and he wanted that his poison be clean, at least—and in it he emptied the powder. Then he went to the pitcher to get water to pour on it; but the water was all frozen, through and through. However, a little thing like that was not going to stop him. He took the rusty poker; held it in the flame of the candle till it was pretty hot, and with it he melted a little of the ice at a time, till he had what water he needed. Never mind the poker, Ernst; put it down. We don't want to heat that one; and you scatter the ashes that Sophie just swept so nicely. Well, he went back to the table and seated himself; this time with the cup before him, and he closed his eyes a moment—not hesitatingly— only while he might bid good-bye to life, as it were. As he sat thus, there suddenly broke upon the stillness, a long low wail, like the voice of a soul that begs. Oh! but it was soft and exquisite, and it sent a quiver through the frame of the poor wretch who heard it. That sweetness of sound seemed to swell and grow broader till it filled the little room with melody such as you never heard in your lives, children. Such a blending of tones! pleading, chiding, singing out in the night. He at the table sat spellbound: now with wide-open eyes; for he was no longer in his cold bleak room. His blood tingled with a genial warmth. Hundreds of lights were blazing. He was a little boy again, happy of heart, seated between father and mother in a grand theater, and listening to the same wonderful music that came to him now. Ah! that would have been a moment to die in. But this enchanting voice had made him forget that he wanted to die. It had brought youth, and love, and trust, back to his old heart."

"Papa Konrad, it must have been the angels, singing on Christmas eve!"

"That is what the poor creature thought at first himself, Sophie. What he did was to get up, and dash his cup of poison into the empty fireplace. Then he fell on his knees and wept, and thanked the good God who had chosen this way to speak to him. When he arose, he crept close, close to the door to listen, for those heavenly sounds were coming from the next room. When the music had ended—I'm sure, I don't know how he found courage to do it—he rapped gently on the door."

"Wasn't he afraid, Papa Konrad? Suppose it *had* been real angels! oh my!"

"Well, he knew it wasn't such angels as we see in the picture books, Ernst. When he knocked a second time, the door opened, and there stood the young man whose picture you see hanging over the mantlepiece. Standing just that way, with his violin under his arm, his long black hair hanging over his forehead, and his dark eyes full of kindness. He looked puzzled at first; then threw the door wide open, and drew the unhappy man into his room. A lamp was burning brightly, and there was a good fire in the grate. Not such a fine one, to be sure, as Ernst has been making us; but it was like the glow of warm sunlight to the desolate old man. The young musician said nothing, but drew his chair up and looked fixedly at his strange guest. Then he arose, went to a little cupboard, and brought out a loaf of bread, some cheese, and a bottle of beer."

"And butter and jam? Papa Konrad?"

"No, Grissel, I'm afraid there was neither butter nor jam; but I'm sure it tasted like nectar and ambrosia. Make me think to tell you about nectar and ambrosia at our little talk next Sunday. Before the poor devil went to bed that night, he had told everything to the young violin-player; and from that moment he never wanted for a friend again."

"That was a grand, rich young man, wasn't he? And he gave the poor old man plenty money?"

"No, he wasn't rich, Ernst. He had only a little himself; but that little he shared with the other till darkness was past. If we only have patience to wait through the night, children, be sure that day will break at the close of it."

"Where is the young man now, Papa Konrad? Is he dead, and has he got real wings on in heaven?"

"Oh! no, Sophie. Thank God he isn't dead! He is coming to eat his Christmas dinner with me to-morrow."

"But I thought that Herr Ludwig, the great leader of the opera, was coming to eat Christmas dinner with you; and that was why you were going to have such a grand dinner; and said that we might come in and have coffee and cake afterwards!"

"Ah! to be sure—to be sure, Papa Konrad is getting old and forgets things. I hear the mother calling. Maybe Santa Claus has come and lighted the Christmas-tree."

Mrs. Mobry's Reason

I

It was in the springtime and under the blossom-laden branches of an apple tree that Editha Payne finally accepted John Mobry for her husband.

For three years she had been refusing him, with an obstinacy that made people wonder only a little less than they marvelled at the persistence of his desire to marry her. She was simply a nobody—an English girl with antecedents shrouded in obscurity; a governess, moreover; not in her first youth, and none too handsome. But John Mobry was of that class of men who, when they want something, usually keep on wanting it and striving for it so long as there is possibility of attainment in view.

Chance brought him to her that spring day out under the blossoms, at a moment when inward forces were at work with her to weaken and undo the determination of a lifetime.

She looked away from him, far away across the green hills that the sun had touched and quickened, and beyond, into the impenetrable mist. Her tired face wore the look of the conquered who has made a brave fight and would rest.

"Well, John, if you want it," she said, placing her hand in his.

And as she did so she formed the inward resolve that her eyes should never again look into the impenetrable mist. But why she had ever rejected him was something which people kept on asking themselves and each other for the length of time that people will ask such things.

The answer came slowly—twenty-five years later. Most people had forgotten by that time that they ever wanted to know why.

II

Again it was springtime.

A young man who had been trying to read, where he lounged in the deep embrasure of a window, turned to say to the girl who sat playing at the piano:

"Naomi, why is it the spring always comes like a revelation—a delicious surprise?"

"Wait, Sigmund," and she played the closing bars of the piece of music that was open before her, then rising, went to join him at the window.

She was a splendid type of physical health and beauty, lithe, supple, firm of flesh, wearing youth's colors in cheek and lip; youth's gloss and glow in the waves of her thick brown hair. Her brown eyes drowsed and gleamed alternately, and questioned often.

"The spring?" she said, "why does it come like a revelation? How should I know? This is surely reversing roles when you question."

She took the book from his hand to glance carelessly through its pages.

"Do you know, you are a very curious young woman," he said, looking at her with something of admiration, but yet superciliously, for he was young, and a college student. "You gave me the same reply this morning when I asked you—what was it, now, I asked you?"

"To define the quality in Chopin's music that charms me. Well," she continued, "I don't know the 'why' of things. That certain sounds, scenes, impressions move me I know, because I feel it. I don't bother about reasons. Remember, Sigmund, I know so little."

"Oh, you want training, no doubt, and it's an immense pity you've never received it. Let us go through a course together this summer. Do you agree to it?"

He was the lordly collegiate, sure of his weapons.

"I don't believe I do, Sigmund," Naomi laughed. "And if I did it would be useless, for mamma never would consent. You know what she thinks of ologies and isms and all that for women."

"Oh, isms and ologies do not constitute solely the training I have in mind."

"Why, my recollection never goes back to any time when books formed an important feature of my life," she interrupted. "I've lived more than half my days under the sky, galloping over the hills, as often as not with the rain stinging my face. Oh, the open air and all that it teems with! There's nothing like it, Sigmund. What color! Look, now, at the purple wrapping those hills away to the east. See the hundred shades of green spreading before us, with the new-plowed fields between making brown dashes and patches. And then the sky, so blue where it frames those white velvet clouds. They'll be red and gold this evening."

"What a greedy eye you have—a veritable savage eye for pure color. Do you know how to use it? to make it serve you?"

"Oh, no, Sigmund," she said. "Music's the only thing I've studied and learned. Mamma couldn't have prevented that if she'd wanted to, I believe. There's nothing that has the meaning for me in this world that sound has. I feel as if the Truth were going to come to me, some day, through the harmony of it. I wonder if anyone else has an ear so tuned and sharpened as I have, to detect the music, not of the spheres, but of earth, subtleties of major and minor chord that the wind strikes upon the tree branches. Have you ever heard the earth breathe, Sigmund?" she asked, with wide eyes that filled with merriment when she saw the astonishment in his.

Then, half laughing, half singing the gay refrain of a comic opera air, she sprang with quick cat-like movement to her feet, and seizing a foil from against the wall, whirled with it into position in the centre of the room.

Her companion had been as quick to follow. They measured their distances with stately grace, and looked a continuous challenge into each other's eyes. Then for five long minutes, as they stood face to face exchanging skillful thrust and parry, no sound was heard but the clink and scrape of the slender steels; on the hard-wood floor the stamp of advancing feet in the charge. It was only when Mrs. Mobry's long, pale face looked in at the cautiously opened door that the engagement ended.

"Why, Naomi," she said, a little apologetically, coming into the room, "I didn't hear the piano and—"

"And you wondered what disaster could have happened," the girl replied, flushed and amused as she replaced her weapon upon the wall. "I was only giving Cousin Sigmund a lesson with the foils, mamma."

"You know your father comes on the early train to-day, Naomi; he'll be disappointed if you're not at the station to meet him, dear."

"And a perfect right he'd have to be disappointed, and bewildered, too. When have I ever failed him?"

And she quitted the room, making, as she left it, a pass at Sigmund with an imaginary weapon, and laughing gaily as she did so.

Mrs. Mobry went to the piano and gathered together the sheets of music that Naomi had left there in some disorder, and arranged them upon the stand. She had the appearance of seeking occupation; a house full of servants left her little or none of a manual sort; for wealth was one of the things which John Mobry had persistently wanted, long ago.

Mrs. Mobry was past fifty, with her hair, that was turning gray, carefully parted and brushed smooth down upon her temples. When she seated herself and began to rock gently, she drew the cape which she wore closely about her thin shoulders.

"Don't you find it chill, Sigmund," she said, "with that window open? I dare say not, though; young blood is warm."

But Sigmund went and closed the window, making no boast that his veins were scintillant. He only said:

"You're right, Aunt Editha; this early spring air is treacherous."

"I wanted to speak with you a moment alone, dear," she commenced at once, coughing uneasily behind her hand. "It may be, and I trust it is, wholly unnecessary, this caution; but it's best to be open, so far as we can be, in this world. And, of course, when young people are thrown together—"

Sigmund, to quote his thoughts, literally, wondered what his aunt was driving at.

"I only want to say—as you perhaps are not aware of it—that it's our intention, and Naomi's, too, that she shall never marry. As you will be with us all summer I thought it best to acquaint you at once with such little family arrangements, so that we may all feel comfortable and avoid unpleasant consequences." Mrs. Mobry smiled feebly as she said this, and smoothed down the hair on her temples with her long thin hands.

"Has Naomi made you such a promise?" Sigmund asked, thinking it a great pity if she had.

"Oh, there's been no promise, but it has been always understood. I've impressed upon her since she was a little child that she is to remain with me always. It looks selfish—I know it looks selfish; your Uncle John even thinks so, though he has never opposed my wish."

"I see rather a natural instinct in this wish of yours than cold selfishness, Aunt Editha. Something you can't overcome, perhaps. I remember now hearing how fearfully cut up you were two years ago when Edward married."

Mrs. Mobry grew a shade paler, and her voice trembled when she said:

"I can't pardon Edward. It was treacherous, marrying in that way, knowing how I opposed it. It was unfortunate that your uncle should have sent him to take charge of the business in Middleburg. That marriage could not have come about if he had been here at my side, where his place was."

"But, Aunt Editha, it isn't such a calamity after all. He has married a charming woman, and seems perfectly happy. If you would consent to visit him, and were to see his content with your bodily eyes I think you would be reconciled to his coup d'état."

Sigmund thought his aunt Editha rather stupidly set in her ideas. But as he had already recognized the possibility of falling in love with his cousin, Naomi, he was not ill-pleased that Mrs. Mobry had so considerately warned him. If he walked into the fire now it would be with open eyes.

Sigmund was the son of Mr. Mobry's sister; a student of medicine, twenty-two years of age, a little run down and overworked, and hoping for recuperation amid these Western hills. He had visited his uncle's family often as a child, when he and his cousin Edward—two years his senior—had been friends. But his absence this time had lasted four years. He had left Naomi an awkward, boisterous girl of fourteen. When he returned he found that she had undergone a seeming re-creation.

He himself was a good-looking young blond fellow, full of hope and belief in his future; though he tried hard to cultivate an interesting cynicism, which he could never succeed in making anyone believe in.

III

Had Mrs. Mobry's intention been that Sigmund should fall in love with her daughter she could not have designed a plan more Machiavellian than the one she employed. But her only thought had been a caution against marriage. Thus there was no cause to grumble, for she had done her work well and surely.

This caution served Sigmund as his only shield—poor fool; all others he set aside at once. It was more than a shield. It was a license, drawn, signed, stamped and delivered to his conscience, which permitted him to live at Naomi's side with his young nature all unbridled to wound itself, after the manner of young unbridled natures.

They lived such a joyous life during those spring and summer days, and did so many things that were delightful! For must it not have been a delight to rise when the morning was yet gray, and to tramp—high-booted both of them—through the brush of the hillside, crisp and silvered with dew? To silently wait with ready rifle for the young covey to start with sudden whirr from the fence corners? To watch the east begin to fire and set the wet earth sparkling?

But perhaps they liked it better, or certainly as well, when they sat side by side in Naomi's wagonette and went jogging to town, three miles away, behind the fat, lazy pony who always wanted to stop and drink when they crossed the shallow ford of the Meramec, where the water ran like liquid crystal over the shining pebbles beneath. He always wanted to stop, too, and rest under the branches of the big walnut tree that marked the limit of the Mobrys' field. It was a whim of Naomi's to let her pony do what he wanted to, and as often as not he wanted to nibble the grass that grew tender along the edges of the road.

It is no wonder then that their little jogs to town consumed an incredible length of time. Yet what had they to do with time but to waste it? And this they did from morning till night. Sometimes upon the river that twines like a silver ribbon through the green slopes of Southern Missouri, seated in Naomi's slender boat, they floated in mid-stream when the stars or moon were over them. They skirted the banks, gliding under the shade of hanging willows when the sun grew hot and lurid, as it did often when the summer days came.

Then Sigmund's blue eyes saw nothing in all the world so good to look upon as Naomi's brown ones, that filled with wonder at the sweet trouble which stirred her when she caught his gaze and answered it.

There was much reading in books, too, during that summer time. There are many things in books beside isms and ologies. The world has always its poets who sing. And, strangely enough, Sigmund could think of no training so fit for Naomi's untrammelled thought as to follow Lancelot in his loves or Juliet in her hot despair. And Naomi often sighed over such tales, and wept sometimes, for Sigmund told them from his heart, and they seemed very real.

Mrs. Mobry's first care—and John Mobry's, too, for that matter—was always Naomi's health; then, Naomi's happiness. These had been from babyhood so fixed and well established that the mother could surely have been forgiven had she permitted her solicitude to wane sometimes. But this she never did. The color must be always there in Naomi's cheek, or she must know why it was not. When the girl grew languid and dreamy—the summer being hot—the mother must know why it was so.

"I'm sure I don't know, mamma. This heavy heat would make anyone's blood run a little sluggishly, I think."

IV

One morning when the family arose and assembled at an early breakfast, it was to find that Naomi had been up long before and had gone for one of her tramps. The gardener had seen her pass when he left his cottage just at daybreak, and she had called to him: "We are no sluggards to lie abed, Heinrich, when the earth has waked up," so he said.

They thought at every moment she would enter, flushed and dishevelled, to take her place at table. Sigmund was restless because she was not there; Mrs. Mobry anxious, as she gazed constantly from the window and listened to every sound. When the meal ended, and John Mobry was forced to leave for the station without giving Naomi the accustomed morning farewell, it was plainly a thing that gave him annoyance and pain, for that early kiss from the daughter he loved was a day's inspiration to him.

Sigmund went in search of her. He was quite sure she would be up on the summit of that nearest hill, seated upon the rocky plateau that he knew. But she was not there, nor in the oak grove, nor in any of the places where he looked. The time was speeding, and the sun had grown fierce. He retraced his steps, sure that he would find her at home when he reached there. Passing an opening in the wood that led down to the river, and where it was narrow, he turned instinctively, thinking that she might be there by the water, where she loved to sit. And there he found her. But she was across the stream in her boat, resting motionless under the willow branches, her big straw hat hanging down over the side of her face.

"Naomi! oh, Naomi!" Sigmund called.

At the sound of his voice she looked up, then seizing the oars she pulled with vigorous strokes across the water toward the spot where he stood waiting for her. She sprang from the boat, heedless of the aid which he offered, and passing him quickly, hastened up the slope, where she seated herself, when she had reached its summit, upon the huge trunk of a fallen tree.

Sigmund followed in some surprise, and went to sit beside her.

"We mustn't linger here too long, Naomi; Aunt Editha is worried about your absence. Why did you stay so long away? You shouldn't do such cruel things."

"Sigmund," she whispered, and drawing nearer to him twined her arms around his neck. "I want you to kiss me, Sigmund."

Had the earth trembled, that Sigmund shook like that? And had the sky and the air grown red before his eyes? Were his arms turned wooden that they should hang at his side, when hers were around him? He was hoping a senseless hope for strength when she kissed him. Then his arms did their office. He could not help it; he was young and so human. But he sought no further kiss. He only sat motionless with Naomi in his arms; her head resting upon his heart where his pulses had gone mad.

"Ah, Sigmund, this is just as I was dreaming it this morning when I awoke. Then I was angry because you were sleeping off there in your room like a senseless log, when I was awake and wanted you. And you slept on and never came to me. How could you do it? I was angry and went away and walked over the hills. I thought you would come after me, but you never did. I wouldn't go back till you came. And just now, I went in the boat, and when I was out there in the middle of the stream— listen, Sigmund—the sun struck me upon the head, with something in its hand—no, no, not in his hand—"

"Naomi!"

"And after that I didn't care, for I know everything now. I know what the birds are saying up in the trees—"

"Naomi, look at me!"

"Like Siegfried when he played upon his pipe under a tree, last winter in town. I can tell you everything that the fishes say in the water. They were talking under the boat when you called me—"

"Naomi! Oh, God—Naomi, look at me!"

He did look into her eyes then—her eyes that he loved so, and there was no more light in them.

"Aunt Editha," said Sigmund, entering his aunt's room, where she was in restless movement, as she had been all morning— "Aunt Editha,

Naomi is in the library. I left her there. She must have been chilled by the early morning air, I'm afraid. And the sun seems to have made her ill—wait—Aunt Editha—," for Mrs. Mobry had clutched Sigmund's arm with fingers like steel, and was staggering toward the library.

"How dare you tell me Naomi's ill? She can't be ill," she gasped; "she was never ill in all her life."

They had reached the library, and facing the door through which they entered Naomi sat upon a lounge. She was playing like a little child, with scraps of paper that she was tearing and placing in rows upon the cushion beside her. An instant more, and Mrs. Mobry lay in Sigmund's arms like one dead.

But when night came she kneeled, sobbing as a culprit might, at her husband's feet, telling him a broken story that he scarcely heeded in his anguish.

"It has been in the blood that is mine for generations, John, and I knew it, and I married you.

"Oh, God! if it might end with me and with her—my stricken dove! But, John," she whispered with a new terror in her eyes, "Edward has already a child. Others will be born to him, and I see the crime of my marriage reaching out to curse me through the lips of generations that will come."

A No-Account Creole

I

One agreeable afternoon in late autumn two young men stood to-gether on Canal Street, closing a conversation that had evidently begun within the club-house which they had just quitted.

"There's big money in it, Offdean," said the elder of the two. "I would n't have you touch it if there was n't. Why, they tell me Patchly's pulled a hundred thousand out of the concern a'ready."

"That may be," replied Offdean, who had been politely attentive to the words addressed to him, but whose face bore a look indicating that he was closed to conviction. He leaned back upon the clumsy stick which he carried, and continued: "It's all true, I dare say, Fitch; but a decision of that sort would mean more to me than you'd believe if I were to tell you. The beggarly twenty-five thousand's all I have, and I want to sleep with it under my pillow a couple of months at least before I drop it into a slot."

"You'll drop it into Harding & Offdean's mill to grind out the pitiful two and a half per cent commission racket; that's what you 'll do in the end, old fellow—see if you don't."

"Perhaps I shall; but it's more than likely I shan't. We'll talk about it when I get back. You know I 'm off to north Louisiana in the morning"—

"No! What the deuce"—

"Oh, business of the firm."

"Write me from Shreveport, then; or wherever it is."

"Not so far as that. But don't expect to hear from me till you see me. I can't say when that will be."

Then they shook hands and parted. The rather portly Fitch boarded a Prytania Street car, and Mr. Wallace Offdean hurried to the bank in order to replenish his portemonnaie, which had been materially lightened at the club through the medium of unpropitious jack-pots and bobtail flushes.

He was a sure-footed fellow, this young Offdean, despite an occasional fall in slippery places. What he wanted, now that he had reached his twenty-sixth year and his inheritance, was to get his feet well planted on solid ground, and to keep his head cool and clear.

With his early youth he had had certain shadowy intentions of shaping his life on intellectual lines. That is, he wanted to; and he meant to use his faculties intelligently, which means more than is at once apparent. Above all, he would keep clear of the maelstroms of sordid work and senseless pleasure in which the average American business man may be said alternately to exist, and which reduce him, naturally, to a rather ragged condition of soul.

Offdean had done, in a temperate way, the usual things which young men do who happen to belong to good society, and are possessed of moderate means and healthy instincts. He had gone to college, had traveled a little at home and abroad, had frequented society and the clubs, and had worked in his uncle's commission-house; in all of which employments he had expended much time and a modicum of energy.

But he felt all through that he was simply in a preliminary stage of being, one that would develop later into something tangible and intelligent, as he liked to tell himself. With his patrimony of twenty-five thousand dollars came what he felt to be the turning-point in his life,—the time when it behooved him to choose a course, and to get himself into proper trim to follow it manfully and consistently.

When Messrs. Harding & Offdean determined to have some one look after what they called "a troublesome piece of land on Red River," Wallace Offdean requested to be intrusted with that special commission of land-inspector.

A shadowy, ill-defined piece of land in an unfamiliar part of his native State, might, he hoped, prove a sort of closet into which he could retire and take counsel with his inner and better self.

II

What Harding & Offdean had called a piece of land on Red River was better known to the people of Natchitoches* parish as "the old Santien place."

In the days of Lucien Santien and his hundred slaves, it had been very splendid in the wealth of its thousand acres. But the war did its work, of course. Then Jules Santien was not the man to mend such damage as the war had left. His three sons were even less able than he had been to bear the weighty inheritance of debt that came to them with the dismantled plantation; so it was a deliverance to all when Harding & Offdean, the New Orleans creditors, relieved them of the place with the responsibility and indebtedness which its ownership had entailed.

Hector, the eldest, and Grégoire, the youngest of these Santien boys, had gone each his way. Placide alone tried to keep a desultory foothold upon the land which had been his and his forefathers'. But he too was given to wandering—within a radius, however, which rarely took him so far that he could not reach the old place in an afternoon of travel, when he felt so inclined.

There were acres of open land cultivated in a slovenly fashion, but so rich that cotton and corn and weed and "cocoa-grass" grew rampant if they had only the semblance of a chance. The negro quarters were at the far end of this open stretch, and consisted of a long row of old and very crippled cabins. Directly back of these a dense wood grew, and held much mystery, and witchery of sound and shadow, and strange lights when the sun shone. Of a gin-house there was left scarcely a trace; only so much as could serve as inadequate shelter to the miserable dozen cattle that huddled within it in winter-time.

A dozen rods or more from the Red River bank stood the dwelling-house, and nowhere upon the plantation had time touched so sadly as here. The steep, black, moss-covered roof sat like an extinguisher above the eight large rooms that it covered, and had come to do its office so poorly that not more than half of these were habitable when the rain fell. Perhaps the live-oaks made too thick and close a shelter about it. The verandas were long and broad and inviting; but it was well to know that the brick pillar was crumbling away under one corner, that the railing was insecure at another, and that still another had long ago been condemned as unsafe. But that, of course, was not the corner in which Wallace Offdean sat the day following his arrival at the Santien place. This one

---

* Pronounced Nack-e-tosh.

was comparatively secure. A gloire-de-Dijon, thick-leaved and charged with huge creamy blossoms, grew and spread here like a hardy vine upon the wires that stretched from post to post. The scent of the blossoms was delicious; and the stillness that surrounded Offdean agreeably fitted his humor that asked for rest. His old host, Pierre Manton, the manager of the place, sat talking to him in a soft, rhythmic monotone; but his speech was hardly more of an interruption than the hum of the bees among the roses. He was saying:—

"If it would been me myse'f, I would nevair grumb'. W'en a chimbly breck, I take one, two de boys; we patch 'im up bes' we know how. We keep on men' de fence', firs' one place, anudder; an' if it would n' be fer dem mule' of Lacroix—*tonnerre!* I don' wan' to talk 'bout dem mule'. But me, I would n' grumb'. It 's Euphrasie, hair. She say dat's all fool nonsense fer rich man lack Hardin'-Offde'n to let a piece o' lan' goin' lack dat."

"Euphrasie?" questioned Offdean, in some surprise; for he had not yet heard of any such person.

"Euphrasie, my li'le chile. Escuse me one minute," Pierre added, remembering that he was in his shirt-sleeves, and rising to reach for his coat, which hung upon a peg near by. He was a small, square man, with mild, kindly face, brown and roughened from healthy exposure. His hair hung gray and long beneath the soft felt hat that he wore. When he had seated himself, Offdean asked:—

"Where is your little child? I have n't seen her," inwardly marveling that a little child should have uttered such words of wisdom as those recorded of her.

"She yonder to Mme. Duplan on Cane River. I been kine espectin' hair sence yistiday—hair an' Placide," casting an unconscious glance down the long plantation road. "But Mme. Duplan she nevair want to let Euphrasie go. You know it's hair raise' Euphrasie sence hair po' ma die', Mr. Offde'n. She teck dat li'le chile, an' raise it, sem lack she raisin' Ninette. But it 's mo' 'an a year now Euphrasie say dat 's all fool nonsense to leave me livin' 'lone lack dat, wid nuttin' 'cep' dem nigger'—an' Placide once a w'ile. An' she came yair bossin'! My goodness!" The old man chuckled, "Dat 's hair been writin' all dem letter' to Hardin'-Offde'n. If it would been me myse'f"—

III

Placide seemed to have had a foreboding of ill from the start when he found that Euphrasie began to interest herself in the condition of the plantation. This ill feeling voiced itself partly when he told her it was none of her lookout if the place went to the dogs. "It 's good enough for Joe Duplan to run things *en grand seigneur*, Euphrasie; that 's w'at 's spoiled you."

Placide might have done much single-handed to keep the old place in better trim, if he had wished. For there was no one more clever than he to do a hand's turn at any and every thing. He could mend a saddle or bridle while he stood whistling a tune. If a wagon required a brace or a bolt, it was nothing for him to step into a shop and turn out one as deftly as the most skilled blacksmith. Any one seeing him at work with plane and rule and chisel would have declared him a born carpenter. And as for mixing paints, and giving a fine and lasting coat to the side of a house or barn, he had not his equal in the country.

This last talent he exercised little in his native parish. It was in a neighboring one, where he spent the greater part of his time, that his fame as a painter was established. There, in the village of Orville, he owned a little shell of a house, and during odd times it was Placide's great delight to tinker at this small home, inventing daily new beauties and conveniences to add to it. Lately it had become a precious possession to him, for in the spring he was to bring Euphrasie there as his wife.

Maybe it was because of his talent, and his indifference in turning it to good, that he was often called "a no-account creole" by thriftier souls than himself. But no-account creole or not, painter, carpenter, blacksmith, and whatever else he might be at times, he was a Santien always, with the best blood in the country running in his veins. And many thought his choice had fallen in very low places when he engaged himself to marry little Euphrasie, the daughter of old Pierre Manton and a problematic mother a good deal less than nobody.

Placide might have married almost any one, too; for it was the easiest thing in the world for a girl to fall in love with him,— sometimes the hardest thing in the world not to, he was such a splendid fellow, such a careless, happy, handsome fellow. And he did not seem to mind in the least that young men who had grown up with him were lawyers now, and planters, and members of Shakespeare clubs in town. No one ever expected anything quite so humdrum as that of the Santien boys. As youngsters, all three had been the despair of the country schoolmaster; then of the private tutor who had come to shackle them, and had failed in his design. And the state of mutiny and revolt that they had brought about at the college of Grand Coteau when their father, in a moment of weak concession to prejudice, had sent them there, is a thing yet remembered in Natchitoches.

And now Placide was going to marry Euphrasie. He could not recall the time when he had not loved her. Somehow he felt that it began the day when he was six years old, and Pierre, his father's overseer, had called him from play to come and make her acquaintance. He was permitted to hold her in his arms a moment, and it was with silent awe that he did so. She was the first whitefaced baby he remembered having seen, and he straightway believed she had been sent to him as a birthday gift to be his little playmate and friend. If he loved her, there was no great wonder; every one did, from the time she took her first dainty step, which was a brave one, too.

She was the gentlest little lady ever born in old Natchitoches parish, and the happiest and merriest. She never cried or whimpered for a hurt. Placide never did, why should she? When she wept, it was when she did what was wrong, or when he did; for that was to be a coward, she felt. When she was ten, and her mother was dead, Mme. Duplan, the Lady Bountiful of the parish, had driven across from her plantation, Les Chêniers, to old Pierre's very door, and there had gathered up this precious little maid, and carried her away, to do with as she would.

And she did with the child much as she herself had been done by. Euphrasie went to the convent soon, and was taught all gentle things, the pretty arts of manner and speech that the ladies of the "Sacred Heart" can teach so well. When she quitted them, she left a trail of love behind her; she always did.

Placide continued to see her at intervals, and to love her always. One day he told her so; he could not help it. She stood under one of the big oaks at Les Chêniers. It was midsummer time, and the tangled sunbeams had enmeshed her in a golden fretwork. When he saw her standing there in the sun's glamour, which was like a glory upon her, he trembled. He seemed to see her for the first time. He could only look at her, and wonder why her hair gleamed so, as it fell in those thick chestnut waves about her ears and neck. He had looked a thousand times into her eyes before; was it only to-day they held that sleepy, wistful light in them that invites love? How had he not seen it before? Why had he not known before that her lips were red, and cut in fine, strong curves? that her flesh was like cream? How had he not seen that she was beautiful? "Euphrasie," he said, taking her hands,—"Euphrasie, I love you!"

She looked at him with a little astonishment. "Yes; I know, Placide." She spoke with the soft intonation of the creole.

"No, you don't, Euphrasie. I did n' know myse'f how much tell jus' now."

Perhaps he did only what was natural when he asked her next if she loved him. He still held her hands. She looked thoughtfully away, unready to answer.

"Do you love anybody better?" he asked jealously. "Any one jus' as well as me?"

"You know I love papa better, Placide, an' Maman Duplan jus' as well."

Yet she saw no reason why she should not be his wife when he asked her to.

Only a few months before this, Euphrasie had returned to live with her father. The step had cut her off from everything that girls of eighteen call pleasure. If it cost her one regret, no one could have guessed it. She went often to visit the Duplans, however; and Placide had gone to bring her home from Les Chêniers the very day of Offdean's arrival at the plantation.

They had traveled by rail to Natchitoches, where they found Pierre's no-top buggy awaiting them, for there was a drive of five miles to be made through the pine woods before the plantation was reached. When they were at their journey's end, and had driven some distance up the long plantation road that led to the house in the rear, Euphrasie exclaimed:—

"W'y, there's some one on the gall'ry with papa, Placide!"

"Yes; I see."

"It looks like some one f'om town. It mus' be Mr. Gus Adams; but I don' see his horse."

" 'T ain't no one f'om town that I know. It 's boun' to be some one f'om the city."

"Oh, Placide, I should n' wonder if Harding & Offdean have sent some one to look after the place at las'," she exclaimed a little excitedly.

They were near enough to see that the stranger was a young man of very pleasing appearance. Without apparent reason, a chilly depression took hold of Placide.

"I tole you it was n' yo' lookout f'om the firs', Euphrasie," he said to her.

IV

Wallace Offdean remembered Euphrasie at once as a young person whom he had assisted to a very high perch on his clubhouse balcony the previous Mardi Gras night. He had thought her pretty and attractive then, and for the space of a day or two wondered who she might be. But he had not made even so fleeting an impression upon her; seeing which, he did not refer to any former meeting when Pierre introduced them.

She took the chair which he offered her, and asked him very simply when he had come, if his journey had been pleasant, and if he had not found the road from Natchitoches in very good condition.

"Mr. Offde'n only come sence yistiday, Euphrasie," interposed Pierre. "We been talk' plenty 'bout de place, him an' me. I been tole 'im all 'bout it—*va!* An' if Mr. Offde'n want to escuse me now, I b'lieve I go he'p Placide wid dat hoss an' buggy;" and he descended the steps slowly, and walked lazily with his bent figure in the direction of the shed beneath which Placide had driven, after depositing Euphrasie at the door.

"I dare say you find it strange," began Offdean, "that the owners of this place have neglected it so long and shamefully. But you see," he added, smiling, "the management of a plantation does n't enter into the routine of a commission merchant's business. The place has already cost them more than they hope to get from it, and naturally they have n't the wish to sink further money in it." He did not know why he was saying these things to a mere girl, but he went on: "I'm authorized to sell the plantation if I can get anything like a reasonable price for it." Euphrasie laughed in a way that made him uncomfortable, and he thought he would say no more at present,—not till he knew her better, anyhow.

"Well," she said in a very decided fashion, "I know you 'll fin' one or two persons in town who 'll begin by running down the lan' till you would n' want it as a gif', Mr. Offdean; and who will en' by offering to take it off yo' han's for the promise of a song, with the lan' as security again."

They both laughed, and Placide, who was approaching, scowled. But before he reached the steps his instinctive sense of the courtesy due to a stranger had banished the look of ill humor. His bearing was so frank and graceful, and his face such a marvel of beauty, with its dark, rich coloring and soft lines, that the well-clipped and groomed Offdean felt his astonishment to be more than half admiration when they shook hands. He knew that the Santiens had been the former owners of this plantation which he had come to look after, and naturally he expected some sort of co-operation or direct assistance from Placide in his efforts at reconstruction. But Placide proved non-committal, and exhibited an indifference and ignorance concerning the condition of affairs that savored surprisingly of affectation.

He had positively nothing to say so long as the talk touched upon matters concerning Offdean's business there. He was only a little less taciturn when more general topics were approached, and directly after supper he saddled his horse and went away. He would not wait until morning, for the moon would be rising about midnight, and he knew the road as well by night as by day. He knew just where the best fords were across the bayous, and the safest paths across the hills. He knew for a certainty whose plantations he might traverse, and whose fences he might derail. But, for that matter, he would derail what he liked, and cross where he pleased.

Euphrasie walked with him to the shed when he went for his horse. She was bewildered at his sudden determination, and wanted it explained.

"I don' like that man," he admitted frankly; "I can't stan' him. Sen' me word w'en he 's gone, Euphrasie."

She was patting and rubbing the pony, which knew her well. Only their dim outlines were discernible in the thick darkness.

"You are foolish, Placide," she replied in French. "You would do better to stay and help him. No one knows the place so well as you"—

"The place is n't mine, and it 's nothing to me," he answered bitterly. He took her hands and kissed them passionately, but stooping, she pressed her lips upon his forehead.

"Oh!" he exclaimed rapturously, "you do love me, Euphrasie?" His arms were holding her, and his lips brushing her hair and cheeks as they eagerly but ineffectually sought hers.

"Of co'se I love you, Placide. Ain't I going to marry you nex' spring? You foolish boy!" she replied, disengaging herself from his clasp.

When he was mounted, he stooped to say, "See yere, Euphrasie, don't have too much to do with that d——Yankee."

"But, Placide, he is n't a—a—'d——Yankee;' he 's a Southerner, like you,—a New Orleans man."

"Oh, well, he looks like a Yankee." But Placide laughed, for he was happy since Euphrasie had kissed him, and he whistled softly as he urged his horse to a canter and disappeared in the darkness.

The girl stood awhile with clasped hands, trying to understand a little sigh that rose in her throat, and that was not one of regret. When she regained the house, she went directly to her room, and left her father talking to Offdean in the quiet and perfumed night.

V

When two weeks had passed, Offdean felt very much at home with old Pierre and his daughter, and found the business that had called him to the country so engrossing that he had given no thought to those personal questions he had hoped to solve in going there.

The old man had driven him around in the no-top buggy to show him how dismantled the fences and barns were. He could see for himself that the house was a constant menace to human life. In the evenings the three would sit out on the gallery and talk of the land and its strong points and its weak ones, till he came to know it as if it had been his own.

Of the rickety condition of the cabins he got a fair notion, for he and Euphrasie passed them almost daily on horseback, on their way to the woods. It was seldom that their appearance together did not rouse comment among the darkies who happened to be loitering about.

La Chatte, a broad black woman with ends of white wool sticking out from under her *tignon*, stood with arms akimbo watching them as they disappeared one day. Then she turned and said to a young woman who sat in the cabin door:—

"Dat young man, ef he want to listen to me, he gwine quit dat ar caperin' roun' Miss 'Phrasie."

The young woman in the doorway laughed, and showed her white teeth, and tossed her head, and fingered the blue beads at her throat, in a way to indicate that she was in hearty sympathy with any question that touched upon gallantry.

"Law! La Chatte, you ain' gwine hinder a gemman f'om payin' intentions to a young lady w'en he a mine to."

"Dat all I got to say," returned La Chatte, seating herself lazily and heavily on the doorstep. "Nobody don' know dem Sanchun boys bettah 'an I does. Did n' I done part raise 'em? W'at you reckon my ha'r all tu'n plumb w'ite dat-a-way ef it warn't dat Placide w'at done it?"

"How come he make yo' ha'r tu'n w'ite, La Chatte?"

"Dev'ment, pu' dev'ment, Rose. Did n' he come in dat same cabin one day, w'en he warn't no bigga 'an dat Pres'dent Hayes w'at you sees gwine 'long de road wid dat cotton sack 'crost 'im? He come an' sets down by de do', on dat same t'ree-laigged stool w'at you's a-settin' on now, wid his gun in his han', an' he say: 'La Chatte, I wants some croquignoles, an' I wants 'em quick, too.' I 'low: 'G' 'way f'om dah, boy. Don' you see I's flutin' yo' ma's petticoat?' He say: 'La Chatte, put 'side dat ar flutin'-i'on an' dat ar petticoat;' an' he cock dat gun an' p'int it to my head. 'Dar de ba'el,' he say; 'git out dat flour, git out dat butta an' dat aigs; step roun' dah, ole 'oman. Dis heah gun don' quit yo' head tell dem croquignoles is on de table, wid a w'ite tableclof an' a cup o' coffee.' Ef I goes to de ba'el, de gun's a-p'intin'. Ef I goes to de fiah, de gun's a-p'intin'. W'en I rolls out de dough, de gun 's a-p'intin'; an' him neva say nuttin', an' me a-trim'lin' like ole Uncle Noah w'en de mis'ry strike 'im."

"Lordy! w'at you reckon he do ef he tu'n roun' an' git mad wid dat young gemman f'om de city?"

"I don' reckon nuttin'; I knows w'at he gwine do,—same w'at his pa done."

"W'at his pa done, La Chatte?"

"G' 'long 'bout yo' business; you 's axin' too many questions." And La Chatte arose slowly and went to gather her party-colored wash that hung drying on the jagged and irregular points of a dilapidated picket-fence.

But the darkies were mistaken in supposing that Offdean was paying attention to Euphrasie. Those little jaunts in the wood were purely of a business character. Offdean had made a contract with a neighboring mill for fencing, in exchange for a certain amount of uncut timber. He had made it his work—with the assistance of Euphrasie—to decide upon what trees he wanted felled, and to mark such for the woodman's axe.

If they sometimes forgot what they had gone into the woods for, it was because there was so much to talk about and to laugh about. Often, when Offdean had blazed a tree with the sharp hatchet which he carried at his pommel, and had further discharged his duty by calling it "a fine piece of timber," they would sit upon some fallen and decaying trunk, maybe to listen to a chorus of mocking-birds above their heads, or to exchange confidences, as young people will.

Euphrasie thought she had never heard any one talk quite so pleasantly as Offdean did. She could not decide whether it was his manner or the tone of his voice, or the earnest glance of his dark and deep-set blue eyes, that gave such meaning to everything he said; for she found herself afterward thinking of his every word.

One afternoon it rained in torrents, and Rose was forced to drag buckets and tubs into Offdean's room to catch the streams that threatened to flood it. Euphrasie said she was glad of it; now he could see for himself.

And when he had seen for himself, he went to join her out on a corner of the gallery, where she stood with a cloak around her, close up against the house. He leaned against the house, too, and they stood thus together, gazing upon as desolate a scene as it is easy to imagine.

The whole landscape was gray, seen through the driving rain. Far away the dreary cabins seemed to sink and sink to earth in abject misery. Above their heads the live-oak branches were beating with sad monotony against the blackened roof. Great pools of water had formed in the yard, which was deserted by every living thing; for the little darkies had scampered away to their cabins, the dogs had run to their kennels, and the hens were puffing big with wretchedness under the scanty shelter of a fallen wagon-body.

Certainly a situation to make a young man groan with ennui, if he is used to his daily stroll on Canal Street, and pleasant afternoons at the club. But Offdean thought it delightful. He only wondered that he had never known, or some one had never told him, how charming a place an old, dismantled plantation can be—when it rains. But as well as he liked it, he could not linger there forever. Business called him back to New Orleans, and after a few days he went away.

The interest which he felt in the improvement of this plantation was of so deep a nature, however, that he found himself thinking of it constantly. He wondered if the timber had all been felled, and how the fencing was coming on. So great was his desire to know such things that much correspondence was required between himself and Euphrasie, and he watched eagerly for those letters that told him of her trials and vexations with carpenters, bricklayers, and shingle-bearers. But in the midst of it, Offdean suddenly lost interest in the progress of work on the plantation. Singularly enough, it happened simultaneously with the arrival of a letter from Euphrasie which announced in a modest postscript that she was going down to the city with the Duplans for Mardi Gras.

VI

When Offdean learned that Euphrasie was coming to New Orleans, he was delighted to think he would have an opportunity to make some return for the hospitality which he had received from her father. He decided at once that she must see everything: day processions and night parades, balls and tableaux, operas and plays. He would arrange for it all, and he went to the length of begging to be relieved of certain duties that had been assigned him at the club, in order that he might feel himself perfectly free to do so.

The evening following Euphrasie's arrival, Offdean hastened to call upon her, away down on Esplanade Street. She and the Duplans were staying there with old Mme. Carantelle, Mrs. Duplan's mother, a delightfully conservative old lady who had not "crossed Canal Street" for many years.

He found a number of people gathered in the long high-ceiled drawing-room,—young people and old people, all talking French, and some talking louder than they would have done if Madame Carantelle had not been so very deaf.

When Offdean entered, the old lady was greeting some one who had come in just before him. It was Placide, and she was calling him Grégoire, and wanting to know how the crops were up on Red River. She met every one from the country with this stereotyped inquiry, which placed her at once on the agreeable and easy footing she liked.

Somehow Offdean had not counted on finding Euphrasie so well provided with entertainment, and he spent much of the evening in trying to persuade himself that the fact was a pleasing one in itself. But he wondered why Placide was with her, and sat so persistently beside her, and danced so repeatedly with her when Mrs. Duplan played upon the piano. Then he could not see by what right these young creoles had already arranged for the Proteus ball, and every other entertainment that he had meant to provide for her.

He went away without having had a word alone with the girl whom he had gone to see. The evening had proved a failure. He did not go to the club as usual, but went to his rooms in a mood which inclined him to read a few pages from a stoic philosopher whom he sometimes affected. But the words of wisdom that had often before helped him over disagreeable places left no impress tonight. They were powerless to banish from his thoughts the look of a pair of brown eyes, or to drown the tones of a girl's voice that kept singing in his soul.

Placide was not very well acquainted with the city; but that made no difference to him so long as he was at Euphrasie's side. His brother Hector, who lived in some obscure corner of the town, would willingly have made his knowledge a more intimate one; but Placide did not choose to learn the lessons that Hector was ready to teach. He asked nothing better than to walk with Euphrasie along the streets, holding her parasol at an agreeable angle over her pretty head, or to sit beside her in the evening at the play, sharing her frank delight.

When the night of the Mardi Gras ball came, he felt like a lost spirit during the hours he was forced to remain away from her. He stood in the dense crowd on the street gazing up at her, where she sat on the club-house balcony amid a bevy of gayly dressed women. It was not easy to distinguish her, but he could think of no more agreeable occupation than to stand down there on the street trying to do so.

She seemed during all this pleasant time to be entirely his own, too. It made him very fierce to think of the possibility of her not being entirely his own. But he had no cause whatever to think this. She had grown conscious and thoughtful of late about him and their relationship. She often communed with herself, and as a result tried to act toward him as an engaged girl would toward her *fiancé.* Yet a wistful look came sometimes into the brown eyes when she walked the streets with Placide, and eagerly scanned the faces of passers-by.

Offdean had written her a note, very studied, very formal, asking to see her a certain day and hour, to consult about matters on the plantation, saying he had found it so difficult to obtain a word with her, that he was forced to adopt this means, which he trusted would not be offensive.

This seemed perfectly right to Euphrasie. She agreed to see him one afternoon—the day before leaving town—in the long, stately drawing-room, quite alone.

It was a sleepy day, too warm for the season. Gusts of moist air were sweeping lazily through the long corridors, rattling the slats of the half-closed green shutters, and bringing a delicious perfume from the courtyard where old Charlot was watering the spreading palms and brilliant par-terres. A group of little children had stood awhile quarreling noisily under the windows, but had moved on down the street and left quietness reigning.

Offdean had not long to wait before Euphrasie came to him. She had lost some of that ease which had marked her manner during their first acquaintance. Now, when she seated herself before him, she showed a disposition to plunge at once into the subject that had brought him there. He was willing enough that it should play some rôle, since it had been his pretext for coming; but he soon dismissed it, and with it much restraint that had held him till now. He simply looked into her eyes, with a gaze that made her shiver a little, and began to complain because she was going away next day and he had seen nothing of her; because he had wanted to do so many things when she came—why had she not let him?

"You fo'get I'm no stranger here," she told him. "I know many people. I've been coming so often with Mme. Duplan. I wanted to see mo' of you, Mr. Offdean"—

"Then you ought to have managed it; you could have done so. It 's—it 's aggravating," he said, far more bitterly than the subject warranted, "when a man has so set his heart upon something."

"But it was n' anything ver' important," she interposed; and they both laughed, and got safely over a situation that would soon have been strained, if not critical.

Waves of happiness were sweeping through the soul and body of the girl as she sat there in the drowsy afternoon near the man whom she loved. It mattered not what they talked about, or whether they talked at all. They were both scintillant with feeling. If Offdean had taken Euphrasie's hands in his and leaned forward and kissed her lips, it would have seemed to both only the rational outcome of things that stirred them. But he did not do this. He knew now that overwhelming passion was taking possession of him. He had not to heap more coals upon the fire; on the contrary, it was a moment to put on the brakes, and he was a young gentleman able to do this when circumstances required.

However, he held her hand longer than he needed to when he bade her good-by. For he got entangled in explaining why he should have to go back to the plantation to see how matters stood there, and he dropped her hand only when the rambling speech was ended.

He left her sitting by the window in a big brocaded armchair. She drew the lace curtain aside to watch him pass in the street. He lifted his hat and smiled when he saw her. Any other man she knew would have done the same thing, but this simple act caused the blood to surge to her cheeks. She let the curtain drop, and sat there like one dreaming. Her eyes, intense with the unnatural light that glowed in them, looked steadily into vacancy, and her lips stayed parted in the half-smile that did not want to leave them.

Placide found her thus, a good while afterward, when he came in, full of bustle, with theatre tickets in his pocket for the last night. She started up, and went eagerly to meet him.

"W'ere have you been, Placide?" she asked with unsteady voice, placing her hands on his shoulders with a freedom that was new and strange to him.

He appeared to her suddenly as a refuge from something, she did not know what, and she rested her hot cheek against his breast. This made him mad, and he lifted her face and kissed her passionately upon the lips.

She crept from his arms after that, and went away to her room, and locked herself in. Her poor little inexperienced soul was torn and sore. She knelt down beside her bed, and sobbed a little and prayed a little. She felt that she had sinned, she did not know exactly in what; but a fine nature warned her that it was in Placide's kiss.

VII

The spring came early in Orville, and so subtly that no one could tell exactly when it began. But one morning the roses were so luscious in Placide's sunny parterres, the peas and bean-vines and borders of strawberries so rank in his trim vegetable patches, that he called out lustily, "No mo' winta, Judge!" to the staid Judge Blount, who went ambling by on his gray pony.

"There 's right smart o' folks don't know it, Santien," responded the judge, with occult meaning that might be applied to certain indebted clients back on the bayou who had not broken land yet. Ten minutes later the judge observed sententiously, and apropos of nothing, to a group that stood waiting for the post-office to open:—

"I see Santien 's got that noo fence o' his painted. And a pretty piece o' work it is," he added reflectively.

"Look lack Placide goin' pent mo' 'an de fence," sagaciously snickered 'Tit-Edouard, a strolling *maigre-échine* of indefinite occupation. "I seen 'im, me, pesterin' wid all kine o' pent on a piece o' bo'd yistiday."

"I knows he gwine paint mo' 'an de fence," emphatically announced Uncle Abner, in a tone that carried conviction. "He gwine paint de house;

dat what he gwine do. Did n' Marse Luke Williams orda de paints? An' did n' I done kyar' 'em up dah myse'f?"

Seeing the deference with which this positive piece of knowledge was received, the judge coolly changed the subject by announcing that Luke Williams's Durham bull had broken a leg the night before in Luke's new pasture ditch,—a piece of news that fell among his hearers with telling, if paralytic effect.

But most people wanted to see for themselves these astonishing things that Placide was doing. And the young ladies of the village strolled slowly by of afternoons in couples and arm in arm. If Placide happened to see them, he would leave his work to hand them a fine rose or a bunch of geraniums over the dazzling white fence. But if it chanced to be 'Tit-Edouard or Luke Williams, or any of the young men of Orville, he pretended not to see them, or to hear the ingratiating cough that accompanied their lingering footsteps.

In his eagerness to have his home sweet and attractive for Euphrasie's coming, Placide had gone less frequently than ever before up to Natchitoches. He worked and whistled and sang until the yearning for the girl's presence became a driving need; then he would put away his tools and mount his horse as the day was closing, and away he would go across bayous and hills and fields until he was with her again. She had never seemed to Placide so lovable as she was then. She had grown more womanly and thoughtful. Her cheek had lost much of its color, and the light in her eyes flashed less often. But her manner had gained a something of pathetic tenderness toward her lover that moved him with an intoxicating happiness. He could hardly wait with patience for that day in early April which would see the fulfillment of his lifelong hopes.

After Euphrasie's departure from New Orleans, Offdean told himself honestly that he loved the girl. But being yet unsettled in life, he felt it was no time to think of marrying, and, like the worldly-wise young gentleman that he was, resolved to forget the little Natchitoches girl. He knew it would be an affair of some difficulty, but not an impossible thing, so he set about forgetting her.

The effort made him singularly irascible. At the office he was gloomy and taciturn; at the club he was a bear. A few young ladies whom he called upon were astonished and distressed at the cynical views of life which he had so suddenly adopted.

When he had endured a week or more of such humor, and inflicted it upon others, he abruptly changed his tactics. He decided not to fight against his love for Euphrasie. He would not marry her,—certainly not; but he would let himself love her to his heart's bent, until that love should die a natural death, and not a violent one as he had designed. He abandoned himself completely to his passion, and dreamed of the girl by day and thought of her by night. How delicious had been the scent of her hair, the warmth of her breath, the nearness of her body, that rainy day when they stood close together upon the veranda! He recalled the glance of her honest, beautiful eyes, that told him things which made his heart beat fast now when he thought of them. And then her voice! Was there another like it when she laughed or when she talked! Was there another woman in the world possessed of so alluring a charm as this one he loved!

He was not bearish now, with these sweet thoughts crowding his brain and thrilling his blood; but he sighed deeply, and worked languidly, and enjoyed himself listlessly.

One day he sat in his room puffing the air thick with sighs and smoke, when a thought came suddenly to him—an inspiration, a very message from heaven, to judge from the cry of joy with which he greeted it. He sent his cigar whirling through the window, over the stone paving of the street, and he let his head fall down upon his arms, folded upon the table.

It had happened to him, as it does to many, that the solution of a vexed question flashed upon him when he was hoping least for it. He positively laughed aloud, and somewhat hysterically. In the space of a moment he saw the whole delicious future which a kind fate had mapped out for him: those rich acres upon the Red River his own, bought and embellished with his inheritance; and Euphrasie, whom he loved, his wife and companion throughout a life such as he knew now he had craved for,—a life that, imposing bodily activity, admits the intellectual repose in which thought unfolds.

Wallace Offdean was like one to whom a divinity had revealed his vocation in life,—no less a divinity because it was love. If doubts assailed him of Euphrasie's consent, they were soon stilled. For had they not spoken over and over to each other the mute and subtle language of reciprocal love—out under the forest trees, and in the quiet night-time on the plantation when the stars shone? And never so plainly as in the stately old drawing-room down on Esplanade Street. Surely no other speech was needed then, save such as their eyes told. Oh, he knew that she loved him; he was sure of it! The knowledge made him all the more eager now to hasten to her, to tell her that he wanted her for his very own.

VIII

If Offdean had stopped in Natchitoches on his way to the plantation, he would have heard something there to astonish him, to say the very least; for the whole town was talking of Euphrasie's wedding, which was to take place in a few days. But he did not linger. After securing a horse at the stable, he pushed on with all the speed of which the animal was capable, and only in such company as his eager thoughts afforded him.

The plantation was very quiet, with that stillness which broods over broad, clean acres that furnish no refuge for so much as a bird that sings. The negroes were scattered about the fields at work, with hoe and plow, under the sun, and old Pierre, on his horse, was far off in the midst of them.

Placide had arrived in the morning, after traveling all night, and had gone to his room for an hour or two of rest. He had drawn the lounge close up to the window to get what air he might through the closed shutters. He was just beginning to doze when he heard Euphrasie's light footsteps approaching. She stopped and seated herself so near that he could have touched her if he had but reached out his hand. Her nearness banished all desire to sleep, and he lay there content to rest his limbs and think of her.

The portion of the gallery on which Euphrasie sat was facing the river, and away from the road by which Offdean had reached the house. After fastening his horse, he mounted the steps, and traversed the broad hall that intersected the house from end to end, and that was open wide. He found Euphrasie engaged upon a piece of sewing. She was hardly aware of his presence before he had seated himself beside her.

She could not speak. She only looked at him with frightened eyes, as if his presence were that of some disembodied spirit.

"Are you not glad that I have come?" he asked her. "Have I made a mistake in coming?" He was gazing into her eyes, seeking to read the meaning of their new and strange expression.

"Am I glad?" she faltered. "I don' know. W'at has that to do? You 've come to see the work, of co'se. It 's—it 's only half done, Mr. Offdean. They would n' listen to me or to papa, an' you did n' seem to care."

"I have n't come to see the work," he said, with a smile of love and confidence. "I am here only to see you,—to say how much I want you, and need you—to tell you how I love you."

She rose, half choking with words she could not utter. But he seized her hands and held her there.

"The plantation is mine, Euphrasie,—or it will be when you say that you will be my wife," he went on excitedly. "I know that you love me"—

"I do not!" she exclaimed wildly. "W'at do you mean? How do you dare," she gasped, "to say such things w'en you know that in two days I shall be married to Placide?" The last was said in a whisper; it was like a wail.

"Married to Placide!" he echoed, as if striving to understand,—to grasp some part of his own stupendous folly and blindness. "I knew nothing of it," he said hoarsely. "Married to Placide! I would never have spoken to you as I did, if I had known. You believe me, I hope? Please say that you forgive me."

He spoke with long silences between his utterances.

"Oh, there is n' anything to fo'give. You 've only made a mistake. Please leave me, Mr. Offdean. Papa is out in the fiel', I think, if you would like to speak with him. Placide is somew'ere on the place."

"I shall mount my horse and go see what work has been done," said Offdean, rising. An unusual pallor had overspread his face, and his mouth was drawn with suppressed pain. "I must turn my fool's errand to some practical good," he added, with a sad attempt at playfulness; and with no further word he walked quickly away.

She listened to his going. Then all the wretchedness of the past months, together with the sharp distress of the moment, voiced itself in a sob: "O God—O my God, he'p me!"

But she could not stay out there in the broad day for any chance comer to look upon her uncovered sorrow.

Placide heard her rise and go to her room. When he had heard the key turn in the lock, he got up, and with quiet deliberation prepared to go out. He drew on his boots, then his coat. He took his pistol from the dressing-bureau, where he had placed it a while before, and after examining its chambers carefully, thrust it into his pocket. He had certain work to do with the weapon before night. But for Euphrasie's presence he might have accomplished it very surely a moment ago, when the hound— as he called him—stood outside his window. He did not wish her to know anything of his movements, and he left his room as quietly as possible, and mounted his horse, as Offdean had done.

"La Chatte," called Placide to the old woman, who stood in her yard at the washtub, "w'ich way did that man go?"

"W'at man dat? I is n' studyin' 'bout no mans; I got 'nough to do wid dis heah washin'. 'Fo' God, I don' know w'at man you 's talkin' 'bout"—

"La Chatte, w'ich way did that man go? Quick, now!" with the deliberate tone and glance that had always quelled her.

"Ef you 's talkin' 'bout dat Noo Orleans man, I could 'a' tole you dat. He done tuck de road to de cocoa-patch," plunging her black arms into the tub with unnecessary energy and disturbance.

"That 's enough. I know now he 's gone into the woods. You always was a liar, La Chatte."

"Dat his own lookout, de smoove-tongue' raskil," soliloquized the woman a moment later. "I done said he did n' have no call to come heah, caperin' roun' Miss 'Phrasie."

Placide was possessed by only one thought, which was a want as well,—to put an end to this man who had come between him and his love. It was the same brute passion that drives the beast to slay when he sees the object of his own desire laid hold of by another.

He had heard Euphrasie tell the man she did not love him, but what of that? Had he not heard her sobs, and guessed what her distress was? It needed no very flexible mind to guess as much, when a hundred signs besides, unheeded before, came surging to his memory. Jealousy held him, and rage and despair.

Offdean, as he rode along under the trees in apathetic despondency, heard some one approaching him on horseback, and turned aside to make room in the narrow pathway.

It was not a moment for punctilious scruples, and Placide had not been hindered by such from sending a bullet into the back of his rival. The only thing that stayed him was that Offdean must know why he had to die.

"Mr. Offdean," Placide said, reining his horse with one hand, while he held his pistol openly in the other, "I was in my room 'w'ile ago, and yeared w'at you said to Euphrasie. I would 'a' killed you then if she had n' been 'longside o' you. I could 'a' killed you jus' now w'en I come up behine you."

"Well, why did n't you?" asked Offdean, meanwhile gathering his faculties to think how he had best deal with this madman.

"Because I wanted you to know who done it, an' w'at he done it for."

"Mr. Santien, I suppose to a person in your frame of mind it will make no difference to know that I 'm unarmed. But if you make any attempt upon my life, I shall certainly defend myself as best I can."

"Defen' yo'se'f, then."

"You must be mad," said Offdean, quickly, and looking straight into Placide's eyes, "to want to soil your happiness with murder. I thought a creole knew better than that how to love a woman."

"By——! are you goin' to learn me how to love a woman?"

"No, Placide," said Offdean eagerly, as they rode slowly along; "your own honor is going to tell you that. The way to love a woman is to think first of her happiness. If you love Euphrasie, you must go to her clean. I love her myself enough to want you to do that. I shall leave this place tomorrow; you will never see me again if I can help it. Is n't that enough for you? I 'm going to turn here and leave you. Shoot me in the back if you like; but I know you won't." And Offdean held out his hand.

"I don' want to shake han's with you," said Placide sulkily. "Go 'way f'om me."

He stayed motionless watching Offdean ride away. He looked at the pistol in his hand, and replaced it slowly in his pocket; then he removed the broad felt hat which he wore, and wiped away the moisture that had gathered upon his forehead.

Offdean's words had touched some chord within him and made it vibrant; but they made him hate the man no less.

"The way to love a woman is to think firs' of her happiness," he muttered reflectively. "He thought a creole knew how to love. Does he reckon he 's goin' to learn a creole how to love?"

His face was white and set with despair now. The rage had all left it as he rode deeper on into the wood.

IX

Offdean rose early, wishing to take the morning train to the city. But he was not before Euphrasie, whom he found in the large hall arranging the breakfast-table. Old Pierre was there too, walking slowly about with hands folded behind him, and with bowed head.

A restraint hung upon all of them, and the girl turned to her father and asked him if Placide were up, seemingly for want of something to say. The old man fell heavily into a chair, and gazed upon her in the deepest distress.

"Oh, my po' li'le Euphrasie! my po' li'le chile! Mr. Offde'n, you ain't no stranger."

"*Bon Dieu!* Papa!" cried the girl sharply, seized with a vague terror. She quitted her occupation at the table, and stood in nervous apprehension of what might follow.

"I yaired people say Placide was one no-'count creole. I nevair want to believe dat, me. Now I know dat 's true. Mr. Offde'n, you ain't no stranger, you."

Offdean was gazing upon the old man in amazement.

"In de night," Pierre continued, "I yaired some noise on de winder. I go open, an' dere Placide, standin' wid his big boot' on, an' his w'ip w'at he knocked wid on de winder, an' his hoss all saddle'. Oh, my po' li'le chile! He say, 'Pierre, I yaired say Mr. Luke William' want his house pent down in Orville. I reckon I go git de job befo' somebody else teck it.' I say, 'You come straight back, Placide?' He say, 'Don' look fer me.' An w'en I ax 'im w'at I goin' tell to my li'le chile, he say, 'Tell Euphrasie Placide know better 'an anybody livin' w'at goin' make her happy.' An' he start 'way; den he come back an' say, 'Tell dat man'—I don' know who he was talk' 'bout—'tell 'im he ain't goin' learn nuttin' to a creole.' *Mon Dieu! Mon Dieu!* I don' know w'at all dat mean."

He was holding the half-fainting Euphrasie in his arms, and stroking her hair.

"I always yaired say he was one no-'count creole. I nevair want to believe dat."

"Don't—don't say that again, papa," she whisperingly entreated, speaking in French. "Placide has saved me!"

"He has save' you f'om w'at, Euphrasie?" asked her father, in dazed astonishment.

"From sin," she replied to him under her breath.

"I don' know w'at all dat mean," the old man muttered, bewildered, as he arose and walked out on the gallery.

Offdean had taken coffee in his room, and would not wait for breakfast. When he went to bid Euphrasie good-by, she sat beside the table with her head bowed upon her arm.

He took her hand and said good-by to her, but she did not look up.

"Euphrasie," he asked eagerly, "I may come back? Say that I may—after a while."

She gave him no answer, and he leaned down and pressed his cheek caressingly and entreatingly against her soft thick hair.

"May I, Euphrasie?" he begged. "So long as you do not tell me no, I shall come back, dearest one."

She still made him no reply, but she did not tell him no.

So he kissed her hand and her cheek,—what he could touch of it, that peeped out from her folded arm,—and went away.

An hour later, when Offdean passed through Natchitoches, the old town was already ringing with the startling news that Placide had been dismissed by his *fiancée*, and the wedding was off, information which the young creole was taking the trouble to scatter broadcast as he went.

For Marse Chouchoute

"An' now, young man, w'at you want to remember is this—an' take it fer yo' motto: 'No monkey-shines with Uncle Sam.' You undastan'? You aware now o' the penalties attached to monkey-shinin' with Uncle Sam. I reckon that 's 'bout all I got to say; so you be on han' promp' to-morrow mornin' at seven o'clock, to take charge o' the United States mail-bag."

This formed the close of a very pompous address delivered by the postmaster of Cloutierville to young Armand Verchette, who had been appointed to carry the mails from the village to the railway station three miles away.

Armand—or Chouchoute, as every one chose to call him, following the habit of the Creoles in giving nicknames—had heard the man a little impatiently.

Not so the negro boy who accompanied him. The child had listened with the deepest respect and awe to every word of the rambling admonition.

"How much you gwine git, Marse Chouchoute?" he asked, as they walked down the village street together, the black boy a little behind. He was very black, and slightly deformed; a small boy, scarcely reaching to the shoulder of his companion, whose castoff garments he wore. But Chouchoute was tall for his sixteen years, and carried himself well.

"W'y, I'm goin' to git thirty dolla' a month, Wash; w'at you say to that? Betta 'an hoein' cotton, ain't it?" He laughed with a triumphant ring in his voice.

But Wash did not laugh; he was too much impressed by the importance of this new function, too much bewildered by the vision of sudden wealth which thirty dollars a month meant to his understanding.

He felt, too, deeply conscious of the great weight of responsibility which this new office brought with it. The imposing salary had confirmed the impression left by the postmaster's words.

"*You* gwine git all dat money? Sakes! W'at you reckon Ma'ame Verchette say? I know she gwine mos' take a fit w'en she heah dat."

But Chouchoute's mother did not "mos' take a fit" when she heard of her son's good fortune. The white and wasted hand which she rested upon the boy's black curls trembled a little, it is true, and tears of emotion came into her tired eyes. This step seemed to her the beginning of better things for her fatherless boy.

They lived quite at the end of this little French village, which was simply two long rows of very old frame houses, facing each other closely across a dusty roadway.

Their home was a cottage, so small and so humble that it just escaped the reproach of being a cabin.

Every one was kind to Madame Verchette. Neighbors ran in of mornings to help her with her work—she could do so little for herself. And often the good priest, Père Antoine, came to sit with her and talk innocent gossip.

To say that Wash was fond of Madame Verchette and her son is to be poor in language to express devotion. He worshiped her as if she were already an angel in Paradise.

Chouchoute was a delightful young fellow; no one could help loving him. His heart was as warm and cheery as his own southern sunbeams. If he was born with an unlucky trick of forgetfulness—or better, thoughtlessness—no one ever felt much like blaming him for it, so much did it seem a part of his happy, careless nature. And why was that faithful watch-dog, Wash, always at Marse Chouchoute's heels, if it were not to be hands and ears and eyes to him, more than half the time?

One beautiful spring night, Chouchoute, on his way to the station, was riding along the road that skirted the river. The clumsy mail-bag that lay before him across the pony was almost empty; for the Cloutierville mail was a meagre and unimportant one at best.

But he did not know this. He was not thinking of the mail, in fact; he was only feeling that life was very agreeable this delicious spring night.

There were cabins at intervals upon the road—most of them darkened, for the hour was late. As he approached one of these, which was more pretentious than the others, he heard the sound of a fiddle, and saw lights through the openings of the house.

It was so far from the road that when he stopped his horse and peered through the darkness he could not recognize the dancers who passed before the open doors and windows. But he knew this was Gros-Léon's ball, which he had heard the boys talking about all the week.

Why should he not go and stand in the doorway an instant and exchange a word with the dancers?

Chouchoute dismounted, fastened his horse to the fence-post, and proceeded towards the house.

The room, crowded with people young and old, was long and low, with rough beams across the ceiling, blackened by smoke and time. Upon the high mantelpiece a single coal-oil lamp burned, and none too brightly.

In a far corner, upon a platform of boards laid across two flour barrels, sat Uncle Ben, playing upon a squeaky fiddle, and shouting the "figures."

"Ah! *v'là* Chouchoute!" some one called.

"Eh! Chouchoute!"

"Jus' in time, Chouchoute; yere 's Miss Léontine waitin' fer a partna."

"S'lute yo' partnas!" Uncle Ben was thundering forth; and Chouchoute, with one hand gracefully behind him, made a profound bow to Miss Léontine, as he offered her the other.

Now Chouchoute was noted far and wide for his skill as a dancer. The moment he stood upon the floor, a fresh spirit seemed to enter into all present. It was with renewed vigor that Uncle Ben intoned his "Balancy all! Fus' fo' fo'ard an' back!"

The spectators drew close about the couples to watch Chouchoute's wonderful performance; his pointing of toes; his pigeonwings in which his feet seemed hardly to touch the floor.

"It take Chouchoute to show 'em de step, *va!*" proclaimed Gros-Léon, with a fat satisfaction, to the audience at large.

"Look 'im! look 'im yonda! Ole Ben got to work hard' 'an dat, if he want to keep up wid Chouchoute, I tell you!"

So it was; encouragement and adulation on all sides, till, from the praise that was showered on him, Chouchoute's head was soon as light as his feet.

At the windows appeared the dusky faces of negroes, their bright eyes gleaming as they viewed the scene within and mingled their loud guffaws with the medley of sound that was already deafening.

The time was speeding. The air was heavy in the room, but no one seemed to mind this. Uncle Ben was calling the figures now with a rhythmic sing-song:—

"Right an' lef' all 'roun'! Swing co'nas!"

Chouchoute turned with a smile to Miss Félicie on his left, his hand extended, when what should break upon his ear but the long, harrowing wail of a locomotive!

Before the sound ceased he had vanished from the room. Miss Félicie stood as he left her, with hand uplifted, rooted to the spot with astonishment.

It was the train whistling for his station, and he a mile and more away! He knew he was too late, and that he could not make the distance; but the sound had been a rude reminder that he was not at his post of duty.

However, he would do what he could now. He ran swiftly to the outer road, and to the spot where he had left his pony.

The horse was gone, and with it the United States mail-bag!

For an instant Chouchoute stood half-stunned with terror. Then, in one quick flash, came to his mind a vision of possibilities that sickened him. Disgrace overtaking him in this position of trust; poverty his portion again; and his dear mother forced to share both with him.

He turned desperately to some negroes who had followed him, seeing his wild rush from the house:—

"Who saw my hoss? W'at you all did with my hoss, say?"

"Who you reckon tech yo' hoss, boy?" grumbled Gustave, a sullen-looking mulatto. "You did n' have no call to lef' 'im in de road, fus' place."

" 'Pear to me like I heahed a hoss a-lopin' down de road jis' now; did n' you, Uncle Jake?" ventured a second.

"Neva heahed nuttin'—nuttin' 't all, 'cep' dat big-mouf Ben yonda makin' mo' fuss 'an a t'unda-sto'm."

"Boys!" cried Chouchoute, excitedly, "bring me a hoss, quick, one of you. I 'm boun' to have one! I 'm boun' to! I 'll give two dolla' to the firs' man brings me a hoss."

Near at hand, in the "lot" that adjoined Uncle Jake's cabin, was his little creole pony, nibbling the cool, wet grass that he found, along the edges and in the corners of the fence.

The negro led the pony forth. With no further word, and with one bound, Chouchoute was upon the animal's back. He wanted neither saddle nor bridle, for there were few horses in the neighborhood that had not been trained to be guided by the simple motions of a rider's body.

Once mounted, he threw himself forward with a certain violent impulse, leaning till his cheek touched the animal's mane.

He uttered a sharp "Hei!" and at once, as if possessed by sudden frenzy, the horse dashed forward, leaving the bewildered black men in a cloud of dust.

What a mad ride it was! On one side was the river bank, steep in places and crumbling away; on the other, an unbroken line of fencing; now in straight lines of neat planking, now treacherous barbed wire, sometimes the zigzag rail.

The night was black, with only such faint light as the stars were shedding. No sound was to be heard save the quick thud of the horse's hoofs upon the hard dirt road, the animal's heavy breathing, and the boy's feverish "hei-hei!" when he fancied the speed slackened.

Occasionally a marauding dog started from the obscurity to bark and give useless chase.

"To the road, to the road, Bon-à-rien!" panted Chouchoute, for the horse in his wild race had approached so closely to the river's edge that the bank crumbled beneath his flying feet. It was only by a desperate lunge and bound that he saved himself and rider from plunging into the water below.

Chouchoute hardly knew what he was pursuing so madly. It was rather something that drove him; fear, hope, desperation.

He was rushing to the station, because it seemed to him, naturally, the first thing to do. There was the faint hope that his own horse had broken rein and gone there of his own accord; but such hope was almost lost in a wretched conviction that had seized him the instant he saw "Gustave the thief" among the men gathered at Gros-Léon's.

"Hei! hei, Bon-à-rien!"

The lights of the railway station were gleaming ahead, and Chouchoute's hot ride was almost at an end.

With sudden and strange perversity of purpose, Chouchoute, as he drew closer upon the station, slackened his horse's speed. A low fence was in his way. Not long before, he would have cleared it at a bound, for Bon-à-rien could do such things. Now he cantered easily to the end of it, to go through the gate which was there.

His courage was growing faint, and his heart sinking within him as he drew nearer and nearer.

He dismounted, and holding the pony by the mane, approached with some trepidation the young station-master, who was taking note of some freight that had been deposited near the tracks.

"Mr. Hudson," faltered Chouchoute, "did you see my pony 'roun' yere anywhere? an'—an' the mail-sack?"

"Your pony's safe in the woods, Chou'te. The mail-bag's on its way to New Orleans"—

"Thank God!" breathed the boy.

"But that poor little fool darkey of yours has about done it for himself, I guess."

"Wash? Oh, Mr. Hudson! w'at 's—w'at 's happen' to Wash?"

"He's inside there, on my mattress. He's hurt, and he's hurt bad; that's what's the matter. You see the ten forty-five had come in, and she did n't make much of a stop; she was just pushing out, when bless me if that little chap of yours did n't come tearing along on Spunky as if Old Harry was behind him.

"You know how No. 22 can pull at the start; and there was that little imp keeping abreast of her 'most under the thing's wheels.

"I shouted at him. I could n't make out what he was up to, when blamed if he did n't pitch the mail-bag clean into the car! Buffalo Bill could n't have done it neater.

"Then Spunky, she shied; and Wash he bounced against the side of that car and back, like a rubber ball, and laid in the ditch till we carried him inside.

"I've wired down the road for Doctor Campbell to come up on 14 and do what he can for him."

Hudson had related these events to the distracted boy while they made their way toward the house.

Inside, upon a low pallet, lay the little negro, breathing heavily, his black face pinched and ashen with approaching death. He had wanted no one to touch him further than to lay him upon the bed.

The few men and colored women gathered in the room were looking upon him with pity mingled with curiosity.

When he saw Chouchoute he closed his eyes, and a shiver passed through his small frame. Those about him thought he was dead. Chouchoute knelt, choking, at his side and held his hand.

"O Wash, Wash! W'at you did that for? W'at made you, Wash?"

"Marse Chouchoute," the boy whispered, so low that no one could hear him but his friend, "I was gwine 'long de big road, pas' Marse Gros-Léon's, an' I seed Spunky tied dah wid de mail. Dar warn't a minute—

I 'clar', Marse Chouchoute, dar warn't a minute—to fotch you. W'at makes my head tu'n 'roun' dat away?"

"Neva mine, Wash; keep still; don't you try to talk," entreated Chouchoute.

"You ain't mad, Marse Chouchoute?"

The lad could only answer with a hand pressure.

"Dar warn't a minute, so I gits top o' Spunky—I neva seed nuttin' cl'ar de road like dat. I come 'long side—de train—an' fling de sack. I seed 'im kotch it, and I don' know nuttin' mo' 'cep' mis'ry, tell I see you—a-comin' frough de do'. Mebby Ma'ame Verchette know some'pin," he murmured faintly, "w'at gwine make my— head quit tu'nin' 'round dat away. I boun' to git well, 'ca'se who—gwine—watch Marse—Chouchoute?"

The Going Away of Liza

The south-bound mail and express had just pulled away from Bludgitt station. There had been an exchange of mail bags; sundry freight marked "Abner Rydon, Bludgitt Station, Missouri" had been deposited upon the platform and that was all. It was Christmas eve, a raw, chill, Christmas eve, and the air was thick with promise of snow.

A few weazened, shivering men stood with hands plunged in their trouser pockets, watching the train come and go. When the station-master dragged the freight under shelter, depositing some of it within the waiting-room, they all tramped into the room too and proceeded to lounge round the rusty red-hot stove.

Presently a light cart drove up along-side the platform, and one of this leisurely band craning his neck to peer through the begrimed window panes, remarked :

"Thur's Abner, now."

Abner Rydon was a stalwart fellow of thirty. He was stern-visaged, with stubborn determination in the set of his square jaw. The casual glance which he offered the assembled group was neither friendly nor inviting.

"It's a wonder you wouldn't of took the two horse wagon, Ab, with them roads." He paid no attention to the insinuation.

"Seems to me you'd fix that thur road and throw a bridge acrost Bludgitt creek," suggested a second. "If I had your money—"

"If you had my money you wouldn't run the county with it more 'an you do your own," replied Abner as he quitted the room, bearing an armful of freight. Returning for more he was met by further friendly advances:

"I seen a man the other day, Ab, says he run acrost Liza-Jane a couple o' weeks ago in town."

Abner turned quickly upon the speaker, and with a sharp blow of his clenched fist sent him sprawling to the floor. He then continued towards the cart, mounted it, and drove rapidly away over the rough and fast-hardening road, and into the woods beyond.

A burst of hilarity greeted the discomfiture of this too daring speaker.

"Oh, Whillikens! *you* seen a man that run acrost Liza-Jane, did you!" "Anything more to say on the subject of Liza-Jane, Si? Ab ain't got so fur you can't ketch up with him."

Si had risen and was rubbing his injured back as best he could.

"The plague-on-it-fool," he muttered; "if he thinks so much o' that red-cheeked huzzy, what in tarnation did he want to turn her loose to Satan fur!"

When the mirth occasioned by this quickly acted scene had subsided, it left the assembly in a pleasant, reminiscent mood that led naturally to the quiet discussion of Abner Rydon's domestic affairs.

"I always said thet harm would come o' the match," remarked the traditional prophet, "time Almiry told me thet Liza-Jane was goin' to marry Abner Rydon. Why, a blind un could 'a seen they wasn't a matched team. First place, thet gal was all fur readin'—constant readin' in them paper-covered books thet come to her through the mail, an' readin's boun' to fill the mind up with one thing another in time.

"When she'd come an' see Almiry she'd out en' tell by the hour how folks lives in town. How the ladies sets in rockin' cheers by the winders all day imbroidryin' things with their white, jewel fingers; an' how they walks up an' down drawin' rooms disdainful; an' rides in open karridges along the boulyvards, bowin' languid to gents a horseback. She got it all out o' them books, an' she called it the higher life, an' said she hankered fur it, to Almiry."

"I was down here to Bludgitt the mornin' she left," interrupted one whose information was more to the point. "Time I seen her I knowed somthin' was up. Her black eyes was fairly snappin' fire, an' her cheeks was blazin' most as red as the ribband round her nake. She never were back'ard with her talk, an' when I ast whur she was bound fur, she up an' let loose again' Ab, an' mother Rydon, an' thur life of drudgery what was no ixistence."

"Ab never turned her out, did he?"

"Turn her out! Abner Rydon ain't the man to turn a dog from his door. No; they had one o' them everlastin' quarrels what's been a im-bitterin' their married life. She out with the hull thing that day down here to Bludgitt. How they fussed, an' how she endid by tellin' him that no woman born could keep on lovin' a man that hadn't no soul above the commonplaces. How he flung back at her that a woman better quit livin' with a man when she quit kerrin' fur him. She said she didn't ask no better, 'fur,' sa' she, 'I hev that within me, Mr. MicBride, thet craves to taste the joys of ixistence. I hev gathered my belongings; my own in-competence is in my pocket, an' I hev shook the dust of the Rydon threshold from off of my feet forever,' was her own words. An' Si Smith might's well learn to-day as tomorrow that Ab Rydon's goin' to knock any man down that mentions the name o' Liza-Jane to him.''

At every fresh gust of wind that struck the north-west angle of the old Rydon farm-house that night, mother Rydon would give a little jump and clasp the arms of her comfortable chair that she occupied at the fire-side.

"Lands, Abner! I hain't hered the wind a blowin' so since the night the pasture fence was laid low, what's it a doin' out o' doors, anyway. Before dark the hull country was covered with snow. Now the sleet's a strikin' like pebbles again' the window panes.''

"That's just it, mother; sleet an' snow an' wind a tryin' to outdo thurselves,'' said Abner, throwing upon the fire a fresh stick that he had brought from the porch, where a pile of evenly-cut fire wood was stacked.

He sat down beside the table upon which a lamp burned brightly, and opened his newspaper. His features seemed much less harsh than when he faced the roomful of loafers down at Bludgitt. There was a kind ring in his voice.

The two seated so cozily together amid their homely surroundings, resembled each other closely. Only the steadfast look in the eyes of the woman had grown patient with age.

"It's a mercy you went fur the goods to-day, Abner, what with Moll's lame foot, an' the mules loaned fur old man Buckthorn's funeral, you never would hev got the cart through them roads tomorrow. Who'd you see down to Bludgitt?''

"The same old lot at the station, a settin' round the stove. It's a puzzle to me how they live. That McBride don't do work enough to keep him in tobacco. Old Joseph—I guess he ain't able to work. But that Si Smith—

why!" he exclaimed excitedly, "the government ought to take holt of it."

"That's thur business, Abner; 'tain't none o' ours," his mother replied rebukingly. "I'd like if you'd read me the noos, now. An' read about them curious animals."

Abner stretched his fine legs out towards the blaze and began to read from the conglomerate contents of his weekly paper. Old Mother Rydon sat upright, knitting and listening. Abner was reading slowly and carefully:

"This singular animal has seldom been seen by the eye of civilized man, familiar as are the native blacks with his habits and peculiar haunts. The writer—fortunately armed with his trusty—"

"Hold, Abner! Hark!"

"What is it, mother?"

"Seems like I heard something at the door latch, and a movin' on the porch."

"The dogs would bark if any one as much as opened the gate, mother. This talk about the animals has got you worked up."

"No such thing. Thur! I hered it again. Go see, Abner; 'tain't goin' to hurt nothin' to look."

Abner approached the door and opened it abruptly. A wild gust of wind came blowing into the room; beating and lashing as it did so, the bedraggled garments of a young woman who was clinging to the door-post.

"My God!" cried Abner starting back. Mother Rydon in astonishment could only utter : "Liza-Jane! for the land sakes!"

The wind literally drove the woman into the room. Abner stayed there with his hand upon the latch, shaken at what seemed this apparition before him.

Liza-Jane stood like a hunted and hungry thing in the great glow of the firelight, her big dark eyes greedily seizing upon every detail of homely and honest comfort that surrounded her. Her cheeks were not round nor red as they had been. Whatever sin or suffering had swept over her had left its impress upon her plastic being.

As Abner looked at her, of all the voices that clamored in his soul to be heard, that of the outraged husband was the loudest.

When mother Rydon endeavored to remove Liza-Jane's wet and tattered shawl the woman clutched it firmly, turning a frightened and beseeching face upon her husband.

"Abner, son, what air you a waitin' fur?" demanded mother Rydon, standing back.

Mother and son looked for a long instant into each other's eyes. Then Abner approached his wife. With unsteady hands he lifted the soaking garment from her shoulders. When he saw that Liza-Jane's arms fell to her side at his approach, and that two shining tears hung beneath the half closed lids, he knelt upon the floor and took the wet and torn shoes from off her feet.

The Maid of Saint Phillippe

Marianne was tall, supple, and strong. Dressed in her worn buckskin trappings she looked like a handsome boy rather than like the French girl of seventeen that she was. As she stepped from the woods the glimmer of the setting sun dazzled her. An instant she raised her hand—palm outward—to shield her eyes from the glare, then she continued to descend the gentle slope and make her way toward the little village of Saint Phillippe that lay before her, close by the waters of the Mississippi.

Marianne carried a gun across her shoulder as easily as a soldier might. Her stride was as untrammelled as that of the stag who treads his native hill-side unmolested. There was something stag-like, too, in the poise of her small head as she turned it from side to side, to snuff the subtle perfume of the Indian summer. But against the red western sky curling columns of thin blue smoke began to ascend from chimneys in the village. This meant that housewives were already busy preparing the evening meal; and the girl quickened her steps, singing softly as she strode along over the tufted meadow where sleek cattle were grazing in numbers.

Less than a score of houses formed the village of Saint Phillippe, and they differed in no wise from one another except in the matter of an additional room when the prosperity of the owner admitted of such. All were of upright logs, standing firmly in the ground, or rising from a low foundation of stone, with two or more rooms clustering round a central stone chimney. Before each was an inviting porch, topped by the projection of the shingled roof.

Gathered upon such a porch, when Marianne walked into the village, were groups of men talking eagerly and excitedly together with much gesture and intensity of utterance.

The place was Sans-Chagrin's tavern; and Marianne stopped beside the fence, seeing that her father, Picoté Laronce, was among the number who crowded the gallery. But it was not he, it was young Jacques Labrie who when he saw her there came down to where she stood.

"Well, what luck, Marianne?" he asked, noting her equipment.

"Oh, not much," she replied, slapping the game-bag that hung rather slack at her side. "Those idle soldiers down at the fort have no better employment than to frighten the game away out of reach. But what does this talk and confusion mean? I thought all the trouble with monsieur le curé was settled. My father stands quiet there in a corner; he seems to be taking no part. What is it all about?"

"The old grievance of a year ago, Marianne. We were content to grumble only so long as the English did not come to claim what is theirs. But we hear to-day they will soon be at Fort Chartres to take possession."

"Never!" she exclaimed. "Have not the Natchez driven them back each time they attempted to ascend the river? And do you think that watchful tribe will permit them now to cross the line?"

"They have not attempted the river this time. They have crossed the great mountains and are coming from the east."

"Ah," muttered the girl with pale exasperation, "that is a monarch to be proud of! Your Louis who sits in his palace at Versailles and gives away his provinces and his people as if they were baubles! Well, what next?"

"Come, Marianne," said the young man as he joined her outside. "Let me walk to your home with you, I will tell you as we go along. Sans-Chagrin, you know, returned this morning from the West Illinois, and he tells astonishing things of the new trading-post over there—Laclede's village."

"The one they call Saint Louis?" she asked half-heartedly, "where old Toussaint of Kaskaskia has taken his family to live?"

"Old Toussaint is far seeing, Marianne, for Sans-Chagrin says the town across the water is growing as if by enchantment. Already it is double the size of Saint Phillippe and Kaskaskia put together. When the English reach Fort Chartres, St. Ange de Bellerive will relinquish the fort to them, and with his men will cross to Laclede's village—all but Captain Vaudry, who has leave to return to France."

"Capt. Alexis Vaudry will return to France!" she echoed in tones that rose and fell like a song of lamentation. "The English are coming from the east! And all this news has come to-day while I hunted in the forest."

"Do you not see what is in the air, Marianne?" he asked, giving her a sideward cautious glance.

They were at her portal now, and as he followed her into the house she half turned to say to him:

"No, Jacques, I can see no way out of it." She sat down languidly at the table, as though heavy fatigue had suddenly weighted her limbs.

"We hate the English," Jacques began emphatically; leaning upon the table as he stood beside her.

"To be sure, we hate the English," she returned, as though the fact were a self-evident one that needed no comment.

"Well, it is only the eastern province of Louisiana that has been granted to England. There is hardly a man in Saint Phillippe who would not rather die than live subject to that country. But there is no reason to do either," he added smiling. "In a week from now, Marianne, Saint Phillippe will be deserted."

"You mean that the people will abandon their homes, and go to the new trading-post?"

"Yes, that is what I mean."

"But I have heard—I am sure I have heard, long ago, that King Louis made a gift of his Louisiana possessions to his cousin of Spain; that they jointly granted the East Illinois to England. So that leaves the West under the Spanish dominion, Jacques."

"But Spain is not England," he explained, a little disconcerted. "No Frenchman who respects himself will live subject to England," he added fiercely. "All are of one mind—to quit Saint Phillippe at once. All save one, Marianne."

"And that one?"

"Your father."

"My father! Ah, I might have known. What does he say?" she questioned eagerly.

"He says he is old; that he has dwelt here many years——"

"That is true," the girl mused. "I was born here in Saint Phillippe; so were you, Jacques."

"He says," continued the young man, "that he could not dispose of his mill and that he would not leave it."

"His mill—his mill! no!" exclaimed Marianne, rising abruptly, "it is not that. Would you know why my father will never leave Saint Phillippe?" approaching as she said this a rear window whose shutters were partly closed, and throwing them wide open. "Come here, Jacques. That is the reason," pointing with her strong shapely arm to where a wooden cross marked the presence of a grave out under the wide-spreading branches of a maple.

They both stood for a while silently gazing across the grassy slope that reflected the last flickering gleams of the setting sun. Then Jacques muttered as if in answer to some unspoken thought:

"Yes, he loved her very dearly. Surely the better part of himself went with her. And you, Marianne?" he questioned gently.

"I, Jacques? Oh, it is only the old whose memories dwell in graves," she replied a little wearily. "My life belongs to my father. I have but to follow his will; whatever that may be."

Then Marianne left Jacques standing by the open window, and went into the adjoining room to divest herself of her hunting raiment. When she returned she was dressed in the garments that had been her mother's once—a short camlet skirt of sober hue; a green laced bodice whose scantiness was redeemed by a muslin kerchief laid in deep folds across the bosom; and upon her head was the white cap of the French working-woman.

Jacques had lighted the fire for her in the big stone chimney, and gone silently away.

It was indeed true. During that autumn of 1765, a handful of English, under command of Captain Sterling of the Highlanders, crossed the Alleghanies and were coming to take peaceful possession of their hitherto inaccessible lands in the Illinois.

To none did this seem a more hated intrusion than to the people of Saint Phillippe. After the excited meeting at Sans-Chagrin's tavern, all went to work with feverish haste to abandon the village which had been the only home that many of them had ever known. Men, women, and children seemed suddenly possessed with demoniac strength to demolish. Doors, windows, and flooring; everything that could serve in building up the new was rifled from the old. For days there was gathering together and hauling away in rough carts constructed for the sole purpose. Cattle were called from the pasture lands and driven in herds to the north-ward.

When the last of these rebellious spirits was gone, Saint Phillippe stood like the skeleton of its former self; and Picoté Laronce with his daughter found themselves alone amid the desolate hearthstones.

"It will be a dreary life, my child, for you," said the old man, gathering Marianne in a close embrace.

"It will not be dreary," she assured him, disengaging herself to look into his eyes. "I shall have much work to do. We shall forget—try to forget—that the English are at our door. And some time when we are rich in peltries, we will go to visit our friends in that great town that they talk so much about. Do not ever think that I am sad, father, because we are alone."

But the silence was very desolate. So was the sight of those abandoned homes, where smiling faces no longer looked from windows, and where the music of children's laughter was heard no more.

Marianne worked and hunted and grew strong and stronger. The old man was more and more like a child to her. When she was not with him, he would sit for hours upon a rude seat under the maple-tree, with a placid look of content in his old, dim eyes.

One day when Captain Vaudry rode up from Fort Chartres, fine as could be in his gay uniform of a French officer, he found Picoté and Marianne sitting in the solitude hand in hand. He had heard how they had remained alone in Saint Phillippe, and he had come to know if it was true, and to persuade them, if he could, to return with him to France— to La Rochelle, where Picoté had formerly lived. But he urged in vain. Picoté knew no home save that in which his wife had dwelt with him, and no resting-place on earth except where she lay. And Marianne said always the same thing—that her father's will was hers.

But when she came in from her hunt one evening and found him stretched in the eternal sleep out under the maple, at once she felt that she was alone, with no will to obey in the world but her own. Then her heart was as strong as oak and her nerves were like iron. Lovingly she carried him into the house. And when she had wept because he was dead, she lit two blessed candles and placed them at his head and she watched with him all through the still night.

At the break of day she barred the doors and windows, and mounting her fleet Indian pony, away she galloped to the fort, five miles below, to seek the aid she needed.

Captain Vaudry, and others as well, made all haste to Saint Phillippe when they learned this sad thing that had befallen Marianne. Word was sent to the good curé of Kaskaskia, and he came too, with prayer and benediction. Jacques was in Kaskaskia when the tidings of Picoté's death reached there, and with all the speed at his command he hurried to Marianne to help her in her need.

So Marianne was not alone. Good and staunch friends were about her.

When Picoté had been laid to rest—under the maple—and the last blessing had been spoken, the good curé turned to Marianne and said:

"My daughter, you will return with me to Kaskaskia. Your father had many friends in that village, and there is not a door but will open to receive you. It would be unseemly, now he is gone, to live alone in Saint Phillippe."

"I thank you, my father," she answered, "but I must pass this night alone, and in thought. If I decide to go to my good friends in Kaskaskia, I shall ride into town early, upon my pony."

Jacques, too, spoke to her, with gentle persuasion: "You know, Marianne, what I want to say, and what my heart is full of. It is not I alone but my father and mother as well to whom you are dear, and who long to have you with us—one of us. Over there in the new village of Saint Louis a new life has begun for all of us. Let me beg that you will not refuse to share it till you have at least tried——"

She held up her hand in token that she had heard enough and turned resolutely from him. "Leave me, my friend," she said, "leave me alone. Follow the curé, there where he goes. If I so determine, you shall hear from me, if not, then think no longer of Marianne."

So another silent night fell upon Saint Phillippe, with Marianne alone in her home. Not even the dead with her now. She did not know that under the shelter of a neighboring porch Captain Vaudry lay like a sentinel wrapped in his mantle.

Near the outer road, but within the inclosure of Marianne's home, was "the great tree of Saint Phillippe" under which a rude table and benches stood. Here Picoté and his daughter had often taken their humble meals, shared with any passer-by that chose to join them.

Seated there in the early morning was Captain Vaudry when Marianne stepped from her door, in her jerkin of buckskin and her gun across her shoulder.

"What are you doing here, Captain Vaudry?" she asked with startled displeasure when she saw him there.

"I have waited, Marianne. You cannot turn me from you as lightly as you have the others." And then with warm entreaty in his voice he talked to her of France:

"Ah, Marianne, you do not know what life is, here in this wild America. Let the curé of Kaskaskia say the words that will make you my wife, and I will take you to a land, child, where men barter with gold, and not with hides and peltries. Where you shall wear jewels and silks and walk upon soft and velvet carpets. Where life can be a round of pleasure. I do not say these things to tempt you; but to let you know that existence holds joys you do not dream of—that may be yours if you will."

"Enough, Captain Alexis Vaudry! I have sometimes thought I should like to know what it is that men call luxury; and sometimes have felt that I should like to live in sweet and gentle intercourse with men and women. Yet these have been but fleeting wishes. I have passed the night in meditation and my choice is made."

"I love you, Marianne." He sat with hands clasped upon the table, and his handsome enraptured eyes gazing up into her face, as she stood before him. But she went on unheedingly:

"I could not live here in Saint Phillippe or there in Kaskaskia. The English shall never be masters of Marianne. Over the river it is no better. The Spaniards may any day they choose give a rude awakening to those stolid beings who are living on in a half-slumber of content——"

"I love you; oh, I love you, Marianne!"

"Do you not know, Captain Vaudry," she said with savage resistance, "I have breathed the free air of forest and stream, till it is in my blood now. I was not born to be the mother of slaves."

"Oh, how can you think of slaves and motherhood! Look into my eyes, Marianne, and think of love."

"I will not look into your eyes, Captain Vaudry," she murmured, letting the quivering lids fall upon her own, "with your talk and your looks of love—of love! You have looked it before, and you have spoken it before till the strength would go from my limbs and leave me feeble as a little child, till my heart would beat like that of one who has been stricken. Go away, with your velvet and your jewels and your love. Go away to your France and to your treacherous kings; they are not for me."

"What do you mean, Marianne?" demanded the young man, grown pale with apprehension. "You deny allegiance to England and Spain; you spurn France with contempt; what is left for you?"

"Freedom is left for me!" exclaimed the girl, seizing her gun that she lifted upon her shoulder. "Marianne goes to the Cherokees! You cannot stay me; you need not try to. Hardships may await me, but let it be death rather than bondage."

While Vaudry sat dumb with pain and motionless with astonishment; while Jacques was hoping for a message; while the good curé was looking eagerly from his door-step for signs of the girl's approach, Marianne had turned her back upon all of them.

With gun across her shoulder she walked up the gentle slope; her brave, strong face turned to the rising sun.

A Wizard from Gettysburg

It was one afternoon in April, not long ago, only the other day, and the shadows had already begun to lengthen.

Bertrand Delmandé, a fine, bright-looking boy of fourteen years,—fifteen, perhaps,—was mounted, and riding along a pleasant country road, upon a little Creole pony, such as boys in Louisiana usually ride when they have nothing better at hand. He had hunted, and carried his gun before him.

It is unpleasant to state that Bertrand was not so depressed as he should have been, in view of recent events that had come about. Within the past week he had been recalled from the college of Grand Coteau to his home, the Bon-Accueil plantation.

He had found his father and his grand-mother depressed over money matters, awaiting certain legal developments that might result in his permanent withdrawal from school. That very day, directly after the early dinner, the two had driven to town, on this very business, to be absent till the late afternoon. Bertrand, then, had saddled Picayune and gone for a long jaunt, such as his heart delighted in.

He was returning now, and had approached the beginning of the great tangled Cherokee hedge that marked the boundary line of Bon-Accueil, and that twinkled with multiple white roses.

The pony started suddenly and violently at something there in the turn of the road, and just under the hedge. It looked like a bundle of rags at first. But it was a tramp, seated upon a broad, flat stone.

Bertrand had no maudlin consideration for tramps as a species; he had only that morning driven from the place one who was making himself unpleasant at the kitchen window.

But this tramp was old and feeble. His beard was long, and as white as new-ginned cotton, and when Bertrand saw him he was engaged in stanching a wound in his bare heel with a fistful of matted grass.

"What's wrong, old man?" asked the boy, kindly.

The tramp looked up at him with a bewildered glance, but did not answer.

"Well," thought Bertrand, "since it's decided that I'm to be a physician some day, I can't begin to practice too early."

He dismounted, and examined the injured foot. It had an ugly gash. Bertrand acted mostly from impulse. Fortunately his impulses were not bad ones. So, nimbly, and as quickly as he could manage it, he had the old man astride Picayune, whilst he himself was leading the pony down the narrow lane.

The dark green hedge towered like a high and solid wall on one side. On the other was a broad, open field, where here and there appeared the flash and gleam of uplifted, polished hoes, that negroes were plying between the even rows of cotton and tender corn.

"This is the State of Louisiana," uttered the tramp, quaveringly.

"Yes, this is Louisiana," returned Bertrand cheerily.

"Yes, I know it is. I've been in all of them since Gettysburg. Sometimes it was too hot, and sometimes it was too cold; and with that bullet in my head—you don't remember? No, you don't remember Gettysburg."

"Well, no, not vividly," laughed Bertrand.

"Is it a hospital? It is n't a factory, is it?" the man questioned.

"Where we're going? Why, no, it's the Delmandé plantation—Bon-Accueil. Here we are. Wait, I 'll open the gate."

This singular group entered the yard from the rear, and not far from the house. A big black woman, who sat just without a cabin door, picking a pile of rusty-looking moss, called out at sight of them:—

"W'at's dat you's bringin' in dis yard, boy? top dat hoss?"

She received no reply. Bertrand, indeed, took no notice of her inquiry.

"Fu' a boy w'at goes to school like you does—whar's yo' sense?" she went on, with a fine show of indignation; then, muttering to herself, "Ma'ame Bertrand an' Marse St. Ange ain't gwine stan' dat, I knows dey ain't. Dah! ef he ain't done sot 'im on de gall'ry, plumb down in his pa's rockin'-cheer!"

Which the boy had done; seated the tramp in a pleasant corner of the veranda, while he went in search of bandages for his wound.

The servants showed high disapproval, the housemaid following

Bertrand into his grandmother's room, whither he had carried his investigations.

"W'at you tearin' yo' gra'ma's closit to pieces dat away, boy?" she complained in her high soprano.

"I'm looking for bandages."

"Den w'y you don't ax fu' ban'ges, an' lef yo' gra'ma's closit 'lone? You want to listen to me; you gwine git shed o' dat tramp settin' dah naxt to de dinin'-room! W'en de silva be missin', 'tain' you w'at gwine git blame, it's me."

"The silver? Nonsense, 'Cindy; the man's wounded, and can't you see he 's out of his head?"

"No mo' outen his head 'an I is. 'T ain' me w'at want to tres' [trust] 'im wid de sto'-room key, ef he is outen his head," she concluded with a disdainful shrug.

But Bertrand's protégé proved so unapproachable in his long-worn rags, that the boy concluded to leave him unmolested till his father's return, and then ask permission to turn the forlorn creature into the bathhouse, and array him afterward in clean, fresh garments.

So there the old tramp sat in the veranda corner, stolidly content, when St. Ange Delmandé and his mother returned from town.

St. Ange was a dark, slender man of middle age, with a sensitive face, and a plentiful sprinkle of gray in his thick black hair; his mother, a portly woman, and an active one for her sixty-five years.

They were evidently in a despondent mood. Perhaps it was for the cheer of her sweet presence that they had brought with them from town a little girl, the child of Madame Delmandé's only daughter, who was married, and lived there.

Madame Delmandé and her son were astonished to find so uninviting an intruder in possession. But a few earnest words from Bertrand reassured them, and partly reconciled them to the man's presence; and it was with wholly indifferent though not unkindly glances that they passed him by when they entered. On any large plantation there are always nooks and corners where, for a night or more, even such a man as this tramp may be tolerated and given shelter.

When Bertrand went to bed that night, he lay long awake thinking of the man, and of what he had heard from his lips in the hushed starlight. The boy had heard of the awfulness of Gettysburg, till it was like something he could feel and quiver at.

On that field of battle this man had received a new and tragic birth.

For all his existence that went before was a blank to him. There, in the black desolation of war, he was born again, without friends or kindred; without even a name he could know was his own. Then he had gone forth a wanderer; living more than half the time in hospitals; toiling when he could, starving when he had to.

Strangely enough, he had addressed Bertrand as "St. Ange," not once, but every time he had spoken to him. The boy wondered at this. Was it because he had heard Madame Delmandé address her son by that name, and fancied it?

So this nameless wanderer had drifted far down to the plantation of Bon-Accueil, and at last had found a human hand stretched out to him in kindness.

When the family assembled at breakfast on the following morning, the tramp was already settled in the chair, and in the corner which Bertrand's indulgence had made familiar to him.

If he had turned partly around, he would have faced the flower garden, with its graveled walks and trim parterres, where a tangle of color and perfume were holding high revelry this April morning; but he liked better to gaze into the back yard, where there was always movement: men and women coming and going, bearing implements of work; little negroes in scanty garments, darting here and there, and kicking up the dust in their exuberance.

Madame Delmandé could just catch a glimpse of him through the long window that opened to the floor, and near which he sat.

Mr. Delmandé had spoken to the man pleasantly; but he and his mother were wholly absorbed by their trouble, and talked constantly of that, while Bertrand went back and forth ministering to the old man's wants. The boy knew that the servants would have done the office with ill grace, and he chose to be cup-bearer himself to the unfortunate creature for whose presence he alone was responsible.

Once, when Bertrand went out to him with a second cup of coffee, steaming and fragrant, the old man whispered:—

"What are they saying in there?" pointing over his shoulder to the dining-room.

"Oh, money troubles that will force us to economize for a while," answered the boy. "What father and *mé-mère* feel worst about is that I shall have to leave college now."

"No, no! St. Ange must go to school. The war's over, the war's over! St. Ange and Florentine must go to school."

"But if there 's no money," the boy insisted, smiling like one who humors the vagaries of a child.

"Money! money!" murmured the tramp. "The war 's over—money! money!"

His sleepy gaze had swept across the yard into the thick of the orchard beyond, and rested there.

Suddenly he pushed aside the light table that had been set before him, and rose, clutching Bertrand's arm.

"St. Ange, you must go to school!" he whispered. "The war 's over," looking furtively around. "Come. Don't let them hear you. Don't let the negroes see us. Get a spade—the little spade that Buck Williams was digging his cistern with."

Still clutching the boy, he dragged him down the steps as he said this, and traversed the yard with long, limping strides, himself leading the way.

From under a shed where such things were to be found, Bertrand selected a spade, since the tramp's whim demanded that he should, and together they entered the orchard.

The grass was thick and tufted here, and wet with the morning dew. In long lines, forming pleasant avenues between, were peach-trees growing, and pear and apple and plum. Close against the fence was the pomegranate hedge, with its waxen blossoms, brick-red. Far down in the centre of the orchard stood a huge pecan-tree, twice the size of any other that was there, seeming to rule like an old-time king.

Here Bertrand and his guide stopped. The tramp had not once hesitated in his movements since grasping the arm of his young companion on the veranda. Now he went and leaned his back against the pecan-tree, where there was a deep knot, and looking steadily before him he took ten paces forward. Turning sharply to the right, he made five additional paces. Then pointing his finger downward, and looking at Bertrand, he commanded:—

"There, dig. I would do it myself, but for my wounded foot. For I 've turned many a spade of earth since Gettysburg. Dig, St. Ange, dig! The war 's over; you must go to school."

Is there a boy of fifteen under the sun who would not have dug, even knowing he was following the insane dictates of a demented man? Bertrand entered with all the zest of his years and his spirit into the curious adventure; and he dug and dug, throwing great spadefuls of the rich, fragrant earth from side to side.

The tramp, with body bent, and fingers like claws clasping his bony knees, stood watching with eager eyes, that never unfastened their steady gaze from the boy's rhythmic motions.

"That 's it!" he muttered at intervals. "Dig, dig! The war 's over. You must go to school, St. Ange."

Deep down in the earth, too deep for any ordinary turning of the soil with spade or plow to have reached it, was a box. It was of tin, apparently, something larger than a cigar box, and bound round and round with twine, rotted now and eaten away in places.

The tramp showed no surprise at seeing it there; he simply knelt upon the ground and lifted it from its long resting place.

Bertrand had let the spade fall from his hands, and was quivering with the awe of the thing he saw. Who could this wizard be that had come to him in the guise of a tramp, that walked in cabalistic paces upon his own father's ground, and pointed his finger like a divining-rod to the spot where boxes—may be treasures—lay? It was like a page from a wonder-book.

And walking behind this white-haired old man, who was again leading the way, something of childish superstition crept back into Bertrand's heart. It was the same feeling with which he had often sat, long ago, in the weird firelight of some negro's cabin, listening to tales of witches who came in the night to work uncanny spells at their will.

Madame Delmandé had never abandoned the custom of washing her own silver and dainty china. She sat, when the breakfast was over, with a pail of warm suds before her that 'Cindy had brought to her, with an abundance of soft linen cloths. Her little granddaughter stood beside her playing, as babies will, with the bright spoons and forks, and ranging them in rows on the polished mahogany. St. Ange was at the window making entries in a note-book, and frowning gloomily as he did so.

The group in the dining-room were so employed when the old tramp came staggering in, Bertrand close behind him.

He went and stood at the foot of the table, opposite to where Madame Delmandé sat, and let fall the box upon it.

The thing in falling shattered, and from its bursting sides gold came, clicking, spinning, gliding, some of it like oil; rolling along the table and off it to the floor, but heaped up, the bulk of it, before the tramp.

"Here's money!" he called out, plunging his old hand in the thick of it. "Who says St. Ange shall not go to school? The war 's over—here 's money! St. Ange, my boy," turning to Bertrand and speaking with quick authority, "tell Buck Williams to hitch Black Bess to the buggy, and go bring Judge Parkerson here."

Judge Parkerson, indeed, who had been dead for twenty years and more!

"Tell him that—that"—and the hand that was not in the gold went up to the withered forehead, "that—Bertrand Delmandé needs him!"

Madame Delmandé, at sight of the man with his box and his gold, had given a sharp cry, such as might follow the plunge of a knife. She lay now in her son's arms, panting hoarsely.

"Your father, St. Ange,—come back from the dead—your father!"

"Be calm, mother!" the man implored. "You had such sure proof of his death in that terrible battle, this *may* not be he."

"I know him! I know your father, my son!" and disengaging herself from the arms that held her, she dragged herself as a wounded serpent might to where the old man stood.

His hand was still in the gold, and on his face was yet the flush which had come there when he shouted out the name Bertrand Delmandé.

"Husband," she gasped, "do you know me—your wife?"

The little girl was playing gleefully with the yellow coin.

Bertrand stood, pulseless almost, like a young Actæon cut in marble.

When the old man had looked long into the woman's imploring face, he made a courtly bow.

"Madame," he said, "an old soldier, wounded on the field of Gettysburg, craves for himself and his two little children your kind hospitality."

A Shameful Affair

I

Mildred Orme, seated in the snuggest corner of the big front porch of the Kraummer farmhouse, was as content as a girl need hope to be.

This was no such farm as one reads about in humorous fiction. Here were swelling acres where the undulating wheat gleamed in the sun like a golden sea. For silver there was the Meramec—or, better, it was pure crystal, for here and there one might look clean through it down to where the pebbles lay like green and yellow gems. Along the river's edge trees were growing to the very water, and in it, sweeping it when they were willows.

The house itself was big and broad, as country houses should be. The master was big and broad, too. The mistress was small and thin, and it was always she who went out at noon to pull the great clanging bell that called the farmhands in to dinner.

From her agreeable corner where she lounged with her Browning or her Ibsen, Mildred watched the woman do this every day. Yet when the clumsy farmhands all came tramping up the steps and crossed the porch in going to their meal that was served within, she never looked at them. Why should she? Farmhands are not so very nice to look at, and she was nothing of an anthropologist. But once when the half dozen men came along, a paper which she had laid carelessly upon the railing was blown across their path. One of them picked it up, and when he had mounted the steps restored it to her. He was young, and brown, of course, as the sun had made him. He had nice blue eyes. His fair hair was dishevelled. His shoulders were broad and square and his limbs strong and clean. A not unpicturesque figure in the rough attire that bared his throat to view and gave perfect freedom to his every motion.

Mildred did not make these several observations in the half second that she looked at him in courteous acknowledgment. It took her as many days to note them all. For she signaled him out each time that he passed her, meaning to give him a condescending little smile, as she knew how. But he never looked at her. To be sure, clever young women of twenty, who are handsome, besides, who have refused their half dozen offers and are settling down to the conviction that life is a tedious affair, are not going to care a straw whether farmhands look at them or not. And Mildred did not care, and the thing would not have occupied her a moment if Satan had not intervened, in offering the employment which natural conditions had failed to supply. It was summer time; she was idle; she was piqued, and that was the beginning of the shameful affair.

"Who are these men, Mrs. Kraummer, that work for you? Where do you pick them up?"

"Oh, ve picks 'em up everyvere. Some is neighbors, some is tramps, and so."

"And that broad-shouldered young fellow—is he a neighbor? The one who handed me my paper the other day—you remember?"

"Gott, no! You might yust as well say he vas a tramp. Aber he vorks like a steam ingine."

"Well, he's an extremely disagreeable-looking man. I should think you'd be afraid to have him about, not knowing him."

"Vat you vant to be 'fraid for?" laughed the little woman. "He don't talk no more un ven he vas deef und dumb. I didn't t'ought you vas sooch a baby."

"But, Mrs. Kraummer, I don't want you to think I'm a baby, as you say—a coward, as you mean. Ask the man if he will drive me to church to-morrow. You see, I'm not so very much afraid of him," she added with a smile.

The answer which this unmannerly farmhand returned to Mildred's request was simply a refusal. He could not drive her to church because he was going fishing.

"Aber," offered good Mrs. Kraummer, "Hans Platzfeldt will drive you to church, oder vereever you vants. He vas a goot boy vat you can trust, dat Hans."

"Oh, thank him very much. But I find I have so many letters to write to-morrow, and it promises to be hot, too. I shan't care to go to church after all."

She could have cried for vexation. Snubbed by a farmhand! a tramp, perhaps. She, Mildred Orme, who ought really to have been with the rest of the family at Narragansett—who had come to seek in this retired spot the repose that would enable her to follow exalted lines of thought. She marvelled at the problematic nature of farmhands.

After sending her the uncivil message already recorded, and as he passed beneath the porch where she sat, he did look at her finally, in a way to make her positively gasp at the sudden effrontery of the man.

But the inexplicable look stayed with her. She could not banish it.

II

It was not so very hot after all, the next day, when Mildred walked down the long narrow footpath that led through the bending wheat to the river. High above her waist reached the yellow grain. Mildred's brown eyes filled with a reflected golden light as they caught the glint of it, as she heard the trill that it answered to the gentle breeze. Anyone who has walked through the wheat in midsummer-time knows that sound.

In the woods it was sweet and solemn and cool. And there beside the river was the wretch who had annoyed her, first, with his indifference, then with the sudden boldness of his glance.

"Are you fishing?" she asked politely and with kindly dignity, which she supposed would define her position toward him. The inquiry lacked not pertinence, seeing that he sat motionless, with a pole in his hand and his eyes fixed on a cork that bobbed aimlessly on the water.

"Yes, madam," was his brief reply.

"It won't disturb you if I stand here a moment, to see what success you will have?"

"No, madam."

She stood very still, holding tight to the book she had brought with her. Her straw hat had slipped disreputably to one side, over the wavy bronze-brown bang that half covered her forehead. Her cheeks were ripe with color that the sun had coaxed there; so were her lips.

All the other farmhands had gone forth in Sunday attire. Perhaps this one had none better than these working clothes that he wore. A feminine commiseration swept her at the thought. He spoke never a word. She wondered how many hours he could sit there, so patiently waiting for fish to come to his hook. For her part, the situation began to pall, and she wanted to change it at last.

"Let me try a moment, please? I have an idea—"

"Yes, madam."

"The man is surely an idiot, with his monosyllables," she commented inwardly. But she remembered that monosyllables belong to a boor's equipment.

She laid her book carefully down and took the pole gingerly that he came to place in her hands. Then it was his turn to stand back and look respectfully and silently on at the absorbing performance.

"Oh!" cried the girl, suddenly, seized with excitement upon seeing the line dragged deep in the water.

"Wait, wait! Not yet."

He sprang to her side. With his eyes eagerly fastened on the tense line, he grasped the pole to prevent her drawing it, as her intention seemed to be. That is, he meant to grasp the pole, but instead, his brown hand came down upon Mildred's white one.

He started violently at finding himself so close to a bronze-brown tangle that almost swept his chin—to a hot cheek only a few inches away from his shoulder, to a pair of young, dark eyes that gleamed for an instant unconscious things into his own.

Then, why ever it happened, or how ever it happened, his arms were holding Mildred and he kissed her lips. She did not know if it was ten times or only once.

She looked around—her face milk-white—to see him disappear with rapid strides through the path that had brought her there. Then she was alone.

Only the birds had seen, and she could count on their discretion. She was not wildly indignant, as many would have been. Shame stunned her. But through it she gropingly wondered if she should tell the Kraummers that her chaste lips had been rifled of their innocence. Publish her own confusion? No! Once in her room she would give calm thought to the situation, and determine then how to act. The secret must remain her own: a hateful burden to bear alone until she could forget it.

III

And because she feared not to forget it, Mildred wept that night. All day long a hideous truth had been thrusting itself upon her that made her ask herself if she could be mad. She feared it. Else why was that kiss the most delicious thing she had known in her twenty years of life? The sting of it had never left her lips since it was pressed into them. The sweet trouble of it banished sleep from her pillow.

But Mildred would not bend the outward conditions of her life to serve any shameful whim that chanced to visit her soul, like an ugly dream. She would avoid nothing. She would go and come as always.

In the morning she found in her chair upon the porch the book she had left by the river. A fresh indignity! But she came and went as she intended to, and sat as usual upon the porch amid her familiar surroundings. When the Offender passed her by she knew it, though her eyes were never lifted. Are there only sight and sound to tell such things? She discerned it by a wave that swept her with confusion and she knew not what besides.

She watched him furtively, one day, when he talked with Farmer Kraummer out in the open. When he walked away she remained like one who has drunk much wine. Then unhesitatingly she turned and began her preparations to leave the Kraummer farmhouse.

When the afternoon was far spent they brought letters to her. One of them read like this:

"My Mildred, deary! I am only now at Narragansett, and so broke up not to find you. So you are down at that Kraummer farm, on the Iron Mountain. Well! What do you think of that delicious crank, Fred Evelyn? For a man must be a crank who does such things. Only fancy! Last year he chose to drive an engine back and forth across the plains. This year he tills the soil with laborers. Next year it will be something else as insane— because he likes to live more lives than one kind, and other Quixotic reasons. We are great chums. He writes me he's grown as strong as an ox. But he hasn't mentioned that you are there. I know you don't get on with him, for he isn't a bit intellectual—detests Ibsen and abuses Tolstoi. He doesn't read 'in books'—says they are spectacles for the short-sighted to look at life through. Don't snub him, dear, or be too hard on him; he has a heart of gold, if he is the first crank in America."

Mildred tried to think—to feel that the intelligence which this letter brought to her would take somewhat of the sting from the shame that tortured her. But it did not. She knew that it could not.

In the gathering twilight she walked again through the wheat that was heavy and fragrant with dew. The path was very long and very narrow. When she was midway she saw the Offender coming toward her. What could she do? Turn and run, as a little child might? Spring into the wheat, as some frightened four-footed creature would? There was nothing but to pass him with the dignity which the occasion clearly demanded.

But he did not let her pass. He stood squarely in the pathway before her, hat in hand, a perturbed look upon his face.

"Miss Orme," he said, "I have wanted to say to you, every hour of the past week, that I am the most consummate hound that walks the earth."

She made no protest. Her whole bearing seemed to indicate that her opinion coincided with his own.

"If you have a father, or brother, or any one, in short, to whom you may say such things—"

"I think you aggravate the offense, sir, by speaking of it. I shall ask you never to mention it again. I want to forget that it ever happened. Will you kindly let me by."

"Oh," he ventured eagerly, "you want to forget it! Then, maybe, since you are willing to forget, you will be generous enough to forgive the offender some day?"

"Some day," she repeated, almost inaudibly, looking seemingly through him, but not at him—"some day—perhaps; when I shall have forgiven myself."

He stood motionless, watching her slim, straight figure lessening by degrees as she walked slowly away from him. He was wondering what she meant. Then a sudden, quick wave came beating into his brown throat and staining it crimson, when he guessed what it might be.

A Rude Awakening

"Take de do' an' go! You year me? Take de do'!"

Lolotte's brown eyes flamed. Her small frame quivered. She stood with her back turned to a meagre supper-table, as if to guard it from the man who had just entered the cabin. She pointed toward the door, to order him from the house.

"You mighty cross to-night, Lolotte. You mus' got up wid de wrong foot to 's mo'nin'. *Hein*, Veveste? *hein*, Jacques, w'at you say?"

The two small urchins who sat at table giggled in sympathy with their father's evident good humor.

"I'm wo' out, me!" the girl exclaimed, desperately, as she let her arms fall limp at her side. "Work, work! Fu w'at? Fu feed de lazies' man in Natchitoches pa'ish."

"Now, Lolotte, you think w'at you sayin'," expostulated her father. "Sylveste Bordon don' ax nobody to feed 'im."

"W'en you brought a poun' of suga in de house?" his daughter retorted hotly, "or a poun' of coffee? W'en did you brought a piece o' meat home, you? An' Nonomme all de time sick. Co'n bread an' po'k, dat's good fu Veveste an' me an' Jacques; but Nonomme? no!"

She turned as if choking, and cut into the round, soggy "pone" of corn bread which was the main feature of the scanty supper.

"Po' li'le Nonomme; we mus' fine some'in' to break dat fevah. You want to kill a chicken once a w'ile fu Nonomme, Lolotte." He calmly seated himself at the table.

"Did n' I done put de las' roostah in de pot?" she cried with exasperation. "Now you come axen me fu kill de hen'! W'ere I goen to fine aigg' to trade wid, w'en de hen' be gone? Is I got one picayune in de house fu trade wid, me?"

"Papa," piped the young Jacques, "w'at dat I yeard you drive in de yard, w'ile go?"

"Dat 's it! W'en Lolotte would n' been talken' so fas', I could tole you 'bout dat job I got fu to-morrow. Dat was Joe Duplan's team of mule' an' wagon, wid t'ree bale' of cotton, w'at you yaird. I got to go soon in de mo'nin' wid dat load to de landin'. An' a man mus' eat w'at got to work; dat's sho."

Lolotte's bare brown feet made no sound upon the rough boards as she entered the room where Nonomme lay sick and sleeping. She lifted the coarse mosquito net from about him, sat down in the clumsy chair by the bedside, and began gently to fan the slumbering child.

Dusk was falling rapidly, as it does in the South. Lolotte's eyes grew round and big, as she watched the moon creep up from branch to branch of the moss-draped live-oak just outside her window. Presently the weary girl slept as profoundly as Nonomme. A little dog sneaked into the room, and socially licked her bare feet. The touch, moist and warm, awakened Lolotte.

The cabin was dark and quiet. Nonomme was crying softly, because the mosquitoes were biting him. In the room beyond, old Sylveste and the others slept. When Lolotte had quieted the child, she went outside to get a pail of cool, fresh water at the cistern. Then she crept into bed beside Nonomme, who slept again.

Lolotte's dreams that night pictured her father returning from work, and bringing luscious oranges home in his pocket for the sick child.

When at the very break of day she heard him astir in his room, a certain comfort stole into her heart. She lay and listened to the faint noises of his preparations to go out. When he had quitted the house, she waited to hear him drive the wagon from the yard.

She waited long, but heard no sound of horse's tread or wagon-wheel. Anxious, she went to the cabin door and looked out. The big mules were still where they had been fastened the night before. The wagon was there, too.

Her heart sank. She looked quickly along the low rafters supporting the roof of the narrow porch to where her father's fishing pole and pail always hung. Both were gone.

" 'T ain' no use, 't ain' no use," she said, as she turned into the house with a look of something like anguish in her eyes.

When the spare breakfast was eaten and the dishes cleared away, Lolotte turned with resolute mien to the two little brothers.

"Veveste," she said to the older, "go see if dey got co'n in dat wagon fu feed dem mule'."

"Yes, dey got co'n. Papa done feed 'em, fur I see de co'n-cob in de trough, me."

"Den you goen he'p me hitch dem mule, to de wagon. Jacques, go down de lane an' ax Aunt Minty if she come set wid Nonomme w'ile I go drive dem mule' to de landin'."

Lolotte had evidently determined to undertake her father's work. Nothing could dissuade her; neither the children's astonishment nor Aunt Minty's scathing disapproval. The fat black negress came laboring into the yard just as Lolotte mounted upon the wagon.

"Git down f'om dah, chile! Is you plumb crazy?" she exclaimed.

"No, I ain't crazy; I'm hungry, Aunt Minty. We all hungry. Somebody got fur work in dis fam'ly."

"Dat ain't no work fur a gal w'at ain't bar' seventeen year ole; drivin' Marse Duplan's mules! W'at I gwine tell yo' pa?"

"Fu me, you kin tell 'im w'at you want. But you watch Nonomme. I done cook his rice an' set it 'side."

"Don't you bodda," replied Aunt Minty; "I got somepin heah fur my boy. I gwine 'ten' to him."

Lolotte had seen Aunt Minty put something out of sight when she came up, and made her produce it. It was a heavy fowl.

"Sence w'en you start raisin' Brahma chicken', you?" Lolotte asked mistrustfully.

"My, but you is a cu'ious somebody! Ev'ything w'at got fedders on its laigs is Brahma chicken wid you. Dis heah ole hen"—

"All de same, you don't got fur give dat chicken to eat to Nonomme. You don't got fur cook 'im in my house."

Aunt Minty, unheeding, turned to the house with blustering inquiry for her boy, while Lolotte drove away with great clatter.

She knew, notwithstanding her injunction, that the chicken would be cooked and eaten. Maybe she herself would partake of it when she came back, if hunger drove her too sharply.

"Nax' thing I'm goen be one rogue," she muttered; and the tears gathered and fell one by one upon her cheeks.

"It *do* look like one Brahma, Aunt Mint," remarked the small and weazened Jacques, as he watched the woman picking the lusty fowl.

"How ole is you?" was her quiet retort.

"I don' know, me."

"Den if you don't know dat much, you betta keep yo' mouf shet, boy."

Then silence fell, but for a monotonous chant which the woman droned as she worked. Jacques opened his lips once more.

"It *do* look like one o' Ma'me Duplan' Brahma, Aunt Mint."

"Yonda, whar I come f'om, befo' de wah"—

"Ole Kaintuck, Aunt Mint?"

"Ole Kaintuck."

"Dat ain't one country like dis yere, Aunt Mint?"

"You mighty right, chile, dat ain't no sech kentry as dis heah. Yonda, in Kaintuck, w'en boys says de word 'Brahma chicken,' we takes an' gags em, an' ties dar han's behines 'em, an' fo'ces 'em ter stan' up watchin' folks settin' down eatin' chicken soup."

Jacques passed the back of his hand across his mouth; but lest the act should not place sufficient seal upon it, he prudently stole away to go and sit beside Nonomme, and wait there as patiently as he could the coming feast.

And what a treat it was! The luscious soup,—a great pot of it,—golden yellow, thickened with the flaky rice that Lolotte had set carefully on the shelf. Each mouthful of it seemed to carry fresh blood into the veins and a new brightness into the eyes of the hungry children who ate of it.

And that was not all. The day brought abundance with it. Their father came home with glistening perch and trout that Aunt Minty broiled deliciously over glowing embers, and basted with the rich chicken fat.

"You see," explained old Sylveste, "w'en I git up to 's mo'nin' an' see it was cloudy, I say to me, 'Sylveste, w'en you go wid dat cotton, rememba you got no tarpaulin. Maybe it rain, an' de cotton was spoil. Betta you go yonda to Lafirme Lake, w'ere de trout was bitin' fas'er 'an mosquito, an' so you git a good mess fur de chil'en.' Lolotte—w'at she goen do yonda? You ought stop Lolotte, Aunt Minty, w'en you see w'at she was want to do."

"Did n' I try to stop 'er? Did n' I ax 'er, 'W'at I gwine tell yo' pa?' An' she 'low, 'Tell 'im to go hang hisse'f, de triflind ole rapscallion! I 's de one w'at 's runnin' dis heah fambly!'"

"Dat don' soun' like Lolotte, Aunt Minty; you mus' yaird 'er crooked; *hein*, Nonomme?"

The quizzical look in his good-natured features was irresistible. Nonomme fairly shook with merriment.

"My head feel so good," he declared. "I wish Lolotte would come, so

I could tole 'er." And he turned in his bed to look down the long, dusty lane, with the hope of seeing her appear as he had watched her go, sitting on one of the cotton bales and guiding the mules.

But no one came all through the hot morning. Only at noon a broad-shouldered young negro appeared in view riding through the dust. When he had dismounted at the cabin door, he stood leaning a shoulder lazily against the jamb.

"Well, heah you is," he grumbled, addressing Sylveste with no mark of respect. "Heah you is, settin' down like comp'ny, an' Marse Joe yonda sont me see if you was dead."

"Joe Duplan boun' to have his joke, him," said Sylveste, smiling un-easily.

"Maybe it look like a joke to you, but 't aint no joke to him, man, to have one o' his wagons smoshed to kindlin', an' his bes' team tearin' t'rough de country. You don't want to let 'im lay han's on you, joke o' no joke."

"*Malédiction!*" howled Sylveste, as he staggered to his feet. He stood for one instant irresolute; then he lurched past the man and ran wildly down the lane. He might have taken the horse that was there, but he went tottering on afoot, a frightened look in his eyes, as if his soul gazed upon an inward picture that was horrible.

The road to the landing was little used. As Sylveste went he could readily trace the marks of Lolotte's wagon-wheels. For some distance they went straight along the road. Then they made a track as if a madman had directed their course, over stump and hillock, tearing the bushes and barking the trees on either side.

At each new turn Sylveste expected to find Lolotte stretched senseless upon the ground, but there was never a sign of her.

At last he reached the landing, which was a dreary spot, slanting down to the river and partly cleared to afford room for what desultory freight might be left there from time to time. There were the wagon-tracks, clean down to the river's edge and partly in the water, where they made a sharp and senseless turn. But Sylveste found no trace of his girl.

"Lolotte!" the old man cried out into the stillness. "Lolotte, *ma fille*, Lolotte!" But no answer came; no sound but the echo of his own voice, and the soft splash of the red water that lapped his feet.

He looked down at it, sick with anguish and apprehension.

Lolotte had disappeared as completely as if the earth had opened and swallowed her. After a few days it became the common belief that the girl had been drowned. It was thought that she must have been hurled from the wagon into the water during the sharp turn that the wheel-tracks indicated, and carried away by the rapid current.

During the days of search, old Sylveste's excitement kept him up. When it was over, an apathetic despair seemed to settle upon him.

Madame Duplan, moved by sympathy, had taken the little four-year-old Nonomme to the plantation Les Chêniers, where the child was awed by the beauty and comfort of things that surrounded him there. He thought always that Lolotte would come back, and watched for her every day; for they did not tell him the sad tidings of her loss.

The other two boys were placed in the temporary care of Aunt Minty; and old Sylveste roamed like a persecuted being through the country. He who had been a type of indolent content and repose had changed to a restless spirit.

When he thought to eat, it was in some humble negro cabin that he stopped to ask for food, which was never denied him. His grief had clothed him with a dignity that imposed respect.

One morning very early he appeared before the planter with a disheveled and hunted look.

"M'sieur Duplan," he said, holding his hat in his hand and looking away into vacancy, "I been try ev'thing. I been try settin' down still on de sto' gall'ry. I been walk, I been run; 't ain' no use. Dey got al'ays some'in' w'at push me. I go fishin', an' it's some'in' w'at push me worser 'an ever. By gracious! M'sieur Duplan, gi' me some work!"

The planter gave him at once a plow in hand, and no plow on the whole plantation dug so deep as that one, nor so fast. Sylveste was the first in the field, as he was the last one there. From dawn to nightfall he worked, and after, till his limbs refused to do his bidding.

People came to wonder, and the negroes began to whisper hints of demoniacal possession.

When Mr. Duplan gave careful thought to the subject of Lolotte's mysterious disappearance, an idea came to him. But so fearful was he to arouse false hopes in the breasts of those who grieved for the girl that to no one did he impart his suspicions save to his wife. It was on the eve of a business trip to New Orleans that he told her what he thought, or what he hoped rather.

Upon his return, which happened not many days later, he went out to where old Sylveste was toiling in the field with frenzied energy.

"Sylveste," said the planter, quietly, when he had stood a moment watching the man at work, "have you given up all hope of hearing from your daughter?"

"I don' know, me; I don' know. Le' me work, M'sieur Duplan."

"For my part, I believe the child is alive."

"You b'lieve dat, you?" His rugged face was pitiful in its imploring lines.

"I know it," Mr. Duplan muttered, as calmly as he could. "Hold up! Steady yourself, man! Come; come with me to the house. There is some one there who knows it, too; some one who has seen her."

The room into which the planter led the old man was big, cool, beautiful, and sweet with the delicate odor of flowers. It was shady, too, for the shutters were half closed; but not so darkened but Sylveste could at once see Lolotte, seated in a big wicker chair.

She was almost as white as the gown she wore. Her neatly shod feet rested upon a cushion, and her black hair, that had been closely cut, was beginning to make little rings about her temples.

"Aie!" he cried sharply, at sight of her, grasping his seamed throat as he did so. Then he laughed like a madman, and then he sobbed.

He only sobbed, kneeling upon the floor beside her, kissing her knees and her hands, that sought his. Little Nonomme was close to her, with a health flush creeping into his cheek. Veveste and Jacques were there, and rather awed by the mystery and grandeur of everything.

"W'ere'bouts you find her, M'sieur Duplan?" Sylveste asked, when the first flush of his joy had spent itself, and he was wiping his eyes with his rough cotton shirt sleeve.

"M'sieur Duplan find me 'way yonda to de city, papa, in de hospital," spoke Lolotte, before the planter could steady his voice to reply. "I did n' know who ev'ybody was, me. I did n' know me, myse'f, tell I tu'n roun' one day an' see M'sieur Duplan, w'at stan'en dere."

"You was boun' to know M'sieur Duplan, Lolotte," laughed Sylveste, like a child.

"Yes, an' I know right 'way how dem mule was git frighten' w'en de boat w'istle fu stop, an' pitch me plumb on de groun'. An' I remema it was one *mulâtresse* w'at call herse'f one chembamed, all de time aside me."

"You must not talk too much, Lolotte," interposed Madame Duplan, coming to place her hand with gentle solicitude upon the girl's forehead, and to feel how her pulse beat.

Then to save the child further effort of speech, she herself related how the boat had stopped at this lonely landing to take on a load of cottonseed. Lolotte had been found stretched insensible by the river, fallen apparently from the clouds, and had been taken on board.

The boat had changed its course into other waters after that trip, and had not returned to Duplan's Landing. Those who had tended Lolotte and left her at the hospital supposed, no doubt, that she would make known her identity in time, and they had troubled themselves no further about her.

"An' dah you is!" almost shouted aunt Minty, whose black face gleamed in the doorway; "dah you is, settin' down, lookin' jis' like w'ite folks!"

"Ain't I always was w'ite folks, Aunt Mint?" smiled Lolotte, feebly.

"G'long, chile. You knows me. I don' mean no harm."

"And now, Sylveste," said Mr. Duplan, as he rose and started to walk the floor, with hands in his pockets, "listen to me. It will be a long time before Lolotte is strong again. Aunt Minty is going to look after things for you till the child is fully recovered. But what I want to say is this: I shall trust these children into your hands once more, and I want you never to forget again that you are their father—do you hear?—that you are a man!"

Old Sylveste stood with his hand in Lolotte's, who rubbed it lovingly against her cheek.

"By gracious! M'sieur Duplan," he answered, "w'en God want to he'p me, I'm goen try my bes'!"

A Harbinger

Bruno did very nice work in black and white; sometimes in green and yellow and red. But he never did anything quite so clever as during that summer he spent in the hills.

The spring-time freshness had stayed, some way. And then there was the gentle Diantha, with hair the color of ripe wheat, who posed for him when he wanted. She was as beautiful as a flower, crisp with morning dew. Her violet eyes were baby-eyes—when he first came. When he went away he kissed her, and she turned red and white and trembled. As quick as thought the baby look went out of her eyes and another flashed into them.

Bruno sighed a good deal over his work that winter. The women he painted were all like mountain-flowers. The big city seemed too desolate for endurance often. He tried not to think of sweet-eyed Diantha. But there was nothing to keep him from remembering the hills; the whirr of the summer breeze through delicate-leafed maples; the bird-notes that used to break clear and sharp into the stillness when he and Diantha were together on the wooded hillside.

So when summer came again, Bruno gathered his bags, his brushes and colors and things. He whistled soft low tunes as he did so. He sang even, when he was not lost in wondering if the sunlight would fall just as it did last June, aslant the green slopes; and if—and if Diantha would quiver red and white again when he called her his sweet own Diantha, as he meant to.

Bruno had made his way through a tangle of underbrush; but before he came quite to the wood's edge, he halted: for there about the little church that gleamed white in the sun, people were gathered—old and young. He thought Diantha might be among them, and strained his eyes to see if she were. But she was not. He did see her though—when the doors of the rustic temple swung open—like a white-robed lily now.

There was a man beside her—it mattered not who; enough that it was one who had gathered this wild flower for his own, while Bruno was dreaming. Foolish Bruno! to have been only love's harbinger after all! He turned away. With hurried strides he descended the hill again, to wait by the big water-tank for a train to come along.

Doctor Chevalier's Lie

The quick report of a pistol rang through the quiet autumn night. It was no unusual sound in the unsavory quarter where Dr. Chevalier had his office. Screams commonly went with it. This time there had been none.

Midnight had already rung in the old cathedral tower.

The doctor closed the book over which he had lingered so late, and awaited the summons that was almost sure to come.

As he entered the house to which he had been called he could not but note the ghastly sameness of detail that accompanied these oft-recurring events. The same scurrying; the same groups of tawdry, frightened women bending over banisters—hysterical, some of them; morbidly curious, others; and not a few shedding womanly tears; with a dead girl stretched somewhere, as this one was.

And yet it was not the same. Certainly she was dead: there was the hole in the temple where she had sent the bullet through. Yet it was different. Other such faces had been unfamiliar to him, except so far as they bore the common stamp of death. This one was not.

Like a flash he saw it again amid other surroundings. The time was little more than a year ago. The place, a homely cabin down in Arkansas, in which he and a friend had found shelter and hospitality during a hunting expedition.

There were others beside. A little sister or two; a father and mother— coarse, and bent with toil, but proud as archangels of their handsome girl, who was too clever to stay in an Arkansas cabin, and who was going away to seek her fortune in the big city.

"The girl is dead," said Doctor Chevalier. "I knew her well, and charge myself with her remains and decent burial."

147

The following day he wrote a letter. One, doubtless, to carry sorrow, but no shame to the cabin down there in the forest.

It told that the girl had sickened and died. A lock of hair was sent and other trifles with it. Tender last words were even invented.

Of course it was noised about that Doctor Chevalier had cared for the remains of a woman of doubtful repute.

Shoulders were shrugged. Society thought of cutting him. Society did not, for some reason or other, so the affair blew over.

A Very Fine Fiddle

When the half dozen little ones were hungry, old Cléophas would take the fiddle from its flannel bag and play a tune upon it. Perhaps it was to drown their cries, or their hunger, or his conscience, or all three. One day Fifine, in a rage, stamped her small foot and clinched her little hands, and declared:

"It 's no two way'! I 'm goin' smash it, dat fiddle, some day in a t'ousan' piece'!"

"You mus' n' do dat, Fifine," expostulated her father. "Dat fiddle been ol'er 'an you an' me t'ree time' put togedder. You done yaird me tell often 'nough 'bout dat *Italien* w'at give it to me w'en he die, 'long yonder befo' de war. An' he say, 'Cléophas, dat fiddle—dat one part my life—w'at goin' live w'en I be dead—*Dieu merci!*' You talkin' too fas', Fifine."

"Well, I 'm goin' do some'in' wid dat fiddle, *va!*" returned the daughter, only half mollified. "Mine w'at I say."

So once when there were great carryings-on up at the big plantation— no end of ladies and gentlemen from the city, riding, driving, dancing, and making music upon all manner of instruments—Fifine, with the fiddle in its flannel bag, stole away and up to the big house where these festivities were in progress.

No one noticed at first the little barefoot girl seated upon a step of the veranda and watching, lynx-eyed, for her opportunity.

"It 's one fiddle I got for sell," she announced, resolutely, to the first who questioned her.

It was very funny to have a shabby little girl sitting there wanting to sell a fiddle, and the child was soon surrounded.

The lustreless instrument was brought forth and examined, first with amusement, but soon very seriously, especially by three gentlemen: one with very long hair that hung down, another with equally long hair that stood up, the third with no hair worth mentioning.

These three turned the fiddle upside down and almost inside out. They thumped upon it, and listened. They scraped upon it, and listened. They walked into the house with it, and out of the house with it, and into remote corners with it. All this with much putting of heads together, and talking together in familiar and unfamiliar languages. And, finally, they sent Fifine away with a fiddle twice as beautiful as the one she had brought, and a roll of money besides!

The child was dumb with astonishment, and away she flew. But when she stopped beneath a big chinaberry-tree, to further scan the roll of money, her wonder was redoubled. There was far more than she could count, more than she had ever dreamed of possessing. Certainly enough to top the old cabin with new shingles; to put shoes on all the little bare feet and food into the hungry mouths. Maybe enough—and Fifine's heart fairly jumped into her throat at the vision—maybe enough to buy Blanchette and her tiny calf that Unc' Siméon wanted to sell!

"It 's jis like you say, Fifine," murmured old Cléophas, huskily, when he had played upon the new fiddle that night. "It 's one fine fiddle; an' like you say, it shine' like satin. But some way or udder, 't ain' de same. Yair, Fifine, take it—put it 'side. I b'lieve, me, I ain' goin' play de fiddle no mo'."

Boulôt and Boulotte

When Boulôt and Boulotte, the little piny-wood twins, had reached the dignified age of twelve, it was decided in family council that the time had come for them to put their little naked feet into shoes. They were two brown-skinned, black-eyed 'Cadian roly-polies, who lived with father and mother and a troop of brothers and sisters halfway up the hill, in a neat log cabin that had a substantial mud chimney at one end. They could well afford shoes now, for they had saved many a picayune through their industry of selling wild grapes, blackberries, and "socoes" to ladies in the village who "put up" such things.

Boulôt and Boulotte were to buy the shoes themselves, and they selected a Saturday afternoon for the important transaction, for that is the great shopping time in Natchitoches Parish. So upon a bright Saturday afternoon Boulôt and Boulotte, hand in hand, with their quarters, their dimes, and their picayunes tied carefully in a Sunday handkerchief, descended the hill, and disappeared from the gaze of the eager group that had assembled to see them go.

Long before it was time for their return, this same small band, with ten year old Seraphine at their head, holding a tiny Seraphin in her arms, had stationed themselves in a row before the cabin at a convenient point from which to make quick and careful observation.

Even before the two could be caught sight of, their chattering voices were heard down by the spring, where they had doubtless stopped to drink. The voices grew more and more audible. Then, through the branches of the young pines, Boulotte's blue sun-bonnet appeared, and Boulôt's straw hat. Finally the twins, hand in hand, stepped into the clearing in full view.

Consternation seized the band.

"You bof crazy *donc*, Boulôt an' Boulotte," screamed Seraphine. "You go buy shoes, an' come home barefeet like you was go!"

Boulôt flushed crimson. He silently hung his head, and looked sheepishly down at his bare feet, then at the fine stout brogans that he carried in his hand. He had not thought of it.

Boulotte also carried shoes, but of the glossiest, with the highest of heels and brightest of buttons. But she was not one to be disconcerted or to look sheepish; far from it.

"You 'spec' Boulôt an' me we got money fur was'e—us?" she retorted, with withering condescension. "You think we go buy shoes fur ruin it in de dus'? *Comment!*"

And they all walked into the house crestfallen; all but Boulotte, who was mistress of the situation, and Seraphin, who did not care one way or the other.

Love on the Bon-Dieu

Upon the pleasant veranda of Père Antoine's cottage, that adjoined the church, a young girl had long been seated, awaiting his return. It was the eve of Easter Sunday, and since early afternoon the priest had been engaged in hearing the confessions of those who wished to make their Easters the following day. The girl did not seem impatient at his delay; on the contrary, it was very restful to her to lie back in the big chair she had found there, and peep through the thick curtain of vines at the people who occasionally passed along the village street.

She was slender, with a frailness that indicated lack of wholesome and plentiful nourishment. A pathetic, uneasy look was in her gray eyes, and even faintly stamped her features, which were fine and delicate. In lieu of a hat, a barège veil covered her light brown and abundant hair. She wore a coarse white cotton "josie," and a blue calico skirt that only half concealed her tattered shoes.

As she sat there, she held carefully in her lap a parcel of eggs securely fastened in a red bandana handkerchief.

Twice already a handsome, stalwart young man in quest of the priest had entered the yard, and penetrated to where she sat. At first they had exchanged the uncompromising "howdy" of strangers, and nothing more. The second time, finding the priest still absent, he hesitated to go at once. Instead, he stood upon the step, and narrowing his brown eyes, gazed beyond the river, off towards the west, where a murky streak of mist was spreading across the sun.

"It look like mo' rain," he remarked, slowly and carelessly.

"We done had 'bout 'nough," she replied, in much the same tone.

"It's no chance to thin out the cotton," he went on.

"An' the Bon-Dieu," she resumed, "it 's on'y to-day you can cross him on foot."

"You live yonda on the Bon-Dieu, *donc?*" he asked, looking at her for the first time since he had spoken.

"Yas, by Nid d'Hibout, m'sieur."

Instinctive courtesy held him from questioning her further. But he seated himself on the step, evidently determined to wait there for the priest. He said no more, but sat scanning critically the steps, the porch, and pillar beside him, from which he occasionally tore away little pieces of detached wood, where it was beginning to rot at its base.

A click at the side gate that communicated with the churchyard soon announced Père Antoine's return. He came hurriedly across the garden-path, between the tall, lusty rosebushes that lined either side of it, which were now fragrant with blossoms. His long, flapping cassock added something of height to his undersized, middle-aged figure, as did the skullcap which rested securely back on his head. He saw only the young man at first, who rose at his approach.

"Well, Azenor," he called cheerily in French, extending his hand. "How is this? I expected you all the week."

"Yes, monsieur; but I knew well what you wanted with me, and I was finishing the doors for Gros-Léon's new house;" saying which, he drew back, and indicated by a motion and look that some one was present who had a prior claim upon Père Antoine's attention.

"Ah, Lalie!" the priest exclaimed, when he had mounted to the porch, and saw her there behind the vines. "Have you been waiting here since you confessed? Surely an hour ago!"

"Yes, monsieur."

"You should rather have made some visits in the village, child."

"I am not acquainted with any one in the village," she returned-ed.

The priest, as he spoke, had drawn a chair, and seated himself beside her, with his hands comfortably clasping his knees. He wanted to know how things were out on the bayou.

"And how is the grandmother?" he asked. "As cross and crabbed as ever? And with that"—he added reflectively—"good for ten years yet! I said only yesterday to Butrand—you know Butrand, he works on Le Blôt's Bon-Dieu place—'And that Madame Zidore: how is it with her, Butrand? I believe God has forgotten her here on earth.' 'It is n't that, your reverence,' said Butrand, 'but it's neither God nor the Devil that wants her!' " And Père Antoine laughed with a jovial frankness that took all sting of ill-nature from his very pointed remarks.

Lalie did not reply when he spoke of her grandmother; she only pressed her lips firmly together, and picked nervously at the red bandana.

"I have come to ask, Monsieur Antoine," she began, lower than she needed to speak—for Azenor had withdrawn at once to the far end of the porch—"to ask if you will give me a little scrap of paper—a piece of writing for Monsieur Chartrand at the store over there. I want new shoes and stockings for Easter, and I have brought eggs to trade for them. He says he is willing, yes, if he was sure I would bring more every week till the shoes are paid for."

With good-natured indifference, Père Antoine wrote the order that the girl desired. He was too familiar with distress to feel keenly for a girl who was able to buy Easter shoes and pay for them with eggs.

She went immediately away then, after shaking hands with the priest, and sending a quick glance of her pathetic eyes towards Azenor, who had turned when he heard her rise, and nodded when he caught the look. Through the vines he watched her cross the village street.

"How is it that you do not know Lalie, Azenor? You surely must have seen her pass your house often. It lies on her way to the Bon-Dieu."

"No, I don't know her; I have never seen her," the young man replied, as he seated himself—after the priest—and kept his eyes absently fixed on the store across the road, where he had seen her enter.

"She is the granddaughter of that Madame Izidore"—

"What! Ma'ame Zidore whom they drove off the island last winter?"

"Yes, yes. Well, you know, they say the old woman stole wood and things,—I don't know how true it is,—and destroyed people's property out of pure malice."

"And she lives now on the Bon-Dieu?"

"Yes, on Le Blôt's place, in a perfect wreck of a cabin. You see, she gets it for nothing; not a negro on the place but has refused to live in it."

"Surely, it can't be that old abandoned hovel near the swamp, that Michon occupied ages ago?"

"That is the one, the very one."

"And the girl lives there with that old wretch?" the young man marveled.

"Old wretch to be sure, Azenor. But what can you expect from a woman who never crosses the threshold of God's house—who even tried to hinder the child doing so as well? But I went to her. I said: 'See here, Madame

Zidore,'—you know it 's my way to handle such people without gloves,—
'you may damn your soul if you choose,' I told her, 'that is a privilege
which we all have; but none of us has a right to imperil the salvation of
another. I want to see Lalie at mass hereafter on Sundays, or you will
hear from me;' and I shook my stick under her nose. Since then the child
has never missed a Sunday. But she is half starved, you can see that. You
saw how shabby she is—how broken her shoes are? She is at Chartrand's
now, trading for new ones with those eggs she brought, poor thing! There
is no doubt of her being ill-treated. Butrand says he thinks Madame Zidore
even beats the child. I don't know how true it is, for no power can make
her utter a word against her grandmother."

Azenor, whose face was a kind and sensitive one, had paled with distress
as the priest spoke; and now at these final words he quivered as though
he felt the sting of a cruel blow upon his own flesh.

But no more was said of Lalie, for Père Antoine drew the young man's
attention to the carpenter-work which he wished to intrust to him. When
they had talked the matter over in all its lengthy details, Azenor mounted
his horse and rode away.

A moment's gallop carried him outside the village. Then came a half-
mile strip along the river to cover. Then the lane to enter, in which stood
his dwelling midway, upon a low, pleasant knoll.

As Azenor turned into the lane, he saw the figure of Lalie far ahead of
him. Somehow he had expected to find her there, and he watched her
again as he had done through Père Antoine's vines. When she passed his
house, he wondered if she would turn to look at it. But she did not. How
could she know it was his? Upon reaching it himself, he did not enter the
yard, but stood there motionless, his eyes always fastened upon the girl's
figure. He could not see, away off there, how coarse her garments were.
She seemed, through the distance that divided them, as slim and delicate
as a flower-stalk. He stayed till she reached the turn of the lane and disappeared into the woods.

Mass had not yet begun when Azenor tiptoed into church on Easter
morning. He did not take his place with the congregation, but stood close
to the holy-water font, and watched the people who entered.

Almost every girl who passed him wore a white mull, a dotted swiss,
or a fresh-starched muslin at least. They were bright with ribbons that
hung from their persons, and flowers that bedecked their hats. Some
carried fans and cambric handkerchiefs. Most of them wore gloves, and

were odorant of *poudre de riz* and nice toilet-waters; while all carried gay little baskets filled with Easter-eggs.

But there was one who came empty-handed, save for the worn prayer-book which she bore. It was Lalie, the veil upon her head, and wearing the blue print and cotton bodice which she had worn the day before.

He dipped his hand into the holy water when she came, and held it out to her, though he had not thought of doing this for the others. She touched his fingers with the tips of her own, making a slight inclination as she did so; and after a deep genuflection before the Blessed Sacrament, passed on to the side. He was not sure if she had known him. He knew she had not looked into his eyes, for he would have felt it.

He was angered against other young women who passed him, because of their flowers and ribbons, when she wore none. He himself did not care, but he feared she might, and watched her narrowly to see if she did.

But it was plain that Lalie did not care. Her face, as she seated herself, settled into the same restful lines it had worn yesterday, when she sat in Père Antoine's big chair. It seemed good to her to be there. Sometimes she looked up at the little colored panes through which the Easter sun was streaming; then at the flaming candles, like stars; or at the embowered figures of Joseph and Mary, flanking the central tabernacle which shrouded the risen Christ. Yet she liked just as well to watch the young girls in their spring freshness, or to sensuously inhale the mingled odor of flowers and incense that filled the temple.

Lalie was among the last to quit the church. When she walked down the clean pathway that led from it to the road, she looked with pleased curiosity towards the groups of men and maidens who were gayly matching their Easter-eggs under the shade of the China-berry trees.

Azenor was among them, and when he saw her coming solitary down the path, he approached her and, with a smile, extended his hat, whose crown was quite lined with the pretty colored eggs.

"You mus' of forgot to bring aiggs," he said. "Take some o' mine."

"Non, merci," she replied, flushing and drawing back.

But he urged them anew upon her. Much pleased, then, she bent her pretty head over the hat, and was evidently puzzled to make a selection among so many that were beautiful.

He picked out one for her,—a pink one, dotted with white clover-leaves.

"Yere," he said, handing it to her, "I think this is the pretties'; an' it look' strong too. I'm sho' it will break all of the res'." And he playfully held out another, half-hidden in his fist, for her to try its strength upon.

But she refused to. She would not risk the ruin of her pretty egg. Then she walked away, without once having noticed that the girls, whom Azenor had left, were looking curiously at her.

When he rejoined them, he was hardly prepared for their greeting; it startled him.

"How come you talk to that girl? She 's real canaille, her," was what one of them said to him.

"Who say' so? Who say she 's canaille? If it's a man, I 'll smash 'is head!" he exclaimed, livid. They all laughed merrily at this.

"An' if it 's a lady, Azenor? W'at you goin' to do 'bout it?" asked another, quizzingly.

" 'T ain' no lady. No lady would say that 'bout a po' girl, w'at she don't even know."

He turned away, and emptying all his eggs into the hat of a little urchin who stood near, walked out of the churchyard. He did not stop to exchange another word with any one; neither with the men who stood all *endimanchés* before the stores, nor the women who were mounting upon horses and into vehicles, or walking in groups to their homes.

He took a short cut across the cotton-field that extended back of the town, and walking rapidly, soon reached his home. It was a pleasant house of few rooms and many windows, with fresh air blowing through from every side; his workshop was beside it. A broad strip of greensward, studded here and there with trees, sloped down to the road.

Azenor entered the kitchen, where an amiable old black woman was chopping onion and sage at a table.

"Tranquiline," he said abruptly, "they 's a young girl goin' to pass yere afta a w'ile. She 's got a blue dress an' w'ite josie on, an' a veil on her head. W'en you see her, I want you to go to the road an' make her res' there on the bench, an' ask her if she don't want a cup o' coffee. I saw her go to communion, me; so she did n't eat any breakfas'. Eve'ybody else f'om out o' town, that went to communion, got invited somew'ere another. It 's enough to make a person sick to see such meanness."

"An' you want me ter go down to de gate, jis' so, an' ax 'er pineblank ef she wants some coffee?" asked the bewildered Tranquiline.

"I don't care if you ask her poin' blank o' not; but you do like I say." Tranquiline was leaning over the gate when Lalie came along.

"Howdy," offered the woman.

"Howdy," the girl returned.

"Did you see a yalla calf wid black spots a t'arin' down de lane, missy?"

"Non; not yalla, an' not with black spot'. *Mais* I see one li'le w'ite calf tie by a rope, yonda 'roun' the ben'."

"Dat warn't hit. Dis heah one was yalla. I hope he done flung hisse'f down de bank an' broke his nake. Sarve 'im right! But whar you come f'om, chile? You look plum wo' out. Set down dah on dat bench, an' le' me fotch you a cup o' coffee."

Azenor had already in his eagerness arranged a tray, upon which was a smoking cup of *café au lait*. He had buttered and jellied generous slices of bread, and was searching wildly for something when Tranquiline re-entered.

"W'at become o' that half of chicken-pie, Tranquiline, that was yere in the *garde manger* yesterday?"

"W'at chicken-pie? W'at *garde manger?*" blustered the woman.

"Like we got mo' 'en one *garde manger* in the house, Tranquiline!"

"You jis' like ole Ma'ame Azenor use' to be, you is! You 'spec' chicken-pie gwine las' etarnal? W'en some'pin done sp'ilt, I flings it 'way. Dat's me—dat's Tranquiline!"

So Azenor resigned himself,—what else could he do?—and sent the tray, incomplete, as he fancied it, out to Lalie.

He trembled at the thought of what he did; he, whose nerves were usually as steady as some piece of steel mechanism.

Would it anger her if she suspected? Would it please her if she knew? Would she say this or that to Tranquiline? And would Tranquiline tell him truly what she said—how she looked?

As it was Sunday, Azenor did not work that afternoon. Instead, he took a book out under the trees, as he often did, and sat reading it, from the first sound of the Vesper bell, that came faintly across the fields, till the Angelus. All that time! He turned many a page, yet in the end did not know what he had read. With his pencil he had traced "Lalie" upon every margin, and was saying it softly to himself.

Another Sunday Azenor saw Lalie at mass—and again. Once he walked with her and showed her the short cut across the cotton-field. She was very glad that day, and told him she was going to work—her grandmother said she might. She was going to hoe, up in the fields with Monsieur Le Blôt's hands. He entreated her not to; and when she asked his reason, he could not tell her, but turned and tore shyly and savagely at the elder-blossoms that grew along the fence.

Then they stopped where she was going to cross the fence from the field into the lane. He wanted to tell her that was his house which they could see not far away; but he did not dare to, since he had fed her there on the morning she was hungry.

"An' you say yo' gran'ma 's goin' to let you work? She keeps you f'om workin', *donc?*" He wanted to question her about her grandmother, and could think of no other way to begin.

"Po' ole grand'mère!" she answered. "I don' b'lieve she know mos' time w'at she 's doin'. Sometime she say' I ain't no betta an' one nigga, an' she fo'ce me to work. Then she say she know I 'm goin' be one canaille like maman, an' she make me set down still, like she would want to kill me if I would move. Her, she on'y want' to be out in the wood', day an' night, day an' night. She ain' got her right head, po' grand'mère. I know she ain't."

Lalie had spoken low and in jerks, as if every word gave her pain. Azenor could feel her distress as plainly as he saw it. He wanted to say something to her—to do something for her. But her mere presence paralyzed him into inactivity—except his pulses, that beat like hammers when he was with her. Such a poor, shabby little thing as she was, too!

"I 'm goin' to wait yere nex' Sunday fo' you, Lalie," he said, when the fence was between them. And he thought he had said something very daring.

But the next Sunday she did not come. She was neither at the appointed place of meeting in the lane, nor was she at mass. Her absence—so unexpected—affected Azenor like a calamity. Late in the afternoon, when he could stand the trouble and bewilderment of it no longer, he went and leaned over Père Antoine's fence. The priest was picking the slugs from his roses on the other side.

"That young girl from the Bon-Dieu," said Azenor—"she was not at mass to-day. I suppose her grandmother has forgotten your warning."

"No," answered the priest. "The child is ill, I hear. Butrand tells me she has been ill for several days from overwork in the fields. I shall go out to-morrow to see about her. I would go to-day, if I could."

"The child is ill," was all Azenor heard or understood of Père Antoine's words. He turned and walked resolutely away, like one who determines suddenly upon action after meaningless hesitation.

He walked towards his home and past it, as if it were a spot that did not concern him. He went on down the lane and into the wood where he had seen Lalie disappear that day.

Here all was shadow, for the sun had dipped too low in the west to send a single ray through the dense foliage of the forest.

Now that he found himself on the way to Lalie's home, he strove to understand why he had not gone there before. He often visited other girls in the village and neighborhood,—why not have gone to her, as well? The answer lay too deep in his heart for him to be more than half-conscious of it. Fear had kept him,—dread to see her desolate life face to face. He did not know how he could bear it.

But now he was going to her at last. She was ill. He would stand upon that dismantled porch that he could just remember. Doubtless Ma'ame Zidore would come out to know his will, and he would tell her that Père Antoine had sent to inquire how Mamzelle Lalie was. No! Why drag in Père Antoine? He would simply stand boldly and say, "Ma'ame Zidore, I learn that Lalie is ill. I have come to know if it is true, and to see her, if I may."

When Azenor reached the cabin where Lalie dwelt, all sign of day had vanished. Dusk had fallen swiftly after the sunset. The moss that hung heavy from great live oak branches was making fantastic silhouettes against the eastern sky that the big, round moon was beginning to light. Off in the swamp beyond the bayou, hundreds of dismal voices were droning a lullaby. Upon the hovel itself, a stillness like death rested.

Oftener than once Azenor tapped upon the door, which was closed as well as it could be, without obtaining a reply. He finally approached one of the small unglazed windows, in which coarse mosquito-netting had been fastened, and looked into the room.

By the moonlight slanting in he could see Lalie stretched upon a bed; but of Ma'ame Zidore there was no sign. "Lalie!" he called softly. "Lalie!"

The girl slightly moved her head upon the pillow. Then he boldly opened the door and entered.

Upon a wretched bed, over which was spread a cover of patched calico, Lalie lay, her frail body only half concealed by the single garment that was upon it. One hand was plunged beneath her pillow; the other, which was free, he touched. It was as hot as flame; so was her head. He knelt sobbing upon the floor beside her, and called her his love and his soul. He begged her to speak a word to him,—to look at him. But she only muttered disjointedly that the cotton was all turning to ashes in the fields, and the blades of the corn were in flames.

If he was choked with love and grief to see her so, he was moved by anger as well; rage against himself, against Père Antoine, against the people upon the plantation and in the village, who had so abandoned a helpless creature to misery and maybe death. Because she had been silent —had not lifted her voice in complaint—they believed she suffered no more than she could bear.

But surely the people could not be utterly without heart. There must be one somewhere with the spirit of Christ. Père Antoine would tell him of such a one, and he would carry Lalie to her,— out of this atmosphere of death. He was in haste to be gone with her. He fancied every moment of delay was a fresh danger threatening her life.

He folded the rude bed-cover over Lalie's naked limbs, and lifted her in his arms. She made no resistance. She seemed only loath to withdraw her hand from beneath the pillow. When she did, he saw that she held lightly but firmly clasped in her encircling fingers the pretty Easter-egg he had given her! He uttered a low cry of exultation as the full significance of this came over him. If she had hung for hours upon his neck telling him that she loved him, he could not have known it more surely than by this sign. Azenor felt as if some mysterious bond had all at once drawn them heart to heart and made them one.

No need now to go from door to door begging admittance for her. She was his. She belonged to him. He knew now where her place was, whose roof must shelter her, and whose arms protect her.

So Azenor, with his loved one in his arms, walked through the forest, surefooted as a panther. Once, as he walked, he could hear in the distance the weird chant which Ma'ame Zidore was crooning—to the moon, may-be—as she gathered her wood.

Once, where the water was trickling cool through rocks, he stopped to lave Lalie's hot cheeks and hands and forehead. He had not once touched his lips to her. But now, when a sudden great fear came upon him because she did not know him, instinctively he pressed his lips upon hers that were parched and burning. He held them there till hers were soft and pliant from the healthy moisture of his own.

Then she knew him. She did not tell him so, but her stiffened fingers relaxed their tense hold upon the Easter bauble. It fell to the ground as she twined her arm around his neck; and he understood.

"Stay close by her, Tranquiline," said Azenor, when he had laid Lalie upon his own couch at home. "I'm goin' for the doctor en' for Père

Antoine. Not because she is goin' to die," he added hastily, seeing the awe that crept into the woman's face at mention of the priest. "She is goin' to live! Do you think I would let my wife die, Tranquiline?"

An Embarrassing Position

COMEDY IN ONE ACT

CHARACTERS

MISS EVA ARTLESS—Brought up on unconventional and startling lines by her eccentric father, a retired army officer.

MR. WILLIS PARKHAM—Wealthy young bachelor. Candidate for a public office.

MR. COOL LATELY—Reporter for the *Paul Pry*.

CATO—Respectable old negro servitor.

SCENE—Snuggery in Willis Parkham's suburban residence.

TIME—11:30 P. M.

Parkham stands with back to open fire lighting cigar. Cato busily engaged removing evidences of a jovial bachelor gathering.

PARKHAM: Never mind, Cato; leave all that till morning.

CATO: Marse Will's, you ten' to yo' business; I g'ine ten' to mine. Dat away to save trouble.

PARKHAM: (*Laughs good naturedly*). It never occurs to you to take liberties, does it Cato?

CATO: I never takes nuttin' w'at don' b'long to me, Marse Will's. But what I despises hits to come in heah of a mornin' an' find de bottles an' glasses scatter roun' like nine pins; de kiards an' poker chips layin' 'bout loose. An' dis heah w'at you all calls a p'litical meetin'!

PARKHAM: (*Seats himself in easy chair and picks up book from table.*) One name'll do as well as another for a poker game, Cato. Now see that everything is well closed. It's turning cold and seems to be blowing a blizzard outside.

CATO: Yas, suh, de groun' all done kiver up wid snow; an' hits fallin' like

164

fedders outen a busted fedder bed. (*Exit with tray, glasses, etc., limping painfully aud affectedly.*)

PARKHAM: (*Settles back in easy chair for a quiet read.*) Talk of being ruled with an iron rod! (*Door bell rings.*) At this hour! a caller! who in perdition can it be! (*Hurries to open the door himself and ushers in a handsome, sprightly young girl holding, with difficulty, a dripping umbrella, hand-bag, cat and small dog—one under each arm. Wears a feathered hat tied under chin, and long costly circular.*)

PARKHAM: (*Excitedly.*) Eva Artless!

EVA: Yes, I knew you'd be astonished. I just knew you would—at this time of night. Here, take my umbrella and bag, please. (*Parkham takes them. Closes umbrella and sets it to one side.*)

PARKHAM: You're right, I'm perfectly amazed.

EVA: I knew you'd be delighted, too.

PARKHAM: (*Uncertainly.*) Oh, I am; charmed. But has anything happened? The Major'll be along presently, I suppose, in a few moments?

EVA: The Major! Do you think I'd have come if the Major were home? Take that telegram from my belt. I can't with Zizi and Booboo. Do you see it, the end sticking up, there?

PARKHAM: This is it? (*Draws paper gingerly from Eva's belt.*)

EVA: That's it. Read it. Read it aloud and see.

PARKHAM: (*Reads telegram.*) "Dearest Eva."

EVA: Just like a letter, "Dearest Eva." Poor, sweet papa; the first telegram I ever had from him. Go on.

PARKHAM: "Dearest Eva"—

EVA: You read that.

PARKHAM: So I did. "Accident and obstruction on tracks below. Shall be detained here till noon tomorrow. Am in despair at thought of you remaining alone till then. May heaven have you in keeping till return of your distracted father."

EVA: "Distracted father." Heigh-ho. Put it back in my belt, please, Willis. (*Parkham replaces the telegram awkwardly and with difficulty.*) So when I got it, naturally, I was distracted, too.

PARKHAM: When did it come?

EVA: About an hour ago. Untie my hat and circular, will you? (*Parkham does as she bids, and places things on chair.*) Thanks. (*Caresses dog and cat alternately.*) My poor Zizi; my sweet Booboo; 'oo was jus' as s'eep'y as 'oo tould be, so 'oo was. Won't you kindly give them a little corner for the night, Willis? You know I *couldn't* leave them behind.

PARKHAM: Let me have them? (*Takes pets by back of the neck—one in each hand, and proceeds towards room to right. Pushes door open and deposits Booboo and Zizi within, closes door and rejoins Eva, who has seated herself.*) May I learn now, Eva, to what I owe the distinction of this unexpected visit?

EVA: Why, as I said before, you owe it to papa's unavoidable absence. Finding that I was destined, for the first time in my life, to spend a night apart from him, and knowing him to be distracted about it, as you read yourself, I naturally sat down to do a little thinking on my own account.

PARKHAM: Oh, you did? A little original thinking, as it were?

EVA: Yes, entirely original. I thought "now, what would papa want me to do under the circumstances?" Why, simply this: "Go and spend the night at the home of one of our friends, Eva."

PARKHAM: Now, I think you are entirely mistaken. I can't for a moment believe that your father would advise you to any such thing.

EVA: (*With mock loftiness.*) Do you presume to know Major Artless better than his own daughter does, Mr. Willis Parkham?

PARKHAM: I know him quite well enough to feel sure of what I say. Since my boyhood, and the death of my own father, I have had much of his confidence, and he has had all of mine.

EVA: (*Emphatically.*) That is precisely it. So in casting about among my father's friends, for a possible night's refuge, I said to myself, "there is no one whom father esteems so highly or loves so well as Willis Parkham."

PARKHAM: (*Aside.*) Would to Heaven he had loved me less. And you mean to tell me, Eva, that you have come here to my house with the intention of spending the night?

EVA: Certainly—that is, part of it, for the night must be half gone. And it's ever such a lark, too—coming through the night and the snow. I just thought to myself how nice it would be to sleep in that lovely guest-chamber of yours.

PARKHAM: (*Forgetting his dilemma.*) It's been all refitted. It's charming; you wouldn't know it.

EVA: Oh—how nice! Then to get up in the morning and take breakfast with you; you on one side the table, I, on the other.

PARKHAM: (*Still forgetful.*) No, I should sit beside you.

EVA: Well, just as you please, but papa always sits opposite—I pouring your coffee—I say "sugar and cream, Willis? how many lumps?"

PARKHAM: (*Still forgetful.*) Two lumps.

EVA: Only two? Then we pass things to each other. I ring for Cato: "Cato, bring hot buttered toast for Marse Willis, and the morning paper at once."

PARKHAM: (*Still forgetful.*) I'm very fond of buttered toast with the morning paper and hot coffee.

EVA: Yes, with coffee; isn't it nice.

PARKHAM: (*Still forgetful.*) It would all be delicious. (*Suddenly remembers.*) But it can't be! (*Dejectedly.*)

EVA: (*Goes to table on which tray rests.*) This talk about breakfast has made me hungry. (*Pours herself small glass of sherry and nibbles cracker with it.*) Why can't it be?

PARKHAM: Believe me when I tell you, simply, that it can't—it mustn't be.

EVA: (*Lays down cracker and glass. Looks down mournfully.*) Then I have made a mistake; you are not glad that I came.

PARKHAM: (*Approaches and takes her hand.*) Oh, don't say that. There's no one in the world whom I want to see always, so much as you. And it's because I do, and because I'm your friend and your father's friend, that I say you had better not be here.

EVA: (*Withdraws her hand coldly. With tears in her voice.*) Very well, I shall leave without delay. You have a telephone, I believe. Will you kindly ring at once for a carriage?

PARKHAM: Why not your own? I would offer mine.

EVA: I wouldn't trouble you so far, sir. My coachman is ill with la grippe. I came in a carriage from the city stand; I can return in one, I'm sure.

PARKHAM: Oh, you didn't come in your own carriage? Your coachman— your servants perhaps do not know that you are here?

EVA: (*Impatiently.*) No one knows I am here, but you. (*Goes toward her cloak, which she tentatively offers to put on. Furtively wipes corner of her eye with pocket handkerchief.*)

PARKHAM: (*Aside—reflectively.*) So no one knows she's here. That presents the matter in a less difficult light. (*Steals a glance towards her dejected figure.*) She shall stay! (*with sudden resolution.*) Her father will understand, and he trusts me absolutely. Her presence here I can manage to keep from the knowledge of others. (*Goes towards her.*) Eva! (*A little penitently.*)

EVA: Well?

PARKHAM: Don't mind please, what I said.

EVA: (*With indignant reproach.*) Don't mind that; you said or implied I would better have staid home! Perhaps you want me to forget that you said I ought not to have come?

PARKHAM: Yes. You'll forget it, won't you?

EVA: Never!

PARKHAM: (*Attempting to take her hand.*) Oh, you will; because I ask you; because I beg you to. I want you to stay to-night under my roof; to sleep in the guest-chamber that you like so. And I want you to believe that it will be doing me a pleasure—an honor, that I shall remember always. You will, Eva? Say that you will?

EVA: (*Relenting.*) It was very unkind, and unfriendly, Willis; papa wouldn't have treated you so.

PARKHAM: Oh, I know it seemed a savage thing to say. Some day perhaps, Eva, I may explain it all, if you will give me the right to. (*Door bell rings. Parkham starts violently. Walks for a moment distractedly about. Aside.*) Heavens! Gadsby! Dodswell! Some idiot that would better never have been born! (*Bell rings second time.*)

EVA: Don't you hear the bell, Willis? Has Cato gone to bed?

PARKHAM: (*Incoherently.*) No; yes—I'll open the door myself. It's a man I'm expecting on important business.

EVA: (*Astonished.*) Important business now? Almost midnight.

PARKHAM: I always—that is I generally attend to business at that hour. May I ask you to go into this room—(*going towards door to right*)—while he is here?

EVA: Why, certainly. Will he be long, do you suppose?

PARKHAM: Only a few moments. (*Bell rings third time. Opens door for Eva. Exit Eva. Parkham then opens folding doors and outer door. Enter, Mr. Cool Lately, stamping and brushing off the snow.*)

COOL LATELY: I've had the pleasure of meeting you before, Mr. Parkham; dare say you have forgotten. Permit me—this card may possibly help to refresh your memory. (*Hands card to Parkham.*)

PARKHAM: (*Reads.*) Mr. Cool Lately.

COOL LATELY: Reporter, occasional paragraphist, and special interviewer on staff of *Paul Pry!*

PARKHAM: I can't recall the name, though your face is not unfamiliar. Let me ask you to state as briefly as you can the business which brings you to my house at so unseasonable an hour.

COOL LATELY: Only too happy to do so, Mr. Parkham. (*Seats himself in a chair indicated by Parkham.*) Since you mention unseasonable hour, my theory is, that hours are all one, or ought to be, to a man in public life.

PARKHAM: I don't know how it may be to a man in public life, but to a man in private life they are certainly not all one.

COOL LATELY: Only your modest way of putting it, Mr. Parkham; for you know you are at present an object of special interest to the public. Your friend, Mr. Dodswell, kindly dropped into the *Paul-Pry* office on his return from the informal political gathering which he tells us assembled here to-night——

PARKHAM: (*Aside.*) Damn Dodswell!

COOL LATELY: And in which you positively decline to represent your party before the convention, and formulated your reasons for doing so. Now——

PARKHAM: It appears to me that Mr. Dodswell's information has fully covered the ground.

COOL LATELY: By no means, my dear Mr. Parkham, by no means. Having this amount of good inside information on hand, naturally we thirsted for more. The hour was late, to be sure, and it was snowing—obstacles, I'll admit; but to men in my profession obstacles exist only to be over-come. I jumped into a cab; away I drove; saw the light in the vesti-bule——

PARKHAM : (*Aside.*) Hang the light in the vestibule——

COOL LATELY: Rang the bell, and here I am. (*Cool Lately has observed through his eye-glasses, rather closely, details of the apartment whilst talking. Parkham sees that he has perceived Eva's cloak and hat on chair.*)

PARKHAM: (*With forced laugh.*) Servants will take liberties in bachelor establishments, Mr. Lately. You see where my house-maid chooses to deposit her toggery during my absence?

COOL LATELY: (*Aside.*) Housemaid is good.

PARKHAM: But, let us make haste to dispose of this little interview as quickly as possible.

COOL LATELY: (*Takes notebook from pocket and sharpens pencil.*) Now, you're talking, Mr. Parkham.

PARKHAM: I suppose you want briefly my political attitude; reasons for declining this nomination; opinions on the tariff, perhaps, in its relations to our American industries——

COOL LATELY: It's clever (*American sense*) of you, Mr. Parkham, to offer these suggestions; but you are not exactly on to it. No, sir. Anyone can have opinions about the tariff and protection and get them into print, for that matter. It's those little intimate details of a man's life—and daily life, that we want—that appeal to the sympathies of our American public. When, where, how were you born. How many servants do you keep? How many horses? What time do you rise in the morning—if in the morning—and what do you eat for your breakfast? These are merely suggestions, of course, which I throw out—which we can elaborate as we go along, and—

EVA: (*Opens door and pokes out her head.*) Pardon me for interruption; but, Willis come here a moment, please. It's about Booboo's bed; he can't sleep on that hard Axminster rug, don't you know? (*Exit Parkham wildly.*)

COOL LATELY: (*Alone.*) Well, Cool Lately, if this find isn't worth a ten dollar raise in your salary, I don't know what is. (*Writes rapidly in note book. Examines circular from all sides, turns it about and feels it. Does same with hat. Finally reads aloud from notes.*) "Corruption in high circles. Mr. Willis Parkham's reasons for declining nomination won't hold water. A lady in the case. Daughter of a well known retired military officer implicated." A good night's work, Cool Lately. (*Replaces book in pocket. Enter Parkham from right.*) Hem-he, (*coughs affectedly.*) I see you have Miss Eva Artless for a guest, Mr. Parkham.

PARKHAM: Miss Artless and her father are doing me that honor, sir.

COOL LATELY: Oh. Ah—really now, that's very singular.

PARKHAM: Not at all singular. It happens often that I entertain such old friends at my house for a day or two.

COOL LATELY: Oh, to be sure. It's nothing. I was merely thinking of a telegram that came into the office an hour or two ago from the G. A. R. reunion at Bolton. Must have been a fake.

PARKHAM: (*Vociferously.*) The lady is *not* Miss Artless!

COOL LATELY: Not Miss Artless! Well, upon my word, I could have sworn it was. Nothing so curious and interesting as these cases of mistaken identity.

PARKHAM: (*Driven to the wall.*) The lady is Mrs. Willis Parkham, my wife! Now will you kindly excuse me, Mr. Lately, from any further conversation, and let me bid you good-night.

COOL LATELY: Why, Mr. Parkham, you must perceive that this is a highly interesting piece of information. Permit me to present my felicitations, and to ask when the happy event was consummated?

PARKHAM: I decline to discuss the subject further. (*Goes towards folding door which he opens.*)

COOL LATELY: I understand then that we have your authority to make public the announcement of your marriage to Miss Eva Artless.

PARKHAM: I have nothing to say. Good evening, Mr. Lately.

COOL LATELY: Good evening, Mr. Parkham. (*Aside.*) A rattling good two-column article, all the same. (*Exit Cool Lately. Parkham drags himself, with a chair, in deepest dejection to front of stage. Seats himself and groans.*) Oh what a situation! *what* a situation! Why couldn't that major have died in his cradle and left this poor girl to be brought up as a rational woman ought to be! But I must act at once. There isn't a moment to lose. Eva Artless has to marry me to-night if she's got to be hypnotized! (*Hurries towards door to left. Opens it and calls.*) Cato! Cato! (*Interval.*) I say, Cato! (*Throws poker, tongs, and finally chair through the door with much clatter.*) Cato!!

CATO: (*Appears, holding candle. Very much in disorder, and half awake.*) Did you heah a rakit, Marse Wills? I was dreamin' dat my po' ole 'oman done come back f'om de distant sho's.

PARKHAM: (*Drags Cato to front of stage.*) Cato, can you be trusted?

CATO: Kin I be trusted! Ef dat aint some'pin putty fur ole Marse Hank Parkham's gran'son to be a axin' Cato! Aint I done ben trested wid mo' gole an' silver 'an you ever sot yo' eyes on?——

PARKHAM: Oh, never mind that story.

CATO:——Dat time down tu de Ridge, w'en we heahed de Yanks a shootin' like all possessed in de hills, an' we knowed dey was a comin',——

PARKHAM: Yes, yes, I know.

CATO:——Ole Marse Hank, he come tu me, an' he 'low "Cato you's de on'iest one on de place w'at I kin tres"——

PARKHAM: (*Simultaneously with Cato's closing lines. Aside.*) By heavens! for once in my life, I shan't hear that story to its close——

CATO: Take dis heah gole, an' dis heah silver——

PARKHAM: Come, listen, Cato. Not another word. There's very important work to be done here before morning, and you've got to do your share of it. You know where the Rev. Dr. Andrews lives?

CATO: De preacher? Like I aint pass by his house an' his chu'ch an' heahed him kiarrin' on mo' times 'an——

PARKHAM: Very well. I want you to go to his house——

CATO: To-morrow mo'nin'?

PARKHAM: Now, to-night. Tell him I must see him at once. If he seems reluctant to come, insist. Tell him it's very urgent.

CATO: I mus'n tell 'im you gwine crazy, Marse Wills?

PARKHAM: Nothing of the sort. But I depend upon you to bring him. Tell him, if it's necessary, that I'm dying, and want the last consolations of the church before breathing my last—anything to make him come. Now go—and be quick.

CATO: (*Aside.*) All de same, I gwine tell 'im I t'inks po' Marse Wills is losin' 'is mine.

(*Exit Cato to left.*)

PARKHAM: (*Alone.*) Now for the ordeal! Willis Parkham, see if you are man enough to win a woman in a quarter of an hour! (*Knocks upon door to right. Eva opens it.*)

EVA: (*Coming upon stage.*) Well, has your friend gone at last? What a time he staid.

PARKHAM: I don't think I said he was my friend.

EVA: No, it's true. You said business acquaintance. What a nice, intelligent face he has.

PARKHAM: I think he has the countenance of a fiend.

EVA: (*Seats herself on ottoman.*) Oh, well, it doesn't matter. But what night-owls we are. It's jolly to be setting up so late, too—but I don't know if papa would like it.

PARKHAM: (*Stands with folded arms and serious air before the girl.*) Eva, there is something very important I want to speak with you about. A matter of paramount importance, I may say.

EVA: Why, I never saw you quite so important before, Willis.

PARKHAM: And I'm sure, there has never before come so critical a moment in my life. I wish to make you an offer of marriage.

EVA: (*Startled, but quickly dissembles her surprise.*) Oh, indeed! Well, I don't know why, but this appears to me a strange time and place you have chosen to make me a proposal of marriage.

PARKHAM: I have chosen neither the time nor the place; both have been forced upon me.

EVA: (*Emphatically.*) Forced upon you! Well, I declare; forced upon you! Perhaps the whole situation has been forced upon you, too?

PARKHAM: It has.

EVA: I am at a perfect loss to understand why you so suddenly, and in the middle of the night, feel forced to make me an offer of marriage. (*With dignity.*) I simply decline it. Consider yourself rejected.

PARKHAM: (*Resolutely.*) No; I'll consider nothing of the sort.

EVA: Just as you like. You needn't to. I consider you rejected, so it amounts to the same thing.

PARKHAM: Please understand, Eva, that I am moved by no purely selfish motives to urge you to become my wife. I am thinking only of you, of your own coming welfare and happiness. The peace of your whole future life may depend upon your marriage to me. There are reasons why you must be my wife—reasons that are not to be set aside.

EVA: (*Has been boiling over. Laughs hysterically.*) And *this* is an offer of marriage! I never had one before! I never want one again! *So* Mr. Willis Parkham, you think that my future happiness depends upon becoming your wife. Well, permit me to inform you, that you are making a curious mistake. The idea of being your wife has never entered my mind. And so little does my future happiness depend upon your society, that I intend to quit it just as soon as I can. (*A conception of his maladroitness has dawned upon Parkham during the above harangue. He seats himself apart with head buried in his hands. He rises finally and goes to stand behind her—but close to her.*)

PARKHAM: Eva——

EVA: (*With affected weariness.*) Oh what is it?

PARKHAM: I have another reason for wanting you to marry me; the strongest reason which any man could have for wanting a woman to be his wife. I suppose it is useless, however, to mention it. I have proven myself so clumsy an idiot, that you can never again think of me save with anger and contempt.

EVA: (*Carelessly.*) Oh, I should like to hear it, all the same—I suppose it is fully as startling as the one you have already expressed.

PARKHAM: You have a perfect right to sneer at so great a fool. I am not asking you now to marry me; I only want to tell you how I love you. (*Bending his head close to hers, fervently.*) Oh, how I love you!

EVA: (*Gives little start of delight, but pretends doubt and indifference.*) Oh, indeed? Another surprising disclosure!

PARKHAM: I knew you'd not believe me. How can I expect you to, after all that has happened?

EVA: No: but these varying moods of yours are interesting. You say you love me.

PARKHAM: To distraction, Eva—

EVA: To distraction! (*Laughs lightly.*) How long, may I ask, have you loved me to distraction?

PARKHAM: (*Distinctly.*) All my life.

EVA: (*Makes figures on the floor with the toe of her boot, for a long moment. Rises suddenly and faces him, seriously and resolutely.*) Willis, how can you say that? You have acted through this whole evening in a way that I can't understand. Now, at the close of it, you tell me that you love me. I want to believe it. But why do you tell me that it has been always? If you do love me, confess, Willis, it has only been for the past hour.

PARKHAM: I have only lived, Eva, for the past hour. (*Eva advances to front and center of stage.*)

PARKHAM: (*Following.*) And you, Eva?

EVA: (*Turns shyly away.*) Oh—I don't know, Willis,—but I believe I have —lived a little longer than that.

(*He takes her in his arms and embraces her tenderly. Cato appears in folding doors. Starts with surprise and turns his back.*)

CATO: Heah's de preacher, Marse Will's!

PARKHAM: Oh, tell the minister to enter, Cato.

EVA: The minister!

PARKHAM: To marry us, Eva.

EVA: Now? To-night?

PARKHAM: Why not to-night rather than to-morrow or a year hence, since we love one another. (*Kisses her hand tenderly.*)

Beyond the Bayou

The bayou curved like a crescent around the point of land on which La Folle's cabin stood. Between the stream and the hut lay a big abandoned field, where cattle were pastured when the bayou supplied them with water enough. Through the woods that spread back into unknown regions the woman had drawn an imaginary line, and past this circle she never stepped. This was the form of her only mania.

She was now a large, gaunt black woman, past thirty-five. Her real name was Jacqueline, but every one on the plantation called her La Folle, because in childhood she had been frightened literally "out of her senses," and had never wholly regained them.

It was when there had been skirmishing and sharpshooting all day in the woods. Evening was near when P'tit Maître, black with powder and crimson with blood, had staggered into the cabin of Jacqueline's mother, his pursuers close at his heels. The sight had stunned her childish reason.

She dwelt alone in her solitary cabin, for the rest of the quarters had long since been removed beyond her sight and knowledge. She had more physical strength than most men, and made her patch of cotton and corn and tobacco like the best of them. But of the world beyond the bayou she had long known nothing, save what her morbid fancy conceived.

People at Bellissime had grown used to her and her way, and they thought nothing of it. Even when "Old Mis'" died, they did not wonder that La Folle had not crossed the bayou, but had stood upon her side of it, wailing and lamenting.

P'tit Maître was now the owner of Bellissime. He was a middle-aged man, with a family of beautiful daughters about him, and a little son whom La Folle loved as if he had been her own. She called him Chéri, and so did every one else because she did.

None of the girls had ever been to her what Chéri was. They had each and all loved to be with her, and to listen to her wondrous stories of things that always happened "yonda, beyon' de bayou."

But none of them had stroked her black hand quite as Chéri did, nor rested their heads against her knee so confidingly, nor fallen asleep in her arms as he used to do. For Chéri hardly did such things now, since he had become the proud possessor of a gun, and had had his black curls cut off.

That summer—the summer Chéri gave La Folle two black curls tied with a knot of red ribbon—the water ran so low in the bayou that even the little children at Bellissime were able to cross it on foot, and the cattle were sent to pasture down by the river. La Folle was sorry when they were gone, for she loved these dumb companions well, and liked to feel that they were there, and to hear them browsing by night up to her own inclosure.

It was Saturday afternoon, when the fields were deserted. The men had flocked to a neighboring village to do their week's trading, and the women were occupied with household affairs,—La Folle as well as the others. It was then she mended and washed her handful of clothes, scoured her house, and did her baking.

In this last employment she never forgot Chéri. To-day she had fashioned croquignoles of the most fantastic and alluring shapes for him. So when she saw the boy come trudging across the old field with his gleaming little new rifle on his shoulder, she called out gayly to him, "Chéri! Chéri!"

But Chéri did not need the summons, for he was coming straight to her. His pockets all bulged out with almonds and raisins and an orange that he had secured for her from the very fine dinner which had been given that day up at his father's house.

He was a sunny-faced youngster of ten. When he had emptied his pockets, La Folle patted his round red cheek, wiped his soiled hands on her apron, and smoothed his hair. Then she watched him as, with his cakes in his hand, he crossed her strip of cotton back of the cabin, and disappeared into the wood.

He had boasted of the things he was going to do with his gun out there.

"You think they got plenty deer in the wood, La Folle?" he had inquired, with the calculating air of an experienced hunter.

"*Non, non!*" the woman laughed. "Don't you look fo' no deer, Chéri. Dat 's too big. But you bring La Folle one good fat squirrel fo' her dinner to-morrow, an' she goin' be satisfi'."

"One squirrel ain't a bite. I'll bring you mo' 'an one, La Folle," he had boasted pompously as he went away.

When the woman, an hour later, heard the report of the boy's rifle close to the wood's edge, she would have thought nothing of it if a sharp cry of distress had not followed the sound.

She withdrew her arms from the tub of suds in which they had been plunged, dried them upon her apron, and as quickly as her trembling limbs would bear her, hurried to the spot whence the ominous report had come.

It was as she feared. There she found Chéri stretched upon the ground, with his rifle beside him. He moaned piteously:—

"I'm dead, La Folle! I'm dead! I'm gone!"

"*Non, non!*" she exclaimed resolutely, as she knelt beside him. "Put you' arm 'roun' La Folle's nake, Chéri. Dat 's nuttin'; dat goin' be nuttin'." She lifted him in her powerful arms.

Chéri had carried his gun muzzle-downward. He had stumbled,—he did not know how. He only knew that he had a ball lodged somewhere in his leg, and he thought that his end was at hand. Now, with his head upon the woman's shoulder, he moaned and wept with pain and fright.

"Oh, La Folle! La Folle! it hurt so bad! I can' stan' it, La Folle!"

"Don't cry, *mon bébé, mon bébé, mon Chéri!*" the woman spoke soothingly as she covered the ground with long strides. "La Folle goin' mine you; Doctor Bonfils goin' come make *mon Chéri* well agin."

She had reached the abandoned field. As she crossed it with her precious burden, she looked constantly and restlessly from side to side. A terrible fear was upon her,—the fear of the world beyond the bayou, the morbid and insane dread she had been under since childhood.

When she was at the bayou's edge she stood there, and shouted for help as if a life depended upon it:—

"Oh, P'tit Maître! P'tit Maître! Venez donc! Au secours! Au secours!"

No voice responded. Chéri's hot tears were scalding her neck. She called for each and every one upon the place, and still no answer came.

She shouted, she wailed; but whether her voice remained unheard or unheeded, no reply came to her frenzied cries. And all the while Chéri moaned and wept and entreated to be taken home to his mother.

La Folle gave a last despairing look around her. Extreme terror was upon her. She clasped the child close against her breast, where he could feel her heart beat like a muffled hammer. Then shutting her eyes, she ran suddenly down the shallow bank of the bayou, and never stopped till she had climbed the opposite shore.

She stood there quivering an instant as she opened her eyes. Then she plunged into the footpath through the trees.

She spoke no more to Chéri, but muttered constantly, "Bon Dieu, ayez pitié La Folle! Bon Dieu, ayez pitié moi!"

Instinct seemed to guide her. When the pathway spread clear and smooth enough before her, she again closed her eyes tightly against the sight of that unknown and terrifying world.

A child, playing in some weeds, caught sight of her as she neared the quarters. The little one uttered a cry of dismay.

"La Folle!" she screamed, in her piercing treble. "La Folle done cross de bayer!"

Quickly the cry passed down the line of cabins.

"Yonda, La Folle done cross de bayou!"

Children, old men, old women, young ones with infants in their arms, flocked to doors and windows to see this awe-inspiring spectacle. Most of them shuddered with superstitious dread of what it might portend. "She totin' Chéri!" some of them shouted.

Some of the more daring gathered about her, and followed at her heels, only to fall back with new terror when she turned her distorted face upon them. Her eyes were bloodshot and the saliva had gathered in a white foam on her black lips.

Some one had run ahead of her to where P'tit Maître sat with his family and guests upon the gallery.

"P'tit Maître! La Folle done cross de bayou! Look her! Look her yonda totin' Chéri!" This startling intimation was the first which they had of the woman's approach.

She was now near at hand. She walked with long strides. Her eyes were fixed desperately before her, and she breathed heavily, as a tired ox.

At the foot of the stairway, which she could not have mounted, she laid the boy in his father's arms. Then the world that had looked red to La Folle suddenly turned black,—like that day she had seen powder and blood.

She reeled for an instant. Before a sustaining arm could reach her, she fell heavily to the ground.

When La Folle regained consciousness, she was at home again, in her own cabin and upon her own bed. The moon rays, streaming in through the open door and windows, gave what light was needed to the old black mammy who stood at the table concocting a tisane of fragrant herbs. It was very late.

Others who had come, and found that the stupor clung to her, had gone again. P'tit Maître had been there, and with him Doctor Bonfils, who said that La Folle might die.

But death had passed her by. The voice was very clear and steady with which she spoke to Tante Lizette, brewing her tisane there in a corner.

"Ef you will give me one good drink tisane, Tante Lizette, I b'lieve I'm goin' sleep, me."

And she did sleep; so soundly, so healthfully, that old Lizette without compunction stole softly away, to creep back through the moonlit fields to her own cabin in the new quarters.

The first touch of the cool gray morning awoke La Folle. She arose, calmly, as if no tempest had shaken and threatened her existence but yesterday.

She donned her new blue cottonade and white apron, for she remembered that this was Sunday. When she had made for herself a cup of strong black coffee, and drunk it with relish, she quitted the cabin and walked across the old familiar field to the bayou's edge again.

She did not stop there as she had always done before, but crossed with a long, steady stride as if she had done this all her life.

When she had made her way through the brush and scrub cottonwood-trees that lined the opposite bank, she found herself upon the border of a field where the white, bursting cotton, with the dew upon it, gleamed for acres and acres like frosted silver in the early dawn.

La Folle drew a long, deep breath as she gazed across the country. She walked slowly and uncertainly, like one who hardly knows how, looking about her as she went.

The cabins, that yesterday had sent a clamor of voices to pursue her, were quiet now. No one was yet astir at Bellissime. Only the birds that darted here and there from hedges were awake, and singing their matins.

When La Folle came to the broad stretch of velvety lawn that surrounded the house, she moved slowly and with delight over the springy turf, that was delicious beneath her tread.

She stopped to find whence came those perfumes that were assailing her senses with memories from a time far gone.

There they were, stealing up to her from the thousand blue violets that peeped out from green, luxuriant beds. There they were, showering down from the big waxen bells of the magnolias far above her head, and from the jessamine clumps around her.

There were roses, too, without number. To right and left palms spread in broad and graceful curves. It all looked like enchantment beneath the sparkling sheen of dew.

When La Folle had slowly and cautiously mounted the many steps that led up to the veranda, she turned to look back at the perilous ascent she had made. Then she caught sight of the river, bending like a silver bow at the foot of Bellissime. Exultation possessed her soul.

La Folle rapped softly upon a door near at hand. Chéri's mother soon cautiously opened it. Quickly and cleverly she dissembled the astonishment she felt at seeing La Folle.

"Ah, La Folle! Is it you, so early?"

"*Oui*, madame. I come ax how my po' li'le Chéri to, 's mo'nin'."

"He is feeling easier, thank you, La Folle. Dr. Bonfils says it will be nothing serious. He's sleeping now. Will you come back when he awakes?"

"*Non*, madame. I'm goin' wait yair tell Chéri wake up." La Folle seated herself upon the topmost step of the veranda.

A look of wonder and deep content crept into her face as she watched for the first time the sun rise upon the new, the beautiful world beyond the bayou.

After the Winter

I

Trézinie, the blacksmith's daughter, stepped out upon the gallery just as M'sieur Michel passed by. He did not notice the girl but walked straight on down the village street.

His seven hounds skulked, as usual, about him. At his side hung his powder-horn, and on his shoulder a gunny-bag slackly filled with game that he carried to the store. A broad felt hat shaded his bearded face and in his hand he carelessly swung his old-fashioned rifle. It was doubtless the same with which he had slain so many people, Trézinie shudderingly reflected. For Cami, the cobbler's son—who must have known—had often related to her how this man had killed two Choctaws, as many Texans, a free mulatto and numberless blacks, in that vague locality known as "the hills."

Older people who knew better took little trouble to correct this ghastly record that a younger generation had scored against him. They themselves had come to half-believe that M'sieur Michel might be capable of anything, living as he had, for so many years, apart from humanity, alone with his hounds in a kennel of a cabin on the hill. The time seemed to most of them fainter than a memory when, a lusty young fellow of twenty-five, he had cultivated his strip of land across the lane from Les Chêniers; when home and toil and wife and child were so many benedictions that he humbly thanked heaven for having given him.

But in the early '60's he went with his friend Duplan and the rest of the "Louisiana Tigers." He came back with some of them. He came to find—well, death may lurk in a peaceful valley lying in wait to ensnare the toddling feet of little ones. Then, there are women—there are wives with thoughts that roam and grow wanton with roaming; women whose pulses are stirred by strange voices and eyes that woo; women who forget the claims of yesterday, the hopes of to-morrow, in the impetuous clutch of to-day.

But that was no reason, some people thought, why he should have cursed men who found their blessings where they had left them—cursed God, who had abandoned him.

Persons who met him upon the road had long ago stopped greeting him. What was the use? He never answered them; he spoke to no one; he never so much as looked into men's faces. When he bartered his game and fish at the village store for powder and shot and such scant food as he needed, he did so with few words and less courtesy. Yet feeble as it was, this was the only link that held him to his fellow-beings.

Strange to say, the sight of M'sieur Michel, though more forbidding than ever that delightful spring afternoon, was so suggestive to Trézinie as to be almost an inspiration.

It was Easter eve and the early part of April. The whole earth seemed teeming with new, green, vigorous life everywhere—except the arid spot that immediately surrounded Trézinie. It was no use; she had tried. Nothing would grow among those cinders that filled the yard; in that atmosphere of smoke and flame that was constantly belching from the forge where her father worked at his trade. There were wagon wheels, bolts and bars of iron, plowshares and all manner of unpleasant-looking things littering the bleak, black yard; nothing green anywhere except a few weeds that would force themselves into fence corners. And Trézinie knew that flowers belong to Easter time, just as dyed eggs do. She had plenty of eggs; no one had more or prettier ones; she was not going to grumble about that. But she did feel distressed because she had not a flower to help deck the altar on Easter morning. And every one else seemed to have them in such abundance! There was 'Dame Suzanne among her roses across the way. She must have clipped a hundred since noon. An hour ago Trézinie had seen the carriage from Les Chêniers pass by on its way to church with Mamzelle Euphrasie's pretty head looking like a picture enframed with the Easter lilies that filled the vehicle.

For the twentieth time Trézinie walked out upon the gallery. She saw M'sieur Michel and thought of the pine hill. When she thought of the hill she thought of the flowers that grew there—free as sunshine. The girl gave a joyous spring that changed to a farandole as her feet twinkled across the rough, loose boards of the gallery.

"Hé, Cami!" she cried, clapping her hands together.

Cami rose from the bench where he sat pegging away at the clumsy sole of a shoe, and came lazily to the fence that divided his abode from Trézinie's.

"Well, w'at?" he inquired with heavy amiability. She leaned far over the railing to better communicate with him.

"You'll go with me yonda on the hill to pick flowers fo' Easter, Cami? I'm goin' to take La Fringante along, too, to he'p with the baskets. W'at you say?"

"No!" was the stolid reply. "I'm boun' to finish them shoe', if it is fo' a nigga."

"Not now," she returned impatiently; "to-morrow mo'nin' at sun-up. An' I tell you, Cami, my flowers'll beat all! Look yonda at 'Dame Suzanne pickin' her roses a'ready. An' Mamzelle Euphrasie she's car'ied her lilies an' gone, her. You tell me all that's goin' be fresh to-moro'!"

"Jus' like you say," agreed the boy, turning to resume his work. "But you want to mine out fo' the ole possum up in the wood. Let M'sieu Michel set eyes on you!" and he raised his arms as if aiming with a gun. "Pim, pam, poum! No mo' Trézinie, no mo' Cami, no mo' La Fringante—all stretch'!"

The possible risk which Cami so vividly foreshadowed but added a zest to Trézinie's projected excursion.

II

It was hardly sun-up on the following morning when the three children —Trézinie, Cami and the little negress, La Fringante—were filling big, flat Indian baskets from the abundance of brilliant flowers that studded the hill.

In their eagerness they had ascended the slope and penetrated deep into the forest without thought of M'sieur Michel or of his abode. Suddenly, in the dense wood, they came upon his hut—low, forbidding, seeming to scowl rebuke upon them for their intrusion.

La Fringante dropped her basket, and, with a cry, fled. Cami looked as if he wanted to do the same. But Trézinie, after the first tremor, saw that the ogre himself was away. The wooden shutter of the one window was closed. The door, so low that even a small man must have stooped to enter it, was secured with a chain. Absolute silence reigned, except for the whirr of wings in the air, the fitful notes of a bird in the treetop.

"Can't you see it's nobody there!" cried Trézinie impatiently.

La Fringante, distracted between curiosity and terror, had crept cautiously back again. Then they all peeped through the wide chinks between the logs of which the cabin was built.

M'sieur Michel had evidently begun the construction of his house by felling a huge tree, whose remaining stump stood in the centre of the hut, and served him as a table. This primitive table was worn smooth by twenty-five years of use. Upon it were such humble utensils as the man required. Everything within the hovel, the sleeping bunk, the one seat, were as rude as a savage would have fashioned them.

The stolid Cami could have stayed for hours with his eyes fastened to the aperture, morbidly seeking some dead, mute sign of that awful pastime with which he believed M'sieur Michel was accustomed to beguile his solitude. But Trézinie was wholly possessed by the thought of her Easter offerings. She wanted flowers and flowers, fresh with the earth and crisp with dew.

When the three youngsters scampered down the hill again there was not a purple verbena left about M'sieur Michel's hut; not a May apple blossom, not a stalk of crimson phlox—hardly a violet.

He was something of a savage, feeling that the solitude belonged to him. Of late there had been forming within his soul a sentiment toward man, keener than indifference, bitter as hate. He was coming to dread even that brief intercourse with others into which his traffic forced him.

So when M'sieur Michel returned to his hut, and with his quick, accustomed eye saw that his woods had been despoiled, rage seized him. It was not that he loved the flowers that were gone more than he loved the stars, or the wind that trailed across the hill, but they belonged to and were a part of that life which he had made for himself, and which he wanted to live alone and unmolested.

Did not those flowers help him to keep his record of time that was passing? They had no right to vanish until the hot May days were upon him. How else should he know? Why had these people, with whom he had nothing in common, intruded upon his privacy and violated it? What would they not rob him of next?

He knew well enough it was Easter; he had heard and seen signs yesterday in the store that told him so. And he guessed that his woods had been rifled to add to the mummery of the day.

M'sieur Michel sat himself moodily down beside his table—centuries old—and brooded. He did not even notice his hounds that were pleading to be fed. As he revolved in his mind the event of the morning—innocent as it was in itself—it grew in importance and assumed a significance not at first apparent. He could not remain passive under pressure of its disturbance. He rose to his feet, every impulse aggressive, urging him to activity. He would go down among those people all gathered together, blacks and whites, and face them for once and all. He did not know what he would say to them, but it would be defiance—something to voice the hate that oppressed him.

The way down the hill, then across a piece of flat, swampy woodland and through the lane to the village was so familiar that it required no attention from him to follow it. His thoughts were left free to revel in the humor that had driven him from his kennel.

As he walked down the village street he saw plainly that the place was deserted save for the appearance of an occasional negress, who seemed occupied with preparing the midday meal. But about the church scores of horses were fastened; and M'sieur Michel could see that the edifice was thronged to the very threshold.

He did not once hesitate, but obeying the force that impelled him to face the people wherever they might be, he was soon standing with the crowd within the entrance of the church. His broad, robust shoulders had forced space for himself, and his leonine head stood higher than any there.

"Take off yo' hat!"

It was an indignant mulatto who addressed him. M'sieur Michel instinctively did as he was bidden. He saw confusedly that there was a mass of humanity close to him, whose contact and atmosphere affected him strangely. He saw his wild-flowers, too. He saw them plainly, in bunches and festoons, among the Easter lilies and roses and geraniums. He was going to speak out, now; he had the right to and he would, just as soon as that clamor overhead would cease.

"Bonté divine! M'sieur Michel!" whispered 'Dame Suzanne tragically to her neighbor. Trézinie heard. Cami saw. They exchanged an electric glance, and tremblingly bowed their heads low.

M'sieur Michel looked wrathfully down at the puny mulatto who had ordered him to remove his hat. Why had he obeyed? That initial act of compliance had somehow weakened his will, his resolution. But he would regain firmness just as soon as that clamor above gave him chance to speak.

It was the organ filling the small edifice with volumes of sound. It was the voices of men and women mingling in the "Gloria in excelsis Deo!"

The words bore no meaning for him apart from the old familiar strain which he had known as a child and chanted himself in that same organ-loft years ago. How it went on and on! Would it never cease! It was like a menace; like a voice reaching out from the dead past to taunt him.

"Gloria in excelsis Deo!" over and over! How the deep basso rolled it out! How the tenor and alto caught it up and passed it on to be lifted by the high, flute-like ring of the soprano, till all mingled again in the wild pæan, "Gloria in excelsis!"

How insistent was the refrain! and where, what, was that mysterious, hidden quality in it; the power which was overcoming M'sieur Michel, stirring within him a turmoil that bewildered him?

There was no use in trying to speak, or in wanting to. His throat could not have uttered a sound. He wanted to escape, that was all. "Bonæ voluntatis,"—he bent his head as if before a beating storm. "Gloria! Gloria! Gloria!" He must fly; he must save himself, regain his hill where sights and odors and sounds and saints or devils would cease to molest him. "In excelsis Deo!" He retreated, forcing his way backward to the door. He dragged his hat down over his eyes and staggered away down the road. But the refrain pursued him—"Pax! pax! pax!"—fretting him like a lash. He did not slacken his pace till the tones grew fainter than an echo, floating, dying away in an "in excelsis!" When he could hear it no longer he stopped and breathed a sigh of rest and relief.

III

All day long M'sieur Michel stayed about his hut engaged in some familiar employment that he hoped might efface the unaccountable impressions of the morning. But his restlessness was unbounded. A longing had sprung up within him as sharp as pain and not to be appeased. At once, on this bright, warm Easter morning the voices that till now had filled his solitude became meaningless. He stayed mute and uncomprehending before them. Their significance had vanished before the driving want for human sympathy and companionship that had reawakened in his soul.

When night came on he walked through the woods down the slant of the hill again.

"It mus' be all fill' up with weeds," muttered M'sieur Michel to himself as he went. "Ah, Bon Dieu! with trees, Michel, with trees—in twenty-five years, man."

He had not taken the road to the village, but was pursuing a different one in which his feet had not walked for many days. It led him along the river bank for a distance. The narrow stream, stirred by the restless breeze, gleamed in the moonlight that was flooding the land.

As he went on and on, the scent of the newplowed earth that had been from the first keenly perceptible, began to intoxicate him. He wanted to kneel and bury his face in it. He wanted to dig into it; turn it over. He wanted to scatter the seed again as he had done long ago, and watch the new, green life spring up as if at his bidding.

When he turned away from the river, and had walked a piece down the lane that divided Joe Duplan's plantation from that bit of land that had once been his, he wiped his eyes to drive away the mist that was making him see things as they surely could not be.

He had wanted to plant a hedge that time before he went away, but he had not done so. Yet there was the hedge before him, just as he had meant it to be, and filling the night with fragrance. A broad, low gate divided its length, and over this he leaned and looked before him in amazement. There were no weeds as he had fancied; no trees except the scattered live oaks that he remembered.

Could that row of hardy fig trees, old, squat and gnarled, be the twigs that he himself had set one day into the ground? One raw December day when there was a fine, cold mist falling. The chill of it breathed again upon him; the memory was so real. The land did not look as if it ever had been plowed for a field. It was a smooth, green meadow, with cattle huddled upon the cool sward, or moving with slow, stately tread as they nibbled the tender shoots.

There was the house unchanged, gleaming white in the moon, seeming to invite him beneath its calm shelter. He wondered who dwelt within it now. Whoever it was he would not have them find him, like a prowler, there at the gate. But he would come again and again like this at night-time, to gaze and refresh his spirit.

A hand had been laid upon M'sieur Michel's shoulder and some one called his name. Startled, he turned to see who accosted him.

"Duplan!"

The two men who had not exchanged speech for so many years stood facing each other for a long moment in silence.

"I knew you would come back some day, Michel. It was a long time to wait, but you have come home at last."

M'sieur Michel cowered instinctively and lifted his hands with expressive deprecatory gesture. "No, no; it's no place for me, Joe; no place!"

"Isn't a man's home a place for him, Michel?" It seemed less a question than an assertion, charged with gentle authority.

"Twenty-five years, Duplan; twenty-five years! It's no use; it's too late."

"You see, I have used it," went on the planter, quietly, ignoring M'sieur Michel's protestations. "Those are my cattle grazing off there. The house has served me many a time to lodge guests or workmen, for whom I had no room at Les Chêniers. I have not exhausted the soil with any crops. I had not the right to do that. Yet am I in your debt, Michel, and ready to settle en bon ami."

The planter had opened the gate and entered the inclosure, leading M'sieur Michel with him. Together they walked toward the house.

Language did not come readily to either—one so unaccustomed to hold intercourse with men; both so stirred with memories that would have rendered any speech painful. When they had stayed long in a silence which was eloquent of tenderness, Joe Duplan spoke:

"You know how I tried to see you, Michel, to speak with you, and you never would."

M'sieur Michel answered with but a gesture that seemed a supplication.

"Let the past all go, Michel. Begin your new life as if the twenty-five years that are gone had been a long night, from which you have only awakened. Come to me in the morning," he added with quick resolution, "for a horse and a plow." He had taken the key of the house from his pocket and placed it in M'sieur Michel's hand.

"A horse?" M'sieur Michel repeated uncertainly; "a plow! Oh, it's too late, Duplan; too late."

"It isn't too late. The land has rested all these years, man; it's fresh, I tell you; and rich as gold. Your crop will be the finest in the land." He held out his hand and M'sieur Michel pressed it without a word in reply, save a muttered "Mon ami."

Then he stood there watching the planter disappear behind the high, clipped hedge.

He held out his arms. He could not have told if it was toward the retreating figure, or in welcome to an infinite peace that seemed to descend upon him and envelop him.

All the land was radiant except the hill far off that was in black shadow against the sky.

The Bênitous' Slave

Old Uncle Oswald believed he belonged to the Bênitous, and there was no getting the notion out of his head. Monsieur tried every way, for there was no sense in it. Why, it must have been fifty years since the Bênitous owned him. He had belonged to others since, and had later been freed. Beside, there was not a Bênitou left in the parish now, except one rather delicate woman, who lived with her little daughter in a corner of Natchitoches town, and constructed "fashionable millinery." The family had dispersed, and almost vanished, and the plantation as well had lost its identity.

But that made no difference to Uncle Oswald. He was always running away from Monsieur—who kept him out of pure kindness—and trying to get back to those Bênitous.

More than that, he was constantly getting injured in such attempts. Once he fell into the bayou and was nearly drowned. Again he barely escaped being run down by an engine. But another time, when he had been lost two days, and finally discovered in an unconscious and half-dead condition in the woods, Monsieur and Doctor Bonfils reluctantly decided that it was time to "do something" with the old man.

So, one sunny spring morning, Monsieur took Uncle Oswald in the buggy, and drove over to Natchitoches with him, intending to take the evening train for the institution in which the poor creature was to be cared for.

It was quite early in the afternoon when they reached town, and Monsieur found himself with several hours to dispose of before train-time. He tied his horses in front of the hotel—the quaintest old stuccoed house, too absurdly unlike a "hotel" for anything—and entered. But he left Uncle Oswald seated upon a shaded bench just within the yard.

There were people occasionally coming in and going out; but no one took the smallest notice of the old negro drowsing over the cane that he held between his knees. The sight was common in Natchitoches.

One who passed in was a little girl about twelve, with dark, kind eyes, and daintily carrying a parcel. She was dressed in blue calico, and wore a stiff white sun-bonnet, extinguisher fashion, over her brown curls.

Just as she passed Uncle Oswald again, on her way out, the old man, half asleep, let fall his cane. She picked it up and handed it back to him, as any nice child would have done.

"Oh, thankee, thankee, missy," stammered Uncle Oswald, all confused at being waited upon by this little lady. "You is a putty li'le gal. W'at 's yo' name, honey?"

"My name 's Susanne; Susanne Bênitou," replied the girl.

Instantly the old negro stumbled to his feet. Without a moment's hesitancy he followed the little one out through the gate, down the street, and around the corner.

It was an hour later that Monsieur, after a distracted search, found him standing upon the gallery of the tiny house in which Madame Bênitou kept "fashionable millinery."

Mother and daughter were sorely perplexed to comprehend the intentions of the venerable servitor, who stood, hat in hand, persistently awaiting their orders.

Monsieur understood and appreciated the situation at once, and he has prevailed upon Madame Bênitou to accept the gratuitous services of Uncle Oswald for the sake of the old darky's own safety and happiness.

Uncle Oswald never tries to run away now. He chops wood and hauls water. He cheerfully and faithfully bears the parcels that Susanne used to carry; and makes an excellent cup of black coffee.

I met the old man the other day in Natchitoches, contentedly stumbling down St. Denis street with a basket of figs that some one was sending to his mistress. I asked him his name.

"My name 's Oswal', Madam; Oswal'—dat's my name. I b'longs to de Bênitous," and some one told me his story then.

A Turkey Hunt

Three of Madame's finest bronze turkeys were missing from the brood. It was nearing Christmas, and that was the reason, perhaps, that even Monsieur grew agitated when the discovery was made. The news was brought to the house by Sévérin's boy, who had seen the troop at noon a half mile up the bayou three short. Others reported the deficiency as even greater. So, at about two in the afternoon, though a cold drizzle had begun to fall, popular feeling in the matter was so strong that all the household forces turned out to search for the missing gobblers.

Alice, the housemaid, went down the river, and Polisson, the yard-boy, went up the bayou. Others crossed the fields, and Artemise was rather vaguely instructed to "go look too."

Artemise is in some respects an extraordinary person. In age she is anywhere between ten and fifteen, with a head not unlike in shape and appearance to a dark chocolate-colored Easter-egg. She talks almost wholly in monosyllables, and has big round glassy eyes, which she fixes upon one with the placid gaze of an Egyptian sphinx.

The morning after my arrival at the plantation, I was awakened by the rattling of cups at my bedside. It was Artemise with the early coffee.

"Is it cold out?" I asked, by way of conversation, as I sipped the tiny cup of ink-black coffee.

"Ya, 'm."

"Where do you sleep, Artemise?" I further inquired, with the same intention as before.

"In uh hole," was precisely what she said, with a pump-like motion of the arm that she habitually uses to indicate a locality. What she meant was that she slept in the hall.

Again, another time, she came with an armful of wood, and having deposited it upon the hearth, turned to stare fixedly at me, with folded hands.

"Did Madame send you to build a fire, Artemise?" I hastened to ask, feeling uncomfortable under the look.

"Ya, 'm."

"Very well; make it."

"Matches!" was all she said.

There happened to be no matches in my room, and she evidently considered that all personal responsibility ceased in face of this first and not very serious obstacle. Pages might be told of her unfathomable ways; but to the turkey hunt.

All afternoon the searching party kept returning, singly and in couples, and in a more or less bedraggled condition. All brought unfavorable reports. Nothing could be seen of the missing fowls. Artemise had been absent probably an hour when she glided into the hall where the family was assembled, and stood with crossed hands and contemplative air beside the fire. We could see by the benign expression of her countenance that she possibly had information to give, if any inducement were offered her in the shape of a question.

"Have you found the turkeys, Artemise?" Madame hastened to ask.

"Ya, 'm."

"You Artemise!" shouted Aunt Florindy, the cook, who was passing through the hall with a batch of newly baked light bread. "She 's a-lyin', mist'ess, if dey ever was! *You* foun' dem turkeys?" turning upon the child. "Whar was you at, de whole blesse' time? Warn't you stan'in' plank up agin de back o' de hen-'ous'? Never budged a inch? Don't jaw me down, gal; don't jaw me!" Artemise was only gazing at Aunt Florindy with un-ruffled calm. "I warn't gwine tell on 'er, but arter dat untroof, I boun' to."

"Let her alone, Aunt Florindy," Madame interfered. "Where are the turkeys, Artemise?"

"Yon'a," she simply articulated, bringing the pump-handle motion of her arm into play.

"Where 'yonder'?" Madame demanded, a little impatiently.

"In uh hen-'ous'!"

Sure enough! The three missing turkeys had been accidentally locked up in the morning when the chickens were fed.

Artemise, for some unknown reason, had hidden herself during the search behind the hen-house, and had heard their muffled gobble.

Old Aunt Peggy

When the war was over, old Aunt Peggy went to Monsieur, and said:—

"Massa, I ain't never gwine to quit yer. I'm gittin' ole an' feeble, an' my days is few in dis heah lan' o' sorrow an' sin. All I axes is a li'le co'ner whar I kin set down an' wait peaceful fu de en'."

Monsieur and Madame were very much touched at this mark of affection and fidelity from Aunt Peggy. So, in the general reconstruction of the plantation which immediately followed the surrender, a nice cabin, pleasantly appointed, was set apart for the old woman. Madame did not even forget the very comfortable rocking-chair in which Aunt Peggy might "set down," as she herself feelingly expressed it, "an' wait fu de en'."

She has been rocking ever since.

At intervals of about two years Aunt Peggy hobbles up to the house, and delivers the stereotyped address which has become more than familiar:—

"Mist'ess, I 's come to take a las' look at you all. Le' me look at you good. Le' me look at de chillun,—de big chillun an' de li'le chillun. Le' me look at de picters an' de photygraphts an' de pianny, an' eve'ything 'fo' it 's too late. One eye is done gone, an' de udder 's a-gwine fas'. Any mo'nin' yo' po' ole Aunt Peggy gwine wake up an' fin' herse'f stone-bline."

After such a visit Aunt Peggy invariably returns to her cabin with a generously filled apron.

The scruple which Monsieur one time felt in supporting a woman for so many years in idleness has entirely disappeared. Of late his attitude towards Aunt Peggy is simply one of profound astonishment,—wonder at the surprising age which an old black woman may attain when she sets her mind to it, for Aunt Peggy is a hundred and twenty-five, so she says.

It may not be true, however. Possibly she is older.

The Lilies

That little vagabond Mamouche amused himself one afternoon by letting down the fence rails that protected Mr. Billy's young crop of cotton and corn. He had first looked carefully about him to make sure there was no witness to this piece of rascality. Then he crossed the lane and did the same with the Widow Angèle's fence, thereby liberating Toto, the white calf who stood disconsolately penned up on the other side.

It was not ten seconds before Toto was frolicking madly in Mr. Billy's crop, and Mamouche—the young scamp—was running swiftly down the lane, laughing fiendishly to himself as he went.

He could not at first decide whether there could be more fun in letting Toto demolish things at his pleasure, or in warning Mr. Billy of the calf's presence in the field. But the latter course commended itself as possessing a certain refinement of perfidy.

"Ho, the'a, you!" called out Mamouche to one of Mr. Billy's hands, when he got around to where the men were at work; "you betta go yon'a an' see 'bout that calf o' Ma'me Angèle; he done broke in the fiel' an' 'bout to finish the crop, him." Then Mamouche went and sat behind a big tree, where, unobserved, he could laugh to his heart's content.

Mr. Billy's fury was unbounded when he learned that Madame Angèle's calf was eating up and trampling down his corn. At once he sent a detachment of men and boys to expel the animal from the field. Others were required to repair the damaged fence; while he himself, boiling with wrath, rode up the lane on his wicked black charger.

But merely to look upon the devastation was not enough for Mr. Billy. He dismounted from his horse, and strode belligerently up to Madame

Angèle's door, upon which he gave, with his riding-whip, a couple of sharp raps that plainly indicated the condition of his mind.

Mr. Billy looked taller and broader than ever as he squared himself on the gallery of Madame Angèle's small and modest house. She herself half-opened the door, a pale, sweet-looking woman, somewhat bewildered, and holding a piece of sewing in her hands. Little Marie Louise was beside her, with big, inquiring, frightened eyes.

"Well, Madam!" blustered Mr. Billy, "this is a pretty piece of work! That young beast of yours is a fence-breaker, Madam, and ought to be shot."

"Oh, non, non, M'sieur. Toto's too li'le; I'm sho he can't break any fence, him."

"Don't contradict me, Madam. I say he's a fence-breaker. There's the proof before your eyes. He ought to be shot, I say, and—don't let it occur again, Madam." And Mr. Billy turned and stamped down the steps with a great clatter of spurs as he went.

Madame Angèle was at the time in desperate haste to finish a young lady's Easter dress, and she could not afford to let Toto's escapade occupy her to any extent, much as she regretted it. But little Marie Louise was greatly impressed by the affair. She went out in the yard to Toto, who was under the fig-tree, looking not half so shamefaced as he ought. The child, with arms clasped around the little fellow's white shaggy neck, scolded him roundly.

"Ain't you shame', Toto, to go eat up Mr. Billy's cotton an' co'n? W'at Mr. Billy ev'a done to you, to go do him that way? If you been hungry, Toto, w'y you did'n' come like always an' put yo' head in the winda? I'm goin' tell yo' maman w'en she come back f'om the woods to 's'evenin', M'sieur."

Marie Louise only ceased her mild rebuke when she fancied she saw a penitential look in Toto's big soft eyes.

She had a keen instinct of right and justice for so young a little maid. And all the afternoon, and long into the night, she was disturbed by the thought of the unfortunate accident. Of course, there could be no question of repaying Mr. Billy with money; she and her mother had none. Neither had they cotton and corn with which to make good the loss he had sustained through them.

But had they not something far more beautiful and precious than cotton and corn? Marie Louise thought with delight of that row of Easter lilies on their tall green stems, ranged thick along the sunny side of the house.

The assurance that she would, after all, be able to satisfy Mr. Billy's just anger, was a very sweet one. And soothed by it, Marie Louise soon fell asleep and dreamt a grotesque dream: that the lilies were having a stately dance on the green in the moonlight, and were inviting Mr. Billy to join them.

The following day, when it was nearing noon, Marie Louise said to her mamma: "Maman, can I have some of the Easter lily, to do with like I want?"

Madame Angèle was just then testing the heat of an iron with which to press out the seams in the young lady's Easter dress, and she answered a shade impatiently:

"Yes, yes; va t'en, chérie," thinking that her little girl wanted to pluck a lily or two.

So the child took a pair of old shears from her mother's basket, and out she went to where the tall, perfumed lilies were nodding, and shaking off from their glistening petals the rain-drops with which a passing cloud had just laughingly pelted them.

Snip, snap, went the shears here and there, and never did Marie Louise stop plying them till scores of those long-stemmed lilies lay upon the ground. There were far more than she could hold in her small hands, so she literally clasped the great bunch in her arms, and staggered to her feet with it.

Marie Louise was intent upon her purpose, and lost no time in its accomplishment. She was soon trudging earnestly down the lane with her sweet burden, never stopping, and only once glancing aside to cast a reproachful look at Toto, whom she had not wholly forgiven.

She did not in the least mind that the dogs barked, or that the darkies laughed at her. She went straight on to Mr. Billy's big house, and right into the dining-room, where Mr. Billy sat eating his dinner all alone.

It was a finely-furnished room, but disorderly—very disorderly, as an old bachelor's personal surroundings sometimes are. A black boy stood waiting upon the table. When little Marie Louise suddenly appeared, with that armful of lilies, Mr. Billy seemed for a moment transfixed at the sight.

"Well—bless—my soul! what's all this? What's all this?" he questioned, with staring eyes.

Marie Louise had already made a little courtesy. Her sunbonnet had fallen back, leaving exposed her pretty round head; and her sweet brown eyes were full of confidence as they looked into Mr. Billy's.

"I'm bring some lilies to pay back fo' yo' cotton an' co'n w'at Toto eat all up, M'sieur."

Mr. Billy turned savagely upon Pompey. "What are you laughing at, you black rascal? Leave the room!"

Pompey, who out of mistaken zeal had doubled himself with merriment, was too accustomed to the admonition to heed it literally, and he only made a pretense of withdrawing from Mr. Billy's elbow.

"Lilies! well, upon my—isn't it the little one from across the lane?"

"Dat's who," affirmed Pompey, cautiously insinuating himself again into favor.

"Lilies! who ever heard the like? Why, the baby's buried under 'em. Set 'em down somewhere, little one; anywhere." And Marie Louise, glad to be relieved from the weight of the great cluster, dumped them all on the table close to Mr. Billy.

The perfume that came from the damp, massed flowers was heavy and almost sickening in its pungency. Mr. Billy quivered a little, and drew involuntarily back, as if from an unexpected assailant, when the odor reached him. He had been making cotton and corn for so many years, he had forgotten there were such things as lilies in the world.

"Kiar 'em out? fling 'em 'way?" questioned Pompey, who had observed his master cunningly.

"Let 'em alone! Keep your hands off them! Leave the room, you out-landish black scamp! Whar are you standing there for? Can't you set the Mamzelle a place at table, and draw up a chair?"

So Marie Louise—perched upon a fine old-fashioned chair, supplemented by a Webster's Unabridged—sat down to dine with Mr. Billy.

She had never eaten in company with so peculiar a gentlemen before; so irascible toward the inoffensive Pompey, and so courteous to herself. But she was not ill at ease, and conducted herself properly as her mamma had taught her how.

Mr. Billy was anxious that she should enjoy her dinner, and began by helping her generously to Jambalaya. When she had tasted it she made no remark, only laid down her fork, and looked composedly before her.

"Why, bless me! what ails the little one? You don't eat your rice."

"It ain't cook', M'sieur," replied Marie Louise politely.

Pompey nearly strangled in his attempt to smother an explosion.

"Of course it isn't cooked," echoed Mr. Billy, excitedly, pushing away his plate. "What do you mean, setting a mess of that sort before human beings? Do you take us for a couple of—of rice-birds? What are you standing there for; can't you look up some jam or something to keep the young one from starving? Where's all that jam I saw stewing a while back, here?"

Pompey withdrew, and soon returned with a platter of black-looking jam. Mr. Billy ordered cream for it. Pompey reported there was none.

"No cream, with twenty-five cows on the plantation if there's one!" cried Mr. Billy, almost springing from his chair with indignation.

"Aunt Printy 'low she sot de pan o' cream on de winda-sell, suh, an' Unc' Jonah come 'long an' tu'n it cl'ar ova; neva lef' a drap in de pan."

But evidently the jam, with or without cream, was as distasteful to Marie Louise as the rice was; for after tasting it gingerly she laid away her spoon as she had done before.

"O, no! little one; you don't tell me it isn't cooked this time," laughed Mr. Billy. "I saw the thing boiling a day and a half. Wasn't it a day and a half, Pompey? if you know how to tell the truth."

"Aunt Printy alluz do cooks her p'esarves tell dey plumb done, sho," agreed Pompey.

"It's burn', M'sieur," said Marie Louise, politely, but decidedly, to the utter confusion of Mr. Billy, who was as mortified as could be at the failure of his dinner to please his fastidious little visitor.

Well, Mr. Billy thought of Marie Louise a good deal after that; as long as the lilies lasted. And they lasted long, for he had the whole household employed in taking care of them. Often he would chuckle to himself: "The little rogue, with her black eyes and her lilies! And the rice wasn't cooked, if you please; and the jam was burnt. And the best of it is, she was right."

But when the lilies withered finally, and had to be thrown away, Mr. Billy donned his best suit, a starched shirt and fine silk necktie. Thus attired, he crossed the lane to carry his somewhat tardy apologies to Madame Angèle and Mamzelle Marie Louise, and to pay them a first visit.

Ripe Figs

Maman-Nainaine said that when the figs were ripe Babette might go to visit her cousins down on the Bayou-Lafourche where the sugar cane grows. Not that the ripening of figs had the least thing to do with it, but that is the way Maman-Nainaine was.

It seemed to Babette a very long time to wait; for the leaves upon the trees were tender yet, and the figs were like little hard, green marbles.

But warm rains came along and plenty of strong sunshine, and though Maman-Nainaine was as patient as the statue of la Madone, and Babette as restless as a humming-bird, the first thing they both knew it was hot summer-time. Every day Babette danced out to where the fig-trees were in a long line against the fence. She walked slowly beneath them, carefully peering between the gnarled, spreading branches. But each time she came disconsolate away again. What she saw there finally was something that made her sing and dance the whole long day.

When Maman-Nainaine sat down in her stately way to breakfast, the following morning, her muslin cap standing like an aureole about her white, placid face, Babette approached. She bore a dainty porcelain platter, which she set down before her godmother. It contained a dozen purple figs, fringed around with their rich, green leaves.

"Ah," said Maman-Nainaine, arching her eyebrows, "how early the figs have ripened this year!"

"Oh," said Babette, "I think they have ripened very late."

"Babette," continued Maman-Nainaine, as she peeled the very plumpest figs with her pointed silver fruit-knife, "you will carry my love to them all down on Bayou-Lafourche. And tell your Tante Frosine I shall look for her at Toussaint—when the chrysanthemums are in bloom."

Croque-Mitaine

There was one thing about the nursery-governess from Paris that did not suit P'tit-Paul. It was her constant reference, in a semi-threatening way, to one Croque-Mitaine, a hideous ogre, said to inhabit the strip of wood just beyond the children's playground.

The darkies knew nothing of such an existence; for P'tit-Paul questioned them:

"You neva saw Croque-Mitaine, you, Unc' Juba?"

"No, honey. Don't you listen tu no sich talk. Dat 'ar wood ain't no mo' haunted 'an my ole 'oman's veg'tible patch. W'y dar hain't no buryin'-groun' din fo' mile' o' heah! You knows dat diz uz well uz I does, boy."

But as Mamzelle's allusions to Croque-Mitaine grew more and more frequent, P'tit-Paul decided to investigate the matter himself, finally.

A favorable occasion soon presented itself. Mamzelle was going to a ball at a neighboring plantation. But before leaving she impressed upon the little ones that they must lie very still and go to sleep, or Croque-Mitaine would stalk from the wood and come to devour them where they lay.

She had hardly gone than P'tit-Paul slipped into his clothes and stole away to go sit at the far end of the play-ground upon a bench there, that commanded a view of the road which was much travelled. It will be seen that beside an inquiring spirit, P'tit-Paul possessed a very courageous one.

The night was beautiful, with a round moon lighting the landscape and a delicious fragrance filling the soft, warm air. Off in the Magnolia-trees the mocking-birds had begun their nightly serenade.

After a half-hour, no one had yet passed by except Uncle Juba who stopped a moment to upbraid the child for "settin' dis so, in de full o' de moon."

Then another half-hour went by and P'tit-Paul was growing drowsy, when suddenly the blood chilled in his veins and the hair fairly rose on his head. For, coming towards him from the wood, was an object more horrible than his eyes had ever beheld or his fancy pictured. It bore the grotesque shape of a man, but its head was that of an unfamiliar beast having great horns and wild tremendous eyes. The monster wielded a pitch-fork in his misshapen hand and Paul doubted not that in a few moments he would feel its cruel prongs piercing his own body.

Besides being almost powerless to run, he felt it would be useless, and reasoned confusedly that perhaps Croque-Mitaine might be conciliated, for he was even then flourishing in his paw what seemed to be a flag of truce.

The shape approached nearer and nearer, and Paul shrunk smaller and smaller in the corner of the bench.

Then a most singular thing happened. Croque-Mitaine stood still in the road, rested his pitch-fork, and removing his hideous face, began to mop his head with the flag of truce! Then P'tit-Paul understood!

He hardly remembers how he reached home.

Next morning he confided his discovery to the little brothers and sisters.

When Mamzelle talks of Croque-Mitaine now, they look at each other and smile slyly and very provokingly. For they know that Croque-Mitaine is only Monsieur Alcée going to a masked ball!

A Little Free-Mulatto*

M'sié Jean-Ba'—that was Aurélia's father—was so especially fine and imposing when he went down to the city, with his glossy beard, his elegant clothes, and gold watch-chain, that he could easily have ridden in the car "For Whites." No one would ever have known the difference. But M'sié Jean-Ba' was too proud to do that. He was very proud. So was Ma'ame Jean-Ba'. And because of that unyielding pride, little Aurélia's existence was not altogether a happy one.

She was not permitted to play with the white children up at the big-house, who would often willingly have had her join their games. Neither was she allowed to associate in any way with the little darkies who frolicked all day long as gleefully as kittens before their cabin doors. There seemed nothing for her to do in the world but to have her shiny hair plaited, or to sit at her mother's knee learning to spell or to patch quilt pieces.

It was well enough so long as she was a baby and crawled about the gallery satisfied to play with a sun-beam. But growing older she pined for some more real companionship.

"La p'tite, 'pear tu me lack she gittin' po', yere lately," remarked M'sié Jean-Ba' solicitously to his wife one day when he noted his little daughter's drooping mien.

"You right, Jean-Ba'; Aurélia a'n't pick up none, the las' year." And they watched the child carefully after that. She seemed to fade like a flower that wants the sun.

Of course M'sié Jean-Ba' could not stand that. So when December

* A term still applied in Louisiana to Mulattoes who were never in slavery.

came, and his contract with the planter had ceased, he gathered his family and all his belongings and went away to live—in paradise.

That is, little Aurélia thinks it is paradise, the change is so wonderful.

There is a constant making and receiving of visits, now. She trudges off every morning to the convent where numbers of little children just like herself are taught by the sisters. Even in the church in which she, her mamma and papa make their Sunday devotions, they breathe an atmosphere which is native to them. And then, such galloping about the country on little creole ponies!

Well, there is no question about it. The happiest little Free-Mulatto in all Louisiana is Aurélia, since her father has moved to "L'Isle des Mulâtres."

Miss McEnders

When Miss Georgie McEnders had finished an elaborately simple toilet of gray and black, she divested herself completely of rings, bangles, brooches—everything to suggest that she stood in friendly relations with fortune. For Georgie was going to read a paper upon "The Dignity of Labor" before the Woman's Reform Club; and if she was blessed with an abundance of wealth, she possessed a no less amount of good taste.

Before entering the neat victoria that stood at her father's too-sumptuous door—and that was her special property—she turned to give certain directions to the coachman. First upon the list from which she read was inscribed: "Look up Mademoiselle Salambre."

"James," said Georgie, flushing a pretty pink, as she always did with the slightest effort of speech, "we want to look up a person named Mademoiselle Salambre, in the southern part of town, on Arsenal street," indicating a certain number and locality. Then she seated herself in the carriage, and as it drove away proceeded to study her engagement list further and to knit her pretty brows in deep and complex thought.

"Two o'clock—look up M. Salambre," said the list. "Three-thirty—read paper before Woman's Ref. Club. Four-thirty—" and here followed cabalistic abbreviations which meant: "Join committee of ladies to investigate moral condition of St. Louis factory-girls. Six o'clock—dine with papa. Eight o'clock—hear Henry George's lecture on Single Tax."

So far, Mademoiselle Salambre was only a name to Georgie McEnders, one of several submitted to her at her own request by her furnishers, Push and Prodem, an enterprising firm charged with the construction of Miss McEnder's very elaborate trousseau. Georgie liked to know the people who worked for her, as far as she could.

She was a charming young woman of twenty-five, though almost too white-souled for a creature of flesh and blood. She possessed ample wealth and time to squander, and a burning desire to do good—to elevate the human race, and start the world over again on a comfortable footing for everybody.

When Georgie had pushed open the very high gate of a very small yard she stood confronting a robust German woman, who, with dress tucked carefully between her knees, was in the act of noisily "redding" the bricks.

"Does M'selle Salambre live here?" Georgie's tall, slim figure was very erect. Her face suggested a sweet peach blossom, and she held a severely simple lorgnon up to her short-sighted blue eyes.

"Ya! ya! aber oop stairs!" cried the woman brusquely and impatiently. But Georgie did not mind. She was used to greetings that lacked the ring of cordiality.

When she had ascended the stairs that led to an upper porch she knocked at the first door that presented itself, and was told to enter by Mlle. Salambre herself.

The woman sat at an opposite window, bending over a bundle of misty white goods that lay in a fluffy heap in her lap. She was not young. She might have been thirty, or she might have been forty. There were lines about her round, piquante face that denoted close acquaintance with struggles, hardships and all manner of unkind experiences.

Georgie had heard a whisper here and there touching the private character of Mlle. Salambre which had determined her to go in person and make the acquaintance of the woman and her surroundings; which latter were poor and simple enough, and not too neat. There was a little child at play upon the floor.

Mlle. Salambre had not expected so unlooked-for an apparition as Miss McEnders, and seeing the girl standing there in the door she removed the eye-glasses that had assisted her in the delicate work, and stood up also.

"Mlle. Salambre, I suppose?" said Georgie, with a courteous inclination.

"Ah! Mees McEndairs! What an agree'ble surprise! Will you be so kind to take a chair." Mademoiselle had lived many years in the city, in various capacities, which brought her in touch with the fashionable set. There were few people in polite society whom Mademoiselle did not know —by sight, at least; and their private histories were as familiar to her as her own.

"You 'ave come to see your the work?" the woman went on with a smile that quite brightened her face. "It is a pleasure to handle such fine, such delicate quality of goods, Mees," and she went and laid several pieces of her handiwork upon the table beside Georgie, at the same time indicating such details as she hoped would call forth her visitor's approval.

There was something about the woman and her surroundings, and the atmosphere of the place, that affected the girl unpleasantly. She shrank instinctively, drawing her invisible mantle of chastity closely about her. Mademoiselle saw that her visitor's attention was divided between the lingerie and the child upon the floor, who was engaged in battering a doll's unyielding head against the unyielding floor.

"The child of my neighbor down-stairs," said Mademoiselle, with a wave of the hand which expressed volumes of unutterable ennui. But at that instant the little one, with instinctive mistrust, and in seeming defiance of the repudiation, climbed to her feet and went rolling and toddling towards her mother, clasping the woman about the knees, and calling her by the endearing title which was her own small right.

A spasm of annoyance passed over Mademoiselle's face, but still she called the child "*Chene*," as she grasped its arm to keep it from falling. Miss McEnders turned every shade of carmine.

"Why did you tell me an untruth?" she asked, looking indignantly into the woman's lowered face. "Why do you call yourself 'Mademoiselle' if this child is yours?"

"For the reason that it is more easy to obtain employment. For reasons that you would not understand," she continued, with a shrug of the shoulders that expressed some defiance and a sudden disregard for consequences. "Life is not all *couleur de rose*, Mees McEndairs; you do not know what life is, you!" And drawing a handkerchief from an apron pocket she mopped an imaginary tear from the corner of her eye, and blew her nose till it glowed again.

Georgie could hardly recall the words or actions with which she quitted Mademoiselle's presence. As much as she wanted to, it had been impossible to stand and read the woman a moral lecture. She had simply thrown what disapproval she could into her hasty leave-taking, and that was all for the moment. But as she drove away, a more practical form of rebuke suggested itself to her not too nimble intelligence—one that she promised herself to act upon as soon as her home was reached.

When she was alone in her room, during an interval between her many engagements, she then attended to the affair of Mlle. Salambre.

Georgie believed in discipline. She hated unrighteousness. When it pleased God to place the lash in her hand she did not hesitate to apply it. Here was this Mlle. Salambre living in her sin. Not as one who is young and blinded by the glamour of pleasure, but with cool and deliberate intention. Since she chose to transgress, she ought to suffer, and be made to feel that her ways were iniquitous and invited rebuke. It lay in Georgie's power to mete out a small dose of that chastisement which the woman deserved, and she was glad that the opportunity was hers.

She seated herself forthwith at her writing table, and penned the following note to her furnishers:

"MESSRS. PUSH & PRODEM.

"*Gentlemen*—Please withdraw from Mademoiselle Salambre all work of mine, and return same to me at once—finished or unfinished.

Yours truly,

GEORGIE McENDERS."

II

On the second day following this summary proceeding, Georgie sat at her writing-table, looking prettier and pinker than ever, in a luxurious and soft-toned robe de chambre that suited her own delicate coloring, and fitted the pale amber tints of her room decorations.

There were books, pamphlets, and writing material set neatly upon the table before her. In the midst of them were two framed photographs, which she polished one after another with a silken scarf that was near.

One of these was a picture of her father, who looked like an Englishman, with his clean-shaved mouth and chin, and closely-cropped side-whiskers, just turning gray. A good-humored shrewdness shone in his eyes. From the set of his thin, firm lips one might guess that he was in the foremost rank in the interesting game of "push" that occupies mankind. One might further guess that his cleverness in using opportunities had brought him there, and that a dexterous management of elbows had served him no less. The other picture was that of Georgie's fiancé, Mr. Meredith Holt, approaching more closely than he liked to his forty-fifth year and an unbecoming corpulence. Only one who knew beforehand that he was a *viveur* could have detected evidence of such in his face, which told little more than that he was a good-looking and amiable man of the world, who might be counted on to do the gentlemanly thing always. Georgie was going to marry him because his personality pleased her; because his easy knowledge of life—such as she apprehended it— commended itself to her approval; because he was likely to interfere in no way with her "work." Yet she might not have given any of these reasons if asked for one. Mr. Meredith Holt was simply an eligible man, whom almost any girl in her set would have accepted for a husband.

Georgie had just discovered that she had yet an hour to spare before starting out with the committee of four to further investigate the moral condition of the factory-girl, when a maid appeared with the announcement that a person was below who wished to see her.

"A person? Surely not a visitor at this hour?"

"I left her in the hall, miss, and she says her name is Mademoiselle Sal-Sal—"

"Oh, yes! Ask her to kindly walk up to my room, and show her the way, please, Hannah."

Mademoiselle Salambre came in with a sweep of skirts that bristled defiance, and a poise of the head that was aggressive in its backward tilt. She seated herself, and with an air of challenge waited to be questioned or addressed.

Georgie felt at ease amid her own familiar surroundings. While she made some idle tracings with a pencil upon a discarded envelope, she half turned to say:

"This visit of yours is very surprising, madam, and wholly useless. I suppose you guess my motive in recalling my work, as I have done."

"Maybe I do, and maybe I do not, Mees McEndairs," replied the woman, with an impertinent uplifting of the eyebrows.

Georgie felt the same shrinking which had overtaken her before in the woman's presence. But she knew her duty, and from that there was no shrinking.

"You must be made to understand, madam, that there is a right way to live, and that there is a wrong way," said Georgie with more conde-scension than she knew. "We cannot defy God's laws with impunity, and without incurring His displeasure. But in His infinite justice and mercy He offers forgiveness, love and protection to those who turn away from evil and repent. It is for each of us to follow the divine way as well as may be. And I am only humbly striving to do His will."

"A most charming sermon, Mees McEndairs!" mademoiselle inter-rupted with a nervous laugh; "it seems a great pity to waste it upon so small an audience. And it grieves me, I cannot express, that I have not the time to remain and listen to its close."

She arose and began to talk volubly, swiftly, in a jumble of French and English, and with a wealth of expression and gesture which Georgie could hardly believe was natural, and not something acquired and rehearsed.

She had come to inform Miss McEnders that she did not want her work; that she would not touch it with the tips of her fingers. And her little, gloved hands recoiled from an imaginary pile of lingerie with unspeakable disgust. Her eyes had traveled nimbly over the room, and had been arrested by the two photographs on the table. Very small, indeed, were her worldly possessions, she informed the young lady; but as Heaven was her witness—not a mouthful of bread that she had not earned. And her parents over yonder in France! As honest as the sunlight! Poor, ah! for that—poor as rats. God only knew how poor; and God only knew how honest. Her eyes remained fixed upon the picture of Horace McEnders. Some people might like fine houses, and servants, and horses, and all the luxury which dishonest wealth brings. Some people might enjoy such surroundings. As for her!—and she drew up her skirts ever so carefully and daintily, as though she feared contamination to her petticoats from the touch of the rich rug upon which she stood.

Georgie's blue eyes were filled with astonishment as they followed the woman's gestures. Her face showed aversion and perplexity.

"Please let this interview come to an end at once," spoke the girl. She would not deign to ask an explanation of the mysterious allusions to ill-gotten wealth. But mademoiselle had not yet said all that she had come there to say.

"If it was only me to say so," she went on, still looking at the likeness, "but, *cher maître!* Go, yourself, Mees McEndairs, and stand for a while on the street and ask the people passing by how your dear papa has made his money, and see what they will say."

Then shifting her glance to the photograph of Meredith Holt, she stood in an attitude of amused contemplation, with a smile of commiseration playing about her lips.

"Mr. Meredith Holt!" she pronounced with quiet, surpressed emphasis —"ah! *c'est un propre, celui la!* You know him very well, no doubt, Mees McEndairs. You would not care to have my opinion of Mr. Meredith Holt. It would make no difference to you, Mees McEndairs, to know that he is not fit to be the husband of a self-respecting bar-maid. Oh! you know a good deal, my dear young lady. You can preach sermons in *merveille!*"

When Georgie was finally alone, there came to her, through all her disgust and indignation, an indefinable uneasiness. There was no misunderstanding the intention of the woman's utterances in regard to the girl's fiancé and her father. A sudden, wild, defiant desire came to her to test the suggestion which Mademoiselle Salambre had let fall.

Yes, she would go stand there on the corner and ask the passers-by how Horace McEnders made his money. She could not yet collect her thoughts for calm reflection; and the house stifled her. It was fully time for her to join her committee of four, but she would meddle no further with morals till her own were adjusted, she thought. Then she quitted the house, very pale, even to her lips that were tightly set.

Georgie stationed herself on the opposite side of the street, on the corner, and waited there as though she had appointed to meet some one.

The first to approach her was a kind-looking old gentleman, very much muffled for the pleasant spring day. Georgie did not hesitate an instant to accost him:

"I beg pardon, sir. Will you kindly tell me whose house that is?" pointing to her own domicile across the way.

"That is Mr. Horace McEnder's residence, Madame," replied the old gentleman, lifting his hat politely.

"Could you tell me how he made the money with which to build so magnificent a home?"

"You should not ask indiscreet questions, my dear young lady," answered the mystified old gentleman, as he bowed and walked away.

The girl let one or two persons pass her. Then she stopped a plumber, who was going cheerily along with his bag of tools on his shoulder.

"I beg pardon," began Georgie again; "but may I ask whose residence that is across the street?"

"Yes'um. That's the McEnderses."

"Thank you; and can you tell me how Mr. McEnders made such an immense fortune?"

"Oh, that ain't my business; but they say he made the biggest pile of it in the Whisky Ring."

So the truth would come to her somehow! These were the people from whom to seek it—who had not learned to veil their thoughts and opinions in polite subterfuge.

When a careless little news-boy came strolling along, she stopped him with the apparent intention of buying a paper from him.

"Do you know whose house that is?" she asked him, handing him a piece of money and nodding over the way.

"W'y, dats ole MicAndrus' house."

"I wonder where he got the money to build such a fine house."

"He stole it; dats w'ere he got it. Thank you," pocketing the change which Georgie declined to take, and he whistled a popular air as he disappeared around the corner.

Georgie had heard enough. Her heart was beating violently now, and her cheeks were flaming. So everybody knew it; even to the street gamins! The men and women who visited her and broke bread at her father's table, knew it. Her co-workers, who strove with her in Christian endeavor, knew. The very servants who waited upon her doubtless knew this, and had their jests about it.

She shrank within herself as she climbed the stairway to her room.

Upon the table there she found a box of exquisite white spring blossoms that a messenger had brought from Meredith Holt, during her absence. Without an instant's hesitation, Georgie cast the spotless things into the wide, sooty, fire-place. Then she sank into a chair and wept bitterly.

Loka

She was a half-breed Indian girl, with hardly a rag to her back. To the ladies of the Band of United Endeavor who questioned her, she said her name was Loka, and she did not know where she belonged, unless it was on Bayou Choctaw.

She had appeared one day at the side door of Frobissaint's "oyster saloon" in Natchitoches, asking for food. Frobissaint, a practical philanthropist, engaged her on the spot as tumbler-washer.

She was not successful at that; she broke too many tumblers. But, as Frobissaint charged her with the broken glasses, he did not mind, until she began to break them over the heads of his customers. Then he seized her by the wrist and dragged her before the Band of United Endeavor, then in session around the corner. This was considerate on Frobissaint's part, for he could have dragged her just as well to the police station.

Loka was not beautiful, as she stood in her red calico rags before the scrutinizing band. Her coarse, black, unkempt hair framed a broad, swarthy face without a redeeming feature, except eyes that were not bad; slow in their movements, but frank eyes enough. She was big-boned and clumsy.

She did not know how old she was. The minister's wife reckoned she might be sixteen. The judge's wife thought that it made no difference. The doctor's wife suggested that the girl have a bath and change before she be handled, even in discussion. The motion was not seconded. Loka's ultimate disposal was an urgent and difficult consideration.

Some one mentioned a reformatory. Every one else objected.

Madame Laballière, the planter's wife, knew a respectable family of 'Cadians living some miles below, who, she thought, would give the girl a home, with benefit to all concerned. The 'Cadian woman was a deserving one, with a large family of small children, who had all her own work to do. The husband cropped in a modest way. Loka would not only be taught to work at the Padues', but would receive a good moral training beside.

That settled it. Every one agreed with the planter's wife that it was a chance in a thousand; and Loka was sent to sit on the steps outside, while the band proceeded to the business next in order.

Loka was afraid of treading upon the little Padues when she first got amongst them,—there were so many of them,—and her feet were like leaden weights, encased in the strong brogans with which the band had equipped her.

Madame Padue, a small, black-eyed, aggressive woman, questioned her in a sharp, direct fashion peculiar to herself.

"How come you don't talk French, you?" Loka shrugged her shoulders.

"I kin talk English good 's anybody; an' lit' bit Choctaw, too," she offered, apologetically.

"*Ma foi*, you kin fo'git yo' Choctaw. Soona the betta for me. Now if you willin', an' ent too lazy an' sassy, we 'll git 'long somehow. *Vrai sauvage ça*," she muttered under her breath, as she turned to initiate Loka into some of her new duties.

She herself was a worker. A good deal more fussy one than her easy-going husband and children thought necessary or agreeable. Loka's slow ways and heavy motions aggravated her. It was in vain Monsieur Padue expostulated:—

"She 's on'y a chile, rememba, Tontine."

"She 's *vrai sauvage*, that 's w'at. It 's got to be work out of her," was Tontine's only reply to such remonstrance.

The girl was indeed so deliberate about her tasks that she had to be urged constantly to accomplish the amount of labor that Tontine required of her. Moreover, she carried to her work a stolid indifference that was exasperating. Whether at the wash-tub, scrubbing the floors, weeding the garden, or learning her lessons and catechism with the children on Sundays, it was the same.

It was only when intrusted with the care of little Bibine, the baby, that Loka crept somewhat out of her apathy. She grew very fond of him. No wonder; such a baby as he was! So good, so fat, and complaisant! He had such a way of clasping Loka's broad face between his pudgy fists and savagely biting her chin with his hard, toothless gums! Such a way of bouncing in her arms as if he were mounted upon springs! At his antics the girl would laugh a wholesome, ringing laugh that was good to hear.

She was left alone to watch and nurse him one day. An accommodating neighbor who had become the possessor of a fine new spring wagon passed by just after the noon-hour meal, and offered to take the whole family on a jaunt to town. The offer was all the more tempting as Tontine had some long-delayed shopping to do; and the opportunity to equip the children with shoes and summer hats could not be slighted. So away they all went. All but Bibine, who was left swinging in his branle with only Loka for company.

This branle consisted of a strong circular piece of cotton cloth, securely but slackly fastened to a large, stout hoop suspended by three light cords to a hook in a rafter of the gallery. The baby who has not swung in a branle does not know the quintessence of baby luxury. In each of the four rooms of the house was a hook from which to hang this swing.

Often it was taken out under the trees. But to-day it swung in the shade of the open gallery; and Loka sat beside it, giving it now and then a slight impetus that sent it circling in slow, sleep-inspiring undulations.

Bibine kicked and cooed as long as he was able. But Loka was humming a monotonous lullaby; the branle was swaying to and fro, the warm air fanning him deliciously; and Bibine was soon fast asleep.

Seeing this, Loka quietly let down the mosquito net, to protect the child's slumber from the intrusion of the many insects that were swarming in the summer air.

Singularly enough, there was no work for her to do; and Tontine, in her hurried departure, had failed to provide for the emergency. The washing and ironing were over; the floors had been scrubbed, and the rooms righted; the yard swept; the chickens fed; vegetables picked and washed. There was absolutely nothing to do, and Loka gave herself up to the dreams of idleness.

As she sat comfortably back in the roomy rocker, she let her eyes sweep lazily across the country. Away off to the right peeped up, from amid densely clustered trees, the pointed roofs and long pipe of the steam-gin of Laballière's. No other habitation was visible except a few low, flat dwellings far over the river, that could hardly be seen.

The immense plantation took up all the land in sight. The few acres that Baptiste Padue cultivated were his own, that Laballière, out of friendly consideration, had sold to him. Baptiste's fine crop of cotton and corn was "laid by" just now, waiting for rain; and Baptiste had gone with the rest of the family to town. Beyond the river and the field and everywhere about were dense woods.

Loka's gaze, that had been slowly traveling along the edge of the horizon, finally fastened upon the woods, and stayed there. Into her eyes came the absent look of one whose thought is projected into the future or the past, leaving the present blank. She was seeing a vision. It had come with a whiff that the strong south breeze had blown to her from the woods.

She was seeing old Marot, the squaw who drank whiskey and plaited baskets and beat her. There was something, after all, in being beaten, if only to scream out and fight back, as at that time in Natchitoches, when she broke a glass on the head of a man who laughed at her and pulled her hair, and called her "fool names."

Old Marot wanted her to steal and cheat, to beg and lie, when they went out with the baskets to sell. Loka did not want to. She did not like to. That was why she had run away—and because she was beaten. But —but ah! the scent of the sassafras leaves hanging to dry in the shade! The pungent camomile! The sound of the bayou tumbling over that old slimy log! Only to lie there for hours and watch the glistening lizards glide in and out was worth a beating.

She knew the birds must be singing in chorus out there in the woods where the gray moss was hanging, and the trumpetvine trailing from the trees, spangled with blossoms. In spirit she heard the songsters.

She wondered if Choctaw Joe and Sambite played dice every night by the campfire, as they used to do; and if they still fought and slashed each other when wild with drink. How good it felt to walk with moccasined feet over the springy turf, under the trees! What fun to trap the squirrels, to skin the otter; to take those swift flights on the pony that Choctaw Joe had stolen from the Texans!

Loka sat motionless; only her breast heaved tumultuously. Her heart was aching with savage homesickness. She could not feel just then that the sin and pain of that life were anything beside the joy of its freedom.

Loka was sick for the woods. She felt she must die if she could not get back to them, and to her vagabond life. Was there anything to hinder her? She stooped and unlaced the brogans that were chafing her feet, removed them and her stockings, and threw the things away from her. She stood up all a-quiver, panting, ready for flight.

But there was a sound that stopped her. It was little Bibine, cooing, sputtering, battling hands and feet with the mosquito net that he had dragged over his face. The girl uttered a sob as she reached down for the baby she had grown to love so, and clasped him in her arms. She could not go and leave Bibine behind.

Tontine began to grumble at once when she discovered that Loka was not at hand to receive them on their return.

"*Bon!*" she exclaimed. "Now w'ere is that Loka? Ah, that girl, she aggravates me too much. Firs' thing she knows I 'm goin' sen' her straight back to them ban' of lady w'ere she come frum."

"Loka!" she called, in short, sharp tones, as she traversed the house and peered into each room. "Lo—ka!" She cried loudly enough to be heard half a mile away when she got out upon the back gallery. Again and again she called.

Baptiste was exchanging the discomfort of his Sunday coat for the accustomed ease of shirt sleeves.

"*Mais* don't git so excite, Tontine," he implored. "I 'm sho she 's yonda to the crib shellin' co'n, or somew'ere like that."

"Run, François, you, an' see to the crib," the mother commanded. "Bibine mus' be starve! Run to the hen-house an' look, Juliette. Maybe she 's fall asleep in some corna. That 'll learn me 'notha time to go trus' *une pareille sauvage* with my baby, *va!*"

When it was discovered that Loka was nowhere in the immediate vicinity, Tontine was furious.

"*Pas possible* she 's walk to Laballière, with Bibine!" she exclaimed.

"I 'll saddle the hoss an' go see, Tontine," interposed Baptiste, who was beginning to share his wife's uneasiness.

"Go, go, Baptiste," she urged. "An' you, boys, run yonda down the road to ole Aunt Judy's cabin an' see."

It was found that Loka had not been seen at Laballière's, nor at Aunt Judy's cabin; that she had not taken the boat, that was still fastened to its moorings down the bank. Then Tontine's excitement left her. She turned pale and sat quietly down in her room, with an unnatural calm that frightened the children.

Some of them began to cry. Baptiste walked restlessly about, anxiously scanning the country in all directions. A wretched hour dragged by. The sun had set, leaving hardly an afterglow, and in a little while the twilight that falls so swiftly would be there.

Baptiste was preparing to mount his horse, to start out again on the round he had already been over. Tontine sat in the same state of intense abstraction when François, who had perched himself among the lofty branches of a chinaberry-tree, called out: "Ent that Loka 'way yon'a, jis' come out de wood? climbin' de fence down by de melon patch?"

It was difficult to distinguish in the gathering dusk if the figure were that of man or beast. But the family was not left long in suspense. Baptiste sped his horse away in the direction indicated by François, and in a little while he was galloping back with Bibine in his arms; as fretful, sleepy and hungry a baby as ever was.

Loka came trudging on behind Baptiste. He did not wait for explanations; he was too eager to place the child in the arms of its mother. The suspense over, Tontine began to cry; that followed naturally, of course. Through her tears she managed to address Loka, who stood all tattered and disheveled in the doorway; "W'ere you been? Tell me that."

"Bibine an' me," answered Loka, slowly and awkwardly, "we was lonesome—we been take lit' 'broad in de wood."

"You did n' know no betta 'an to take 'way Bibine like that? W'at Ma'ame Laballière mean, anyhow, to sen' me such a objec' like you, I want to know?"

"You go'n' sen' me 'way?" asked Loka, passing her hand in a hopeless fashion over her frowzy hair.

"*Par exemple!* straight you march back to that ban' w'ere you come from. To give me such a fright like that! *pas possible.*"

"Go slow, Tontine; go slow," interposed Baptiste.

"Don' sen' me 'way frum Bibine," entreated the girl, with a note in her voice like a lament.

"To-day," she went on, in her dragging manner, "I want to run 'way bad, an' take to de wood; an' go yonda back to Bayou Choctaw to steal an' lie agin. It 's on'y Bibine w'at hole me back. I could n' lef' 'im. I could n' do dat. An' we jis' go take lit' 'broad in de wood, das all, him an' me. Don' sen' me 'way like dat!"

Baptiste led the girl gently away to the far end of the gallery, and spoke soothingly to her. He told her to be good and brave, and he would right the trouble for her. He left her standing there and went back to his wife.

"Tontine," he began, with unusual energy, "you got to listen to the truth—once fo' all." He had evidently determined to profit by his wife's lachrymose and wilted condition to assert his authority.

"I want to say who 's masta in this house—it 's me," he went on. Tontine did not protest; only clasped the baby a little closer, which encouraged him to proceed.

"You been grind that girl too much. She ent a bad girl—I been watch her close, 'count of the chil'ren; she ent bad. All she want, it 's li'le mo' rope. You can't drive a ox with the same gearin' you drive a mule. You got to learn that, Tontine."

He approached his wife's chair and stood beside her.

"That girl, she done tole us how she was temp' to-day to turn *canaille*— like we all temp' sometime'. W'at was it save her? That li'le chile w'at you hole in yo' arm. An' now you want to take her guarjun angel 'way f'om her? *Non, non, ma femme,*" he said, resting his hand gently upon his wife's head. "We got to rememba she ent like you an' me, po' thing; she 's one Injun, her."

At the 'Cadian Ball

Bobinôt, that big, brown, good-natured Bobinôt, had no intention of going to the ball, even though he knew Calixta would be there. For what came of those balls but heartache, and a sickening disinclination for work the whole week through, till Saturday night came again and his tortures began afresh? Why could he not love Ozéina, who would marry him to-morrow; or Fronie, or any one of a dozen others, rather than that little Spanish vixen? Calixta's slender foot had never touched Cuban soil; but her mother's had, and the Spanish was in her blood all the same. For that reason the prairie people forgave her much that they would not have overlooked in their own daughters or sisters.

Her eyes,—Bobinôt thought of her eyes, and weakened,—the bluest, the drowsiest, most tantalizing that ever looked into a man's; he thought of her flaxen hair that kinked worse than a mulatto's close to her head; that broad, smiling mouth and tiptilted nose, that full figure; that voice like a rich contralto song, with cadences in it that must have been taught by Satan, for there was no one else to teach her tricks on that 'Cadian prairie. Bobinôt thought of them all as he plowed his rows of cane.

There had even been a breath of scandal whispered about her a year ago, when she went to Assumption,—but why talk of it? No one did now. "C'est Espagnol, ça," most of them said with lenient shoulder-shrugs. "Bon chien tient de race," the old men mumbled over their pipes, stirred by recollections. Nothing was made of it, except that Fronie threw it up to Calixta when the two quarreled and fought on the church steps after mass one Sunday, about a lover. Calixta swore roundly in fine 'Cadian French and with true Spanish spirit, and slapped Fronie's face. Fronie had slapped her back; "Tiens, cocotte, va!" "Espèce de lionèse; prends ça, et ça!" till the curé himself was obliged to hasten and make peace between them. Bobinôt thought of it all, and would not go to the ball.

But in the afternoon, over at Friedheimer's store, where he was buying a trace-chain, he heard some one say that Alcée Laballière would be there. Then wild horses could not have kept him away. He knew how it would be—or rather he did not know how it would be—if the handsome young planter came over to the ball as he sometimes did. If Alcée happened to be in a serious mood, he might only go to the card-room and play a round or two; or he might stand out on the galleries talking crops and politics with the old people. But there was no telling. A drink or two could put the devil in his head,—that was what Bobinôt said to himself, as he wiped the sweat from his brow with his red bandanna; a gleam from Calixta's eyes, a flash of her ankle, a twirl of her skirts could do the same. Yes, Bobinôt would go to the ball.

That was the year Alcée Laballière put nine hundred acres in rice. It was putting a good deal of money into the ground, but the returns promised to be glorious. Old Madame Laballière, sailing about the spacious galleries in her white *volante*, figured it all out in her head. Clarisse, her goddaughter, helped her a little, and together they built more air-castles than enough. Alcée worked like a mule that time; and if he did not kill himself, it was because his constitution was an iron one. It was an every-day affair for him to come in from the field well-nigh exhausted, and wet to the waist. He did not mind if there were visitors; he left them to his mother and Clarisse. There were often guests: young men and women who came up from the city, which was but a few hours away, to visit his beautiful kinswoman. She was worth going a good deal farther than that to see. Dainty as a lily; hardy as a sunflower; slim, tall, graceful, like one of the reeds that grew in the marsh. Cold and kind and cruel by turn, and everything that was aggravating to Alcée.

He would have liked to sweep the place of those visitors, often. Of the men, above all, with their ways and their manners; their swaying of fans like women, and dandling about hammocks. He could have pitched them over the levee into the river, if it had n't meant murder. That was Alcée. But he must have been crazy the day he came in from the rice-field, and, toil-stained as he was, clasped Clarisse by the arms and panted a volley of hot, blistering love-words into her face. No man had ever spoken love to her like that.

"Monsieur!" she exclaimed, looking him full in the eyes, without a quiver. Alcée's hands dropped and his glance wavered before the chill of her calm, clear eyes.

"*Par exemple!*" she muttered disdainfully, as she turned from him, deftly adjusting the careful toilet that he had so brutally disarranged.

That happened a day or two before the cyclone came that cut into the rice like fine steel. It was an awful thing, coming so swiftly, without a moment's warning in which to light a holy candle or set a piece of blessed palm burning. Old madame wept openly and said her beads, just as her son Didier, the New Orleans one, would have done. If such a thing had happened to Alphonse, the Laballière planting cotton up in Natchitoches, he would have raved and stormed like a second cyclone, and made his surroundings unbearable for a day or two. But Alcée took the misfortune differently. He looked ill and gray after it, and said nothing. His speech-lessness was frightful. Clarisse's heart melted with tenderness; but when she offered her soft, purring words of condolence, he accepted them with mute indifference. Then she and her nénaine wept afresh in each other's arms.

A night or two later, when Clarisse went to her window to kneel there in the moonlight and say her prayers before retiring, she saw that Bruce, Alcée's negro servant, had led his master's saddle-horse noiselessly along the edge of the sward that bordered the gravel-path, and stood holding him near by. Presently, she heard Alcée quit his room, which was beneath her own, and traverse the lower portico. As he emerged from the shadow and crossed the strip of moonlight, she perceived that he carried a pair of well-filled saddle-bags which he at once flung across the animal's back. He then lost no time in mounting, and after a brief exchange of words with Bruce, went cantering away, taking no precaution to avoid the noisy gravel as the negro had done.

Clarisse had never suspected that it might be Alcée's custom to sally forth from the plantation secretly, and at such an hour; for it was nearly midnight. And had it not been for the telltale saddle-bags, she would only have crept to bed, to wonder, to fret and dream unpleasant dreams. But her impatience and anxiety would not be held in check. Hastily unbolting the shutters of her door that opened upon the gallery, she stepped outside and called softly to the old negro.

"Gre't Peter! Miss Clarisse. I was n' sho it was a ghos' o' w'at, stan'in' up dah, plumb in de night, dataway."

He mounted halfway up the long, broad flight of stairs. She was standing at the top.

"Bruce, w'ere has Monsieur Alcée gone?" she asked.

"W'y, he gone 'bout he business, I reckin," replied Bruce, striving to be non-committal at the outset.

"W'ere has Monsieur Alcée gone?" she reiterated, stamping her bare foot. "I won't stan' any nonsense or any lies; mine, Bruce."

"I don' ric'lic ez I eva tole you lie *yit*, Miss Clarisse. Mista Alcée, he all broke up, sho."

"W'ere—has—he gone? Ah, Sainte Vierge! faut de la patience! butor, va!"

"W'en I was in he room, a-breshin' off he clo'es to-day," the darkey began, settling himself against the stair-rail, "he look dat speechless an' down, I say, 'You 'pear to me like some pussun w'at gwine have a spell o' sickness, Mista Alcée.' He say, 'You reckin?' 'I dat he git up, go look hisse'f stiddy in de glass. Den he go to de chimbly an' jerk up de quinine bottle an' po' a gre't hoss-dose on to he han'. An' he swalla dat mess in a wink, an' wash hit down wid a big dram o' w'iskey w'at he keep in he room, aginst he come all soppin' wet outen de fiel'.

"He 'lows, 'No, I ain' gwine be sick, Bruce.' Den he square off. He say, 'I kin mak out to stan' up an' gi' an' take wid any man I knows, lessen hit 's John L. Sulvun. But w'en God A'mighty an' a 'oman jines fo'ces agin me, dat 's one too many fur me.' I tell 'im, 'Jis so,' whils' I 'se makin' out to bresh a spot off w'at ain' dah, on he coat colla. I tell 'im, 'You wants li'le res', suh.' He say, 'No, I wants li'le fling; dat w'at I wants; an' I gwine git it. Pitch me a fis'ful o' clo'es in dem 'ar saddle-bags.' Dat w'at he say. Don't you bodda, missy. He jis' gone a-caperin' yonda to de Cajun ball. Uh—uh—de skeeters is fair' a-swarmin' like bees roun' yo' foots!"

The mosquitoes were indeed attacking Clarisse's white feet savagely. She had unconsciously been alternately rubbing one foot over the other during the darkey's recital.

"The 'Cadian ball," she repeated contemptuously. "Humph! *Par exemple!* Nice conduc' for a Laballière. An' he needs a saddle-bag, fill' with clothes, to go to the 'Cadian ball!"

"Oh, Miss Clarisse; you go on to bed, chile; git yo' soun' sleep. He 'low he come back in couple weeks o' so. I kiarn be repeatin' lot o' truck w'at young mans say, out heah face o' young gal."

Clarisse said no more, but turned and abruptly reëntered the house.

"You done talk too much wid yo' mouf a'ready, you ole fool nigga, you," muttered Bruce to himself as he walked away.

Alcée reached the ball very late, of course—too late for the chicken gumbo which had been served at midnight.

The big, low-ceiled room—they called it a hall—was packed with men and women dancing to the music of three fiddles. There were broad galleries all around it. There was a room at one side where sober-faced men were playing cards. Another, in which babies were sleeping, was called *le parc aux petits*. Any one who is white may go to a 'Cadian ball, but he must pay for his lemonade, his coffee and chicken gumbo. And he must behave himself like a 'Cadian. Grosbœuf was giving this ball. He had been giving them since he was a young man, and he was a middle-aged one, now. In that time he could recall but one disturbance, and that was caused by American railroaders, who were not in touch with their surroundings and had no business there. "Ces maudits gens du raiderode," Grosbœuf called them.

Alcée Laballière's presence at the ball caused a flutter even among the men, who could not but admire his "nerve" after such misfortune befalling him. To be sure, they knew the Laballières were rich—that there were resources East, and more again in the city. But they felt it took a *brave homme* to stand a blow like that philosophically. One old gentleman, who was in the habit of reading a Paris newspaper and knew things, chuckled gleefully to everybody that Alcée's conduct was altogether *chic*, *mais chic*. That he had more *panache* than Boulanger. Well, perhaps he had.

But what he did not show outwardly was that he was in a mood for ugly things to-night. Poor Bobinôt alone felt it vaguely. He discerned a gleam of it in Alcée's handsome eyes, as the young planter stood in the doorway, looking with rather feverish glance upon the assembly, while he laughed and talked with a 'Cadian farmer who was beside him.

Bobinôt himself was dull-looking and clumsy. Most of the men were. But the young women were very beautiful. The eyes that glanced into Alcée's as they passed him were big, dark, soft as those of the young heifers standing out in the cool prairie grass.

But the belle was Calixta. Her white dress was not nearly so handsome or well made as Fronie's (she and Fronie had quite forgotten the battle on the church steps, and were friends again), nor were her slippers so stylish as those of Ozéina; and she fanned herself with a handkerchief, since she had broken her red fan at the last ball, and her aunts and uncles were not willing to give her another. But all the men agreed she was at her best to-night. Such animation! and abandon! such flashes of wit!

"Hé, Bobinôt! *Mais* w'at 's the matta? W'at you standin' *planté là* like ole Ma'ame Tina's cow in the bog, you?"

That was good. That was an excellent thrust at Bobinôt, who had forgotten the figure of the dance with his mind bent on other things, and it started a clamor of laughter at his expense. He joined good-naturedly. It was better to receive even such notice as that from Calixta than none at all. But Madame Suzonne, sitting in a corner, whispered to her neighbor that if Ozéina were to conduct herself in a like manner, she should immediately be taken out to the mule-cart and driven home. The women did not always approve of Calixta.

Now and then were short lulls in the dance, when couples flocked out upon the galleries for a brief respite and fresh air. The moon had gone down pale in the west, and in the east was yet no promise of day. After such an interval, when the dancers again assembled to resume the interrupted quadrille, Calixta was not among them.

She was sitting upon a bench out in the shadow, with Alcée beside her. They were acting like fools. He had attempted to take a little gold ring from her finger; just for the fun of it, for there was nothing he could have done with the ring but replace it again. But she clinched her hand tight. He pretended that it was a very difficult matter to open it. Then he kept the hand in his. They seemed to forget about it. He played with her earring, a thin crescent of gold hanging from her small brown ear. He caught a wisp of the kinky hair that had escaped its fastening, and rubbed the ends of it against his shaven cheek.

"You know, last year in Assumption, Calixta?" They belonged to the younger generation, so preferred to speak English.

"Don't come say Assumption to me, M'sieur Alcée. I done yeard Assumption till I 'm plumb sick."

"Yes, I know. The idiots! Because you were in Assumption, and I happened to go to Assumption, they must have it that we went together. But it was nice—*hein*, Calixta?—in Assumption?"

They saw Bobinôt emerge from the hall and stand a moment outside the lighted doorway, peering uneasily and searchingly into the darkness. He did not see them, and went slowly back.

"There is Bobinôt looking for you. You are going to set poor Bobinôt crazy. You 'll marry him some day; *hein*, Calixta?"

"I don't say no, me," she replied, striving to withdraw her hand, which he held more firmly for the attempt.

"But come, Calixta; you know you said you would go back to Assumption, just to spite them."

"No, I neva said that, me. You mus' dreamt that."

"Oh, I thought you did. You know I 'm going down to the city."

"W'en?"

"To-night."

"Betta make has'e, then; it 's mos' day."

"Well, to-morrow 'll do."

"W'at you goin' do, yonda?"

"I don't know. Drown myself in the lake, maybe; unless you go down there to visit your uncle."

Calixta's senses were reeling; and they well-nigh left her when she felt Alcée's lips brush her ear like the touch of a rose.

"Mista Alcée! Is dat Mista Alcée?" the thick voice of a negro was asking; he stood on the ground, holding to the banister-rails near which the couple sat.

"W'at do you want now?" cried Alcée impatiently. "Can't I have a moment of peace?"

"I ben huntin' you high an' low, suh," answered the man. "Dey—dey some one in de road, onda de mulbare-tree, want see you a minute."

"I would n't go out to the road to see the Angel Gabriel. And if you come back here with any more talk, I 'll have to break your neck." The negro turned mumbling away.

Alcée and Calixta laughed softly about it. Her boisterousness was all gone. They talked low, and laughed softly, as lovers do.

"Alcée! Alcée Laballière!"

It was not the negro's voice this time; but one that went through Alcée's body like an electric shock, bringing him to his feet.

Clarisse was standing there in her riding-habit, where the negro had stood. For an instant confusion reigned in Alcée's thoughts, as with one who awakes suddenly from a dream. But he felt that something of serious import had brought his cousin to the ball in the dead of night.

"W'at does this mean, Clarisse?" he asked.

"It means something has happen' at home. You mus' come."

"Happened to maman?" he questioned, in alarm.

"No; nénaine is well, and asleep. It is something else. Not to frighten you. But you mus' come. Come with me, Alcée."

There was no need for the imploring note. He would have followed the voice anywhere.

She had now recognized the girl sitting back on the bench.

"Ah, c'est vous, Calixta? Comment ça va, mon enfant?"

"Tcha va b'en; et vous, mam'zélle?"

Alcée swung himself over the low rail and started to follow Clarisse, without a word, without a glance back at the girl. He had forgotten he was leaving her there. But Clarisse whispered something to him, and he turned back to say "Good-night, Calixta," and offer his hand to press through the railing. She pretended not to see it.

"How come that? You settin' yere by yo'se'f, Calixta?" It was Bobinôt who had found her there alone. The dancers had not yet come out. She looked ghastly in the faint, gray light struggling out of the east.

"Yes, that's me. Go yonda in the *parc aux petits* an' ask Aunt Olisse fu' my hat. She knows w'ere 't is. I want to go home, me."

"How you came?"

"I come afoot, with the Cateaus. But I 'm goin' now. I ent goin' wait fu' 'em. I 'm plumb wo' out, me."

"Kin I go with you, Calixta?"

"I don' care."

They went together across the open prairie and along the edge of the fields, stumbling in the uncertain light. He told her to lift her dress that was getting wet and bedraggled; for she was pulling at the weeds and grasses with her hands.

"I don' care; it 's got to go in the tub, anyway. You been sayin' all along you want to marry me, Bobinôt. Well, if you want, yet, I don' care, me."

The glow of a sudden and overwhelming happiness shone out in the brown, rugged face of the young Acadian. He could not speak, for very joy. It choked him.

"Oh well, if you don' want," snapped Calixta, flippantly, pretending to be piqued at his silence.

"*Bon Dieu!* You know that makes me crazy, w'at you sayin'. You mean that, Calixta? You ent goin' turn roun' agin?"

"I neva tole you that much *yet*, Bobinôt. I mean that. *Tiens*," and she held out her hand in the business-like manner of a man who clinches a bargain with a hand-clasp. Bobinôt grew bold with happiness and asked Calixta to kiss him. She turned her face, that was almost ugly after the night's dissipation, and looked steadily into his.

"I don' want to kiss you, Bobinôt," she said, turning away again, "not to-day. Some other time. *Bonté divine!* ent you satisfy, *yet!*"

"Oh, I 'm satisfy, Calixta," he said.

Riding through a patch of wood, Clarisse's saddle became ungirted, and she and Alcée dismounted to readjust it.

For the twentieth time he asked her what had happened at home.

"But, Clarisse, w'at is it? Is it a misfortune?"

"Ah Dieu sait! It 's only something that happen' to me."

"To you!"

"I saw you go away las' night, Alcée, with those saddle-bags," she said, haltingly, striving to arrange something about the saddle, "an' I made Bruce tell me. He said you had gone to the ball, an' wouldn' be home for weeks an' weeks. I thought, Alcée—maybe you were going to—to Assumption. I got wild. An' then I knew if you did n't come back, *now*, to-night, I could n't stan' it,—again."

She had her face hidden in her arm that she was resting against the saddle when she said that.

He began to wonder if this meant love. But she had to tell him so, before he believed it. And when she told him, he thought the face of the Universe was changed—just like Bobinôt. Was it last week the cyclone had well-nigh ruined him? The cyclone seemed a huge joke, now. It was he, then, who, an hour ago was kissing little Calixta's ear and whispering nonsense into it. Calixta was like a myth, now. The one, only, great reality in the world was Clarisse standing before him, telling him that she loved him.

In the distance they heard the rapid discharge of pistol-shots; but it did not disturb them. They knew it was only the negro musicians who had gone into the yard to fire their pistols into the air, as the custom is, and to announce "*le bal est fini.*"

A Visit to Avoyelles

Every one who came up from Avoyelles had the same story to tell of Mentine. *Cher Maître!* but she was changed. And there were babies, more than she could well manage; as good as four already. Jules was not kind except to himself. They seldom went to church, and never anywhere upon a visit. They lived as poorly as pine-woods people. Doudouce had heard the story often, the last time no later than that morning.

"Ho-a!" he shouted to his mule plumb in the middle of the cotton row. He had staggered along behind the plow since early morning, and of a sudden he felt he had had enough of it. He mounted the mule and rode away to the stable, leaving the plow with its polished blade thrust deep in the red Cane River soil. His head felt like a windmill with the recollections and sudden intentions that had crowded it and were whirling through his brain since he had heard the last story about Mentine.

He knew well enough Mentine would have married him seven years ago had not Jules Trodon come up from Avoyelles and captivated her with his handsome eyes and pleasant speech. Doudouce was resigned then, for he held Mentine's happiness above his own. But now she was suffering in a hopeless, common, exasperating way for the small comforts of life. People had told him so. And somehow, to-day, he could not stand the knowledge passively. He felt he must see those things they spoke of with his own eyes. He must strive to help her and her children if it were possible.

Doudouce could not sleep that night. He lay with wakeful eyes watching the moonlight creep across the bare floor of his room; listening to sounds that seemed unfamiliar and weird down among the rushes along the bayou. But towards morning he saw Mentine as he had seen her last in her white wedding gown and veil. She looked at him with appealing eyes and held out her arms for protection,—for rescue, it seemed to him. That dream determined him. The following day Doudouce started for Avoyelles.

Jules Trodon's home lay a mile or two from Marksville. It consisted of three rooms strung in a row and opening upon a narrow gallery. The whole wore an aspect of poverty and dilapidation that summer day, towards noon, when Doudouce approached it. His presence outside the gate aroused the frantic barking of dogs that dashed down the steps as if to attack him. Two little brown barefooted children, a boy and girl, stood upon the gallery staring stupidly at him. "Call off you' dogs," he requested; but they only continued to stare.

"Down, Pluto! down, Achille!" cried the shrill voice of a woman who emerged from the house, holding upon her arm a delicate baby of a year or two. There was only an instant of unrecognition.

"*Mais* Doudouce, that ent you, *comment!* Well, if any one would tole me this mornin'! Git a chair, 'Tit Jules. That 's Mista Doudouce, f'om 'way yonda Natchitoches w'ere yo' maman use' to live. *Mais*, you ent change'; you' lookin' well, Doudouce."

He shook hands in a slow, undemonstrative way, and seated himself clumsily upon the hide-bottomed chair, laying his broad-rimmed felt hat upon the floor beside him. He was very uncomfortable in the cloth Sunday coat which he wore.

"I had business that call' me to Marksville," he began, "an' I say to myse'f, '*Tiens*, you can't pass by without tell' 'em all howdy.'"

"*Par exemple!* w'at Jules would said to that! *Mais*, you' lookin' well; you ent change', Doudouce."

"An' you' lookin' well, Mentine. Jis' the same Mentine." He regretted that he lacked talent to make the lie bolder.

She moved a little uneasily, and felt upon her shoulder for a pin with which to fasten the front of her old gown where it lacked a button. She had kept the baby in her lap. Doudouce was wondering miserably if he would have known her outside her home. He would have known her sweet, cheerful brown eyes, that were not changed; but her figure, that had looked so trim in the wedding gown, was sadly misshapen. She was brown, with skin like parchment, and piteously thin. There were lines, some deep as if old age had cut them, about the eyes and mouth.

"An' how you lef' 'em all, yonda?" she asked, in a high voice that had grown shrill from screaming at children and dogs.

"They all well. It 's mighty li'le sickness in the country this yea'. But they been lookin' fo' you up yonda, straight along, Mentine."

"Don't talk, Doudouce, it 's no chance; with that po' wo' out piece o' lan' w'at Jules got. He say, anotha yea' like that, he 's goin' sell out, him."

The children were clutching her on either side, their persistent gaze always fastened upon Doudouce. He tried without avail to make friends with them. Then Jules came home from the field, riding the mule with which he had worked, and which he fastened outside the gate.

"Yere 's Doudouce f'om Natchitoches, Jules," called out Mentine, "he stop' to tell us howdy, *en passant*." The husband mounted to the gallery and the two men shook hands; Doudouce listlessly, as he had done with Mentine; Jules with some bluster and show of cordiality.

"Well, you' a lucky man, you," he exclaimed with his swagger air, "able to broad like that, *encore!* You could n't do that if you had half a dozen mouth' to feed, *allez!*"

"Non, j'te garantis!" agreed Mentine, with a loud laugh. Doudouce winced, as he had done the instant before at Jules's heartless implication. This husband of Mentine surely had not changed during the seven years, except to grow broader, stronger, handsomer. But Doudouce did not tell him so.

After the mid-day dinner of boiled salt pork, corn bread and molasses, there was nothing for Doudouce but to take his leave when Jules did.

At the gate, the little boy was discovered in dangerous proximity to the mule's heels, and was properly screamed at and rebuked.

"I reckon he likes hosses," Doudouce remarked. "He take' afta you, Mentine. I got a li'le pony yonda home," he said, addressing the child, "w'at ent no use to me. I 'm goin' sen' 'im down to you. He 's a good, tough li'le mustang. You jis' can let 'im eat grass an' feed 'im a han'ful o' co'n, once a w'ile. An' he 's gentle, yes. You an' yo' ma can ride 'im to church, Sundays. *Hein!* you want?"

"W'at you say, Jules?" demanded the father. "W'at you say?" echoed Mentine, who was balancing the baby across the gate. " 'Tit sauvage, va!"

Doudouce shook hands all around, even with the baby, and walked off in the opposite direction to Jules, who had mounted the mule. He was bewildered. He stumbled over the rough ground because of tears that were blinding him, and that he had held in check for the past hour.

He had loved Mentine long ago, when she was young and attractive, and he found that he loved her still. He had tried to put all disturbing thought of her away, on that wedding-day, and he supposed he had succeeded. But he loved her now as he never had. Because she was no longer beautiful, he loved her. Because the delicate bloom of her existence had been rudely brushed away; because she was in a manner fallen; because she was Mentine, he loved her; fiercely, as a mother loves an afflicted child. He would have liked to thrust that man aside, and gather up her and her children, and hold them and keep them as long as life lasted.

After a moment or two Doudouce looked back at Mentine, standing at the gate with her baby. But her face was turned away from him. She was gazing after her husband, who went in the direction of the field.

Ma'ame Pélagie

When the war began, there stood on Côte Joyeuse an imposing mansion of red brick, shaped like the Pantheon. A grove of majestic live-oaks surrounded it.

Thirty years later, only the thick walls were standing, with the dull red brick showing here and there through a matted growth of clinging vines. The huge round pillars were intact; so to some extent was the stone flagging of hall and portico. There had been no home so stately along the whole stretch of Côte Joyeuse. Every one knew that, as they knew it had cost Philippe Valmêt sixty thousand dollars to build, away back in 1840. No one was in danger of forgetting that fact, so long as his daughter Pélagie survived. She was a queenly, white-haired woman of fifty. "Ma'ame Pélagie," they called her, though she was unmarried, as was her sister Pauline, a child in Ma'ame Pélagie's eyes; a child of thirty-five.

The two lived alone in a three-roomed cabin, almost within the shadow of the ruin. They lived for a dream, for Ma'ame Pélagie's dream, which was to rebuild the old home.

It would be pitiful to tell how their days were spent to accomplish this end; how the dollars had been saved for thirty years and the picayunes hoarded; and yet, not half enough gathered! But Ma'ame Pélagie felt sure of twenty years of life before her, and counted upon as many more for her sister. And what could not come to pass in twenty—in forty—years?

Often, of pleasant afternoons, the two would drink their black coffee, seated upon the stone-flagged portico whose canopy was the blue sky of Louisiana. They loved to sit there in the silence, with only each other and the sheeny, prying lizards for company, talking of the old times and planning for the new; while light breezes stirred the tattered vines high up among the columns, where owls nested.

"We can never hope to have all just as it was, Pauline," Ma'ame Pélagie would say; "perhaps the marble pillars of the salon will have to be replaced by wooden ones, and the crystal candelabra left out. Should you be willing, Pauline?"

"Oh, yes Sesoeur, I shall be willing." It was always, "Yes, Sesoeur," or "No, Sesoeur," "Just as you please, Sesoeur," with poor little Mam'selle Pauline. For what did she remember of that old life and that old splendor? Only a faint gleam here and there; the half-consciousness of a young, uneventful existence; and then a great crash. That meant the nearness of war; the revolt of slaves; confusion ending in fire and flame through which she was borne safely in the strong arms of Pélagie, and carried to the log cabin which was still their home. Their brother, Léandre, had known more of it all than Pauline, and not so much as Pélagie. He had left the management of the big plantation with all its memories and traditions to his older sister, and had gone away to dwell in cities. That was many years ago. Now, Léandre's business called him frequently and upon long journeys from home, and his motherless daughter was coming to stay with her aunts at Côte Joyeuse.

They talked about it, sipping their coffee on the ruined portico. Mam'selle Pauline was terribly excited; the flush that throbbed into her pale, nervous face showed it; and she locked her thin fingers in and out incessantly.

"But what shall we do with La Petite, Sesoeur? Where shall we put her? How shall we amuse her? Ah, Seigneur!"

"She will sleep upon a cot in the room next to ours," responded Ma'ame Pélagie, "and live as we do. She knows how we live, and why we live; her father has told her. She knows we have money and could squander it if we chose. Do not fret, Pauline; let us hope La Petite is a true Valmêt."

Then Ma'ame Pélagie rose with stately deliberation and went to saddle her horse, for she had yet to make her last daily round through the fields; and Mam'selle Pauline threaded her way slowly among the tangled grasses toward the cabin.

The coming of La Petite, bringing with her as she did the pungent atmosphere of an outside and dimly known world, was a shock to these two, living their dream-life. The girl was quite as tall as her aunt Pélagie, with dark eyes that reflected joy as a still pool reflects the light of stars; and her rounded cheek was tinged like the pink crêpe myrtle. Mam'selle

Pauline kissed her and trembled. Ma'ame Pélagie looked into her eyes with a searching gaze, which seemed to seek a likeness of the past in the living present.

And they made room between them for this young life.

II

La Petite had determined upon trying to fit herself to the strange, narrow existence which she knew awaited her at Côte Joyeuse. It went well enough at first. Sometimes she followed Ma'ame Pélagie into the fields to note how the cotton was opening, ripe and white; or to count the ears of corn upon the hardy stalks. But oftener she was with her aunt Pauline, assisting in household offices, chattering of her brief past, or walking with the older woman arm-in-arm under the trailing moss of the giant oaks.

Mam'selle Pauline's steps grew very buoyant that summer, and her eyes were sometimes as bright as a bird's, unless La Petite were away from her side, when they would lose all other light but one of uneasy expectancy. The girl seemed to love her well in return, and called her endearingly Tan'tante. But as the time went by, La Petite became very quiet,—not listless, but thoughtful, and slow in her movements. Then her cheeks began to pale, till they were tinged like the creamy plumes of the white crêpe myrtle that grew in the ruin.

One day when she sat within its shadow, between her aunts, holding a hand of each, she said: "Tante Pélagie, I must tell you something, you and Tan'tante." She spoke low, but clearly and firmly. "I love you both, —please remember that I love you both. But I must go away from you. I can't live any longer here at Côte Joyeuse."

A spasm passed through Mam'selle Pauline's delicate frame. La Petite could feel the twitch of it in the wiry fingers that were intertwined with her own. Ma'ame Pélagie remained unchanged and motionless. No human eye could penetrate so deep as to see the satisfaction which her soul felt. She said: "What do you mean, Petite? Your father has sent you to us, and I am sure it is his wish that you remain."

"My father loves me, tante Pélagie, and such will not be his wish when he knows. Oh!" she continued with a restless movement, "it is as though a weight were pressing me backward here. I must live another life; the life I lived before. I want to know things that are happening from day to day over the world, and hear them talked about. I want my music, my books, my companions. If I had known no other life but this one of privation, I suppose it would be different. If I had to live this life, I should make the best of it. But I do not have to; and you know, tante Pélagie, you do not need to. It seems to me," she added in a whisper, "that it is a sin against myself. Ah, Tan'tante!—what is the matter with Tan'tante?"

It was nothing; only a slight feeling of faintness, that would soon pass. She entreated them to take no notice; but they brought her some water and fanned her with a palmetto leaf.

But that night, in the stillness of the room, Mam'selle Pauline sobbed and would not be comforted. Ma'ame Pélagie took her in her arms.

"Pauline, my little sister Pauline," she entreated, "I never have seen you like this before. Do you no longer love me? Have we not been happy together, you and I?"

"Oh, yes, Sesoeur."

"Is it because La Petite is going away?"

"Yes, Sesoeur."

"Then she is dearer to you than I!" spoke Ma'ame Pélagie with sharp resentment. "Than I, who held you and warmed you in my arms the day you were born; than I, your mother, father, sister, everything that could cherish you. Pauline, don't tell me that."

Mam'selle Pauline tried to talk through her sobs.

"I can't explain it to you, Sesoeur. I don't understand it myself. I love you as I have always loved you; next to God. But if La Petite goes away I shall die. I can't understand,—help me, Sesoeur. She seems—she seems like a saviour; like one who had come and taken me by the hand and was leading me somewhere—somewhere I want to go."

Ma'ame Pélagie had been sitting beside the bed in her peignoir and slippers. She held the hand of her sister who lay there, and smoothed down the woman's soft brown hair. She said not a word, and the silence was broken only by Mam'selle Pauline's continued sobs. Once Ma'ame Pélagie arose to mix a drink of orange-flower water, which she gave to her sister, as she would have offered it to a nervous, fretful child. Almost an hour passed before Ma'ame Pélagie spoke again. Then she said:—

"Pauline, you must cease that sobbing, now, and sleep. You will make yourself ill. La Petite will not go away. Do you hear me? Do you understand? She will stay, I promise you."

Mam'selle Pauline could not clearly comprehend, but she had great faith in the word of her sister, and soothed by the promise and the touch of Ma'ame Pélagie's strong, gentle hand, she fell asleep.

III

Ma'ame Pélagie, when she saw that her sister slept, arose noiselessly and stepped outside upon the low-roofed narrow gallery. She did not linger there, but with a step that was hurried and agitated, she crossed the distance that divided her cabin from the ruin.

The night was not a dark one, for the sky was clear and the moon resplendent. But light or dark would have made no difference to Ma'ame Pélagie. It was not the first time she had stolen away to the ruin at night-time, when the whole plantation slept; but she never before had been there with a heart so nearly broken. She was going there for the last time to dream her dreams; to see the visions that hitherto had crowded her days and nights, and to bid them farewell.

There was the first of them, awaiting her upon the very portal; a robust old whitehaired man, chiding her for returning home so late. There are guests to be entertained. Does she not know it? Guests from the city and from the near plantations. Yes, she knows it is late. She had been abroad with Félix, and they did not notice how the time was speeding. Félix is there; he will explain it all. He is there beside her, but she does not want to hear what he will tell her father.

Ma'ame Pélagie had sunk upon the bench where she and her sister so often came to sit. Turning, she gazed in through the gaping chasm of the window at her side. The interior of the ruin is ablaze. Not with the moon-light, for that is faint beside the other one—the sparkle from the crystal candelabra, which negroes, moving noiselessly and respectfully about, are lighting, one after the other. How the gleam of them reflects and glances from the polished marble pillars!

The room holds a number of guests. There is old Monsieur Lucien Santien, leaning against one of the pillars, and laughing at something which Monsieur Lafirme is telling him, till his fat shoulders shake. His son Jules is with him—Jules, who wants to marry her. She laughs. She wonders if Félix has told her father yet. There is young Jérôme Lafirme playing at checkers upon the sofa with Léandre. Little Pauline stands annoying them and disturbing the game. Léandre reproves her. She begins to cry, and old black Clémentine, her nurse, who is not far off, limps across the room to pick her up and carry her away. How sensitive the little one is! But she trots about and takes care of herself better than she did a year or two ago, when she fell upon the stone hall floor and raised a great "bo-bo" on her forehead. Pélagie was hurt and angry enough about it; and she ordered rugs and buffalo robes to be brought and laid thick upon the tiles, till the little one's steps were surer.

"Il ne faut pas faire mal à Pauline." She was saying it aloud—"faire mal à Pauline."

But she gazes beyond the salon, back into the big dining hall, where the white crèpe myrtle grows. Ha! how low that bat has circled. It has struck Ma'ame Pélagie full on the breast. She does not know it. She is beyond there in the dining hall, where her father sits with a group of friends over their wine. As usual they are talking politics. How tiresome! She has heard them say "la guerre" oftener than once. La guerre. Bah! She and Félix have something pleasanter to talk about, out under the oaks, or back in the shadow of the oleanders.

But they were right! The sound of a cannon, shot at Sumter, has rolled across the Southern States, and its echo is heard along the whole stretch of Côte Joyeuse.

Yet Pélagie does not believe it. Not till La Ricaneuse stands before her with bare, black arms akimbo, uttering a volley of vile abuse and of brazen impudence. Pélagie wants to kill her. But yet she will not believe. Not till Félix comes to her in the chamber above the dining hall—there where that trumpet vine hangs—comes to say good-by to her. The hurt which the big brass buttons of his new gray uniform pressed into the tender flesh of her bosom has never left it. She sits upon the sofa, and he beside her, both speechless with pain. That room would not have been altered. Even the sofa would have been there in the same spot, and Ma'ame Pélagie had meant all along, for thirty years, all along, to lie there upon it some day when the time came to die.

But there is no time to weep, with the enemy at the door. The door has been no barrier. They are clattering through the halls now, drinking the wines, shattering the crystal and glass, slashing the portraits.

One of them stands before her and tells her to leave the house. She slaps his face. How the stigma stands out red as blood upon his blanched cheek!

Now there is a roar of fire and the flames are bearing down upon her motionless figure. She wants to show them how a daughter of Louisiana can perish before her conquerors. But little Pauline clings to her knees in an agony of terror. Little Pauline must be saved.

"Il ne faut pas faire mal à Pauline." Again she is saying it aloud—
"faire mal à Pauline."

The night was nearly spent; Ma'ame Pélagie had glided from the
bench upon which she had rested, and for hours lay prone upon the stone
flagging, motionless. When she dragged herself to her feet it was to walk
like one in a dream. About the great, solemn pillars, one after the other,
she reached her arms, and pressed her cheek and her lips upon the
senseless brick.

"Adieu, adieu!" whispered Ma'ame Pélagie.

There was no longer the moon to guide her steps across the familiar
pathway to the cabin. The brightest light in the sky was Venus, that
swung low in the east. The bats had ceased to beat their wings about the
ruin. Even the mocking-bird that had warbled for hours in the old
mulberry-tree had sung himself asleep. That darkest hour before the day
was mantling the earth. Ma'ame Pélagie hurried through the wet, clinging
grass, beating aside the heavy moss that swept across her face, walking
on toward the cabin—toward Pauline. Not once did she look back upon
the ruin that brooded like a huge monster—a black spot in the darkness
that enveloped it.

IV

Little more than a year later the transformation which the old Valmêt
place had undergone was the talk and wonder of Côte Joyeuse. One
would have looked in vain for the ruin; it was no longer there; neither
was the log cabin. But out in the open, where the sun shone upon it, and
the breezes blew about it, was a shapely structure fashioned from woods
that the forests of the State had furnished. It rested upon a solid foundation
of brick.

Upon a corner of the pleasant gallery sat Léandre smoking his afternoon
cigar, and chatting with neighbors who had called. This was to be his
pied à terre now; the home where his sisters and his daughter dwelt. The
laughter of young people was heard out under the trees, and within the
house where La Petite was playing upon the piano. With the enthusiasm
of a young artist she drew from the keys strains that seemed marvelously
beautiful to Mam'selle Pauline, who stood enraptured near her. Mam'selle
Pauline had been touched by the re-creation of Valmêt. Her cheek was as

full and almost as flushed as La Petite's. The years were falling away from her.

Ma'ame Pélagie had been conversing with her brother and his friends. Then she turned and walked away; stopping to listen awhile to the music which La Petite was making. But it was only for a moment. She went on around the curve of the veranda, where she found herself alone. She stayed there, erect, holding to the banister rail and looking out calmly in the distance across the fields.

She was dressed in black, with the white kerchief she always wore folded across her bosom. Her thick, glossy hair rose like a silver diadem from her brow. In her deep, dark eyes smouldered the light of fires that would never flame. She had grown very old. Years instead of months seemed to have passed over her since the night she bade farewell to her visions.

Poor Ma'ame Pélagie! How could it be different! While the outward pressure of a young and joyous existence had forced her footsteps into the light, her soul had stayed in the shadow of the ruin.

Désirée's Baby

As the day was pleasant, Madame Valmondé drove over to L'Abri to see Désirée and the baby.

It made her laugh to think of Désirée with a baby. Why, it seemed but yesterday that Désirée was little more than a baby herself; when Monsieur in riding through the gateway of Valmondé had found her lying asleep in the shadow of the big stone pillar.

The little one awoke in his arms and began to cry for "Dada." That was as much as she could do or say. Some people thought she might have strayed there of her own accord, for she was of the toddling age. The prevailing belief was that she had been purposely left by a party of Texans, whose canvas-covered wagon, late in the day, had crossed the ferry that Coton Maïs kept, just below the plantation. In time Madame Valmondé abandoned every speculation but the one that Désirée had been sent to her by a beneficent Providence to be the child of her affection, seeing that she was without child of the flesh. For the girl grew to be beautiful and gentle, affectionate and sincere,—the idol of Valmondé.

It was no wonder, when she stood one day against the stone pillar in whose shadow she had lain asleep, eighteen years before, that Armand Aubigny riding by and seeing her there, had fallen in love with her. That was the way all the Aubignys fell in love, as if struck by a pistol shot. The wonder was that he had not loved her before; for he had known her since his father brought him home from Paris, a boy of eight, after his mother died there. The passion that awoke in him that day, when he saw her at the gate, swept along like an avalanche, or like a prairie fire, or like anything that drives headlong over all obstacles.

Monsieur Valmondé grew practical and wanted things well considered:

that is, the girl's obscure origin. Armand looked into her eyes and did not care. He was reminded that she was nameless. What did it matter about a name when he could give her one of the oldest and proudest in Louisiana? He ordered the *corbeille* from Paris, and contained himself with what patience he could until it arrived; then they were married.

Madame Valmondé had not seen Désirée and the baby for four weeks. When she reached L'Abri she shuddered at the first sight of it, as she always did. It was a sad looking place, which for many years had not known the gentle presence of a mistress, old Monsieur Aubigny having married and buried his wife in France, and she having loved her own land too well ever to leave it. The roof came down steep and black like a cowl, reaching out beyond the wide galleries that encircled the yellow stuccoed house. Big, solemn oaks grew close to it, and their thick-leaved, far-reaching branches shadowed it like a pall. Young Aubigny's rule was a strict one, too, and under it his negroes had forgotten how to be gay, as they had been during the old master's easy-going and indulgent lifetime.

The young mother was recovering slowly, and lay full length, in her soft white muslins and laces, upon a couch. The baby was beside her, upon her arm, where he had fallen asleep, at her breast. The yellow nurse woman sat beside a window fanning herself.

Madame Valmondé bent her portly figure over Désirée and kissed her, holding her an instant tenderly in her arms. Then she turned to the child.

"This is not the baby!" she exclaimed, in startled tones. French was the language spoken at Valmondé in those days.

"I knew you would be astonished," laughed Désirée, "at the way he has grown. The little *cochon de lait!* Look at his legs, mamma, and his hands and fingernails,—real finger-nails. Zandrine had to cut them this morning. Is n't it true, Zandrine?"

The woman bowed her turbaned head majestically, "Mais si, Madame."

"And the way he cries," went on Désirée, "is deafening. Armand heard him the other day as far away as La Blanche's cabin."

Madame Valmondé had never removed her eyes from the child. She lifted it and walked with it over to the window that was lightest. She scanned the baby narrowly, then looked as searchingly at Zandrine, whose face was turned to gaze across the fields.

"Yes, the child has grown, has changed," said Madame Valmondé, slowly, as she replaced it beside its mother. "What does Armand say?"

Désirée's face became suffused with a glow that was happiness itself.

"Oh, Armand is the proudest father in the parish, I believe, chiefly because it is a boy, to bear his name; though he says not,—that he would have loved a girl as well. But I know it is n't true. I know he says that to please me. And mamma," she added, drawing Madame Valmondé's head down to her, and speaking in a whisper, "he has n't punished one of them —not one of them—since baby is born. Even Négrillon, who pretended to have burnt his leg that he might rest from work—he only laughed, and said Négrillon was a great scamp. Oh, mamma, I 'm so happy; it frightens me."

What Désirée said was true. Marriage, and later the birth of his son had softened Armand Aubigny's imperious and exacting nature greatly. This was what made the gentle Désirée so happy, for she loved him desperately. When he frowned she trembled, but loved him. When he smiled, she asked no greater blessing of God. But Armand's dark, handsome face had not often been disfigured by frowns since the day he fell in love with her.

When the baby was about three months old, Désirée awoke one day to the conviction that there was something in the air menacing her peace. It was at first too subtle to grasp. It had only been a disquieting suggestion; an air of mystery among the blacks; unexpected visits from far-off neighbors who could hardly account for their coming. Then a strange, an awful change in her husband's manner, which she dared not ask him to explain. When he spoke to her, it was with averted eyes, from which the old love-light seemed to have gone out. He absented himself from home; and when there, avoided her presence and that of her child, without excuse. And the very spirit of Satan seemed suddenly to take hold of him in his dealings with the slaves. Désirée was miserable enough to die.

She sat in her room, one hot afternoon, in her *peignoir*, listlessly drawing through her fingers the strands of her long, silky brown hair that hung about her shoulders. The baby, half naked, lay asleep upon her own great mahogany bed, that was like a sumptuous throne, with its satin-lined half-canopy. One of La Blanche's little quadroon boys—half naked too— stood fanning the child slowly with a fan of peacock feathers. Désirée's eyes had been fixed absently and sadly upon the baby, while she was striving to penetrate the threatening mist that she felt closing about her. She looked from her child to the boy who stood beside him, and back again; over and over. "Ah!" It was a cry that she could not help; which she was not conscious of having uttered. The blood turned like ice in her veins, and a clammy moisture gathered upon her face.

She tried to speak to the little quadroon boy; but no sound would come, at first. When he heard his name uttered, he looked up, and his mistress was pointing to the door. He laid aside the great, soft fan, and obediently stole away, over the polished floor, on his bare tiptoes.

She stayed motionless, with gaze riveted upon her child, and her face the picture of fright.

Presently her husband entered the room, and without noticing her, went to a table and began to search among some papers which covered it.

"Armand," she called to him, in a voice which must have stabbed him, if he was human. But he did not notice. "Armand," she said again. Then she rose and tottered towards him. "Armand," she panted once more, clutching his arm, "look at our child. What does it mean? tell me."

He coldly but gently loosened her fingers from about his arm and thrust the hand away from him. "Tell me what it means!" she cried despairingly.

"It means," he answered lightly, "that the child is not white; it means that you are not white."

A quick conception of all that this accusation meant for her nerved her with unwonted courage to deny it. "It is a lie; it is not true, I am white! Look at my hair, it is brown; and my eyes are gray, Armand, you know they are gray. And my skin is fair," seizing his wrist. "Look at my hand; whiter than yours, Armand," she laughed hysterically.

"As white as La Blanche's," he returned cruelly; and went away leaving her alone with their child.

When she could hold a pen in her hand, she sent a despairing letter to Madame Valmondé.

"My mother, they tell me I am not white. Armand has told me I am not white. For God's sake tell them it is not true. You must know it is not true. I shall die. I must die. I cannot be so unhappy, and live."

The answer that came was as brief:

"My own Désirée: Come home to Valmondé; back to your mother who loves you. Come with your child."

When the letter reached Désirée she went with it to her husband's study, and laid it open upon the desk before which he sat. She was like a stone image: silent, white, motionless after she placed it there.

In silence he ran his cold eyes over the written words. He said nothing. "Shall I go, Armand?" she asked in tones sharp with agonized suspense.

"Yes, go."

"Do you want me to go?"

"Yes, I want you to go."

He thought Almighty God had dealt cruelly and unjustly with him; and felt, somehow, that he was paying Him back in kind when he stabbed thus into his wife's soul. Moreover he no longer loved her, because of the unconscious injury she had brought upon his home and his name.

She turned away like one stunned by a blow, and walked slowly towards the door, hoping he would call her back.

"Good-by, Armand," she moaned.

He did not answer her. That was his last blow at fate.

Désirée went in search of her child. Zandrine was pacing the sombre gallery with it. She took the little one from the nurse's arms with no word of explanation, and descending the steps, walked away, under the live-oak branches.

It was an October afternoon; the sun was just sinking. Out in the still fields the negroes were picking cotton.

Désirée had not changed the thin white garment nor the slippers which she wore. Her hair was uncovered and the sun's rays brought a golden gleam from its brown meshes. She did not take the broad, beaten road which led to the far-off plantation of Valmondé. She walked across a deserted field, where the stubble bruised her tender feet, so delicately shod, and tore her thin gown to shreds.

She disappeared among the reeds and willows that grew thick along the banks of the deep, sluggish bayou; and she did not come back again.

Some weeks later there was a curious scene enacted at L'Abri. In the centre of the smoothly swept back yard was a great bonfire. Armand Aubigny sat in the wide hallway that commanded a view of the spectacle; and it was he who dealt out to a half dozen negroes the material which kept this fire ablaze.

A graceful cradle of willow, with all its dainty furbishings, was laid upon the pyre, which had already been fed with the richness of a priceless *layette*. Then there were silk gowns, and velvet and satin ones added to these; laces, too, and embroideries; bonnets and gloves; for the *corbeille* had been of rare quality.

The last thing to go was a tiny bundle of letters; innocent little scribblings that Désirée had sent to him during the days of their espousal. There was the remnant of one back in the drawer from which he took them. But it was not Désirée's; it was part of an old letter from his mother to his father. He read it. She was thanking God for the blessing of her husband's love:—

"But, above all," she wrote, "night and day, I thank the good God for having so arranged our lives that our dear Armand will never know that his mother, who adores him, belongs to the race that is cursed with the brand of slavery."

Caline

The sun was just far enough in the west to send inviting shadows. In the centre of a small field, and in the shade of a haystack which was there, a girl lay sleeping. She had slept long and soundly, when something awoke her as suddenly as if it had been a blow. She opened her eyes and stared a moment up in the cloudless sky. She yawned and stretched her long brown legs and arms, lazily. Then she arose, never minding the bits of straw that clung to her black hair, to her red bodice, and the blue cotonade skirt that did not reach her naked ankles.

The log cabin in which she dwelt with her parents was just outside the enclosure in which she had been sleeping. Beyond was a small clearing that did duty as a cotton field. All else was dense wood, except the long stretch that curved round the brow of the hill, and in which glittered the steel rails of the Texas and Pacific road.

When Caline emerged from the shadow she saw a long train of passenger coaches standing in view, where they must have stopped abruptly. It was that sudden stopping which had awakened her; for such a thing had not happened before within her recollection, and she looked stupid, at first, with astonishment. There seemed to be something wrong with the engine; and some of the passengers who dismounted went forward to investigate the trouble. Others came strolling along in the direction of the cabin, where Caline stood under an old gnarled mulberry tree, staring. Her father had halted his mule at the end of the cotton row, and stood staring also, leaning upon his plow.

There were ladies in the party. They walked awkwardly in their high-heeled boots over the rough, uneven ground, and held up their skirts mincingly. They twirled parasols over their shoulders, and laughed immoderately at the funny things which their masculine companions were saying.

They tried to talk to Caline, but could not understand the French patois with which she answered them.

One of the men—a pleasant-faced youngster—drew a sketch book from his pocket and began to make a picture of the girl. She stayed motionless, her hands behind her, and her wide eyes fixed earnestly upon him.

Before he had finished there was a summons from the train; and all went scampering hurriedly away. The engine screeched, it sent a few lazy puffs into the still air, and in another moment or two had vanished, bearing its human cargo with it.

Caline could not feel the same after that. She looked with new and strange interest upon the trains of cars that passed so swiftly back and forth across her vision, each day; and wondered whence these people came, and whither they were going.

Her mother and father could not tell her, except to say that they came from "loin là bas," and were going "Djieu sait é où."

One day she walked miles down the track to talk with the old flagman, who stayed down there by the big water tank. Yes, he knew. Those people came from the great cities in the north, and were going to the city in the south. He knew all about the city; it was a grand place. He had lived there once. His sister lived there now; and she would be glad enough to have so fine a girl as Caline to help her cook and scrub, and tend the babies. And he thought Caline might earn as much as five dollars a month, in the city.

So she went; in a new cotonade, and her Sunday shoes; with a sacredly guarded scrawl that the flagman sent to his sister.

The woman lived in a tiny, stuccoed house, with green blinds, and three wooden steps leading down to the banquette. There seemed to be hundreds like it along the street. Over the house tops loomed the tall masts of ships, and the hum of the French market could be heard on a still morning.

Caline was at first bewildered. She had to readjust all her preconceptions to fit the reality of it. The flagman's sister was a kind and gentle task-mistress. At the end of a week or two she wanted to know how the girl liked it all. Caline liked it very well, for it was pleasant, on Sunday afternoons, to stroll with the children under the great, solemn sugar sheds; or to sit upon the compressed cotton bales, watching the stately steamers, the graceful boats, and noisy little tugs that plied the waters of the Mississippi. And it filled her with agreeable excitement to go to the

French market, where the handsome Gascon butchers were eager to present their compliments and little Sunday bouquets to the pretty Acadian girl; and to throw fistfuls of *lagniappe* into her basket.

When the woman asked her again after another week if she were still pleased, she was not so sure. And again when she questioned Caline the girl turned away, and went to sit behind the big, yellow cistern, to cry unobserved. For she knew now that it was not the great city and its crowds of people she had so eagerly sought; but the pleasant-faced boy, who had made her picture that day under the mulberry tree.

The Return of Alcibiade

Mr. Fred Bartner was sorely perplexed and annoyed to find that a wheel and tire of his buggy threatened to part company.

"Ef you want," said the negro boy who drove him, "we kin stop yonda at ole M'sié Jean Ba's an' fix it; he got de bes' blacksmif shop in de pa'ish on his place."

"Who in the world is old Monsieur Jean Ba," the young man inquired.

"How come, suh, you don' know old M'sié Jean Baptiste Plochel? He ole, ole. He sorter quare in he head ev' sence his son M'sié Alcibiade got kill' in de wah. Yonda he live'; whar you sees dat che'okee hedge takin' up half de road."

Little more than twelve years ago, before the "Texas and Pacific" had joined the cities of New Orleans and Shreveport with its steel bands, it was a common thing to travel through miles of central Louisiana in a buggy. Fred Bartner, a young commission merchant of New Orleans, on business bent, had made the trip in this way by easy stages from his home to a point on Cane River, within a half day's journey of Natchitoches. From the mouth of Cane River he had passed one plantation after another,—large ones and small ones. There was nowhere sight of anything like a town, except the little hamlet of Cloutierville, through which they had sped in the gray dawn. "Dat town, hit's ole, ole; mos' a hund'ed year' ole, dey say. Uh, uh, look to me like it heap ol'r an' dat," the darkey had commented. Now they were within sight of Monsieur Jean Ba's towering Cherokee hedge.

It was Christmas morning, but the sun was warm and the air so soft and mild that Bartner found the most comfortable way to wear his light overcoat was across his knees. At the entrance to the plantation he dismounted and the negro drove away toward the smithy which stood on the edge of the field.

From the end of the long avenue of magnolias that led to it, the house which confronted Bartner looked grotesquely long in comparison with its height. It was one story, of pale, yellow stucco; its massive wooden shutters were a faded green. A wide gallery, topped by the overhanging roof, encircled it.

At the head of the stairs a very old man stood. His figure was small and shrunken, his hair long and snow-white. He wore a broad, soft felt hat, and a brown plaid shawl across his bent shoulders. A tall, graceful girl stood beside him; she was clad in a warm-colored blue stuff gown. She seemed to be expostulating with the old gentleman, who evidently wanted to descend the stairs to meet the approaching visitor. Before Bartner had had time to do more than lift his hat, Monsieur Jean Ba had thrown his trembling arms about the young man and was exclaiming in his quavering old tones: "À la fin! mon fils! à la fin!" Tears started to the girl's eyes and she was rosy with confusion. "Oh, escuse him, sir; please escuse him," she whisperingly entreated, gently striving to disengage the old gentleman's arms from around the astonished Bartner. But a new line of thought seemed fortunately to take possession of Monsieur Jean Ba, for he moved away and went quickly, pattering like a baby, down the gallery. His fleecy white hair streamed out on the soft breeze, and his brown shawl flapped as he turned the corner.

Bartner, left alone with the girl, proceeded to introduce himself and to explain his presence there.

"Oh! Mr. Fred Bartna of New Orleans? The commission merchant!" she exclaimed, cordially extending her hand. "So well known in Natchitoches parish. Not *our* merchant, Mr. Bartna," she added, naïvely, "but jus' as welcome, all the same, at my gran'father's."

Bartner felt like kissing her, but he only bowed and seated himself in the big chair which she offered him. He wondered what was the longest time it could take to mend a buggy tire.

She sat before him with her hands pressed down into her lap, and with an eagerness and pretty air of being confidential that were extremely engaging, explained the reasons for her grandfather's singular behavior.

Years ago, her uncle Alcibiade, in going away to the war, with the cheerful assurance of youth, had promised his father that he would return to eat Christmas dinner with him. He never returned. And now, of late years, since Monsieur Jean Ba had begun to fail in body and mind, that old, unspoken hope of long ago had come back to live anew in his heart. Every Christmas Day he watched for the coming of Alcibiade.

"Ah! if you knew, Mr. Bartna, how I have endeavor' to distrac' his mine from that thought! Weeks ago, I tole to all the negroes, big and li'le, 'If one of you dare to say the word, Christmas gif', in the hearing of Monsieur Jean Baptiste, you will have to answer it to me.' "

Bartner could not recall when he had been so deeply interested in a narration.

"So las' night, Mr. Bartna, I said to grandpère, 'Pépère, you know to-morrow will be the great feas' of la Trinité; we will read our litany together in the morning and say a *chapelet*.' He did not answer a word; *il est malin, oui*. But this morning at daylight he was rapping his cane on the back gallery, calling together the negroes. Did they not know it was Christmas Day, an' a great dinner mus' be prepare' for his son Alcibiade, whom he was especting!"

"And so he has mistaken me for his son Alcibiade. It is very unfortunate," said Bartner, sympathetically. He was a good-looking, honest-faced young fellow.

The girl arose, quivering with an inspiration. She approached Bartner, and in her eagerness laid her hand upon his arm.

"Oh, Mr. Bartna, if you will do me a favor! The greates' favor of my life!"

He expressed his absolute readiness.

"Let him believe, jus' for this one Christmas day, that you are his son. Let him have that Christmas dinner with Alcibiade, that he has been longing for so many year'."

Bartner's was not a puritanical conscience, but truthfulness was a habit as well as a principle with him, and he winced. "It seems to me it would be cruel to deceive him; it would not be"—he did not like to say "right," but she guessed that he meant it.

"Oh, for that," she laughed, "you may stay as w'ite as snow, Mr. Bartna. *I* will take all the sin on my conscience. I assume all the responsibility on my shoulder'."

"Esmée!" the old man was calling as he came trotting back, "Esmée, my child," in his quavering French, "I have ordered the dinner. Go see to the arrangements of the table, and have everything faultless."

The dining-room was at the end of the house, with windows opening upon the side and back galleries. There was a high, simply carved wooden mantelpiece, bearing a wide, slanting, old-fashioned mirror that reflected the table and its occupants. The table was laden with an overabundance. Monsieur Jean Ba sat at one end, Esmée at the other, and Bartner at the side.

Two *"grif"* boys, a big black woman and a little mulatto girl waited upon them; there was a reserve force outside within easy call, and the little black and yellow faces kept bobbing up constantly above the window-sills. Windows and doors were open, and a fire of hickory branches blazed on the hearth.

Monsieur Jean Ba ate little, but that little greedily and rapidly; then he stayed in rapt contemplation of his guest.

"You will notice, Alcibiade, the flavor of the turkey," he said. "It is dressed with pecans; those big ones from the tree down on the bayou. I had them gathered expressly." The delicate and rich flavor of the nut was indeed very perceptible.

Bartner had a stupid impression of acting on the stage, and had to pull himself together every now and then to throw off the stiffness of the amateur actor. But this discomposure amounted almost to paralysis when he found Mademoiselle Esmée taking the situation as seriously as her grandfather.

"*Mon Dieu!* uncle Alcibiade, you are not eating! *Mais* w'ere have you lef' your appetite? Corbeau, fill your young master's glass. Doralise, you are neglecting Monsieur Alcibiade; he is without bread."

Monsieur Jean Ba's feeble intelligence reached out very dimly; it was like a dream which clothes the grotesque and unnatural with the semblance of reality. He shook his head up and down with pleased approbation of Esmée's "Uncle Alcibiade," that tripped so glibly on her lips. When she arranged his after-dinner *brûlot*,—a lump of sugar in a flaming teaspoonful of brandy, dropped into a tiny cup of black coffee,—he reminded her, "Your Uncle Alcibiade takes two lumps, Esmée. The scamp! he is fond of sweets. Two or three lumps, Esmée." Bartner would have relished his *brûlot* greatly, prepared so gracefully as it was by Esmée's deft hands, had it not been for that superfluous lump.

After dinner the girl arranged her grandfather comfortably in his big armchair on the gallery, where he loved to sit when the weather permitted. She fastened his shawl about him and laid a second one across his knees. She shook up the pillow for his head, patted his sunken cheek and kissed his forehead under the soft-brimmed hat. She left him there with the sun warming his feet and old shrunken knees.

Esmée and Bartner walked together under the magnolias. In walking they trod upon the violet borders that grew rank and sprawling, and the subtle perfume of the crushed flowers scented the air deliciously. They stooped and plucked handfuls of them. They gathered roses, too, that were blooming yet against the warm south end of the house; and they chattered and laughed like children. When they sat in the sunlight upon the low steps to arrange the flowers they had broken, Bartner's conscience began to prick him anew.

"You know," he said, "I can't stay here always, as well as I should like to. I shall have to leave presently; then your grandfather will discover that we have been deceiving him,—and you can see how cruel that will be."

"Mr. Bartna," answered Esmée, daintily holding a rosebud up to her pretty nose, "W'en I awoke this morning an' said my prayers, I prayed to the good God that He would give one happy Christmas day to my gran'father. He has answered my prayer; an' He does not sen' his gif's incomplete. He will provide.

"Mr. Bartna, this morning I agreed to take all responsibility on my shoulder', you remember? Now, I place all that responsibility on the shoulder' of the blessed Virgin."

Bartner was distracted with admiration; whether for this beautiful and consoling faith, or its charming votary, was not quite clear to him.

Every now and then Monsieur Jean Ba would call out, "Alcibiade, *mon fils!*" and Bartner would hasten to his side. Sometimes the old man had forgotten what he wanted to say. Once it was to ask if the salad had been to his liking, or if he would, perhaps, not have preferred the turkey *aux truffes*.

"Alcibiade, *mon fils!*" Again Bartner amiably answered the summons. Monsieur Jean Ba took the young man's hand affectionately in his, but limply, as children hold hands. Bartner's closed firmly around it.

"Alcibiade, I am going to take a little nap now. If Robert McFarlane comes while I am sleeping, with more talk of wanting to buy Nég Séverin, tell him I will sell none of my slaves; not the least little *négrillon*. Drive him from the place with the shot-gun. Don't be afraid to use the shot-gun, Alcibiade,—when I am asleep,—if he comes."

Esmée and Bartner forgot that there was such a thing as time, and that it was passing. There were no more calls of "Alcibiade, *mon fils!*" As the sun dipped lower and lower in the west, its light was creeping, creeping up and illuming the still body of Monsieur Jean Ba. It lighted his waxen hands, folded so placidly in his lap; it touched his shrunken bosom. When it reached his face, another brightness had come there before it,—the glory of a quiet and peaceful death.

Bartner remained over night, of course, to add what assistance he could to that which kindly neighbors offered.

In the early morning, before taking his departure, he was permitted to see Esmée. She was overcome with sorrow, which he could hardly hope to assuage, even with the keen sympathy which he felt.

"And may I be permitted to ask, Mademoiselle, what will be your plans for the future?"

"Oh," she moaned, "I cannot any longer remain upon the ole plantation, which would not be home without grandpère. I suppose I shall go to live in New Orleans with my *tante* Clémentine." The last was spoken in the depths of her handkerchief.

Bartner's heart bounded at this intelligence in a manner which he could not but feel was one of unbecoming levity. He pressed her disengaged hand warmly, and went away.

The sun was again shining brightly, but the morning was crisp and cool; a thin wafer of ice covered what had yesterday been pools of water in the road. Bartner buttoned his coat about him closely. The shrill whistles of steam cotton-gins sounded here and there. One or two shivering negroes were in the field gathering what shreds of cotton were left on the dry, naked stalks. The horses snorted with satisfaction, and their strong hoof-beats rang out against the hard ground.

"Urge the horses," Bartner said; "they 've had a good rest and we want to push on to Natchitoches."

"You right, suh. We done los' a whole blesse' day,—a plumb day."

"Why, so we have," said Bartner, "I had n't thought of it."

In and Out of Old Natchitoches

Precisely at eight o'clock every morning except Saturdays and Sundays, Mademoiselle Suzanne St. Denys Godolph would cross the railroad trestle that spanned Bayou Boispourri. She might have crossed in the flat which Mr. Alphonse Laballière kept for his own convenience; but the method was slow and unreliable; so, every morning at eight, Mademoiselle St. Denys Godolph crossed the trestle.

She taught public school in a picturesque little white frame structure that stood upon Mr. Laballière's land, and hung upon the very brink of the bayou.

Laballière himself was comparatively a new-comer in the parish. It was barely six months since he decided one day to leave the sugar and rice to his brother Alcée, who had a talent for their cultivation, and to try his hand at cotton-planting. That was why he was up in Natchitoches parish on a piece of rich, high, Cane River land, knocking into shape a tumbled-down plantation that he had bought for next to nothing.

He had often during his perambulations observed the trim, graceful figure stepping cautiously over the ties, and had sometimes shivered for its safety. He always exchanged a greeting with the girl, and once threw a plank over a muddy pool for her to step upon. He caught but glimpses of her features, for she wore an enormous sun-bonnet to shield her complexion, that seemed marvelously fair; while loosely-fitting leather gloves protected her hands. He knew she was the school-teacher, and also that she was the daughter of that very pig-headed old Madame St. Denys Godolph who was hoarding her barren acres across the bayou as a miser hoards gold. Starving over them, some people said. But that was nonsense; nobody starves on a Louisiana plantation, unless it be with suicidal intent.

These things he knew, but he did not know why Mademoiselle St. Denys Godolph always answered his salutation with an air of chilling hauteur that would easily have paralyzed a less sanguine man.

The reason was that Suzanne, like every one else, had heard the stories that were going the rounds about him. People said he was entirely too much at home with the free mulattoes.* It seems a dreadful thing to say, and it would be a shocking thing to think of a Laballière; but it was n't true.

When Laballière took possession of his land, he found the plantation-house occupied by one Giestin and his swarming family. It was past reckoning how long the free mulatto and his people had been there. The house was a six-room, long, shambling affair, shrinking together from decrepitude. There was not an entire pane of glass in the structure; and the Turkey-red curtains flapped in and out of the broken apertures. But there is no need to dwell upon details; it was wholly unfit to serve as a civilized human habitation; and Alphonse Laballière would no sooner have disturbed its contented occupants than he would have scattered a family of partridges nesting in a corner of his field. He established himself with a few belongings in the best cabin he could find on the place, and, without further ado, proceeded to supervise the building of house, of gin, of this, that, and the other, and to look into the hundred details that go to set a neglected plantation in good working order. He took his meals at the free mulatto's, quite apart from the family, of course; and they attended, not too skillfully, to his few domestic wants.

Some loafer whom he had snubbed remarked one day in town that Laballière had more use for a free mulatto than he had for a white man. It was a sort of catching thing to say, and suggestive, and was repeated with the inevitable embellishments.

One morning when Laballière sat eating his solitary breakfast, and being waited upon by the queenly Madame Giestin and a brace of her weazened boys, Giestin himself came into the room. He was about half the size of his wife, puny and timid. He stood beside the table, twirling his felt hat aimlessly and balancing himself insecurely on his high-pointed boot-heels.

"Mr. Laballière," he said, "I reckon I tell you; it 's betta you git shed o' me en' my fambly. Jis like you want, yas."

"What in the name of common sense are you talking about?" asked

* A term still applied in Louisiana to mulattoes who were never in slavery, and whose families in most instances were themselves slave owners.

Laballière, looking up abstractedly from his New Orleans paper. Giestin wriggled uncomfortably.

"It 's heap o' story goin' roun' 'bout you, if you want b'lieve me." And he snickered and looked at his wife, who thrust the end of her shawl into her mouth and walked from the room with a tread like the Empress Eugenie's, in that elegant woman's palmiest days.

"Stories!" echoed Laballière, his face the picture of astonishment. "Who—where—what stories?"

"Yon'a in town en' all about. It 's heap o' tale goin' roun', yas. They say how come you mighty fon' o' mulatta. You done shoshiate wid de mulatta down yon'a on de suga plantation, tell you can't res' lessen it 's mulatta roun' you."

Laballière had a distressingly quick temper. His fist, which was a strong one, came down upon the wobbling table with a crash that sent half of Madame Giestin's crockery bouncing and crashing to the floor. He swore an oath that sent Madame Giestin and her father and grandmother, who were all listening in the next room, into suppressed convulsions of mirth.

"Oh, ho! so I 'm not to associate with whom I please in Natchitoches parish. We 'll see about that. Draw up your chair, Giestin. Call your wife and your grandmother and the rest of the tribe, and we 'll breakfast together. By thunder! if I want to hobnob with mulattoes, or negroes or Choctaw Indians or South Sea savages, whose business is it but my own?"

"I don' know, me. It 's jis like I tell you, Mr. Laballière," and Giestin selected a huge key from an assortment that hung against the wall, and left the room.

A half hour later, Laballière had not yet recovered his senses. He appeared suddenly at the door of the schoolhouse, holding by the shoulder one of Giestin's boys. Mademoiselle St. Denys Godolph stood at the opposite extremity of the room. Her sunbonnet hung upon the wall, now, so Laballière could have seen how charming she was, had he not at the moment been blinded by stupidity. Her blue eyes that were fringed with dark lashes reflected astonishment at seeing him there. Her hair was dark like her lashes, and waved softly about her smooth, white forehead.

"Mademoiselle," began Laballière at once, "I have taken the liberty of bringing a new pupil to you."

Mademoiselle St. Denys Godolph paled suddenly and her voice was unsteady when she replied:—

"You are too considerate, Monsieur. Will you be so kine to give me

the name of the scholar whom you desire to int'oduce into this school?"
She knew it as well as he.

"What 's your name, youngster? Out with it!" cried Laballière,
striving to shake the little free mulatto into speech; but he stayed as
dumb as a mummy.

"His name is André Giestin. You know him. He is the son"—

"Then, Monsieur," she interrupted, "permit me to remine you that
you have made a se'ious mistake. This is not a school conducted fo' the
education of the colored population. You will have to go elsew'ere with
yo' protégé."

"I shall leave my protégé right here, Mademoiselle, and I trust you 'll
give him the same kind attention you seem to accord to the others;"
saying which Laballière bowed himself out of her presence. The little
Giestin, left to his own devices, took only the time to give a quick, wary
glance round the room, and the next instant he bounded through
the open door, as the nimblest of four-footed creatures might have
done.

Mademoiselle St. Denys Godolph conducted school during the hours
that remained, with a deliberate calmness that would have seemed
ominous to her pupils, had they been better versed in the ways of young
women. When the hour for dismissal came, she rapped upon the table to
demand attention.

"Chil'ren," she began, assuming a resigned and dignified mien, "you
all have been witness to-day of the insult that has been offered to yo'
teacher by the person upon whose lan' this schoolhouse stan's. I have
nothing further to say on that subjec'. I only shall add that to-morrow yo'
teacher shall sen' the key of this schoolhouse, together with her resignation,
to the gentlemen who compose the school-boa'd." There followed visible
disturbance among the young people.

"I ketch that li'le m'latta, I make 'im see sight', yas," screamed one.

"Nothing of the kine, Mathurin, you mus' take no such step, if only out
of consideration fo' my wishes. The person who has offered the affront I
consider beneath my notice. André, on the other han', is a chile of good
impulse, an' by no means to blame. As you all perceive, he has shown
mo' taste and judgment than those above him, f'om whom we might have
espected good breeding, at least."

She kissed them all, the little boys and the little girls, and had a kind
word for each. "*Et toi, mon petit Numa, j'espère qu'un autre*"—She could not
finish the sentence, for little Numa, her favorite, to whom she had never

been able to impart the first word of English, was blubbering at a turn of
affairs which he had only miserably guessed at.

She locked the schoolhouse door and walked away towards the bridge.
By the time she reached it, the little 'Cadians had already disappeared
like rabbits, down the road and through and over the fences.

Mademoiselle St. Denys Godolph did not cross the trestle the following
day, nor the next nor the next. Laballière watched for her; for his big
heart was already sore and filled with shame. But more, it stung him with
remorse to realize that he had been the stupid instrument in taking the
bread, as it were, from the mouth of Mademoiselle St. Denys Godolph.

He recalled how unflinchingly and haughtily her blue eyes had challenged his own. Her sweetness and charm came back to him and he dwelt
upon them and exaggerated them, till no Venus, so far unearthed, could
in any way approach Mademoiselle St. Denys Godolph. He would have
liked to exterminate the Giestin family, from the great-grandmother down
to the babe unborn.

Perhaps Giestin suspected this unfavorable attitude, for one morning he
piled his whole family and all his effects into wagons, and went away;
over into that part of the parish known as *l'Isle des Mulâtres*.

Laballière's really chivalrous nature told him, beside, that he owed an
apology, at least, to the young lady who had taken his whim so seriously.
So he crossed the bayou one day and penetrated into the wilds where
Madame St. Denys Godolph ruled.

An alluring little romance formed in his mind as he went; he fancied
how easily it might follow the apology. He was almost in love with Mademoiselle St. Denys Godolph when he quitted his plantation. By the
time he had reached hers, he was wholly so.

He was met by Madame mère, a sweet-eyed, faded woman, upon whom
old age had fallen too hurriedly to completely efface all traces of youth.
But the house was old beyond question; decay had eaten slowly to the
heart of it during the hours, the days, and years that it had been standing.

"I have come to see your daughter, Madame," began Laballière, all
too bluntly; for there is no denying he was blunt.

"Mademoiselle St. Denys Godolph is not presently at home, sir," Madame replied. "She is at the time in New Orleans. She fills there a place
of high trus' an' employment, Monsieur Laballière."

When Suzanne had ever thought of New Orleans, it was always in
connection with Hector Santien, because he was the only soul she knew

who dwelt there. He had had no share in obtaining for her the position she had secured with one of the leading dry-goods firms; yet it was to him she addressed herself when her arrangements to leave home were completed.

He did not wait for her train to reach the city, but crossed the river and met her at Gretna. The first thing he did was to kiss her, as he had done eight years before when he left Natchitoches parish. An hour later he would no more have thought of kissing Suzanne than he would have tendered an embrace to the Empress of China. For by that time he had realized that she was no longer twelve nor he twenty-four.

She could hardly believe the man who met her to be the Hector of old. His black hair was dashed with gray on the temples; he wore a short, parted beard and a small moustache that curled. From the crown of his glossy silk hat down to his trimly-gaitered feet, his attire was faultless. Suzanne knew her Natchitoches, and she had been to Shreveport and even penetrated as far as Marshall, Texas, but in all her travels she had never met a man to equal Hector in the elegance of his mien.

They entered a cab, and seemed to drive for an interminable time through the streets, mostly over cobble-stones that rendered conversation difficult. Nevertheless he talked incessantly, while she peered from the windows to catch what glimpses she could, through the night, of that New Orleans of which she had heard so much. The sounds were bewildering; so were the lights, that were uneven, too, serving to make the patches of alternating gloom more mysterious.

She had not thought of asking him where he was taking her. And it was only after they crossed Canal and had penetrated some distance into Royal Street, that he told her. He was taking her to a friend of his, the dearest little woman in town. That was Maman Chavan, who was going to board and lodge her for a ridiculously small consideration.

Maman Chavan lived within comfortable walking distance of Canal Street, on one of those narrow, intersecting streets between Royal and Chartres. Her house was a tiny, single-story one, with overhanging gable, heavily shuttered door and windows and three wooden steps leading down to the banquette. A small garden flanked it on one side, quite screened from outside view by a high fence, over which appeared the tops of orange trees and other luxuriant shrubbery.

She was waiting for them—a lovable, fresh-looking, white-haired, black-eyed, small, fat little body, dressed all in black. She understood no English; which made no difference. Suzanne and Hector spoke but French to each other.

Hector did not tarry a moment longer than was needed to place his young friend and charge in the older woman's care. He would not even stay to take a bite of supper with them. Maman Chavan watched him as he hurried down the steps and out into the gloom. Then she said to Suzanne: "That man is an angel, Mademoiselle, *un ange du bon Dieu.*"

"Women, my dear Maman Chavan, you know how it is with me in regard to women. I have drawn a circle round my heart, so—at pretty long range, mind you—and there is not one who gets through it, or over it or under it."

"*Blagueur, va!*" laughed Maman Chavan, replenishing her glass from the bottle of sauterne.

It was Sunday morning. They were breakfasting together on the pleasant side gallery that led by a single step down to the garden. Hector came every Sunday morning, an hour or so before noon, to breakfast with them. He always brought a bottle of sauterne, a paté, or a mess of artichokes or some tempting bit of *charcuterie*. Sometimes he had to wait till the two women returned from hearing mass at the cathedral. He did not go to mass himself. They were both making a Novena on that account, and had even gone to the expense of burning a round dozen of candles before the good St. Joseph, for his conversion. When Hector accidentally discovered the fact, he offered to pay for the candles, and was distressed at not being permitted to do so.

Suzanne had been in the city more than a month. It was already the close of February, and the air was flower-scented, moist, and deliciously mild.

"As I said: women, my dear Maman Chavan"—

"Let us hear no more about women!" cried Suzanne, impatiently. "*Cher Maître!* but Hector can be tiresome when he wants. Talk, talk; to say what in the end?"

"Quite right, my cousin; when I might have been saying how charming you are this morning. But don't think that I have n't noticed it," and he looked at her with a deliberation that quite unsettled her. She took a letter from her pocket and handed it to him.

"Here, read all the nice things mamma has to say of you, and the love messages she sends to you." He accepted the several closely written sheets from her and began to look over them.

"*Ah, la bonne tante,*" he laughed, when he came to the tender passages that referred to himself. He had pushed aside the glass of wine that he had only partly filled at the beginning of breakfast and that he had scarcely touched. Maman Chavan again replenished her own. She also lighted a cigarette. So did Suzanne, who was learning to smoke. Hector did not smoke; he did not use tobacco in any form, he always said to those who offered him cigars.

Suzanne rested her elbows on the table, adjusted the ruffles about her wrists, puffed awkwardly at her cigarette that kept going out, and hummed the Kyrie Eleison that she had heard so beautifully rendered an hour before at the Cathedral, while she gazed off into the green depths of the garden. Maman Chavan slipped a little silver medal toward her, accompanying the action with a pantomime that Suzanne readily understood. She, in turn, secretly and adroitly transferred the medal to Hector's coat-pocket. He noticed the action plainly enough, but pretended not to.

"Natchitoches has n't changed," he commented. "The everlasting *can-cans!* when will they have done with them? This is n't little Athénaïse Miché, getting married! *Sapristi!* but it makes one old! And old Papa Jean-Pierre only dead now? I thought he was out of purgatory five years ago. And who is this Laballière? One of the Laballières of St. James?"

"St. James, *mon cher*. Monsieur Alphonse Laballière; an aristocrat from the 'golden coast.' But it is a history, if you will believe me. *Figurez vous*, Maman Chavan,—*pensez donc, mon ami*"—And with much dramatic fire, during which the cigarette went irrevocably out, she proceeded to narrate her experiences with Laballière.

"Impossible!" exclaimed Hector when the climax was reached; but his indignation was not so patent as she would have liked it to be.

"And to think of an affront like that going unpunished!" was Maman Chavan's more sympathetic comment.

"Oh, the scholars were only too ready to offer violence to poor little André, but that, you can understand, I would not permit. And now, here is mamma gone completely over to him; entrapped, God only knows how!"

"Yes," agreed Hector, "I see he has been sending her tamales and *boudin blanc*."

"*Boudin blanc*, my friend! If it were only that! But I have a stack of letters, so high,—I could show them to you,—singing of Laballière, Laballière, enough to drive one distracted. He visits her constantly. He is a man of attainment, she says, a man of courage, a man of heart; and the best of company. He has sent her a bunch of fat robins as big as a tub"—

"There is something in that—a good deal in that, mignonne," piped Maman Chavan, approvingly.

"And now *boudin blanc!* and she tells me it is the duty of a Christian to forgive. Ah, no; it 's no use; mamma's ways are past finding out."

Suzanne was never in Hector's company elsewhere than at Maman Chavan's. Beside the Sunday visit, he looked in upon them sometimes at dusk, to chat for a moment or two. He often treated them to theatre tickets, and even to the opera, when business was brisk. Business meant a little notebook that he carried in his pocket, in which he sometimes dotted down orders from the country people for wine, that he sold on commission. The women always went together, unaccompanied by any male escort; trotting along, arm in arm, and brimming with enjoyment.

That same Sunday afternoon Hector walked with them a short distance when they were on their way to vespers. The three walking abreast almost occupied the narrow width of the banquette. A gentleman who had just stepped out of the Hotel Royal stood aside to better enable them to pass. He lifted his hat to Suzanne, and cast a quick glance, that pictured stupe-faction and wrath, upon Hector.

"It 's he!" exclaimed the girl, melodramatically seizing Maman Chavan's arm.

"Who, he?"

"Laballière!"

"No!"

"Yes!"

"A handsome fellow, all the same," nodded the little lady, approvingly. Hector thought so too. The conversation again turned upon Laballière, and so continued till they reached the side door of the cathedral, where the young man left his two companions.

In the evening Laballière called upon Suzanne. Maman Chavan closed the front door carefully after he entered the small parlor, and opened the side one that looked into the privacy of the garden. Then she lighted the lamp and retired, just as Suzanne entered.

The girl bowed a little stiffly, if it may be said that she did anything stiffly. "Monsieur Laballière." That was all she said.

"Mademoiselle St. Denys Godolph," and that was all he said. But ceremony did not sit easily upon him.

"Mademoiselle," he began, as soon as seated, "I am here as the bearer of a message from your mother. You must understand that otherwise I would not be here."

"I do understan', sir, that you an' maman have become very warm frien's during my absence," she returned, in measured, conventional tones.

"It pleases me immensely to hear that from you," he responded, warmly; "to believe that Madame St. Denys Godolph is my friend."

Suzanne coughed more affectedly than was quite nice, and patted her glossy braids. "The message, if you please, Mr. Laballière."

"To be sure," pulling himself together from the momentary abstraction into which he had fallen in contemplating her. "Well, it 's just this; your mother, you must know, has been good enough to sell me a fine bit of land—a deep strip along the bayou"—

"Impossible! *Mais* w'at sorcery did you use to obtain such a thing of my mother, Mr. Laballière? Lan' that has been in the St. Denys Godolph family since time untole!"

"No sorcery whatever, Mademoiselle, only an appeal to your mother's intelligence and common sense; and she is well supplied with both. She wishes me to say, further, that she desires your presence very urgently and your immediate return home."

"My mother is unduly impatient, surely," replied Suzanne, with chilling politeness.

"May I ask, mademoiselle," he broke in, with an abruptness that was startling, "the name of the man with whom you were walking this afternoon?"

She looked at him with unaffected astonishment, and told him: "I hardly understan' yo' question. That gentleman is Mr. Hector Santien, of one of the firs' families of Natchitoches; a warm ole frien' an' far distant relative of mine."

"Oh, that 's his name, is it, Hector Santien? Well, please don't walk on the New Orleans streets again with Mr. Hector Santien."

"Yo' remarks would be insulting if they were not so highly amusing, Mr. Laballière."

"I beg your pardon if I am insulting; and I have no desire to be amusing," and then Laballière lost his head. "You are at liberty to walk the streets with whom you please, of course," he blurted, with ill-suppressed passion, "but if I encounter Mr. Hector Santien in your company again, in public, I shall wring his neck, then and there, as I would a chicken; I shall break every bone in his body"—Suzanne had arisen.

"You have said enough, sir. I even desire no explanation of yo' words."

"I did n't intend to explain them," he retorted, stung by the insinuation.

"You will escuse me further," she requested icily, motioning to retire.

"Not till—oh, not till you have forgiven me," he cried impulsively, barring her exit; for repentance had come swiftly this time.

But she did not forgive him. "I can wait," she said. Then he stepped aside and she passed by him without a second glance.

She sent word to Hector the following day to come to her. And when he was there, in the late afternoon, they walked together to the end of the vine-sheltered gallery,—where the air was redolent with the odor of spring blossoms.

"Hector," she began, after a while, "some one has told me I should not be seen upon the streets of New Orleans with you."

He was trimming a long rose-stem with his sharp penknife. He did not stop nor start, nor look embarrassed, nor anything of the sort.

"Indeed!" he said.

"But, you know," she went on, "if the saints came down from heaven to tell me there was a reason for it, I could n't believe them."

"You would n't believe them, *ma petite Suzanne?*" He was getting all the thorns off nicely, and stripping away the heavy lower leaves.

"I want you to look me in the face, Hector, and tell me if there is any reason."

He snapped the knife-blade and replaced the knife in his pocket; then he looked in her eyes, so unflinchingly, that she hoped and believed it presaged a confession of innocence that she would gladly have accepted. But he said indifferently: "Yes, there are reasons."

"Then I say there are not," she exclaimed excitedly; "you are amusing yourself—laughing at me, as you always do. There are no reasons that I will hear or believe. You will walk the streets with me, will you not, Hector?" she entreated, "and go to church with me on Sunday; and, and—oh, it 's nonsense, nonsense for you to say things like that!"

He held the rose by its long, hardy stem, and swept it lightly and caressingly across her forehead, along her cheek, and over her pretty mouth and chin, as a lover might have done with his lips. He noticed how the red rose left a crimson stain behind it.

She had been standing, but now she sank upon the bench that was there, and buried her face in her palms. A slight convulsive movement of the muscles indicated a suppressed sob.

"Ah, Suzanne, Suzanne, you are not going to make yourself unhappy about a *bon à rien* like me. Come, look at me; tell me that you are not." He drew her hands down from her face and held them a while, bidding her good-by. His own face wore the quizzical look it often did, as if he were laughing at her.

"That work at the store is telling on your nerves, *mignonne*. Promise me that you will go back to the country. That will be best."

"Oh, yes; I am going back home, Hector."

"That is right, little cousin," and he patted her hands kindly, and laid them both down gently into her lap.

He did not return; neither during the week nor the following Sunday. Then Suzanne told Maman Chavan she was going home. The girl was not too deeply in love with Hector; but imagination counts for something, and so does youth.

Laballière was on the train with her. She felt, somehow, that he would be. And yet she did not dream that he had watched and waited for her each morning since he parted from her.

He went to her without preliminary of manner or speech, and held out his hand; she extended her own unhesitatingly. She could not understand why, and she was a little too weary to strive to do so. It seemed as though the sheer force of his will would carry him to the goal of his wishes.

He did not weary her with attentions during the time they were together. He sat apart from her, conversing for the most time with friends and acquaintances who belonged in the sugar district through which they traveled in the early part of the day.

She wondered why he had ever left that section to go up into Natchitoches. Then she wondered if he did not mean to speak to her at all. As if he had read the thought, he went and sat down beside her.

He showed her, away off across the country, where his mother lived, and his brother Alcée, and his cousin Clarisse.

On Sunday morning, when Maman Chavan strove to sound the depth of Hector's feeling for Suzanne, he told her again: "Women, my dear Maman Chavan, you know how it is with me in regard to women,"— and he refilled her glass from the bottle of sauterne.

"*Farceur va!*" and Maman Chavan laughed, and her fat shoulders quivered under the white *volante* she wore.

A day or two later, Hector was walking down Canal Street at four in the afternoon. He might have posed, as he was, for a fashion-plate. He looked not to the right nor to the left; not even at the women who passed by. Some of them turned to look at him.

When he approached the corner of Royal, a young man who stood there nudged his companion.

"You know who that is?" he said, indicating Hector.

"No; who?"

"Well, you are an innocent. Why, that 's Deroustan, the most notorious gambler in New Orleans."

Mamouche

Mamouche stood within the open doorway, which he had just entered. It was night; the rain was falling in torrents, and the water trickled from him as it would have done from an umbrella, if he had carried one.

Old Doctor John-Luis, who was toasting his feet before a blazing hickory-wood fire, turned to gaze at the youngster through his spectacles. Marshall, the old negro who had opened the door at the boy's knock, also looked down at him, and indignantly said:

"G'long back on de gall'ry an' drip yo'se'f! W'at Cynthy gwine say tomorrow w'en she see dat flo' mess' up dat away?"

"Come to the fire and sit down," said Doctor John-Luis.

Doctor John-Luis was a bachelor. He was small and thin; he wore snuff-colored clothes that were a little too large for him, and spectacles. Time had not deprived him of an abundant crop of hair that had once been red, and was not now more than half-bleached.

The boy looked irresolutely from master to man; then went and sat down beside the fire on a splint-bottom chair. He sat so close to the blaze that had he been an apple he would have roasted. As he was but a small boy, clothed in wet rags, he only steamed.

Marshall grumbled audibly, and Doctor John-Luis continued to inspect the boy through his glasses.

"Marsh, bring him something to eat," he commanded, tentatively.

Marshall hesitated, and challenged the child with a speculating look.

"Is you wi'te o' is you black?" he asked. "Dat w'at I wants ter know 'fo' I kiar' victuals to yo in de settin'-room."

"I'm w'ite, me," the boy responded, promptly.

"I ain't disputin'; go ahead. All right fer dem w'at wants ter take yo' wud fer it." Doctor John-Luis coughed behind his hand and said nothing.

Marshall brought a platter of cold food to the boy, who rested the dish upon his knees and ate from it with keen appetite.

"Where do you come from?" asked Doctor John-Luis, when his caller stopped for breath. Mamouche turned a pair of big, soft, dark eyes upon his questioner.

"I come frum Cloutierville this mo'nin'. I been try to git to the twenty-fo'-mile ferry w'en de rain ketch me."

"What were you going to do at the twenty-four-mile ferry?"

The boy gazed absently into the fire. "I don' know w'at I was goin' to do yonda to the twenty-fo'-mile ferry," he said.

"Then you must be a tramp, to be wandering aimlessly about the country in that way!" exclaimed the doctor.

"No; I don' b'lieve I'm a tramp, me." Mamouche was wriggling his toes with enjoyment of the warmth and palatable food.

"Well, what's your name?" continued Doctor John-Luis.

"My name it's Mamouche."

" 'Mamouche.' Fiddlesticks! That's no name."

The boy looked as if he regretted the fact, while not being able to help it.

"But my pa, his name it was Mathurin Peloté," he offered in some palliation.

"Peloté! Peloté!" mused Doctor John-Luis. "Any kin to Théodule Peloté who lived formerly in Avoyelles parish?"

"W'y, yas!" laughed Mamouche. "Théodule Peloté, it was my gran'-pa."

"Your grandfather? Well, upon my word!" He looked again, critically, at the youngster's rags. "Then Stéphanie Galopin must have been your grandmother!"

"Yas," responded Mamouche, complacently; "that who was my gran'-ma. She die two year ago down by Alexandria."

"Marsh," called Doctor John-Luis, turning in his chair, "bring him a mug of milk and another piece of pie!"

When Mamouche had eaten all the good things that were set before him, he found that one side of him was quite dry, and he transferred himself over to the other corner of the fire so as to turn to the blaze the side which was still wet.

The action seemed to amuse Doctor John-Luis, whose old head began to fill with recollections.

"That reminds me of Théodule," he laughed. "Ah, he was a great fellow, your father, Théodule!"

"My gran'pa," corrected Mamouche.

"Yes, yes, your grandfather. He was handsome; I tell you, he was good-looking. And the way he could dance and play the fiddle and sing! Let me see, how did that song go that he used to sing when we went out serenading: 'A ta—à ta—'

> ' A ta fenêtre
> Daignes paraître—tra la la la!' "

Doctor John-Luis' voice, even in his youth, could not have been agreeable; and now it bore no resemblance to any sound that Mamouche had ever heard issue from a human throat. The boy kicked his heels and rolled sideward on his chair with enjoyment. Doctor John-Luis laughed even more heartily, finished the stanza, and sang another one through.

"That's what turned the girls' heads, I tell you, my boy," said he, when he had recovered his breath; "that fiddling and dancing and tra la la."

During the next hour the old man lived again through his youth; through any number of alluring experiences with his friend Théodule, that merry fellow who had never done a steady week's work in his life; and Stéphanie, the pretty Acadian girl, whom he had never wholly understood, even to this day.

It was quite late when Doctor John-Luis climbed the stairs that led from the sitting-room up to his bedchamber. As he went, followed by the ever attentive Marshall, he was singing:

> "A ta fenêtre
> Daignes paraître,"

but very low, so as not to awaken Mamouche, whom he left sleeping upon a bed that Marshall at his order had prepared for the boy beside the sitting-room fire.

At a very early hour next morning Marshall appeared at his master's bedside with the accustomed morning coffee.

"What is he doing?" asked Doctor John-Luis, as he sugared and stirred the tiny cup of black coffee.

"Who dat, sah?"

"Why, the boy, Mamouche. What is he doing?"

"He gone, sah. He done gone."

"Gone!"

"Yas, sah. He roll his bed up in de corner; he onlock de do'; he gone. But de silver an' ev'thing dah; he ain't kiar' nuttin' off."

"Marshall," snapped Doctor John-Luis, ill-humoredly, "there are times when you don't seem to have sense and penetration enough to talk about! I think I'll take another nap," he grumbled, as he turned his back upon Marshall. "Wake me at seven."

It was no ordinary thing for Doctor John-Luis to be in a bad humor, and perhaps it is not strictly true to say that he was now. He was only in a little less amiable mood than usual when he pulled on his high rubber boots and went splashing out in the wet to see what his people were doing.

He might have owned a large plantation had he wished to own one, for a long life of persistent, intelligent work had left him with a comfortable fortune in his old age; but he preferred the farm on which he lived contentedly and raised an abundance to meet his modest wants.

He went down to the orchard, where a couple of men were busying themselves in setting out a line of young fruit-trees.

"Tut, tut, tut!" They were doing it all wrong; the line was not straight; the holes were not deep. It was strange that he had to come down there and discover such things with his old eyes!

He poked his head into the kitchen to complain to Prudence about the ducks that she had not seasoned properly the day before, and to hope that the accident would never occur again.

He tramped over to where a carpenter was working on a gate; securing it—as he meant to secure all the gates upon his place—with great patent clamps and ingenious hinges, intended to baffle utterly the designs of the evil-disposed persons who had lately been tampering with them. For there had been a malicious spirit abroad, who played tricks, it seemed, for pure wantonness upon the farmers and planters, and caused them infinite annoyance.

As Dr. John-Luis contemplated the carpenter at work, and remembered how his gates had recently all been lifted from their hinges one night and left lying upon the ground, the provoking nature of the offense dawned upon him as it had not done before. He turned swiftly, prompted by a sudden determination, and re-entered the house.

Then he proceeded to write out in immense black characters a half-dozen placards. It was an offer of twenty-five dollars' reward for the capture of the person guilty of the malicious offence already described.

These placards were sent abroad with the same eager haste that had conceived and executed them.

After a day or two, Doctor John-Luis' ill humor had resolved itself into a pensive melancholy.

"Marsh," he said, "you know, after all, it's rather dreary to be living alone as I do, without any companion—of my own color, you understand."

"I knows dat, sah. It sho' am lonesome," replied the sympathetic Marshall.

"You see, Marsh, I've been thinking lately," and Doctor John-Luis coughed, for he disliked the inaccuracy of that "lately." "I've been thinking that this property and wealth that I've worked so hard to accumulate, are after all doing no permanent, practical good to any one. Now, if I could find some well-disposed boy whom I might train to work, to study, to lead a decent, honest life—a boy of good heart who would care for me in my old age; for I am still comparatively—hem—not old? hey, Marsh?"

"Dey ain't one in de pa'ish hole yo' own like you does, sah."

"That's it. Now, can you think of such a boy? Try to think."

Marshall slowly scratched his head and looked reflective.

"If you can think of such a boy," said Doctor John-Luis, "you might bring him here to spend an evening with me, you know, without hinting at my intentions, of course. In that way I could sound him; study him up, as it were. For a step of such importance is not to be taken without due consideration, Marsh."

Well, the first whom Marshall brought was one of Baptiste Choupic's boys. He was a very timid child, and sat on the edge of his chair, fearfully. He replied in jerky monosyllables when Doctor John-Luis spoke to him, "Yas, sah—no, sah," as the case might be; with a little nervous bob of the head.

His presence made the doctor quite uncomfortable. He was glad to be rid of the boy at nine o'clock, when he sent him home with some oranges and a few sweetmeats.

Then Marshall had Theodore over; an unfortunate selection that evinced little judgment on Marshall's part. Not to mince matters, the boy was painfully forward. He monopolized the conversation; asked impertinent questions and handled and inspected everything in the room. Dr. John-Luis sent him home with an orange and not a single sweet.

Then there was Hyppolite, who was too ugly to be thought of; and

Cami, who was heavy and stupid, and fell asleep in his chair with his mouth wide open. And so it went. If Doctor John-Luis had hoped in the company of any of these boys to repeat the agreeable evening he had passed with Mamouche, he was sadly deceived.

At last he instructed Marshall to discontinue the search of that ideal companion he had dreamed of. He was resigned to spend the remainder of his days without one.

Then, one day when it was raining again, and very muddy and chill, a red-faced man came driving up to Doctor John-Luis' door in a dilapidated buggy. He lifted a boy from the vehicle, whom he held with a vise-like clutch, and whom he straightway dragged into the astonished presence of Doctor John-Luis.

"Here he is, sir," shouted the red-faced man. "We've got him at last! Here he is."

It was Mamouche, covered with mud, the picture of misery. Doctor John-Luis stood with his back to the fire. He was startled, and visibly and painfully moved at the sight of the boy.

"Is it possible!" he exclaimed. "Then it was you, Mamouche, who did this mischievous thing to me? Lifting my gates from their hinges; letting the chickens in among my flowers to ruin them; and the hogs and cattle to trample and uproot my vegetables!"

"Ha! ha!" laughed the red-faced man, "that game's played out, now;" and Doctor John-Luis looked as if he wanted to strike him.

Mamouche seemed unable to reply. His lower lip was quivering.

"Yas, it's me!" he burst out. "It's me w'at take yo' gates off the hinge. It's me w'at turn loose Mr. Morgin's hoss, w'en Mr. Morgin was passing *veillée* wid his sweetheart. It's me w'at take down Ma'ame Angèle's fence, an' lef her calf loose to tramp in Mr. Billy's cotton. It's me w'at play like a ghos' by the graveyard las' Toussaint to scare the darkies passin' in the road. It's me w'at—"

The confession had burst out from the depth of Mamouche's heart like a torrent, and there is no telling when it would have stopped if Doctor John-Luis had not enjoined silence.

"And pray tell me," he asked, as severely as he could, "why you left my house like a criminal, in the morning, secretly?"

The tears had begun to course down Mamouche's brown cheeks.

"I was 'shame' of myse'f, that's w'y. If you wouldn' gave me no suppa, an' no bed, an' no fire, I don' say. I wouldn' been 'shame' then."

"Well, sir," interrupted the red-faced man, "you've got a pretty square case against him, I see. Not only for malicious trespass, but of theft. See this bolt?" producing a piece of iron from his coat pocket. "That's what gave him away."

"I en't no thief!" blurted Mamouche, indignantly. "It's one piece o' iron w'at I pick up in the road."

"Sir," said Doctor John-Luis with dignity, "I can understand how the grandson of Théodule Peloté might be guilty of such mischievous pranks as this boy has confessed to. But I know that the grandson of Stéphanie Galopin could not be a thief."

And he at once wrote out the check for twenty-five dollars, and handed it to the red-faced man with the tips of his fingers.

It seemed very good to Doctor John-Luis to have the boy sitting again at his fireside; and so natural, too. He seemed to be the incarnation of unspoken hopes; the realization of vague and fitful memories of the past.

When Mamouche kept on crying, Doctor John-Luis wiped away the tears with his own brown silk handkerchief.

"Mamouche," he said, "I want you to stay here; to live here with me always. To learn how to work; to learn how to study; to grow up to be an honorable man. An honorable man, Mamouche, for I want you for my own child."

His voice was pretty low and husky when he said that.

"I shall not take the key from the door tonight," he continued. "If you do not choose to stay and be all this that I say, you may open the door and walk out. I shall use no force to keep you."

"What is he doing, Marsh?" asked Doctor John-Luis the following morning, when he took the coffee that Marshall had brought to him in bed.

"Who dat, sah?"

"Why, the boy Mamouche, of course. What is he doing?"

Marshall laughed.

"He kneelin' down dah on de flo'. He keep on sayin', 'Hail, Mary, full o' grace, de Lord is wid dee. Hail, Mary, full o' grace'—t'ree, fo' times, sah. I tell 'im, 'W'at you sayin' yo' prayer dat away, boy?' He 'low dat w'at his gran'ma larn 'im, ter keep outen mischief. W'en de devil say, 'Take dat gate offen de hinge; do dis; do dat,' he gwine say t'ree Hail Mary, an' de devil gwine tu'n tail an' run."

"Yes, yes," laughed Doctor John-Luis. "That's Stéphanie all over."

"An' I tell 'im: See heah, boy, you drap a couple o' dem Hail Mary, an' quit studyin' 'bout de devil, an' sot yo'se'f down ter wuk. Dat the oniest way to keep outen mischief."

"What business is it of yours to interfere?" broke in Doctor John-Luis, irritably. "Let the boy do as his grandmother instructed him."

"I ain't desputin', sah," apologized Marshall.

"But you know, Marsh," continued the doctor, recovering his usual amiability. "I think we'll be able to do something with the boy. I'm pretty sure of it. For, you see, he has his grandmother's eyes; and his grandmother was a very intelligent woman; a clever woman, Marsh. Her one great mistake was when she married Théodule Peloté."

Madame Célestin's Divorce

Madame Célestin always wore a neat and snugly fitting calico wrapper when she went out in the morning to sweep her small gallery. Lawyer Paxton thought she looked very pretty in the gray one that was made with a graceful Watteau fold at the back: and with which she invariably wore a bow of pink ribbon at the throat. She was always sweeping her gallery when lawyer Paxton passed by in the morning on his way to his office in St. Denis Street.

Sometimes he stopped and leaned over the fence to say good-morning at his ease; to criticise or admire her rosebushes; or, when he had time enough, to hear what she had to say. Madame Célestin usually had a good deal to say. She would gather up the train of her calico wrapper in one hand, and balancing the broom gracefully in the other, would go tripping down to where the lawyer leaned, as comfortably as he could, over her picket fence.

Of course she had talked to him of her troubles. Every one knew Madame Célestin's troubles.

"Really, madame," he told her once, in his deliberate, calculating, lawyer-tone, "it 's more than human nature—woman's nature—should be called upon to endure. Here you are, working your fingers off"—she glanced down at two rosy finger-tips that showed through the rents in her baggy doeskin gloves—"taking in sewing; giving music lessons; doing God knows what in the way of manual labor to support yourself and those two little ones"—Madame Célestin's pretty face beamed with satisfaction at this enumeration of her trials.

"You right, Judge. Not a picayune, not one, not one, have I lay my eyes on in the pas' fo' months that I can say Célestin give it to me or sen' it to me."

"The scoundrel!" muttered lawyer Paxton in his beard.

"An' *pourtant*," she resumed, "they say he 's making money down roun' Alexandria w'en he wants to work."

"I dare say you have n't seen him for months?" suggested the lawyer.

"It 's good six month' since I see a sight of Célestin," she admitted.

"That 's it, that 's what I say; he has practically deserted you; fails to support you. It wouldn't surprise me a bit to learn that he has ill treated you."

"Well, you know, Judge," with an evasive cough, "a man that drinks —w'at can you expec'? An' if you would know the promises he has made me! Ah, If I had as many dolla' as I had promise from Célestin, I would n' have to work, *je vous garantis*."

"And in my opinion, Madame, you would be a foolish woman to endure it longer, when the divorce court is there to offer you redress."

"You spoke about that befo', Judge; I 'm goin' think about that divo'ce. I believe you right."

Madame Célestin thought about the divorce and talked about it, too; and lawyer Paxton grew deeply interested in the theme.

"You know, about that divo'ce, Judge," Madame Célestin was waiting for him that morning, "I been talking to my family an' my frien's, an' it 's me that tells you, they all plumb agains' that divo'ce."

"Certainly, to be sure; that 's to be expected, Madame, in this community of Creoles. I warned you that you would meet with opposition, and would have to face it and brave it."

"Oh, don't fear, I 'm going to face it! Maman says it 's a disgrace like it 's neva been in the family. But it 's good for Maman to talk, her. W'at trouble she ever had? She says I mus' go by all means consult with Père Duchéron—it 's my confessor, you undastan'—Well, I 'll go, Judge, to please Maman. But all the confessor' in the worl' ent goin' make me put up with that conduc' of Célestin any longa."

A day or two later, she was there waiting for him again. "You know, Judge, about that divo'ce."

"Yes, yes," responded the lawyer, well pleased to trace a new determination in her brown eyes and in the curves of her pretty mouth. "I suppose you saw Père Duchéron and had to brave it out with him, too."

"Oh, fo' that, a perfec' sermon, I assho you. A talk of giving scandal an' bad example that I thought would neva en'! He says, fo' him, he wash' his hands; I mus' go see the bishop."

"You won't let the bishop dissuade you, I trust," stammered the lawyer more anxiously than he could well understand.

"You don't know me yet, Judge," laughed Madame Célestin with a turn of the head and a flirt of the broom which indicated that the interview was at an end.

"Well, Madame Célestin! And the bishop!" Lawyer Paxton was standing there holding to a couple of the shaky pickets. She had not seen him. "Oh, it 's you, Judge?" and she hastened towards him with an *empressement* that could not but have been flattering.

"Yes, I saw Monseigneur," she began. The lawyer had already gathered from her expressive countenance that she had not wavered in her determination. "Ah, he 's a eloquent man. It 's not a mo' eloquent man in Natchitoches parish. I was fo'ced to cry, the way he talked to me about my troubles; how he undastan's them, an' feels for me. It would move even you, Judge, to hear how he talk' about that step I want to take; its danga, its temptation. How it is the duty of a Catholic to stan' everything till the las' extreme. An' that life of retirement an' self-denial I would have to lead,—he tole me all that."

"But he has n't turned you from your resolve, I see," laughed the lawyer complacently.

"For that, no," she returned emphatically. "The bishop don't know w'at it is to be married to a man like Célestin, an' have to endu' that conduc' like I have to endu' it. The Pope himse'f can't make me stan' that any longer, if you say I got the right in the law to sen' Célestin sailing."

A noticeable change had come over lawyer Paxton. He discarded his work-day coat and began to wear his Sunday one to the office. He grew solicitous as to the shine of his boots, his collar, and the set of his tie. He brushed and trimmed his whiskers with a care that had not before been apparent. Then he fell into a stupid habit of dreaming as he walked the streets of the old town. It would be very good to take unto himself a wife, he dreamed. And he could dream of no other than pretty Madame Célestin filling that sweet and sacred office as she filled his thoughts, now. Old Natchitoches would not hold them comfortably, perhaps; but the world was surely wide enough to live in, outside of Natchitoches town.

His heart beat in a strangely irregular manner as he neared Madame Célestin's house one morning, and discovered her behind the rosebushes, as usual plying her broom. She had finished the gallery and steps and was sweeping the little brick walk along the edge of the violet border.

"Good-morning, Madame Célestin."

"Ah, it 's you, Judge? Good-morning." He waited. She seemed to be · doing the same. Then she ventured, with some hesitancy, "You know, Judge, about that divo'ce. I been thinking,—I reckon you betta neva mine about that divo'ce." She was making deep rings in the palm of her gloved hand with the end of the broomhandle, and looking at them critically. Her face seemed to the lawyer to be unusually rosy; but maybe it was only the reflection of the pink bow at the throat. "Yes, I reckon you need n' mine. You see, Judge, Célestin came home las' night. An' he 's promise me on his word an' honor he 's going to turn ova a new leaf."

An Idle Fellow

I am tired. At the end of these years I am very tired. I have been studying in books the languages of the living and those we call dead. Early in
the fresh morning I have studied in books, and throughout the day when
the sun was shining; and at night when there were stars, I have lighted
my oil-lamp and studied in books. Now my brain is weary and I want
rest.

I shall sit here on the door-step beside my friend Paul. He is an idle
fellow with folded hands. He laughs when I upbraid him, and bids me,
with a motion, hold my peace. He is listening to a thrush's song that
comes from the blur of yonder apple-tree. He tells me the thrush is singing
a complaint. She wants her mate that was with her last blossom-time and
builded a nest with her. She will have no other mate. She will call for
him till she hears the notes of her beloved-one's song coming swiftly towards her across forest and field.

Paul is a strange fellow. He gazes idly at a billowy white cloud that
rolls lazily over and over along the edge of the blue sky.

He turns away from me and the words with which I would instruct
him, to drink deep the scent of the clover-field and the thick perfume
from the rose-hedge.

We rise from the door-step and walk together down the gentle slope of
the hill; past the apple-tree, and the rose-hedge; and along the border of
the field where wheat is growing. We walk down to the foot of the gentle
slope where women and men and children are living.

Paul is a strange fellow. He looks into the faces of people who pass us
by. He tells me that in their eyes he reads the story of their souls. He
knows men and women and the little children, and why they look this

way and that way. He knows the reasons that turn them to and fro and cause them to go and come. I think I shall walk a space through the world with my friend Paul. He is very wise, he knows the language of God which I have not learned.

A Matter of Prejudice

Madame Carambeau wanted it strictly understood that she was not to be disturbed by Gustave's birthday party. They carried her big rocking-chair from the back gallery, that looked out upon the garden where the children were going to play, around to the front gallery, which closely faced the green levee bank and the Mississippi coursing almost flush with the top of it.

The house—an old Spanish one, broad, low and completely encircled by a wide gallery—was far down in the French quarter of New Orleans. It stood upon a square of ground that was covered thick with a semi-tropical growth of plants and flowers. An impenetrable board fence, edged with a formidable row of iron spikes, shielded the garden from the prying glances of the occasional passer-by.

Madame Carambeau's widowed daughter, Madame Cécile Lalonde, lived with her. This annual party, given to her little son, Gustave, was the one defiant act of Madame Lalonde's existence. She persisted in it, to her own astonishment and the wonder of those who knew her and her mother.

For old Madame Carambeau was a woman of many prejudices—so many, in fact, that it would be difficult to name them all. She detested dogs, cats, organ-grinders, white servants and children's noises. She despised Americans, Germans and all people of a different faith from her own. Anything not French had, in her opinion, little right to existence.

She had not spoken to her son Henri for ten years because he had married an American girl from Prytania street. She would not permit green tea to be introduced into her house, and those who could not or would not drink coffee might drink tisane of *fleur de Laurier* for all she cared.

Nevertheless, the children seemed to be having it all their own way that day, and the organ-grinders were let loose. Old madame, in her retired corner, could hear the screams, the laughter and the music far more distinctly than she liked. She rocked herself noisily, and hummed "Partant pour la Syrie."

She was straight and slender. Her hair was white, and she wore it in puffs on the temples. Her skin was fair and her eyes blue and cold.

Suddenly she became aware that footsteps were approaching, and threatening to invade her privacy—not only footsteps, but screams! Then two little children, one in hot pursuit of the other, darted wildly around the corner near which she sat.

The child in advance, a pretty little girl, sprang excitedly into Madame Carambeau's lap, and threw her arms convulsively around the old lady's neck. Her companion lightly struck her a "last tag," and ran laughing gleefully away.

The most natural thing for the child to do then would have been to wriggle down from madame's lap, without a "thank you" or a "by your leave," after the manner of small and thoughtless children. But she did not do this. She stayed there, panting and fluttering, like a frightened bird.

Madame was greatly annoyed. She moved as if to put the child away from her, and scolded her sharply for being boisterous and rude. The little one, who did not understand French, was not disturbed by the reprimand, and stayed on in madame's lap. She rested her plump little cheek, that was hot and flushed, against the soft white linen of the old lady's gown.

Her cheek was very hot and very flushed. It was dry, too, and so were her hands. The child's breathing was quick and irregular. Madame was not long in detecting these signs of disturbance.

Though she was a creature of prejudice, she was nevertheless a skillful and accomplished nurse, and a connoisseur in all matters pertaining to health. She prided herself upon this talent, and never lost an opportunity of exercising it. She would have treated an organ-grinder with tender consideration if one had presented himself in the character of an invalid.

Madame's manner toward the little one changed immediately. Her arms and her lap were at once adjusted so as to become the most comfortable of resting places. She rocked very gently to and fro. She fanned the child softly with her palm leaf fan, and sang "Partant pour la Syrie" in a low and agreeable tone.

The child was perfectly content to lie still and prattle a little in that language which madame thought hideous. But the brown eyes were soon swimming in drowsiness, and the little body grew heavy with sleep in madame's clasp.

When the little girl slept Madame Carambeau arose, and treading carefully and deliberately, entered her room, that opened near at hand upon the gallery. The room was large, airy and inviting, with its cool matting upon the floor, and its heavy, old, polished mahogany furniture. Madame, with the child still in her arms, pulled a bell-cord; then she stood waiting, swaying gently back and forth. Presently an old black woman answered the summons. She wore gold hoops in her ears, and a bright bandanna knotted fantastically on her head.

"Louise, turn down the bed," commanded madame. "Place that small, soft pillow below the bolster. Here is a poor little unfortunate creature whom Providence must have driven into my arms." She laid the child carefully down.

"Ah, those Americans! Do they deserve to have children? Understanding as little as they do how to take care of them!" said madame, while Louise was mumbling an accompanying assent that would have been unintelligible to any one unacquainted with the negro patois.

"There, you see, Louise, she is burning up," remarked madame; "she is consumed. Unfasten the little bodice while I lift her. Ah, talk to me of such parents! So stupid as not to perceive a fever like that coming on, but they must dress their child up like a monkey to go play and dance to the music of organ-grinders.

"Haven't you better sense, Louise, than to take off a child's shoe as if you were removing the boot from the leg of a cavalry officer?" Madame would have required fairy fingers to minister to the sick. "Now go to Mamzelle Cécile, and tell her to send me one of those old, soft, thin nightgowns that Gustave wore two summers ago."

When the woman retired, madame busied herself with concocting a cooling pitcher of orange-flower water, and mixing a fresh supply of *eau sédative* with which agreeably to sponge the little invalid.

Madame Lalonde came herself with the old, soft nightgown. She was a pretty, blonde, plump little woman, with the deprecatory air of one whose will has become flaccid from want of use. She was mildly distressed at what her mother had done.

"But, mamma! But, mamma, the child's parents will be sending the carriage for her in a little while. Really, there was no use. Oh dear! oh dear!"

If the bedpost had spoken to Madame Carambeau, she would have paid more attention, for speech from such a source would have been at least surprising if not convincing. Madame Lalonde did not possess the faculty of either surprising or convincing her mother.

"Yes, the little one will be quite comfortable in this," said the old lady, taking the garment from her daughter's irresolute hands.

"But, mamma! What shall I say, what shall I do when they send? Oh, dear; oh, dear!"

"That is your business," replied madame, with lofty indifference. "My concern is solely with a sick child that happens to be under my roof. I think I know my duty at this time of life, Cécile."

As Madame Lalonde predicted, the carriage soon came, with a stiff English coachman driving it, and a red-cheeked Irish nurse-maid seated inside. Madame would not even permit the maid to see her little charge. She had an original theory that the Irish voice is distressing to the sick.

Madame Lalonde sent the girl away with a long letter of explanation that must have satisfied the parents; for the child was left undisturbed in Madame Carambeau's care. She was a sweet child, gentle and affectionate. And, though she cried and fretted a little throughout the night for her mother, she seemed, after all, to take kindly to madame's gentle nursing. It was not much of a fever that afflicted her, and after two days she was well enough to be sent back to her parents.

Madame, in all her varied experience with the sick, had never before nursed so objectionable a character as an American child. But the trouble was that after the little one went away, she could think of nothing really objectionable against her except the accident of her birth, which was, after all, her misfortune; and her ignorance of the French language, which was not her fault.

But the touch of the caressing baby arms; the pressure of the soft little body in the night; the tones of the voice, and the feeling of the hot lips when the child kissed her, believing herself to be with her mother, were impressions that had sunk through the crust of madame's prejudice and reached her heart.

She often walked the length of the gallery, looking out across the wide, majestic river. Sometimes she trod the mazes of her garden where the solitude was almost that of a tropical jungle. It was during such moments that the seed began to work in her soul—the seed planted by the innocent and undesigning hands of a little child.

The first shoot that it sent forth was Doubt. Madame plucked it away once or twice. But it sprouted again, and with it Mistrust and Dissatisfaction. Then from the heart of the seed, and amid the shoots of Doubt and Misgiving, came the flower of Truth. It was a very beautiful flower, and it bloomed on Christmas morning.

As Madame Carambeau and her daughter were about to enter her carriage on that Christmas morning, to be driven to church, the old lady stopped to give an order to her black coachman, François. François had been driving these ladies every Sunday morning to the French Cathedral for so many years—he had forgotten exactly how many, but ever since he had entered their service, when Madame Lalonde was a little girl. His astonishment may therefore be imagined when Madame Carambeau said to him:

"François, to-day you will drive us to one of the American churches."

"Plait-il, madame?" the negro stammered, doubting the evidence of his hearing.

"I say, you will drive us to one of the American churches. Any one of them," she added, with a sweep of her hand. "I suppose they are all alike," and she followed her daughter into the carriage.

Madame Lalonde's surprise and agitation were painful to see, and they deprived her of the ability to question, even if she had possessed the courage to do so.

François, left to his fancy, drove them to St. Patrick's Church on Camp street. Madame Lalonde looked and felt like the proverbial fish out of its element as they entered the edifice. Madame Carambeau, on the contrary, looked as if she had been attending St. Patrick's church all her life. She sat with unruffled calm through the long service and through a lengthy English sermon, of which she did not understand a word.

When the mass was ended and they were about to enter the carriage again, Madame Carambeau turned, as she had done before, to the coachman.

"François," she said, coolly, "you will now drive us to the residence of my son, M. Henri Carambeau. No doubt Mamzelle Cécile can inform you where it is," she added, with a sharply penetrating glance that caused Madame Lalonde to wince.

Yes, her daughter Cécile knew, and so did François, for that matter. They drove out St. Charles avenue—very far out. It was like a strange city to old madame, who had not been in the American quarter since the town had taken on this new and splendid growth.

The morning was a delicious one, soft and mild; and the roses were all in bloom. They were not hidden behind spiked fences. Madame appeared not to notice them, or the beautiful and striking residences that lined the avenue along which they drove. She held a bottle of smelling-salts to her nostrils, as though she were passing through the most unsavory instead of the most beautiful quarter of New Orleans.

Henri's house was a very modern and very handsome one, standing a little distance away from the street. A well-kept lawn, studded with rare and charming plants, surrounded it. The ladies, dismounting, rang the bell, and stood out upon the banquette, waiting for the iron gate to be opened.

A white maid-servant admitted them. Madame did not seem to mind. She handed her a card with all proper ceremony, and followed with her daughter to the house.

Not once did she show a sign of weakness; not even when her son, Henri, came and took her in his arms and sobbed and wept upon her neck as only a warm-hearted Creole could. He was a big, good-looking, honest-faced man, with tender brown eyes like his dead father's and a firm mouth like his mother's.

Young Mrs. Carambeau came, too, her sweet, fresh face transfigured with happiness. She led by the hand her little daughter, the "American child" whom madame had nursed so tenderly a month before, never suspecting the little one to be other than an alien to her.

"What a lucky chance was that fever! What a happy accident!" gurgled Madame Lalonde.

"Cécile, it was no accident, I tell you; it was Providence," spoke madame, reprovingly, and no one contradicted her.

They all drove back together to eat Christmas dinner in the old house by the river. Madame held her little granddaughter upon her lap; her son Henri sat facing her, and beside her was her daughter-in-law.

Henri sat back in the carriage and could not speak. His soul was possessed by a pathetic joy that would not admit of speech. He was going back again to the home where he was born, after a banishment of ten long years.

He would hear again the water beat against the green levee-bank with a sound that was not quite like any other that he could remember. He would sit within the sweet and solemn shadow of the deep and overhanging roof; and roam through the wild, rich solitude of the old garden, where he had played his pranks of boyhood and dreamed his dreams of youth. He would listen to his mother's voice calling him, "mon fils," as it had always done before that day he had had to choose between mother and wife. No; he could not speak.

But his wife chatted much and pleasantly—in a French, however, that must have been trying to old madame to listen to.

"I am so sorry, ma mère," she said, "that our little one does not speak French. It is not my fault, I assure you," and she flushed and hesitated a little. "It—it was Henri who would not permit it."

"That is nothing," replied madame, amiably, drawing the child close to her. "Her grandmother will teach her French; and she will teach her grandmother English. You see, I have no prejudices. I am not like my son. Henri was always a stubborn boy. Heaven only knows how he came by such a character!"

Azélie

Azélie crossed the yard with slow, hesitating steps. She wore a pink sunbonnet and a faded calico dress that had been made the summer before, and was now too small for her in every way. She carried a large tin pail on her arm. When within a few yards of the house she stopped under a chinaberry-tree, quite still, except for the occasional slow turning of her head from side to side.

Mr. Mathurin, from his elevation upon the upper gallery, laughed when he saw her; for he knew she would stay there, motionless, till some one noticed and questioned her.

The planter was just home from the city, and was therefore in an excellent humor, as he always was, on getting back to what he called *le grand air*, the space and stillness of the country, and the scent of the fields. He was in shirtsleeves, walking around the gallery that encircled the big square white house. Beneath was a brick-paved portico upon which the lower rooms opened. At wide intervals were large whitewashed pillars that supported the upper gallery.

In one corner of the lower house was the store, which was in no sense a store for the general public, but maintained only to supply the needs of Mr. Mathurin's "hands."

"Eh bien! what do you want, Azélie?" the planter finally called out to the girl in French. She advanced a few paces, and, pushing back her sunbonnet, looked up at him with a gentle, inoffensive face—"to which you would give the good God without confession," he once described it.

"Bon jou', M'si' Mathurin," she replied; and continued in English: "I come git a li'le piece o' meat. We plumb out o' meat home."

"Well, well, the meat is n' going to walk to you, my chile: it has n' got feet. Go fine Mr. 'Polyte. He's yonda mending his buggy unda the shed." She turned away with an alert little step, and went in search of Mr. 'Polyte.

"That's you again!" the young man exclaimed, with a pretended air of annoyance, when he saw her. He straightened himself, and looked down at her and her pail with a comprehending glance. The sweat was standing in shining beads on his brown, good-looking face. He was in his shirt-sleeves, and the legs of his trousers were thrust into the tops of his fine, high-heeled boots. He wore his straw hat very much on one side, and had an air that was altogether *fanfaron*. He reached to a back pocket for the store key, which was as large as the pistol that he sometimes carried in the same place. She followed him across the thick, tufted grass of the yard with quick, short steps that strove to keep pace with his longer, swinging ones.

When he had unlocked and opened the heavy door of the store, there escaped from the close room the strong, pungent odor of the varied wares and provisions massed within. Azélie seemed to like the odor, and, lifting her head, snuffed the air as people sometimes do upon entering a conservatory filled with fragrant flowers.

A broad ray of light streamed in through the open door, illumining the dingy interior. The double wooden shutters of the windows were all closed, and secured on the inside by iron hooks.

"Well, w'at you want, Azélie?" asked 'Polyte, going behind the counter with an air of hurry and importance. "I ain't got time to fool. Make has'e; say w'at you want."

Her reply was precisely the same that she had made to Mr. Mathurin.

"I come git a li'le piece o' meat. We plumb out o' meat home."

He seemed exasperated.

"Bonté! w'at you all do with meat yonda? You don't reflec' you about to eat up yo' crop befo' it's good out o' the groun', you all. I like to know w'y yo' pa don't go he'p with the killin' once aw'ile, an' git some fresh meat fo' a change."

She answered in an unshaded, unmodulated voice that was penetrating, like a child's: "Popa he do go he'p wid the killin'; but he say he can't work 'less he got salt meat. He got plenty to feed—him. He's got to hire he'p wid his crop, an' he's boun' to feed 'em; they won't year no diffe'nt. An' he's got gra'ma to feed, an' Sauterelle, an' me—"

"An' all the lazy-bone 'Cadians in the country that know w'ere they goin' to fine the coffee-pot always in the corna of the fire," grumbled 'Polyte.

With an iron hook he lifted a small piece of salt meat from the pork barrel, weighed it, and placed it in her pail. Then she wanted a little coffee. He gave it to her reluctantly. He was still more loath to let her have sugar; and when she asked for lard, he refused flatly.

She had taken off her sunbonnet, and was fanning herself with it, as she leaned with her elbows upon the counter, and let her eyes travel lingeringly along the well-lined shelves. 'Polyte stood staring into her face with a sense of aggravation that her presence, her manner, always stirred up in him.

The face was colorless but for the red, curved line of the lips. Her eyes were dark, wide, innocent, questioning eyes, and her black hair was plastered smooth back from the forehead and temples. There was no trace of any intention of coquetry in her manner. He resented this as a token of indifference toward his sex, and thought it inexcusable.

"Well, Azélie, if it's anything you don't see, ask fo' it," he suggested, with what he flattered himself was humor. But there was no responsive humor in Azélie's composition. She seriously drew a small flask from her pocket.

"Popa say, if you want to let him have a li'le dram, 'count o' his pains that's 'bout to cripple him."

"Yo' pa knows as well as I do we don't sell w'isky. Mr. Mathurin don't carry no license."

"I know. He say if you want to give 'im a li'le dram, he's willin' to do some work fo' you."

"No! Once fo' all, no!" And 'Polyte reached for the day-book, in which to enter the articles he had given to her.

But Azélie's needs were not yet satisfied. She wanted tobacco; he would not give it to her. A spool of thread; he rolled one up, together with two sticks of peppermint candy, and placed it in her pail. When she asked for a bottle of coal-oil, he grudgingly consented, but assured her it would be useless to cudgel her brain further, for he would positively let her have nothing more. He disappeared toward the coal-oil tank, which was hidden from view behind the piled-up boxes on the counter. When she heard him searching for an empty quart bottle, and making a clatter with the tin funnels, she herself withdrew from the counter against which she had been leaning.

After they quitted the store, 'Polyte, with a perplexed expression upon his face, leaned for a moment against one of the whitewashed pillars, watching the girl cross the yard. She had folded her sunbonnet into a pad, which she placed beneath the heavy pail that she balanced upon her head. She walked upright, with a slow, careful tread. Two of the yard dogs that had stood a moment before upon the threshold of the store door, quivering and wagging their tails, were following her now, with a little businesslike trot. 'Polyte called them back.

The cabin which the girl occupied with her father, her grandmother, and her little brother Sauterelle, was removed some distance from the plantation house, and only its pointed roof could be discerned like a speck far away across the field of cotton, which was all in bloom. Her figure soon disappeared from view, and 'Polyte emerged from the shelter of the gallery, and started again toward his interrupted task. He turned to say to the planter, who was keeping up his measured tramp above:

"Mr. Mathurin, ain't it 'mos' time to stop givin' credit to Arsène Pauché. Look like that crop o' his ain't goin' to start to pay his account. I don't see, me, anyway, how you come to take that triflin' Li'le river gang on the place."

"I know it was a mistake, 'Polyte, but que voulez-vous?" the planter returned, with a good-natured shrug. "Now they are yere, we can't let them starve, my frien'. Push them to work all you can. Hole back all supplies that are not necessary, an' nex' year we will let some one else enjoy the privilège of feeding them," he ended, with a laugh.

"I wish they was all back on Li'le river," 'Polyte muttered under his breath as he turned and walked slowly away.

Directly back of the store was the young man's sleeping-room. He had made himself quite comfortable there in his corner. He had screened his windows and doors; planted Madeira vines, which now formed a thick green curtain between the two pillars that faced his room; and had swung a hammock out there, in which he liked well to repose himself after the fatigues of the day.

He lay long in the hammock that evening, thinking over the day's happenings and the morrow's work, half dozing, half dreaming, and wholly possessed by the charm of the night, the warm, sweeping air that blew through the long corridor, and the almost unbroken stillness that enveloped him.

At times his random thoughts formed themselves into an almost inaudible speech: "I wish she would go 'way f'om yere."

One of the dogs came and thrust his cool, moist muzzle against 'Polyte's cheek. He caressed the fellow's shaggy head. "I don't know w'at's the matta with her," he sighed; "I don' b'lieve she's got good sense."

It was a long time afterward that he murmured again: "I wish to God she'd go 'way f'om yere!"

The edge of the moon crept up—a keen, curved blade of light above the dark line of the cotton-field. 'Polyte roused himself when he saw it. "I didn' know it was so late," he said to himself—or to his dog. He entered his room at once, and was soon in bed, sleeping soundly.

It was some hours later that 'Polyte was roused from his sleep by—he did not know what; his senses were too scattered and confused to determine at once. There was at first no sound; then so faint a one that he wondered how he could have heard it. A door of his room communicated with the store, but this door was never used, and was almost completely blocked by wares piled up on the other side. The faint noise that 'Polyte heard, and which came from within the store, was followed by a flare of light that he could discern through the chinks, and that lasted as long as a match might burn.

He was now fully aware that some one was in the store. How the intruder had entered he could not guess, for the key was under his pillow with his watch and his pistol.

As cautiously as he could he donned an extra garment, thrust his bare feet into slippers, and crept out into the portico, pistol in hand.

The shutters of one of the store windows were open. He stood close to it, and waited, which he considered surer and safer than to enter the dark and crowded confines of the store to engage in what might prove a bootless struggle with the intruder.

He had not long to wait. In a few moments some one darted through the open window as nimbly as a cat. 'Polyte staggered back as if a heavy blow had stunned him. His first thought and his first exclamation were: "My God! how close I come to killin' you!"

It was Azélie. She uttered no cry, but made one quick effort to run when she saw him. He seized her arm and held her with a brutal grip. He put the pistol back into his pocket. He was shaking like a man with the palsy. One by one he took from her the parcels she was carrying, and flung them back into the store. There were not many: some packages of tobacco, a cheap pipe, some fishing-tackle, and the flask which she had brought with her in the afternoon. This he threw into the yard. It was still empty, for she had not been able to find the "key" to the whisky-barrel.

"So—so, you a thief!" he muttered savagely under his breath.

"You hurtin' me, Mr. 'Polyte," she complained, squirming. He some-what relaxed, but did not relinquish, his hold upon her.

"I ain't no thief," she blurted.

"You was stealin'," he contradicted her sharply.

"I wasn' stealin'. I was jus' takin' a few li'le things you all too mean to gi' me. You all treat my popa like he was a dog. It's on'y las' week Mr. Mathurin sen' 'way to the city to fetch a fine buckboa'd fo' Son Ambroise, an' he's on'y a nigga, après tout. An' my popa he want a picayune tobacco? It's 'No'—" She spoke loud in her monotonous, shrill voice. 'Polyte kept saying: "Hush, I tell you! Hush! Somebody'll year you. Hush! It's enough you broke in the sto'—how you got in the sto'?" he added, looking from her to the open window.

"It was w'en you was behine the boxes to the coal-oil tank—I unhook' it," she explained sullenly.

"An' you don' know I could sen' you to Baton Rouge fo' that?" He shook her as though trying to rouse her to a comprehension of her grievous fault.

"Jus' fo' a li'le picayune o' tobacco!" she whimpered.

He suddenly abandoned his hold upon her, and left her free. She mechanically rubbed the arm that he had grasped so violently.

Between the long row of pillars the moon was sending pale beams of light. In one of these they were standing.

"Azélie," he said, "go 'way f'om yere quick; some one might fine you yere. W'en you want something in the sto', fo' yo'se'f or fo' yo' pa—I don' care—ask me fo' it. But you—but you can't neva set yo' foot inside that sto' again. Go 'way f'om yere quick as you can, I tell you!"

She tried in no way to conciliate him. She turned and walked away over the same ground she had crossed before. One of the big dogs started to follow her. 'Polyte did not call him back this time. He knew no harm could come to her, going through those lonely fields, while the animal was at her side.

He went at once to his room for the store key that was beneath his pillow. He entered the store, and refastened the window. When he had made everything once more secure, he sat dejectedly down upon a bench that was in the portico. He sat for a long time motionless. Then, over-come by some powerful feeling that was at work within him, he buried his face in his hands and wept, his whole body shaken by the violence of his sobs.

After that night 'Polyte loved Azélie desperately. The very action which should have revolted him had seemed, on the contrary, to inflame him with love. He felt that love to be a degradation—something that he was almost ashamed to acknowledge to himself; and he knew that he was hopelessly unable to stifle it.

He watched now in a tremor for her coming. She came very often, for she remembered every word he had said; and she did not hesitate to ask him for those luxuries which she considered necessities to her "popa's" existence. She never attempted to enter the store, but always waited outside, of her own accord, laughing, and playing with the dogs. She seemed to have no shame or regret for what she had done, and plainly did not realize that it was a disgraceful act. 'Polyte often shuddered with disgust to discern in her a being so wholly devoid of moral sense.

He had always been an industrious, bustling fellow, never idle. Now there were hours and hours in which he did nothing but long for the sight of Azélie. Even when at work there was that gnawing want at his heart to see her, often so urgent that he would leave everything to wander down by her cabin with the hope of seeing her. It was even something if he could catch a glimpse of Sauterelle playing in the weeds, or of Arsène lazily dragging himself about, and smoking the pipe which rarely left his lips now that he was kept so well supplied with tobacco.

Once, down the bank of the bayou, when 'Polyte came upon Azélie unexpectedly, and was therefore unprepared to resist the shock of her sudden appearance, he seized her in his arms, and covered her face with kisses. She was not indignant; she was not flustered or agitated, as might have been a susceptible, coquettish girl; she was only astonished, and annoyed.

"W'at you doin', Mr. 'Polyte?" she cried, struggling. "Leave me 'lone, I say! Leave me go!"

"I love you, I love you, I love you!" he stammered helplessly over and over in her face.

"You mus' los' yo' head," she told him, red from the effort of the struggle, when he released her.

"You right, Azélie; I b'lieve I los' my head," and he climbed up the bank of the bayou as fast as he could.

After that his behavior was shameful, and he knew it, and he did not care. He invented pretexts that would enable him to touch her hand with his. He wanted to kiss her again, and told her she might come into the store as she used to do. There was no need for her to unhook a window now; he gave her whatever she asked for, charging it always to his own account on the books. She permitted his caresses without returning them, and yet that was all he seemed to live for now. He gave her a little gold ring.

He was looking eagerly forward to the close of the season, when Arsène would go back to Little River. He had arranged to ask Azélie to marry him. He would keep her with him when the others went away. He longed to rescue her from what he felt to be the demoralizing influences of her family and her surroundings. 'Polyte believed he would be able to awaken Azélie to finer, better impulses when he should have her apart to himself.

But when the time came to propose it, Azélie looked at him in amazement. "Ah, b'en, no. I ain't goin' to stay yere wid you, Mr. 'Polyte; I'm goin' yonda on Li'le river wid my popa."

This resolve frightened him, but he pretended not to believe it.

"You jokin', Azélie; you mus' care a li'le about me. It looked to me all along like you cared some about me."

"An' my popa, donc? Ah, b'en, no."

"You don' rememba how lonesome it is on Li'le river, Azélie," he pleaded. "W'enever I think 'bout Li'le river it always make me sad—like I think about a graveyard. To me it's like a person mus' die, one way or otha, w'en they go on Li'le river. Oh, I hate it! Stay with me, Azélie; don' go 'way f'om me."

She said little, one way or the other, after that, when she had fully understood his wishes, and her reserve led him to believe, since he hoped it, that he had prevailed with her and that she had determined to stay with him and be his wife.

It was a cool, crisp morning in December that they went away. In a ramshackle wagon, drawn by an ill-mated team, Arsène Pauché and his family left Mr. Mathurin's plantation for their old familiar haunts on Little river. The grandmother, looking like a witch, with a black shawl tied over her head, sat upon a roll of bedding in the bottom of the wagon. Sauterelle's bead-like eyes glittered with mischief as he peeped over the side. Azélie, with the pink sunbonnet completely hiding her round young face, sat beside her father, who drove.

'Polyte caught one glimpse of the group as they passed in the road. Turning, he hurried into his room, and locked himself in.

It soon became evident that 'Polyte's services were going to count for little. He himself was the first to realize this. One day he approached the planter, and said: "Mr. Mathurin, befo' we start anotha year togetha, I betta tell you I'm goin' to quit." 'Polyte stood upon the steps, and leaned back against the railing. The planter was a little above on the gallery.

"W'at in the name o' sense are you talking about, 'Polyte!" he exclaimed in astonishment.

"It's jus' that; I'm boun' to quit."

"You had a better offer?"

"No; I ain't had no offa."

"Then explain yo'se'f, my frien'—explain yo'se'f," requested Mr. Mathurin, with something of offended dignity. "If you leave me, w'ere are you going?"

'Polyte was beating his leg with his limp felt hat. "I reckon I jus' as well go yonda on Li'le river—w'ere Azélie," he said.

A Lady of Bayou St. John

The days and the nights were very lonely for Madame Delisle. Gustave, her husband, was away yonder in Virginia somewhere, with Beauregard, and she was here in the old house on Bayou St. John, alone with her slaves.

Madame was very beautiful. So beautiful, that she found much diversion in sitting for hours before the mirror, contemplating her own loveliness; admiring the brilliancy of her golden hair, the sweet languor of her blue eyes, the graceful contours of her figure, and the peach-like bloom of her flesh. She was very young. So young that she romped with the dogs, teased the parrot, and could not fall asleep at night unless old black Manna-Loulou sat beside her bed and told her stories.

In short, she was a child, not able to realize the significance of the tragedy whose unfolding kept the civilized world in suspense. It was only the immediate effect of the awful drama that moved her: the gloom that, spreading on all sides, penetrated her own existence and deprived it of joyousness.

Sépincourt found her looking very lonely and disconsolate one day when he stopped to talk with her. She was pale, and her blue eyes were dim with unwept tears. He was a Frenchman who lived near by. He shrugged his shoulders over this strife between brothers, this quarrel which was none of his; and he resented it chiefly upon the ground that it made life uncomfortable; yet he was young enough to have had quicker and hotter blood in his veins.

When he left Madame Delisle that day, her eyes were no longer dim, and a something of the dreariness that weighted her had been lifted away. That mysterious, that treacherous bond called sympathy, had revealed them to each other.

He came to her very often that summer, clad always in cool, white duck, with a flower in his buttonhole. His pleasant brown eyes sought hers with warm, friendly glances that comforted her as a caress might comfort a disconsolate child. She took to watching for his slim figure, a little bent, walking lazily up the avenue between the double line of magnolias.

They would sit sometimes during whole afternoons in the vine-sheltered corner of the gallery, sipping the black coffee that Manna-Loulou brought to them at intervals; and talking, talking incessantly during the first days when they were unconsciously unfolding themselves to each other. Then a time came—it came very quickly—when they seemed to have nothing more to say to one another.

He brought her news of the war; and they talked about it listlessly, between long intervals of silence, of which neither took account. An occasional letter came by round-about ways from Gustave—guarded and saddening in its tone. They would read it and sigh over it together.

Once they stood before his portrait that hung in the drawing-room and that looked out at them with kind, indulgent eyes. Madame wiped the picture with her gossamer handkerchief and impulsively pressed a tender kiss upon the painted canvas. For months past the living image of her husband had been receding further and further into a mist which she could penetrate with no faculty or power that she possessed.

One day at sunset, when she and Sépincourt stood silently side by side, looking across the *marais*, aflame with the western light, he said to her: "*M'amie*, let us go away from this country that is so *triste*. Let us go to Paris, you and me."

She thought that he was jesting, and she laughed nervously. "Yes, Paris would surely be gayer than Bayou St. John," she answered. But he was not jesting. She saw it at once in the glance that penetrated her own; in the quiver of his sensitive lip and the quick beating of a swollen vein in his brown throat.

"Paris, or anywhere—with you—ah, *bon Dieu!*" he whispered, seizing her hands. But she withdrew from him, frightened, and hurried away into the house, leaving him alone.

That night, for the first time, Madame did not want to hear Manna-Loulou's stories, and she blew out the wax candle that till now had burned nightly in her sleeping-room, under its tall, crystal globe. She had suddenly become a woman capable of love or sacrifice. She would not hear Manna-Loulou's stories. She wanted to be alone, to tremble and to weep.

In the morning her eyes were dry, but she would not see Sépincourt when he came. Then he wrote her a letter.

"I have offended you and I would rather die!" it ran. "Do not banish me from your presence that is life to me. Let me lie at your feet, if only for a moment, in which to hear you say that you forgive me."

Men have written just such letters before, but Madame did not know it. To her it was a voice from the unknown, like music, awaking in her a delicious tumult that seized and held possession of her whole being.

When they met, he had but to look into her face to know that he need not lie at her feet craving forgiveness. She was waiting for him beneath the spreading branches of a live-oak that guarded the gate of her home like a sentinel.

For a brief moment he held her hands, which trembled. Then he folded her in his arms and kissed her many times. "You will go with me, *m'amie?* I love you—oh, I love you! Will you not go with me, *m'amie?*"

"Anywhere, anywhere," she told him in a fainting voice that he could scarcely hear.

But she did not go with him. Chance willed it otherwise. That night a courier brought her a message from Beauregard, telling her that Gustave, her husband, was dead.

When the new year was still young, Sépincourt decided that, all things considered, he might, without any appearance of indecent haste, speak again of his love to Madame Delisle. That love was quite as acute as ever; perhaps a little sharper, from the long period of silence and waiting to which he had subjected it. He found her, as he had expected, clad in deepest mourning. She greeted him precisely as she had welcomed the curé, when the kind old priest had brought to her the consolations of religion—clasping his two hands warmly, and calling him *"cher ami."* Her whole attitude and bearing brought to Sépincourt the poignant, the bewildering conviction that he held no place in her thoughts.

They sat in the drawing-room before the portrait of Gustave, which was draped with his scarf. Above the picture hung his sword, and beneath it was an embankment of flowers. Sépincourt felt an almost irresistible impulse to bend his knee before this altar, upon which he saw foreshadowed the immolation of his hopes.

There was a soft air blowing gently over the *marais.* It came to them through the open window, laden with a hundred subtle sounds and scents of the springtime. It seemed to remind Madame of something far, far away, for she gazed dreamily out into the blue firmament. It fretted Sépincourt with impulses to speech and action which he found it impossible to control.

"You must know what has brought me," he began impulsively, drawing his chair nearer to hers. "Through all these months I have never ceased to love you and to long for you. Night and day the sound of your dear voice has been with me; your eyes"—

She held out her hand deprecatingly. He took it and held it. She let it lie unresponsive in his.

"You cannot have forgotten that you loved me not long ago," he went on eagerly, "that you were ready to follow me anywhere,—anywhere; do you remember? I have come now to ask you to fulfill that promise; to ask you to be my wife, my companion, the dear treasure of my life."

She heard his warm and pleading tones as though listening to a strange language, imperfectly understood.

She withdrew her hand from his, and leaned her brow thoughtfully upon it.

"Can you not feel—can you not understand, *mon ami*," she said calmly, "that now such a thing—such a thought, is impossible to me?"

"Impossible?"

"Yes, impossible. Can you not see that now my heart, my soul, my thought—my very life, must belong to another? It could not be different."

"Would you have me believe that you can wed your young existence to the dead?" he exclaimed with something like horror. Her glance was sunk deep in the embankment of flowers before her.

"My husband has never been so living to me as he is now," she replied with a faint smile of commiseration for Sépincourt's fatuity. "Every object that surrounds me speaks to me of him. I look yonder across the *marais*, and I see him coming toward me, tired and toil-stained from the hunt. I see him again sitting in this chair or in that one. I hear his familiar voice, his footsteps upon the galleries. We walk once more together beneath the magnolias; and at night in dreams I feel that he is there, there, near me. How could it be different! Ah! I have memories, memories to crowd and fill my life, if I live a hundred years!"

Sépincourt was wondering why she did not take the sword from her altar and thrust it through his body here and there. The effect would have been infinitely more agreeable than her words, penetrating his soul like fire. He arose confused, enraged with pain.

"Then, Madame," he stammered, "there is nothing left for me but to take my leave. I bid you adieu."

"Do not be offended, *mon ami*," she said kindly, holding out her hand. "You are going to Paris, I suppose?"

"What does it matter," he exclaimed desperately, "where I go?"

"Oh, I only wanted to wish you *bon voyage*," she assured him amiably.

Many days after that Sépincourt spent in the fruitless mental effort of trying to comprehend that psychological enigma, a woman's heart.

Madame still lives on Bayou St. John. She is rather an old lady now, a very pretty old lady, against whose long years of widowhood there has never been a breath of reproach. The memory of Gustave still fills and satisfies her days. She has never failed, once a year, to have a solemn high mass said for the repose of his soul.

La Belle Zoraïde

The summer night was hot and still; not a ripple of air swept over the *marais*. Yonder, across Bayou St. John, lights twinkled here and there in the darkness, and in the dark sky above a few stars were blinking. A lugger that had come out of the lake was moving with slow, lazy motion down the bayou. A man in the boat was singing a song.

The notes of the song came faintly to the ears of old Manna-Loulou, herself as black as the night, who had gone out upon the gallery to open the shutters wide.

Something in the refrain reminded the woman of an old, half-forgotten Creole romance, and she began to sing it low to herself while she threw the shutters open:—

> "Lisett' to kité la plaine,
> Mo perdi bonhair à moué;
> Ziés à moué semblé fontaine,
> Dépi mo pa miré toué."

And then this old song, a lover's lament for the loss of his mistress, floating into her memory, brought with it the story she would tell to Madame, who lay in her sumptuous mahogany bed, waiting to be fanned and put to sleep to the sound of one of Manna-Loulou's stories. The old negress had already bathed her mistress's pretty white feet and kissed them lovingly, one, then the other. She had brushed her mistress's beautiful hair, that was as soft and shining as satin, and was the color of Madame's wedding-ring. Now, when she reëntered the room, she moved softly toward the bed, and seating herself there began gently to fan Madame Delisle.

Manna-Loulou was not always ready with her story, for Madame would hear none but those which were true. But to-night the story was all there in Manna-Loulou's head—the story of la belle Zoraïde—and she told it to her mistress in the soft Creole patois, whose music and charm no English words can convey.

"La belle Zoraïde had eyes that were so dusky, so beautiful, that any man who gazed too long into their depths was sure to lose his head, and even his heart sometimes. Her soft, smooth skin was the color of *café-au-lait.* As for her elegant manners, her *svelte* and graceful figure, they were the envy of half the ladies who visited her mistress, Madame Delarivière.

"No wonder Zoraïde was as charming and as dainty as the finest lady of la rue Royale: from a toddling thing she had been brought up at her mistress's side; her fingers had never done rougher work than sewing a fine muslin seam; and she even had her own little black servant to wait upon her. Madame, who was her godmother as well as her mistress, would often say to her:—

" 'Remember, Zoraïde, when you are ready to marry, it must be in a way to do honor to your bringing up. It will be at the Cathedral. Your wedding gown, your *corbeille,* all will be of the best; I shall see to that myself. You know, M'sieur Ambroise is ready whenever you say the word; and his master is willing to do as much for him as I shall do for you. It is a union that will please me in every way.'

"M'sieur Ambroise was then the body servant of Doctor Langlé. La belle Zoraïde detested the little mulatto, with his shining whiskers like a white man's, and his small eyes, that were cruel and false as a snake's. She would cast down her own mischievous eyes, and say:—

" 'Ah, nénaine, I am so happy, so contented here at your side just as I am. I don't want to marry now; next year, perhaps, or the next.' And Madame would smile indulgently and remind Zoraïde that a woman's charms are not everlasting.

"But the truth of the matter was, Zoraïde had seen le beau Mézor dance the Bamboula in Congo Square. That was a sight to hold one rooted to the ground. Mézor was as straight as a cypress-tree and as proud looking as a king. His body, bare to the waist, was like a column of ebony and it glistened like oil.

"Poor Zoraïde's heart grew sick in her bosom with love for le beau Mézor from the moment she saw the fierce gleam of his eye, lighted by the inspiring strains of the Bamboula, and beheld the stately movements of his splendid body swaying and quivering through the figures of the dance.

"But when she knew him later, and he came near her to speak with her, all the fierceness was gone out of his eyes, and she saw only kindness in them and heard only gentleness in his voice; for love had taken possession of him also, and Zoraïde was more distracted than ever. When Mézor was not dancing Bamboula in Congo Square, he was hoeing sugar-cane, barefooted and half naked, in his master's field outside of the city. Doctor Langlé was his master as well as M'sieur Ambroise's.

"One day, when Zoraïde kneeled before her mistress, drawing on Madame's silken stockings, that were of the finest, she said:

" 'Nénaine, you have spoken to me often of marrying. Now, at last, I have chosen a husband, but it is not M'sieur Ambroise; it is le beau Mézor that I want and no other.' And Zoraïde hid her face in her hands when she had said that, for she guessed, rightly enough, that her mistress would be very angry. And, indeed, Madame Delarivière was at first speechless with rage. When she finally spoke it was only to gasp out, exasperated:—

" 'That negro! that negro! Bon Dieu Seigneur, but this is too much!'

" 'Am I white, nénaine?' pleaded Zoraïde.

" 'You white! *Malheureuse!* You deserve to have the lash laid upon you like any other slave; you have proven yourself no better than the worst.'

" 'I am not white,' persisted Zoraïde, respectfully and gently. 'Doctor Langlé gives me his slave to marry, but he would not give me his son. Then, since I am not white, let me have from out of my own race the one whom my heart has chosen.'

"However, you may well believe that Madame would not hear to that. Zoraïde was forbidden to speak to Mézor, and Mézor was cautioned against seeing Zoraïde again. But you know how the negroes are, Ma'zélle Titite," added Manna-Loulou, smiling a little sadly. "There is no mistress, no master, no king nor priest who can hinder them from loving when they will. And these two found ways and means.

"When months had passed by, Zoraïde, who had grown unlike herself, —sober and preoccupied,—said again to her mistress:—

" 'Nénaine, you would not let me have Mézor for my husband; but I have disobeyed you, I have sinned. Kill me if you wish, nénaine: forgive me if you will; but when I heard le beau Mézor say to me, "Zoraïde, mo l'aime toi," I could have died, but I could not have helped loving him.'

"This time Madame Delarivière was so actually pained, so wounded at hearing Zoraïde's confession, that there was no place left in her heart for anger. She could utter only confused reproaches. But she was a woman of action rather than of words, and she acted promptly. Her first step was to induce Doctor Langlé to sell Mézor. Doctor Langlé, who was a widower, had long wanted to marry Madame Delarivière, and he would willingly have walked on all fours at noon through the Place d'Armes if she wanted him to. Naturally he lost no time in disposing of le beau Mézor, who was sold away into Georgia, or the Carolinas, or one of those distant countries far away, where he would no longer hear his Creole tongue spoken, nor dance Calinda, nor hold la belle Zoraïde in his arms.

"The poor thing was heartbroken when Mézor was sent away from her, but she took comfort and hope in the thought of her baby that she would soon be able to clasp to her breast.

"La belle Zoraïde's sorrows had now begun in earnest. Not only sorrows but sufferings, and with the anguish of maternity came the shadow of death. But there is no agony that a mother will not forget when she holds her first-born to her heart, and presses her lips upon the baby flesh that is her own, yet far more precious than her own.

"So, instinctively, when Zoraïde came out of the awful shadow she gazed questioningly about her and felt with her trembling hands upon either side of her. 'Où li, mo piti a moin? (Where is my little one?)' she asked imploringly. Madame who was there and the nurse who was there both told her in turn, 'To piti à toi, li mouri' ('Your little one is dead'), which was a wicked falsehood that must have caused the angels in heaven to weep. For the baby was living and well and strong. It had at once been removed from its mother's side, to be sent away to Madame's plantation, far up the coast. Zoraïde could only moan in reply, 'Li mouri, li mouri,' and she turned her face to the wall.

"Madame had hoped, in thus depriving Zoraïde of her child, to have her young waiting-maid again at her side free, happy, and beautiful as of old. But there was a more powerful will than Madame's at work—the will of the good God, who had already designed that Zoraïde should grieve with a sorrow that was never more to be lifted in this world. La belle Zoraïde was no more. In her stead was a sad-eyed woman who mourned night and day for her baby. 'Li mouri, li mouri,' she would sigh over and over again to those about her, and to herself when others grew weary of her complaint.

"Yet, in spite of all, M'sieur Ambroise was still in the notion to marry her. A sad wife or a merry one was all the same to him so long as that wife was Zoraïde. And she seemed to consent, or rather submit, to the approaching marriage as though nothing mattered any longer in this world.

"One day, a black servant entered a little noisily the room in which Zoraïde sat sewing. With a look of strange and vacuous happiness upon her face, Zoraïde arose hastily. 'Hush, hush,' she whispered, lifting a warning finger, 'my little one is asleep; you must not awaken her.'

"Upon the bed was a senseless bundle of rags shaped like an infant in swaddling clothes. Over this dummy the woman had drawn the mosquito bar, and she was sitting contentedly beside it. In short, from that day Zoraïde was demented. Night nor day did she lose sight of the doll that lay in her bed or in her arms.

"And now was Madame stung with sorrow and remorse at seeing this terrible affliction that had befallen her dear Zoraïde. Consulting with Doctor Langlé, they decided to bring back to the mother the real baby of flesh and blood that was now toddling about, and kicking its heels in the dust yonder upon the plantation.

"It was Madame herself who led the pretty, tiny little "griffe" girl to her mother. Zoraïde was sitting upon a stone bench in the courtyard, listening to the soft splashing of the fountain, and watching the fitful shadows of the palm leaves upon the broad, white flagging.

" 'Here,' said Madame, approaching, 'here, my poor dear Zoraïde, is your own little child. Keep her; she is yours. No one will ever take her from you again.'

"Zoraïde looked with sullen suspicion upon her mistress and the child before her. Reaching out a hand she thrust the little one mistrustfully away from her. With the other hand she clasped the rag bundle fiercely to her breast; for she suspected a plot to deprive her of it.

"Nor could she ever be induced to let her own child approach her; and finally the little one was sent back to the plantation, where she was never to know the love of mother or father.

"And now this is the end of Zoraïde's story. She was never known again as la belle Zoraïde, but ever after as Zoraïde la folle, whom no one ever wanted to marry—not even M'sieur Ambroise. She lived to be an old woman, whom some people pitied and others laughed at—always clasping her bundle of rags—her 'piti.'

"Are you asleep, Ma'zélle Titite?"

"No, I am not asleep; I was thinking. Ah, the poor little one, Man Loulou, the poor little one! better had she died!"

But this is the way Madame Delisle and Manna-Loulou really talked to each other:—

"Vou pré droumi, Ma'zélle Titite?"

"Non, pa pré droumi; mo yapré zongler. Ah, la pauv' piti, Man Loulou. La pauv' piti! Mieux li mouri!"

At Chênière Caminada

I

There was no clumsier looking fellow in church that Sunday morning than Antoine Bocaze—the one they called Tonie. But Tonie did not really care if he were clumsy or not. He felt that he could speak intelligibly to no woman save his mother; but since he had no desire to inflame the hearts of any of the island maidens, what difference did it make?

He knew there was no better fisherman on the Chênière Caminada than himself, if his face was too long and bronzed, his limbs too unmanageable and his eyes too earnest—almost too honest.

It was a midsummer day, with a lazy, scorching breeze blowing from the Gulf straight into the church windows. The ribbons on the young girls' hats fluttered like the wings of birds, and the old women clutched the flapping ends of the veils that covered their heads.

A few mosquitoes, floating through the blistering air, with their nipping and humming fretted the people to a certain degree of attention and consequent devotion. The measured tones of the priest at the altar rose and fell like a song: "Credo in unum Deum patrem omnipotentem" he chanted. And then the people all looked at one another, suddenly electrified.

Some one was playing upon the organ whose notes no one on the whole island was able to awaken; whose tones had not been heard during the many months since a passing stranger had one day listlessly dragged his fingers across its idle keys. A long, sweet strain of music floated down from the loft and filled the church.

It seemed to most of them—it seemed to Tonie standing there beside his old mother—that some heavenly being must have descended upon the Church of Our Lady of Lourdes and chosen this celestial way of communicating with its people.

But it was no creature from a different sphere; it was only a young lady from Grand Isle. A rather pretty young person with blue eyes and nut-brown hair, who wore a dotted lawn of fine texture and fashionable make, and a white Leghorn sailor-hat.

Tonie saw her standing outside of the church after mass, receiving the priest's voluble praises and thanks for her graceful service.

She had come over to mass from Grand Isle in Baptiste Beaudelet's lugger, with a couple of young men, and two ladies who kept a pension over there. Tonie knew these two ladies—the widow Lebrun and her old mother—but he did not attempt to speak with them; he would not have known what to say. He stood aside gazing at the group, as others were doing, his serious eyes fixed earnestly upon the fair organist.

Tonie was late at dinner that day. His mother must have waited an hour for him, sitting patiently with her coarse hands folded in her lap, in that little still room with its "brick-painted" floor, its gaping chimney and homely furnishings.

He told her that he had been walking—walking he hardly knew where, and he did not know why. He must have tramped from one end of the island to the other; but he brought her no bit of news or gossip. He did not know if the Cotures had stopped for dinner with the Avendettes; whether old Pierre François was worse, or better, or dead, or if lame Philibert was drinking again this morning. He knew nothing; yet he had crossed the village, and passed every one of its small houses that stood close together in a long jagged line facing the sea; they were gray and battered by time and the rude buffets of the salt sea winds.

He knew nothing though the Cotures had all bade him "good day" as they filed into Avendette's, where a steaming plate of crab gumbo was waiting for each. He had heard some woman screaming, and others saying it was because old Pierre François had just passed away. But he did not remember this, nor did he recall the fact that lame Philibert had staggered against him when he stood absently watching a "fiddler" sidling across the sun-baked sand. He could tell his mother nothing of all this; but he said he had noticed that the wind was fair and must have driven Baptiste's boat, like a flying bird, across the water.

Well, that was something to talk about, and old Ma'me Antoine, who was fat, leaned comfortably upon the table after she had helped Tonie to his courtbouillon, and remarked that she found Madame was getting old. Tonie thought that perhaps she was aging and her hair was getting whiter. He seemed glad to talk about her, and reminded his mother of old Madame's kindness and sympathy at the time his father and brothers had perished. It was when he was a little fellow, ten years before, during a squall in Barataria Bay.

Ma'me Antoine declared that she could never forget that sympathy, if she lived till Judgment Day; but all the same she was sorry to see that Madame Lebrun was also not so young or fresh as she used to be. Her chances of getting a husband were surely lessening every year; especially with the young girls around her, budding each spring like flowers to be plucked. The one who had played upon the organ was Mademoiselle Duvigné, Claire Duvigné, a great belle, the daughter of the famous lawyer who lived in New Orleans, on Rampart street. Ma'me Antoine had found that out during the ten minutes she and others had stopped after mass to gossip with the priest.

"Claire Duvigné," muttered Tonie, not even making a pretense to taste his courtbouillon, but picking little bits from the half loaf of crusty brown bread that lay beside his plate. "Claire Duvigné; that is a pretty name. Don't you think so, mother? I can't think of anyone on the Chênière who has so pretty a one, nor at Grand Isle, either, for that matter. And you say she lives on Rampart street?"

It appeared to him a matter of great importance that he should have his mother repeat all that the priest had told her.

II

Early the following morning Tonie went out in search of lame Philibert, than whom there was no cleverer workman on the island when he could be caught sober.

Tonie had tried to work on his big lugger that lay bottom upward under the shed, but it had seemed impossible. His mind, his hands, his tools refused to do their office, and in sudden desperation he desisted. He found Philibert and set him to work in his own place under the shed. Then he got into his small boat with the red lateen-sail and went over to Grand Isle.

There was no one at hand to warn Tonie that he was acting the part of a fool. He had, singularly, never felt those premonitory symptoms of love which afflict the greater portion of mankind before they reach the age which he had attained. He did not at first recognize this powerful impulse that had, without warning, possessed itself of his entire being. He obeyed it without a struggle, as naturally as he would have obeyed the dictates of hunger and thirst.

Tonie left his boat at the wharf and proceeded at once to Mme. Lebrun's pension, which consisted of a group of plain, stoutly built cottages that stood in mid island, about half a mile from the sea.

The day was bright and beautiful with soft, velvety gusts of wind blowing from the water. From a cluster of orange trees a flock of doves ascended, and Tonie stopped to listen to the beating of their wings and follow their flight toward the water oaks whither he himself was moving.

He walked with a dragging, uncertain step through the yellow, fragrant camomile, his thoughts traveling before him. In his mind was always the vivid picture of the girl as it had stamped itself there yesterday, connected in some mystical way with that celestial music which had thrilled him and was vibrating yet in his soul.

But she did not look the same to-day. She was returning from the beach when Tonie first saw her, leaning upon the arm of one of the men who had accompanied her yesterday. She was dressed differently—in a dainty blue cotton gown. Her companion held a big white sunshade over them both. They had exchanged hats and were laughing with great abandonment.

Two young men walked behind them and were trying to engage her attention. She glanced at Tonie, who was leaning against a tree when the group passed by; but of course she did not know him. She was speaking English, a language which he hardly understood.

There were other young people gathered under the water oaks—girls who were, many of them, more beautiful than Mlle. Duvigné; but for Tonie they simply did not exist. His whole universe had suddenly become converted into a glamorous background for the person of Mlle. Duvigné, and the shadowy figures of men who were about her.

Tonie went to Mme. Lebrun and told her he would bring her oranges next day from the Chênière. She was well pleased, and commissioned him to bring her other things from the stores there, which she could not procure at Grand Isle. She did not question his presence, knowing that these summer days were idle ones for the Chênière fishermen. Nor did she seem surprised when he told her that his boat was at the wharf, and would be there every day at her service. She knew his frugal habits, and supposed he wished to hire it, as others did. He intuitively felt that this could be the only way.

And that is how it happened that Tonie spent so little of his time at the Chênière Caminada that summer. Old Ma'me Antoine grumbled enough about it. She herself had been twice in her life to Grand Isle and once to Grand Terre, and each time had been more than glad to get back to the Chênière. And why Tonie should want to spend his days, and even his nights, away from home, was a thing she could not comprehend, especially as he would have to be away the whole winter; and meantime there was much work to be done at his own hearthside and in the company of his own mother. She did not know that Tonie had much, much more to do at Grand Isle than at the Chênière Caminada.

He had to see how Claire Duvigné sat upon the gallery in the big rocking chair that she kept in motion by the impetus of her slender, slippered foot; turning her head this way and that way to speak to the men who were always near her. He had to follow her lithe motions at tennis or croquet, that she often played with the children under the trees. Some days he wanted to see how she spread her bare, white arms, and walked out to meet the foam-crested waves. Even here there were men with her. And then at night, standing alone like a still shadow under the stars, did he not have to listen to her voice when she talked and laughed and sang? Did he not have to follow her slim figure whirling through the dance, in the arms of men who must have loved her and wanted her as he did. He did not dream that they could help it more than he could help it. But the days when she stepped into his boat, the one with the red lateen sail, and sat for hours within a few feet of him, were days that he would have given up for nothing else that he could think of.

III

There were always others in her company at such times, young people with jests and laughter on their lips. Only once she was alone.

She had foolishly brought a book with her, thinking she would want to read. But with the breath of the sea stinging her she could not read a line. She looked precisely as she had looked the day he first saw her, standing outside of the church at Chênière Caminada.

She laid the book down in her lap, and let her soft eyes sweep dreamily along the line of the horizon where the sky and water met. Then she looked straight at Tonie, and for the first time spoke directly to him.

She called him Tonie, as she had heard others do, and questioned him about his boat and his work. He trembled, and answered her vaguely and stupidly. She did not mind, but spoke to him anyhow, satisfied to talk herself when she found that he could not or would not. She spoke French, and talked about the Chênière Caminada, its people and its church. She talked of the day she had played upon the organ there, and complained of the instrument being woefully out of tune.

Tonie was perfectly at home in the familiar task of guiding his boat before the wind that bellied its taut, red sail. He did not seem clumsy and awkward as when he sat in church. The girl noticed that he appeared as strong as an ox.

As she looked at him and surprised one of his shifting glances, a glimmer of the truth began to dawn faintly upon her. She remembered how she had encountered him daily in her path, with his earnest, devouring eyes always seeking her out. She recalled—but there was no need to recall anything. There are women whose perception of passion is very keen; they are the women who most inspire it.

A feeling of complacency took possession of her with this conviction. There was some softness and sympathy mingled with it. She would have liked to lean over and pat his big, brown hand, and tell him she felt sorry and would have helped it if she could. With this belief he ceased to be an object of complete indifference in her eyes. She had thought, awhile before, of having him turn about and take her back home. But now it was really piquant to pose for an hour longer before a man—even a rough fisherman—to whom she felt herself to be an object of silent and consuming devotion. She could think of nothing more interesting to do on shore.

She was incapable of conceiving the full force and extent of his infatuation. She did not dream that under the rude, calm exterior before her a man's heart was beating clamorously, and his reason yielding to the savage instinct of his blood.

"I hear the Angelus ringing at Chênière, Tonie," she said. "I didn't know it was so late; let us go back to the island." There had been a long silence which her musical voice interrupted.

Tonie could now faintly hear the Angelus bell himself. A vision of the church came with it, the odor of incense and the sound of the organ. The girl before him was again that celestial being whom our Lady of Lourdes had once offered to his immortal vision.

It was growing dusk when they landed at the pier, and frogs had begun to croak among the reeds in the pools. There were two of Mlle. Duvigné's usual attendants anxiously awaiting her return. But she chose to let Tonie assist her out of the boat. The touch of her hand fired his blood again.

She said to him very low and half-laughing, "I have no money tonight, Tonie; take this instead," pressing into his palm a delicate silver chain, which she had worn twined about her bare wrist. It was purely a spirit of coquetry that prompted the action, and a touch of the sentimentality which most women possess. She had read in some romance of a young girl doing something like that.

As she walked away between her two attendants she fancied Tonie pressing the chain to his lips. But he was standing quite still, and held it buried in his tightly-closed hand; wanting to hold as long as he might the warmth of the body that still penetrated the bauble when she thrust it into his hand.

He watched her retreating figure like a blotch against the fading sky. He was stirred by a terrible, an overmastering regret, that he had not clasped her in his arms when they were out there alone, and sprung with her into the sea. It was what he had vaguely meant to do when the sound of the Angelus had weakened and palsied his resolution. Now she was going from him, fading away into the mist with those figures on either side of her, leaving him alone. He resolved within himself that if ever again she were out there on the sea at his mercy, she would have to perish in his arms. He would go far, far out where the sound of no bell could reach him. There was some comfort for him in the thought.

But as it happened, Mlle. Duvigné never went out alone in the boat with Tonie again.

IV

It was one morning in January. Tonie had been collecting a bill from one of the fishmongers at the French Market, in New Orleans, and had turned his steps toward St. Philip street. The day was chilly; a keen wind was blowing. Tonie mechanically buttoned his rough, warm coat and crossed over into the sun.

There was perhaps not a more wretched-hearted being in the whole district, that morning, than he. For months the woman he so hopelessly loved had been lost to his sight. But all the more she dwelt in his thoughts, preying upon his mental and bodily forces until his unhappy condition became apparent to all who knew him. Before leaving his home for the winter fishing grounds he had opened his whole heart to his mother, and told her of the trouble that was killing him. She hardly expected that he would ever come back to her when he went away. She feared that he would not, for he had spoken wildly of the rest and peace that could only come to him with death.

That morning when Tonie had crossed St. Philip street he found himself accosted by Madame Lebrun and her mother. He had not noticed them approaching, and, moreover, their figures in winter garb appeared unfamiliar to him. He had never seen them elsewhere than at Grand Isle and the Chênière during the summer. They were glad to meet him, and shook his hand cordially. He stood as usual a little helplessly before them. A pulse in his throat was beating and almost choking him, so poignant were the recollections which their presence stirred up.

They were staying in the city this winter, they told him. They wanted to hear the opera as often as possible, and the island was really too dreary with everyone gone. Madame Lebrun had left her son there to keep order and superintend repairs, and so on.

"You are both well?" stammered Tonie.

"In perfect health, my dear Tonie," Madame Lebrun replied. She was wondering at his haggard eyes and thin, gaunt cheeks; but possessed too much tact to mention them.

"And—the young lady who used to go sailing—is she well?" he inquired lamely.

"You mean Mlle. Favette? She was married just after leaving Grand Isle."

"No; I mean the one you called Claire—Mamzelle Duvigné—is she well?"

Mother and daughter exclaimed together: "Impossible! You haven't heard? Why, Tonie," madame continued, "Mlle. Duvigné died three weeks ago! But that was something sad, I tell you . . . Her family heart-broken . . . Simply from a cold caught by standing in thin slippers, waiting for her carriage after the opera . . . . What a warning!"

The two were talking at once. Tonie kept looking from one to the other. He did not know what they were saying, after madame had told him, "Elle est morte."

As in a dream he finally heard that they said good-by to him, and sent their love to his mother.

He stood still in the middle of the banquette when they had left him, watching them go toward the market. He could not stir. Something had happened to him—he did not know what. He wondered if the news was killing him.

Some women passed by, laughing coarsely. He noticed how they laughed and tossed their heads. A mockingbird was singing in a cage which hung from a window above his head. He had not heard it before.

Just beneath the window was the entrance to a barroom. Tonie turned and plunged through its swinging doors. He asked the bartender for whisky. The man thought he was already drunk, but pushed the bottle toward him nevertheless. Tonie poured a great quantity of the fiery liquor into a glass and swallowed it at a draught. The rest of the day he spent among the fishermen and Barataria oystermen; and that night he slept soundly and peacefully until morning.

He did not know why it was so; he could not understand. But from that day he felt that he began to live again, to be once more a part of the moving world about him. He would ask himself over and over again why it was so, and stay bewildered before this truth that he could not answer or explain, and which he began to accept as a holy mystery.

One day in early spring Tonie sat with his mother upon a piece of drift-wood close to the sea.

He had returned that day to the Chênière Caminada. At first she thought he was like his former self again, for all his old strength and courage had returned. But she found that there was a new brightness in his face which had not been there before. It made her think of the Holy Ghost descending and bringing some kind of light to a man.

She knew that Mademoiselle Duvigné was dead, and all along had feared that this knowledge would be the death of Tonie. When she saw him come back to her like a new being, at once she dreaded that he did not know. All day the doubt had been fretting her, and she could bear the uncertainty no longer.

"You know, Tonie—that young lady whom you cared for—well, some one read it to me in the papers—she died last winter." She had tried to speak as cautiously as she could.

"Yes, I know she is dead. I am glad."

It was the first time he had said this in words, and it made his heart beat quicker.

Ma'me Antoine shuddered and drew aside from him. To her it was somehow like murder to say such a thing.

"What do you mean? Why are you glad?" she demanded, indignantly.

Tonie was sitting with his elbows on his knees. He wanted to answer his mother, but it would take time; he would have to think. He looked out across the water that glistened gem-like with the sun upon it, but there was nothing there to open his thought. He looked down into his open palm and began to pick at the callous flesh that was hard as a horse's hoof. Whilst he did this his ideas began to gather and take form.

"You see, while she lived I could never hope for anything," he began, slowly feeling his way. "Despair was the only thing for me. There were always men about her. She walked and sang and danced with them. I knew it all the time, even when I didn't see her. But I saw her often enough. I knew that some day one of them would please her and she would give herself to him—she would marry him. That thought haunted me like an evil spirit."

Tonie passed his hand across his forehead as if to sweep away anything of the horror that might have remained there.

"It kept me awake at night," he went on. "But that was not so bad; the worst torture was to sleep, for then I would dream that it was all true.

"Oh, I could see her married to one of them—his wife—coming year after year to Grand Isle and bringing her little children with her! I can't tell you all that I saw—all that was driving me mad! But now"—and Tonie clasped his hands together and smiled as he looked again across the water—"she is where she belongs; there is no difference up there; the curé has often told us there is no difference between men. It is with the soul that we approach each other there. Then she will know who has loved her best. That is why I am so contented. Who knows what may happen up there?"

Ma'me Antoine could not answer. She only took her son's big, rough hand and pressed it against her.

"And now, ma mère," he exclaimed, cheerfully, rising, "I shall go light the fire for your bread; it is a long time since I have done anything for you," and he stooped and pressed a warm kiss on her withered old cheek.

With misty eyes she watched him walk away in the direction of the big brick oven that stood open-mouthed under the lemon trees.

A Gentleman of Bayou Têche

It was no wonder Mr. Sublet, who was staying at the Hallet plantation, wanted to make a picture of Evariste. The 'Cadian was rather a picturesque subject in his way, and a tempting one to an artist looking for bits of "local color" along the Têche.

Mr. Sublet had seen the man on the back gallery just as he came out of the swamp, trying to sell a wild turkey to the housekeeper. He spoke to him at once, and in the course of conversation engaged him to return to the house the following morning and have his picture drawn. He handed Evariste a couple of silver dollars to show that his intentions were fair, and that he expected the 'Cadian to keep faith with him.

"He tell' me he want' put my picture in one fine '*Mag*'zine,'" said Evariste to his daughter, Martinette, when the two were talking the matter over in the afternoon. "W'at fo' you reckon he want' do dat?" They sat within the low, homely cabin of two rooms, that was not quite so comfortable as Mr. Hallet's negro quarters.

Martinette pursed her red lips that had little sensitive curves to them, and her black eyes took on a reflective expression.

"Mebbe he yeard 'bout that big fish w'at you ketch las' winta in Carancro lake. You know it was all wrote about in the 'Suga Bowl.'" Her father set aside the suggestion with a deprecatory wave of the hand.

"Well, anyway, you got to fix yo'se'f up," declared Martinette, dismissing further speculation; "put on yo' otha pant'loon an' yo' good coat; an' you betta ax Mr. Léonce to cut yo' hair, an' yo' w'sker' a li'le bit."

"It 's w'at I say," chimed in Evariste. "I tell dat gent'man I 'm goin' make myse'f fine. He say', 'No, no,' like he ent please'. He want' me like

I come out de swamp. So much betta if my pant'loon' an' coat is tore, he say, an' color' like de mud." They could not understand these eccentric wishes on the part of the strange gentleman, and made no effort to do so.

An hour later Martinette, who was quite puffed up over the affair, trotted across to Aunt Dicey's cabin to communicate the news to her. The negress was ironing; her irons stood in a long row before the fire of logs that burned on the hearth. Martinette seated herself in the chimney corner and held her feet up to the blaze; it was damp and a little chilly out of doors. The girl's shoes were considerably worn and her garments were a little too thin and scant for the winter season. Her father had given her the two dollars he had received from the artist, and Martinette was on her way to the store to invest them as judiciously as she knew how.

"You know, Aunt Dicey," she began a little complacently after listening awhile to Aunt Dicey's unqualified abuse of her own son, Wilkins, who was dining-room boy at Mr. Hallet's, "you know that stranger gentleman up to Mr. Hallet's? he want' to make my popa's picture; an' he say' he goin' put it in one fine *Mag*'zine yonda."

Aunt Dicey spat upon her iron to test its heat. Then she began to snicker. She kept on laughing inwardly, making her whole fat body shake, and saying nothing.

"W'at you laughin' 'bout, Aunt Dice?" inquired Martinette mistrustfully.

"I is n' laughin', chile!"

"Yas, you' laughin'."

"Oh, don't pay no 'tention to me. I jis studyin' how simple you an' yo' pa is. You is bof de simplest somebody I eva come 'crost."

"You got to say plumb out w'at you mean, Aunt Dice," insisted the girl doggedly, suspicious and alert now.

"Well, dat w'y I say you is simple," proclaimed the woman, slamming down her iron on an inverted, battered pie pan, "jis like you says, dey gwine put yo' pa's picture yonda in de picture paper. An' you know w'at readin' dey gwine sot down on'neaf dat picture?" Martinette was intensely attentive. "Dey gwine sot down on'neaf: 'Dis heah is one dem low-down 'Cajuns o' Bayeh Têche!' "

The blood flowed from Martinette's face, leaving it deathly pale; in another instant it came beating back in a quick flood, and her eyes smarted with pain as if the tears that filled them had been fiery hot.

"I knows dem kine o' folks," continued Aunt Dicey, resuming her interrupted ironing. "Dat stranger he got a li'le boy w'at ain't none too

big to spank. Dat li'le imp he come a hoppin' in heah yistiddy wid a kine
o' box on'neaf his arm. He say' 'Good mo'nin', madam. Will you be so
kine an' stan' jis like you is dah at yo' i'onin', an' lef me take yo' picture?'
I 'lowed I gwine make a picture outen him wid dis heah flati'on, ef he
don' cl'ar hisse'f quick. An' he say he baig my pardon fo' his intrudement.
All dat kine o' talk to a ole nigga 'oman! Dat plainly sho' he don' know
his place."

"W'at you want 'im to say, Aunt Dice?" asked Martinette, with an
effort to conceal her distress.

"I wants 'im to come in heah an' say: 'Howdy, Aunt Dicey! will you be
so kine and go put on yo' noo calker dress an' yo' bonnit w'at you w'ars
to meetin', an' stan' 'side f'om dat i'onin'-boa'd w'ilse I gwine take yo
photygraph.' Dat de way fo' a boy to talk w'at had good raisin'."

Martinette had arisen, and began to take slow leave of the woman.
She turned at the cabin door to observe tentatively: "I reckon it's Wilkins
tells you how the folks they talk, yonda up to Mr. Hallet's."

She did not go to the store as she had intended, but walked with a
dragging step back to her home. The silver dollars clicked in her pocket
as she walked. She felt like flinging them across the field; they seemed to
her somehow the price of shame.

The sun had sunk, and twilight was settling like a silver beam upon
the bayou and enveloping the fields in a gray mist. Evariste, slim and
slouchy, was waiting for his daughter in the cabin door. He had lighted
a fire of sticks and branches, and placed the kettle before it to boil. He
met the girl with his slow, serious, questioning eyes, astonished to see her
empty-handed.

"How come you did n' bring nuttin' f'om de sto', Martinette?"

She entered and flung her gingham sunbonnet upon a chair. "No, I
did n' go yonda;" and with sudden exasperation: "You got to go take
back that money; you mus' n' git no picture took."

"But, Martinette," her father mildly interposed, "I promise' 'im; an'
he's goin' give me some mo' money w'en he finish."

"If he give you a ba'el o' money, you mus' n' git no picture took. You
know w'at he want to put un'neath that picture, fo' ev'body to read?"
She could not tell him the whole hideous truth as she had heard it distorted
from Aunt Dicey's lips; she would not hurt him that much. "He's goin'
to write: 'This is one *'Cajun* o' the Bayou Têche.' " Evariste winced.

"How you know?" he asked.

"I yeard so. I know it's true."

The water in the kettle was boiling. He went and poured a small quantity upon the coffee which he had set there to drip. Then he said to her: "I reckon you jus' as well go care dat two dolla' back, tomo' mo'nin'; me, I 'll go yonda ketch a mess o' fish in Carancro lake."

Mr. Hallet and a few masculine companions were assembled at a rather late breakfast the following morning. The dining-room was a big, bare one, enlivened by a cheerful fire of logs that blazed in the wide chimney on massive andirons. There were guns, fishing tackle, and other implements of sport lying about. A couple of fine dogs strayed unceremoniously in and out behind Wilkins, the negro boy who waited upon the table. The chair beside Mr. Sublet, usually occupied by his little son, was vacant, as the child had gone for an early morning outing and had not yet returned.

When breakfast was about half over, Mr. Hallet noticed Martinette standing outside upon the gallery. The dining-room door had stood open more than half the time.

"Is n't that Martinette out there, Wilkins?" inquired the jovial-faced young planter.

"Dat 's who, suh," returned Wilkins. "She ben standin' dah sence mos' sun-up; look like she studyin' to take root to de gall'ry."

"What in the name of goodness does she want? Ask her what she wants. Tell her to come in to the fire."

Martinette walked into the room with much hesitancy. Her small, brown face could hardly be seen in the depths of the gingham sun-bonnet. Her blue cottonade skirt scarcely reached the thin ankles that it should have covered.

"Bonjou'," she murmured, with a little comprehensive nod that took in the entire company. Her eyes searched the table for the "stranger gentleman," and she knew him at once, because his hair was parted in the middle and he wore a pointed beard. She went and laid the two silver dollars beside his plate and motioned to retire without a word of explanation.

"Hold on, Martinette!" called out the planter, "what 's all this pantomime business? Speak out, little one."

"My popa don't want any picture took," she offered, a little timorously. On her way to the door she had looked back to say this. In that fleeting glance she detected a smile of intelligence pass from one to the other of the group. She turned quickly, facing them all, and spoke out, excitement making her voice bold and shrill: "My popa ent one low-down 'Cajun. He ent goin' to stan' to have that kine o' writin' put down un'neath his picture!"

She almost ran from the room, half blinded by the emotion that had helped her to make so daring a speech.

Descending the gallery steps she ran full against her father who was ascending, bearing in his arms the little boy, Archie Sublet. The child was most grotesquely attired in garments far too large for his diminutive person—the rough jeans clothing of some negro boy. Evariste himself had evidently been taking a bath without the preliminary ceremony of removing his clothes, that were now half dried upon his person by the wind and sun.

"Yere you' li'le boy," he announced, stumbling into the room. "You ought not lef dat li'le chile go by hisse'f *comme ça* in de pirogue." Mr. Sublet darted from his chair; the others following suit almost as hastily. In an instant, quivering with apprehension, he had his little son in his arms. The child was quite unharmed, only somewhat pale and nervous, as the consequence of a recent very serious ducking.

Evariste related in his uncertain, broken English how he had been fishing for an hour or more in Carancro lake, when he noticed the boy paddling over the deep, black water in a shell-like pirogue. Nearing a clump of cypress-trees that rose from the lake, the pirogue became entangled in the heavy moss that hung from the tree limbs and trailed upon the water. The next thing he knew, the boat had overturned, he heard the child scream, and saw him disappear beneath the still, black surface of the lake.

"W'en I done swim to de sho' wid 'im," continued Evariste, "I hurry yonda to Jake Baptiste's cabin, an' we rub 'im an' warm 'im up, an' dress 'im up dry like you see. He all right now, M'sieur; but you mus'n lef 'im go no mo' by hisse'f in one pirogue."

Martinette had followed into the room behind her father. She was feeling and tapping his wet garments solicitously, and begging him in French to come home. Mr. Hallet at once ordered hot coffee and a warm breakfast for the two; and they sat down at the corner of the table, making no manner of objection in their perfect simplicity. It was with visible reluctance and ill-disguised contempt that Wilkins served them.

When Mr. Sublet had arranged his son comfortably, with tender care, upon the sofa, and had satisfied himself that the child was quite uninjured, he attempted to find words with which to thank Evariste for this service which no treasure of words or gold could pay for. These warm and heart-felt expressions seemed to Evariste to exaggerate the importance of his action, and they intimidated him. He attempted shyly to hide his face as well as he could in the depths of his bowl of coffee.

"You will let me make your picture now, I hope, Evariste," begged Mr. Sublet, laying his hand upon the 'Cadian's shoulder. "I want to place it among things I hold most dear, and shall call it 'A hero of Bayou Têche.' " This assurance seemed to distress Evariste greatly.

"No, no," he protested, "it 's nuttin' hero' to take a li'le boy out de water. I jus' as easy do dat like I stoop down an' pick up a li'le chile w'at fall down in de road. I ent goin' to 'low dat, me. I don't git no picture took, *va!*"

Mr. Hallet, who now discerned his friend's eagerness in the matter, came to his aid.

"I tell you, Evariste, let Mr. Sublet draw your picture, and you yourself may call it whatever you want. I 'm sure he 'll let you."

"Most willingly," agreed the artist.

Evariste glanced up at him with shy and child-like pleasure. "It 's a bargain?" he asked.

"A bargain," affirmed Mr. Sublet.

"Popa," whispered Martinette, "you betta come home an' put on yo' otha pant'loon' an' yo' good coat."

"And now, what shall we call the much talked-of picture?" cheerily inquired the planter, standing with his back to the blaze.

Evariste in a business-like manner began carefully to trace on the table-cloth imaginary characters with an imaginary pen; he could not have written the real characters with a real pen—he did not know how.

"You will put on'neat' de picture," he said, deliberately, " 'Dis is one picture of Mista Evariste Anatole Bonamour, a gent'man of de Bayou Têche.' "

In Sabine

The sight of a human habitation, even if it was a rude log cabin with a mud chimney at one end, was a very gratifying one to Grégoire.

He had come out of Natchitoches parish, and had been riding a great part of the day through the big lonesome parish of Sabine. He was not following the regular Texas road, but, led by his erratic fancy, was pushing toward the Sabine River by circuitous paths through the rolling pine forests.

As he approached the cabin in the clearing, he discerned behind a palisade of pine saplings an old negro man chopping wood.

"Howdy, Uncle," called out the young fellow, reining his horse. The negro looked up in blank amazement at so unexpected an apparition, but he only answered: "How you do, suh," accompanying his speech by a series of polite nods.

"Who lives yere?"

"Hit 's Mas' Bud Aiken w'at live' heah, suh."

"Well, if Mr. Bud Aiken c'n affo'd to hire a man to chop his wood, I reckon he won't grudge me a bite o' suppa an' a couple hours' res' on his gall'ry. W'at you say, ole man?"

"I say dit Mas' Bud Aiken don't hires me to chop 'ood. Ef I don't chop dis heah, his wife got it to do. Dat w'y I chops 'ood, suh. Go right 'long in, suh; you g'ine fine Mas' Bud some'eres roun', ef he ain't drunk an' gone to bed."

Grégoire, glad to stretch his legs, dismounted, and led his horse into the small inclosure which surrounded the cabin. An unkempt, vicious-looking little Texas pony stopped nibbling the stubble there to look maliciously at him and his fine sleek horse, as they passed by. Back of the hut, and running plumb up against the pine wood, was a small, ragged specimen of a cotton-field.

Grégoire was rather undersized, with a square, well-knit figure, upon which his clothes sat well and easily. His corduroy trousers were thrust into the legs of his boots; he wore a blue flannel shirt; his coat was thrown across the saddle. In his keen black eyes had come a puzzled expression, and he tugged thoughtfully at the brown moustache that lightly shaded his upper lip.

He was trying to recall when and under what circumstances he had before heard the name of Bud Aiken. But Bud Aiken himself saved Grégoire the trouble of further speculation on the subject. He appeared suddenly in the small doorway, which his big body quite filled; and then Grégoire remembered. This was the disreputable so-called "Texan" who a year ago had run away with and married Baptiste Choupic's pretty daughter, 'Tite Reine, yonder on Bayou Pierre, in Natchitoches parish. A vivid picture of the girl as he remembered her appeared to him: her trim rounded figure; her piquant face with its saucy black coquettish eyes; her little exacting, imperious ways that had obtained for her the nickname of 'Tite Reine, little queen. Grégoire had known her at the 'Cadian balls that he sometimes had the hardihood to attend.

These pleasing recollections of 'Tite Reine lent a warmth that might otherwise have been lacking to Grégoire's manner, when he greeted her husband.

"I hope I fine you well, Mr. Aiken," he exclaimed cordially, as he approached and extended his hand.

"You find me damn' porely, suh; but you 've got the better o' me, ef I may so say." He was a big good-looking brute, with a straw-colored "horse-shoe" moustache quite concealing his mouth, and a several days' growth of stubble on his rugged face. He was fond of reiterating that women's admiration had wrecked his life, quite forgetting to mention the early and sustained influence of "Pike's Magnolia" and other brands, and wholly ignoring certain inborn propensities capable of wrecking unaided any ordinary existence. He had been lying down, and looked frouzy and half asleep.

"Ef I may so say, you 've got the better o' me, Mr.—er"—

"Santien, Grégoire Santien. I have the pleasure o' knowin' the lady you married, suh; an' I think I met you befo',—somew'ere o' 'nother," Grégoire added vaguely.

"Oh," drawled Aiken, waking up, "one o' them Red River Sanchuns!"

and his face brightened at the prospect before him of enjoying the society of one of the Santien boys. "Mortimer!" he called in ringing chest tones worthy a commander at the head of his troop. The negro had rested his axe and appeared to be listening to their talk, though he was too far to hear what they said.

"Mortimer, come along here an' take my frien' Mr. Sanchun's hoss. Git a move thar, git a move!" Then turning toward the entrance of the cabin he called back through the open door: "Rain!" it was his way of pronouncing 'Tite Reine's name. "Rain!" he cried again peremptorily; and turning to Grégoire: "she 's 'tendin' to some or other housekeepin' truck." 'Tite Reine was back in the yard feeding the solitary pig which they owned, and which Aiken had mysteriously driven up a few days before, saying he had bought it at Many.

Grégoire could hear her calling out as she approached: "I 'm comin', Bud. Yere I come. W'at you want, Bud?" breathlessly, as she appeared in the door frame and looked out upon the narrow sloping gallery where stood the two men. She seemed to Grégoire to have changed a good deal. She was thinner, and her eyes were larger, with an alert, uneasy look in them; he fancied the startled expression came from seeing him there unexpectedly. She wore cleanly homespun garments, the same she had brought with her from Bayou Pierre; but her shoes were in shreds. She uttered only a low, smothered exclamation when she saw Grégoire.

"Well, is that all you got to say to my frien' Mr. Sanchun? That 's the way with them Cajuns," Aiken offered apologetically to his guest; "ain't got sense enough to know a white man when they see one." Grégoire took her hand.

"I 'm mighty glad to see you, 'Tite Reine," he said from his heart. She had for some reason been unable to speak; now she panted somewhat hysterically:—

"You mus' escuse me, Mista Grégoire. It 's the truth I did n' know you firs', stan'in' up there." A deep flush had supplanted the former pallor of her face, and her eyes shone with tears and ill-concealed excitement.

"I thought you all lived yonda in Grant," remarked Grégoire carelessly, making talk for the purpose of diverting Aiken's attention away from his wife's evident embarrassment, which he himself was at a loss to understand.

"Why, we did live a right smart while in Grant; but Grant ain't no parish to make a livin' in. Then I tried Winn and Caddo a spell; they was n't no better. But I tell you, suh, Sabine 's a damn' sight worse than any of 'em. Why, a man can't git a drink o' whiskey here without going out of the parish fer it, or across into Texas. I 'm fixin' to sell out an' try Vernon."

Bud Aiken's household belongings surely would not count for much in the contemplated "selling out." The one room that constituted his home was extremely bare of furnishing,—a cheap bed, a pine table, and a few chairs, that was all. On a rough shelf were some paper parcels representing the larder. The mud daubing had fallen out here and there from between the logs of the cabin; and into the largest of these apertures had been thrust pieces of ragged bagging and wisps of cotton. A tin basin outside on the gallery offered the only bathing facilities to be seen. Notwithstanding these drawbacks, Grégoire announced his intention of passing the night with Aiken.

"I 'm jus' goin' to ask the privilege o' layin' down yere on yo' gall'ry to-night, Mr. Aiken. My hoss ain't in firs'-class trim; an' a night's res' ain't goin' to hurt him o' me either." He had begun by declaring his intention of pushing on across the Sabine, but an imploring look from 'Tite Reine's eyes had stayed the words upon his lips. Never had he seen in a woman's eyes a look of such heartbroken entreaty. He resolved on the instant to know the meaning of it before setting foot on Texas soil. Grégoire had never learned to steel his heart against a woman's eyes, no matter what language they spoke.

An old patchwork quilt folded double and a moss pillow which 'Tite Reine gave him out on the gallery made a bed that was, after all, not too uncomfortable for a young fellow of rugged habits.

Grégoire slept quite soundly after he laid down upon his improvised bed at nine o'clock. He was awakened toward the middle of the night by some one gently shaking him. It was 'Tite Reine stooping over him; he could see her plainly, for the moon was shining. She had not removed the clothing she had worn during the day; but her feet were bare and looked wonderfully small and white. He arose on his elbow, wide awake at once. "W'y, 'Tite Reine! w'at the devil you mean? w'ere 's yo' husban'?"

"The house kin fall on 'im, 't en goin' wake up Bud w'en he 's sleepin'; he drink' too much." Now that she had aroused Grégoire, she stood up, and sinking her face in her bended arm like a child, began to cry softly. In an instant he was on his feet.

"My God, 'Tite Reine! w'at 's the matta? you got to tell me w'at 's the matta." He could no longer recognize the imperious 'Tite Reine, whose will had been the law in her father's household. He led her to the edge of the low gallery and there they sat down.

Grégoire loved women. He liked their nearness, their atmosphere; the tones of their voices and the things they said; their ways of moving and turning about; the brushing of their garments when they passed him by pleased him. He was fleeing now from the pain that a woman had inflicted upon him. When any overpowering sorrow came to Grégoire he felt a singular longing to cross the Sabine River and lose himself in Texas. He had done this once before when his home, the old Santien place, had gone into the hands of creditors. The sight of 'Tite Reine's distress now moved him painfully.

"W'at is it, 'Tite Reine? tell me w'at it is," he kept asking her. She was attempting to dry her eyes on her coarse sleeve. He drew a handkerchief from his back pocket and dried them for her.

"They all well, yonda?" she asked, haltingly, "my popa? my moma? the chil'en?" Grégoire knew no more of the Baptiste Choupic family than the post beside him. Nevertheless he answered: "They all right well, 'Tite Reine, but they mighty lonesome of you."

"My popa, he got a putty good crop this yea'?"

"He made right smart o' cotton fo' Bayou Pierre."

"He done haul it to the relroad?"

"No, he ain't quite finish pickin'."

"I hope they all ent sole 'Putty Girl'?" she inquired solicitously.

"Well, I should say not! Yo' pa says they ain't anotha piece o' hossflesh in the pa'ish he 'd want to swap fo' 'Putty Girl.' " She turned to him with vague but fleeting amazement,—"Putty Girl" was a cow!

The autumn night was heavy about them. The black forest seemed to have drawn nearer; its shadowy depths were filled with the gruesome noises that inhabit a southern forest at night time.

"Ain't you 'fraid sometimes yere, 'Tite Reine?" Grégoire asked, as he felt a light shiver run through him at the weirdness of the scene.

"No," she answered promptly, "I ent 'fred o' nothin' 'cep' Bud."

"Then he treats you mean? I thought so!"

"Mista Grégoire," drawing close to him and whispering in his face, "Bud 's killin' me." He clasped her arm, holding her near him, while an expression of profound pity escaped him. "Nobody don' know, 'cep' Unc' Mort'mer," she went on. "I tell you, he beats me; my back an' arms— you ought to see—it 's all blue. He would 'a' choke' me to death one day w'en he was drunk, if Unc' Mort'mer had n' make 'im lef go—with his axe ov' his head." Grégoire glanced back over his shoulder toward the room where the man lay sleeping. He was wondering if it would really be a criminal act to go then and there and shoot the top of Bud Aiken's head off. He himself would hardly have considered it a crime, but he was not sure of how others might regard the act.

"That 's w'y I wake you up, to tell you," she continued. "Then sometime' he plague me mos' crazy; he tell me 't ent no preacher, it 's a Texas drummer w'at marry him an' me; an' w'en I don' know w'at way to turn no mo', he say no, it 's a Meth'dis' archbishop, an' keep on laughin' 'bout me, an' I don' know w'at the truth!"

Then again, she told how Bud had induced her to mount the vicious little mustang "Buckeye," knowing that the little brute would n't carry a woman; and how it had amused him to witness her distress and terror when she was thrown to the ground.

"If I would know how to read an' write, an' had some pencil an' paper, it 's long 'go I would wrote to my popa. But it 's no pos'office, it 's no relroad,—nothin' in Sabine. An' you know, Mista Grégoire, Bud say he 's goin' carry me yonda to Vernon, an' fu'ther off yet,—'way yonda, an' he 's goin' turn me loose. Oh, don' leave me yere, Mista Grégoire! don' leave me behine you!" she entreated, breaking once more into sobs.

" 'Tite Reine," he answered, "do you think I 'm such a low-down scound'el as to leave you yere with that"—He finished the sentence mentally, not wishing to offend the ears of 'Tite Reine.

They talked on a good while after that. She would not return to the room where her husband lay; the nearness of a friend had already emboldened her to inward revolt. Grégoire induced her to lie down and rest upon the quilt that she had given to him for a bed. She did so, and broken down by fatigue was soon fast asleep.

He stayed seated on the edge of the gallery and began to smoke cigarettes which he rolled himself of périque tobacco. He might have gone in and shared Bud Aiken's bed, but preferred to stay there near 'Tite Reine. He watched the two horses, tramping slowly about the lot, cropping the dewy wet tufts of grass.

Grégoire smoked on. He only stopped when the moon sank down behind the pine-trees, and the long deep shadow reached out and enveloped him. Then he could no longer see and follow the filmy smoke from his cigarette, and he threw it away. Sleep was pressing heavily upon him. He stretched himself full length upon the rough bare boards of the gallery and slept until day-break.

Bud Aiken's satisfaction was very genuine when he learned that Grégoire proposed spending the day and another night with him. He had already recognized in the young creole a spirit not altogether uncongenial to his own.

'Tite Reine cooked breakfast for them. She made coffee; of course there was no milk to add to it, but there was sugar. From a meal bag that stood in the corner of the room she took a measure of meal, and with it made a pone of corn bread. She fried slices of salt pork. Then Bud sent her into the field to pick cotton with old Uncle Mortimer. The negro's cabin was the counterpart of their own, but stood quite a distance away hidden in the woods. He and Aiken worked the crop on shares.

Early in the day Bud produced a grimy pack of cards from behind a parcel of sugar on the shelf. Grégoire threw the cards into the fire and replaced them with a spic and span new "deck" that he took from his saddlebags. He also brought forth from the same receptacle a bottle of whiskey, which he presented to his host, saying that he himself had no further use for it, as he had "sworn off" since day before yesterday, when he had made a fool of himself in Cloutierville.

They sat at the pine table smoking and playing cards all the morning, only desisting when 'Tite Reine came to serve them with the gumbo-filé that she had come out of the field to cook at noon. She could afford to treat a guest to chicken gumbo, for she owned a half dozen chickens that Uncle Mortimer had presented to her at various times. There were only two spoons, and 'Tite Reine had to wait till the men had finished before eating her soup. She waited for Grégoire's spoon, though her husband was the first to get through. It was a very childish whim.

In the afternoon she picked cotton again; and the men played cards, smoked, and Bud drank.

It was a very long time since Bud Aiken had enjoyed himself so well, and since he had encountered so sympathetic and appreciative a listener to the story of his eventful career. The story of 'Tite Reine's fall from the horse he told with much spirit, mimicking quite skillfully the way in which she had complained of never being permitted "to teck a li'le pleasure," whereupon he had kindly suggested horseback riding. Grégoire enjoyed the story amazingly, which encouraged Aiken to relate many more of a similar character. As the afternoon wore on, all formality of address between the two had disappeared: they were "Bud" and

"Grégoire" to each other, and Grégoire had delighted Aiken's soul by promising to spend a week with him. 'Tite Reine was also touched by the spirit of recklessness in the air; it moved her to fry two chickens for supper. She fried them deliciously in bacon fat. After supper she again arranged Grégoire's bed out on the gallery.

The night fell calm and beautiful, with the delicious odor of the pines floating upon the air. But the three did not sit up to enjoy it. Before the stroke of nine, Aiken had already fallen upon his bed unconscious of everything about him in the heavy drunken sleep that would hold him fast through the night. It even clutched him more relentlessly than usual, thanks to Grégoire's free gift of whiskey.

The sun was high when he awoke. He lifted his voice and called imperiously for 'Tite Reine, wondering that the coffee-pot was not on the hearth, and marveling still more that he did not hear her voice in quick response with its, "I 'm comin', Bud. Yere I come." He called again and again. Then he arose and looked out through the back door to see if she were picking cotton in the field, but she was not there. He dragged himself to the front entrance. Grégoire's bed was still on the gallery, but the young fellow was nowhere to be seen.

Uncle Mortimer had come into the yard, not to cut wood this time, but to pick up the axe which was his own property, and lift it to his shoulder.

"Mortimer," called out Aiken, "whur 's my wife?" at the same time advancing toward the negro. Mortimer stood still, waiting for him. "Whur 's my wife an' that Frenchman? Speak out, I say, before I send you to h—l."

Uncle Mortimer never had feared Bud Aiken; and with the trusty axe upon his shoulder, he felt a double hardihood in the man's presence. The old fellow passed the back of his black, knotty hand unctuously over his lips, as though he relished in advance the words that were about to pass them. He spoke carefully and deliberately:

"Miss Reine," he said, "I reckon she mus' of done struck Natchitoches pa'ish sometime to'ard de middle o' de night, on dat 'ar swif' hoss o' Mr. Sanchun's."

Aiken uttered a terrific oath. "Saddle up Buckeye," he yelled, "before I count twenty, or I 'll rip the black hide off yer. Quick, thar! Thur ain't nothin' fourfooted top o' this earth that Buckeye can't run down." Uncle Mortimer scratched his head dubiously, as he answered:—

"Yas, Mas' Bud, but you see, Mr. Sanchun, he done cross de Sabine befo' sun-up on Buckeye."

A Respectable Woman

Mrs. Baroda was a little provoked to learn that her husband expected his friend, Gouvernail, up to spend a week or two on the plantation.

They had entertained a good deal during the winter; much of the time had also been passed in New Orleans in various forms of mild dissipation. She was looking forward to a period of unbroken rest, now, and undisturbed tête-à-tête with her husband, when he informed her that Gouvernail was coming up to stay a week or two.

This was a man she had heard much of but never seen. He had been her husband's college friend; was now a journalist, and in no sense a society man or "a man about town," which were, perhaps, some of the reasons she had never met him. But she had unconsciously formed an image of him in her mind. She pictured him tall, slim, cynical; with eye-glasses, and his hands in his pockets; and she did not like him. Gouvernail was slim enough, but he wasn't very tall nor very cynical; neither did he wear eye-glasses nor carry his hands in his pockets. And she rather liked him when he first presented himself.

But why she liked him she could not explain satisfactorily to herself when she partly attempted to do so. She could discover in him none of those brilliant and promising traits which Gaston, her husband, had often assured her that he possessed. On the contrary, he sat rather mute and receptive before her chatty eagerness to make him feel at home and in face of Gaston's frank and wordy hospitality. His manner was as courteous toward her as the most exacting woman could require; but he made no direct appeal to her approval or even esteem.

Once settled at the plantation he seemed to like to sit upon the wide portico in the shade of one of the big Corinthian pillars, smoking his cigar lazily and listening attentively to Gaston's experience as a sugar planter.

"This is what I call living," he would utter with deep satisfaction, as the air that swept across the sugar field caressed him with its warm and scented velvety touch. It pleased him also to get on familiar terms with the big dogs that came about him, rubbing themselves sociably against his legs. He did not care to fish, and displayed no eagerness to go out and kill grosbecs when Gaston proposed doing so.

Gouvernail's personality puzzled Mrs. Baroda, but she liked him. Indeed, he was a lovable, inoffensive fellow. After a few days, when she could understand him no better than at first, she gave over being puzzled and remained piqued. In this mood she left her husband and her guest, for the most part, alone together. Then finding that Gouvernail took no manner of exception to her action, she imposed her society upon him, accompanying him in his idle strolls to the mill and walks along the batture. She persistently sought to penetrate the reserve in which he had unconsciously enveloped himself.

"When is he going—your friend?" she one day asked her husband. "For my part, he tires me frightfully."

"Not for a week yet, dear. I can't understand; he gives you no trouble."

"No. I should like him better if he did; if he were more like others, and I had to plan somewhat for his comfort and enjoyment."

Gaston took his wife's pretty face between his hands and looked tenderly and laughingly into her troubled eyes. They were making a bit of toilet sociably together in Mrs. Baroda's dressing-room.

"You are full of surprises, ma belle," he said to her. "Even I can never count upon how you are going to act under given conditions." He kissed her and turned to fasten his cravat before the mirror.

"Here you are," he went on, "taking poor Gouvernail seriously and making a commotion over him, the last thing he would desire or expect."

"Commotion!" she hotly resented. "Nonsense! How can you say such a thing? Commotion, indeed! But, you know, you said he was clever."

"So he is. But the poor fellow is run down by overwork now. That's why I asked him here to take a rest."

"You used to say he was a man of ideas," she retorted, unconciliated. "I expected him to be interesting, at least. I'm going to the city in the morning to have my spring gowns fitted. Let me know when Mr. Gouvernail is gone; I shall be at my Aunt Octavie's."

That night she went and sat alone upon a bench that stood beneath a live oak tree at the edge of the gravel walk.

She had never known her thoughts or her intentions to be so confused. She could gather nothing from them but the feeling of a distinct necessity to quit her home in the morning.

Mrs. Baroda heard footsteps crunching the gravel; but could discern in the darkness only the approaching red point of a lighted cigar. She knew it was Gouvernail, for her husband did not smoke. She hoped to remain unnoticed, but her white gown revealed her to him. He threw away his cigar and seated himself upon the bench beside her; without a suspicion that she might object to his presence.

"Your husband told me to bring this to you, Mrs. Baroda," he said, handing her a filmy, white scarf with which she sometimes enveloped her head and shoulders. She accepted the scarf from him with a murmur of thanks, and let it lie in her lap.

He made some commonplace observation upon the baneful effect of the night air at that season. Then as his gaze reached out into the darkness, he murmured, half to himself:

" 'Night of south winds—night of the large few stars!
Still nodding night—' "

She made no reply to this apostrophe to the night, which indeed, was not addressed to her.

Gouvernail was in no sense a diffident man, for he was not a self-conscious one. His periods of reserve were not constitutional, but the result of moods. Sitting there beside Mrs. Baroda, his silence melted for the time.

He talked freely and intimately in a low, hesitating drawl that was not unpleasant to hear. He talked of the old college days when he and Gaston had been a good deal to each other; of the days of keen and blind ambitions and large intentions. Now there was left with him, at least, a philosophic acquiescence to the existing order—only a desire to be permitted to exist, with now and then a little whiff of genuine life, such as he was breathing now.

Her mind only vaguely grasped what he was saying. Her physical being was for the moment predominant. She was not thinking of his words, only drinking in the tones of his voice. She wanted to reach out her hand in the darkness and touch him with the sensitive tips of her fingers upon the face or the lips. She wanted to draw close to him and whisper against his cheek—she did not care what—as she might have done if she had not been a respectable woman.

The stronger the impulse grew to bring herself near him, the further, in fact, did she draw away from him. As soon as she could do so without an appearance of too great rudeness, she rose and left him there alone.

Before she reached the house, Gouvernail had lighted a fresh cigar and ended his apostrophe to the night.

Mrs. Baroda was greatly tempted that night to tell her husband—who was also her friend—of this folly that had seized her. But she did not yield to the temptation. Beside being a respectable woman she was a very sensible one; and she knew there are some battles in life which a human being must fight alone.

When Gaston arose in the morning, his wife had already departed. She had taken an early morning train to the city. She did not return till Gouvernail was gone from under her roof.

There was some talk of having him back during the summer that followed. That is, Gaston greatly desired it; but this desire yielded to his wife's strenuous opposition.

However, before the year ended, she proposed, wholly from herself, to have Gouvernail visit them again. Her husband was surprised and delighted with the suggestion coming from her.

"I am glad, chère amie, to know that you have finally overcome your dislike for him; truly he did not deserve it."

"Oh," she told him, laughingly, after pressing a long, tender kiss upon his lips, "I have overcome everything! you will see. This time I shall be very nice to him."

Tante Cat'rinette

It happened just as every one had predicted. Tante Cat'rinette was beside herself with rage and indignation when she learned that the town authorities had for some reason condemned her house and intended to demolish it.

"Dat house w'at Vieumaite gi' me his own se'f, out his own mout', w'en he gi' me my freedom! All wrote down en règle befo' de cote! Bon dieu Seigneur, w'at dey talkin' 'bout!"

Tante Cat'rinette stood in the doorway of her home, resting a gaunt black hand against the jamb. In the other hand she held her corncob pipe. She was a tall, large-boned woman of a pronounced Congo type. The house in question had been substantial enough in its time. It contained four rooms: the lower two of brick, the upper ones of adobe. A dilapidated gallery projected from the upper story and slanted over the narrow banquette, to the peril of passers-by.

"I don't think I ever heard why the property was given to you in the first place, Tante Cat'rinette," observed Lawyer Paxton, who had stopped in passing, as so many others did, to talk the matter over with the old negress. The affair was attracting some attention in town, and its development was being watched with a good deal of interest. Tante Cat'rinette asked nothing better than to satisfy the lawyer's curiosity.

"Vieumaite all time say Cat'rinette wort' gole to 'im; de way I make dem nigga' walk chalk. But," she continued, with recovered seriousness, "w'en I nuss 'is li'le gal w'at all de doctor' 'low it 's goin' die, an' I make it well, me, den Vieumaite, he can't do 'nough, him. He name' dat li'le gal Cat'rine fo' me. Das Miss Kitty w'at marry Miché Raymond yon' by Gran' Eco'. Den he gi' me my freedom; he got plenty slave', him;

337

one don' count in his pocket. An' he gi' me dat house w'at I'm stan'in' in de do'; he got plenty house' an' lan', him. Now dey want pay me t'ousan' dolla', w'at I don' axen' fo', an' tu'n me out dat house! I waitin' fo' 'em, Miché Paxtone," and a wicked gleam shot into the woman's small, dusky eyes. "I got my axe grine fine. Fus' man w'at touch Cat'rinette fo' tu'n her out dat house, he git 'is head bus' like I bus' a gode."

"Dat's nice day, ainty, Miché Paxtone? Fine wedda fo' dry my close." Upon the gallery above hung an array of shirts, which gleamed white in the sunshine, and flapped in the rippling breeze.

The spectacle of Tante Cat'rinette defying the authorities was one which offered much diversion to the children of the neighborhood. They played numberless pranks at her expense; daily serving upon her fictitious notices purporting to be to the last degree official. One youngster, in a moment of inspiration, composed a couplet, which they recited, sang, shouted at all hours, beneath her windows.

> "Tante Cat'rinette, she go in town;
> W'en she come back, her house pull' down."

So ran the production. She heard it many times during the day, but, far from offending her, she accepted it as a warning,—a prediction, as it were,—and she took heed not to offer to fate the conditions for its fulfillment. She no longer quitted her house even for a moment, so great was her fear and so firm her belief that the town authorities were lying in wait to possess themselves of it. She would not cross the street to visit a neighbor. She waylaid passers-by and pressed them into service to do her errands and small shopping. She grew distrustful and suspicious, ever on the alert to scent a plot in the most innocent endeavor to induce her to leave the house.

One morning, as Tante Cat'rinette was hanging out her latest batch of washing, Eusèbe, a "free mulatto" from Red River, stopped his pony beneath her gallery.

"Hé, Tante Cat'rinette!" he called up to her.

She turned to the railing just as she was, in her bare arms and neck that gleamed ebony-like against the unbleached cotton of her chemise. A coarse skirt was fastened about her waist, and a string of many-colored beads knotted around her throat. She held her smoking pipe between her yellow teeth.

"How you all come on, Miché Eusèbe?" she questioned, pleasantly.

"We all middlin', Tante Cat'rinette. But Miss Kitty, she putty bad

off out yon'a. I see Mista Raymond dis mo'nin' w'en I pass by his house;
he say look like de feva don' wan' to quit 'er. She been axen' fo' you all
t'rough de night. He 'low he reckon I betta tell you. Nice wedda we got
fo' plantin', Tante Cat'rinette."

"Nice wedda fo' lies, Miché Eusèbe," and she spat contemptuously
down upon the banquette. She turned away without noticing the man
further, and proceeded to hang one of Lawyer Paxton's fine linen shirts
upon the line.

"She been axen' fo' you all t'rough de night."

Somehow Tante Cat'rinette could not get that refrain out of her head.
She would not willingly believe that Eusèbe had spoken the truth, but—
"She been axen fo' you all t'rough de night—all t'rough de night." The
words kept ringing in her ears, as she came and went about her daily
tasks. But by degrees she dismissed Eusèbe and his message from her
mind. It was Miss Kitty's voice that she could hear in fancy following
her, calling out through the night, "W'ere Tante Cat'rinette? W'y
Tante Cat'rinette don' come? W'y she don' come—w'y she don'
come?"

All day the woman muttered and mumbled to herself in her Creole
patois; invoking council of "Vieumaite," as she always did in her troubles.
Tante Cat'rinette's religion was peculiarly her own; she turned to heaven
with her grievances, it is true, but she felt that there was no one in
Paradise with whom she was quite so well acquainted as with "Vieumaite."

Late in the afternoon she went and stood on her doorstep, and looked
uneasily and anxiously out upon the almost deserted street. When a little
girl came walking by,—a sweet child with a frank and innocent face,
upon whose word she knew she could rely,—Tante Cat'rinette invited
her to enter.

"Come yere see Tante Cat'rinette, Lolo. It's long time you en't come
see Tante Cat'rine; you gittin' proud." She made the little one sit down,
and offered her a couple of cookies, which the child accepted with pretty
avidity.

"You putty good li'le gal, you, Lolo. You keep on go confession all de
time?"

"Oh, yes. I'm goin' make my firs' communion firs' of May, Tante
Cat'rinette." A dog-eared catechism was sticking out of Lolo's apron
pocket.

"Das right; be good li'le gal. Mine yo' maman ev't'ing she say; an' neva tell no story. It's nuttin' bad in dis worl' like tellin' lies. You know Eusèbe?"

"Eusèbe?"

"Yas; dat li'le ole Red River free m'latto. Uh, uh! dat one man w'at kin tell lies, yas! He come tell me Miss Kitty down sick yon'a. You ev' yeard such big story like dat, Lolo?"

The child looked a little bewildered, but she answered promptly, " 'Tain't no story, Tante Cat'rinette. I yeard papa sayin', dinner time, Mr. Raymond sen' fo' Dr. Chalon. An' Dr. Chalon says he ain't got time to go yonda. An' papa says it's because Dr. Chalon on'y want to go w'ere it's rich people; an' he's 'fraid Mista Raymond ain' goin' pay 'im."

Tante Cat'rinette admired the little girl's pretty gingham dress, and asked her who had ironed it. She stroked her brown curls, and talked of all manner of things quite foreign to the subject of Eusèbe and his wicked propensity for telling lies.

She was not restless as she had been during the early part of the day, and she no longer mumbled and muttered as she had been doing over her work.

At night she lighted her coal-oil lamp, and placed it near a window where its light could be seen from the street through the half-closed shutters. Then she sat herself down, erect and motionless, in a chair.

When it was near upon midnight, Tante Cat'rinette arose, and looked cautiously, very cautiously, out of the door. Her house lay in the line of deep shadow that extended along the street. The other side was bathed in the pale light of the declining moon. The night was agreeably mild, profoundly still, but pregnant with the subtle quivering life of early spring. The earth seemed asleep and breathing,—a scent-laden breath that blew in soft puffs against Tante Cat'rinette's face as she emerged from the house. She closed and locked her door noiselessly; then she crept slowly away, treading softly, stealthily as a cat, in the deep shadow.

There were but few people abroad at that hour. Once she ran upon a gay party of ladies and gentlemen who had been spending the evening over cards and anisette. They did not notice Tante Cat'rinette almost effacing herself against the black wall of the cathedral. She breathed freely and ventured from her retreat only when they had disappeared from view. Once a man saw her quite plainly, as she darted across a narrow strip of moonlight. But Tante Cat'rinette need not have gasped with fright as she did. He was too drunk to know if she were a thing of flesh, or only one of the fantastic, maddening shadows that the moon was casting across his path to bewilder him. When she reached the outskirts of the town, and had to cross the broad piece of open country which stretched out toward the pine wood, an almost paralyzing terror came over her. But she crouched low, and hurried through the marsh and weeds, avoiding the open road. She could have been mistaken for one of the beasts browsing there where she passed.

But once in the Grand Ecore road that lay through the pine wood, she felt secure and free to move as she pleased. Tante Cat'rinette straightened herself, stiffened herself in fact, and unconsciously assuming the attitude of the professional sprinter, she sped rapidly beneath the Gothic interlacing branches of the pines. She talked constantly to herself as she went, and to the animate and inanimate objects around her. But her speech, far from intelligent, was hardly intelligible.

She addressed herself to the moon, which she apostrophized as an impertinent busybody spying upon her actions. She pictured all manner of troublesome animals, snakes, rabbits, frogs, pursuing her, but she defied them to catch Cat'rinette, who was hurrying toward Miss Kitty. "Pa capab trapé Cat'rinette, vouzot; mo pé couri vite coté Miss Kitty." She called up to a mocking-bird warbling upon a lofty limb of a pine tree, asking why it cried out so, and threatening to secure it and put it into a cage. "Ca to pé crié comme ça, ti céléra? Arete, mo trapé zozos la, mo mété li dan ain bon lacage." Indeed, Tante Cat'rinette seemed on very familiar terms with the night, with the forest, and with all the flying, creeping, crawling things that inhabit it. At the speed with which she traveled she soon had covered the few miles of wooded road, and before long had reached her destination.

The sleeping-room of Miss Kitty opened upon the long outside gallery, as did all the rooms of the unpretentious frame house which was her home. The place could hardly be called a plantation; it was too small for that. Nevertheless Raymond was trying to plant; trying to teach school between times, in the end room; and sometimes, when he found himself in a tight place, trying to clerk for Mr. Jacobs over in Campte, across Red River.

Tante Cat'rinette mounted the creaking steps, crossed the gallery, and entered Miss Kitty's room as though she were returning to it after a few moments' absence. There was a lamp burning dimly upon the high mantelpiece. Raymond had evidently not been to bed; he was in shirt sleeves, rocking the baby's cradle. It was the same mahogany cradle which had held Miss Kitty thirty-five years before, when Tante Cat'rinette

had rocked it. The cradle had been bought then to match the bed,—
that big, beautiful bed on which Miss Kitty lay now in a restless half
slumber. There was a fine French clock on the mantel, still telling the
hours as it had told them years ago. But there were no carpets or rugs
on the floors. There was no servant in the house.

Raymond uttered an exclamation of amazement when he saw Tante
Cat'rinette enter.

"How you do, Miché Raymond?" she said, quietly. "I yeard Miss
Kitty been sick; Eusèbe tell me dat dis mo'nin'."

She moved toward the bed as lightly as though shod with velvet, and
seated herself there. Miss Kitty's hand lay outside the coverlid; a shapely
hand, which her few days of illness and rest had not yet softened. The
negress laid her own black hand upon it. At the touch Miss Kitty instinctively turned her palm upward.

"It's Tante Cat'rinette!" she exclaimed, with a note of satisfaction in
her feeble voice. "W'en did you come, Tante Cat'rinette? They all said
you wouldn' come."

"I'm goin' come ev'y night, cher coeur, ev'y night tell you be well.
Tante Cat'rinette can't come daytime no mo'."

"Raymond tole me about it. They doin' you mighty mean in town,
Tante Cat'rinette."

"Nev' mine, ti chou. I know how take care dat w'at Vieumaite gi' me.
You go sleep now. Cat'rinette goin' set yere an' mine you. She goin' make
you well like she all time do. We don' wan' no céléra doctor. We drive
'em out wid a stick, dey come roun' yere."

Miss Kitty was soon sleeping more restfully than she had done since
her illness began. Raymond had finally succeeded in quieting the baby,
and he tiptoed into the adjoining room, where the other children lay, to
snatch a few hours of much-needed rest for himself. Cat'rinette sat faithfully beside her charge, administering at intervals to the sick woman's
wants.

But the thought of regaining her home before daybreak, and of the
urgent necessity for doing so, did not leave Tante Cat'rinette's mind for
an instant.

In the profound darkness, the deep stillness of the night that comes
before dawn, she was walking again through the woods, on her way back
to town.

The mocking-birds were asleep, and so were the frogs and the snakes;
and the moon was gone, and so was the breeze. She walked now in utter

silence but for the heavy guttural breathing that accompanied her rapid footsteps. She walked with a desperate determination along the road, every foot of which was familiar to her.

When she at last emerged from the woods, the earth about her was faintly, very faintly, beginning to reveal itself in the tremulous, gray, uncertain light of approaching day. She staggered and plunged onward with beating pulses quickened by fear.

A sudden turn, and Tante Cat'rinette stood facing the river. She stopped abruptly, as if at command of some unseen power that forced her. For an instant she pressed a black hand against her tired, burning eyes, and stared fixedly ahead of her.

Tante Cat'rinette had always believed that Paradise was up there overhead where the sun and stars and moon are, and that "Vieumaite" inhabited that region of splendor. She never for a moment doubted this. It would be difficult, perhaps unsatisfying, to explain why Tante Cat'rinette, on that particular morning, when a vision of the rising day broke suddenly upon her, should have believed that she stood in face of a heavenly revelation. But why not, after all? Since she talked so familiarly herself to the unseen, why should it not respond to her when the time came?

Across the narrow, quivering line of water, the delicate budding branches of young trees were limned black against the gold, orange,— what word is there to tell the color of that morning sky! And steeped in the splendor of it hung one pale star; there was not another in the whole heaven.

Tante Cat'rinette stood with her eyes fixed intently upon that star, which held her like a hypnotic spell. She stammered breathlessly:

"Mo pé couté, Vieumaite. Cat'rinette pé couté." (I am listening, Vieumaite. Cat'rinette hears you.)

She stayed there motionless upon the brink of the river till the star melted into the brightness of the day and became part of it.

When Tante Cat'rinette entered Miss Kitty's room for the second time, the aspect of things had changed somewhat. Miss Kitty was with much difficulty holding the baby while Raymond mixed a saucer of food for the little one. Their oldest daughter, a child of twelve, had come into the room with an apronful of chips from the woodpile, and was striving to start a fire on the hearth, to make the morning coffee. The room seemed bare and almost squalid in the daylight.

"Well, yere Tante Cat'rinette come back," she said, quietly announcing herself.

They could not well understand why she was back; but it was good to have her there, and they did not question.

She took the baby from its mother, and, seating herself, began to feed it from the saucer which Raymond placed beside her on a chair.

"Yas," she said, "Cat'rinette goin' stay; dis time she en't nev' goin' 'way no mo'.'"

Husband and wife looked at each other with surprised, questioning eyes.

"Miché Raymond," remarked the woman, turning her head up to him with a certain comical shrewdness in her glance, "if somebody want len' you t'ousan' dolla', w'at you goin' say? Even if it's ole nigga 'oman?"

The man's face flushed with sudden emotion. "I would say that person was our bes' frien', Tante Cat'rinette. An'," he added, with a smile, "I would give her a mortgage on the place, of co'se, to secu' her f'om loss."

"Das right," agreed the woman practically. "Den Cat'rinette goin' len' you t'ousan' dolla'. Dat w'at Vieumaite give her, dat b'long to her; don' b'long to nobody else. An' we go yon'a to town, Miché Raymond, you an' me. You care me befo' Miché Paxtone. I want 'im fo' put down in writin' befo' de cote dat w'at Cat'rinette got, it fo' Miss Kitty w'en I be dead."

Miss Kitty was crying softly in the depths of her pillow.

"I en't got no head fo' all dat, me," laughed Tante Cat'rinette, good humoredly, as she held a spoonful of pap up to the baby's eager lips. "It's Vieumaite tell me all dat clair an' plain dis mo'nin', w'en I comin' 'long de Gran' Eco' road."

A Dresden Lady in Dixie

Madame Valtour had been in the sitting-room some time before she noticed the absence of the Dresden china figure from the corner of the mantel-piece, where it had stood for years. Aside from the intrinsic value of the piece, there were some very sad and tender memories associated with it. A baby's lips that were now forever still had loved once to kiss the painted "pitty 'ady"; and the baby arms had often held it in a close and smothered embrace.

Madame Valtour gave a rapid, startled glance around the room, to see perchance if it had been misplaced; but she failed to discover it.

Viny, the house-maid, when summoned, remembered having carefully dusted it that morning, and was rather indignantly positive that she had not broken the thing to bits and secreted the pieces.

"Who has been in the room during my absence?" questioned Madame Valtour, with asperity. Viny abandoned herself to a moment's reflection.

"Pa-Jeff comed in yere wid de mail—" If she had said St. Peter came in with the mail, the fact would have had as little bearing on the case from Madame Valtour's point of view.

Pa-Jeff's uprightness and honesty were so long and firmly established as to have become proverbial on the plantation. He had not served the family faithfully since boyhood and been all through the war with "old Marse Valtour" to descend at his time of life to tampering with household bric-a-brac.

"Has any one else been here?" Madame Valtour naturally inquired.

"On'y Agapie w'at brung you some Creole aiggs. I tole 'er to sot 'em down in de hall. I don' know she comed in de settin'-room o' not."

Yes, there they were; eight, fresh "Creole eggs" reposing on the muslin in the sewing basket. Viny herself had been seated on the gallery brushing her mistress' gowns during the hours of that lady's absence, and could think of no one else having penetrated to the sitting-room.

Madame Valtour did not entertain the thought that Agapie had stolen the relic. Her worst fear was, that the girl, finding herself alone in the room, had handled the frail bit of porcelain and inadvertently broken it.

Agapie came often to the house to play with the children and amuse them—she loved nothing better. Indeed, no other spot known to her on earth so closely embodied her confused idea of paradise, as this home with its atmosphere of love, comfort and good cheer. She was, herself, a cheery bit of humanity, overflowing with kind impulses and animal spirits.

Madame Valtour recalled the fact that Agapie had often admired this Dresden figure (but what had she not admired!); and she remembered having heard the girl's assurance that if ever she became possessed of "fo' bits" to spend as she liked, she would have some one buy her just such a china doll in town or in the city.

Before night, the fact that the Dresden lady had strayed from her proud eminence on the sitting-room mantel, became, through Viny's indiscreet babbling, pretty well known on the place.

The following morning Madame Valtour crossed the field and went over to the Bedauts' cabin. The cabins on the plantation were not grouped; but each stood isolated upon the section of land which its occupants cultivated. Pa-Jeff's cabin was the only one near enough to the Bedauts to admit of neighborly intercourse.

Seraphine Bedaut was sitting on her small gallery, stringing red peppers, when Madame Valtour approached.

"I'm so distressed, Madame Bedaut," began the planter's wife, abruptly. But the 'Cadian woman arose politely and interrupted, offering her visitor a chair.

"Come in, set down, Ma'me Valtour."

"No, no; it's only for a moment. You know, Madame Bedaut, yesterday when I returned from making a visit, I found that an ornament was missing from my sitting-room mantel-piece. It's a thing I prize very, very much—" with sudden tears filling her eyes—"and I would not willingly part with it for many times its value." Seraphine Bedaut was listening, with her mouth partly open, looking, in truth, stupidly puzzled.

"No one entered the room during my absence," continued Madame

Valtour, "but Agapie." Seraphine's mouth snapped like a steel trap and her black eyes gleamed with a flash of anger.

"You wan' say Agapie stole some'in' in yo' house!" she cried out in a shrill voice, tremulous from passion.

"No; oh no! I'm sure Agapie is an honest girl and we all love her; but you know how children are. It was a small Dresden figure. She may have handled and broken the thing and perhaps is afraid to say so. She may have thoughtlessly misplaced it; oh, I don't know what! I want to ask if she saw it."

"Come in; you got to come in, Ma'me Valtour," stubbornly insisted Seraphine, leading the way into the cabin. "I sen' 'er to de house yistiddy wid some Creole aiggs," she went on in her rasping voice, "like I all time do, because you all say you can't eat dem sto' aiggs no mo'. Yere de basket w'at I sen' 'em in," reaching for an Indian basket which hung against the wall—and which was partly filled with cotton seed.

"Oh, never mind," interrupted Madame Valtour, now thoroughly distressed at witnessing the woman's agitation.

"Ah, bien non. I got to show you, Agapie en't no mo' thief 'an yo' own child'en is." She led the way into the adjoining room of the hut.

"Yere all her things w'at she 'muse herse'f wid," continued Seraphine, pointing to a soapbox which stood on the floor just beneath the open window. The box was filled with an indescribable assortment of odds and ends, mostly doll-rags. A catechism and a blue-backed speller poked dog-eared corners from out of the confusion; for the Valtour children were making heroic and patient efforts toward Agapie's training.

Seraphine cast herself upon her knees before the box and dived her thin brown hands among its contents. "I wan' show you; I goin' show you," she kept repeating excitedly. Madame Valtour was standing beside her.

Suddenly the woman drew forth from among the rags, the Dresden lady, as dapper, sound, and smiling as ever. Seraphine's hand shook so violently that she was in danger of letting the image fall to the floor. Madame Valtour reached out and took it very quietly from her. Then Seraphine rose tremblingly to her feet and broke into a sob that was pitiful to hear.

Agapie was approaching the cabin. She was a chubby girl of twelve. She walked with bare, callous feet over the rough ground and bare-headed under the hot sun. Her thick, short, black hair covered her head like a mane. She had been dancing along the path, but slackened her pace upon catching sight of the two women who had returned to the gallery. But when she perceived that her mother was crying she darted impetuously forward. In an instant she had her arms around her mother's neck, clinging so tenaciously in her youthful strength as to make the frail woman totter.

Agapie had seen the Dresden figure in Madame Valtour's possession and at once guessed the whole accusation.

"It en't so! I tell you, maman, it en't so! I neva touch' it. Stop cryin'; stop cryin'!" and she began to cry most piteously herself.

"But Agapie, we fine it in yo' box," moaned Seraphine through her sobs.

"Then somebody put it there. Can't you see somebody put it there? 'Ten't so, I tell you."

The scene was extremely painful to Madame Valtour. Whatever she might tell these two later, for the time she felt herself powerless to say anything befitting, and she walked away. But she turned to remark, with a hardness of expression and intention which she seldom displayed: "No one will know of this through me. But, Agapie, you must not come into my house again; on account of the children; I could not allow it."

As she walked away she could hear Agapie comforting her mother with renewed protestations of innocence.

Pa-Jeff began to fail visibly that year. No wonder, considering his great age, which he computed to be about one hundred. It was, in fact, some ten years less than that, but a good old age all the same. It was seldom that he got out into the field; and then, never to do any heavy work—only a little light hoeing. There were days when the "misery" doubled him up and nailed him down to his chair so that he could not set foot beyond the door of his cabin. He would sit there courting the sunshine and blinking, as he gazed across the fields with the patience of the savage.

The Bedauts seemed to know almost instinctively when Pa-Jeff was sick. Agapie would shade her eyes and look searchingly towards the old man's cabin.

"I don' see Pa-Jeff this mo'nin'," or "Pa-Jeff en't open his winda," or "I didn' see no smoke yet yonda to Pa-Jeff's." And in a little while the girl would be over there with a pail of soup or coffee, or whatever there was at hand which she thought the old negro might fancy. She had lost all the color out of her cheeks and was pining like a sick bird.

She often sat on the steps of the gallery and talked with the old man while she waited for him to finish his soup from her tin pail.

"I tell you, Pa-Jeff, its neva been no thief in the Bedaut family. My pa say he couldn' hole up his head if he think I been a thief, me. An' maman say it would make her sick in bed, she don' know she could ever git up. Sosthène tell me the chil'en been cryin' fo' me up yonda. Li'le Lulu cry so hard M'sieur Valtour want sen' afta me, an' Ma'me Valtour say no."

And with this, Agapie flung herself at length upon the gallery with her face buried in her arms, and began to cry so hysterically as seriously to alarm Pa-Jeff. It was well he had finished his soup, for he could not have eaten another mouthful.

"Hole up yo' head, chile. God save us! W'at you kiarrin' on dat away?" he exclaimed in great distress. "You gwine to take a fit? Hole up yo' head."

Agapie rose slowly to her feet, and drying her eyes upon the sleeve of her "josie," reached out for the tin bucket. Pa-Jeff handed it to her, but without relinquishing his hold upon it.

"War hit you w'at tuck it?" he questioned in a whisper. "I isn' gwine tell; you knows I isn' gwine tell." She only shook her head, attempting to draw the pail forcibly away from the old man.

"Le' me go, Pa-Jeff. W'at you doin'! Gi' me my bucket!"

He kept his old blinking eyes fastened for a while questioningly upon her disturbed and tear-stained face. Then he let her go and she turned and ran swiftly away towards her home.

He sat very still watching her disappear; only his furrowed old face twitched convulsively, moved by an unaccustomed train of reasoning that was at work in him.

"She w'ite, I is black," he muttered calculatingly. "She young, I is ole; sho I is ole. She good to Pa-Jeff like I her own kin an' color." This line of thought seemed to possess him to the exclusion of every other. Late in the night he was still muttering.

"Sho I is ole. She good to Pa-Jeff, yas."

A few days later, when Pa-Jeff happened to be feeling comparatively well, he presented himself at the house just as the family had assembled at their early dinner. Looking up suddenly, Monsieur Valtour was astonished to see him standing there in the room near the open door. He leaned upon his cane and his grizzled head was bowed upon his breast. There was general satisfaction expressed at seeing Pa-Jeff on his legs once more.

"Why, old man, I'm glad to see you out again," exclaimed the planter, cordially, pouring a glass of wine, which he instructed Viny to hand to the old fellow. Pa-Jeff accepted the glass and set it solemnly down upon a small table near by.

"Marse Albert," he said, "I is come heah to-day fo' to make a statement of de rights an' de wrongs w'at is done hang heavy on my soul dis heah long time. Arter you heahs me an' de missus heahs me an' de chillun an' ev'body, den ef you says: 'Pa-Jeff you kin tech yo' lips to dat glass o' wine,' all well an' right.' "

His manner was impressive and caused the family to exchange surprised and troubled glances. Foreseeing that his recital might be long, a chair was offered to him, but he declined it.

"One day," he began, "w'en I ben hoein' de madam's flower bed close to de fence, Sosthène he ride up, he say: 'Heah, Pa-Jeff, heah de mail.' I takes de mail f'om 'im an' I calls out to Viny w'at settin' on de gallery: 'Heah Marse Albert's mail, gal; come git it.'

"But Viny she answer, pert-like—des like Viny: 'You is got two laigs, Pa-Jeff, des well as me.' I ain't no han' fo' disputin' wid gals, so I brace up an' I come 'long to de house an' goes on in dat settin'-room dah, naix' to de dinin'-room. I lays dat mail down on Marse Albert's table; den I looks roun'.

"Ev'thing do look putty, sho! De lace cu'tains was a-flappin' an' de flowers was a-smellin' sweet, an' de pictures a-settin' back on de wall. I keep on lookin' roun'. To reckly my eye hit fall on de li'le gal w'at al'ays sets on de een' o' de mantel-shelf. She do look mighty sassy dat day, wid 'er toe a-stickin' out, des so; an' holdin' her skirt des dat away; an' lookin' at me wid her head twis'.

"I laff out. Viny mus' heahed me. I say, 'g'long 'way f'om dah, gal.' She keep on smilin'. I reaches out my han'. Den Satan an' de good Sperrit, dey begins to wrastle in me. De Sperrit say: 'You ole fool-nigga, you; mine w'at you about.' Satan keep on shovin' my han'—des so— keep on shovin'. Satan he mighty powerful dat day, an' he win de fight. I kiar dat li'le trick home in my pocket."

Pa-Jeff lowered his head for a moment in bitter confusion. His hearers were moved with distressful astonishment. They would have had him stop the recital right there, but Pa-Jeff resumed, with an effort:

"Come dat night I heah tell how dat li'le trick, wo'th heap money; how madam, she cryin' 'cause her li'le blessed lamb was use' to play wid dat, an' kiar-on ov' it. Den I git scared. I say, 'w'at I gwine do?' An' up jump Satan an' de Sperrit a-wrastlin' again.

"De Sperrit say: 'Kiar hit back whar it come f'om, Pa-Jeff.' Satan 'low: 'Fling it in de bayeh, you ole fool.' De Sperrit say: 'You won't fling dat in de bayeh, whar de madam kain't neva sot eyes on hit no mo'?' Den Satan he kine give in; he 'low he plumb sick o' disputin' so long; tell me go hide it some 'eres whar dey nachelly gwine fine it. Satan he win dat fight.

"Des w'en de day g'ine break, I creeps out an' goes 'long de fiel' road. I pass by Ma'me Bedaut's house. I riclic how dey says li'le Bedaut gal ben in de sittin'-room, too, day befo'. De winda war open. Ev'body sleepin'. I tres' in my head, des like a dog w'at shame hisse'f. I sees dat box o' rags befo' my eyes; an' I drops dat li'le imp'dence 'mongst dem rags.

"Mebby yo' all t'ink Satan an' de Sperrit lef' me 'lone, arter dat?" continued Pa-Jeff, straightening himself from the relaxed position in which his members seemed to have settled.

"No, suh; dey ben desputin' straight 'long. Las' night dey come nigh onto en'in' me up. De Sperrit say: 'Come 'long, I gittin' tired dis heah, you g'long up yonda an' tell de truf an' shame de devil.' Satan 'low: 'Stay whar you is; you heah me!' Dey clutches me. Dey twis'es an' twines me. Dey dashes me down an' jerks me up. But de Sperrit he win dat fight in de en', an' heah I is, mist'ess, master, chillun'; heah I is."

Years later Pa-Jeff was still telling the story of his temptation and fall. The negroes especially seemed never to tire of hearing him relate it. He enlarged greatly upon the theme as he went, adding new and dramatic features which gave fresh interest to its every telling.

Agapie grew up to deserve the confidence and favors of the family. She redoubled her acts of kindness toward Pa-Jeff; but somehow she could not look into his face again.

Yet she need not have feared. Long before the end came, poor old Pa-Jeff, confused, bewildered, believed the story himself as firmly as those who had heard him tell it over and over for so many years.

The Story of an Hour

Knowing that Mrs. Mallard was afflicted with a heart trouble, great care was taken to break to her as gently as possible the news of her husband's death.

It was her sister Josephine who told her, in broken sentences; veiled hints that revealed in half concealing. Her husband's friend Richards was there, too, near her. It was he who had been in the newspaper office when intelligence of the railroad disaster was received, with Brently Mallard's name leading the list of "killed." He had only taken the time to assure himself of its truth by a second telegram, and had hastened to forestall any less careful, less tender friend in bearing the sad message.

She did not hear the story as many women have heard the same, with a paralyzed inability to accept its significance. She wept at once, with sudden, wild abandonment, in her sister's arms. When the storm of grief had spent itself she went away to her room alone. She would have no one follow her.

There stood, facing the open window, a comfortable, roomy armchair. Into this she sank, pressed down by a physical exhaustion that haunted her body and seemed to reach into her soul.

She could see in the open square before her house the tops of trees that were all aquiver with the new spring life. The delicious breath of rain was in the air. In the street below a peddler was crying his wares. The notes of a distant song which some one was singing reached her faintly, and countless sparrows were twittering in the eaves.

There were patches of blue sky showing here and there through the clouds that had met and piled one above the other in the west facing her window.

She sat with her head thrown back upon the cushion of the chair, quite motionless, except when a sob came up into her throat and shook her, as a child who has cried itself to sleep continues to sob in its dreams.

She was young, with a fair, calm face, whose lines bespoke repression and even a certain strength. But now there was a dull stare in her eyes, whose gaze was fixed away off yonder on one of those patches of blue sky. It was not a glance of reflection, but rather indicated a suspension of intelligent thought.

There was something coming to her and she was waiting for it, fearfully. What was it? She did not know; it was too subtle and elusive to name. But she felt it, creeping out of the sky, reaching toward her through the sounds, the scents, the color that filled the air.

Now her bosom rose and fell tumultuously. She was beginning to recognize this thing that was approaching to possess her, and she was striving to beat it back with her will—as powerless as her two white slender hands would have been.

When she abandoned herself a little whispered word escaped her slightly parted lips. She said it over and over under her breath: "free, free, free!" The vacant stare and the look of terror that had followed it went from her eyes. They stayed keen and bright. Her pulses beat fast, and the coursing blood warmed and relaxed every inch of her body.

She did not stop to ask if it were or were not a monstrous joy that held her. A clear and exalted perception enabled her to dismiss the suggestion as trivial.

She knew that she would weep again when she saw the kind, tender hands folded in death; the face that had never looked save with love upon her, fixed and gray and dead. But she saw beyond that bitter moment a long procession of years to come that would belong to her absolutely. And she opened and spread her arms out to them in welcome.

There would be no one to live for her during those coming years; she would live for herself. There would be no powerful will bending hers in that blind persistence with which men and women believe they have a right to impose a private will upon a fellow-creature. A kind intention or a cruel intention made the act seem no less a crime as she looked upon it in that brief moment of illumination.

And yet she had loved him—sometimes. Often she had not. What did it matter! What could love, the unsolved mystery, count for in face of this possession of self-assertion which she suddenly recognized as the strongest impulse of her being!

"Free! Body and soul free!" she kept whispering.

Josephine was kneeling before the closed door with her lips to the key-hole, imploring for admission. "Louise, open the door! I beg; open the door—you will make yourself ill. What are you doing, Louise? For heaven's sake open the door."

"Go away. I am not making myself ill." No; she was drinking in a very elixir of life through that open window.

Her fancy was running riot along those days ahead of her. Spring days, and summer days, and all sorts of days that would be her own. She breathed a quick prayer that life might be long. It was only yesterday she had thought with a shudder that life might be long.

She arose at length and opened the door to her sister's importunities. There was a feverish triumph in her eyes, and she carried herself unwittingly like a goddess of Victory. She clasped her sister's waist, and together they descended the stairs. Richards stood waiting for them at the bottom.

Some one was opening the front door with a latchkey. It was Brently Mallard who entered, a little travel-stained, composedly carrying his grip-sack and umbrella. He had been far from the scene of accident, and did not even know there had been one. He stood amazed at Josephine's piercing cry; at Richards' quick motion to screen him from the view of his wife.

But Richards was too late.

When the doctors came they said she had died of heart disease—of joy that kills.

Lilacs

Mme. Adrienne Farival never announced her coming; but the good nuns knew very well when to look for her. When the scent of the lilac blossoms began to permeate the air, Sister Agathe would turn many times during the day to the window; upon her face the happy, beatific expression with which pure and simple souls watch for the coming of those they love.

But it was not Sister Agathe; it was Sister Marceline who first espied her crossing the beautiful lawn that sloped up to the convent. Her arms were filled with great bunches of lilacs which she had gathered along her path. She was clad all in brown; like one of the birds that come with the spring, the nuns used to say. Her figure was rounded and graceful, and she walked with a happy, buoyant step. The cabriolet which had conveyed her to the convent moved slowly up the gravel drive that led to the imposing entrance. Beside the driver was her modest little black trunk, with her name and address printed in white letters upon it: "Mme. A. Farival, Paris." It was the crunching of the gravel which had attracted Sister Marceline's attention. And then the commotion began.

White-capped heads appeared suddenly at the windows; she waved her parasol and her bunch of lilacs at them. Sister Marceline and Sister Marie Anne appeared, fluttered and expectant at the doorway. But Sister Agathe, more daring and impulsive than all, descended the steps and flew across the grass to meet her. What embraces, in which the lilacs were crushed between them! What ardent kisses! What pink flushes of happiness mounting the cheeks of the two women!

Once within the convent Adrienne's soft brown eyes moistened with tenderness as they dwelt caressingly upon the familiar objects about her, and noted the most trifling details. The white, bare boards of the floor had lost nothing of their luster. The stiff, wooden chairs, standing in rows against the walls of hall and parlor, seemed to have taken on an extra polish since she had seen them, last lilac time. And there was a new picture of the Sacré-Coeur hanging over the hall table. What had they done with Ste. Catherine de Sienne, who had occupied that position of honor for so many years? In the chapel—it was no use trying to deceive her—she saw at a glance that St. Joseph's mantle had been embellished with a new coat of blue, and the aureole about his head freshly gilded. And the Blessed Virgin there neglected! Still wearing her garb of last spring, which looked almost dingy by contrast. It was not just—such partiality! The Holy Mother had reason to be jealous and to complain.

But Adrienne did not delay to pay her respects to the Mother Superior, whose dignity would not permit her to so much as step outside the door of her private apartments to welcome this old pupil. Indeed, she was dignity in person; large, uncompromising, unbending. She kissed Adrienne without warmth, and discussed conventional themes learnedly and prosaically during the quarter of an hour which the young woman remained in her company.

It was then that Adrienne's latest gift was brought in for inspection. For Adrienne always brought a handsome present for the chapel in her little black trunk. Last year it was a necklace of gems for the Blessed Virgin, which the Good Mother was only permitted to wear on extra occasions, such as great feast days of obligation. The year before it had been a precious crucifix—an ivory figure of Christ suspended from an ebony cross, whose extremities were tipped with wrought silver. This time it was a linen embroidered altar cloth of such rare and delicate workmanship that the Mother Superior, who knew the value of such things, chided Adrienne for the extravagance.

"But, dear Mother, you know it is the greatest pleasure I have in life— to be with you all once a year, and to bring some such trifling token of my regard."

The Mother Superior dismissed her with the rejoinder: "Make yourself at home, my child. Sister Thérèse will see to your wants. You will occupy Sister Marceline's bed in the end room, over the chapel. You will share the room with Sister Agathe."

There was always one of the nuns detailed to keep Adrienne company during her fortnight's stay at the convent. This had become almost a fixed regulation. It was only during the hours of recreation that she found herself with them all together. Those were hours of much harmless merry-making under the trees or in the nuns' refectory.

This time it was Sister Agathe who waited for her outside of the Mother Superior's door. She was taller and slenderer than Adrienne, and perhaps ten years older. Her fair blonde face flushed and paled with every passing emotion that visited her soul. The two women linked arms and went together out into the open air.

There was so much which Sister Agathe felt that Adrienne must see. To begin with, the enlarged poultry yard, with its dozens upon dozens of new inmates. It took now all the time of one of the lay sisters to attend to them. There had been no change made in the vegetable garden, but— yes there had; Adrienne's quick eye at once detected it. Last year old Philippe had planted his cabbages in a large square to the right. This year they were set out in an oblong bed to the left. How it made Sister Agathe laugh to think Adrienne should have noticed such a trifle! And old Philippe, who was nailing a broken trellis not far off, was called forward to be told about it.

He never failed to tell Adrienne how well she looked, and how she was growing younger each year. And it was his delight to recall certain of her youthful and mischievous escapades. Never would he forget that day she disappeared; and the whole convent in a hubbub about it! And how at last it was he who discovered her perched among the tallest branches of the highest tree on the grounds, where she had climbed to see if she could get a glimpse of Paris! And her punishment afterwards!—half of the Gospel of Palm Sunday to learn by heart!

"We may laugh over it, my good Philippe, but we must remember that Madame is older and wiser now."

"I know well, Sister Agathe, that one ceases to commit follies after the first days of youth." And Adrienne seemed greatly impressed by the wisdom of Sister Agathe and old Philippe, the convent gardener.

A little later when they sat upon a rustic bench which overlooked the smiling landscape about them, Adrienne was saying to Sister Agathe, who held her hand and stroked it fondly:

"Do you remember my first visit, four years ago, Sister Agathe? and what a surprise it was to you all!"

"As if I could forget it, dear child!"

"And I! Always shall I remember that morning as I walked along the boulevard with a heaviness of heart—oh, a heaviness which I hate to recall. Suddenly there was wafted to me the sweet odor of lilac blossoms.

A young girl had passed me by, carrying a great bunch of them. Did you ever know, Sister Agathe, that there is nothing which so keenly revives a memory as a perfume—an odor?"

"I believe you are right, Adrienne. For now that you speak of it, I can feel how the odor of fresh bread—when Sister Jeanne bakes—always makes me think of the great kitchen of ma tante de Sierge, and crippled Julie, who sat always knitting at the sunny window. And I never smell the sweet scented honeysuckle without living again through the blessed day of my first communion."

"Well, that is how it was with me, Sister Agathe, when the scent of the lilacs at once changed the whole current of my thoughts and my despondency. The boulevard, its noises, its passing throng, vanished from before my senses as completely as if they had been spirited away. I was standing here with my feet sunk in the green sward as they are now. I could see the sunlight glancing from that old white stone wall, could hear the notes of birds, just as we hear them now, and the humming of insects in the air. And through all I could see and could smell the lilac blossoms, nodding invitingly to me from their thick-leaved branches. It seems to me they are richer than ever this year, Sister Agathe. And do you know, I became like an *enragée;* nothing could have kept me back. I do not remember now where I was going; but I turned and retraced my steps homeward in a perfect fever of agitation: 'Sophie! my little trunk—quick—the black one! A mere handful of clothes! I am going away. Don't ask me any questions. I shall be back in a fortnight.' And every year since then it is the same. At the very first whiff of a lilac blossom, I am gone! There is no holding me back."

"And how I wait for you, and watch those lilac bushes, Adrienne! If you should once fail to come, it would be like the spring coming without the sunshine or the song of birds.

"But do you know, dear child, I have sometimes feared that in moments of despondency such as you have just described, I fear that you do not turn as you might to our Blessed Mother in heaven, who is ever ready to comfort and solace an afflicted heart with the precious balm of her sympathy and love."

"Perhaps I do not, dear Sister Agathe. But you cannot picture the annoyances which I am constantly submitted to. That Sophie alone, with her detestable ways! I assure you she of herself is enough to drive me to St. Lazare."

"Indeed, I do understand that the trials of one living in the world must be very great, Adrienne; particularly for you, my poor child, who have to bear them alone, since Almighty God was pleased to call to himself your dear husband. But on the other hand, to live one's life along the lines which our dear Lord traces for each one of us, must bring with it resignation and even a certain comfort. You have your household duties, Adrienne, and your music, to which, you say, you continue to devote yourself. And then, there are always good works—the poor—who are always with us—to be relieved; the afflicted to be comforted."

"But, Sister Agathe! Will you listen! Is it not La Rose that I hear moving down there at the edge of the pasture? I fancy she is reproaching me with being an ingrate, not to have pressed a kiss yet on that white forehead of hers. Come, let us go."

The two women arose and walked again, hand in hand this time, over the tufted grass down the gentle decline where it sloped toward the broad, flat meadow, and the limpid stream that flowed cool and fresh from the woods. Sister Agathe walked with her composed, nunlike tread; Adrienne with a balancing motion, a bounding step, as though the earth responded to her light footfall with some subtle impulse all its own.

They lingered long upon the foot-bridge that spanned the narrow stream which divided the convent grounds from the meadow beyond. It was to Adrienne indescribably sweet to rest there in soft, low converse with this gentle-faced nun, watching the approach of evening. The gurgle of the running water beneath them; the lowing of cattle approaching in the distance, were the only sounds that broke upon the stillness, until the clear tones of the angelus bell pealed out from the convent tower. At the sound both women instinctively sank to their knees, signing themselves with the sign of the cross. And Sister Agathe repeated the customary invocation, Adrienne responding in musical tones:

"The Angel of the Lord declared unto Mary,
    And she conceived by the Holy Ghost—"
and so forth, to the end of the brief prayer, after which they arose and retraced their steps toward the convent.

It was with subtle and naïve pleasure that Adrienne prepared herself that night for bed. The room which she shared with Sister Agathe was immaculately white. The walls were a dead white, relieved only by one florid print depicting Jacob's dream at the foot of the ladder, upon which angels mounted and descended. The bare floors, a soft yellow-white, with two little patches of gray carpet beside each spotless bed. At the head of the white-draped beds were two *bénitiers* containing holy water absorbed in sponges.

Sister Agathe disrobed noiselessly behind her curtains and glided into bed without having revealed, in the faint candlelight, as much as a shadow of herself. Adrienne pattered about the room, shook and folded her garments with great care, placing them on the back of a chair as she had been taught to do when a child at the convent. It secretly pleased Sister Agathe to feel that her dear Adrienne clung to the habits acquired in her youth.

But Adrienne could not sleep. She did not greatly desire to do so. These hours seemed too precious to be cast into the oblivion of slumber.

"Are you not asleep, Adrienne?"

"No, Sister Agathe. You know it is always so the first night. The excitement of my arrival—I don't know what—keeps me awake."

"Say your 'Hail, Mary,' dear child, over and over."

"I have done so, Sister Agathe; it does not help."

"Then lie quite still on your side and think of nothing but your own respiration. I have heard that such inducement to sleep seldom fails."

"I will try. Good night, Sister Agathe."

"Good night, dear child. May the Holy Virgin guard you."

An hour later Adrienne was still lying with wide, wakeful eyes, listening to the regular breathing of Sister Agathe. The trailing of the passing wind through the treetops, the ceaseless babble of the rivulet were some of the sounds that came to her faintly through the night.

The days of the fortnight which followed were in character much like the first peaceful, uneventful day of her arrival, with the exception only that she devoutly heard mass every morning at an early hour in the convent chapel, and on Sundays sang in the choir in her agreeable, cultivated voice, which was heard with delight and the warmest appreciation.

When the day of her departure came, Sister Agathe was not satisfied to say good-by at the portal as the others did. She walked down the drive beside the creeping old cabriolet, chattering her pleasant last words. And then she stood—it was as far as she might go—at the edge of the road, waving good-by in response to the fluttering of Adrienne's handkerchief. Four hours later Sister Agathe, who was instructing a class of little girls for their first communion, looked up at the classroom clock and murmured: "Adrienne is at home now."

Yes, Adrienne was at home. Paris had engulfed her.

At the very hour when Sister Agathe looked up at the clock, Adrienne, clad in a charming negligé, was reclining indolently in the depths of a luxurious armchair. The bright room was in its accustomed state of picturesque disorder. Musical scores were scattered upon the open piano. Thrown carelessly over the backs of chairs were puzzling and astonishing-looking garments.

In a large gilded cage near the window perched a clumsy green parrot. He blinked stupidly at a young girl in street dress who was exerting herself to make him talk.

In the centre of the room stood Sophie, that thorn in her mistress's side. With hands plunged in the deep pockets of her apron, her white starched cap quivering with each emphatic motion of her grizzled head, she was holding forth, to the evident ennui of the two young women. She was saying:

"Heaven knows I have stood enough in the six years I have been with Mademoiselle; but never such indignities as I have had to endure in the past two weeks at the hands of that man who calls himself a manager! The very first day—and I, good enough to notify him at once of Mademoiselle's flight—he arrives like a lion; I tell you, like a lion. He insists upon knowing Mademoiselle's whereabouts. How can I tell him any more than the statue out there in the square? He calls me a liar! Me, me—a liar! He declares he is ruined. The public will not stand La Petite Gilberta in the role which Mademoiselle has made so famous—La Petite Gilberta, who dances like a jointed wooden figure and sings like a *traînée* of a *café chantant*. If I were to tell La Gilberta that, as I easily might, I guarantee it would not be well for the few straggling hairs which he has left on that miserable head of his!

"What could he do? He was obliged to inform the public that Mademoiselle was ill; and then began my real torment! Answering this one and that one with their cards, their flowers, their dainties in covered dishes! which, I must admit, saved Florine and me much cooking. And all the while having to tell them that the physician had advised for Mademoiselle a rest of two weeks at some watering-place, the name of which I had forgotten!"

Adrienne had been contemplating old Sophie with quizzical, half-closed eyes, and pelting her with hot-house roses which lay in her lap, and which she nipped off short from their graceful stems for that purpose. Each rose struck Sophie full in the face; but they did not disconcert her or once stem the torrent of her talk.

"Oh, Adrienne!" entreated the young girl at the parrot's cage. "Make her hush; please do something. How can you ever expect Zozo to talk? A dozen times he has been on the point of saying something! I tell you, she stupefies him with her chatter."

"My good Sophie," remarked Adrienne, not changing her attitude, "you see the roses are all used up. But I assure you, anything at hand goes," carelessly picking up a book from the table beside her. "What is this? Mons. Zola! Now I warn you, Sophie, the weightiness, the heaviness of Mons. Zola are such that they cannot fail to prostrate you; thankful you may be if they leave you with energy to regain your feet."

"Mademoiselle's pleasantries are all very well; but if I am to be shown the door for it—if I am to be crippled for it—I shall say that I think Mademoiselle is a woman without conscience and without heart. To torture a man as she does! A man? No, an angel!

"Each day he has come with sad visage and drooping mien. 'No news, Sophie?'

" 'None, Monsieur Henri.' 'Have you no idea where she has gone?' 'Not any more than the statue in the square, Monsieur.' 'Is it perhaps possible that she may not return at all?' with his face blanching like that curtain.

"I assure him you will be back at the end of the fortnight. I entreat him to have patience. He drags himself, *désolé*, about the room, picking up Mademoiselle's fan, her gloves, her music, and turning them over and over in his hands. Mademoiselle's slipper, which she took off to throw at me in the impatience of her departure, and which I purposely left lying where it fell on the chiffonier—he kissed it—I saw him do it—and thrust it into his pocket, thinking himself unobserved.

"The same song each day. I beg him to eat a little good soup which I have prepared. 'I cannot eat, my dear Sophie.' The other night he came and stood long gazing out of the window at the stars. When he turned he was wiping his eyes; they were red. He said he had been riding in the dust, which had inflamed them. But I knew better; he had been crying.

"*Ma foi!* in his place I would snap my finger at such cruelty. I would go out and amuse myself. What is the use of being young!"

Adrienne arose with a laugh. She went and seizing old Sophie by the shoulders shook her till the white cap wobbled on her head.

"What is the use of all this litany, my good Sophie? Year after year the same! Have you forgotten that I have come a long, dusty journey by rail, and that I am perishing of hunger and thirst? Bring us a bottle of Château Yquem and a biscuit and my box of cigarettes." Sophie had freed herself, and was retreating toward the door. "And, Sophie! If Monsieur Henri is still waiting, tell him to come up."

It was precisely a year later. The spring had come again, and Paris was intoxicated.

Old Sophie sat in her kitchen discoursing to a neighbor who had come in to borrow some trifling kitchen utensil from the old *bonne*.

"You know, Rosalie, I begin to believe it is an attack of lunacy which seizes her once a year. I wouldn't say it to everyone, but with you I know it will go no further. She ought to be treated for it; a physician should be consulted; it is not well to neglect such things and let them run on.

"It came this morning like a thunder clap. As I am sitting here, there had been no thought or mention of a journey. The baker had come into the kitchen—you know what a gallant he is—with always a girl in his eye. He laid the bread down upon the table and beside it a bunch of lilacs. I didn't know they had bloomed yet. 'For Mam'selle Florine, with my regards,' he said with his foolish simper.

"Now, you know I was not going to call Florine from her work in order to present her the baker's flowers. All the same, it would not do to let them wither. I went with them in my hand into the dining room to get a majolica pitcher which I had put away in the closet there, on an upper shelf, because the handle was broken. Mademoiselle, who rises early, had just come from her bath, and was crossing the hall that opens into the dining room. Just as she was, in her white *peignoir*, she thrust her head into the dining room, snuffling the air and exclaiming, 'What do I smell?'

"She espied the flowers in my hand and pounced upon them like a cat upon a mouse. She held them up to her, burying her face in them for the longest time, only uttering a long 'Ah!'

"Sophie, I am going away. Get out the little black trunk; a few of the plainest garments I have; my brown dress that I have not yet worn."

" 'But, Mademoiselle,' I protested, 'you forget that you have ordered a breakfast of a hundred francs for tomorrow.'

" 'Shut up!' she cried, stamping her foot.

" 'You forget how the manager will rave,' I persisted, 'and vilify me. And you will go like that without a word of adieu to Monsieur Paul, who is an angel if ever one trod the earth.'

"I tell you, Rosalie, her eyes flamed.

" 'Do as I tell you this instant,' she exclaimed, 'or I will strangle you—with your Monsieur Paul and your manager and your hundred francs!' "

"Yes," affirmed Rosalie, "it is insanity. I had a cousin seized in the same way one morning, when she smelled calf's liver frying with onions. Before night it took two men to hold her."

"I could well see it was insanity, my dear Rosalie, and I uttered not another word as I feared for my life. I simply obeyed her every command in silence. And now—whiff, she is gone! God knows where. But between us, Rosalie—I wouldn't say it to Florine—but I believe it is for no good. I, in Monsieur Paul's place, should have her watched. I would put a detective upon her track.

"Now I am going to close up; barricade the entire establishment. Monsieur Paul, the manager, visitors, all—all may ring and knock and shout themselves hoarse. I am tired of it all. To be vilified and called a liar—at my age, Rosalie!"

Adrienne left her trunk at the small railway station, as the old cabriolet was not at the moment available; and she gladly walked the mile or two of pleasant roadway which led to the convent. How infinitely calm, peaceful, penetrating was the charm of the verdant, undulating country spreading out on all sides of her! She walked along the clear smooth road, twirling her parasol; humming a gay tune; nipping here and there a bud or a waxlike leaf from the hedges along the way; and all the while drinking deep draughts of complacency and content.

She stopped, as she had always done, to pluck lilacs in her path.

As she approached the convent she fancied that a whitecapped face had glanced fleetingly from a window; but she must have been mistaken. Evidently she had not been seen, and this time would take them by surprise. She smiled to think how Sister Agathe would utter a little joyous cry of amazement, and in fancy she already felt the warmth and tenderness of the nun's embrace. And how Sister Marceline and the others would laugh, and make game of her puffed sleeves! For puffed sleeves had come into fashion since last year; and the vagaries of fashion always afforded infinite merriment to the nuns. No, they surely had not seen her.

She ascended lightly the stone steps and rang the bell. She could hear the sharp metallic sound reverberate through the halls. Before its last note had died away the door was opened very slightly, very cautiously by a lay sister who stood there with downcast eyes and flaming cheeks. Through the narrow opening she thrust forward toward Adrienne a package and a letter, saying, in confused tones: "By order of our Mother Superior." After which she closed the door hastily and turned the heavy key in the great lock.

Adrienne remained stunned. She could not gather her faculties to grasp the meaning of this singular reception. The lilacs fell from her arms to the stone portico on which she was standing. She turned the note and the parcel stupidly over in her hands, instinctively dreading what their contents might disclose.

The outlines of the crucifix were plainly to be felt through the wrapper of the bundle, and she guessed, without having courage to assure herself, that the jeweled necklace and the altar cloth accompanied it.

Leaning against the heavy oaken door for support, Adrienne opened the letter. She did not seem to read the few bitter reproachful lines word by word—the lines that banished her forever from this haven of peace, where her soul was wont to come and refresh itself. They imprinted themselves as a whole upon her brain, in all their seeming cruelty—she did not dare to say injustice.

There was no anger in her heart; that would doubtless possess her later, when her nimble intelligence would begin to seek out the origin of this treacherous turn. Now, there was only room for tears. She leaned her forehead against the heavy oaken panel of the door and wept with the abandonment of a little child.

She descended the steps with a nerveless and dragging tread. Once as she was walking away, she turned to look back at the imposing façade of the convent, hoping to see a familiar face, or a hand, even, giving a faint token that she was still cherished by some one faithful heart. But she saw only the polished windows looking down at her like so many cold and glittering and reproachful eyes.

In the little white room above the chapel, a woman knelt beside the bed on which Adrienne had slept. Her face was pressed deep in the pillow in her efforts to smother the sobs that convulsed her frame. It was Sister Agathe.

After a short while, a lay sister came out of the door with a broom, and swept away the lilac blossoms which Adrienne had let fall upon the portico.

The Night Came Slowly

I am losing my interest in human beings; in the significance of their lives and their actions. Some one has said it is better to study one man than ten books. I want neither books nor men; they make me suffer. Can one of them talk to me like the night—the Summer night? Like the stars or the caressing wind?

The night came slowly, softly, as I lay out there under the maple tree. It came creeping, creeping stealthily out of the valley, thinking I did not notice. And the outlines of trees and foliage nearby blended in one black mass and the night came stealing out from them, too, and from the east and west, until the only light was in the sky, filtering through the maple leaves and a star looking down through every cranny.

The night is solemn and it means mystery.

Human shapes flitted by like intangible things. Some stole up like little mice to peep at me. I did not mind. My whole being was abandoned to the soothing and penetrating charm of the night.

The katydids began their slumber song: they are at it yet. How wise they are. They do not chatter like people. They tell me only: "sleep, sleep, sleep." The wind rippled the maple leaves like little warm love thrills.

Why do fools cumber the Earth! It was a man's voice that broke the necromancer's spell. A man came to-day with his "Bible Class." He is detestable with his red cheeks and bold eyes and coarse manner and speech. What does he know of Christ? Shall I ask a young fool who was born yesterday and will die tomorrow to tell me things of Christ? I would rather ask the stars: they have seen him.

Juanita

To all appearances and according to all accounts, Juanita is a character who does not reflect credit upon her family or her native town of Rock Springs. I first met her there three years ago in the little back room behind her father's store. She seemed very shy, and inclined to efface herself; a heroic feat to attempt, considering the narrow confines of the room; and a hopeless one, in view of her five-feet-ten, and more than two-hundred pounds of substantial flesh, which, on that occasion, and every subsequent one when I saw her, was clad in a soiled calico "Mother Hubbard."

Her face, and particularly her mouth had a certain fresh and sensuous beauty, though I would rather not say "beauty" if I might say anything else.

I often saw Juanita that summer, simply because it was so difficult for the poor thing not to be seen. She usually sat in some obscure corner of their small garden, or behind an angle of the house, preparing vegetables for dinner or sorting her mother's flower-seed.

It was even at that day said, with some amusement, that Juanita was not so unattractive to men as her appearance might indicate; that she had more than one admirer, and great hopes of marrying well if not brilliantly.

Upon my return to the "Springs" this summer, in asking news of the various persons who had interested me three years ago, Juanita came naturally to my mind, and her name to my lips. There were many ready to tell me of Juanita's career since I had seen her.

The father had died and she and the mother had had ups and downs, but still continued to keep the store. Whatever else happened, however, Juanita had never ceased to attract admirers, young and old. They hung on her fence at all hours; they met her in the lanes; they penetrated to the store and back to the living-room. It was even talked about that a gentleman in a plaid suit had come all the way from the city by train for no other purpose than to call upon her. It is not astonishing, in face of these persistent attentions, that speculation grew rife in Rock Springs as to whom and what Juanita would marry in the end.

For a while she was said to be engaged to a wealthy South Missouri farmer, though no one could guess when or where she had met him. Then it was learned that the man of her choice was a Texas millionaire who possessed a hundred white horses, one of which spirited animals Juanita began to drive about that time.

But in the midst of speculation and counter speculation on the subject of Juanita and her lovers, there suddenly appeared upon the scene a one-legged man; a very poor and shabby, and decidedly one-legged man. He first became known to the public through Juanita's soliciting sub-scriptions towards buying the unhappy individual a cork-leg.

Her interest in the one-legged man continued to show itself in various ways, not always apparent to a curious public; as was proven one morning when Juanita became the mother of a baby, whose father, she announced, was her husband, the one-legged man. The story of a wander-ing preacher was told; a secret marriage in the State of Illinois; and a lost certificate.

However that may be, Juanita has turned her broad back upon the whole race of masculine bipeds, and lavishes the wealth of her undivided affections upon the one-legged man.

I caught a glimpse of the curious couple when I was in the village. Juanita had mounted her husband upon a dejected looking pony which she herself was apparently leading by the bridle, and they were moving up the lane towards the woods, whither, I am told, they often wander in this manner. The picture which they presented was a singular one; she with a man's big straw hat shading her inflamed moon-face, and the breeze bellying her soiled "Mother Hubbard" into monstrous proportions. He puny, helpless, but apparently content with his fate which had not even vouchsafed him the coveted cork-leg.

They go off thus to the woods together where they may love each other away from all prying eyes save those of the birds and the squirrels. But what do the squirrels care!

For my part I never expected Juanita to be more respectable than a squirrel; and I don't see how any one else could have expected it.

Cavanelle

I was always sure of hearing something pleasant from Cavanelle across the counter. If he was not mistaking me for the freshest and prettiest girl in New Orleans, he was reserving for me some bit of silk, or lace, or ribbon of a nuance marvelously suited to my complexion, my eyes or my hair! What an innocent, delightful humbug Cavanelle was! How well I knew it and how little I cared! For when he had sold me the confection or bit of dry-goods in question, he always began to talk to me of his sister Mathilde, and then I knew that Cavanelle was an angel.

I had known him long enough to know why he worked so faithfully, so energetically and without rest—it was because Mathilde had a voice. It was because of her voice that his coats were worn till they were out of fashion and almost out at elbows. But for a sister whose voice needed only a little training to rival that of the nightingale, one might do such things without incurring reproach.

"You will believe, madame, that I did not know you las' night at the opera? I remark' to Mathilde, 'tiens! Mademoiselle Montreville,' an' I only rec'nize my mistake when I finally adjust my opera glass . . . . . . I guarantee you will be satisfied, madame. In a year from now you will come an' thank me for having secu' you that bargain in a poult-de-soie . . . . . Yes, yes; as you say, Tolville was in voice. But," with a shrug of the narrow shoulders and a smile of commiseration that wrinkled the lean olive cheeks beneath the thin beard, "but to hear that cavatina render' as I have heard it render' by Mathilde, is another affair! A quality, madame, that moves, that penetrates. Perhaps not yet enough volume, but that will accomplish itself with time, when she will become more robus' in health. It is my intention to sen' her for the summer to

Gran' Isle; that good air an' surf bathing will work miracles. An artiste, voyez vous, it is not to be treated like a human being of every day; it needs des petits soins; perfec' res' of body an' mind; good red wine an' plenty . . . . . oh yes, madame, the stage; that is our intention; but never with my consent in light opera. Patience is what I counsel to Mathilde. A little more stren'th; a little dev'lopment of the chest to give that soupçon of compass which is lacking, an' gran' opera is what I aspire for my sister."

I was curious to know Mathilde and to hear her sing; and thought it a great pity that a voice so marvelous as she doubtless possessed should not gain the notice that might prove the step toward the attainment of her ambition. It was such curiosity and a half-formed design or desire to interest myself in her career that prompted me to inform Cavanelle that I should greatly like to meet his sister; and I asked permission to call upon her the following Sunday afternoon.

Cavanelle was charmed. He otherwise would not have been Cavanelle. Over and over I was given the most minute directions for finding the house. The green car—or was it the yellow or blue one? I can no longer remember. But it was near Goodchildren street, and would I kindly walk this way and turn that way? At the corner was an ice dealer's. In the middle of the block, their house—one-story; painted yellow; a knocker; a banana tree nodding over the side fence. But indeed, I need not look for the banana tree, the knocker, the number or anything, for if I but turn the corner in the neighborhood of five o'clock I would find him planted at the door awaiting me.

And there he was! Cavanelle himself; but seeming to me not himself; apart from the entourage with which I was accustomed to associate him. Every line of his mobile face, every gesture emphasized the welcome which his kind eyes expressed as he ushered me into the small parlor that opened upon the street.

"Oh, not that chair, madame! I entreat you. This one, by all means. Thousan' times more comfortable."

"Mathilde! Strange; my sister was here but an instant ago. Mathilde! Où es tu donc?" Stupid Cavanelle! He did not know when I had already guessed it—that Mathilde had retired to the adjoining room at my approach, and would appear after a sufficient delay to give an appropriate air of ceremony to our meeting.

And what a frail little piece of mortality she was when she did appear! At beholding her I could easily fancy that when she stepped outside of the yellow house, the zephyrs would lift her from her feet and, given a proper adjustment of the balloon sleeves, gently waft her in the direction of Goodchildren street, or wherever else she might want to go.

Hers was no physique for grand opera—certainly no stage presence; apparently so slender a hold upon life that the least tension might snap it. The voice which could hope to overcome these glaring disadvantages would have to be phenomenal.

Mathilde spoke English imperfectly, and with embarrassment, and was glad to lapse into French. Her speech was languid, unaffectedly so; and her manner was one of indolent repose; in this respect offering a striking contrast to that of her brother. Cavanelle seemed unable to rest. Hardly was I seated to his satisfaction than he darted from the room and soon returned followed by a limping old black woman bringing in a sirop d'orgeat and layer cake on a tray.

Mathilde's face showed feeble annoyance at her brother's want of savoir vivre in thus introducing the refreshments at so early a stage of my visit.

The servant was one of those cheap black women who abound in the French quarter, who speak Creole patois in preference to English, and who would rather work in a petit ménage in Goodchildren street for five dollars a month than for fifteen in the fourth district. Her presence, in some unaccountable manner, seemed to reveal to me much of the inner working of this small household. I pictured her early morning visit to the French market, where picayunes were doled out sparingly, and lagniappes gathered in with avidity.

I could see the neatly appointed dinner table; Cavanelle extolling his soup and bouillie in extravagant terms; Mathilde toying with her papabotte or chicken-wing, and pouring herself a demi-verre from her very own half-bottle of St. Julien; Pouponne, as they called her, mumbling and grumbling through habit, and serving them as faithfully as a dog through instinct. I wondered if they knew that Pouponne "played the lottery" with every spare "quarter" gathered from a judicious management of lagniappe. Perhaps they would not have cared, or have minded, either, that she as often consulted the Voudoo priestess around the corner as her father confessor.

My thoughts had followed Pouponne's limping figure from the room, and it was with an effort I returned to Cavanelle twirling the piano stool this way and that way. Mathilde was languidly turning over musical scores, and the two warmly discussing the merits of a selection which she had evidently decided upon.

The girl seated herself at the piano. Her hands were thin and anæmic, and she touched the keys without firmness or delicacy. When she had played a few introductory bars, she began to sing. Heaven only knows what she sang; it made no difference then, nor can it make any now.

The day was a warm one, but that did not prevent a creepy chilliness seizing hold of me. The feeling was generated by disappointment, anger, dismay and various other disagreeable sensations which I cannot find names for. Had I been intentionally deceived and misled? Was this some impertinent pleasantry on the part of Cavanelle? Or rather had not the girl's voice undergone some hideous transformation since her brother had listened to it? I dreaded to look at him, fearing to see horror and astonishment depicted on his face. When I did look, his expression was earnestly attentive and beamed approval of the strains to which he measured time by a slow, satisfied motion of the hand.

The voice was thin to attenuation, I fear it was not even true. Perhaps my disappointment exaggerated its simple deficiencies into monstrous defects. But it was an unsympathetic voice that never could have been a blessing to possess or to listen to.

I cannot recall what I said at parting—doubtless conventional things which were not true. Cavanelle politely escorted me to the car, and there I left him with a hand-clasp which from my side was tender with sympathy and pity.

"Poor Cavanelle! poor Cavanelle!" The words kept beating time in my brain to the jingle of the car bells and the regular ring of the mules' hoofs upon the cobble stones. One moment I resolved to have a talk with him in which I would endeavor to open his eyes to the folly of thus casting his hopes and the substance of his labor to the winds. The next instant I had decided that chance would possibly attend to Cavanelle's affair less clumsily than I could. "But all the same," I wondered, "is Cavanelle a fool? is he a lunatic? is he under a hypnotic spell?" And then—strange that I did not think of it before—I realized that Cavanelle loved Mathilde intensely, and we all know that love is blind, but a god just the same.

Two years passed before I saw Cavanelle again. I had been absent that length of time from the city. In the meanwhile Mathilde had died. She and her little voice—the apotheosis of insignificance—were no more. It was perhaps a year after my visit to her that I read an account of her death in a New Orleans paper. Then came a momentary pang of commiseration for my good Cavanelle. Chance had surely acted here the part of a skillful though merciless surgeon; no temporizing, no half measures. A deep, sharp thrust of the scalpel; a moment of agonizing pain; then rest, rest; convalescence; health; happiness! Yes, Mathilde had been dead a year and I was prepared for great changes in Cavanelle.

He had lived like a hampered child who does not recognize the restrictions hedging it about, and lives a life of pathetic contentment in the midst of them. But now all that was altered. He was, doubtless, regaling himself with the half-bottles of St. Julien, which were never before for him; with, perhaps, an occasional petit souper at Moreau's, and there was no telling what little pleasures beside.

Cavanelle would certainly have bought himself a suit of clothes or two of modern fit and finish. I would find him with a brightened eye, a fuller cheek, as became a man of his years; perchance, even, a waxed moustache! So did my imagination run rampant with me.

And after all, the hand which I clasped across the counter was that of the self-same Cavanelle I had left. It was no fuller, no firmer. There were even some additional lines visible through the thin, brown beard.

"Ah, my poor Cavanelle! you have suffered a grievous loss since we parted." I saw in his face that he remembered the circumstance of our last meeting, so there was no use in avoiding the subject. I had rightly conjectured that the wound had been a cruel one, but in a year such wounds heal with a healthy soul.

He could have talked for hours of Mathilde's unhappy taking-off, and if the subject had possessed for me the same touching fascination which it held for him, doubtless, we would have done so, but—

"And how is it now, mon ami? Are you living in the same place? running your little ménage as before, my poor Cavanelle?"

"Oh, yes, madame, except that my Aunt Félicie is making her home with me now. You have heard me speak of my aunt—No? You never have heard me speak of my Aunt Félicie Cavanelle of Terrebonne! That, madame, is a noble woman who has suffer' the mos' cruel affliction, an' deprivation, since the war.—No, madame, not in good health, unfortunately, by any means. It is why I esteem that a blessed privilege to give her declining years those little comforts, ces petits soins, that is a woman's right to expec' from men."

I knew what "des petits soins" meant with Cavanelle; doctors' visits, little jaunts across the lake, friandises of every description showered upon "Aunt Félicie," and he himself relegated to the soup and bouillie which typified his prosaic existence.

I was unreasonably exasperated with the man for awhile, and would not even permit myself to notice the beauty in texture and design of the mousseline de laine which he had spread across the counter in tempting folds. I was forced to restrain a brutal desire to say something stinging and cruel to him for his fatuity.

However, before I had regained the street, the conviction that Cavanelle was a hopeless fool seemed to reconcile me to the situation and also afforded me some diversion.

But even this estimate of my poor Cavanelle was destined not to last. By the time I had seated myself in the Prytania street car and passed up my nickel, I was convinced that Cavanelle was an angel.

Regret

Mamzelle Aurélie possessed a good strong figure, ruddy cheeks, hair that was changing from brown to gray, and a determined eye. She wore a man's hat about the farm, and an old blue army overcoat when it was cold, and sometimes topboots.

Mamzelle Aurélie had never thought of marrying. She had never been in love. At the age of twenty she had received a proposal, which she had promptly declined, and at the age of fifty she had not yet lived to regret it.

So she was quite alone in the world, except for her dog Ponto, and the negroes who lived in her cabins and worked her crops, and the fowls, a few cows, a couple of mules, her gun (with which she shot chicken-hawks), and her religion.

One morning Mamzelle Aurélie stood upon her gallery, contemplating, with arms akimbo, a small band of very small children who, to all intents and purposes, might have fallen from the clouds, so unexpected and bewildering was their coming, and so unwelcome. They were the children of her nearest neighbor, Odile, who was not such a near neighbor, after all.

The young woman had appeared but five minutes before, accompanied by these four children. In her arms she carried little Elodie; she dragged Ti Nomme by an unwilling hand; while Marcéline and Marcélette followed with irresolute steps.

Her face was red and disfigured from tears and excitement. She had been summoned to a neighboring parish by the dangerous illness of her mother; her husband was away in Texas—it seemed to her a million miles away; and Valsin was waiting with the mule-cart to drive her to the station.

"It's no question, Mamzelle Aurélie; you jus' got to keep those young-sters fo' me tell I come back. Dieu sait, I would n' botha you with 'em if it was any otha way to do! Make 'em mine you, Mamzelle Aurélie; don' spare 'em. Me, there, I'm half crazy between the chil'ren, an' Léon not home, an' maybe not even to fine po' maman alive encore!"—a harrowing possibility which drove Odile to take a final hasty and con-vulsive leave of her disconsolate family.

She left them crowded into the narrow strip of shade on the porch of the long, low house; the white sunlight was beating in on the white old boards; some chickens were scratching in the grass at the foot of the steps, and one had boldly mounted, and was stepping heavily, solemnly, and aimlessly across the gallery. There was a pleasant odor of pinks in the air, and the sound of negroes' laughter was coming across the flowering cotton-field.

Mamzelle Aurélie stood contemplating the children. She looked with a critical eye upon Marcéline, who had been left staggering beneath the weight of the chubby Elodie. She surveyed with the same calculating air Marcélette mingling her silent tears with the audible grief and rebellion of Ti Nomme. During those few contemplative moments she was collecting herself, determining upon a line of action which should be identical with a line of duty. She began by feeding them.

If Mamzelle Aurélie's responsibilities might have begun and ended there, they could easily have been dismissed; for her larder was amply provided against an emergency of this nature. But little children are not little pigs; they require and demand attentions which were wholly un-expected by Mamzelle Aurélie, and which she was ill prepared to give.

She was, indeed, very inapt in her management of Odile's children during the first few days. How could she know that Marcélette always wept when spoken to in a loud and commanding tone of voice? It was a peculiarity of Marcélette's. She became acquainted with Ti Nomme's passion for flowers only when he had plucked all the choicest gardenias and pinks for the apparent purpose of critically studying their botanical construction.

" 'Tain't enough to tell 'im, Mamzelle Aurélie," Marcéline instructed her; "you got to tie 'im in a chair. It's w'at maman all time do w'en he's bad: she tie 'im in a chair." The chair in which Mamzelle Aurélie tied Ti Nomme was roomy and comfortable, and he seized the opportunity to take a nap in it, the afternoon being warm.

At night, when she ordered them one and all to bed as she would have shooed the chickens into the hen-house, they stayed uncomprehending before her. What about the little white nightgowns that had to be taken from the pillow-slip in which they were brought over, and shaken by some strong hand till they snapped like ox-whips? What about the tub of water which had to be brought and set in the middle of the floor, in which the little tired, dusty, sunbrowned feet had every one to be washed sweet and clean? And it made Marcéline and Marcélette laugh merrily —the idea that Mamzelle Aurélie should for a moment have believed that Ti Nomme could fall asleep without being told the story of *Croque-mitaine* or *Loup-garou*, or both; or that Elodie could fall asleep at all without being rocked and sung to.

"I tell you, Aunt Ruby," Mamzelle Aurélie informed her cook in confidence; "me, I'd rather manage a dozen plantation' than fo' chil'ren. It's terrassent! Bonté! Don't talk to me about chil'ren!"

" 'Tain' ispected sich as you would know airy thing 'bout 'em, Mamzelle Aurélie. I see dat plainly yistiddy w'en I spy dat li'le chile playin' wid yo' baskit o' keys. You don' know dat makes chillun grow up hard-headed, to play wid keys? Des like it make 'em teeth hard to look in a lookin'-glass. Them's the things you got to know in the raisin' an' manigement o' chillun."

Mamzelle Aurélie certainly did not pretend or aspire to such subtle and far-reaching knowledge on the subject as Aunt Ruby possessed, who had "raised five an' bared (buried) six" in her day. She was glad enough to learn a few little mother-tricks to serve the moment's need.

Ti Nomme's sticky fingers compelled her to unearth white aprons that she had not worn for years, and she had to accustom herself to his moist kisses—the expressions of an affectionate and exuberant nature. She got down her sewing-basket, which she seldom used, from the top shelf of the armoire, and placed it within the ready and easy reach which torn slips and buttonless waists demanded. It took her some days to become accustomed to the laughing, the crying, the chattering that echoed through the house and around it all day long. And it was not the first or the second night that she could sleep comfortably with little Elodie's hot, plump body pressed close against her, and the little one's warm breath beating her cheek like the fanning of a bird's wing.

But at the end of two weeks Mamzelle Aurélie had grown quite used to these things, and she no longer complained.

It was also at the end of two weeks that Mamzelle Aurélie, one evening, looking away toward the crib where the cattle were being fed, saw Valsin's blue cart turning the bend of the road. Odile sat beside the mulatto, upright and alert. As they drew near, the young woman's beaming face indicated that her homecoming was a happy one.

But this coming, unannounced and unexpected, threw Mamzelle Aurélie into a flutter that was almost agitation. The children had to be gathered. Where was Ti Nomme? Yonder in the shed, putting an edge on his knife at the grindstone. And Marcéline and Marcélette? Cutting and fashioning doll-rags in the corner of the gallery. As for Elodie, she was safe enough in Mamzelle Aurélie's arms; and she had screamed with delight at sight of the familiar blue cart which was bringing her mother back to her.

The excitement was all over, and they were gone. How still it was when they were gone! Mamzelle Aurélie stood upon the gallery, looking and listening. She could no longer see the cart; the red sunset and the blue-gray twilight had together flung a purple mist across the fields and road that hid it from her view. She could no longer hear the wheezing and creaking of its wheels. But she could still faintly hear the shrill, glad voices of the children.

She turned into the house. There was much work awaiting her, for the children had left a sad disorder behind them; but she did not at once set about the task of righting it. Mamzelle Aurélie seated herself beside the table. She gave one slow glance through the room, into which the evening shadows were creeping and deepening around her solitary figure. She let her head fall down upon her bended arm, and began to cry. Oh, but she cried! Not softly, as women often do. She cried like a man, with sobs that seemed to tear her very soul. She did not notice Ponto licking her hand.

The Kiss

It was still quite light out of doors, but inside with the curtains drawn and the smouldering fire sending out a dim, uncertain glow, the room was full of deep shadows.

Brantain sat in one of these shadows; it had overtaken him and he did not mind. The obscurity lent him courage to keep his eyes fastened as ardently as he liked upon the girl who sat in the firelight.

She was very handsome, with a certain fine, rich coloring that belongs to the healthy brune type. She was quite composed, as she idly stroked the satiny coat of the cat that lay curled in her lap, and she occasionally sent a slow glance into the shadow where her companion sat. They were talking low, of indifferent things which plainly were not the things that occupied their thoughts. She knew that he loved her—a frank, blustering fellow without guile enough to conceal his feelings, and no desire to do so. For two weeks past he had sought her society eagerly and persistently. She was confidently waiting for him to declare himself and she meant to accept him. The rather insignificant and unattractive Brantain was enormously rich; and she liked and required the entourage which wealth could give her.

During one of the pauses between their talk of the last tea and the next reception the door opened and a young man entered whom Brantain knew quite well. The girl turned her face toward him. A stride or two brought him to her side, and bending over her chair—before she could suspect his intention, for she did not realize that he had not seen her visitor—he pressed an ardent, lingering kiss upon her lips.

Brantain slowly arose; so did the girl arise, but quickly, and the new-comer stood between them, a little amusement and some defiance struggling with the confusion in his face.

"I believe," stammered Brantain, "I see that I have stayed too long. I—I had no idea—that is, I must wish you good-by." He was clutching his hat with both hands, and probably did not perceive that she was extending her hand to him, her presence of mind had not completely deserted her; but she could not have trusted herself to speak.

"Hang me if I saw him sitting there, Nattie! I know it's deuced awkward for you. But I hope you'll forgive me this once—this very first break. Why, what's the matter?"

"Don't touch me; don't come near me," she returned angrily. "What do you mean by entering the house without ringing?"

"I came in with your brother, as I often do," he answered coldly, in self-justification. "We came in the side way. He went upstairs and I came in here hoping to find you. The explanation is simple enough and ought to satisfy you that the misadventure was unavoidable. But do say that you forgive me, Nathalie," he entreated, softening.

"Forgive you! You don't know what you are talking about. Let me pass. It depends upon—a good deal whether I ever forgive you."

At that next reception which she and Brantain had been talking about she approached the young man with a delicious frankness of manner when she saw him there.

"Will you let me speak to you a moment or two, Mr. Brantain?" she asked with an engaging but perturbed smile. He seemed extremely unhappy; but when she took his arm and walked away with him, seeking a retired corner, a ray of hope mingled with the almost comical misery of his expression. She was apparently very outspoken.

"Perhaps I should not have sought this interview, Mr. Brantain; but —but, oh, I have been very uncomfortable, almost miserable since that little encounter the other afternoon. When I thought how you might have misinterpreted it, and believed things"—hope was plainly gaining the ascendancy over misery in Brantain's round, guileless face—"of course, I know it is nothing to you, but for my own sake I do want you to understand that Mr. Harvy is an intimate friend of long standing. Why, we have always been like cousins—like brother and sister, I may say. He is my brother's most intimate associate and often fancies that he is entitled to the same privileges as the family. Oh, I know it is absurd, uncalled for, to tell you this; undignified even," she was almost weeping, "but it makes so much difference to me what you think of—of me." Her voice had grown very low and agitated. The misery had all disappeared from Brantain's face.

"Then you do really care what I think, Miss Nathalie? May I call you Miss Nathalie?" They turned into a long, dim corridor that was lined on either side with tall, graceful plants. They walked slowly to the very end of it. When they turned to retrace their steps Brantain's face was radiant and hers was triumphant.

Harvy was among the guests at the wedding; and he sought her out in a rare moment when she stood alone.

"Your husband," he said, smiling, "has sent me over to kiss you."

A quick blush suffused her face and round polished throat. "I suppose it's natural for a man to feel and act generously on an occasion of this kind. He tells me he doesn't want his marriage to interrupt wholly that pleasant intimacy which has existed between you and me. I don't know what you've been telling him," with an insolent smile, "but he has sent me here to kiss you."

She felt like a chess player who, by the clever handling of his pieces, sees the game taking the course intended. Her eyes were bright and tender with a smile as they glanced up into his; and her lips looked hungry for the kiss which they invited.

"But, you know," he went on quietly, "I didn't tell him so, it would have seemed ungrateful, but I can tell you. I've stopped kissing women; it's dangerous."

Well, she had Brantain and his million left. A person can't have everything in this world; and it was a little unreasonable of her to expect it.

Ozème's Holiday

Ozème often wondered why there was not a special dispensation of providence to do away with the necessity for work. There seemed to him so much created for man's enjoyment in this world, and so little time and opportunity to profit by it. To sit and do nothing but breathe was a pleasure to Ozème; but to sit in the company of a few choice companions, including a sprinkling of ladies, was even a greater delight; and the joy which a day's hunting or fishing or picnicking afforded him is hardly to be described. Yet he was by no means indolent. He worked faithfully on the plantation the whole year long, in a sort of methodical way; but when the time came around for his annual week's holiday, there was no holding him back. It was often decidedly inconvenient for the planter that Ozème usually chose to take his holiday during some very busy season of the year.

He started out one morning in the beginning of October. He had borrowed Mr. Laballière's buckboard and Padue's old gray mare, and a harness from the negro Séverin. He wore a light blue suit which had been sent all the way from St. Louis, and which had cost him ten dollars; he had paid almost as much again for his boots; and his hat was a broad-rimmed gray felt which he had no cause to be ashamed of. When Ozème went "broading," he dressed—well, regardless of cost. His eyes were blue and mild; his hair was light, and he wore it rather long; he was clean shaven, and really did not look his thirty-five years.

Ozème had laid his plans weeks beforehand. He was going visiting along Cane River; the mere contemplation filled him with pleasure. He counted upon reaching Fédeaus' about noon, and he would stop and dine there. Perhaps they would ask him to stay all night. He really did not hold to staying all night, and was not decided to accept if they did ask him. There were only the two old people, and he rather fancied the notion of pushing on to Beltrans', where he would stay a night, or even two, if urged. He was quite sure that there would be something agreeable going on at Beltrans', with all those young people—perhaps a fish-fry, or possibly a ball!

Of course he would have to give a day to Tante Sophie and another to Cousine Victoire; but none to the St. Annes unless entreated—after St. Anne reproaching him last year with being a fainéant for broading at such a season! At Cloutierville, where he would linger as long as possible, he meant to turn and retrace his course, zigzagging back and forth across Cane River so as to take in the Duplans, the Velcours, and others that he could not at the moment recall. A week seemed to Ozème a very, very little while in which to crowd so much pleasure.

There were steam-gins at work; he could hear them whistling far and near. On both sides of the river the fields were white with cotton, and everybody in the world seemed busy but Ozème. This reflection did not distress or disturb him in the least; he pursued his way at peace with himself and his surroundings.

At Lamérie's cross-roads store, where he stopped to buy a cigar, he learned that there was no use heading for Fédeaus', as the two old people had gone to town for a lengthy visit, and the house was locked up. It was at Fédeaus' that Ozème had intended to dine.

He sat in the buckboard, given up to a moment or two of reflection. The result was that he turned away from the river, and entered the road that led between two fields back to the woods and into the heart of the country. He had determined upon taking a short cut to the Beltrans' plantation, and on the way he meant to keep an eye open for old Aunt Tildy's cabin, which he knew lay in some remote part of this cut-off. He remembered that Aunt Tildy could cook an excellent meal if she had the material at hand. He would induce her to fry him a chicken, drip a cup of coffee, and turn him out a pone of corn-bread, which he thought would be sumptuous enough fare for the occasion.

Aunt Tildy dwelt in the not unusual log cabin, of one room, with its chimney of mud and stone, and its shallow gallery formed by the jutting of the roof. In close proximity to the cabin was a small cotton-field, which from a long distance looked like a field of snow. The cotton was bursting and overflowing foam-like from bolls on the drying stalk. On the lower branches it was hanging ragged and tattered, and much of it had already fallen to the ground. There were a few chinaberry-trees in the yard before the hut, and under one of them an ancient and rusty-looking mule was eating corn from a wood trough. Some common little Creole chickens were scratching about the mule's feet and snatching at the grains of corn that occasionally fell from the trough.

Aunt Tildy was hobbling across the yard when Ozème drew up before the gate. One hand was confined in a sling; in the other she carried a tin pan, which she let fall noisily to the ground when she recognized him. She was broad, black, and misshapen, with her body bent forward almost at an acute angle. She wore a blue cottonade of large plaids, and a bandana awkwardly twisted around her head.

"Good God A'mighty, man! Whar you come from?" was her startled exclamation at beholding him.

"F'om home, Aunt Tildy; w'ere else do you expec'?" replied Ozème, dismounting composedly.

He had not seen the old woman for several years—since she was cooking in town for the family with which he boarded at the time. She had washed and ironed for him, atrociously, it is true, but her intentions were beyond reproach if her washing was not. She had also been clumsily attentive to him during a spell of illness. He had paid her with an occasional bandana, a calico dress, or a checked apron, and they had always considered the account between themselves square, with no sentimental feeling of gratitude remaining on either side.

"I like to know," remarked Ozème, as he took the gray mare from the shafts, and led her up to the trough where the mule was—"I like to know w'at you mean by makin' a crop like that an' then lettin' it go to was'e? Who you reckon's goin' to pick that cotton? You think maybe the angels goin' to come down an' pick it fo' you, an' gin it an' press it, an' then give you ten cents a poun' fo' it, hein?"

"Ef de Lord don' pick it, I don' know who gwine pick it, Mista Ozème. I tell you, me an' Sandy we wuk dat crap day in an' day out; it's him done de mos' of it."

"Sandy? That little—"

"He ain' dat li'le Sandy no mo' w'at you rec'lec's; he 'mos' a man, an' he wuk like a man now. He wuk mo' 'an fittin' fo' his strenk, an' now he layin' in dah sick—God A'mighty knows how sick. An' me wid a risin' twell I bleeged to walk de flo' o' nights, an' don' know ef I ain' gwine to lose de han' atter all."

"W'y, in the name o' conscience, you don' hire somebody to pick?"

"Whar I got money to hire? An' you knows well as me ev'y chick an' chile is pickin' roun' on de plantations an' gittin' good pay."

The whole outlook appeared to Ozème very depressing, and even menacing, to his personal comfort and peace of mind. He foresaw no prospect of dinner unless he should cook it himself. And there was that Sandy—he remembered well the little scamp of eight, always at his grandmother's heels when she was cooking or washing. Of course he would have to go in and look at the boy, and no doubt dive into his traveling-bag for quinine, without which he never traveled.

Sandy was indeed very ill, consumed with fever. He lay on a cot covered up with a faded patchwork quilt. His eyes were half closed, and he was muttering and rambling on about hoeing and bedding and cleaning and thinning out the cotton; he was hauling it to the gin, wrangling about weight and bagging and ties and the price offered per pound. That bale or two of cotton had not only sent Sandy to bed, but had pursued him there, holding him through his fevered dreams, and threatening to end him. Ozème would never have known the black boy, he was so tall, so thin, and seemingly so wasted, lying there in bed.

"See yere, Aunt Tildy," said Ozème, after he had, as was usual with him when in doubt, abandoned himself to a little reflection; "between us—you an' me—we got to manage to kill an' cook one o' those chickens I see scratchin' out yonda, fo' I'm jus' about starved. I reckon you ain't got any quinine in the house? No; I didn't suppose an instant you had. Well, I'm goin' to give Sandy a good dose o' quinine to-night, an' I'm goin' stay an' see how that'll work on 'im. But sun-up, min' you, I mus' get out o' yere."

Ozème had spent more comfortable nights than the one passed in Aunt Tildy's bed, which she considerately abandoned to him.

In the morning Sandy's fever was somewhat abated, but had not taken a decided enough turn to justify Ozème in quitting him before noon, unless he was willing "to feel like a dog," as he told himself. He appeared before Aunt Tildy stripped to the undershirt, and wearing his second-best pair of trousers.

"That's a nice pickle o' fish you got me in, ol' woman. I guarantee, nex' time I go abroad, 'tain't me that'll take any cut-off. W'ere's that cotton-basket an' cotton-sack o' yo's?"

"I knowed it!" chanted Aunt Tildy—"I knowed de Lord war gwine sen' somebody to holp me out. He war n' gwine let de crap was'e atter he give Sandy an' me de strenk to make hit. De Lord gwine shove you 'long de row, Mista Ozème. De Lord gwine give you plenty mo' fingers an' han's to pick dat cotton nimble an' clean."

"Neva you min' w'at the Lord's goin' to do; go get me that cotton-sack. An' you put that poultice like I tol' you on yo' han', an' set down there an' watch Sandy. It looks like you are 'bout as helpless as a' ol' cow tangled up in a potato-vine."

Ozème had not picked cotton for many years, and he took to it a little awkwardly at first; but by the time he had reached the end of the first row the old dexterity of youth had come back to his hands, which flew rapidly back and forth with the motion of a weaver's shuttle; and his ten fingers became really nimble in clutching the cotton from its dry shell. By noon he had gathered about fifty pounds. Sandy was not then quite so well as he had promised to be, and Ozème concluded to stay that day and one more night. If the boy were no better in the morning, he would go off in search of a doctor for him, and he himself would continue on down to Tante Sophie's; the Beltrans' was out of the question now.

Sandy hardly needed a doctor in the morning. Ozème's doctoring was beginning to tell favorably; but he would have considered it criminal indifference and negligence to go away and leave the boy to Aunt Tildy's awkward ministrations just at the critical moment when there was a turn for the better; so he stayed that day out, and picked his hundred and fifty pounds.

On the third day it looked like rain, and a heavy rain just then would mean a heavy loss to Aunt Tildy and Sandy, and Ozème again went to the field, this time urging Aunt Tildy with him to do what she might with her one good hand.

"Aunt Tildy," called out Ozème to the bent old woman moving ahead of him between the white rows of cotton, "if the Lord gets me safe out o' this ditch, 't ain't to-morro' I'll fall in anotha with my eyes open, I bet you."

"Keep along, Mista Ozème; don' grumble, don' stumble; de Lord's a-watchin' you. Look at yo' Aunt Tildy; she doin' mo' wid her one han' 'an you doin' wid yo' two, man. Keep right along, honey. Watch dat cotton how it fallin' in yo' Aunt Tildy's bag."

"I am watchin' you, ol' woman; you don' fool me. You got to work that han' o' yo's spryer than you doin', or I'll take the rawhide. You done fo'got w'at the rawhide tas'e like, I reckon"—a reminder which amused Aunt Tildy so powerfully that her big negro-laugh resounded over the whole cotton-patch, and even caused Sandy, who heard it, to turn in his bed.

The weather was still threatening on the succeeding day, and a sort of dogged determination or characteristic desire to see his undertakings carried to a satisfactory completion urged Ozème to continue his efforts to drag Aunt Tildy out of the mire into which circumstances seemed to have thrust her.

One night the rain did come, and began to beat softly on the roof of the old cabin. Sandy opened his eyes, which were no longer brilliant with the fever flame. "Granny," he whispered, "de rain! Des listen, granny; de rain a-comin', an' I ain' pick dat cotton yit. W'at time it is? Gi' me my pants—I got to go—"

"You lay whar you is, chile alive. Dat cotton put aside clean and dry. Me an' de Lord an' Mista Ozème done pick dat cotton."

Ozème drove away in the morning looking quite as spick and span as the day he left home in his blue suit and his light felt drawn a little over his eyes.

"You want to take care o' that boy," he instructed Aunt Tildy at parting, "an' get 'im on his feet. An', let me tell you, the nex' time I start out to broad, if you see me passin' in this yere cut-off, put on yo' specs an' look at me good, because it won't be me; it'll be my ghos', ol' woman."

Indeed, Ozème, for some reason or other, felt quite shamefaced as he drove back to the plantation. When he emerged from the lane which he had entered the week before, and turned into the river road, Lamérie, standing in the store door, shouted out:

"Hé, Ozème! you had good times yonda? I bet you danced holes in the sole of them new boots."

"Don't talk, Lamérie!" was Ozème's rather ambiguous reply, as he flourished the remainder of a whip over the old gray mare's sway-back, urging her to a gentle trot.

When he reached home, Bodé, one of Padue's boys, who was assisting him to unhitch, remarked:

"How come you didn' go yonda down de coas' like you said, Mista Ozème? Nobody didn' see you in Cloutierville, an' Mailitte say you neva cross' de twenty-fo'-mile ferry, an' nobody didn' see you no place."

Ozème returned, after his customary moment of reflection:

"You see, it's 'mos' always the same thing on Cane riva, my boy; a man gets tired o' that à la fin. This time I went back in the woods, 'way yonda in the Fédeau cut-off; kin' o' campin' an' roughin' like, you might say. I tell you, it was sport, Bodé."

A Sentimental Soul

Lacodie stayed longer than was his custom in Mamzelle Fleurette's little store that evening. He had been tempted by the vapid utterances of a conservative bellhanger to loudly voice his radical opinions upon the rights and wrongs of humanity at large and his fellow-workingmen in particular. He was quite in a tremble when he finally laid his picayune down upon Mamzelle Fleurette's counter and helped himself to *l'Abeille* from the top of the diminished pile of newspapers which stood there.

He was small, frail and hollow-chested, but his head was magnificent with its generous adornment of waving black hair; its sunken eyes that glowed darkly and steadily and sometimes flamed, and its moustaches which were formidable.

"Eh bien, Mamzelle Fleurette, à demain, à demain!" and he waved a nervous good-bye as he let himself quickly and noiselessly out.

However violent Lacodie might be in his manner toward conservatives, he was always gentle, courteous and low-voiced with Mamzelle Fleurette, who was much older than he, much taller; who held no opinions, and whom he pitied, and even in a manner revered. Mamzelle Fleurette at once dismissed the bellhanger, with whom, on general principles, she had no sympathy.

She wanted to close the store, for she was going over to the cathedral to confession. She stayed a moment in the doorway watching Lacodie walk down the opposite side of the street. His step was something between a spring and a jerk, which to her partial eyes seemed the perfection of motion. She watched him until he entered his own small low doorway, over which hung a huge wooden key painted red, the emblem of his trade.

For many months now, Lacodie had been coming daily to Mamzelle Fleurette's little notion store to buy the morning paper, which he only bought and read, however, in the afternoon. Once he had crossed over with his box of keys and tools to open a cupboard, which would unlock for no inducements of its owner. He would not suffer her to pay him for the few moments' work; it was nothing, he assured her; it was a pleasure; he would not dream of accepting payment for so trifling a service from a camarade and fellow-worker. But she need not fear that he would lose by it, he told her with a laugh; he would only charge an extra quarter to the rich lawyer around the corner, or to the top-lofty druggist down the street when these might happen to need his services, as they sometimes did. This was an alternative which seemed far from right and honest to Mamzelle Fleurette. But she held a vague understanding that men were wickeder in many ways than women; that ungodliness was constitutional with them, like their sex, and inseparable from it.

Having watched Lacodie until he disappeared within his shop, she retired to her room, back of the store, and began her preparations to go out. She brushed carefully the black alpaca skirt, which hung in long nun-like folds around her spare figure. She smoothed down the brown, ill-fitting basque, and readjusted the old-fashioned, rusty black lace collar which she always wore. Her sleek hair was painfully and suspiciously black. She powdered her face abundantly with poudre de riz before starting out, and pinned a dotted black lace veil over her straw bonnet. There was little force or character or anything in her withered face, except a pathetic desire and appeal to be permitted to exist.

Mamzelle Fleurette did not walk down Chartres street with her usual composed tread; she seemed preoccupied and agitated. When she passed the locksmith's shop over the way and heard his voice within, she grew tremulously self-conscious, fingering her veil, swishing the black alpaca and waving her prayer book about with meaningless intention.

Mamzelle Fleurette was in great trouble; trouble which was so bitter, so sweet, so bewildering, so terrifying! It had come so stealthily upon her she had never suspected what it might be. She thought the world was growing brighter and more beautiful; she thought the flowers had re-doubled their sweetness and the birds their song, and that the voices of her fellow-creatures had grown kinder and their faces truer.

The day before Lacodie had not come to her for his paper. At six o'clock he was not there, at seven he was not there, nor at eight, and then she knew he would not come. At first, when it was only a little past the time of his coming, she had sat strangely disturbed and distressed in the rear of the store, with her back to the door. When the door opened she turned with fluttering expectancy. It was only an unhappy-looking child, who wanted to buy some foolscap, a pencil and an eraser. The next to come in was an old mulatresse, who was bringing her prayer beads for Mamzelle Fleurette to mend. The next was a gentleman, to buy the *Courier des États Unis*, and then a young girl, who wanted a holy picture for her favorite nun at the Ursulines; it was everybody but Lacodie.

A temptation assailed Mamzelle Fleurette, almost fierce in its intensity, to carry the paper over to his shop herself, when he was not there at seven. She conquered it from sheer moral inability to do anything so daring, so unprecedented. But to-day, when he had come back and had stayed so long discoursing with the bellhanger, a contentment, a rapture, had settled upon her being which she could no longer ignore or mistake. She loved Lacodie. That fact was plain to her now, as plain as the conviction that every reason existed why she should not love him. He was the husband of another woman. To love the husband of another woman was one of the deepest sins which Mamzelle Fleurette knew; murder was perhaps blacker, but she was not sure. She was going to confession now. She was going to tell her sin to Almighty God and Father Fochelle, and ask their forgiveness. She was going to pray and beg the saints and the Holy Virgin to remove the sweet and subtle poison from her soul. It was surely a poison, and a deadly one, which could make her feel that her youth had come back and taken her by the hand.

II

Mamzelle Fleurette had been confessing for many years to old Father Fochelle. In his secret heart he often thought it a waste of his time and her own that she should come with her little babblings, her little nothings to him, calling them sins. He felt that a wave of the hand might brush them away, and that it in a manner compromised the dignity of holy absolution to pronounce the act over so innocent a soul.

To-day she had whispered all her shortcomings into his ear through the grating of the confessional; he knew them so well! There were many other penitents waiting to be heard, and he was about to dismiss her with a hasty blessing when she arrested him, and in hesitating, faltering accents told him of her love for the locksmith, the husband of another woman.

A slap in the face would not have startled Father Fochelle more forcibly or more painfully. What soul was there on earth, he wondered, so hedged about with innocence as to be secure from the machinations of Satan! Oh, the thunder of indignation that descended upon Mamzelle Fleurette's head! She bowed down, beaten to earth beneath it. Then came questions, one, two, three, in quick succession, that made Mamzelle Fleurette gasp and clutch blindly before her. Why was she not a shadow, a vapor, that she might dissolve from before those angry, penetrating eyes; or a small insect, to creep into some crevice and there hide herself forevermore?

"Oh, father! no, no, no!" she faltered, "he knows nothing, nothing. I would die a hundred deaths before he should know, before anyone should know, besides yourself and the good God of whom I implore pardon."

Father Fochelle breathed more freely, and mopped his face with a flaming bandana, which he took from the ample pocket of his soutane. But he scolded Mamzelle Fleurette roundly, unpityingly; for being a fool, for being a sentimentalist. She had not committed mortal sin, but the occasion was ripe for it; and look to it she must that she keep Satan at bay with watchfulness and prayer. "Go, my child, and sin no more."

Mamzelle Fleurette made a detour in regaining her home by which she would not have to pass the locksmith's shop. She did not even look in that direction when she let herself in at the glass door of her store.

Some time before, when she was yet ignorant of the motive which prompted the act, she had cut from a newspaper a likeness of Lacodie, who had served as foreman of the jury during a prominent murder trial. The likeness happened to be good, and quite did justice to the locksmith's fine physiognomy with its leonine hirsute adornment. This picture Mamzelle Fleurette had kept hitherto between the pages of her prayer book. Here, twice a day, it looked out at her; as she turned the leaves of the holy mass in the morning, and when she read her evening devotions before her own little home altar, over which hung a crucifix and a picture of the Empress Eugénie.

Her first action upon entering her room, even before she unpinned the dotted veil, was to take Lacodie's picture from her prayer book and place it at random between the leaves of a "Dictionnaire de la Langue Française," which was the undermost of a pile of old books that stood on the corner of the mantelpiece. Between night and morning, when she would approach the holy sacrament, Mamzelle Fleurette felt it to be her duty to thrust Lacodie from her thoughts by every means and device known to her.

The following day was Sunday, when there was no occasion or opportunity for her to see the locksmith. Moreover, after partaking of holy communion, Mamzelle Fleurette felt invigorated; she was conscious of a new, if fictitious, strength to combat Satan and his wiles.

On Monday, as the hour approached for Lacodie to appear, Mamzelle Fleurette became harassed by indecision. Should she call in the young girl, the neighbor who relieved her on occasion, and deliver the store into the girl's hands for an hour or so? This might be well enough for once in a while, but she could not conveniently resort to this subterfuge daily. After all, she had her living to make, which consideration was paramount. She finally decided that she would retire to her little back room and when she heard the store door open she would call out:

"Is it you, Monsieur Lacodie? I am very busy; please take your paper and leave your cinq sous on the counter." If it happened not to be Lacodie she would come forward and serve the customer in person. She did not, of course, expect to carry out this performance each day; a fresh device would no doubt suggest itself for tomorrow. Mamzelle Fleurette proceeded to carry out her programme to the letter.

"Is it you, Monsieur Lacodie?" she called out from the little back room, when the front door opened. "I am very busy; please take your paper—"

"Ce n'est pas Lacodie, Mamzelle Fleurette. C'est moi, Augustine."

It was Lacodie's wife, a fat, comely young woman, wearing a blue veil thrown carelessly over her kinky black hair, and carrying some grocery parcels clasped close in her arms. Mamzelle Fleurette emerged from the back room, a prey to the most contradictory emotions; relief and disappointment struggling for the mastery with her.

"No Lacodie to-day, Mamzelle Fleurette," Augustine announced with a certain robust ill-humor; "he is there at home shaking with a chill till the very window panes rattle. He had one last Friday" (the day he had not come for his paper) "and now another and a worse one to-day. God knows, if it keeps on—well, let me have the paper; he will want to read it to-night when his chill is past."

Mamzelle Fleurette handed the paper to Augustine, feeling like an old woman in a dream handing a newspaper to a young woman in a dream. She had never thought of Lacodie having chills or being ill. It seemed very strange. And Augustine was no sooner gone than all the ague remedies she had ever heard of came crowding to Mamzelle Fleurette's mind; an egg in black coffee—or was it a lemon in black coffee? or an egg in vinegar? She rushed to the door to call Augustine back, but the young woman was already far down the street.

III

Augustine did not come the next day, nor the next, for the paper. The unhappy looking child who had returned for more foolscap, informed Mamzelle Fleurette that he had heard his mother say that Monsieur Lacodie was very sick, and the bellhanger had sat up all night with him. The following day Mamzelle Fleurette saw Choppin's coupé pass clattering over the cobblestones and stop before the locksmith's door. She knew that with her class it was only in a case of extremity that the famous and expensive physician was summoned. For the first time she thought of death. She prayed all day, silently, to herself, even while waiting upon customers.

In the evening she took an *Abeille* from the top of the pile on the counter, and throwing a light shawl over her head, started with the paper over to the locksmith's shop. She did not know if she were committing a sin in so doing. She would ask Father Fochelle on Saturday, when she went to confession. She did not think it could be a sin; she would have called long before on any other sick neighbor, and she intuitively felt that in this distinction might lie the possibility of sin.

The shop was deserted except for the presence of Lacodie's little boy of five, who sat upon the floor playing with the tools and contrivances which all his days he had coveted, and which all his days had been denied to him. Mamzelle Fleurette mounted the narrow stairway in the rear of the shop which led to an upper landing and then into the room of the married couple. She stood a while hesitating upon this landing before venturing to knock softly upon the partly open door through which she could hear their voices.

"I thought," she remarked apologetically to Augustine, "that perhaps Monsieur Lacodie might like to look at the paper and you had no time to come for it, so I brought it myself."

"Come in, come in, Mamzelle Fleurette. It's Mamzelle Fleurette who comes to inquire about you, Lacodie," Augustine called out loudly to her husband, whose half consciousness she somehow confounded with deafness.

Mamzelle Fleurette drew mincingly forward, clasping her thin hands together at the waist line, and she peeped timorously at Lacodie lying lost amid the bedclothes. His black mane was tossed wildly over the pillow and lent a fictitious pallor to the yellow waxiness of his drawn features. An approaching chill was sending incipient shudders through his frame, and making his teeth claque. But he still turned his head courteously in Mamzelle Fleurette's direction.

"Bien bon de votre part, Mamzelle Fleurette—mais c'est fini. J'suis flambé, flambé, flambé!"

Oh, the pain of it! to hear him in such extremity thanking her for her visit, assuring her in the same breath that all was over with him. She wondered how Augustine could hear it so composedly. She whisperingly inquired if a priest had been summoned.

"Inutile; il n'en veut pas," was Augustine's reply. So he would have no priest at his bedside, and here was a new weight of bitterness for Mamzelle Fleurette to carry all her days.

She flitted back to her store through the darkness, herself like a slim shadow. The November evening was chill and misty. A dull aureole shot out from the feeble gas jet at the corner, only faintly and for an instant illumining her figure as it glided rapidly and noiselessly along the banquette. Mamzelle Fleurette slept little and prayed much that night. Saturday morning Lacodie died. On Sunday he was buried and Mamzelle Fleurette did not go to the funeral, because Father Fochelle told her plainly she had no business there.

It seemed inexpressibly hard to Mamzelle Fleurette that she was not permitted to hold Lacodie in tender remembrance now that he was dead. But Father Fochelle, with his practical insight, made no compromise with sentimentality; and she did not question his authority, or his ability to master the subtleties of a situation utterly beyond reach of her own powers.

It was no longer a pleasure for Mamzelle Fleurette to go to confession as it had formerly been. Her heart went on loving Lacodie and her soul went on struggling; for she made this delicate and puzzling distinction between heart and soul, and pictured the two as set in a very death struggle against each other.

"I cannot help it, father. I try, but I cannot help it. To love him is like breathing; I do not know how to help it. I pray, and pray, and it does no good, for half of my prayers are for the repose of his soul. It surely cannot be a sin, to pray for the repose of his soul?"

Father Fochelle was heartily sick and tired of Mamzelle Fleurette and her stupidities. Oftentimes he was tempted to drive her from the confessional, and forbid her return until she should have regained a rational state of mind. But he could not withhold absolution from a penitent who, week after week, acknowledged her shortcoming and strove with all her faculties to overcome it and atone for it.

IV

Augustine had sold out the locksmith's shop and the business, and had removed further down the street over a bakery. Out of her window she had hung a sign, "Blanchisseuse de Fin." Often, in passing by, Mamzelle Fleurette would catch a glimpse of Augustine up at the window, plying the irons; her sleeves rolled to the elbows, baring her round, white arms, and the little black curls all moist and tangled about her face. It was early spring then, and there was a languor in the air; an odor of jasmine in every passing breeze; the sky was blue, unfathomable, and fleecy white; and people along the narrow street laughed, and sang, and called to one another from windows and doorways. Augustine had set a pot of rose-geranium on her window sill and hung out a bird cage.

Once, Mamzelle Fleurette in passing on her way to confession heard her singing roulades, vying with the bird in the cage. Another time she saw the young woman leaning with half her body from the window, exchanging pleasantries with the baker standing beneath on the banquette.

Still, a little later, Mamzelle Fleurette began to notice a handsome young fellow often passing the store. He was jaunty and debonnaire and wore a rich watchchain, and looked prosperous. She knew him quite well as a fine young Gascon, who kept a stall in the French Market, and from whom she had often bought charcuterie. The neighbors told her the young Gascon was paying his addresses to Mme. Lacodie. Mamzelle Fleurette shuddered. She wondered if Lacodie knew! The whole situation seemed suddenly to shift its base, causing Mamzelle Fleurette to stagger. What ground would her poor heart and soul have to do battle upon now?

She had not yet had time to adjust her conscience to the altered conditions when one Saturday afternoon, as she was about to start out to confession, she noticed an unusual movement down the street. The bellhanger, who happened to be presenting himself in the character of a customer, informed her that it was nothing more nor less than Mme.

Lacodie returning from her wedding with the Gascon. He was black and bitter with indignation, and thought she might at least have waited for the year to be out. But the charivari was already on foot; and Mamzelle need not feel alarmed if, in the night, she heard sounds and clamor to rouse the dead as far away as Metairie ridge.

Mamzelle Fleurette sank down in a chair, trembling in all her members. She faintly begged the bellhanger to pour her a glass of water from the stone pitcher behind the counter. She fanned herself and loosened her bonnet strings. She sent the bellhanger away.

She nervously pulled off her rusty black kid gloves, and ten times more nervously drew them on again. To a little customer, who came in for chewing gum, she handed a paper of pins.

There was a great, a terrible upheaval taking place in Mamzelle Fleurette's soul. She was preparing for the first time in her life to take her conscience into her own keeping.

When she felt herself sufficiently composed to appear decently upon the street, she started out to confession. She did not go to Father Fochelle. She did not even go to the Cathedral; but to a church which was much farther away, and to reach which she had to spend a picayune for car fare.

Mamzelle Fleurette confessed herself to a priest who was utterly new and strange to her. She told him all her little venial sins, which she had much difficulty in bringing to a number of any dignity and importance whatever. Not once did she mention her love for Lacodie, the dead husband of another woman.

Mamzelle Fleurette did not ride back to her home; she walked. The sensation of walking on air was altogether delicious; she had never experienced it before. A long time she stood contemplative before a shop window in which were displayed wreaths, mottoes, emblems, designed for the embellishment of tombstones. What a sweet comfort it would be, she reflected, on the 1st of November to carry some such delicate offering to Lacodie's last resting place. Might not the sole care of his tomb devolve upon her, after all! The possibility thrilled her and moved her to the heart. What thought would the merry Augustine and her lover-husband have for the dead lying in cemeteries!

When Mamzelle Fleurette reached home she went through the store directly into her little back room. The first thing which she did, even before unpinning the dotted lace veil, was to take the "Dictionnaire de la Langue Française" from beneath the pile of old books on the mantelpiece.

It was not easy to find Lacodie's picture hidden somewhere in its depths. But the search afforded her almost a sensuous pleasure; turning the leaves slowly back and forth.

When she had secured the likeness she went into the store and from her showcase selected a picture frame—the very handsomest there; one of those which sold for thirty-five cents.

Into the frame Mamzelle Fleurette neatly and deftly pasted Lacodie's picture. Then she re-entered her room and deliberately hung it upon the wall—between the crucifix and the portrait of Empress Eugènie—and she did not care if the Gascon's wife ever saw it or not.

Her Letters

I

She had given orders that she wished to remain undisturbed and more-over had locked the doors of her room.

The house was very still. The rain was falling steadily from a leaden sky in which there was no gleam, no rift, no promise. A generous wood fire had been lighted in the ample fireplace and it brightened and illu-mined the luxurious apartment to its furthermost corner.

From some remote nook of her writing desk the woman took a thick bundle of letters, bound tightly together with strong, coarse twine, and placed it upon the table in the centre of the room.

For weeks she had been schooling herself for what she was about to do. There was a strong deliberation in the lines of her long, thin, sensitive face; her hands, too, were long and delicate and blue-veined.

With a pair of scissors she snapped the cord binding the letters together. Thus released the ones which were top-most slid down to the table and she, with a quick movement thrust her fingers among them, scattering and turning them over till they quite covered the broad surface of the table.

Before her were envelopes of various sizes and shapes, all of them addressed in the handwriting of one man and one woman. He had sent her letters all back to her one day when, sick with dread of possibilities, she had asked to have them returned. She had meant, then, to destroy them all, his and her own. That was four years ago, and she had been feeding upon them ever since; they had sustained her, she believed, and kept her spirit from perishing utterly.

But now the days had come when the premonition of danger could no longer remain unheeded. She knew that before many months were past she would have to part from her treasure, leaving it unguarded. She shrank from inflicting the pain, the anguish which the discovery of those letters would bring to others; to one, above all, who was near to her, and whose tenderness and years of devotion had made him, in a manner, dear to her.

She calmly selected a letter at random from the pile and cast it into the roaring fire. A second one followed almost as calmly, with the third her hand began to tremble; when, in a sudden paroxysm she cast a fourth, a fifth, and a sixth into the flames in breathless succession.

Then she stopped and began to pant—for she was far from strong, and she stayed staring into the fire with pained and savage eyes. Oh, what had she done! What had she not done! With feverish apprehension she began to search among the letters before her. Which of them had she so ruthlessly, so cruelly put out of her existence? Heaven grant, not the first, that very first one, written before they had learned, or dared to say to each other "I love you." No, no; there it was, safe enough. She laughed with pleasure, and held it to her lips. But what if that other most precious and most imprudent one were missing! in which every word of untempered passion had long ago eaten its way into her brain; and which stirred her still to-day, as it had done a hundred times before when she thought of it. She crushed it between her palms when she found it. She kissed it again and again. With her sharp white teeth she tore the far corner from the letter, where the name was written; she bit the torn scrap and tasted it between her lips and upon her tongue like some god-given morsel.

What unbounded thankfulness she felt at not having destroyed them all! How desolate and empty would have been her remaining days without them; with only her thoughts, illusive thoughts that she could not hold in her hands and press, as she did these, to her cheeks and her heart.

This man had changed the water in her veins to wine, whose taste had brought delirium to both of them. It was all one and past now, save for these letters that she held encircled in her arms. She stayed breathing softly and contentedly, with the hectic cheek resting upon them.

She was thinking, thinking of a way to keep them without possible ultimate injury to that other one whom they would stab more cruelly than keen knife blades.

At last she found the way. It was a way that frightened and bewildered her to think of at first, but she had reached it by deduction too sure to admit of doubt. She meant, of course, to destroy them herself before the end came. But how does the end come and when? Who may tell? She would guard against the possibility of accident by leaving them in charge of the very one who, above all, should be spared a knowledge of their contents.

She roused herself from the stupor of thought and gathered the scattered letters once more together, binding them again with the rough twine. She wrapped the compact bundle in a thick sheet of white polished paper. Then she wrote in ink upon the back of it, in large, firm characters:

"I leave this package to the care of my husband. With perfect faith in his loyalty and his love, I ask him to destroy it unopened."

It was not sealed; only a bit of string held the wrapper, which she could remove and replace at will whenever the humor came to her to pass an hour in some intoxicating dream of the days when she felt she had lived.

II

If he had come upon that bundle of letters in the first flush of his poignant sorrow there would not have been an instant's hesitancy. To destroy it promptly and without question would have seemed a welcome expression of devotion—a way of reaching her, of crying out his love to her while the world was still filled with the illusion of her presence. But months had passed since that spring day when they had found her stretched upon the floor, clutching the key of her writing desk, which she appeared to have been attempting to reach when death overtook her.

The day was much like that day a year ago when the leaves were falling and rain pouring steadily from a leaden sky which held no gleam, no promise. He had happened accidentally upon the package in that remote nook of her desk. And just as she herself had done a year ago, he carried it to the table and laid it down there, standing, staring with puzzled eyes at the message which confronted him:

"I leave this package to the care of my husband. With perfect faith in his loyalty and his love, I ask him to destroy it unopened."

She had made no mistake; every line of his face—no longer young—spoke loyalty and honesty, and his eyes were as faithful as a dog's and as loving. He was a tall, powerful man, standing there in the firelight, with shoulders that stooped a little, and hair that was growing somewhat thin and gray, and a face that was distinguished, and must have been handsome when he smiled. But he was slow. "Destroy it unopened," he re-read, half-aloud, "but why unopened?"

He took the package again in his hands, and turning it about and feeling it, discovered that it was composed of many letters tightly packed together.

So here were letters which she was asking him to destroy unopened. She had never seemed in her lifetime to have had a secret from him. He knew her to have been cold and passionless, but true, and watchful of his comfort and his happiness. Might he not be holding in his hands the secret of some other one, which had been confided to her and which she had promised to guard? But, no, she would have indicated the fact by some additional word or line. The secret was her own, something contained in these letters, and she wanted it to die with her.

If he could have thought of her as on some distant shadowy shore waiting for him throughout the years with outstretched hands to come and join her again, he would not have hesitated. With hopeful confidence he would have thought "in that blessed meeting-time, soul to soul, she will tell me all; till then I can wait and trust." But he could not think of her in any far-off paradise awaiting him. He felt that there was no smallest part of her anywhere in the universe, more than there had been before she was born into the world. But she had embodied herself with terrible significance in an intangible wish, uttered when life still coursed through her veins; knowing that it would reach him when the annihilation of death was between them, but uttered with all confidence in its power and potency. He was moved by the splendid daring of the act, which at the same time exalted him and lifted him above the head of common mortals.

What secret save one could a woman choose to have die with her? As quickly as the suggestion came to his mind, so swiftly did the man-instinct of possession stir in his blood. His fingers cramped about the package in his hands, and he sank into a chair beside the table. The agonizing suspicion that perhaps another had shared with him her thoughts, her affections, her life, deprived him for a swift instant of honor and reason. He thrust the end of his strong thumb beneath the string which, with a single turn would have yielded—"with perfect faith in your loyalty and your love." It was not the written characters addressing themselves to the eye; it was like a voice speaking to his soul. With a tremor of anguish he bowed his head down upon the letters.

A half-hour passed before he lifted his head. An unspeakable conflict had raged within him, but his loyalty and his love had conquered. His face was pale and deep-lined with suffering, but there was no more hesitancy to be seen there.

He did not for a moment think of casting the thick package into the flames to be licked by the fiery tongues, and charred and half-revealed to his eyes. That was not what she meant. He arose, and taking a heavy bronze paper-weight from the table, bound it securely to the package. He walked to the window and looked out into the street below. Darkness had come, and it was still raining. He could hear the rain dashing against the window-panes, and could see it falling through the dull yellow rim of light cast by the lighted street lamp.

He prepared himself to go out, and when quite ready to leave the house thrust the weighted package into the deep pocket of his top-coat.

He did not hurry along the street as most people were doing at that hour, but walked with a long, slow, deliberate step, not seeming to mind the penetrating chill and rain driving into his face despite the shelter of his umbrella.

His dwelling was not far removed from the business section of the city; and it was not a great while before he found himself at the entrance of the bridge that spanned the river—the deep, broad, swift, black river dividing two States. He walked on and out to the very centre of the structure. The wind was blowing fiercely and keenly. The darkness where he stood was impenetrable. The thousands of lights in the city he had left seemed like all the stars of heaven massed together, sinking into some distant mysterious horizon, leaving him alone in a black, boundless universe.

He drew the package from his pocket and leaning as far as he could over the broad stone rail of the bridge, cast it from him into the river. It fell straight and swiftly from his hand. He could not follow its descent through the darkness, nor hear its dip into the water far below. It vanished silently; seemingly into some inky unfathomable space. He felt as if he were flinging it back to her in that unknown world whither she had gone.

III

An hour or two later he sat at his table in the company of several men whom he had invited that day to dine with him. A weight had settled upon his spirit, a conviction, a certitude that there could be but one secret which a woman would choose to have die with her. This one thought was possessing him. It occupied his brain, keeping it nimble and alert with suspicion. It clutched his heart, making every breath of existence a fresh moment of pain.

The men about him were no longer the friends of yesterday; in each one he discerned a possible enemy. He attended absently to their talk. He was remembering how she had conducted herself toward this one and that one; striving to recall conversations, subtleties of facial expression that might have meant what he did not suspect at the moment, shades of meaning in words that had seemed the ordinary interchange of social amenities.

He led the conversation to the subject of women, probing these men for their opinions and experiences. There was not one but claimed some infallible power to command the affections of any woman whom his fancy might select. He had heard the empty boast before from the same group and had always met it with good-humored contempt. But to-night every flagrant, inane utterance was charged with a new meaning, revealing possibilities that he had hitherto never taken into account.

He was glad when they were gone. He was eager to be alone, not from any desire or intention to sleep. He was impatient to regain her room, that room in which she had lived a large portion of her life, and where he had found those letters. There must surely be more of them somewhere, he thought; some forgotten scrap, some written thought or expression lying unguarded by an inviolable command.

At the hour when he usually retired for the night he sat himself down before her writing desk and began the search of drawers, slides, pigeon-holes, nooks and corners. He did not leave a scrap of anything unread. Many of the letters which he found were old; some he had read before; others were new to him. But in none did he find a faintest evidence that his wife had not been the true and loyal woman he had always believed her to be. The night was nearly spent before the fruitless search ended. The brief, troubled sleep which he snatched before his hour for rising was freighted with feverish, grotesque dreams, through all of which he could hear and could see dimly the dark river rushing by, carrying away his heart, his ambitions, his life.

But it was not alone in letters that women betrayed their emotions, he thought. Often he had known them, especially when in love, to mark fugitive, sentimental passages in books of verse or prose, thus expressing and revealing their own hidden thought. Might she not have done the same?

Then began a second and far more exhausting and arduous quest than the first, turning, page by page, the volumes that crowded her room—books of fiction, poetry, philosophy. She had read them all; but nowhere, by the shadow of a sign, could he find that the author had echoed the secret of her existence—the secret which he had held in his hands and had cast into the river.

He began cautiously and gradually to question this one and that one, striving to learn by indirect ways what each had thought of her. Foremost he learned she had been unsympathetic because of her coldness of manner. One had admired her intellect; another her accomplishments; a third had thought her beautiful before disease claimed her, regretting, however, that her beauty had lacked warmth of color and expression. She was praised by some for gentleness and kindness, and by others for cleverness and tact. Oh, it was useless to try to discover anything from men! He might have known. It was women who would talk of what they knew.

They did talk, unreservedly. Most of them had loved her; those who had not had held her in respect and esteem.

IV

And yet, and yet, "there is but one secret which a woman would choose to have die with her," was the thought which continued to haunt him and deprive him of rest. Days and nights of uncertainty began slowly to unnerve him and to torture him. An assurance of the worst that he dreaded would have offered him peace most welcome, even at the price of happiness.

It seemed no longer of any moment to him that men should come and go; and fall or rise in the world; and wed and die. It did not signify if money came to him by a turn of chance or eluded him. Empty and meaningless seemed to him all devices which the world offers for man's entertainment. The food and the drink set before him had lost their flavor. He did not longer know or care if the sun shone or the clouds lowered about him. A cruel hazard had struck him there where he was weakest, shattering his whole being, leaving him with but one wish in his soul, one gnawing desire, to know the mystery which he had held in his hands and had cast into the river.

One night when there were no stars shining he wandered, restless, upon the streets. He no longer sought to know from men and women what they dared not or could not tell him. Only the river knew. He went and stood again upon the bridge where he had stood many an hour since that night when the darkness then had closed around him and engulfed his manhood.

Only the river knew. It babbled, and he listened to it, and it told him nothing, but it promised all. He could hear it promising him with caressing voice, peace and sweet repose. He could hear the sweep, the song of the water inviting him.

A moment more and he had gone to seek her, and to join her and her secret thought in the immeasurable rest.

Odalie Misses Mass

Odalie sprang down from the mulecart, shook out her white skirts, and firmly grasping her parasol, which was blue to correspond with her sash, entered Aunt Pinky's gate and proceeded towards the old woman's cabin. She was a thick-waisted young thing who walked with a firm tread and carried her head with a determined poise. Her straight brown hair had been rolled up over night in papillotes, and the artificial curls stood out in clusters, stiff and uncompromising beneath the rim of her white chip hat. Her mother, sister and brother remained seated in the cart before the gate.

It was the fifteenth of August, the great feast of the Assumption, so generally observed in the Catholic parishes of Louisiana. The Chotard family were on their way to mass, and Odalie had insisted upon stopping to "show herself" to her old friend and protegée, Aunt Pinky.

The helpless, shrivelled old negress sat in the depths of a large, rudely-fashioned chair. A loosely hanging unbleached cotton gown enveloped her mite of a figure. What was visible of her hair beneath the bandana turban, looked like white sheep's wool. She wore round, silver-rimmed spectacles, which gave her an air of wisdom and respectability, and she held in her hand the branch of a hickory sapling, with which she kept mosquitoes and flies at bay, and even chickens and pigs that sometimes penetrated the heart of her domain.

Odalie walked straight up to the old woman and kissed her on the cheek.

"Well, Aunt Pinky, yere I am," she announced with evident self-complacency, turning herself slowly and stiffly around like a mechanical dummy. In one hand she held her prayer-book, fan and handkerchief, in the other the blue parasol, still open; and on her plump hands were blue cotton mitts. Aunt Pinky beamed and chuckled; Odalie hardly expected her to be able to do more.

"Now you saw me," the child continued. "I reckon you satisfied. I mus' go; I ain't got a minute to was'e." But at the threshold she turned to inquire, bluntly:

"W'ere's Pug?"

"Pug," replied Aunt Pinky, in her tremulous old-woman's voice. "She's gone to chu'ch; done gone; she done gone," nodding her head in seeming approval of Pug's action.

"To church!" echoed Odalie with a look of consternation settling in her round eyes.

"She gone to chu'ch," reiterated Aunt Pinky. "Say she kain't miss chu'ch on de fifteent'; de debble gwine pester her twell jedgment, she miss chu'ch on de fifteent'."

Odalie's plump cheeks fairly quivered with indignation and she stamped her foot. She looked up and down the long, dusty road that skirted the river. Nothing was to be seen save the blue cart with its dejected looking mule and patient occupants. She walked to the end of the gallery and called out to a negro boy whose black bullet-head showed up in bold relief against the white of the cotton patch:

"He, Baptiste! w'ere's yo' ma? Ask yo' ma if she can't come set with Aunt Pinky."

"Mammy, she gone to chu'ch," screamed Baptiste in answer.

"Bonté! w'at's taken you all darkies with yo' 'church' to-day? You come along yere Baptiste an' set with Aunt Pinky. That Pug! I'm goin' to make yo' ma wear her out fo' that trick of hers—leavin' Aunt Pinky like that."

But at the first intimation of what was wanted of him, Baptiste dipped below the cotton like a fish beneath water, leaving no sight nor sound of himself to answer Odalie's repeated calls. Her mother and sister were beginning to show signs of impatience.

"But, I can't go," she cried out to them. "It's nobody to stay with Aunt Pinky. I can't leave Aunt Pinky like that, to fall out of her chair, maybe, like she already fell out once."

"You goin' to miss mass on the fifteenth, you, Odalie! W'at you thinkin' about?" came in shrill rebuke from her sister. But her mother offering no objection, the boy lost not a moment in starting the mule forward at a brisk trot. She watched them disappear in a cloud of dust;

and turning with a dejected, almost tearful countenance, re-entered the room.

Aunt Pinky seemed to accept her reappearance as a matter of course; and even evinced no surprise at seeing her remove her hat and mitts, which she laid carefully, almost religiously, on the bed, together with her book, fan and handkerchief.

Then Odalie went and seated herself some distance from the old woman in her own small, low rocking-chair. She rocked herself furiously, making a great clatter with the rockers over the wide, uneven boards of the cabin floor; and she looked out through the open door.

"Puggy, she done gone to chu'ch; done gone. Say de debble gwine pester her twell jedgment—"

"You done tole me that, Aunt Pinky; neva mine; don't le's talk about it."

Aunt Pinky thus rebuked, settled back into silence and Odalie continued to rock and stare out of the door.

Once she arose, and taking the hickory branch from Aunt Pinky's nerveless hand, made a bold and sudden charge upon a little pig that seemed bent upon keeping her company. She pursued him with flying heels and loud cries as far as the road. She came back flushed and breathless and her curls hanging rather limp around her face; she began again to rock herself and gaze silently out of the door.

"You gwine make yo' fus' c'mmunion?"

This seemingly sober inquiry on the part of Aunt Pinky at once shattered Odalie's ill-humor and dispelled every shadow of it. She leaned back and laughed with wild abandonment.

"Mais w'at you thinkin' about, Aunt Pinky? How you don't remember I made my firs' communion las' year, with this same dress w'at maman let out the tuck," holding up the altered skirt for Aunt Pinky's inspection. "An' with this same petticoat w'at maman added this ruffle an' crochet' edge; excep' I had a w'ite sash."

These evidences proved beyond question convincing and seemed to satisfy Aunt Pinky. Odalie rocked as furiously as ever, but she sang now, and the swaying chair had worked its way nearer to the old woman.

"You gwine git mar'ied?"

"I declare, Aunt Pinky," said Odalie, when she had ceased laughing and was wiping her eyes, "I declare, sometime' I think you gittin' plumb foolish. How you expec' me to git married w'en I'm on'y thirteen?"

Evidently Aunt Pinky did not know why or how she expected anything so preposterous; Odalie's holiday attire that filled her with contemplative rapture, had doubtless incited her to these vagaries.

The child now drew her chair quite close to the old woman's knee after she had gone out to the rear of the cabin to get herself some water and had brought a drink to Aunt Pinky in the gourd dipper.

There was a strong, hot breeze blowing from the river, and it swept fitfully and in gusts through the cabin, bringing with it the weedy smell of cacti that grew thick on the bank, and occasionally a shower of reddish dust from the road. Odalie for a while was greatly occupied in keeping in place her filmy skirt, which every gust of wind swelled balloon-like about her knees. Aunt Pinky's little black, scrawny hand had found its way among the droopy curls, and strayed often caressingly to the child's plump neck and shoulders.

"You riclics, honey, dat day yo' granpappy say it wur pinchin' times an' he reckin he bleege to sell Yallah Tom an' Susan an' Pinky? Don' know how come he think 'bout Pinky, 'less caze he sees me playin' an' trapsin' roun' wid you alls, day in an' out. I riclics yit how you tu'n w'ite like milk an' fling yo' arms roun' li'le black Pinky; an' you cries out you don' wan' no saddle-mar'; you don' wan' no silk dresses and fing' rings an' sich; an' don' wan' no idication; des wants Pinky. An' you cries an' screams an' kicks, an' 'low you gwine kill fus' pusson w'at dar come an' buy Pinky an' kiars her off. You riclics dat, honey?"

Odalie had grown accustomed to these flights of fancy on the part of her old friend; she liked to humor her as she chose to sometimes humor very small children; so she was quite used to impersonating one dearly beloved but impetuous, "Paulette," who seemed to have held her place in old Pinky's heart and imagination through all the years of her suffering life.

"I rec'lec' like it was yesterday, Aunt Pinky. How I scream an' kick an' maman gave me some med'cine; an' how you scream an' kick an' Susan took you down to the quarters an' give you 'twenty'."

"Das so, honey; des like you says," chuckled Aunt Pinky. "But you don' riclic dat time you cotch Pinky cryin' down in de holler behine de gin; an' you say you gwine give me 'twenty' ef I don' tell you w'at I cryin' 'bout?"

"I rec'lec' like it happen'd to-day, Aunt Pinky. You been cryin' because you want to marry Hiram, ole Mr. Benitou's servant."

"Das true like you says, Miss Paulette; an' you goes home an' cries and kiars on an' won' eat, an' breaks dishes, an' pesters yo' gran'pap 'tell he bleedge to buy Hi'um f'om de Benitous."

"Don't talk, Aunt Pink! I can see all that jus' as plain!" responded Odalie sympathetically, yet in truth she took but a languid interest in these reminiscences which she had listened to so often before.

She leaned her flushed cheek against Aunt Pinky's knee.

The air was rippling now, and hot and caressing. There was the hum of bumble bees outside; and busy mud-daubers kept flying in and out through the door. Some chickens had penetrated to the very threshold in their aimless roamings, and the little pig was approaching more cautiously. Sleep was fast overtaking the child, but she could still hear through her drowsiness the familiar tones of Aunt Pinky's voice.

"But Hi'um, he done gone; he nuva come back; an' Yallah Tom nuva come back; an' ole Marster an' de chillun—all gone—nuva come back. Nobody nuva come back to Pinky 'cep you, my honey. You ain' gwine 'way f'om Pinky no mo', is you, Miss Paulette?"

"Don' fret, Aunt Pinky—I'm goin'—to stay with—you."

"No pussun nuva come back 'cep' you."

Odalie was fast asleep. Aunt Pinky was asleep with her head leaning back on her chair and her fingers thrust into the mass of tangled brown hair that swept across her lap. The chickens and little pig walked fearlessly in and out. The sunlight crept close up to the cabin door and stole away again.

Odalie awoke with a start. Her mother was standing over her arousing her from sleep. She sprang up and rubbed her eyes. "Oh, I been asleep!" she exclaimed. The cart was standing in the road waiting. "An' Aunt Pinky, she's asleep, too."

"Yes, chérie, Aunt Pinky is asleep," replied her mother, leading Odalie away. But she spoke low and trod softly as gentle-souled women do, in the presence of the dead.

Polydore

It was often said that Polydore was the stupidest boy to be found "from the mouth of Cane river plumb to Natchitoches." Hence it was an easy matter to persuade him, as meddlesome and mischievous people sometimes tried to do, that he was an overworked and much abused individual.

It occurred one morning to Polydore to wonder what would happen if he did not get up. He hardly expected the world to stop turning on its axis; but he did in a way believe that the machinery of the whole plantation would come to a standstill.

He had awakened at the usual hour,—about daybreak,—and instead of getting up at once, as was his custom, he re-settled himself between the sheets. There he lay, peering out through the dormer window into the gray morning that was deliciously cool after the hot summer night, listening to familiar sounds that came from the barn-yard, the fields and woods beyond, heralding the approach of day.

A little later there were other sounds, no less familiar or significant; the roll of the wagon-wheels; the distant call of a negro's voice; Aunt Siney's shuffling step as she crossed the gallery, bearing to Mamzelle Adélaïde and old Monsieur José their early coffee.

Polydore had formed no plan and had thought only vaguely upon results. He lay in a half-slumber awaiting developments, and philosophically resigned to any turn which the affair might take. Still he was not quite ready with an answer when Jude came and thrust his head in at the door.

"Mista Polydore! O Mista Polydore! You 'sleep?"

"W'at you want?"

"Dan 'low he ain' gwine wait yonda wid de wagon all day. Say does you inspect 'im to pack dat freight f'om de landing by hisse'f?"

"I reckon he got it to do, Jude. I ain' going to get up, me."

"You ain' gwine git up?"

"No; I'm sick. I'm going stay in bed. Go 'long and le' me sleep."

The next one to invade Polydore's privacy was Mamzelle Adélaïde herself. It was no small effort for her to mount the steep, narrow stairway to Polydore's room. She seldom penetrated to these regions under the roof. He could hear the stairs creak beneath her weight, and knew that she was panting at every step. Her presence seemed to crowd the small room; for she was stout and rather tall, and her flowing muslin wrapper swept majestically from side to side as she walked.

Mamzelle Adélaïde had reached middle age, but her face was still fresh with its mignon features; and her brown eyes at the moment were round with astonishment and alarm.

"W'at's that I hear, Polydore? They tell me you're sick!" She went and stood beside the bed, lifting the mosquito bar that settled upon her head and fell about her like a veil.

Polydore's eyes blinked, and he made no attempt to answer. She felt his wrist softly with the tips of her fingers, and rested her hand for a moment on his low forehead beneath the shock of black hair.

"But you don't seem to have any fever, Polydore!"

"No," hesitatingly, feeling himself forced to make some reply. "It's a kine of—a kine of pain, like you might say. It kitch me yere in the knee, and it goes 'long like you stickin' a knife clean down in my heel. Aie! Oh, lala!" expressions of pain wrung from him by Mamzelle Adélaïde gently pushing aside the covering to examine the afflicted member.

"My patience! but that leg is swollen, yes, Polydore." The limb, in fact, seemed dropsical, but if Mamzelle Adélaïde had bethought her of comparing it with the other one, she would have found the two corresponding in their proportions to a nicety. Her kind face expressed the utmost concern, and she quitted Polydore feeling pained and ill at ease.

For one of the aims of Mamzelle Adélaïde's existence was to do the right thing by this boy, whose mother, a 'Cadian hill woman, had begged her with dying breath to watch over the temporal and spiritual welfare of her son; above all, to see that he did not follow in the slothful footsteps of an over-indolent father.

Polydore's scheme worked so marvellously to his comfort and pleasure that he wondered at not having thought of it before. He ate with keen relish the breakfast which Jude brought to him on a tray. Even old Monsieur José was concerned, and made his way up to Polydore, bringing a number of picture-papers for his entertainment, a palm-leaf fan and a cow-bell, with which to summon Jude when necessary and which he placed within easy reach.

As Polydore lay on his back fanning luxuriously, it seemed to him that he was enjoying a foretaste of paradise. Only once did he shudder with apprehension. It was when he heard Aunt Siney, with lifted voice, recommending to "wrop the laig up in bacon fat; de oniest way to draw out de misery."

The thought of a healthy leg swathed in bacon fat on a hot day in July was enough to intimidate a braver heart than Polydore's. But the suggestion was evidently not adopted, for he heard no more of the bacon fat. In its stead he became acquainted with the not unpleasant sting of a soothing liniment which Jude rubbed into the leg at intervals during the day.

He kept the limb propped on a pillow, stiff and motionless, even when alone and unobserved. Toward evening he fancied that it really showed signs of inflammation, and he was quite sure it pained him.

It was a satisfaction to all to see Polydore appear down-stairs the following afternoon. He limped painfully, it is true, and clutched wildly at anything in his way that offered a momentary support. His acting was clumsily overdrawn; and by less guileless souls than Mamzelle Adélaïde and her father would have surely been suspected. But these two only thought with deep concern of means to make him comfortable.

They seated him on the shady back gallery in an easy-chair, with his leg propped up before him.

"He inhe'its dat rheumatism," proclaimed Aunt Siney, who affected the manner of an oracle. "I see dat boy's granpap, many times, all twis' up wid rheumatism twell his head sot down on his body, hine side befo'. He got to keep outen de jew in de mo'nin's, and he 'bleege to w'ar red flannen."

Monsieur José, with flowing white locks enframing his aged face, leaned upon his cane and contemplated the boy with unflagging attention. Polydore was beginning to believe himself a worthy object as a center of interest.

Mamzelle Adélaïde had but just returned from a long drive in the open buggy, from a mission which would have fallen to Polydore had he not been disabled by this unlooked-for illness. She had thoughtlessly driven across the country at an hour when the sun was hottest, and now she sat panting and fanning herself; her face, which she mopped incessantly with her handkerchief, was inflamed from the heat.

Mamzelle Adélaïde ate no supper that night, and went to bed early, with a compress of *eau sédative* bound tightly around her head. She thought it was a simple headache, and that she would be rid of it in the morning; but she was not better in the morning.

She kept her bed that day, and late in the afternoon Jude rode over to town for the doctor, and stopped on the way to tell Mamzelle Adélaïde's married sister that she was quite ill, and would like to have her come down to the plantation for a day or two.

Polydore made round, serious eyes and forgot to limp. He wanted to go for the doctor in Jude's stead; but Aunt Siney, assuming a brief authority, forced him to sit still by the kitchen door and talked further of bacon fat.

Old Monsieur José moved about uneasily and restlessly, in and out of his daughter's room. He looked vacantly at Polydore now, as if the stout young boy in blue jeans and a calico shirt were a sort of a transparency.

A dawning anxiety, coupled to the inertia of the past two days, deprived Polydore of his usual healthful night's rest. The slightest noises awoke him. Once it was the married sister breaking ice down on the gallery. One of the hands had been sent with the cart for ice late in the afternoon; and Polydore himself had wrapped the huge chunk in an old blanket and set it outside of Mamzelle Adélaïde's door.

Troubled and wakeful, he arose from bed and went and stood by the open window. There was a round moon in the sky, shedding its pale glamor over all the country; and the live-oak branches, stirred by the restless breeze, flung quivering, grotesque shadows slanting across the old roof. A mocking-bird had been singing for hours near Polydore's window, and farther away there were frogs croaking. He could see as through a silvery gauze the level stretch of the cotton-field, ripe and white; a gleam of water beyond,—that was the bend of the river,—and farther yet, the gentle rise of the pine hill.

There was a cabin up there on the hill that Polydore remembered well. Negroes were living in it now, but it had been his home once. Life had been pinched and wretched enough up there with the little chap. The bright days had been the days when his godmother, Mamzelle Adélaïde, would come driving her old white horse over the pine needles and crackling fallen twigs of the deserted hill-road. Her presence was connected with the earliest recollections of whatever he had known of comfort and well-being.

And one day when death had taken his mother from him, Mamzelle Adélaïde had brought him home to live with her always. Now she was sick down there in her room; very sick, for the doctor had said so, and the married sister had put on her longest face.

Polydore did not think of these things in any connected or very intelligent way. They were only impressions that penetrated him and made his heart swell, and the tears well up to his eyes. He wiped his eyes on the sleeve of his night-gown. The mosquitoes were stinging him and raising great welts on his brown legs. He went and crept back under the mosquito-bar, and soon he was asleep and dreaming that his *nénaine* was dead and he left alone in the cabin upon the pine hill.

In the morning, after the doctor had seen Mamzelle Adélaïde, he went and turned his horse into the lot and prepared to stay with his patient until he could feel it would be prudent to leave her.

Polydore tiptoed into her room and stood at the foot of the bed. Nobody noticed now whether he limped or not. She was talking very loud, and he could not believe at first that she could be as ill as they said, with such strength of voice. But her tones were unnatural, and what she said conveyed no meaning to his ears.

He understood, however, when she thought she was talking to his mother. She was in a manner apologizing for his illness; and seemed to be troubled with the idea that she had in a way been the indirect cause of it by some oversight or neglect.

Polydore felt ashamed, and went outside and stood by himself near the cistern till some one told him to go and attend to the doctor's horse.

Then there was confusion in the household, when mornings and afternoons seemed turned around; and meals, which were scarcely tasted, were served at irregular and unseasonable hours. And there came one awful night, when they did not know if Mamzelle Adélaïde would live or die.

Nobody slept. The doctor snatched moments of rest in the hammock. He and the priest, who had been summoned, talked a little together with professional callousness about the dry weather and the crops.

Old monsieur walked, walked, like a restless, caged animal. The married sister came out on the gallery every now and then and leaned up against the post and sobbed in her handkerchief. There were many negroes around, sitting on the steps and standing in small groups in the yard.

Polydore crouched on the gallery. It had finally come to him to comprehend the cause of his *nénaine's* sickness—that drive in the sweltering afternoon, when he was shamming illness. No one there could have comprehended the horror of himself, the terror that possessed him, squatting there outside her door like a savage. If she died—but he could not think of that. It was the point at which his reason was stunned and seemed to swoon.

A week or two later Mamzelle Adélaïde was sitting outside for the first time since her convalescence began. They had brought her own rocker around to the side where she could get a sight and whiff of the flower-garden and the blossom-laden rose-vine twining in and out of the banisters. Her former plumpness had not yet returned, and she looked much older, for the wrinkles were visible.

She was watching Polydore cross the yard. He had been putting up his pony. He approached with his heavy, clumsy walk; his round, simple face was hot and flushed from the ride. When he had mounted to the gallery he went and leaned against the railing, facing Mamzelle Adélaïde, mopping his face, his hands and neck with his handkerchief. Then he removed his hat and began to fan himself with it.

"You seem to be perfec'ly cu'ed of yo' rheumatism, Polydore. It doesn' hurt you any mo', my boy?" she questioned.

He stamped the foot and extended the leg violently, in proof of its perfect soundness.

"You know w'ere I been, *nénaine?*" he said. "I been to confession."

"That's right. Now you mus' rememba and not take a drink of water to-morrow morning, as you did las' time, and miss yo' communion, my boy. You are a good child, Polydore, to go like that to confession without bein' told."

"No, I ain' good," he returned, doggedly. He began to twirl his hat on one finger. "Père Cassimelle say he always yeard I was stupid, but he never knew befo' how bad I been."

"Indeed!" muttered Mamzelle Adélaïde, not over well pleased with the priest's estimate of her protégé.

"He gave me a long penance," continued Polydore. "The 'Litany of the Saint' and the 'Litany of the Blessed Virgin,' and three 'Our Father' and three 'Hail Mary' to say ev'ry mo'ning fo' a week. But he say' that ain' enough."

"My patience! W'at does he expec' mo' from you, I like to know?" Polydore was now creasing and scanning his hat attentively.

"He say' w'at I need, it's to be wo' out with the raw-hide. He say' he knows M'sieur José is too ole and feeble to give it to me like I deserve; and if you want, he say' he's willing to give me a good tas'e of the raw-hide himse'f."

Mamzelle Adélaïde found it impossible to disguise her indignation:

"Père Cassimelle sho'ly fo'gets himse'f, Polydore. Don't repeat to me any further his inconsid'ate remarks."

"He's right, *nénaine*. Père Cassimelle is right."

Since the night he crouched outside her door, Polydore had lived with the weight of his unconfessed fault oppressing every moment of existence. He had tried to rid himself of it in going to Father Cassimelle; but that had only helped by indicating the way. He was awkward and unaccustomed to express emotions with coherent speech. The words would not come.

Suddenly he flung his hat to the ground, and falling on his knees, began to sob, with his face pressed down in Mamzelle Adélaïde's lap. She had never seen him cry before, and in her weak condition it made her tremble.

Then somehow he got it out; he told the whole story of his deceit. He told it simply, in a way that bared his heart to her for the first time. She said nothing; only held his hand close and stroked his hair. But she felt as if a kind of miracle had happened. Hitherto her first thought in caring for this boy had been a desire to fulfill his dead mother's wishes.

But now he seemed to belong to herself, and to be her very own. She knew that a bond of love had been forged that would hold them together always.

"I know I can't he'p being stupid," sighed Polydore, "but it's no call fo' me to be bad."

"Neva mine, Polydore; neva mine, my boy," and she drew him close to her and kissed him as mothers kiss.

Dead Men's Shoes

It never occurred to any person to wonder what would befall Gilma now that "le vieux Gamiche" was dead. After the burial people went their several ways, some to talk over the old man and his eccentricities, others to forget him before nightfall, and others to wonder what would become of his very nice property, the hundred-acre farm on which he had lived for thirty years, and on which he had just died at the age of seventy.

If Gilma had been a child, more than one motherly heart would have gone out to him. This one and that one would have bethought them of carrying him home with them; to concern themselves with his present comfort, if not his future welfare. But Gilma was not a child. He was a strapping fellow of nineteen, measuring six feet in his stockings, and as strong as any healthy youth need be. For ten years he had lived there on the plantation with Monsieur Gamiche; and he seemed now to have been the only one with tears to shed at the old man's funeral.

Gamiche's relatives had come down from Caddo in a wagon the day after his death, and had settled themselves in his house. There was Septime, his nephew, a cripple, so horribly afflicted that it was distressing to look at him. And there was Septime's widowed sister, Ma'me Brozé, with her two little girls. They had remained at the house during the burial, and Gilma found them still there upon his return.

The young man went at once to his room to seek a moment's repose. He had lost much sleep during Monsieur Gamiche's illness; yet, he was in fact more worn by the mental than the bodily strain of the past week.

But when he entered his room, there was something so changed in its aspect that it seemed no longer to belong to him. In place of his own apparel which he had left hanging on the row of pegs, there were a few shabby little garments and two battered straw hats, the property of the Brozé children. The bureau drawers were empty, there was not a vestige of anything belonging to him remaining in the room. His first impression was that Ma'me Brozé had been changing things around and had assigned him to some other room.

But Gilma understood the situation better when he discovered every scrap of his personal effects piled up on a bench outside the door, on the back or "false" gallery. His boots and shoes were under the bench, while coats, trousers and underwear were heaped in an indiscriminate mass together.

The blood mounted to his swarthy face and made him look for the moment like an Indian. He had never thought of this. He did not know what he had been thinking of; but he felt that he ought to have been prepared for anything; and it was his own fault if he was not. But it hurt. This spot was "home" to him against the rest of the world. Every tree, every shrub was a friend; he knew every patch in the fences; and the little old house, gray and weather-beaten, that had been the shelter of his youth, he loved as only few can love inanimate things. A great enmity arose in him against Ma'me Brozé. She was walking about the yard, with her nose in the air, and a shabby black dress trailing behind her. She held the little girls by the hand.

Gilma could think of nothing better to do than to mount his horse and ride away—anywhere. The horse was a spirited animal of great value. Monsieur Gamiche had named him "Jupiter" on account of his proud bearing, and Gilma had nicknamed him "Jupe," which seemed to him more endearing and expressive of his great attachment to the fine creature. With the bitter resentment of youth, he felt that "Jupe" was the only friend remaining to him on earth.

He had thrust a few pieces of clothing in his saddlebags and had requested Ma'me Brozé, with assumed indifference, to put his remaining effects in a place of safety until he should be able to send for them.

As he rode around by the front of the house, Septime, who sat on the gallery all doubled up in his uncle Gamiche's big chair, called out:

"Hé, Gilma! w'ere you boun' fo'?"

"I'm goin' away," replied Gilma, curtly, reining his horse.

"That's all right; but I reckon you might jus' as well leave that hoss behine you."

"The hoss is mine," returned Gilma, as quickly as he would have returned a blow.

"We'll see 'bout that li'le later, my frien'. I reckon you jus' well turn 'im loose."

Gilma had no more intention of giving up his horse than he had of parting with his own right hand. But Monsieur Gamiche had taught him prudence and respect for the law. He did not wish to invite disagreeable complications. So, controlling his temper by a supreme effort, Gilma dismounted, unsaddled the horse then and there, and led it back to the stable. But as he started to leave the place on foot, he stopped to say to Septime:

"You know, Mr. Septime, that hoss is mine; I can collec' a hundred aff'davits to prove it. I'll bring them yere in a few days with a statement f'om a lawyer; an' I'll expec' the hoss an' saddle to be turned over to me in good condition."

"That's all right. We'll see 'bout that. Won't you stay fo' dinna?"

"No, I thank you, suh; Ma'me Brozé already ask' me." And Gilma strode away, down the beaten footpath that led across the sloping grassplot toward the outer road.

A definite destination and a settled purpose ahead of him seemed to have revived his flagging energies of an hour before. It was with no trace of fatigue that he stepped out bravely along the wagon-road that skirted the bayou.

It was early spring, and the cotton had already a good stand. In some places the negroes were hoeing. Gilma stopped alongside the rail fence and called to an old negress who was plying her hoe at no great distance.

"Hello, Aunt Hal'fax! see yere."

She turned, and immediately quitted her work to go and join him, bringing her hoe with her across her shoulder. She was largeboned and very black. She was dressed in the deshabille of the field.

"I wish you'd come up to yo' cabin with me a minute, Aunt Hally," he said; "I want to get an aff'davit f'om you."

She understood, after a fashion, what an affidavit was; but she couldn't see the good of it.

"I ain't got no aff'davis, boy; you g'long an' don' pesta me."

" 'Twon't take you any time, Aunt Hal'fax. I jus' want you to put yo' mark to a statement I'm goin' to write to the effec' that my hoss, Jupe, is my own prop'ty; that you know it, an' willin' to swear to it."

"Who say Jupe don' b'long to you?" she questioned cautiously, leaning on her hoe.

He motioned toward the house.

"Who? Mista Septime and them?"

"Yes."

"Well, I reckon!" she exclaimed, sympathetically.

"That's it," Gilma went on; "an' nex' thing they'll be sayin' yo' ole mule, Policy, don't b'long to you."

She started violently.

"Who say so?"

"Nobody. But I say, nex' thing, that' w'at they'll be sayin'."

She began to move along the inside of the fence, and he turned to keep pace with her, walking on the grassy edge of the road.

"I'll jus' write the aff'davit, Aunt Hally, an' all you got to do"—

"You know des well as me dat mule mine. I done paid ole Mista Gamiche fo' 'im in good cotton; dat year you falled outen de puckhorn tree; an' he write it down hisse'f in his 'count book."

Gilma did not linger a moment after obtaining the desired statement from Aunt Halifax. With the first of those "hundred affidavits" that he hoped to secure, safe in his pocket, he struck out across the country, seeking the shortest way to town.

Aunt Halifax stayed in the cabin door.

" 'Relius," she shouted to a little black boy out in the road, "does you see Pol'cy anywhar? G'long, see ef he 'roun' de ben'. Wouldn' s'prise me ef he broke de fence an' got in yo' pa's corn ag'in." And, shading her eyes to scan the surrounding country, she muttered, uneasily: "Whar dat mule?"

The following morning Gilma entered town and proceeded at once to Lawyer Paxton's office. He had no difficulty in obtaining the testimony of blacks and whites regarding his ownership of the horse; but he wanted to make his claim as secure as possible by consulting the lawyer and returning to the plantation armed with unassailable evidence.

The lawyer's office was a plain little room opening upon the street. Nobody was there, but the door was open; and Gilma entered and took a seat at the bare round table and waited. It was not long before the lawyer came in; he had been in conversation with some one across the street.

"Good-morning, Mr. Pax'on," said Gilma, rising.

The lawyer knew his face well enough, but could not place him, and only returned: "Good-morning, sir—good-morning."

"I come to see you," began Gilma plunging at once into business, and drawing his handful of nondescript affidavits from his pocket, "about a matter of prope'ty, about regaining possession of my hoss that Mr. Septime, ole Mr. Gamiche's nephew, is holdin' f'om me yonder."

The lawyer took the papers and, adjusting his eye-glasses, began to look them through.

"Yes, yes," he said; "I see."

"Since Mr. Gamiche died on Tuesday"—began Gilma.

"Gamiche died!" repeated Lawyer Paxton, with astonishment. "Why, you don't mean to tell me that vieux Gamiche is dead? Well, well. I hadn't heard of it; I just returned from Shreveport this morning. So le vieux Gamiche is dead, is he? And you say you want to get possession of a horse. What did you say your name was?" drawing a pencil from his pocket.

"Gilma Germain is my name, suh."

"Gilma Germain," repeated the lawyer, a little meditatively, scanning his visitor closely. "Yes, I recall your face now. You are the young fellow whom le vieux Gamiche took to live with him some ten or twelve years ago."

"Ten years ago las' November, suh."

Lawyer Paxton arose and went to his safe, from which, after unlocking it, he took a legal-looking document that he proceeded to read carefully through to himself.

"Well, Mr. Germain, I reckon there won't be any trouble about regaining possession of the horse," laughed Lawyer Paxton. "I'm pleased to inform you, my dear sir, that our old friend, Gamiche, has made you sole heir to his property; that is, his plantation, including live stock, farming implements, machinery, household effects, etc. Quite a pretty piece of property," he proclaimed leisurely, seating himself comfortably for a long talk. "And I may add, a pretty piece of luck, Mr. Germain, for a young fellow just starting out in life; nothing but to step into a dead man's shoes! A great chance—great chance. Do you know, sir, the moment you mentioned your name, it came back to me like a flash, how le vieux Gamiche came in here one day, about three years ago, and wanted to make his will"—And the loquacious lawyer went on with his reminiscences and interesting bits of information, of which Gilma heard scarcely a word.

He was stunned, drunk, with the sudden joy of possession; the thought of what seemed to him great wealth, all his own—his own! It seemed as if a hundred different sensations were holding him at once, and as if a thousand intentions crowded upon him. He felt like another being who would have to readjust himself to the new conditions, presenting themselves so unexpectedly. The narrow confines of the office were stifling, and it seemed as if the lawyer's flow of talk would never stop. Gilma arose abruptly, and with a half-uttered apology, plunged from the room into the outer air.

Two days later Gilma stopped again before Aunt Halifax's cabin, on his way back to the plantation. He was walking as before, having declined to avail himself of any one of the several offers of a mount that had been tendered him in town and on the way. A rumor of Gilma's great good fortune had preceded him, and Aunt Halifax greeted him with an almost triumphal shout as he approached.

"God knows you desarve it, Mista Gilma! De Lord knows you does, suh! Come in an' res' yo'se'f, suh. You, 'Relius! git out dis heah cabin; crowdin' up dat away!" She wiped off the best chair available and offered it to Gilma.

He was glad to rest himself and glad to accept Aunt Halifax's proffer of a cup of coffee, which she was in the act of dripping before a small fire. He sat as far as he could from the fire, for the day was warm; he mopped his face, and fanned himself with his broad-rimmed hat.

"I des' can't he'p laughin' w'en I thinks 'bout it," said the old woman, fairly shaking, as she leaned over the hearth. "I wakes up in de night, even, an' has to laugh."

"How's that, Aunt Hal'fax," asked Gilma, almost tempted to laugh himself at he knew not what.

"G'long, Mista Gilma! like you don' know! It's w'en I thinks 'bout Septime an' them like I gwine see 'em in dat wagon to-mor' mo'nin', on' dey way back to Caddo. Oh, lawsy!"

"That isn' so ver' funny, Aunt Hal'fax," returned Gilma, feeling himself ill at ease as he accepted the cup of coffee which she presented to him with much ceremony on a platter. "I feel pretty sorry for Septime, myse'f."

"I reckon he know now who Jupe b'long to," she went on, ignoring his expression of sympathy; "no need to tell him who Pol'cy b'long to, nuther. An' I tell you, Mista Gilma," she went on, leaning upon the table without seating herself, "dey gwine back to hard times in Caddo. I heah tell dey nuva gits 'nough to eat, yonda. Septime, he can't do nuttin' 'cep' set still all twis' up like a sarpint. An' Ma'me Brozé, she do some kine sewin'; but don't look like she got sense 'nough to do dat halfway. An' dem li'le gals, dey 'bleege to run bar'foot mos' all las' winta', twell dat li'les' gal, she got her heel plum fros' bit, so dey tells me. Oh, lawsy! How dey gwine look to-mor', all trapsin' back to Caddo!''

Gilma had never found Aunt Halifax's company so intensely disagreeable as at that moment. He thanked her for the coffee, and went away so suddenly as to startle her. But her good humor never flagged. She called out to him from the doorway:

"Oh, Mista Gilma! You reckon dey knows who Pol'cy b'longs to now?''

He somehow did not feel quite prepared to face Septime; and he lingered along the road. He even stopped a while to rest, apparently, under the shade of a huge cottonwood tree that overhung the bayou. From the very first, a subtle uneasiness, a self-dissatisfaction had mingled with his elation, and he was trying to discover what it meant.

To begin with, the straightforwardness of his own nature had inwardly resented the sudden change in the bearing of most people toward himself. He was trying to recall, too, something which the lawyer had said; a little phrase, out of that multitude of words, that had fallen in his consciousness. It had stayed there, generating a little festering sore place that was beginning to make itself irritatingly felt. What was it, that little phrase? Something about—in his excitement he had only half heard it— something about dead men's shoes.

The exuberant health and strength of his big body; the courage, virility, endurance of his whole nature revolted against the expression in itself, and the meaning which it conveyed to him. Dead men's shoes! Were they not for such afflicted beings as Septime? as that helpless, dependent woman up there? as those two little ones, with their poorly fed, poorly clad bodies and sweet, appealing eyes? Yet he could not determine how he would act and what he would say to them.

But there was no room left in his heart for hesitancy when he came to face the group. Septime was still crouched in his uncle's chair; he seemed never to have left it since the day of the funeral. Ma'me Brozé had been crying, and so had the children—out of sympathy, perhaps.

"Mr. Septime," said Gilma, approaching, "I brought those aff'davits about the hoss. I hope you about made up yo' mind to turn it over without further trouble."

Septime was trembling, bewildered, almost speechless.

"W'at you mean?" he faltered, looking up with a shifting, sideward glance. "The whole place b'longs to you. You tryin' to make a fool out o' me?"

"Fo' me," returned Gilma, "the place can stay with Mr. Gamiche's own flesh an' blood. I'll see Mr. Pax'on again an' make that according to the law. But I want my hoss."

Gilma took something besides his horse—a picture of le vieux Gamiche, which had stood on his mantelpiece. He thrust it into his pocket. He also took his old benefactor's walking-stick and a gun.

As he rode out of the gate, mounted upon his well-beloved "Jupe," the faithful dog following, Gilma felt as if he had awakened from an intoxicating but depressing dream.

Athénaïse

I

Athénaïse went away in the morning to make a visit to her parents, ten miles back on rigolet de Bon Dieu. She did not return in the evening, and Cazeau, her husband, fretted not a little. He did not worry much about Athénaïse, who, he suspected, was resting only too content in the bosom of her family; his chief solicitude was manifestly for the pony she had ridden. He felt sure those "lazy pigs," her brothers, were capable of neglecting it seriously. This misgiving Cazeau communicated to his servant, old Félicité, who waited upon him at supper.

His voice was low pitched, and even softer than Félicité's. He was tall, sinewy, swarthy, and altogether severe looking. His thick black hair waved, and it gleamed like the breast of a crow. The sweep of his mustache, which was not so black, outlined the broad contour of the mouth. Beneath the under lip grew a small tuft which he was much given to twisting, and which he permitted to grow, apparently for no other purpose. Cazeau's eyes were dark blue, narrow and overshadowed. His hands were coarse and stiff from close acquaintance with farming tools and implements, and he handled his fork and knife clumsily. But he was distinguished looking, and succeeded in commanding a good deal of respect, and even fear sometimes.

He ate his supper alone, by the light of a single coal-oil lamp that but faintly illuminated the big room, with its bare floor and huge rafters, and its heavy pieces of furniture that loomed dimly in the gloom of the apartment. Félicité, ministering to his wants, hovered about the table like a little, bent, restless shadow.

She served him with a dish of sunfish fried crisp and brown. There was nothing else set before him beside the bread and butter and the bottle of red wine which she locked carefully in the buffet after he had poured his second glass. She was occupied with her mistress's absence, and kept reverting to it after he had expressed his solicitude about the pony.

"Dat beat me! on'y marry two mont', an' got de head turn' a'ready to go 'broad. C'est pas Chrétien, tenez!"

Cazeau shrugged his shoulders for answer, after he had drained his glass and pushed aside his plate. Félicité's opinion of the unchristianlike behavior of his wife in leaving him thus alone after two months of marriage weighed little with him. He was used to solitude, and did not mind a day or a night or two of it. He had lived alone ten years, since his first wife died, and Félicité might have known better than to suppose that he cared. He told her she was a fool. It sounded like a compliment in his modulated, caressing voice. She grumbled to herself as she set about clearing the table, and Cazeau arose and walked outside on the gallery; his spur, which he had not removed upon entering the house, jangled at every step.

The night was beginning to deepen, and to gather black about the clusters of trees and shrubs that were grouped in the yard. In the beam of light from the open kitchen door a black boy stood feeding a brace of snarling, hungry dogs; further away, on the steps of a cabin, some one was playing the accordion; and in still another direction a little negro baby was crying lustily. Cazeau walked around to the front of the house, which was square, squat and one-story.

A belated wagon was driving in at the gate, and the impatient driver was swearing hoarsely at his jaded oxen. Félicité stepped out on the gallery, glass and polishing towel in hand, to investigate, and to wonder, too, who could be singing out on the river. It was a party of young people paddling around, waiting for the moon to rise, and they were singing Juanita, their voices coming tempered and melodious through the distance and the night.

Cazeau's horse was waiting, saddled, ready to be mounted, for Cazeau had many things to attend to before bed-time; so many things that there was not left to him a moment in which to think of Athénaïse. He felt her absence, though, like a dull, insistent pain.

However, before he slept that night he was visited by the thought of her, and by a vision of her fair young face with its drooping lips and sullen and averted eyes. The marriage had been a blunder; he had only to look into her eyes to feel that, to discover her growing aversion. But it was a thing not by any possibility to be undone. He was quite prepared to make the best of it, and expected no less than a like effort on her part. The less she revisited the rigolet, the better. He would find means to keep her at home hereafter.

These unpleasant reflections kept Cazeau awake far into the night, notwithstanding the craving of his whole body for rest and sleep. The moon was shining, and its pale effulgence reached dimly into the room, and with it a touch of the cool breath of the spring night. There was an unusual stillness abroad; no sound to be heard save the distant, tireless, plaintive notes of the accordion.

II

Athénaïse did not return the following day, even though her husband sent her word to do so by her brother, Montéclin, who passed on his way to the village early in the morning.

On the third day Cazeau saddled his horse and went himself in search of her. She had sent no word, no message, explaining her absence, and he felt that he had good cause to be offended. It was rather awkward to have to leave his work, even though late in the afternoon,—Cazeau had always so much to do; but among the many urgent calls upon him, the task of bringing his wife back to a sense of her duty seemed to him for the moment paramount.

The Michés, Athénaïse's parents, lived on the old Gotrain place. It did not belong to them; they were "running" it for a merchant in Alexandria. The house was far too big for their use. One of the lower rooms served for the storing of wood and tools; the person "occupying" the place before Miché having pulled up the flooring in despair of being able to patch it. Upstairs, the rooms were so large, so bare, that they offered a constant temptation to lovers of the dance, whose importunities Madame Miché was accustomed to meet with amiable indulgence. A dance at Miché's and a plate of Madame Miché's gumbo filé at midnight were pleasures not to be neglected or despised, unless by such serious souls as Cazeau.

Long before Cazeau reached the house his approach had been observed, for there was nothing to obstruct the view of the outer road; vegetation was not yet abundantly advanced, and there was but a patchy, straggling stand of cotton and corn in Miché's field.

Madame Miché, who had been seated on the gallery in a rocking-chair, stood up to greet him as he drew near. She was short and fat, and wore a black skirt and loose muslin sack fastened at the throat with a hair brooch. Her own hair, brown and glossy, showed but a few threads of silver. Her round pink face was cheery, and her eyes were bright and good humored. But she was plainly perturbed and ill at ease as Cazeau advanced.

Montéclin, who was there too, was not ill at ease, and made no attempt to disguise the dislike with which his brother-in-law inspired him. He was a slim, wiry fellow of twenty-five, short of stature like his mother, and resembling her in feature. He was in shirt-sleeves, half leaning, half sitting, on the insecure railing of the gallery, and fanning himself with his broad-rimmed felt hat.

"Cochon!" he muttered under his breath as Cazeau mounted the stairs,—"sacré cochon!"

"Cochon" had sufficiently characterized the man who had once on a time declined to lend Montéclin money. But when this same man had had the presumption to propose marriage to his well-beloved sister, Athénaïse, and the honor to be accepted by her, Montéclin felt that a qualifying epithet was needed fully to express his estimate of Cazeau.

Miché and his oldest son were absent. They both esteemed Cazeau highly, and talked much of his qualities of head and heart, and thought much of his excellent standing with city merchants.

Athénaïse had shut herself up in her room. Cazeau had seen her rise and enter the house at perceiving him. He was a good deal mystified, but no one could have guessed it when he shook hands with Madame Miché. He had only nodded to Montéclin, with a muttered "Comment ça va?"

"Tiens! something tole me you were coming to-day!" exclaimed Madame Miché, with a little blustering appearance of being cordial and at ease, as she offered Cazeau a chair.

He ventured a short laugh as he seated himself.

"You know, nothing would do," she went on, with much gesture of her small, plump hands, "nothing would do but Athénaïse mus' stay las' night fo' a li'le dance. The boys wouldn' year to their sister leaving."

Cazeau shrugged his shoulders significantly, telling as plainly as words that he knew nothing about it.

"Comment! Montéclin didn' tell you we were going to keep Athénaïse?" Montéclin had evidently told nothing.

"An' how about the night befo'," questioned Cazeau, "an' las' night? It isn't possible you dance every night out yere on the Bon Dieu!"

Madame Miché laughed, with amiable appreciation of the sarcasm; and turning to her son, "Montéclin, my boy, go tell yo' sister that Monsieur Cazeau is yere."

Montéclin did not stir except to shift his position and settle himself more securely on the railing.

"Did you year me, Montéclin?"

"Oh yes, I yeard you plain enough," responded her son, "but you know as well as me it's no use to tell 'Thénaïse anything. You been talkin' to her yo'se'f since Monday; an' pa's preached himse'f hoa'se on the subject; an' you even had uncle Achille down yere yesterday to reason with her. W'en 'Thénaïse said she wasn' goin' to set her foot back in Cazeau's house, she meant it."

This speech, which Montéclin delivered with thorough unconcern, threw his mother into a condition of painful but dumb embarrassment. It brought two fiery red spots to Cazeau's cheeks, and for the space of a moment he looked wicked.

What Montéclin had spoken was quite true, though his taste in the manner and choice of time and place in saying it were not of the best. Athénaïse, upon the first day of her arrival, had announced that she came to stay, having no intention of returning under Cazeau's roof. The announcement had scattered consternation, as she knew it would. She had been implored, scolded, entreated, stormed at, until she felt herself like a dragging sail that all the winds of heaven had beaten upon. Why in the name of God had she married Cazeau? Her father had lashed her with the question a dozen times. Why indeed? It was difficult now for her to understand why, unless because she supposed it was customary for girls to marry when the right opportunity came. Cazeau, she knew, would make life more comfortable for her; and again, she had liked him, and had even been rather flustered when he pressed her hands and kissed them, and kissed her lips and cheeks and eyes, when she accepted him.

Montéclin himself had taken her aside to talk the thing over. The turn of affairs was delighting him.

"Come, now, 'Thénaïse, you mus' explain to me all about it, so we can settle on a good cause, an' secu' a separation fo' you. Has he been mistreating an' abusing you, the sacré cochon?" They were alone together in her room, whither she had taken refuge from the angry domestic elements.

"You please to reserve yo' disgusting expressions, Montéclin. No, he has not abused me in any way that I can think."

"Does he drink? Come 'Thénaïse, think well over it. Does he ever get drunk?"

"Drunk! Oh, mercy, no,—Cazeau never gets drunk."

"I see; it's jus' simply you feel like me; you hate him."

"No, I don't hate him," she returned reflectively; adding with a sudden impulse, "It's jus' being married that I detes' an' despise. I hate being Mrs. Cazeau, an' would want to be Athénaïse Miché again. I can't stan' to live with a man; to have him always there; his coats an' pantaloons hanging in my room; his ugly bare feet—washing them in my tub, befo' my very eyes, ugh!" She shuddered with recollections, and resumed, with a sigh that was almost a sob: "Mon Dieu, mon Dieu! Sister Marie Angélique knew w'at she was saying; she knew me better than myse'f w'en she said God had sent me a vocation an' I was turning deaf ears. W'en I think of a blessed life in the convent, at peace! Oh, w'at was I dreaming of!" and then the tears came.

Montéclin felt disconcerted and greatly disappointed at having obtained evidence that would carry no weight with a court of justice. The day had not come when a young woman might ask the court's permission to return to her mamma on the sweeping ground of a constitutional disinclination for marriage. But if there was no way of untying this Gordian knot of marriage, there was surely a way of cutting it.

"Well, 'Thénaise, I'm mighty durn sorry you got no better groun's 'an w'at you say. But you can count on me to stan' by you w'atever you do. God knows I don' blame you fo' not wantin' to live with Cazeau."

And now there was Cazeau himself, with the red spots flaming in his swarthy cheeks, looking and feeling as if he wanted to thrash Montéclin into some semblance of decency. He arose abruptly, and approaching the room which he had seen his wife enter, thrust open the door after a hasty preliminary knock. Athénaïse, who was standing erect at a far window, turned at his entrance.

She appeared neither angry nor frightened, but thoroughly unhappy, with an appeal in her soft dark eyes and a tremor on her lips that seemed to him expressions of unjust reproach, that wounded and maddened him at once. But whatever he might feel, Cazeau knew only one way to act toward a woman.

"Athénaïse, you are not ready?" he asked in his quiet tones. "It's getting late; we havn' any time to lose."

She knew that Montéclin had spoken out, and she had hoped for a wordy interview, a stormy scene, in which she might have held her own as she had held it for the past three days against her family, with Montéclin's aid. But she had no weapon with which to combat subtlety. Her husband's looks, his tones, his mere presence, brought to her a sudden sense of hopelessness, an instinctive realization of the futility of rebellion against a social and sacred institution.

Cazeau said nothing further, but stood waiting in the doorway. Madame Miché had walked to the far end of the gallery, and pretended to be occupied with having a chicken driven from her parterre. Montéclin stood by, exasperated, fuming, ready to burst out.

Athénaïse went and reached for her riding skirt that hung against the wall. She was rather tall, with a figure which, though not robust, seemed perfect in its fine proportions. "La fille de son père," she was often called, which was a great compliment to Miché. Her brown hair was brushed all fluffily back from her temples and low forehead, and about her features and expression lurked a softness, a prettiness, a dewiness, that were perhaps too childlike, that savored of immaturity.

She slipped the riding-skirt, which was of black alpaca, over her head, and with impatient fingers hooked it at the waist over her pink linen-lawn. Then she fastened on her white sunbonnet and reached for her gloves on the mantelpiece.

"If you don' wan' to go, you know w'at you got to do, 'Thénaïse," fumed Montéclin. "You don' set yo' feet back on Cane River, by God, unless you want to,—not w'ile I'm alive."

Cazeau looked at him as if he were a monkey whose antics fell short of being amusing.

Athénaïse still made no reply, said not a word. She walked rapidly past her husband, past her brother; bidding good-bye to no one, not even to her mother. She descended the stairs, and without assistance from any one mounted the pony, which Cazeau had ordered to be saddled upon his arrival. In this way she obtained a fair start of her husband, whose departure was far more leisurely, and for the greater part of the way she managed to keep an appreciable gap between them. She rode almost madly at first, with the wind inflating her skirt balloon-like about her knees, and her sunbonnet falling back between her shoulders.

At no time did Cazeau make an effort to overtake her until traversing an old fallow meadow that was level and hard as a table. The sight of a great solitary oak-tree, with its seemingly immutable outlines, that had been a landmark for ages—or was it the odor of elderberry stealing up from the gully to the south? or what was it that brought vividly back to Cazeau, by some association of ideas, a scene of many years ago? He had passed that old live-oak hundreds of times, but it was only now that the memory of one day came back to him. He was a very small boy that day, seated before his father on horse-back. They were proceeding slowly, and Black Gabe was moving on before them at a little dog-trot. Black Gabe had run away, and had been discovered back in the Gotrain swamp. They had halted beneath this big oak to enable the negro to take breath; for Cazeau's father was a kind and considerate master, and every one had agreed at the time that Black Gabe was a fool, a great idiot indeed, for wanting to run away from him.

The whole impression was for some reason hideous, and to dispel it Cazeau spurred his horse to a swift gallop. Overtaking his wife, he rode the remainder of the way at her side in silence.

It was late when they reached home. Félicité was standing on the grassy edge of the road, in the moonlight, waiting for them.

Cazeau once more ate his supper alone; for Athénaïse went to her room, and there she was crying again.

III

Athénaïse was not one to accept the inevitable with patient resignation, a talent born in the souls of many women; neither was she the one to accept it with philosophical resignation, like her husband. Her sensibilities were alive and keen and responsive. She met the pleasurable things of life with frank, open appreciation, and against distasteful conditions she rebelled. Dissimulation was as foreign to her nature as guile to the breast of a babe, and her rebellious outbreaks, by no means rare, had hitherto been quite open and aboveboard. People often said that Athénaïse would know her own mind some day, which was equivalent to saying that she was at present unacquainted with it. If she ever came to such knowledge, it would be by no intellectual research, by no subtle analyses or tracing the motives of actions to their source. It would come to her as the song to the bird, the perfume and color to the flower.

Her parents had hoped—not without reason and justice—that marriage would bring the poise, the desirable pose, so glaringly lacking in Athénaïse's character. Marriage they knew to be a wonderful and powerful agent in the development and formation of a woman's character; they had seen its effect too often to doubt it.

"And if this marriage does nothing else," exclaimed Miché in an outburst of sudden exasperaton, "it will rid us of Athénaïse; for I am at the end of my patience with her! You have never had the firmness to manage her,"—he was speaking to his wife,—"I have not had the time, the leisure, to devote to her training; and what good we might have accomplished, that maudit Montéclin—Well, Cazeau is the one! It takes just such a steady hand to guide a disposition like Athénaïse's, a master hand, a strong will that compels obedience."

And now, when they had hoped for so much, here was Athénaïse, with gathered and fierce vehemence, beside which her former outbursts appeared mild, declaring that she would not, and she would not, and she would not continue to enact the role of wife to Cazeau. If she had had a reason! as Madame Miché lamented; but it could not be discovered that she had any sane one. He had never scolded, or called names, or deprived her of comforts, or been guilty of any of the many reprehensible acts commonly attributed to objectionable husbands. He did not slight nor neglect her. Indeed, Cazeau's chief offense seemed to be that he loved her, and Athénaïse was not the woman to be loved against her will. She called marriage a trap set for the feet of unwary and unsuspecting girls, and in round, unmeasured terms reproached her mother with treachery and deceit.

"I told you Cazeau was the man," chuckled Miché, when his wife had related the scene that had accompanied and influenced Athénaïse's departure.

Athénaïse again hoped, in the morning, that Cazeau would scold or make some sort of a scene, but he apparently did not dream of it. It was exasperating that he should take her acquiescence so for granted. It is true he had been up and over the fields and across the river and back long before she was out of bed, and he may have been thinking of something else, which was no excuse, which was even in some sense an aggravation. But he did say to her at breakfast, "That brother of yo's, that Montéclin, is unbearable."

"Montéclin? Par exemple!"

Athénaïse, seated opposite to her husband, was attired in a white morning wrapper. She wore a somewhat abused, long face, it is true,— an expression of countenance familiar to some husbands,—but the expression was not sufficiently pronounced to mar the charm of her youthful freshness. She had little heart to eat, only playing with the food before her, and she felt a pang of resentment at her husband's healthy appetite.

"Yes, Montéclin," he reasserted. "He's developed into a firs'-class nuisance; an' you better tell him, Athénaïse,—unless you want me to tell him,—to confine his energies after this to matters that concern him. I have no use fo' him or fo' his interference in w'at regards you an' me alone."

This was said with unusual asperity. It was the little breach that Athenaïse had been watching for, and she charged rapidly: "It's strange, if you detes' Montéclin so heartily, that you would desire to marry his sister." She knew it was a silly thing to say, and was not surprised when he told her so. It gave her a little foothold for further attack, however. "I don't see, anyhow, w'at reason you had to marry me, w'en there were so many others," she complained, as if accusing him of persecution and injury. "There was Marianne running after you fo' the las' five years till it was disgraceful; an' any one of the Dortrand girls would have been glad to marry you. But no, nothing would do; you mus' come out on the rigolet fo' me." Her complaint was pathetic, and at the same time so amusing that Cazeau was forced to smile.

"I can't see w'at the Dortrand girls or Marianne have to do with it," he rejoined; adding, with no trace of amusement, "I married you because I loved you; because you were the woman I wanted to marry, an' the only one. I reckon I tole you that befo'. I thought—of co'se I was a fool fo' taking things fo' granted—but I did think that I might make you happy in making things easier an' mo' comfortable fo' you. I expected— I was even that big a fool—I believed that yo' coming yere to me would be like the sun shining out of the clouds, an' that our days would be like w'at the story-books promise after the wedding. I was mistaken. But I can't imagine w'at induced you to marry me. W'atever it was, I reckon you foun' out you made a mistake, too. I don' see anything to do but make the best of a bad bargain, an' shake han's over it." He had arisen from the table, and, approaching, held out his hand to her. What he had said was commonplace enough, but it was significant, coming from Cazeau, who was not often so unreserved in expressing himself.

Athénaïse ignored the hand held out to her. She was resting her chin in her palm, and kept her eyes fixed moodily upon the table. He rested his hand, that she would not touch, upon her head for an instant, and walked away out of the room.

She heard him giving orders to workmen who had been waiting for him out on the gallery, and she heard him mount his horse and ride away. A hundred things would distract him and engage his attention during the day. She felt that he had perhaps put her and her grievance from his thoughts when he crossed the threshold; whilst she—

Old Félicité was standing there holding a shining tin pail, asking for flour and lard and eggs from the storeroom, and meal for the chicks.

Athénaïse seized the bunch of keys which hung from her belt and flung them at Félicité's feet.

"Tiens! tu vas les garder comme tu as jadis fait. Je ne veux plus de ce train là, moi!"

The old woman stooped and picked up the keys from the floor. It was really all one to her that her mistress returned them to her keeping, and refused to take further account of the ménage.

IV

It seemed now to Athénaïse that Montéclin was the only friend left to her in the world. Her father and mother had turned from her in what appeared to be her hour of need. Her friends laughed at her, and refused to take seriously the hints which she threw out,—feeling her way to discover if marriage were as distasteful to other women as to herself. Montéclin alone understood her. He alone had always been ready to act for her and with her, to comfort and solace her with his sympathy and his support. Her only hope for rescue from her hateful surroundings lay in Montéclin. Of herself she felt powerless to plan, to act, even to conceive a way out of this pitfall into which the whole world seemed to have conspired to thrust her.

She had a great desire to see her brother, and wrote asking him to come to her. But it better suited Montéclin's spirit of adventure to appoint a meeting-place at the turn of the lane, where Athénaïse might appear to be walking leisurely for health and recreation, and where he might seem to be riding along, bent on some errand of business or pleasure.

There had been a shower, a sudden downpour, short as it was sudden, that had laid the dust in the road. It had freshened the pointed leaves of the live-oaks, and brightened up the big fields of cotton on either side of the lane till they seemed carpeted with green, glittering gems.

Athénaïse walked along the grassy edge of the road, lifting her crisp skirts with one hand, and with the other twirling a gay sunshade over her bare head. The scent of the fields after the rain was delicious. She inhaled long breaths of their freshness and perfume, that soothed and quieted her for the moment. There were birds splashing and spluttering in the pools, pluming themselves on the fence-rails, and sending out little sharp cries, twitters, and shrill rhapsodies of delight.

She saw Montéclin approaching from a great distance,—almost as far away as the turn of the woods. But she could not feel sure it was he; it appeared too tall for Montéclin, but that was because he was riding a large horse. She waved her parasol to him; she was so glad to see him. She had never been so glad to see Montéclin before; not even the day when he had taken her out of the convent, against her parents' wishes, because she had expressed a desire to remain there no longer. He seemed to her, as he drew near, the embodiment of kindness, of bravery, of chivalry, even of wisdom; for she had never known Montéclin at a loss to extricate himself from a disagreeable situation.

He dismounted, and, leading his horse by the bridle, started to walk beside her, after he had kissed her affectionately and asked her what she was crying about. She protested that she was not crying, for she was laughing, though drying her eyes at the same time on her handkerchief, rolled in a soft mop for the purpose.

She took Montéclin's arm, and they strolled slowly down the lane; they could not seat themselves for a comfortable chat, as they would have liked, with the grass all sparkling and bristling wet.

Yes, she was quite as wretched as ever, she told him. The week which had gone by since she saw him had in no wise lightened the burden of her discontent. There had even been some additional provocations laid upon her, and she told Montéclin all about them,—about the keys, for instance, which in a fit of temper she had returned to Félicité's keeping; and she told how Cazeau had brought them back to her as if they were something she had accidentally lost, and he had recovered; and how he had said, in that aggravating tone of his, that it was not the custom on Cane river for the negro servants to carry the keys, when there was a mistress at the head of the household.

But Athénaïse could not tell Montéclin anything to increase the disrespect which he already entertained for his brother-in-law; and it was then he unfolded to her a plan which he had conceived and worked out for her deliverance from this galling matrimonial yoke.

It was not a plan which met with instant favor, which she was at once ready to accept, for it involved secrecy and dissimulation, hateful alternatives, both of them. But she was filled with admiration for Montéclin's resources and wonderful talent for contrivance. She accepted the plan; not with the immediate determination to act upon it, rather with the intention to sleep and to dream upon it.

Three days later she wrote to Montéclin that she had abandoned herself to his counsel. Displeasing as it might be to her sense of honesty, it would yet be less trying than to live on with a soul full of bitterness and revolt, as she had done for the past two months.

V

When Cazeau awoke, one morning at his usual very early hour, it was to find the place at his side vacant. This did not surprise him until he discovered that Athénaïse was not in the adjoining room, where he had often found her sleeping in the morning on the lounge. She had perhaps gone out for an early stroll, he reflected, for her jacket and hat were not on the rack where she had hung them the night before. But there were other things absent,—a gown or two from the armoire; and there was a great gap in the piles of lingerie on the shelf; and her traveling-bag was missing, and so were her bits of jewelry from the toilet tray—and Athénaïse was gone!

But the absurdity of going during the night, as if she had been a prisoner, and he the keeper of a dungeon! So much secrecy and mystery, to go sojourning out on the Bon Dieu! Well, the Michés might keep their daughter after this. For the companionship of no woman on earth would he again undergo the humiliating sensation of baseness that had overtaken him in passing the old oak-tree in the fallow meadow.

But a terrible sense of loss overwhelmed Cazeau. It was not new or sudden; he had felt it for weeks growing upon him, and it seemed to culminate with Athénaïse's flight from home. He knew that he could again compel her return as he had done once before,— compel her to return to the shelter of his roof, compel her cold and unwilling submission to his love and passionate transports; but the loss of self-respect seemed to him too dear a price to pay for a wife.

He could not comprehend why she had seemed to prefer him above others; why she had attracted him with eyes, with voice, with a hundred womanly ways, and finally distracted him with love which she seemed, in her timid, maidenly fashion, to return. The great sense of loss came from the realization of having missed a chance for happiness,—a chance that would come his way again only through a miracle. He could not think of himself loving any other woman, and could not think of Athénaïse ever—even at some remote date—caring for him.

He wrote her a letter, in which he disclaimed any further intention of forcing his commands upon her. He did not desire her presence ever again in his home unless she came of her free will, uninfluenced by family or friends; unless she could be the companion he had hoped for in marrying her, and in some measure return affection and respect for the love which he continued and would always continue to feel for her. This letter he sent out to the rigolet by a messenger early in the day. But she was not out on the rigolet, and had not been there.

The family turned instinctively to Montéclin, and almost literally fell upon him for an explanation; he had been absent from home all night. There was much mystification in his answers, and a plain desire to mislead in his assurances of ignorance and innocence.

But with Cazeau there was no doubt or speculation when he accosted the young fellow. "Montéclin, w'at have you done with Athénaïse?" he questioned bluntly. They had met in the open road on horseback, just as Cazeau ascended the river bank before his house.

"W'at have you done to Athénaïse?" returned Montéclin for answer.

"I don't reckon you've considered yo' conduct by any light of decency an' propriety in encouraging yo' sister to such an action, but let me tell you"—

"Voyons! you can let me alone with yo' decency an' morality an' fiddlesticks. I know you mus' 'a' done Athénaïse pretty mean that she can't live with you; an' fo' my part, I'm mighty durn glad she had the spirit to quit you."

"I ain't in the humor to take any notice of yo' impertinence, Montéclin; but let me remine you that Athénaïse is nothing but a chile in character; besides that, she's my wife, an' I hole you responsible fo' her safety an' welfare. If any harm of any description happens to her, I'll strangle you, by God, like a rat, and fling you in Cane river, if I have to hang fo' it!" He had not lifted his voice. The only sign of anger was a savage gleam in his eyes.

"I reckon you better keep yo' big talk fo' the women, Cazeau," replied Montéclin, riding away.

But he went doubly armed after that, and intimated that the precaution was not needless, in view of the threats and menaces that were abroad touching his personal safety.

VI

Athénaïse reached her destination sound of skin and limb, but a good deal flustered, a little frightened, and altogether excited and interested by her unusual experiences.

Her destination was the house of Sylvie, on Dauphine Street, in New Orleans,—a three-story gray brick, standing directly on the banquette, with three broad stone steps leading to the deep front entrance. From the second-story balcony swung a small sign, conveying to passers-by the intelligence that within were *"chambres garnies."*

It was one morning in the last week of April that Athénaïse presented herself at the Dauphine Street house. Sylvie was expecting her, and introduced her at once to her apartment, which was in the second story of the back ell, and accessible by an open, outside gallery. There was a yard below, paved with broad stone flagging; many fragrant flowering shrubs and plants grew in a bed along the side of the opposite wall, and others were distributed about in tubs and green boxes.

It was a plain but large enough room into which Athénaïse was ushered, with matting on the floor, green shades and Nottingham-lace curtains at the windows that looked out on the gallery, and furnished with a cheap walnut suit. But everything looked exquisitely clean, and the whole place smelled of cleanliness.

Athénaïse at once fell into the rocking-chair, with the air of exhaustion and intense relief of one who has come to the end of her troubles. Sylvie, entering behind her, laid the big traveling-bag on the floor and deposited the jacket on the bed.

She was a portly quadroon of fifty or there-about, clad in an ample *volante* of the old-fashioned purple calico so much affected by her class. She wore large golden hoop-earrings, and her hair was combed plainly, with every appearance of effort to smooth out the kinks. She had broad, coarse features, with a nose that turned up, exposing the wide nostrils, and that seemed to emphasize the loftiness and command of her bearing, —a dignity that in the presence of white people assumed a character of respectfulness, but never of obsequiousness. Sylvie believed firmly in maintaining the color line, and would not suffer a white person, even a child, to call her "Madame Sylvie,"—a title which she exacted religiously, however, from those of her own race.

"I hope you be please' wid yo' room, madame," she observed amiably. "Dat's de same room w'at yo' brother, M'sieur Miché, all time like w'en he come to New Orlean'. He well, M'sieur Miché? I receive' his letter las' week, an' dat same day a gent'man want I give 'im dat room. I say, 'No, dat room already ingage'.' Ev-body like dat room on 'count it so quite (quiet). M'sieur Gouvernail, dere in nax' room, you can't pay 'im! He been stay t'ree year' in dat room; but all fix' up fine wid his own furn'ture an' books, 'tel you can't see! I say to 'im plenty time', 'M'sieur Gouvernail, w'y you don't take dat t'ree-story front, now, long it's empty?' He tells me, 'Leave me 'lone, Sylvie; I know a good room w'en I fine it, me.' "

She had been moving slowly and majestically about the apartment, straightening and smoothing down bed and pillows, peering into ewer and basin, evidently casting an eye around to make sure that everything was as it should be.

"I sen' you some fresh water, madame," she offered upon retiring from the room. "An' w'en you want an't'ing, you jus' go out on de gall'ry an' call Pousette: she year you plain,—she right down dere in de kitchen."

Athénaïse was really not so exhausted as she had every reason to be after that interminable and circuitous way by which Montéclin had seen fit to have her conveyed to the city.

Would she ever forget that dark and truly dangerous midnight ride along the "coast" to the mouth of Cane river! There Montéclin had parted with her, after seeing her aboard the St. Louis and Shreveport packet which he knew would pass there before dawn. She had received instructions to disembark at the mouth of Red river, and there transfer to the first south-bound steamer for New Orleans; all of which instructions she had followed implicitly, even to making her way at once to Sylvie's upon her arrival in the city. Montéclin had enjoined secrecy and much caution; the clandestine nature of the affair gave it a savor of adventure which was highly pleasing to him. Eloping with his sister was only a little less engaging than eloping with some one else's sister.

But Montéclin did not do the *grand seigneur* by halves. He had paid Sylvie a whole month in advance for Athénaïse's board and lodging. Part of the sum he had been forced to borrow, it is true, but he was not niggardly.

Athénaïse was to take her meals in the house, which none of the other lodgers did; the one exception being that Mr. Gouvernail was served with breakfast on Sunday mornings.

Sylvie's clientèle came chiefly from the southern parishes; for the most part, people spending but a few days in the city. She prided herself upon the quality and highly respectable character of her patrons, who came and went unobtrusively.

The large parlor opening upon the front balcony was seldom used. Her guests were permitted to entertain in this sanctuary of elegance,—but they never did. She often rented it for the night to parties of respectable and discreet gentlemen desiring to enjoy a quiet game of cards outside the bosom of their families. The second-story hall also led by a long window out on the balcony. And Sylvie advised Athénaïse, when she grew weary of her back room, to go and sit on the front balcony, which was shady in the afternoon, and where she might find diversion in the sounds and sights of the street below.

Athénaïse refreshed herself with a bath, and was soon unpacking her few belongings, which she ranged neatly away in the bureau drawers and the armoire.

She had revolved certain plans in her mind during the past hour or so. Her present intention was to live on indefinitely in this big, cool, clean back room on Dauphine street. She had thought seriously, for moments, of the convent, with all readiness to embrace the vows of poverty and chastity; but what about obedience? Later, she intended, in some roundabout way, to give her parents and her husband the assurance of her safety and welfare; reserving the right to remain unmolested and lost to them. To live on at the expense of Montéclin's generosity was wholly out of the question, and Athénaïse meant to look about for some suitable and agreeable employment.

The imperative thing to be done at present, however, was to go out in search of material for an inexpensive gown or two; for she found herself in the painful predicament of a young woman having almost literally nothing to wear. She decided upon pure white for one, and some sort of a sprigged muslin for the other.

VII

On Sunday morning, two days after Athénaïse's arrival in the city, she went in to breakfast somewhat later than usual, to find two covers laid at table instead of the one to which she was accustomed. She had been to mass, and did not remove her hat, but put her fan, parasol, and prayer-book aside. The dining-room was situated just beneath her own apartment, and, like all rooms of the house, was large and airy; the floor was covered with a glistening oil-cloth.

The small, round table, immaculately set, was drawn near the open window. There were some tall plants in boxes on the gallery outside; and Pousette, a little, old, intensely black woman, was splashing and dashing buckets of water on the flagging, and talking loud in her Creole patois to no one in particular.

A dish piled with delicate river-shrimps and crushed ice was on the table; a caraffe of crystal-clear water, a few *hors d'œuvres*, beside a small golden-brown crusty loaf of French bread at each plate. A half-bottle of wine and the morning paper were set at the place opposite Athénaïse.

She had almost completed her breakfast when Gouvernail came in and seated himself at table. He felt annoyed at finding his cherished privacy invaded. Sylvie was removing the remains of a mutton-chop from before Athénaïse, and serving her with a cup of café au lait.

"M'sieur Gouvernail," offered Sylvie in her most insinuating and impressive manner, "you please leave me make you acquaint' wid Madame Cazeau. Dat's M'sieur Miché's sister; you meet 'im two t'ree time', you rec'lec', an' been one day to de race wid 'im. Madame Cazeau, you please leave me make you acquaint' wid M'sieur Gouvernail."

Gouvernail expressed himself greatly pleased to meet the sister of Monsieur Miché, of whom he had not the slightest recollection. He inquired after Monsieur Miché's health, and politely offered Athénaïse a part of his newspaper,—the part which contained the Woman's Page and the social gossip.

Athénaïse faintly remembered that Sylvie had spoken of a Monsieur Gouvernail occupying the room adjoining hers, living amid luxurious surroundings and a multitude of books. She had not thought of him further than to picture him a stout, middle-aged gentleman, with a bushy beard turning gray, wearing large gold-rimmed spectacles, and stooping somewhat from much bending over books and writing material. She had confused him in her mind with the likeness of some literary celebrity that she had run across in the advertising pages of a magazine.

Gouvernail's appearance was, in truth, in no sense striking. He looked older than thirty and younger than forty, was of medium height and weight, with a quiet, unobtrusive manner which seemed to ask that he be let alone. His hair was light brown, brushed carefully and parted in the middle. His mustache was brown, and so were his eyes, which had a mild, penetrating quality. He was neatly dressed in the fashion of the day; and his hands seemed to Athénaïse remarkably white and soft for a man's.

He had been buried in the contents of his newspaper, when he suddenly realized that some further little attention might be due to Miché's sister. He started to offer her a glass of wine, when he was surprised and relieved to find that she had quietly slipped away while he was absorbed in his own editorial on Corrupt Legislation.

Gouvernail finished his paper and smoked his cigar out on the gallery. He lounged about, gathered a rose for his buttonhole, and had his regular Sunday-morning confab with Pousette, to whom he paid a weekly stipend for brushing his shoes and clothing. He made a great pretense of haggling over the transaction, only to enjoy her uneasiness and garrulous excitement.

He worked or read in his room for a few hours, and when he quitted the house, at three in the afternoon, it was to return no more till late at night. It was his almost invariable custom to spend Sunday evenings out in the American quarter, among a congenial set of men and women,— *des esprits forts*, all of them, whose lives were irreproachable, yet whose opinions would startle even the traditional "sapeur," for whom "nothing is sacred." But for all his "advanced" opinions, Gouvernail was a liberal-minded fellow; a man or woman lost nothing of his respect by being married.

When he left the house in the afternoon, Athénaïse had already ensconced herself on the front balcony. He could see her through the jalousies when he passed on his way to the front entrance. She had not yet grown lonesome or homesick; the newness of her surroundings made them sufficiently entertaining. She found it diverting to sit there on the front balcony watching people pass by, even though there was no one to talk to. And then the comforting, comfortable sense of not being married!

She watched Gouvernail walk down the street, and could find no fault with his bearing. He could hear the sound of her rockers for some little distance. He wondered what the "poor little thing" was doing in the city, and meant to ask Sylvie about her when he should happen to think of it.

VIII

The following morning, towards noon, when Gouvernail quitted his room, he was confronted by Athénaïse, exhibiting some confusion and trepidation at being forced to request a favor of him at so early a stage of their acquaintance. She stood in her doorway, and had evidently been sewing, as the thimble on her finger testified, as well as a long-threaded needle thrust in the bosom of her gown. She held a stamped but unaddressed letter in her hand.

And would Mr. Gouvernail be so kind as to address the letter to her brother, Mr. Montéclin Miché? She would hate to detain him with explanations this morning,—another time, perhaps,—but now she begged that he would give himself the trouble.

He assured her that it made no difference, that it was no trouble whatever; and he drew a fountain pen from his pocket and addressed the letter at her dictation, resting it on the inverted rim of his straw hat. She wondered a little at a man of his supposed erudition stumbling over the spelling of "Montéclin" and "Miché."

She demurred at overwhelming him with the additional trouble of posting it, but he succeeded in convincing her that so simple a task as the posting of a letter would not add an iota to the burden of the day. Moreover, he promised to carry it in his hand, and thus avoid any possible risk of forgetting it in his pocket.

After that, and after a second repetition of the favor, when she had told him that she had had a letter from Montéclin, and looked as if she wanted to tell him more, he felt that he knew her better. He felt that he knew her well enough to join her out on the balcony, one night, when he found her sitting there alone. He was not one who deliberately sought the society of women, but he was not wholly a bear. A little commiseration for Athénaïse's aloneness, perhaps some curiosity to know further what manner of woman she was, and the natural influence of her feminine charm were equal unconfessed factors in turning his steps towards the balcony when he discovered the shimmer of her white gown through the open hall window.

It was already quite late, but the day had been intensely hot, and neighboring balconies and doorways were occupied by chattering groups of humanity, loath to abandon the grateful freshness of the outer air. The voices about her served to reveal to Athénaïse the feeling of loneliness that was gradually coming over her. Notwithstanding certain dormant impulses, she craved human sympathy and companionship.

She shook hands impulsively with Gouvernail, and told him how glad she was to see him. He was not prepared for such an admission, but it pleased him immensely, detecting as he did that the expression was as sincere as it was outspoken. He drew a chair up within comfortable conversational distance of Athénaïse, though he had no intention of talking more than was barely necessary to encourage Madame—He had actually forgotten her name!

He leaned an elbow on the balcony rail, and would have offered an opening remark about the oppressive heat of the day, but Athénaïse did not give him the opportunity. How glad she was to talk to some one, and how she talked!

An hour later she had gone to her room, and Gouvernail stayed smoking on the balcony. He knew her quite well after that hour's talk. It was not so much what she had said as what her half saying had revealed to his quick intelligence. He knew that she adored Montéclin, and he suspected that she adored Cazeau without being herself aware of it. He had gathered that she was self-willed, impulsive, innocent, ignorant, unsatisfied, dissatisfied; for had she not complained that things seemed all wrongly arranged in this world, and no one was permitted to be happy in his own way? And he told her he was sorry she had discovered that primordial fact of existence so early in life.

He commiserated her loneliness, and scanned his bookshelves next morning for something to lend her to read, rejecting everything that offered itself to his view. Philosophy was out of the question, and so was poetry; that is, such poetry as he possessed. He had not sounded her literary tastes, and strongly suspected she had none; that she would have rejected The Duchess as readily as Mrs. Humphry Ward. He compromised on a magazine.

It had entertained her passably, she admitted, upon returning it. A New England story had puzzled her, it was true, and a Creole tale had offended her, but the pictures had pleased her greatly, especially one which had reminded her so strongly of Montéclin after a hard day's ride that she was loath to give it up. It was one of Remington's Cowboys, and Gouvernail insisted upon her keeping it,—keeping the magazine.

He spoke to her daily after that, and was always eager to render her some service or to do something towards her entertainment.

One afternoon he took her out to the lake end. She had been there once, some years before, but in winter, so the trip was comparatively new and strange to her. The large expanse of water studded with pleasure-boats, the sight of children playing merrily along the grassy palisades, the music, all enchanted her. Gouvernail thought her the most beautiful woman he had ever seen. Even her gown—the sprigged muslin—appeared to him the most charming one imaginable. Nor could anything be more becoming than the arrangement of her brown hair under the white sailor hat, all rolled back in a soft puff from her radiant face. And she carried her parasol and lifted her skirts and used her fan in ways that seemed quite unique and peculiar to herself, and which he considered almost worthy of study and imitation.

They did not dine out there at the water's edge, as they might have done, but returned early to the city to avoid the crowd. Athénaïse wanted to go home, for she said Sylvie would have dinner prepared and would be expecting her. But it was not difficult to persuade her to dine instead in the quiet little restaurant that he knew and liked, with its sanded floor, its secluded atmosphere, its delicious menu, and its obsequious waiter wanting to know what he might have the honor of serving to "monsieur et madame." No wonder he made the mistake, with Gouvernail assuming such an air of proprietorship! But Athénaïse was very tired after it all; the sparkle went out of her face, and she hung draggingly on his arm in walking home.

He was reluctant to part from her when she bade him good-night at her door and thanked him for the agreeable evening. He had hoped she would sit outside until it was time for him to regain the newspaper office. He knew that she would undress and get into her peignoir and lie upon her bed; and what he wanted to do, what he would have given much to do, was to go and sit beside her, read to her something restful, soothe her, do her bidding, whatever it might be. Of course there was no use in thinking of that. But he was surprised at his growing desire to be serving her. She gave him an opportunity sooner than he looked for.

"Mr. Gouvernail," she called from her room, "will you be so kine as to call Pousette an' tell her she fo'got to bring my ice-water?"

He was indignant at Pousette's negligence, and called severely to her over the banisters. He was sitting before his own door, smoking. He knew that Athénaïse had gone to bed, for her room was dark, and she had opened the slats of the door and windows. Her bed was near a window.

Pousette came flopping up with the ice-water, and with a hundred excuses: "Mo pa oua vou à tab c'te lanuite, mo cri vou pé gagni déja là-bas; parole! Vou pas cri conté ça Madame Sylvie?" She had not seen Athénaïse at table, and thought she was gone. She swore to this, and hoped Madame Sylvie would not be informed of her remissness.

A little later Athénaïse lifted her voice again: "Mr. Gouvernail, did you remark that young man sitting on the opposite side from us, coming in, with a gray coat an' a blue ban' aroun' his hat?"

Of course Gouvernail had not noticed any such individual, but he assured Athénaïse that he had observed the young fellow particularly.

"Don't you think he looked something,—not very much, of co'se,— but don't you think he had a little faux-air of Montéclin?"

"I think he looked strikingly like Montéclin," asserted Gouvernail, with the one idea of prolonging the conversation. "I meant to call your attention to the resemblance, and something drove it out of my head."

"The same with me," returned Athénaïse. "Ah, my dear Montéclin! I wonder w'at he is doing now?"

"Did you receive any news, any letter from him to-day?" asked Gouvernail, determined that if the conversation ceased it should not be through lack of effort on his part to sustain it.

"Not to-day, but yesterday. He tells me that maman was so distracted with uneasiness that finally, to pacify her, he was fo'ced to confess that he knew w'ere I was, but that he was boun' by a vow of secrecy not to reveal it. But Cazeau has not noticed him or spoken to him since he threaten' to throw po' Montéclin in Cane river. You know Cazeau wrote me a letter the morning I lef', thinking I had gone to the rigolet. An' maman opened it, an' said it was full of the mos' noble sentiments, an' she wanted Montéclin to sen' it to me; but Montéclin refuse' poin' blank, so he wrote to me."

Gouvernail preferred to talk of Montéclin. He pictured Cazeau as unbearable, and did not like to think of him.

A little later Athénaïse called out, "Good-night, Mr. Gouvernail."

"Good-night," he returned reluctantly. And when he thought that she was sleeping, he got up and went away to the midnight pandemonium of his newspaper office.

IX

Athénaïse could not have held out through the month had it not been for Gouvernail. With the need of caution and secrecy always uppermost in her mind, she made no new acquaintances, and she did not seek out persons already known to her; however, she knew so few, it required little effort to keep out of their way. As for Sylvie, almost every moment of her time was occupied in looking after her house; and, moreover, her deferential attitude towards her lodgers forbade anything like the gossipy chats in which Athénaïse might have condescended sometimes to indulge with her land-lady. The transient lodgers, who came and went, she never had occasion to meet. Hence she was entirely dependent upon Gouvernail for company.

He appreciated the situation fully; and every moment that he could spare from his work he devoted to her entertainment. She liked to be out of doors, and they strolled together in the summer twilight through the mazes of the old French quarter. They went again to the lake end, and stayed for hours on the water; returning so late that the streets through which they passed were silent and deserted. On Sunday morning he arose at an unconscionable hour to take her to the French market, knowing that the sights and sounds there would interest her. And he did not join the intellectual coterie in the afternoon, as he usually did, but placed himself all day at the disposition and service of Athénaïse.

Notwithstanding all, his manner toward her was tactful, and evinced intelligence and a deep knowledge of her character, surprising upon so brief an acquaintance. For the time he was everything to her that she would have him; he replaced home and friends. Sometimes she wondered if he had ever loved a woman. She could not fancy him loving any one passionately, rudely, offensively, as Cazeau loved her. Once she was so naïve as to ask him outright if he had ever been in love, and he assured her promptly that he had not. She thought it an admirable trait in his character, and esteemed him greatly therefor.

He found her crying one night, not openly or violently. She was leaning over the gallery rail, watching the toads that hopped about in the moonlight, down on the damp flagstones of the courtyard. There was an oppressively sweet odor rising from the cape jessamine. Pousette was down there, mumbling and quarreling with some one, and seeming to be having it all her own way,—as well she might, when her companion was only a black cat that had come in from a neighboring yard to keep her company.

Athénaïse did admit feeling heart-sick, body-sick, when he questioned her; she supposed it was nothing but homesick. A letter from Montéclin had stirred her all up. She longed for her mother, for Montéclin; she was sick for a sight of the cotton-fields, the scent of the ploughed earth, for the dim, mysterious charm of the woods, and the old tumble-down home on the Bon Dieu.

As Gouvernail listened to her, a wave of pity and tenderness swept through him. He took her hands and pressed them against him. He wondered what would happen if he were to put his arms around her.

He was hardly prepared for what happened, but he stood it courageously. She twined her arms around his neck and wept outright on his shoulder; the hot tears scalding his cheek and neck, and her whole body shaken in his arms. The impulse was powerful to strain her to him; the temptation was fierce to seek her lips; but he did neither.

He understood a thousand times better than she herself understood it that he was acting as substitute for Montéclin. Bitter as the conviction was, he accepted it. He was patient; he could wait. He hoped some day to hold her with a lover's arms. That she was married made no particle of difference to Gouvernail. He could not conceive or dream of it making a difference. When the time came that she wanted him,—as he hoped and believed it would come,—he felt he would have a right to her. So long as she did not want him, he had no right to her,—no more than her husband had. It was very hard to feel her warm breath and tears upon his cheek, and her struggling bosom pressed against him and her soft arms clinging to him and his whole body and soul aching for her, and yet to make no sign.

He tried to think what Montéclin would have said and done, and to act accordingly. He stroked her hair, and held her in a gentle embrace, until the tears dried and the sobs ended. Before releasing herself she kissed him against the neck; she had to love somebody in her own way! Even that he endured like a stoic. But it was well he left her, to plunge into the thick of rapid, breathless, exacting work till nearly dawn.

Athénaïse was greatly soothed, and slept well. The touch of friendly hands and caressing arms had been very grateful. Henceforward she would not be lonely and unhappy, with Gouvernail there to comfort her.

X

The fourth week of Athénaïse's stay in the city was drawing to a close. Keeping in view the intention which she had of finding some suitable and agreeable employment, she had made a few tentatives in that direction. But with the exception of two little girls who had promised to take piano lessons at a price that would be embarrassing to mention, these attempts had been fruitless. Moreover, the homesickness kept coming back, and Gouvernail was not always there to drive it away.

She spent much of her time weeding and pottering among the flowers down in the courtyard. She tried to take an interest in the black cat, and a mockingbird that hung in a cage outside the kitchen door, and a disreputable parrot that belonged to the cook next door, and swore hoarsely all day long in bad French.

Beside, she was not well; she was not herself, as she told Sylvie. The climate of New Orleans did not agree with her. Sylvie was distressed to learn this, as she felt in some measure responsible for the health and well-being of Monsieur Miché's sister; and she made it her duty to inquire closely into the nature and character of Athénaïse's malaise.

Sylvie was very wise, and Athénaïse was very ignorant. The extent of her ignorance and the depth of her subsequent enlightenment were bewildering. She stayed a long, long time quite still, quite stunned, after her interview with Sylvie, except for the short, uneven breathing that ruffled her bosom. Her whole being was steeped in a wave of ecstasy. When she finally arose from the chair in which she had been seated, and looked at herself in the mirror, a face met hers which she seemed to see for the first time, so transfigured was it with wonder and rapture.

One mood quickly followed another, in this new turmoil of her senses, and the need of action became uppermost. Her mother must know at once, and her mother must tell Montéclin. And Cazeau must know. As she thought of him, the first purely sensuous tremor of her life swept over her. She half whispered his name, and the sound of it brought red blotches into her cheeks. She spoke it over and over, as if it were some new, sweet sound born out of darkness and confusion, and reaching her for the first time. She was impatient to be with him. Her whole passionate nature was aroused as if by a miracle.

She seated herself to write to her husband. The letter he would get in the morning, and she would be with him at night. What would he say? How would he act? She knew that he would forgive her, for had he not written a letter?—and a pang of resentment toward Montéclin shot through her. What did he mean by withholding that letter? How dared he not have sent it?

Athénaïse attired herself for the street, and went out to post the letter which she had penned with a single thought, a spontaneous impulse. It would have seemed incoherent to most people, but Cazeau would understand.

She walked along the street as if she had fallen heir to some magnificent inheritance. On her face was a look of pride and satisfaction that passersby noticed and admired. She wanted to talk to some one, to tell some person; and she stopped at the corner and told the oyster-woman, who was Irish, and who God-blessed her, and wished prosperity to the race of Cazeaus for generations to come. She held the oyster-woman's fat, dirty little baby in her arms and scanned it curiously and observingly, as if a baby were a phenomenon that she encountered for the first time in life. She even kissed it!

Then what a relief it was to Athénaïse to walk the streets without dread of being seen and recognized by some chance acquaintance from Red river! No one could have said now that she did not know her own mind.

She went directly from the oyster-woman's to the office of Harding & Offdean, her husband's merchants; and it was with such an air of partnership, almost proprietorship, that she demanded a sum of money on her husband's account, they gave it to her as unhesitatingly as they would have handed it over to Cazeau himself. When Mr. Harding, who knew her, asked politely after her health, she turned so rosy and looked so conscious, he thought it a great pity for so pretty a woman to be such a little goose.

Athénaïse entered a dry-goods store and bought all manner of things, —little presents for nearly everybody she knew. She bought whole bolts of sheerest, softest, downiest white stuff; and when the clerk, in trying to meet her wishes, asked if she intended it for infant's use, she could have sunk through the floor, and wondered how he might have suspected it.

As it was Montéclin who had taken her away from her husband, she wanted it to be Montéclin who should take her back to him. So she wrote him a very curt note,—in fact it was a postal card,—asking that he meet her at the train on the evening following. She felt convinced that after what had gone before, Cazeau would await her at their own home; and she preferred it so.

Then there was the agreeable excitement of getting ready to leave, of packing up her things. Pousette kept coming and going, coming and going; and each time that she quitted the room it was with something that Athénaïse had given her,—a handkerchief, a petticoat, a pair of stockings with two tiny holes at the toes, some broken prayer-beads, and finally a silver dollar.

Next it was Sylvie who came along bearing a gift of what she called "a set of pattern',"—things of complicated design which never could have been obtained in any new-fangled bazaar or pattern-store, that Sylvie had acquired of a foreign lady of distinction whom she had nursed years before at the St. Charles hotel. Athénaïse accepted and handled them with reverence, fully sensible of the great compliment and favor, and laid them religiously away in the trunk which she had lately acquired.

She was greatly fatigued after the day of unusual exertion, and went early to bed and to sleep. All day long she had not once thought of Gouvernail, and only did think of him when aroused for a brief instant by the sound of his foot-falls on the gallery, as he passed in going to his room. He had hoped to find her up, waiting for him.

But the next morning he knew. Some one must have told him. There was no subject known to her which Sylvie hesitated to discuss in detail with any man of suitable years and discretion.

Athénaïse found Gouvernail waiting with a carriage to convey her to the railway station. A momentary pang visited her for having forgotten him so completely, when he said to her, "Sylvie tells me you are going away this morning."

He was kind, attentive, and amiable, as usual, but respected to the utmost the new dignity and reserve that her manner had developed since yesterday. She kept looking from the carriage window, silent, and embarrassed as Eve after losing her ignorance. He talked of the muddy streets and the murky morning, and of Montéclin. He hoped she would find everything comfortable and pleasant in the country, and trusted she would inform him whenever she came to visit the city again. He talked as if afraid or mistrustful of silence and himself.

At the station she handed him her purse, and he bought her ticket, secured for her a comfortable section, checked her trunk, and got all the bundles and things safely aboard the train. She felt very grateful. He pressed her hand warmly, lifted his hat, and left her. He was a man of intelligence, and took defeat gracefully; that was all. But as he made his way back to the carriage, he was thinking, "By heaven, it hurts, it hurts!"

XI

Athénaïse spent a day of supreme happiness and expectancy. The fair sight of the country unfolding itself before her was balm to her vision and to her soul. She was charmed with the rather unfamiliar, broad, clean sweep of the sugar plantations, with their monster sugar-houses, their rows of neat cabins like little villages of a single street, and their impressive homes standing apart amid clusters of trees. There were sudden glimpses of a bayou curling between sunny, grassy banks, or creeping sluggishly out from a tangled growth of wood, and brush, and fern, and poison-vines, and palmettos. And passing through the long stretches of monotonous woodlands, she would close her eyes and taste in anticipation the moment of her meeting with Cazeau. She could think of nothing but him.

It was night when she reached her station. There was Montéclin, as she had expected, waiting for her with a two-seated buggy, to which he had hitched his own swift-footed, spirited pony. It was good, he felt, to have her back on any terms; and he had no fault to find since she came of her own choice. He more than suspected the cause of her coming; her eyes and her voice and her foolish little manner went far in revealing the secret that was brimming over in her heart. But after he had deposited her at her own gate, and as he continued his way toward the rigolet, he could not help feeling that the affair had taken a very disappointing, an ordinary, a most commonplace turn, after all. He left her in Cazeau's keeping.

Her husband lifted her out of the buggy, and neither said a word until they stood together within the shelter of the gallery. Even then they did not speak at first. But Athénaïse turned to him with an appealing gesture. As he clasped her in his arms, he felt the yielding of her whole body against him. He felt her lips for the first time respond to the passion of his own.

The country night was dark and warm and still, save for the distant notes of an accordion which some one was playing in a cabin away off. A little negro baby was crying somewhere. As Athénaïse withdrew from her husband's embrace, the sound arrested her.

"Listen, Cazeau! How Juliette's baby is crying! Pauvre ti chou, I wonder w'at is the matter with it?"

Two Summers and Two Souls

I

He was a fine, honest-looking fellow; young, impetuous, candid; and he was bidding her good-bye.

It was in the country, where she lived, and where her soul and senses were slowly unfolding, like the languid petals of some white and fragrant blossom.

Five weeks—only five weeks he had known her. They seemed to him a flash, an eternity, a rapturous breath, an existence—a re-creation of light and life, and soul and senses. He tried to tell her something of this when the hour of parting came. But he could only say that he loved her; nothing else that he wanted to say seemed to mean so much as this. She was glad, and doubtful, and afraid, and kept reiterating:

"Only five weeks! so short! and love and life are so long."

"Then you don't love me!"

"I don't know. I want to be with you—near you."

"Then you do love me!"

"I don't know. I thought love meant something different—powerful, overwhelming. No. I am afraid to say."

He talked like a mad man then, and troubled and bewildered her with his incoherence. He begged for love as a mendicant might beg for alms, without reserve and without shame, and the passion within him gave an unnatural ring to his voice and a new, strange look to his eyes that chilled her unawakened senses and sent her shivering within herself.

"No, no, no!" was all she could say to him.

He willed not to believe it; he had felt so sure of her. And she was not one to play fast and loose, with those honest eyes whose depths had convinced while they ensnared him.

455

"Don't send me away like this," he pleaded, "without a crumb of hope to feed on and keep me living."

She dismissed him with a promise that it might not be final. "Who knows! I will think; but leave me alone. Don't trouble me; and I will see—Good-bye."

He did not once look back after leaving her, but walked straight on with a step that was quick and firm from habit. But he was almost blind and senseless from pain.

She stayed watching him cross the lawn and the long stretch of meadow beyond. She watched him till the deepening shadows of the coming night crept between them. She stayed troubled, uncertain; tearful because she did not know!

II

"I remember quite well the words I told you a year ago when we parted," she wrote to him. "I told you I did not know, I wanted to think, I even wanted to pray, but I believe I did not tell you that. And now, will you believe me when I say that I have not been able to think— hardly to pray. I have only been able to feel. When you went away that day you seemed to leave me in an empty world. I kept saying to myself, 'to-morrow or next day it will be different; it will be with me as it was before he came.' Then your letters coming—three of them, one upon the other—gave voice to the empty places. You were everywhere after that. And still I doubted, and I was cautious; for it has seemed to me that the love which is to hold two beings together through life must be love indeed.

"But what is the use of saying more than that I love you. I would not care to live without you; I think I could not. Come back to me."

III

When this letter reached him he was in preparation for a journey with a party of friends. It came with a batch of business letters, and in the midst of the city's rush and din which he had meant in another day to leave behind him.

He was all unprepared for its coming and unable at once to master the shock of it, that bewildered and unnerved him.

Then came back to him the recollection of pain—a remembrance always faint and unreal; but there was complete inability to revive the conditions that had engendered it.

How he had loved her and how he had suffered! especially during those first days, and even months, when he slept and waked dreaming of her; when his letters remained unanswered, and when existence was but a name for bitter endurance.

How long had it lasted? Could he tell? The end began when he could wake in the morning without the oppression, and free from the haunting pain. The end was that day, that hour or second, when he thought of her without emotion and without regret; as he thought of her now, with unstirred pulses. There was even with him now the touch of something keener than indifference—something engendered by revolt.

It was as if one loved, and dead and forgotten had returned to life; with the strange illusion that the rush of existence had halted while she lay in her grave; and with the still more singular delusion that love is eternal.

He did not hesitate as though confronted by a problem. He did not think of leaving the letter unnoticed. He did not think of telling her the truth. If he thought of these expedients, it was only to dismiss them.

He simply went to her. As he would have gone unflinchingly to meet the business obligation that he knew would leave him bankrupt.

The Unexpected

When Randall, for a brief absence, left his Dorothea, whom he was to marry after a time, the parting was bitter; the enforced separation seemed to them too cruel an ordeal to bear. The good-by dragged with lingering kisses and sighs, and more kisses and more clinging till the last wrench came.

He was to return at the close of the month. Daily letters, impassioned and interminable, passed between them.

He did not return at the close of the month; he was delayed by illness. A heavy cold, accompanied by fever, contracted in some unaccountable way, held him to his bed. He hoped it would be over and that he would rejoin her in a week. But this was a stubborn cold, that seemed not to yield to familiar treatment; yet the physician was not discouraged, and promised to have him on his feet in a fortnight.

All this was torture to the impatient Dorothea; and if her parents had permitted, she surely would have hastened to the bedside of her beloved.

For a long interval he could not write himself. One day he seemed better; another day a "fresh cold" seized him with relentless clutch; and so a second month went by, and Dorothea had reached the limit of her endurance.

Then a tremulous scrawl came from him, saying he would be obliged to pass a season at the south; but he would first revisit his home, if only for a day, to clasp his dearest one to his heart, to appease the hunger for her presence, the craving for her lips that had been devouring him through all the fever and pain of this detestable illness.

Dorothea had read his impassioned letters almost to tatters. She had sat daily gazing for hours upon his portrait, which showed him to be an almost perfect specimen of youthful health, strength and manly beauty.

She knew he would be altered in appearance—he had prepared her, and had even written that she would hardly know him. She expected to see him ill and wasted; she would not seem shocked; she would not let him see astonishment or pain in her face. She was in a quiver of anticipation, a sensuous fever of expectancy till he came.

She sat beside him on the sofa, for after the first delirious embrace he had been unable to hold himself upon his tottering feet, and had sunk exhausted in a corner of the sofa. He threw his head back upon the cushions and stayed, with closed eyes, panting; all the strength of his body had concentrated in the clasp—the grasp with which he clung to her hand.

She stared at him as one might look upon a curious apparition which inspired wonder and mistrust rather than fear. This was not the man who had gone away from her; the man she loved and had promised to marry. What hideous transformation had he undergone, or what devilish transformation was she undergoing in contemplating him? His skin was waxy and hectic, red upon the cheek-bones. His eyes were sunken; his features pinched and prominent; and his clothing hung loosely upon his wasted frame. The lips with which he had kissed her so hungrily, and with which he was kissing her now, were dry and parched, and his breath was feverish and tainted.

At the sight and the touch of him something within her seemed to be shuddering, shrinking, shriveling together, losing all semblance of what had been. She felt as if it was her heart; but it was only her love.

"This is the way my Uncle Archibald went—in a gallop—you know." He spoke with a certain derision and in little gasps, as if breath were failing him. "There's no danger of that for me, of course, once I get south; but the doctors won't answer for me if I stay here during the coming fall and winter."

Then he held her in his arms with what seemed to be a frenzy of passion; a keen and quickened desire beside which his former and healthful transports were tempered and lukewarm by comparison.

"We need not wait, Dorothea," he whispered. "We must not put it off. Let the marriage be at once, and you will come with me and be with me. Oh, God! I feel as if I would never let you go; as if I must hold you in my arms forever, night and day, and always!"

She attempted to withdraw from his embrace. She begged him not to think of it, and tried to convince him that it was impossible.

"I would only be a hindrance, Randall. You will come back well and strong; it will be time enough then," and to herself she was saying: "never, never, never!" There was a long silence, and he had closed his eyes again.

"For another reason, my Dorothea," and then he waited again, as one hesitates through shame or through fear, to speak. "I am quite—almost sure I shall get well; but the strongest of us cannot count upon life. If the worst should come I want you to have all I possess; what fortune I have must be yours, and marriage will make my wish secure. Now I'm getting morbid." He ended with a laugh that died away in a cough which threatened to wrench the breath from his body, and which brought the attendant, who had waited without, quickly to his side.

Dorothea watched him from the window descend the steps, leaning upon the man's arm, and saw him enter his carriage and fall helpless and exhausted as he had sunk an hour before in the corner of her sofa.

She was glad there was no one present to compel her to speak. She stayed at the window as if dazed, looking fixedly at the spot where the carriage had stood. A clock on the mantel striking the hour finally roused her, and she realized that there would soon be people appearing whom she would be forced to face and speak to.

Fifteen minutes later Dorothea had changed her house gown, had mounted her "wheel," and was fleeing as if Death himself pursued her.

She sped along the familiar roadway, seemingly borne on by some force other than mechanical—some unwonted energy—a stubborn impulse that lighted her eyes, set her cheeks aflame, bent her supple body to one purpose—that was, swiftest flight.

How far, and how long did she go? She did not know; she did not care. The country about her grew unfamiliar. She was on a rough, unfrequented road, where the birds in the wayside bushes seemed unafraid. She could perceive no human habitation; an old fallow field, a stretch of wood, great trees bending thick-leaved branches, languidly, and flinging long, inviting shadows aslant the road; the weedy smell of summer; the drone of the insects; the sky and the clouds, and the quivering, lambent air. She was alone with nature; her pulses beating in unison with its sensuous throb, as she stopped and stretched herself upon the sward. Every muscle, nerve, fibre abandoned itself to the delicious sensation of rest that overtook and crept tingling through the whole length of her body.

She had never spoken a word after bidding him good-by; but now she seemed disposed to make confidants of the tremulous leaves, or the crawling and hopping insects, or the big sky into which she was staring.

"Never!" she whispered, "not for all his thousands! Never, never! not for millions!"

Two Portraits

I

THE WANTON

Alberta having looked not very long into life, had not looked very far. She put out her hands to touch things that pleased her and her lips to kiss them. Her eyes were deep brown wells that were drinking, drinking impressions and treasuring them in her soul. They were mysterious eyes and love looked out of them.

Alberta was very fond of her mama who was really not her mama; and the beatings which alternated with the most amiable and generous indulgence, were soon forgotten by the little one, always hoping that there would never be another, as she dried her eyes.

She liked the ladies who petted her and praised her beauty, and the artists who painted it naked, and the student who held her upon his knee and fondled and kissed her while he taught her to read and spell.

There was a cruel beating about that one day, when her mama happened to be in the mood to think her too old for fondling. And the student had called her mama some very vile names in his wrath, and had asked the woman what else she expected.

There was nothing very fixed or stable about her expectations—whatever they were—as she had forgotten them the following day, and Alberta, consoled with a fantastic bracelet for her plump little arm and a shower of bonbons, installed herself again upon the student's knee. She liked nothing better, and in time was willing to take the beating if she might hold his attentions and her place in his affections and upon his knee.

Alberta cried very bitterly when he went away. The people about her seemed to be always coming and going. She had hardly the time to fix her affections upon the men and the women who came into her life before they were gone again.

Her mama died one day—very suddenly; a self-inflicted death, she heard the people say. Alberta grieved sorely, for she forgot the beatings and remembered only the outbursts of a torrid affection. But she really did not belong anywhere then, nor to anybody. And when a lady and gentleman took her to live with them, she went willingly as she would have gone anywhere, with any one. With them she met with more kindness and indulgence than she had ever known before in her life.

There were no more beatings; Alberta's body was too beautiful to be beaten—it was made for love. She knew that herself; she had heard it since she had heard anything. But now she heard many things and learned many more. She did not lack for instruction in the wiles—the ways of stirring a man's desire and holding it. Yet she did not need instruction—the secret was in her blood and looked out of her passionate, wanton eyes and showed in every motion of her seductive body.

At seventeen she was woman enough, so she had a lover. But as for that, there did not seem to be much difference. Except that she had gold now—plenty of it with which to make herself appear more beautiful, and enough to fling with both hands into the laps of those who came whining and begging to her.

Alberta is a most beautiful woman, and she takes great care of her body, for she knows that it brings her love to squander and gold to squander.

Some one has whispered in her ear:

"Be cautious, Alberta. Save, save your gold. The years are passing. The days are coming when youth slips away, when you will stretch out your hands for money and for love in vain. And what will be left for you but—"

Alberta shrunk in horror before the pictured depths of hideous degradation that would be left for her. But she consoles herself with the thought that such need never be—with death and oblivion always within her reach.

Alberta is capricious. She gives her love only when and where she chooses. One or two men have died because of her withholding it. There is a smooth-faced boy now who teases her with his resistance; for Alberta does not know shame or reserve.

One day he seems to half-relent and another time he plays indifference, and she frets and she fumes and rages.

But he had best have a care; for since Alberta has added much wine to her wantonness she is apt to be vixenish; and she carries a knife.

II

THE NUN

Alberta having looked not very long into life, had not looked very far. She put out her hands to touch things that pleased her, and her lips to kiss them. Her eyes were deep brown wells that were drinking, drinking impressions and treasuring them in her soul. They were mysterious eyes and love looked out of them.

It was a very holy woman who first took Alberta by the hand. The thought of God alone dwelt in her mind, and his name and none other was on her lips.

When she showed Alberta the creeping insects, the blades of grass, the flowers and trees; the rain-drops falling from the clouds; the sky and the stars and the men and women moving on the earth, she taught her that it was God who had created all; that God was great, was good, was the Supreme Love.

And when Alberta would have put out her hands and her lips to touch the great and all-loving God, it was then the holy woman taught her that it is not with the hands and lips and eyes that we reach God, but with the soul; that the soul must be made perfect and the flesh subdued. And what is the soul but the inward thought? And this the child was taught to keep spotless—pure, and fit as far as a human soul can be, to hold intercourse with the all-wise and all-seeing God.

Her existence became a prayer. Evil things approached her not. The inherited sin of the blood must have been washed away at the baptismal font; for all the things of this world that she encountered—the pleasures, the trials and even temptations, but turned her gaze within, through her soul up to the fountain of all love and every beatitude.

When Alberta had reached the age when with other women the languor of love creeps into the veins and dreams begin, at such a period an overpowering impulse toward the purely spiritual possessed itself of her. She could no longer abide the sights, the sounds, the accidental happenings of life surrounding her, that tended but to disturb her contemplation of the heavenly existence.

It was then she went into the convent—the white convent on the hill that overlooks the river; the big convent whose long, dim corridors echo with the soft tread of a multitude of holy women; whose atmosphere of chastity, poverty and obedience penetrates to the soul through benumbed senses.

But of all the holy women in the white convent, there is none so saintly as Alberta. Any one will tell you that who knows them. Even her pious guide and counsellor does not equal her in sanctity. Because Alberta is endowed with the powerful gift of a great love that lifts her above common mortals, close to the invisible throne. Her ears seem to hear sounds that reach no other ears; and what her eyes see, only God and herself know. When the others are plunged in meditation, Alberta is steeped in an oblivious ecstasy. She kneels before the Blessed Sacrament with stiffened, tireless limbs; with absorbing eyes that drink in the holy mystery till it is a mystery no longer, but a real flood of celestial love deluging her soul. She does not hear the sound of bells nor the soft stir of disbanding numbers. She must be touched upon the shoulder; roused, awakened.

Alberta does not know that she is beautiful. If you were to tell her so she would not blush and utter gentle protest and reproof as might the others. She would only smile, as though beauty were a thing that concerned her not. But she is beautiful, with the glow of a holy passion in her dark eyes. Her face is thin and white, but illumined from within by a light which seems not of this world.

She does not walk upright; she could not, overpowered by the Divine Presence and the realization of her own nothingness. Her hands, slender and blue-veined, and her delicate fingers seem to have been fashioned by God to be clasped and uplifted in prayer.

It is said—not broadcast, it is only whispered—that Alberta sees visions. Oh, the beautiful visions! The first of them came to her when she was rapped in suffering, in quivering contemplation of the bleeding and agonizing Christ. Oh, the dear God! Who loved her beyond the power of man to describe, to conceive. The God-Man, the Man-God, suffering, bleeding, dying for her, Alberta, a worm upon the earth; dying that she might be saved from sin and transplanted among the heavenly delights. Oh, if she might die for him in return! But she could only abandon herself to his mercy and his love. "Into thy hands, Oh Lord! Into thy hands!"

She pressed her lips upon the bleeding wounds and the Divine Blood transfigured her. The Virgin Mary enfolded her in her mantle. She could not describe in words the ecstasy; that taste of the Divine love which only the souls of the transplanted could endure in its awful and complete intensity. She, Alberta, had received this sign of Divine favor; this foretaste of heavenly bliss. For an hour she had swooned in rapture; she had lived in Christ. Oh, the beautiful visions!

The visions come often to Alberta now, refreshing and strengthening her soul; it is being talked about a little in whispers.

And it is said that certain afflicted persons have been helped by her prayers. And others having abounding faith, have been cured of bodily ailments by the touch of her beautiful hands.

Fedora

Fedora had determined upon driving over to the station herself for Miss Malthers.

Though one or two of them looked disappointed—notably her brother —no one opposed her. She said the brute was restive, and shouldn't be trusted to the handling of the young people.

To be sure Fedora was old enough, from the standpoint of her sister Camilla and the rest of them. Yet no one would ever have thought of it but for her own persistent affectation and idiotic assumption of superior years and wisdom. She was thirty.

Fedora had too early in life formed an ideal and treasured it. By this ideal she had measured such male beings as had hitherto challenged her attention, and needless to say she had found them wanting. The young people—her brothers' and sisters' guests, who were constantly coming and going that summer—occupied her to a great extent, but failed to interest her. She concerned herself with their comforts—in the absence of her mother—looked after their health and well-being; contrived for their amusements, in which she never joined. And, as Fedora was tall and slim, and carried her head loftily, and wore eye-glasses and a severe expression, some of them—the silliest—felt as if she were a hundred years old. Young Malthers thought she was about forty.

One day when he stopped before her out in the gravel walk to ask her some question pertaining to the afternoon's sport, Fedora, who was tall, had to look up into his face to answer him. She had known him eight years, since he was a lad of fifteen, and to her he had never been other than the lad of fifteen.

But that afternoon, looking up into his face, the sudden realization came home to her that he was a man—in voice, in attitude, in bearing, in every sense—a man.

In an absorbing glance, and with unaccountable intention, she gathered in every detail of his countenance as though it were a strange, new thing to her, presenting itself to her vision for the first time. The eyes were blue, earnest, and at the moment a little troubled over some trivial affair that he was relating to her. The face was brown from the sun, smooth, with no suggestion of ruddiness, except in the lips, that were strong, firm and clean. She kept thinking of his face, and every trick of it after he passed on.

From that moment he began to exist for her. She looked at him when he was near by, she listened for his voice, and took notice and account of what he said. She sought him out; she selected him when occasion permitted. She wanted him by her, though his nearness troubled her. There was uneasiness, restlessness, expectation when he was not there within sight or sound. There was redoubled uneasiness when he was by —there was inward revolt, astonishment, rapture, self-contumely; a swift, fierce encounter betwixt thought and feeling.

Fedora could hardly explain to her own satisfaction why she wanted to go herself to the station for young Malthers' sister. She felt a desire to see the girl, to be near her; as unaccountable, when she tried to analyze it, as the impulse which drove her, and to which she often yielded, to touch his hat, hanging with others upon the hall pegs, when she passed it by. Once a coat which he had discarded hung there too. She handled it under pretense of putting it in order. There was no one near, and, obeying a sudden impulse, she buried her face for an instant in the rough folds of the coat.

Fedora reached the station a little before train time. It was in a pretty nook, green and fragrant, set down at the foot of a wooded hill. Off in a clearing there was a field of yellow grain, upon which the sinking sunlight fell in slanting, broken beams. Far down the track there were some men at work, and the even ring of their hammers was the only sound that broke upon the stillness. Fedora loved it all—sky and woods and sunlight; sounds and smells. But her bearing—elegant, composed, reserved—betrayed nothing emotional as she tramped the narrow platform, whip in hand, and occasionally offered a condescending word to the mail man or the sleepy agent.

Malthers' sister was the only soul to disembark from the train. Fedora had never seen her before; but if there had been a hundred, she would have known the girl. She was a small thing; but aside from that, there was the coloring; there were the blue, earnest eyes; there, above all, was the firm, full curve of the lips; the same setting of the white, even teeth. There was the subtle play of feature, the elusive trick of expression, which she had thought peculiar and individual in the one, presenting themselves as family traits.

The suggestive resemblance of the girl to her brother was vivid, poignant even to Fedora, realizing, as she did with a pang, that familiarity and custom would soon blur the image.

Miss Malthers was a quiet, reserved creature, with little to say. She had been to college with Camilla, and spoke somewhat of their friendship and former intimacy. She sat lower in the cart than Fedora, who drove, handling whip and rein with accomplished skill.

"You know, dear child," said Fedora, in her usual elderly fashion, "I want you to feel completely at home with us." They were driving through a long, quiet, leafy road, into which the twilight was just beginning to creep. "Come to me freely and without reserve—with all your wants; with any complaints. I feel that I shall be quite fond of you."

She had gathered the reins into one hand, and with the other free arm she encircled Miss Malthers' shoulders.

When the girl looked up into her face, with murmured thanks, Fedora bent down and pressed a long, penetrating kiss upon her mouth.

Malthers' sister appeared astonished, and not too well pleased. Fedora, with seemingly unruffled composure, gathered the reins, and for the rest of the way stared steadily ahead of her between the horses' ears.

Vagabonds

Valcour was waiting. A negro who had come to the store for rations told me that he was down below around the bend and wanted to see me. It never would have entered my mind to put myself the least bit out of the way for the sake of a rendezvous with Valcour; he might have waited till the crack of doom. But it was the hour for my afternoon walk and I did not mind stopping on the way, to see what the vagabond wanted with me.

The weather was a little warm for April, and of course it had been raining. But with the shabby skirt which I wore and the clumsy old boots, the wet and the mud distressed me not at all; beside, I walked along the grassy edge of the road. The river was low and sluggish between its steep embankments that were like slimy pit-falls. Valcour was sitting on the fallen trunk of a tree near the water, waiting.

I saw at a glance that he was sober; though his whole appearance gave evidence of his having been drunk at no very remote period. His clothes, his battered hat, his skin, his straggling beard which he never shaved, were all of one color—the color of clay. He made but the faintest offer to rise at my approach; and I saved him the complete effort by seating myself at once beside him on the log. I was glad that he showed no disposition to shake hands, for his hands were far from clean; and moreover he might have discovered the dollar bill which I had slipped into my glove in case of emergencies. He greeted me with his usual:

"How you come on, cousin?"

There exists a tradition outside the family that Valcour is a relation of ours. I am the only one, somehow, who does not strenuously deny the charge.

"Me, I'm well enough, Valcour."

I long ago discovered that there is no need of wasting fine language on Valcour. Such effort could only evince a pride and affectation from which I am happily free.

"W'at you mean," I continued, "by sending me word you want to see me. You don' think fo' an instant I'd come down here o' purpose to see an object like you."

Valcour laughed. He is the only soul who discovers any intention of humor in my utterances. He refuses to take me seriously.

"An' w'at you doing with yo'self these days?" I asked.

"Oh, me, I been jobbin' roun' some, up the coas'. But I yeard 'bout a chance down in Alexandria if I c'n make out to git down there."

"Of course not a picayune in sight," I grumbled. "An' I tell you, I ain't much better off myself. Look at those shoes"—holding my feet out for his inspection—"an' this dress; an' take a look at those cabins an' fences—ready to fall to pieces."

"I ent no mine to ask you fo' money, cousin," he cheerfully assured me.

"All the same, I bet you a' plumb broke," I insisted. With some little difficulty—for his grasp was unsteady—he drew from his trousers pocket a few small coins which he held out before me. I was glad to see them and thrust the dollar bill further into my glove.

"Just about the price of a quart, Valcour," I calculated. "I reckon it's no use warning a *vaurien* like you agains' whiskey; it's boun' to be the end of you some o' these days."

"It make' a man crazy, that w'iskey," he admitted. "Wouldn' been fo' that w'iskey, I neva would got in that peck o' trouble yonda on Bayou Derbonne. Me, I don' rec'lec' a thing till I fine myse'f layin' on doctor Jureau's gall'ry."

"That *was* a nice mess," I told him, "getting yo'self filled plumb full of buckshot fo' trying to kiss another man's wife. You must a' been pretty drunk anyway, to want to kiss Joe Poussin's wife."

Valcour, again mistaking cynicism for humor, almost rolled off the log in his hilarious appreciation of the insinuation. His laugh was contagious and I could not help joining him. "*Hein*, Valcour?" I persisted, "a man mus' be pretty drunk, or mighty hard pushed, *va!*"

"You right," he returned between attacks of mirth, "a man got to be hard push', sho', that want' to kiss Joe Poussin's wife; 'less he been blin' drunk like me."

At the end of a half hour (how could I have stood the vagabond so long!) I reminded Valcour that the way to Alexandria lay across the river; and I expressed a hope that the walking was fair.

I had asked him how he fared, what he ate and where, and how he slept. There was his gun beside him—for a wonder he had never sold it for drink—and were the woods not filled with feathered and antlered game? And sometimes there was a chicken roosting low, and always there was a black wench ready to cook it. As for sleeping—in the winter time, better not have asked him. Grand Dieu! that was hard. But with the summer coming on, why, a man could sleep anywhere that the mosquitoes would let him.

I called him names; but all the same I could not help thinking that it must be good to prowl sometimes; to get close to the black night and lose oneself in its silence and mystery.

He waited for the flat that had been crossing and recrossing a little distance away, and when it touched the bank he said good-by—as he had greeted me—stolidly and indifferently. He went slipping and slumping down the slimy embankment, ankle deep in mud.

I stayed for pure idleness watching the flat cross the river. Valcour made no offer to help the ferryman with an oar; but rested his arms indolently on the rail of the boat and stared into the muddy stream.

I turned to continue my walk. I was glad the vagabond did not want money. But for the life of me I don't know what he wanted, or why he wanted to see me.

Madame Martel's Christmas Eve

Madame Martel was alone in the house. Even the servants upon one pretext and another had deserted her. She did not care; nothing mattered.

She was a slender, blond woman, dressed in deep mourning. As she sat looking into the fire, holding in her hand an old letter that she had been reading, the naturally sorrowful expression of her face was sharpened by acute and vivid memories. The tears kept welling up to her eyes and she kept wiping them away with a fine, black-bordered cambric handkerchief. Occasionally she would turn to the table beside her and picking up an old ambrotype that lay there amid the pile of letters, she would gaze and gaze with misty eyes upon the picture; choking back the sobs; seeming to hold them in with the black-bordered handkerchief that she pressed to her mouth.

The room in which she sat was cheerful, with its open wood-fire and its fine old-fashioned furniture that betokened taste as well as comfort and wealth. Over the mantel-piece hung the pleasing, handsome portrait of a man in his early prime.

But Madame Martel was alone. Not only the servants were absent but even her children were away. Instead of coming home for Christmas, Gustave had accepted the invitation of a college friend to spend the holidays in Assumption.

He had learned by experience that his mother preferred to be alone at this season and he respected her wishes. Adélaïde, his older sister, had of course gone to Iberville to be with her uncle Achille's family, where there was no end of merrymaking all the year round. And even little Lulu was glad to get away for a few days from the depressing atmosphere which settled upon their home at the approach of Christmas.

Madame Martel was one of those women—not rare among Creoles—who make a luxury of grief. Most people thought it peculiarly touching that she had never abandoned mourning for her husband, who had been dead six years, and that she never intended to lay it aside.

More than one woman had secretly resolved, in the event of a like bereavement, to model her own widowhood upon just such lines. And there were men who felt that death would lose half its sting if, in dying they might bear away with them the assurance of being mourned so faithfully, so persistently as Madame Martel mourned her departed husband.

It was especially at the season of Christmas that she indulged to the utmost in her poignant memories and abandoned herself to a very intoxication of grief. For her husband had possessed a sunny, cheerful temperament—the children resembled him—and it had often seemed to her that he had chiefly welcomed in Christmas the pretext to give rein to his own boyish exuberance of spirit. A thousand recollections crowded upon her. She could see his beaming face; she could hear the clear ring of his laughter, joining the little ones in their glee as every fresh delight of the day unfolded itself.

The room had grown oppressive; for it was really not cold out of doors—hardly cold enough for the fire that was burning there on the hearth. Madame Martel arose and went and poured herself a glass of water. Her throat was parched and her head was beginning to ache. The pitcher was heavy and her thin hand shook a little as she poured the water. She went into her sleeping-room for a fresh, dry handkerchief, and she cooled her face, which was hot and inflamed, with a few puffs of *poudre de riz*.

She was nervous and unstrung. She had been dwelling so persistently on the thought of her husband that she felt as if he must be there in the house. She felt as if the years had rolled backward and given her again her own. If she were to go into the playroom, surely she would find the Christmas-tree there, all ablaze, as it was that last Christmas that he was with them. He would be there holding little Lulu in his arms. She could almost hear the ring of voices and the patter of little feet.

Madame Martel, suffocating with memories, threw a light shawl over her shoulders and stepped out upon the gallery, leaving the door ajar. There was a faint moonlight that seemed rather a misty effulgence enveloping the whole landscape. Through the tangle of her garden she could see the lights of the village a little distance away. And there were sounds that reached her: there was music somewhere; and occasional shouts of merriment and laughter; and some one was lustily blowing a horn not far away.

She walked slowly and with a measured tramp, up and down. She lingered a while at the south end of the gallery where there were roses hanging still untouched by the frost, and she stayed there looking before her into the shadowy depths that seemed to picture the gloom of her own existence. Her acute grief of a while before had passed, but a terrible loneliness had settled upon her spirit.

Her husband was forever gone, and now the children even seemed to be slipping out of her life, cut off by want of sympathy. Perhaps it was in the nature of things; she did not know; it was very hard to bear; and her heart suddenly turned savage and hungry within her for human companionship—for some expression of human love.

Little Lulu was not far away: on the other side of the village, about a half mile or so. She was staying there with old and intimate friends of her mother, in a big, hospitable house where there were lots of young people and much good cheer in store for the holidays.

With the thought of Lulu's nearness the desire came to Madame Martel to see the child, to have the little one with her again at home. She would go herself on the instant and fetch Lulu back. She wondered how she could ever have suffered the child to leave her.

Acting at once upon the impulse that moved her, Madame Martel hastily descended the stairs and walked hurriedly down the path that led between two lines of tall Magnolias to the outer road.

There was quite a bit of desolate road to traverse, but she did not fear. She knew every soul for miles around and was sure of not being molested.

The moon had grown brighter. It was not so misty now and she could see plainly ahead of her and all about her. There was the end of the plank walk a rod or so away. Here was the wedge of a cotton field to pass, still covered with its gaunt, dry stalks to which ragged shreds of cotton clung here and there. Off against the woods a mile away, a railroad train was approaching. She could not hear it yet; she could only see the swiftly moving line of lights against the dark background of forest.

Madame Martel had drawn her black shawl up over her head and she looked like a slim nun moving along through the moonlight. A few stragglers on their way to the station made room for her; and the jest and laughter died on their lips as she passed by. People respected her as a sort of mystery; as something above them, and to be taken very seriously.

Old Uncle Wisdom made a profound bow as he stumbled down from the plank walk to give her the right of way. His wife was with him and he dragged his granddaughter, Tildy, by a willing hand. They were on their way to the station to meet Tildy's "maw" who was coming to spend Christmas with them in the shanty yonder on the rim of the bayou.

Through the open door of a cabin that she passed came the scraping notes of a fiddle, and people were dancing within. The sounds were distressing to her sensitive, musical ear and she hurried by. A big wagon load of people swung into the country road, out for a moonlight drive. In the village proper there was much flitting about; people greeting each other or bidding good-bye in door-ways and on steps and galleries. The very air seemed charged with a cheerful excitement.

When Madame Martel reached the big house at the far end of town, she made her way at once to the front door and entered, after a faint knock that never could have been heard amid the hubbub that reigned within.

There she stood within the entrance of the big hall that was thronged with people. Lights were hanging from the huge rafters; the whitewashed walls were decorated with cedar branches and mistletoe. Some one was playing a lively air upon the piano, to which no one was paying any attention except two young Convent girls who were waltzing together with much difficulty in one corner.

There were old ladies and gentlemen all seeming to be talking at once. There was a young mother, loath to quit the scene, foolishly striving to put her baby to sleep in the midst of it. A few little darkies were leaning against the whitewashed wall, clinging each to an orange which some one had given them. But above all there was the laughter and voices of children; and just as Madame Martel appeared in the doorway, Lulu, with flaming cheeks and sparkling eyes, was twirling a plate in the middle of the room.

"*Tiens!* Madame Martel!"

If the cry had been "*tiens! un revenant*—a spirit from the other world!" it could not have had a more instantaneous, depressing effect upon the whole assembly. The piano ceased playing; the Convent girls stopped waltzing; the old people stopped talking and the young ones stopped laughing; only the plate in the middle of the floor seemed not to care and it went on whirling.

But the surprise—the suspense were only momentary. People crowded around Madame Martel with expressions of satisfaction at seeing her and all wanted her to do something: to take off her shawl; to sit down; to look at the baby; to accept a bit of refreshment.

"No, no!" in her gentle, deprecatory voice. She begged they would excuse her—she had only come—it was about Lulu. The child had not seemed entirely well in the morning when she left home. Madame Martel thought that she had better take her back; she hoped that Lulu would be willing to return with her.

A perfect storm of protest! And Lulu the very picture of despair! The child had approached her mother and clung to her, imploring to be permitted to remain as if begging for very existence.

"Of course your mama will let you stay, now that she sees you are well and amusing yourself," asserted a comfortably fat old lady with a talent for arranging matters. "Your mama would never be so selfish!"

"Selfish!" She had not thought of it as selfish; and she at once felt willing to endure any suffering rather than afflict others with her own selfish desires.

Surely Lulu could remain if she wished to; and she gave the child a passionate embrace as she let her go. But she herself could not be induced to linger for a moment. She would not accept the offer of an escort home. She went as she had come—alone.

Hardly had Madame Martel turned her back than she could hear that they were at it again. The piano began playing and all the noises started up afresh.

The simple and rather natural choice of the child to remain with her young companions, took somewhat the aspect of a tragedy to Madame Martel as she made her way homeward. It was not so much the fact itself as the significance of the fact. She felt as if she had driven love out of her life and she kept repeating to herself: "I have driven love away; I have driven it away." And at the same time she seemed to feel a reproach from her dear, dead husband that she had looked for consolation and hoped for comfort aside from his cherished memory.

She would go back home now to her old letters, to her thoughts, to her tears. How he and he alone had always understood her! It seemed as if he understood her now; as if he were with her now in spirit as she hurried through the night back to her desolate home.

Madame Martel, upon quitting the sitting-room where she had been poring over her old letters, had lowered the light on the table. Now, as she mounted the front stairs, the room appeared to her to be brighter than the flare of the dying embers could have made it; and mechanically approaching the window that opened upon the gallery, she looked in.

She did not scream, or cry out at what she saw. She only gave a gasp that seemed to wrench her whole body and she clutched blindly at the window jamb for support. She saw that the light under its tempered shade had been raised; the embers had fallen into a dull, glowing heap between the andirons. And there before the fire, in her own armchair, sat her husband. How well she knew him!

She could not see his face, but his leg was stretched out toward the fire, his head was bent, and he sat motionless looking at something that he held in his hand.

She closed her eyes; she knew that when she opened them the vision would be gone. With swift retrospection she remembered all the stories she had ever heard of optical illusions: all the tricks that an over-excited brain is apt to play upon one. She realized that she had been nervous, overwrought, and this was the revenge of her senses: disclosing to her this vision of her husband. How familiar to her was the poise of his head, the sweep of arm and set of his shoulder. And when she opened her eyes he would be no longer there; the chair would again be empty. She pressed her fingers for an instant hard upon her eyeballs, then looked again.

The chair was not empty! He was still there but his face was turned now toward the table, completely away from her and a hand rested upon the pile of letters there. How significant the action!

Madame Martel straightened, steeled herself. "I am losing my mind," she whispered hoarsely, "I am seeing visions."

It did not occur to her to call for help. Help? Against what! She knew the servants were away, and even if they were not she shrank from disclosing what she believed to be this morbid condition of mind to the ignorant and unsympathetic.

"I will go in," she resolved, "place my hand upon—the shoulder; and it will be over; the illusion will vanish."

In fancy she went through the whole sensation of placing her hand upon a visible, intangible something that would melt away, vanish like smoke before her eyes. An involuntary shudder passed through her frame from head to foot.

As she glided noiselessly into the room in her black garb, Madame Martel, with that light, filmy hair, her wide-open, fearful blue eyes, looked far more like a "spirit" than the substantial figure seated in her armchair before the fire.

She had not time to place her hand upon the shoulder of her ghastly visitant. Before she reached the chair he had turned. She tottered, and springing forward he seized her in his arms.

"Mother! mother! mother! what is it? Are you ill?" He was kissing her hair, her forehead and closed, quivering eyes.

"Wait, Gustave. In a moment, dear son—it will be all right." She was, in fact, rather faint from the shock. He placed her upon the sofa and after bringing her a glass of water seated himself beside her.

"Idiot that I am!" he exclaimed. "I wanted to surprise you and here I've almost thrown you into a swoon." She was looking at him with eyes full of tenderness but for some reason she did not tell him the whole story of her surprise.

How glad she was to see him—her big, manly son of nineteen. And how like his father at that age! The age at which the old ambrotype had been taken; the picture that she had been weeping over and that Gustave was looking at when she first discovered him there.

"Of course you came on the evening train, Gustave?" she asked him quietly.

"Yes, only a while ago. I got to thinking—well, I had enough of Assumption last year. And after all there's no place for a fellow at Christmas like home."

"You knew that I wanted you, Gustave. Confess; you knew it." Madame was hoping for a little disclosure of thought transference—mental telepathy—occultism in short. But he disabused her.

"No," he said. "I'm afraid I was purely selfish, mother. I know that you prefer to be alone at this season," in that tone of subdued respect which was always assumed in approaching the subject of Madame Martel's sorrow. "I came because I couldn't help it; because I couldn't stay away. I wanted to see you, to be with you, mother."

"You know, Gustave, it won't be gay here at home," she said nestling closer to him.

"Oh, well, if we can't be gay, there's nothing to keep us from being happy, mom."

And she was, very, very happy as she rubbed her cheek against his rough coat sleeve and felt the warm, firm pressure of his hand.

The Recovery

She was a woman of thirty-five, possessing something of youthfulness. It was not the bloom, the softness, nor delicacy of coloring which had once been hers; those were all gone. It lurked rather in the expression of her sensitive face, which was at once appealing, pathetic, confiding.

For fifteen years she had lived in darkness with closed lids. By one of those seeming miracles of science, and by slow and gradual stages, the light had been restored to her. Now, for the first time in many years, she opened her eyes upon the full, mellow brightness of a June day.

She was alone. She had asked to be alone at the very first. Glad almost to ecstasy, she was yet afraid. She wanted first to see the light from her open window; to look at the dumb inanimate objects around her before gazing into the dear familiar faces that were stamped with sharp and vivid impress upon her mind.

And how beautiful was the world from her open window!

"Oh, my God!" she whispered, overcome. Her prayer could get no further. There were no words to utter her rapture and thanksgiving at beholding the blue unfathomable June sky; the rolling meadows, russet and green, reaching deep into the purple distance. Close beside her window the maple leaves rippled in the sun; flowers, rich and warm in color, blossomed beneath, and radiant-winged butterflies hovered sensuous in mid-air.

"The world has not changed," she murmured; "it has only grown more beautiful. Oh, I had forgotten how beautiful!"

Within her room were all the dear, dumb companions comforting her. How well she remembered them all! her mahogany table, bright and polished, just as it had stood fifteen years ago, with a crystal vase of roses and a few books ranged upon it. The sight of chairs, beds, pictures gave her keen joy. The carpet and draperies, even—with their designs as much like the old ones as could be—seemed to her the same.

She touched with caressing fingers the French clock upon the mantel with its pompous little bronze figure of a last-century gentleman posing in buckles and frills beside the dial. She greeted him as an old friend, and delicately wiped his little bronze face with her soft handkerchief. As a child she had thought him an imposing figure. At a later and over-discriminating age she had patronized him as a poor bit of art. Now, nothing could have induced her to part with the old French clock and its little bronze bonhomme.

The mirror was over there in the corner. She had not forgotten it; oh, no, she had not forgotten, only she grew tremulous at the thought of it standing there. She held back, as a young girl who is going to confession is ashamed and afraid, and invites delay. But she had not forgotten.

"This is folly," she uttered suddenly, passing the handkerchief nervously over her face. With quick resolution she crossed the room and faced her reflected image in the glass.

"Mother!" she cried, involuntarily, turning swiftly; but she was still alone. It had happened like a flash—an unreasoning impulse that knew not control or direction. She at once recovered herself and drew a deep breath. Again she wiped her forehead, that was a little clammy. She clutched the back of a low chair with her shaking hands and looked once more into the mirror. The veins in her wrists swelled like cords and throbbed.

You or I or anyone looking upon that same picture in the glass would have seen a rather well-preserved, stately blonde woman of thirty-five or more. Only God knows what she saw. It was something that held her with terrible fascination.

The eyes, above all, seemed to speak to her. Afflicted as they had been, they alone belonged to that old, other self that had somewhere vanished. She questioned, she challenged them. And while she looked down into their depths she drew into her soul all the crushing weight of the accumulated wisdom of years.

"They lied; they all lied to me," she said, half aloud, never taking her eyes from those others. "Mother, sisters, Robert—all, all of them lied."

When the eyes in the glass had nothing more to tell her, she turned away from them. The pathos of her face had vanished; there was no longer the appeal that had been there a while ago; neither was there confidence.

The following day she walked abroad leaning upon the arm of the man whose untiring devotion to her had persisted for years. She would not fulfill her promise to marry him when blindness had overtaken her. He had endured the years of probation, wanting no other woman for his wife; living at her side when he could, and bringing himself close to her inner life by a warm, quick, watchful sympathy born of much love.

He was older than she—a man of splendid physique. The slim stripling of fifteen years ago was hardly the promise of this man of forty. His face had settled into a certain ruggedness accentuated by a few strong lines, and white hairs were beginning to show among the black ones on the temples.

They walked across the level stretch of lawn toward a sheltered garden seat no great distance away. She had spoken little since that moment of revelation before her mirror. Nothing had startled her after that. She was prepared for the changes which the years had wrought in all of them —mother, sisters, friends.

She seemed to be silently absorbing things, and would have lingered in ecstasy before a flower, or with her gaze penetrating the dense foliage beyond. Her senses had long been sharpened to the sounds and odors of the good, green world, and now her restored vision completed a sensuous impression such as she had never dreamed could be borne in upon a human consciousness.

He led her away to the bench. He fancied that seated he could better hold her attention to what was in his mind to say to her.

He took her hand in his. She was used to this and did not draw it away, but let it lie there.

"Do you remember the old plans, Jane?" he began, almost at once, "all that we were to have done, to have seen, all that we were going to live together? How we had chosen to start away in the early spring time upon our travels—you and I—and only come back with the frosts of winter. You have not forgotten, dearest?" He bent his face down over her hand and kissed it. "The spring is over; but we have the summer with us, and God willing, the autumn and winter left to us. Tell me, Jane—tell me—speak to me!" he entreated.

She looked into his face and then away, and back again, uncertainly.

"I—oh, Robert," she said, gropingly, "wait—I—the sight of things confuses me," and with a faint smile, "I am not used; I must go back into the dark to think."

He still held her hand, but she turned half away from him and buried her face in her arm that she leaned upon the back of the garden seat.

What could she hope to gather from the darkness that the light had not given her! She might hope, and she might wait and she might pray; but hope and prayer and waiting would avail her nothing.

The blessed light had given her back the world, life, love; but it had robbed her of her illusions; it had stolen away her youth.

He drew close to her, pressing his face near hers for his answer; and all that he heard was a little low sob.

A Night in Acadie

There was nothing to do on the plantation so Telèsphore, having a few dollars in his pocket, thought he would go down and spend Sunday in the vicinity of Marksville.

There was really nothing more to do in the vicinity of Marksville than in the neighborhood of his own small farm; but Elvina would not be down there, nor Amaranthe, nor any of Ma'me Valtour's daughters to harass him with doubt, to torture him with indecision, to turn his very soul into a weather-cock for love's fair winds to play with.

Telèsphore at twenty-eight had long felt the need of a wife. His home without one was like an empty temple in which there is no altar, no offering. So keenly did he realize the necessity that a dozen times at least during the past year he had been on the point of proposing marriage to almost as many different young women of the neighborhood. Therein lay the difficulty, the trouble which Telèsphore experienced in making up his mind. Elvina's eyes were beautiful and had often tempted him to the verge of a declaration. But her skin was over swarthy for a wife; and her movements were slow and heavy; he doubted she had Indian blood, and we all know what Indian blood is for treachery. Amaranthe presented in her person none of these obstacles to matrimony. If her eyes were not so handsome as Elvina's, her skin was fine, and being slender to a fault, she moved swiftly about her household affairs, or when she walked the country lanes in going to church or to the store. Telèsphore had once reached the point of believing that Amaranthe would make him an excellent wife. He had even started out one day with the intention of declaring himself, when, as the god of chance would have it, Ma'me Valtour espied him passing in the road and enticed him to enter and

partake of coffee and "baignés." He would have been a man of stone to
have resisted, or to have remained insensible to the charms and accomplishments of the Valtour girls. Finally there was Ganache's widow,
seductive rather than handsome, with a good bit of property in her own
right. While Telèsphore was considering his chances of happiness or even
success with Ganache's widow, she married a younger man.

From these embarrassing conditions, Telèsphore sometimes felt himself
forced to escape; to change his environment for a day or two and thereby
gain a few new insights by shifting his point of view.

It was Saturday morning that he decided to spend Sunday in the
vicinity of Marksville, and the same afternoon found him waiting at the
country station for the south-bound train.

He was a robust young fellow with good, strong features and a somewhat
determined expression—despite his vacillations in the choice of a wife.
He was dressed rather carefully in navy-blue "store clothes" that fitted
well because anything would have fitted Telèsphore. He had been freshly
shaved and trimmed and carried an umbrella. He wore—a little tilted
over one eye—a straw hat in preference to the conventional gray felt;
for no other reason than that his uncle Telèsphore would have worn a
felt, and a battered one at that. His whole conduct of life had been
planned on lines in direct contradistinction to those of his uncle Telèsphore, whom he was thought in early youth to greatly resemble. The
elder Telèsphore could not read nor write, therefore the younger had
made it the object of his existence to acquire these accomplishments.
The uncle pursued the avocations of hunting, fishing and moss-picking;
employments which the nephew held in detestation. And as for carrying
an umbrella, "Nonc" Telèsphore would have walked the length of the
parish in a deluge before he would have so much as thought of one. In
short, Telèsphore, by advisedly shaping his course in direct opposition
to that of his uncle, managed to lead a rather orderly, industrious, and
respectable existence.

It was a little warm for April but the car was not uncomfortably
crowded and Telèsphore was fortunate enough to secure the last available
window-seat on the shady side. He was not too familiar with railway
travel, his expeditions being usually made on horse-back or in a buggy,
and the short trip promised to interest him.

There was no one present whom he knew well enough to speak to: the
district attorney, whom he knew by sight, a French priest from Natchitoches and a few faces that were familiar only because they were native.

But he did not greatly care to speak to anyone. There was a fair stand of cotton and corn in the fields and Telèsphore gathered satisfaction in silent contemplation of the crops, comparing them with his own.

It was toward the close of his journey that a young girl boarded the train. There had been girls getting on and off at intervals and it was perhaps because of the bustle attending her arrival that this one attracted Telèsphore's attention.

She called good-bye to her father from the platform and waved good-bye to him through the dusty, sun-lit window pane after entering, for she was compelled to seat herself on the sunny side. She seemed inwardly excited and preoccupied save for the attention which she lavished upon a large parcel that she carried religiously and laid reverentially down upon the seat before her.

She was neither tall nor short, nor stout nor slender; nor was she beautiful, nor was she plain. She wore a figured lawn, cut a little low in the back, that exposed a round, soft nuque with a few little clinging circlets of soft, brown hair. Her hat was of white straw, cocked up on the side with a bunch of pansies, and she wore gray lisle-thread gloves. The girl seemed very warm and kept mopping her face. She vainly sought her fan, then she fanned herself with her handkerchief, and finally made an attempt to open the window. She might as well have tried to move the banks of Red river.

Telèsphore had been unconsciously watching her the whole time and perceiving her straight he arose and went to her assistance. But the window could not be opened. When he had grown red in the face and wasted an amount of energy that would have driven the plow for a day, he offered her his seat on the shady side. She demurred—there would be no room for the bundle. He suggested that the bundle be left where it was and agreed to assist her in keeping an eye upon it. She accepted Telèsphore's place at the shady window and he seated himself beside her.

He wondered if she would speak to him. He feared she might have mistaken him for a Western drummer, in which event he knew that she would not; for the women of the country caution their daughters against speaking to strangers on the trains. But the girl was not one to mistake an Acadian farmer for a Western traveling man. She was not born in Avoyelles parish for nothing.

"I wouldn' want anything to happen to it," she said.

"It's all right w'ere it is," he assured her, following the direction of her glance, that was fastened upon the bundle.

"The las' time I came over to Foché's ball I got caught in the rain on my way up to my cousin's house, an' my dress! J' vous réponds! it was a sight. Li'le mo', I would miss the ball. As it was, the dress looked like I'd wo' it weeks without doin'-up."

"No fear of rain to-day," he reassured her, glancing out at the sky, "but you can have my umbrella if it does rain; you jus' as well take it as not."

"Oh, no! I wrap' the dress roun' in toile-cirée this time. You goin' to Foché's ball? Didn' I meet you once yonda on Bayou Derbanne? Looks like I know yo' face. You mus' come f'om Natchitoches pa'ish."

"My cousins, the Fédeau family, live yonda. Me, I live on my own place in Rapides since '92."

He wondered if she would follow up her inquiry relative to Foché's ball. If she did, he was ready with an answer, for he had decided to go to the ball. But her thoughts evidently wandered from the subject and were occupied with matters that did not concern him, for she turned away and gazed silently out of the window.

It was not a village; it was not even a hamlet at which they descended. The station was set down upon the edge of a cotton field. Near at hand was the post office and store; there was a section house; there were a few cabins at wide intervals, and one in the distance the girl informed him was the home of her cousin, Jules Trodon. There lay a good bit of road before them and she did not hesitate to accept Telèsphore's offer to bear her bundle on the way.

She carried herself boldly and stepped out freely and easily, like a negress. There was an absence of reserve in her manner; yet there was no lack of womanliness. She had the air of a young person accustomed to decide for herself and for those about her.

"You said yo' name was Fédeau?" she asked, looking squarely at Telèsphore. Her eyes were penetrating—not sharply penetrating, but earnest and dark, and a little searching. He noticed that they were handsome eyes; not so large as Elvina's, but finer in their expression. They started to walk down the track before turning into the lane leading to Trodon's house. The sun was sinking and the air was fresh and invigorating by contrast with the stifling atmosphere of the train.

"You said yo' name was Fédeau?" she asked.

"No," he returned. "My name is Telèsphore Baquette."

"An' my name; it's Zaïda Trodon. It looks like you ought to know me; I don' know w'y."

"It looks that way to me, somehow," he replied. They were satisfied to recognize this feeling—almost conviction—of pre-acquaintance, without trying to penetrate its cause.

By the time they reached Trodon's house he knew that she lived over on Bayou de Glaize with her parents and a number of younger brothers and sisters. It was rather dull where they lived and she often came to lend a hand when her cousin's wife got tangled in domestic complications; or, as she was doing now, when Foché's Saturday ball promised to be unusually important and brilliant. There would be people there even from Marksville, she thought; there were often gentlemen from Alexandria. Telèsphore was as unreserved as she, and they appeared like old acquaintances when they reached Trodon's gate.

Trodon's wife was standing on the gallery with a baby in her arms, watching for Zaïda; and four little bare-footed children were sitting in a row on the step, also waiting; but terrified and struck motionless and dumb at sight of a stranger. He opened the gate for the girl but stayed outside himself. Zaïda presented him formally to her cousin's wife, who insisted upon his entering.

"Ah, b'en, pour ça! you got to come in. It's any sense you goin' to walk yonda to Foché's! Ti Jules, run call yo' pa." As if Ti Jules could have run or walked even, or moved a muscle!

But Telèsphore was firm. He drew forth his silver watch and looked at it in a business-like fashion. He always carried a watch; his uncle Telèsphore always told the time by the sun, or by instinct, like an animal. He was quite determined to walk on to Foché's, a couple of miles away, where he expected to secure supper and a lodging, as well as the pleasing distraction of the ball.

"Well, I reckon I see you all to-night," he uttered in cheerful anticipation as he moved away.

"You'll see Zaïda; yes, an' Jules," called out Trodon's wife good-humoredly. "Me, I got no time to fool with balls, J' vous réponds! with all them chil'ren."

"He's good-lookin'; yes," she exclaimed, when Telèsphore was out of ear-shot. "An' dressed! it's like a prince. I didn' know you knew any Baquettes, you, Zaïda."

"It's strange you don' know 'em yo' se'f, cousine." Well, there had been no question from Ma'me Trodon, so why should there be an answer from Zaïda?

Telèsphore wondered as he walked why he had not accepted the invitation to enter. He was not regretting it; he was simply wondering what could have induced him to decline. For it surely would have been agreeable to sit there on the gallery waiting while Zaïda prepared herself for the dance; to have partaken of supper with the family and afterward accompanied them to Foché's. The whole situation was so novel, and had presented itself so unexpectedly that Telèsphore wished in reality to become acquainted with it, accustomed to it. He wanted to view it from this side and that in comparison with other, familiar situations. The girl had impressed him—affected him in some way; but in some new, unusual way, not as the others always had. He could not recall details of her personality as he could recall such details of Amaranthe or the Valtours, of any of them. When Telèsphore tried to think of her he could not think at all. He seemed to have absorbed her in some way and his brain was not so occupied with her as his senses were. At that moment he was looking forward to the ball; there was no doubt about that. Afterwards, he did not know what he would look forward to; he did not care; afterward made no difference. If he had expected the crash of doom to come after the dance at Foché's, he would only have smiled in his thankfulness that it was not to come before.

There was the same scene every Saturday at Foché's! A scene to have aroused the guardians of the peace in a locality where such commodities abound. And all on account of the mammoth pot of gumbo that bubbled, bubbled, bubbled out in the open air. Foché in shirt-sleeves, fat, red and enraged, swore and reviled, and stormed at old black Douté for her extravagance. He called her every kind of a name of every kind of animal that suggested itself to his lurid imagination. And every fresh invective that he fired at her she hurled it back at him while into the pot went the chickens and the pans-full of minced ham, and the fists-full of onion and sage and piment rouge and piment vert. If he wanted her to cook for pigs he had only to say so. She knew how to cook for pigs and she knew how to cook for people of les Avoyelles.

The gumbo smelled good, and Telèsphore would have liked a taste of it. Douté was dragging from the fire a stick of wood that Foché had officiously thrust beneath the simmering pot, and she muttered as she hurled it smouldering to one side:

"Vaux mieux y s'méle ces affairs, lui; si non!" But she was all courtesy as she dipped a steaming plate for Telèsphore; though she assured him it would not be fit for a Christian or a gentleman to taste till midnight.

Telèsphore having brushed, "spruced" and refreshed himself, strolled about, taking a view of the surroundings. The house, big, bulky and weather-beaten, consisted chiefly of galleries in every stage of decrepitude and dilapidation. There were a few chinaberry trees and a spreading live oak in the yard. Along the edge of the fence, a good distance away, was a line of gnarled and distorted mulberry trees; and it was there, out in the road, that the people who came to the ball tied their ponies, their wagons and carts.

Dusk was beginning to fall and Telèsphore, looking out across the prairie, could see them coming from all directions. The little Creole ponies galloping in a line looked like hobby horses in the faint distance; the mule-carts were like toy wagons. Zaïda might be among those people approaching, flying, crawling ahead of the darkness that was creeping out of the far wood. He hoped so, but he did not believe so; she would hardly have had time to dress.

Foché was noisily lighting lamps, with the assistance of an inoffensive mulatto boy whom he intended in the morning to butcher, to cut into sections, to pack and salt down in a barrel, like the Colfax woman did to her old husband—a fitting destiny for so stupid a pig as the mulatto boy. The negro musicians had arrived: two fiddlers and an accordion player, and they were drinking whiskey from a black quart bottle which was passed socially from one to the other. The musicians were really never at their best till the quart bottle had been consumed.

The girls who came in wagons and on ponies from a distance wore, for the most part, calico dresses and sun-bonnets. Their finery they brought along in pillow-slips or pinned up in sheets and towels. With these they at once retired to an upper room; later to appear be-ribboned and be-furbelowed; their faces masked with starch powder, but never a touch of rouge.

Most of the guests had assembled when Zaïda arrived—"dashed up" would better express her coming—in an open, two-seated buckboard, with her cousin Jules driving. He reined the pony suddenly and viciously before the time-eaten front steps, in order to produce an impression upon those who were gathered around. Most of the men had halted their vehicles outside and permitted their women folk to walk up from the mulberry trees.

But the real, the stunning effect was produced when Zaïda stepped upon the gallery and threw aside her light shawl in the full glare of half a dozen kerosene lamps. She was white from head to foot—literally, for her slippers even were white. No one would have believed, let alone suspected that they were a pair of old black ones which she had covered with pieces of her first communion sash. There is no describing her dress, it was fluffy, like a fresh powder-puff, and stood out. No wonder she had handled it so reverentially! Her white fan was covered with spangles that she herself had sewed all over it; and in her belt and in her brown hair were thrust small sprays of orange blossom.

Two men leaning against the railing uttered long whistles expressive equally of wonder and admiration.

"Tiens! t'es pareille comme ain mariée, Zaïda," cried out a lady with a baby in her arms. Some young women tittered and Zaïda fanned herself. The women's voices were almost without exception shrill and piercing; the men's, soft and low-pitched.

The girl turned to Telèsphore, as to an old and valued friend:

"Tiens! c'est vous?" He had hesitated at first to approach, but at this friendly sign of recognition he drew eagerly forward and held out his hand. The men looked at him suspiciously, inwardly resenting his stylish appearance, which they considered intrusive, offensive and demoralizing.

How Zaïda's eyes sparkled now! What very pretty teeth Zaïda had when she laughed, and what a mouth! Her lips were a revelation, a promise; something to carry away and remember in the night and grow hungry thinking of next day. Strictly speaking, they may not have been quite all that; but in any event, that is the way Telèsphore thought about them. He began to take account of her appearance: her nose, her eyes, her hair. And when she left him to go in and dance her first dance with cousin Jules, he leaned up against a post and thought of them: nose, eyes, hair, ears, lips and round, soft throat.

Later it was like Bedlam.

The musicians had warmed up and were scraping away indoors and calling the figures. Feet were pounding through the dance; dust was flying. The women's voices were piped high and mingled discordantly, like the confused, shrill clatter of waking birds, while the men laughed boisterously. But if some one had only thought of gagging Foché, there would have been less noise. His good humor permeated everywhere, like an atmosphere. He was louder than all the noise; he was more visible than the dust. He called the young mulatto (destined for the knife) "my boy" and sent him flying hither and thither. He beamed upon Douté as he tasted the gumbo and congratulated her: "C'est toi qui s'y connais, ma fille! 'cré tonnerre!"

Telèsphore danced with Zaïda and then he leaned out against the post; then he danced with Zaïda, and then he leaned against the post. The mothers of the other girls decided that he had the manners of a pig.

It was time to dance again with Zaïda and he went in search of her. He was carrying her shawl, which she had given him to hold.

"W'at time is it?" she asked him when he had found and secured her. They were under one of the kerosene lamps on the front gallery and he drew forth his silver watch. She seemed to be still laboring under some suppressed excitement that he had noticed before.

"It's fo'teen minutes pas' twelve," he told her exactly.

"I wish you'd fine out w'ere Jules is. Go look yonda in the card-room if he's there, an' come tell me." Jules had danced with all the prettiest girls. She knew it was his custom after accomplishing this agreeable feat, to retire to the card-room.

"You'll wait yere till I come back?" he asked.

"I'll wait yere; you go on." She waited but drew back a little into the shadow. Telèsphore lost no time.

"Yes, he's yonda playin' cards with Foché an' some others I don' know," he reported when he had discovered her in the shadow. There had been a spasm of alarm when he did not at once see her where he had left her under the lamp.

"Does he look—look like he's fixed yonda fo' good?"

"He's got his coat off. Looks like he's fixed pretty comf'table fo' the nex' hour or two."

"Gi' me my shawl."

"You cole?" offering to put it around her.

"No, I ain't cole." She drew the shawl about her shoulders and turned as if to leave him. But a sudden generous impulse seemed to move her, and she added:

"Come along yonda with me."

They descended the few rickety steps that led down to the yard. He followed rather than accompanied her across the beaten and trampled sward. Those who saw them thought they had gone out to take the air. The beams of light that slanted out from the house were fitful and uncertain, deepening the shadows. The embers under the empty gumbo-pot glared red in the darkness. There was a sound of quiet voices coming from under the trees.

Zaïda, closely accompanied by Telèsphore, went out where the vehicles and horses were fastened to the fence. She stepped carefully and held up her skirts as if dreading the least speck of dew or of dust.

"Unhitch Jules' ho'se an' buggy there an' turn 'em 'roun' this way, please." He did as instructed, first backing the pony, then leading it out to where she stood in the half-made road.

"You goin' home?" he asked her, "betta let me water the pony."

"Neva mine." She mounted and seating herself grasped the reins. "No, I ain't goin' home," she added. He, too, was holding the reins gathered in one hand across the pony's back.

"W'ere you goin'?" he demanded.

"Neva you mine w'ere I'm goin'."

"You ain't goin' anyw'ere this time o' night by yo'se'f?"

"W'at you reckon I'm 'fraid of?" she laughed. "Turn loose that ho'se," at the same time urging the animal forward. The little brute started away with a bound and Telèsphore, also with a bound, sprang into the buckboard and seated himself beside Zaïda.

"You ain't goin' anyw'ere this time o' night by yo'se'f." It was not a question now, but an assertion, and there was no denying it. There was even no disputing it, and Zaïda recognizing the fact drove on in silence.

There is no animal that moves so swiftly across a 'Cadian prairie as the little Creole pony. This one did not run nor trot; he seemed to reach out in galloping bounds. The buckboard creaked, bounced, jolted and swayed. Zaïda clutched at her shawl while Telèsphore drew his straw hat further down over his right eye and offered to drive. But he did not know the road and she would not let him. They had soon reached the woods.

If there is any animal that can creep more slowly through a wooded road than the little Creole pony, that animal has not yet been discovered in Acadie. This particular animal seemed to be appalled by the darkness of the forest and filled with dejection. His head drooped and he lifted his feet as if each hoof were weighted with a thousand pounds of lead. Any one unacquainted with the peculiarities of the breed would sometimes have fancied that he was standing still. But Zaïda and Telèsphore knew better. Zaïda uttered a deep sigh as she slackened her hold on the reins and Telèsphore, lifting his hat, let it swing from the back of his head.

"How you don' ask me w'ere I'm goin'?" she said finally. These were the first words she had spoken since refusing his offer to drive.

"Oh, it don' make any diff'ence w'ere you goin'."

"Then if it don' make any diff'ence w'ere I'm goin', I jus' as well tell you." She hesitated, however. He seemed to have no curiosity and did not urge her.

"I'm goin' to get married," she said.

He uttered some kind of an exclamation; it was nothing articulate—more like the tone of an animal that gets a sudden knife thrust. And now he felt how dark the forest was. An instant before it had seemed a sweet, black paradise; better than any heaven he had ever heard of.

"W'y can't you get married at home?" This was not the first thing that occurred to him to say, but this was the first thing he said.

"Ah, b'en oui! with perfec' mules fo' a father an' mother! it's good enough to talk."

"W'y couldn' he come an' get you? W'at kine of a scound'el is that to let you go through the woods at night by yo'se'f?"

"You betta wait till you know who you talkin' about. He didn' come an' get me because he knows I ain't 'fraid; an' because he's got too much pride to ride in Jules Trodon's buckboard afta he done been put out o' Jules Trodon's house."

"W'at's his name an' w'ere you goin' to fine 'im?"

"Yonda on the other side the woods up at ole Wat Gibson's—a kine of justice of the peace or something. Anyhow he's goin' to marry us. An' afta we done married those têtes-de-mulets yonda on bayou de Glaize can say w'at they want."

"W'at's his name?"

"André Pascal."

The name meant nothing to Telèsphore. For all he knew, André Pascal might be one of the shining lights of Avoyelles; but he doubted it.

"You betta turn 'roun'," he said. It was an unselfish impulse that prompted the suggestion. It was the thought of this girl married to a man whom even Jules Trodon would not suffer to enter his house.

"I done give my word," she answered.

"W'at's the matta with 'im? W'y don't yo' father and mother want you to marry 'im?"

"W'y? Because it's always the same tune! W'en a man's down eve'y-body's got stones to throw at 'im. They say he's lazy. A man that will walk from St. Landry plumb to Rapides lookin' fo' work; an' they call that lazy! Then, somebody's been spreadin' yonda on the Bayou that he drinks. I don' b'lieve it. I neva saw 'im drinkin', me. Anyway, he won't drink afta he's married to me; he's too fon' of me fo' that. He say he'll blow out his brains if I don' marry 'im."

"I reckon you betta turn roun'."

"No, I done give my word." And they went creeping on through the woods in silence.

"W'at time is it?" she asked after an interval. He lit a match and looked at his watch.

"It's quarta to one. W'at time did he say?"

"I tole 'im I'd come about one o'clock. I knew that was a good time to get away f'om the ball."

She would have hurried a little but the pony could not be induced to do so. He dragged himself, seemingly ready at any moment to give up the breath of life. But once out of the woods he made up for lost time. They were on the open prairie again, and he fairly ripped the air; some flying demon must have changed skins with him.

It was a few minutes of one o'clock when they drew up before Wat Gibson's house. It was not much more than a rude shelter, and in the dim starlight it seemed isolated, as if standing alone in the middle of the black, far-reaching prairie. As they halted at the gate a dog within set up a furious barking; and an old negro who had been smoking his pipe at that ghostly hour, advanced toward them from the shelter of the gallery. Telèsphore descended and helped his companion to alight.

"We want to see Mr. Gibson," spoke up Zaïda. The old fellow had already opened the gate. There was no light in the house.

"Marse Gibson, he yonda to ole Mr. Bodel's playin' kairds. But he neva' stay atter one o'clock. Come in, ma'am; come in, suh; walk right 'long in." He had drawn his own conclusions to explain their appearance. They stood upon the narrow porch waiting while he went inside to light the lamp.

Although the house was small, as it comprised but one room, that room was comparatively a large one. It looked to Telèsphore and Zaïda very large and gloomy when they entered it. The lamp was on a table that stood against the wall, and that held further a rusty looking ink bottle, a pen and an old blank book. A narrow bed was off in the corner. The brick chimney extended into the room and formed a ledge that served as mantel shelf. From the big, low-hanging rafters swung an assortment of fishing tackle, a gun, some discarded articles of clothing and a string of red peppers. The boards of the floor were broad, rough and loosely joined together.

Telèsphore and Zaïda seated themselves on opposite sides of the table and the negro went out to the wood pile to gather chips and pieces of bois-gras with which to kindle a small fire.

It was a little chilly; he supposed the two would want coffee and he knew that Wat Gibson would ask for a cup the first thing on his arrival.

"I wonder w'at's keepin' 'im," muttered Zaïda impatiently. Telèsphore looked at his watch. He had been looking at it at intervals of one minute straight along.

"It's ten minutes pas' one," he said. He offered no further comment.

At twelve minutes past one Zaïda's restlessness again broke into speech.

"I can't imagine, me, w'at's become of André! He said he'd be yere sho' at one." The old negro was kneeling before the fire that he had kindled, contemplating the cheerful blaze. He rolled his eyes toward Zaïda.

"You talkin' 'bout Mr. André Pascal? No need to look fo' him. Mr. André he b'en down to de P'int all day raisin' Cain."

"That's a lie," said Zaïda. Telèsphore said nothing.

"Tain't no lie, ma'am; he b'en sho' raisin' de ole Nick." She looked at him, too contemptuous to reply.

The negro told no lie so far as his bald statement was concerned. He was simply mistaken in his estimate of André Pascal's ability to "raise Cain" during an entire afternoon and evening and still keep a rendezvous with a lady at one o'clock in the morning. For André was even then at hand, as the loud and menacing howl of the dog testified. The negro hastened out to admit him.

André did not enter at once; he stayed a while outside abusing the dog and communicating to the negro his intention of coming out to shoot the animal after he had attended to more pressing business that was awaiting him within.

Zaïda arose, a little flurried and excited when he entered. Telèsphore remained seated.

Pascal was partially sober. There had evidently been an attempt at dressing for the occasion at some early part of the previous day, but such evidences had almost wholly vanished. His linen was soiled and his whole appearance was that of a man who, by an effort, had aroused himself from a debauch. He was a little taller than Telèsphore, and more loosely put together. Most women would have called him a handsomer man. It was easy to imagine that when sober, he might betray by some subtle grace of speech or manner, evidences of gentle blood.

"W'y did you keep me waitin', André? w'en you knew—" she got no further, but backed up against the table and stared at him with earnest, startled eyes.

"Keep you waiting, Zaïda? my dear li'le Zaïdé, how can you say such a thing! I started up yere an hour ago an' that—w'ere's that damned ole Gibson?" He had approached Zaïda with the evident intention of embracing her, but she seized his wrist and held him at arm's length away. In casting his eyes about for old Gibson his glance alighted upon Telèsphore.

The sight of the 'Cadian seemed to fill him with astonishment. He stood back and began to contemplate the young fellow and lose himself in speculation and conjecture before him, as if before some unlabeled wax figure. He turned for information to Zaïda.

"Say, Zaïda, w'at you call this? W'at kine of damn fool you got sitting yere? Who let him in? W'at you reckon he's lookin' fo'? trouble?"

Telèsphore said nothing; he was awaiting his cue from Zaïda.

"André Pascal," she said, "you jus' as well take the do' an' go. You might stan' yere till the day o' judgment on yo' knees befo' me; an' blow out yo' brains if you a mine to. I ain't neva goin' to marry you."

"The hell you ain't!"

He had hardly more than uttered the words when he lay prone on his back. Telèsphore had knocked him down. The blow seemed to complete the process of sobering that had begun in him. He gathered himself together and rose to his feet; in doing so he reached back for his pistol. His hold was not yet steady, however, and the weapon slipped from his grasp and fell to the floor. Zaïda picked it up and laid it on the table behind her. She was going to see fair play.

The brute instinct that drives men at each other's throat was awake and stirring in these two. Each saw in the other a thing to be wiped out of his way—out of existence if need be. Passion and blind rage directed the blows which they dealt, and steeled the tension of muscles and clutch of fingers. They were not skillful blows, however.

The fire blazed cheerily; the kettle which the negro had placed upon the coals was steaming and singing. The man had gone in search of his master. Zaïda had placed the lamp out of harm's way on the high mantel ledge and she leaned back with her hands behind her upon the table.

She did not raise her voice or lift her finger to stay the combat that was acting before her. She was motionless, and white to the lips; only her eyes seemed to be alive and burning and blazing. At one moment she felt that André must have strangled Telèsphore; but she said nothing. The next instant she could hardly doubt that the blow from Telèsphore's doubled fist could be less than a killing one; but she did nothing.

How the loose boards swayed and creaked beneath the weight of the struggling men! the very old rafters seemed to groan; and she felt that the house shook.

The combat, if fierce, was short, and it ended out on the gallery whither they had staggered through the open door—or one had dragged the other—she could not tell. But she knew when it was over, for there was a long moment of utter stillness. Then she heard one of the men descend the steps and go away, for the gate slammed after him. The other went out to the cistern; the sound of the tin bucket splashing in the water reached her where she stood. He must have been endeavoring to remove traces of the encounter.

Presently Telèsphore entered the room. The elegance of his apparel had been somewhat marred; the men over at the 'Cadian ball would hardly have taken exception now to his appearance.

"W'ere is André?" the girl asked.

"He's gone," said Telèsphore.

She had never changed her position and now when she drew herself up her wrists ached and she rubbed them a little. She was no longer pale; the blood had come back into her cheeks and lips, staining them crimson. She held out her hand to him. He took it gratefully enough, but he did not know what to do with it; that is, he did not know what he might dare to do with it, so he let it drop gently away and went to the fire.

"I reckon we betta be goin', too," she said. He stooped and poured some of the bubbling water from the kettle upon the coffee which the negro had set upon the hearth.

"I'll make a li'le coffee firs'," he proposed, "an' anyhow we betta wait till ole man w'at's-his-name comes back. It wouldn't look well to leave his house that way without some kine of excuse or explanation."

She made no reply, but seated herself submissively beside the table.

Her will, which had been overmastering and aggressive, seemed to have grown numb under the disturbing spell of the past few hours. An illusion had gone from her, and had carried her love with it. The absence of regret revealed this to her. She realized, but could not comprehend it, not knowing that the love had been part of the illusion. She was tired in body and spirit, and it was with a sense of restfulness that she sat all drooping and relaxed and watched Telèsphore make the coffee.

He made enough for them both and a cup for old Wat Gibson when he should come in, and also one for the negro. He supposed the cups, the sugar and spoons were in the safe over there in the corner, and that is where he found them.

When he finally said to Zaïda, "Come, I'm going to take you home now," and drew her shawl around her, pinning it under the chin, she was like a little child and followed whither he led in all confidence.

It was Telèsphore who drove on the way back, and he let the pony cut no capers, but held him to a steady and tempered gait. The girl was still quiet and silent; she was thinking tenderly—a little tearfully of those two old têtes-de-mulets yonder on Bayou de Glaize.

How they crept through the woods! and how dark it was and how still!

"W'at time it is?" whispered Zaïda. Alas! he could not tell her; his watch was broken. But almost for the first time in his life, Telèsphore did not care what time it was.

A Pair of Silk Stockings

Little Mrs. Sommers one day found herself the unexpected possessor of fifteen dollars. It seemed to her a very large amount of money, and the way in which it stuffed and bulged her worn old *porte-monnaie* gave her a feeling of importance such as she had not enjoyed for years.

The question of investment was one that occupied her greatly. For a day or two she walked about apparently in a dreamy state, but really absorbed in speculation and calculation. She did not wish to act hastily, to do anything she might afterward regret. But it was during the still hours of the night when she lay awake revolving plans in her mind that she seemed to see her way clearly toward a proper and judicious use of the money.

A dollar or two should be added to the price usually paid for Janie's shoes, which would insure their lasting an appreciable time longer than they usually did. She would buy so and so many yards of percale for new shirt waists for the boys and Janie and Mag. She had intended to make the old ones do by skilful patching. Mag should have another gown. She had seen some beautiful patterns, veritable bargains in the shop windows. And still there would be left enough for new stockings—two pairs apiece —and what darning that would save for a while! She would get caps for the boys and sailor-hats for the girls. The vision of her little brood looking fresh and dainty and new for once in their lives excited her and made her restless and wakeful with anticipation.

The neighbors sometimes talked of certain "better days" that little Mrs. Sommers had known before she had ever thought of being Mrs. Sommers. She herself indulged in no such morbid retrospection. She had no time—no second of time to devote to the past. The needs of the present absorbed her every faculty. A vision of the future like some dim, gaunt monster sometimes appalled her, but luckily to-morrow never comes.

Mrs. Sommers was one who knew the value of bargains; who could stand for hours making her way inch by inch toward the desired object that was selling below cost. She could elbow her way if need be; she had learned to clutch a piece of goods and hold it and stick to it with persistence and determination till her turn came to be served, no matter when it came.

But that day she was a little faint and tired. She had swallowed a light luncheon—no! when she came to think of it, between getting the children fed and the place righted, and preparing herself for the shopping bout, she had actually forgotten to eat any luncheon at all!

She sat herself upon a revolving stool before a counter that was comparatively deserted, trying to gather strength and courage to charge through an eager multitude that was besieging breast-works of shirting and figured lawn. An all-gone limp feeling had come over her and she rested her hand aimlessly upon the counter. She wore no gloves. By degrees she grew aware that her hand had encountered something very soothing, very pleasant to touch. She looked down to see that her hand lay upon a pile of silk stockings. A placard near by announced that they had been reduced in price from two dollars and fifty cents to one dollar and ninety-eight cents; and a young girl who stood behind the counter asked her if she wished to examine their line of silk hosiery. She smiled, just as if she had been asked to inspect a tiara of diamonds with the ultimate view of purchasing it. But she went on feeling the soft, sheeny luxurious things—with both hands now, holding them up to see them glisten, and to feel them glide serpent-like through her fingers.

Two hectic blotches came suddenly into her pale cheeks. She looked up at the girl.

"Do you think there are any eights-and-a-half among these?"

There were any number of eights-and-a-half. In fact, there were more of that size than any other. Here was a light-blue pair; there were some lavender, some all black and various shades of tan and gray. Mrs. Sommers selected a black pair and looked at them very long and closely. She pretended to be examining their texture, which the clerk assured her was excellent.

"A dollar and ninety-eight cents," she mused aloud. "Well, I'll take this pair." She handed the girl a five-dollar bill and waited for her change and for her parcel. What a very small parcel it was! It seemed lost in the depths of her shabby old shopping-bag.

Mrs. Sommers after that did not move in the direction of the bargain counter. She took the elevator, which carried her to an upper floor into the region of the ladies' waiting-rooms. Here, in a retired corner, she exchanged her cotton stockings for the new silk ones which she had just bought. She was not going through any acute mental process or reasoning with herself, nor was she striving to explain to her satisfaction the motive of her action. She was not thinking at all. She seemed for the time to be taking a rest from that laborious and fatiguing function and to have abandoned herself to some mechanical impulse that directed her actions and freed her of responsibility.

How good was the touch of the raw silk to her flesh! She felt like lying back in the cushioned chair and reveling for a while in the luxury of it. She did for a little while. Then she replaced her shoes, rolled the cotton stockings together and thrust them into her bag. After doing this she crossed straight over to the shoe department and took her seat to be fitted.

She was fastidious. The clerk could not make her out; he could not reconcile her shoes with her stockings, and she was not too easily pleased. She held back her skirts and turned her feet one way and her head another way as she glanced down at the polished, pointed-tipped boots. Her foot and ankle looked very pretty. She could not realize that they belonged to her and were a part of herself. She wanted an excellent and stylish fit, she told the young fellow who served her, and she did not mind the difference of a dollar or two more in the price so long as she got what she desired.

It was a long time since Mrs. Sommers had been fitted with gloves. On rare occasions when she had bought a pair they were always "bargains," so cheap that it would have been preposterous and unreasonable to have expected them to be fitted to the hand.

Now she rested her elbow on the cushion of the glove counter, and a pretty, pleasant young creature, delicate and deft of touch, drew a long-wristed "kid" over Mrs. Sommer's hand. She smoothed it down over the wrist and buttoned it neatly, and both lost themselves for a second or two in admiring contemplation of the little symmetrical gloved hand. But there were other places where money might be spent.

There were books and magazines piled up in the window of a stall a few paces down the street. Mrs. Sommers bought two high-priced magazines such as she had been accustomed to read in the days when she had been accustomed to other pleasant things. She carried them without wrapping. As well as she could she lifted her skirts at the crossings. Her stockings and boots and well fitting gloves had worked marvels in her bearing—had given her a feeling of assurance, a sense of belonging to the well-dressed multitude.

She was very hungry. Another time she would have stilled the cravings for food until reaching her own home, where she would have brewed herself a cup of tea and taken a snack of anything that was available. But the impulse that was guiding her would not suffer her to entertain any such thought.

There was a restaurant at the corner. She had never entered its doors; from the outside she had sometimes caught glimpses of spotless damask and shining crystal, and soft-stepping waiters serving people of fashion.

When she entered her appearance created no surprise, no consternation, as she had half feared it might. She seated herself at a small table alone, and an attentive waiter at once approached to take her order. She did not want a profusion; she craved a nice and tasty bite—a half dozen blue-points, a plump chop with cress, a something sweet—a crème-frappée, for instance; a glass of Rhine wine, and after all a small cup of black coffee.

While waiting to be served she removed her gloves very leisurely and laid them beside her. Then she picked up a magazine and glanced through it, cutting the pages with a blunt edge of her knife. It was all very agreeable. The damask was even more spotless than it had seemed through the window, and the crystal more sparkling. There were quiet ladies and gentlemen, who did not notice her, lunching at the small tables like her own. A soft, pleasing strain of music could be heard, and a gentle breeze was blowing through the window. She tasted a bite, and she read a word or two, and she sipped the amber wine and wiggled her toes in the silk stockings. The price of it made no difference. She counted the money out to the waiter and left an extra coin on his tray, whereupon he bowed before her as before a princess of royal blood.

There was still money in her purse, and her next temptation presented itself in the shape of a matinée poster.

It was a little later when she entered the theatre, the play had begun and the house seemed to her to be packed. But there were vacant seats here and there, and into one of them she was ushered, between brilliantly dressed women who had gone there to kill time and eat candy and display their gaudy attire. There were many others who were there solely for the play and acting. It is safe to say there was no one present who bore quite the attitude which Mrs. Sommers did to her surroundings. She gathered in the whole—stage and players and people in one wide impression, and absorbed it and enjoyed it. She laughed at the comedy and wept—she and the gaudy woman next to her wept over the tragedy. And they talked a little together over it. And the gaudy woman wiped her eyes and sniffled on a tiny square of filmy, perfumed lace and passed little Mrs. Sommers her box of candy.

The play was over, the music ceased, the crowd filed out. It was like a dream ended. People scattered in all directions. Mrs. Sommers went to the corner and waited for the cable car.

A man with keen eyes, who sat opposite to her, seemed to like the study of her small, pale face. It puzzled him to decipher what he saw there. In truth, he saw nothing—unless he were wizard enough to detect a poignant wish, a powerful longing that the cable car would never stop anywhere, but go on and on with her forever.

Nég Créol

At the remote period of his birth he had been named César François Xavier, but no one ever thought of calling him anything but Chicot, or Nég, or Maringouin. Down at the French market, where he worked among the fishmongers, they called him Chicot, when they were not calling him names that are written less freely than they are spoken. But one felt privileged to call him almost anything, he was so black, lean, lame, and shriveled. He wore a head-kerchief, and whatever other rags the fishermen and their wives chose to bestow upon him. Throughout one whole winter he wore a woman's discarded jacket with puffed sleeves.

Among some startling beliefs entertained by Chicot was one that "Michié St. Pierre et Michié St. Paul" had created him. Of "Michié bon Dieu" he held his own private opinion, and not a too flattering one at that. This fantastic notion concerning the origin of his being he owed to the early teaching of his young master, a lax believer, and a great *farceur* in his day. Chicot had once been thrashed by a robust young Irish priest for expressing his religious views, and at another time knifed by a Sicilian. So he had come to hold his peace upon that subject.

Upon another theme he talked freely and harped continuously. For years he had tried to convince his associates that his master had left a progeny, rich, cultured, powerful, and numerous beyond belief. This prosperous race of beings inhabited the most imposing mansions in the city of New Orleans. Men of note and position, whose names were familiar to the public, he swore were grandchildren, great-grandchildren, or, less frequently, distant relatives of his master, long deceased. Ladies who came to the market in carriages, or whose elegance of attire attracted the attention and admiration of the fishwomen, were all *des 'tites cousines* to his former master, Jean Boisduré. He never looked for recognition from any of these superior beings, but delighted to discourse by the hour upon their dignity and pride of birth and wealth.

Chicot always carried an old gunny-sack, and into this went his earnings. He cleaned stalls at the market, scaled fish, and did many odd offices for the itinerant merchants, who usually paid in trade for his service. Occasionally he saw the color of silver and got his clutch upon a coin, but he accepted anything, and seldom made terms. He was glad to get a handkerchief from the Hebrew, and grateful if the Choctaws would trade him a bottle of *filé* for it. The butcher flung him a soup bone, and the fishmonger a few crabs or a paper bag of shrimps. It was the big *mulatresse, vendeuse de café*, who cared for his inner man.

Once Chicot was accused by a shoe-vender of attempting to steal a pair of ladies' shoes. He declared he was only examining them. The clamor raised in the market was terrific. Young Dagoes assembled and squealed like rats; a couple of Gascon butchers bellowed like bulls. Matteo's wife shook her fist in the accuser's face and called him incomprehensible names. The Choctaw women, where they squatted, turned their slow eyes in the direction of the fray, taking no further notice; while a police-man jerked Chicot around by the puffed sleeve and brandished a club. It was a narrow escape.

Nobody knew where Chicot lived. A man—even a nég créol—who lives among the reeds and willows of Bayou St. John, in a deserted chicken-coop constructed chiefly of tarred paper, is not going to boast of his habitation or to invite attention to his domestic appointments. When, after market hours, he vanished in the direction of St. Philip street, limping, seemingly bent under the weight of his gunny-bag, it was like the disappearance from the stage of some petty actor whom the audience does not follow in imagination beyond the wings, or think of till his return in another scene.

There was one to whom Chicot's coming or going meant more than this. In *la maison grise* they called her La Chouette, for no earthly reason unless that she perched high under the roof of the old rookery and scolded in shrill sudden outbursts. Forty or fifty years before, when for a little while she acted minor parts with a company of French players (an escapade that had brought her grandmother to the grave), she was known as Mademoiselle de Montallaine. Seventy-five years before she had been christened Aglaé Boisduré.

No matter at what hour the old negro appeared at her threshold,

Mamzelle Aglaé always kept him waiting till she finished her prayers. She opened the door for him and silently motioned him to a seat, returning to prostrate herself upon her knees before a crucifix, and a shell filled with holy water that stood on a small table; it represented in her imagination an altar. Chicot knew that she did it to aggravate him; he was convinced that she timed her devotions to begin when she heard his footsteps on the stairs. He would sit with sullen eyes contemplating her long, spare, poorly clad figure as she knelt and read from her book or finished her prayers. Bitter was the religious warfare that had raged for years between them, and Mamzelle Aglaé had grown, on her side, as intolerant as Chicot. She had come to hold St. Peter and St. Paul in such utter detestation that she had cut their pictures out of her prayer-book.

Then Mamzelle Aglaé pretended not to care what Chicot had in his bag. He drew forth a small hunk of beef and laid it in her basket that stood on the bare floor. She looked from the corner of her eye, and went on dusting the table. He brought out a handful of potatoes, some pieces of sliced fish, a few herbs, a yard of calico, and a small pat of butter wrapped in lettuce leaves. He was proud of the butter, and wanted her to notice it. He held it out and asked her for something to put it on. She handed him a saucer, and looked indifferent and resigned, with lifted eyebrows.

"Pas d' sucre, Nég?"

Chicot shook his head and scratched it, and looked like a black picture of distress and mortification. No sugar! But tomorrow he would get a pinch here and a pinch there, and would bring as much as a cupful.

Mamzelle Aglaé then sat down, and talked to Chicot uninterruptedly and confidentially. She complained bitterly, and it was all about a pain that lodged in her leg; that crept and acted like a live, stinging serpent, twining about her waist and up her spine, and coiling round the shoulder-blade. And then *les rheumatismes* in her fingers! He could see for himself how they were knotted. She could not bend them; she could hold nothing in her hands, and had let a saucer fall that morning and broken it in pieces. And if she were to tell him that she had slept a wink through the night, she would be a liar, deserving of perdition. She had sat at the window *la nuit blanche*, hearing the hours strike and the market-wagons rumble. Chicot nodded, and kept up a running fire of sympathetic comment and suggestive remedies for rheumatism and insomnia: herbs, or *tisanes*, or *grigris*, or all three. As if he knew! There was Purgatory Mary, a perambulating soul whose office in life was to pray for the shades in purgatory,—she had brought Mamzelle Aglaé a bottle of *eau de Lourdes*, but so little of it! She might have kept her water of Lourdes, for all the good it did,—a drop! Not so much as would cure a fly or a mosquito! Mamzelle Aglaé was going to show Purgatory Mary the door when she came again, not only because of her avarice with the Lourdes water, but, beside that, she brought in on her feet dirt that could only be removed with a shovel after she left.

And Mamzelle Aglaé wanted to inform Chicot that there would be slaughter and bloodshed in *la maison grise* if the people below stairs did not mend their ways. She was convinced that they lived for no other purpose than to torture and molest her. The woman kept a bucket of dirty water constantly on the landing with the hope of Mamzelle Aglaé falling over it or into it. And she knew that the children were instructed to gather in the hall and on the stairway, and scream and make a noise and jump up and down like galloping horses, with the intention of driving her to suicide. Chicot should notify the policeman on the beat, and have them arrested, if possible, and thrust into the parish prison, where they belonged.

Chicot would have been extremely alarmed if he had ever chanced to find Mamzelle Aglaé in an uncomplaining mood. It never occurred to him that she might be otherwise. He felt that she had a right to quarrel with fate, if ever mortal had. Her poverty was a disgrace, and he hung his head before it and felt ashamed.

One day he found Mamzelle Aglaé stretched on the bed, with her head tied up in a handkerchief. Her sole complaint that day was, "Aïe—aïe—aïe! Aïe—aïe—aïe!" uttered with every breath. He had seen her so before, especially when the weather was damp.

"Vous pas bézouin tisane, Mamzelle Aglaé? Vous pas veux mo cri gagni docteur?"

She desired nothing. "Aïe—aïe—aïe!"

He emptied his bag very quietly, so as not to disturb her; and he wanted to stay there with her and lie down on the floor in case she needed him, but the woman from below had come up. She was an Irishwoman with rolled sleeves.

"It's a shtout shtick I'm afther giving her, Nég, and she do but knock on the flure it's me or Janie or wan of us that'll be hearing her."

"You too good, Brigitte. Aïe—aïe—aïe! Une goutte d'eau sucré, Nég! That Purg'tory Marie,—you see hair, ma bonne Brigitte, you tell hair go say li'le prayer là-bas au Cathédral. Aïe—aïe—aïe!"

Nég could hear her lamentation as he descended the stairs. It followed him as he limped his way through the city streets, and seemed part of the city's noise; he could hear it in the rumble of wheels and jangle of car-bells, and in the voices of those passing by.

He stopped at Mimotte the Voudou's shanty and bought a *grigri*—a cheap one for fifteen cents. Mimotte held her charms at all prices. This he intended to introduce next day into Mamzelle Aglaé's room,—somewhere about the altar,—to the confusion and discomfort of "Michié bon Dieu," who persistently declined to concern himself with the welfare of a Boisduré.

At night, among the reeds on the bayou, Chicot could still hear the woman's wail, mingled now with the croaking of the frogs. If he could have been convinced that giving up his life down there in the water would in any way have bettered her condition, he would not have hesitated to sacrifice the remnant of his existence that was wholly devoted to her. He lived but to serve her. He did not know it himself; but Chicot knew so little, and that little in such a distorted way! He could scarcely have been expected, even in his most lucid moments, to give himself over to self-analysis.

Chicot gathered an uncommon amount of dainties at market the following day. He had to work hard, and scheme and whine a little; but he got hold of an orange and a lump of ice and a *chou-fleur*. He did not drink his cup of *café au lait*, but asked Mimi Lambeau to put it in the little new tin pail that the Hebrew notion-vender had just given him in exchange for a mess of shrimps. This time, however, Chicot had his trouble for nothing. When he reached the upper room of *la maison grise*, it was to find that Mamzelle Aglaé had died during the night. He set his bag down in the middle of the floor, and stood shaking, and whined low like a dog in pain.

Everything had been done. The Irishwoman had gone for the doctor, and Purgatory Mary had summoned a priest. Furthermore, the woman had arranged Mamzelle Aglaé decently. She had covered the table with a white cloth, and had placed it at the head of the bed, with the crucifix and two lighted candles in silver candlesticks upon it; the little bit of ornamentation brightened and embellished the poor room. Purgatory Mary, dressed in shabby black, fat and breathing hard, sat reading half audibly from a prayerbook. She was watching the dead and the silver candlesticks, which she had borrowed from a benevolent society, and for which she held herself responsible. A young man was just leaving,—a reporter snuffing the air for items, who had scented one up there in the top room of *la maison grise.*

All the morning Janie had been escorting a procession of street Arabs up and down the stairs to view the remains. One of them—a little girl, who had had her face washed and had made a species of toilet for the occasion—refused to be dragged away. She stayed seated as if at an entertainment, fascinated alternately by the long, still figure of Mamzelle Aglaé, the mumbling lips of Purgatory Mary, and the silver candlesticks.

"Will ye get down on yer knees, man, and say a prayer for the dead!" commanded the woman.

But Chicot only shook his head, and refused to obey. He approached the bed, and laid a little black paw for a moment on the stiffened body of Mamzelle Aglaé. There was nothing for him to do here. He picked up his old ragged hat and his bag and went away.

"The black h'athen!" the woman muttered. "Shut the dure, child."

The little girl slid down from her chair, and went on tiptoe to shut the door which Chicot had left open. Having resumed her seat, she fastened her eyes upon Purgatory Mary's heaving chest.

"You, Chicot!" cried Matteo's wife the next morning. "My man, he read in paper 'bout woman name' Boisduré, use' b'long to big-a famny. She die roun' on St. Philip—po', same-a like church rat. It's any them Boisdurés you alla talk 'bout?"

Chicot shook his head in slow but emphatic denial. No, indeed, the woman was not of kin to his Boisdurés. He surely had told Matteo's wife often enough—how many times did he have to repeat it!—of their wealth, their social standing. It was doubtless some Boisduré of *les Attakapas;* it was none of his.

The next day there was a small funeral procession passing a little distance away,—a hearse and a carriage or two. There was the priest who had attended Mamzelle Aglaé, and a benevolent Creole gentleman whose father had know the Boisdurés in his youth. There was a couple of player-folk, who, having got wind of the story, had thrust their hands into their pockets.

"Look, Chicot!" cried Matteo's wife. "Yonda go the fune'al. Mus-a be that-a Boisduré woman we talken 'bout yesaday."

But Chicot paid no heed. What was to him the funeral of a woman who had died in St. Philip street? He did not even turn his head in the direction of the moving procession. He went on scaling his red-snapper.

Aunt Lympy's Interference

The day was warm, and Melitte, cleaning her room, strayed often to the south window that looked out toward the Annibelles' place. She was a slender young body of eighteen with skirts that escaped the ground and a pink-sprigged shirt-waist. She had the beauty that belongs to youth—the freshness, the dewiness—with healthy brown hair that gleamed and honest brown eyes that could be earnest as well as merry.

Looking toward the Annibelles' place, Melitte could see but a speck of the imposing white house through the trees. Men were at work in the field, head and shoulders above the cotton. She could occasionally hear them laugh or shout. The air came in little broken waves from the south, bringing the hot, sweet scent of flowers and sometimes the good smell of the plowed earth.

Melitte always cleaned her room thoroughly on Saturday, because it was her only free day; of late she had been conducting a small school which stood down the road at the far end of the Annibelle place.

Almost every morning, as she trudged to school, she saw Victor Annibelle mending the fence; always mending it, but why so much nailing and bracing were required, no one but himself knew. The spectacle of the young man so persistently at work was one to distress Melitte in the goodness of her soul.

"My! but you have trouble with yo' fence, Victor," she called out to him in passing.

His good-looking face changed from a healthy brown to the color of one of his own cotton blooms; and never a phrase could his wits find till she was out of ear-shot; for Melitte never stopped to talk. She would but fling him a pleasant word, turning her face to him framed, buried, in a fluted pink sunbonnet.

He had not always been so diffident—when they were youngsters, for instance, and he lent her his pony, or came over to thrash the pecan-tree for her. Now it was different. Since he had been long away from home and had returned at twenty-two, she gave herself the airs and graces of a young lady.

He did not dare to call her "Melitte," he was ashamed to call her "Miss," so he called her nothing, and hardly spoke to her.

Sometimes Victor went over to visit in the evenings, when he would be amiably entertained by Melitte, her brother, her brother's wife, her two little nieces and one little nephew. On Saturdays the young man was apparently less concerned about the condition of his fences, and passed frequently up and down the road on his white horse.

Melitte thought it was perhaps he, calling upon some pretext, when the little tot of a nephew wabbled in to say that some one wanted to see her on the front gallery. She gave a flurried glance at the mirror and divested her head of the dust-cloth.

"It's Aunt Lympy!" exclaimed the two small nieces, who had followed in the wake of the toddling infant.

"She won't say w'at she wants, *ti tante*," pursued one of them. "She don't look pleased, an' she sittin' down proud as a queen in the big chair."

There, in fact, Melitte found Aunt Lympy, proud and unbending in all the glory of a flowered "challie" and a black grenadine shawl edged with a purple satin quilling; she was light-colored. Two heavy bands of jet-black hair showed beneath her bandanna and covered her ears down to the gold hoop earrings.

"W'y, Aunt Lympy!" cried the girl, cordially, extending both hands. "Didn't I hear you were in Alexandria?"

"Tha's true, ma' Melitte." Aunt Lympy spoke slowly and with emphasis. "I ben in Alexandria nussin' Judge Morse's wife. She well now, an' I ben sence Chuseday in town. Look like Severin git 'long well 'idout me, an' I ant hurry to go home." Her dusky eyes glowed far from cheerfully.

"I yeard some'in' yonda in town," the woman went on, "w'at I don' wan' to b'lieve. An' I say to myse'f, 'Olympe, you don' listen to no sich tale tell you go axen ma' Melitte.' "

"Something you heard about me, Aunt Lympy?" Melitte's eyes were wide.

"I don' wan' to spick about befo' de chillun," said Aunt Lympy.

"I yeard yonda in town, ma' Melitte," she went on after the children had gone, "I yeard you was turn school-titcher! Dat ant true?"

The question in her eyes was almost pathetic.

"Oh!" exclaimed Melitte; an utterance that expressed relief, surprise, amusement, commiseration, affirmation.

"Den it's true," Aunt Lympy almost whispered; "a De Broussard turn school-titcher!" The shame of it crushed her into silence.

Melitte felt the inutility of trying to dislodge the old family servant's deep-rooted prejudices. All her effort was directed toward convincing Aunt Lympy of her complete self-satisfaction in this new undertaking.

But Aunt Lympy did not listen. She had money in her reticule, if that would do any good. Melitte gently thrust it away. She changed the subject, and kindly offered the woman a bit of refreshment. But Aunt Lympy would not eat, drink, unbend, nor lend herself to the subterfuge of small talk. She said good-by, with solemnity, as we part from those in sore affliction. When she had mounted into her ramshackle open buggy the old vehicle looked somev.ay like a throne.

Scarcely a week after Aunt Lympy's visit Melitte was amazed by receiving a letter from her uncle, Gervais Leplain, of New Orleans. The tone of the letter was sad, self-condemnatory, reminiscent. A flood of tender recollection of his dead sister seemed to have suddenly overflowed his heart and glided from the point of his pen.

He was asking Melitte to come to them there in New Orleans and be as one of his own daughters, who were quite as eager to call her "sister" as he was desirous of subscribing himself always henceforward, her father. He sent her a sum of money to supply her immediate wants, and informed her that he and one of his daughters would come for her in person at an early date.

Never a word was said of a certain missive dictated and sent to him by Aunt Lympy, every line of which was either a stinging rebuke or an appeal to the memory of his dead sister, whose child was tasting the bitter dregs of poverty. Melitte would never have recognized the overdrawn picture of herself.

From the very first there seemed to be no question about her accepting the offer of her uncle. She had literally not time to lift her voice in protest, before relatives, friends, acquaintances throughout the country raised a very clamor of congratulation. What luck! What a chance! To form one of the Gervais Leplain household!

Perhaps Melitte did not know that they lived in the most sumptuous style in la rue Esplanade, with a cottage across the lake; and they travelled—they spent summers at the North! Melitte would see the great, the big, the beautiful world! They already pictured little Melitte gowned *en Parisienne;* they saw her name figuring in the society columns of the Sunday papers! as attending balls, dinners, luncheons and card parties.

The whole proceeding had apparently stunned Melitte. She sat with folded hands; except that she put the money carefully aside to return to her uncle. She would in no way get it confounded with her own small hoard; that was something precious and apart, not to be contaminated by gift-money.

"Have you written to yo' uncle to thank him, Melitte?" asked the sister-in-law.

Melitte shook her head. "No; not yet."

"But, Melitte!"

"Yes; I know."

"Do you want yo' brother to write?"

"No! Oh, no!"

"Then don't put it off a day longer, Melitte. Such rudeness! W'at will yo' Uncle Gervais an' yo' cousins think!"

Even the babies that loved her were bitten with this feverish ambition for Melitte's worldly advancement. " 'Taint you, *ti tante,* that's goin' to wear a sunbonnet any mo', or calico dresses, or an apron, or feed the chickens!"

"Then you want *ti tante* to go away an' leave you all?"

They were not ready to answer, but hung their heads in meditative silence, which lasted until the full meaning of *ti tante's* question had penetrated the inner consciousness of the little man, whereupon he began to howl, loud and deep and long.

Even the curé, happy to see the end of a family estrangement, took Melitte's acceptance wholly for granted. He visited her and discoursed at length and with vivid imagination upon the perils and fascinations of "the city's" life, presenting impartially, however, its advantages, which he hoped she would use to the betterment of her moral and intellectual faculties. He recommended to her a confessor at the cathedral who had travelled with him from France so many years ago.

"It's time you were dismissing an' closing up that school of yo's,

Melitte," advised her sister-in-law, puzzled and disturbed, as Melitte was preparing to leave for the schoolhouse.

She did not answer. She seemed to have been growing sullen and ill-humored since her great piece of good luck; but perhaps she did not hear, with the pink sunbonnet covering her pink ears.

Melitte was sensible of a strong attachment for the things about her—the dear, familiar things. She did not fully realize that her surroundings were poor and pinched. The thought of entering upon a different existence troubled her.

Why was every one, with single voice, telling her to "go"? Was it that no one cared? She did not believe this, but chose to nourish the fancy. It furnished her a pretext for tears.

Why should she not go, and live in ease, free from responsibility and care? Why should she stay where no soul had said, "I can't bear to have you go, Melitte?"

If they had only said, "I shall miss you, Melitte," it would have been something—but no! Even Aunt Lympy, who had nursed her as a baby, and in whose affection she had always trusted—even she had made her appearance and spent a whole day upon the scene, radiant, dispensing compliments, self-satisfied, as one who feels that all things are going well in her royal possessions.

"Oh, I'll go! I will go!" Melitte was saying a little hysterically to herself as she walked. The familiar road was a brown and green blur, for the tears in her eyes.

Victor Annibelle was not mending his fence that morning; but there he was, leaning over it as Melitte came along. He had hardly expected she would come, and at that hour he should have been back in the swamp with the men who were hired to cut timber; but the timber could wait, and the men could wait, and so could the work. It did not matter. There would be days enough to work when Melitte was gone.

She did not look at him; her head was down and she walked steadily on, carrying her bag of books. In a moment he was over the fence; he did not take the time to walk around to the gate; and with a few long strides he had joined her.

"Good morning, Melitte." She gave a little start, for she had not heard him approaching.

"Oh—good morning. How is it you are not at work this morning?"

"I'm going a little later. An' how is it you are at work, Melitte? I didn't expect to see you passing by again."

"Then you were going to let me leave without coming to say good-by?" she returned with an attempt at sprightliness.

And he, after a long moment's hesitation, "Yes, I believe I was. W'en do you go?"

"When do you go! When do you go!" There it was again! Even he was urging her. It was the last straw.

"Who said I was going?" She spoke with quick exasperation. It was warm, and he would have lingered beneath the trees that here and there flung a pleasant shade, but she led him a pace through the sun.

"Who said?" he repeated after her. "W'y, I don't know—everybody. You are going, of co'se?"

"Yes."

She walked slowly and then fast in her agitation, wondering why he did not leave her instead of remaining there at her side in silence.

"Oh, I can't bear to have you go, Melitte!"

They were so near the school it seemed perfectly natural that she should hurry forward to join the little group that was there waiting for her under a tree. He made no effort to follow her. He expected no reply; the expression that had escaped him was so much a part of his unspoken thought, he was hardly conscious of having uttered it.

But the few spoken words, trifling as they seemed, possessed a power to warm and brighten greater than that of the sun and the moon. What mattered now to Melitte if the hours were heavy and languid; if the children were slow and dull! Even when they asked, "W'en are you going, Miss Melitte?" she only laughed and said there was plenty of time to think of it. And were they so anxious to be rid of her? she wanted to know. She some way felt that it would not be so very hard to go now. In the afternoon, when she had dismissed the scholars, she lingered a while in the schoolroom. When she went to close the window, Victor Annibelle came up and stood outside with his elbows on the sill.

"Oh!" she said, with a start, "why are you not working this hour of the day?" She was conscious of reiteration and a sad lack of imagination or invention to shape her utterances. But the question suited his intention well enough.

"I haven't worked all day," he told her. "I haven't gone twenty paces from this schoolhouse since you came into it this morning." Every particle of diffidence that had hampered his intercourse with her during the past few months had vanished.

"I'm a selfish brute," he blurted, "but I reckon it's instinct fo' a man to fight fo' his happiness just as he would fight fo' his life."

"I mus' be going, Victor. Please move yo' arms an' let me close the window."

"No, I won't move my arms till I say w'at I came here to say." And seeing that she was about to withdraw, he seized her hand and held it. "If you go away, Melitte—if you go I—oh! I don't want you to go. Since morning—I don't know w'y—something you said—or some way, I have felt that maybe you cared a little; that you might stay if I begged you. Would you, Melitte—would you?"

"I believe I would, Victor. Oh—never mind my hand; don't you see I must shut the window?"

So after all Melitte did not go to the city to become a *grande dame*. Why? Simply because Victor Annibelle asked her not to. The old people when they heard it shrugged their shoulders and tried to remember that they, too, had been young once; which is, sometimes, a very hard thing for old people to remember. Some of the younger ones thought she was right, and many of them believed she was wrong to sacrifice so brilliant an opportunity to shine and become a woman of fashion.

Aunt Lympy was not altogether dissatisfied; she felt that her interference had not been wholly in vain.

The Blind Man

A man carrying a small red box in one hand walked slowly down the street. His old straw hat and faded garments looked as if the rain had often beaten upon them, and the sun had as many times dried them upon his person. He was not old, but he seemed feeble; and he walked in the sun, along the blistering asphalt pavement. On the opposite side of the street there were trees that threw a thick and pleasant shade; people were all walking on that side. But the man did not know, for he was blind, and moreover he was stupid.

In the red box were lead pencils, which he was endeavoring to sell. He carried no stick, but guided himself by trailing his foot along the stone copings or his hand along the iron railings. When he came to the steps of a house he would mount them. Sometimes, after reaching the door with great difficulty, he could not find the electric button, whereupon he would patiently descend and go his way. Some of the iron gates were locked—their owners being away for the summer—and he would consume much time in striving to open them, which made little difference, as he had all the time there was at his disposal.

At times he succeeded in finding the electric button; but the man or maid who answered the bell needed no pencil, nor could they be induced to disturb the mistress of the house about so small a thing.

The man had been out long and had walked very far, but had sold nothing. That morning some one who had finally grown tired of having him hanging around had equipped him with this box of pencils, and sent him out to make his living. Hunger, with sharp fangs, was gnawing at his stomach and a consuming thirst parched his mouth and tortured him. The sun was broiling. He wore too much clothing—a vest and coat over his shirt. He might have removed these and carried them on his arm or thrown them away; but he did not think of it. A kind-hearted woman who saw him from an upper window felt sorry for him, and wished that he would cross over into the shade.

The man drifted into a side street, where there was a group of noisy, excited children at play. The color of the box which he carried attracted them and they wanted to know what was in it. One of them attempted to take it away from him. With the instinct to protect his own and his only means of sustenance, he resisted, shouted at the children and called them names. A policeman coming around the corner and seeing that he was the centre of a disturbance, jerked him violently around by the collar; but upon perceiving that he was blind, considerately refrained from clubbing him and sent him on his way. He walked on in the sun.

During his aimless rambling he turned into a street where there were monster electric cars thundering up and down, clanging wild bells and literally shaking the ground beneath his feet with their terrific impetus. He started to cross the street.

Then something happened—something horrible happened that made the women faint and the strongest men who saw it grow sick and dizzy. The motorman's lips were as gray as his face, and that was ashen gray; and he shook and staggered from the superhuman effort he had put forth to stop his car.

Where could the crowds have come from so suddenly, as if by magic? Boys on the run, men and women tearing up on their wheels to see the sickening sight; doctors dashing up in buggies as if directed by Providence.

And the horror grew when the multitude recognized in the dead and mangled figure one of the wealthiest, most useful and most influential men of the town—a man noted for his prudence and foresight. How could such a terrible fate have overtaken him? He was hastening from his business house—for he was late—to join his family, who were to start in an hour or two for their summer home on the Atlantic coast. In his hurry he did not perceive the other car coming from the opposite direction, and the common, harrowing thing was repeated.

The blind man did not know what the commotion was all about. He had crossed the street, and there he was, stumbling on in the sun, trailing his foot along the coping.

A Vocation and a Voice

I

"Is this Adams avenue?" asked a boy whose apparel and general appearance marked him as belonging to the lower ranks of society. He had just descended from a street car which had left the city an hour before, and was now depositing its remnant of passengers at the entrance of a beautiful and imposing suburban park.

"Adams avenue?" returned the conductor. "No this is Woodland Park. Can't you see it ain't any avenue? Adams is two miles northeast o'here. Th' Adams Avenue car turned north on Dennison, just ahead of us, a half hour ago. You must a' taken the wrong car."

The boy was for a moment perplexed and undecided. He stood a while staring towards the northeast, then, thrusting his hands into his pockets, he turned and walked into the park.

He was rather tall, though he had spoken with the high, treble voice of a girl. His trousers were too short and so were the sleeves of his ill-fitting coat. His brown hair, under a shabby, felt cap, was longer than the prevailing fashion demanded, and his eyes were dark and quiet; they were not alert and seeking mischief, as the eyes of boys usually are.

The pockets into which he had thrust his hands were empty—quite empty; there was not so much as a penny in either of them. This was a fact which gave him cause for some reflection, but apparently no uneasiness. Mrs. Donnelly had given him but the five cents; and her mother, to whom he had been sent to deliver a message of some domestic purport, was expected to pay his return fare. He realized that his own lack of attention had betrayed him into the strait in which he found himself, and that his own ingenuity would have to extricate him. The only device which presented itself to him as possible, was to walk back to "The Patch," or out to Mrs. Donnelly's mother's.

It would be night before he could reach either place; he did not know the way anywhere; he was not accustomed to long and sustained walks. These considerations, which he accepted as final, gave him a comfortable sense of irresponsibility.

It was the late afternoon of an October day. The sun was warm and felt good to his shoulders through the old coat which he wore. There was a soft breeze blowing, seemingly from every quarter, playing fantastic tricks with the falling and fallen leaves that ran before him helter-skelter as he walked along the beaten, gravel path. He thought they looked like little live things, birds with disabled wings making the best of it in a mad frolic. He could not catch up with them; they ran on before him. There was a fine sweep of common to one side which gave an impression of space and distance, and men and boys were playing ball there. He did not turn in that direction or even more than glance at the ball-players, but wandered aimlessly across the grass towards the water and sat down upon a bench.

With him was a conviction that it would make no difference to any one whether he got back to "The Patch" or not. The Donnelly household, of which he formed an alien member, was overcrowded for comfort. The few dimes which he earned did not materially swell its sources of income. The seat which he occupied in the parish school for an hour or two each day would not remain long vacant in his absence. There were a dozen boys or more of his neighborhood who would serve Mass as ably as he, and who could run Father Doran's errands and do the priest's chores as capably. These reflections embodied themselves in a vague sense of being unessential which always dwelt with him, and which permitted him, at that moment, to abandon himself completely to the novelty and charm of his surroundings.

He stayed there a very long time, seated on the bench, quite still, blinking his eyes at the rippling water which sparkled in the rays of the setting sun. Contentment was penetrating him at every pore. His eyes gathered all the light of the waning day and the russet splendor of the Autumn foliage. The soft wind caressed him with a thousand wanton touches, and the scent of the earth and the trees—damp, aromatic,— came pleasantly to him mingled with the faint odor of distant burning leaves. The blue-gray smoke from a smoldering pile of leaves rolled in lazy billows among the birches on a far slope.

How good it was to be out in the open air. He would have liked to stay there always, far from the noise and grime of "The Patch." He wondered if Heaven might not be something like this, and if Father Doran was not misled in his conception of a celestial city paved with gold.

He sat blinking in the sun, almost purring with contentment. There were young people out in boats and others making merry on the grass near by. He looked at them, but felt no desire to join in their sports. The young girls did not attract him more than the boys or the little children. He had lapsed into a blessed state of tranquility and contemplation which seemed native to him. The sordid and puerile impulses of an existence which was not living had retired into a semi-oblivion in which he seemed to have no share. He belonged under God's sky in the free and open air.

When the sun had set and the frogs were beginning to croak in the waste places, the boy got up and stretched and relaxed his muscles which had grown cramped from sitting so long and so still. He felt that he would like to wander, even then, further into the Park, which looked to his unaccustomed eye like a dense forest across the water of the artificial lake. He would like to penetrate beyond into the open country where there were fields and hills and long stretches of wood. As he turned to leave the place he determined within himself that he would speak to Father Doran and ask the priest to assist him in obtaining employment somewhere in the country, somewhere that he might breathe as freely and contentedly as he had been doing for the past hour here in Woodland Park.

II

In order to regain "The Patch" there was nothing for the boy to do but follow the track of the car which had brought him so far from his destination. He started out resolutely, walking between the tracks, taking great strides with his long, growing legs and looking wistfully after each car as he stepped out of the way of its approach. Here and there he passed an imposing mansion in the dusk, splendid and isolated. There were long stretches of vacant land which enterprising dealers had laid out in building lots. Sometimes he left the track and walked along the line of a straggling fence behind which were market-gardens, the vegetables all in stiff geometrical designs and colorless in the uncertain light.

There were few people abroad; an occasional carriage rolled by, and workingmen, more fortunate than he, occupied the cars that went jangling along. He sat for awhile at the back of a slow-moving wagon, dropping down into the dust when it turned out of his course.

The boy, as he labored along in the semi-darkness that was settling about him, at once became conscious that he was very hungry. It was the odor of frying bacon and the scent of coffee somewhere near that had suddenly made him aware of the fact.

At no great distance from the road he saw a canvas-covered wagon and a small tent, the rude paraphernalia of "movers." A woman was occupied in vigorously beating with a stick a strip of burning grass which had caught from the fire with which she had been cooking her evening meal. The boy ran to her assistance, and, thrusting her aside, lest her garments should become ignited, he began stamping the incipient blaze until he had succeeded in extinguishing it. The woman threw aside her stick and standing upright wiped her whole face indiscriminately with her bended arm.

"Damn him," she said, "I wish the whole thing had took fire and burnt up," and turning upon the boy, "did you see a man anywhere coming this way, leading a couple of mules?"

She was robust and young—twenty or thereabouts—and comely, in a certain rude, vigorous fashion. She wore a yellow-cotton handkerchief bound around her head somewhat in the manner of a turban.

Yes, the boy had seen a man watering two mules at the trough before a road-house some distance away. He remembered it because the man was talking loud in some sort of a foreign, unfamiliar accent to a group of men standing by.

"That's him; damn him," she reiterated, and, moving towards the fire where she had been cooking; "want something to eat?" she asked, kindly enough.

The boy was not shocked at her language; he had not been brought up in "The Patch" for nothing. He only thought she had a more emphatic way of expressing herself than good manners or morals demanded. He did not swear himself; he had no positive leaning towards the emphatic, and moreover it was a custom not held in high esteem by Father Doran, whose teachings had not been wholly thrown away upon the boy.

Her offer of food was tempting and gratifying. A premonition that she was a woman who might take a first refusal as final, determined him to overcome all natural shyness and frankly accept without mincing.

"I'm mighty hungry," he admitted, turning with her towards the frying-pan and coffee-pot that rested upon the coals near the tent. She went inside and presently emerged bearing a brace of tin cups and a half loaf of bread. He had seated himself upon an inverted pine box; she gave him two slices of bread interlarded with bacon and a mug of coffee. Then, serving herself with the same homely fare, she sat down upon a second box and proceeded to eat her bread and bacon with great relish and to drain her cup of coffee.

It was quite dark now, save for the dim light of a road lamp nearby and the dull glow of the embers. The stars were coming out and the breeze was beating capriciously about the common, blowing the soiled canvas of the tent and buffeting a strip of cotton cambric that was loosely stretched between two poles at the edge of the road. The boy, looking up, remembered that he had read the inscription on the cambric, as he passed in the car: "The Egyptian Fortune Teller," in huge black letters on a yellow back-ground. It was fashioned to arrest the eye.

"Yes," said the woman, following his upward glance, "I'm a fortune-teller. Want your fortune told? But I don't talk like this here when I'm telling fortunes reg'lar. I talk a kind of Egyptian accent. That's his notion," motioning contemptuously with her head, down the road. "Because my skin's dark and my eyes, he goes to work and calls me 'The Egyptian Maid, the Wonder of the Orient.' I guess if my hair was yellow he'd call me 'The Swiss Fortune Teller,' or something like that and make me talk some kind of a *nicks-com-araus*. Only there's too many Dutch in this here country; they'd ketch on."

"You bet," said the boy.

The expression smacked of sympathy and reached her, some way. She looked up quickly and laughed. They both laughed. She had taken his cup from him and she was beating the two tins softly together, her arms resting on her knees.

"Where do you come from?" she asked with an awakened interest.

He told her he had come from Woodland Park, and how he had got there and why he was tramping it back to "The Patch." He even told her he was in no haste to regain "The Patch"; that it made no difference whether he ever got back or not; that he detested the crowded city and hoped soon to obtain employment in the country and stay there the rest of his life. These opinions and intentions took positive shape with him in the telling.

A notion or two got into her head as she listened to him. He seemed a companionable boy, though he was a good five years younger than herself. She thought of the long, slow journey ahead of her, the dreary road, the lonely hill-side, of those times in which her only human associate was a man who more than half the while was drunk and abusive.

"Come, go 'long with us," she said abruptly.

"Why?" he demanded. "What for? To do what?"

"Oh! there's lots of things you could do—help around, tell fortune maybe—'taint hard when you once get the hang of it, sell his old herbs and things when he's too drunk to talk. Why, lots o' things. Here, I ought to be pulling up stakes right now. Wait till you hear him when he comes back and finds I ain't done a thing! Hope I may die if I lay a finger to a stick of the measly truck," and she flung the tin cups, one after the other, into the open tent and maintained her careless, restful position on the soap box.

"Let me," offered the boy. "What you got to do? I'll do it." And he arose willingly, prompted by a decent feeling that he should do something in return for his supper.

"You can jerk them poles up and roll up the sign and stick it in the wagon; we're going to pull out of here in the morning. Then those pots and things got to be hooked under the wagon. Leave out the coffee pot."

While the boy busied himself in following her various instructions she talked on:

"I guess he's drunk down there—him and his mules! He thinks more of them mules than he does of me and the whole world put together. Because he paid two hundred and ten dollars for 'em he thinks they are made out o' some precious composition that's never been duplicated outside of Paradise. Oh! I'm about sick of playing second fiddle to a team of mules. Mr. Man 'll wake up some o' these here mornings and find that I've cut an' run. Here! let that frying pan alone. He forgets I been used to better things than living in a tent. I sung in the chorus of an opera when I wasn't more than sixteen. Some people said if I'd had means to cultivate my voice I'd be—well, I wouldn't be here to-day, I can tell you."

The object of scorn and contumely was even then approaching; a short, broad-girted man, leading his sleek bay mules—splendid looking animals —and talking to them as he came along. In the dim light the boy could see that his hair, as well as his beard, was long, curly and greasy; that he wore a slouch felt hat over a knotted red handkerchief and small golden hoops in his ears. His dialect, when he spoke, was as indescribable as his origin was undiscernable. He might have been Egyptian, for aught the boy could guess, or Zulu—something foreign and bestial for all he knew.

The woman's name, originally Susan, had been changed to Suzima to meet the exigencies of her oriental character. The Beast pronounced it "Tzutzima."

"You can thank this here boy," she began by way of greeting. "If it hadn't been for him you wouldn't a found nothing here but a pile of ashes."

"So!" exclaimed the man in his greasy guttural, with utter lack of interest.

"Yes, 'so'! The whole blamed shooting-match was afire when he come along and put it out. If it hadn't been for him you wouldn't 'a found nothing here but a pile of ashes. He says he'll go along with us in the morning if we like. Looks like he knows how to work."

"That's good," agreed the man, "bring 'im along. Plenty of room where we live."

Usually "pulling up" time was one of contention between these two, each maintaining that the brunt of the work should be borne by the other. So the presence and timely services of the boy seemed to introduce a certain unlooked-for harmony into this unconventional *menage*. Suzima arose and went over to join the man, still occupied with the well-being of his mules. He was smoking a short-stemmed pipe, which indicated that he had—wherever he got it—a sufficiency of food and drink, and would not trouble her on that score. They chatted pleasantly together.

When they retired into the tent for the night, the boy crept into the wagon, as he was instructed to do. It was broad and roomy and there he slept at ease the night through on a folded cotton "comforter."

III

They wandered toward the south, idly, listlessly. The days were a gorgeous, golden processional, good and warm with sunshine, and languorous. There were ten, twelve, twenty such days when the earth, sky, wind and water, light and color and sun, and men's souls and their senses and the odor and breath of animals mingled and melted into the harmony of a joyful existence.

They wandered toward the south; the two vagabonds and the boy.

He felt as if he had been transplanted into another sphere, into a native element from which he had all along been excluded. The sight of the country was beautiful to him and his whole being expanded in the space and splendor of it. He liked the scent of the earth and the dry, rotting leaves, the sound of snapping twigs and branches, and the shrill songs of birds. He liked the feel of the soft, springy turf beneath his feet when he walked, or of the rolling pebbles when he mounted a stony hillside.

Gutro, otherwise the Beast, drove his mules and talked to them, watered, washed and curried them; lavished upon them a care prompted by a wealth of affection and esteem. The boy was not permitted to touch the animals; he might not even think of them with their owner's knowledge or consent. But he had plenty else to do, with Suzima shifting the greater part of her work and duties upon him.

"I've got some time to sew now, thank heaven!" she said, and with a coarse thimble upon her clumsy finger and a needle threaded long, she sat at the back of the wagon or on a log in the warm air and constructed, with bits of cotton cloth, awkward-fashioned garments for the boy to wear next to his skin that she might wash those which he had on.

They moved along while the days were pleasant. Suzima must have felt glad as they went; for often-times, as she walked beside the slow-moving wagon through the still woods, she lifted her voice and sang. The boy thought he had never heard anything more beautiful than the full, free notes that came from her throat, filling the vast, woody temple with melody. It was always the same stately refrain from some remembered opera that she sang as she walked.

But on moonlight nights or when resting beside the camp fire, she brought forth a disabled guitar, and to a strumming accompaniment sang low, pleasant things, popular airs and little bits from the lighter operas. The boy sometimes joined her with his fluty girl voice, and it pleased her very well.

If Gutro was sober he took a degree of interest in the performance and made suggestions which proved that he was not devoid of a certain taste and rude knowledge of music.

But when Gutro was drunk, everyone, everything suffered but the mules. Suzima defied him and suffered the more for her defiance. She went about wincing and rubbing her shoulders and calling him vile names under her breath. But she would not let him beat the boy. She had a tender feeling for helpless and dependent things. She often exclaimed with impulsive pity over the dead and bleeding birds which they brought in from the forest. Gutro was teaching the boy to handle a gun, and many a tasty morsel they procured for their sylvan feasts. Sometimes they picked nuts like squirrels, gathering pecans when they reached the South country.

When it rained they sat bundled and huddled in the wagon under the streaming canopy, Gutro driving and swearing at the elements. Suzima was miserable when it rained and would not sing and would hardly talk. The boy was not unhappy. He peeped out at the water running in the ruts, and liked the sound of the beating rain on the canvas and the noise and crash of the storm in the forest.

"Look, Suzima! Look at the rain coming across the hill, yonder, in sheets! It'll be along here in three minutes."

"Maybe you like it," she would grumble. "I don't," and she would draw her shawl closer and crouch further in the wagon.

Often they traveled at night, when the moon shone; sometimes when it rained. They went creeping, the mules feeling their way cautiously, surely, through the darkness, along the unfamiliar roads. Suzima and the boy slept then in the bottom of the wagon on the folded "comforter." He often wished, at such times, that the wagon was broader or that Suzima would not take up so much room. Sometimes they quarreled about it, shoving, elbowing each other like children in a trundle bed. Gutro, in a rage, would turn and threaten to throw them both into the road and leave them there to perish.

IV

The boy felt no little astonishment when he made Suzima's acquaintance in her official capacity of a fortune teller. It was a sunny afternoon and they had halted at the edge of a small country town and stopped there to rest, to make ready for a fresh start in the morning. Their presence created no little stir, and aroused some curiosity. Small children assembled and followed with absorbing interest the boy's activity in hoisting the sign, stretching the tent and setting forth the various and unique living utensils.

Gutro, robed in a long, loose robe of dingy scarlet and black, arranged, with much precision, upon an improvised table of boards, a quantity of vari-colored herbs and powders, unfailing remedies for any and every ailment which mankind had yet discovered or conceived. He was no faith healer, Gutro. He believed in the efficacy of things that grew, that could be seen and felt and tasted; green and bitter and yellow things. Some he had gathered at risk of life and limb on the steep ascents of the Himalayas. Others he had collected under the burning suns of Egypt; secret and mysterious, unknown save to himself and a little band of compatriots on the banks of the Nile. So he said. And the best of it, or the worst of it, was that those who listened believed and bought and felt secure in the possession of a panacea for their ailments.

Suzima, giving an extra twist to her yellow turban, sat at the door of the tent with a "lap-board," such as housewives use, extended across her knees. Upon this she laid out in bewildering array a pack of cards covered with pictures and mythical designs: a key, a ring, a letter or a coffin, a fine lady in a train and a finer gentleman on horseback. Suzima could tell fortunes by the cards or without the cards, off-hand, any way. The dialect which she assumed was not alone indescribable, but, for the most part, unintelligible, and required frequent interpretations from Gutro. There was no native Egyptian in that Southwest country to challenge her say and it passed muster and carried conviction. The boy could not withhold a feeling of admiration for her resources and powers of invention.

Suzima was over-blunt in her occult revelations to the negroes and farm-hands who loitered to learn somewhat of their destiny. But later, when youths and maidens from the village began to assemble and linger, half ashamed, wholly eager, then was Suzima all sentiment and sympathy, even delicacy. Oh! the beautiful fortunes that she told! How she lifted the veil of a golden future for each! For Suzima dealt not with the past. She would have scorned to have taken silver for telling anyone that which they already knew. She sent them away with confidence and a sweet agitation. One little maid sickened with apprehension when Suzima predicted for her a journey in the very near future. For the maid was even then planning a trip into Western Texas, and what might not this woman with the penetrating vision next foretell! Perhaps the appalling day and hour of her death.

Together Suzima and the boy sang their songs. It was the only part of the programme in which he took any part. He had refused to wear any foreign headgear or fantastic garb, or to twist his tongue into deceitful and misleading utterances. But he sang, standing behind Suzima bending over her guitar. There was more color in his face and lips now than when he had sat dreaming in Woodland Park. His eyes looked straight into the hazy distance, over the heads of the small gathering of people. Some of them looking at his upturned face, thought it was very beautiful. There was a tranquil light shining, glowing rather, from within; something which they saw without comprehending, as they saw the glow in the western sky.

At night, when everything was still, the boy walked abroad. He was not afraid of the night or of strange places and people. To step his foot out in the darkness, he did not know where, was like tempting the Unknown. Walking thus he felt as if he were alone and holding communion with something mysterious, greater than himself, that reached out from the far distance to touch him—something he called God. Whenever he had gone alone into the parish church at dusk and knelt before the red light of the tabernacle, he had known a feeling akin to this. The boy was not innocent or ignorant. He knew the ways of men and viewed them with tranquil indifference, as something external to which no impulse within him responded. His soul had passed through dark places untouched, just as his body was passing now, unharmed, through the night, where there were pitfalls into which his feet, some way, did not wander.

V

Along in January the vagabonds felt that they would like to settle down for a time and lead a respectable existence, if only for the sake of novelty. Perhaps they would never have been so tempted if they had not stumbled upon a dismantled cabin pre-empted by a family of pigs whose ejection was but a matter of bluff and bluster joined to some physical persuasion. There was no door to the cabin, but there was part of a roof and a suggestion of chimney. And the wanderers were not over-exacting in their requirements, especially with no landlord at hand, to bow to his whims and fancies.

So they settled down to a domestic existence which some way proved to be not so united a one as their life on the road.

Near at hand was a big field where negroes were engaged during the day in clearing away stubble, some in plowing and others in bedding up cotton seed on the dry and unyielding parts.

Gutro, with the mules ever foremost in his mind, went out on the very first day and negotiated for their hire with the owner of the plantation, offering to throw himself in for *lagniappe*. A mule takes to the plow like the proverbial fish to water; then these were fine fellows with the brawn and muscle for freight hauling. When the planter took them for a month,

Gutro followed and stuck to them and stayed by them. He sat on the wagon when they were driven to the landing. He kept his beady eyes upon them when they pulled the plow, and he was there at hand to note the quality and quantity of the provender dealt out to them. It would have been an evil hour for the negro who had dared, in his presence, to misuse or abuse one or the other of the animals.

Suzima and the boy went nosing about in search of bits of lumber with which to improve the condition of their temporary abode. But a stray plank was not easy to find, with everybody around patching fences, so they did not pursue their search with stubborn persistence, but went, instead, down the bank of the bayou and tried to catch some fish. The negroes told them that if they wanted fish they would have to go back to the lake; but they decided to drag crawfishes from the ditches along the field. The canvas-covered wagon marked them as "movers," and no one questioned or disturbed them.

That first night, when it came bedtime, they were unable to dispute the possession of the cabin with the fleas and, vanquished, they returned to the shelter of the tent. Next morning Suzima sent the boy to the village, a mile away, to learn, if possible, something about the disposition of that particular breed of fleas, and to acquaint himself with a method by which they might be induced to temper their aggressive activity.

It was Saturday. The boy discerned that there was a church in the village, and a pastor, who, arrayed in cassock, happened to be walking through his garden adjacent to the parsonage.

He went and spoke over the fence to the priest, who looked approachable, who was surely more approachable for him than would have been any other soul in that locality whom he might have encountered and addressed.

The priest was kind, sociable and communicative. He knew much about fleas, their habits and vices, and withheld nothing of enlightenment upon the subject from the boy. In turn he expressed some curiosity himself and a desire for information touching the particular stamp of young vagabond who had come sauntering along the road and who addressed him so cavalierly over his own fence. He was gratified to hear that the boy was a Catholic. He was astonished to discover that he could serve Mass, and amazed to hear that he liked to do so. What an anomaly! A boy who liked to serve Mass, who did not have to be coaxed, cajoled, almost lassoed and dragged in to do service at the Holy Sacrifice! And so he would be on hand betimes in the morning, would he? They parted friends, agreeably impressed, one with the other.

The boy was well pleased to find himself once more and so unexpectedly brought in touch with the religious life and the sacred office. As he traversed the road on his way back to the cabin he kept rehearsing the service half audibly.

"*Judica me, Deus, et discerna causam meam, de gente non sancta—ab homine iniquo et doloso erue me*"—and so forth.

He told Suzima he was going to the village to attend Mass the following morning.

"Go on," she said, "it won't hurt you. I've known people that were helped a sight by prayer-meeting. I'll go along too."

A part of her present scheme of respectability was a temporary discontinuance of the "Egyptian accent" and a suspension of professional performances. The yellow sign was not unfurled. She determined to contribute nothing during that restful month towards the household expenses. When she went into the village to church the following morning, with the boy, she had laid aside her yellow turban and wore a folded veil over her head. She looked not unlike some of the 'Cadian women who were there. But her carriage was freer and there was a vigorous vitality in her movements and in the gleam of her eyes that the milder 'Cadians did not possess. The little church, with its mixed congregation of whites and blacks interested her, and as she sat uncomfortably on the edge of the pew, her hands folded in her lap, she shifted her eyes constantly from one object to the other. But when the boy appeared with the priest before the altar, clad in his long white vestments, she was spell-bound with astonishment and admiration and her attention was not once again diverted from him. How tall he looked and how beautiful! He made her think of the picture of an angel. And when she saw him go through the maneuvers of serving with skill and ease, and heard his clear responses in a language which was not familiar to her, she was seized by a sudden respect and consideration which had not before entered into her feelings for him.

"Oh! it's out of sight!" she told him after Mass. "You got to wear one of them gowns on the road and talk that language: the Egyptian ain't in it."

"That's Latin," he said with a little bridling pride. "It only belongs in church, and I ain't going to talk it on the road for you or anybody. What's more, the vestments belong in church, too, and I wouldn't wear 'em outside to save my life. Why, it'd be a sin."

"A sin," marveled Suzima, who knew no delicate shades of distinction in the matter of sinfulness. "Oh pshaw! I didn't mean no harm."

They took their midday meal with the priest, who felt an interest in them and kindly offered them a share of his plain and wholesome fare. Suzima sat stiff and awkward at table, staring, for the most part, straight out of the open door, into the yard, where there were chickens scratching around and a little calf tied under a tree.

The boy feared for her own sake that she might forget herself and drop into the careless, emphatic speech which was habitual with her. But he need not have feared. Suzima spoke not at all, except in monosyllables, when she was politely addressed by the priest. She was plainly ill at ease. When the old gentleman arose to procure something from a side table, she winked at the boy and gave him a playful kick under the table. He returned the kick, not as a confederate, but a little viciously, as one who might say, "be quiet will you, and behave yourself in the company of your betters."

For a whole half day and more Suzima had been eminently respectable —almost too respectable for her own comfort. On their way back to the hut, as they passed a desolate strip of woodland, she gave a sudden impatient movement of the shoulders, as if to throw off some burden that had been weighing upon them, and lifting her voice she sang. There was even a ring of defiance in the vibrant notes. She sang the one stately refrain that had grown familiar to the boy and that he heard sometimes in his dreams.

"Oh!" he exclaimed impetuously. "I'd rather hear you sing than anything in the world, Suzima."

It was not often that she received words of admiration or praise and the boy's impulsive outburst touched her. She took hold of his hand and swung it as they went along.

"Say!" she called out to him that night, as she flung him his comforter, "it's good the Beast wasn't along. He don't know how to behave in company. He'd a' given the whole snap away, damn him."

VI

Suzima's approval of the boy in sanctuary robes was explainable in view of the contrast offered by his appearance in everyday habiliments. She had done the best for his shabby garments with clumsy darns and patches. But what was her poor best, with himself doing the worst for them with broadening girth and limbs and hardening flesh and swelling muscles! There was no vestige of pallor now in his cheeks. Suzima often told him that he was not worth his salt, because his voice, which had been girlish and melodious, was no better now than the sound of a cracked pot. He was sometimes sensitive and did not like to be told such things. He tried to master the waverings and quaverings, but it was of no use, so he gave over joining Suzima in her songs.

The priest at the village did not mind so trifling a thing as the breaking of a boy's voice—a thing, moreover, which could not be helped—but he was concerned over the shabbiness and general misfit of his attire, and thereupon grew compassionate. He found employment for him in a store of the village and the boy, in exchange for his services, received a suit of clothes, taken down, brand new, from the shelf and folded in sharp creases. They were not of the best or finest, but they were adequate, covering his body completely and offering ample room for a fair play of limb and muscle.

He walked away each morning to the village, leaving Suzima alone, and he did not return till evening. His dinner he took at noon with the priest, and the two grew chatty and intimate over their soup. He confided to his venerable friend, when questioned, that he knew nothing of his companions of the road, absolutely nothing, except that they were Gutro and Suzima, who wandered across country in a covered wagon selling drugs and telling fortunes for a livelihood.

A shake of the head and a shrug of the shoulders can be very expressive and the boy read disapproval in these involuntary gestures of his old companion. Within his very own soul—that part of him which thought, compared, weighing considerations—there was also disapproval, but, some way, he was always glad to find Suzima sauntering down the road at evening to meet him. Walking beside her, he told her how his whole day had been spent, without reserve, as he would have spoken in the confessional.

"I don't know what the Beast's thinking about," she grumbled. "It's time to be pulling out of this here."

"I can't go till I'm through paying for my clothes," he told her determinedly.

"I got a few dollars that'll pay for these things," she told him. "They mighty poor stuff for the price, any way you look at it."

Poor stuff or not they had to be paid for, and this boy stood firm in his resolution to work out the balance due.

He brought religious newspapers and sometimes a book, which the priest gave him.

"What you want with them?" questioned Suzima, mistrustfully.

"Why, to read when I get a chance. A feller's got to read sometime, I guess." He put them carefully away in his pack, as he cared not to read by the flickering light of a candle or the uncertain flare of the brushwood in the dilapidated chimney. Suzima looked suspiciously upon these signs of ambition for enlightenment, especially as the papers and books were not of a character to entertain her. She examined them during the boy's absence.

One day she came to his encounter quite at the edge of the village, radiant, greeting him with a sounding slap on the shoulder. She was not so tall as the boy, but she felt he was an insignificant personage never-theless, when not arrayed in canonicals, one whom she might patronize and with whom she might assume the liberty of equality and *camaraderie*, when so inclined.

"What you say? We going to pull out in the morning. He came back to-day with the mules. He made the devil of a noise when he didn't find you here to pack up, but I pitched in myself, and we got everything ready for an early start."

"Then I must go right back and tell them," said the boy, halting in the road.

"Don't need to tell nobody," she assured him. "You don't owe them nothing." The suit of clothes was, in fact, paid for and, moreover, he carried a small surplus in his pocket.

"No, but I got to go back," he insisted doggedly. He remembered quite distinctly—aside from Suzima reminding him of it—that he had not thought it essential "to go back" four months ago, when he decided to cast his lot with the wayfarers. But he was not now the child of four months ago. A sense of honor was overtaking him, with other manly qualities. He was quite determined to return to the village and bid good-bye to friends and acquaintances he had made there.

"Then I'll wait here," said Suzima, not too well pleased, seating herself on a low, grassy knoll at the edge of the road.

It was already getting dusk in the village. The store was closed, but the proprietor was still loitering near, and the boy went up and spoke to him and took his leave of him. He shook hands with an old gray-haired negro sitting on the porch, and bade goodbye to the children and boys of his own age who were standing about in groups.

The priest had just come in from his barnyard and smelled of the stable and cow. He met the boy on the gallery that was dim with the dying daylight filtering through the vines. Within, an old negress was lighting a lamp.

"I come to say goodbye," said the boy, removing his hat and extending his hand. "We going to start again in the morning." There was an excited ring in his voice that was noticeable.

"Going to start in the morning!" repeated the priest in his slow, careful, broken English. "Oh! no, you must not go."

The boy gave a start and withdrew his hand from the man's grasp, holding it thereafter to himself.

"I got to go," he said, making a motion to retire, "and it's getting kind of late now. I ought to be back."

"But, my friend, wait a moment," urged the priest, detaining him with a touch on the arm. "Sit down. Let us talk over it together." The boy seated himself reluctantly on the upper step of the gallery. He had too great reverence for the old man in his sacred character to refuse out-right. But his thoughts were not here, nor was his heart, with the breath of Spring abroad beating softly in his face, and the odors of Spring assailing his senses.

"I got to go," he murmured, anticipating and forestalling his companion. Yet he could not but agree with him. Yes, he wanted to lead an upright, clean existence before God and man. To be sure he meant to settle down, some day, to a respectable employment that would offer him time and opportunity to gather instruction. He liked the village, the people, the life which he had led there. Above all he liked the man whose kindly spirit had been moved to speak and act in his behalf. But the stars were beginning to shine and he thought of the still nights in the forest. A savage instinct stirred within him and revolted against the will of this man who was seeking to detain him.

"I must go," he said again rising resolutely. "I want to go."

"Then, if you must, God bless you and be with you, my son. Forget not your Creator in the days of your youth."

"No—no—never!"

"And bear in mind and in heart always the holy teachings of the church, my child."

"Oh, yes—always. Good-bye, sir; good-bye, and thank you, sir."

He had seen indistinctly the shadowy form of Suzima lurking nearby, waiting for him.

VII

And now the wayfarers traveled northward following in the wake of Spring that turned to meet them radiant at every stage.

Many were the drugs and nostrums that Gutro sold as they went; for languor was on every side and people were running hither and thither with their complaints.

"It is the Spring," said the old people and the wise ones, with shrugs, as if to say: "The Spring is no great matter to worry over; it will pass." And then along came Gutro in the nick of time with powders that cleanse the blood and specifics that clear the brain, renew the "system" and reconstruct men and women, making them as it were perfect and whole.

When people are languid and tired they dream—what else can they do? Those day dreams that weave fantastic tricks with that time to come which belongs to them, which they can do with as they choose—in dreams! The young man rested at the plow and lost himself in thoughts of the superlatively fair one whom he had met the winter past in a distant county and whose image arose before him now to trouble him and to move him to devise ways to draw near to her. The maiden dropped the sewing from her hands to dream of she knew not what, and not knowing, it troubled her the more.

Then along came Suzima, the interpreter of dreams, with her mystic cards and Egyptian wisdom that penetrated and revealed.

The boy, on his side, was not idle. He knew the catch-penny trade; a job here and a helpful turn there that brought him small pieces of silver, which he always turned over to Suzima. But he, too, had his dreaming time. His imagination was much stirred by the tales which Gutro told at night beside the camp fire. There was matter for speculation upon the amount of invention which entered into the telling of those personal experiences.

But what of that? It was the time when the realities of life clothe themselves in the garb of romance, when Nature's decoys are abroad; when the tempting bait is set and the golden-meshed net is cast for the unwary. What mattered if Gutro's tales were true or not? They were true enough for the season. Some of them left the boy not so tranquil. He began to remember and see, in a new, dawning light, things and people past.

He sometimes brought forth the books and papers which the priest had given him, and tried to read, lying flat on the grass, resting upon his elbows. But he could not find what he sought in the printed page, and he drowsed over it. The woods were full of lights and shades and alive with the flutter and songs of birds. The boy wandered about, for the most part alone, always moving on, restless, expectant, looking for that which lured and eluded him, which he could not overtake.

He would rather have dreamed or done anything that noonday than taken the mules to water. But here was Gutro, who was part human, after all, not wholly a beast, writhing in the clutch of twinges that have attacked more decent men than he. The fellow sat upon a stretched blanket beneath a tree, a huge leg extended, rendered helpless by a sharp and sudden pain which was well nigh unbearable. He could only sit and glare at the afflicted member and curse it.

"Try some of your own magic ointment," suggested the boy; then he turned and swore at the boy. And where was Suzima? Down at the pool, at the foot of the hill, washing the clothes. Oh! the wretch! Oh! the vile woman, to be washing clothes and he here with a hideous fate overtaking him, and the mules there, with lolling tongues, panting for water!

If the boy were not an idiot and a villain (and Gutro strongly suspected him of being both), he might be trusted to lead the valued animals to water. But he must have a care, a hundred cares, for that matter. One of the mules, he must remember, stumbled in going down hill; the other picked up loose stones in his hoof as he went. Then this one should not drink so much as he wanted, while the other should be urged to drink more than he seemed to want. The boy whistled a soft accompaniment to the litany of Gutro's instructions. He had no respect for the man and meant to tell him so some day. He walked away, leading the mules, meaning to deal with them as he saw fit, paying no attention whatever to the stumbling propensity or the instinct for picking up stones.

The air was heavy and hot as a day in summer. Not a leaf stirred on the branches above his head, and not a sound could be heard save the soft splash of the water down at the pool. He felt oppressed and unhappy; he did not know why, and his legs ached as he took long, slow strides down the grassy incline that led through a scattered wood to the water. He wondered what Suzima would say when she saw him for the first time intrusted to care for the mules.

She had finished her washing of the clothes. They were lying, wrung tight, in a small pile, on the pebbly bank. She was seated, naked, upon a broad, flat stone, washing herself, her feet in the water that reached almost up to her round, glistening knees.

He saw her as one sees an object in a flash from a dark sky—sharply, vividly. Her image, against the background of tender green, ate into his brain and into his flesh with the fixedness and intensity of white-hot iron.

"Oh! the devil!" she exclaimed, reaching back hurriedly for the first garment that her hands fell upon, and drawing it across her shoulders. But she need not have troubled to cover herself. After that first flash, he did not look again. He kept his face turned from her, leading the mules to the water's edge, and staring down into the pool as they drank. There was no use to look at her; he held her as real and alive in his imagination as she was in the flesh, seated upon the stone.

She said not a word after the first impetuous exclamation. She did not go on with her ablutions, but sat drawn together, clutching the garment over her bosom and staring at him.

When the mules were satisfied he turned and led them up the hill again; but his every action was mechanical. There was a cold moisture on his forehead, and, involuntarily, he took off his hat and wiped his face with his shirt sleeve. His face, all his skin, to the very soles of his feet, was burning and pricking, and every pulse in his body was beating, clamoring, sounding in his ears like confused, distant drum-taps. He shook all over as he dragged his unwilling limbs up the ascent.

The sight of Gutro, bestial, seated helpless there upon the grass, seemed to turn the current of his passion in a new direction. He let the mules go and stood a moment, silent and quivering, before the man. It was only a moment's hesitation in which he seemed to be gathering all his forces to loosen in a torrent of invective and abuse. Where did the rage come from that maddened him? For the first time in his life he uttered oaths and curses that would have made Suzima herself quail. Gutro was suffocating; casting about for any object that his hands fell upon to hurl at the boy.

When the youth's senseless passion had spent itself, he stayed a moment, panting like a wounded animal, then, turning, fled into the woods. When he had gone far and deep into the forest, he threw himself down upon the ground and sobbed.

VIII

Suzima treated the boy as she had never done before. She was less kind to him. She was cross and sulked for a time. It grieved him. He wanted to explain, to tell her that it was not his fault, but he did not dare to approach the subject, while she ignored it. Yet he felt that her ill-humor towards him was unreasonable. There was no renewal of his rage against Gutro, but he did not feel bound to apologize to that individual. Gutro doubted not that the boy was going mad and communicated his misgiving to Suzima. He related to her the scene which had transpired the day she was washing the clothes down at the pool, and intimated that it would be safe to get rid of so dangerous a character.

She had listened, scowling, but interested. Then she told Gutro a few uncomplimentary things on her own account.

The Beast was on his legs again. The pangs and twinges had gone as suddenly and mysteriously as they had come. But he was fearful of a second visitation, and determined to push on towards some point where he might procure professional and skillful treatment. Gutro was in no sense brave, nor was he foolhardy.

There came along some moonlight about that time and the vagabonds took advantage of it to travel by night.

It was the first night out; so beautiful, so still! The wagon moved along the white stony road, its white canopy gleaming in the white moonlight as it crept in and out of the shadows. The iron pots and pans hooked beneath the wagon swung to and fro with a monotonous, scraping sound.

Gutro sat huddled in a heap on the outside seat, half asleep as was his custom when he drove the mules at night. Suzima lay in the wagon and the youth walked on behind it. She, too, had walked some distance—not beside him as she used to, but more abreast of the wagon. She had been singing as she walked along and the echo of her song came back from a distant hillside. But getting tired at last she had sprung into the wagon and now she lay there. She had taken off her shoes and stockings and her bare feet peeped out, gleaming in the moonlight. The youth saw them and looked at them as he walked behind.

He wondered how long he could walk thus—if he could walk the night through. He would not go and sit beside Gutro; the physical repulsion which he felt for the man was too real to admit of such close contact. And there is a question whether Gutro would have permitted it, suspecting the boy, as he did, of being a dangerous and malicious character.

The boy walked on, stumbling. He was troubled, he was distracted and his breath failed him. He wanted sometimes to rush forward and take Suzima's feet between his hands, and then, on the other hand he wanted to turn and flee.

It was in response to neither of these impulses, but in submission to a sudden determination moving him, seemingly, without his volition, that he sprang into the wagon. He sat down at the back with his feet dangling.

The night was cool and pleasant. They were crawling along the edge of a hill, and the whole valley beneath spread out before them more soft, more radiant, more beautiful than brush could ever picture or voice ever tell. The boy did not know that it was pleasant and cool or that the valley was gleaming all for him in a magic splendor. He only knew that Suzima's bare feet were near him, touching him.

He supposed she was asleep. He drew himself up in the wagon and laid there beside her, rigid, faint, and quivering by turns. Suzima was not asleep. Turning, she folded her arms about him and drew him close to her. She held him fast with her arms and with her lips.

IX

A few days had wrought great changes with the boy. That which he had known before he now comprehended, and with comprehension sympathy awoke. He seemed to have been brought in touch with the universe of men and all things that live. He cared more than ever for the creeping and crawling things, for the beautiful voiceless life that met him at every turn; in sky, in rock, in stream, in the trees and grass and flowers that silently unfolded the mysterious, inevitable existence.

But most of all he cared for Suzima. He talked and laughed and played with her. He watched her as she walked and turned about, and as she worked, helping her where he could. And when she sang her voice penetrated his whole being and seemed to complete the new and bewildering existence that had overtaken him.

There were a thousand new lights in Suzima's eyes that he watched for. She made pretty speeches that sounded in his ears as soft as the slow beating of the south wind. She had become something precious and apart from all things in the world and not to be confounded with them. She was the embodiment of desire and the fulfillment of life.

Suzima was defiant one day because Gutro was drunk. She was always defiant then—when he was brutal and nagging. The boy was near at hand, restless, quivering with apprehension of he knew not what. They had stopped to take their rude meal beneath the shade of a tree. Suzima and the boy were gathering up the utensils they had used. Gutro was hooking the mules to the wagon. He talked and nagged and Suzima talked and defied.

"Hush, Suzima," the boy kept whispering. "Oh, hush!"

Suddenly, the man, in a rage, turned to strike her with a halter that he held uplifted, but, quicker than he, the boy was ready with a pointed hunting knife that he seized from the ground.

It was only a scratch that he gave after all, for the woman had thrown herself against him with a force that diverted his deadly aim.

Gutro quaked and reeled with fright; he staggered and stood swaying, livid, with hanging jaw. Then, with a sudden revulsion of feeling that came with the dawn of illumination, he began to laugh. Oh, how he laughed! his oily, choking laugh! till the very woods resounded with the vile clamor of it. He leaned up against the wagon holding the fat cushion of his side and pointing a stub of finger. Suzima was red with consciousness, and scowling.

The boy said nothing, but sat down upon the grass. He was not red, like Suzima, but pale and bewildered. He lent no further hand in assisting their departure.

"Go on," he said, when they were ready to start.

"Come," said Suzima, making room for him in the wagon.

"Go on," he told her again. She thought that he would follow, taking a cut through the woods, as he often did. The wagon moved slowly away; the boy stayed leaning on his elbow, picking at the grass.

He had always supposed that he could live in the world a blameless life. He took no merit for he could not recognize within himself a propensity toward evil. He had never dreamed of a devil lurking unknown to him, in his blood, that would some day blind him, disable his will and direct his hands to deeds of violence. For he could not remember that he had willed. He knew that he had seen black and scarlet flashes before his eyes and he was conscious of an impulse which directed him to kill. He had as good as committed a crime for which they hang men. He stayed picking at the grass. An overwhelming confusion of thoughts, fears, intentions crowded upon him. He felt as if he had encountered some hideous being with whom he was not acquainted and who had said to him: "I am yourself." He shrank from trusting himself with this being alone. His soul turned toward the refuge of spiritual help, and he prayed to God and the saints and the Virgin Mary to save him and to direct him.

A mile or more back on the road they had passed an imposing structure built upon a hill. A gilded cross surmounted the pile. There were vine-yards covering the slope, gardens and flowers and vegetables, highly and skillfully cultivated. The boy had noticed, when he passed, black-robed figures at work among the vines and in the meadow down along the fence.

The boy arose from the ground and walked away. He did not follow in the direction of the wagon. He turned and walked toward the building on the hill surmounted by a gilded cross.

X

Brother Ludovic was so strong, so stalwart, that the boys of the institution often wished he might be permitted to give an exhibition of his prowess or to enter a contest of some sort whereby they might shine in the reflected honor of his achievements. Some said it all came of sleeping with open windows, winter and summer, because he could not abide the confinement of four walls. Others thought it came of chopping trees. For when he wielded his axe, which was twice the size of any other man's, the forest resounded with the blows. He was not one to dilly-dally about the grape vines or the flower beds, like a woman, mincing with a hoe. He had begun that way, they told each other, but he was soon away in the forest felling trees and out in the fields breaking the stubborn lands. So he had grown to be the young marvel of strength who now excited their youthful imaginations and commanded their respect. He had no mind for books, so they had heard—but what of that! He knew by name every bird and bush and tree, and all the rocks that are buried in the earth and all the soil that covered them. He was a friend of all the seasons and all the elements. He was a hero of the wood, to the vivid imagination of the young.

In reality he was still a youth, hardly past the age when men are permitted to have a voice and a will in the direction of government of the state. There was a stubborn growth of beard upon his face, which he shaved clean every morning and which wore the purple shadow again before night.

He often felt that he had been born anew, the day whereupon he had entered the gate of this holy refuge. That hideous, evil spectre of himself lurking outside, ready at any moment to claim him should he venture within its reach, was, for a long time, a menace to him. But he had come to dread it no longer, secure in the promise of peace which his present life held out to him.

The dreams of the youth found their object among the saintly and celestial beings presented to his imagination constantly, and to his pious contemplation. The bodily energy of youth spent itself in physical labor that taxed his endurance to the utmost. By day he worked, he studied, he assisted in the guidance and instruction of boys.

At night he slept a sleep of exhaustion, complete oblivion. Sometimes, at the approach of dawn, when his slumber lightened, some disturbing vision would weave itself into a dream to fool his fancy. Half asleep, half waking, he roamed the woods again, following, following, never overtaking a woman—that one woman he had known—who lured him.

"Come, come on!" she would say while the white-topped wagon drew her always further and further away, out of his reach. But he knew a prayer—a dozen prayers—which could dispel any trick that a dream might put upon him.

XI

Brother Ludovic had a great fancy, all his own, and one whose execution he was permitted to undertake. It was to build, with his own hands, a solid stone wall around the "Refuge." The idea had come to him like an inspiration, and it took hold of his imagination with the fixedness of a settled purpose in life. He was in a fever till he had begun his work: hauling the stones, laying them in position, binding them firm with sand and mortar. He liked to speculate upon the number of years that it would take him to complete the task. He liked to picture himself an old man, grown feeble with age, living upon this peaceful summit all enclosed by the solid stone wall built with the strength of his youth and manhood.

The Brothers were greatly interested and at the outset would collect together during the hours of recess, in small bands, and crossing vineyard and meadow, would repair to the scene of his labor.

"You'll not be telling me it's yourself that lifted the stone, Brother Ludovic?" and each would take turn in vain attempt to heave some monster which the younger man had laid in position. What would Brother Ludovic have done by the end of the year? was a never failing source of amiable controversy among them all. He worked on like the ant.

XII

It was a spring day, just such another day as when he had first entered at the gate. The breeze lashed his gown about his legs as he quitted the group that had assembled after dinner to take their customary exercise around the brick-paved walk.

"It's a prison he'll be putting us in, with his stone wall!" called out a little jovial Brother in spectacles. Brother Ludovic laughed as he walked away, clutching at his hat. He descended the slope, taking long strides. So nearly perfect was his bodily condition that he was never conscious of the motion of limb or the movement of muscle that propelled him.

The wheat was already high in the meadow. He touched it with his finger-tips as he walked through, gathering up his narrow skirt as far as the knees. There were yellow butterflies floating on ahead, and grasshoppers sprang aside in noisy confusion.

He had obtained permission to work the whole afternoon and the prospect elated him. He often wondered whether it were really the work which he enjoyed or the opportunity to be out in the open air, close to the earth and the things growing thereon.

There was a good bit of wall well started. Brother Ludovic stood for a while contemplating with satisfaction the result of his labor; then he set to work with stone and mortar and trowel. There was ease in his every movement and energy in the steady glow of his dark eyes.

Suddenly Brother Ludovic stopped, lifting his head with the mute quivering attention of some animal in the forest, startled at the scent of approaching danger. What had come over him? Was there some invisible, malicious spirit abroad, that for pure wantonness had touched him, floating by, and transported him to other times and scenes? The air was hot and heavy, the leaves were motionless upon the trees. He was walking with aching limbs down a grassy incline, leading the mules to water. He could hear soft splashing at the pool. An image that had once been branded into his soul, that had grown faint and blurred, unfolded before his vision with the poignancy of life. Was he mad?

The moon was shining, and there was a valley that lay in peaceful slumber all bathed in its soft radiance. A white-topped wagon was creeping along a white, stony road, in and out of the shadows. An iron pot scraped as it swung beneath.

He knew now that he had pulses, for they were clamoring, and flesh, for it tingled and burned as if pricked with nettles.

He had heard the voice of a woman singing the catchy refrain from an opera; the voice and song that he heard sometimes in dreams, which vanished at the first holy exhortation. The sound was faint and distant, but it was approaching, coming nearer and nearer. The trowel fell from Brother Ludovic's hand and he leaned upon the wall and listened; not now like a frightened animal at the approach of danger.

The voice drew nearer and nearer; the woman drew nearer and nearer. She was coming; she was here. She was there, passing in the road beneath, leading by the bridle a horse attached to a small, light wagon. She was alone, walking with uplifted throat, singing her song.

He watched her as she passed. He sprang upon the bit of wall he had built and stood there, the breeze lashing his black frock. He was conscious of nothing in the world but the voice that was calling him and the cry of his own being that responded. Brother Ludovic bounded down from the wall and followed the voice of the woman.

A Mental Suggestion

I

"When you meet Pauline this morning she will be charming; she will be quite the most attractive woman in the room and the only one worthy of your attention and consideration."

This was the mental suggestion which Don Graham brought to bear upon his friend Faverham as the two were making their morning toilet together. Graham was a college professor, a hard working young fellow with a penchant for psychic research. He attended hypnotic seances and thereby had acquired a hypnotic power by no means trifling, which he sometimes exercised with marked success, especially upon his friend Faverham. When Faverham, getting up in the morning discovered that his black sack coat had assumed a vivid scarlet hue, he did not lament the fact or hesitate to put it on and present himself in public wearing so conspicuous a garment. He simply went to the telephone and rang up Graham:

"Hello! there—you blamed idiot! Stop monkeying with my coat!" Sometimes the message ran:

"Hello! This is the second morning I have n't been able to stand my bath—" or "here's my coffee spoiled again! By thunder! I want this thing to stop right here!" Whereupon a little group of professors at the other end of the "phone" would be moved by a current of gratification hardly to be understood by those who have never known the success of a scientific demonstration.

Faverham himself was not a hard worker. With plenty of money and a good deal of charm, he dispensed both lavishly and was a great favorite with both women and men. There was one privilege which he assumed at all times; he persistently avoided people, places and things which bored him. One being among others on earth who thoroughly bored Faverham, was Pauline, the fiancée of his friend Graham. Pauline was a brown little body with fluffy hair and eye glasses, possessed of an investigating turn of mind and much energy of manner in the pursuit of mental problems. She "went in" for art which she studied with a scientific spirit and acquired by mathematical tabulation. She was the type of woman that Faverham detested. Her mental poise was a rebuke to him; there was constant rebuff in her lack of the coquettish, the captivating, the feminine. He supposed she and Graham were born for each other and he could not help feeling sorry for his friend. Needless to say Faverham avoided Pauline and, so far as his instinctive courtesy permitted, snubbed her.

He and his friend were down at Cedar Branch where a number of pleasant and interesting people were spending the month of October.

On that particular October Monday morning, Graham was returning to his engagements in the city and Faverham meant to stay on at the Branch so long as he could do so without being bored. There were a number of jolly, congenial girls who contributed somewhat to his entertainment, and beside the fishing was good; so were the bathing and driving.

As Graham stood before the mirror tying his cravat, the disturbing thought came to him that his little Pauline would have a dreary time during his two weeks' absence. With the exception of a German lady who collected butterflies and stuck pins through them, there was not a thoroughly congenial soul to keep her company. Graham thought of the driving, the sailing, the dancing in all of which Faverham was the leading and moving spirit and the temptation came to him to silently utter the suggestion which would convert Pauline from an object of indifference in Faverham's eyes to a captivating young woman. Under some pretext he approached and laid his hand upon Faverham who was lacing his boot. "When you meet Pauline this morning at breakfast she will be charming; she will be quite the most attractive woman in the room and the only one worthy of your attention and consideration."

There were a number of people assembled in the large dining room when Graham and Faverham entered. Some were already seated while others were standing chatting in small groups. Pauline was near a window reading a letter, absorbed in its contents which she hastened to communicate to her friend, after a hurried and absent-minded greeting. The letter was from an art-dealer, and all about a certain "example of

Early Flemish" which he had obtained for her. Pauline was collecting facsimiles of the various "schools" and "periods" of painting with the precision and exactitude which characterized all her efforts. The acquisition of this bit of "Early Flemish" which she had been pursuing with unusual activity, settled her into a comfortable condition of mind.

Graham sat beside her and they brought their heads together and chatted psychology and art over their oatmeal. Faverham sat opposite. He kept looking at her. He was talking to the Tennis-Girl next to him and listening to Pauline.

"Miss Edmonds," he said abruptly, leaning forward so as to arrest her attention, "you must have Graham bring you around to my apartments when we're all in town again. I have a few pieces by the Glasgow men which I picked up last summer in Scotland and a bit of Persian tapestry that seems like a Hornel with the color toned down. Perhaps you would like to look at them."

Pauline flushed with surprise and pleasure. The Tennis-Girl drew back and stared at him. The Golf-Girl threw a pellet of bread at him from the far end of the table and Graham smiled and chuckled inwardly and took some mental notes.

Faverham maintained a lively conversation with Pauline across the table during the entire repast, while inwardly he was thinking:

"How wonderfully that soft brown suits her complexion and eyes! And what very sweet eyes she has behind those glasses. What depth! what animation! Could any thing be more captivating than that unstudied, spontaneous manner? and what a bright intelligence! By Jove! it puts a fellow on his mettle." Graham had reason to congratulate himself upon the success of his experiment.

Great was his astonishment however upon leaving table to see Faverham saunter away in company with the Tennis-Girl, evincing no particle of further interest in Pauline.

"How is this?" thinks Graham. "Ah-ha! to be sure! I suggested that he should think Pauline charming and captivating when he met her at breakfast. I must renew and qualify the suggestion."

When he went away, carrying his valise and things, Pauline accompanied him to the gate which was a good stretch from the big, rambling house. He maintained a peculiar and rigid silence as they strolled down the gravel path that was already covered with fallen leaves. Pauline looked questioningly up at him.

"I wish, dear," he said, "you would abandon your thought to me;

project all your mental energy into mine and let it follow and help the direction of my suggestion." The Golf-Girl might have doubted the sanity of such a speech; not Pauline; she was used to him. As he withdrew to go and shake hands with Faverham who was near-by, she converted her mind, so far as she was able, into a vacuous blank, abandoning it to his intention. The mental suggestion which Graham rapidly formulated as he held Faverham's hand, ran somewhat in this wise:

"Pauline is charming, intelligent, honest, sincere. She has depths in her nature that are worth sounding." He and the girl then walked silently together down to the gate and parted there with a mute pressure of hands.

He looked back as he went down the road. Pauline had turned and was regaining the house. Faverham had abandoned the tennis group and was crossing the lawn to join her. Graham took some fresh mental notes and patted himself metaphorically upon the back.

II

In a letter which Pauline wrote a few days later to Graham, she said:

"I have not yet begun my notes on the Renaissance and I should have finished them by now! I deserve a scolding and hope you will not spare me. The truth is, I have been an idle girl and am quite ashamed of myself. You must have asked your friend Mr. Faverham to pay me a little attention. Were you afraid I should be bored? It was a misdirected kindness, dear, for he causes me to waste much time; he wanted to read Tennyson to me this morning out under the big maple when I had gone to begin those everlasting notes! I prevailed upon him to substitute Browning. I had to save something from this wreck of time! He is a delightful reader; his voice is mellow and withal intelligent, not merely musical. He was amazed at the beauty, the insight, the philosophy of our dear Browning. 'Where have you been?' I asked him in some surprise. 'Oh! in good company,' he avowed, 'but will you take me on a voyage of discovery and make me acquainted with the immortals?' But enough—If you have not yet seen Lilienthal about the Tintoretto" &c &c.

After a short interval she wrote:

"I am growing frivolous. I positively danced last night! You did not know I could dance? Oh! but I can; for I learned some pretty steps two winters ago when our 'Manners and Customs' class took up the history of dancing."

It was a week later that she said in a letter:

"I am distrustful of pleasures and emotions which reach one through other than intellectual channels. I received a singular impression a night or two ago. The evening was warm for October, and as there was a big, bright moon shining, Mr. Faverham, who had taken me for a sail, ventured to remain out longer than his usual hour for turning in. It was very late and very still. There was not a sound but the lapping of the little wavelets as the boat cut through the water, and the occasional flapping of the sail. The aromatic odor of the pines and firs wafted to us from the shore was very acute. I someway felt as if I were some other one, living in some other age and some other place. All that has heretofore made up the substance of my life seemed far away and unreal. All thought, ambition, energy had left me. I wanted to stay there forever upon the water, drifting, drifting along, not caring—I recognize that the whole experience was sensuous and therefore to be mistrusted."

Near the end of the two weeks there was a queer, rambling little note that seemed to Graham wholly out of character and irrelevant:

"You are staying away very long. I feel that I need you, to interpret me to myself if for nothing else. I fear there are forces in life against which the intellectual training makes no provision. Why are we placed at the mercy of emotions? What are the books for after all if we can snatch from them no weapon with which to meet and combat unsuspected and undreamed of subtleties of existence? Oh dear! Oh dear! Come back and help me disentangle it all." Graham was puzzled and uneasy.

III

He returned to the Branch with the full intention of reclaiming his own. He was gratified with the success of his experiment, which at the same time had been the means of procuring for Pauline a period of diversion such as he believed would benefit her. His intention was to remove the suggestion he had put upon Faverham when everything would, of course, be as it was before.

If his love for the girl had been of the blind, passionate, exacting sort, perhaps he would have done so, even against the odds of changed conditions which met him.

"It may be a passing infatuation," she admitted with pathetic frankness. "I do not know; I have never felt anything like it before. If you wish—if you think it best and wisest to hold me to my promise you will find me ready to fulfill it. But as things are now, I must tell you that my whole temperament seems to have undergone a change. I—I sometimes —oh! I love him!"

She did not hide her face upon reaching the climax of her confession as most girls would have done, but looked out straight before her. They were sitting under the big maple where Faverham had read Browning to her; and the day was already beginning to fade. There was a light in her face that he had never seen there before; a glow such as he had never been able to kindle; whose source lay deeper in her soul than he had ever reached.

He took her small hand and stroked it quietly. His own hands were cold and moist. He said nothing except:

"You are quite free, dear; entirely free from any promise to me; don't bother; don't mind in the least." He might have said much more, but it did not seem to him worth while. He was letting go of things as he sat there so quietly: of some hopes, a few plans, pictures, intentions, and his whole being was undergoing the wrench of separation.

She said nothing. Love is selfish. She was tasting the exultation of liberty and shrank from inflicting the panacea of conventional phrase or utterance upon a wounded soul.

There were more things than one to trouble Graham. How had his suggestion held and how would it hold? There was no doubt that Faverham was still under the influence of the spell, as Graham detected at once upon first meeting him. The suggestion seemed to have got beyond the professor's control. He shuddered to think of the consequences; yet no course presented itself to him as acceptable but one of inactivity. There was nothing to do but hold off and let the experiment work itself out as it would.

Faverham said to him that night:

"I'm going away in the morning, old fellow. I'm a devilish nice sort of friend if you only knew it. Spare me the shame of explaining. When we meet again in town I hope I shall have pulled myself sufficiently together to understand a certain aberration of mind or morals—or—or—hang me if I know what I'm talking about!"

"I leave in the morning myself," returned Graham. "I may as well tell you that Pauline and I have discovered that we are not of that singleness of thought and that oneness of heart which offer the traditional pretext for two beings to cast their lots in common. We might go up to town together in the morning, if you like."

IV

A few months later Faverham and Pauline were married. Their marriage seemed to mark the culmination of a certain tortuous doubt that possessed itself of the young professor and rendered his days intolerable. "If, if, if!" kept buzzing in his brain: during hours of work; while he walked or rested or read; even throughout the night when he slept.

He remembered Faverham's former dislike for the woman he had married. He realized that the aversion had been dispelled by means of a force whose limitations were as yet unknown; of whose possibilities he himself was wholly ignorant, and whose subtleties were beyond the control of his capacity. "How long will the suggestion hold?" This was the thought which preyed upon him. What if Faverham should awake some morning detesting the woman at his side! What if his infatuation should fade by degrees, imperceptibly; leaving her wrecked, stripped and shivering, to feed upon bitterness till the end of her days!

He visited them often during the first months of their marriage. People who knew them said their union was an ideal one; and for once, people were right. Unconscious impulses were tempering, acting, counteracting each other, inevitably working towards the moulding of these two into the ideal "one" of the poets' dreams.

Graham, when he was with them, watched them stealthily, with a certain cat-like intensity which, had they been less occupied with each other, they might have noticed and resented. It was always with a temporary relief he quitted them; a feeling of thankfulness that the lighted fuse had not yet reached the dynamite in the cellar.

But the torture of uncertainty became almost unbearable and once or twice he went to them with the full intention of removing the suggestion; to see what would happen, and have done with it. But the sight of their content, their mutual sympathy, palsied his resolution, and he left as he had gone to them, the prey of doubt and sharp uneasiness.

One day Graham reasoned it all out with himself. The state of worry in which he lived had become unbearable. He determined to that

evening, remove the suggestion which he had fixed upon Faverham six
months before. If he found that he could do so, then it would easily
follow that he could again renew it, if he thought best. But if the disillusion had to come finally to Faverham, why not have it come now, at
once, at the outset of their married life, before Pauline had too firmly
taken the habit of loving and while he, Graham, might still hold enough
of the old influence to offer a balm to her intellect and her imagination
if not to her heart.

Graham, that night, realized more keenly than ever the change which
Pauline had undergone. He looked at her often as they sat at table, unable to define what was yet so apparent. She was a pretty woman now.
There was color in her face whose contour was softened and embellished
by a peculiarly happy arrangement of her brown hair. The pince-nez
which she had substituted for the rather formidable spectacles, while
depriving her face somewhat of its former student-air, lent it a piquancy
that was very attractive. Her gown was rich as her husband's purse could
buy and its colors were marvelously soft, indefinable, harmonious, making
of the garment a distinct part of herself and her surroundings.

Graham seemed to take his place and fit into this small ménage as
an essential and valued part of it. He certainly felt in no trifling degree
responsible for its existence. That night he felt like some patriarch of
old about to immolate a cherished object upon the altar of science—a
victim to the insatiable God of the Inevitable.

It was not during that pleasant moment of dining, but later in the
evening that Graham chose to tempt once more the power which he had
played with and which, like some venomous, unknown reptile had stung
and wounded him.

They sat drowsily before the remnant of a wood-fire that had spent
itself, and glowed now, and flamed fitfully. Faverham had been reading
aloud by the light of a single lamp, soft lines whose beauty had melted
and entered into their souls like an ointment, soothing them to inward
contemplation rather than moving them to speech and wordy discussion.
The book yet hung from his hand as he stared into the glow of embers.
There was a flurry of rain beating against the window panes. Graham,
buried in the cushioned depths of an arm chair, gazed at Faverham.
Pauline had arisen and she walked slowly to and fro in the apartment,
her garments making a soft, pleasant rustle as she moved in and out of
the shadows. Graham felt that the moment had come.

He arose and went towards the lamp to light the cigar which he took from his pocket. As he stood beside the table he rested a hand carelessly upon the shoulder of his friend.

"Pauline is the woman she was six months ago. She is not charming or attractive," he suggested silently. "Pauline is the woman she was six months ago when she first went to Cedar Branch." Graham lit his cigar at the lamp and returned to his chair in the shadow.

Faverham shivered as if a cold breath had swept by him, and drew his lounge a little nearer the fire. He turned his head and looked at his wife as she passed in her slow walk. Again he gazed into the fire, then restlessly back at his wife; over and over. Graham kept his eyes fixed upon him, silently repeating the suggestion.

Suddenly Faverham arose letting the book fall unnoticed to the floor. Impetuously he approached his wife and taking her in his arms as if he had been alone with her, he held her close, while passionately, almost rudely, he kissed her flushed and startled face, over and over, hungrily. She was panting, and red with confusion and annoyance when he finally released her from his ardent embrace.

"Polly, Polly!" he entreated, "forgive me," for she went and hid her face in the cushion of a chair; "don't mind, dearest. Graham knows how much I love you." He turned and walked towards the fire. He was agitated and passed his hand in an unmeaning fashion across his forehead.

"I don't know when I've made such an ass of myself," he said apologetically in a low tone to Graham. "I hope you'll forgive the tactless display of emotion. The truth is, I feel hardly responsible for it myself; more as if I had obeyed some imperative impulse driving me to an emphatic expression. I admit it was ill-timed," he laughed; "overmastering love is my only excuse."

Graham did not stay much longer. A sense of relief—release, was overpowering him. But he was baffled; he wanted to be alone to puzzle the phenomenon out according to his lights.

He did not lift his umbrella, but rather welcomed the dash of rain in his face as he strode along the glistening pavement. There was a good bit of a walk before him and it was only towards the end of it, when the rain had stopped and a few little stars were blinking down at him, that the truth finally dawned. He remembered that six months ago he had suggested to Faverham that Pauline was charming, captivating, intelligent, honest, worthy of study. But what about love? He had said nothing of that. Love had come unbidden, without a "will you?" or a "by your leave"; and there was love in possession, holding his own against any power of the universe. It was indeed a great illumination to Graham.

He gave rein to his imagination. Recalling Faverham's singular actions under the last hypnotic suggestion, he hugged the fancy that the two forces, love, and the imperative suggestion had waged a short, fierce conflict within the man's subconsciousness, and love had triumphed. He positively believed this.

Graham looked up at the little winking stars and they looked down at him. He bowed in acknowledgement to the supremacy of the moving power which is love; which is life.

Suzette

Ma'me Zidore thrust her head in at the window to tell Suzette that Michel Jardeau was dead.

"Ah, bon Dieu!" cried the girl, clasping her hands, "c' pauv' Michel!"

Ma'me Zidore had heard the news from one of Chartrand's "hands" who was passing with his wagon through the cut-off when she was gathering wood. Her old back was at that moment bent beneath the fagots. She spoke loud and noisily in shrill outbursts. With her unsteady, claw-like fingers she kept brushing aside the wisp of wiry gray hair that fell across her withered cheek.

She knew the story from beginning to end. Michel had boarded the Grand Ecore flat that very morning at daybreak. Jules Bat, the ferry man, had found him waiting on the bank to cross when he carried the doctor over to see Racell's sick child. He could not say whether Michel were drunk or not; he was gruff and ill-humored and seemed to be half asleep. Ma'me Zidore thought it highly probable that the young man had been carousing all night and was still under the influence of liquor when he lost his balance and fell into the water. A half dozen times Jules Bat had called out to him, warning him of his danger, for he persisted in standing at the open end of the boat. Then all in one miserable second over he went like a log. The water was high and turbid as a boiling caldron. Jules Bat saw no more of him than if he had been so many pounds of lead dropped into Red River.

A few people had assembled at their gates across the way, having gathered from snatches of the old woman's penetrating tones that something of interest had happened. She left Suzette standing at the window and crossed the road slant-wise, her whole gaunt frame revealing itself through her scanty, worn garments as the soft, swift breeze struck her old body.

"Michel Jardeau est mort!" she croaked, telling her news so suddenly that the women all cried out in dismay, and little Pavie Ombre, who was just reviving from a spell of sickness, uttered not a sound, but swayed to and fro and sank gently down on her knees in a white, dead faint.

Suzette retired into the room and approaching the tiny mirror that hung above the chest of drawers proceeded to finish her toilet, in which task she had been interrupted by Ma'me Zidore's abrupt announcement of Michel Jardeau's death.

The girl every little while muttered under her breath:

"C' pauv' Michel." Yet her eyes were quite dry; they gleamed, but not with tears. Regret over the loss of "poor Michel" was in nowise distracting her attention from the careful arrangement of a bunch of carnations in the coils of her lustrous brown hair.

Yet she was thinking of him and wondering why she did not care.

A year ago—not so long as that—she had loved him desperately. It began that day at the barbecue when, seized with sudden infatuation, he stayed beside her the whole day long; turning her head with his tones, his glances, and soft touches. Before that day he had seemed to care for little Pavie Ombre who had come out of her faint and was now wailing and sobbing across the way, indifferent to those who might hear her in passing along the road. But after that day he cared no longer for Pavie Ombre or any woman on earth besides Suzette. What a weariness that love had finally become to her, only herself knew.

Why did he persist? why could he not have understood? His attentions had fretted her beyond measure; it was torture to feel him there every Sunday at Mass with his eyes fastened upon her during the entire service. It was not her fault that he had grown desperate—that he was dead.

She turned her head this way and that way before the small glass noting the effect of the carnations in her hair. She gave light touches to the trimmings about her neck and waist, and adjusted the puffed sleeves of her white gown. She moved about the small room with a certain suppressed agitation, returning often to the mirror, and sometimes straying to the window.

Suzette was standing there when a sound arrested her attention—the distant tramp of an advancing herd of cattle. It was what she had been waiting for; what she had been listening for. Yet she trembled through her whole supple frame when she heard it, and the color began to mount into her cheeks. She stayed there at the window looking like a painted picture in its frame.

The house was small and low and stood a little back, with no inclosing fence about the grass plot that reached from the window quite to the edge of the road.

All was still, save for the tramp of the advancing herd. There was no dust, for it had rained during the morning; and Suzette could see them now, approaching with slow, swinging motion and tossing of long horns. Mothers had run out, gathering and snatching their little ones from the road. Baptiste, one of the drivers, shouted hoarsely, cracking his long whip, while a couple of dogs tore madly around snapping and barking.

The other driver, a straight-backed young fellow, sat his horse with familiar ease and carelessness. He wore a white flannel shirt, coarse trousers and leggings and a broad-brimmed gray felt. From the moment his figure appeared in sight, Suzette did not remove her eyes from him. The glow in her cheeks was resplendent now.

She was feeling in anticipation the penetration of his glance, the warmth of his smile when he should see her. He would ride up to the window, no doubt, to say good-by, and she would give him the carnations as a remembrance to keep till he came back.

But what did he mean? She turned a little chill with apprehension. Why, at that precious moment should he bother about the unruly beast that seemed bent upon making trouble? And there was that idiot, that pig of a Baptiste pulling up on the other side of him—talking to him, holding his attention. Mère de Dieu! how she hated and could have killed the fool!

With a single impulse there was a sudden quickened movement of the herd—a dash forward. Then they went! with lowered, tossing heads, rounding the bend that sloped down to the ford.

He had passed! He had not looked at her! He had not thought of her! He would be gone three weeks—three eternities! and every hour freighted with the one bitter remembrance of his indifference!

Suzette turned from the window—her face gray and pinched, with all the warmth and color gone out of it. She flung herself upon the bed and there she cried and moaned with wrenching sobs between.

The carnations drooped from their fastening and lay like a blood-stain upon her white neck.

The Locket

I

One night in autumn a few men were gathered about a fire on the slope of a hill. They belonged to a small detachment of Confederate forces and were awaiting orders to march. Their gray uniforms were worn beyond the point of shabbiness. One of the men was heating something in a tin cup over the embers. Two were lying at full length a little distance away, while a fourth was trying to decipher a letter and had drawn close to the light. He had unfastened his collar and a good bit of his flannel shirt front.

"What's that you got around your neck, Ned?" asked one of the men lying in the obscurity.

Ned—or Edmond—mechanically fastened another button of his shirt and did not reply. He went on reading his letter.

"Is it your sweet heart's picture?"

"Taint no gal's picture," offered the man at the fire. He had removed his tin cup and was engaged in stirring its grimy contents with a small stick. "That's a charm; some kind of hoodoo business that one o' them priests gave him to keep him out o' trouble. I know them Cath'lics. That's how come Frenchy got permoted an never got a scratch sence he's been in the ranks. Hey, French! aint I right?" Edmond looked up absently from his letter.

"What is it?" he asked.

"Aint that a charm you got round your neck?"

"It must be, Nick," returned Edmond with a smile. "I don't know how I could have gone through this year and a half without it."

The letter had made Edmond heart sick and home sick. He stretched himself on his back and looked straight up at the blinking stars. But he

560

was not thinking of them nor of anything but a certain spring day when the bees were humming in the clematis; when a girl was saying good bye to him. He could see her as she unclasped from her neck the locket which she fastened about his own. It was an old fashioned golden locket bearing miniatures of her father and mother with their names and the date of their marriage. It was her most precious earthly possession. Edmond could feel again the folds of the girl's soft white gown, and see the droop of the angel-sleeves as she circled her fair arms about his neck. Her sweet face, appealing, pathetic, tormented by the pain of parting, appeared before him as vividly as life. He turned over, burying his face in his arm and there he lay, still and motionless.

The profound and treacherous night with its silence and semblance of peace settled upon the camp. He dreamed that the fair Octavie brought him a letter. He had no chair to offer her and was pained and embarrassed at the condition of his garments. He was ashamed of the poor food which comprised the dinner at which he begged her to join them.

He dreamt of a serpent coiling around his throat, and when he strove to grasp it the slimy thing glided away from his clutch. Then his dream was clamor.

"Git your duds! you! Frenchy!" Nick was bellowing in his face. There was what appeared to be a scramble and a rush rather than any regulated movement. The hill side was alive with clatter and motion; with sudden up-springing lights among the pines. In the east the dawn was unfolding out of the darkness. Its glimmer was yet dim in the plain below.

"What's it all about?" wondered a big black bird perched in the top of the tallest tree. He was an old solitary and a wise one, yet he was not wise enough to guess what it was all about. So all day long he kept blinking and wondering.

The noise reached far out over the plain and across the hills and awoke the little babes that were sleeping in their cradles. The smoke curled up toward the sun and shadowed the plain so that the stupid birds thought it was going to rain; but the wise one knew better.

"They are children playing a game," thought he. "I shall know more about it if I watch long enough."

At the approach of night they had all vanished away with their din and smoke. Then the old bird plumed his feathers. At last he had understood! With a flap of his great, black wings he shot downward, circling toward the plain.

A man was picking his way across the plain. He was dressed in the garb of a clergyman. His mission was to administer the consolations of religion to any of the prostrate figures in whom there might yet linger a spark of life. A negro accompanied him, bearing a bucket of water and a flask of wine.

There were no wounded here; they had been borne away. But the retreat had been hurried and the vultures and the good Samaritans would have to look to the dead.

There was a soldier—a mere boy—lying with his face to the sky. His hands were clutching the sward on either side and his finger nails were stuffed with earth and bits of grass that he had gathered in his despairing grasp upon life. His musket was gone; he was hatless and his face and clothing were begrimed. Around his neck hung a gold chain and locket. The priest, bending over him, unclasped the chain and removed it from the dead soldier's neck. He had grown used to the terrors of war and could face them unflinchingly; but its pathos, someway, always brought the tears to his old, dim eyes.

The angelus was ringing half a mile away. The priest and the negro knelt and murmured together the evening benediction and a prayer for the dead.

II

The peace and beauty of a spring day had descended upon the earth like a benediction. Along the leafy road which skirted a narrow, tortuous stream in central Louisiana, rumbled an old fashioned cabriolet, much the worse for hard and rough usage over country roads and lanes. The fat, black horses went in a slow, measured trot, notwithstanding constant urging on the part of the fat, black coachman. Within the vehicle were seated the fair Octavie and her old friend and neighbor, Judge Pillier, who had come to take her for a morning drive.

Octavie wore a plain black dress, severe in its simplicity. A narrow belt held it at the waist and the sleeves were gathered into close fitting wristbands. She had discarded her hoopskirt and appeared not unlike a nun. Beneath the folds of her bodice nestled the old locket. She never displayed it now. It had returned to her sanctified in her eyes; made precious as material things sometimes are by being forever identified with a significant moment of one's existence.

A hundred times she had read over the letter with which the locket had come back to her. No later than that morning she had again pored over it. As she sat beside the window, smoothing the letter out upon her knee, heavy and spiced odors stole in to her with the songs of birds and the humming of insects in the air.

She was so young and the world was so beautiful that there came over her a sense of unreality as she read again and again the priest's letter. He told of that autumn day drawing to its close, with the gold and the red fading out of the west, and the night gathering its shadows to cover the faces of the dead. Oh! She could not believe that one of those dead was her own! with visage uplifted to the gray sky in an agony of supplication. A spasm of resistance and rebellion seized and swept over her. Why was the spring here with its flowers and its seductive breath if he was dead! Why was she here! What further had she to do with life and the living!

Octavie had experienced many such moments of despair, but a blessed resignation had never failed to follow, and it fell then upon her like a mantle and enveloped her.

"I shall grow old and quiet and sad like poor Aunt Tavie," she murmured to herself as she folded the letter and replaced it in the secretary. Already she gave herself a little demure air like her Aunt Tavie. She walked with a slow glide in unconscious imitation of Mademoiselle Tavie whom some youthful affliction had robbed of earthly compensation while leaving her in possession of youth's illusions.

As she sat in the old cabriolet beside the father of her dead lover, again there came to Octavie the terrible sense of loss which had assailed her so often before. The soul of her youth clamored for its rights; for a share in the world's glory and exultation. She leaned back and drew her veil a little closer about her face. It was an old black veil of her Aunt Tavie's. A whiff of dust from the road had blown in and she wiped her cheeks and her eyes with her soft, white handkerchief, a homemade handkerchief, fabricated from one of her old fine muslin petticoats.

"Will you do me the favor, Octavie," requested the judge in the courteous tone which he never abandoned, "to remove that veil which you wear. It seems out of harmony, someway, with the beauty and promise of the day."

The young girl obediently yielded to her old companion's wish and unpinning the cumbersome, sombre drapery from her bonnet, folded it neatly and laid it upon the seat in front of her.

"Ah! that is better; far better!" he said in a tone expressing unbounded relief. "Never put it on again, dear." Octavie felt a little hurt; as if he wished to debar her from share and parcel in the burden of affliction which had been placed upon all of them. Again she drew forth the old muslin handkerchief.

They had left the big road and turned into a level plain which had formerly been an old meadow. There were clumps of thorn trees here and there, gorgeous in their spring radiance. Some cattle were grazing off in the distance in spots where the grass was tall and luscious. At the far end of the meadow was the towering lilac hedge, skirting the lane that led to Judge Pillier's house, and the scent of its heavy blossoms met them like a soft and tender embrace of welcome.

As they neared the house the old gentleman placed an arm around the girl's shoulders and turning her face up to him he said: "Do you not think that on a day like this, miracles might happen? When the whole earth is vibrant with life, does it not seem to you, Octavie, that heaven might for once relent and give us back our dead?" He spoke very low, advisedly, and impressively. In his voice was an old quaver which was not habitual and there was agitation in every line of his visage. She gazed at him with eyes that were full of supplication and a certain terror of joy.

They had been driving through the lane with the towering hedge on one side and the open meadow on the other. The horses had somewhat quickened their lazy pace. As they turned into the avenue leading to the house, a whole choir of feathered songsters fluted a sudden torrent of melodious greeting from their leafy hiding places.

Octavie felt as if she had passed into a stage of existence which was like a dream, more poignant and real than life. There was the old gray house with its sloping eaves. Amid the blur of green, and dimly, she saw familiar faces and heard voices as if they came from far across the fields, and Edmond was holding her. Her dead Edmond; her living Edmond, and she felt the beating of his heart against her and the agonizing rapture of his kisses striving to awake her. It was as if the spirit of life and the awakening spring had given back the soul to her youth and bade her rejoice.

It was many hours later that Octavie drew the locket from her bosom and looked at Edmond with a questioning appeal in her glance.

"It was the night before an engagement," he said. "In the hurry of the encounter, and the retreat next day, I never missed it till the fight was over. I thought of course I had lost it in the heat of the struggle, but it was stolen."

"Stolen," she shuddered, and thought of the dead soldier with his face uplifted to the sky in an agony of supplication.

Edmond said nothing; but he thought of his messmate; the one who had lain far back in the shadow; the one who had said nothing.

A Morning Walk

Archibald had been up many hours. He had breakfasted, and now he was taking a morning stroll along the village street, which was little other than a high ledge cut into the mountain-side.

He was forty or thereabout, but did not resent being thought older, and never corrected the miscalculations of acquaintances when they added a half-score years to his age. He was tall, with broad shoulders, a straight back, and legs that took long, energetic strides. His hair was light and rather thin; his face strong and rugged from exposure, and his eyes narrow and observant. He beat about with his stick as he walked, turning over pebbles and small stones, and sometimes uprooting a weed or flower that grew in his path.

The village sprawled along the gradual slope of a mountain side. The few streets rising one above the other were irregular in their tortuous effort to cuddle up to the houses that were built hap-hazard and wide apart. Flights of wooden steps, black and weather-stained, connected the streets with each other. Fruit trees were in bloom, making a pink and white blur against the blue sky and the gray, rocky slopes. Birds were piping in the hedges. It had rained, but the sun was shining now and riotous odors were abroad; they met him with every velvety gust that softly beat into his face. Now and again he straightened his shoulders and shook his head with an impatient movement, as might some proud animal which rebels against an unaccustomed burden.

The spring was nothing new to him, nor were its sounds, its perfumes, its colors; nor was its tender and caressing breath; but, for some unaccountable reason, these were reaching him to-day through unfamiliar channels.

Archibald had started out for a walk, not because the day was beautiful and alluring but for the healthful exercise, and for the purpose of gathering into his lungs the amount of pure oxygen needed to keep his body in good working condition. For he leaned decidedly toward practical science; of sentiment he knew little, except what he gathered from a class of speculative philosophers. He liked to read musty books about musty peoples long since gathered to the earth and the elements. He liked to observe insect life at close range, and when he gathered flowers it was usually to dismember their delicate, sweet bodies for the purpose of practical and profitable investigation.

But, strangely enough, he saw only the color of the blossoms this morning, and noted their perfumes. The butterflies floated unmolested within his reach, and the jumping grasshoppers were not afraid. The spring day was saying "good morning" to him in a new, delicious way, while the blood in his veins beat a response.

A little ahead of him Archibald suddenly observed a huge bunch of white lilies ascending apparently from the sepulchral depths of the earth. In fact they were ascending one of the steep flights of wooden steps which led up from the street below. A young girl's face could be seen between the long stems and the blossoms. In another moment she stood on the edge of the road, panting a little. She was pretty, as healthful girls of twenty usually are. She was unusually pretty at that moment; her face, peeping over the lilies, was like another flower that had gathered its hues from the roseate dawn and the glimmer of the dew.

"Good morning, Mr. Archibald," she called in her sweet, high, village voice.

"Good morning, Jane; good morning," he responded with unusual cordiality.

"Oh! it isn't Jane," she laughed, "it's Lucy. L-U-C-Y Lucy. Last week you persistently thought I was my sister Amanda. This morning I am my cousin Jane. Tomorrow I suppose it will be 'good morning, Mrs. Brockett;' or 'Howdy, Granny Ball!' "

A more delicately attuned ear than Archibald's might have detected a lurking note of vexation in the girl's saucy speech. He flushed with annoyance at his own awkwardness. Yesterday he would have smiled with condescending inattention, and probably called her "Amelia" at their next meeting.

"Yes," she was thinking, as they walked together down the road, "if I were a stone or a weed or some nasty old beetle or other, he would know my name well enough." She was one of a group of girls whom he had seen grow up in almost daily association with his own nieces and nephews at home. It was not to be expected that he could disassociate them. He regretted that there had been made no arbitrary classification of the family of "Girls," whereby a man of studious instincts and mental preoccupation might be able to identify the individual at sight, and even name it at a moment's notice. However, he felt quite sure that he would not soon forget that it was Lucy who carried the lilies and bade him good morning, like a second vision of spring.

"Let me carry your flowers," he offered; not through any tardy spirit of gallantry; solely because he knew better than she how to handle a bunch of blossoms, and it pained him to see the big wax-like petals bruised and jostled. The odor of the flowers was heavy and penetrating, like the fumes of a subtle intoxicant that reached Archibald's brain, and wrought and wove fantastic thoughts and visions there. He looked down into the girl's face, and her soft, curved lips made him think of peaches that he had bitten; of grapes that he had tasted; of a cup's rim from which he had sometimes sipped wine.

They walked down the grassy slope, the girl chatting the while, and Archibald saying little. Lucy was on her way to church. It was Easter morning, and the bells had been calling and clamoring to them as they went along. At the vestibule door she turned and delivered him of his burden of flowers. But Archibald did not leave there, as she expected he would. He followed her into the church; he did not know why, and for once he did not care to investigate his motives. When she had disposed of the lilies, turning them over to a sanctuary boy, she came and seated herself with the congregation, and Archibald, who had stood waiting, placed himself beside her. He assumed no reverential attitude, nor did he bow his head with any pretense of devotion. His presence caused much wonder, and glances and whispers of speculation were exchanged. Archibald did not notice, and would not have minded them if he had noticed.

The day was warm, and some of the stained glass windows were open. The sunlight came in, and the shadows of quivering leaves played upon the casement through which he gazed. A bird was singing among the branches.

During the prayers he was inattentive, and to the singing he lent no ear. But when the minister turned to address the assembly, Archibald wondered what he was going to say. The man stayed a long moment with his slow, earnest glance sweeping the congregation, then he uttered solemnly and impressively: "I am the Resurrection and the Life."

Another long moment of silence followed; and, lifting his head, he reiterated in louder, clearer tones than before, "I am the Resurrection and the Life."

This was his text. It fell upon ears that had heard it before. It crept into the consciousness of Archibald, sitting there. As he gathered it into his soul a vision of life came with it; the poet's vision, of the life that is within and the life that is without, pulsing in unison, breathing the harmony of an undivided existence.

He listened to no further words of the minister. He entered into himself and he preached unto himself a sermon in his own heart, as he gazed from the window through which the song came and where the leafy shadows quivered.

An Egyptian Cigarette

My friend, the Architect, who is something of a traveler, was showing us various curios which he had gathered during a visit to the Orient.

"Here is something for you," he said, picking up a small box and turning it over in his hand. "You are a cigarette-smoker; take this home with you. It was given to me in Cairo by a species of fakir, who fancied I had done him a good turn."

The box was covered with glazed, yellow paper, so skillfully gummed as to appear to be all one piece. It bore no label, no stamp—nothing to indicate its contents.

"How do you know they are cigarettes?" I asked, taking the box and turning it stupidly around as one turns a sealed letter and speculates before opening it.

"I only know what he told me," replied the Architect, "but it is easy enough to determine the question of his integrity." He handed me a sharp, pointed paper-cutter, and with it I opened the lid as carefully as possible.

The box contained six cigarettes, evidently hand-made. The wrappers were of pale-yellow paper, and the tobacco was almost the same color. It was of finer cut than the Turkish or ordinary Egyptian, and threads of it stuck out at either end.

"Will you try one now, Madam?" asked the Architect, offering to strike a match.

"Not now and not here," I replied, "after the coffee, if you will permit me to slip into your smoking-den. Some of the women here detest the odor of cigarettes."

The smoking-room lay at the end of a short, curved passage. Its

570

appointments were exclusively Oriental. A broad, low window opened out upon a balcony that overhung the garden. From the divan upon which I reclined, only the swaying tree-tops could be seen. The maple leaves glistened in the afternoon sun. Beside the divan was a low stand which contained the complete paraphernalia of a smoker. I was feeling quite comfortable, and congratulated myself upon having escaped for a while the incessant chatter of the women that reached me faintly.

I took a cigarette and lit it, placing the box upon the stand just as the tiny clock, which was there, chimed in silvery strokes the hour of five.

I took one long inspiration of the Egyptian cigarette. The gray-green smoke arose in a small puffy column that spread and broadened, that seemed to fill the room. I could see the maple leaves dimly, as if they were veiled in a shimmer of moonlight. A subtle, disturbing current passed through my whole body and went to my head like the fumes of disturbing wine. I took another deep inhalation of the cigarette.

"Ah! the sand has blistered my cheek! I have lain here all day with my face in the sand. To-night, when the everlasting stars are burning, I shall drag myself to the river."

He will never come back.

Thus far I followed him; with flying feet; with stumbling feet; with hands and knees, crawling; and outstretched arms, and here I have fallen in the sand.

The sand has blistered my cheek; it has blistered all my body, and the sun is crushing me with hot torture. There is shade beneath yonder cluster of palms.

I shall stay here in the sand till the hour and the night comes.

I laughed at the oracles and scoffed at the stars when they told that after the rapture of life I would open my arms inviting death, and the waters would envelop me.

Oh! how the sand blisters my cheek! and I have no tears to quench the fire. The river is cool and the night is not far distant.

I turned from the gods and said: "There is but one; Bardja is my god." That was when I decked myself with lilies and wove flowers into a garland and held him close in the frail, sweet fetters.

He will never come back. He turned upon his camel as he rode away. He turned and looked at me crouching here and laughed, showing his gleaming white teeth.

Whenever he kissed me and went away he always came back again.

Whenever he flamed with fierce anger and left me with stinging words, he always came back. But to-day he neither kissed me nor was he angry. He only said:

"Oh! I am tired of fetters, and kisses, and you. I am going away. You will never see me again. I am going to the great city where men swarm like bees. I am going beyond, where the monster stones are rising heavenward in a monument for the unborn ages. Oh! I am tired. You will see me no more."

And he rode away on his camel. He smiled and showed his cruel white teeth as he turned to look at me crouching here.

How slow the hours drag! It seems to me that I have lain here for days in the sand, feeding upon despair. Despair is bitter and it nourishes resolve.

I hear the wings of a bird flapping above my head, flying low, in circles.

The sun is gone.

The sand has crept between my lips and teeth and under my parched tongue.

If I raise my head, perhaps I shall see the evening star.

Oh! the pain in my arms and legs! My body is sore and bruised as if broken. Why can I not rise and run as I did this morning? Why must I drag myself thus like a wounded serpent, twisting and writhing?

The river is near at hand. I hear it—I see it—Oh! the sand! Oh! the shine! How cool! how cold!

The water! the water! In my eyes, my ears, my throat! It strangles me! Help! will the gods not help me?

Oh! the sweet rapture of rest! There is music in the Temple. And here is fruit to taste. Bardja came with the music—The moon shines and the breeze is soft—A garland of flowers—let us go into the King's garden and look at the blue lily, Bardja.

The maple leaves looked as if a silvery shimmer enveloped them. The gray-green smoke no longer filled the room. I could hardly lift the lids of my eyes. The weight of centuries seemed to suffocate my soul that struggled to escape, to free itself and breathe.

I had tasted the depths of human despair.

The little clock upon the stand pointed to a quarter past five. The cigarettes still reposed in the yellow box. Only the stub of the one I had smoked remained. I had laid it in the ash tray.

As I looked at the cigarettes in their pale wrappers, I wondered what other visions they might hold for me; what might I not find in their mystic fumes? Perhaps a vision of celestial peace; a dream of hopes fulfilled; a taste of rapture, such as had not entered into my mind to conceive.

I took the cigarettes and crumpled them between my hands. I walked to the window and spread my palms wide. The light breeze caught up the golden threads and bore them writhing and dancing far out among the maple leaves.

My friend, the Architect, lifted the curtain and entered, bringing me a second cup of coffee.

"How pale you are!" he exclaimed, solicitously. "Are you not feeling well?"

"A little the worse for a dream," I told him.

A Family Affair

The moment that the wagon rattled out of the yard away to the station, Madame Solisainte settled herself into a state of nervous expectancy.

She was superabundantly fat; and her body accommodated itself to the huge chair in which she sat, filling up curves and crevices like water poured into a mould. She was clad in an ample muslin *peignoir* sprigged with brown. Her cheeks were flabby, her mouth thin-lipped and decisive. Her eyes were small, watchful, and at the same time timid. Her brown hair, streaked with gray, was arranged in a bygone fashion, a narrow mesh being drawn back from the centre of the forehead to conceal a bald spot, and the sides plastered down smooth over her small, close ears.

The room in which she sat was large and uncarpeted. There were handsome and massive pieces of furniture decorating the apartment, and a magnificent brass clock stood on the mantelpiece.

Madame Solisainte sat at a back window which overlooked the yard, the brick kitchen—a little removed from the house—and the field road which led down to the negro quarters. She was unable to leave her chair. It was an affair of importance to get her out of bed in the morning, and an equally arduous task to put her back there at night.

It was a sore affliction to the old woman to be thus incapacitated during her latter years, and rendered unable to watch and control her household affairs. She was sure that she was being robbed continuously and on all sides. This conviction was nourished and kept alive by her confidential servant, Dimple, a very black girl of sixteen, who trod softly about on her bare feet and had thereby made herself unpopular in the kitchen and down at the quarters.

The notion had entered Madame Solisainte's head to have one of her nieces come up from New Orleans and stay with her. She thought it would be doing the niece and her family a great kindness, and would furthermore be an incalculable saving to herself in many ways, and far cheaper than hiring a housekeeper.

There were four nieces, not too well off, with whom she was indifferently acquainted. In selecting one of these to make her home on the plantation she exercised no choice, leaving that matter to her sister and the girls, to be settled among them.

It was Bosey who consented to go to her aunt. Her mother spelled her name Bosé. She herself spelled it Bosey. But as often as not she was called plain Bose. It was she who was sent, because, as her mother wrote to Madame Solisainte, Bosé was a splendid manager, a most excellent housekeeper, and moreover possessed a temperament of such rare amiability that none could help being cheered and enlivened by her presence.

What she did not write was that none of the other girls would entertain the notion for an instant of making even a temporary abiding place with their *Tante* Félicie. And Bosey's consent was only wrung from her with the understanding that the undertaking was purely experimental, and that she bound herself by no cast-iron obligations.

Madame Solisainte had sent the wagon to the station for her niece, and was impatiently awaiting its return.

"It's no sign of the wagon yet, Dimple? You don't see it? You don't year it coming?"

"No'um; 'tain't no sign. De train des 'bout lef' de station. I yeard it w'istle." Dimple stood on the back porch beside her mistress' open window. She wore a calico dress so skimp and inadequate that her growing figure was bursting through the rents and apertures. She was constantly pinning it at the back of the waist with a bent safety-pin which was forever giving way. The task of pinning her dress and biting the old brass safety-pin into shape occupied a great deal of her time.

"It's true," Madame said. "I recommend to Daniel to drive those mule' very slow in this hot weather. They are not strong, those mule'."

"He drive 'em slow 'nough long 's he's in the fiel' road!" exclaimed Dimple. "Time he git roun' in de big road whar you kain't see 'im—uh! uh! he make' dem mule' fa'r' lope!"

Madame tightened her lips and blinked her eyes. She rarely replied otherwise to these disclosures of Dimple, but they sank into her soul and festered there.

The cook—in reality a big-boned field hand—came in with pans and pails to get out the things for supper. Madame kept her provisions right there under her nose in a large closet, or cupboard, which she had had built in the side of the room. A small supply of butter was in a jar that stood on the hearth, and the eggs were kept in a basket that hung on a peg near by.

Dimple came in and unlocked the cupboard, taking the keys from her mistress' bag. She gave out a little flour, a little meal, a cupful of coffee, some sugar and a piece of bacon. Four eggs were wanted for a pudding, but Madame thought that two would be enough, finally compromising, however, upon three.

Miss Bosey Brantonniere arrived at her aunt's house with three trunks, a large, circular, tin bathtub, a bundle of umbrellas and sunshades, and a small dog. She was a pretty, energetic-looking girl, with her chin in the air, tastefully dressed in the latest fashion, and dispersing an atmosphere of bustle and importance about her. Daniel had driven her up the field road, depositing her at the back entrance, where Madame, from her window, commanded a complete view of her arrival.

"I thought you would have sent the carriage for me, *Tante* Félicie, but Daniel tells me you have no carriage," said the girl after the first greetings were over. She had had her trunks taken to her room, the tub slipped under the bed, and now she sat fondling the dog and talking to *Tante* Félicie.

The old lady shook her head dismally and her lips curled into a disparaging smile.

"Oh! no, no! The ol' carriage 'as been sol' ages ago to Zéphire Lablatte. It was falling to piece' in the shed. Me—I never stir f'um w'ere you see me; it is good two year' since I 'ave been inside the church, let alone to go *en promenade*."

"Well, I'm going to take all care and bother off your shoulders, *Tante* Félicie," uttered the girl cheerfully. "I'm going to brighten things up for you, and we'll see how quickly you'll improve. Why, in less than two months I'll have you on your feet, going about as spry as anybody."

Madame was far less hopeful. "My ol' mother was the same," she replied with dejected resignation. "Nothing could 'elp her. She lived many year' like you see me; your mamma mus' 'ave often tol' you."

Mrs. Brantonniere had never related to the girls anything disparaging concerning their Aunt Félicie, but other members of the family had been less considerate, and Bosey had often been told of her aunt's avarice and grasping ways. How she had laid her clutch upon her mother's belongings, taking undisputed possession by the force of audacity alone. The girl could not help thinking it must have been while her grandmother sat so helpless in her huge chair that *Tante* Félicie had made herself mistress of the situation. But she was not one to harbor malice. She felt very sorry for *Tante* Félicie, so afflicted in her childless old age.

Madame lay long awake that night troubled someway over the advent of this niece from New Orleans, who was not precisely what she had expected. She did not like the excess of trunks, the bathtub and the dog, all of which savored of extravagance. Nor did she like the chin in the air, which indicated determination and promised trouble.

Dimple was warned next morning to say nothing to her mistress concerning a surprise which Miss Bosey had in store for her. This surprise was that, instead of being deposited in her accustomed place at the back window, where she could keep an eye upon her people, Madame was installed at the front-room window that looked out toward the live oaks and along a leafy, sleepy road that was seldom used.

"*Jamais! Jamais!* it will never do! *Pas possible!*" cried out the old lady with helpless excitement when she perceived what was about to be done to her.

"You'll do just as I say, *Tante* Félicie," said Bosey, with sprightly determination. "I'm here to take care of you and make you comfortable, and I'm going to do it. Now, instead of looking out on that hideous back yard, full of dirty little darkies, and pigs and chickens wallowing round, here you have this sweet, peaceful view whenever you look out of the window. Now, here comes Dimple with the magazines and things. Bring them right here, Dimple, and lay them on the table beside Ma'me Félicie. I brought these up from the city expressly for you, *Tante*, and I have a whole trunkful more when you are through with them."

Dimple was entering, staggering with arms full of books and periodicals of all sizes, shapes and colors. The strain of carrying the weight of literature had caused the safety-pin to give way, and Dimple greatly feared it might have fallen and been lost.

"So, *Tante* Félicie, you'll have nothing to do but read and enjoy yourself. Here are some French books mamma sent you, something by Daudet, something by Maupassant and a lot more. Here, let me brighten up your spectacles." She brightened the old lady's glasses with a piece of thin tissue paper which fell from one of the books.

"And now, Madame Solisainte, you give me all the keys! Turn them right over, and I'll go out and make myself thoroughly acquainted with everything." Madame spasmodically clutched the bag that swung to the arm of her chair.

"Oh! a whole bagful!" exclaimed the girl, gently but firmly disengaging it from her aunt's claw-like fingers. "My, what an undertaking I have before me! Dimple had better show me round this morning until I get thoroughly acquainted. You can knock on the floor with your stick when you want her. Come along, Dimple. Fasten your dress." The girl was scanning the floor for the safety-pin, which she found out in the hall.

During all of Madame Solisainte's days no one had ever spoken to her with the authority which this young woman assumed. She did not know what to make of it. She felt that she should have revolted at once against being thus banished to the front room. She should have spoken out and maintained possession of her keys when demanded, with the spirit of a highway robber, to give them up. She pounded her stick on the floor with loud and sudden energy. Dimple appeared with inquisitive eyes.

"Dimple," said Madame, "tell Miss Bosé to please 'ave the kin'ness an sen' me back my bag of key'."

Dimple vanished and returned almost on the instant.

"Miss Bosey 'low don't you bodda. Des you go on lookin' at de picters. She ain' gwine let nuttin' happen to de keys."

After an uneasy interval Madame recalled the girl.

"Dimple, if you could look in the bag an' bring me my armoire key— you know it—the brass one. Do not let on as though I would want that key in partic'lar."

"De bag hangin' on her arm. She got de string twis' roun' her wris'," reported Dimple presently. Madame Félicie inwardly fumed with impotent rage.

"W'at is she doing, Dimple?" she asked uneasily.

"She got de cubbud do's fling wide open. She standin' on a cha'r lookin' in de corners an' behin' eve'ything."

"Dimple!" called out Bosey from the far room. And away flew Dimple, who had not been so pleasingly agitated since the previous Christmas.

After a little while, of her own accord she stole noiselessly back into the room where Madame Félicie sat in speechless wrath beside the table of books. She closed the door behind her, rolled her eyes, and spoke in a hoarse whisper:

"She done fling 'way de barrel o' meal; 'low it all fill up wid weevils."

"Weevil'!" cried out her mistress.

"Yas'um, weevils; 'low it plumb sp'ilt. 'Low it on'y fitten fo' de chickens an' hogs; 'tain't fitten fo' folks. She done make Dan'el roll it out on de gal'ry."

"Weevil'!" reiterated Madame Félicie, tremulous with suppressed excitement. "Bring me some of that meal in a saucer, Dimple. Don't let on anything."

She and Dimple bent over the cup of meal which the girl brought concealed under her skirt.

"Do you see any weevil', you, Dimple?"

"No'um." Dimple smelled it, and Madame felt the sample of meal and rolled a pinch or two between her fingers. It was lumpy, musty and old.

"She got'Susan out dah helpin' her," insinuated Dimple, "an' Sam an' Dan'el; all helpin' her."

"*Bon Dieu!* it won't be a grain of sugar left, a bar of soap—nothing! nothing! Go watch, Dimple. Don't stan' there like a stick."

"She 'low she gwine sen' Susan back to wuk in de fiel'," went on Dimple, heedless of her mistress' admonition. "She 'low Susan don' know how to cook. Susan say she willin' to go back, her. An' Miss Bosey, she ax Dan'el ef he know a fus'-class cook, w'at kin brile chicken an' steak an' make good soup, an' waffles, an' rolls, an' fricassée, an' dessert, an' custud, an sich."

She passed her tongue over a slobbering lip. "Dan'el say his wife Mandy done cook fo' de pa'tic'lest people in town, but she don' wuk cheap 'nough fo' Ma'me Félicie. An' Miss Bosey, she 'low it don' make no odd' 'bout de price, 'long she git hole o' somebody w'at know how to cook."

Madame's fingers worked nervously at the illuminated cover of a magazine. She said nothing. Only tightened her lips and blinked her small eyes.

When Bosey thrust her head in at the door to inquire how "*Tantine*" was getting on, the old lady fumbled at the books with a pretense of having been occupied with looking at them.

"That's right, *Tante* Félicie! You look as comfortable as can be. I wanted to make you a nice glass of lemonade, but Susan tells me there isn't a lemon on the place. I told Fannie's boy to bring up half a box of lemons from Lablatte's store in the handcart. There's nothing healthier than lemonade in summer. And he's going to bring a chunk of ice, too. We'll have to order ice from town after this." She had on a white apron over her gingham dress, and her sleeves were rolled to the elbows.

"I detes' lemonade; it is bad for *mon estomac*," interposed Madame vehemently. "We 'ave no use in the worl' for lemon', an' there is no place vere to keep ice. Tell Fannie's boy never min' about lemon' an' ice."

"Oh, he's gone long ago! And as for the ice, why, Daniel says he can make me a box lined with sawdust—he made one for Doctor Godfrey. We can keep it under the back porch." And away she went, the embodiment of the thoroughgoing, bustling little housewife. Somewhat past noon, Dimple came in with an air of importance, removed the books, and spread a white damask cloth upon the table. It was like spreading a red cloth before a sullen bull. Madame's eyes glared at the cloth.

"W'ere did you get that?" she asked as if she would have annihilated Dimple on the spot.

"Miss Bosey, she tuck it out de big press; tuck some mo' out; 'low she kain't eat on dat meal-sack w'at we alls calls de table-clot'e." The damask cloth bore the initials of Madame's mother, embroidered in a corner.

"She done kilt two dem young pullets in de *basse-cour*," went on Dimple, like a croaking raven. "Mandy come lopin' up f'om de quarters time Dan'el told 'er. She yonder, rarin' roun' in de kitchen. Dey done sent fo' some sto' lard an' bakin' powders down to Lablatte's. Fannie's boy, he ben totin' all mornin'. De cubbud done look lak a sto'."

"Dimple!" called Bosey in the distance.

When she returned it was with a pompous air, her head uplifted, and stepping carefully like a fat chicken. She bore a tray weighted with a repast such as she had never before in her life served to Madame Solisainte.

Mandy had outdone herself. She had broiled the breast of a pullet to a turn. She had fried the potatoes after a New Orleans receipt, and had made a pudding of richest ingredients of her own invention which had given her a name in the parish. There were two milky-looking poached eggs, and the biscuits were as light as snowflakes and the color of gold. The forks and spoons were of massive silver, also bearing the initials of Madame's mother. They had been reclaimed from the press with the table linen.

Under this new, strange influence Madame Solisainte seemed to have been deprived of the power of asserting her will. There was an occasional outburst like the flare of a smouldering fire, but she was outwardly timid and submissive. Only when she was alone with her young handmaid did she speak her mind.

Bosey took special care in arranging her aunt's toilet one morning not long after her arrival. She fastened a sheer white 'kerchief (which she found in the press) about the old lady's neck. She powdered her face from her own box of *duvet de cygne* ; and she gave her a fine linen handkerchief (which she also found in the press), sprinkling it from the bottle of cologne water which she had brought from New Orleans. She filled the vase upon the table with fresh flowers, and dusted and rearranged the books there.

Madame had been moving forward the bookmark in the novel to pretend that she was reading it.

These unusual preparations were explained an hour or two later, when Bosey introduced into Madame Solisainte's presence their neighbor, Doctor Godfrey. He was a youngish, good-looking man, with a loud, cheery voice and a superabundance of animal spirits. He seemed to carry about with him the very atmosphere of health and to dispense it broadcast in invisible waves.

"Do you see, *Tante* Félicie, how I think of everything? When I saw, last night, the suffering you endured at being put to bed, I decided that you ought to be under a physician's treatment. So the first thing I did this morning was to send a messenger for Doctor Godfrey, and here he is!"

Madame glared at him as he drew up a chair on the opposite side of the table and began to talk about how long it was since he had seen her.

"I do not need a physician!" she cried in tones of exasperation, looking from one to the other. "All the physician' in the worl' cannot 'elp me. My mother was the same; she try all the physician' of the parish. She went to the 'ot spring', to *la Nouvelle Orleans*, an' she die' at las' in this chair. Nothing will 'elp me."

"That is for me to say, Madame Solisainte," said the Doctor, with cheerful assurance. "It is a good idea of your niece's that you should place yourself under a physician's care. I don't say mine, understand—there are many excellent physicians in the parish—but some one ought to look after you, if it is only to keep you in comfortable condition."

Madame blinked at him under lowered brows. She was thinking of his bill for this visit, and determined that he should not make a second one. She saw ruin staring her in the face, and felt as if she were being borne along on a raging torrent of extravagance to meet it.

Bosey had already explained Madame's symptoms to the Doctor, and he said he would send or bring over a preparation which Madame Solisainte must take night and morning till he saw fit to alter or discontinue it. Then he glanced at the magazines, while he and the girl engaged in a lively conversation across Madame's chair. His eyes sparkled with animation as he looked at Bosey, as fresh and sweet in her pink dimity gown as one of the flowers there on the table.

He came very often, and Madame grew sick with apprehension and uncertainty, unable to distinguish between his professional and social visits. At first she refused to take his medicine until Bosey stood over her one evening with a spoonful, gently but firmly expressing a determination to stand there till morning, if necessary, and Madame consented to swallow the mixture. The Doctor took Bosey out driving in his new buggy behind two fast trotters. The first time, after she had driven away, Madame Félicie charged Dimple to go into Miss Bosey's room and search everywhere for the bag of keys. But they were not to be found.

"She mus' kiard 'em wid 'er. She all time got 'em twis' roun' 'er arm. I believe she sleep wid 'em twis' roun' 'er arm," offered Dimple in explanation of her failure.

Unable to find the keys, she turned to examining the young girl's dainty belongings—such as were not under lock. She crept back into Madame Félicie's room, carrying a lace-frilled parasol which she silently held out for Madame's inspection. The lace was simple and inexpensive, but the old woman shuddered at sight of it as if it had been the rarest d'Alençon.

Perceiving the impression created by the gay sunshade, Dimple next brought in a pair of slippers with spangled toes, a fine pair of stockings that hung on the back of a chair, an embroidered petticoat, and finally a silk waist. She brought the articles one by one, with a certain solemnity rendered doubly impressive by her silence.

Dimple was wearing her best dress—a red calico with ruffles and puffed sleeves (Miss Bosey had compelled her to discard the other). As a consequence of this holiday attire Dimple gave herself Sunday airs, and passed her time hanging to the gallery post or doubling her body across the bannister rail.

Bosey grew more and more prolific in devices for her Aunt Félicie's comfort and entertainment. She invited Madame's old friends to visit her, singly and in groups; to spend the day—in some instances several days.

She began to have company herself. The young gentlemen and girls of the parish came from miles around to pay their respects. She was of a hospitable turn, and dispensed iced lemonade on such occasions, and sangaree—Lablatte having ordered a case of red wine from the city. There was constant baking of cakes going on in the kitchen, Daniel's wife surpassing all her former efforts in that direction.

Bosey gave lawn parties, with the Chinese lanterns all festooned among the oaks, with three musicians from the quarters playing the fiddle, the guitar and accordion on the gallery, right under Madame Solisainte's nose. She gave a ball and dressed *Tante* Félicie up for the occasion in a silk *peignoir* which she had had made in the city as a surprise.

The Doctor took Bosey driving or horseback riding every other day. He all but lived at Madame Solisainte's, and was in danger of losing all his practice, till Bosey, in mercy, promised to marry him.

She kept her engagement a secret from *Tante* Félicie, pursuing her avocation of the ministering angel up to the very day of her departure for the city to make preparations for her approaching marriage.

A beatitude, a beneficent joy settled upon Madame when Bosey announced her engagement to the Doctor and her intention to leave the plantation that afternoon.

"Oh! You can't imagine, *Tante* Félicie, how I regret to leave you—just as I was getting things so comfortably and pleasantly settled about you, too. If you want, perhaps Fifine or sister Adèle would come——"

"No! no!" cried Madame in shrill protest. "Nothing of the kin'! I insist, let them stay w'ere they are. I am ole; I am use' to my ways. It is not 'ard for me to be alone. I will not year of it!"

Madame could have sung for very joy as she listened all morning to the bustle of her niece's packing. She even petted doggie in her exuberance, for she had aimed many a blow at him with her stick when he had had the temerity to trust himself alone with her.

The trunks and the bathtub were sent away at noon. The clatter accompanying their departure sounded like sweet music in Madame Solisainte's ears. It was with almost a feeling of affection that she embraced her niece when the girl came and kissed her good-by. The Doctor was going to drive his *fiancée* to the station in his buggy.

He told Madame Félicie that he felt like an archangel. In reality, he looked demented with happiness and excitement. She was as suave as honey to him. She was thinking that in the character of a nephew he would not have the indelicacy to present a bill for professional services.

The Doctor hurried out to turn the horses and to get ready the lap-robe to spread over the knees of his divinity. Bosey looked as dainty as the day she had made her appearance, in the same brown linen gown and jaunty traveling hat. There was a fathomless look in her blue eyes.

"And now, *Tante* Félicie," she said finally, "here is your bag of keys. You will find everything in perfect order, and I hope you will be satisfied. All the purchases have been entered in the book—you will find Lablatte's bills and everything correct. But, by the way, *Tante* Félicie, I want to tell you—I have made an equal division of grandmother's silver and table linen and jewels which I found in the strong box, and sent them to mamma. You know yourself it was only just; mamma had as much right to them as you. So, good-by, *Tante* Félicie. You are quite sure you wouldn't like to have sister Adèle?"

"*Voleuse! voleuse! voleuse!*" she heard her aunt's voice lifted after her in a shrill scream. It followed her as far as the leafy road beyond the live oaks.

Madame Solisainte trembled with excitement and agitation. She looked into the bag and counted the keys. They were all there.

"*Voleuse!*" she kept muttering. She was convinced that Bosey had robbed her of everything she possessed. The jewels were gone, she was sure of it—all gone. Her mother's watch and chain; bracelets, rings, ear-rings, everything gone. All the silver; the table, the bed linen, her mother's clothes—ah! that was why she had brought those three trunks!

Madame Solisainte clutched the brass key and glared at it with eyes wild with apprehension. She pounded her stick upon the floor till the rafters rang. But at that time of the afternoon—the hours between dinner and supper—the yard was deserted. And Dimple, still under the delusion created by the red ruffles and puffed sleeves, was strolling leisurely toward the station to see Miss Bosey off.

Madame pounded and called. In her wrath she overturned the table and sent the books and magazines flying in all directions. She sat a while a prey to the most violent agitation, the most turbulent misgivings, that made the pulses throb in her head and the blood course through her body as though the devil himself were at the valve.

"Robbed! Robbed! Robbed!" she repeated. "My gold; the rings; the necklace! I might have known! Oh! fool! Ah! *cher maître! pas possible!*"

Her head quivered as with a palsy upon its fat bulk. She clutched the arm of her chair and attempted to rise; her effort was fruitless. A second attempt, and she drew herself a few inches out of the chair and fell back again. A third effort, in which her whole big body shook and swayed like a vessel which has sprung a leak, and Madame Solisainte stood upon her feet.

She grasped the cane there at hand and stood helpless, screaming for Dimple. Then she began to walk—or rather drag her feet along the floor, slowly and with painful effort, shaking and leaning heavily upon her stick.

Madame did not think it strange or miraculous that she should be moving thus upon her tottering limbs, which for two years had refused to do their office. Her whole attention was bent upon reaching the press in her bedroom across the hall. She clutched the brass key; she had let all the other keys go, and she said nothing now but "*Volé, volé, volé!*"

Madame Solisainte managed to reach the room without other assistance than the chairs in her way afforded her, and the walls along which she propped her body as she sidled along. Her first thought upon unlocking the press was for her gold. Yes, there it was, all of it, in little piles as she had so often arranged it. But half the silver was gone; half the jewels and table linen.

When the servants began to congregate in the yard, they discovered Madame Félicie standing upon the gallery waiting for them. They uttered exclamations of wonder and consternation. Dimple became hysterical, and began to cry and scream out.

"Go an' fin' Richmond," said Madame to Daniel, and without comment or question he hurried off in search of the overseer.

"I will 'ave the law! Ah! *par exemple! pas possible!* to be rob' in that way! I will 'ave the law. Tell Lablatte I will not pay the bills. Mandy, go back to the quarters, an' sen' Susan to the kitchen. Dimple! Go an' carry all those book' an' magazine' up in the attic, an' put on you' other dress. Do not let me fin' you array in those flounce' again! *Pas possible! volé comme ça!* I will 'ave the law!"

Elizabeth Stock's One Story

Elizabeth Stock, an unmarried woman of thirty-eight, died of consumption during the past winter at the St. Louis City Hospital. There were no unusually pathetic features attending her death. The physicians say she showed hope of rallying till placed in the incurable ward, when all courage seemed to leave her, and she relapsed into a silence that remained unbroken till the end.

In Stonelift, the village where Elizabeth Stock was born and raised, and where I happen to be sojourning this summer, they say she was much given over to scribbling. I was permitted to examine her desk, which was quite filled with scraps and bits of writing in bad prose and impossible verse. In the whole conglomerate mass, I discovered but the following pages which bore any semblance to a connected or consecutive narration.

Since I was a girl I always felt as if I would like to write stories. I never had that ambition to shine or make a name; first place because I knew what time and labor it meant to acquire a literary style. Second place, because whenever I wanted to write a story I never could think of a plot. Once I wrote about old Si' Shepard that got lost in the woods and never came back, and when I showed it to Uncle William he said : "Why, Elizabeth, I reckon you better stick to your dress making : this here ain't no story; everybody knows about old Si' Shepard."

No, the trouble was with plots. Whenever I tried to think of one, it always turned out to be something that some one else had thought about before me. But here back awhile, I heard of great inducements offered for an acceptable story, and I said to myself : "Elizabeth Stock, this is your chance. Now or never!" And I laid awake most a whole week; and walked about days in a kind of dream, turning and twisting things in my mind just like I often saw old ladies twisting quilt patches around to compose a design. I tried to think of a railroad story with a wreck, but couldn' t. No more could I make a tale out of a murder, or money getting stolen, or even mistaken identity; for the story had to be original, entertaining, full of action and Goodness knows what all. It was no use. I gave it up. But now that I got my pen in my hand and sitting here kind of quiet and peaceful at the south window, and the breeze so soft carrying the autumn leaves along, I feel as I'd like to tell how I lost my position, mostly through my own negligence, I'll admit that.

My name is Elizabeth Stock. I'm thirty-eight years old and unmarried, and not afraid or ashamed to say it. Up to a few months ago I been postmistress of this village of Stonelift for six years, through one administration and a half—up to a few months ago.

Often seems like the village was most too small; so small that people were bound to look into each other's lives, just like you see folks in crowded tenements looking into each other's windows. But I was born here in Stonelift and I got no serious complaints. I been pretty comfortable and contented most of my life. There ain't more than a hundred houses all told, if that, counting stores, churches, postoffice, and even Nathan Brightman's palatial mansion up on the hill. Looks like Stonelift wouldn't be anything without that.

He's away a good part of the time, and his family; but he's done a lot for this community, and they always appreciated it, too.

But I leave it to any one—to any woman especially, if it ain't human nature in a little place where everybody knows every one else, for the postmistress to glance at a postal card once in a while. She could hardly help it. And besides, seems like if a person had anything very particular and private to tell, they'd put it under a sealed envelope.

Anyway, the train was late that day. It was the breaking up of winter, or the beginning of spring; kind of betwixt and between; along in March. It was most night when the mail came in that ought have been along at 5:15. The Brightman girls had been down with their pony-cart, but had got tired waiting and had been gone more than an hour.

It was chill and dismal in the office. I had let the stove go out for fear of fire. I was cold and hungry and anxious to get home to my supper. I gave out everybody's mail that was waiting; and for the thousandth time told Vance Wallace there was nothing for him. He'll come and ask as regular as clockwork. I got that mail assorted and put aside in a hurry.

There was no dilly dallying with postal cards, and how I ever come to give a second look at Nathan Brightman's postal, Heaven only knows!

It was from St. Louis, written with pencil in large characters and signed, "Collins," nothing else; just "Collins." It read:

"Dear Brightman: Be on hand tomorrow, Tuesday at 10. A. M. promptly. Important meeting of the board. Your own interest demands your presence. Whatever you do, don't fail. In haste, Collins."

I went to the door to see if there was anyone left standing around: but the night was so raw and chill, every last one of the loungers had disappeared. Vance Wallace would of been willing enough to hang about to see me home; but that was a thing I'd broken him of long ago. I locked things up and went on home, just ashivering as I went, it was that black and penetrating—worse than a downright freeze, I thought.

After I had had my supper and got comfortably fixed front of the fire, and glanced over the St. Louis paper and was just starting to read my seaside Library novel, I got thinking, somehow, about that postal card of Nath Brightman's. To a person that knew B. from hill's foot, it was just as plain as day that if that card laid on there in the office, Mr. Brightman would miss that important meeting in St. Louis in the morning. It wasn't anything to me, of course, except it made me uncomfortable and I couldn't rest or get my mind fixed on the story I was reading. Along about nine o'clock, I flung aside the book and says to myself:

"Elizabeth Stock, you a fool, and you know it." There ain't much use telling how I put on my rubbers and waterproof, covered the fire with ashes, took my umbrella and left the house.

I carried along the postoffice key and went on down and got out that postal card—in fact, all of the Brightman's mail—wasn't any use leaving part of it, and started for "the house on the hill" as we mostly call it. I don't believe anything could of induced me to go if I had known before hand what I was undertaking. It was drizzling and the rain kind of turned to ice when it struck the ground. If it hadn't been for the rubbers, I'd of taken more than one fall. As it was, I took one good and hard one on the footbridge. The wind was sweeping down so swiftly from the Northwest, looked like it carried me clean off my feet before I could clutch the handrail. I found out about that time that the stitches had come out of my old rubbers that I'd sewed about a month before, and letting the water in soaking my feet through and through. But I'd got more than good and started and I wouldn't think of turning around.

Nathan Brightman has got kind of steps cut along the side of the hill, going zig-zag. What you would call a gradual ascent, and making it easy to climb. That is to say, in good weather. But Lands! There wasn't anything easy that night, slipping back one step for every two; clutching at the frozen twigs along the path; and having to use my umbrella half the time for a walking stick; like a regular Alpine climber. And my heart would most stand still at the way the cedar trees moaned and whistled like doleful organ tones; and sometimes sighing deep and soft like dying souls in pain.

Then I was a fool for not putting on something warm underneath that mackintosh. I could of put on my knitted wool jacket just as easy as not. But the day had been so mild, it bamboozled us into thinking spring was here for good; especially when we were all looking and longing for it; and the orchards ready to bud, too.

But I forgot all the worry and unpleasantness of the walk when I saw how Nath Brightman took on over me bringing him that postal card. He made me sit down longside the fire and dry my feet, and kept saying:

"Why, Miss Elizabeth, it was exceedingly obliging of you; on such a night, too. Margaret, my dear"—that was his wife—"mix a good stiff toddy for Miss Elizabeth, and see that she drinks it."

I never could stand the taste or smell of alcohol. Uncle William says if I'd of had any sense and swallowed down that toddy like medicine, it might of saved the day.

Anyhow, Mr. Brightman had the girls scampering around getting his grip packed; one bringing his big top coat, another his muffler and umbrella; and at the same time here they were all three making up a list of a thousand and one things they wanted him to bring down from St. Louis.

Seems like he was ready in a jiffy, and by that time I was feeling sort of thawed out and I went along with him. It was a mighty big comfort to have him, too. He was as polite as could be, and kept saying:

"Mind out, Miss Elizabeth! Be careful here; slow now. My! but it's cold! Goodness knows what damage this won't do to the fruit trees." He walked to my very door with me, helping me along. Then he went on to the station. When the midnight express came tearing around the bend, rumbling like thunder and shaking the very house, I'd got my clothes changed and was drinking a hot cup of tea side the fire I'd started up. There was a lot of comfort knowing that Mr. Brightman had got aboard that train. Well, we all more or less selfish creatures in this world! I don't believe I'd of slept a wink that night if I'd of left that postal card lying in the office.

Uncle William will have it that this heavy cold all came of that walk; though he got to admit with me that this family been noted for weak lungs as far back as I ever heard of.

Anyway, I'd been sick on and off all spring; sometimes hardly able to stand on my feet when I'd drag myself down to that postoffice. When one morning, just like lightning out of a clear sky, here comes an official document from Washington, discharging me from my position as postmistress of Stonelift. I shook all over when I read it, just like I had a chill; and I felt sick at my stomach and my teeth chattered. No one was in the office when I opened that document except Vance Wallace, and I made him read it and I asked him what he made out it meant. Just like when you can't understand a thing because you don't want to. He says:

"You've lost your position, Lizabeth. That what it means; they've passed you up."

I took it away from him kind of dazed, and says:

"We got to see about it. We got to go see Uncle William; see what he says. Maybe it's a mistake."

"Uncle Sam don't make mistakes," said Vance. "We got to get up a petition in this here community; that's what I reckon we better do, and send it to the government."

Well, it don't seem like any use to dwell on this subject. The whole community was indignant, and pronounced it an outrage. They decided, in justice to me, I had to find out what I got that dismissal for. I kind of thought it was for my poor health, for I would of had to send in my resignation sooner or later, with these fevers and cough. But we got information it was for incompetence and negligence in office, through certain accusations of me reading postal cards and permitting people to help themselves to their own mail. Though I don't know as that ever happened except with Nathan Brightman always reaching over and saying :

"Don't disturb yourself, Miss Elizabeth," when I'd be sorting out letters and he could reach his mail in the box just as well as not.

But that's all over and done for. I been out of office two months now, on the 26th. There's a young man named Collins, got the position. He's the son of some wealthy, influential St. Louis man; a kind of delicate, poetical-natured young fellow that can't get along in business, and they used their influence to get him the position when it was vacant. They thinks it's the very place for him. I reckon 'tis. I hope in my soul he'll prosper. He's a quiet, nice-mannered young man. Some of the community thought of boycotting him. It was Vance Wallace started the notion. I told them they must be demented, and I up and told Vance Wallace he was a fool.

"I know I'm a fool, Lizabeth Stock," he said, "I always been a fool for hanging round you for the past twenty years."

The trouble with Vance is, he's got no intellect. I believe in my soul Uncle William's got more. Uncle William advised me to go up to St. Louis and get treated. I been up there. The doctor said, with this cough and short breath, if I know what's good for me I'll spend the winter in the South. But the truth is, I got no more money, or so little it don't count. Putting Danny to school and other things here lately, hasn't left me much to brag of. But I oughtn't be blamed about Danny; he's the only one of sister Martha's boys that seemed to me capable. And full of ambition to study as he was! It would have felt sinful of me, not to. Of course, I've taken him out, now I've lost my position. But I got him in with Filmore Green to learn the grocery trade, and maybe it's all for the best; who knows!

But indeed, indeed, I don't know what to do. Seems like I've come to the end of the rope. O! it's mighty pleasant here at this south window. The breeze is just as soft and warm as May, and the leaves look like birds flying. I'd like to sit right on here and forget every thing and go to sleep and never wake up. Maybe it's sinful to make that wish. After all, what I got to do is leave everything in the hands of Providence, and trust to luck.

The Storm

A Sequel to "The 'Cadian Ball"

I

The leaves were so still that even Bibi thought it was going to rain. Bobinôt, who was accustomed to converse on terms of perfect equality with his little son, called the child's attention to certain sombre clouds that were rolling with sinister intention from the west, accompanied by a sullen, threatening roar. They were at Friedheimer's store and decided to remain there till the storm had passed. They sat within the door on two empty kegs. Bibi was four years old and looked very wise.

"Mama'll be 'fraid, yes," he suggested with blinking eyes.

"She'll shut the house. Maybe she got Sylvie helpin' her this evenin'," Bobinôt responded reassuringly.

"No; she ent got Sylvie. Sylvie was helpin' her yistiday," piped Bibi.

Bobinôt arose and going across to the counter purchased a can of shrimps, of which Calixta was very fond. Then he returned to his perch on the keg and sat stolidly holding the can of shrimps while the storm burst. It shook the wooden store and seemed to be ripping great furrows in the distant field. Bibi laid his little hand on his father's knee and was not afraid.

II

Calixta, at home, felt no uneasiness for their safety. She sat at a side window sewing furiously on a sewing machine. She was greatly occupied and did not notice the approaching storm. But she felt very warm and often stopped to mop her face on which the perspiration gathered in beads. She unfastened her white sacque at the throat. It began to grow dark, and suddenly realizing the situation she got up hurriedly and went about closing windows and doors.

Out on the small front gallery she had hung Bobinôt's Sunday clothes to air and she hastened out to gather them before the rain fell. As she stepped outside, Alcée Laballière rode in at the gate. She had not seen him very often since her marriage, and never alone. She stood there with Bobinôt's coat in her hands, and the big rain drops began to fall. Alcée rode his horse under the shelter of a side projection where the chickens had huddled and there were plows and a harrow piled up in the corner.

"May I come and wait on your gallery till the storm is over, Calixta?" he asked.

"Come 'long in, M'sieur Alcée."

His voice and her own startled her as if from a trance, and she seized Bobinôt's vest. Alcée, mounting to the porch, grabbed the trousers and snatched Bibi's braided jacket that was about to be carried away by a sudden gust of wind. He expressed an intention to remain outside, but it was soon apparent that he might as well have been out in the open: the water beat in upon the boards in driving sheets, and he went inside, closing the door after him. It was even necessary to put something beneath the door to keep the water out.

"My! what a rain! It's good two years sence it rain' like that," exclaimed Calixta as she rolled up a piece of bagging and Alcée helped her to thrust it beneath the crack.

She was a little fuller of figure than five years before when she married; but she had lost nothing of her vivacity. Her blue eyes still retained their melting quality; and her yellow hair, dishevelled by the wind and rain, kinked more stubbornly than ever about her ears and temples.

The rain beat upon the low, shingled roof with a force and clatter that threatened to break an entrance and deluge them there. They were in the dining room—the sitting room—the general utility room. Adjoining was her bed room, with Bibi's couch along side her own. The door stood open, and the room with its white, monumental bed, its closed shutters, looked dim and mysterious.

Alcée flung himself into a rocker and Calixta nervously began to gather up from the floor the lengths of a cotton sheet which she had been sewing.

"If this keeps up, *Dieu sait* if the levees goin' to stan' it!" she exclaimed.

"What have you got to do with the levees?"

"I got enough to do! An' there's Bobinôt with Bibi out in that storm—if he only didn' left Friedheimer's!"

"Let us hope, Calixta, that Bobinôt's got sense enough to come in out of a cyclone."

She went and stood at the window with a greatly disturbed look on her face. She wiped the frame that was clouded with moisture. It was stiflingly hot. Alcée got up and joined her at the window, looking over her shoulder. The rain was coming down in sheets obscuring the view of far-off cabins and enveloping the distant wood in a gray mist. The playing of the lightning was incessant. A bolt struck a tall chinaberry tree at the edge of the field. It filled all visible space with a blinding glare and the crash seemed to invade the very boards they stood upon.

Calixta put her hands to her eyes, and with a cry, staggered backward. Alcée's arm encircled her, and for an instant he drew her close and spasmodically to him.

"*Bonté!*" she cried, releasing herself from his encircling arm and retreating from the window, "the house'll go next! If I only knew w'ere Bibi was!" She would not compose herself; she would not be seated. Alcée clasped her shoulders and looked into her face. The contact of her warm, palpitating body when he had unthinkingly drawn her into his arms, had aroused all the old-time infatuation and desire for her flesh.

"Calixta," he said, "don't be frightened. Nothing can happen. The house is too low to be struck, with so many tall trees standing about. There! aren't you going to be quiet? say, aren't you?" He pushed her hair back from her face that was warm and steaming. Her lips were as red and moist as pomegranate seed. Her white neck and a glimpse of her full, firm bosom disturbed him powerfully. As she glanced up at him the fear in her liquid blue eyes had given place to a drowsy gleam that unconsciously betrayed a sensuous desire. He looked down into her eyes and there was nothing for him to do but to gather her lips in a kiss. It reminded him of Assumption.

"Do you remember—in Assumption, Calixta?" he asked in a low voice broken by passion. Oh! she remembered; for in Assumption he had kissed her and kissed and kissed her; until his senses would well nigh fail, and to save her he would resort to a desperate flight. If she was not an immaculate dove in those days, she was still inviolate; a passionate creature whose very defenselessness had made her defense, against which his honor forbade him to prevail. Now—well, now—her lips seemed in a manner free to be tasted, as well as her round, white throat and her whiter breasts.

They did not heed the crashing torrents, and the roar of the elements made her laugh as she lay in his arms. She was a revelation in that dim, mysterious chamber; as white as the couch she lay upon. Her firm, elastic flesh that was knowing for the first time its birthright, was like a creamy lily that the sun invites to contribute its breath and perfume to the undying life of the world.

The generous abundance of her passion, without guile or trickery, was like a white flame which penetrated and found response in depths of his own sensuous nature that had never yet been reached.

When he touched her breasts they gave themselves up in quivering ecstasy, inviting his lips. Her mouth was a fountain of delight. And when he possessed her, they seemed to swoon together at the very borderland of life's mystery.

He stayed cushioned upon her, breathless, dazed, enervated, with his heart beating like a hammer upon her. With one hand she clasped his head, her lips lightly touching his forehead. The other hand stroked with a soothing rhythm his muscular shoulders.

The growl of the thunder was distant and passing away. The rain beat softly upon the shingles, inviting them to drowsiness and sleep. But they dared not yield.

The rain was over; and the sun was turning the glistening green world into a palace of gems. Calixta, on the gallery, watched Alcée ride away. He turned and smiled at her with a beaming face; and she lifted her pretty chin in the air and laughed aloud.

III

Bobinôt and Bibi, trudging home, stopped without at the cistern to make themselves presentable.

"My! Bibi, w'at will yo' mama say! You ought to be ashame'. You oughtn' put on those good pants. Look at 'em! An' that mud on yo' collar! How you got that mud on yo' collar, Bibi? I never saw such a boy!" Bibi was the picture of pathetic resignation. Bobinôt was the embodiment of serious solicitude as he strove to remove from his own person and his son's the signs of their tramp over heavy roads and through wet fields. He scraped the mud off Bibi's bare legs and feet with a stick and carefully removed all traces from his heavy brogans. Then, prepared for the worst—the meeting with an over-scrupulous housewife, they entered cautiously at the back door.

Calixta was preparing supper. She had set the table and was dripping coffee at the hearth. She sprang up as they came in.

"Oh, Bobinôt! You back! My! but I was uneasy. W'ere you been during the rain? An' Bibi? he ain't wet? he ain't hurt?" She had clasped Bibi and was kissing him effusively. Bobinôt's explanations and apologies which he had been composing all along the way, died on his lips as Calixta felt him to see if he were dry, and seemed to express nothing but satisfaction at their safe return.

"I brought you some shrimps, Calixta," offered Bobinôt, hauling the can from his ample side pocket and laying it on the table.

"Shrimps! Oh, Bobinôt! you too good fo' anything! and she gave him a smacking kiss on the cheek that resounded. "*J'vous réponds*, we'll have a feas' to night! umph-umph!"

Bobinôt and Bibi began to relax and enjoy themselves, and when the three seated themselves at table they laughed much and so loud that anyone might have heard them as far away as Laballière's.

IV

Alcée Laballière wrote to his wife, Clarisse, that night. It was a loving letter, full of tender solicitude. He told her not to hurry back, but if she and the babies liked it at Biloxi, to stay a month longer. He was getting on nicely; and though he missed them, he was willing to bear the separation a while longer—realizing that their health and pleasure were the first things to be considered.

V

As for Clarisse, she was charmed upon receiving her husband's letter. She and the babies were doing well. The society was agreeable; many of her old friends and acquaintances were at the bay. And the first free breath since her marriage seemed to restore the pleasant liberty of her maiden days. Devoted as she was to her husband, their intimate conjugal life was something which she was more than willing to forego for a while.

So the storm passed and every one was happy.

The Godmother

Tante Elodie attracted youth in some incomprehensible way. It was seldom there was not a group of young people gathered about her fire in winter or sitting with her in summer, in the pleasant shade of the live-oaks that screened the gallery.

There were several persons forming a half circle around her generous chimney early one evening in February. There were Madame Nicolas' two tiny little girls who sat on the floor and played with a cat the whole time; Madame Nicolas herself, who only came for the little girls and insisted on hurrying away because it was time to put the children to bed, and who, moreover, was expecting a caller. There was a fair, blonde girl, one of the younger teachers at the Normal school. Gabriel Lucaze offered to escort her home when she got up to go, after Madame Nicolas' departure. But she had already accepted the company of a silent, studious looking youth who had come there in the hope of meeting her. So they all went away but young Gabriel Lucaze, Tante Elodie's godson, who stayed and played cribbage with her. They played at a small table on which were a shaded lamp, a few magazines and a dish of *pralines* which the lady took great pleasure in nibbling during the reflective pauses of the game. They had played one game and were nearing the end of the second. He laid a queen upon the table.

"Fifteen-two" she said, playing a five.

"Twenty, and a pair."

"Twenty-five. Six points for me."

"Its a 'go.' "

"Thirty-one and out. That is the second game I've won. Will you play another rubber, Gabriel?"

"Not much, Tante Elodie, when you are playing in such luck. Besides, I've got to get out, it's half-past-eight." He had played recklessly, often glancing at the bronze clock which reposed majestically beneath its crystal globe on the mantle-piece. He prepared at once to leave, going before the gilt-framed, oval mirror to fold and arrange a silk muffler beneath his great coat.

He was rather good looking. That is, he was healthy looking; his face a little florid, and hair almost black. It was short and curly and parted on one side. His eyes were fine when they were not bloodshot, as they sometimes were. His mouth might have been better. It was not disagreeable or unpleasant, but it was unsatisfactory and drooped a little at the corners. However, he was good to look at as he crossed the muffler over his chest. His face was unusually alert. Tante Elodie looked at him in the glass.

"Will you be warm enough, my boy? It has turned very cold since six o'clock."

"Plenty warm. Too warm."

"Where are you going?"

"Now, Tante Elodie," he said, turning, and laying a hand on her shoulder; he was holding his soft felt hat in the other. "It is always 'where are you going?' 'Where have you been?' I have spoiled you. I have told you too much. You expect me to tell you everything; consequently, I must sometimes tell you fibs. I am going to confession. There! are you satisfied?" and he bent down and gave her a hearty kiss.

"I am satisfied, provided you go to the right priestess to confession; not up the hill, mind you!"

"Up the hill" meant up at the Normal School with Tante Elodie. She was a very conservative person. "The Normal" seemed to her an unpardonable innovation, with its teachers from Minnesota, from Iowa, from God-knows-where, bringing strange ways and manners to the old town. She was one, also, who considered the emancipation of slaves a great mistake. She had many reasons for thinking so and was often called upon to enumerate this in her wordy arguments with her many opponents.

II

Tante Elodie distinctly heard the Doctor leave the Widow Nicolas' at a quarter past ten. He visited the handsome and attractive young woman two evenings in the week and always left at the same hour. Tante Elodie's double glass doors opened upon the wide upper gallery. Around the angle of the gallery were the apartments of Madame Nicolas. Any one visiting the widow was obliged to pass Tante Elodie's door. Beneath was a store occasionally occupied by some merchant or other, but oftener vacant. A stairway led down from the porch to the yard where two enormous live-oaks grew and cast a dense shade upon the gallery above, making it an agreeable retreat and resting place on hot summer afternoons. The high, wooden yard-gate opened directly upon the street.

A half hour went by after the Doctor passed her door. Tante Elodie played "solitaire." Another half hour followed and still Tante Elodie was not sleepy nor did she think of going to bed. It was very near midnight when she began to prepare her night toilet and to cover the fire.

The room was very large with heavy rafters across the ceiling. There was an enormous bed over in the corner; a four-posted mahogany covered with a lace spread which was religiously folded every night and laid on a chair. There were some old ambrotypes and photographs about the room; a few comfortable but simple rocking chairs and a broad fire place in which a big log sizzled. It was an attractive room for anyone, not because of anything that was in it except Tante Elodie herself. She was far past fifty. Her hair was still soft and brown and her eyes bright and vivacious. Her figure was slender and nervous. There were many lines in her face, but it did not look care-worn. Had she her youthful flesh, she would have looked very young.

Tante Elodie had spent the evening in munching *pralines* and reading by lamp-light some old magazines that Gabriel Lucaze had brought her from the club.

There was a romance connected with her early days. Romances serve but to feed the imagination of the young; they add nothing to the sum of truth. No one realized this fact more strongly than Tante Elodie herself. While she tacitly condoned the romance, perhaps for the sake of the sympathy it bred, she never thought of Justin Lucaze but with a feeling of gratitude towards the memory of her parents who had prevented her marrying him thirty-five years before. She could have no connection between her deep and powerful affection for young Gabriel Lucaze and her old-time, brief passion for his father. She loved the boy above everything on earth. There was none so attractive to her as he; none so thoughtful of her pleasures and pains. In his devotion there was no trace of a duty-sense; it was the spontaneous expression of affection and seeming dependence.

After Tante Elodie had turned down her bed and undressed, she drew a grey flannel *peignoir* over her nightgown and knelt down to say her prayers; kneeling before a rocker with her bare feet turned to the fire. Prayers were no trifling matter with her. Besides those which she knew by heart, she read litanies and invocations from a book and also a chapter of "The Following of Christ." She had said her *Notre Père*, her *Salve Marie* and *Je crois en Dieu* and was deep in the litany of the Blessed Virgin when she fancied she heard footsteps on the stairs. The night was breathlessly still; it was very late.

"*Vierge des Vierges: Priez pour nous. Mère de Dieu: Priez—*"

Surely there was a stealthy step upon the gallery, and now a hand at her door, striving to lift the latch. Tante Elodie was not afraid. She felt the utmost security in her home and had no dread of mischievous intruders in the peaceful old town. She simply realized that there was some one at her door and that she must find out who it was and what they wanted. She got up from her knees, thrust her feet into her slippers that were near the fire and, lowering the lamp by which she had been reading her litanies, approached the door. There was the very softest rap upon the pane. Tante Elodie unbolted and opened the door the least bit.

"*Qui est là?*" she asked.

"Gabriel." He forced himself into the room before she had time to fully open the door to him.

III

Gabriel strode past her towards the fire, mechanically taking off his hat, and sat down in the rocker before which she had been kneeling. He sat on the prayer books she had left there. He removed them and laid them upon the table. Seeming to realize in a dazed way that it was not their accustomed place, he threw the two books on a nearby chair.

Tante Elodie raised the lamp and looked at him. His eyes were bloodshot, as they were when he drank or experienced any unusual emotion or excitement. But he was pale and his mouth drooped excessively, and twitched with the effort he made to control it. The top button was wrenched from his coat and his muffler was disarranged. Tante Elodie was grieved to the soul, seeing him thus. She thought he had been drinking.

"Gabriel, w'at is the matter?" she asked imploringly. "Oh, my poor child, w'at is the matter?" He looked at her in a fixed way and passed a hand over his head. He tried to speak, but his voice failed, as with one who experiences stage fright. Then he articulated, hoarsely, swallowing nervously between the slow words:

"I—killed a man—about an hour ago—yonder in the old Nigger-Luke Cabin." Tante Elodie's two hands went suddenly down to the table and she leaned heavily upon them for support.

"You did not; you did not," she panted. "You are drinking. You do not know w'at you are saying. Tell me, Gabriel, who 'as been making you drink? Ah! they will answer to me! You do not know w'at you are saying. *Boute!* how can you know!" She clutched him and the torn button that hung in the button-hole fell to the floor.

"I don't know why it happened," he went on, gazing into the fire with unseeing eyes, or rather with eyes that saw what was pictured in his mind and not what was before them.

"I've been in cutting scrapes and shooting scrapes that never amounted to anything, when I was just as crazy mad as I was to-night. But I tell you, Tante Elodie, he's dead. I've got to get away. But how are you going to get out of a place like this, when every dog and cat"—His effort had spent itself, and he began to tremble with a nervous chill; his teeth chattered and his lips could not form an utterance.

Tante Elodie, stumbling rather than walking, went over to a small buffet and pouring some brandy into a glass, gave it to him. She took a little herself. She looked much older in the *peignoir* and the handkerchief tied around her head. She sat down beside Gabriel and took his hand. It was cold and clammy.

"Tell me everything," she said with determination, "everything; without delay; and do not speak so loud. We shall see what must be done. Was it a negro? Tell me everything."

"No, it was a white man, you don't know, from Conshotta, named Everson. He was half drunk; a hulking bully as strong as an ox, or I could have licked him. He tortured me until I was frantic. Did you ever see a cat torment a mouse? The mouse can't do anything but lose its head. I lost my head, but I had my knife; that big hornhandled knife."

"Where is it?" she asked sharply. He felt his back pocket.

"I don't know." He did not seem to care, or to realize the importance of the loss.

"Go on; make haste; tell me the whole story. You went from here—you went—go on."

"I went down the river a piece," he said, throwing himself back in the chair and keeping his eyes fixed upon one burning ember on the hearth, "down to Symund's store where there was a game of cards. A lot of the fellows were there. I played a little and didn't drink anything, and stopped at ten. I was going"—He leaned forward with his elbows on his knees and his hands hanging between. "I was going to see a woman at eleven o'clock; it was the only time I could see her. I came along and when I got by the old Nigger-Luke Cabin I lit a match and looked at my watch. It was too early and it wouldn't do to hang around. I went into the cabin and started a blaze in the chimney with some fine wood I found there. My feet were cold and I sat on an empty soap-box before the fire to dry them. I remember I kept looking at my watch. It was twenty-five minutes to eleven when Everson came into the cabin. He was half drunk and his face was red and looked like a beast. He had left the game and had followed me. I hadn't spoken of where I was going. But he said he knew I was off for a lark and he wanted to go along. I said he couldn't go where I was going, and there was no use talking. He kept it up. At a quarter to eleven I wanted to go, and he went and stood in the doorway.

" 'If I don't go, you don't go', he said, and he kept it up. When I tried to pass him he pushed me back like I was a feather. He didn't get mad. He laughed all the time and drank whiskey out of a bottle he had in his pocket. If I hadn't got mad and lost my head, I might have fooled him or played some trick on him—if I had used my wits. But I didn't know any more what I was doing than the day I threw the inkstand at old Dainean's head when he switched me and made fun of me before the whole school.

"I stooped by the fire and looked at my watch; he was talking all kinds of foulishness I can't repeat. It was eleven o'clock. I was in a killing rage and made a dash for the door. His big body and his big arm were there like an iron bar, and he laughed. I took out my knife and stuck it into him. I don't believe he knew at first that I had touched him, for he kept on laughing; then he fell over like a pig, and the old cabin shook."

Gabriel had raised his clinched hand with an intensely dramatic movement when he said, "I stuck it into him." Then he let his head fall back against the chair and finished the concluding sentences of his story with closed eyes.

"How do you know he is dead?" asked Tante Elodie, whose voice sounded hard and monotonous.

"I only walked ten steps away and went back to see. He was dead. Then I came here. The best thing is to go give myself up, I reckon, and tell the whole story like I've told you. That's about the best thing I can do if I want any peace of mind."

"Are you crazy, Gabriel! You have not yet regained your senses. Listen to me. Listen to me and try to understand what I say."

Her face was full of a hard intelligence he had not seen there before; all the soft womanliness had for the moment faded out of it.

"You 'ave not killed the man Everson," she said deliberately. "You know nothing about 'im. You do not know that he left Symund's or that he followed you. You left at ten o'clock. You came straight in town, not feeling well. You saw a light in my window, came here; rapped on the door; I let you in and gave you something for cramps in the stomach and made you warm yourself and lie down on the sofa. Wait a moment. Stay still there."

She got up and went shuffling out the door, around the angle of the gallery and tapped on Madame Nicolas' door. She could hear the young woman jump out of bed bewildered, asking, "Who is there? Wait! What is it?"

"It is Tante Elodie." The door was unbolted at once.

"Oh! how I hate to trouble you, *cherie*. Poor Gabriel 'as been at my room for hours with the most severe cramps. Nothing I can do seems to relieve 'im. Will you let me 'ave the morphine which Doctor left with you for old Betsy's rheumatism? Ah! thank you. I think a quarter of a grain will relieve 'im. Poor boy! Such suffering! I am so sorry dear, to disturb you. Do not stand by the door, you will take cold. Good night."

Tante Elodie persuaded Gabriel, if the club were still open, to look in there on his way home. He had a room in a relative's house. His mother was dead and his father lived on a plantation several miles from town. Gabriel feared that his nerve would fail him. But Tante Elodie had him up again with a glass of brandy. She said that he must get the fact lodged in his mind that he was innocent. She inspected the young man carefully before he went away, brushing and arranging his toilet. She sewed the missing button on his coat. She had noticed some blood upon his right hand. He himself had not seen it. With a wet towel she washed his face and hands as though he were a little child. She brushed his hair and sent him away with a thousand reiterated precautions.

IV

Tante Elodie was not overcome in any way after Gabriel left her. She did not indulge in a hysterical moment, but set about accomplishing some purpose which she had evidently had in her mind. She dressed herself again; quickly, nervously, but with much precision. A shawl over her head and a long, black cape across her shoulders made her look like a nun. She quitted her room. It was very dark and very still out of doors. There was only a whispering wail among the live-oak leaves.

Tante Elodie stole noiselessly down the steps and out the gate. If she had met anyone, she intended to say she was suffering with toothache and was going to the doctor or druggist for relief.

But she met not a soul. She knew every plank, every uneven brick of the side walk; every rut of the way, and might have walked with her eyes closed. Strangely enough she had forgotten to pray. Prayer seemed to belong to her moments of contemplation; while now she was all action; prompt, quick, decisive action.

It must have been near upon two o'clock. She did not meet a cat or a dog on her way to the Nigger-Luke Cabin. The hut was well out of town and isolated from a group of tumbled-down shanties some distance off, in which a lazy set of negroes lived. There was not the slightest feeling of fear or horror in her breast. There might have been, had she not already been dominated and possessed by the determination that Gabriel must be shielded from ignominy—maybe, worse.

She glided into the low cabin like a shadow, hugging the side of the open door. She would have stumbled over the dead man's feet if she had not stepped so cautiously. The embers were burning so low that they gave but a faint glow in the sinister cabin with its obscure corners, its black, hanging cobwebs and the dead man lying twisted as he had fallen with his face on his arm.

Once in the cabin the woman crept towards the body on her hands and knees. She was looking for something in the dusky light; something she could not find. Crawling towards the fire over the uneven, creaking boards, she stirred the embers the least bit with a burnt stick that had fallen to one side. She dared not make a blaze. Then she dragged herself once more towards the lifeless body. She pictured how the knife had been thrust in; how it had fallen from Gabriel's hand; how the man had come down like a felled ox. Yes, the knife could not be far off, but she could not discover a trace of it. She slipped her fingers beneath the body and felt all along. The knife lay up under his arm pit. Her hand scraped his chin as she withdrew it. She did not mind. She was exultant at getting the knife. She felt like some other being, possessed by Satan. Some fiend in human shape, some spirit of murder. A cricket began to sing on the hearth.

Tante Elodie noticed the golden gleam of the murdered man's watch chain, and a sudden thought invaded her. With deft, though unsteady fingers, she unhooked the watch and chain. There was money in his pockets. She emptied them, turning the pockets inside out. It was difficult to reach his left hand pockets, but she did so. The money, a few bank notes and some silver coins, together with the watch and knife she tied in her handkerchief. Then she hurried away, taking a long stride across the man's body in order to reach the door.

The stars were like shining pieces of gold upon dark velvet. So Tante Elodie thought as she looked up at them an instant.

There was the sound of disorderly voices away off in the negro shanties. Clasping the parcel close to her breast she began to run. She ran, ran, as fast as some fleet fourfooted creature, ran, panting. She never stopped till she reached the gate that let her in under the live-oaks. The most intent listener could not have heard her as she mounted the stairs; as she let herself in at the door; as she bolted it. Once in the room she began to totter. She was sick to her stomach and her head swam. Instinctively she reached out towards the bed, and fell fainting upon it, face downward.

The gray light of dawn was coming in at her windows. The lamp on the table had burned out. Tante Elodie groaned as she tried to move. And again she groaned with mental anguish, this time as the events of the past night came back to her, one by one, in all their horrifying details. Her labor of love, begun the night before, was not yet ended. The parcel containing the watch and money were there beneath her, pressing into her bosom. When she managed to regain her feet the first thing which she did was to rekindle the fire with splinters of pine and pieces of hickory that were at hand in her wood box. When the fire was burning briskly, Tante Elodie took the paper money from the little bundle and burned it. She did not notice the denomination of the bills, there were five or six, she thrust them into the blaze with the poker and watched them burn. The few loose pieces of silver she put in her purse, apart from her own money; there was sixty-five cents in small coin. The watch she placed between her mattresses; then, seized with misgiving, took it out. She gazed around the room, seeking a safe hiding place and finally put the watch into a large, strong stocking which she pinned securely around her waist beneath her clothing. The knife she washed carefully, drying it with pieces of newspaper which she burned. The water in which she had washed it she also threw in a corner of the large fire place upon a heap of ashes. Then she put the knife into the pocket of one of Gabriel's coats which she had cleaned and mended for him; it was hanging in her closet.

She did all this slowly and with great effort, for she felt very sick. When the unpleasant work was over it was all she could do to undress and get beneath the covers of her bed.

She knew that when she did not appear at breakfast Madame Nicolas would send to investigate the cause of her absence. She took her meals with the young widow around the corner of the gallery. Tante Elodie was not rich. She received a small income from the remains of what had once been a magnificent plantation adjoining the lands which Justin Lucaze owned and cultivated. But she lived frugally, with a hundred small cares and economies and rarely felt the want of extra money except when the generosity of her nature prompted her to help an afflicted neighbor, or to bestow a gift upon some one of whom she was fond. It often seemed to Tante Elodie that all the affection of her heart was centered upon her young protégé, Gabriel; that what she felt for others was simply an emanation—rays, as it were, from this central sun of love that shone for him alone.

In the midst of twinges, of nervous tremors, her thoughts were with him. It was impossible for her to think of anything else. She was filled with unspeakable dread that he might betray himself. She wondered what he had done after he left her: what he was doing at that moment? She wanted to see him again alone, to insist anew upon the necessity of his self-assertion of innocence.

As she expected, Mrs. Wm. Nicolas came around at the breakfast hour to see what was the matter. She was an active woman, very pretty and fresh looking, with willing, deft hands and the kindest voice and eyes. She was distressed at the spectacle of poor Tante Elodie extended in bed with her head tied up, and looking pale and suffering.

"Ah! I suspected it!" she exclaimed, "coming out in the cold on the gallery last night to get morphine for Gabriel; *ma foi!* as if he could not go to the drug store for his morphine! Where have you pain? Have you any fever, Tante Elodie?"

"It is nothing, *chérie*. I believe I am only tired and want to rest for a day in bed."

"Then you must rest as long as you want. I will look after your fire and see that you have what you need. I will bring your coffee at once. It is a beautiful day; like spring. When the sun gets very warm I will open the window."

V

All day long Gabriel did not appear, and she dared not make inquiries about him. Several persons came in to see her, learning that she was sick. The midnight murder in the Nigger-Luke Cabin seemed to be the favorite subject of conversation among her visitors. They were not greatly excited over it as they might have been were the man other than a comparative stranger. But the subject seemed full of interest, enhanced by the mystery surrounding it. Madame Nicolas did not risk to speak of it.

"That is not a fit conversation for a sick-room. Any doctor—anybody with sense will tell you. For Mercy's sake! change the subject."

But Fifine Delonce could not be silenced.

"And now it appears," she went on with renewed animation, "it appears he was playing cards down at Symund's store. That shows how they pass their time—those boys! It's a scandal! But nobody can remember when he left. Some say at nine, some say it was past eleven. He sort of went away like he didn't want them to notice."

"Well, we didn't know the man. My patience! there are murders every day. If we had to keep up with them, *ma foi!* Who is going to Lucie's card party to-morrow? I hear she did not invite her cousin Claire. They have fallen out again it seems." And Madame Nicolas, after speaking, went to give Tante Elodie a drink of *Tisane.*

"Mr. Ben's got about twenty darkies from Niggerville, holding them on suspicion," continued Fifine, dancing on the edge of her chair. "Without doubt the man was enticed to the cabin and murdered and robbed there. Not a picayune left in his pockets! only his pistol—that they didn't take, all loaded, in his back pocket, that he might have used, and his watch gone! Mr. Ben thinks his brother in Conshotta, that's very well off, is going to offer a big reward."

"What relation was the man to you, Fifine?" asked Madame Nicolas, sarcastically.

"He was a human being, Amelia; you have no heart, no feeling. If it makes a woman that hard to associate with a doctor, then thank God—well—as I was saying, if they can catch those two strange section hands that left town last night—but you better bet they're not such fools to keep that watch. But old Uncle Marte said he saw little foot prints like a woman's, early this morning, but no one wanted to listen to him or pay any attention, and the crowd tramped them out in little or no time. None of the boys want to let on; they don't want us to know which ones were playing cards at Symund's. Was Gabriel at Symund's, Tante Elodie?"

Tante Elodie coughed painfully and looked blankly as though she had only heard her name and had been inattentive to what was said.

"For pity sake leave Tante Elodie out of this! it's bad enough she has to listen, suffering as she is. Gabriel spent the evening here, on Tante Elodie's sofa, very sick with cramps. You will have to pursue your detective work in some other quarter, my dear."

A little girl came in with a huge bunch of blossoms. There was some bustle attending the arrangement of the flowers in vases, and in the midst of it, two or three ladies took their leave.

"I wonder if they're going to send the body off to-night, or if they're going to keep it for the morning train," Fifine was heard to speculate, before the door closed upon her.

Tante Elodie could not sleep that night. The following day she had some fever and Madame Nicolas insisted upon her seeing the doctor. He gave her a sleeping draught and some fever drops and said she would be all right in a few days; for he could find nothing alarming in her condition.

By a supreme effort of the will she got up on the third day hoping in the accustomed routine of her daily life to get rid, in part, of the uneasiness and unhappiness that possessed her.

The sun shone warm in the afternoon and she went and stood on the gallery watching for Gabriel to pass. He had not been near her. She was wounded, alarmed, miserable at his silence and absence; but determined to see him. He came down the street, presently, never looking up, with his hat drawn over his eyes.

"Gabriel!" she called. He gave a start and glanced around.

"Come up; I want to see you a moment."

"I haven't time now, Tante Elodie."

"Come in!" she said sharply.

"All right, you'll have to fix it up with Morrison," and he opened the gate and went in. She was back in her room by the time he reached it, and in her chair, trembling a little and feeling sick again.

"Gabriel, if you 'ave no heart, it seems to me you would 'ave some intelligence; a moment's reflection would show you the folly of altering your 'abits so suddenly. Did you not know I was sick? did you not guess my uneasiness?"

"I haven't guessed anything or known anything but a taste of hell," he said, not looking at her. Her heart bled afresh for him and went out to him in full forgiveness. "You were right," he went on, "it would have been horrible to saying anything. There is no suspicion. I'll never say anything unless some one should be falsely accused."

"There will be no possible evidence to accuse anyone," she assured him. "Forget it, forget it. Keep on as though it was something you had dreamed. Not only for the outside, but within yourself. Do not accuse yourself of that act, but the actions, the conduct, the ungovernable temper that made it possible. Promise me it will be a lesson to you, Gabriel; and God, who reads men's hearts, will not call it a crime, but an accident which your unbridled nature invited. I will forget it. You must forget it. 'Ave you been to the office?"

"To-day; not yesterday. I don't know what I did yesterday, but look for the knife—after they—I couldn't go while he was there—and I thought every minute some one was coming to accuse me. And when I realized they weren't—I don't know—I drank too much, I think. Reading law! I might as well have been reading Hebrew. If Morrison thinks —See here Tante Elodie, are there any spots on this coat? Can you see anything here in the light?"

"There are no spots anywhere. Stop thinking of it, I implore you." But he pulled off the coat and flung it across a chair. He went to the closet to get his other coat which he knew hung there. Tante Elodie, still feeble and suffering, in the depths of her chair, was not quick enough, could think of no way to prevent it. She had at first put the knife in his pocket with the intention of returning it to him. But now she dreaded to have him find it, and thus discover the part she had played in the sickening dream.

He buttoned up his coat briskly and started away.

"Please burn it," he said, looking at the garment on the chair, "I never want to see it again."

VI

When it became distinctly evident that no slightest suspicion would be attached to him for the killing of Everson; when he plainly realized that there was no one upon whom the guilt could be fastened, Gabriel thought he would regain his lost equilibrium. If in no other way, he fancied he could reason himself back into it. He was suffering, but he someway had no fear that his present condition of mind would last. He thought it would pass away like a malignant fever. It would have to pass away or it would have to kill him.

From Tante Elodie's he went over to Morrison's office where he was reading law. Morrison and his partner were out of town and he had the office to himself. He had been there all morning. There was nothing for him to do now but to see anyone who called on business, and to go on with his reading. He seated himself and spread his book before him, but he looked into the street through the open door. Then he got up and shut the door. He again fastened his eyes upon the pages before him, but his mind was traveling other ways. For the hundredth time he was going over every detail of the fatal night, and trying to justify himself in his own heart.

If it had been an open and fair fight there would have been no trouble in squaring himself with his conscience; if the man had shown the slightest disposition to do him bodily harm, but he had not. On the other hand, he asked himself, what constituted a murder? Why, there was Morrison himself who had once fired at Judge Filips on that very street. His ball had gone wide of the mark, and subsequently he and Filips had adjusted their difficulties and become friends. Was Morrison any less a murderer because his weapon had missed?

Suppose the knife had swerved, had penetrated the arm, had inflicted a harmless scratch or flesh wound, would he be sitting there now, calling himself names? But he would try to think it all out later. He could not bear to be there alone, he never liked to be alone, and now he could not endure it. He closed the book without the slightest recollection of a line his eyes had followed. He went and gazed up and down the street, then he locked the office and walked away.

The fact of Everson having been robbed was very puzzling to Gabriel. He thought about it as he walked along the street.

The complete change that had taken place in his emotions, his sentiments, did not astonish him in the least: we accept such phenomena without question. A week ago—not so long as that—he was in love with the fair-haired girl up at the Normal. He was undeniably in love with her. He knew the symptoms. He wanted to marry her and meant to ask her whenever his position justified him in doing so.

Now, where had that love gone? He thought of her with indifference. Still, he was seeking her at that moment, through habit, without any special motive. He had no positive desire to see her; to see any one; and yet he could not endure to be alone. He had no desire to see Tante Elodie. She wanted him to forget and her presence made him remember.

The girl was walking under the beautiful trees, and she stood and waited for him, when she saw him mounting the hill. As he looked at her, his fondness for her and his intentions toward her, appeared now, like child's play. Life was something terrible of which she had no conception. She seemed to him as harmless, as innocent, as insignificant as a little bird.

"Oh! Gabriel," she exclaimed. "I had just written you a note. Why haven't you been here? It was foolish to get offended. I wanted to explain: I couldn't get out of it the other night, at Tante Elodie's, when he asked me. You know I couldn't, and that I would rather have come with you." Was it possible he would have taken this seriously a week ago?

"Delonce is a good fellow; he's a decent fellow. I don't blame you. That's all right." She was hurt at his easy complaisance. She did not wish to offend him, and here she was grieved because he was not offended.

"Will you come indoors to the fire?" she asked.

"No; I just strolled up for a minute." He leaned against a tree and looked bored, or rather, preoccupied with other things than herself. It was not a week ago that he wanted to see her every day; when he said the hours were like minutes that he passed beside her. "I just strolled up to tell you that I am going away."

"Oh! going away?" and the pink deepened in her cheeks, and she tried to look indifferent and to clasp her glove tighter. He had not the slightest intention of going away when he mounted the hill. It came to him like an inspiration.

"Where are you going?"

"Going to look for work in the city."

"And what about your law studies?"

"I have no talent for the law; it's about time I acknowledged it. I want to get into something that will make me hustle. I wouldn't mind—I'd like to get something to do on a railroad that would go tearing through the country night and day. What's the matter?" he asked, perceiving the tears that she could not conceal.

"Nothing's the matter," she answered with dignity, and a sense of seeming proud.

He took her word for it and, instead of seeking to console her, went rambling on about the various occupations in which he should like to engage for a while.

"When are you going?"

"Just as soon as I can."

"Shall I see you again?"

"Of course. Good-bye. Don't stay out here too long; you might take cold." He listlessly shook hands with her and descended the hill with long rapid strides.

He would not intentionally have hurt her. He did not realize that he was wounding her. It would have been as difficult for him to revive his passion for her as to bring Everson back to life. Gabriel knew there could be fresh horror added to the situation. Discovery would have added to it; a false accusation would have deepened it. But he never dreamed of the new horror coming as it did, through Tante Elodie, when he found the knife in his pocket. It took a long time to realize what it meant; and then he felt as if he never wanted to see her again. In his mind, her action identified itself with his crime, and made itself a hateful, hideous part of it, which he could not endure to think of, and of which he could not help thinking.

It was the one thing which had saved him, and yet he felt no gratitude. The great love which had prompted the deed did not soften him. He could not believe that any man was worth loving to such length, or worth saving at such a price. She seemed, to his imagination, less a woman than a monster, capable of committing, in cold-blood, deeds, which he himself could only accomplish in blind rage. For the first time, Gabriel wept. He threw himself down upon the ground in the deepening twilight and wept as he never had before in his life. A terrible sense of loss overpowered him; as if someone dearer than a mother had been taken out of the reach of his heart; as if a refuge had gone from him. The last spark of human affection was dead within him. He knew it as he was losing it. He wept at the loss which left him alone with his thoughts.

VII

Tante Elodie was always chilly. It was warm for the last of April, and the women at Madame Nicolas' wedding were all in airy summer attire. All but Tante Elodie, who wore her black silk, her old silk with a white lace fichu, and she held an embroidered handkerchief and a fan in her hand.

Fifine Delonce had been over in the morning to take up the seams in the dress, for, as she expressed herself, it was miles too loose for Tante Elodie's figure. She appeared to be shrivelling away to nothing. She had not again been sick in bed since that little spell in February; but she was plainly wasting and was very feeble. Her eyes, though, were as bright as ever;

sometimes they looked as hard as flint. The doctor, whom Madame Nicolas insisted upon her seeing occasionally, gave a name to her disease; it was a Greek name and sounded convincing. She was taking a tonic especially prepared for her, from a large bottle, three times a day.

Fifine was a great gossip. When and how she gathered her news nobody could tell. It was always said she knew ten times more than the weekly paper would dare to print. She often visited Tante Elodie, and she told her news of everyone; among others of Gabriel.

It was she who told that he had abandoned the study of the law. She told Tante Elodie when he started for the city to look for work and when he came back from the fruitless search.

"Did you know that Gabriel is working on the railroad, now? Fireman! Think of it! What a comedown from reading law in Morrison's office. If I were a man, I'd try to have more strength of character than to go to the dogs on account of a girl; an insignificant somebody from Kansas! Even if she is going to marry my brother, I must say it was no way to treat a boy—leading him on, especially a boy like Gabriel, that any girl would have been glad—Well, it's none of my business; only I'm sorry he took it like he did. Drinking himself to death, they say."

That morning, as she was taking up the seams of the silk dress, there was fresh news of Gabriel. He was tired of the railroad, it seemed. He was down on his father's place herding cattle, breaking in colts, drinking like a fish.

"I wouldn't have such a thing on my conscience! Goodness me! I couldn't sleep at nights if I was that girl."

Tante Elodie always listened with a sad, resigned smile. It did not seem to make any difference whether she had Gabriel or not. He had broken her heart and he was killing her. It was not his crime that had broken her heart; it was his indifference to her love and his turning away from her.

It was whispered about that Tante Elodie had grown indifferent to her religion. There was no truth in it. She had not been to confession for two months; but otherwise she followed closely the demands made upon her; redoubling her zeal in church work and attending mass each morning.

At the wedding she was holding quite a little reception of her own in the corner of the gallery. The air was mild and pleasant. Young people flocked about her and occasionally the radiant bride came out to see if she were comfortable and if there was anything she wanted to eat or drink.

A young girl leaning over the railing suddenly exclaimed "*Tiens!* someone is dead. I didn't know any one was sick." She was watching the approach of a man who was coming down the street, distributing, according to the custom of the country, a death notice from door to door.

He wore a long black coat and walked with a measured tread. He was as expressionless as an automaton; handing the little slips of paper at every door; not missing one. The girl, leaning over the railing, went to the head of the stairs to receive the notice when he entered Tante Elodie's gate.

The small, single sheet, which he gave her, was bordered in black and decorated with an old-fashioned wood cut of a weeping willow beside a grave. It was an announcement on the part of Monsieur Justin Lucaze of the death of his only son, Gabriel, who had been instantly killed, the night before, by a fall from his horse.

If the automaton had had any sense of decency, he might have skipped the house of joy, in which there was a wedding feast, in which there was the sound of laughter, the click of glasses, the hum of merry voices, and a vision of sweet women with their thoughts upon love and marriage and earthly bliss. But he had no sense of decency. He was as indifferent and relentless as Death, whose messenger he was.

The sad news, passed from lip to lip, cast a shadow as if a cloud had flitted across the sky. Tante Elodie alone stayed in its shadow. She sank deeper down into the rocker, more shrivelled than ever. They all remembered Tante Elodie's romance and respected her grief.

She did not speak any more, or even smile, but wiped her forehead with the old lace handkerchief and sometimes closed her eyes. When she closed her eyes she pictured Gabriel dead, down there on the plantation, with his father watching beside him. He might have betrayed himself had he lived. There was nothing now to betray him. Even the shining gold watch lay deep in a gorged ravine where she had flung it when she once walked through the country alone at dusk.

She thought of her own place down there beside Justin's, all dismantled, with bats beating about the eaves and negroes living under the falling roof.

Tante Elodie did not seem to want go in doors again. The bride and groom went away. The guests went away, one by one, and all the little children. She stayed there alone in the corner, under the deep shadow of the oaks while the stars came out to keep her company.

A Little Country Girl

Ninette was scouring the tin milk-pail with sand and lye-soap, and bringing it to a high polish. She used for that purpose the native scrub-brush, the fibrous root of the palmetto, which she called *latanier*. The long table on which the tins were ranged, stood out in the yard under a mulberry tree. It was there that the pots and kettles were washed, the chickens, the meats and vegetables cut up and prepared for cooking.

Occasionally a drop of water fell with a faint splash on the shining surface of the tin; whereupon Ninette would wipe it away and carrying the corner of her checked apron up to her eyes, she would wipe them and proceed with her task. For the drops were falling from Ninette's eyes; trickling down her cheeks and sometimes dropping from the end of her nose.

It was all because two disagreeable old people, who had long outlived their youth, no longer believed in the circus as a means of cheering the human heart; nor could they see the use of it.

Ninette had not even mentioned the subject to them. Why should she? She might as well have said : "Grandfather and Grandmother, with your permission and a small advance of fifty cents, I should like, after my work is done, to make a visit to one of the distant planets this afternoon."

It was very warm and Ninette's face was red with heat and ill-humor. Her hair was black and straight and kept falling over her face. It was an untidy length; her grandmother having decided to let it grow, about six months before. She was barefooted and her calico skirt reached a little above her thick, brown ankles.

Even the negroes were all going to the circus. Suzan's daughter, who was known as Black-Gal, had lingered beside the table a moment on her way through the yard.

"You ain't gwine to de suckus?" she inquired with condescension.

"No," and bread-pan went bang on the table.

"We all's goin'. Pap an' Mammy an' all us is goin'," with a complacent air and a restful pose against the table.

"Where you all goin' to get the money, I like to know."

"Oh, Mr. Ben advance' Mammy a dollar on de crap; an' Joe, he got six bits lef' f'om las' pickin'; an' pap sole a ole no'count plow to Dennis. We all's goin'."

"Joe say he seed 'em pass yonder back Mr. Ben's lane. Dey a elephant mos' as big as dat corn-crib, walkin' long des like he somebody. An' a whole pa'cel wild critters shet up in a cage. An' all kind o' dogs an' hosses; an' de ladies rarin' an' pitchin' in red skirts all fill' up wid gole an' diamonds.

"We all's goin'. Did you ax yo' gran'ma? How come you don't ax yo' gran'pap?"

"That's my business; 'tain't none o' yo's, Black-Gal. You better be gettin' yonder home, tendin' to yo' work, I think."

"I ain't got no work, 'cep' iron out my pink flounce' dress fo' de suckus." But she took herself off with an air of lofty contempt, swinging her tattered skirts. It was after that that Ninette's tears began to drop and spatter.

Resentment rose and rose within her like a leaven, causing her to ferment with wickedness and to make all manner of diabolical wishes in regard to the circus. The worst of these was that she wished it would rain.

"I hope to goodness it'll po' down rain; po' down rain; po' down rain!" She uttered the wish with the air of a young Medusa pronouncing a blighting curse.

"I like to see 'em all drippin' wet. Black-Gal with her pink flounces, all drippin' wet." She spoke these wishes in the very presence of her grandfather and grandmother, for they understood not a word of English; and she used that language to express her individual opinion on many occasions.

"What do you say, Ninette?" asked her grandmother. Ninette had brought in the last of the tin pails and was ranging them on a shelf in the kitchen.

"I said I hoped it would rain," she answered, wiping her face and fanning herself with a pie pan as though the oppressive heat had suggested the desire for a change of weather.

"You are a wicked girl," said her grandmother, turning on her, "when you know your grandfather has acres and acres of cotton ready to fall, that the rain would ruin. He's angry enough, too, with every man, woman and child leaving the fields to-day to take themselves off to the village. There ought to be a law to compel them to pick their cotton; those trifling creatures! Ah! it was different in the good old days."

Ninette possessed a sensitive soul, and she believed in miracles. For instance, if she were to go to the circus that afternoon she would consider it a miracle. Hope follows on the heels of Faith. And the white-winged goddess—which is Hope—did not leave her, but prompted her to many little surreptitious acts of preparation in the event of the miracle coming to pass.

She peeped into the clothes-press to see that her gingham dress was where she had folded and left it the Sunday before, after Mass. She inspect- ed her shoes and got out a clean pair of stockings which she hid beneath the pillow. In the tin basin behind the house, she scrubbed her face and neck till they were red as a boiled crawfish. And her hair, which was too short to plait, she plastered and tied back with a green ribbon; it stood out in a little bristling, stiff tail.

The noon hour had hardly passed, than an unusual agitation began to be visible throughout the surrounding country. The fields were deserted. People, black and white, began passing along the road in squads and detachments. Ponies were galloping on both sides of the river, carrying two and as many as three, on their backs. Blue and green carts with rampant mules; top-buggies and no-top buggies; family carriages that groaned with age and decrepitude; heavy wagons filled with piccaninnies made a passing procession that nothing short of a circus in town could have accounted for.

Grandfather Bézeau was too angry to look at it. He retired to the hall, where he sat gloomily reading a two-weeks-old paper. He looked about ninety years old; he was in reality, not more than seventy.

Grandmother Bézeau stayed out on the gallery, apparently to cast ridicule and contempt upon the heedless and extravagant multitude; in reality, to satisfy a womanly curiosity and a natural interest in the affairs of her neighbors.

As for Ninette, she found it difficult to keep her attention fixed upon her task of shelling peas and her inward supplications that something might happen.

Something *did* happen. Jules Perrault, with a family load in his big farm-wagon, stopped before their gate. He handed the reins to one of the children and he, himself, got down and came up to the gallery where Ninette and her grandmother were sitting.

"What's this! what's this!" he cried out in French, "Ninette not going to the circus? not even ready to go?"

"*Par exemple!*" exclaimed the old lady, looking daggers over her spectacles. She was binding the leg of a wounded chicken that squawked and fluttered with terror.

" '*Par exemple*' or no '*par exemple*' she's going and she's going with me; and her grandfather will give her the money. Run in, little one; get ready; make haste, we shall be late." She looked appealingly at her grandmother who said nothing, being ashamed to say what she felt in the face of her neighbor, Perrault, of whom she stood a little in awe. Ninette, taking silence for consent, darted into the house to get ready.

And when she came out, wonder of wonders! There was her grandfather taking his purse from his pocket. He was drawing it out slowly and painfully, with a hideous grimace, as though it were some vital organ that he was extracting. What arguments could Mons. Perrault have used! They were surely convincing. Ninette had heard them in wordy discussion as she nervously laced her shoes; dabbed her face with flour; hooked the gingham dress; and balanced upon her head a straw "flat" whose roses looked as though they had stayed out over night in a frost.

But no triumphant queen on her throne could have presented a more beaming and joyful countenance than did Ninette when she ascended and seated herself in the big wagon in the midst of the Perrault family. She at once took the baby from Mme. Perrault and held it and felt supremely happy.

The more the wagon jolted and bounced, the more did it convey to her a sense of reality; and less did it seem like a dream. They passed Black-Gal and her family in the road, trudging ankle-deep in dust. Fortunately the girl was barefooted; though the pink flounces were all there, and she carried a green parasol. Her mother was *semi-décolletée* and her father wore a heavy winter coat; while Joe had secured piecemeal, a species of cake-walk costume for the occasion. It was with a feeling of lofty disdain that Ninette passed and left the Black-Gal family in a cloud of dust.

Even after they reached the circus grounds, which were just outside the the village, Ninette continued to carry the baby. She would willingly have carried three babies, had such a thing been possible. The infant took a wild and noisy interest in the merry-go-round with its hurdy-gurdy accompaniment. Oh! that she had had more money! that she might have mounted one of those flying horses and gone spinning round in a whirl of ecstasy!

There were side-shows, too. She would have liked to see the lady who weighed six hundred pounds and the gentleman who tipped the scales at fifty. She would have wanted to peep in at the curious monster, captured after a desperate struggle in the wilds of Africa. Its picture, in red and green on the flapping canvas, was surely not like anything she had ever seen or even heard of.

The lemonade was tempting: the pop-corn, the peanuts, the oranges were delights that she might only gaze upon and sigh for. Mons. Perrault took them straight to the big tent, bought the tickets and entered.

Ninette's pulses were thumping with excitement. She sniffed the air, heavy with the smell of saw-dust and animals, and it lingered in her nostrils like some delicious odor. Sure enough! There was the elephant which Black-Gal had described. A chain was about his ponderous leg and he kept reaching out his trunk for tempting morsels. The wild creatures were all there in cages, and the people walked solemnly around, looking at them; awed by the unfamiliarity of the scene.

Ninette never forgot that she had the baby in her arms. She talked to it, and it listened and looked with round, staring eyes. Later on she felt as if she were a person of distinction assisting at some royal pageant when the be-spangled Knights and Ladies in plumes and flowing robes went prancing round on their beautiful horses.

The people all sat on the circus benches and Ninette's feet hung down, because an irritable old lady objected to having them thrust into the small of her back. Mme. Perrault offered to take the baby, but Ninette clung to it. It was something to which she might communicate her excitement. She squeezed it spasmodically when her emotions became uncontrollable.

"Oh! *bébé*! I believe I'm goin' to split my sides! Oh, la! la! if gran'ma could see that, I know she'd laugh herse'f sick." It was none other than the clown who was producing this agreeable impression upon Ninette. She had only to look at his chalky face to go into contortions of mirth.

No one had noticed a gathering obscurity, and the ominous growl of thunder made every one start with disappointment or apprehension. A flash and a second clap, that was like a crash, followed. It came just as the ring-master was cracking his whip with a "hip-la! hip-la!" at the bareback rider, and the clown was standing on his head. There was a sinister roar; a terrific stroke of the wind; the center pole swayed and snapped; the great canvas swelled and beat the air with bellowing resistance.

Pandemonium reigned. In the confusion Ninette found herself down beneath piled up benches. Still clutching the baby, she proceeded to crawl out of an opening in the canvas. She stayed huddled up against the fallen tent, thinking her end had come, while the baby shrieked lustily.

The rain poured in sheets. The cries and howls of the frightened animals were like unearthly sounds. Men called and shouted; children screamed; women went into hysterics and the negroes were having fits.

Ninette got on her knees and prayed God to keep her and the baby and everyone from injury and to take them safely home. It was thus that Mons. Perrault discovered her and the baby, half covered by the fallen tent.

She did not seem to recover from the shock. Days afterward, Ninette was going about in a most unhappy frame of mind, with a wretched look upon her face. She was often discovered in tears.

When her condition began to grow monotonous and depressing, her grandmother insisted upon knowing the cause of it. Then it was that she confessed her wickedness and claimed the guilt of having caused the terrible catastrophe at the circus.

It was her fault that a horse had been killed; it was her fault if an old gentleman had had a collar-bone broken and a lady an arm dislocated. She was the cause of several persons having been thrown into fits and hysterics. All her fault! She it was who had called the rain down upon their heads and thus had she been punished!

It was a very delicate matter for grandmother Bézeau to pronounce upon—far too delicate. So the next day she went and explained it all to the priest and got him to come over and talk to Ninette.

The girl was at the table under the mulberry tree peeling potatoes when the priest arrived. He was a jolly little man who did not like to take things too seriously. So he advanced over the short, tufted grass, bowing low to the ground and making deep salutations with his hat.

"I am overwhelmed," he said, "at finding myself in the presence of the wonderful Magician! who has but to call upon the rain and down it comes. She whistles for the wind and—there it is! Pray, what weather will you give us this afternoon, fair Sorceress?"

Then he became serious and frowning, straightened himself and rapped his stick upon the table.

"What foolishness is this I hear? look at me; look at me!" for she was covering her face, "and who are you, I should like to know, that you dare think you can control the elements!"

Well, they made a great deal of fuss of Ninette and she felt ashamed. But Mons. Perrault came over; he understood best of all. He took grandmother and grandfather aside and told them the girl was morbid from staying so much with old people, and never associating with those of her own age. He was very impressive and convincing. He frightened them, for he hinted vaguely at terrible consequences to the child's intellect.

He must have touched their hearts, for they both consented to let her go to a birthday party over at his house the following day. Grandfather Bézeau even declared that *if it was necessary* he would contribute towards providing her with a suitable toilet for the occasion.

A Reflection

Some people are born with a vital and responsive energy. It not only enables them to keep abreast of the times; it qualifies them to furnish in their own personality a good bit of the motive power to the mad pace. They are fortunate beings. They do not need to apprehend the significance of things. They do not grow weary nor miss step, nor do they fall out of rank and sink by the wayside to be left contemplating the moving procession.

Ah! that moving procession that has left me by the road-side! Its fantastic colors are more brilliant and beautiful than the sun on the undulating waters. What matter if souls and bodies are falling beneath the feet of the ever-pressing multitude! It moves with the majestic rhythm of the spheres. Its discordant clashes sweep upward in one harmonious tone that blends with the music of other worlds—to complete God's orchestra.

It is greater than the stars—that moving procession of human energy; greater than the palpitating earth and the things growing thereon. Oh! I could weep at being left by the wayside; left with the grass and the clouds and a few dumb animals. True, I feel at home in the society of these symbols of life's immutability. In the procession I should feel the crushing feet, the clashing discords, the ruthless hands and stifling breath. I could not hear the rhythm of the march.

Salve! ye dumb hearts. Let us be still and wait by the roadside.

Ti Démon

"It's this way," said Ti Démon to Aristides Bonneau—"If I go yonda with you to Symond's sto', it'll be half pas' eight befo' I git out to Marianne an' she'll sho' be gone to bed—an' she won' know how come I missed goin'."

Every Saturday afternoon Ti Démon, as did many others along the Cadian Bayou, laid aside hoe and plow—turned the mule loose and all primped up—*endimanché* as they say down there—betook himself to town on his ragged pony, his one luxury. After putting the pony in the lot adjoining Gamarché's store—he would go about town making his necessary purchases, gazing in at the windows, finally picking up a ribbon or a cornet of candy for his Marianne. At half past six he invariably betook himself to Marianne's who lived with her mother a little beyond the outskirts of town. She was his fiancée. He was going to marry her at the close of summer when the crops were gathered, and he was happy in a certain unemotional way that took things for granted.

His name was Plaisance, but his mother called him Ti Démon when he was a baby and kept her awake bawling at night, and the name stuck to him. It had lost all significance, however, in his growing goodness, and in the bovine mildness that characterized his youth years the name identified itself with his personality and became almost a synonym for gentleness.

At half past six, instead of being out at Marianne's, he was lounging in the drug store where he had allowed himself to be persuaded into a rendez-vouz with Aristides. He was a square clumsy fellow with sunburnt hair and skin—features that were not bad and eyes that were decidedly good as they reflected a peaceful soul. Gazing down into the show case of the drug store, Ti Démon longed to be rich, more on Marianne's account than his own for the things arrayed before him were such as appealed distinctly to the feminine taste—green and yellow perfumes in bottles—hand mirrors—toilet powders—savon fin—dainty writing paper —a hundred costly nothings which the Druggist had little hope or chance of selling before Christmas. Ti Démon felt that a bale of cotton would hardly more than cover the price of a full and free and reckless indulgence —of the longings which assailed him through Marianne as he gazed down into the drug store show case.

Aristides soon joined him and together they left the store and walked down the main street of the town, across the foot-bridge that covered a deep ravine and down the hill toward a motley group of shanties—one of which was Symond's store, not so much a store as a resort for young men whose erratic inclinations sometimes led them to seek more spirited diversion than the domestic and social circle offered them. Perhaps no other man in town could so have tempted and prevailed with Ti Démon. It flattered his self-complacency to be seen walking down the street with Aristides whose distinction of manner was unquestionable, whose grace and amiability made him an object of envy with the men and a creature to be worshiped by susceptible women. By contrast Ti Démon was all the more conscious of his own lurching plowman's walk, his awkward stoop and broad heavy hands that looked as if they might do the office of sledge hammers if occasion required.

The foul smelling coal oil lamps had been lighted in Symond's back room when they reached there. Several men were already gathered playing cards around rude tables whose grimy tops bore the stale and fresh marks of liquor glasses. Aristides and Ti Démon had strolled down for a social game of seven-up and a convivial hour among friends and acquaintances. For the young farmer had expressed a determination to leave at 8 o'clock and rejoin Marianne who he knew would be wondering and perhaps grieving at his absence. But at 8 o'clock Ti Démon was more excited than he had ever been in his life. His big fist was coming down on the table with a reckless disregard for the fate of the jingling glasses and his big horse laugh, mellowed by numerous toddies, resounded and stirred a pleasing animation about him. The game of seven-up had been changed to poker. Ti Démon formed one of the seven men at his table, and though he was acquainted with the game, having played on rare occasions, never before had the fluctuations of the game so excited him. It was the hoarse tones of the clock in the store adjoining, striking 10 that brought him partially to his senses and reminded him of his disregarded intentions. "Leave me out this time, I got to go," said Ti Démon rising, conscious of stiffened joints. "I ain't winnin' and I ain't losin' to talk about, so it don't make no difference. Where's my hat—w'at become o' Mr. Aristides?"

"W'ere yo' sense, Ti Démon, Aristides lef' a couple hours ago—he tole you he was goin' and you didn' pay any attention. Yo' hat's on yo' head w'ere it ought to be. Deal them cards over again—you dealt a han' to Ti Démon, it's goin' to spoil the draw. I'm glad he's gone—he makes mo' noise than Symond's donkey—"

Ti Démon managed to get out on the gallery with a great clatter of brogans and overturning of chairs. He was clumsy and noisy. Once out of doors, he drew a deep long breath of the fresh spring night. Looking across the hollow and far up the opposite slope he could see a light in the window of Marianne's house. He vaguely wondered if she had gone to bed. He vaguely hoped she might be still sitting out on the gallery with her mother. The night was so beautiful that it might well tempt any one to steal a few hours from sleep, and linger out under the sky to taste the delight of it. He left the shanty and started off in the direction of Marianne's cottage. He was conscious of some unsteadiness of gait. He knew he was not entirely sober but was confident of his ability to disguise that fact from Marianne, if he should be fortunate enough to find her still up. He was seized as he had never been in his life before, by a flood of tenderness, a conscious longing for the girl that he had been brought to fully realize perhaps by his moment of weakness and disloyalty, perhaps as much by the subtle spirit of the caressing night, the soft effulgence the moon was shedding over the country, the poignant odors of the spring. The good familiar scent of new plowed earth assailed him and made him think of his big field on the bayou—of his home—and Marianne, as she would be, at picking time, coming down between the tall rows of white bursting cotton to meet him. The thought was like a vivid picture flashed and imprinted upon his brain. It was so sweet a thought that he would not give it up, but kept it with him in his walk and treasured it and fondled it.

Then up the slope stood the poor little cottage a good bit back from the road. It was an upward, grassy road with a few faint wagon tracks. There was a row of trees at irregular intervals along the fence, and they cast deep shadows across the white moonlight. Ascending the road, Ti Démon saw two people approaching—advancing toward him—walking slowly arm in arm. At first he did not recognize them, passing slowly in and out, in and out of the shadows. But when they stopped in the moonlight to pick some white blossoms hanging over the fence, he knew them. It was Aristides and Marianne. The young man fixed a white spray in the girl's heavy black braids. He seemed to linger over the pleasing task, then arm in arm they resumed their walk—continued to approach Ti Démon. With the first flash of recognition came madness. As vividly as the powerful picture of love and domestic peace had imprinted upon his mind— just as sharply now came in a blinding flash the conviction of trickery and deceit. Marianne, not devoid of coquetry, could see no harm in accepting the attentions of Aristides or any other agreeable youth in the absence of her fiancé. It was with no feeling of guiltiness that she perceived him approaching. On the contrary, she framed a reproach in her mind and uttered it as he came near—"You takin' yo' time to night, I mus' say, Ti Démon." But with an utter disregard for her words—a terrible purpose in his newly aroused consciousness, in speechless wrath he tore her companion from her side and fell upon him with those big broad fists that could do the service of sledge hammers when occasion required.

"You crazy! Ti Démon! Help—*Au secours—au secours*—you crazy— Ti Démon," shrieked Marianne hanging upon him in fear and desperation.

There was hardly a shred of soul left in Aristides' shapely body when help came—negroes running from near cabins at the sound of Marianne's screams. The force of numbers against him alone prevailed with Ti Démon to desist in his deadly work. He left Marianne bruised and weeping, Aristides battered and bleeding, lying unconscious on the ground in the moonlight, and the negroes all standing there in helpless indecision— and he went limping away—down the slope across the hollow over the footbridge that crossed the ravine and back into town. He took his pony from the lot where he had left it, mounted and rode in a gentle canter back to his home on the Cadian Bayou.

Of course Marianne never viewed him after that—she would not trust her life in the keeping of so murderous a madman. Nor did she marry Aristides, who in truth never had any intention of asking her. But a girl with so sweet a manner, with tender eyes and dark and glossy braids had but the trouble of choosing among the Cadian youths along the bayou. That was Ti Démon's one and only demoniacal outburst during his life, but it affected the community in an inexplicable way. Some one said that

Aristides said he was going to shoot Ti Démon at sight. So Ti Démon got permission to carry a pistol—a rusty old blunderbuss that was a sore trial and inconvenience for so peaceable a man to lug around with him. Aristides, whatever he might have said, had no intention of molesting him—he never prosecuted his assailant as he might have done, and even got into a way of turning up one street when he saw Ti Démon coming down the other. "He's a dangerous man, that Cadian," said Aristides; "mark my words, he'll kill his man befo' he's through." The negroes who had been witnesses to the encounter on the moonlit slope described it in language that made children and timid women shriek and tremble and made men look to their firearms. As for Marianne she always begged to be spared describing the horror of it. People began to believe he had been well named after all—"*il est bien nommé Ti Démon, va!*" said women to each other.

"You can't fool with Ti Démon—he don' say much, him, but w'en he gits mad, mine out!" It somehow got into the air and stayed there— other men fought and brawled and bled and quietly resumed their roles of law-abiding citizens—not so with Ti Démon. Little children got into the way of scrambling into the house when they saw him coming. Years later he was sometimes pointed out to strangers by those of a younger generation who had no distinctive idea of the nature of his crimes. "You see that ol' fellow—he's bad as they make 'em—he's dangerous him— they call 'm Ti Démon."

A December Day in Dixie

The train was an hour and a half late. I failed to hear any complaints on that score from the few passengers who disembarked with me at Cypress Junction at 6:30 A.M. and confronted an icy blast that would better have stayed where it came from. But there was Emile Sautier's saloon just across the tracks, flaunting an alluring sign that offered to hungry wayfarers ham and eggs, fried chicken, oysters and delicious coffee at any hour.

Emile's young wife was as fat and dirty as a little pig that has slept over time in an untidy sty. Possibly she had slept under the stove; the night must have been cold. She told us Emile had come home "boozy" the night before from town. She told it before his very face and he never said a word—only went ahead pouring coal-oil on the fire that wouldn't burn. She wore over her calico dress a heavy cloth jacket with huge pearl buttons and enormous puffed sleeves, and a tattered black-white "nubia" twined about her head and shoulders as if she were contemplating a morning walk. It is impossible for me to know what her intentions were. She stood in the doorway with her little dirty, fat, ring-bedecked hands against the frame, seeming to guard the approach to an adjacent apartment in which there was a cooking stove, a bed and other articles of domestic convenience.

"Yas, he come home boozy, Emile, he don' care, him; dat's nuttin to him w'at happen'."

In his indifference to fate, the youth had lost an eye, a summer or two ago, and now he was saving no coal-oil for the lamps.

We were clamoring for coffee. Any one of us was willing to forego the fried chicken, that was huddled outside under a slanting, icy board; or the oysters, that had never got off the train; or the ham that was grunting beneath the house; or the eggs, which were possibly out where the chicken was; but we did want coffee.

Emile made us plenty of it, black as ink, since no one cared for the condensed milk which he offered with the sugar.

We could hear the chattering of a cherub in the next room where the bed and cook stove were. And when the piggish little mother went in to dress it, what delicious prattle of Cadian French! what gurgling and suppressed laughter! One of my companions—there were three of us, two Natchitoches men and myself—one of them related an extraordinary experience which the infant had endured a month or two before. He had fallen into an old unused cistern a great distance from the house. In falling through the tangled brush that covered it, he had been caught beneath the arms by some protecting limbs, and thus insecurely sustained he had called and wailed for two hours before help came.

"Yas," said his mother who had come back into the room, " 'is face was black like de stove w'en we fine 'im. An' de cistern was all fill' up wid lizard' an' snake'. It was one big snake all curl' up on de udder en' de branch, lookin' at 'im de whole time." His little swarthy, rosy moon-face beamed cheerfully at us from over his mother's shoulder, and his black eyes glittered like a squirrel's. I wondered how he had lived through those two hours of suffering and terror. But the little children's world is so unreal, that no doubt it is often difficult for them to distinguish between the life of the imagination and of reality.

The earth was covered with two inches of snow, as white, as dazzling, as soft as northern snow and a hundred times more beautiful. Snow upon and beneath the moss-draped branches of the forests; snow along the bayou's edges, powdering the low, pointed, thick palmetto growths; white snow and the fields and fields of white cotton bursting from dry bolls. The Natchitoches train sped leisurely through the white, still country, and I longed for some companion to sit beside me who would feel the marvelous and strange beauty of the scene as I did. My neighbor was a gentleman of too practical a turn.

"Oh! the cotton and the snow!" I almost screamed as the first vision of a white cotton field appeared.

"Yes, the lazy rascals; won't pick a lock of it; cotton at 4 cts, what's the use they say."

"What's the use," I agreed. How cold and inky black the negroes looked, standing in the white patches.

"Cotton's in the fields all along here and down through the bayou Natchez country."

"Oh! it isn't earthly—its Fairyland!"

"Don't know what the planters are going to do, unless they turn half the land into pasture and start raising cattle. What you going to do with that Cane river plantation of yours?"

"God knows. I wonder if it looks like this. Do you think they've picked the cotton—Do you think one could ever forget—"

Well, some kind soul should have warned us not to go into Natchitoches town. The people were all stark mad. The snow had gone to their heads.

"Keep them curtains shut tight," said the driver of the rumbling old hack. "They don't know what they about; they jus' as lief pelt you to death as not."

The horses plunged in their break neck speed; the driver swore deep under his breath; pim! pam! the missiles rained against the protecting curtains; the shrieks and yells outside were demoniac, blood curdling.— There was no court that day—the judges and lawyers were rolling in the snow with the boys and girls. There was no school that day; the professors at the Normal—those from the North-states, were showing off and getting the worst of it. The nuns up on the hill and their little charges were like march hares. Barred doors were no protection if an unguarded window had been forgotten. The sanctity of home and person was a myth to be demolished with pelting, melting, showering, suffocating snow.

But the next day the sun came out and the snow all went away, except where bits of it lay here and there in protected roof angles. The magnolia leaves gleamed and seemed to smile in the sunshine. Hardy rose-vines clinging to old stuccoed pillars plumed themselves and bristled their leaves with satisfaction. And the violets peeped out to see if it was all over.

"Ah! this is a southern day," I uttered with deep gratification as I leisurely crossed the bridge afoot. A warm, gentle breeze was stirring. On the opposite side, a dear old lady was standing in her dear old door-way waiting for me.

The Gentleman from New Orleans

Mr. and Mrs. Thomas Bénoîte, commonly known as Mr. and Mrs. Buddie Bénoîte, were so devoted a couple it seemed an unusual pity that anything so sombre as a cloud should ever shadow their domestic serenity. That is what Sophronie would have said if she had put her thoughts into words. It grieved her beyond measure whenever this amiable couple, for example, got upon the subject of Mrs. Buddie's family, a family which, having strongly objected, with some reason, to the marriage in the first place, would in the second place have gladly forgiven and forgotten when things turned out so happily.

But Buddie Bénoîte was neither forgiving nor forgetting, and had a sinister way of oiling his shot gun after a too emphatic conversation regarding family ties and obligations. There were minor differences too, upon the training of the children and the treatment of domestic animals which were not serious and furnished zest to what might otherwise have been too colorless an existence.

There hung no cloud however over this engaging family the morning they started off to the barbecue in Mr. Buddie's big spring wagon. He, his wife, three small children, a couple of neighbors and a huge hemper were as much of a load as the mules could be expected to draw. Mr. Buddie was good looking, energetic, a little too stout and blustering; characteristics which were overemphasized by contrast with his wife, too faded for her years and showing a certain lack of self assertion which her husband regarded as the perfection of womanliness. But one and all beamed happy anticipation as they drove away with noisy clatter.

The morning was still fresh; the sun had not yet dried the dew that shone like a silvery frost on the spears of grass and rested like a mantle of gems on the hardy rose bushes. Sophronie stood shading her eyes and watching them till they were out of sight. She bore not the slightest ill will at being left behind. She was good-natured, and reflected that some one had to stay and watch the premises. To be sure there was old Aunt Crissy, rather the worse for rheumatism. But with the best intentions in the world, what was to prevent Aunt Crissy, if left alone, from setting fire to the house with a coal from her pipe?

No, Sophronie did not complain, but cherished a sense of importance after they were gone. So many things to remember! and so inconsiderate of them to expect her to remember them all! She was not to forget the milk, the calves, the chickens, the dogs. She was to remember to lay the sheets to bleach; to remember if Mr. Sneckbauer from New Orleans stopped in passing, to be polite and to apologize for Mr. Buddie's absence. Mr. Sneckbauer was a commercial representative making the parish rounds and he was due any moment of any day that week.

Sophronie rattled the keys and bustled around at a great rate. She made up the beds and threw things about on the sunny galleries to air. Aunt Crissy was quite impressed:—" 'Tain't right," she grumbled, "leave a nice, pert gal like you behine an' take demse'fs off to de barb'cue des so."

"Oh, well; every dog its day, Aunt Crissy," said Sophronie pounding a pillow into shape; "my turn 'll come some these times. 'Tain't much fun anyhow to go to a barbecue in a wagon with a lot of chil'ren an' ol' people."

"I know w'at you studyin' 'bout," laughed Aunt Crissy; "you got yo' mine sot on settin' up 'side a nice young man behine a fas' trotter like in Kaintuck yonda."

"You losin' yo' time, Aunt Crissy. Go sit down an' shell those peas. I'll have you here on my han's cryin' misery before you get through."

Aunt Crissy reluctantly retired, deploring Sophronie's unwillingness to profit by so excellent an opportunity for cheerful conversation.

Pitty-pot, pitty-pat went Sophronie's little feet. Now she was flying down to the yard shooing the chickens; again she was dragging the pillows in out of the sun. Swish, swash! went the broom over the bare floors. Bing, bang! opening windows; closing shutters. Clitter, clatter! filling water jars and buckets at the cistern. It's a pity there was no one more appreciative than Aunt Crissy and the ducks to witness such a display of comeliness and youthful energy.

"She mus' a' walked ten miles sence dey gone," grumbled the old woman shelling the peas with her knotty fingers. "W'at you gwine have fo' dinner, Miss Phrony?" she called out.

"I'll jus' take some milk an' something cold, Aunt Crissy. You got yo' bacon an' greens. I don't want to bother with dinner."

It was nearly noon when Sophronie, freshened up, neat as a pin in her blue calico, seated herself to her sewing within the shade of the gallery. But the tribulations of this young housewife were seemingly endless. From afar she had seen a buggy coming down the long, country road. She gazed at it with the natural speculation of the country girl, never dreaming that it would stop there at the gate.

But stop it did. The buggy was old and weather worn. The horse, while an honest enough looking animal, would never have carried off the blue ribbon at a horse show. A thin, blond man in a long linen duster and a soft gray hat got down and divided his attention between his horse and a brace of dogs that viciously challenged his presence.

"Oh, my!" wailed Sophronie; "the gentleman from New Orleans! An' I can't even remember his name to save me. W'y couldn't he waited till tomorrow! You! Jet! *Passez!* Maje! Go back there! Come in, suh; they won't touch you; don't be afraid."

He opened the gate and came forward with a long, slow stride; pulling at his straggling, straw-colored beard.

"Please come in, suh; come right in. Brother Buddie was expecting you all week. It's too bad; they gone since mornin' to the barbecue."

"Family all gone?" he asked with a slow, bashful drawl, seating himself with an uneasy look.

"Yes, the chil'ren an' all. But you make yo'se'f at home."

He pushed back his broad hat, tilted his chair and crossed his legs; nevertheless he did not appear at ease. Sophronie, after the formalities of his reception were over, felt it would be a relief to him if she excused herself and went away to see about preparing some dinner for him.

"He's come, Aunt Crissy; the gentleman from New Orleans. Here, take a glass of fresh water to him an' come back quick as yo' ol' legs'll bring you."

Nothing could have been more welcome to Aunt Crissy than this pleasing distraction. She pinned a clean kerchief about her neck, gave an extra twist to her bandana and started out to the guest with a cool glass of sparkling water on a tray. She was almost bent double, exaggerating her infirmities as was her custom on special occasions. The gentleman from New Orleans thanked her, wiped his beard on a red cotton handkerchief that he abstracted from the depths of the linen duster, and relapsed into silence.

She eyed him closely while he drank. On her way back to the kitchen she passed through the rooms turning the keys on the closet doors and putting small articles of value out of sight.

Sophronie was already busy with the chicken which had been prepared for the evening meal when Aunt Crissy returned to the kitchen.

"W'at he said 'is name was?" she asked bluntly.

"Oh! I didn't ask him, Aunt Crissy. Here, pour some water on the peas. He knows we know his name; I wasn't goin' to let on I'd forgotten it. Watch the chicken w'ile I go set the table. An' I think I better get out a bottle of wine. Brother Buddie wouldn't be pleased if we didn't treat 'im right."

"W'at he said 'is name was?"

"You enough to try the patience of a saint, Aunt Crissy!"

"Don' look to me like a gemman f'om Noo O'leans."

"Oh! you know so many gentlemen from New Orleans an' from Shreveport an' Baton Rouge an' New York! You can tell one from the other if any body can!"

Aunt Crissy at this pointed rebuke considered all responsibility removed and set stolidly about watching the bubbling pots, while Sophronie busied herself in the dining room, spreading out the very best of everything.

The gentleman from New Orleans laid his felt hat down on the floor beside him when he seated himself at table. He still wore the linen duster because he had no coat beneath it, and he still seemed shy and reluctant to talk.

"You reckon they'll be home before night?" he asked. It was the third time he had put the same question to Sophronie.

"Yes indeed. They wouldn't think of stayin' out with the chil'ren after dark. He'p yo'se'f to mo' wine, suh; it's good wine; it was made in the parish on Mr. Billy Botton's place. Not good as you get in New Orleans, of course, but it's good wine."

"Let's see; there's two children, ain't there?"

"Three. The las' little boy is jus' a year ol'. They beautiful chil'ren, an' jus' as good! The ol'es' boy's got a will of his own, though; he takes after brother Buddie." Later she suggested, with the purpose of discovering whether he intended to stay or not: "If you decide to wait you can put yo' buggy in the shed." The respectable horse had already been provided for.

"Well, I reckon I'll wait s'long as I came this far."

"You can take a walk over the place," prompted Sophronie. "Brother Buddie's put in a new press; an' he's got some o' the fines' cotton fo' miles aroun', down the far end o' the field."

She was delighted to find that her suggestion met with approval. Though a healthy and energetic girl, the strain of entertaining this difficult visitor was beginning to tell on her nerves. She had offered him papers to read which he never looked at. She gave him books with the same result. Conversation was too one-sided to please even a talkative young person.

It was with intense relief that she saw him take his way down the field path, followed by the dogs that had made friends. The linen duster flapped like a skirt about his ankles, and he looked with some show of interest from side to side. Aunt Crissy's gaze followed him with smouldering disapproval. But she washed the dishes in silence and when through, sat in grim silence smoking her pipe on the bench outside the kitchen door.

Sophronie retreated to her room, drew the shutters and lay down to take a nap. She certainly needed the rest.

"Now, if he comes back too soon," she thought with a certain reckless desperation, "he'll have to entertain himself the best he can."

It was not yet dark when the barbecue party came back, thoroughly tired and disheartened, except Mr. Buddie whose spirits seemed to be not in the least impaired. His wife's face was white and drawn, with the premature lines brought strongly out by fatigue. Her pale hair fell on either side in wisps, and she offered altogether a pathetic picture, struggling with the fretful children. The wagon went on, to convey the two neighbors to their home, and the Bénoîte family struggled to the house, Sophronie who had been on the watch, carrying the baby.

"The gentleman from New Orleans is here," she announced to her brother.

"Mr. Sneckbauer! w'en did he come?"

"This mornin'. I gave him dinner. He went out to take a walk an' he hasn't come back yet."

"My, my! did you receive him well?" questioned Mr. Buddie with evident anxiety; "did you give him a good dinner and did Sam put up his buggy? Mr. Sneckbauer's here, Millie," to his wife, "go primp up a little an' fix up the chil'ren. You showed him to his room, Phronie? Did Crissy see that he had everything he needed?"

"Yes, I invited him to make himse'f comfortable, but he didn't seem to want anything in particular. He's been gone a long time; I'll reckon he'll soon be back."

Mr. Buddie performed quite a bit of toilet on his own account, anxious that the family should make a good impression upon Mr. Sneckbauer. His little daughter who was the idol of his heart, toddled after his every step as he came and went about the room, clinging to his legs, hanging to his loosened suspenders. The two were inseparable friends; and when Mr. Buddie had put the last touch by getting into a spic and span blue linen coat, he gathered the importunate little one up in his arms and tenderly brushed the curls away from her dimpled face.

"He's coming, brother Buddie," said Sophronie thrusting her head in at the door. "Sister Millie's out on the back gallery; hurry up!"

When Mr. Buddy reached the gallery he saw the tall, lean figure approaching, already close at hand. Mrs. Buddie stood pale and apparently stricken with some powerful emotion. Then she uttered a cry, and as if possessed of wings, she was down the steps, had crossed the short bit of sward and the next instant she was lost in the arms of the stranger and was sobbing with the utter abandon of a child. He lifted her small person bodily from the ground and for a moment she was quite enfolded in the flapping duster.

"Bud Bénoîte," began the visitor without preliminary, "I know it's common talk you got your shotgun fixed for the first Parkins that steps foot on your land. I respected your wishes; I never feared your gun; now blaze away. I was bound to see my daughter if I had to die for it." Mrs. Buddie had never relinquished her clutch about his neck with her face buried upon his shoulder.

The scene was so unexpected to Buddie Bénoîte that it found him wholly unprepared. He could find no words. The wrath which he had always expected would blaze up at sight of a Parkins, was somehow dispelled by factors that he had not considered. The sight of his wife's great emotion was a painful revelation. The realization that the tie which united those two clinging to each other out there was the same that bound his own to the cherished baby in his arms, was an overwhelming realization. His impulses were not slow. He hastened forward and held out his hand to his wife's father.

Sophronie had sunk into a chair. She was astounded at her mistake, and trying to comprehend it. She feared at first she had committed a crime. A moment later she began to believe she had brilliantly managed a difficult situation.

"Her mother's failing pretty smart," went on Parkins, caressing Mrs. Buddie's cheek but showing not half so much emotion now as Mr. Buddie who was frankly shedding tears. "She couldn't stand the trip from Winn; but she felt the same as me; we'd got to see Millie; we couldn't stand it no longer; neither could her brothers. The last words she says was, 'Si Parkins you fetch my girl to me if you got to bring her across Bud Benoîte's dead body; if we wait any longer it might be too late.' "

Mr. Buddie in his entire change of sentiment felt like placing a pistol in Mr. Parkins' hand and requesting that gentleman to use him as a target. But he happily realized that there is a limit even to belated courtesy.

Aunt Crissy was trying to make herself heard; she had hobbled around from the front of the house: "Marse Buddie, oh, Marse Buddie; de gen'-man f'om Noo O'leans is roun' at de front gate."

And there he was, Mr. Sneckbauer, in a finely varnished buggy drawn by two bays that shone with health and good grooming; a young darky driving him; a tightly packed suit case strapped behind; himself, dapper, wide awake, affable.

But Mr. Sneckbauer was not the guest of honor that night at Mr. Buddie's table, notwithstanding the fresh and pleasing atmosphere which his presence brought with it.

Sophronie was delighted to think the one cloud over the domestic paradise had been removed. She could not help regretting, however, that the gentleman from New Orleans and the gentleman from Winn had not reversed the order of their coming. What a charming day she might have spent in providing hospitality to so agreeable a personage! She avoided Aunt Crissy's eye. There was a triumphant light in it which interpreted meant: "I know a gentleman when I see one."

"Yo' father can drive you an' the baby in his buggy," said Mr. Buddie after supper with the air of arranging for a second barbecue. "I'll take the other chil'ren with me in the light wagon."

His wife looked up with startled enquiry.

"To Winn," he replied; "we'll start in the mornin'."

Sophronie wondered if she were again going to be left behind, and began to feel a little discouraged.

Charlie

Six of Mr. Laborde's charming daughters had been assembled for the past half hour in the study room. The seventh, Charlotte, or Charlie as she was commonly called, had not yet made her appearance. The study was a very large corner room with openings leading out upon the broad upper gallery.

Hundreds of birds were singing out in the autumn foliage. A little stern-wheeler was puffing and sputtering, making more commotion than a man-o'-war as she rounded the bend. The river was almost under the window—just on the other side of the high green levee.

At one of the windows, seated before a low table covered with kindergarten paraphernalia were the twins, nearing six, Paula and Pauline, who were but a few weeks old when their mother died. They were round-faced youngsters with white pinafores and chubby hands. They peeped out at the little snorting stern-wheeler and whispered to each other about it. The eldest sister, Julia, a slender girl of nineteen, rapped upon her desk. She was diligently reading her English Literature. Her hands were as white as lilies and she wore a blue ring and a soft white gown. The other sisters were Charlotte, the absentee, just past her seventeenth birthday, Amanda, Irene and Fidelia; girls of sixteen, fourteen and ten who looked neat and trim in their ginghams; with shining hair plaited on either side and tied with large bows of ribbon.

Each girl occupied a separate desk. There was a broad table at one end of the room before which Miss Melvern the governess seated herself when she entered. She was tall, with a refined though determined expression. The "Grandfather's Clock" pointed to a quarter of nine as she came in. Her pupils continued to work in silence while she busied herself in arranging the contents of the table.

The little stern-wheeler had passed out of sight though not out of hearing. But again the attention of the twins was engaged with something outside and again their curly heads met across the table.

"Paula," called Miss Melvern, "I don't think it is quite nice to whisper in that way and interrupt your sisters at their work. What are you two looking at out of the window?"

"Looking at Charlie," spoke Paula quite bravely while Pauline glanced down timidly and picked her fingers. At the mention of Charlie, Miss Melvern's face assumed a severe expression and she cautioned the little girls to confine their attention to the task before them.

The sight of Charlie galloping along the green levee summit on a big black horse, as if pursued by demons, was surely enough to distract the attention of any one from any thing.

Presently there was a clatter of hoofs upon the ground below, the voice of a girl pitched rather high was heard and the apologetic, complaining whine of a young negro.

"I didn' have no time, Miss Charlie. It's hones', I never had no time. I tole Marse Laborde you gwine git mad an' fuss. You c'n ax Aleck."

"Get mad and fuss! Didn't have time! Look at that horse's back—look at it. I'll give you time and something else in the bargain. Just let me catch Tim's back looking like that again, sir."

The twins were plainly agitated, and kept looking alternately at Miss Melvern's imperturbable face and at the door through which they expected their sister to enter.

A quick footstep sounded along the corridor, the door was thrown hurriedly open, and in came Charlie. She looked right up at the clock, uttered an exclamation of disgust, jerked off her little cloth cap and started toward her desk. She was robust and pretty well grown for her age. Her hair was cut short and was so damp with perspiration that it clung to her head and looked almost black. Her face was red and overheated at the moment. She wore a costume of her own devising, something between bloomers and a divided skirt which she called her "trouserlets." Canvas leggings, dusty boots and a single spur completed her costume.

"Charlotte!" called Miss Melvern arresting the girl. Charlie stood still and faced the governess. She felt in both side pockets of her trouserlets for a handkerchief which she finally abstracted from a hip pocket. It was not a very white or fresh looking handkerchief; nevertheless she wiped her face with it.

"If you remember," said Miss Melvern, "the last time you came in late to study—which was only the day before yesterday—I told you that if it occurred again I should have to speak to your father. It's getting to be an almost every day affair, and I cannot consent to have your sisters repeatedly interrupted in this way. Take your books and go elsewhere to study until I can see your father." Charlie was gazing dejectedly at the polished floor and continuing to mop her face with the soiled handkerchief. She started to blurt out an apology, checked herself and crossing over to her desk provided herself with a few books and some scraps of paper.

"I'd rather you wouldn't speak to father this once," she appealed, but Miss Melvern only motioned with her head toward the door and the girl went out; not sullenly, but lugubriously. The twins looked at each other with serious eyes while Irene frowned savagely behind the pages of her geography.

It was not many moments before a young black girl came and thrust her head in at the door, rolling two great eyes which she had under very poor control.

"Miss Charlie 'low, please sen' her pencil w'at she lef' behine; an' if Miss Julia wants to give her some dem smove sheets o' paper; an' she be obleege if Miss Irene len' her de fountain pen, des dis once."

Irene darted forward, but subsided at a glance from Miss Melvern. That lady handed the black emissary a pencil and tablet from the table.

Before very long she was back again interrupting the exercises to lay a bulky wad before the governess. It was an elaborate description of the unavoidable adventures which had retarded Charlie's appearance in the study room.

"That will do, Blossom," said Miss Melvern severely, motioning the girl to be gone.

"She wants me to wait fo' an' answer," responded Blossom settling herself comfortably against the door jamb.

"That will do, Blossom," with distinct emphasis, whereupon Blossom reluctantly took her leave. But before long she was back again, nothing daunted and solemnly placed in Miss Melvern's unwilling hand a single folded sheet. Whereupon she retired with a slow dignity which convinced the twins that a telling and important strike had been accomplished by the absent Charlie. This time it was a poem—an original poem, and it began:

"Relentless Fate, and thou, relentless Friend!"

Its composition had cost Charlie much laborious breathing and some hard wrung drops from her perspiring brow. Charlie had a way, when strongly moved, of expressing herself in verse. She was greatly celebrated for two notable achievements in her life. One was the writing of a lengthy ode upon the occasion of her Grandmother's seventieth birthday; but she was perhaps more distinguished for having once saved the levee during a time of perilous overflow when her father was away. It was a story in which an unloaded revolver played a part, demoralized negroes and earth-filled gunny sacks. It got into the papers and made a heroine of her for a week or two.

On the other hand, it would be difficult to enumerate Charlie's short-comings. She never seemed to do anything that anyone except her father approved of. Yet she was popularly described as not having a mean bone in her body.

Charlie was seated in a tilted chair, her heels on the rung, and in the intervals of composition her attention was greatly distracted by her surroundings. She sat outside on the brick or "false gallery" that formed a sort of long corridor at the back of the house. There was always a good deal going on out there. The kitchen was a little removed from the house. There was a huge live oak under whose spreading branches a few negro children were always playing—a few clucking chickens always scratching in the dust. People who rode in from the field always fastened their horses there. A young negro was under the tree, sharpening his axe at the grindstone while the big fat cook stood in the kitchen door abusing him in unmeasured terms. He was her own child, so she enjoyed the privilege of dealing with him as harshly as the law allowed.

"W'at you did wid dat gode (gourd) you, Demins! You kiar water to de grine stone wid it! I tell you, boy, dey be kiarrin' water in yo' skull time I git tho' wid you. Fetch dat gode back heah whar it b'longs. I gwine break eve'y bone in yo' body, an' I gwine tu'n you over to yo' pa: he make jelly outen yo' hide an taller."

The fat woman's vituperations were interrupted by the shock of a well-aimed missile squarely striking her broad body.

"If there are going to be any bones broken around here, I'll take a hand in it and I'll begin with you, Aunt Maryllis. What do you mean by making such a racket when you see me studying out here?"

"I gwine tell yo' pa, Miss Charlie. Dis time I gwine tell 'im sho'. Marse Laborde ain' gwine let you keep on cripplin' his han's scand'lous like you does. You, Demins! run 'long to de cabin, honey, an' fetch yo' mammy de spirits o' camphire." She turned back in the kitchen bent almost double, holding her hand sprawled over her ponderous side.

It was indeed very trying to Charlie to be thus interrupted in her second stanza as she was vainly striving after a suitable rhyme for "persecution." And again there was Aurendele, the 'Cadian girl, stalking across the yard with a brace of chickens to sell. She had them tied together at the legs with a strip of cotton cloth and they hung from her hand head downward motionless.

"He! what do you want? Aurendele!" Charlie called out. The girl piped shrilly back from the depths of a gingham sunbonnet.

"I lookin' fo' Ma'me Philomel, see if she want buy couple fine pullets. They fine, yes," she reiterated holding them out for Charlie's inspection. "We raise 'em from that Plymouth Rock. They ain't no Creole chicken, them, they good breed, you c'n see fo' yo'se'f."

"Plymouth fiddlesticks! You'd better hold on to them and try to sell them to the circus as curiosities: 'The feathered skeletons.' Here, Demins! turn these martyrs loose. Give them water and corn and rub some oil on their legs . . .

"No, Aurendele, I was only joking. I don't know how you can part with those Plymouth Rocks; you'll feel the separation and it'll go hard with your mother and the children. What do you want for them?"

Aurendele only wanted a little coffee and flour, a piece of fine soap, some blue ribbon such as her sister Odélia had bought at the store and a yard of "cross-bars" for a sunbonnet for Nannouche.

Charlie directed the girl to Ma'me Philomel. "And you ought to know better," she added, "than to stand here talking when you see I'm busy with my lessons."

"You please escuse me, Miss Charlie, I didn' know you was busy. W'ere you say I c'n fine Ma'me Philomel?"

And Charlie went back to the closing stanza which was something of an exhortation: "Let me not look again upon thy face While frowning mood, of joy usurps the place."

The poem being finished, signed and duly delivered by Blossom, the sister of Demins, Charlie felt that she had brought her intellectual labors to a fitting close.

A moment before, a negro had wheeled into the yard on a hand-cart

Charlie's new bicycle. It had been deposited at the landing by the little stern-wheeler earlier in the morning, and to witness and superintend its debarkation had been the cause of Charlie's tardiness in the class room. Now, with the assistance of Demins and Blossom the wheel was unpacked and adjusted under the live oak. It was a beauty, of very latest construction. Charlie had traded her old wheel with Uncle Ruben for an afflicted pony which she had great hope of saving and training for speed. The discarded bicycle was intended as a gift for Uncle Ruben's bride. Since its presentation the bride had not been seen in public.

Charlie mounted and gave an exhibition of her skill to a delighted audience of negroes, chickens and a few dogs. Then she decided that she would ride out in search of her father. It was not on her own account that she had entreated Miss Melvern's silence, it was on his. She realized that she was a difficult and perhaps annoying problem for him, and did not relish the idea of adding to his perplexity.

As Charlie wheeled past the kitchen she peeped furtively in at the window. Aunt Maryllis was kneading a lump of dough with one hand while the other was still clapped to her side. Charlie felt remorseful and wondered whether Aunt Maryllis would rather have fifty cents or a new bandana! But the gate was open, and away she went, down the long inviting level road that led to the sugar mill.

II

Miss Melvern in a moment of exasperation had once asked Charlie if she were wholly devoid of a moral sense. The expression was rather cruelly forceful, but the provocation had been unusually trying. And Charlie was so far devoid of the sense in question as not to be stung by the implication. She really felt that nothing made much difference so long as her father was happy. Her actions were reprehensible in her own eyes only so far as they interfered with his peace of mind. Therefore a great part of her time was employed in apologetic atonement and the framing of vast and unattainable resolutions.

An easy solution would have been to send Charlie away to boarding school. But upon the point of separation from any of his daughters, Mr. Laborde had set his heart with stubborn determination. He had once vaguely entertained the expedient of a second marriage, but was quite willing to abandon the idea on the strength of a touching petition framed by Charlie and signed by the seven sisters—the twins setting down their marks with heavy emphasis. And then Charlie could ride and shoot and fish; she was untiring and fearless. In many ways she filled the place of that ideal son he had always hoped for and that had never come.

He was standing at the mill holding the bridle of his horse and watching Charlie's approach with complicated interest. He was preposterously young looking—slender, with a clean shaved face and deep set blue eyes like Charlie's, and dark brown hair. The gray hairs on his temples might have been counted and often were, by the twins, perched on either arm of his chair.

"Well, Dad, how do you like it? Isn't it a beaut!" Charlie exclaimed as she flung herself off her wheel and wiped her steaming face with her bended arm. Mr. Laborde took a fresh linen handkerchief from his pocket and passed it over her face as if she had been a little child.

"If I hadn't been down at the landing this morning, goodness knows what they would have done with it. What do you suppose? That idiot of a Lulin swore it wasn't aboard. If I hadn't gone aboard myself and found it—well—that's why I happened to be late again. Miss Melvern is going to speak to you." A grieved and troubled look swept into his face, and was more stinging than if he had upbraided her. This way there was no excuse—no denial that she could make.

"And what are you doing out here now? Why aren't you in with the others at work?" he questioned.

"She sent me away—she's getting tired." Charlie's face was a picture of impotent regret as she looked down and uprooted a clump of grass with the toe of her clumsy boot. "I worked some, though, and then I just *had* to see about the wheel. I couldn't have trusted Demins."

It was one of the occasions when she regretted that her father was not a more talkative man. His silences gave her no opportunity to defend herself. When he rode away and left her there she noticed that he did not hold his chin in the air with his glance directed across the fields as usual, but looked meditatively between his horse's ears. Then she knew that he was perplexed again.

Charlie just wished that Miss Melvern with her rules and regulations was back in Pennsylvania where she came from. What was the use of learning tasks one week only to forget them the next? What was the use of hammering a lot of dates and figures into her head beclouding her intelligence and imagination? Wasn't it enough to have six well educated daughters!

But troubled thoughts, doubts, misgivings found no refuge in Charlie's bosom and they glanced away from her as lightly as winged messengers. Her father was plainly hurt and had not invited her to join him as he sometimes did. Miss Melvern had declined to entertain her apologies and, she knew, would not admit her into the class room. Anyway she felt that God must have intended people to be out of doors on a day like that, or why should he have given it to them? Like many older and more intelligent than herself, Charlie sometimes aspired to a knowledge of God's ways.

Far down the lane on the edge of a field was the Bichous' cabin—the parents of Aurendele, from whom Charlie had that morning purchased the chickens. Youngsters were swarming to their noontide meal and the odor within of frying bacon made Charlie sensible of the fact that she was hungry. She rode into the enclosure with an air of proprietorship which no one ever dreamed of resenting, and informed the Bichou family that she had come to dine with them.

"I thought you was *so* busy, Miss Charlie," remarked Aurendele with fine sarcasm.

"You mustn't think so hard, Aurendele. That's what Tinette's baby died of last week."

Aurendele had obtained the yard of "cross-bar" and was cutting out the sun bonnet for Nannouche who happened to have a good complexion which her relatives thought it expedient to preserve.

"Tinette's baby died o' the measles!" screamed Nannouche who knew everything.

"That's what I said. If she had only thought she didn't have the measles instead of thinking so hard that she did, she wouldn't have died. That's a new religion; but you haven't got sense enough to understand it. You haven't an idea above corn bread and molasses."

Charlie seemed not to have many ideas above corn bread and molasses herself when she sat down to dine with the Bichous. She shared the children's *couche couche* in the homely little yellow bowl like the rest of them—and did not disdain to partake of a goodly share of salt pork and greens with which Father Bichou regaled himself. His wife stood up at the head of the table serving every one with her long bare arms that had a tremendous reach.

Charlie made herself exceedingly entertaining by furnishing a condensed chronicle of the news in the great world, colored by her own lively imagination. They had a way of believing everything she said—which was a powerful temptation that many a sterner spirit would have found difficult to resist.

She was on the most intimate and friendly terms with the children and it was Xenophore who procured a fine hickory stick for her when, after dinner she expressed a desire to have one. She trimmed it down to her liking, seated on the porch rail.

"There are lots of bears where I'm going; maybe tigers," she threw off indifferently as she whittled away.

"W'ere you goin'?" demanded Xenophore with round eyed credulity.

"Yonder in the woods."

"I never yeared they any tigers in the wood. Bears, yes. Mr. Gail killed one w'en I been a baby."

"When you 'been a baby,' what do you call yourself now? But tigers or bears, it's all the same to me. I haven't killed quite as many tigers; but tigers die harder. And then if the stick goes back on me, why, I have my diamond ring."

"Yo' diamon' ring!" echoed Xenophore fixing his eyes solemnly on a shining cluster that adorned Charlie's middle finger.

"You see if I find myself in a tight place all I have to do is to turn the ring three times, repeat a Latin verse, and presto! I disappear like smoke. A tiger wouldn't know me from a hickory sapling."

She got down off the rail, brandished the stick around to test its quality, buckled her belt a bit tighter and announced that she would be off. She asked the Bichous to look after her wheel.

"And don't you attempt to ride it, Aurendele," she cautioned. "You might break your head and you'd be sure to break the wheel."

"I got plenty to do, me, let alone ridin' yo' bicyc'," retorted the girl with lofty indifference.

"It wouldn't matter so much about the head—there are plenty to spare around here—but there isn't another wheel like that in America; and I reckon you heard about Ruben's bride."

"W'at about Ruben's bride?"

"Well, never mind about what, but you keep off that wheel."

Charlie started off down the lane with a brisk step.

"W'ere she goin'?" demanded Mother Bichou looking after her. "My! my! she's a piece, that Charlie! W'ere she goin'?"

"She goin' yonder in the wood," replied Xenophore from the abundance of his knowledge. Ma'me Bichou still gazed after the retreating figure of the girl.

"You better go 'long behine her, you, Xenophore."

Xenophore did not wait to be told twice. In three seconds he was off, after Charlie; his little blue-jeaned legs and brown feet moving rapidly beneath the shade thrown by the circle of his enormous straw hat.

The strip of wood toward which Charlie was directing her steps was by no means of the wild and gloomy character of other woods further away. It was hardly more than a breathing spot, a solemn, shady grove inviting dreams and repose. Along its edge there was a road which led to the station. Charlie had reached the wood before she perceived that Xenophore was at her heels. She turned and seized the youngster by the shoulder giving him a vigorous shake.

"What do you mean by following me? If I was anxious for your company I would have invited you, or I could have stayed at the cabin and enjoyed your society. Speak up, why are you tagging along after me like this?"

"Maman sen' me, it's her sen' me behine you."

"Oh, I see; for an escort, a protector. But tell the truth, Xenophore, you came to see me kill the tigers and bears; own up. And just to punish you I'm not going to disturb them. I'm not even going in the direction where they stay."

Xenophore's face clouded, but he continued to follow, confident that despite her disappointing resolutions in regard to the wild beasts, Charlie would furnish diversion of some sort or other. They walked on for a while in silence and when they came to a fallen tree, Charlie sat herself down and Xenophore flopped himself beside her, his brown little hands folded over the blue jeans, and peeping up at her from under the brim of his enormous hat.

"I tell you what it is Xenophore, usually, when I come in the woods, after slaying a panther or so, I sit down and write a poem or two. That's why I came out here to day—to write a poem. There are lots of things troubling me, and nothing comforts me like that. But Tennyson himself couldn't write poetry with a little impish 'Cadian staring at him like this. I tell you what let's do, Xenophore," and she pulled a pad of paper from some depths of her trouserlets. "I think I'll practise my shooting; I'm getting a little rusty; only hit nine alligators out of ten last week in bayou Bonfils."

"It's pretty good, nine out o' ten," proclaimed Xenophore with an appreciative bob.

"Do you think so?" in amazement, "why I never think about the nine, only about the one I missed," and she proceeded to tear into little squares portions of the tablet Miss Melvern had sent her by Blossom in the morning. Handing a slip to Xenophore:

"Go stick this to that big tree yonder, as high as you can reach, and come back here." The youngster obeyed with alacrity. Charlie, taking from her back pocket a small pistol which no one on earth knew she possessed except her sister Irene, began to shoot at the mark, keeping Xenophore trotting back and forth to report results. Some of the shots were wide of the mark, and it was with the utmost reluctance that Xenophore admitted these failures.

There was a sudden loud, peremptory cry uttered near at hand.

"Stop that shooting, you idiots!" A young man came stalking through the bushes as if he had popped out of the ground.

"You young scamp! I'll thrash the life out of you," he exclaimed, mistaking Charlie for a boy at first. "Oh! I beg pardon. This is great sport for a girl, I must say. Don't you know you might have killed me? That last ball passed so near that—that—"

"That it hit you!" cried Charlie perceiving with her quick and practised glance a red blotch on the sleeve of his white shirt, above the elbow. He had been walking briskly and carried his coat across his arm. At her exclamation he looked down, turned pale, and then foolishly laughed at the idea of being wounded and not knowing it, or else in appreciation of his deliverance from an untimely death.

"It's no laughing matter," she said with a proffered motion to be of some assistance.

"It might have been worse," he cheerfully admitted, reaching for his handkerchief. With Charlie's help he bound the ugly gash, for the ball had plowed pretty deep into the flesh.

The girl was conscience stricken and too embarrassed to say much. But she invited the victim of her folly to accompany her to Les Palmiers.

That was precisely his original destination, he was pleased to tell her. He was on a business mission from a New Orleans firm. The beauty of the day had tempted him to take a short cut through the woods.

His name was Walton—Firman Walton, which information, together with his business card he conveyed to Charlie as they walked along. Xenophore kept well abreast, his little heart fluttering with excitement over the stirring adventure.

Charlie glanced absently at the card, as though it had nothing to do with the situation, and proceeded to roll it into a narrow cylinder while a troubled look spread over her face.

"I'm dreadfully sorry," she said. "I'm always getting into trouble, no matter what I do. I don't know what father'll say this time—about the gun, and hitting you and all that. He won't forgive me this time!" Her expression was one of abject wretchedness. He glanced down at her with amused astonishment.

"The hurt wasn't anything," he said. "I shall say nothing about it— absolutely nothing; and we'll give this young man a quarter to hold his tongue." She shook her head hopelessly.

"It'll have to be dressed and looked after."

"Please don't think of it," he entreated, "and say nothing more about it."

At half past one the family assembled at dinner. It was always Julia who presided at table. She looked very womanly with her long braid of light-brown hair wound round and round till it formed a coil as large as a dessert plate. Her father sat at the opposite end of the table and the children, the governess and Madame Philomel were dispersed on either side. There were always a few extra places set for unexpected guests. Uncle Ruben, in a white linen apron served the soup and carved the meats at a side table while the plates and dishes were passed around by Demins and a young mulatto girl.

The dining room was on the ground floor and opened upon the false gallery where Charlie had spent a portion of her morning in composition. The absence of that young person from her accustomed place at table was immediately observed and commented upon by her father.

"Where's Charlie" he asked, of everybody—of nobody in particular.

Julia looked a little helpless, the others nonplussed, while Pauline picked her fingers in painful embarrassment. Madame Philomel, who was fat and old fashioned, thought that the new bicycle would easily account for her absence.

"If Charlotte appears befo' sundown, it will be a subjec' of astonishment," she said with an air of conviction and irresponsibility. Every one assumed an air of irresponsibility in regard to Charlie which was annoying to Mr. Laborde as it implied that the whole burden of responsibility lay upon his own shoulders, and he was conscious of not bearing it gracefully. He had spent the half hour before dinner in consultation with Miss Melvern, who prided herself upon her firmness—as if firmness were heaven's first law. Mr. Laborde was in a position to convey to her

Charlie's latest resolutions, in which Miss Melvern placed but a small degree of faith. Mr. Laborde himself believed firmly in the ultimate integrity of his daughter's intentions. Miss Melvern's strongest point of objection was the pernicious example which Charlie furnished to her well-meaning sisters, and the interruptions occasioned by her misdirected impulses. Her tardiness of the morning, though not a great fault in itself, was the culmination of a long line of offenses. It might in fact be said that it was the last straw *but one*. Miss Melvern was inclined to think it *was* the last straw. But as hers was not the back which bore the brunt of the burden, she was not wholly qualified to judge. Mr. Laborde began to perceive that there might be a last straw.

Blossom, who assumed the role of a privileged character—the velvet footed Blossom stepped softly into the dining room and spoke, while her glance revolved and fixed itself upon the ceiling.

"Yonder Miss Charlie comin' 'long de fiel' road wid a young gent'man. Nary one ain't ridin' de bicycle—des steppin' out slow a-shovin' it 'long. 'Tain't Mr. Gus an' 'tain't Mr. Joe Slocum. 'Tain't nobody we all knows." Whereupon Blossom withdrew, being less anxious to witness the effect of her announcement than to assist at the arrival of Charlie, the gentleman and the bicycle.

Though accustomed to face situations, this young gentleman exhibited some natural trepidation at being ushered unexpectedly into the bosom of a dining family. He was good looking, intelligent looking. His appearance in itself was a guarantee of his respectability.

"This is Mr. Walton, dad," announced Charlie without preliminary, "he was coming to see you anyhow. He took a short cut through the woods and—and I shot him by mistake in the arm. Better have some antiseptic and stuff on it before he sits down. I had my dinner with the Bichous."

III

There seemed to be a universal, tacit understanding that Charlie was in disgrace, that she herself had deposited the last straw and that there would be results. The silence and outward calm with which her father had met this latest offense were ominous. She was made to stand and deliver her firearm together with her ammunition.

"Take care, father, it's loaded," she cautioned as she placed it upon his writing table.

She was informed that she would not be expected to join the others in the class room and was instructed to go and get her wardrobe in order and to discard her trouserlets as soon as possible.

Mr. Walton was not taken into the family confidence, but he realized that his coming was in the nature of a catastrophe. Having dispatched the business which brought him he would have continued on his way, but the scratch on his arm was rather painful, and that night he had some fever. Mr. Laborde insisted upon his remaining a few days. He knew the young man's people in New Orleans and did business with the firm which he represented.

To young Walton the place seemed charming—like a young ladies' Seminary. And well it might. Madame Philomel taught the girls music and drawing; accomplishments which she had herself acquired at the Ursulines in her youth. During the afternoon hour there was nearly always to be heard the sound of the piano: exercises and scales, interspersed with variations upon the Operas.

"Who is playing the piano?" asked Walton. He leaned against a pillar of the portico, his arm in a sling, and caressing a big dog with the other hand. Charlie sat dejectedly on the step. She still wore the trouserlets, having been unable to procure at so short notice anything that she considered suitable.

"The piano?" she echoed, looking up. "Fidelia, I suppose. It all sounds alike to me except that Fidelia plays the loudest. She's so clumsy and heavy-handed."

Fidelia in fact was thickwaisted and breathed hard. She was given over to afflictions of the throat and made to take exercise which, being lazy, she did not like to do.

"What a lot of you there are," said the young fellow. "Your eldest sister is beautiful, isn't she! It seems to me she's the most beautiful girl I almost ever saw."

"She has a right to be beautiful. She looks like dad and has a character like Aunt Clementine. Aunt Clementine is a perfect angel. If ever there was a saint on earth—Hi, Pitts! catch 'im! catch 'im Pitts!" The dog bounded away after a pig that had mysteriously escaped from its pen and made its way around to the front, prospecting.

Julia, with Amanda and Irene had driven away a while before in the ample barouche. Nothing could have been daintier than Julia in a soft blue "jaconette" that brightened her color and brought out the blue of her eyes.

"Why didn't you go along driving?" asked Walton when the dog had darted away and he seated himself beside Charlie on the step.

"They're going over to Colimarts to take a dancing lesson."

"Don't you like to dance?"

"I haven't time. Maybe if I liked to, I'd find time. Madame Philomel made a row about me not taking dancing and music and all that, and Dad said I might do as I liked about it. So Ma'me Philo stopped interfering. 'I 'ave nothing to say!' that's her attitude now towards poor me."

"I'm awfully sorry," said the young man earnestly.

"Sorry! about the dancing? pshaw! what difference—"

"No—no, sorry about the accident of the other day. I'm afraid, perhaps it's going to get you into trouble."

"It'll get me into trouble all right; I see it coming."

"I hope you'll forgive me," he asked persistently, as though he had been the offender.

"It wasn't your fault," she said with condescension. "If it hadn't been that it would have been something else. I don't know what's going to happen; boarding school I'm afraid."

A small figure came gliding around the corner of the house. It was Xenophore, blue jeans, legs, hat and all. He came quietly and seated himself on a step at some little distance.

"What do you want?" she asked in French.

"Nothing."

They both laughed at the youngster. Far from being offended he smiled and peered slyly up from under his hat.

"Mr. Gus sen' word howdy," piped Xenophore a little later apropos of nothing, breaking right into the conversation.

"W'ere you saw Mr. Gus?" asked Charlie, falling into the 'Cadian speech as she sometimes did when talking to the Bichous.

"He pass yonder by de house on 'is ho'se. He say 'How you come on, Xenophore; w'en you see Miss Charlie?' I say, 'I see Miss Charlie to s'mornin',' an' he say 'Tell Miss Charlie howdy fo' me.'"

Then Xenophore arose and turning mechanically, glided noiselessly around the corner of the house.

It was dusk and the moon was already shining in the river and breaking with a pale glow through the magnolia leaves when the girls came home from their dancing lesson. It was nearing the supper hour so they did not linger, and Charlie went with them into the house, bent upon making a bit of toilet for the evening. She was secretly in hopes that Amanda would lend her a dress. Julia's gowns were quite too young-ladified; they touched the ground, often with a graceful sweep. One of Amanda's would have done nicely. But Amanda looked sidewise from her long, narrow, dark eyes when Charlie approached her with the request and blankly refused. Irene grew excited and indignant.

"Don't ask her, Charlie; why do you ask her? She thinks her clothes are made of diamonds and pearls, too good for Queen Victoria! What about my pink gingham if I ripped out the tucks?"

"Oh! it's no use," wailed Charlie. "There isn't time to rip anything and I could never get into it."

They were in Amanda's room, Irene and Charlie seated on a box lounge and Amanda decorating herself before the mirror. She had laid her own evening toilet on the bed and carefully locked closet, wardrobe and bureau drawers. She always kept things locked and had an ostentatious way of carrying her highly polished keys that were on a ring. Charlie gazed at her sister's reflected image with a sort of despair but with no trace of malice.

"If there's a thing I hate, it's to have people sit and stare when I'm dressing," remarked Amanda. The two girls got up and went out and Amanda locked the door behind them.

"Why not wear your Sunday dress, Charlie?" offered Irene as they walked down the long hall, arm in arm.

"You know what Julia said about its being so short and the sleeves so old fashioned and she wouldn't be seen at church with me if I wore it again. So I gave it to Aurendele the other day."

But it was Julia who came to the rescue. She fastened and pinned and tucked up one of her own gowns on Charlie and the effect, if not completely happy, could not have been called a distinct failure.

No one remarked upon the metamorphosis when she appeared thus arrayed at table. Miss Melvern and Madame Philomel were far too polite to seem to notice. The twins only beamed their approval and astonishment. Fidelia gasped and stared, closed her lips tight and sought Miss Melvern's glance for direction. Blossom alone expressed herself in a smothered explosion in the door way, and went outside and clung to a post for support.

To Mr. Laborde there was something poignant in the sight of his beloved daughter in this unfamiliar garb. It seemed a dismal part of the unhappy situation which had given him such heartache to solve—for he had solved it. He avoided looking at Charlie and wore an expression which reminded them all of the time he heard of his brother's death in Old Mexico.

Mr. Laborde had that evening reached a conclusion which was communicated to Charlie directly after supper when the others strolled out upon the veranda and she went with him to his study. She was to go to New Orleans and enter a private school noted for its excellent discipline. Two weeks at Aunt Clementine's would enable her to be fitted out as became her age, sex and condition in life. Julia was to go to the city with her, to see that she was properly equipped and later her father would join her and accompany her to the Young Ladies' Seminary.

She fingered the lace ruffle on Julia's sleeve as she looked down and listened to her father's admonitions.

"I'm sorry to give you all this worry, dad," she said, "but I'm not going to make any more promises; it's a farce, the way I've persistently broken them. I hope I shan't give you any more trouble." He took her in his arms, and kissed her fervently. Charlie was exceedingly astonished to discover that the arrangement planned by her father was not so distasteful as it would have seemed a while ago. It was not at all distasteful and she secretly marvelled.

When she and her father rejoined the others on the veranda they found that a visitor had arrived, Mr. Gus Bradley, the son of a neighboring planter and an intimate friend of the family. He had been painfully disconcerted at finding a stranger when he had expected to meet only familiar faces and the effect was not happy. Mr. Gus was so shy that it had never yet been discovered whom his visits at Les Palmiers were intended for. It was, however, generally believed that he favored Charlie on account of the messages which he so often sent her through Xenophore and others. He had given her a fine dog and a riding whip. But he had also made the twins a present of a gentle Shetland pony, and he had sent Amanda his photograph! He was a big fellow and awkward only from shyness and when in company, for in the saddle or out in the road or the fields he had a fine, free carriage. His hair was light and fine and his face smooth and looked as if it belonged to a far earlier period of society and had no connection with the fevered and modern present day.

The moon sent a great flood of light in upon the group—the only shadows were cast by the big round pillars and the fantastic quivering vines. Amanda sat by herself, tip toeing in a hammock and picking a tune on the mandolin. Madame Philomel was telling the twins a marvelous story in French about *Croque Mitaine*. Fidelia was drinking in words of wisdom at Miss Melvern's feet. It was Irene who was entertaining Mr. Gus and endeavoring to account to him in veiled whispers for young Walton's presence on the scene. She might have spoken as loud as she liked for the young gentleman in question was entirely absorbed in Julia's conversation and had ears for nothing else.

"I'm not going to stay," said Mr. Gus, almost apologetically. "I only rode over for a minute. I wanted to see your sister Charlie. I had something important to tell her."

"She'll be out pretty soon; she's inside talking to father."

When Charlie came out she went and seated herself beside Irene on the long bench that stood by the railing. Mr. Gus was near by in a camp chair. He was so flustered at seeing Charlie in frills and furbelows that he could scarcely articulate.

"I didn't know you," he blurted.

"Oh, well, I have to begin some time."

Irene got up and left them alone, remembering Mr. Gus's admission of an important communication for Charlie's ears alone.

"I haven't long to stay," he began. "I heard about Tim's shoulder and brought you a recipe for gall. It's the finest thing ever was. You'll find all the ingredients in your father's workshop, and you'd better mix it yourself; don't trust any one else. If you'd like, I'll put it up myself and bring it around tomorrow."

Irene off in the distance was positively agitated. She firmly believed Charlie was receiving her first proposal.

"Thank you, Mr. Gus, but it's no use," said Charlie. "Some one else is going to look after Tim from now on; I'm going away."

"Going away!"

"Yes, going to the Seminary in the city. Dad thinks it's best; I suppose it is."

He found absolutely nothing to say, but his mobile face took on a crestfallen look that the moonlight made pathetic; and Irene from her corner of observation, concluded that he had been rejected as she knew he would.

"I'll send dear old Pitts back. You keep him for me. I reckon they wouldn't let me have him in the Seminary."

"I'll come for him tomorrow," responded Mr. Gus with dreary eagerness. "When do you go?"

"In a day or two. The sooner the better as long as there's no getting out of it."

Two days later Charlie left the plantation accompanied by her sister Julia, young Walton and Madame Philomel. They boarded the little sputtering stern-wheeler about nine in the morning. It seemed as if the whole plantation, blacks and whites, had turned out to bid her *bon voyage*. The sisters were in tears. Even Amanda seemed moved and Irene was frankly hysterical. Miss Melvern was under a big sunshade with Fidelia, and the twins held their father's hands. All the Bichous had come; Aurendele in Charlie's "Sunday dress," Xenophore, round eyed, serious, unable to cry, unable to laugh, apprehending calamity. Mr. Gus galloped up with a huge bouquet of flowers, striving to appear as if it were wholly by accident.

Charlie was completely overcome. She would not go up to the cabin but stayed dejectedly seated on a cotton bale, alternately wiping her eyes and waving her handkerhcief until it was too limp to flutter.

IV

The change, or rather the revolution in Charlie's character at this period was so violent and pronounced that for a while it rendered Julia helpless. The trouble which Julia had anticipated was entirely of an opposite nature from the one which confronted her and it took her some time to realize the situation and ajust herself to it. As it happened, the combined efforts of both Aunt Clementine and Julia were insufficient to keep Charlie within bounds; to give her a proper appreciation of values after the feminine instinct had been aroused in her.

The diamond ring she had always with her. It was her mother's engagement ring. Hitherto she had worn it for the tender associations which made her love the bauble. Now she began to look upon it as an adornment. She possessed a round gold locket containing her mother's and father's pictures. This she suspended from her neck by a long thin gold chain. Such family jewels as had by inheritance descended to her, seemed to the young thing insufficient to proclaim the gentle quality of sex. She would have cajoled her father into extravagances. She wanted lace and embroideries upon her garments; and she longed to bedeck herself with ribbons and *passementeries* which the shops displayed in such tempting array.

Her short cropped hair was a sore grievance to Charlie when she viewed herself in the mirror and she resorted to the disfiguring curling irons with results which were, to say the least, appalling to Julia who came in one afternoon and discovered her entertaining young Walton with her head looking like a prize chrysanthemum.

"I can't understand her, Aunt," Julia confided to her Aunt Clementine with tears in her blue eyes. "It's bad enough as it is, but just imagine what a spectacle she would make of herself if we permitted it. I'm afraid she's a little out of her senses. I'd almost rather think that than to believe she could develop such vulgar instincts."

Aunt Clementine would do no more than shrug her shoulders and look placidly and blamelessly perplexed. She was quite sure that Charlie did not take after any member of her side of the family; so the blame of heredity, if any, had naturally to be traced to other sides of the family.

Through mild and firm coercion Charlie was brought to understand that such excessive ornamentation as she favored would not for a moment be tolerated by the disciplinarians at the Seminary. When finally that young person was admitted to the refined precincts—save for the diamond ring and the locket, in the matter of which she had taken a stubborn stand—no fault could have been found with her appearance which was in every way consistent with that of the well mannered girl of seventeen.

She had spent a delightful fortnight. Aunt Clementine who was at once a lady of fashion and a person of gentle refinement had provided entertainment such as Charlie had not yet encountered outside of novels of high life: her Aunt Clementine's *ménage* having not before been to her liking.

They drove, they visited and received calls, dined and went to the opera. There was much shopping, perambulating and trying on of gowns and hats. There was a perpetual flutter, and indescribable excitement awaiting her at every turn. Young Walton was persistent in his attentions to the sisters, but as there were other and many claims upon Julia it was oftener Charlie who entertained him, walked abroad with him and even accompanied him on one occasion to Church.

The first moment that Charlie found herself alone in the privacy of her own room at the Seminary, she devoted that moment to unburdening her soul. She sat beside the window and looked out a while. There was not much inspiration to be gathered from the big red brick building opposite. But her inspiration was not dependent upon anything extraneous; it was bubbling up inside of her and generating an energy that found a vent in its natural channel.

Equipped with a very fine pen point and the filmiest sheet of filmy writing paper, Charlie wrote some lines of poetry in the smallest possible cramped hand. She did not hesitate or bite her pen or frown, seeking for words and rhymes. She had made it all up beforehand and its rhythm kept time with the beating of her heart. Poor little thing! Let her alone. It would be cruel to tell the whole story. When the lines were written she folded the sheet over and over and over, making it as flat and thin as possible. Then with her hat pin she picked out the little glass frame that contained her mother's picture in the locket, and laying the scrap of poetry in the cover, replaced the picture.

As the young girls at the Seminary were all of gentle breeding they gave no pronounced exhibition of their astonishment at Charlie's lack of accomplishments. She herself felt her shortcomings keenly and read their guarded wonder. With dogged determination she had made up her mind to transform herself from a hoyden to a fascinating young lady, if persistence and hard work could do it.

As for hard work, there was enough of it! Hoeing, or chopping cane seemed child's play compared with the excruciating intricacies which the piano offered her. She began to have some respect for Fidelia's ponderous talent and even wondered at the twins. After some lessons in drawing, the instructor disinterestedly advised her to save her money. He was gloomy about it. The spirit of commercialism, he said, had not touched him to the crass extent of countenancing robbery. With some sinking of heart, Charlie let the drawing go, but when it came to dancing, she would yield not an inch. She practised the steps in the narrow confines of her room, and when opportunity favored her, she waltzed and two-stepped up and down the long corridors. Some of the girls took pity and gave her private instructions, for which she offered tempting inducements to their cupidity in the shape of chocolate bon-bons and stick-pins.

She was immensely liked, though they had small respect for her abilities until one day it fell upon them with the startling bewilderment of lightning from a clear sky that Charlie was a poet. It happened in this wise: The fête of the foundress of the Seminary was to be celebrated and the young ladies were desired to write addresses in her honor, the worthiest of these addresses to be selected and delivered in the venerable lady's presence upon the date in question.

It was so much easier for Charlie to write twenty or fifty lines of verse than pages and pages of prose.

When the announcement of the award was made in a most flattering little speech to the assembled classes by the lady directress, the girls were stupefied, and Charlie herself almost as well pleased as if she had been able to play a minuet upon the piano or go through the figures of a dance without blundering.

"Did you ever!" "Well, I knew there was something in her!"

"I told you she wasn't as stupid as she looks!"

"Why didn't she say so!" were a few of the comments passed upon Charlie's suddenly unearthed talent.

A group besieged her in her room that afternoon.

"Out with them!" cried the spokesman, armed with a box of chocolate creams, "every last of them. Where do you keep them? Hand over the key of that desk. You're a barefaced impostor, if you want to know it."

They seated themselves on chairs, stools, the lounge, the floor and the bed—as many as could crowd in a row, and awaited with the pleased expectancy of girls ready to extract entertainment from any situation that presents itself.

Charlie had no thought of reluctance. She brought forth the mass of manuscript and delivered it over to the chocolate bearer who had a sonorous voice and a reputation as an elocutionist.

One by one the poems were read, with fictitious fire, with melting pathos as the occasion called for, while silently the chocolates were passed around and around.

Charlie rocked violently and tried to look indifferent. Her hair was long enough to tie back now with a bow of ribbon. On her forehead she wore a few little curls made with the curling irons, and as she glanced in the mirror while she rocked she wondered if her face would ever get beautiful and silky white. Charlie took no part in the athletic sports such as tennis and basket ball, though urged to do so. She was given over to putting some kind of greasy stuff on her hands at night and slept in a pair of her father's old gloves.

"Well," commented the reader, laying down the leaves.

"Moonlight on the Mississippi."

"This is the finest thing I ever read. I wish you'd give me this, I'd like to send it to mother. And all I've got to say for you is that you are a large sized goose. The idea of keeping such poetry as that cooped up here! Why don't you go to work and publish those things in the Magazines, I'd like to know. I tell you, they'd jump at the—well! I like this! Empty! where are all those chocolates gone? The next time I go halves in a box of chocolates you people'll know it!"

It need not be supposed that Charlie saw nothing of her home folks during her stay at the Seminary. They came in squads and detachments. Julia must have been spending much time with her Aunt Clementine, for the two not infrequently drove around in Aunt Clementine's victoria upon which occasions Charlie was very proud of her sister's beauty and air of distinctintion which the other girls did not fail to observe and rave over.

Amanda and Irene came down from the plantation with their father expressly to see her. The girls who caught a glimpse of them did not hesitate to pronounce Mr. Laborde the handsomest man they had ever set eyes upon; Amanda a most striking and fascinating personality. But of Irene they held their estimate in reserve, as the poor girl had seemed demented, laughing in the midst of tears, weeping to an accompaniment of laughter.

Once Miss Melvern made her appearance with Fidelia. It was a great pleasure to introduce the governess to the faculty and the methods, while Fidelia trod heavily and seriously at her side, crimson under the scrutiny of so many strange eyes.

Last came Madame Philomel one morning with the twins and whom beside but Aurendele and Xenophore! She wore a beautiful new bonnet, a sprigged challie dress with a black mantilla and kid gloves. The young ladies who were growing more and more interested in Charlie's family with every fresh installment, to quote them literally, lost their minds over the twins who were like two chubby rosy-cheeked angels in spotless white.

"It's positively paralyzing!"

"How do you tell them apart?"

"I must have a sketch of them."

"How do they know themselves, which is which?"

"Oh! *we* know them of course," said Charlie with laudable pride, "but strangers can tell by their difference of manner: Pauline is timid and Paula dreadfully mischievous. Would you believe it? She fooled dad one day by hanging her head and picking her fingers when he asked her an embarrassing question. There was no trouble at this juncture in discovering which was which."

Aurendele, still wearing Charlie's "Sunday dress" which was getting sadly small for her and a sailor hat of Irene's, was alert, but overawed and unable to remember the multitude of things she had stored up in her brain to communicate to Charlie. And as for Xenophore, he felt there had been a convulsion of nature and he was powerless to place the responsibility. To be sitting there in "store clothes," brogans, twirling in his hands a little felt hat no bigger than a plate, Miss Charlie in hair ribbons and dressed like a girl! He was speechless. It was only toward the close of the visit that he uttered his first word.

"Mr. Gus sen' word 'howdy.' "

"W'en you saw Mr. Gus?" asked Charlie laughing.

"He pass by the house an' he say, 'How you come on, Xenophore! w'at you all year f'om Miss Charlie?' I tell 'im I'm goin' to the city to see you an' he say, 'Tell Miss Charlie howdy fo' me.' "

But when her father came alone one morning quite early—he had remained over night in the city that he might be early—and carried her off with him for the day, her delight knew no bounds. He did not tell her in so many words how hungry he was for her, but he showed it in a hundred ways. He was like a school boy on a holiday; it was like a conspiracy; there was a flavor of secrecy about it too. They did not go near Aunt Clementine's. They saw no one they knew except Young Walton who was busy over accounts in the commission office where Mr. Laborde stopped to supply himself with money enough to pay his way. The young fellow turned crimson with unexpected pleasure when he saw them. He was eager to know if any other members of the family were in the city. He showed a disposition to be excused from the office and to join them, a suggestion which Mr. Laborde did not favor, which rather alarmed him and hurried his departure. Moreover he could see that Charlie did not like the young man, and he could not blame her for that, all things considered! She gave her whole attention to her gloves and the clasp of her parasol while there.

It was well they provided themselves with money. Charlie needed every thing she could think of and what she forgot her father remembered. He carried her jacket and assisted her over the crossings like an experienced cavalier. He helped her to select a new sailor hat and saw that she put it on straight. Not approving of her hat pin he bought her another, besides handkerchiefs, a fan, stick pins, presents for the girls and the favorite teachers, books of poetry, and the latest novels. The maid at the Seminary was kept busy all afternoon carrying in bundles.

They went to the lake to eat breakfast; a second breakfast to be sure, but such exceedingly young persons could not be expected to restrict themselves to the conventional order in the matter of refreshment. It was a great delight to be abroad: the air was soft and moist and the warm sun of early March brought out the scent of the earth and of distant gardens and the weedy smell from the still pools.

They were almost alone at the lake end save for the habitual fishermen and sportsmen, the *restaurateurs* and lazy looking *garçons*. Their small table was out where the capricious breeze beat about them, and they sat looking across the glistening water, watching the slow sails and feeling like a couple of bees in clover.

Charlie drew off a glove, looked at her hand and silently held it out for her father's inspection, right under his eyes.

"What do you think of that, dad?" she asked finally. He gazed at the hand and rubbed his cheek, meditatively, as he would have pulled his moustache if he had had one.

"Just take a good look at it. Notice anything?" He took her hand, scrutinizing the ring.

"No stones missing, are there?"

"I don't mean the ring, but the hand," turning her palm uppermost. "Feel that. You know what it used to be. Ever feel anything softer than that?"

He held the hand fondly in both of his, but she withdrew it, holding it at arm's length.

"Now, dad, I want your candid opinion; don't say anything you don't believe; but do you think it's as white as—Julia's, for instance?"

He narrowed his eyes, surveying the little hand that gleamed in the sun, like a connoisseur sizing up a picture.

"I don't want to be hasty," he said quizzically. "I'm not too sure that I remember, and I shouldn't like to do Julia's hand an injustice, but my opinion is that yours is whiter."

She threw an arm around his neck and hugged him, to the astonishment of a lame oysterman and a little Brazilian monkey that squealed in his cage with amusement.

"It's all right, Charlie dear, but you know you mustn't think too much about the hands and all that. Take care of the head, too, and the temper."

"Don't fret, dad," tapping her forehead under the rim of the 'sailor,' "the head's coming right up to the front: history, literature, ologies, everything but dates and figures; getting right in here; consumed with ambition. And the girls didn't think I'd ever learn to dance until I gave them a double shuffle and a Coonpine! Now I'm giving lessons. Never mind! some of these days they'll be asking your permission to make me queen of the Carnival. And as for temper! Why, it's ridiculous, dad. I'm beginning to—to bleat!"

Well, it was a day full to the brim. In the afternoon they heard a wonderful pianist play. It gave Charlie a feeling of exaltation, a new insight; the music somehow filled her soul with its power.

It was nearly dark when she embraced her father and bade him good bye. For weeks the memory of that day lasted.

It was in the full flush of April that a telegram came summoning Charlie home at once. Terror seized her like some tangible thing. She feared some one was dead.

Her father had been injured, they told her. Not fatally, but he wanted her.

V

It was one of those terrible catastrophes which seem so impossible, so uncalled for when they come home to us, that stupefy with grief and regret; an accident at the sugar mill; a bit of perilous repairing in which he chose to assume the risk rather than expose others to danger. It was hard to say what had happened to him. He was alive; that was all, but torn, maimed and unconscious. The surgeon, who was coming as fast as steam and the iron wheels could bring him, would tell them more of it. The surgeon was on the train with Charlie and so was the professional nurse. They seemed to her like monsters; because he read a newspaper and conversed with the conductor about crops and the weather; and the other, demure in her grey dress and close bonnet, displayed an interest in a group of children who were traveling with their mother.

Charlie could not speak. Her brain was confused with horror and her thoughts were beyond control. Every thing had lost significance but her grief and nothing was real but her despair. Emotion stupefied her when she thought that he would not be there at the station waiting for her with outstretched arms and beaming visage; that she would perhaps never see him again as he had been that day at the lake, robust and beautiful, clasping her with loving arms when he said good bye in the soft twilight. She became keenly conscious of the rhythm of the iron wheels that seemed to mock her and keep time to the throbbing in her head and bosom.

There was a hush upon the whole plantation. Silent embraces; serious faces and tearful eyes greeted her. It seemed inexpressibly hard that she should be kept from him while the surgeon and the nurse were hurried to his side. A physician was already there, and so was Mr. Gus.

During the hour or more that followed, Charlie sat alone on the upper gallery. Madame Philomel with Julia and Amanda were indoors praying upon their knees. The others were speechless with anxiety. Charlie alone was quiet and dull. It had rained and there was a delicious freshness in the air, the birds were mad with joy among the dripping leaves that glistened with the filtering rays of the setting sun. She sat and stared at the water still pouring from a tin spout.

The twins came and leaned their heads against her. She took Pauline into her lap and fastened the child's shoestring that had come untied. She stared at them both with absent-minded eyes. Then Irene came and led them away. The water had stopped flowing from the spout and Charlie fixed her eyes upon the peacock that moved with low trailing plumage over the wet grass.

There was a sweet, sickening odor stealing from the house, more penetrating than the scent of the rain-washed flowers. She groaned as the fumes of the anesthetic reached her. She leaned her elbows upon the rail and with her head clasped in her hands, stared down at the gravel before the steps.

Someone came out upon the porch and stood beside her; it was Mr. Gus, all his shyness submerged for the moment in quick sympathy.

"Poor old Charlie," he said softly and took her hand.

"Is he dead, Mr. Gus? have they killed him?" she asked dully.

"He isn't dead. He won't die if he can help it."

"What have they done to him?"

"Never mind now, Charlie; just thank God that he is left to us."

A deep prayer of thankfulness went up from every heart. The crushing pressure was lifted, and they rejoiced that it was to be life rather than death—life at any price.

With the changed conditions that so soon make themselves familiar, a new character was stamped upon the family life at Les Palmiers. There was a quiet and unconscious readjustment. The center of responsibility shifted and sought as it were to find lodgment for a time in every individual breast. The family took turns in watching at the bedside after the quiet woman in grey had gone. Then it was that even Demins showed fine mettle in those days. Money might have paid his services, it could never balance his devotion.

Charlie forgot that she was young and that the sun was shining out of doors and the voices of the woods and fields awaited her. But between sick-watches she took again to the task of beautifying her outward and inward being. She sought after becoming arrangements of her hair; over the kitchen fire she mixed ointments for the whitening of her skin; and while committing to memory tasks that filled her sisters with admiration, she polished her pointed nails till they rivalled the pearly rose of the conch-shells which Mme. Philomel kept upon either side of her hearth.

It was getting pretty warm and systematic work in the class room had been abandoned. Miss Melvern went away on her annual home visit and Aunt Clementine came up to the plantation to condole and to read the riot-act.

Her brother was sufficiently recovered to be scolded, to listen to the truth as Aunt Clementine defined her plain talk. It was high time he gave over thinking he might keep his daughters always like a bouquet of flowers, in a bunch, as it were, on the family hearth. He was not quite equal to the task of disagreeing with her. She had plans for separating these blossoms so that they might disseminate their sweetness even across the seas. Julia and Amanda should accompany her abroad in the Autumn. A winter in Paris and Rome, not to mention Florence, would accomplish more for them than years in the class room. Aunt Clementine saw great possibilities of a fine lady in Amanda. The girl presented more crude, promising material than Julia even. A year at the Seminary for Irene, and Charlie—

"Please leave me out of your calculations, Aunt," said Charlie with a flash of her old rebellious nature. "Dad'll have something to say when he's able to bother about it, and in the meantime I propose to take care of myself and the youngsters and of Dad, and this meeting's got to end right here. When he is strong enough to talk back, Aunt Clementine, you may come and have it out with him." Aunt Clementine had always considered the girl coarse and she surveyed the girl with compassion.

"Charlie, remember to whom you are speaking," said Julia with gentle rebuke. But they all filed out of the sick room, Amanda with a calm exultation in her face—and left Charlie to smoothe the pillow and quiet the nerves of the convalescent.

Julia seemed to be always more than ready to accept an invitation from her aunt. Life in the country began apparently to weary her, and, without too much urging she accompanied Aunt Clementine back to the city.

Young Walton had been up to Les Palmiers on a visit of sympathy and had had a conversation alone with Mr. Laborde which had been to the last degree satisfactory. Charlie wore her pink organdie and her grandmother's pearls during his visit and puffed her hair.

It was a week or so after Julia's departure for the city that the remaining sisters were all assembled on the false gallery one forenoon awaiting the return of Demins with the mail. Twice a day it was Demins' duty to fetch and carry the family mail from and to the station. Amanda's familiarity with keys seemed to entitle her to the office of locking and unlocking the canvas bag and it was she who distributed the mail.

There was a letter from Julia for each one of the sisters, under separate cover; even the twins got one between them. A proceeding so unfamiliar on the part of the undemonstrative Julia caused more than a flutter of wonder and comment. Envelopes were torn open, exclamations followed: rejoicing, dismay, elation, consternation! Engaged! Julia engaged! and the sky still in its place overhead and not crumbling about their ears!

Charlie alone said nothing at first, then in a voice hideous with anger: "She's a deceitful hypocrite, she's no sister of mine, I hate her!" She turned and went into the house leaving Julia's letter lying upon the bricks. Pauline began to utter little choking sobs at once. Fidelia grew red with indecision and dismay.

"She can't bear him," said Irene with shame-faced apology.

"Charlie's a goose," remarked Amanda picking up the letter and folding it back into its envelope, "let's go and hear what father has to say."

A little later Charlie in her trouserlets, boots and leggings, mounted black Tim and galloped madly away, no one knew where.

"Look like ol' Nick took hol' o' Miss Charlie again," commented Aunt Maryllis leaning from the kitchen window.

"She mad 'cause Miss Julia g'in git ma'rid to de young man w'at she shot," said Blossom. "I yeard 'em. Miss Irene 'low Miss Charlie f'or hate dat man like pizen."

At the sound of Tim's pounding hoofs upon the road, Xenophore darted from the cabin door. And at sight of Charlie rushing past in the old familiar guise of a whirlwind, the youngster threw himself flat down and rolled in the dust with glee, even though he knew his mother would whip the dust from his jeans without the trouble of removing them from his small person.

No one ever knew where Charlie ate her dinner that day. She did not quite kill Tim but it took days of care to set him on his accustomed legs again. She did not join the family at the evening meal and remained apart in her own room, refusing admittance to those who sought to reach her.

In her mad ride Charlie had thrown off the savage impulse which had betrayed itself in such bitter denunciation of her sister. Shame and regret had followed and now she was steeped in humiliation such as she had never felt before. She did not feel worthy to approach her father or her sisters. The girlish infatuation which had blinded her was swept away in the torrents of a deeper emotion, and left her a woman.

It was trivial, perhaps, for her to take the little poem from the back of her mother's miniature and holding it on the point of a hat pin, consume it in the flame of a match.

During the stillness of the night when she could not sleep, she crept out of bed and lit her lamp, shading it so that its glimmer could not be detected from without.

Removing the precious diamond ring from her finger she began to polish and brighten it till the glittering stones were scintillant in their dazzling whiteness. The task over, she put the ring in a little blue velvet cover which she took from her bureau drawer and laid it upon the pin cushion. Then Charlie went back to bed and slept till the sun was high in the heavens.

She had little to say at breakfast the next morning and there was no one who felt privileged to question her. With the others she gathered on the false gallery to wait for the mail as she had done the day before. When her letters were handed to her she also took her father's mail and turned to go with it.

"Girls," she said bravely, half turning. "I want to tell you I am ashamed of what I said yesterday. I hope you'll forget it. I mean to try to make you forget it." That was all. She went on up to her father.

He was stretched upon a cot near the window, like a pale shadow of himself.

"Where have you been all this time, Charlie?" he asked, with reproachful eyes. She stood over his cot couch for a moment silent.

"I've been climbing a high mountain, dad." He was used to her flights of speech when they were alone.

"And what did you see from the top, little girl?" he questioned with a smile.

"I saw the new moon. But here are your letters, dad." She drew a low chair and sat close, close to his bed.

"Isn't Gus coming up?" he asked. Mr. Gus came each morning to offer his services in reading or answering letters.

"I'm jealous of Mr. Gus," she said. "I know as much as he, more perhaps when it comes to writing letters. I know as much about the plantation as you do, dad; you know I do. And from now on I'm going to be—to be your right hand—your poor right hand," she almost sobbed sinking her face in the pillow. The arm that was left to him he folded around her and pressed his lips to her brow.

"Look, Dad," she exclaimed, cheerfully recovering herself and plunging her hand in her pocket. "What do you think of this for a wedding present for Julia?" She held the open blue velvet case before his eyes.

"You rave! nonsense. I thought you prized it more than any of your possessions; more than Tim even."

"I do. That's why I give it. There'd be no value in giving a thing I didn't prize," she said inconsequentially.

While she was writing out the card of presentation at the table, Mr. Gus came in and Charlie joined him at the bed side.

"This little woman has an idea she can run the plantation, Gus, till I get on my feet," said Mr. Laborde more cheerfully than he had spoken since his accident. "What do you think about it?"

Mr. Gus turned a fine pink under his burned skin.

"If she says so, I don't doubt it," he agreed, "and I'm always ready to lend a hand; you know that. I'm going towards the mill now, and if Charlie cares—I see her horse saddled out there," peering from the window as if the sight of the horse saddled, awaiting its rider, was something he had not perceived before.

"Here are your letters, dad. One of the girls will come up and get them ready for you and when I come back I'll answer them. I'll save Mr. Gus that much."

From his window Mr. Laborde watched the two mount their horses under the live oak tree.

Aunt Maryllis was standing in the kitchen door holding a small tin cup.

"Miss Charlie," she called out, "heah dis heah grease you mix' up fo' yo' han's; w'at I gwine do wid it?"

"Throw it away, Aunt Maryllis," cried Charlie over her shoulder.

The old woman sniffed at the cup. It smelled good. She thrust the tip of a knotty black finger into the creamy white mixture and rubbed it on her hand. Then she deliberately hid the tin in a piece of newspaper and set it away on the chimney shelf.

There is no telling what would have become of Les Palmiers that

summer if it had not been for Charlie and Mr. Gus. It was precisely a
year since Charlie had been hustled away to the boarding school in a
state of semi-disgrace. Now, with all the dignity and grace which the
term implied, she was mistress of Les Palmiers.

Julia was married and away on her wedding journey prior to making
her home in the city. Amanda was qualifying in Paris under the tutelage
of Aunt Clementine to enter the lists as a fine lady of fashion. The others
were back in the class room with Miss Melvern in her old place. Mr.
Laborde had recuperated slowly from the terrible shock to his nervous
system six months before; and though he was getting about, he spent
much time reclining in the long lounge in the upper hall.

It was a moonlight night and very quiet. He could sometimes faintly
hear the lap of the great river, and he caught the low hum of voices
below. It was Mr. Gus and Charlie conversing in the lower veranda.
Mr. Gus was stripping a long, thin branch of its thorns and leaves and
tangling his speech into incoherence.

"There's no hurry. I just mentioned it, Charlie, because I—couldn't
help it."

"No, there's no hurry," agreed Charlie leaning back against a pillar
and gazing up at the sky. "I couldn't dream of leaving Dad without a
right arm."

"Of course not; I couldn't expect it. But then couldn't he have two
right arms!"

"And then the twins. I've come to be a sort of mother to them rather
than a sister; and you see I'd have to wait till they grew up."

"Yes, I suppose so. About how old are the twins now?"

"Nearly seven. But we'll talk of all that some other time. Didn't you
hear Dad cough? That's a sly way he has of attracting my attention. He
doesn't like to call me outright." Mr. Gus was beating the switch upon
the gravel.

"There's something I wanted to ask you."

"I know. You want to ask me not to call you 'Mr.' Gus any more."

"How did you know?"

"I am a clairvoyant. And besides you want to ask me if I like you
pretty well."

"You *are* a clairvoyant!"

"It seems to me I've always liked you better than any one, and that
I'll keep on liking you more and more. So there! Good night." She ran
lightly away into the house and left him in an ecstasy in the moonlight.

"Is that you, Charlie?" asked her father at the sound of her light footfall. She came and took his hand, leaning fondly over him as he lay in the soft, dim light.

"Did you want anything, Dad?"

"I only wanted to know if you were there."

The White Eagle

It was not an eagle of flesh and feathers but a cast-iron bird poised with extended wings and wearing an expression which, in a human being, would have passed for wisdom. He stood conspicuously upon the lawn of an old homestead. In the spring, if any white paint went the rounds, he came in for his share of it, otherwise he had to be content with a coat of whitewash such as the sheds and fences were treated to.

But he was always proud; in the summer standing spotless on the green with a background of climbing roses; when the leaves fell softly and he began to show unsightly spots here and there; when the snow wrapped him like a shroud, or the rain beat upon him and the wind struck at him with wild fury—he was always proud.

A small child could sit in the shadow of his wings. There was one who often did on sunny days while her soul drank the unconscious impressions of childhood. Later she grew sensible of her devotion for the white eagle and she often caressed his venerable head or stroked his wings in passing on the lawn.

But people die and children squabble over estates, large or small. This estate was not large, but the family was, and it seemed but a pittance that fell to the share of each. The girl secured her portion and the white eagle beside; no one else wanted it. She moved her belongings up the street into a pleasant room of a neighbor who rented lodgings. The eagle was set down in the back yard under an apple tree, and for a while he succeeded in keeping the birds away. But they grew accustomed to his brooding presence and often alighted on his outspread wings after their mischievous onslaughts upon the apples. Indeed he seemed to be of no earthly use except to have sheltered the unconscious summer dreams of a small child.

671

People wondered at the young woman's persistence in carting him about with her when she moved from place to place. Her want of perspicacity might have explained this eccentricity. It explained many other things, chiefly the misfortune which overtook her of losing her small share of the small estate. But that is such an ordinary human experience, it seems useless to mention it; and, besides, the white eagle had nothing to do with it.

There was finally no place for him save in a corner of her narrow room, that was otherwise crowded with a bed, a chair or two, a table and a sewing machine, that always stood by the window. Oftentimes when she sewed at the machine, or else from her bed before she arose in the early dawn, she fancied the white eagle blinked at her from his sombre corner on the floor, an effect produced by remnants of white paint that still stuck in his deep eye sockets.

The years went by, slowly, swiftly, haltingly as they marked off the uneven progress of her life. No mate came to seek her out. Her hair began to grizzle. Her skin got dry and waxlike upon her face and hands. Her chest grew shrunken from eternal bending over the sewing machine and lack of pure, fresh air. The white eagle was always there in the gloomy corner. He helped her to remember; or, better, he never permitted her to forget. Sometimes little children in the house penetrated to her room, and amused themselves with him. Once they made a Christmas spectacle of him with a cocked hat and bits of tawdry tinsel suspended from his wings.

When the woman—no longer young—grew sick and had a fierce fever, she uttered a shriek in the night which brought a straggler inquiring at her bedside. The eagle had blinked and blinked, had left his corner and come and perched upon her, pecking at her bosom. That was the last she knew of her white eagle in this life. She died, and a close relative, with some sentiment and possessing the means of transportation, came from a distance and laid her out suitably and buried her decently in the old cemetery on the side of the hill. It was far up on the very crest, overlooking a vast plain that reached out to the horizon.

None of her belongings, save perhaps the sewing machine, were of a character to arouse family interest. No one knew what to do with the white eagle. The suggestion that it be thrown into the ash-bin was not favorably received by the sentimental relative, who happened to remember a small, barefooted child seated in the summer grass within the shadow of its outstretched wings.

So the white eagle was carted for the last time up the hill to the old cemetery and placed like a tombstone at the head of her grave. He has stood there for years. Sometimes little children in spring throw wreaths of clover-blossoms over him. The blossoms dry and rot and fall to pieces in time. The grave has sunk unkept to the level. The grass grows high above it in the summer time. With the sinking grave the white eagle has dipped forward as if about to take his flight. But he never does. He gazes across the vast plain with an expression which in a human being would pass for wisdom.

The Wood-Choppers

Enough rain had fallen all day—and was still falling—to dampen the most sanguine spirits. The little frame schoolhouse beside the bayou sat in water like Noah's ark. The pelting rain upon the shingle roof and the raucous quacking of ducks outside seriously interfered with the routine of the work.

Léontine concluded that the cause of education would be in no way imperiled if she dismissed, a little earlier than usual, the four small boys who were her only pupils that day. All the little girls had stayed at home.

From the doorway she watched the barefooted youngsters go splashing homeward, with their jean trousers rolled high above the knees. Then she herself, with bent head, seeming to charge the elements with her big cotton umbrella, turned toward home.

She was well-equipped against an ordinary rain, so far as mackintosh and rubber shoes went, but best of all, she carried a stout heart. She tried to think only of the snug fireside toward which she was making her laborious way ankle-deep in mud and running water.

Her home was nearly half a mile away; a poor little bit of a Southern house, standing pretty close to the road that skirted the river. A few cabins were far in the distance, set down in a level field that bristled with gaunt, denuded cotton-stalks.

Léontine let herself in at the gate. She found the cow waiting there, and let her in, too, after making sure that the calf was secure. Then she mounted the few wobbly steps to the gallery, where she removed her dripping mackintosh and the rubber shoes that had been next to no protection at all.

Léontine's look of anticipation, as she opened the house door and hurried in, was suddenly turned to dismay when she saw her mother at the fireplace scraping together a few red ashes between the andirons, while Mandy, a very small black girl, was kneeling on the hearth with an apronful of wet chips.

"Why, mother!" the girl cried in French. "What are you doing without a fire on a day like this? Do you want to catch your death of cold?"

Her white-haired mother, feeble-looking and much bent, turned with a quaver that was like an apologetic appeal.

"There is no wood cut, my child; none, none, none," and she continued to scrape the embers with the tongs.

"No wood cut!" echoed Léontine, forgetting her soaking and be-draggled condition. "Where's Peter? Didn't Peter come?"

"No Peter all day. I sent Mandy through the rain to hunt him up. His wife says he is working over at Aaron's store, hauling freight. She says he told François to come, but François has not come; no one has come."

"I see François," piped up Mandy. "François 'low he ain't 'bleege to do somethin' des because Unc' Peter say so."

Léontine hesitated a moment, and then slipped on her mackintosh again. Right through the driving rain the girl went to the wood-pile.

"Léontine! Léontine, come back! Are you crazy? You are losing your mind! Oh dear! dear!" cried the mother, wringing her poor, delicate hands.

"Go in and shut the door, mother! Shut the door!" The door was shut, and Léontine proceeded to get the ax, which was under the shelter of the back gallery—a stout, sharp ax.

She had sometimes chopped kindling and bits of light wood, and she did not believe that this would be much harder. It certainly looked like child's play when Peter wielded the ax.

She selected the slimmest stick she could conveniently pull into place and arrange for action, and pretty soon she was hard at work. She knew just as well as if she were looking into the house that her mother was weeping, and that Mandy was standing with folded hands, gazing upon the doleful spectacle.

"Pim! pam!" began the ax. "Bing! bang!" it resounded, and Léontine, with swinging arms, was presently in a fine glow.

If every blow had counted, she would soon have had a neat stack of firewood at hand; but the trouble was that the strokes, in the most un-accountable manner, never fell twice in the same spot.

Many another girl, in a like predicament, might have felt discouraged; not Léontine. The knack of wood-chopping was something she believed she might acquire in time, and there was a beginning to everything.

A buggy drawn by two stout mules came slowly splashing along the road. It stopped opposite to where she was so lustily at work. A head peered over the protecting curtain, and a masterful voice called out:

"Hey, there, girl! What are you up to? Are the men Indians in this parish, that they let the women chop wood?"

Léontine looked up, and seeing that the man was a total stranger, she would have reddened if she could have become any redder than she was. Turning, she went on wielding the ax without replying.

"Stop that chopping and go along into the house out of the rain! You ought to be ashamed of yourself!"

As there was no use in trying to turn red, Léontine turned purple and went on chopping.

The man alighted from his buggy without another word, came in at the gate, and was soon standing beside her at the wood-pile. He wore a long, thick overcoat and a black slouch hat, and looked to Léontine like a bearded tyrant.

"This won't do," he said, quietly and firmly taking the ax out of her hand. "What are you doing this for? Isn't there any black fellow around these diggings to chop your wood?"

Léontine was what they sometimes, in that region, call "spunky." She tried to look dignified and offended, but, with mortification, realized that the atmospheric conditions somewhat thwarted her design.

"You are a stranger, sir," she began.

"No, I'm not. I live six miles below here, just moved, and I'm there to stay."

"Peter cuts wood for us," she explained, somewhat mollified. "He didn't come to-day, and I found my mother without a fire and suffering with cold when I returned from school a while ago. Will you kindly let me continue my work? I have no time to waste in conversation."

"Trot along in, trot along in, mademoiselle, and get into some dry clothes," was the man's only reply.

Realizing the futility of standing out in the rain arguing, not to say quarreling, with an eccentric, perhaps insane, stranger, Léontine left him and went into the house. She found her mother and Mandy, agitated by the liveliest curiosity, peering through the window.

"I don't know him," she answered to her mother's question. "I don't know what he intends to do," in further reply. "Maybe murder us all; you'd better lock the door." And she went into the adjoining bedroom to divest herself of the saturated garments that felt like leaden weights upon her.

"Dey look like Mr. Slocum's mules an' buggy," ventured Mandy, whose attention was divided between the man and his equipage.

"You're right, Mandy. It must be the young man that bought the Slocum place and everything on it."

Léontine soon heard the ax fairly singing out at the wood-pile. Then a sepulchral whisper reached her from Mandy through the keyhole:

"Miss L'ontine, he's choppin' wood!"

"Well, let him chop; who cares?"

A while later, when her toilet was almost completed, Mandy's stealthy voice was again projected into the room:

"Miss L'ontine, he done got a big pile chop'. He kiarin' it on de gal'ry."

Léontine hardly knew how to cope with the situation. She wished that her mother were possessed of more strength of character. But she knew just as well as anything that her mother would be polite to him, without the least assertion of offended dignity.

As Léontine emerged from her room blooming, all freshly attired in a neat, dark skirt and white shirt-waist, the stranger appeared in the door-way leading from the back gallery.

"Pardon me, ladies," he said, with an easy inclination. "My name's Willet. I live six miles below here—Slocum place. Just want to be neighborly. I'll give you you lots of chances of returning the compliment. Have you people got any kindling, any light wood around here that could start a fire?" His eyes had been attracted to the gaping, empty fireplace.

Madame hastened to inform him, deprecatingly:

"Aaron promise' to sen' me a load las' week, monsieur, but his oxen got cripple' in the cut-off."

"Never mind, mother," interrupted Léontine, in French. "You needn't explain to him; it isn't necessary."

The intruder, undismayed at the knowledge that they were "talking about him," cast a searching eye around, and unceremoniously started out to the buggy, returning with an empty pine box which he had taken from under the seat.

He broke the box on the hearth with his stout boot heel, and in less than five minutes there was a glorious blaze roaring up the cavernous chimney.

"Now that looks more cheerful!" he exclaimed, brushing off his hands. "I'll bid you good day, mademoiselle; good-by, madame," interrupting her voluble acknowledgements. "Don't let mademoiselle chop wood any more. In the first place, she doesn't know how, and in the second place— she doesn't know how."

Then he went brusquely away, entered his buggy, and started the mules at a brisk trot, probably to make up for lost time.

Léontine looked after him in a blaze of indignation.

"Truly a gentleman and a man of noble heart!" madame exclaimed. "Mandy, put the water on for coffee, and also a few sweet potatoes in the ashes."

If Léontine hoped to have seen the last of this stranger, with his unconventional ways, she was greatly mistaken. Scarcely a day passed that she did not find, on her return from school, evidences of his continued assiduity in her and her mother's behalf—a basket of fruit, a haunch of venison or a wild turkey hanging out on the meat hook. Some indication of neighborly regard was forever confronting her.

When he called one Sunday afternoon, having obtained her mother's permission to do so, she was at first the small personification of dignity and reserve. This time he had brought a book with him, and some magazines, and the girl, hungry for such things, must have been of stone not to have melted somewhat under this benign influence.

The subject of wood-chopping seemed by mutual consent to be eliminated from their conversation. Further reference to the theme was moreover entirely unnecessary, since Peter and François, for some mysterious cause, fairly fought with each other over the privilege of chopping wood and rendering themselves generally useful about the place.

"What a noble soul!" madame often exclaimed. "And in my opinion there is none in the parish to compare with him in looks." Léontine was silent, but it was not the silence of contradiction.

Once she said, with great show of emotion:

"Mother, you must put a stop to Mr. Willet's constant visits and attentions. Some day he will be bringing a wife home to his plantation. Some one who may look down on us, who will be disagreeable, whom we will dislike. I'm *sure* we will dislike her. Such men always marry women whom people dislike!"

Madame did not even seem to listen to this harangue. She only ordered Mandy to throw another stick upon the fire.

One afternoon it was raining very hard, and madame was watching through the misty panes for the return of her daughter. It was George Willet's buggy that stopped at the door, and it was the young planter himself who helped Léontine to alight. They came into the room beaming with some unexpressed secret. To the astonishment of all—none more than Mandy—Mr. Willet walked up to the old lady, threw his arms round her and gave her a hearty kiss.

"It's all right, mother," laughed Léontine, and Mr. Willet, gaily echoing her words, cried, "It's all right, mother!"

When they were married in the spring and moved over to the big plantation, there was but one of Léontine's possessions that George Willet laid personal claim to. That was the heavy old ax. He bore it away himself in a sort of triumph, proclaiming that as long as he lived it should hold a place of honor in his establishment.

Polly

Polly particularly disliked to have her mail addressed to the real estate office in which she was employed as assistant bookkeeper. She pushed aside the businesslike letter which confronted her one morning when she had mounted the high stool before her desk.

What Polly did like was to find letters awaiting her at her boarding-house in the evening, when she might, in the privacy of her room, enjoy reading the news from home or from friends scattered over the western hemisphere.

There was one weekly letter to which Polly especially looked forward. She always read it slowly, as she would have eaten ice-cream, making the delight of it last as long as possible. There was in every one of those letters a cheerful reference to something which was going to happen "when Ferguson opens up in St. Jo"; something that made Polly look as bright as a sparrow on a maple branch.

What was *not* going to happen when Ferguson opened up in St. Jo? Polly was going to get a better position; or rather, some one else, named George, was going to get a better position, and incidentally through George Polly was going to get a position which every well-meaning girl, at some time of her life, looks forward to as the beginning of better things.

When the noon hour came Polly laid aside her brown paper cuffs, put on her jacket, stabbed a hat-pin through her cloth hat, and thrusting the businesslike letter into her hand-bag, went out to luncheon.

It was not until Polly was entirely through with her frugal repast that she opened the businesslike letter to see what it was all about. She first saw that it enclosed a check for one hundred dollars, payable to the order of Polly McQuade. Then she saw that it was a letter from her Uncle Ben.

It is to be regretted that Uncle Ben's letter cannot be omitted here, so lacking was it in elegance or refinement of expression. It was from Fort Worth, and it read:

"Dear Little Polly. Your Uncle Ben has struck it rich in a small way, and the first treat he gives himself is to send you the enclosed—with conditions. You are to spend every red cent of it. No rainy-day fund will be tolerated by your Uncle B. Just you go to the stores and blow it all in—just take a fling with it. I want to give you the opportunity to feel what it's like to spend money for once in your life. Let me know when Ferguson opens up in St. Jo, and this little transaction will be duplicated. How are you getting on? Love to your mother and the girls. Affectionately, your Uncle Ben."

"Uncle Ben! Dear, dear Uncle Ben!" exclaimed Polly, with subdued emotion. This was an event in her life, and she met it with prompt decision. She had no intention of disregarding her Uncle Ben's conditions. She at once gave the waiter ten cents, which left a balance in her favor of ninety-nine dollars and ninety cents.

She went straight back to the office and asked the junior partner for an afternoon off. It was the first favor she had asked, and while the junior partner realized the indelicacy of refusing it, he was appalled.

"A *whole* afternoon! And so near the end of the month!"

"Yes, please." A most unfeminine Polly thus to keep her own counsel bottled and bubbling up inside her. Most girls would have—but never mind the other girls; this is about Polly.

It did not take her the whole afternoon to spend that hundred dollars. Uncle Ben would have been rather startled at her promptness in following his wishes. She had often lingered before the shop windows, and in imagination had sometimes spent as much as this and even more. It was as easy as if she had had a list written out beforehand.

A complete dinner-set of dainty but bygone pattern, $15, reduced from $25.

Sitting-room rug, $20.

Sitting-room lamp, $3.98, reduced from $5.75.

Books, $21.50.

Table-cloth and napkins, $5.

Sitting-room curtains, $6 (great bargain).

Order on a Filmore coal dealer for one hundred bushels of coal to be delivered to Mrs. Louise McQuade, $12.

Order on a Filmore grocer for supplies amounting to $10, to be delivered to Mrs. Louise McQuade.

A telegram to Filmore, 25 cents.

"Will be home Saturday evening to visit over Sunday. Polly."

A gorgeous cravat for Uncle Ben, a box of candy for the girls, a dozen linen handkerchiefs for mother, express charges, and a fifty-mile round-trip ticket to Filmore more than cleared up Polly's obligations to Uncle Ben.

Polly lay feverishly awake that night picturing the wonder of the family when this hundred dollars' worth of solid comfort began to descend upon them. The next day she sent a second telegram:

"Don't get excited. It's only me. Will explain Saturday. Polly."

Polly, in the bosom of her family on Saturday evening, could only laugh and laugh. She did not at once take off her wraps, but sat on the sofa beside her mother, doubling up with mirth. Her sister Phoebe, still a schoolgirl, was trying to tell her all about it.

"The whole town turned out, Polly, after the station-master had circulated the news that Mrs. McQuade had bought out St. Louis. When the things began to arrive, Mr. Fulton had to come over to keep order and hold back the crowd. In the midst up drives Smith: 'And where do you want the groceries put, Mrs. McQuade?' Groceries! And mum on the eve of nervous prostration! And there was Murphy at the back with two wagons shoveling coal into the shed till the planks gave way, and old Hiram so excited he couldn't find the hatchet and nails. Mr. Fulton's dog had three fits, and old Peter Neely's rheumatism left him in the effort he made to hobble down here, and it's never come back!"

Polly was hugging her mother, who was small, like herself, with gray hair. She looked like Polly with the light of youth grown dim within her.

Isabel, the tall and elegant older sister, who taught school, was looking at Polly with plain disapproval.

"Will you tell me, Polly McQuade, if you've taken leave of your senses?" she asked.

"Senses!" echoed Polly, with round eyes.

"Yes, senses! Have you lost them?"

"Well," said Polly, "I felt I'd left something behind, but I was afraid it was my tooth-brush."

"You're so good at figuring," continued Isabel, "will you kindly figure out how many winters you've been wearing that brown jacket?"

Polly stared down, disconcerted, at the brown jacket; then she began to thump her head with her knuckles, exclaiming:

"Stupid! Stupid!"

"Well, it's to be hoped," went on Isabel, "you have supplied yourself with shoes, stockings, underclothes, a suit, hat, gloves—" but by this time Polly had fled to make a bit of toilet for the evening, which was to be given over to sociability. Isabel had invited the guests, and had written a note to George to be of the number.

The evening which Isabel intended to devote to conversation and music was, it must be confessed, given up chiefly to inspecting the new appointments and expatiating upon their value and serviceable qualities.

The young people hovered over the books like bees over a clover path in June. The ladies could hardly be induced to leave the pantry after they had been given a glimpse of the new dinner-set with its dainty but bygone pattern, while Mr. Fulton was fascinated—absolutely bewitched by the lamp. He studied its mechanism with intense interest, and declared that nothing of the kind had ever been seen in Filmore, despite his wife's opinion that it was the counterpart of the one Laura Bliss had received for a wedding present.

After the hour of eight Polly's spirits began to descend lower and lower as the moments passed. Her laughter ceased, then silence seized her. Her eyes began to dim, and if her hair had only turned gray she would have looked exactly like her mother.

At ten o'clock she was about to plead a headache, which was no pretense, when he came! She heard the beat of his horse's hoofs upon the freezing ground blocks and blocks away. She heard them above the monotonous intonations of the druggist, who was reading selections from Browning as well as he could, with old Mr. Fulton turning the lamp-wick up and down at his pleasure.

How flushed and tall and fine he looked when he came into the room! Polly saw all the heroes of romance embodied in this one blond young man. He had been called away by a telegram early in the day, but had never believed he would not be back in good time for the party.

They wanted him to go out and look at the dishes; to survey the books and carpet; old Mr. Fulton called his attention to the lamp; but he would look at nothing but Polly. He went and sat beside her and took her hand in face of all the company.

"I have a great piece of news," he said, "that is, great to me, and I hope of interest to Polly. Ferguson's going to open up in St. Jo on the first of January!"

There was a general exclamation of delight, for this bold statement seemed to carry its own information to all. Mrs. McQuade went over and kissed her small daughter and George, and the others felt that congratulations were in order.

"Now, Miss Polly," whispered Isabel, "don't you wish you had it back?"

"What back?"

"Uncle Ben's check."

"Then I shouldn't have been here to hear it. I should only have heard it through a letter."

"Heard what?"

"Why, that—that Ferguson's going to open up in St. Jo."

It was with great regret that Lord & Pellem had to let Polly go a month later. Where could they find another like her? they asked each other. The senior partner, with an original sense of humor, presented her with a wedding gift in the firm's name: a small brass teakettle containing pieces of money aggregating a month's salary. And he sent it with the humorous injunction: "Polly, put the kettle on!"

The Impossible Miss Meadows

I

As Miss Meadows was a person of no consequence whatever, Mrs. Hyleigh sent the second best trap over to the railway station for her. The coachman was instructed to bring her trunk or whatever belongings she had, by the same conveyance. Mrs. Hyleigh, a couple of daughters, a son and his college chum were seated on the piazza of their summer home overlooking one of the beautiful Wisconsin lakes.

"One of us ought to have gone over to meet Miss Miller; the bishop won't like it," said Evadne who sat in a hammock, munching caramels and reading "The Triumph of Death."

"Meadows, not Miller," corrected Mrs. Hyleigh, "and what the bishop likes or doesn't like is no concern of yours, my dear, when it comes to the management of my own household." Mrs. Hyleigh was large and decided. Her hair was white and rolled back in a symmetrical and un-comprising pompadour. Cushions of fat had obliterated all lines of beauty from her face which was red with a suggestion of purple under the skin.

"I don't see why he chose to saddle her on us," whimpered Mildred who fumbled with a long gold chain and gazed ill-humoredly across the water. "Goodness knows we do enough church work in town; and the Sheltons coming on Thursday, too. I don't see what possessed him, or where we're going to put her. She can't room with Florence Shelton; that's a cinch."

"Mother, I wish you'd make Mildred stop that slang. You don't realize what it sounds like. If I was running this family—" and the boy whose name was Max and whose age was nineteen, finished his sentence with a sweeping glance of disapproval which seemed to include the entire

685

household, the lake, the boating, the neighbors and the whole surrounding country. He and his friend had played a little tennis that day, a little golf, had taken the naphta launch around the lake, driven ten miles across country and back, and they were then exchanging remarks upon the monotony of existence at a Wisconsin summer resort.

Mrs. Hyleigh heard little of what went on around her; her mind was always somewhere else, and she now gazed at a nasturtium-bed, planning an alteration in its shape and going through a mental interview with the gardener. It was at the request of the bishop that Mrs. Hyleigh had invited Miss Meadows for a few days' sojourn at Far Niente. The reverend gentleman had represented the young woman as the daughter of an humble and impoverished English clergyman, whose death had thrown her upon the world and her own resources. A long spell of illness had left the poor creature with shattered nerves which a week or two of wholesome country air would, it was hoped, restore to a healthful condition. The bishop was keenly sensible of Mrs. Hyleigh's kindness in the matter, and gave her the pleasing assurance that her reward would not be overlooked.

Miss Meadows, even with Max's assistance, descended awkwardly and timidly from the high trap when William pulled up a short distance from the house. She was tall, thin and stoop-shouldered with a flat chest. She wore a black alpaca skirt and a cheap, ill-fitting shirt waist. A leather belt that encircled her waist, slanted downward at the back, and her skirt band hung a little below it. The young lady's shoes were shabby, so were her gloves and so also were the sailor hat and bit of black dotted veil that covered the most ordinary and uninteresting features. Her voice alone when she spoke was not commonplace. It was rich and singy with the suggestion of a brogue.

"We are glad to have you come, Miss Meadows," said Mrs. Hyleigh with her stereotyped amiability; forgetting for the moment that she was not addressing a person of fashion or distinction. She had gone to the edge of the piazza to meet her visitor.

"This is my daughter, Evadne, who will see that the maid shows you to your room. And my older daughter—Mildred, dear?" Mildred arose, mumbled, and fell back into her chair. The boys were duly presented. After the briefest talk concerning the journey from Chicago, Miss Meadows followed Evadne like an embarrassed house-maid seeking an engagement.

"Another Klondike!" groaned Max.

"Hard lines," responded his friend; and clasping their knees they looked wearily toward the distant tennis court.

Mrs. Hyleigh and her daughter looked at each other.

"Well?" uttered the girl in a tone which implied: "I told you so."

"She's impossible! utterly impossible!" sighed Mrs. Hyleigh.

II

No one knew precisely what to make of Miss Meadows. She was homely as original sin; not so well dressed as the housemaid; wholly colorless and flat, but always in evidence; Mildred surveyed her with smothered rage, redoubled as the day of the Sheltons' coming drew near. In a vague unreasoning way she held her creed, indirectly through the bishop, responsible for a long line of discomforts which seemed to culminate in what she called the saddling of Miss Meadows; and she began to think there might be truths worth investigating in Agnosticism. She was a pale, anemic beauty who held her father and mother in condescending tolerance, the college boys in supreme contempt, and everything but the Sheltons in placid indifference.

Evadne, with some compassion and a natural consideration for the looks of things, tried a few improving touches upon Miss Meadows. With the aid of a safety pin, she fastened the girl's sagging skirt band to the belt of her shirt waist, and suggested an unobtrusive bustle.

"You see, a person of your build—well—it's too bad about your hair, isn't it—"

"Yes," replied Miss Meadows looking in the glass and passing a nerveless hand over her thin short blond hair. "It comes of the typhoid—but it seems to be coming out no thicker for that," with a profound sigh. There was all the beauty of vigorous youth and health in the face that glanced into the mirror over Miss Meadows' shoulder.

"Never mind," exclaimed the girl cheerfully, endeavouring to straighten back Miss Meadows' shoulders. "Brace up and look pleasant. You must get some color into your cheeks before you go back to town. I'm going to take you driving and sailing and teach you tennis, if you don't know it. Your folks won't recognize you, the time I get through with you."

Miss Meadows smiled in a way that lighted her whole face showing a row of fine teeth and a sudden light in her eyes. But in a second the light and the smile faded and she looked as dull and commonplace as ever.

She began at the very start to carry a piece of embroidery about with her and was forever losing her thimble or her scissors.

"Have you any relations in this country?" asked Mrs. Hyleigh the morning following the girl's arrival at Far Niente. They were alone together on the piazza. She laid down her embroidery and shook her head lugubriously, beginning to sway in the rocking chair, with a forward bob of the head.

"Father died eight months ago, the Friday past," clutching at the coarse handkerchief which lay in her lap. "He was all I had, save for an uncle in the north. There was very little, ma'm, indeed very little left when he was gone; and what with paying the pitiful debts, nothing left except from the furniture. Barely enough to bring me to New York. Me uncle thought there'd be more chance on this side, and Dr. Whitemar gave me a letter to the bishop in Chicago. But when I got there the typhoid took me before I ever so much as set me eye on his Grace." Here she passed a hand over her thin light hair and pressed the handkerchief to her lips.

It was indeed too bad. Mrs. Hyleigh felt uncomfortably moved; but really wished she might have helped the girl in some more agreeable way to herself, than entertaining her in the height of the season at Far Niente.

"There, there, my dear; we'll see what can be done. What does the bishop propose?"

"A nursery governess is about all I'm equal to, ma'm," going back to her work with a resigned air. "His Grace thinks he can place me with a family on the North Side when I get back. Indeed me pride's all gone. For it isn't me ancestor who fought for Charles II that can help me now!"

Mrs. Hyleigh, too, heaved a deep sigh. She couldn't have told if it was over the ragged condition of her nasturtium-bed or the utter impossibility of counting upon Charles II or his followers to alleviate the present distress of Miss Meadows. She dimly felt it incumbent upon her to return the young person to the bishop in a better condition than she had received her.

"Well," she said rising, "you must get about. Don't mope over that fancy work. The boys'll see that you have a good time and Evadne'll look after you."

"The boys," engaged in a game of "go bang" just within the hall way, and overhearing all, fell in a heap against each other and uttered a simultaneous groan. A moment later they were leaving the house swiftly and noiselessly by a rear exit.

ESSAYS AND COMMENTS

The Western Association of Writers

Provincialism in the best sense of the word stamps the character of this association of writers, who gather chiefly from the State of Indiana and meet annually at Spring Fountain Park. It is an ideally beautiful spot, a veritable garden of Eden in which the disturbing fruit of the tree of knowledge still hangs unplucked. The cry of the dying century has not reached this body of workers, or else it has not been comprehended. There is no doubt in their souls, no unrest: apparently an abiding faith in God as he manifests himself through the sectional church, and an overmastering love of their soil and institutions.

Most of them are singers. Their native streams, trees, bushes and birds, the lovely country life about them, form the chief burden of their often too sentimental songs.

Occasionally the voice of one of them reaches out across the prairies and is heard by the world beyond. For this is the soil, these are the conditions, and the Western Association of Writers are the typical human group which have given us James Whitcomb Riley, Mrs. Catherwood and Lew Wallace.

Among these people are to be found an earnestness in the acquirement and dissemination of book-learning, a clinging to past and conventional standards, an almost Creolean sensitiveness to criticism and a singular ignorance of, or disregard for, the value of the highest art forms.

There is a very, very big world lying not wholly in northern Indiana, nor does it lie at the antipodes, either. It is human existence in its subtle, complex, true meaning, stripped of the veil with which ethical and conventional standards have draped it. When the Western

691

Association of Writers with their earnestness of purpose and poetic insights shall have developed into students of true life and true art, who knows but they may produce a genius such as America has not yet known.

"Crumbling Idols" by Hamlin Garland

Mr. Garland seems not content that the idols whereof he speaks are crumbling. He attempts to hasten their demolition with hammer-strokes that resound and make much noise, even if they accomplish nothing in that work of destruction which moves too slowly for his impatient humor.

In these twelve essays on art, however, the author has sounded a true note if not a new one, which would be more forcible were it less insistent; which would ring clearer were it not accompanied by a clamor and bluster often distressing to sensitive ears. He suggests—what no one who has thought upon the subject is ready to dispute—that the youthful artist should free himself from the hold of conventionalism; that he should go direct to those puissant sources, Life and Nature, for inspiration and turn his back upon models furnished by man; in a word, that he should be creative and not imitative. But Mr. Garland undervalues the importance of the past in art and exaggerates the significance of the present.

Human impulses do not change and can not so long as men and women continue to stand in the relation to one another which they have occupied since our knowledge of their existence began. It is why Æschylus is true, and Shakespeare is true to-day, and why Ibsen will not be true in some remote to-morrow, however forcible and representative he may be for the hour, because he takes for his themes social problems which by their very nature are mutable. And, notwithstanding Mr. Garland's opinion to the contrary, social problems, social environments, local color and the rest of it are not *of themselves* motives to insure the survival of a writer who employs them.

The author of "Crumbling Idols" would even lightly dismiss from the artist's consideration such primitive passions as love, hate, etc. He declares that in real life people do not talk love. How does he know? I feel very sorry for Mr. Garland.

An excellent chapter in the book deals with impressionism in painting. It will be found interesting and even instructive to many who have rather vague and confused notions of what impressionism means. Mr. Garland has gone over heart and soul to the Impressionists. He feels and sees with them; being in close sympathy with their individualism; their abandonment of the traditional and conventional in the interest of "truth." He admits that he himself has discovered certain "purple shadows" by looking at a stretch of sand, with his head turned top-side down! It is doubtful if many of us would exhibit an equal zeal in pursuing anything so elusive as a shadow; but the incident goes to prove Mr. Garland's earnestness and sincerity of purpose.

His attitude in regard to the East as a literary center is to be deplored; and his expressions in that respect seem exaggerated and uncalled for. The fact remains that Chicago is not yet a literary center, nor is St. Louis (!), nor San Francisco, nor Denver, nor any of those towns in whose behalf he drops into prophecy. There can no good come of abusing Boston and New York. On the contrary, as "literary centers" they have rendered incalculable service to the reading world by bringing to light whatever there has been produced of force and originality in the West and South since the war.

The book is one which all Western art lovers should read. Mr. Garland is surely a representative Western man of letters. He is too young to assume the role of prophet becomingly; and he somehow gives the impression of a man who has not yet "lived," but he is vigorous and sincere, and he is one of us.

The Real Edwin Booth

The October *Century* opens with a selection of private letters of the late Edwin Booth, preceded by a brief preface from his daughter, Mrs. Grossman. The article bears the title, "The Real Edwin Booth," and forms part of a collection to be published later in book form.

If Booth were able to-day to take up the magazine and re-read these letters, never intended for the public eye, it is easy to fancy him quoting from one of them, "I shrink from the indelicacy."

Never has the world known a man more wrapped about in a mantle of sensitiveness and reserve than was Edwin Booth; and it seems a pity that in his case the public might not have respected the mute appeal for privacy which his whole existence expressed.

Judging from the selection before us one can hardly hope that these letters will throw any new light upon the man's relation to his life work—which could give some excuse for their being, so far as the public is concerned. They simply show us a man who seems fond of his daughter and of his friends; they lay bare the poignant sorrow of a husband for the loss of a well-beloved wife; they indicate that he possessed some heart, so far as the written word can represent so abstract a thing as a human heart; and they evince little or no power of mind or depth of character. No, it is not here that we are to look for the real Edwin Booth, in a puerile collection of letters, expressions wrung from him by the conventional demands of his daily life.

The *real* Edwin Booth gave himself to the public through his art. Those of us who most felt its magnetic power are the ones who knew him best, and as he would have wished to be known. His art was his closest and most precious possession. Through it he was great, he was individual, he was a force that appealed to and acted upon the finer responsive chords of every human intelligence that heard him. It was the medium through which he expressed himself. He possessed no other form of expression by which to make himself known.

If he might to-day turn over the leaves of this collection of letters, it would surely be with that sad, "pale smile" which we all remember, and no doubt with a spoken reproach to all of us—public, daughter and publishers: "Why look you, how unworthy a thing you make of me."

Emile Zola's "Lourdes"

I once heard a devotee of impressionism admit, in looking at a picture by Monet, that, while he himself had never seen in nature the peculiar yellows and reds therein depicted, he was convinced that Monet had painted them because he saw them and because they were true. With something of a kindred faith in the sincerity of all Mons. Zola's work, I am yet not at all times ready to admit its truth, which is only equivalent to saying that our points of view differ, that truth rests upon a shifting basis and is apt to be kaleidoscopic.

"Lourdes" seems to me to be a mistake, not in its conception, but in its treatment. It cannot be called a failure, because Mons. Zola has not failed in his intention to give to the world an exhaustive history of Bernadette's Lourdes. But that history could have been as direct, and surely more effective, had it been made subordinate to some powerful narrative, such as Mons. Zola is so well able to invent.

As it is, the story is the merest thread of a story running loosely through the 400 pages, and more than two-thirds of the time swamped beneath a mass of prosaic data, offensive and nauseous description and rampant sentimentality.

In no former work has Mons. Zola so glaringly revealed his constructive methods. Not for an instant, from first to last, do we lose sight of the author and his note-book and of the disagreeable fact that his design is to instruct us. Pierre, the hero of the book, seems to be also the victim, the passive medium chosen by the author to convey information to his readers. This young man (an unbeliever) is inspired with an inordinate tenderness for the memory of Bernadette, solely that he may chance to be carrying her history in his coat pocket that he may read it to the

697

pilgrims journeying on the "white train" towards Lourdes, and that the reader may in this way become acquainted with it himself. Once at Lourdes, the movements of this young priest come to be looked upon by the reader with uneasiness and misgiving. If he happen to walk abroad, we need not suppose it is to take the air, or that it is for any other purpose than to be waylaid by one of the many individuals who seem to swarm in Lourdes, ever on the watch for willing ears in which to empty the overflowing vials of their information. If he sits for a moment contemplative before the Grotto, the insidious man of knowledge is soon there beside him, conveying to him by pages and pages information which we know that Mons. Zola acquired in the same way and thus subtly conveys to us.

We are told that Pierre goes to the barber's to be shaved, but we know better by this time; we know that he goes for some other purpose, which soon reveals itself when the intelligent barber tells in round terms what he thinks of certain clerical abuses prevailing at Lourdes, and we are certain that we are hearing what the author himself thinks of those things. Such handling of a subject is unpardonable in Mons. Zola.

The style all through, however, is masterly, and there are descriptive bits which are superb, notably the description of a candle-light procession winding its tortuous way in and out among the hills: "Au ciel il semblait y avoir moins d'étoiles. Une voie lactée était tombée de la haut roulant son pondroiement de mondes, et qui continuait sur la terre la ronde des astres."

Very powerfully conceived and described is the scene before the Grotto, leading up to Marie Guersaint's remarkable cure. The writer here touches a fine psychological point, though not a new one—the possibility of the combined will-power of a mass of humanity forcing nature to subserve its ends. A French savant has already reminded us that "the psychology of a multitude of men is not the psychology of the individual." The subject is attractive, and Mons. Zola might have made more of it.

"Lourdes" has been roundly denounced by Catholics and, I think, the ban of the Church set upon it. I cannot see why. It is a book which I think a good Catholic would greatly enjoy reading, the only and easy condition being to set aside Mons. Zola's point of view and color his facts with one's own. He has a thorough knowledge of Catholicism, extending to the most trifling mannerisms of its votaries, and this part of his subject he handles delicately and captivatingly.

But the book will doubtless thrust him a step further away from the goal of his hopes and ambitions—the French Academy.

It is hard to understand in Mons. Zola this persistent desire to be admitted to the Academy. One would suppose he would be content, even proud, to stand outside of its doors in the company of Alphonse Daudet.

Confidences

There is somewhere registered in my consciousness a vow that I would never be confidential except for the purpose of misleading. But consistency is a pompous and wearisome burden to bear always and there is often relief in casting it aside.

Having determined therefore to be inconsistent and talk about myself, I devised an ingenious plan by which I might do so without being detected in the offense.

I disguised myself as a gentleman smoking cigars with my feet on the table. Opposite me was another gentleman (who furnished the cigars) entrapping me into disclosures by well turned questions, after the manner of the middle men at the "Minstrels." A person of sounder judgment than myself convinced me that the device was more clumsy than clever, and likely to bewilder rather than to deceive. He appreciated what he supposed to be the underlying notion of my diffidence and intimated that he readily understood I might be ashamed of myself. In this he is mistaken. Like the colored gentleman in the Passemala I am sometimes "afraid o' myse'f" but never ashamed.

About eight years ago there fell accidentally into my hands a volume of Maupassant's tales. These were new to me. I had been in the woods, in the fields, groping around; looking for something big, satisfying, convincing, and finding nothing but—myself; a something neither big nor satisfying but wholly convincing. It was at this period of my emerging from the vast solitude in which I had been making my own acquaintance, that I stumbled upon Maupassant. I read his stories and marvelled at them. Here was life, not fiction; for where were the plots, the old fashioned mechanism and stage trapping that in a vague, unthinking way I had fancied were essential to the art of story making. Here was a man who had escaped from tradition and authority, who had entered into himself and looked out upon life through his own being and with his own eyes; and who, in a direct and simple way, told us what he saw. When a man does this, he gives us the best that he can; something valuable for it is genuine and spontaneous. He gives us his impressions. Some one told me the other day that Maupassant had gone out of fashion. I was not grieved to hear it. He has never seemed to me to belong to the multitude, but rather to the individual. He is not one whom we gather in crowds to listen to—whom we follow in procession—with beating of brass instruments. He does not move us to throw ourselves into the throng—having the integral of an unthinking whole to shout his praise. I even like to think that he appeals to me alone. You probably like to think that he reaches you exclusively. A whole multitude may be secretly nourishing the belief in regard to him for all I know. Someway I like to cherish the delusion that he has spoken to no one else so directly, so intimately as he does to me. He did not say, as another might have done, "do you see these are charming stories of mine? take them into your closet—study them closely—mark their combination—observe the method, the manner of their putting together—and if ever you are moved to write stories you can do no better than to imitate . . .

[Here two pages of the MS. are missing.]

. . .my head on the side when I heard it and abandoned myself to poetic reflection. She often tells me that I have no soul (some people will tell you anything) and that my work consequently lacks that dignity as well as charm—which the spiritual impulse infuses into fiction. "You have eyes, ears, nose, fingers and—senses—nothing else; you are a brute, you have no soul," and—being rather fond of me—she weeps about it—in her lace handkerchief. In vain have I represented to her that at an early and credulous age I was told that the soul was a round, white, luminous substance or—copying some misunderstood portion of my anatomy—beautiful and luminous in a state of grace, but spotted black and hideous by sin—every fresh offense adding a new disfigurement, and that I have never been able wholly to disassociate the idea of soul from that first material impression. But she accepts no apology. She says that any kind of a soul—no matter how material—is better than none at all. She sometimes makes me feel that I am stubbornly and persistently rejecting some beautiful and precious adornment that has been offered to me as a velvet cushion.

She still urges me to cultivate the religious impulse—as though it were to be acquired like a foreign language! We have many a pretty quarrel upon this and kindred subjects. My dear Madame Précieuse—I have discovered my limitations and I have saved myself much worry and torment by recognizing and accepting them as final. I can gain nothing by cultivating faculties that are not my own—I can reach nothing by running after it—but I find that many things come to me here in my corner.

Some wise man has promulgated an eleventh commandment—"thou shalt not preach," which interpreted means "thou shalt not instruct thy neighbor." It is a commandment about as difficult to observe as the other ten—for the preacher is always with us—he is omnipresent. "Thou shalt parcel thy day off into sections—and with mathematical precision," said one of these well-meaning Preachers—"so many hours shalt thou abandon thyself to thought—and to writing—so many to household duties—to social enjoyment—to ministering to thy afflicted fellow creatures." I hearkened to the voice of the teachers and the result was stagnation and untold misery—until in the spirit of revolt I turned to and played "solitaire" during my thinking hours—and whist during my "ministering to my [afflicted fellow creatures?] -hours and scribbled a little during my social enjoyment hour, until I succeeded in introducing the harmonious discord which had reigned my days before I had listened to the Voice.

But there are always voices.—And one of them said: "thou art passing stupid—go forth and gather wisdom in the intellectual atmosphere of clubs, in those centers of thought where questions are debated and knowledge is disseminated like the kind rain upon the parched earth." I listened to the Voice of the teachers and hastened forth to enroll myself among the thinkers and disseminators of knowledge and propounders of questions. But much as the kitchen maid must feel who suddenly finds herself introduced into a drawing room of fine fashionables did I feel in these intellectual gatherings. The amount of knowledge—massed, seething around me, emphasized and made clear to me my own density. I trembled for fear my profound ignorance on all subjects might accidentally be detected, causing me to serve as an object lesson and finally the subject of a discourse. I escaped as hurriedly as I decently could from the intellectual atmosphere—back to my corner where no question and no fine language can reach me—and am slowly, after years, regaining in some degree my self-respect.

In the Confidence of a Story-Writer

There is registered somewhere in my consciousness a vow that I will never be confidential except for the purpose of misleading. But consistency is a pompous and wearisome burden, and I seek relief by casting it aside; for, like the colored gentleman in the Passemala, I am sometimes "afraid o' myse'f," but never ashamed.

I have discovered my limitations, and I have saved myself much worry and torment by accepting them as final. I can gain nothing but tribulation by cultivating faculties that are not my own. I cannot reach anything by running after it, but I find that many pleasant and profitable things come to me here in my corner.

Some wise man has promulgated an eleventh commandment, "Thou shalt not preach," which, interpreted, means, "Thou shalt not instruct thy neighbor as to what he should do." But the Preacher is always with us. Said one to me: "Thou shalt parcel off thy day into mathematical sections. So many hours shalt thou abandon thyself to thought, so many to writing; a certain number shalt thou devote to household duties, to social enjoyment, to ministering to thy afflicted fellow creatures." I listened to the voice of the Preacher, and the result was stagnation all along the line of "hours" and unspeakable bitterness of spirit. In brutal revolt I turned to and played solitaire during my "thinking hour," and whist when I should have been ministering to the afflicted. I scribbled a little during my "social enjoyment" period, and shattered the "household duties" into fragments of every conceivable fraction of time, with which I besprinkled the entire day as from a pepper-box. In this way I succeeded in reëstablishing the harmonious discord and confusion which had surrounded me before I listened to the voice, and which seems necessary to my physical and mental well-being.

But there are many voices preaching. Said another one to me: "Go forth and gather wisdom in the intellectual atmosphere of clubs,—in those centres of thought where questions are debated and knowledge is disseminated." Once more giving heed, I hurried to enroll myself among the thinkers, and dispensers of knowledge, and propounders of questions. And very much out of place did I feel in these intellectual gatherings. I escaped by some pretext, and regained my corner, where no "questions" and no fine language can reach me.

There is far too much gratuitous advice bandied about, regardless of personal aptitude and wholly confusing to the individual point of view.

I had heard so often reiterated that "genius is a capacity for taking pains" that the axiom had become lodged in my brain with the fixedness of a fundamental truth. I had never hoped or aspired to be a genius. But one day the thought occurred to me, "I will take pains." Thereupon I proceeded to lie awake at night plotting a tale that should convince my limited circle of readers that I could rise above the commonplace. As to choice of "time," the present century offered too prosaic a setting for a tale intended to stir the heart and the imagination. I selected the last century. It is true I know little of the last century, and have a feeble imagination. I read volumes bearing upon the history of the times and people that I proposed to manipulate, and pored over folios depicting costumes and household utensils then in use, determined to avoid inaccuracy. For the first time in my life I took notes,—copious notes,—and carried them bulging in my jacket pockets, until I felt as if I were wearing Zola's coat. I have never seen a craftsman at work upon a fine piece of mosaic, but I fancy that he must handle the delicate bits much as I handled the words in that story, picking, selecting, grouping, with an eye to color and to artistic effect,—never satisfied. The story completed, I was very, very weary; but I had the satisfaction of feeling that for once in my life I had worked hard, I had achieved something great, I had taken pains.

But the story failed to arouse enthusiasm among the editors. It is at present lying in my desk. Even my best friend declined to listen to it, when I offered to read it to her.

I am more than ever convinced that a writer should be content to use his own faculty, whether it be a faculty for taking pains or a faculty for reaching his effects by the most careless methods. Every writer, I fancy, has his group of readers who understand, who are in sympathy with his thoughts or impressions or whatever he gives them. And he who is content to reach his own group, without ambition to be heard beyond it, attains, in my opinion, somewhat to the dignity of a philosopher.

As You Like It

I

I have a young friend who occasionally drops in on his way from school to toast his feet before my sitting-room fire. He startled me one time by asking me abruptly to give him a subject for an essay. I was standing at the window looking at a man shoveling coal across the street. I like to look out of the window; there is a good deal of unadulterated human nature that passes along during the length of a day. Of course I do not live in Westmoreland Place. At the mention of "essay," I turned with some interest and went to join him at the fireside. "A subject, my dear! That is not so very easy to think of on the spur of the moment. But whatever you do let it be original. Give your own impressions, for goodness sake! However lame or poor, they ought to be of more value than any second-hand material you may chance to gather."

"I know what you mean," he replied; "but that isn't what they want."

"Well, I suppose you know what they want better than I do"; so we talked of other things. The subject which he chose was either "The Condition of Our Army" or "Naval Resources in the Event of War With Spain." I don't know which. He is just seventeen, a "game," plucky boy in a stand-up fight, I am told. But I doubt if his combative experiences have qualified him to discourse knowledge upon the subject of "Standing Armies," and I am quite sure his nautical impressions have been gathered at Crève Cœur Lake. But, as he said, he knew what they wanted, and he gave it to them.

It was only the other day that the same very young friend wanted me to suggest a title for an oration. It was a positive shock to me.

"An oration!" I cried. "Good heavens! Call it something else."

"Can't call it anything else; got to call it an 'oration'; that's what it is."

"But, my child, I know less, much less, about the nature of an oration than does the cook down in the kitchen."

"Oh, the oration's written all right; got it here in my pocket. What I want is a title for it."

It has been many a long day since I listened to an oration. The last one, I think, was from Archbishop Ryan, who was then "Father Ryan," and pastor of the Annunciation Church, on Sixth street. It was an imposing piece of work, but at this late day I forget what it was all about. Naturally I was rather curious to hear what my young companion had written, and with a pretty reluctance he drew a few folded sheets from his pocket and began to read. The paper was short, in which respect it was an improvement upon former orations which I had listened to. It was delicious to hear the roll of his sentences and the thunder of his climaxes. He had caught the very essence and spirit of the thing. It was a good composition, and I told him so. But there was no truth in it from beginning to end, and I told him so.

"It's all right for you to roast orations," he said, a little nettled, putting the paper back in his pocket. "But I tell you what, they're a mighty good thing; it teaches a fellow how to stand up and talk and say what he's got to say. It's a mighty good thing for a fellow that's going to be a lawyer."

"So you're going to be a lawyer?" I laughed. "Then I'll have to like you all I can now, for I shan't like you when you're a lawyer."

"Don't you like lawyers?"

"No."

"Why?"

"Oh, I don't know. Maybe because they're given over to orations. I can't say just why."

"What do you like?"

"Well, I think a poet's rather a likable sort of a person."

"Pshaw! You know I can't write poetry."

"I didn't say anything about writing poetry. Then the philosopher isn't bad at times."

"Philosopher! What good is philosophy when a fellow wants to get on in the world and make a living and make a mark?"

"I wasn't talking about the successful person; I was talking about the person I like. Then there's the loafer. Sometimes I've discovered a charming companion in a loafer."

"Oh, I see you're roasting me. Well, I'm not a poet or a philosopher, and, thank heavens, I ain't a loafer."

"But you are all three, my dear, and that's why I like you. Do you know what illusions are?"

"Let's see. An illusion is when—"

"No, you don't. We never know what illusions are till we have lost them. They belong to youth, and they are poetry and philosophy, and vagabondage, and everything delightful. And they last till men and the world, life and the institutions, come along with—but gracious! I forgot whom I was talking to. Run on and get your skates. I hear there's great sport out at Forest Park."

II

It has lately been my unhappy experience to make the acquaintance of a gentleman who said:

"Look this way; that way, please; to the right; to the left; up; now, down." And while striving to follow these conflicting instructions as nimbly as they were given, it was further my miserable fate to have a glance of ten million candle-power turned upon my defenseless right eye. The very wastes and caverns of my inner thought must have been resolved by the searching probe.

"Only a little inflammation," he said politely; "the eye needs rest." I quite agreed with him.

"And what mustn't I do for it, doctor?"

"You must not read, write, nor sew."

"Thank you. And may I clean out closets; go see people; play whist; and think upon my sins and the means of escaping the penalty thereof?"

"Next, please!"

The snub direct from a professional gentleman in the discharge of his duty!

Well, the newspapers remain unread; letters are lying unanswered, and the boys are sewing on their own buttons. Women who are in the full enjoyment of these several delights and privileges will not, I trust, withhold their sympathy and a prayer for my speedy restoration.

Yet have I not lacked the kindly ministrations of well-meaning souls. One sweet woman has sent me a green eye-shade, fashioned with her own deft fingers. A second has brought me a homeopathic specific of such subtle quality and insidious efficacy that there seems to me to be no excuse for blindness upon the face of the earth unless she has been mis-informed. Another willing friend has sought to induce me to visit with her a gentleman by the name of Sullivan, who—well, never mind what he does. And yet another has come and read to me the MS. of an address which she will soon deliver before an Intellectual Society for the Pre-vention of Cruelty to Adults.

There is something very pleasing and restful in being read to. If the reader happen to be a sympathetic personality and the volume anything half so attractive as Alexander Kielland's little stories, then the charm is complete. Speaking of Kielland—but let me say that the courteous editor of THE CRITERION, obeying some misguided impulse, has kindly placed at my disposal a couple of columns of this entertaining journal, in which to exploit my opinions upon books and writers, and matters and things pertaining thereto.

The mistake which the editor of THE CRITERION made was in not giving an imperative command. When a person is politely offered *carte blanche* to discourse upon "matters and things," that person is going to talk about herself and her own small doings, unless she is old enough to know better. One must be very old indeed to be old enough to know better.

A second mistake—if I may be permitted to mention mistakes and the editor of THE CRITERION in the same breath—a second mistake was in supposing that I had any opinions. Very long ago I could do nothing with them; nobody wanted them; they were not self-supporting, and perished of inanition. Since then I have sometimes thought of cultivating a few—a batch of sound, marketable opinions, in anticipation of just such an emergency, but I neglected to do so. Of course there are such things as transplanted opinions; then one may know them, even steal them; there are lots of ways; but what is the use? I did not tell all this to the editor of THE CRITERION beforehand, because I might have lost the opportunity of telling it to the public.

But, speaking of Kielland, I am not going to advise anyone to read his stories; I would not be guilty of advising anyone to do anything. I only want to say that they possess a subtle quality that suited the ear, the understanding, the mood with which I listened to them. The book, "Tales of Two Countries," is not new; it was published, I think, in '91 or earlier. There is no rush upon the libraries to obtain it. There are no newspapers discussing it, and, so far as I can be certain, no medico-literary societies dissecting it for the purpose of ascertaining what it died of.

Norwegian translations always seem to possess a certain crudeness, not usually found in translations from the Spanish, German, French, or Italian. A something—it must be an idiomatic simplicity for which the English translator seemed unable to find in our language any corresponding expression. It is essential, in order to enjoy these tales of Kielland, to distrust our own point of view; to set aside all prejudice as to nicety of technique; to abandon ourselves to the spirit of the narrator, and project ourselves into the very atmosphere of the subject.

In "Pharaoh," the first tale in the volume, there is a fine psychological touch. The beautiful countess is being conveyed in her carriage to some imperial ball. She was always beautiful, but she was not always a countess. Her beauty had been the means of lifting her from the ranks of the "people," in which she was born. The carriage is slowly, and with difficulty, making its way through a dense throng of grumbling, hungry-eyed humanity; shoving and jostling each other to get snatched glimpses of that luxurious existence filing by; further from their reach than heaven itself. As the beautiful woman gazes out at this surging sea of up-turned faces, her heart, her very soul goes out to them; not with any sympathy born of compassion, but with the sympathy of blood. She wants to be where she belongs, out there with the growling multitude. A quick hate is born within her for the jewels upon her arms, the soft fabrics that enfold her, for the palace in which she is shortly to enter, and the people of rank whom she will find there. That is all the story; but it is enough.

And how I wish some one would paint a picture of the poor little mountebank "At The Fair!" The screaming, unhappy little being is crying behind the tent, his face buried in the grimy canvas, so as to stifle his sobs that they be not heard on the other side. He has a yellow and a red leg, and he stands on his yellow leg "like a stork," with the red one doubled up under him. "*Maman m'a pris mon sou*," he wails between sobs. His mother has taken his sou!

The story of "Two Friends" is one of the most subtle delineations of character which I ever read. It is not told as I like stories to be told; but that, perhaps, is because it is Norwegian. I stayed quite still after hearing it, quite still for a long time, pretending to be asleep, thinking of it, wondering at it.

III

Several years ago I read in *Lippincott's Magazine* a story by Ruth McEnery Stuart, entitled "Carlotta's Intended." It was the novelette of the number, a tale of such marked excellence that it left an impression upon my mind which has never been disturbed. The character, the dialect of the dagoes with whom it deals, and of the Irish cobbler who plays so important a rôle, are singularly true to nature. Their fidelity must appear striking to anyone who has lived in New Orleans in familiar touch with the life which the author so graphically depicts in this story.

Since then I have read Mrs. Stuart's stories, as they frequently appeared in the magazines, and I have never failed to find the same wholesome, human note sounding through and through them. Mrs. Stuart's work deals mainly with the negroes and "poor whites" of Louisiana, her native state.

Her humor is rich and plentiful, with nothing finical or feminine about it. Few of our women writers have equalled her in this respect. Even Page and Harris among the men have not surpassed her in the portrayal of that child-like exuberance which is so pronounced a feature of negro character, and which has furnished so much that is deliciously humorous and pathetic to our recent literature.

I had sometimes thought that if ever I met Mrs. Stuart I would talk to her about her stories. I would seek a further acquaintance with sweet Carlotta; with some of the whole-souled darkies; above all, with that delightful "Sonny," whom we have recently come to know through the pages of the *Century Magazine*. I have met Mrs. Stuart, and did not speak of her stories.

It was a week or two ago—maybe longer—at all events the morning of the big snow, that I went to call upon her out in the suburbs, where she was visiting with friends. There was something peculiarly beautiful about that one day's snow. There was so much of it; an abundance so thick, soft, clinging, that for three hours or more the world seemed transformed into fairyland. People moved noiselessly along like dream-figures. There was no rumble of wheel or beat of hoof as carriages rolled by; a spell of silence had fallen upon the earth during the night. A spell of peace, too, and quietude which the silent, white snow brings, and which I would have liked to hold and cling to—till the snow melted, anyway.

But there was present with me the disturbing anticipation of meeting

an unfamiliar personality—a celebrity, moreover. I had met a few celeb-
rities, and they had never failed to depress me.

There is no question about Mrs. Stuart being a celebrity. Her achievements have entitled her to that distinction, and as such she is recognized
throughout the length and breadth of these United States—everywhere,
except in one small parish in Louisiana. I am quite sure that when
Mrs. Stuart occasionally wanders back to *Les Avoyelles* there comes
sauntering up to her some black wench or other, who accosts her with:

"G'long Mis' Ruth! you knows des well as me, we all colo'ed people
we don' talk dat away lack you makes us talk in yo' books!" And I am
greatly mistaken in this guess work if some old chap from Bayou de Glaize
hasn't said more than once, "Hit seems Ruth MicHenry's took to writin'
books. But land! they ain't like no books I ever seen! Thes about common
eve'y day talk an' people!" In short, Mrs. Stuart is a prophet outside
of *Les Avoyelles*.

But pshaw! I should have known better than to have been bothered
at the thought of meeting her. I might have known that a woman
possessing so great an abundance of the saving grace—which is humor
—was not going to take herself seriously, or to imagine for a moment
that I intended to take her seriously.

Mrs. Stuart is not one whose work overshadows her personality. That
—I subsequently discovered in thinking the matter over—was the reason
I failed to speak to her of her stories—possibly failed to think of them
while in her presence. Her voice in conversation (I did not hear her read)
has a melting quality that penetrates the senses, as some soothing ointment goes through the skin. Her eyes do the rest—complete the charm
begun by voice, expression, and a thoroughly natural and sympathetic
manner. Sympathy and insight are the qualities, I believe, which make
her stories lovable, which make them linger in the memory like pleasant
human experiences—happy realities that we are loath to part with. I
fancy there are no sharp edges to this woman's soul, no unsheathed prejudices dwelling therein wherewith to inflict wound, or prick, or stab
upon her fellow-man or woman.

Mrs. Stuart, in fact, is a delightful womanly woman. I just wanted
to sit there beside her all the rest of the day, while the snow melted out
of doors and the world waked up from its fantastic, voiceless snow-dream.
I know she would not have bored me the whole day long. I know she
does not inflict the penalty of speech upon sympathetic companionship.
Failing in this desire, I should have liked to spirit Mrs. Stuart away—

out through a window or a defenseless back door. I wanted to take her up and set her down beside my sitting-room fire; to lock the door against receptions, luncheons, and the clamor of many voices. I would have had her sleep and rest there for a week, for a month, for a year!

But I could do nothing of all this. I could only carry away with me her sweet voice and the memory of a captivating presence, which lingered with me the whole day like the echo of some delicious strain of music that one cannot and would not banish.

This may be all wrong. If it is, I trust Mrs. Stuart herself will set me right. But for this once I should hate to be wrong.

IV

A while ago there was lying upon my table a book, which for some inscrutable reason has been withdrawn, I am told, from circulation at our libraries. The spectacle of this book lying in evidence communicated a severe shock to the susceptibilities of a woman who was calling upon me.

"Oh! how can you!" she exclaimed, "with so many young people about!"

The question of how much or how little knowledge of life should be withheld from the youthful mind is one which need only be touched upon here. It is a subject about which there exists a diversity of opinion with the conservative element no doubt, greatly in preponderance. As a rule the youthful, untrained nature is left to gather wisdom as it comes along in a thousand-and-one ways and in whatever form it may present itself to the intelligent, the susceptible, the observant. In this respect experience is perhaps an abler instructor than direct enlightenment from man or woman; for it works by suggestion. There are many phases and features of life which cannot, or rather should not be expounded, demonstrated, presented to the youthful imagination as cold facts, for it is safe to assert they are not going to be accepted as such. It is moreover robbing youth of its privilege to gather wisdom as the bee gathers honey.

The book referred to a moment ago is a ponderous and formidable looking affair at best. There is nothing alluring in its title or in its sombre black binding. It has the outward appearance of a Congressional Record, and it might easily have escaped the attention of the young person if some reviewers, a few gossips and the libraries had seen fit to let it work out its own damnation. I read the book and then I laid it upon the table.

"Any good?" asked one or two youngsters who have a propensity for getting at the inside of an interesting novel.

"Unutterably tiresome," I said, "but you might like it."

"Oh! thank you."

So there it remained unmolested till the reviewers and others began to get in their work. Then a sudden interest in that volume awoke among people I knew, moving them to borrow; and the young folks began to pick it up and turn it over, in some instances attempting to read it. If any one of them succeeded in reading it from start to finish (which I believe is not the case) he is to be congratulated upon the achievement of having surmounted obstacles the like of which have never before confronted the seeker after entertainment.

From beginning to end there is not a gleam of humor in the book. From beginning to end there is not a line, a thought, a suggestion which could be called seductive. Its brutality is an obvious and unhappy imitation of the great French realist. The characters are so plainly constructed with the intention of illustrating the purposes of the author, that they do not for a moment convey any impression of reality. A gloom which is never lightened pervades the pages. The art is so poor that scenes intended to be impressive are at best but grotesque. The whole exposition is colorless. The hero arouses so little sympathy that at the close one does not care whether he lives or dies; he might be put upon the rack and submitted to unspeakable torture, and I am sure nobody would object; for no one minds much about the spilling of sawdust or the wrenching of rubber joints! A villainous brute of a woman commits deeds that ought by right (if the author knows his craft) to make the hair of the person who reads of them stand on end; but somehow they don't. You will just keep on munching a cream chocolate, or wondering if the postman has gone by or if there is coal on the furnace.

The book is detestably bad; it is unpardonably dull; and immoral, chiefly because it is not true.

It seems rather irrelevant and late in the day to say all this about *Jude the Obscure*. It is only sympathy for the young person which moves me to do so. I hate to know that deceptions are being practised upon him. He has been led to believe that the work is dangerous and alluring. Failing to obtain it at the libraries he is quite convinced that it is pernicious and altogether delightful, whereupon he hurries, in some instances, to the nearest book store and spends his week's allowance in procuring it. I feel very sorry to think that he should part with so many good silver quarters and receive nothing in return but disappointment and disillusion.

After all, that investigating spirit in the young person is in no sense peculiar, or is it to be wondered at or condemned. It is a characteristic shared in common with the rest of the human race, to seek to unravel mysteries and things hidden and denied. There are the scientists, probing the heavens for its secrets, delving in the depths of the earth for what they may discover. And what about explorers, Theosophists, Hoodoos?

I should like to say to the young people that books which are withheld from their perusal are usually not worth reading. They are not worth bothering about or going to any trouble or expense to obtain. If they are written by thoughtful men, they are not addressed to the youthful imagination and are not fashioned to be comprehended by such. If they are written by other than thoughtful people, there is apt to be no truth in them, and they cannot appeal to lovers of sincerity of any age or condition.

I once knew a very young person who, while rummaging in a bureau drawer discovered a volume secreted in its disordered profundity. The book was obviously in hiding, and no other than she herself was the important personage from whom it was being hidden! She at once locked the door, abstracted the volume, and sat herself down to its perusal. Expectation was rampant within her. She had been scenting mysteries in the air, and the hour of illumination was at hand! The book was something obscure, metaphysical, hysterical. It was dull reading, but she persevered. She would greatly rather have been up in the attic reading *Ivanhoe*. But no one had hidden *Ivanhoe* in the far depths of a bureau drawer—*Voilà!*

V

A good many of us who were alive back in the seventies are wondering why under the canopy Mrs. Mackin, or "Sallie Britton" as we all remember her, should have written her memoirs. Though for my part I find it quite natural that a woman should want to write her memoirs, and enjoy doing so; even a common, every-day person, let alone "A Society Woman on Two Continents."

When I learned, a week or two ago, that Sallie, who was my contemporary, had been writing memoirs, I was seized with an insane desire to do likewise. I remembered how she used to come up on St. Ange Avenue from her home around on Chouteau to ask my mother's permission for me to stay all night with her. A request which was never granted, because Sallie was not a Catholic! And to-day, here she is, not only a Catholic, but actually receiving a golden rose from the Pope! While I—Well, I doubt if the Holy Father has ever heard of me, or if he would give me a golden rose if he had.

Still I was set upon the idea of the memoirs, and at once started out to make a beginning. But a very serious obstacle met me. I found that my memory was of that order which retains only the most useless rubbish, while all recollections of those charming episodes—those delightful experiences which I, no doubt, shared in common with others of my age and condition—had completely deserted me.

It was then that I bethought me of a friend, one of the reminiscent kind, whose "don't-you-remembers" and "it-was-in-the-summer-of-seventy-sixes" had often startled me with their unerring precision and cocksureness. I sent for him. He came. He was delighted with my project.

"Memoirs!" he exclaimed, rubbing his hands together, "Capital idea! You want me to help you out? First rate notion of yours," seating himself in the corner of the sofa. I had taken a seat at no great distance away, pencil and pad in hand, ready for business.

"What I want," I told him, "is for you to spur my memory; remind me of all manner of pleasant little past events calculated to give sparkle to the pages of a memoir—so now!"

"Well," he said, leaning with his elbows on his knees, "you've got to begin at the beginning. Let's see: suppose you tell about the time I took you to—"

"These are not your memoirs; they are mine," I reminded him rather coldly.

"Oh! all right. Then you might write of how you tore down the union flag from the front porch when the Yanks tied it up there; and of the night the prisoners escaped from the Gratiot street prison and hid in the lilac bushes, and we all—you all went out with lanterns—"

"You must think I want to write war papers, don't you?"

"What *do* you want to write?"

"Why, I don't know exactly. I want to tell of interesting and entertaining things; whether I received much attention, and whether I was a great belle or not; that sort of thing. Do you remember if I ever met any people of distinction?"

"Distinction?"

"Yes. Grand dukes or anything of that kind.—Didn't I dance with the Prince of Wales somewhere about '70 at the Home Circle?"

"Prince of Wales never went to the Home Circle. The Prince of Wales never came over here in the seventies. It must have been some one else you met. It'd be kind of funny, though, to tell about the night you went to Mrs. Maffitt's party on Sixth and Olive, and slipped down the stone steps trying to get away from—"

"I thought Barr's was on Sixth and Olive."

"Oh! did you? No; it used to be, but it's been moved out to 44th and West Pine."

I saw he was offended. But indeed, for the life of me I can never remember "the old church that used to stand on the corner where the Skylark building now stands," and so forth. For all I know to the contrary the Union Trust has always been where it is now; and it seems to me that nothing but the Century building has ever stood on Seventh and Olive. Or is it Seventh and Olive? I tried to conciliate my friend.

"Wouldn't it be rather interesting to relate the story of that drive, in which the horses ran away and threw me down an embankment?"

"It wasn't you; it was your cousin who was thrown down the embankment."

His face was settling into a gloomy cast. I quietly laid aside my pencil and pad.

"I guess you'd better stick to inventions," he suggested.

"I guess I had," I replied submissively.

Speaking of editors—though I don't know that I was speaking of them. I must have been thinking of them in connection with Sallie Britton's memoirs, and wondering whether she ever "submitted" them for publication, or how she did it. But editors are really a singular class of men; they have such strange and incomprehensible ways with them.

I once submitted a story to a prominent New York editor, who returned it promptly with the observation that "the public is getting very tired of that sort of thing." I felt very sorry for the public; but I wasn't willing to take one man's word for it, so I clapped the offensive document into an envelope and sent it away again—this time to a well-known Boston editor.

"I am delighted with the story," read the letter of acceptance, which came a few weeks later, "and so, I am sure, will be our readers." (!)

When an editor says a thing like that it is at his own peril. I at once sent him another tale, thinking thereby to increase his delight and add to it ten-fold.

"Can you call this a story, dear madam?" he asked when he sent it back. "Really, there seems to me to be no story at all; what is it all about?" I could see his pale smile.

It was getting interesting, like playing at battledore and shuttlecock. Off went the would-be story by the next mail to the New York editor—the one who so considerately gauged the ennui of the public.

"It is a clever and excellent piece of work," he wrote me; "the story is well told." I wonder if the editor, the writer, and the public are ever at one.

VI

We are told that Macaulay was in the habit of swallowing a book almost at a gulp; just as the ogres used to swallow little children, clothes and all. One longs for a like super-human capacity when confronted by the bewildering and tempting variety of wares which the book-stands are offering us to-day. Among the magazines there are always the old reliables. We almost know beforehand what they are going to say. In all events, we know in advance that, while they are going to entertain us, possibly to amuse and instruct us, they are not going to shock us. They hold no surprises in reserve; we should very likely resent the innovation if they were to take upon themselves any such new departure.

It is to the newer booklets, chiplets, clap-traplets, that we must turn for sensations; there we may get them in abundance. These candidates for popular favor are employing every device, legitimate and illegitimate, to attract notice to themselves. They appear in every imaginable form, color and garb, mincing before the public, and they make their little bows. Some of them are like ladies with painted cheeks, whose beauty is not even skin deep. But many of them are worth knowing. They come from the new land where "the modern" holds sway. If we keep them company for awhile we may find ourselves a little blown and dizzy from the unaccustomed pace, but, on the whole, invigorated.

Messrs. Houghton, Mifflin & Co. of Boston and New York have recently published a new book by Joel Chandler Harris, entitled *Sister Jane*.

This is a story which has come perilously near being ruined by a plot. It is astonishing that Mr. Harris has not discovered at this late day that he has nothing to do with clap-trap. It doubtless often happens that a writer, when he happens to be a man of genius, is unconscious of his own power. His work is so wholly the result of impulse, so natural an expression of himself, that he accepts it as a matter of course, along with other spiritual or physical phenomena of his being. So, on the other hand, is he unable to realize his limitations, or to recognize the extent of his failure when he adopts an external suggestion and tries to make it his own.

In *Sister Jane* Mr. Harris has given us another confirmation of his genius; not alone by what he has done, but as well by that which he has failed to accomplish. If he were not a genius—if he were simply a clever craftsman—he might have taken that lamentable plot and made something of it. A child is stolen; a child who exists for no other reason than to be stolen. He is spirited away for purposes of revenge by a man created for that special rôle of abduction. There is a hypocritical villain, the father of an illegitimate child, who is talked about all through the book, yet whose acquaintance we make only in the final pages. There is everything weak, unjointed, melodramatic about the plot. Absurdities accumulate and grow into a tower of folly which should be an everlasting reproach. Pages might be written concerning Mr. Harris' mistake in this direction. But it is pleasanter to talk of Mr. Harris' achievements in *Sister Jane*.

A singular feature of the book is that the real characters in it have absolutely nothing to do with the furtherance of the plot; they are the author's own, and every one of them is a masterpiece of his creative genius. Sister Jane herself; William Warnum, who tells the story; Mrs. Bishears, Mandy, Jincy Meadows, Brother Cosby and Grandsir Roach, Free Betsey and the two old demented sisters; the baby Klibs and even the negro Mose, are people who will live so long as creatures of the imagination continue to haunt our fancy.

There are chapters in *Sister Jane* that stand out like flaming torches. "Free Betsey Runs the Cards" is a gem; as well as "Two Old Friends and Another." "Jincy in the New Ground" is a little bit of fiction whose poetry and poignant charm Mr. Harris himself has never surpassed.

Mr. Harris is not a novelist. He has not the constructive faculty that goes to the making of even the mediocre novel; while he lacks the "vision" which gives us the great novel. But he has the quaint and fanciful imagination of the poet; he has the power to depict character in its outward manifestations, unsurpassed by any American writer of the present day and equalled by few.

Let us hope that he will tell us more of those old-time people in their quiet, sleepy corner of Middle Georgia. We shall not demand a plot; just a record of their plain and simple lives is all we want.

There is so much being said now-a-days about mental energy and its compelling force or quality, that one cannot avoid at times taking the subject under consideration.

The other day the thoughts of millions of people were at one and the same moment occupied with the great fist fight, its participants and its results. I could not help wondering whether this accumulated mental force, projected at a given time upon a common object, could fail to affect in some way the men against whom it was directed. I have had this notion before, in regard to events which have claimed the simultaneous attention of a whole nation. It seems to me, for instance, that the united impulse of horror which went out from millions of souls must in some subtle way have reached Guiteau's inner consciousness, after his crime, and made itself felt. But this is something for the psychologists; I had better stop, or I shall have them laughing at me. *

* The reference is to Charles J. Guiteau, who was hanged in 1882 for his murder of President Garfield, but who was still discussed in the press in 1897. (Editor's note.)

On Certain Brisk, Bright Days

On certain brisk, bright days I like to walk from my home, near Thirty-fourth street, down to the shopping district. After a few such experiments I begin to fancy that I have the walking habit. Doubtless I convey the same impression to acquaintances who see me from the car window "hot-footing" it down Olive street or Washington avenue. But in my sub-consciousness, as my friend Mrs. R— would say, I know that I have not the walking habit.

Eight or nine years ago I began to write stories—short stories which appeared in the magazines, and I forthwith began to suspect I had the writing habit. The public shared this impression, and called me an author. Since then, though I have written many short stories and a novel or two, I am forced to admit that I have not the writing habit. But it is hard to make people with the questioning habit believe this.

"Now, where, when, why, what do you write?" are some of the questions that I remember. How do I write? On a lapboard with a block of paper, a stub pen and a bottle of ink bought at the corner grocery, which keeps the best in town.

Where do I write? In a Morris chair beside the window, where I can see a few trees and a patch of sky, more or less blue.

When do I write? I am greatly tempted here to use slang and reply "any old time," but that would lend a tone of levity to this bit of confidence, whose seriousness I want to keep intact if possible. So I shall say I write in the morning, when not too strongly drawn to struggle with the intricacies of a pattern, and in the afternoon, if the temptation to try a new furniture polish on an old table leg is not too powerful to be denied; sometimes at night, though as I grow older I am more and more inclined to believe that night was made for sleep.

"Why do I write?" is a question which I have often asked myself and never very satisfactorily answered. Story-writing—at least with me—is the spontaneous expression of impressions gathered goodness knows where. To seek the source, the impulse of a story is like tearing a flower to pieces for wantonness.

What do I write? Well, not everything that comes into my head, but much of what I have written lies between the covers of my books.

There are stories that seem to write themselves, and others which positively refuse to be written—which no amount of coaxing can bring to anything. I do not believe any writer has ever made a "portrait" in fiction. A trick, a mannerism, a physical trait or mental characteristic go a very short way towards portraying the complete individual in real life who suggests the individual in the writer's imagination. The "material" of a writer is to the last degree uncertain, and I fear not marketable. I have been told stories which were looked upon as veritable gold mines by the generous narrators who placed them at my disposal. I have been taken to spots supposed to be alive with local color. I have been introduced to excruciating characters with frank permission to use them as I liked, but never, in any single instance, has such material been of the slightest service. I am completely at the mercy of unconscious selection. To such an extent is this true, that what is called the polishing up process has always proved disastrous to my work, and I avoid it, preferring the integrity of crudities to artificialities.

How hard it is for one's acquaintances and friends to realize that one's books are to be taken seriously, and that they are subject to the same laws which govern the existence of others' books! I have a son who is growing wroth over the question: "Where can I find your mother's books, or latest book?"

"The very next time any one asks me that question," he exclaimed excitedly, "I am going to tell them to try the stock yards!"

I hope he won't. He might thus offend a possible buyer. Politeness, besides being a virtue, is sometimes an art. I am often met with the same question, and I always try to be polite. "My latest book? Why, you will find it, no doubt, at the bookseller's or the libraries."

"The libraries! Oh, no, they don't keep it." She hadn't thought of the bookseller's. It's real hard to think of everything! Sometimes I feel as if I should like to get a good, remunerative job to do the thinking for some people. This may sound conceited, but it isn't. If I had space (I have plenty of time; time is my own, but space belongs to the *Post-Dispatch*), I should like to demonstrate satisfactorily that it is not conceited.

I trust it will not be giving away professional secrets to say that many readers would be surprised, perhaps shocked, at the questions which some newspaper editors will put to a defenseless woman under the guise of flattery.

For instance: "How many children have you?" This form is subtle and greatly to be commended in dealing with women of shy and retiring propensities. A woman's reluctance to speak of her children has not yet been chronicled. I have a good many, but they'd be simply wild if I dragged them into this. I might say something of those who are at a safe distance—the idol of my soul in Kentucky; the light of my eye off in Colorado; the treasure of his mother's heart in Louisiana—but I mistrust the form of their displeasure, with poisoned candy going through the mails.

"Do you smoke cigarettes?" is a question which I consider impertinent, and I think most women will agree with me. Suppose I do smoke cigarettes? Am I going to tell it out in meeting? Suppose I don't smoke cigarettes. Am I going to admit such a reflection upon my artistic integrity, and thereby bring upon myself the contempt of the guild?

In answering questions in which an editor believes his readers to be interested, the victim cannot take herself too seriously.

POEMS

If It Might Be

If it might be that thou didst need my life;
Now on the instant would I end this strife
'Twixt hope and fear, and glad the end I'd meet
With wonder only, to find death so sweet.

If it might be that thou didst need my love;
To love thee dear, my life's fond work would prove.
All time, to tender watchfulness I'd give;
And count it happiness, indeed, to live.

Psyche's Lament

O let all darkness fall upon mine eyes:
    I want no more of light!
Since Helios in the blazing skies
    Cannot make day so bright
As my lost one did make for me the night!

O, sombre sweetness; black-enfolden charms,
    Come to me once again!
Leave me not desolate; with empty arms
    That seeking, strive in vain
To clasp a void where warmest Love hath lain.

Now is no heart beat pulsing into mine
    Since he is gone. I see,
I feel but the cursed lights that shine—
    That made my Love to flee.
O Love, O God, O Night come back to me!

727

The Song Everlasting

The birds are telling it over and over;
    So are the flowers.
The bees have been humming it out in the clover
    For hours and hours.
    Awake, Love!

The thousand tongued voices of nature are ringing.
    Awake Love!
And list to the song that my soul is singing.
    Awake Love!

You and I

How many years since we walked, you and I,
Under the stars and the April sky;
You were young then, I was not older;
Then you were shy, nor was I bolder.
Was it love did we feel? was it life did we live?
It was springtime indeed, but can springtime give
The fullness of life and of love? Completest
When living and loving and roses are sweetest!
Shall we walk together once more, you and I,
Under the stars and the summer sky?

It Matters All

A little more or less of health?
    What does it matter!

A little more or less of wealth?
   A boon to scatter!
But more or less of love your own to call,
   It matters all!

In Dreams Throughout the Night

In dreams throughout the night, dear,
   Thy voice I heard;
A tenderest love and longing
   Freighted each blessed word.

All through the night in dreams, love,
   Thine eyes were there;
And hid in the depth of their fondness
   I read a silent prayer.

O, how should I answer thine eyes, dear,
   But with my own!
And how respond to the voice I love
   Save with an answering tone.

Good Night

Good night, good night!
Good-by it shall not be;
For all the days that come and go, dear love,
'Twixt now and happiness, 'twixt thee and me,
Shall moments dark, oblivious prove.

Until I look into thy tender eyes,

And hear again thy voice, no light,
No day will break, for me no sun will rise—
My own, my well-beloved—good night, good night!

If Some Day

If some day I, with casual, wanton glance
Should for a moment's space thine eyes ensnare;
    Or more, if I should dare
To rest my finger tips upon thy sleeve,
Or, grown more bold, upon thy swarthy cheek;
    If further I should seek
With honey-trick of tone thy name to call,
Breathing it soft, in meaning whisper low,
    Then wouldst thou know?

Is there no subtler sense, that holds not commerce
With the glancing eyes, the touch, the tone?
    Whereby alone
I would convey to thee some faintest gleam
Of what I dare not look, or speak, or dream!

To Carrie B.

Your greeting filled me with distress.
I've pondered long and sore to guess
What 'twould express.

Ah, Lady fair! can you not see:
From gentlemen of high degree
I always flee!

To Hider Schuyler—

I send a dozen wishes.
Let's say the first is "health."
(I send a dozen kisses!)
And the last we'll call it wealth.
The others—you must choose some.
I'm poor at counting wishes.
I'd be pretty sure to lose some—
But I double up the kisses!

To "Billy" with a Box of Cigars

These may be, without question,
Rather bad for your digestion.
But the Powers have not sent me
To preach sermons; they've but lent me
A keen desire to please you
Now and always without end,
And a little wish to tease you
With the fondness of a friend.

To Mrs. R.

I do not know you out upon the street
    Where people meet.
We talk as women talk; shall I confess?
    I know you less.
I hear you play, and touched by the wondrous spell—
    I know you well—

Let the Night Go

The night is gone, the year and yesterday;
The dozen little hours I had stole
And hid within the shadow of my soul
To play with by the way.

Let the night go! the year and yesterday!
I've kept one little hour from the past:
A pretty thing—a bauble to hold fast
And play with—by the way.

There's Music Enough

There's music enough in the wood to-day,
   O, me! O, my!
With Love a-piping his same old lay:
   We live, we die!
But tomorrow's a million miles away
When the world is green and the month is May.

An Ecstasy of Madness

There's an ecstasy of madness
Where the March Hares dwell;
A delirium of gladness
Too wild to tell.

The Moon has gone a-maying
And the Sun's so far!
O! what's the use of staying
With a blinking star!

Let us join hands this instant
And fly a-top the hill,
And whether near or distant,
We'll ne'er stop still

Or we find the Moon that's Maying
And the Sun so far,
That left us here a-praying
To a blinking star.

I Wanted God

I wanted God. In heaven and earth I sought,
And lo! I found him in my inmost thought.

The Haunted Chamber

Of course 'twas an excellent story to tell
Of a fair, frail, passionate woman who fell.
It may have been false, it may have been true.
That was nothing to me—it was less to you.
But with bottle between us, and clouds of smoke
From your last cigar, 'twas more of a joke
Than a matter of sin or a matter of shame
That a woman had fallen, and nothing to blame,
So far as you or I could discover,

But her beauty, her blood and an ardent lover.
But when you were gone and the lights were low
And the breeze came in with the moon's pale glow,
The far, faint voice of a woman, I heard,
'Twas but a wail, and it spoke no word.
It rose from the depths of some infinite gloom
And its tremulous anguish filled the room.
Yet the woman was dead and could not deny,
But women forever will whine and cry.
So now I must listen the whole night through
To the torment with which I had nothing to do—
But women forever will whine and cry
And men forever must listen—and sigh—

Life

A day with a splash of sunlight,
Some mist and a little rain.
A life with a dash of love-light,
Some dreams and a touch of pain.
To love a little and then to die!
To live a little and never know why!

Because—

Because they must, the birds sing.
The earth turns new in Spring
Because it must—'Tis only man
That does because he can
And knowing good from ill,
Chooses because he will—

To the Friend of My Youth: To Kitty

It is not all of life
To cling together while the years glide past.
It is not all of love
To walk with clasped hands from first to last.
That mystic garland which the spring did twine
Of scented lilac and the new-blown rose,
Faster than chains will hold my soul to thine
Thro' joy, and grief, thro' life—unto its close.

NOVELS

AT
FAULT

PART I

I

The Mistress of Place-Du-Bois

When Jérôme Lafirme died, his neighbors awaited the results of his sudden taking off with indolent watchfulness. It was a matter of unusual interest to them that a plantation of four thousand acres had been left unincumbered to the disposal of a handsome, inconsolable, childless Creole widow of thirty. A *bêtise* of some sort might safely be looked for. But time passing, the anticipated folly failed to reveal itself; and the only wonder was that Thérèse Lafirme so successfully followed the methods of her departed husband.

Of course Thérèse had wanted to die with her Jérôme, feeling that life without him held nothing that could reconcile her to its further endurance. For days she lived alone with her grief; shutting out the appeals that came to her from the demoralized "hands," and unmindful of the disorder that gathered about her. Till Uncle Hiram came one day with a respectful tender of sympathy, offered in the guise of a reckless misquoting of Scripture—and with a grievance.

"Mistuss," he said, "I 'lowed 'twar best to come to de house an' tell you; fur Massa he alluz did say 'Hi'urm, I counts on you to keep a eye open endurin' my appersunce; 'you ricollic, marm?'" addressing an expanse of black bordered cambric that veiled the features of his mistress. "Things is a goin' wrong; dat dey is. I don't wants to name no names 'doubt I'se 'bleeged to; but dey done start a kiarrin' de cotton seed off de place, and dats how."

If Hiram's information had confined itself to the bare statement of things "goin' wrong," such intimation, of its nature vague and susceptible of uncertain interpretation, might have failed to rouse Thérèse from her lethargy of grief. But that wrong doing presented as a tangible abuse and defiance of authority, served to move her to action. She felt at once the weight and sacredness of a trust, whose acceptance brought consolation and awakened unsuspected powers of doing.

In spite of Uncle Hiram's parting prediction "de cotton 'll be a goin' naxt" no more seed was hauled under cover of darkness from Place-du-Bois.

The short length of this Louisiana plantation stretched along Cane River, meeting the water when that stream was at it highest, with a thick growth of cotton-wood trees; save where a narrow convenient opening had been cut into their midst, and where further down the pine hills started in abrupt prominence from the water and the dead level of land on either side of them. These hills extended in a long line of gradual descent far back to the wooded borders of Lac du Bois; and within the circuit which they formed on the one side, and the irregular half circle of a sluggish bayou on the other, lay the cultivated open ground of the plantation—rich in its exhaustless powers of reproduction.

Among changes which the railroad brought soon after Jérôme Lafirme's death, and which were viewed by many as of questionable benefit, was one which drove Thérèse to seek another domicile. The old homestead that nestled to the hill side and close to the water's edge, had been abandoned to the inroads of progressive civilization; and Mrs. Lafirme had rebuilt many rods away from the river and beyond sight of the mutilated dwelling, converted now into a section house. In building, she avoided the temptations offered by modern architectural innovations, and clung to the simplicity of large rooms and broad verandas : a style whose merits had stood the test of easy-going and comfort-loving generations.

The negro quarters were scattered at wide intervals over the land, breaking with picturesque irregularity into the systematic division of field from field; and in the early spring-time gleaming in their new coat of whitewash against the tender green of the sprouting cotton and corn.

Thérèse loved to walk the length of the wide verandas, armed with her field-glass, and to view her surrounding possessions with comfortable satisfaction. Then her gaze swept from cabin to cabin; from patch to patch; up to the pine-capped hills, and down to the station which squatted a brown and ugly intruder within her fair domain.

She had made pouting resistance to this change at first, opposing it step by step with a conservatism that yielded only to the resistless. She pictured a visionary troop of evils coming in the wake of the railroad, which, in her eyes no conceivable benefits could mitigate. The occasional tramp, she foresaw as an army; and the travelers whom chance deposited at the store that adjoined the station, she dreaded as an endless procession of intruders forcing themselves upon her privacy.

Grégoire, the young nephew of Mrs. Lafirme, whose duty on the plantation was comprehended in doing as he was bid, qualified by a propensity for doing as he liked, rode up from the store one day in the reckless fashion peculiar to Southern youth, breathless with the information that a stranger was there wishing audience with her.

Thérèse at once bristled with objections. Here was a confirmation of her worst dread. But encouraged by Grégoire's reiteration "he 'pear to me like a nice sort o' person," she yielded a grudging assent to the interview.

She sat within the wide hall-way beyond the glare and heat that were beating mercilessly down upon the world out of doors, engaged in a light work not so exacting as to keep her thoughts and glance from wandering. Looking through the wide open back doors, the picture which she saw was a section of the perfect lawn that encircled the house for an acre around, and from which Hiram was slowly raking the leaves cast from a clump of tall magnolias. Beneath the spreading shade of an umbrella-China tree, lay the burly Hector, but half awake to the possible nearness of tramps; and Betsy, a piece of youthful ebony in blue cottonade, was crossing leisurely on her way to the poultry yard; unheeding the scorching sun-rays that she thought were sufficiently parried by the pan of chick feed that she balanced adroitly on her bushy black head.

At the front, the view at certain seasons would have been clear and unbroken: to the station, the store, and out-lying hills. But now she could see beyond the lawn only a quivering curtain of rich green which the growing corn spread before the level landscape, and above whose swaying heads appeared occasionally the top of an advancing white sun-shade.

Thérèse was of a roundness of figure suggesting a future of excessive fullness if not judiciously guarded; and she was fair, with a warm whiteness that a passing thought could deepen into color. The waving blonde hair, gathered in an abundant coil on top of her head, grew away with a pretty sweep from the temples, the low forehead and nape of the white neck that showed above a frill of soft lace. Her eyes were blue, as certain gems are; that deep blue that lights, and glows, and tells things of the soul. When David Hosmer presented himself, they were intense only with expectancy and the color was in her cheek like the blush in a shell.

He was a tall individual of perhaps forty; thin and sallow. His black hair was streaked abundantly with grey, and his face marked with premature lines; left there by care, no doubt, and, by a too close attention to what men are pleased to call the main chances of life.

"A serious one," was Thérèse's first thought in looking at him. "A man who has never learned to laugh or who has forgotten how." Though plainly feeling the effects of the heat, he did not seem to appreciate the relief offered by the grateful change into this shadowy, sweet smelling, cool retreat; used as he was to ignore the comforting things of life when presented to him as irrelevant to that dominant main chance. He accepted under protest a glass of ice water from the wide-eyed Betsy, and suffered a fan to be thrust into his hand, seemingly to save his time or his timidity by its possibly unheeded rejection.

"Lor'-zee folks," exclaimed the observant Betsy on re-entering the kitchen, "dey'se a man in yonda, look like he gwine eat somebody up. I was fur gittin' 'way quick me."

It can be readily imagined that Hosmer lost little time in preliminary small talk. He introduced himself vaguely as from the West; then perceiving the need of being more specific as from Saint Louis. She had guessed he was no Southerner. He had come to Mrs. Lafirme on the part of himself and others with a moneyed offer for the privilege of cutting timber from her land for a given number of years. The amount named was alluring, but here was proposed another change and she felt plainly called on for resistance.

The company which he represented had in view the erection of a saw-mill some two miles back in the woods, close beside the bayou and at a convenient distance from the lake. He was not wordy, nor was he eager in urging his plans; only in a quiet way insistent in showing points to be considered in her own favor which she would be likely herself to overlook.

Mrs. Lafirme, a clever enough business woman, was moved by no undue haste to give her answer. She begged for time to think the matter over, which Hosmer readily agreed to; expressing a hope that a favorable answer be sent to him at Natchitoches, where he would await her convenience. Then resisting rather than declining all further hospitality, he again took his way through the scorching fields.

Thérèse wanted but time to become familiar with this further change. Alone she went out to her beloved woods, and at the hush of mid-day, bade a tearful farewell to the silence.

II

At the Mill

David Hosmer sat alone in his little office of roughly fashioned pine board. So small a place, that with his desk and his clerk's desk, a narrow bed in one corner, and two chairs, there was scant room for a man to more than turn himself comfortably about. He had just dispatched his clerk with the daily bundle of letters to the post-office, two miles away in the Lafirme store, and he now turned with the air of a man who had well earned his moment of leisure, to the questionable relaxation of adding columns and columns of figures.

The mill's unceasing buzz made pleasant music to his ears and stirred reflections of a most agreeable nature. A year had gone by since Mrs. Lafirme had consented to Hosmer's proposal; and already the business more than gave promise of justifying the venture. Orders came in from the North and West more rapidly than they could be filled. That "Cypresse Funerall" which stands in grim majesty through the dense forests of Louisiana had already won its just recognition; and Hosmer's appreciation of a successful business venture was showing itself in a little more pronounced stoop of shoulder, a deepening of pre-occupation and a few additional lines about mouth and forehead.

Hardly had the clerk gone with his letters than a light footstep sounded on the narrow porch; the quick tap of a parasol was heard on the door-sill; a pleasant voice asking, "Any admission except on business?" and Thérèse crossed the small room and seated herself beside Hosmer's desk before giving him time to arise.

She laid her hand and arm,—bare to the elbow—across his work, and said, looking at him reproachfully :—

"Is this the way you keep a promise?"

"A promise?" he questioned, smiling awkwardly and looking furtively at the white arm, then very earnestly at the ink-stand beyond.

"Yes. Didn't you promise to do no work after five o'clock?"

"But this is merely pastime," he said, touching the paper, yet leaving it undisturbed beneath the fair weight that was pressing it down. "My work is finished: you must have met Henry with the letters."

"No, I suppose he went through the woods; we came on the hand-car. Oh, dear! It's an ungrateful task, this one of reform," and she leaned back, fanning leisurely, whilst he proceeded to throw the contents of his desk into hopeless disorder by pretended efforts at arrangement.

"My husband used sometimes to say, and no doubt with reason," she continued, "that in my eagerness for the rest of mankind to do right, I was often in danger of losing sight of such necessity for myself."

"Oh, there could be no fear of that," said Hosmer with a short laugh. There was no further pretext for continued occupation with his pens and pencils and rulers, so he turned towards Thérèse, rested an arm on the desk, pulled absently at his black moustache, and crossing his knee, gazed with deep concern at the toe of his boot, and set of his trouser about the ankle.

"You are not what my friend Homeyer would call an individualist," he ventured, "since you don't grant a man the right to follow the promptings of his character."

"No, I'm no individualist, if to be one is to permit men to fall into hurtful habits without offering protest against it. I'm losing faith in that friend Homeyer, who I strongly suspect is a mythical apology for your own short-comings."

"Indeed he's no myth; but a friend who is fond of going into such things and allows me the benefit of his deeper perceptions."

"You having no time, well understood. But if his influence has had the merit of drawing your thoughts from business once in a while we won't quarrel with it."

"Mrs. Lafirme," said Hosmer, seeming moved to pursue the subject, and addressing the spray of white blossoms that adorned Thérèse's black hat, "you admit, I suppose, that in urging your views upon me, you have in mind the advancement of my happiness?"

"Well understood."

"Then why wish to substitute some other form of enjoyment for the one which I find in following my inclinations?"

"Because there is an unsuspected selfishness in your inclinations that works harm to yourself and to those around you. I want you to know," she continued warmly, "the good things of life that cheer and warm, that are always at hand."

"Do you think the happiness of Melicent or—or others could be materially lessened by my fondness for money getting?" he asked dryly, with a faint elevation of eyebrow.

"Yes, in proportion as it deprives them of a charm which any man's society loses, when pursuing one object in life, he grows insensible to every other. But I'll not scold any more. I've made myself troublesome enough for one day. You haven't asked about Melicent. It's true," she laughed, "I haven't given you much chance. She's out on the lake with Grégoire."

"Ah?"

"Yes, in the pirogue. A dangerous little craft, I'm afraid; but she tells me she can swim. I suppose it's all right."

"Oh, Melicent will look after herself."

Hosmer had great faith in his sister Melicent's ability to look after herself; and it must be granted that the young lady fully justified his belief in her.

"She enjoys her visit more than I thought she would," he said.

"Melicent's a dear girl," replied Thérèse cordially, "and a wise one too in guarding herself against a somber influence that I know," with a meaning glance at Hosmer, who was preparing to close his desk.

She suddenly perceived the picture of a handsome boy, far back in one of the pigeon-holes, and with the familiarity born of country intercourse, she looked intently at it, remarking upon the boy's beauty.

"A child whom I loved very much," said Hosmer. "He's dead," and he closed the desk, turning the key in the lock with a sharp click which seemed to add—"and buried."

Thérèse then approached the open door, leaned her back against its casing, and turned her pretty profile towards Hosmer, who, it need not be supposed, was averse to looking at it—only to being caught in the act.

"I want to look in at the mill before work closes," she said; and not waiting for an answer she went on to ask—moved by some association of ideas :—

"How is Joçint doing?"

"Always unruly, the foreman tells me. I don't believe we shall be able to keep him."

Hosmer then spoke a few words through the telephone which connected with the agent's desk at the station, put on his great slouch hat, and thrusting keys and hands into his pocket, joined Thérèse in the door-way.

Quitting the office and making a sharp turn to the left, they came in direct sight of the great mill. She quickly made her way past the huge piles of sawed timber, not waiting for her companion, who loitered at each step of the way, with observant watchfulness. Then mounting the steep stairs that led to the upper portions of the mill, she went at once to her favorite spot, quite on the edge of the open platform that overhung the dam. Here she watched with fascinated delight the great logs hauled dripping from the water, following each till it had changed to the clean symmetry of sawed planks. The unending work made her giddy. For no one was there a moment of rest, and she could well understand the open revolt of the surly Joçint; for he rode the day long on that narrow car, back and forth, back and forth, with his heart in the pine hills and knowing that his little Creole pony was roaming the woods in vicious idleness and his rifle gathering an unsightly rust on the cabin wall at home.

The boy gave but ugly acknowledgment to Thérèse's amiable nod; for he thought she was one upon whom partly rested the fault of this intrusive Industry which had come to fire the souls of indolent fathers with a greedy ambition for gain, at the sore expense of revolting youth.

III

In the Pirogue

"You got to set mighty still in this pirogue," said Grégoire, as with a long oar-stroke he pulled out into mid stream.

"Yes, I know," answered Melicent complacently, arranging herself opposite him in the long narrow boat: all sense of danger which the situation might arouse being dulled by the attractiveness of a new experience.

Her resemblance to Hosmer ended with height and slenderness of figure, olive tinted skin, and eyes and hair which were of that dark brown often miscalled black; but unlike his, her face was awake with an eagerness to know and test the novelty and depth of unaccustomed sensation. She had thus far lived an unstable existence, free from the weight of responsibilities, with a notion lying somewhere deep in her consciousness that the world must one day be taken seriously; but that contingency was yet too far away to disturb the harmony of her days.

She had eagerly responded to her brother's suggestion of spending a summer with him in Louisiana. Hitherto, having passed her summers North, West, or East as alternating caprice prompted, she was ready at a word to fit her humor to the novelty of a season at the South. She enjoyed in advance the startling effect which her announced intention produced upon her intimate circle at home; thinking that her whim deserved the distinction of eccentricity with which they chose to invest it. But Melicent was chiefly moved by the prospect of an uninterrupted sojourn with her brother, whom she loved blindly, and to whom she attributed qualities of mind and heart which she thought the world had discovered to use against him.

"You got to set mighty still in this pirogue."

"Yes, I know; you told me so before," and she laughed.

"W'at are you laughin' at?" asked Grégoire with amused but uncertain expectancy.

"Laughing at you, Grégoire; how can I help it?" laughing again.

"Betta wait tell I do somethin' funny, I reckon. Ain't this a putty sight?" he added, referring to the dense canopy of an overarching tree, beneath which they were gliding, and whose extreme branches dipped quite into the slow moving water.

The scene had not attracted Melicent. For she had been engaged in observing her companion rather closely; his personality holding her with a certain imaginative interest.

The young man whom she so closely scrutinized was slightly undersized, but of close and brawny build. His hands were not so refinedly white as those of certain office bred young men of her acquaintance, yet they were not coarsened by undue toil : it being somewhat an axiom with him to do nothing that an available "nigger" might do for him.

Close fitting, high-heeled boots of fine quality incased his feet, in whose shapeliness he felt a pardonable pride; for a young man's excellence was often measured in the circle which he had frequented, by the possession of such a foot. A peculiar grace in the dance and a talent for bold repartee were further characteristics which had made Grégoire's departure keenly felt among certain belles of upper Red River. His features were handsome, of sharp and refined cut, and his eyes black and brilliant as eyes of an alert and intelligent animal sometimes are. Melicent could not reconcile his voice to her liking; it was too softly low and feminine, and carried a note of pleading or pathos, unless he argued with his horse, his dog, or a "nigger," at which times, though not unduly raised, it acquired a biting quality that served the purpose of relieving him from further form of insistence.

He pulled rapidly and in silence down the bayou, that was now so entirely sheltered from the open light of the sky by the meeting branches above, as to seem a dim leafy tunnel fashioned by man's ingenuity. There were no perceptible banks, for the water spread out on either side of them, further than they could follow its flashings through the rank underbrush. The dull plash of some object falling into the water, or the wild call of a lonely bird were the only sounds that broke upon the stillness, beside the monotonous dipping of the oars and the occasional low undertones of their own voices. When Grégoire called the girl's attention to an object near by, she fancied it was the protruding stump of a decaying tree; but reaching for his revolver and taking quiet aim, he drove a ball into the black upturned nozzle that sent it below the surface with an angry splash.

"Will he follow us?" she asked, mildly agitated.

"Oh no; he's glad 'nough to git out o' the way. You betta put down yo' veil," he added a moment later.

Before she could ask a reason—for it was not her fashion to obey at word of command—the air was filled with the doleful hum of a gray swarm of mosquitoes, which attacked them fiercely.

"You didn't tell me the bayou was the refuge of such savage creatures," she said, fastening her veil closely about face and neck, but not before she had felt the sharpness of their angry sting.

"I reckoned you'd 'a knowed all about it: seems like you know everything." After a short interval he added, "you betta take yo' veil off."

She was amused at Grégoire's authoritative tone and she said to him laughing, yet obeying his suggestion, which carried a note of command: "you shall tell me always, why I should do things."

"All right," he replied; "because they ain't any mo' mosquitoes; because I want you to see somethin' worth seein' afta while; and because I like to look at you," which he was doing, with the innocent boldness of a forward child. "Ain't that 'nough reasons?"

"More than enough," she replied shortly.

The rank and clustering vegetation had become denser as they went on, forming an impenetrable tangle on either side, and pressing so closely above that they often needed to lower their heads to avoid the blow of some drooping branch. Then a sudden and unlooked for turn in the bayou carried them out upon the far-spreading waters of the lake, with the broad canopy of the open sky above them.

"Oh," cried Melicent, in surprise. Her exclamation was like a sigh of relief which comes at the removal of some pressure from body or brain.

The wildness of the scene caught upon her erratic fancy, speeding it for a quick moment into the realms of romance. She was an Indian maiden of the far past, fleeing and seeking with her dusky lover some wild and solitary retreat on the borders of this lake, which offered them no seeming foot-hold save such as they would hew themselves with axe or tomahawk. Here and there, a grim cypress lifted its head above the water, and spread wide its moss covered arms inviting refuge to the great black-winged buzzards that circled over and about it in mid-air. Nameless voices—weird sounds that awake in a Southern forest at twilight's approach,—were crying a sinister welcome to the settling gloom.

"This is a place thet can make a man sad, I tell you," said Grégoire, resting his oars, and wiping the moisture from his forehead. "I wouldn't want to be yere alone, not fur any money."

"It is an awful place," replied Melicent with a little appreciative shudder; adding "do you consider me a bodily protection?" and feebly smiling into his face.

"Oh; I ain't 'fraid o' any thing I can see an on'erstan'. I can han'le mos' any thing thet's got a body. But they do tell some mighty queer tales 'bout this lake an' the pine hills yonda."

"Queer—how?"

"W'y, ole McFarlane's buried up there on the hill; an' they's folks 'round yere says he walks about o' nights; can't res' in his grave fur the niggas he's killed."

"Gracious! and who was old McFarlane?"

"The meanest w'ite man thet ever lived, seems like. Used to own this place long befo' the Lafirmes got it. They say he's the person that Mrs. W'at's her name wrote about in Uncle Tom's Cabin."

"Legree? I wonder if it could be true?" Melicent asked with interest.

"Thet's w'at they all say: ask any body."

"You'll take me to his grave, won't you Grégoire," she entreated.

"Well, not this evenin'—I reckon not. It'll have to be broad day, an' the sun shinin' mighty bright w'en I take you to ole McFarlane's grave."

They had retraced their course and again entered the bayou, from which the light had now nearly vanished, making it needful that they watch carefully to escape the hewn logs that floated in numbers upon the water.

"I didn't suppose you were ever sad, Grégoire," Melicent said gently.

"Oh my! yes;" with frank acknowledgment. "You ain't ever seen me w'en I was real lonesome. 'Tain't so bad sence you come. But times w'en I git to thinkin' 'bout home, I'm boun' to cry—seems like I can't he'p it."

"Why did you ever leave home?" she asked sympathetically.

"You see w'en father died, fo' year ago, mother she went back to France, t'her folks there; she never could stan' this country—an' lef' us boys to manage the place. Hec, he took charge the firs' year an' run it in debt. Placide an' me did'n' have no betta luck the naxt year. Then the creditors come up from New Orleans an' took holt. That's the time I packed my duds an' lef'."

"And you came here?"

"No, not at firs'. You see the Santien boys had a putty hard name in the country. Aunt Thérèse, she'd fallen out with father years ago 'bout the way, she said, he was bringin' us up. Father, he wasn't the man to take nothin' from nobody. Never 'lowed any of us to come down yere. I was in Texas, goin' to the devil I reckon, w'en she sent for me, an' yere I am."

"And here you ought to stay, Grégoire."

"Oh, they ain't no betta woman in the worl' then Aunt Thérèse, w'en you do like she wants. See 'em yonda waitin' fur us? Reckon they thought we was drowned."

IV

A Small Interruption

When Melicent came to visit her brother, Mrs. Lafirme persuaded him to abandon his uncomfortable quarters at the mill and take up his residence in the cottage, which stood just beyond the lawn of the big house. This cottage had been furnished *de pied en cap* many years before, in readiness against an excess of visitors, which in days gone by was not of infrequent occurrence at Place-du-Bois. It was Melicent's delighted intention to keep house here. And she foresaw no obstacle in the way of procuring the needed domestic aid in a place which was clearly swarming with idle women and children.

"Got a cook yet, Mel?" was Hosmer's daily enquiry on returning home, to which Melicent was as often forced to admit that she had no cook, but was not without abundant hope of procuring one.

Betsy's Aunt Cynthy had promised with a sincerity which admitted not of doubt, that "de Lord willin' " she would "be on han' Monday, time to make de mornin' coffee." Which assurance had afforded Melicent a Sunday free of disturbing doubts concerning the future of her undertaking. But who may know what the morrow will bring forth? Cynthy had been "tuck sick in de night." So ran the statement of the wee pickaninny who appeared at Melicent's gate many hours later than morning coffee time: delivering his message in a high voice of complaint, and disappearing like a vision without further word.

Uncle Hiram, then called to the breach, had staked his patriarchal honor on the appearance of his niece Suze on Tuesday. Melicent and Thérèse meeting Suze some days later in a field path, asked the cause of her bad faith. The girl showed them all the white teeth which nature had lavished on her, saying with the best natured laugh in the world: "I don' know how come I didn' git dere Chewsday like I promise."

If the ladies were not disposed to consider that an all-sufficient reason, so much the worse, for Suze had no other to offer.

From Mose's wife, Minervy, better things might have been expected. But after a solemn engagement to take charge of Melicent's kitchen on Wednesday, the dusky matron suddenly awoke to the need of "holpin' Mose hoe out dat co'n in the stiff lan'."

Thérèse, seeing that the girl was really eager to play in the brief rôle of housekeeper had used her powers, persuasive and authoritative, to procure servants for her, but without avail. She herself was not without an abundance of them, from the white-haired Hiram, whose position on the place had long been a sinecure, down to the little brown legged tot Mandy, much given to falling asleep in the sun, when not chasing venturesome poultry off forbidden ground, or stirring gentle breezes with an enormous palm leaf fan about her mistress during that lady's after dinner nap.

When pressed to give a reason for this apparent disinclination of the negroes to work for the Hosmers, Nathan, who was at the moment being interviewed on the front veranda by Thérèse and Melicent, spoke out.

"Dey 'low 'roun' yere, dat you's mean to de black folks, ma'am: dat what dey says—I don' know me."

"Mean," cried Melicent, amazed, "in what way, pray?"

"Oh, all sort o' ways," he admitted, with a certain shy brazenness; determined to go through with the ordeal.

"Dey 'low you wants to cut de little gals' plaits off, an' sich—I don' know me."

"Do you suppose, Nathan," said Thérèse attempting but poorly to hide her amusement at Melicent's look of dismay, "that Miss Hosmer would bother herself with darkies' plaits?"

"Dat's w'at I tink m'sef. Anyways, I'll sen' Ar'minty 'roun' to-morrow, sho."

Melicent was not without the guilty remembrance of having one day playfully seized one of the small Mandy's bristling plaits, daintily between finger and thumb, threatening to cut them all away with the scissors which she carried. Yet she could not but believe that there was some deeper motive underlying this systematic reluctance of the negroes to give their work in exchange for the very good pay which she offered. Thérèse soon enlightened her with the information that the negroes were very averse to working for Northern people whose speech, manners, and attitude towards themselves were unfamiliar. She was given the consoling assurance of not being the only victim of this boycott, as Thérèse recalled many examples of strangers whom she knew to have met with a like cavalier treatment at the darkies' hands.

Needless to say, Araminty never appeared.

Hosmer and Melicent were induced to accept Mrs. Lafirme's generous hospitality; and one of that lady's many supernumeraries was detailed each morning to "do up" Miss Melicent's rooms, but not without the previous understanding that the work formed part of Miss T'rèse's system.

Nothing which had happened during the year of his residence at Place-du-Bois had furnished Hosmer such amusement as these misadventures of his sister Melicent, he having had no like experience with his mill hands.

It is not unlikely that his good humor was partly due to the acceptable arrangement which assured him the daily society of Thérèse, whose presence was growing into a need with him.

V

In the Pine Woods

When Grégoire said to Melicent that there was no better woman in the world than his Aunt Thérèse, "W'en you do like she wants," the statement was so incomplete as to leave one in uncomfortable doubt of the expediency of venturing within the influence of so exacting a nature. True, Thérèse required certain conduct from others, but she was willing to further its accomplishment by personal efforts, even sacrifices—that could leave no doubt of the pure unselfishness of her motive. There was hardly a soul at Place-du-Bois who had not felt the force of her will and yielded to its gentle influence.

The picture of Joçint as she had last seen him, stayed with her, till it gave form to a troubled desire moving her to see him again and speak with him. He had always been an unruly subject, inclined to a surreptitious defiance of authority. Repeatedly had he been given work on the plantation and as many times dismissed for various causes. Thérèse would have long since removed him had it not been for his old father Morico, whose long life spent on the place had established a claim upon her tolerance.

In the late afternoon, when the shadows of the magnolias were stretching in grotesque lengths across the lawn, Thérèse stood waiting for Uncle Hiram to bring her sleek bay Beauregard around to the front. The dark close fitting habit which she wore lent brilliancy to her soft blonde coloring; and there was no mark of years about her face or figure, save the settling of a thoughtful shadow upon the eyes, which joys and sorrows that were past and gone had left there.

As she rode by the cottage, Melicent came out on the porch to wave a laughing good-bye. The girl was engaged in effacing the simplicity of her rooms with certain bizarre decorations that seemed the promptings of a disordered imagination. Yards of fantastic calico had been brought up from the store, which Grégoire with hammer and tacks was amiably forming into impossible designs at the prompting of the girl. The little darkies had been enlisted to bring their contributions of palm branches, pine cones, ferns, and bright hued bird wings—and a row of those small recruits stood on the porch, gaping in wide-mouthed admiration at a sight that stirred within their breasts such remnant of savage instinct as past generations had left there in dormant survival.

One of the small audience permitted her attention to be drawn for a moment from the gorgeous in-door spectacle, to follow the movements of her mistress.

"Jis' look Miss T'rèse how she go a lopin' down de lane. Dere she go—dere she go—now she gone," and she again became contemplative.

Thérèse, after crossing the railroad, for a space kept to the brow of the hill where stretched a well defined road, which by almost imperceptible degrees led deeper and always higher into the woods. Presently, leaving this road and turning into a bridle path where an unpracticed eye would have discovered no sign of travel, she rode on until reaching a small clearing among the pines, in the center of which stood a very old and weather beaten cabin.

Here she dismounted, before Morico knew of her presence, for he sat with his back partly turned to the open door. As she entered and greeted him, he arose from his chair, all trembling with excitement at her visit; the long white locks, straggling and unkept, falling about his brown visage that had grown old and weather beaten with his cabin. Sinking down into his seat—the hide covered chair that had been worn smooth by years of usefulness—he gazed well pleased at Thérèse, who seated herself beside him.

"Ah, this is quite the handsomest you have made yet, Morico," she said addressing him in French, and taking up the fan that he was curiously fashioning of turkey feathers.

"I am taking extra pains with it," he answered, looking complacently at his handiwork and smoothing down the glossy feathers with the ends of his withered old fingers. "I thought the American lady down at the house might want to buy it."

Thérèse could safely assure him of Melicent's willingness to seize on the trophy.

Then she asked why Joçint had not been to the house with news of him. "I have had chickens and eggs for you, and no way of sending them."

At mention of his son's name, the old man's face clouded with displeasure and his hand trembled so that he was at some pains to place the feather which he was at the moment adding to the widening fan.

"Joçint is a bad son, madame, when even you have been able to do nothing with him. The trouble that boy has given me no one knows; but let him not think I am too old to give him a sound drubbing."

Joçint meanwhile had returned from the mill and seeing Thérèse's horse fastened before his door, was at first inclined to skulk back into the woods; but an impulse of defiance moved him to enter, and gave to his ugly countenance a look that was far from agreeable as he mumbled a greeting to Thérèse. His father he did not address. The old man looked from son to visitor with feeble expectancy of some good to come from her presence there.

Joçint's straight and coarse black hair hung in a heavy mop over his low retreating forehead, almost meeting the ill-defined line of eyebrow that straggled above small dusky black eyes, that with the rest of his physique was an inheritance from his Indian mother.

Approaching the safe or *garde manger*, which was the most prominent piece of furniture in the room, he cut a wedge from the round loaf of heavy soggy corn bread that he found there, added a layer of fat pork, and proceeded to devour the unpalatable morsel with hungry relish.

"That is but poor fare for your old father, Joçint," said Thérèse, looking steadily at the youth.

"Well, I got no chance* me, fu' go fine nuttin in de 'ood" (woods), he answered purposely in English, to annoy his father who did not understand the language.

"But you are earning enough to buy him something better; and you know there is always plenty at the house that I am willing to spare him."

"I got no chance me fu' go to de 'ouse neider," he replied deliberately, after washing down the scant repast with a long draught from the tin bucket which he had replenished at the cistern before entering. He swallowed the water regardless of the "wiggles" whose presence was plainly visible.

"What does he say?" asked Morico scanning Thérèse's face appealingly.

"He only says that work at the mill keeps him a good deal occupied," she said with attempted carelessness.

As she finished speaking, Joçint put on his battered felt hat, and strode

* Meaning "time."

out the back door; his gun on his shoulder and a yellow cur following close at his heels.

Thérèse remained a while longer with the old man, hearing sympathetically the long drawn story of his troubles, and cheering him as no one else in the world was able to do, then she went away.

Joçint was not the only one who had seen Beauregard fastened at Morico's door. Hosmer was making a tour of inspection that afternoon through the woods, and when he came suddenly upon Thérèse some moments after she had quitted the cabin, the meeting was not so wholly accidental as that lady fancied it was.

If there could be a situation in which Hosmer felt more than in another at ease in Thérèse's company, it was the one in which he found himself. There was no need to seek occupation for his hands, those members being sufficiently engaged with the management of his horse. His eyes found legitimate direction in following the various details which a rider is presumed to observe; and his manner freed from the necessity of self direction took upon itself an ease which was occasional enough to mark it as noteworthy.

She told him of her visit. At mention of Joçint's name he reddened: then followed the acknowledgment that the youth in question had caused him to lose his temper and forget his dignity during the afternoon.

"In what way?" asked Thérèse. "It would be better to dismiss him than to rail at him. He takes reproof badly and is extremely treacherous."

"Mill hands are not plentiful, or I should send him off at once. Oh, he is an unbearable fellow. The men told me of a habit he has of letting the logs roll off the carriage, causing a good deal of annoyance and delay in replacing them. I was willing enough to believe it might be accidental, until I caught him today in the very act. I am thankful not to have knocked him down."

Hosmer felt exhilarated. The excitement of his encounter with Joçint had not yet died away; this softly delicious atmosphere; the subtle aroma of the pines; his unlooked for meeting with Thérèse—all combined to stir him with unusual emotions.

"What a splendid creature Beauregard is," he said, smoothing the animal's glossy mane with the end of his riding whip. The horses were walking slowly in step, and close together.

"Of course he is," said Thérèse proudly, patting the arched neck of her favorite. "Beauregard is a blooded animal, remember. He quite throws poor Nelson in the shade," looking pityingly at Hosmer's heavily built iron-grey.

"Don't cast any slurs on Nelson, Mrs. Lafirme. He's done me service that's worthy of praise—worthy of better treatment than he gets."

"I know. He deserves the best, poor fellow. When you go away you should turn him out to pasture, and forbid any one to use him."

"It would be a good idea; but—I'm not so certain about going away."

"Oh I beg your pardon. I fancied your movements were directed by some unchangeable laws."

"Like the planets in their orbits? No, there is no absolute need of my going; the business which would have called me away can be done as readily by letter. If I heed my inclination it certainly holds me here."

"I don't understand that. It's natural enough that I should be fond of the country; but you—I don't believe you've been away for three months, have you? and city life certainly has its attractions."

"It's beastly," he answered decidedly. "I greatly prefer the country— this country; though I can imagine a condition under which it would be less agreeable; insupportable, in fact."

He was looking fixedly at Thérèse, who let her eyes rest for an instant in the unaccustomed light of his, while she asked "and the condition?"

"If you were to go away. Oh! it would take the soul out of my life."

It was now her turn to look in all directions save the one in which his glance invited her. At a slight and imperceptible motion of the bridle, well understood by Beauregard, the horse sprang forward into a quick canter, leaving Nelson and his rider to follow as they could.

Hosmer overtook her when she stopped to let her horse drink at the side of the hill where the sparkling spring water came trickling from the moist rocks, and emptied into the long out-scooped trunk of a cypress, that served as trough. The two horses plunged their heads deep in the clear water; the proud Beauregard quivering with satisfaction, as arching his neck and shaking off the clinging moisture, he waited for his more deliberate companion.

"Doesn't it give one a sympathetic pleasure," said Thérèse, "to see the relish with which they drink?"

"I never thought of it," replied Hosmer, cynically. His face was unusually flushed, and diffidence was plainly seizing him again.

Thérèse was now completely mistress of herself, and during the remainder of the ride she talked incessantly, giving him no chance for more than the briefest answers.

VI

Melicent Talks

"David Hosmer, you are the most supremely unsatisfactory man existing."

Hosmer had come in from his ride, and seating himself in the large wicker chair that stood in the center of the room, became at once absorbed in reflections. Being addressed, he looked up at his sister, who sat sidewards on the edge of a table slightly removed, swaying a dainty slippered foot to and fro in evident impatience.

"What crime have I committed now, Melicent, against your code?" he asked, not fully aroused from his reverie.

"You've committed nothing; your sin is one of omission. I absolutely believe you go through the world with your eyes, to all practical purposes, closed. Don't you notice anything; any change?"

"To be sure I do," said Hosmer, relying on a knowledge lent him by previous similar experiences, and taking in the clinging artistic drapery that enfolded her tall spare figure, "you've a new gown on. I didn't think to mention it, but I noticed it all the same."

This admission of a discernment that he had failed to make evident, aroused Melicent's uncontrolled mirth.

"A new gown!" and she laughed heartily. "A threadbare remnant! A thing that holds by shreds and tatters."

She went behind her brother's chair, taking his face between her hands, and turning it upward, kissed him on the forehead. With his head in such position, he could not fail to observe the brilliant folds of muslin that were arranged across the ceiling to simulate the canopy of a tent. Still holding his face, she moved it sidewards, so that his eyes, knowing now what office was expected of them, followed the line of decorations about the room.

"It's immense, Mel; perfectly immense. When did you do it all?"

"This afternoon, with Grégoire's help," she answered, looking proudly at her work. "And my poor hands are in such condition! But really, Dave," she continued, seating herself on the side of his chair, with an arm about his neck, and he leaning his head back on the improvised cushion, "I wonder that you ever got on in business, observing things as little as you do."

"Oh, that's different."

"Well, I don't believe you see half that you ought to," adding naively, "How did you and Mrs. Lafirme happen to come home together this evening?"

The bright lamp-light made the flush quite evident that arose to his face under her near gaze.

"We met in the woods; she was coming from Morico's."

"David, do you know that woman is an angel. She's simply the most perfect creature I ever knew."

Melicent's emphasis of speech was a thing so recurrent, so singularly her own, as to startle an unaccustomed hearer.

"That opinion might carry some weight, Mel, if I hadn't heard it scores of times from you, and of as many different women."

"Indeed you have not. Mrs. Lafirme is exceptional. Really, when she stands at the end of the veranda, giving orders to those darkies, her face a little flushed, she's positively a queen."

"As far as queenliness may be compatible with the angelic state," replied Hosmer, but not ill pleased with Melicent's exaggerated praise of Thérèse.

Neither had heard a noiseless step approaching, and they only became aware of an added human presence, when Mandy's small voice was heard to issue from Mandy's small body which stood in the mingled light and shadow of the door-way.

"Aunt B'lindy 'low supper on de table gittin' cole."

"Come here, Mandy," cried Melicent, springing after the child. But Mandy was flying back through the darkness. She was afraid of Melicent.

Laughing heartily, the girl disappeared into her bedroom, to make some needed additions to her toilet; and Hosmer, waiting for her, returned to his interrupted reflections. The words which he had spoken during a moment of emotion to Thérèse, out in the piny woods, had served a double purpose with him. They had shown him more plainly than he had quite been certain of, the depth of his feeling for her; and also had they settled his determination. He was not versed in the reading of a woman's nature, and he found himself at a loss to interpret Thérèse's actions. He recalled how she had looked away from him when he had spoken the few tender words that were yet whirling in his memory; how she had impetuously ridden ahead,—leaving him to follow alone; and her incessant speech that had forced him into silence. All of which might or might not be symptoms in his favor. He remembered her kind solicitude for his comfort and happiness during the past year; but he as readily recalled that he had not been the only recipient of such favors. His reflections led to no certainty, except that he loved her and meant to tell her so.

Thérèse's door being closed, and moreover locked, Aunt Belindy, the stout negress who had superintended the laying of supper, felt free to give low speech to her wrath as she went back and forth between dining-room and kitchen.

"Suppa gittin' dat cole 'tain' gwine be fittin' fu' de dogs te' tech. Believe half de time w'ite folks ain't got no feelin's, no how. If dey speck I'se gwine stan' up heah on my two feet all night, dey's foolin' dey sef. I ain't gwine do it. Git out dat doo' you Mandy! you want me dash dis heah coffee pot at you—blockin' up de doo's dat away? W'ar dat good fu' nuttin Betsy? Look yonda, how she done flung dem dere knife an forks on de table. Jis let Miss T'rèse kotch'er. Good God A'mighty, Miss T'rèse mus' done gone asleep. G'long dar an' see."

There was no one on the plantation who would have felt at liberty to enter Thérèse's bedroom without permission, the door being closed; yet she had taken the needless precaution of bringing lock and bolt to the double security of her moment of solitude. The first announcement of supper had found her still in her riding habit, with head thrown back upon the cushion of her lounging chair, and her mind steeped in a semi-stupor that it would be injustice to her brighter moments to call reflection.

Thérèse was a warm-hearted woman, and a woman of clear mental vision; a combination not found so often together as to make it ordinary. Being a woman of warm heart, she had loved her husband with the devotion which good husbands deserve; but being a clear-headed woman, she was not disposed to rebel against the changes which Time brings, when so disposed, to the human sensibilities. She was not steeped in that agony of remorse which many might consider becoming in a widow of five years' standing at the discovery that her heart which had fitted well the holding of a treasure, was not narrowed to the holding of a memory,—the treasure being gone.

Mandy's feeble knock at the door was answered by her mistress in person who had now banished all traces of her ride and its resultant cogitations.

The two women, with Hosmer and Grégoire, sat out on the veranda after supper as their custom was during these warm summer evenings. There was no attempt at sustained conversation; they talked by snatches to and at one another, of the day's small events; Melicent and Grégoire having by far the most to say. The girl was half reclining in the hammock which she kept in a slow, unceasing motion by the impetus of her slender foot; he sitting some distance removed on the steps. Hosmer was noticeably silent; even Joçint as a theme failing to rouse him to more than a few words of dismissal. His will and tenacity were controlling him to one bent. He had made up his mind that he had something to say to Mrs. Lafirme, and he was impatient at any enforced delay in the telling.

Grégoire slept now in the office of the mill, as a measure of precaution. To-night, Hosmer had received certain late telegrams that necessitated a return to the mill, and his iron-grey was standing outside in the lane with Grégoire's horse, awaiting the pleasure of his rider. When Grégoire quitted the group to go and throw the saddles across the patient animals, Melicent, who contemplated an additional hour's chat with Thérèse, crossed over to the cottage to procure a light wrap for her sensitive shoulders against the chill night air. Hosmer, who had started to the assistance of Grégoire, seeing that Thérèse had remained alone, standing at the top of the stairs, approached her. Remaining a few steps below her, and looking up into her face, he held out his hand to say good-night, which was an unusual proceeding, for they had not shaken hands since his return to Place-du-Bois three months before. She gave him her soft hand to hold and as the warm, moist palm met his, it acted like a charged electric battery turning its subtle force upon his sensitive nerves.

"Will you let me talk to you to-morrow?" he asked.

"Yes, perhaps; if I have time."

"Oh, you will make the time. I can't let the day go by without telling you many things that you ought to have known long ago." The battery was still doing its work. "And I can't let the night go by without telling you that I love you."

Grégoire called out that the horses were ready. Melicent was approaching in her diaphanous envelope, and Hosmer reluctantly let drop Thérèse's hand and left her.

As the men rode away, the two women stood silently following their diminishing outlines into the darkness and listening to the creaking of the saddles and the dull regular thud of the horses' feet upon the soft earth, until the sounds grew inaudible, when they turned to the inner shelter of the veranda. Melicent once more possessed herself of the hammock in which she now reclined fully, and Thérèse sat near enough beside her to intertwine her fingers between the tense cords.

"What a great difference in age there must be between you and your brother," she said, breaking the silence.

"Yes—though he is younger and I older than you perhaps think. He was fifteen and the only child when I was born. I am twenty-four, so he of course is thirty-nine."

"I certainly thought him older."

"Just imagine, Mrs. Lafirme, I was only ten when both my parents died. We had no kindred living in the West, and I positively rebelled against being separated from David; so you see he's had the care of me for a good many years."

"He appears very fond of you."

"Oh, not only that, but you've no idea how splendidly he's done for me in every way. Looked after my interest and all that, so that I'm perfectly independent. Poor Dave," she continued, heaving a profound sigh, "he's had more than his share of trouble, if ever a man had. I wonder when his day of compensation will come."

"Don't you think," ventured Thérèse, "that we make too much of our individual trials. We are all so prone to believe our own burden heavier than our neighbor's."

"Perhaps—but there can be no question about the weight of David's. I'm not a bit selfish about him though; poor fellow, I only wish he'd marry again."

Melicent's last words stung Thérèse like an insult. Her native pride rebelled against the reticence of this man who had shared her confidence while keeping her in ignorance of so important a feature of his own life. But her dignity would not permit a show of disturbance; she only asked :—

"How long has his wife been dead?"

"Oh," cried Melicent, in dismay. "I thought you knew of course; why— she isn't dead at all—they were divorced two years ago."

The girl felt intuitively that she had yielded to an indiscretion of speech. She could not know David's will in the matter, but since he had all along left Mrs. Lafirme in ignorance of his domestic trials, she concluded it was not for her to enlighten that lady further. Her next remark was to call Thérèse's attention to the unusual number of glow-worms that were flashing through the darkness, and to ask the sign of it, adding "every thing seems to be the sign of something down here."

"Aunt Belindy might tell you," replied Thérèse, "I only know that I feel the signs of being very sleepy after that ride through the woods to-day. Don't mind if I say good night?"

"Certainly not. Good night, dear Mrs. Lafirme. Let me stay here till David comes back; I should die of fright, to go to the cottage alone."

VII

Painful Disclosures

Thérèse possessed an independence of thought exceptional enough when considered in relation to her life and its surrounding conditions. But as a woman who lived in close contact with her fellow-beings she was little given to the consideration of abstract ideas, except in so far as they touched the individual man. If ever asked to give her opinion of divorce, she might have replied that the question being one which did not immediately concern her, its remoteness had removed it from the range of her inquiry. She felt vaguely that in many cases it might be a blessing; conceding that it must not infrequently be a necessity, to be appealed to however only in an extremity beyond which endurance could scarcely hold. With the prejudices of her Catholic education coloring her sentiment, she instinctively shrank when the theme confronted her as one having even a remote reference to her own clean existence. There was no question with her of dwelling upon the matter; it was simply a thing to be summarily dismissed and as far as possible effaced from her remembrance.

Thérèse had not reached the age of thirty-five without learning that life presents many insurmountable obstacles which must be accepted, whether with the callousness of philosophy, the revolt of weakness or the dignity of self-respect. The following morning, the only sign which she gave of her mental disturbance, was an appearance that might have succeeded a night of unrefreshing sleep.

Hosmer had decided that his interview with Mrs. Lafirme should not be left further to the caprice of accident. An hour or more before noon he rode up from the mill knowing it to be a time when he would likely find her alone. Not seeing her he proceeded to make inquiry of the servants; first appealing to Betsy.

"I don' know whar Miss T'rèse," with a rising inflection on the "whar."

"I yain't seed her sence mornin', time she sont Unc' Hi'um yonda to old Norico wid de light bread an' truck," replied the verbose Betsy. "Aunt B'lindy, you know whar Miss T'rèse?"

"How you want me know? standin' up everlastin' in de kitchen a bakin' light-bread fu' lazy trash det betta be in de fiel' wurkin' a crap like people, stid o' 'pendin' on yeda folks."

Mandy, who had been a silent listener, divining that she had perhaps better make known certain information that was exclusively her own, piped out:—

"Miss T'rèse shet up in de parla; 'low she want we all lef' er 'lone."

Having as it were forced an entrance into the stronghold where Thérèse had supposed herself secure from intrusion, Hosmer at once seated himself beside her.

This was a room kept for the most part closed during the summer days, when the family lived chiefly on the verandas or in the wide open hall. There lingered about it the foreign scent of cool clean matting, mingled with a faint odor of rose which came from a curious Japanese jar that stood on the ample hearth. Through the green half-closed shutters the air came in gentle ripples, sweeping the filmy curtains back and forth in irregular undulations. A few tasteful pictures hung upon the walls, alternating with family portraits, for the most part stiff and unhandsome, except in the case of such as were of so remote date that age gave them a claim upon the interest and admiration of a far removed generation.

It was not entirely clear to the darkies whether this room were not a sort of holy sanctuary, where one should scarce be permitted to breathe, except under compulsion of a driving necessity.

"Mrs. Lafirme," began Hosmer, "Melicent tells me that she made you acquainted last night with the matter which I wished to talk to you about to-day."

"Yes," Thérèse replied, closing the book which she had made a pretense of reading, and laying it down upon the window-sill near which she sat; adding very simply, "Why did you not tell me long ago, Mr. Hosmer?"

"God knows," he replied; the sharp conviction breaking upon him, that this disclosure had some how changed the aspect of life for him. "Natural reluctance to speak of a thing so painful—native reticence—I don't know what. I hope you forgive me; that you will let it make no difference in whatever regard you may have for me."

"I had better tell you at once that there must be no repetition of—of what you told me last night."

Hosmer had feared it. He made no protest in words; his revolt was inward and showed itself only in an added pallor and increased rigidity of face lines. He arose and went to a near window, peering for a while aimlessly out between the partly open slats.

"I hadn't thought of your being a Catholic," he said, finally turning towards her with folded arms.

"Because you have never seen any outward signs of it. But I can't leave you under a false impression: religion doesn't influence my reason in this."

"Do you think then that a man who has had such misfortune, should be debarred the happiness which a second marriage could give him?"

"No, nor a woman either, if it suit her moral principle, which I hold to be something peculiarly one's own."

"That seems to me to be a prejudice," he replied. "Prejudices may be set aside by an effort of the will," catching at a glimmer of hope.

"There are some prejudices which a woman can't afford to part with, Mr. Hosmer," she said a little haughtily, "even at the price of happiness. Please say no more about it, think no more of it."

He seated himself again, facing her; and looking at him all her sympathetic nature was moved at sight of his evident trouble.

"Tell me about it. I would like to know every thing in your life," she said, feelingly.

"It's very good of you," he said, holding a hand for a moment over his closed eyes. Then looking up abruptly, "It was a painful enough experience, but I never dreamed that it could have had this last blow in reserve for me."

"When did you marry?" she asked, wishing to start him with the story which she fancied he would feel better for the telling.

"Ten years ago. I am a poor hand to analyze character: my own or another's. My reasons for doing certain things have never been quite clear to me; or I have never schooled myself to inquiry into my own motives for action. I have been always thoroughly the business man. I don't make a boast of it, but I have no reason to be ashamed of the admission. Socially, I have mingled little with my fellow-beings, especially with women, whose society has had little attraction for me; perhaps, because I have never been thrown much into it, and I was nearly thirty when I first met my wife."

"Was it in St. Louis?" Thérèse asked.

"Yes. I had been inveigled into going on a river excursion," he said, plunging into the story, "Heaven knows how. Perhaps I was feeling unwell—I really can't remember. But at all events I met a friend who introduced me early in the day to a young girl—Fanny Larimore. She was a pretty little thing, not more than twenty, all pink and white and merry blue eyes and stylish clothes. Whatever it was, there was something about her that kept me at her side all day. Every word and movement of hers had an exaggerated importance for me. I fancied such things had never been said or done quite in the same way before."

"You were in love," sighed Thérèse. Why the sigh she could not have told.

"I presume so. Well, after that, I found myself thinking of her at the most inopportune moments. I went to see her again and again—my first impression deepened, and in two weeks I had asked her to marry me. I can safely say, we knew nothing of each other's character. After marriage, matters went well enough for a while." Hosmer here arose, and walked the length of the room.

"Mrs. Lafirme," he said, "can't you understand that it must be a painful thing for a man to disparage one woman to another: the woman who has been his wife to the woman he loves? Spare me the rest."

"Please have no reservations with me; I shall not misjudge you in any case," an inexplicable something was moving her to know what remained to be told.

"It wasn't long before she attempted to draw me into what she called society," Hosmer continued. "I am little versed in defining shades of distinction between classes, but I had seen from the beginning that Fanny's associates were not of the best social rank by any means. I had vaguely expected her to turn from them, I suppose, when she married. Naturally, I resisted anything so distasteful as being dragged through rounds of amusement that had no sort of attraction whatever for me. Besides, my business connections were extending, and they claimed the greater part of my time and thoughts.

"A year after our marriage our boy was born." Here Hosmer ceased speaking for a while, seemingly under pressure of a crowding of painful memories.

"The child whose picture you have at the office?" asked Thérèse.

"Yes," and he resumed with plain effort: "It seemed for a while that the baby would give its mother what distraction she sought so persistently away from home; but its influence did not last and she soon grew as restless as before. Finally there was nothing that united us except the child. I can't really say that we were united through him, but our love for the boy was the one feeling that we had in common. When he was three years old, he died. Melicent had come to live with us after leaving school. She was a high-spirited girl full of conceits as she is now, and in her exaggerated way became filled with horror of what she called the mésalliance I had made. After a month she went away to live with friends. I didn't oppose her. I saw little of my wife, being often away from home; but as feebly observant as I was, I had now and again marked a peculiarity of manner about her that vaguely troubled me. She seemed to avoid me and we grew more and more divided.

One day I returned home rather early. Melicent was with me. We found Fanny in the dining-room lying on the sofa. As we entered, she looked at us wildly and in striving to get up grasped aimlessly at the back of a chair. I felt on a sudden as if there were some awful calamity threatening my existence. I suppose, I looked helplessly at Melicent, managing to ask her what was the matter with my wife. Melicent's black eyes were flashing indignation. 'Can't you see she's been drinking. God help you,' she said. Mrs. Lafirme, you know now the reason which drove me away from home and kept me away. I never permitted my wife to want for the comforts of life during my absence; but she sued for divorce some years ago and it was granted, with alimony which I doubled. You know the miserable story now. Pardon me for dragging it to such a length. I don't see why I should have told it after all."

Thérèse had remained perfectly silent; rigid at times, listening to Hosmer often with closed eyes.

He waited for her to speak, but she said nothing for a while till finally: "Your—your wife is still quite young—do her parents live with her?"

"Oh no, she has none. I suppose she lives alone."

"And those habits; you don't know if she continues them?"

"I dare say she does. I know nothing of her, except that she receipts for the amount paid her each month."

The look of painful thought deepened on Thérèse's face but her questions having been answered, she again became silent.

Hosmer's eyes were imploring her for a look, but she would not answer them.

"Haven't you a word to say to me?" he entreated.

"No, I have nothing to say, except what would give you pain."

"I can bear anything from you," he replied, at a loss to guess her meaning.

"The kindest thing I can say, Mr. Hosmer, is, that I hope you have acted blindly. I hate to believe that the man I care for, would deliberately act the part of a cruel egotist."

"I don't understand you."

"I have learned one thing through your story, which appears very plain to me," she replied. "You married a woman of weak character. You furnished her with every means to increase that weakness, and shut her out absolutely from your life and yourself from hers. You left her then as practically without moral support as you have certainly done now, in deserting her. It was the act of a coward." Thérèse spoke the last words with intensity.

"Do you think that a man owes nothing to himself?" Hosmer asked, in resistance to her accusation.

"Yes. A man owes to his manhood, to face the consequences of his own actions."

Hosmer had remained seated. He did not even with glance follow Thérèse who had arisen and was moving restlessly about the room. He had so long seen himself as a martyr; his mind had become so habituated to the picture, that he could not of a sudden look at a different one, believing that it could be the true one. Nor was he eager to accept a view of the situation that would place him in his own eyes in a contemptible light. He tried to think that Thérèse must be wrong; but even admitting a doubt of her being right, her words carried an element of truth that he was not able to shut out from his conscience. He felt her to be a woman with moral perceptions keener than his own and his love, which in the past twenty-four hours had grown to overwhelm him, moved him now to a blind submission.

"What would you have me do, Mrs. Lafirme?"

"I would have you do what is right," she said eagerly, approaching him.

"O, don't present me any questions of right and wrong; can't you see that I'm blind?" he said, self accusingly. "What ever I do, must be because you want it; because I love you."

She was standing beside him and he took her hand.

"To do a thing out of love for you, would be the only comfort and strength left me."

"Don't say that," she entreated. "Love isn't everything in life; there is something higher."

"God in heaven, there shouldn't be!" he exclaimed, passionately pressing her hand to his forehead, his cheek, his lips.

"Oh, don't make it harder for me," Thérèse said softly, attempting to withdraw her hand.

It was her first sign of weakness, and he seized on it for his advantage. He arose quickly—unhesitatingly—and took her in his arms.

For a moment that was very brief, there was danger that the task of renunciation would not only be made harder, but impossible, for both; for it was in utter blindness to everything but love for each other, that their lips met.

The great plantation bell was clanging out the hour of noon; the hour for sweet and restful enjoyment; but to Hosmer, the sound was like the voice of a derisive demon, mocking his anguish of spirit, as he mounted his horse, and rode back to the mill.

VIII

Treats of Melicent

Melicent knew that there were exchanges of confidence going on between her brother and Mrs. Lafirme, from which she was excluded. She had noted certain lengthy conferences held in remote corners of the verandas. The two had deliberately withdrawn one moonlight evening to pace to and fro the length of gravel walk that stretched from door front to lane; and Melicent had fancied that they rather lingered when under the deep shadow of the two great live-oaks that overarched the gate. But that of course was fancy; a young girl's weakness to think the world must go as she would want it to.

She was quite sure of having heard Mrs. Lafirme say "I will help you." Could it be that David had fallen into financial straights and wanted assistance from Thérèse? No, that was improbable and furthermore, distasteful, so Melicent would not burden herself with the suspicion. It was far more agreeable to believe that affairs were shaping themselves according to her wishes regarding her brother and her friend. Yet her mystification was in no wise made clearer, when David left them to go to St. Louis.

Melicent was not ready or willing to leave with him. She had not had her "visit out" as she informed him, when he proposed it to her. To remain in the cottage during his absence was out of the question, so she removed herself and all her pretty belongings over to the house, taking possession of one of the many spare rooms. The act of removal furnished her much entertainment of a mild sort, into which, however, she successfully infused something of her own intensity by making the occasion one to bring a large detachment of the plantation force into her capricious service.

Melicent was going out, and she stood before her mirror to make sure that she looked properly. She was black from head to foot. From the great ostrich plume that nodded over her wide-brimmed hat, to the pointed toe of the patent leather boot that peeped from under her gown—a filmy gauzy thing setting loosely to her slender shapely figure. She laughed at the somberness of her reflection, which she at once set about relieving with a great bunch of geraniums—big and scarlet and long-stemmed, that she thrust slantwise through her belt.

Melicent, always charming, was very pretty when she laughed. She thought so herself and laughed a second time into the depths of her dark handsome eyes. One corner of the large mouth turned saucily upward, and the lips holding their own crimson and all that the cheeks were lacking, parted only a little over the gleaming whiteness of her teeth. As she looked at herself critically, she thought that a few more pounds of flesh would have well become her. It had been only the other day that her slimness was altogether to her liking; but at present she was in love with plumpness as typified in Mrs. Lafirme. However, on the whole, she was not ill pleased with her appearance, and gathering up her gloves and parasol, she quitted the room.

It was "broad day," one of the requirements which Grégoire had named as essential for taking Melicent to visit old McFarlane's grave. But the sun was not "shining mighty bright," the second condition, and whose absence they were willing enough to overlook, seeing that the month was September.

They had climbed quite to the top of the hill, and stood on the very brink of the deep toilsome railroad cut all fringed with matted grass and young pines, that had but lately sprung there. Up and down the track, as far as they could see on either side the steel rails glittered on into gradual dimness. There were patches of the field before them, white with bursting cotton which scores of negroes, men, women and children were dexterously picking and thrusting into great bags that hung from their shoulders and dragged beside them on the ground; no machine having yet been found to surpass the sufficiency of five human fingers for wrenching the cotton from its tenacious hold. Elsewhere, there were squads "pulling fodder" from the dry corn stalks; hot and distasteful work enough. In the nearest field, where the cotton was young and green, with no show of ripening, the overseer rode slowly between the rows, sprinkling plentifully the dry powder of paris green from two muslin bags attached to the ends of a short pole that lay before him across the saddle.

Grégoire's presence would be needed later in the day, when the cotton was hauled to gin to be weighed; when the mules were brought to stable, to see them properly fed and cared for, and the gearing all put in place. In the meanwhile he was deliciously idle with Melicent.

They retreated into the woods, soon losing sight of everything but the trees that surrounded them and the underbrush, that was scant and scattered over the turf which the height of the trees permitted to grow green and luxuriant.

There, on the far slope of the hill they found McFarlane's grave, which they knew to be such only by the battered and weather-worn cross of wood, that lurched disreputably to one side—there being no hand in all the world that cared enough to make it straight—and from which all lettering had long since been washed away. This cross was all that marked the abiding place of that mist-like form, so often seen at dark to stalk down the hill with threatening stride, or of moonlight nights to cross the lake in a pirogue, whose substance though visible was nought; with sound of dipping oars that made no ripple on the lake's smooth surface. On stormy nights, some more gifted with spiritual insight than their neighbors, and with hearing better sharpened to delicate intonations of the supernatural, had not only seen the mist figure mounted and flying across the hills, but had heard the panting of the blood-hounds, as the invisible pack swept by in hot pursuit of the slave so long ago at rest.

But it was "broad day," and here was nothing sinister to cause Melicent the least little thrill of awe. No owl, no bat, no ill-omened creature hovering near; only a mocking bird high up in the branches of a tall pine tree, gushing forth his shrill staccatoes as blithely as though he sang paeans to a translated soul in paradise.

"Poor old McFarlane," said Melicent, "I'll pay a little tribute to his memory; I dare say his spirit has listened to nothing but abuse of himself there in the other world, since it left his body here on the hill;" and she took one of the long-stemmed blood-red flowers and laid it beside the toppling cross.

"I reckon he's in a place w'ere flowers don't git much waterin', if they got any there."

"Shame to talk so cruelly; I don't believe in such places."

"You don't believe in hell?" he asked in blank surprise.

"Certainly not. I'm a Unitarian."

"Well, that's new to me," was his only comment.

"Do you believe in spirits, Grégoire? I don't—in day time."

"Neva mine 'bout spirits," he answered, taking her arm and leading her off, "let's git away f'om yere."

They soon found a smooth and gentle slope where Melicent sat herself comfortably down, her back against the broad support of a tree trunk, and Grégoire lay prone upon the ground with—his head in Melicent's lap.

When Melicent first met Grégoire, his peculiarities of speech, so unfamiliar to her, seemed to remove him at once from the possibility of her consideration. She was not then awake to certain fine psychological differences distinguishing man from man; precluding the possibility of naming and classifying him in the moral as one might in the animal kingdom. But short-comings of language, which finally seemed not to detract from a definite inheritance of good breeding, touched his personality as a physical deformation might, adding to it certainly no charm, yet from its pathological aspect not without a species of fascination, for a certain order of misregulated mind.

She bore with him, and then she liked him. Finally, whilst indulging in a little introspection; making a diagnosis of various symptoms, indicative by no means of a deep-seated malady, she decided that she was in love with Grégoire. But the admission embraced the understanding with herself, that nothing could come of it. She accepted it as a phase of that relentless fate which in pessimistic moments she was inclined to believe pursued her.

It could not be thought of, that she should marry a man whose eccentricity of speech would certainly not adapt itself to the requirements of polite society.

He had kissed her one day. Whatever there was about the kiss—possibly an over exuberance—it was not to her liking, and she forbade that he ever repeat it, under pain of losing her affection. Indeed, on the few occasions when Melicent had been engaged, kissing had been excluded as superfluous to the relationship, except in the case of the young lieutenant out at Fort Leavenworth who read Tennyson to her, as an angel might be supposed to read, and who in moments of rapturous self-forgetfulness, was permitted to kiss her under the ear: a proceeding not positively distasteful to Melicent, except in so much as it tickled her.

Grégoire's hair was soft, not so dark as her own, and possessed an inclination to curl about her slender fingers.

"Grégoire," she said, "you told me once that the Santien boys were a hard lot; what did you mean by that?"

"Oh no," he answered, laughing good-humoredly up into her eyes, "you did'n year me right. W'at I said was that we had a hard name in the country. I don' see w'y eitha, excep' we all'ays done putty much like we wanted. But my! a man can live like a saint yere at Place-du-Bois, they ain't no temptations o' no kine."

"There's little merit in your right doing, if you have no temptations to withstand," delivering the time worn aphorism with the air and tone of a pretty sage, giving utterance to an inspired truth.

Melicent felt that she did not fully know Grégoire; that he had always been more or less under restraint with her, and she was troubled by something other than curiosity to get at the truth concerning him. One day when she was arranging a vase of flowers at a table on the back porch, Aunt Belindy, who was scouring knives at the same table, had followed Grégoire with her glance, when he walked away after exchanging a few words with Melicent.

"God! but dats a diffunt man sence you come heah."

"Different?" questioned the girl eagerly, and casting a quick sideward look at Aunt Belindy.

"Lord yas honey, 'f you warn't heah dat same Mista Grégor 'd be in Centaville ev'y Sunday, a raisin' Cain. Humph—I knows 'im."

Melicent would not permit herself to ask more, but picked up her vase of flowers and walked with it into the house; her comprehension of Grégoire in no wise advanced by the newly acquired knowledge that he was liable to "raise Cain" during her absence—a proceeding which she could not too hastily condemn, considering her imperfect apprehension of what it might imply.

Meanwhile she would not allow her doubts to interfere with the kindness which she lavished on him, seeing that he loved her to desperation. Was he not at this very moment looking up into her eyes, and talking of his misery and her cruelty? turning his face downward in her lap—as she knew to cry —for had she not already seen him lie on the ground in an agony of tears, when she had told him he should never kiss her again?

And so they lingered in the woods, these two curious lovers, till the shadows grew so deep about old McFarlane's grave that they passed it by with hurried step and averted glance.

IX

Face to Face

After a day of close and intense September heat, it had rained during the night. And now the morning had followed chill and crisp, yet with possibilities of a genial sunshine breaking through the mist that had risen at dawn from the great sluggish river and spread itself through the mazes of the city.

The change was one to send invigorating thrills through the blood, and to quicken the step; to make one like the push and jostle of the multitude that thronged the streets; to make one in love with intoxicating life, and impatient with the grudging dispensation that had given to mankind no wings wherewith to fly.

But with no reacting warmth in his heart, the change had only made Hosmer shiver and draw his coat closer about his chest, as he pushed his way through the hurrying crowd.

The St. Louis Exposition was in progress with all its many allurements that had been heralded for months through the journals of the State.

Hence, the unusual press of people on the streets this bright September morning. Home people, whose air of ownership to the surroundings classified them at once, moving unobservantly about their affairs. Women and children from the near and rich country towns, in for the Exposition and their fall shopping; wearing gowns of ultra fashionable tendencies; leaving in their toilets nothing to expediency; taking no chances of so much as a ribbon or a loop set in disaccordance with the book.

There were whole families from across the bridge, hurrying towards the Exposition. Fathers and mothers, babies and grandmothers, with baskets of lunch and bundles of provisional necessities, in for the day.

Nothing would escape their observation nor elude their criticism, from the creations in color lining the walls of the art gallery, to the most intricate mechanism of inventive genius in the basement. All would pass inspection, with drawing of comparison between the present, the past year and the "year before," likely in a nasal drawl with the R's brought sharply out, leaving no doubt as to their utterance.

The newly married couple walking serenely through the crowd, young, smiling, up-country, hand-in-hand; well pleased with themselves, with their new attire and newer jewelry, would likely have answered Hosmer's "beg pardon" with amiability if he had knocked them down. But he had only thrust them rather violently to one side in his eagerness to board the cable car that was dashing by, with no seeming willingness to stay its mad flight. He still possessed the agility in his unpracticed limbs to swing himself on the grip, where he took a front seat, well buttoned up as to top-coat, and glad of the bodily rest that his half hour's ride would bring him.

The locality in which he descended presented some noticeable changes since he had last been there. Formerly, it had been rather a quiet street, with a leisurely horse car depositing its passengers two blocks away to the north from it; awaking somewhat of afternoons when hordes of children held possession. But now the cable had come to disturb its long repose, adding in the office, nothing to its attractiveness.

There was the drug store still at the corner, with the same proprietor, tilted back in his chair as of old, and as of old reading his newspaper with only the change which a newly acquired pair of spectacles gave to his appearance. The "drug store boy" had unfolded into manhood, plainly indicated by the mustache that in adding adornment and dignity to his person, had lifted him above the menial office of window washing. A task relegated to a mustacheless urchin with a leaning towards the surreptitious abstraction of caramels and chewing gum in the intervals of such manual engagements as did not require the co-operation of a strategic mind.

Where formerly had been the vacant lot "across the street," the Sunday afternoon elysium of the youthful base ball fiend from Biddle Street, now stood a row of brand new pressed-brick "flats." Marvelous must have been the architectural ingenuity which had contrived to unite so many dwellings into so small a space. Before each spread a length of closely clipped grass plot, and every miniature front door wore its fantastic window furnishing; each set of decorations having seemingly fired the next with efforts of surpassing elaboration.

The house at which Hosmer rang—a plain two-storied red brick, standing close to the street—was very old-fashioned in face of its modern opposite neighbors, and the recently metamorphosed dwelling next door, that with added porches and appendages to tax man's faculty of conjecture, was no longer recognizable for what it had been. Even the bell which he pulled was old-fashioned and its tingle might be heard throughout the house long after the servant had opened the door, if she were only reasonably alert to the summons. Its reverberations were but dying away when Hosmer asked if Mrs. Larimore were in. Mrs. Larimore was in; an admission which seemed to hold in reserve a defiant "And what if she is, sir."

Hosmer was relieved to find the little parlor into which he was ushered, with its adjoining dining-room, much changed. The carpets which he and Fanny had gone out together to buy during the early days of their housekeeping, were replaced by rugs that lay upon the bare, well polished floors. The wall paper was different; so were the hangings. The furniture had been newly re-covered. Only the small household gods were as of old: things—trifles—that had never much occupied or impressed him, and that now, amid their altered surroundings stirred no sentiment in him of either pleased or sad remembrance.

It had not been his wish to take his wife unawares, and he had previously written her of his intended coming, yet without giving her a clue for the reason of it.

There was an element of the bull-dog in Hosmer. Having made up his mind, he indulged in no regrets, in no nursing of if's and and's, but stood like a brave soldier to his post, not a post of danger, true—but one well supplied with discomfiting possibilities.

And what had Homeyer said of it? He had railed of course as usual, at the submission of a human destiny to the exacting and ignorant rule of what he termed moral conventionalities. He had startled and angered Hosmer with his denunciation of Thérèse's sophistical guidance. Rather— he proposed—let Hosmer and Thérèse marry, and if Fanny were to be redeemed—though he pooh-poohed the notion as untenable with certain views of what he called the rights to existence: the existence of wrongs— sorrows—diseases—death—let them all go to make up the conglomerate whole—and let the individual man hold on to his personality. But if she must be redeemed—granting this point to their littleness, let the redemption come by different ways than those of sacrifice: let it be an outcome from the capability of their united happiness.

Hosmer did not listen to his friend Homeyer. Love was his god now, and Thérèse was Love's prophet.

So he was sitting in this little parlor waiting for Fanny to come.

She came after an interval that had been given over to the indulgence of a little feminine nervousness. Through the open doors Hosmer could hear her coming down the back stairs; could hear that she halted mid-way. Then she passed through the dining-room, and he arose and went to meet her, holding out his hand, which she was not at once ready to accept, being flustered and unprepared for his manner in whichever way it might direct itself.

They sat opposite each other and remained for a while silent; he with astonishment at sight of the "merry blue eyes" faded and sunken into deep, dark round sockets; at the net-work of little lines all traced about the mouth and eyes, and spreading over the once rounded cheeks that were now hollow and evidently pale or sallow, beneath a layer of rouge that had been laid on with an unsparing hand. Yet was she still pretty, or pleasing, especially to a strong nature that would find an appeal in the pathetic weakness of her face. There was no guessing at what her figure might be, it was disguised under a very fashionable dress, and a worsted shawl covered her shoulders, which occasionally quivered as with an inward chill. She spoke first, twisting the end of this shawl.

"What did you come for, David? why did you come now?" with peevish resistance to the disturbance of his coming.

"I know I have come without warrant," he said, answering her implication. "I have been led to see—no matter how—that I made mistakes in the past, and what I want to do now is to right them, if you will let me."

This was very unexpected to her, and it startled her, but neither with pleasure nor pain; only with an uneasiness which showed itself in her face.

"Have you been ill?" he asked suddenly as the details of change in her appearance commenced to unfold themselves to him.

"Oh no, not since last winter, when I had pneumonia so bad. They thought I was going to die. Dr. Franklin said I would 'a died if Belle Worthington hadn't 'a took such good care of me. But I don't see what you mean coming now. It'll be the same thing over again: I don't see what's the use, David."

"We won't talk about the use, Fanny. I want to take care of you for the rest of your life—or mine—as I promised to do ten years ago; and I want you to let me do it."

"It would be the same thing over again," she reiterated, helplessly.

"It will not be the same," he answered positively. "I will not be the same, and that will make all the difference needful."

"I don't see what you want to do it for, David. Why we'd haf to get married over again and all that, wouldn't we?"

"Certainly," he answered with a faint smile. "I'm living in the South now, in Louisiana, managing a sawmill down there,"

"Oh, I don't like the South. I went down to Memphis, let's see, it was last spring, with Belle and Lou Dawson, after I'd been sick; and I don't see how a person can live down there."

"You would like the place where I'm living. It's a fine large plantation, and the lady who owns it would be the best of friends to you. She knew why I was coming, and told me to say she would help to make your life a happy one if she could."

"It's her told you to come," she replied in quick resentment. "I don't see what business it is of hers."

Fanny Larimore's strength of determination was not one to hold against Hosmer's will set to a purpose, during the hour or more that they talked, he proposing, she finally acquiescing. And when he left her, it was with a gathering peace in her heart to feel that his nearness was something that would belong to her again; but differently as he assured her. And she believed him, knowing that he would stand to his promise.

Her life was sometimes very blank in the intervals of street perambulations and matinées and reading of morbid literature. That elation which she had felt over her marriage with Hosmer ten years before, had soon died away, together with her weak love for him, when she began to dread him and defy him. But now that he said he was ready to take care of her and be good to her, she felt great comfort in her knowledge of his honesty.

X

Fanny's Friends

It was on the day following Hosmer's visit, that Mrs. Lorenzo Worthington, familiarly known to her friends as Belle Worthington, was occupied in constructing a careful and extremely elaborate street toilet before her dressing bureau which stood near the front window of one of the "flats" opposite Mrs. Larimore's. The Nottingham curtain screened her effectually from the view of passers-by without hindering her frequent observance of what transpired in the street.

The lower portion of this lady's figure was draped, or better, seemingly supported, by an abundance of stiffly starched white petticoats that rustled audibly at her slightest movement. Her neck was bare, as were the well shaped arms that for the past five minutes had been poised in mid-air, in the arrangement of a front of exquisitely soft blonde curls, which she had taken from her "top drawer" and was adjusting, with the aid of a multitude of tiny invisible hair-pins, to her own very smoothly brushed hair. Yellow hair it was, with a suspicious darkness about the roots, and a streakiness about the back, that to an observant eye would have more than hinted that art had assisted nature in coloring Mrs. Worthington's locks.

Dressed, and evidently waiting with forced patience for the termination of these overhead maneuvers of her friend, sat Lou,—Mrs. Jack Dawson,— a woman whom most people called handsome. If she were handsome, no one could have told why, for her beauty was a thing which could not be defined. She was tall and thin, with hair, eyes, and complexion of a brownish neutral tint, and bore in face and figure, a stamp of defiance which probably accounted for a certain eccentricity in eschewing hair dyes and cosmetics. Her face was full of little irregularities; a hardly perceptible cast in one eye; the nose drawn a bit to one side, and the mouth twitched decidedly to the other when she talked or laughed. It was this misproportion which gave a piquancy to her expression and which in charming people, no doubt made them believe her handsome.

Mrs. Worthington's coiffure being completed, she regaled herself with a deliberate and comprehensive glance into the street, and the outcome of her observation was the sudden exclamation.

"Well I'll be switched! come here quick Lou. If there ain't Fanny Larimore getting on the car with Dave Hosmer!"

Mrs. Dawson approached the window, but without haste; and in no wise sharing her friend's excitement, gave utterance to her calm opinion.

"They've made it up, I'll bet you what you want."

Surprise seemed for the moment to have deprived Mrs. Worthington of further ability to proceed with her toilet, for she had fallen into a chair as limply as her starched condition would permit, her face full of speculation.

"See here, Belle Worthington, if we've got to be at the 'Lympic at two o'clock, you'd better be getting a move on yourself."

"Yes, I know; but I declare, you might knock me down with a feather."

A highly overwrought figure of speech on the part of Mrs. Worthington, seeing that the feather which would have prostrated her must have met a resistance of some one hundred and seventy-five pounds of solid avoirdupois.

"After all she said about him, too!" seeking to draw her friend into some participation in her own dumbfoundedness.

"Well, you ought to know Fanny Larimore's a fool, don't you?"

"Well, but I just can't get over it; that's all there is about it." And Mrs. Worthington went about completing the adornment of her person in a state of voiceless stupefaction.

In full garb, she presented the figure of a splendid woman; trim and tight in a black silk gown of expensive quality, heavy with jets which hung and shone, and jangled from every available point of her person. Not a thread of her yellow hair was misplaced. She shone with cleanliness, and her broad expressionless face and meaningless blue eyes were set to a good-humored readiness for laughter, which would be wholesome if not musical. She exhaled a fragrance of patchouly or jockey-club, or something odorous and "strong" that clung to every article of her apparel, even to the yellow kid gloves which she would now be forced to put on during her ride in the car. Mrs. Dawson, attired with equal richness and style, showed more of individuality in her toilet.

As they quitted the house she observed to her friend:

"I wish you'd let up on that smell; it's enough to sicken a body."

"I know you don't like it, Lou," was Mrs. Worthington's apologetic and half disconcerted reply, "and I was careful as could be. Give you my word, I didn't think you could notice it."

"Notice it? Gee!" responded Mrs. Dawson.

These were two ladies of elegant leisure, the conditions of whose lives, and the amiability of whose husbands, had enabled them to develop into finished and professional time-killers.

Their intimacy with each other, as also their close acquaintance with Fanny Larimore, dated from a couple of years after that lady's marriage, when they had met as occupants of the same big up-town boarding house. The intercourse had never since been permitted to die out. Once, when the two former ladies were on a visit to Mrs. Larimore, seeing the flats in course of construction, they were at once assailed with the desire to abandon their hitherto nomadic life, and settle to the responsibilities of housekeeping; a scheme which they carried into effect as soon as the houses became habitable.

There was a Mr. Lorenzo Worthington; a gentleman employed for many years past in the custom house. Whether he had been overlooked, which his small unobtrusive, narrow-chested person made possible—or whether his many-sided usefulness had rendered him in a manner indispensable to his employers, does not appear; but he had remained at his post during the various changes of administration that had gone by since his first appointment.

During intervals of his work—intervals often occurring of afternoon hours, when he had been given night work—he was fond of sitting at the sunny kitchen window, with his long thin nose, and shortsighted eyes plunged between the pages of one of his precious books: a small hoard of which he had collected at some cost and more self-denial.

One of the grievances of his life was the necessity under which he found himself of protecting his treasure from the Philistine abuse and contempt of his wife. When they moved into the flat, Mrs. Worthington, during her husband's absence, had ranged them all, systematically enough, on the top shelf of the kitchen closet to "get them out of the way." But at this he had protested, and taken a positive stand, to which his wife had so far yielded as to permit that they be placed on the top shelf of the bedroom closet;

averring that to have them laying around was a thing that she would not do, for they spoilt the looks of any room.

He had not foreseen the possibility of their usefulness being a temptation to his wife in so handy a receptacle.

Seeking once a volume of Ruskin's Miscellanies, he discovered that it had been employed to support the dismantled leg of a dressing bureau. On another occasion, a volume of Schopenhauer, which he had been at much difficulty and expense to procure, Emerson's Essays, and two other volumes much prized, he found had served that lady as weights to hold down a piece of dry goods which she had sponged and spread to dry on an available section of roof top.

He was glad enough to transport them all back to the safer refuge of the kitchen closet, and pay the hired girl a secret stipend to guard them.

Mr. Worthington regarded women as being of peculiar and unsuitable conformation to the various conditions of life amid which they are placed; with strong moral proclivities, for the most part subservient to a weak and inadequate mentality.

It was not his office to remodel them; his rôle was simply to endure with patience the vagaries of an order of human beings, who after all, offered an interesting study to a man of speculative habit, apart from their usefulness as propagators of the species.

As regards this last qualification, Mrs. Worthington had done less than her fair share, having but one child, a daughter of twelve, whose training and education had been assumed by an aunt of her father's, a nun of some standing in the Sacred Heart Convent.

Quite a different type of man was Jack Dawson, Lou's husband. Short, round, young, blonde, good looking and bald—as what St. Louis man past thirty is not? he rejoiced in the agreeable calling of a traveling salesman.

On the occasions when he was at home; once in two weeks—sometimes seldomer—never oftener—the small flat was turned inside out and upside down. He filled it with noise and merriment. If a theater party were not on hand, it was a spin out to Forest park behind a fast team, closing with a wine supper at a road-side restaurant. Or a card party would be hastily gathered to which such neighbors as were congenial were bid in hot haste; deficiencies being supplied from his large circle of acquaintances who happened not to be on the road, and who at the eleventh hour were rung up by telephone. On such occasions Jack's voice would be heard loud in anecdote, introduced in some such wise as "When I was in Houston,

Texas, the other day," or "Tell you what it is, sir, those fellers over in Albuquerque are up to a thing or two."

One of his standing witticisms was to inquire in a stage whisper of Belle or Lou—whether the little gal over the way had taken the pledge yet.

This gentleman and his wife were on the most amiable of terms together, barring the small grievance that he sometimes lost money at poker. But as losing was exceptional with him, and as he did not make it a matter of conscience to keep her at all times posted as to the fluctuations of his luck, this grievance had small occasion to show itself.

What he thought of his wife, might best be told in his own language: that Lou was up to the mark and game every time; feminine characteristics which he apparently held in high esteem.

The two ladies in question had almost reached the terminus of their ride, when Mrs. Worthington remarked incidentally to her friend, "It was nothing in the God's world but pure sass brought those two fellers to see you last night, Lou."

Mrs. Dawson bit her lip and the cast in her eye became more accentuated, as it was apt to do when she was ruffled.

"I notice you didn't treat 'em any too cool yourself," she retorted.

"Oh, they weren't my company, or I'd a give 'em a piece of my mind pretty quick. You know they're married, and they know you're married, and they hadn't a bit o' business there."

"They're perfect gentlemen, and I don't see what business 'tis of yours, anyway."

"Oh that's a horse of another color," replied Mrs. Worthington, bridling and relapsing into injured silence for the period of ten seconds, when she resumed, "I hope they ain't going to poke themselves at the matinée."

"Likely they will 's long as they gave us the tickets."

One of the gentlemen was at the matinée: Mr. Bert Rodney, but he certainly had not "poked" himself there. He never did any thing vulgar or in bad taste. He had only "dropped in!" Exquisite in dress and manner, a swell of the upper circles, versed as was no one better in the code of gentlemanly etiquette—he was for the moment awaiting disconsolately the return of his wife and daughter from Narragansett.

He took a vacant seat behind the two ladies, and bending forward began to talk to them in his low and fascinating drawl.

Mrs. Worthington, who often failed to accomplish her fierce designs, was as gracious towards him as if she had harbored no desire to give him a piece of her mind; but she was resolute in her refusal to make one of a proposed supper party.

A quiet sideward look from Mrs. Dawson, told Mr. Rodney as plainly as words, that in the event of his *partie-carrée* failing him, he might count upon her for a *tête-à-tête*.

XI

The Self-Assumed Burden

The wedding was over. Hosmer and Fanny had been married in the small library of their Unitarian minister whom they had found intent upon the shaping of his Sunday sermon.

Out of deference, he had been briefly told the outward circumstances of the case, which he knew already; for these two had been formerly members of his congregation, and gossip had not been reluctant in telling their story. Hosmer, of course, had drifted away from his knowledge, and in late years, he had seen little of Fanny, who when moved to attend church at all usually went to the Redemptorist's Rock Church with her friend Belle Worthington. This lady was a good Catholic to the necessary extent of hearing a mass on Sundays, abstaining from meat on Fridays and Ember days, and making her "Easters." Which concessions were not without their attendant discomforts, counterbalanced, however, by the soothing assurance which they gave her of keeping on the safe side.

The minister had been much impressed with the significance of this re-marriage which he was called upon to perform, and had offered some few and well chosen expressions of salutary advice as to its future guidance. The sexton and housekeeper had been called in as witnesses. Then Hosmer had taken Fanny back home in a cab as she requested, because of her eyes that were red and swollen.

Inside the little hall-way he took her in his arms and kissed her, calling her "my child." He could not have told why, except that it expressed the responsibility he accepted of bearing all things that a father must bear from the child to whom he has given life.

"I should like to go out for an hour, Fanny; but if you would rather not, I shall stay."

"No, David, I want to be alone," she said, turning into the little parlor, with eyes big and heavy from weariness and inward clashing emotions.

Along the length of Lindell avenue from Grand avenue west to Forest park, reaches for two miles on either side of the wide and well kept gravel drive a smooth stone walk, bordered its full extent with a double row of trees which were young and still uncertain, when Hosmer walked between them.

Had it been Sunday, he would have found himself making one of a fashionable throng of promenaders; it being at that time a fad with society people to walk to Forest park and back of a Sunday afternoon. Driving was then considered a respectable diversion only on the six work days of the week.

But it was not Sunday and this inviting promenade was almost deserted. An occasional laborer would walk clumsily by; apathetic; swinging his tin bucket and bearing some implement of toil with the yellow clay yet clinging to it. Or it might be a brace of strong-minded girls walking with long and springing stride, which was then fashionable; looking not to the right nor left; indulging in no exchange of friendly and girlish chatter, but grimly intent upon the purpose of their walk.

A steady line of vehicles was pushing on towards the park at the moderate speed which the law required. On both sides the wide boulevard tasteful dwellings, many completed, but most of them in course of construction, were in constant view. Hosmer noted every thing, but absently; and yet he was not pre-occupied with thought. He felt himself to be hurrying away from something that was fast overtaking him, and his faculties for the moment were centered in the mere act of motion. It is said that motion is pleasurable to man. No doubt, in connection with a healthy body and free mind, movement brings to the normal human being a certain degree of enjoyment. But where the healthful conditions are only physical, rapid motion changes from a source of pleasure to one of mere expediency.

So long as Hosmer could walk he kept a certain pressing consciousness at bay. He would have liked to run if he had dared. Since he had entered the park there were constant trains of cars speeding somewhere overhead; he could hear them at near intervals clashing over the stone bridge. And there was not a train which passed that he did not long to be at the front of it to measure and let out its speed. What a mad flight he would have given it, to make men hold their breath with terror! How he would have driven it till its end was death and chaos!—so much the better.

There suddenly formed in Hosmer's mind a sentence—sharp and distinct. We are all conscious of such quick mental visions whether of words or pictures, coming sometimes from a hidden and untraceable source, making us quiver with awe at this mysterious power of mind manifesting itself with the vividness of visible matter.

"It was the act of a coward."

Those were the words which checked him, and forbade him to go farther: which compelled him to turn about and face the reality of his convictions.

It is no unusual sight, that of a man lying full length in the soft tender grass of some retired spot of Forest park—with his face hidden in his folded arms. To the few who may see him, if they speculate at all about him he sleeps or he rests his body after a day's fatigue. "Am I never to be the brave man?" thought Hosmer, "always the coward, flying even from my own thoughts?"

How hard to him was this unaccustomed task of dealing with moral difficulties, which all through his life before, however lightly they had come, he had shirked and avoided! He realized now, that there was to be no more of that. If he did not wish his life to end in disgraceful ship-wreck, he must take command and direction of it upon himself.

He had felt himself capable of stolid endurance since love had declared itself his guide and helper. But now—only to-day—something beside had crept into his heart. Not something to be endured, but a thing to be strangled and thrust away. It was the demon of hate; so new, so awful, so loathsome, he doubted that he could look it in the face and live.

Here was the problem of his new existence.

The woman who had formerly made his life colorless and empty he had quietly turned his back upon, carrying with him a pity that was not untender. But the woman who had unwittingly robbed him of all possi-bility of earthly happiness—he hated her. The woman who for the remainder of a life-time was to be in all the world the nearest thing to him, he hated her. He hated this woman of whom he must be careful, to whom he must be tender, and loyal and generous. And to give no sign or word but of kindness; to do no action that was not considerate, was the task which destiny had thrust upon his honor.

He did not ask himself if it were possible of accomplishment. He had flung hesitancy away, to make room for the all-powerful "Must be."

He walked slowly back to his home. There was no need to run now; nothing pursued him. Should he quicken his pace or drag himself ever so slowly, it could henceforth make no difference. The burden from which he had fled was now banded upon him and not to be loosed, unless he fling himself with it into forgetfulness.

XII

Severing Old Ties

Returning from the matinée, Belle and her friend Lou Dawson, before entering their house, crossed over to Fanny's. Mrs. Worthington tried the door and finding it fastened, rang the bell, then commenced to beat a tattoo upon the pane with her knuckles; an ingenuous manner which she had of announcing her identity. Fanny opened to them herself, and the three walked into the parlor.

"I haven't seen you for a coon's age, Fanny," commenced Belle, "where on earth have you been keeping yourself?"

"You saw me yesterday breakfast time, when you came to borrow the wrapper pattern," returned Fanny, in serious resentment to her friend's exaggeration.

"And much good the old wrapper pattern did me: a mile too small every way, no matter how much I let out the seams. But see here—"

"Belle's the biggest idiot about her size: there's no convincing her she's not a sylph."

"*Thank* you, Mrs. Dawson."

"Well, it's a fact. Didn't you think Furgeson's scales were all wrong the other day because you weighed a hundred and eighty pounds?"

"O that's the day I had that heavy rep on."

"Heavy nothing. We were coming over last night, Fanny, but we had company," continued Mrs. Dawson.

"Who d'you have?" asked Fanny mechanically and glad of the respite.

"Bert Rodney and Mr. Grant. They're so anxious to meet you. I'd 'a sent over for you, but Belle—"

"See here, Fanny, what the mischief was Dave Hosmer doing here to-day, and going down town with you and all that sort o' thing?"

Fanny flushed uneasily. "Have you seen the evening paper?" she asked.

"How d'you want us to see the paper? we just come from the matinée."

"David came yesterday," Fanny said working nervously at the window shade. "He'd wrote me a note the postman brought right after you left with the pattern. When you saw us getting on the car, we were going down to Dr. Martin's, and we've got married again."

Mrs. Dawson uttered a long, low whistle by way of comment. Mrs. Worthington gave vent to her usual "Well I'll be switched," which she was capable of making expressive of every shade of astonishment, from the lightest to the most pronounced; at the same time unfastening the bridle of her bonnet which plainly hindered her free respiration after such a shock.

"Say that Fanny isn't sly, after that, Belle."

"Sly? My God, she's a fool! If ever a woman had a snap! and to go to work and let a man get around her like that."

Mrs. Worthington seemed powerless to express herself in anything but disconnected exclamations.

"What are you going to do, Fanny?" asked Lou, who having aired all the astonishment which she cared to show, in her whistle, was collected enough to want her natural curiosity satisfied.

"David's living down South. I guess we'll go down there pretty soon. Soon's he can get things fixed up here."

"Where—down South?"

"Oh, I don't know. Somewheres in Louisiana."

"It's to be hoped in New Orleans," spoke Belle didactically, "that's the only decent place in Louisiana where a person could live."

"No, 'tain't in New Orleans. He's got a saw mill somewheres down there."

"Heavens and earth! a saw mill?" shrieked Belle. Lou was looking calmly resigned to the startling news.

"Oh, I ain't going to live in a saw mill. I wisht you'd all let me alone, any way," she returned pettishly. "There's a lady keeps a plantation, and that's where he lives."

"Well of all the rigmaroles! a lady, and a saw mill and a plantation. It's my opinion that man could make you believe black's white, Fanny Larimore."

As Hosmer approached his house, he felt mechanically in his pocket for his latch key; so small a trick having come back to him with the old habit of misery. Of course he found no key. His ring startled Fanny, who at once sprang from her seat to open the door for him; but having taken a few steps, she hesitated and irresolutely re-seated herself. It was only his second ring that the servant unamiably condescended to answer.

"So you're going to take Fanny away from us, Mr. Hosmer," said

Belle, when he had greeted them and seated himself beside Mrs. Dawson on the small sofa that stood between the door and window. Fanny sat at the adjoining window, and Mrs. Worthington in the center of the room; which was indeed so small a room that any one of them might have reached out and almost touched the hand of the others.

"Yes, Fanny has agreed to go South with me," he answered briefly. "You're looking well, Mrs. Worthington."

"Oh, Law yes, I'm never sick. As I tell Mr. Worthington, he'll never get rid of me, unless he hires somebody to murder me. But I tell you what, you came pretty near not having any Fanny to take away with you. She was the sickest woman! Did you tell him about it, Fanny? Come to think of it, I guess the climate down there'll be the very thing to bring her round."

Mrs. Dawson without offering apology interrupted her friend to inquire of Hosmer if his life in the South were not of the most interesting, and begging that he detail them something of it; with a look to indicate that she felt the deepest concern in anything that touched him.

A masculine presence had always the effect of rousing Mrs. Dawson into an animation which was like the glow of a slumbering ember, when a strong pressure of air is brought to bear upon it.

Hosmer had always considered her an amiable woman, with rather delicate perceptions; frivolous, but without the vulgarisms of Mrs. Worthington, and consequently a less objectionable friend for Fanny. He answered, looking down into her eyes, which were full of attentiveness.

"My life in the South is not one that you would think interesting. I live in the country where there are no distractions such as you ladies call amusements—and I work pretty hard. But it's the sort of life that one grows attached to and finds himself longing for again if he have occasion to change it."

"Yes, it must be very satisfying," she answered; for the moment perfectly sincere.

"Oh very!" exclaimed Mrs. Worthington, with a loud and aggressive laugh. "It would just suit you to a T, Lou, but how it's going to satisfy Fanny! Well, I've got nothing to say about it, thanks be; it don't concern me."

"If Fanny finds that she doesn't like it after a fair trial, she has the privilege of saying so, and we shall come back again," he said looking at his wife whose elevation of eyebrow, and droop of mouth gave her the expression of martyred resignation, which St. Lawrence might have worn, when invited to make himself comfortable on the gridiron—so had Mrs. Worthington's words impressed her with the force of their prophetic meaning.

Mrs. Dawson politely hoped that Hosmer would not leave before Jack came home; it would distress Jack beyond everything to return and find that he had missed an old friend whom he thought so much of.

Hosmer could not say precisely when they would leave. He was in present negotiation with a person who wanted to rent the house, furnished; and just as soon as he could arrange a few business details, and Fanny could gather such belongings as she wished to take with her they would go.

"You seem mighty struck on Dave Hosmer, all of a sudden," remarked Mrs. Worthington to her friend, as the two crossed over the street. "A feller without any more feelings than a stick; it's what I always said about him."

"Oh, I always did like Hosmer," replied Mrs. Dawson. "But I thought he had more sense than to tie himself to that little gump again, after he'd had the luck to get rid of her."

A few days later Jack came home. His return was made palpable to the entire neighborhood; for no cab ever announced itself with quite the dash and clatter and bang of door that Jack's cabs did.

The driver had staggered behind him under the weight of the huge yellow valise, and had been liberally paid for the service.

Immediately the windows were thrown wide open, and the lace curtains drawn aside until no smallest vestige of them remained visible from the street. A condition of things which Mrs. Worthington upstairs bitterly resented, and naturally, spoiling as it necessarily did, the general *coup d'œil* of the flat to passers-by. But Mrs. Dawson had won her husband's esteem by just such acts as this one of amiable permission to ventilate the house according to methods of his own and essentially masculine; regardless of dust that might be flying, or sun that might be shining with disastrous results to the parlor carpet.

Clouds of tobacco smoke were seen to issue from the open windows. Those neighbors whose openings commanded a view of the Dawson's alley-gate might have noted the hired girl starting for the grocery with unusual animation of step, and returning with her basket well stocked with beer and soda bottles—a provision made against a need for "dutch-cocktails," likely to assail Jack during his hours of domesticity.

In the evening the same hired girl, breathless from the multiplicity of errands which she had accomplished during the day, appeared at the Hosmers with a message that Mrs. Dawson wanted them to "come over."

They were preparing to leave on the morrow, but concluded that they could spare a few moments in which to bid adieu to their friends.

Jack met them at the very threshold, with warm and hearty hand-shaking, and loud protest when he learned that they had not come to spend the evening and that they were going away next day.

"Great Scott! you're not leaving to-morrow? And I ain't going to have a chance to get even with Mrs. Hosmer on that last deal? By Jove, she knows how to do it," he said, addressing Hosmer and holding Fanny familiarly by the elbow. "Drew to the middle, sir, and hang me, if she didn't fill. Takes a woman to do that sort o' thing; and me a laying for her with three aces. Hello there, girls! here's Hosmer and Fanny," in response to which summons his wife and Mrs. Worthington issued from the depths of the dining-room, where they had been engaged in preparing certain refreshments for the expected guests.

"See here, Lou, we'll have to fix it up some way to go and see them off to-morrow. If you'd manage to lay over till Thursday I could join you as far as Little Rock. But no, that's a fact," he added reflectively, "I've got to be in Cincinnati on Thursday."

They had all entered the parlor, and Mrs. Worthington suggested that Hosmer go up and make a visit to her husband, whom he would find up there "poring over those everlasting books."

"I don't know what's got into Mr. Worthington lately," she said, "he's getting that religious. If it ain't the Bible he's poring over, well it's something or other just as bad."

The brightly burning light guided Hosmer to the kitchen, where he found Lorenzo Worthington seated beside his student-lamp at the table, which was covered with a neat red cloth. On the gas-stove was spread a similar cloth and the floor was covered with a shining oil-cloth.

Mr. Worthington was startled, having already forgotten that his wife had told him of Hosmer's return to St. Louis.

"Why, Mr. Hosmer, is this you? come, come into the parlor, this is no place," shaking Hosmer's hand and motioning towards the parlor.

"No, it's very nice and cozy here, and I have only a moment to stay," said Hosmer, seating himself beside the table on which the other had laid his book, with his spectacles between the pages to mark his place. Mr. Worthington then did a little hemming and hawing preparatory to saying something fitting the occasion; not wishing to be hasty in offering the old established form of congratulation, in a case whose peculiarity afforded him no precedential guide. Hosmer came to his relief by observing quite naturally that he and his wife had come over to say goodbye, before leaving for the South, adding "no doubt Mrs. Worthington has told you."

"Yes, yes, and I'm sure we're very sorry to lose you; that is, Mrs. Larimore—I should say Mrs. Hosmer. Isabella will certainly regret her departure, I see them always together, you know."

"You cling to your old habit, I see, Mr. Worthington," said Hosmer, indicating his meaning by a motion of the hand towards the book on the table.

"Yes, to a certain extent. Always within the forced limits, you understand. At this moment I am much interested in tracing the history of various religions which are known to us; those which have died out, as well as existing religions. It is curious, indeed, to note the circumstances of their birth, their progress and inevitable death; seeming to follow the course of nations in such respect. And the similitude which stamps them all, is also a feature worthy of study. You would perhaps be surprised, sir, to discover the points of resemblance which indicate in them a common origin. To observe the slight differences, indeed technical differences, distinguishing the Islam from the Hebrew, or both from the Christian religion. The creeds are obviously ramifications from the one deep-rooted trunk which we call religion. Have you ever thought of this, Mr. Hosmer?"

"No, I admit that I've not gone into it. Homeyer would have me think that all religions are but mythological creations invented to satisfy a species of sentimentality—a morbid craving in man for the unknown and undemonstrable."

"That is where he is wrong; where I must be permitted to differ from him. As you would find, my dear sir, by following carefully the history of mankind, that the religious sentiment is implanted, a true and legitimate attribute of the human soul—with peremptory right to its existence. Whatever may be faulty in the creeds—that makes no difference, the foundation is there and not to be dislodged. Homeyer, as I understand him from your former not infrequent references, is an Iconoclast, who would tear down and leave devastation behind him; building up nothing. He would deprive a clinging humanity of the supports about which she twines herself, and leave her helpless and sprawling upon the earth."

"No, no, he believes in a natural adjustment," interrupted Hosmer.

"In an innate reserve force of accommodation. What we commonly call laws in nature, he styles accidents—in society, only arbitrary methods of expediency, which, when they outlive their usefulness to an advancing and exacting civilization, should be set aside. He is a little impatient to always wait for the inevitable natural adjustment."

"Ah, my dear Mr. Hosmer, the world is certainly to-day not prepared to stand the lopping off and wrenching away of old traditions. She must take her stand against such enemies of the conventional. Take religion away from the life of man—"

"Well, I knew it—I was just as sure as preaching," burst out Mrs. Worthington, as she threw open the door and confronted the two men—resplendent in "baby blue" and much steel ornamentation. "As I tell Mr. Worthington, he ought to turn Christian Brother or something and be done with it."

"No, no, my dear; Mr. Hosmer and I have merely been interchanging a few disjointed ideas."

"I'll be bound they were disjointed. I guess Fanny wants you, Mr. Hosmer. If you listen to Mr. Worthington he'll keep you here till daylight with his ideas."

Hosmer followed Mrs. Worthington down-stairs and into Mrs. Dawson's. As he entered the parlor he heard Fanny laughing gaily, and saw that she stood near the sideboard in the dining-room, just clicking her glass of punch to Jack Dawson's, who was making a gay speech on the occasion of her new marriage.

They did not leave when they had intended. Need the misery of that one day be told?

But on the evening of the following day, Fanny peered with pale, haggard face from the closed window of the Pullman car as it moved slowly out of Union depôt, to see Lou and Jack Dawson smiling and waving good-bye, Belle wiping her eyes and Mr. Worthington looking blankly along the line of windows, unable to see them without his spectacles, which he had left between the pages of his Schopenhauer on the kitchen table at home.

PART II

I

Fanny's First Night at Place-Du-Bois

The journey South had not been without attractions for Fanny. She had that consciousness so pleasing to the feminine mind of being well dressed; for her husband had been exceedingly liberal in furnishing her the means to satisfy her fancy in that regard. Moreover the change holding out a promise of novelty, irritated her to a feeble expectancy. The air, that came to her in puffs through the car window, was deliciously soft and mild; steeped with the rich languor of the Indian summer, that had already touched the tree tops, the sloping hill-side, and the very air, with russet and gold.

Hosmer sat beside her, curiously inattentive to his newspaper; observant of her small needs, and anticipating her timid half expressed wishes. Was there some mysterious power that had soon taught the man such methods to a woman's heart, or was he not rather on guard and schooling himself for the rôle which was to be acted out to the end? But as the day was approaching its close, Fanny became tired and languid; a certain mistrust was creeping into her heart with the nearing darkness. It had grown sultry and close, and the view from the car window was no longer cheerful, as they whirled through forests, gloomy with trailing moss, or sped over an unfamiliar country whose features were strange and held no promise of a welcome for her.

They were nearing Place-du-Bois, and Hosmer's spirits had risen almost to the point of gaiety as he began to recognize the faces of those who loitered about the stations at which they stopped. At the Centerville station, five miles before reaching their own, he had even gone out on the platform to shake hands with the rather mystified agent who had not known of his absence. And he had waved a salute to the little French priest of Centerville who stood out in the open beside his horse, booted, spurred and all equipped for bad weather, waiting for certain consignments which were to come with the train, and who answered Hosmer's greeting with a sober and uncompromising sweep of the hand. When the whistle sounded for Place-du-Bois, it was nearly dark. Hosmer hurried Fanny on to the platform, where stood Henry, his clerk. There were a great many negroes loitering about, some of whom offered him a cordial "how'dy Mr. Hosma," and pushing through was Grégoire, meeting them with the ease of a courtier, and acknowledging Hosmer's introduction of his wife, with a friendly hand shake.

"Aunt Thérèse sent the buggy down fur you," he said, "we had rain this mornin' and the road's putty heavy. Come this way. Mine out fur that ba'el, Mrs. Hosma, it's got molasses in. Hiurm bring that buggy ova yere."

"What's the news, Grégoire?" asked Hosmer, as they waited for Hiram to turn the horses about.

"Jus' about the same's ev'a. Miss Melicent wasn't ver' well a few days back; but she's some betta. I reckon you're all plum wore out," he added, taking in Fanny's listless attitude, and thinking her very pretty as far as he could discover in the dim light.

They drove directly to the cottage, and on the porch Thérèse was waiting for them. She took Fanny's two hands and pressed them warmly between her own; then led her into the house with an arm passed about her waist. She shook hands with Hosmer, and stood for a while in cheerful conversation, before leaving them.

The cottage was fully equipped for their reception, with Minervy in possession of the kitchen and the formerly reluctant Suze as housemaid: though Thérèse had been silent as to the methods which she had employed to prevail with these unwilling damsels.

Hosmer then went out to look after their baggage, and when he returned, Fanny sat with her head pillowed on the sofa, sobbing bitterly. He knelt beside her, putting his arm around her, and asked the cause of her distress.

"Oh it's so lonesome, and dreadful, I don't believe I can stand it," she answered haltingly through her tears.

And here was he thinking it was so home-like and comforting, and tasting the first joy that he had known since he had gone away.

"It's all strange and new to you, Fanny; try to bear up for a day or two. Come now, don't be a baby—take courage. It will all seem quite different by and by, when the sun shines."

A knock at the door was followed by the entrance of a young colored boy carrying an armful of wood.

"Miss T'rèse sont me kin'le fiar fu' Miss Hosma; 'low he tu'nin' cole," he said depositing his load on the hearth; and Fanny, drying her eyes, turned to watch him at his work.

He went very deliberately about it, tearing off thin slathers from the fat pine, and arranging them into a light frame-work, beneath a topping of kindling and logs that he placed on the massive brass andirons. He crawled about on hands and knees, picking up the stray bits of chips and moss that had fallen from his arms when he came in. Then sitting back on his heels he looked meditatively into the blaze which he had kindled and scratched his nose with a splinter of pine wood. When Hosmer presently left the room, he rolled his big black eyes towards Fanny, without turning his head, and remarked in a tone plainly inviting conversation "yo' all come f'om way yonda?"

He was intensely black, and if Fanny had been a woman with the slightest sense of humor, she could not but have been amused at the picture which he presented in the revealing fire-light with his elfish and ape like body much too small to fill out the tattered and ill-fitting garments that hung about it. But she only wondered at him and his rags, and at his motive for addressing her.

"We're come from St. Louis," she replied, taking him with a seriousness which in no wise daunted him.

"Yo' all brung de rain," he went on sociably, leaving off the scratching of his nose, to pass his black yellow-palmed hand slowly through the now raging fire, a feat which filled her with consternation. After prevailing upon him to desist from this salamander like exhibition, she was moved to ask if he were not very poor to be thus shabbily clad.

"No 'um," he laughed, "I got some sto' close yonda home. Dis yere coat w'at Mista Grégor gi'me," looking critically down at its length, which swept the floor as he remained on his knees. "He done all to'e tu pieces time he gi' him tu me, whar he scuffle wid Joçint yonda tu de mill. Mammy 'low she gwine mek him de same like new w'en she kin kotch de time."

The entrance of Minervy bearing a tray temptingly arranged with a dainty supper, served to silence the boy, who at seeing her, threw himself upon all fours and appeared to be busy with the fire. The woman, a big raw-boned field hand, set her burden awkwardly down on a table, and after staring comprehensively around, addressed the boy in a low rich voice, "Dar ain't no mo' call to bodda wid dat fiar, you Sampson; how come Miss T'rèse sont you lazy piece in yere tu buil' fiar?"

"Don' know how come," he replied, vanishing with an air of the utmost self-depreciation.

Hosmer and Fanny took tea together before the cheerful fire and he told her something of methods on the plantation, and made her further acquainted with the various people whom she had thus far encountered.

She listened apathetically; taking little interest in what he said, and asking few questions. She did express a little bewilderment at the servant problem. Mrs. Lafirme, during their short conversation, had deplored her inability to procure more than two servants for her; and Fanny could not understand why it should require so many to do the work which at home was accomplished by one. But she was tired—very tired, and early sought her bed, and Hosmer went in quest of his sister whom he had not yet seen.

Melicent had been told of his marriage some days previously, and had been thrown into such a state of nerves by the intelligence, as to seriously alarm those who surrounded her and whose experience with hysterical girls had been inadequate.

Poor Grégoire had betaken himself with the speed of the wind to the store to procure bromide, valerian, and whatever else should be thought available in prevailing with a malady of this distressing nature. But she was "some betta," as he told Hosmer, who found her walking in the darkness of one of the long verandas, all enveloped in filmy white wool. He was a little prepared for a cool reception from her, and ten minutes before she might have received him with a studied indifference. But her mood had veered about and touched the point which moved her to fall upon his neck, and in a manner, condole with him; seasoning her sympathy with a few tears.

"Whatever possessed you, David? I have been thinking, and thinking, and I can see no reason which should have driven you to do this thing. Of course I can't meet her; you surely don't expect it?"

He took her arm and joined her in her slow walk.

"Yes, I do expect it, Melicent, and if you have the least regard for me, I expect more. I want you to be good to her, and patient, and show yourself her friend. No one can do such things more amiably than you, when you try."

"But David, I had hoped for something so different."

"You couldn't have expected me to marry Mrs. Lafirme, a Catholic," he said, making no pretense of misunderstanding her.

"I think that woman would have given up religion—anything for you."

"Then you don't know her, little sister."

It must have been far in the night when Fanny awoke suddenly. She could not have told whether she had been awakened by the long, wailing cry of a traveler across the narrow river, vainly trying to rouse the ferryman; or the creaking of a heavy wagon that labored slowly by in the road and moved Hector to noisy enquiry. Was it not rather the pattering rain that the wind was driving against the window panes? The lamp burned dimly upon the high old-fashioned mantel-piece and her husband had thoughtfully placed an improvised screen before it, to protect her against its disturbance. He himself was not beside her, nor was he in the room. She slid from her bed and moved softly on her bare feet over to the open sitting-room door.

The fire had all burned away. Only the embers lay in a glowing heap, and while she looked, the last stick that lay across the andirons, broke through its tapering center and fell amongst them, stirring a fitful light by which she discovered her husband seated and bowed like a man who has been stricken. Uncomprehending, she stood a moment speechless, then crept back noiselessly to bed.

II

"Neva to See You!"

Thérèse judged it best to leave Fanny a good deal to herself during her first days on the plantation, without relinquishing a certain watchful supervision of her comfort, and looking in on her for a few moments each day. The rain which had come with them continued fitfully and Fanny remained in doors, clad in a warm handsome gown, her small slippered feet cushioned before the fire, and reading the latest novel of one of those prolific female writers who turn out their unwholesome intellectual sweets so tirelessly, to be devoured by the girls and women of the age.

Melicent, who always did the unexpected, crossed over early on the morning after Fanny's arrival; penetrated to her sleeping room and embraced her effusively, even as she lay in bed, calling her "poor dear Fanny" and cautioning her against getting up on such a morning.

The tears which had come to Fanny on arriving, and which had dried on her cheek when she turned to gaze into the cheer of the great wood fire, did not return. Everybody seemed to be making much of her, which was a new experience in her life; she having always felt herself as of little consequence, and in a manner, overlooked. The negroes were overawed at the splendor of her toilettes and showed a respect for her in proportion to the money value which these toilettes reflected. Each morning Grégoire left at her door his compliments with a huge bouquet of brilliant and many colored crysanthemums, and enquiry if he could serve her in any way. And Hosmer's time, that was not given to work, was passed at her side; not in brooding or pre-occupied silence, but in talk that invited her to friendly response.

With Thérèse, she was at first shy and diffident, and over watchful of herself. She did not forget that Hosmer had told her "The lady knows why I have come" and she resented that knowledge which Thérèse possessed of her past intimate married life.

Melicent's attentions did not last in their ultra-effusiveness, but she found Fanny less objectionable since removed from her St. Louis surroundings; and the evident consideration with which she had been accepted at Place-du-Bois seemed to throw about her a halo of sufficient distinction to impel the girl to view her from a new and different standpoint.

But the charm of plantation life was letting go its hold upon Melicent. Grégoire's adoration alone, and her feeble response to it were all that kept her.

"I neva felt anything like this befo'," he said, as they stood together and their hands touched in reaching for a splendid rose that hung invitingly from its tall latticed support out in mid lawn. The sun had come again and dried the last drop of lingering moisture on grass and shrubbery.

"W'en I'm away f'om you, even fur five minutes, 't seems like I mus' hurry quick, quick, to git back again; an' w'en I'm with you, everything 'pears all right, even if you don't talk to me or look at me. Th' otha day, down at the gin," he continued, "I was figurin' on some weights an' wasn't thinkin' about you at all, an' all at once I remember'd the one time I'd kissed you. Goodness! I couldn't see the figures any mo', my head swum and the pencil mos' fell out o' my han'. I neva felt anything like it: hones', Miss Melicent, I thought I was goin' to faint fur a minute."

"That's very unwise, Grégoire," she said, taking the roses that he handed her to add to the already large bunch. "You must learn to think of me calmly: our love must be something like a sacred memory—a sweet recollection to help us through life when we are apart."

"I don't know how I'm goin' to stan' it. Neva to see you! neva—my God!" he gasped, paling and crushing between his nervous fingers the flower she would have taken from him.

"There is nothing in this world that one cannot grow accustomed to, dear," spoke the pretty philosopher, picking up her skirts daintily with one hand and passing the other through his arm—the hand which held the flowers, whose peculiar perfume ever afterwards made Grégoire shiver through a moment of pain that touched very close upon rapture.

He was more occupied than he liked during those busy days of harvesting and ginning, that left him only brief and snatched intervals of Melicent's society. If he could have rested in the comfort of being sure of her, such moments of separation would have had their compensation in reflective anticipation. But with his undisciplined desires and hot-blooded eagerness, her half-hearted acknowledgments and inadequate concessions, closed her about with a chilling barrier that staggered him with its problematic nature. Feeling himself her equal in the aristocracy of blood, and her master in the knowledge and strength of loving, he resented those half understood reasons which removed him from the possibility of being anything to her. And more, he was angry with himself for acquiescing in that self understood agreement. But it was only in her absence that these thoughts disturbed him. When he was with her, his whole being rejoiced in her existence and there was no room for doubt or dread.

He felt himself regenerated through love, and as having no part in that other Grégoire whom he only thought of to dismiss with unrecognition.

The time came when he could ill conceal his passion from others. Thérèse became conscious of it, through an unguarded glance. The unhappiness of the situation was plain to her; but to what degree she could not guess. It was certainly so deplorable that it would have been worth while to have averted it. Yet, she felt great faith in the power of time and absence to heal such wounds even to the extent of leaving no tell-tale scar.

"Grégoire, my boy," she said to him, speaking in French, and laying her hand on his, when they were alone together. "I hope that your heart is not too deep in this folly."

He reddened and asked, "What do you mean, aunt?"

"I mean, that unfortunately, you are in love with Melicent. I do not know how much longer she will remain here, but taking any possibility for granted, let me advise you to leave the place for a while; go back to your home, or take a little trip to the city."

"No, I could not."

"Force yourself to it."

"And lose days, perhaps weeks, of being near her? No, no, I could not do that, aunt. There will be plenty time for that in the rest of my life," he said, trying to speak calmly and forcing his voice to a harshness which the nearness of tears made needful.

"Does she know? Have you told her?"

"Oh yes, she knows how much I love her."

"And she does not love you," said Thérèse, seeming rather to assert than to question.

"No, she does not. No matter what she says—she does not. I can feel that here," he answered, striking his breast. "Oh aunt, it is terrible to think of her going away; forever, perhaps; of never seeing her. I could not stand it." And he stood the strain no longer, but sobbed and wept with his aunt's consoling arms around him.

Thérèse, knowing that Melicent would not tarry much longer with them, thought it not needful to approach her on the subject. Had it been otherwise, she would not have hesitated to beg the girl to desist from this unprofitable amusement of tormenting a human heart.

III

A Talk Under the Cedar Tree

Day by day, Fanny threw off somewhat of the homesickness which had weighted her at coming. Not by any determined effort of the will, nor by any resolve to make the best of things. Outside influences meeting half-way the workings of unconscious inward forces, were the agents that by degrees were gently ridding her of the acute pressure of dissatisfaction, which up to the present, she had stolidly borne without any personal effort to cast it off.

Thérèse affected her forcibly. This woman so wholesome, so fair and strong; so un-American as to be not ashamed to show tenderness and sympathy with eye and lip, moved Fanny like a new and pleasing experience. When Thérèse touched her caressingly, or gently stroked her limp hand, she started guiltily, and looked furtively around to make sure that none had witnessed an exhibition of tenderness that made her flush, and the first time found her unresponsive. A second time, she awkwardly returned the hand pressure, and later, these mildly sensuous exchanges prefaced the outpouring of all Fanny's woes, great and small.

"I don't say that I always done what was right, Mrs. Laferm, but I guess David's told you just what suited him about me. You got to remember there's always two sides to a story."

She had been to the poultry yard with Thérèse, who had introduced her to its feathery tenants, making her acquainted with stately Brahmas and sleek Plymouth-Rocks and hardy little "Creole chickens"*—not much to look at, but very palatable when converted into *fricassée*.

Returning, they seated themselves on the bench that encircled a massive cedar—spreading and conical. Hector, who had trotted attendance upon them during their visit of inspection, cast himself heavily down at his mistress' feet and after glancing knowingly up into her face, looked placidly forth at Sampson, gathering garden greens on the other side of a low dividing fence.

"You see if David'd always been like he is now, I don't know but things 'd been different. Do you suppose he ever went any wheres with me, or even so much as talked to me when he came home? There was always that everlasting newspaper in his pocket, and he'd haul it out the first thing. Then I used to read the paper too sometimes, and when I'd go to talk to him about what I read, he'd never even looked at the same things. Goodness knows what he read in the paper, I never could find out; but here'd be the edges all covered over with figuring. I believe it's the only thing he ever thought or dreamt about; that eternal figuring on every bit of paper he could lay hold of, till I was tired picking them up all over the house. Belle Worthington used to say it'd of took an angel to stand him. I mean his throwing papers around that way. For as far as his never talking went, she couldn't find any fault with that; Mr. Worthington was just as bad, if he wasn't worse. But Belle's not like me; I don't believe she'd let poor Mr. Worthington talk in the house if he wanted to."

She gradually drifted away from her starting point, and like most people who have usually little to say, became very voluble, when once she passed into the humor of talking. Thérèse let her talk unchecked. It seemed to do her good to chatter about Belle and Lou, and Jack Dawson, and about her home life, of which she unknowingly made such a pitiable picture to her listener.

"I guess David never let on to you about himself," she said moodily,

* Native products are called "Creole" in Louisiana: Creole chickens, Creole eggs, Creole butter, Creole ponies, etc.

having come back to the sore that rankled: the dread that Thérèse had laid all the blame of the rupture on her shoulders.

"You're mistaken, Mrs. Hosmer. It was a knowledge of his own short-comings that prompted your husband to go back and ask your forgiveness. You must grant, there's nothing in his conduct now that you could reproach him with. And," she added, laying her hand gently on Fanny's arm, "I know you'll be strong, and do your share in this reconciliation—do what you can to please him."

Fanny flushed uneasily under Thérèse's appealing glance.

"I'm willing to do anything that David wants," she replied, "I made up my mind to that from the start. He's a mighty good husband now, Mrs. Laferm. Don't mind what I said about him. I was afraid you thought that—"

"Never mind," returned Thérèse kindly, "I know all about it. Don't worry any farther over what I may think. I believe in you and in him, and I know you'll both be brave and do what's right."

"There isn't anything so very hard for David to do," she said, depressed with a sense of her inadequate strength to do the task which she had set herself. "He's got no faults to give up. David never did have any faults. He's a true, honest man; and I was a coward to say those things about him."

Melicent and Grégoire were coming across the lawn to join the two, and Fanny, seeing them approach, suddenly chilled and wrapt herself about in her mantle of reserve.

"I guess I better go," she said, offering to rise, but Thérèse held out a detaining hand.

"You don't want to go and sit alone in the cottage; stay here with me till Mr. Hosmer comes back from the mill."

Grégoire's face was a study. Melicent, who did what she wanted with him, had chosen this afternoon, for some inscrutable reason, to make him happy. He carried her shawl and parasol; she herself bearing a veritable armful of flowers, leaves, red berried sprigs, a tangle of richest color. They had been in the woods and she had bedecked him with garlands and festoons of autumn leaves, till he looked a very Satyr; a character which his flushed, swarthy cheeks, and glittering animal eyes did not belie.

They were laughing immoderately, and their whole bearing still reflected their exuberant gaiety as they joined Thérèse and Fanny.

"What a 'Mater Dolorosa' Fanny looks!" exclaimed Melicent, throwing herself into a picturesque attitude on the bench beside Thérèse, and resting her feet on Hector's broad back.

Fanny offered no reply, but to look helplessly resigned; an expression which Melicent knew of old, and which had always the effect of irritating her. Not now, however, for the curve of the bench around the great cedar tree removed her from the possibility of contemplating Fanny's doleful visage, unless she made an effort to that end, which she was certainly not inclined to do.

"No, Grégoire," she said, flinging a rose into his face when he would have seated himself beside her, "go sit by Fanny and do something to make her laugh; only don't tickle her; David mightn't like it. And here's Mrs. Lafirme looking almost as glum. Now, if David would only join us with that 'pale cast of thought' that he bears about usually, what a merry go round we'd have."

"When Melicent looks at the world laughing, she wants it to laugh back at her," said Thérèse, reflecting something of the girl's gaiety.

"As in a looking-glass, well isn't that square?" she returned, falling into slang, in her recklessness of spirit.

Endeavoring to guard her treasure of flowers from Thérèse, who was without ceremony making a critical selection among them of what pleased her, Melicent slid around the bench, bringing herself close to Grégoire and begging his protection against the Vandalism of his aunt. She looked into his eyes for an instant as though asking him for love instead of so slight a favor and he grasped her arm, pressing it till she cried out from the pain: which act, on his side, served to drive her again around to Thérèse.

"Guess what we are going to do to-morrow: you and I and all of us; Grégoire and David and Fanny and everybody?"

"Going to Bedlam along with you?" Thérèse asked.

"Mrs. Lafirme is in need of a rebuke, which I shall proceed to administer," thrusting a crumpled handful of rose leaves down the neck of Thérèse's dress, and laughing joyously in her scuffle to accomplish the punishment.

"No, madam; I don't go to Bedlam; I drive others there. Ask Grégoire what we're going to do. Tell them, Grégoire."

"They ain't much to tell. We'a goin' hoss back ridin'."

"Not me; I can't ride," wailed Fanny.

"You can get up Torpedo for Mrs. Hosmer, can't you, Grégoire?" asked Thérèse.

"Certainly. W'y you could ride ole Torpedo, Mrs. Hosma, if you neva saw a hoss in yo' life. A li'l chile could manage him."

Fanny turned to Thérèse for further assurance and found all that she looked for.

"We'll go up on the hill and see that dear old Morico, and I shall take along a comb, and comb out that exquisite white hair of his and then I shall focus him, seated in his low chair and making one of those cute turkey fans."

"Ole Morico ain't goin' to let you try no monkeyshines on him; I tell you that befo' han'," said Grégoire, rising and coming to Melicent to rid him of his sylvan ornamentations, for it was time for him to leave them. When he turned away, Melicent rose and flung all her flowery wealth into Thérèse's lap, and following took his arm.

"Where are you going?" asked Thérèse.

"Going to help Grégoire feed the mules," she called back looking over her shoulder; the sinking sun lighting her handsome mischievous face.

Thérèse proceeded to arrange the flowers with some regard to graceful symmetry; and Fanny did not regain her talkative spirit that Melicent's coming had put to flight, but sat looking silent and listlessly into the distance.

As Thérèse glanced casually up into her face she saw it warmed by a sudden faint glow—an unusual animation, and following her gaze, she saw that Hosmer had returned and was entering the cottage.

"I guess I better be going," said Fanny rising, and this time Thérèse no longer detained her.

IV

Thérèse Crosses the River

To shirk any serious duties of life would have been entirely foreign to Thérèsc's methods or even instincts. But there did come to her moments of rebellion—or repulsion, against the small demands that presented themselves with an unfailing recurrence; and from such, she at times indulged herself with the privilege of running away. When Fanny left her alone—a pathetic little droop took possession of the corners of her mouth that might not have come there if she had not been alone. She laid the flowers, only half arranged, on the bench beside her, as a child would put aside a toy that no longer interested it. She looked towards the house and could see the servants going back and forth. She knew if she entered, she would be met by appeals from one and the other. The overseer would soon be along, with his crib keys, and stable keys; his account of the day's doings and consultations for to-morrow's work, and for the moment, she would have none of it.

"Come, Hector—come, old boy," she said rising abruptly; and crossing the lawn she soon gained the gravel path that led to the outer road. This road brought her by a mild descent to the river bank. The water, seldom stationary for any long period, was at present running low and sluggishly between its red banks.

Tied to the landing was a huge flat-boat, that was managed by the aid of a stout cable reaching quite across the river; and beside it nestled a small light skiff. In this Thérèse seated herself, and proceeded to row across the stream, Hector plunging into the water and swimming in advance of her.

The banks on the opposite shore were almost perpendicular; and their summit to be reached only by the artificial road that had been cut into them: broad and of easy ascent. This river front was a standing worry to Thérèse, for when the water was high and rapid, the banks caved constantly, carrying away great sections from the land. Almost every year, the fences in places had to be moved back, not only for security, but to allow a margin for the road that on this side followed the course of the small river.

High up and perilously near the edge, stood a small cabin. It had once been far removed from the river, which had now, however, eaten its way close up to it—leaving no space for the road-way. The house was somewhat more pretentious than others of its class, being fashioned of planed painted boards, and having a brick chimney that stood fully exposed at one end. A great rose tree climbed and spread generously over one side, and the big red roses grew by hundreds amid the dark green setting of their leaves.

At the gate of this cabin Thérèse stopped, calling out, *"Grosse tante!— oh, Grosse tante!"*

The sound of her voice brought to the door a negress—coal black and so enormously fat that she moved about with evident difficulty. She was dressed in a loosely hanging purple calico garment of the mother Hubbard type—known as a *volante* amongst Louisiana Creoles; and on her head was knotted and fantastically twisted a bright *tignon*. Her glistening good-natured countenance illumined at the sight of Thérèse.

"*Quo faire to pas woulez rentrer, Tite maîtresse?*" and Thérèse answered in the same Creole dialect: "Not now, *Grosse tante*—I shall be back in half an hour to drink a cup of coffee with you." No English words can convey the soft music of that speech, seemingly made for tenderness and endearment.

As Thérèse turned away from the gate, the black woman re-entered the house, and as briskly as her cumbersome size would permit, began preparations for her mistress' visit. Milk and butter were taken from the safe; eggs, from the India rush basket that hung against the wall; and flour, from the half barrel that stood in convenient readiness in the corner: for *Tite maîtresse* was to be treated to a dish of *croquignoles*. Coffee was always an accomplished fact at hand in the chimney corner.

Grosse tante, or more properly, Marie Louise, was a Creole—Thérèse's nurse and attendant from infancy, and the only one of the family servants who had come with her mistress from New Orleans to Place-du-Bois at that lady's marriage with Jérôme Lafirme. But her ever increasing weight had long since removed her from the possibility of usefulness, otherwise than in supervising her small farm yard. She had little use for "*ces néges Américains*," as she called the plantation hands—a restless lot forever shifting about and changing quarters.

It was seldom now that she crossed the river; only two occasions being considered of sufficient importance to induce her to such effort. One was in the event of her mistress' illness, when she would install herself at her bedside as a fixture, not to be dislodged by any less inducement than Thérèse's full recovery. The other was when a dinner of importance was to be given: then Marie Louise consented to act as *chef de cuisine*, for there was no more famous cook than she in the State; her instructor having been no less a personage than old Lucien Santien—a *gourmet* famed for his ultra Parisian tastes.

Seated at the base of a great China-berry on whose gnarled protruding roots she rested an arm languidly, Thérèse looked out over the river and gave herself up to doubts and misgivings. She first took exception with herself for that constant interference in the concerns of other people. Might not this propensity be carried too far at times? Did the good accruing counterbalance the personal discomfort into which she was often driven by her own agency? What reason had she to know that a policy of non-interference in the affairs of others might not after all be the judicious one? As much as she tried to vaguely generalize, she found her reasoning applying itself to her relation with Hosmer.

The look which she had surprised in Fanny's face had been a painful revelation to her. Yet could she have expected other, and should she have hoped for less, than that Fanny should love her husband and he in turn should come to love his wife?

Had she married Hosmer herself! Here she smiled to think of the storm of indignation that such a marriage would have roused in the parish. Yet, even facing the impossibility of such contingency, it pleased her to indulge in a short dream of what might have been.

If it were her right instead of another's to watch for his coming and rejoice at it! Hers to call him husband and lavish on him the love that awoke so strongly when she permitted herself, as she was doing now, to invoke it! She felt what capability lay within her of rousing the man to new interests in life. She pictured the dawn of an unsuspected happiness coming to him: broadening; illuminating; growing in him to answer to her own big-heartedness.

Were Fanny, and her own prejudices, worth the sacrifice which she and Hosmer had made? This was the doubt that bade fair to unsettle her; that called for a sharp, strong out-putting of the will before she could bring herself to face the situation without its accessions of personalities. Such communing with herself could not be condemned as a weakness with Thérèse, for the effect which it left upon her strong nature was one of added courage and determination.

When she reached Marie Louise's cabin again, twilight, which is so brief in the South, was giving place to the night.

Within the cabin, the lamp had already been lighted, and Marie Louise was growing restless at Thérèse's long delay.

"Ah *Grosse tante*, I'm so tired," she said, falling into a chair near the door; not relishing the warmth of the room after her quick walk, and wishing to delay as long as possible the necessity of sitting at table. At another time she might have found the dish of golden brown *croquignoles* very tempting with its accessory of fragrant coffee; but not to-day.

"Why do you run about so much, *Tite maîtresse?* You are always going this way and that way; on horseback, on foot—through the house. Make those lazy niggers work more. You spoil them. I tell you if it was old mistress that had to deal with them, they would see something different."

She had taken all the pins from Thérèse's hair which fell in a gleaming, heavy mass; and with her big soft hands she was stroking her head as gently as if those hands had been of the whitest and most delicate.

"I know that look in your eyes, it means headache. It's time for me to make you some more *eau sédative*—I am sure you haven't any more; you've given it away as you give away every thing."

"*Grosse tante*," said Thérèse seated at table and sipping her coffee; *Grosse tante* also drinking her cup—but seated apart, "I am going to insist on having your cabin moved back; it is silly to be so stubborn about such a small matter. Some day you will find yourself out in the middle of the river—and what am I going to do then?—no one to nurse me when I am sick—no one to scold me—nobody to love me."

"Don't say that, *Tite maîtresse*, all the world loves you—it isn't only Marie Louise. But no. You must remember the last time poor Monsieur Jérôme moved me, and said with a laugh that I can never forget, 'well, *Grosse tante*, I know we have got you far enough this time out of danger,' away back in Dumont's field you recollect? I said then, Marie Louise will move no more; she's too old. If the good God does not want to take care of me, then it's time for me to go."

"Ah but, *Grosse tante*, remember—God does not want all the trouble on his own shoulders," Thérèse answered humoring the woman, in her conception of the Deity. "He wants us to do our share, too."

"Well, I have done my share. Nothing is going to harm Marie Louise. I thought about all that, do not fret. So the last time Père Antoine passed in the road—going down to see that poor Pierre Pardou at the Mouth— I called him in, and he blessed the whole house inside and out, with holy water—notice how the roses have bloomed since then—and gave me medals of the holy Virgin to hang about. Look over the door, *Tite maîtresse*, how it shines, like a silver star."

"If you will not have your cabin removed, *Grosse tante*, then come live with me. Old Hatton has wanted work at Place-du-Bois, the longest time. We will have him build you a room wherever you choose, a pretty little house like those in the city."

"*Non—non, Tite maîtresse, Marie Louise 'prè créver icite avé tous son butin, si faut*" (no, no, *Tite maîtresse*, Marie Louise will die here with all her belongings if it must be).

The servants were instructed that when their mistress was not at home at a given hour, her absence should cause no delay in the household arrangements. She did not choose that her humor or her movements be hampered by a necessity of regularity which she owed to no one. When she reached home supper had long been over.

Nearing the house she heard the scraping of Nathan's violin, the noise of shuffling feet and unconstrained laughter. These festive sounds came from the back veranda. She entered the dining-room, and from its obscurity looked out on a curious scene. The veranda was lighted by a lamp suspended from one of its pillars. In a corner sat Nathan; serious, dignified, scraping out a monotonous but rhythmic minor strain to which two young negroes from the lower quarters—famous dancers—were keeping time in marvelous shuffling and pigeon-wings; twisting their supple joints into astonishing contortions and the sweat rolling from their black visages. A crowd of darkies stood at a respectful distance an appreciative and encouraging audience. And seated on the broad rail of the veranda were Melicent and Grégoire, patting Juba and singing a loud accompaniment to the breakdown.

Was this the Grégoire who had only yesterday wept such bitter tears on his aunt's bosom?

Thérèse turning away from the scene, the doubt assailed her whether it were after all worth while to strive against the sorrows of life that can be so readily put aside.

V

One Afternoon

Whatever may have been Torpedo's characteristics in days gone by, at this advanced period in his history he possessed none so striking as a stoical inaptitude for being moved. Another of his distinguishing traits was a propensity for grazing which he was prone to indulge at inopportune moments. Such points taken in conjunction with a gait closely resembling that of the camel in the desert, might give much cause to wonder at Thérèse's motive in recommending him as a suitable mount for the unfortunate Fanny, were it not for his wide-spread reputation of angelic inoffensiveness.

The ride which Melicent had arranged and in which she held out such promises of a "lark" proved after all but a desultory affair. For with Fanny making but a sorry equestrian debut and Hosmer creeping along at her side; Thérèse unable to hold Beauregard within conventional limits, and Melicent and Grégoire vanishing utterly from the scene, sociability was a feature entirely lacking to the excursion.

"David, I can't go another step: I just can't, so that settles it."

The look of unhappiness in Fanny's face and attitude, would have moved the proverbial stone.

"I think if you change horses with me, Fanny, you'll find it more comfortable, and we'll turn about and go home."

"I wouldn't get on that horse's back, David Hosmer, if I had to die right here in the woods, I wouldn't."

"Do you think you could manage to walk back that distance then? I can lead the horses," he suggested as a *pis aller*.

"I guess I'll haf to; but goodness knows if I'll ever get there alive."

They were far up on the hill, which spot they had reached by painfully slow and labored stages, each refraining from mention of a discomfort that might interfere with the supposed enjoyment of the other, till Fanny's note of protest.

Hosmer cast about him for some expedient that might lighten the unpleasantness of the situation, when a happy thought occurred to him.

"If you'll try to bear up, a few yards further, you can dismount at old Morico's cabin and I'll hurry back and get the buggy. It can be driven this far anyway: and it's only a short walk from here through the woods."

So Hosmer set her down before Morico's door: her long riding skirt, borrowed for the occasion, twisting awkwardly around her legs, and every joint in her body aching.

Partly by pantomimic signs interwoven with a few French words which he had picked up within the last year, Hosmer succeeded in making himself understood to the old man, and rode away leaving Fanny in his care.

Morico fussily preceded her into the house and placed a great clumsy home-made rocker at her disposal, into which she cast herself with every appearance of bodily distress. He then busied himself in tidying up the room out of deference to his guest; gathering up the scissors, waxen thread and turkey feathers which had fallen from his lap in his disturbance, and laying them on the table. He knocked the ashes from his corn-cob pipe which he now rested on a projection of the brick chimney that extended into the room and that served as mantel-piece. All the while he cast snatched glances at Fanny, who sat pale and tired. Her appearance seemed to move him to make an effort towards relieving it. He took a key from his pocket and unlocking a side of the *garde manger*, drew forth a small flask of whisky. Fanny had closed her eyes and was not aware of his action, till she heard him at her elbow saying in his feeble quavering voice:—

"*Tenez madame; goutez un peu: ça va vous faire du bien,*" and opening her eyes she saw that he held a glass half filled with strong "toddy" for her acceptance.

She thrust out her hand to ward it away as though it had been a reptile that menaced her with its sting.

Morico looked nonplussed and a little abashed: but he had much faith in the healing qualities of his remedy and urged it on her anew. She trembled a little, and looked away with rather excited eyes.

"*Je vous assure madame, ça ne peut pas vous faire du mal.*"

Fanny took the glass from his hand, and rising went and placed it on the table, then walked to the open door and looked eagerly out, as though hoping for the impossibility of her husband's return.

She did not seat herself again, but walked restlessly about the room, intently examining its meager details. The circuit of inspection bringing her again to the table, she picked up Morico's turkey fan, looking at it long and critically. When she laid it down, it was to seize the glass of "toddy" which she unhesitatingly put to her lips and drained at a draught. All uneasiness and fatigue seemed to leave her on the instant as though by magic. She went back to her chair and reseated herself composedly. Her eyes now rested on her old host with a certain quizzical curiosity strange to them.

He was plainly demoralized by her presence, and still made pretense of occupying himself with the arrangement of the room.

Presently she said to him: "Your remedy did me more good than I'd expected," but not understanding her, he only smiled and looked at her blankly.

She laughed good-humoredly back at him, then went to the table and poured from the flask which he had left standing there, liquor to the depth of two fingers, this time drinking it more deliberately. After that she tried to talk to Morico and thought it very amusing that he could not understand her.

Presently Joçint came home and accepted her presence there very indifferently. He went to the *garde manger* to stay his hunger, much as he had done on the occasion of Thérèse's visit; talked in grum abrupt utterances to his father, and disappeared into the adjoining room where

Fanny could hear him and occasionally see him polishing and oiling his cherished rifle.

Morico, more accustomed to foreign sounds in the woods than she, was the first to detect the approach of Grégoire, whom he went out hurriedly to meet, glad of the relief from the supposed necessity of entertaining his puzzling visitor. When he was fairly out of the room, she arose quickly, approached the table and reaching for the flask of liquor, thrust it hastily into her pocket, then went to join him. At the moment that Grégoire came up, Joçint issued from a side door and stood looking at the group.

"Well, Mrs. Hosma, yere I am. I reckon you was tired waitin'. The buggy's yonda in the road."

He shook hands cordially with Morico saying something to him in French which made the old man laugh heartily.

"Why didn't David come? I thought he said he was coming; that's the way he does," said Fanny complainingly.

"That's a po' compliment to me, Mrs. Hosma. Can't you stan' my company for that li'le distance?" returned Grégoire gallantly. "Mr. Hosma had a good deal to do w'en he got back, that's w'y he sent me. An' we betta hurry up if we expec' to git any suppa' to-night. Like as not you'll fine your kitchen cleaned out."

Fanny looked her inquiry for his meaning.

"Why, don't you know this is 'Tous-saint' eve*—w'en the dead git out o' their graves an' walk about? You wouldn't ketch a nigga out o' his cabin to-night afta dark to save his soul. They all gittin' ready now to hustle back to the quartas."

"That's nonsense," said Fanny, drawing on her gloves, "you ought to have more sense than to repeat such things."

Grégoire laughed, looking surprised at her unusual energy of speech and manner. Then he turned to Joçint, whose presence he had thus far ignored, and asked in a peremptory tone:

"W'at did Woodson say 'bout watchin' at the mill to-night? Did you ask him like I tole you?"

"Yaas, me ax um: ee' low ee an' goin'. Say how Sylveste d'wan' watch lak alluz. Say ee an' goin'. Me don' blem 'im neida, don' ketch me out de 'ouse night lak dat fu no man."

"*Sacré imbécile*," muttered Grégoire, between his teeth, and vouchsafed

* All-Saints—Halloween.

him no other answer, but nodded to Morico and turned away. Fanny followed with a freedom of movement quite unlike that of her coming.

Morico went into the house and coming back hastily to the door called to Joçint:

"Bring back that flask of whisky that you took off the table."

"You're a liar: you know I have no use for whisky. That's one of your damned tricks to make me buy you more." And he seated himself on an over-turned tub and with his small black eyes half closed, looked moodily out into the solemn darkening woods. The old man showed no resentment at the harshness and disrespect of his son's speech, being evidently used to such. He passed his hand slowly over his white long hair and turned bewildered into the house.

"Is it just this same old thing year in and year out, Grégoire? Don't any one ever get up a dance, or a card party or anything?"

"Jus' as you say; the same old thing f'om one yea's en' to the otha. I used to think it was putty lonesome myse'f w'en I firs' come yere. Then you see they's no neighbo's right roun' yere. In Natchitoches now; that's the place to have a right down good time. But see yere; I didn' know you was fon' o' dancin' an' such things."

"Why, of course, I just dearly love to dance. But it's as much as my life's worth to say that before David; he's such a stick; but I guess you know that by this time," with a laugh, as he had never heard from her before—so unconstrained; at the same time drawing nearer to him and looking merrily into his face.

"The little lady's been having a 'toddy' at Morico's, that makes her lively," thought Grégoire. But the knowledge did not abash him in the least. He accommodated himself at once to the situation with that adaptability common to the American youth, whether of the South, North, East or West.

"Where abouts did you leave David when you come away?" she asked with a studied indifference.

"Hol' on there, Buckskin—w'ere you takin' us? W'y, I lef' him at the sto' mailin' lettas."

"Had the others all got back? Mrs. Laferm? Melicent? did they all stop at the store, too?"

"Who? Aunt Thrérèse? no, she was up at the house w'en I lef'—I reckon Miss Melicent was there too. Talkin' 'bout fun,—it's to git into one o' them big spring wagons on a moonlight night, like they do in Centaville sometimes; jus' packed down with young folks—and start out fur a dance up the coast. They ain't nothin' to beat it as fah as fun goes."

"It must be just jolly. I guess you're a pretty good dancer, Grégoire?"

"Well—'taint fur me to say. But they ain't many can out dance me: not in Natchitoches pa'ish, anyway. I can say that much."

If such a thing could have been, Fanny would have startled Grégoire more than once during the drive home. Before its close she had obtained a promise from him to take her up to Natchitoches for the very next entertainment,—averring that she didn't care what David said. If he wanted to bury himself that was his own look out. And if Mrs. Laferm took people to be angels that they could live in a place like that, and give up everything and not have any kind of enjoyment out of life, why, she was mistaken and that's all there was to it. To all of which freely expressed views Grégoire emphatically assented.

Hosmer had very soon disembarrassed himself of Torpedo, knowing that the animal would unerringly find his way to the corn crib by supper time. He continued his own way now untrammelled, and at an agreeable speed which soon brought him to the spring at the road side. Here he found Thérèse, half seated against a projection of rock, in her hand a bunch of ferns which she had evidently dismounted to gather, and holding Beauregard's bridle while he munched at the cool wet tufts of grass that grew everywhere.

As Hosmer rode up at a rapid pace, he swung himself from his horse almost before the animal came to a full stop. He removed his hat, mopped his forehead, stamped about a little to relax his limbs and turned to answer the enquiry with which Thérèse met him.

"Left her at Morico's. I'll have to send the buggy back for her."

"I can't forgive myself for such a blunder," said Thérèse regretfully, "indeed I had no idea of that miserable beast's character. I never was on him you know—only the little darkies, and they never complained: they'd as well ride cows as not."

"Oh, it's mainly from her being unaccustomed to riding, I believe."

This was the first time that Hosmer and Thérèse had met alone since his return from St. Louis. They looked at each other with full consciousness of what lay in the other's mind. Thérèse felt that however adroitly another woman might have managed the situation, for herself, it would have been a piece of affectation to completely ignore it at this moment.

"Mr. Hosmer, perhaps I ought to have said something before this, to you—about what you've done."

"Oh, yes, congratulated me—complimented me," he replied with a pretense at a laugh.

"Well, the latter, perhaps. I think we all like to have our good and right actions recognized for their worth."

He flushed, looked at her with a smile, then laughed out-right—this time it was no pretense.

"So I've been a good boy; have done as my mistress bade me and now I'm to receive a condescending little pat on the head—and of course must say thank you. Do you know, Mrs. Lafirme—and I don't see why a woman like you oughtn't to know it—it's one of those things to drive a man mad, the sweet complaisance with which women accept situations, or inflict situations that it takes the utmost of a man's strength to endure."

"Well, Mr. Hosmer," said Thérèse plainly discomposed, "you must concede you decided it was the right thing to do."

"I didn't do it because I thought it was right, but because you thought it was right. But that makes no difference."

"Then remember your wife is going to do the right thing herself—she admitted as much to me."

"Don't you fool yourself, as Melicent says, about what Mrs. Hosmer means to do. I take no account of it. But you take it so easily; so as a matter of course. That's what exasperates me. That you, you, you, shouldn't have a suspicion of the torture of it; the loathsomeness of it. But how could you—how could any woman understand it? Oh forgive me, Thérèse—I wouldn't want you to. There's no brute so brutal as a man," he cried, seeing the pain in her face and knowing he had caused it. "But you know you promised to help me—oh I'm talking like an idiot."

"And I do," returned Thérèse, "that is, I want to, I mean to."

"Then don't tell me again that I have done right. Only look at me sometimes a little differently than you do at Hiram or the gate post. Let me once in a while see a look in your face that tells me that you understand—if it's only a little bit."

Thérèse thought it best to interrupt the situation; so, pale and silently she prepared to mount her horse. He came to her assistance of course, and when she was seated she drew off her loose riding glove and held out her hand to him. He pressed it gratefully, then touched it with his lips; then turned it and kissed the half open palm.

She did not leave him this time, but rode at his side in silence with a frown and little line of thought between her blue eyes.

As they were nearing the store she said diffidently: "Mr. Hosmer, I wonder if it wouldn't be best for you to put the mill in some one else's charge—and go away from Place-du-Bois."

"I believe you always speak with a purpose, Mrs. Lafirme: you have somebody's ultimate good in view, when you say that. Is it your own, or mine or whose is it?"

"Oh! not mine."

"I will leave Place-du-Bois, certainly, if you wish it."

As she looked at him she was forced to admit that she had never seen him look as he did now. His face, usually serious, had a whole unwritten tragedy in it. And she felt altogether sore and puzzled and exasperated over man's problematic nature.

"I don't think it should be left entirely to me to say. Doesn't your own reason suggest a proper course in the matter?"

"My reason is utterly unable to determine anything in which you are concerned. Mrs. Lafirme," he said checking his horse and laying a re-straining hand on her bridle, "let me speak to you one moment. I know you are a woman to whom one may speak the truth. Of course, you remember that you prevailed upon me to go back to my wife. To you it seemed the right thing—to me it seemed certainly hard—but no more nor less than taking up the old unhappy routine of life, where I had left it when I quitted her. I reasoned much like a stupid child who thinks the colors in his kaleidoscope may fall twice into the same design. In place of the old, I found an entirely new situation—horrid, sickening, requiring such a strain upon my energies to live through it, that I believe it's an absurdity to waste so much moral force for so poor an aim—there would be more dignity in putting an end to my life. It doesn't make it any the more bearable to feel that the cause of this unlooked for change lies within myself—my altered feelings. But it seems to me that I have the right to ask you not to take yourself out of my life; your moral support; your bodily atmosphere. I hope not to give way to the weakness of speaking of these things again: but before you leave me, tell me, do you understand a little better why I need you?"

"Yes, I understand now; and I thank you for talking so openly to me. Don't go away from Place-du-Bois: it would make me very wretch-ed."

She said no more and he was glad of it, for her last words held almost the force of action for him; as though she had let him feel for an instant her heart beat against his own with an echoing pain.

Their ways now diverged. She went in the direction of the house and he to the store where he found Grégoire, whom he sent for his wife.

VI

One Night

"Grégoire was right: do you know those nasty creatures have gone and left every speck of the supper dishes unwashed? I've got half a mind to give them both warning to-morrow morning."

Fanny had come in from the kitchen to the sitting-room, and the above homily was addressed to her husband who stood lighting his cigar. He had lately taken to smoking.

"You'd better do nothing of the kind; you wouldn't find it easy to replace them. Put up a little with their vagaries: this sort of thing only happens once a year."

"How do you know it won't be something else just as ridiculous to-morrow? And that idiot of a Minervy; what do you suppose she told me when I insisted on her staying to wash up things? She says, last whatever you call it, her husband wanted to act hard-headed and staid out after dark, and when he was crossing the bayou, the spirits jerked him off his horse and dragged him up and down in the water, till he was nearly drowned. I don't see what you're laughing at; I guess you'd like to make out that they're in the right."

Hosmer was perfectly aware that Fanny had had a drink, and he rightly guessed that Morico had given it to her. But he was at a loss to account for the increasing symptoms of intoxication that she showed. He tried to persuade her to go to bed; but his efforts to that end remained unheeded, till she had eased her mind of an accumulation of grievances, mostly fancied. He had much difficulty in preventing her from going over to give Melicent a piece of her mind about her lofty airs and arrogance in thinking herself better than other people. And she was very eager to tell Thérèse that she meant to do as she liked; and would stand no poking of noses in her business. It was a good while before she fell into a heavy sleep, after shedding a few maudlin tears over the conviction that he intended to leave her again, and clinging to his neck with beseeching enquiry whether he loved her.

He went out on the veranda feeling much as if he had been wrestling with a strong adversary who had mastered him, and whom he was glad to be freed of, even at the cost of coming inglorious from the conflict. The night was so dark, so hushed, that if ever the dead had wished to step from their graves and take a stroll above ground, they could not have found a more fitting hour. Hosmer walked very long in the soothing quiet. He would have liked to walk the night through. The last three hours had been like an acute physical pain, that was over for the moment, and that being over, left his mind free to return to the delicious consciousness, that he had needed to be reminded of, that Thérèse loved him after all. When his measured tread upon the veranda finally ceased to mark the passing hours, a quiet that was almost pulseless fell upon the plantation. Place-du-Bois slept. Perhaps the only night in the year that some or other of the negroes did not lurk in fence corners, or make exchange of nocturnal visits.

But out in the hills there was no such unearthly stillness reigning. Those restless wood-dwellers, that never sleep, were sending startling gruesome calls to each other. Bats were flapping and whirling and darting hither and thither; the gliding serpent making quick rustle amid the dry, crisp leaves, and over all sounded the murmur of the great pine trees, telling their mystic secrets to the night.

A human creature was there too, feeling a close fellowship with these spirits of night and darkness; with no more fear in his heart than the unheeded serpent crossing his path. Every inch of the ground he knew. He wanted no daylight to guide him. Had his eyes been blinded he would no doubt have bent his body close to earth and scented his way along like the human hound that he was. Over his shoulder hung the polished rifle that sent dull and sudden gleamings into the dark. A large tin pail swung from his hand. He was very careful of this pail—or its contents, for he feared to lose a drop. And when he accidentally struck an intervening tree and spilled some upon the ground, he muttered a curse against his own awkwardness.

Twice since leaving his cabin up in the clearing, he had turned to drive back his yellow skulking dog that followed him. Each time the brute had fled in abject terror, only to come creeping again into his master's footsteps, when he thought himself forgotten. Here was a companion whom neither Joçint nor his mission required. Exasperated, he seated himself on a fallen tree and whistled softly. The dog, who had been holding back, dashed to his side, trembling with eagerness, and striving to twist his head around to lick the hand that patted him. Joçint's other hand glided quickly into his pocket, from which he drew forth a coil of thin rope that he flung deftly over the animal's head, drawing it close and tight about the homely, shaggy throat. So quickly was the action done, that no sound was uttered, and Joçint continued his way untroubled by his old and faithful friend, whom he left hanging to the limb of a tree.

He was following the same path that he traversed daily to and from the mill, and which soon brought him out into the level with its soft tufted grass and clumps of squat thorn trees. There was no longer the protecting wood to screen him; but of such there was no need, for the darkness hung about him like the magic mantle of story. Nearing the mill he grew cautious, creeping along with the tread of a stealthy beast, and halting at intervals to listen for sounds that he wished not to hear. He knew there was no one on guard tonight. A movement in the bushes near by, made him fall quick and sprawling to earth. It was only Grégoire's horse munching the soft grass. Joçint drew near and laid his hand on the horse's back. It was hot and reeking with sweat. Here was a fact to make him more wary. Horses were not found in such condition from quietly grazing of a cool autumn night. He seated himself upon the ground, with his hands clasped about his knees, all doubled up in a little heap, and waited there with the patience of the savage, letting an hour go by, whilst he made no movement.

The hour past, he stole towards the mill, and began his work of sprinkling the contents of his pail here and there along the dry timbers at well calculated distances, with care that no drop should be lost. Then, he drew together a great heap of crisp shavings and slathers, plentifully besprinkling it with what remained in the can. When he had struck a match against his rough trousers and placed it carefully in the midst of this small pyramid, he found that he had done his work but too surely. The quick flame sprang into life, seizing at once all it could reach. Leaping over intervals; effacing the darkness that had shrouded him; seeming to mock him as a fool and point him out as a target for heaven and earth to hurl destruction at if they would. Where should he hide himself? He only thought now of how he might have done the deed differently, and with safety to himself. He stood with great beams and loose planks surrounding him; quaking with a premonition of evil. He wanted to fly in one direction; then thought it best to follow the opposite; but a force outside of himself seemed to hold him fast to one spot. When turning suddenly about, he knew it was too late, he felt that all was lost, for there was Grégoire, not twenty paces away—covering him with the muzzle of a pistol and—cursed luck—his own rifle along with the empty pail in the raging fire.

Thérèse was passing a restless night. She had lain long awake, dwelling on the insistent thoughts that the day's happenings had given rise to. The sleep which finally came to her was troubled by dreams—demoniac—grotesque. Hosmer was in a danger from which she was striving with physical effort to rescue him, and when she dragged him painfully from the peril that menaced him, she turned to see that it was Fanny whom she had saved—laughing at her derisively, and Hosmer had been left to perish. The dream was agonizing; like an appalling nightmare. She awoke in a fever of distress, and raised herself in bed to shake off the unnatural impression which such a dream can leave. The curtains were drawn aside from the window that faced her bed, and looking out she saw a long tongue of flame, reaching far up into the sky—away over the tree tops and the whole Southern horizon a glow. She knew at once that the mill was burning, and it was the affair of a moment with her to spring from her bed and don slippers and wrapper. She knocked on Melicent's door to acquaint her with the startling news; then hurried out into the back yard and rang the plantation bell.

Next she was at the cottage rousing Hosmer. But the alarm of the bell had already awakened him, and he was dressed and out on the porch almost as soon as Thérèse had called. Melicent joined them, highly agitated, and prepared to contribute her share towards any scene that might be going forward. But she found little encouragement for heroics with Hosmer. In saddling his horse rather hastily he was as unmoved as though preparing for an uneventful morning canter. He stood at the foot of the stairs preparing to mount when Grégoire rode up as if pursued by furies; checking his horse with a quick, violent wrench that set it quivering in its taut limbs.

"Well," said Hosmer, "I guess it's done for. How did it happen? who did it?"

"Joçint's work," answered Grégoire bitingly.

"The damned scoundrel," muttered Hosmer, "where is he?"

"Don' botha 'bout Joçint; he ain't goin' to set no mo' mill afire," saying which, he turned his horse and the two rode furiously away.

Melicent grasped Thérèse's arm convulsively.

"What does he mean?" she asked in a frightened whisper.

"I—I don't know," Thérèse faltered. She had clasped her hands spasmodically together, at Grégoire's words, trembling with horror of what must be their meaning.

"May be he arrested him," suggested the girl.

"I hope so. Come; let's go to bed: there's no use staying out here in the cold and dark."

Hosmer had left the sitting-room door open, and Thérèse entered. She approached Fanny's door and knocked twice: not brusquely, but sufficiently loud to be heard from within, by any one who was awake. No answer came, and she went away, knowing that Fanny slept.

The unusual sound of the bell, ringing two hours past midnight—that very deadest hour of the night—had roused the whole plantation. On all sides squads of men and a few venturesome women were hurrying towards the fire; the dread of supernatural encounters overcome for the moment by such strong reality and by the confidence lent them in each other's company.

There were many already gathered around the mill, when Grégoire and Hosmer reached it. All effort to save anything had been abandoned as useless. The books and valuables had been removed from the office. The few householders—mill-hands—whose homes were close by, had carried their scant belongings to places of safety, but everything else was given over to the devouring flames.

The heat from this big raging fire was intense, and had driven most of the gaping spectators gradually back—almost into the woods. But there, to one side, where the fire was rapidly gaining, and making itself already uncomfortably felt, stood a small awe-stricken group talking in whispers; their ignorance and superstition making them irresolute to lay a hand upon the dead Joçint. His body lay amongst the heavy timbers, across a huge beam, with arms outstretched and head hanging down upon the ground. The glazed eyes were staring up into the red sky, and on his swarthy visage was yet the horror which had come there, when he looked in the face of death.

"In God's name, what are you doing?" cried Hosmer. "Can't some of you carry that boy's body to a place of safety?"

Grégoire had followed, and was looking down indifferently at the dead. "Come, len' a han' there; this is gittin' too durn hot," he said, stooping to raise the lifeless form. Hosmer was preparing to help him. But there was some one staggering through the crowd; pushing men to right and left. With now a hand upon the breast of both Hosmer and Grégoire, and thrusting them with such force and violence, as to lay them prone amongst the timbers. It was the father. It was old Morico. He had awakened in the night and missed his boy. He had seen the fire; indeed close enough that he could hear its roaring; and he knew everything. The whole story was plain to him as if it had been told by a revealing angel. The strength of his youth had come back to speed him over the ground.

"Murderers!" he cried looking about him with hate in his face. He did not know who had done it; no one knew yet, and he saw in every man he looked upon the possible slayer of his child.

So here he stood over the prostrate figure; his old gray jeans hanging loosely about him; wild eyed—with bare head clasped between his claw-like hands, which the white disheveled hair swept over. Hosmer approached again, offering gently to help him carry his son away.

"Stand back," he hurled at him. But he had understood the offer. His boy must not be left to burn like a log of wood. He bent down and strove to lift the heavy body, but the effort was beyond his strength. Seeing this he stooped again and this time grasped it beneath the arms; then slowly, draggingly, with halting step, began to move backward.

The fire claimed no more attention. All eyes were fastened upon this weird picture; a sight which moved the most callous to offer again and again assistance, that was each time spurned with an added defiance.

Hosmer stood looking on, with folded arms; moved by the grandeur and majesty of the scene. The devouring element, loosed in its awful recklessness there in the heart of this lonely forest. The motley group of black and white standing out in the great red light, powerless to do more than wait and watch. But more was he stirred to the depths of his being, by the sight of this human tragedy enacted before his eyes.

Once, the old man stops in his backward journey. Will he give over? has his strength deserted him? is the thought that seizes every on-looker. But no—with renewed effort he begins again his slow retreat, till at last a sigh of relief comes from the whole watching multitude. Morico with his burden has reached a spot of safety. What will he do next? They watch in breathless suspense. But Morico does nothing. He only stands immovable as a carved image. Suddenly there is a cry that reaches far above the roar of fire and crash of falling timbers: "*Mon fils! mon garçon!*" and the old man totters and falls backward to earth, still clinging to the lifeless body of his son. All hasten towards him. Hosmer reaches him first. And when he gently lifts the dead Joçint, the father this time makes no hinderance, for he too has gone beyond the knowledge of all earthly happenings.

VII

Melicent Leaves Place-Du-Bois

There had been no witness to the killing of Joçint; but there were few who did not recognize Grégoire's hand in the affair. When met with the accusation, he denied it, or acknowledged it, or evaded the charge with a jest, as he felt for the moment inclined. It was a deed characteristic of any one of the Santien boys, and if not altogether laudable—Joçint having been at the time of the shooting unarmed—yet was it thought in a measure justified by the heinousness of his offense, and beyond dispute, a benefit to the community.

Hosmer reserved the expression of his opinion. The occurrence once over, with the emotions which it had awakened, he was inclined to look at it from one of those philosophic stand-points of his friend Homeyer. Heredity and pathology had to be considered in relation with the slayer's character. He saw in it one of those interesting problems of human existence that are ever turning up for man's contemplation, but hardly for the exercise of man's individual judgment. He was conscious of an inward repulsion which this action of Grégoire's awakened in him,— much the same as a feeling of disgust for an animal whose instinct drives it to the doing of violent deeds,—yet he made no difference in his manner towards him.

Thérèse was deeply distressed over this double tragedy: feeling keenly the unhappy ending of old Morico. But her chief sorrow came from the callousness of Grégoire, whom she could not move even to an avowal of regret. He could not understand that he should receive any thing but praise for having rid the community of so offensive and dangerous a personage as Joçint; and seemed utterly blind to the moral aspect of his deed.

An event at once so exciting and dramatic as this conflagration, with the attendant deaths of Morico and his son, was much discussed amongst the negroes. They were a good deal of one opinion in regard to Joçint having been only properly served in getting "w'at he done ben lookin' fu' dis long time." Grégoire was rather looked upon as a clever instrument in the Lord's service; and the occurrence pointed a moral which they were not likely to forget.

The burning of the mill entailed much work upon Hosmer, to which he turned with a zest—an absorption that for the time excluded everything else.

Melicent had shunned Grégoire since the shooting. She had a-voided speaking with him—even looking at him. During the turmoil which closely followed upon the tragic event, this change in the girl had escaped his notice. On the next day he suspected it only. But the third day brought him the terrible conviction. He did not know that she was making preparations to leave for St. Louis, and quite accidentally overheard Hosmer giving an order to one of the unemployed mill hands to call for her baggage on the following morning before train time.

As much as he had expected her departure, and looked painfully forward to it, this certainty—that she was leaving on the morrow and without a word to him—bewildered him. He abandoned at once the work that was occupying him.

"I didn' know Miss Melicent was goin' away tomorrow," he said in a strange pleading voice to Hosmer.

"Why, yes," Hosmer answered, "I thought you knew. She's been talking about it for a couple of days."

"No, I didn' know nothin' 'tall 'bout it," he said, turning away and reaching for his hat, but with such nerveless hand that he almost dropped it before placing it on his head.

"If you're going to the house," Hosmer called after him, "tell Melicent that Woodson won't go for her trunks before morning. She thought she'd need to have them ready to-night."

"Yes, if I go to the house. I don' know if I'm goin' to the house or not," he replied, walking listlessly away.

Hosmer looked after the young man, and thought of him for a moment: of his soft voice and gentle manner—perplexed that he should be the same who had expressed in confidence the single regret that he had not been able to kill Joçint more than once.

Grégoire went directly to the house, and approached that end of the veranda on which Melicent's room opened. A trunk had already been packed and fastened and stood outside, just beneath the low-silled window that was open. Within the room, and also beneath the window, was another trunk, before which Melicent kneeled, filling it more or less systematically from an abundance of woman's toggery that lay in a cumbrous heap on the floor beside her. Grégoire stopped at the window to tell her, with a sad attempt at indifference:

"Yo' brotha says don't hurry packin'; Woodson ain't goin' to come fur your trunks tell mornin'."

"All right, thank you," glancing towards him for an instant carelessly and going on with her work.

"I didn' know you was goin' away."

"That's absurd: you knew all along I was going away," she returned, with countenance as expressionless as feminine subtlety could make it.

"W'y don't you let somebody else do that? Can't you come out yere a w'ile?"

"No, I prefer doing it myself; and I don't care to go out."

What could he do? what could he say? There were no convenient depths in his mind from which he might draw at will, apt and telling speeches to taunt her with. His heart was swelling and choking him, at sight of the eyes that looked anywhere, but in his own; at sight of the lips that he had one time kissed, pressed into an icy silence. She went on with her task of packing, unmoved. He stood a while longer, silently watching her, his hat in his hands that were clasped behind him, and a stupor of grief holding him vise-like. Then he walked away. He felt somewhat as he remembered to have felt oftentimes as a boy, when ill and suffering, his mother would put him to bed and send him a cup of bouillon perhaps, and a little negro to sit beside him. It seemed very cruel to him now that some one should not do something for him—that he should be left to suffer this way. He walked across the lawn over to the cottage, where he saw Fanny pacing slowly up and down the porch.

She saw him approach and stood in a patch of sunlight to wait for him. He really had nothing to say to her as he stood grasping two of the balustrades and looking up at her. He wanted somebody to talk to him about Melicent.

"Did you know Miss Melicent was goin' away?"

Had it been Hosmer or Thérèse asking her the question she would have replied simply "yes," but to Grégoire she said "yes; thank Goodness," as frankly as though she had been speaking to Belle Worthington. "I don't see what's kept her down here all this time, anyway."

"You don't like her?" he asked, stupefied at the strange possibility of any one not loving Melicent to distraction.

"No. You wouldn't either, if you knew her as well as I do. If she likes a person she goes on like a lunatic over them as long as it lasts; then good-bye John! she'll throw them aside as she would an old dress."

"Oh, I believe she thinks a heap of Aunt Thérèse."

"All right; you'll see how much she thinks of Aunt Thérèse. And the people she's been engaged to! There ain't a worse flirt in the city of

St. Louis; and always some excuse or other to break it off at the last minute. I haven't got any use for her, Lord knows. There ain't much love lost between us."

"Well, I reckon she knows they ain't anybody born, good enough fur her?" he said, thinking of those engagements that she had shattered.

"What was David doing?" Fanny asked abruptly.

"Writin' lettas at the sto'."

"Did he say when he was coming?"

"No."

"Do you guess he'll come pretty soon?"

"No, I reckon not fur a good w'ile."

"Is Melicent with Mrs. Laferm?"

"No; she's packin' her things."

"I guess I'll go sit with Mrs. Laferm, d'you think she'll mind?"

"No, she'll be glad to have you."

Fanny crossed over to go join Thérèse. She liked to be with her when there was no danger of interruption from Melicent, and Grégoire went wandering aimlessly about the plantation.

He staked great hopes on what the night might bring for him. She would melt, perhaps, to the extent of a smile or one of her old glances. He was almost cheerful when he seated himself at table; only he and his aunt and Melicent. He had never seen her look so handsome as now, in a woolen gown that she had not worn before, of warm rich tint, that brought out a certain regal splendor that he had not suspected in her. A something that she seemed to have held in reserve till this final moment. But she had nothing for him—nothing. All her conversation was addressed to Thérèse; and she hurried away from table at the close of the meal, under pretext of completing her arrangements for departure.

"Doesn't she mean to speak to me?" he asked fiercely of Thérèse.

"Oh, Grégoire, I see so much trouble around me; so many sad mistakes, and I feel so powerless to right them; as if my hands were tied. I can't help you in this; not now. But let me help you in other ways. Will you listen to me?"

"If you want to help me, Aunt," he said stabbing his fork into a piece of bread before him, "go and ask her if she doesn't mean to talk to me: if she won't come out on the gallery a minute."

"Grégoire wants to know if you won't go out and speak to him a moment, Melicent," said Thérèse entering the girl's room. "Do as you wish, of course. But remember you are going away to-morrow; you'll likely never see him again. A friendly word from you now, may do more good than you imagine. I believe he's as unhappy at this moment as a creature can be!"

Melicent looked at her horrified. "I don't understand you at all, Mrs. Lafirme. Think what he's done; murdered a defenseless man! How can you have him near you—seated at your table? I don't know what nerves you have in your bodies, you and David. There's David, hobnobbing with him. Even that Fanny talking to him as if he were blameless. Never! If he were dying I wouldn't go near him."

"Haven't you a spark of humanity in you?" asked Thérèse, flushing violently.

"Oh, this is something physical," she replied, shivering, "let me alone."

Thérèse went out to Grégoire, who stood waiting on the veranda. She only took his hand and pressed it telling him good-night, and he knew that it was a dismissal.

There may be lovers, who, under the circumstances, would have felt sufficient pride to refrain from going to the depot on the following morning, but Grégoire was not one of them. He was there. He who only a week before had thought that nothing but her constant presence could reconcile him with life, had narrowed down the conditions for his life's happiness now to a glance or a kind word. He stood close to the steps of the Pullman car that she was about to enter, and as she passed him he held out his hand, saying "Good-bye." But he held his hand to no purpose. She was much occupied in taking her valise from the conductor who had hoisted her up, and who was now shouting in stentorian tones "All aboard," though there was not a soul with the slightest intention of boarding the train but herself.

She leaned forward to wave good-bye to Hosmer, and Fanny, and Thérèse, who were on the platform; then she was gone.

Grégoire stood looking stupidly at the vanishing train.

"Are you going back with us?" Hosmer asked him. Fanny and Thérèse had walked ahead.

"No," he replied, looking at Hosmer with ashen face, "I got to go fine my hoss."

VIII

With Loose Rein

"De Lord be praised fu' de blessin's dat he showers down 'pon us," was Uncle Hiram's graceful conclusion of his supper, after which he pushed his empty plate aside regretfully, and addressed Aunt Belindy. " 'Pears to me, Belindy, as you reached a pint wid dem bacon an' greens to-night, dat you never tetched befo'. De pint o' de flavorin' is w'at I alludes to."

"All de same, dat ain't gwine to fetch no mo'," was the rather uncivil reply to this neat compliment to her culinary powers.

"Dah!" cried the youthful Betsy, who formed one of the trio gathered together in the kitchen at Place-du-Bois. "Jis listen (to) Unc' Hiurm! Aunt B'lindy neva tetched a han' to dem bacon an' greens. She tole me out o' her own mouf to put'em on de fiar; she warn't gwine pesta wid 'em."

"Warn't gwine pesta wid 'em?" administering a cuff on the ear of the too communicative Betsy, that sent her sprawling across the table. "T'inks I'se gwine pesta wid you—does you? Messin' roun' heah in de kitchin' an' ain't tu'ned down a bed or drawed a bah, or done a lick o' yo' night wurk yit."

"I is done my night wurk, too," returned Betsy whimpering but defiantly, as she retreated beyond reach of further blows from Aunt Belindy's powerful right hand.

"Dat harshness o' yourn, Belindy, is wat's a sourin' yo' tempa, an' a turnin' of it intur gall an' wormwood. Does you know wat de Scripture tells us of de wrathful woman?"

"Whar I got time to go a foolin' wid Scripture? W'at I wants to know; whar dat Pierson boy, he don't come. He ben gone time 'nough to walk to Natch'toches an' back."

"Ain't dat him I years yonda tu de crib?" suggested Betsy, coming to join Aunt Belindy in the open doorway.

"You heahs mos' too much fu' yo' own good, you does, gal."

But Betsy was right. For soon a tall, slim negro, young and coal black, mounted the stairs and came into the kitchen, where he deposited a meal bag filled with various necessities that he had brought from Centerville. He was one of the dancers who had displayed their skill before Melicent and Grégoire. Uncle Hiram at once accosted him.

"Well, Pierson, we jest a ben a wonderin' consarnin' you. W'at was de 'casion o' dat long delay?"

"De 'casion? W'y man alive, I couldn't git a dog gone soul in de town to wait on me."

"Dat boy kin lie, yas," said Aunt Belindy, "God A'mighty knows ever time I ben to Centaville dem sto' keepas ain't done a blessed t'ing but settin' down."

"Settin' down—Lord! dey warn't settin' down to-day; you heah me."

"W'at dey doin' ef dey ain't settin' down, Unc' Pierson?" asked Betsy with amiable curiosity.

"You jis drap dat 'uncle,' you," turning wrathfully upon the girl, "sence w'en you start dat new trick?"

"Lef de chile 'lone, Pierson, lef 'er alone. Come heah, Betsy, an' set by yo' Uncle Hiurm."

From the encouraging nearness of Uncle Hiram, she ventured to ask "w'at you 'low dey doin' ef dey ain't settin' down?" this time without adding the offensive title.

"Dey flyin' 'roun', Lord! dey hidin' dey sef! dey gittin' out o' de way, I tell you. Grégor jis ben a raisin' ole Cain in Centaville."

"I know'd it; could a' tole you dat mese'f. My Lan'! but dats a piece, dat Grégor," Aunt Belindy enunciated between paroxysms of laughter, seating herself with her fat arms resting on her knees, and her whole bearing announcing pleased anticipation.

"Dat boy neva did have no car' fur de salvation o' his soul," groaned Uncle Hiram.

"W'at he ben a doin' yonda?" demanded Aunt Belindy impatiently.

"Well," said Pierson, assuming a declamatory air and position in the middle of the large kitchen, "he lef' heah—w'at time he lef heah, Aunt B'lindy?"

"He done lef' fo' dinna, 'caze I seed 'im a lopin' to'ads de riva, time I flung dat Sampson boy out o' de doo', bringin' dem greens in heah 'dout washin' of 'em."

"Dat's so; it war good dinna time w'en he come a lopin' in town. Dat hoss look like he ben swimmin' in Cane Riva, he done ride him so hard. He fling he se'f down front o' Grammont's sto' an' he come a stompin' in, look like gwine hu't somebody. Ole Grammont tell him, 'How you come on, Grégor? Come ova tu de house an' eat dinna wid us: de ladies be pleas tu see you.'"

"Humph," muttered Aunt Belindy, "dem Grammont gals be glad to see any t'ing dat got breeches on; lef 'lone good lookin' piece like dat Grégor."

"Grégor, he neva sey, 'Tank you dog,' jis' fling he big dolla down on de counta an' 'low 'don't want no dinna: gimme some w'iskey.' "

"Yas, yas, Lord," from Aunt Belindy.

"Ole Grammont, he push de bottle to'ads 'im, an' I 'clar to Goodness ef he didn' mos fill dat tumbla to de brim, an' drink it down, neva blink a eye. Den he tu'n an treat ev'y las' w'ite man stan'in' roun'; dat ole kiarpenta man; de blacksmif; Marse Verdon. He keep on a treatin'; Grammont, he keep a handin' out de w'iskey; Grégor he keep on a drinkin' an a treatin'—Grammont, he keep a handin' out; don't make no odds tu him s'long uz dat bring de money in de draw. I ben a stan'in' out on de gallery, me, a peekin' in. An' Grégor, he cuss and swar an' he kiarry on, an 'low he want play game poka. Den dey all goes a trompin' in de back room an' sets down roun' de table, an' I comes a creepin' in, me, whar I kin look frough de doo', an dar dey sets an' plays an Grégor, he drinks w'iskey an' he wins de money. An' arta w'ile Marse Verdon, he little eyes blinkin', he 'low', 'y' all had a shootin' down tu Place-du-Bois, *hein* Grégor?' Grégor, he neva say nuttin': he jis' draw he pistol slow out o' he pocket an' lay it down on de table; an' he look squar in Marse Verdon eyes. Man! ef you eva seed some pussun tu'n' w'ite!"

"Reckon dat heifa 'Milky' look black side li'le Verdon dat time," chuckled Aunt Belindy.

"Jis' uz w'ite uz Unc' Hiurm's shurt an' a trimblin', an' neva say no mo' 'bout shootin'. Den ole Grammont, he kine o' hang back an' say, 'You git de jestice de peace, 'hine you, kiarrin' conceal' weepons dat a-way, Grégor.' "

"Dat ole Grammont, he got to git he gab in ef he gwine die fu' it," interrupted Aunt Belindy.

"Grégor say—'I don't 'lows to kiarr no conceal' weepons,' an he draw nudda pistol slow out o' he udda pocket an' lay et on de table. By dat time he gittin' all de money, he crammin' de money in he pocket; an' dem fellas dey gits up one arta d'udda kine o' shy-like, an' sneaks out. Den Grégor, he git up an come out o' de room, he coat 'crost he arm, an' de pistols a stickin' out an him lookin' sassy tell ev'y body make way, same ef he ben Jay Goul'. Ef he look one o' 'em in de eye dey outs wid, 'Howdy, Grégor—how you come on, Grégor?' jis' uz pelite uz a peacock, an' him neva take no trouble to yansa 'em. He jis' holla out fu' somebody bring dat hoss tu de steps, an' him stan'in' 's big uz life, waitin'. I gits tu de hoss fus', me, an' leads 'im up, an' he gits top dat hoss stidy like he ain't tetch a drap, an' he fling me big dolla."

"Whar de dolla, Mista Pierson?" enquired Betsy.

"De dolla in my pocket, an' et gwine stay dah. Didn' ax you fu' no 'Mista Pierson.' Whar yu' all tink he went on dat hoss?"

"How you reckon we knows whar he wint; we wasn't dah," replied Aunt Belindy.

"He jis' went a lopin' twenty yards down to Chartrand's sto'. I goes on 'hine 'im see w'at he gwine do. Dah he git down f'um de hoss an' go a stompin' in de sto'—eve'ybody stan'in' back jis' same like fu' Jay Goul', an' he fling bill down on de counta an' 'low, 'Fill me up a bottle, Chartrand, I'se gwine travelin'.' Den he 'lows, 'You treats eve'y las' man roun' heah at my 'spence, black an' w'ite—nuttin' fu' me,' an' he fole he arms an' lean back on de counta, jis' so. Chartrand, he look skeerd, he say 'François gwine wait on you.' But Grégor, he 'low he don't wants no rusty skileton a waitin' on him w'en he treat, 'Wait on de gemmen yo'se'f—step up gemmen.' Chartrand 'low, 'Damn ef nigga gwine drink wid w'ite man in dat sto',' all same he kine git 'hine box tu say dat."

"Lord, Lord, de ways o' de transgressor!" groaned Uncle Hiram.

"You want to see dem niggas sneaking 'way," resumed Pierson, "dey knows Grégor gwine fo'ce 'em drink; dey knows Chartrand gwine make it hot fu' 'em art'ards ef dey does. Grégor he spie me jis' I'se tryin' glide frough de doo' an he call out, 'Yonda a gemmen f'um Place-du-Bois; Pierson, come heah; you'se good 'nough tu drink wid any w'ite man, 'cept me; you come heah, take drink wid Mr. Louis Chartrand.'

"I 'lows don't wants no drink, much 'bleege, Marse Grégor'. 'Yis, you wants drink,' an' 'id dat he draws he pistol. 'Mista Chartrand want drink, too. I done owe Mista Chartrand somethin' dis long time; I'se gwine pay 'im wid a treat,' he say. Chartrand look like he on fiar, he so red, he so mad, he swell up same like ole bull frog."

"Dat make no odd," chuckled Aunt Belindy, "he gwine drink wid nigga ef Grégor say so."

"Yes, he drink, Lord, only he cuss me slow, an' 'low he gwine break my skull."

"Lordy! I knows you was jis' a trimblin', Mista Pierson."

"Warn't trimblin' no mo' 'en I'se trimblin' dis minute, an' you drap dat 'Mista.' Den w'at you reckon? Yonda come Père Antoine; he come an' stan' in de doo' an' he hole up he han'; look like he ain't 'feard no body an' he 'low: 'Grégor Sanchun, how is you dar' come in dis heah

peaceful town frowin' of it into disorda an' confusion? Ef you isn't 'feard
o' man; hasn't you got no fear o' God A'mighty wat punishes?' "

"Grégor, he look at 'im an' he say cool like, 'Howdy, Père Antoine;
how you come on?' He got he pistol w'at he draw fu' make Chartrand
drink wid dis heah nigga,—he foolin' wid it an' a rubbin' it up and down
he pants, an' he 'low 'Dis a gemmen w'at fit to drink wid a Sanchun—
w'at'll you have?' But Père Antoine, he go on makin' a su'mon same like
he make in chu'ch, an' Grégor, he lean he two arm back on de counta—
kine o' smilin' like, an' he say, 'Chartrand, whar dat bottle I orda you
put up?' Chartrand bring de bottle; Grégor, he put de bottle in he coat
pocket wat hang on he arm—car'ful.

"Père Antoine, he go on preachin', he say, 'I tell you dis young man,
you 'se on de big road w'at leads tu hell.'

"Den Grégor straight he se'f up an' walk close to Père Antoine an' he
say, 'Hell an' damnation dar ain't no sich a place. I reckon she know;
w'at you know side o' her. She say dar ain't no hell, an' ef you an' de
Archbishop an' de Angel Gabriel come along an' 'low dey a hell, you all
liars,' an' he say, 'Make way dah, I'se a gittin' out o' heah; dis ain't no
town fittin' to hol' a Sanchun. Make way ef you don' wants to go to
Kingdom come fo' yo' time.'

"Well, I 'lows dey did make way. Only Père Antoine, he look mighty
sorry an' down cas'.

"Grégor go out dat sto' taking plenty room, an' walkin' car'ful like,
an' he swing he se'f on de hoss; den he lean down mos' flat an' stick he
spurs in dat hoss an' he go tar'in' like de win' down street, out o' de town,
a firin' he pistol up in de a'r.' "

Uncle Hiram had listened to the foregoing recital with troubled countenance, and with many a protesting groan. He now shook his old white
head, and heaved a deep sigh. "All dat gwine come hard an' heavy on
de madam. She don't desarve it—God knows, she don't desarve it."

"How you, ole like you is, kin look fu' somethin' diffunt, Unc' Hiurm?"
observed Aunt Belindy philosophically. "Don't you know Grégor gwine
be Grégor tell he die? Dat's all dar is 'bout it."

Betsy arose with the sudden recollection that she had let the time pass
for bringing in Miss Thérèse's hot water, and Pierson went to the stove
to see what Aunt Belindy had reserved for him in the shape of supper.

IX

The Reason Why

Sampson, the young colored boy who had lighted Fanny's fire on the first day of her arrival at Place-du-Bois, and who had made such insinuating advances of friendliness towards her, had continued to attract her notice and good will. He it was who lighted her fires on such mornings as they were needed. For there had been no winter. In mid-January, the grass was fresh and green; trees and plants were putting forth tender shoots, as if in welcome to spring; roses were blossoming, and it was a veritable atmosphere of Havana rather than of central Louisiana that the dwellers at Place-du-Bois were enjoying. But finally winter made tardy assertion of its rights. One morning broke raw and black with an icy rain falling, and young Sampson arriving in the early bleakness to attend to his duties at the cottage, presented a picture of human distress to move the most hardened to pity. Though dressed comfortably in the clothing with which Fanny had apparelled him—he was ashen. Save for the chattering of his teeth, his body seemed possessed of a paralytic inability to move. He knelt before the empty fire-place as he had done on that first day, and with deep sighs and groans went about his work. Then he remained long before the warmth that he had kindled; even lying full length upon the soft rug, to bask in the generous heat that permeated and seemed to thaw his stiffened limbs.

Next, he went quietly into the bedroom to attend to the fire there. Hosmer and Fanny were still sleeping. He approached a decorated basket that hung against the wall; a receptacle for old newspapers and odds and ends. He drew something from his rather capacious coat pocket, and, satisfying himself that Hosmer slept, thrust it in the bottom of the basket, well covered by the nondescript accumulation that was there.

The house was very warm and cheerful when they arose, and after breakfasting Hosmer felt unusually reluctant to quit his fire-side and face the inclement day; for an unaccustomed fatigue hung upon his limbs and his body was sore, as from the effect of bruises. But he went, nevertheless, well incased in protective rubber; and as he turned away from the house, Fanny hastened to the hanging basket, and fumbling nervously in its depths, found what the complaisant Sampson had left for her.

The cold rain had gradually changed into a fine mist, that in descending, spread an icy coat upon every object that it touched. When Hosmer returned at noon, he did not leave the house again.

During the afternoon Thérèse knocked at Fanny's door. She was enveloped in a long hooded cloak, her face glowing from contact with the sharp moist air, and myriad crystal drops clinging to her fluffy blonde hair that looked very golden under the dark hood that covered it. She wanted to learn how Fanny accepted this unpleasant change of atmospheric conditions, intending to bear her company for the remainder of the day if she found her depressed, as was often the case.

"Why, I didn't know you were home," she said, a little startled, to Hosmer who opened the door to her. "I came over to show Mrs. Hosmer something pretty that I don't suppose she ever saw before." It was a branch from a rose-tree, bearing two open blossoms and a multitude of buds, creamy pink, all encased in an icy transparency that gleamed like diamonds. "Isn't it exquisite?" she said, holding the spray up for Fanny's admiration. But she saw at a glance that the spirit of Disorder had descended and settled upon the Hosmer household.

The usually neat room was in a sad state of confusion. Some of the pictures had been taken from the walls, and were leaning here and there against chairs and tables. The mantel ornaments had been removed and deposited at random and in groups about the room. On the hearth was a pail of water in which swam a huge sponge; and Fanny sat beside the center-table that was piled with her husband's wearing apparel, holding in her lap a coat which she had evidently been passing under inspection. Her hair had escaped from its fastenings; her collar was hooked awry; her face was flushed and her whole bearing indicated her condition.

Hosmer took the frozen spray from Thérèse's hand, and spoke a little about the beauty of the trees, especially the young cedars that he had passed out in the hills on his way home.

"It's all well and good to talk about flowers and things, Mrs. Laferm— sit down please—but when a person's got the job that I've got on my hands, she's something else to think about. And David here smoking one cigar after another. He knows all I've got to do, and goes and sends those darkies home right after dinner."

Thérèse was so shocked that for a while she could say nothing; till for Hosmer's sake she made a quick effort to appear at ease.

"What have you to do, Mrs. Hosmer? Let me help you, I can give you the whole afternoon," she said with an appearance of being ready for any thing that was at hand to be done.

Fanny turned the coat over in her lap, and looked down helplessly at a stain on the collar, that she had been endeavoring to remove; at the same time pushing aside with patient repetition the wisp of hair that kept falling over her cheek.

"Belle Worthington'll be here before we know it; her and her husband and that Lucilla of hers. David knows how Belle Worthington is, just as well as I do; there's no use saying he don't. If she was to see a speck of dirt in this house or on David's clothes, or anything, why we'd never hear the last of it. I got a letter from her," she continued, letting the coat fall to the floor, whilst she endeavored to find her pocket.

"Is she coming to visit you?" asked Thérèse who had taken up a feather brush, and was dusting and replacing the various ornaments that were scattered through the room.

"She's going down to Muddy Graw (Mardi-Gras) her and her husband and Lucilla and she's going to stop here a while. I had that letter—I guess I must of left it in the other room."

"Never mind," Thérèse hastened to say, seeing that her whole energies were centered on finding the letter.

"Let me look," said Hosmer, making a movement towards the bedroom door, but Fanny had arisen and holding out a hand to detain him she went into the room herself, saying she knew where she'd left it.

"Is this the reason you've kept yourself shut up here in the house so often?" Thérèse asked of Hosmer, drawing near him. "Never telling me a word of it," she went on, "it wasn't right; it wasn't kind."

"Why should I have put any extra burden on you?" he answered, looking down at her, and feeling a joy in her presence there, that seemed like a guilty indulgence in face of his domestic shame.

"Don't stay," Thérèse said. "Leave me here. Go to your office or over to the house—leave me alone with her."

Fanny returned, having found the letter, and spoke with increased vehemence of the necessity of having the house in perfect trim against the arrival of Belle Worthington, from whom they would never hear the last, and so forth.

"Well, your husband is going out, and that will give us a chance to get things righted," said Thérèse encouragingly. "You know men are always in the way at such times."

"It's what he ought to done before; and left Suze and Minervy here," she replied with grudging acquiescence.

After repeated visits to the bedroom, under various pretexts, Fanny grew utterly incapable to do more than sit and gaze stupidly at Thérèse, who busied herself in bringing the confusion of the sitting-room into some order.

She continued to talk disjointedly of Belle Worthington and her well-known tyrannical characteristics in regard to cleanliness; finishing by weeping mildly at the prospect of her own inability to ever reach the high standard required by her exacting friend.

It was far in the afternoon—verging upon night, when Thérèse succeeded in persuading her that she was ill and should go to bed. She gladly seized upon the suggestion of illness; assuring Thérèse that she alone had guessed her affliction: that whatever was thought singular in her behavior must be explained by that sickness which was past being guessed at—then she went to bed.

It was late when Hosmer left his office; a rough temporary shanty, put together near the ruined mill.

He started out slowly on his long cold ride. His physical malaise of the morning had augmented as the day went on, and he was beginning to admit to himself that he was "in for it."

But the cheerless ride was lightened by a picture that had been with him through the afternoon, and that moved him in his whole being, as the moment approached when it might be changed to reality. He knew Fanny's habits; knew that she would be sleeping now. Thérèse would not leave her there alone in the house—of that he was sure. And he pictured Thérèse at this moment seated at his fire-side. He would find her there when he entered. His heart beat tumultuously at the thought. It was a very weak moment with him, possibly, one in which his unnerved condition stood for some account. But he felt that when he saw her there, waiting for him, he would cast himself at her feet and kiss them. He would crush her white hands against his bosom. He would bury his face in her silken hair. She should know how strong his love was, and he would hold her in his arms till she yield back tenderness to his own. But —Thérèse met him on the steps. As he was mounting them, she was descending; wrapped in her long cloak, her pretty head covered by the dark hood.

"Oh, are you going?" he asked.

She heard the note of entreaty in his voice.

"Yes," she answered, "I shouldn't have left her before you came; but I knew you were here; I heard your horse's tread a moment ago. She's asleep. Good night. Take courage and have a brave heart," she said, pressing his hand a moment in both hers, and was gone.

The room was as he had pictured it; order restored and the fire blazing brightly. On the table was a pot of hot tea and a tempting little supper laid. But he pushed it all aside and buried his face down upon the table into his folded arms, groaning aloud. Physical suffering; thwarted love, and at the same time a feeling of self-condemnation, made him wish that life were ended for him.

Fanny awoke close upon morning, not knowing what had aroused her. She was for a little while all bewildered and unable to collect herself. She soon learned the cause of her disturbance. Hosmer was tossing about and his outstretched arm lay across her face, where it had evidently been flung with some violence. She took his hand to move it away, and it burned her like a coal of fire. As she touched him he started and began to talk incoherently. He evidently fancied himself dictating a letter to some insurance company, in no pleased terms—of which Fanny caught but snatches. Then:

"That's too much, Mrs. Lafirme; too much—too much—Don't let Grégoire burn—take him from the fire, some one. Thirty day's credit—shipment made on tenth," he rambled on at intervals in his troubled sleep.

Fanny trembled with apprehension as she heard him. Surely he has brain fever she thought, and she laid her hand gently on his burning forehead. He covered it with his own, muttering "Thérèse, Thérèse—so good—let me love you."

X

Perplexing Things

"Lucilla!"

The pale, drooping girl started guiltily at her mother's sharp exclamation, and made an effort to throw back her shoulders. Then she bit her nails nervously, but soon desisted, remembering that that also, as well as yielding to a relaxed tendency of the spinal column, was a forbidden indulgence.

"Put on your hat and go on out and get a breath of fresh air; you're as white as milk-man's cream."

Lucilla rose and obeyed her mother's order with the precision of a soldier, following the directions of his commander.

"How submissive and gentle your daughter is," remarked Thérèse.

"Well, she's got to be, and she knows it. Why, I haven't got to do more than look at that girl most times for her to understand what I want. You didn't notice, did you, how she straightened up when I called 'Lucilla' to her? She knows by the tone of my voice what she's got to do."

"Most mothers can't boast of having such power over their daughters."

"Well, I'm not the woman to stand any shenanigans from a child of mine. I could name you dead loads of women that are just completely walked over by their children. It's a blessing that boy of Fanny's died, between you and I; its what I've always said. Why, Mrs. Laferm, she couldn't any more look after a youngster than she could after a baby elephant. By the by, what do you guess is the matter with her, any way?"

"How, the matter?" Thérèse asked; the too ready blood flushing her face and neck as she laid down her work and looked up at Mrs. Worthington.

"Why, she's acting mighty queer, that's all I can say for her."

"I haven't been able to see her for some time," Thérèse returned, going back to her sewing, "but I suppose she got a little upset and nervous over her husband; he had a few days of very serious illness before you came."

"Oh, I've seen her in all sorts of states and conditions, and I've never seen her like that before. Why, she does nothing in the God's world but whine and sniffle, and wish she was dead; it's enough to give a person the horrors. She can't make out she's sick; I never saw her look better in my life. She must of gained ten pounds since she come down here."

"Yes," said Thérèse, "she was looking so well, and—and I thought everything was going well with her too, but—" and she hesitated to go on.

"Oh, I know what you want to say. You can't help that. No use bothering your brains about that—now you just take my advice," exclaimed Mrs. Worthington brusquely.

The she laughed so loud and suddenly that Thérèse, being already nervous, pricked her finger with her needle till the blood came; a mishap which decided her to lay aside her work.

"If you never saw a fish out of water, Mrs. Laferm, do take a peep at Mr. Worthington astride that horse; it's enough to make a cat expire!"

Mrs. Worthington was on the whole rather inclined to take her husband seriously. As often as he might excite her disapproval, it was seldom that he aroused her mirth. So it may be gathered that his appearance in this unfamiliar rôle of horseman was of the most mirth-provoking.

He and Hosmer were dismounting at the cottage, which decided Mrs.

Worthington to go and look after them; Fanny for the time being—in her opinion—not having "the gumption to look after a sick kitten."

"This is what I call solid comfort," she said looking around the well appointed sitting-room, before quitting it.

"You ought to be a mighty happy woman, Mrs. Laferm; only I'd think you'd die of lonesomeness, sometimes."

Thérèse laughed, and told her not to forget that she expected them all over in the evening.

"You can depend on me; and I'll do my best to drag Fanny over; so-long."

When left alone, Thérèse at once relapsed into the gloomy train of reflections that had occupied her since the day she had seen with her bodily eyes something of the wretched life that she had brought upon the man she loved. And yet that wretchedness in its refinement of cruelty and immorality she could not guess and was never to know. Still, she had seen enough to cause her to ask herself with a shudder "was I right— was I right?"

She had always thought this lesson of right and wrong a very plain one. So easy of interpretation that the simplest minded might solve it if they would. And here had come for the first time in her life a staggering doubt as to its nature. She did not suspect that she was submitting one of those knotty problems to her unpracticed judgment that philosophers and theologians delight in disagreeing upon, and her inability to unravel it staggered her. She tried to convince herself that a very insistent sting of remorse which she felt, came from selfishness—from the pain that her own heart suffered in the knowledge of Hosmer's unhappiness. She was not callous enough to quiet her soul with the balm of having intended the best. She continued to ask herself only "was I right?" and it was by the answer to that question that she would abide, whether in the stony content of accomplished righteousness, or in an enduring remorse that pointed to a goal in whose labyrinthine possibilities her soul lost itself and fainted away.

Lucilla went out to get a breath of fresh air as her mother had commanded, but she did not go far to seek it. Not further than the end of the back veranda, where she stood for some time motionless, before beginning to occupy herself in a way which Aunt Belindy, who was watching her from the kitchen window, considered highly problematical. The negress was wiping a dish and giving it a fine polish in her absence of mind. When her curiosity could no longer contain itself she called out:

"W'ats dat you'se doin' dah, you li'le gal? Come heah an' le' me see."

Lucilla turned with the startled look which seemed to be usual with her when addressed.

"Le' me see," repeated Aunt Belindy pleasantly.

Lucilla approached the window and handed the woman a small square of stiff writing paper which was stuck with myriad tiny pin-holes; some of which she had been making when interrupted by Aunt Belindy.

"W'at in God A'Mighty's name you call dat 'ar?" the darkey asked examining the paper critically, as though expecting the riddle would solve itself before her eyes.

"Those are my acts I've been counting," the girl replied a little gingerly.

"Yo' ax? I don' see nuttin' 'cep' a piece o' papah plum fill up wid holes. W'at you call ax?"

"Acts—acts. Don't you know what acts are?"

"How you want me know? I neva ben to no school whar you larn all dat."

"Why, an act is something you do that you don't want to do—or something you don't want to do, that you do—I mean that you don't do. Or if you want to eat something and don't. Or an aspiration; that's an act, too."

"Go long! W'ats dat—asp'ration?"

"Why, to say any kind of little prayer; or if you invoke our Lord, or our Blessed Lady, or one of the saints, that's an aspiration. You can make them just as quick as you can think—you can make hundreds and hundreds in a day."

"My Lan'! Dat's w'at you'se studyin' 'bout w'en you'se steppin' 'roun' heah like a droopy pullet? An' I t'ought you was studyin' 'bout dat beau you lef' yonda to Sent Lous."

"You mustn't say such things to me; I'm going to be a religious."

"How dat gwine henda you have a beau ef you'se religious?"

"The religious never get married," turning very red, "and don't live in the world like others."

"Look heah, chile, you t'inks I'se fool? Religion—no religion, whar you gwine live ef you don' live in de worl'? Gwine live up in de moon?"

"You're a very ignorant person," replied Lucilla, highly offended. "A religious devotes her life to God, and lives in the convent."

"Den w'y you neva said 'convent'? I knows all 'bout convent. W'at you gwine do wid dem ax w'en de papah done all fill up?" handing the singular tablet back to her.

"Oh," replied Lucilla, "when I have thousands and thousands I gain twenty-five years' indulgence."

"Is dat so?"

"Yes," said the girl; and divining that Aunt Belindy had not understood, "twenty-five years that I don't have to go to purgatory. You see most people have to spend years and years in purgatory, before they can get to Heaven."

"How you know dat?"

If Aunt Belindy had asked Lucilla how she knew that the sun shone, she could not have answered with more assurance "because I know" as she turned and walked rather scornfully away.

"W'at dat kine o' fool talk dey larns gals up yonda tu Sent Lous? An' huh ma a putty woman; yas, bless me; all dress up fittin' to kill. Don' 'pear like she studyin' 'bout ax."

XI

A Social Evening

Mr. and Mrs. Joseph Duplan with their little daughter Ninette, who had been invited to Place-du-Bois for supper, as well as for the evening, were seated with Thérèse in the parlor, awaiting the arrival of the cottage guests. They had left their rather distant plantation, Les Chênières, early in the afternoon, wishing as usual to make the most of these visits, which, though infrequent, were always so much enjoyed.

The room was somewhat altered since that summer day when Thérèse had sat in its cool shadows, hearing the story of David Hosmer's life. Only with such difference, however, as the change of season called for; imparting to it a rich warmth that invited to sociability and friendly confidences. In the depths of the great chimney glowed with a steady and dignified heat, the huge back-log, whose disposal Uncle Hiram had superintended in person; and the leaping flames from the dry hickories that surrounded it, lent a very genial light to the grim-visaged Lafirmes who looked down from their elevation on the interesting group gathered about the hearth.

Conversation had never once flagged with these good friends; for, aside from much neighborhood gossip to be told and listened to, there was the always fertile topic of "crops" to be discussed in all its bearings, that touched, in its local and restricted sense, the labor question, cultivation, freight rates, and the city merchant.

With Mrs. Duplan there was a good deal to be said about the unusual mortality among "Plymouth-Rocks" owing to an alarming prevalence of "pip," which malady, however, that lady found to be gradually yielding to a heroic treatment introduced into her *basse-cour* by one Coulon, a piney wood sage of some repute as a mystic healer.

This was a delicate refined little woman, somewhat old-fashioned and stranded in her incapability to keep pace with the modern conduct of life; but giving her views with a pretty self-confidence, that showed her a ruler in her peculiar realm.

The young Ninette had extended herself in an easy chair, in an attitude of graceful abandonment, the earnest brown eyes looking eagerly out from under a tangle of auburn hair, and resting with absorbed admiration upon her father, whose words and movements she followed with un-flagging attentiveness. The fastidious little miss was clad in a dainty gown that reached scarcely below the knees; revealing the shapely limbs that were crossed and extended to let the well shod feet rest upon the polished brass fender.

Thérèse had given what information lay within her range, concerning the company which was expected. But her confidences had plainly been insufficient to prepare Mrs. Duplan for the startling effect produced by Mrs. Worthington on that little woman in her black silk of a by-gone fashion; so splendid was Mrs. Worthington's erect and imposing figure, so blonde her blonde hair, so bright her striking color and so comprehensive the sweep of her blue and scintillating gown. Yet was Mrs. Worthington not at ease, as might be noticed in the unnatural quaver of her high-pitched voice and the restless motion of her hands, as she seated herself with an arm studiedly resting upon the table near by.

Hosmer had met the Duplans before; on the occasion of a former visit to Place-du-Bois and again at Les Chênières when he had gone to see the planter on business connected with the lumber trade.

Fanny was a stranger to them and promised to remain such; for she acknowledged her presentation with a silent bow and retreated as far from the group as a decent concession to sociability would permit.

Thérèse with her pretty Creole tact was not long in bringing these seemingly incongruent elements into some degree of harmony. Mr. Duplan in his courteous and rather lordly way was presently imparting to Mrs. Worthington certain reminiscences of a visit to St. Louis twenty-five years before, when he and Mrs. Duplan had rather hastily traversed that interesting town during their wedding journey. Mr. Duplan's manner had a singular effect upon Mrs. Worthington, who became dignified, subdued, and altogether unnatural in her endeavor to adjust herself to it.

Mr. Worthington seated himself beside Mrs. Duplan and was soon trying to glean information, in his eager short-sighted way, of psychological interest concerning the negro race; such effort rather bewildering that good lady, who could not bring herself to view the negro as an interesting or suitable theme to be introduced into polite conversation.

Hosmer sat and talked good-naturedly to the little girls, endeavoring to dispel the shyness with which they seemed inclined to view each other —and Thérèse crossed the room to join Fanny.

"I hope you're feeling better," she ventured, "you should have let me help you while Mr. Hosmer was ill."

Fanny looked away, biting her lip, the sudden tears coming to her eyes. She answered with unsteady voice, "Oh, I was able to look after my husband myself, Mrs. Laferm."

Thérèse reddened at finding herself so misunderstood. "I meant in your housekeeping, Mrs. Hosmer; I could have relieved you of some of that worry, whilst you were occupied with your husband."

Fanny continued to look unhappy; her features taking on that peculiar downward droop which Thérèse had come to know and mistrust.

"Are you going to New Orleans with Mrs. Worthington?" she asked, "she told me she meant to try and persuade you."

"No; I'm not going. Why?" looking suspiciously in Thérèse's face.

"Well," laughed Thérèse, "only for the sake of asking, I suppose. I thought you'd enjoy Mardi-Gras, never having seen it."

"I'm not going anywheres unless David goes along," she said, with an impertinent ring in her voice, and with a conviction that she was administering a stab and a rebuke. She had come prepared to watch her husband and Mrs. Lafirme, her heart swelling with jealous suspicion as she looked constantly from one to the other, endeavoring to detect signs of an understanding between them. Failing to discover such, and loth to be robbed of her morbid feast of misery, she set her failure down to their pre-determined subtlety. Thérèse was conscious of a change in Fanny's attitude, and felt herself unable to account for it otherwise than by whim, which she knew played a not unimportant rôle in directing the manner of a large majority of women. Moreover, it was not a moment to lose herself in speculation concerning this woman's capricious behavior. Her guests held the first claim upon her attentions. Indeed, here was Mrs. Worthington even now loudly demanding a pack of cards. "Here's a gentleman never heard of six-handed euchre. If you've got a pack of cards, Mrs. Laferm, I guess I can show him quick enough that it can be done."

"Oh, I don't doubt Mrs. Worthington's ability to make any startling and pleasing revelations," rejoined the planter good humoredly, and gallantly following Mrs. Worthington who had risen with the view of putting into immediate effect her scheme of initiating these slow people into the unsuspected possibilities of euchre; a game which, however adaptable in other ways, could certainly not be indulged in by seven persons. After each one proffering, as is usual on such occasions, his readiness to assume the character of on-looker, Mr. Worthington's claim to entire indifference, if not inability—confirmed by his wife—was accepted as the most sincere, and that gentleman was excluded and excused.

He watched them as they seated themselves at table, even lending assistance, in his own awkward way, to range the chairs in place. Then he followed the game for a while, standing behind Fanny to note the outcome of her reckless offer of "five on hearts," with only three trumps in hand, and every indication of little assistance from her partners, Mr. Duplan and Belle Worthington.

At one end of the room was a long, low, well-filled book-case. Here had been the direction of Mr. Worthington's secret and stolen glances the entire evening. And now towards this point he finally transported himself by gradual movements which he believed appeared unstudied and indifferent. He was confronted by a good deal of French—to him an unfamiliar language. Here a long row of Balzac; then, the Waverley Novels in faded red cloth of very old date. Racine, Molière, Bulwer following in more modern garb; Shakespeare in a compass that promised very small type. His quick trained glance sweeping along the shelves, contracted into a little frown of resentment while he sent his hand impetuously through his scant locks, standing them quite on end.

On the very lowest shelf were five imposing volumes in dignified black and gold, bearing the simple inscription "Lives of the Saints—Rev. A. Butler." Upon one of them, Mr. Worthington seized, opening it at hazard. He had fallen upon the history of St. Monica, mother of the great St. Austin—a woman whose habits it appears had been so closely guarded in her childhood by a pious nurse, that even the quenching of her natural thirst was permitted only within certain well defined bounds. This mentor used to say "you are now for drinking water, but when you come to be mistress of the cellar, water will be despised, but the habit of drinking will stick by you." Highly interesting, Mr. Worthington thought, as he brushed his hair all down again the right way and seated himself the better to learn the fortunes of the good St. Monica who, curiously enough, notwithstanding those early incentives to temperance, "insensibly contracted an inclination to wine," drinking "whole cups of it with pleasure as it came in her way." A "dangerous intemperance" which it finally pleased Heaven to cure through the instrumentality of a maid servant taunting her mistress with being a "wine bibber."

Mr. Worthington did not stop with the story of Saint Monica. He lost himself in those details of asceticism, martyrdom, superhuman possibilities which man is capable of attaining under peculiar conditions of life— something he had not yet "gone into."

The voices at the card table would certainly have disturbed a man with less power of mind concentration. For Mrs. Worthington in this familiar employment was herself again—*con fuoco*. Here was Mr. Duplan in high spirits; his wife putting forth little gushes of bird-like exaltation as the fascinations of the game revealed themselves to her. Even Hosmer and Thérèse were drawn for the moment from their usual preoccupation. Fanny alone was the ghost of the feast. Her features never relaxed from their settled gloom. She played at hap-hazard, listlessly throwing down the cards or letting them fall from her hands, vaguely asking what were trumps at inopportune moments; showing that inattentiveness so exasperating to an eager player and which oftener than once drew a sharp rebuke from Belle Worthington.

"Don't you wish we could play," said Ninette to her companion from her comfortable perch beside the fire, and looking longingly towards the card table.

"Oh, no," replied Lucilla briefly, gazing into the fire, with hands folded in her lap. Thin hands, showing up very white against the dull colored "convent uniform" that hung in plain, severe folds about her and reached to her very ankles.

"Oh, don't you? I play often at home when company comes. And I play cribbage and *vingt-et-un* with papa and win lots of money from him."

"That's wrong."

"No, it isn't; papa wouldn't do it if it was wrong," she answered decidedly. "Do you go to the convent?" she asked, looking critically at

Lucilla and drawing a little nearer, so as to be confidential. "Tell me about it," she continued, when the other had replied affirmatively. "Is it very dreadful? you know they're going to send me soon."

"Oh, it's the best place in the world," corrected Lucilla as eagerly as she could.

"Well, mamma says she was just as happy as could be there, but you see that's so awfully long ago. It must have changed since then."

"The convent never changes: it's always the same. You first go to chapel to mass early in the morning."

"Ugh!" shuddered Ninette.

"Then you have studies," continued Lucilla. "Then breakfast, then recreation, then classes, and there's meditation."

"Oh, well," interrupted Ninette, "I believe anything most would suit you, and mamma when she was little; but if I don't like it—see here, if I tell you something will you promise never, never, to tell?"

"Is it any thing wrong?"

"Oh, no, not very; it isn't a real mortal sin. Will you promise?"

"Yes," agreed Lucilla; curiosity getting something the better of her pious scruples.

"Cross your heart?"

Lucilla crossed her heart carefully, though a little reluctantly.

"Hope you may die?"

"Oh!" exclaimed the little convent girl aghast.

"Oh, pshaw," laughed Ninette, "never mind. But that's what Polly always says when she wants me to believe her: 'hope I may die, Miss Ninette.' Well, this is it: I've been saving up money for the longest time, oh ever so long. I've got eighteen dollars and sixty cents, and when they send me to the convent, if I don't like it, I'm going to run away." This last and startling revelation was told in a tragic whisper in Lucilla's ear, for Betsy was standing before them with a tray of chocolate and coffee that she was passing around.

"I yeard you," proclaimed Betsy with mischievous inscrutable countenance.

"You didn't," said Ninette defiantly, and taking a cup of coffee.

"Yas, I did, I yeard you," walking away.

"See here, Betsy," cried Ninette recalling the girl, "you're not going to tell, are you?"

"Dun know ef I isn't gwine tell. Dun know ef I isn't gwine tell Miss Duplan dis yere ver' minute."

"Oh Betsy," entreated Ninette, "I'll give you this dress if you don't. I don't want it any more."

Betsy's eyes glowed, but she looked down unconcernedly at the pretty gown.

"Don't spec it fit me. An' you know Miss T'rèse ain't gwine let me go flyin' roun' wid my laigs stickin' out dat away."

"I'll let the ruffle down, Betsy," eagerly proposed Ninette.

"Betsy!" called Thérèse a little impatiently.

"Yas, 'um—I ben waitin' fu' de cups."

Lucilla had made many an aspiration—many an "act" the while. This whole evening of revelry, and now this last act of wicked conspiracy seemed to have tainted her soul with a breath of sin which she would not feel wholly freed from, till she had cleansed her spirit in the waters of absolution.

The party broke up at a late hour, though the Duplans had a long distance to go, and, moreover, had to cross the high and turbid river to reach their carriage which had been left on the opposite bank, owing to the difficulty of the crossing.

Mr. Duplan took occasion of a moment aside to whisper to Hosmer with the air of a connoisseur, "fine woman that Mrs. Worthington of yours."

Hosmer laughed at the jesting implication, whilst disclaiming it, and Fanny looked moodily at them both, jealously wondering at the cause of their good humor.

Mrs. Duplan, under the influence of a charming evening passed in such agreeable and distinguished company, was full of amiable bustle in leaving and had many pleasant parting words to say to each, in her pretty broken English.

"Oh, yes, ma'am," said Mrs. Worthington to that lady, who had taken admiring notice of the beautiful silver "Holy Angels" medal that hung from Lucilla's neck and rested against the dark gown. "Lucilla takes after Mr. Worthington as far as religion goes—kind of different though, for I must say it ain't often he darkens the doors of a church."

Mrs. Worthington always spoke of her husband present as of a husband absent. A peculiarity which he patiently endured, having no talent for repartee, that he had at one time thought of cultivating. But that time was long past.

The Duplans were the first to leave. Then Thérèse stood for a while on the veranda in the chill night air watching the others disappear across the lawn. Mr. and Mrs. Worthington and Lucilla had all shaken hands with her in saying good night. Fanny followed suit limply and grudgingly. Hosmer buttoned his coat impatiently and only lifted his hat to Thérèse as he helped his wife down the stairs.

Poor Fanny! she had already taken exception at that hand pressure which was to come and for which she watched, and now her whole small being was in a jealous turmoil—because there had been none.

XII

Tidings That Sting

Thérèse felt that the room was growing oppressive. She had been sitting all morning alone before the fire, passing in review a great heap of household linen that lay piled beside her on the floor, alternating this occupation with occasional careful and tender offices bestowed upon a wee lamb that had been brought to her some hours before, and that now lay wounded and half lifeless upon a pile of coffee sacks before the blaze.

A fire was hardly needed, except to dispel the dampness that had even made its insistent way indoors, covering walls and furniture with a clammy film. Outside, the moisture was dripping from the glistening magnolia leaves and from the pointed polished leaves of the live-oaks, and the sun that had come out with intense suddenness was drawing it steaming from the shingled roof-tops.

When Thérèse, finally aware of the closeness of the room, opened the door and went out on the veranda, she saw a man, a stranger, riding towards the house and she stood to await his approach. He belonged to what is rather indiscriminately known in that section of the State as the "piney-woods" genus. A rawboned fellow, lank and long of leg; as ungroomed with his scraggy yellow hair and beard as the scrubby little Texas pony which he rode. His big soft felt hat had done unreasonable service as a head-piece; and the "store clothes" that hung upon his lean person could never in their remotest freshness have masqueraded under the character of "all wool." He was in transit, as the bulging saddle-bags that hung across his horse indicated, as well as the rough brown blanket strapped behind him to the animal's back. He rode up close to the rail of the veranda near which Thérèse stood, and nodded to her without offering to raise or touch his hat. She was prepared for the drawl with which he addressed her, and even guessed at what his first words would be.

"You're Mrs. Laferm I 'low?"

Thérèse acknowledged her identity with a bow.

"My name's Jimson; Rufe Jimson," he went on, settling himself on the pony and folding his long knotty hands over the hickory switch that he carried in guise of whip.

"Do you wish to speak to me? won't you dismount?" Thérèse asked.

"I hed my dinner down to the store," he said taking her proposal as an invitation to dine, and turning to expectorate a mouth full of tobacco juice before continuing. "Capital sardines them air," passing his hand over his mouth and beard in unctuous remembrance of the oily dainties.

"I'm just from Cornstalk, Texas, on mu way to Grant. An' them roads as I've traversed isn't what I'd call the best in a fair and square talk."

His manner bore not the slightest mark of deference. He spoke to Thérèse as he might have spoken to one of her black servants, or as he would have addressed a princess of royal blood if fate had ever brought him into such unlikely contact, so clearly was the sense of human equality native to him.

Thérèse knew her animal, and waited patiently for his business to unfold itself.

"I reckon thar hain't no ford hereabouts?" he asked, looking at her with a certain challenge.

"Oh, no; its even difficult crossing in the flat," she answered.

"Wall, I hed calc'lated continooing on this near side. Reckon I could make it?" challenging her again to an answer.

"There's no road on this side," she said, turning away to fasten more securely the escaped branches of a rose-bush that twined about a column near which she stood.

Whether there were a road on this side or on the other side, or no road at all, appeared to be matter of equal indifference to Mr. Jimson, so far as his manner showed. He continued imperturbably "I 'lowed to stop here on a little matter o' business. 'Tis some out o' mu way; more'n I'd calc'lated. You couldn't tell the ixact distance from here to Colfax, could you?"

Thérèse rather impatiently gave him the desired information, and begged that he would disclose his business with her.

"Wall," he said, "onpleasant news 'll keep most times tell you're ready fur it. Thet's my way o' lookin' at it."

"Unpleasant news for me?" she inquired, startled from her indifference and listlessness.

"Rather onpleasant ez I take it. I hain't a makin' no misstatement to persume thet Grégor Sanchun was your nephew?"

"Yes, yes," responded Thérèse, now thoroughly alarmed, and approaching as close to Mr. Rufe Jimson as the dividing rail would permit, "What of him, please?"

He turned again to discharge an accumulation of tobacco juice into a thick border of violets, and resumed.

"You see a hot-blooded young feller, ez wouldn't take no more 'an give no odds, stranger or no stranger in the town, he couldn't ixpect civil treatment; leastways not from Colonel Bill Klayton. Ez I said to Tozier—"

"Please tell me as quickly as possible what has happened," demanded Thérèse with trembling eagerness; steadying herself with both hands on the railing before her.

"You see it all riz out o' a little altercation 'twixt him and Colonel Klayton in the colonel's store. Some says he'd ben drinkin'; others denies it. Howsomever they did hev words risin' out o' the colonel addressing your nephew under the title o' 'Frenchy'; which most takes ez a insufficient cause for rilin'."

"He's dead?" gasped Thérèse, looking at the dispassionate Texan with horrified eyes.

"Wall, yes," an admission which he seemed not yet willing to leave unqualified; for he went on "It don't do to alluz speak out open an' above boards, leastways not thar in Cornstalk. But I'll 'low to you, it's my opinion the colonel acted hasty. It's true 'nough, the young feller hed drawed, but ez I said to Tozier, thet's no reason to persume it was his intention to use his gun."

So Grégoire was dead. She understood it all now. The manner of his death was plain to her as if she had seen it, out there in some disorderly settlement. Killed by the hand of a stranger with whom perhaps the taking of a man's life counted as little as it had once counted with his victim. This flood of sudden and painful intelligence staggered her, and leaning against the column she covered her eyes with both hands, for a while forgetting the presence of the man who had brought the sad tidings.

But he had never ceased his monotonous unwinding. "Thar hain't no manner o' doubt, marm," he was saying, "thet he did hev the sympathy o' the intire community—ez far ez they was free to express it—barrin' a few. Fur he was a likely young chap, that warn't no two opinions o' that. Free with his money—alluz ready to set up fur a friend. Here's a bit o' writin' thet'll larn you more o' the pertic'lars," drawing a letter from his pocket, "writ by the Catholic priest, by name of O'Dowd. He 'lowed you mought want proyer meetin's and sich."

"Masses," corrected Thérèse, holding out her hand for the letter. With the other hand she was wiping away the tears that had gathered thick in her eyes.

"Thar's a couple more little tricks thet he sont," continued Rufe Jimson, apparently dislocating his joints to reach the depths of his trouser pocket, from which he drew a battered pocket book wrapped around with an infinity of string. From the grimy folds of this receptacle he took a small paper parcel which he placed in her hand. It was partly unfastened, and as she opened it fully, the pent-up tears came blindingly—for before her lay a few curling rings of soft brown hair, and a pair of scapulars, one of which was pierced by a tell-tale bullet hole.

"Won't you dismount?" she presently asked again, this time a little more kindly.

"No, marm," said the Texan, jerking his hitherto patient pony by the bridle till it performed feats of which an impartial observer could scarcely have suspected it.

"Don't reckon I could make Colfax before dark, do you?"

"Hardly," she said, turning away, "I'm much obliged to you, Mr. Jimson, for having taken this trouble—if the flat is on the other side, you need only call for it."

"Wall, good day, marm—I wish you luck," he added, with a touch of gallantry which her tears and sweet feminine presence had inspired. Then turning, he loped his horse rapidly forward, leaning well back in the saddle and his elbows sawing the air.

XIII

Melicent Hears the News

It was talked about and wept about at Place-du-Bois, that Grégoire should be dead. It seemed to them all so unbelievable. Yet, whatever hesitancy they had in accepting the fact of his death, was perforce removed by the convincing proof of Father O'Dowd's letter.

None could remember but sweetness and kindness of him. Even Nathan, who had been one day felled to earth by a crowbar in Grégoire's hand, had come himself to look at that deed as not altogether blamable in light of the provocation that had called it forth.

Fanny remembered those bouquets which had been daily offered to her forlornness at her arrival; and the conversations in which they had understood each other so well. The conviction that he was gone away beyond the possibility of knowing him further, moved her to tears. Hosmer, too, was grieved and shocked, without being able to view the event in the light of a calamity.

No one was left unmoved by the tidings which brought a lowering cloud even upon the brow of Aunt Belindy, to rest there the whole day. Deep were the mutterings she hurled at a fate that could have been so short- sighted as to remove from earth so bright an ornament as Grégoire. Her grief further spent much of itself upon the inoffensive Betsy, who, for some inscrutable reason was for twenty-four hours debarred entrance to the kitchen.

Thérèse seated at her desk, devoted a morning to the writing of letters, acquainting various members of the family with the unhappy intelligence. She wrote first to Madame Santien, living now her lazy life in Paris, with eyes closed to the duties that lay before her and heart choked up with an egoism that withered even the mother instincts. It was very difficult to withhold the reproach which she felt inclined to deal her; hard to refrain from upbraiding a selfishness which for a life-time had appeared to Thérèse as criminal.

It was a matter less nice, less difficult, to write to the brothers—one up on the Red River plantation living as best he could; the other idling on the New Orleans streets. But it was after all a short and simple story to tell. There was no lingering illness to describe; no moment even of consciousness in which harrowing last words were to be gathered and recorded. Only a hot senseless quarrel to be told about; the speeding of a bullet with very sure aim, and—quick death.

Of course, masses must be said. Father O'Dowd was properly instructed. Père Antoine in Centerville was addressed on the subject. The Bishop of Natchitoches, respectfully asked to perform this last sad office for the departed soul. And the good old priest and friend at the New Orleans Cathedral, was informed of her desires. Not that Thérèse held very strongly to this saying of masses for the dead; but it had been a custom holding for generations in the family and which she was not disposed to abandon now, even if she had thought of it.

The last letter was sent to Melicent. Thérèse made it purposely short and pointed, with a bare statement of facts—a dry, unemotional telling, that sounded heartless when she read it over; but she let it go.

*   *   *

Melicent was standing in her small, quaint sitting-room, her back to the fire, and her hands clasped behind her. How handsome was this Melicent! Pouting now, and with eyes half covered by the dark shaded lids, as they gazed moodily out at the wild snowflakes that were hurrying like crazy things against the warm window pane and meeting their end there. A loose tea-gown clung in long folds about her. A dull colored thing, save for the two broad bands of sapphire plush hanging straight before, from throat to toe. Melicent was plainly dejected; not troubled, nor sad, only dejected, and very much bored; a condition that had made her yawn several times while she looked at the falling snow.

She was philosophizing a little. Wondering if the world this morning were really the unpleasant place that it appeared, or if these conditions of unpleasantness lay not rather within her own mental vision; a train of thought that might be supposed to have furnished her some degree of entertainment had she continued in its pursuit. But she chose rather to dwell on her causes of unhappiness, and thus convince herself that that unhappiness was indeed outside of her and around her and not by any possibility to be avoided or circumvented. There lay now a letter in her desk from David, filled with admonitions if not reproof which she felt to be not entirely unjust, on the disagreeable subject of Expenses. Looking around the pretty room she conceded to herself that here had been temptations which she could not reasonably have been expected to with-stand. The temptation to lodge herself in this charming little flat; furnish it after her own liking; and install that delightful little old poverty-stricken English woman as keeper of Proprieties, with her irresistible white starched caps and her altogether delightful way of inquiring daily after that "poor, dear, kind Mr. Hosmer." It had all cost a little more than she had fore-seen. But the worst of it, the very worst of it was, that she had already begun to ask herself if, for instance, it were not very irritating to see every day, that same branching palm, posing by the window, in that same yellow jardinière. If those draperies that confronted her were not becom-ing positively offensive in the monotony of their solemn folds. If the cuteness and quaintness of the poverty-stricken little English woman were not after all a source of entertainment that she would willingly forego on occasion. The answer to these questions was a sigh that ended in another yawn.

Then Melicent threw herself into a low easy chair by the table, took up her visiting book, and bending lazily with her arms resting on her knees, began to turn over its pages. The names which she saw there recalled to her mind an entertainment at which she had assisted on the previous afternoon. A progressive euchre party; and the remembrance of what she had there endured now filled her soul with horror.

She thought of those hundred cackling women—of course women are never cackling, it was Melicent's exaggerated way of expressing herself—packed into those small overheated rooms, around those twenty-five little tables; and how by no chance had she once found herself with a congenial set. And how that Mrs. Van Wycke had cheated! It was plain to Melicent that she had taken advantage of having fat Miss Bloomdale for a partner, who went to euchre parties only to show her hands and rings. And little Mrs. Brinke playing against her. Little Mrs. Brinke! A woman who only the other day had read an original paper entitled: "An Hour with Hegel" before her philosophy class; who had published that dry mystical affair "Light on the Inscrutable in Dante." How could such a one by any possibility be supposed to observe the disgusting action of Mrs. Van Wycke in throwing off on her partner's trump and swooping down on the last trick with her right bower? Melicent would have thought it beneath her to more than look her contempt as Mrs. Van Wycke rose with a triumphant laugh to take her place at a higher table, dragging the plastic Bloomdale with her. But she did mutter to herself now, "nasty thief."

"Johannah," Melicent called to her maid who sat sewing in the next room.

"Yes, Miss."

"You know Mrs. Van Wycke?"

"Mrs. Van Wycke, Miss? the lady with the pinted nose that I caught a-feeling of the curtains?"

"Yes, when she calls again I'm not at home. Do you understand? not at home."

"Yes, Miss."

It was gratifying enough to have thus summarily disposed of Mrs. Van Wycke; but it was a source of entertainment which was soon ended. Melicent continued to turn over the pages of her visiting book during which employment she came to the conclusion that these people whom she frequented were all very tiresome. All, all of them, except Miss Drake who had been absent in Europe for the past six months. Perhaps Mrs. Manning too, who was so seldom at home when Melicent called. Who when at home, usually rushed down with her bonnet on, breathless with "I can only spare you a moment, dear. It's very sweet of you to come." She was always just going to the "Home" where things had got into such a muddle whilst she was away for a week. Or it was that "Hospital" meeting where she thought certain members were secretly conniving at her removal from the presidency which she had held for so many years. She was always reading minutes at assemblages which Melicent knew nothing about; or introducing distinguished guests to Guild room meetings. Altogether Melicent saw very little of Mrs. Manning.

"Johannah, don't you hear the bell?"

"Yes, Miss," said Johannah, coming into the room and depositing a gown on which she had been working, on the back of a chair. "It's that postman," she said, as she fastened her needle to the bosom of her dress. "And such a one as he is, thinking that people must fly when he so much as touches the bell, and going off a writing of 'no answer to bell,' and me with my hand on the very door-knob."

"I notice that always happens when I'm out, Johannah; he's ringing again."

It was Thérèse's letter, and as Melicent turned it about and looked critically at the neatly written address, it was not without a hope that the reading of it might furnish her a moment's diversion. She did not faint. The letter did not "fall from her nerveless clasp." She rather held it very steadily. But she grew a shade paler and looked long into the fire. When she had read it three times she folded it slowly and carefully and locked it away in her desk.

"Johannah."

"Yes, Miss."

"Put that gown away; I shan't need it."

"Yes, Miss; and all the beautiful passmantry that you bought?"

"It makes no difference, I shan't use it. What's become of that black camel's-hair that Mrs. Gauche spoiled so last winter?"

"It's laid away, Miss, the same in the cedar chest as the day it came home from her hands and no more fit, that I'd be a shame meself and no claims to a dress-maker. And there's many a lady that she never would have seen a cent, let alone making herself pay for the spiling of it."

"Well, well, Johannah, never mind. Get it out, we'll see what can be done with it. I've had some painful news, and I shall wear mourning for a long, long time."

"Oh, Miss, it's not Mr. David! nor yet one of those sweet relations in Utica? leastways not I hope that beautiful Miss Gertrude, with such hair as I never see for the goldness of it and not dyed, except me cousin that's a nun, that her mother actually cried when it was cut off?"

"No, Johannah; only a very dear friend."

There were a few social engagements to be cancelled; and regrets to be sent out, which she attended to immediately. Then she turned again to look long into the fire. That crime for which she had scorned him, was wiped out now by expiation. For a long time—how long she could not yet determine—she would wrap herself in garb of mourning and move about in sorrowing—giving evasive answer to the curious who questioned her. Now might she live again through those summer months with Grégoire—those golden afternoons in the pine woods—whose aroma even now came back to her. She might look again into his loving brown eyes; feel beneath her touch the softness of his curls. She recalled a day when he had said, "Neva to see you—my God!" and how he had trembled. She recalled—strangely enough and for the first time—that one kiss, and a little tremor brought the hot color to her cheek.

Was she in love with Grégoire now that he was dead? Perhaps. At all events, for the next month, Melicent would not be bored.

XIV

A Step Too Far

Who of us has not known the presence of Misery? Perhaps as those fortunate ones whom he has but touched as he passed them by. It may be that we see but a promise of him as we look into the prophetic faces of children; into the eyes of those we love, and the awfulness of life's possibilities presses into our souls. Do we fly him? hearing him gain upon us panting close at our heels, till we turn from the desperation of uncertainty to grapple with him? In close scuffle we may vanquish him. Fleeing, we may elude him. But what if he creep into the sanctuary of our lives, with his subtle omnipresence, that we do not see in all its horror till we are disarmed; thrusting the burden of his companionship upon us to the end! However we turn he is there. However we shrink he is there. However we come or go, or sleep or wake he is before us. Till the keen sense grows dull with apathy at looking on him, and he becomes like the familiar presence of sin.

Into such callousness had Hosmer fallen. He had ceased to bruise his soul in restless endeavor of resistance. When the awful presence bore too closely upon him, he would close his eyes and brave himself to endurance. Yet Fate might have dealt him worse things.

But a man's misery is after all his own, to make of it what he will or what he can. And shall we be fools, wanting to lighten it with our platitudes?

My friend, your trouble I know weighs. That you should be driven by earthly needs to drag the pinioned spirit of your days through rut and mire. But think of the millions who are doing the like. Or is it your boy, that part of your own self and that other dearer self, who is walking in evil ways? Why, I know a man whose son was hanged the other day; hanged on the gibbet; think of it. If you be quivering while the surgeon cuts away that right arm, remember the poor devil in the hospital yesterday who had both his sawed off.

Oh, have done, with your mutilated men and your sons on gibbets! What are they to me? My hurt is greater than all, because it is my own. If it be only that day after day I must look with warm entreaty into eyes that are cold. Let it be but that peculiar trick of feature which I have come to hate, seen each morning across the breakfast table. That recurrent pin-prick: it hurts. The blow that lays the heart in twain: it kills. Let be mine which will; it is the one that counts.

If Misery kill a man, that ends it. But Misery seldom deals so summarily with his victims. And while they are spared to earth, we find them usually sustaining life after the accepted fashion.

Hosmer was seated at table, having finished his breakfast. He had also finished glancing over the contents of a small memorandum book, which he replaced in his pocket. He then looked at his wife sitting opposite him, but turned rather hastily to gaze with a certain entreaty into the big kind eyes of the great shaggy dog who stood—the shameless beggar—at his side.

"I knew there was something wrong," he said abruptly, with his eyes still fixed on the dog, and his fingers thrust into the animal's matted wool, "Where's the mail this morning?"

"I don't know if that stupid boy's gone for it or not. I told him. You can't depend on any one in a place like this."

Fanny had scarcely touched the breakfast before her, and now pushed aside her cup still half filled with coffee.

"Why, how's that? Sampson seems to do the right thing."

"Yes, Sampson; but he ain't here. That boy of Minervy's been doing his work all morning."

Minervy's boy was even now making his appearance, carrying a good sized bundle of papers and letters, with which he walked boldly up to Hosmer, plainly impressed with the importance of this new rôle.

"Well, colonel; so you've taken Sampson's place?" Hosmer observed, receiving the mail from the boy's little black paws.

"My name's Major, suh. Maje; dats my name. I ain't tuck Sampson's place: no, suh."

"Oh, he's having a day off—" Hosmer went on, smiling quizzingly at the dapper little darkey, and handing him a red apple from the dish of fruit standing in the center of the table. Maje received it with a very unmilitary bob of acknowledgment.

"He yonda home 'cross de riva, suh. He ben too late fu' kotch de flat's mornin'. An' he holla an' holla. He know dey warn't gwine cross dat flat 'gin jis' fu' Sampson."

Hosmer had commenced to open his letters. Fanny with her elbows on the table, asked the boy—with a a certain uneasiness in her voice— "Ain't he coming at all to-day? Don't he know all the work he's got to do? His mother ought to make him."

"Don't reckon. Dat away Sampson: he git mad he stay mad," with which assurance Maje vanished through the rear door, towards the region of the kitchen, to seek more substantial condiments than the apple which he still clutched firmly.

One of the letters was for Fanny, which her husband handed her. When he had finished reading his own, he seemed disposed to linger, for he took from the fruit dish the mate to the red apple he had given Maje, and commenced to peel it with his clasp knife.

"What has our friend Belle Worthington to say for herself?" he inquired good humoredly. "How does she get on with those Creoles down there?"

"You know as well as I do, Belle Worthington ain't going to mix with Creoles. She can't talk French if she wanted to. She says Muddy-Graw don't begin to compare with the Veiled Prophets. It's just what I thought —with their 'Muddy-Graw,' " Fanny added, contemptuously.

"Coming from such high authority, we'll consider that verdict a final clincher," Hosmer laughed a little provokingly.

Fanny was looking again through the several sheets of Belle Worthington's letter. "She says if I'll agree to go back with her, she'll pass this way again."

"Well, why don't you? A little change wouldn't hurt."

" 'Tain't because I want to stay here, Lord knows. A God-forsaken place like this. I guess you'd be glad enough," she added, with voice shaking a little at her own boldness.

He closed his knife, placed it in his pocket, and looked at his wife, completely puzzled.

The power of speech had come to her, for she went on, in an unnatural tone, however, and fumbling nervously with the dishes before her. "I'm fool enough about some things, but I ain't quite such a fool as that."

"What are you talking about, Fanny?"

"That woman wouldn't ask anything better than for me to go to St. Louis."

Hosmer was utterly amazed. He leaned his arms on the table, clasping his hands together and looked at his wife.

"That woman? Belle Worthington? What *do* you mean, any way?"

"I don't mean Belle Worthington," she said excitedly, with two deep red spots in her cheeks. "I'm talking about Mrs. Laferm."

He thrust his hand into his pockets and leaned back in his chair. No amazement now, but very pale, and with terrible concentration of glance.

"Well, then, don't talk about Mrs. Lafirme," he said very slowly, not taking his eyes from her face.

"I will talk about her, too. She ain't worth talking about," she blurted incoherently. "It's time for somebody to talk about a woman passing herself off for a saint, and trying to take other women's husbands—"

"Shut up!" cried Hosmer maddened with sudden fury, and rising violently from his chair.

"I won't shut up," Fanny cried excitedly back at him; rising also. "And what's more I won't stay here and have you making love under my very eyes to a woman that's no better than she ought to be."

She meant to say more, but Hosmer grasped her arm with such a grasp, that had it been her throat she would never have spoken more. The other hand went to his pocket, with fingers clutching the clasp knife there.

"By heaven—I'll—kill you!" every word weighted with murder, panted close in her terrified face. What she would have uttered died upon her pale lips, when her frightened eyes beheld the usually calm face of her husband distorted by a passion of which she had not dreamed.

"David," she faltered, "let go my arm."

Her voice broke the spell that held him, and brought him again to his senses. His fingers slowly relaxed their tense hold. A sigh that was something between a moan and a gasp came with his deliverance and shook him. All the horror now was in his own face as he seized his hat and hurried speechless away.

Fanny remained for a little while dazed. Hers was not the fine nature that would stay cruelly stunned after such a scene. Her immediate terror being past, the strongest resultant emotion was one of self-satisfaction at having spoken out her mind.

But there was a stronger feeling yet, moving and possessing her; crowding out every other. A pressing want that only Sampson's coming would relieve, and which bade fair to drive her to any extremity if it were not appeased.

XV

A Fateful Solution

Hosmer passed the day with a great pain at his heart. His hasty and violent passion of the morning had added another weight for his spirit to drag about, and which he could not cast off. No feeling of resentment remained with him; only wonder at his wife's misshapen knowledge and keen self-rebuke of his own momentary forgetfulness. Even knowing Fanny as he did, he could not rid himself of the haunting dread of having wounded her nature cruelly. He felt much as a man who in a moment of anger inflicts an irreparable hurt upon some small, weak, irresponsible creature, and must bear regret for his madness. The only reparation that lay within his power—true, one that seemed inadequate—was an open and manly apology and confession of wrong. He would feel better when it was made. He would perhaps find relief in discovering that the wound he had inflicted was not so deep—so dangerous as he feared.

With such end in view he came home early in the afternoon. His wife was not there. The house was deserted. Even the servants had disappeared. It took but a moment for him to search the various rooms and find them one after the other, unoccupied. He went out on the porch and looked around. The raw air chilled him. The wind was blowing violently, bringing dashes of rain along with it from massed clouds that hung leaden between sky and earth. Could she have gone over to the house? It was unlikely, for he knew her to have avoided Mrs. Lafirme of late, with a persistence that had puzzled him to seek its cause, which had only fully revealed itself in the morning. Yet, where else could she be? An undefined terror was laying hold of him. His sensitive nature, in exaggerating its own heartlessness, was blindly overestimating the delicacy of hers. To what may he not have driven her? What hitherto untouched chord may he not have started into painful quivering? Was it for him to gauge the endurance of a woman's spirit? Fanny was not now the wife whom he hated; his own act of the morning had changed her into the human being, the weak creature whom he had wronged.

In quitting the house she must have gone unprepared for the inclement weather, for there hung her heavy wrap in its accustomed place, with her umbrella beside it. He seized both and buttoning his own great coat about him, hurried away and over to Mrs. Lafirme's. He found that lady in the sitting-room.

"Isn't Fanny here?" he asked abruptly, with no word of greeting.

"No," she answered looking up at him, and seeing the evident uneasiness in his face. "Isn't she at home? Is anything wrong?"

"Oh, everything is wrong," he returned desperately, "But the immediate wrong is that she has disappeared—I must find her."

Thérèse arose at once and called to Betsy who was occupied on the front veranda.

"Yas, um," the girl answered to her mistress' enquiry. "I seed ma'am Hosma goin' to'ads de riva good hour 'go. She mus' crost w'en Nathan tuck dat load ova. I yain't seed 'er comin' back yit."

Hosmer left the house hastily, hardly reassured by Betsy's information. Thérèse's glance—speculating and uneasy—followed his hurrying figure till it disappeared from sight.

The crossing was an affair of extreme difficulty, and which Nathan was reluctant to undertake until he should have gathered a "load" that would justify him in making it. In his estimation, Hosmer did not meet such requirement, even taken in company with the solitary individual who had been sitting on his horse with Egyptian patience for long unheeded moments, the rain beating down upon his back, while he waited the ferryman's pleasure. But Nathan's determination was not proof against the substantial inducements which Hosmer held out to him; and soon they were launched, all hands assisting in the toilsome passage.

The water, in rising to an unaccustomed height, had taken on an added and tremendous swiftness. The red turbid stream was eddying and bulging and hurrying with terrific swiftness between its shallow banks, striking with an immensity of power against the projection of land on which stood Marie Louise's cabin, and rebounding in great circling waves that spread and lost themselves in the seething turmoil. The cable used in crossing the unwieldly flat had long been submerged and the posts which held it wrenched from their fastenings. The three men, each with his long heavy oar in hand began to pull up stream, using a force that brought the swelling veins like iron tracings upon their foreheads where the sweat had gathered as if the day were midsummer. They made their toilsome way by slow inches, that finally landed them breathless and exhausted on the opposite side.

What could have been the inducement to call Fanny out on such a day and such a venture? The answer came only too readily from Hosmer's reproaching conscience. And now, where to seek her? There was nothing to guide him; to indicate the course she might have taken. The rain was falling heavily and in gusts and through it he looked about at the small cabins standing dreary in their dismantled fields. Marie Louise's was the nearest at hand and towards it he directed his steps.

The big good-natured negress had seen his approach from the window, for she opened the door to him before he had time to knock, and entering he saw Fanny seated before the fire holding a pair of very wet smoking feet to dry. His first sensation was one of relief at finding her safe and housed. His next, one of uncertainty as to the kind and degree of resentment which he felt confident must now show itself. But this last was soon dispelled, for turning, she greeted him with a laugh. He would have rather a blow. That laugh said so many things—too many things. True, it removed the dread which had been haunting him all day, but it shattered what seemed to have been now his last illusion regarding this woman. That unsounded chord which he feared he had touched was after all but one in harmony with the rest of her common nature. He saw too at a glance that her dominant passion had been leading and now controlled her. And by one of those rapid trains of thought in which odd and detached fancies, facts, impressions and observations form themselves into an orderly sequence leading to a final conviction—all was made plain to him that before had puzzled him. She need not have told him her reason for crossing the river, he knew it. He dismissed at once the attitude with which he had thought to approach her. Here was no forgiveness to be asked of dulled senses. No bending in expiation of faults committed. He was here as master.

"Fanny, what does this mean?" he asked in cold anger; with no heat now, no passion.

"Yaas, me tell madame, she goin' fur ketch cole si she don' mine out. Dat not fur play dat kine wedder, no. Teck chair, M'sieur; dry you'se'f leet beet. Me mek you one cup coffee."

Hosmer declined the good Marie Louise's kind proffer of coffee, but he seated himself and waited for Fanny to speak.

"You know if you want a thing done in this place, you've got to do it yourself. I've heard you say it myself, time and time again about those people at the mill," she said.

"Could it have been so urgent as to call you out on a day like this, and with such a perilous crossing? Couldn't you have found some one else to come for you?"

"Who? I'd like to know. Just tell me who? It's nothing to you if we're without servants, but I'm not going to stand it. I ain't going to let Sampson act like that without knowing what he means," said Fanny sharply.

"Dat Samp*son*, he one leet dev'," proffered Marie Louise, with laudable design of shifting blame upon the easy shoulders of Sampson, in event of the domestic jar which she anticipated. "No use try do nuttin' 'id Samp*son*, M'sieur."

"I had to know something, one way or the other," Fanny said in a tone which carried apology, rather by courtesy than by what she considered due.

Hosmer walked to the window where he looked out upon the dreary, desolate scene, little calculated to cheer him. The river was just below; and from this window he could gaze down upon the rushing current as it swept around the bend further up and came striking against this projection with a force all its own. The rain was falling still; steadily, blindingly, with wild clatter against the shingled roof so close above their heads. It coursed in little swift rivulets down the furrows of the almost perpendicular banks. It mingled in a demon dance with the dull, red water. There was something inviting to Hosmer in the scene. He wanted to be outside there making a part of it. He wanted to feel that rain and wind beating upon him. Within, it was stifling, maddening; with his wife's presence there, charging the room with an atmosphere of hate that was possessing him and beginning to course through his veins as it had never done before.

"Do you want to go home?" he asked bluntly, turning half around.

"You must be crazy," she replied, with a slow, upward glance out the window, then down at her feet that were still poised on the low stool that Marie Louise had placed for her.

"You'd better come." He could not have said what moved him, unless it were recklessness and defiance.

"I guess you're dreaming, or something, David. You go on home if you want. Nobody asked you to come after me any way. I'm able to take care of myself, I guess. Ain't you going to take the umbrella?" she added, seeing him start for the door empty handed.

"Oh, it doesn't matter about the rain," he answered without a look back as he went out and slammed the door after him.

"M'sieur look lak he not please," said Marie Louise, with plain regret at the turn of affairs. "You see he no lak you go out in dat kine wedder, me know dat."

"Oh, bother," was Fanny's careless reply. "This suits me well enough; I don't care how long it lasts."

She was in Marie Louise's big rocker, balancing comfortably back and forth with a swing that had become automatic. She felt "good," as she would have termed it herself; her visit to Sampson's hut having not been without results tending to that condition. The warmth of the room was very agreeable in contrast to the bleakness of out-doors. She felt free and moved to exercise a looseness of tongue with the amiable old negress which was not common with her. The occurrences of the morning were gradually withdrawing themselves into a distant perspective that left her in the attitude of a spectator rather than that of an actor. And she laughed and talked with Marie Louise, and rocked, and rocked herself on into drowsiness.

Hosmer had no intention of returning home without his wife. He only wanted to be out under the sky; he wanted to breathe, to use his muscles again. He would go and help cross the flat if need be; an occupation that promised him relief in physical effort. He joined Nathan, whom he found standing under a big live-oak, disputing with an old colored woman who wanted to cross to get back to her family before supper time.

"You didn' have no call to come ova in de fus' place," he was saying to her, "you womens is alluz runnin' back'ards and for'ards like skeard rabbit in de co'n fiel'."

"I don' stan' no sich talk is dat f'om you. Ef you kiant tin' to yo' business o' totin' folks w'en dey wants, you betta quit. You done cheat Mose out o' de job, anyways; we all knows dat."

"Mine out, woman, you gwine git hu't. Jis' le'me see Mose han'le dat 'ar flat onct: Jis' le'me. He lan' you down to de Mouf 'fo' you knows it."

"Let me tell you, Nathan," said Hosmer, looking at his watch, "say you wait a quarter of an hour and if no one else comes, we'll cross Aunt Agnes anyway."

"Dat 'nudda t'ing ef you wants to go back, suh."

Aunt Agnes was grumbling now at Hosmer's proposal that promised to keep her another quarter of an hour from her expectant family, when a big lumbering creaking wagon drove up, with its load of baled cotton all covered with tarpaulins.

"Dah!" exclaimed Nathan at sight of the wagon, "ef I'd 'a listened to yo' jawin'—what?"

"Ef you'd listen to me, you'd 'tin' to yo' business betta 'an you does," replied Aunt Agnes, raising a very battered umbrella over her grotesquely apparelled figure, as she stepped from under the shelter of the tree to take her place in the flat.

But she still met with obstacles, for the wagon must needs go first. When it had rolled heavily into place with much loud and needless swearing on the part of the driver who, being a white man, considered Hosmer's presence no hindrance, they let go the chain, and once again pulled out. The crossing was even more difficult now, owing to the extra weight of the wagon.

"I guess you earn your money, Nathan," said Hosmer bending and quivering with the efforts he put forth.

"Yas, suh, I does; an' dis job's wuf mo' 'an I gits fu' it."

"All de same you done lef' off wurking crap sence you start it," mumbled Aunt Agnes.

"You gwine git hu't, woman; I done tole you dat; don' wan' listen," returned Nathan with halting breath.

"Who gwine hu't me?"

Whether from tardy gallantry or from pre-occupation with his arduous work, Nathan offered no reply to this challenge, and his silence left Aunt Agnes in possession of the field.

They were in full mid-stream. Hosmer and the teamster were in the fore end of the boat; Nathan in the rear, and Aunt Agnes standing in the center between the wagon and the protecting railing, against which she leaned her clasped hands that still upheld the semblance of umbrella.

The ill-mated horses stood motionless, letting fall their dejected heads with apathetic droop. The rain was dripping from their glistening coats, and making a great patter as it fell upon the tarpaulins covering the cotton bales.

Suddenly came an exclamation: "Gret God!" from Aunt Agnes, so genuine in its amazement and dismay, that the three men with one accord looked quickly up at her, then at the point on which her terrified gaze was fixed. Almost on the instant of the woman's cry, was heard a shrill, piercing, feminine scream.

What they saw was the section of land on which stood Marie Louise's cabin, undermined—broken away from the main body and gradually gliding into the water. It must have sunk with a first abrupt wrench, for the brick chimney was shaken from its foundation, the smoke issuing in dense clouds from its shattered sides, the house toppling and the roof caving. For a moment Hosmer lost his senses. He could but look, as if at some awful apparition that must soon pass from sight and leave him again in possession of his reason. The leaning house was half submerged when Fanny appeared at the door, like a figure in a dream; seeming a natural part of the awfulness of it. He only gazed on. The two negroes uttered loud lamentations.

"Pull with the current!" cried the teamster, first to regain his presence of mind. It had needed but this, to awaken Hosmer to the situation.

"Leave off," he cried at Nathan, who was wringing his hands. "Take hold that oar or I'll throw you overboard." The trembling ashen negro obeyed on the instant.

"Hold fast—for God's sake—hold fast!" he shouted to Fanny, who was clinging with swaying figure to the door post. Of Marie Louise there was no sign.

The caved bank now remained fixed; but Hosmer knew that at any instant it was liable to disappear before his riveted gaze.

How heavy the flat was! And the horses had caught the contagion of terror and were plunging madly.

"Whip those horses and their load into the river," called Hosmer, "we've got to lighten at any price."

"Them horses an' cotton's worth money," interposed the alarmed teamster.

"Force them into the river, I say; I'll pay you twice their value."

"You 'low to pay fur the cotton, too?"

"Into the river with them or I'll brain you!" he cried, maddened at the weight and delay that were holding them back.

The frightened animals seemed to ask nothing more than to plunge into the troubled water; dragging their load with them.

They were speeding rapidly towards the scene of catastrophe; but to Hosmer they crawled—the moments were hours. "Hold on! hold fast!" he called again and again to his wife. But even as he cried out, the detached section of earth swayed, lurched to one side—plunged to the other, and the whole mass was submerged—leaving the water above it in wild agitation.

A cry of horror went up from the spectators—all but Hosmer. He cast aside his oar—threw off his coat and hat; worked an instant without avail at his wet clinging boots, and with a leap was in the water, swimming towards the spot where the cabin had gone down. The current bore him on without much effort of his own. The flat was close up with him; but he could think of it no longer as a means of rescue. Detached pieces of timber from the ruined house were beginning to rise to the surface. Then something floating softly on the water: a woman's dress, but too far for him to reach it.

When Fanny appeared again, Hosmer was close beside her. His left arm was quickly thrown about her. She was insensible, and he remembered that it was best so, for had she been in possession of her reason, she might have struggled and impeded his movements. He held her fast—close to him and turned to regain the shore. Another horrified shriek went up from the occupants of the flat-boat not far away, and Hosmer knew no more—for a great plunging beam struck him full upon the forehead.

When consciousness came back to him, he found that he lay extended in the flat, which was fastened to the shore. The confused sound of many voices mingled with a ringing din that filled his ears. A warm stream was trickling down over his cheek. Another body lay beside him. Now they were lifting him. Thérèse's face was somewhere—very near, he saw it dimly and that it was white—and he fell again into insensibility.

XVI

To Him Who Waits

The air was filled with the spring and all its promises. Full with the sound of it, the smell of it, the deliciousness of it. Such sweet air; soft and strong, like the touch of a brave woman's hand. The air of an early March day in New Orleans. It was folly to shut it out from nook or cranny. Worse than folly the lady thought who was making futile endeavors to open the car window near which she sat. Her face had grown pink with the effort. She had bit firmly into her red nether lip, making it all the redder; and then sat down from the unaccomplished feat to look ruefully at the smirched finger tips of her Parisian gloves. This flavor of Paris was well about her; in the folds of her graceful wrap that set to her fine shoulders. It was plainly a part of the little black velvet toque that rested on her blonde hair. Even the umbrella and one small valise which she had just laid on the seat opposite her, had Paris written plain upon them.

These were impressions which the little grey-garbed conventional figure, some seats removed, had been noting since the striking lady had entered the car. Points likely to have escaped a man, who—unless a minutely observant one,—would only have seen that she was handsome and worthy of an admiration that he might easily fancy rising to devotion.

Beside herself and the little grey-garbed figure was an interesting family group at the far end of the car. A husband, but doubly a father, surrounded and sat upon by a small band of offspring. A wife—presumably a mother—absorbed with the view of the outside world and the elaborate gold chain that hung around her neck.

The presence of a large valise, an overcoat, a cane and an umbrella disposed on another seat, bespoke a further occupant, likely to be at present in the smoking car.

The train pushed out from the depot. The porter finally made tardy haste to the assistance of the lady who had been attempting to open the window, and when the fresh morning air came blowing in upon her Thérèse leaned back in her seat with a sigh of content.

There was a full day's journey before her. She would not reach Place-du-Bois before dark, but she did not shrink from those hours that were to be passed alone. She rather welcomed the quiet of them after a visit to New Orleans full of pleasant disturbances. She was eager to be home again. She loved Place-du-Bois with a love that was real; that had grown deep since it was the one place in the world which she could connect with the presence of David Hosmer. She had often wondered—indeed was wondering now—if the memory of those happenings to which he belonged would ever grow strange and far away to her. It was a trick of memory with which she indulged herself on occasion, this one of retrospection. Beginning with that June day when she had sat in the hall and watched the course of a white sunshade over the tops of the bending corn.

Such idle thoughts they were with their mingling of bitter and sweet— leading nowhere. But she clung to them and held to them as if to a refuge which she might again and again return to.

The picture of that one terrible day of Fanny's death, stood out in sharp prominent lines; a touch of the old agony always coming back as she remembered how she had believed Hosmer dead too—lying so pale and bleeding before her. Then the parting which had held not so much of sorrow as of awe and bewilderment in it: when sick, wounded and broken he had gone away at once with the dead body of his wife; when the two had clasped hands without words that dared be uttered.

But that was a year ago. And Thérèse thought many things might come about in a year. Anyhow, might not such length of time be hoped to rub the edge off a pain that was not by its nature lasting?

That time of acute trouble seemed to have thrown Hosmer back upon his old diffidence. The letter he wrote her after a painful illness which prostrated him on his arrival in St. Louis, was stiff and formal, as men's letters are apt to be, though it had breathed an untold story of loyalty which she had felt at the time, and still cherished. Other letters—a few— had gone back and forth between them, till Hosmer had gone away to the sea-shore with Melicent, to recuperate, and June coming, Thérèse had sailed from New Orleans for Paris, whither she had passed six months.

Things had not gone well at Place-du-Bois during her absence, the impecunious old kinsman whom she had left in charge, having a decided preference for hunting the *Gros-Bec* and catching trout in the lake to supervising the methods of a troublesome body of blacks. So Thérèse had had much to engage her thoughts from the morbid channel into which those of a more idle woman might have drifted.

She went occasionally enough to the mill. There at least she was always sure to hear Hosmer's name—and what a charm the sound of it had for her. And what a delight it was to her eyes when she caught sight of an envelope lying somewhere on desk or table of the office, addressed in his handwriting. That was a weakness which she could not pardon herself; but which staid with her, seeing that the same trifling cause never failed to awaken the same unmeasured delight. She had even trumped up an excuse one day for carrying off one of Hosmer's business letters—indeed of the dryest in substance, and which, when half-way home, she had torn into the smallest bits and scattered to the winds, so overcome was she by a sense of her own absurdity.

Thérèse had undergone the ordeal of having her ticket scrutinized, commented upon and properly punched by the suave conductor. The little conventional figure had given over the contemplation of Parisian styles and betaken herself to the absorbing pages of a novel which she read through smoked glasses. The husband and father had peeled and distributed his second outlay of bananas amongst his family. It was at this moment that Thérèse, looking towards the door, saw Hosmer enter the car.

She must have felt his presence somewhere near; his being there and coming towards her was so much a part of her thoughts. She held out her hand to him and made place beside her, as if he had left her but a half hour before. All the astonishment was his. But he pressed her hand and took the seat she offered him.

"You knew I was on the train?" he asked.

"Oh, no, how should I?"

Then naturally followed question and answer.

Yes, he was going to Place-du-Bois.

No, the mill did not require his presence; it had been very well managed during his absence.

Yes, she had been to New Orleans. Had had a very agreeable visit. Beautiful weather for city dwellers. But such dryness. So disastrous to the planters.

Yes—quite likely there would be rain next month: there usually was in April. But indeed there was need of more than April showers for that stiff land—that strip along the bayou, if he remembered? Oh, he remembered quite well, but for all that he did not know what she was talking about. She did not know herself. Then they grew silent; not from any feeling of the absurdity of such speech between them, for each had but listened to the other's voice. They became silently absorbed by the consciousness of each other's nearness. She was looking at his hand that rested on his knee, and thinking it fuller than she remembered it before.

She was aware of some change in him which she had not the opportunity to define; but this firmness and fullness of the hand was part of it. She looked up into his face then, to find the same change there, together with a new content. But what she noted beside was the dull scar on his forehead, coming out like a red letter when his eyes looked into her own. The sight of it was like a hurt. She had forgotten it might be there, telling its story of pain through the rest of his life.

"Thérèse," Hosmer said finally, "won't you look at me?"

She was looking from the window. She did not turn her head, but her hand went out and met his that was on the seat close beside her. He held it firmly; but soon with an impatient movement drew down the loose wristlet of her glove and clasped his fingers around her warm wrist.

"Thérèse," he said again; but more unsteadily, "look at me."

"Not here," she answered him, "not now, I mean." And presently she drew her hand away from him and held it for a moment pressed firmly over her eyes. Then she looked at him with brave loving glance.

"It's been so long," she said, with the suspicion of a sigh.

"Too long," he returned, "I couldn't have borne it but for you—the thought of you always present with me; helping me to take myself out of the past. That was why I waited—till I could come to you free. Have you an idea, I wonder, how you have been a promise, and can be the fulfillment of every good that life may give to a man?"

"No, I don't know," she said a little hopelessly, taking his hand again, "I have seen myself at fault in following what seemed the only right. I feel as if there were no way to turn for the truth. Old supports appear to be giving way beneath me. They were so secure before. It commenced, you remember—oh, you know when it must have begun. But do you think, David, that it's right we should find our happiness out of that past of pain and sin and trouble?"

"Thérèse," said Hosmer firmly, "the truth in its entirety isn't given to man to know—such knowledge, no doubt, would be beyond human endurance. But we make a step towards it, when we learn that there is rottenness and evil in the world, masquerading as right and morality—when we learn to know the living spirit from the dead letter. I have not cared to stop in this struggle of life to question. You, perhaps, wouldn't dare to alone. Together, dear one, we will work it out. Be sure there is a way—we may not find it in the end, but we will at least have tried."

XVII

Conclusion

One month after their meeting on the train, Hosmer and Thérèse had gone together to Centerville where they had been made one, as the saying goes, by the good Père Antoine; and without more ado, had driven back to Place-du-Bois: Mr. and Mrs. Hosmer. The event had caused more than the proverbial nine days' talk. Indeed, now, two months after, it was still the absorbing theme that occupied the dwellers of the parish: and such it promised to remain till supplanted by something of sufficient dignity and importance to usurp its place.

But of the opinions, favorable and other, that were being exchanged regarding them and their marriage, Hosmer and Thérèse heard little and would have cared less, so absorbed were they in the overmastering happiness that was holding them in thralldom. They could not yet bring themselves to look at it calmly—this happiness. Even the intoxication of it seemed a thing that promised to hold. Through love they had sought each other, and now the fulfillment of that love had brought more than tenfold its promise to both. It was a royal love; a generous love and a rich one in its revelation. It was a magician that had touched life for them and changed it into a glory. In giving them to each other, it was moving them to the fullness of their own capabilities. Much to do in two little months; but what cannot love do?

"Could it give a woman more than this?" Thérèse was saying softly to herself. Her hands were clasped as in prayer and pressed together against her bosom. Her head bowed and her lips touching the intertwined fingers. She spoke of her own emotion; of a certain sweet turmoil that was stirring within her, as she stood out in the soft June twilight waiting for her husband to come. Waiting to hear the new ring in his voice that was like a song of joy. Waiting to see that new strength and courage in his face, of whose significance she lost nothing. To see the new light that had come in his eyes with happiness. All gifts which love had given her.

"Well, at last," she said, going to the top of the steps to meet him when he came. Her welcome was in her eyes.

"At last," he echoed, with a sigh of relief; pressing her hand which she held out to him and raising it to his lips.

He did not let it go, but passed it through his arm, and together they turned to walk up and down the veranda.

"You didn't expect me at noon, did you?" he asked, looking down at her.

"No; you said you'd be likely not to come; but I hoped for you all the same. I thought you'd manage it some way."

"No," he answered her, laughing, "my efforts failed. I used even strategy. Held out the temptation of your delightful Creole dishes and all that. Nothing was of any avail. They were all business and I had to be all business too, the whole day long. It was horribly stupid."

She pressed his arm significantly.

"And do you think they will put all that money into the mill, David? Into the business?"

"No doubt of it, dear. But they're shrewd fellows: didn't commit themselves in any way. Yet I could see they were impressed. We rode for hours through the woods this morning and they didn't leave a stick of timber unscrutinized. We were out on the lake, too, and they were like ferrets into every cranny of the mill."

"But won't that give you more to do?"

"No, it will give me less: division of labor, don't you see? It will give me more time to be with you."

"And to help with the plantation," his wife suggested.

"No, no, Madame Thérèse," he laughed, "I'll not rob you of your occupation. I'll put no bungling hand into your concerns. I know a sound piece of timber when I see it; but I should hardly be able to tell a sample of Sea Island cotton from the veriest low middling."

"Oh, that's absurd, David. Do you know you're getting to talk such nonsense since we're married; you remind me sometimes of Melicent."

"Of Melicent? Heaven forbid! Why, I have a letter from her," he said, feeling in his breast pocket. "The size and substance of it have actually weighted my pocket the whole day."

"Melicent talking weighty things? That's something new," said Thérèse interested.

"Is Melicent ever anything else than new?" he enquired.

They went and sat together on the bench at the corner of the veranda, where the fading Western light came over their shoulders. A quizzical smile came into his eyes as he unfolded his sister's letter—with Thérèse still holding his arm and sitting very close to him.

"Well," he said, glancing over the first few pages—his wife following—

"she's given up her charming little flat and her quaint little English woman: concludes I was right about the expense, etc., etc. But here comes the gist of the matter," he said, reading from the letter—" 'I know you won't object to the trip, David, I have my heart so set on it. The expense will be trifling, seeing there are four of us to divide carriage hire, restaurant and all that: and it counts.

"If you only knew Mrs. Griesmann I'd feel confident of your consent. You'd be perfectly fascinated with her. She's one of those highly gifted women who knows everything. She's very much interested in me. Thinks to have found that I have a quick comprehensive intellectualism (she calls it) that has been misdirected. I think there is something in that, David; you know yourself I never did care really for society. She says it's impossible to ever come to a true knowledge of life as it is—which should be every one's aim—without studying certain fundamental truths and things.' "

"Oh," breathed Thérèse, overawed.

"But wait—but listen," said Hosmer, " 'Natural History and all that —and we're going to take that magnificent trip through the West—the Yosemite and so forth. It appears the flora of California is especially interesting and we're to carry those delicious little tin boxes strapped over our shoulders to hold specimens. Her son and daughter are both, in their way, striking. He isn't handsome; rather the contrary; but so serene and collected—so intensely bitter—his mother tells me he's a pessimist. And the daughter really puts me to shame, child as she is, with the amount of her knowledge. She labels all her mother's specimens in Latin. Oh, I feel there's so much to be learned. Mrs. Griesmann thinks I ought to wear glasses during the trip. Says we often require them without knowing it ourselves—that they are so restful. She has some theory about it. I'm trying a pair, and see a great deal better through them than I expected to. Only they don't hold on very well, especially when I laugh.

"Who do you suppose seized on to me in Vandervoort's the other day, but that impertinent Mrs. Belle Worthington! Positively took me by the coat and commenced to gush about dear sister Thérèse. She said: 'I tell you what, my dear—' called me my dear at the highest pitch, and that odious Mrs. Van Wycke behind us listening and pretending to examine a lace handkerchief. 'That Mrs. Lafirme's a trump,' she said—'too good for most any man. Hope you won't take offense, but I must say, your brother David's a perfect stick—it's what I always said.' Can you conceive of such shocking impertinence?'

"Well; Belle Worthington does possess the virtue of candor," said Hosmer amused and folding the letter. "That's about all there is, except a piece of scandal concerning people you don't know; that wouldn't interest you."

"But it would interest me," Thérèse insisted, with a little wifely resentment that her husband should have a knowledge of people that excluded her.

"Then you shall hear it," he said, turning to the letter again. "Let's see—'conceive—shocking impertinence—' oh, here it is.

" 'Don't know if you have learned the horrible scandal; too dreadful to talk about. I shall send you the paper. I always knew that Lou Dawson was a perfidious creature—and Bert Rodney! You never did like him, David; but he was always so much the gentleman in his manners—you must admit that. Who could have dreamed it of him. Poor Mrs. Rodney is after all the one to be pitied. She is utterly prostrated. Refuses to see even her most intimate friends. It all came of those two vile wretches thinking Jack Dawson out of town when he wasn't; for he was right there following them around in their perambulations. And the outcome is that Mr. Rodney has his beauty spoiled they say forever; the shot came very near being fatal. But poor, poor Mrs. Rodney!

"Well, good-bye, you dearest David mine. How I wish you both knew Mrs. Griesmann. Give that sweet sister Thérèse as many kisses as she will stand for me.

MELICENT.' "

This time Hosmer put the letter into his pocket, and Thérèse asked with a little puzzled air: "What do you suppose is going to become of Melicent, anyway, David?"

"I don't know, love, unless she marries my friend Homeyer."

"Now, David, you are trying to mystify me. I believe there's a streak of perversity in you after all."

"Of course there is; and here comes Mandy to say that 'suppa's gittin' cole.' "

"Aunt B'lindy 'low suppa on de table gittin' cole," said Mandy, retreating at once from the fire of their merriment.

Thérèse arose and held her two hands out to her husband.

He took them but did not rise; only leaned further back on the seat and looked up at her.

"Oh, supper's a bore; don't you think so?" he asked.

"No, I don't," she replied. "I'm hungry, and so are you. Come, David."

"But look, Thérèse, just when the moon has climbed over the top of that live-oak? We can't go now. And then Melicent's request; we must think about that."

"Oh, surely not, David," she said, drawing back.

"Then let me tell you something," and he drew her head down and whispered something in her pink ear that he just brushed with his lips. It made Thérèse laugh and turn very rosy in the moonlight.

Can that be Hosmer? Is this Thérèse? Fie, fie. It is time we were leaving them.

THE
AWAKENING

I

A green and yellow parrot, which hung in a cage outside the door, kept repeating over and over:

"*Allez vous-en! Allez vous-en! Sapristi!* That's all right!"

He could speak a little Spanish, and also a language which nobody understood, unless it was the mocking-bird that hung on the other side of the door, whistling his fluty notes out upon the breeze with maddening persistence.

Mr. Pontellier, unable to read his newspaper with any degree of comfort, arose with an expression and an exclamation of disgust. He walked down the gallery and across the narrow "bridges" which connected the Lebrun cottages one with the other. He had been seated before the door of the main house. The parrot and the mocking-bird were the property of Madame Lebrun, and they had the right to make all the noise they wished. Mr. Pontellier had the privilege of quitting their society when they ceased to be entertaining.

He stopped before the door of his own cottage, which was the fourth one from the main building and next to the last. Seating himself in a wicker rocker which was there, he once more applied himself to the task of reading the newspaper. The day was Sunday; the paper was a day old. The Sunday papers had not yet reached Grand Isle. He was already acquainted with the market reports, and he glanced restlessly over the editorials and bits of news which he had not had time to read before quitting New Orleans the day before.

Mr. Pontellier wore eye-glasses. He was a man of forty, of medium height and rather slender build; he stooped a little. His hair was brown and straight, parted on one side. His beard was neatly and closely trimmed.

Once in a while he withdrew his glance from the newspaper and looked about him. There was more noise than ever over at the house. The main building was called "the house," to distinguish it from the cottages. The chattering and whistling birds were still at it. Two young girls, the Farival twins, were playing a duet from "Zampa" upon the piano. Madame Lebrun was bustling in and out, giving orders in a high key to a yard-boy whenever she got inside the house, and directions in an equally high voice to a dining-room servant whenever she got outside. She was a fresh, pretty woman, clad always in white with elbow sleeves. Her starched skirts crinkled as she came and went. Farther down, before one of the cottages, a lady in black was walking demurely up and down, telling her beads. A good many persons of the *pension* had gone over to the *Chênière Caminada* in Beaudelet's lugger to hear mass. Some young people were out under the water-oaks playing croquet. Mr. Pontellier's two children were there —sturdy little fellows of four and five. A quadroon nurse followed them about with a far-away, meditative air.

Mr. Pontellier finally lit a cigar and began to smoke, letting the paper drag idly from his hand. He fixed his gaze upon a white sunshade that was advancing at snail's pace from the beach. He could see it plainly between the gaunt trunks of the water-oaks and across the stretch of yellow camomile. The gulf looked far away, melting hazily into the blue of the horizon. The sunshade continued to approach slowly. Beneath its pink-lined shelter were his wife, Mrs. Pontellier, and young Robert Lebrun. When they reached the cottage, the two seated themselves with some appearance of fatigue upon the upper step of the porch, facing each other, each leaning against a supporting post.

"What folly! to bathe at such an hour in such heat!" exclaimed Mr. Pontellier. He himself had taken a plunge at daylight. That was why the morning seemed long to him.

"You are burnt beyond recognition," he added, looking at his wife as one looks at a valuable piece of personal property which has suffered some damage. She held up her hands, strong, shapely hands, and surveyed them critically, drawing up her lawn sleeves above the wrists. Looking at them reminded her of her rings, which she had given to her husband before leaving for the beach. She silently reached out to him, and he, understanding, took the rings from his vest pocket and dropped them into her open palm. She slipped them upon her fingers; then clasping her knees, she looked across at Robert and began to laugh. The rings sparkled upon her fingers. He sent back an answering smile.

"What is it?" asked Pontellier, looking lazily and amused from one to the other. It was some utter nonsense; some adventure out there in the water, and they both tried to relate it at once. It did not seem half so amusing when told. They realized this, and so did Mr. Pontellier. He yawned and stretched himself. Then he got up, saying he had half a mind to go over to Klein's hotel and play a game of billiards.

"Come go along, Lebrun," he proposed to Robert. But Robert admitted quite frankly that he preferred to stay where he was and talk to Mrs. Pontellier.

"Well, send him about his business when he bores you, Edna," instructed her husband as he prepared to leave.

"Here, take the umbrella," she exclaimed, holding it out to him. He accepted the sunshade, and lifting it over his head descended the steps and walked away.

"Coming back to dinner?" his wife called after him. He halted a moment and shrugged his shoulders. He felt in his vest pocket; there was a ten-dollar bill there. He did not know; perhaps he would return for the early dinner and perhaps he would not. It all depended upon the company which he found over at Klein's and the size of "the game." He did not say this, but she understood it, and laughed, nodding good-by to him.

Both children wanted to follow their father when they saw him starting out. He kissed them and promised to bring them back bonbons and peanuts.

II

Mrs. Pontellier's eyes were quick and bright; they were a yellowish brown, about the color of her hair. She had a way of turning them swiftly upon an object and holding them there as if lost in some inward maze of contemplation or thought.

Her eyebrows were a shade darker than her hair. They were thick and almost horizontal, emphasizing the depth of her eyes. She was rather handsome than beautiful. Her face was captivating by reason of a certain frankness of expression and a contradictory subtle play of features. Her manner was engaging.

Robert rolled a cigarette. He smoked cigarettes because he could not afford cigars, he said. He had a cigar in his pocket which Mr. Pontellier had presented him with, and he was saving it for his after-dinner smoke.

This seemed quite proper and natural on his part. In coloring he was not unlike his companion. A clean-shaved face made the resemblance more pronounced than it would otherwise have been. There rested no shadow of care upon his open countenance. His eyes gathered in and reflected the light and languor of the summer day.

Mrs. Pontellier reached over for a palm-leaf fan that lay on the porch and began to fan herself, while Robert sent between his lips light puffs from his cigarette. They chatted incessantly: about the things around them; their amusing adventure out in the water—it had again assumed its entertaining aspect; about the wind, the trees, the people who had gone to the *Chênière;* about the children playing croquet under the oaks, and the Farival twins, who were now performing the overture to "The Poet and the Peasant."

Robert talked a good deal about himself. He was very young, and did not know any better. Mrs. Pontellier talked a little about herself for the same reason. Each was interested in what the other said. Robert spoke of his intention to go to Mexico in the autumn, where fortune awaited him. He was always intending to go to Mexico, but some way never got there. Meanwhile he held on to his modest position in a mercantile house in New Orleans, where an equal familiarity with English, French and Spanish gave him no small value as a clerk and correspondent.

He was spending his summer vacation, as he always did, with his mother at Grand Isle. In former times, before Robert could remember, "the house" had been a summer luxury of the Lebruns. Now, flanked by its dozen or more cottages, which were always filled with exclusive visitors from the "*Quartier Français,*" it enabled Madame Lebrun to maintain the easy and comfortable existence which appeared to be her birthright.

Mrs. Pontellier talked about her father's Mississippi plantation and her girlhood home in the old Kentucky blue-grass country. She was an American woman, with a small infusion of French which seemed to have been lost in dilution. She read a letter from her sister, who was away in the East, and who had engaged herself to be married. Robert was interested, and wanted to know what manner of girls the sisters were, what the father was like, and how long the mother had been dead.

When Mrs. Pontellier folded the letter it was time for her to dress for the early dinner.

"I see Léonce isn't coming back," she said, with a glance in the direction whence her husband had disappeared. Robert supposed he was not, as there were a good many New Orleans club men over at Klein's.

When Mrs. Pontellier left him to enter her room, the young man descended the steps and strolled over toward the croquet players, where, during the half-hour before dinner, he amused himself with the little Pontellier children, who were very fond of him.

III

It was eleven o'clock that night when Mr. Pontellier returned from Klein's hotel. He was in an excellent humor, in high spirits, and very talkative. His entrance awoke his wife, who was in bed and fast asleep when he came in. He talked to her while he undressed, telling her anecdotes and bits of news and gossip that he had gathered during the day. From his trousers pockets he took a fistful of crumpled bank notes and a good deal of silver coin, which he piled on the bureau indiscriminately with keys, knife, handkerchief, and whatever else happened to be in his pockets. She was overcome with sleep, and answered him with little half utterances.

He thought it very discouraging that his wife, who was the sole object of his existence, evinced so little interest in things which concerned him, and valued so little his conversation.

Mr. Pontellier had forgotten the bonbons and peanuts for the boys. Notwithstanding he loved them very much, and went into the adjoining room where they slept to take a look at them and make sure that they were resting comfortably. The result of his investigation was far from satisfactory. He turned and shifted the youngsters about in bed. One of them began to kick and talk about a basket full of crabs.

Mr. Pontellier returned to his wife with the information that Raoul had a high fever and needed looking after. Then he lit a cigar and went and sat near the open door to smoke it.

Mrs. Pontellier was quite sure Raoul had no fever. He had gone to bed perfectly well, she said, and nothing had ailed him all day. Mr. Pontellier was too well acquainted with fever symptoms to be mistaken. He assured her the child was consuming at that moment in the next room.

He reproached his wife with her inattention, her habitual neglect of the children. If it was not a mother's place to look after children, whose on earth was it? He himself had his hands full with his brokerage business. He could not be in two places at once; making a living for his family on the street, and staying at home to see that no harm befell them. He talked in a monotonous, insistent way.

Mrs. Pontellier sprang out of bed and went into the next room. She soon came back and sat on the edge of the bed, leaning her head down on the pillow. She said nothing, and refused to answer her husband when he questioned her. When his cigar was smoked out he went to bed, and in half a minute he was fast asleep.

Mrs. Pontellier was by that time thoroughly awake. She began to cry a little, and wiped her eyes on the sleeve of her *peignoir*. Blowing out the candle, which her husband had left burning, she slipped her bare feet into a pair of satin *mules* at the foot of the bed and went out on the porch, where she sat down in the wicker chair and began to rock gently to and fro.

It was then past midnight. The cottages were all dark. A single faint light gleamed out from the hallway of the house. There was no sound abroad except the hooting of an old owl in the top of a water-oak, and the everlasting voice of the sea, that was not uplifted at that soft hour. It broke like a mournful lullaby upon the night.

The tears came so fast to Mrs. Pontellier's eyes that the damp sleeve of her *peignoir* no longer served to dry them. She was holding the back of her chair with one hand; her loose sleeve had slipped almost to the shoulder of her uplifted arm. Turning, she thrust her face, steaming and wet, into the bend of her arm, and she went on crying there, not caring any longer to dry her face, her eyes, her arms. She could not have told why she was crying. Such experiences as the foregoing were not uncommon in her married life. They seemed never before to have weighed much against the abundance of her husband's kindness and a uniform devotion which had come to be tacit and self-understood.

An indescribable oppression, which seemed to generate in some unfamiliar part of her consciousness, filled her whole being with a vague anguish. It was like a shadow, like a mist passing across her soul's summer day. It was strange and unfamiliar; it was a mood. She did not sit there inwardly upbraiding her husband, lamenting at Fate, which had directed her footsteps to the path which they had taken. She was just having a good cry all to herself. The mosquitoes made merry over her, biting her firm, round arms and nipping at her bare insteps.

The little stinging, buzzing imps succeeded in dispelling a mood which might have held her there in the darkness half a night longer.

The following morning Mr. Pontellier was up in good time to take the rockaway which was to convey him to the steamer at the wharf. He was returning to the city to his business, and they would not see him again at the Island till the coming Saturday. He had regained his composure, which seemed to have been somewhat impaired the night before. He was eager to be gone, as he looked forward to a lively week in Carondelet Street.

Mr. Pontellier gave his wife half of the money which he had brought away from Klein's hotel the evening before. She liked money as well as most women, and accepted it with no little satisfaction.

"It will buy a handsome wedding present for Sister Janet!" she exclaimed, smoothing out the bills as she counted them one by one.

"Oh! we'll treat Sister Janet better than that, my dear," he laughed, as he prepared to kiss her good-by.

The boys were tumbling about, clinging to his legs, imploring that numerous things be brought back to them. Mr. Pontellier was a great favorite, and ladies, men, children, even nurses, were always on hand to say good-by to him. His wife stood smiling and waving, the boys shouting, as he disappeared in the old rockaway down the sandy road.

A few days later a box arrived for Mrs. Pontellier from New Orleans. It was from her husband. It was filled with *friandises*, with luscious and toothsome bits—the finest of fruits, *patés*, a rare bottle or two, delicious syrups, and bonbons in abundance.

Mrs. Pontellier was always very generous with the contents of such a box; she was quite used to receiving them when away from home. The *patés* and fruit were brought to the dining-room; the bonbons were passed around. And the ladies, selecting with dainty and discriminating fingers and a little greedily, all declared that Mr. Pontellier was the best husband in the world. Mrs. Pontellier was forced to admit that she knew of none better.

IV

It would have been a difficult matter for Mr. Pontellier to define to his own satisfaction or any one else's wherein his wife failed in her duty toward their children. It was something which he felt rather than perceived, and he never voiced the feeling without subsequent regret and ample atonement.

If one of the little Pontellier boys took a tumble whilst at play, he was not apt to rush crying to his mother's arms for comfort; he would more likely pick himself up, wipe the water out of his eyes and the sand out of his mouth, and go on playing. Tots as they were, they pulled together and stood their ground in childish battles with doubled fists and uplifted voices, which usually prevailed against the other mother-tots. The quadroon nurse was looked upon as a huge encumbrance, only good to button up waists and panties and to brush and part hair; since it seemed to be a law of society that hair must be parted and brushed.

In short, Mrs. Pontellier was not a mother-woman. The mother-women seemed to prevail that summer at Grand Isle. It was easy to know them, fluttering about with extended, protecting wings when any harm, real or imaginary, threatened their precious brood. They were women who idolized their children, worshiped their husbands, and esteemed it a holy privilege to efface themselves as individuals and grow wings as ministering angels.

Many of them were delicious in the rôle; one of them was the embodiment of every womanly grace and charm. If her husband did not adore her, he was a brute, deserving of death by slow torture. Her name was Adèle Ratignolle. There are no words to describe her save the old ones that have served so often to picture the bygone heroine of romance and the fair lady of our dreams. There was nothing subtle or hidden about her charms; her beauty was all there, flaming and apparent: the spungold hair that comb nor confining pin could restrain; the blue eyes that were like nothing but sapphires; two lips that pouted, that were so red one could only think of cherries or some other delicious crimson fruit in looking at them. She was growing a little stout, but it did not seem to detract an iota from the grace of every step, pose, gesture. One would not have wanted her white neck a mite less full or her beautiful arms more slender. Never were hands more exquisite than hers, and it was a joy to look at them when she threaded her needle or adjusted her gold thimble to her taper middle finger as she sewed away on the little nightdrawers or fashioned a bodice or a bib.

Madame Ratignolle was very fond of Mrs. Pontellier, and often she took her sewing and went over to sit with her in the afternoons. She was sitting there the afternoon of the day the box arrived from New Orleans. She had possession of the rocker, and she was busily engaged in sewing upon a diminutive pair of night-drawers.

She had brought the pattern of the drawers for Mrs. Pontellier to cut out—a marvel of construction, fashioned to enclose a baby's body so effectually that only two small eyes might look out from the garment, like an Eskimo's. They were designed for winter wear, when treacherous drafts came down chimneys and insidious currents of deadly cold found their way through key-holes.

Mrs. Pontellier's mind was quite at rest concerning the present material needs of her children, and she could not see the use of anticipating and making winter night garments the subject of her summer meditations. But she did not want to appear unamiable and uninterested, so she had brought forth newspapers, which she spread upon the floor of the gallery, and under Madame Ratignolle's directions she had cut a pattern of the impervious garment.

Robert was there, seated as he had been the Sunday before, and Mrs. Pontellier also occupied her former position on the upper step, leaning listlessly against the post. Beside her was a box of bonbons, which she held out at intervals to Madame Ratignolle.

That lady seemed at a loss to make a selection, but finally settled upon a stick of nougat, wondering if it were not too rich; whether it could possibly hurt her. Madame Ratignolle had been married seven years. About every two years she had a baby. At that time she had three babies, and was beginning to think of a fourth one. She was always talking about her "condition." Her "condition" was in no way apparent, and no one would have known a thing about it but for her persistence in making it the subject of conversation.

Robert started to reassure her, asserting that he had known a lady who had subsisted upon nougat during the entire—but seeing the color mount into Mrs. Pontellier's face he checked himself and changed the subject.

Mrs. Pontellier, though she had married a Creole, was not thoroughly at home in the society of Creoles; never before had she been thrown so intimately among them. There were only Creoles that summer at Lebrun's. They all knew each other, and felt like one large family, among whom existed the most amicable relations. A characteristic which distinguished them and which impressed Mrs. Pontellier most forcibly was their entire absence of prudery. Their freedom of expression was at first incomprehensible to her, though she had no difficulty in reconciling it with a lofty chastity which in the Creole woman seems to be inborn and unmistakable.

Never would Edna Pontellier forget the shock with which she heard Madame Ratignolle relating to old Monsieur Farival the harrowing story of one of her *accouchements*, withholding no intimate detail. She was growing accustomed to like shocks, but she could not keep the mounting color back from her cheeks. Oftener than once her coming had interrupted the droll story with which Robert was entertaining some amused group of married women.

A book had gone the rounds of the *pension*. When it came her turn to read it, she did so with profound astonishment. She felt moved to read the book in secret and solitude, though none of the others had done so—to hide it from view at the sound of approaching footsteps. It was openly criticised and freely discussed at table. Mrs. Pontellier gave over being astonished, and concluded that wonders would never cease.

V

They formed a congenial group sitting there that summer afternoon —Madame Ratignolle sewing away, often stopping to relate a story or incident with much expressive gesture of her perfect hands; Robert and Mrs. Pontellier sitting idle, exchanging occasional words, glances or smiles which indicated a certain advanced stage of intimacy and *camaraderie.*

He had lived in her shadow during the past month. No one thought anything of it. Many had predicted that Robert would devote himself to Mrs. Pontellier when he arrived. Since the age of fifteen, which was eleven years before, Robert each summer at Grand Isle had constituted himself the devoted attendant of some fair dame or damsel. Sometimes it was a young girl, again a widow; but as often as not it was some interesting married woman.

For two consecutive seasons he lived in the sunlight of Mademoiselle Duvigné's presence. But she died between summers; then Robert posed as an inconsolable, prostrating himself at the feet of Madame Ratignolle for whatever crumbs of sympathy and comfort she might be pleased to vouchsafe.

Mrs. Pontellier liked to sit and gaze at her fair companion as she might look upon a faultless Madonna.

"Could any one fathom the cruelty beneath that fair exterior?" murmured Robert. "She knew that I adored her once, and she let me adore her. It was 'Robert, come; go; stand up; sit down; do this; do that; see if the baby sleeps; my thimble, please, that I left God knows where. Come and read Daudet to me while I sew.'"

"*Par example!* I never had to ask. You were always there under my feet, like a troublesome cat."

"You mean like an adoring dog. And just as soon as Ratignolle appeared on the scene, then it *was* like a dog. '*Passez! Adieu! Allez vous-en!*'"

"Perhaps I feared to make Alphonse jealous," she interjoined, with excessive naïveté. That made them all laugh. The right hand jealous of the left! The heart jealous of the soul! But for that matter, the Creole husband is never jealous; with him the gangrene passion is one which has become dwarfed by disuse.

Meanwhile Robert, addressing Mrs. Pontellier, continued to tell of his one time hopeless passion for Madame Ratignolle; of sleepless nights, of consuming flames till the very sea sizzled when he took his daily plunge. While the lady at the needle kept up a little running, contemptuous comment:

"Blagueur—farceur—gros bête, va!"

He never assumed this serio-comic tone when alone with Mrs. Pontellier. She never knew precisely what to make of it; at that moment it was impossible for her to guess how much of it was jest and what proportion was earnest. It was understood that he had often spoken words of love to Madame Ratignolle, without any thought of being taken seriously. Mrs. Pontellier was glad he had not assumed a similar rôle toward herself. It would have been unacceptable and annoying.

Mrs. Pontellier had brought her sketching materials, which she sometimes dabbled with in an unprofessional way. She liked the dabbling. She felt in it satisfaction of a kind which no other employment afforded her.

She had long wished to try herself on Madame Ratignolle. Never had that lady seemed a more tempting subject than at that moment, seated there like some sensuous Madonna, with the gleam of the fading day enriching her splendid color.

Robert crossed over and seated himself upon the step below Mrs. Pontellier, that he might watch her work. She handled her brushes with a certain ease and freedom which came, not from long and close acquaintance with them, but from a natural aptitude. Robert followed her work with close attention, giving forth little ejaculatory expressions of appreciation in French, which he addressed to Madame Ratignolle.

"Mais ce n'est pas mal! Elle s'y connait, elle a de la force, oui."

During his oblivious attention he once quietly rested his head against Mrs. Pontellier's arm. As gently she repulsed him. Once again he repeated the offense. She could not but believe it to be thoughtlessness on his part; yet that was no reason she should submit to it. She did not remonstrate, except again to repulse him quietly but firmly. He offered no apology.

The picture completed bore no resemblance to Madame Ratignolle. She was greatly disappointed to find that it did not look like her. But it was a fair enough piece of work, and in many respects satisfying.

Mrs. Pontellier evidently did not think so. After surveying the sketch critically she drew a broad smudge of paint across its surface, and crumpled the paper between her hands.

The youngsters came tumbling up the steps, the quadroon following at the respectful distance which they required her to observe. Mrs. Pontellier made them carry her paints and things into the house. She sought to detain them for a little talk and some pleasantry. But they were greatly in earnest. They had only come to investigate the contents of the bonbon box. They accepted without murmuring what she chose to give them, each holding out two chubby hands scoop-like, in the vain hope that they might be filled; and then away they went.

The sun was low in the west, and the breeze soft and languorous that came up from the south, charged with the seductive odor of the sea. Children, freshly befurbelowed, were gathering for their games under the oaks. Their voices were high and penetrating.

Madame Ratignolle folded her sewing, placing thimble, scissors and thread all neatly together in the roll, which she pinned securely. She complained of faintness. Mrs. Pontellier flew for the cologne water and a fan. She bathed Madame Ratignolle's face with cologne, while Robert plied the fan with unnecessary vigor.

The spell was soon over, and Mrs. Pontellier could not help wondering if there were not a little imagination responsible for its origin, for the rose tint had never faded from her friend's face.

She stood watching the fair woman walk down the long line of galleries with the grace and majesty which queens are sometimes supposed to possess. Her little ones ran to meet her. Two of them clung about her white skirts, the third she took from its nurse and with a thousand endearments bore it along in her own fond, encircling arms. Though, as everybody well knew, the doctor had forbidden her to lift so much as a pin!

"Are you going bathing?" asked Robert of Mrs. Pontellier. It was not so much a question as a reminder.

"Oh, no," she answered, with a tone of indecision. "I'm tired; I think not." Her glance wandered from his face away toward the Gulf, whose sonorous murmur reached her like a loving but imperative entreaty.

"Oh, come!" he insisted. "You mustn't miss your bath. Come on. The water must be delicious; it will not hurt you. Come."

He reached up for her big, rough straw hat that hung on a peg outside the door, and put it on her head. They descended the steps, and walked away together toward the beach. The sun was low in the west and the breeze was soft and warm.

VI

Edna Pontellier could not have told why, wishing to go to the beach with Robert, she should in the first place have declined, and in the second place have followed in obedience to one of the two contradictory impulses which impelled her.

A certain light was beginning to dawn dimly within her,—the light which, showing the way, forbids it.

At that early period it served but to bewilder her. It moved her to dreams, to thoughtfulness, to the shadowy anguish which had overcome her the midnight when she had abandoned herself to tears.

In short, Mrs. Pontellier was beginning to realize her position in the universe as a human being, and to recognize her relations as an individual to the world within and about her. This may seem like a ponderous weight of wisdom to descend upon the soul of a young woman of twenty-eight—perhaps more wisdom than the Holy Ghost is usually pleased to vouchsafe to any woman.

But the beginning of things, of a world especially, is necessarily vague, tangled, chaotic, and exceedingly disturbing. How few of us ever emerge from such beginning! How many souls perish in its tumult!

The voice of the sea is seductive; never ceasing, whispering, clamoring, murmuring, inviting the soul to wander for a spell in abysses of solitude; to lose itself in mazes of inward contemplation.

The voice of the sea speaks to the soul. The touch of the sea is sensuous, enfolding the body in its soft, close embrace.

VII

Mrs. Pontellier was not a woman given to confidences, a characteristic hitherto contrary to her nature. Even as a child she had lived her own small life all within herself. At a very early period she had apprehended instinctively the dual life—that outward existence which conforms, the inward life which questions.

That summer at Grand Isle she began to loosen a little the mantle of reserve that had always enveloped her. There may have been—there must have been—influences, both subtle and apparent, working in their several ways to induce her to do this; but the most obvious was the influence of Adèle Ratignolle. The excessive physical charm of the Creole had first attracted her, for Edna had a sensuous susceptibility to beauty. Then the candor of the woman's whole existence, which every one might read, and which formed so striking a contrast to her own habitual reserve—this might have furnished a link. Who can tell what metals the gods use in forging the subtle bond which we call sympathy, which we might as well call love.

The two women went away one morning to the beach together, arm in arm, under the huge white sunshade. Edna had prevailed upon Madame Ratignolle to leave the children behind, though she could not induce her to relinquish a diminutive roll of needlework, which Adèle begged to be allowed to slip into the depths of her pocket. In some unaccountable way they had escaped from Robert.

The walk to the beach was no inconsiderable one, consisting as it did of a long, sandy path, upon which a sporadic and tangled growth that bordered it on either side made frequent and unexpected inroads. There were acres of yellow camomile reaching out on either hand. Further away still, vegetable gardens abounded, with frequent small plantations of orange or lemon trees intervening. The dark green clusters glistened from afar in the sun.

The women were both of goodly height, Madame Ratignolle possessing the more feminine and matronly figure. The charm of Edna Pontellier's physique stole insensibly upon you. The lines of her body were long, clean and symmetrical; it was a body which occasionally fell into splendid poses; there was no suggestion of the trim, stereotyped fashion-plate about it. A casual and indiscriminating observer, in passing, might not cast a second glance upon the figure. But with more feeling and discernment he would have recognized the noble beauty of its modeling, and the graceful severity of poise and movement, which made Edna Pontellier different from the crowd.

She wore a cool muslin that morning—white, with a waving vertical line of brown running through it; also a white linen collar and the big straw hat which she had taken from the peg outside the door. The hat rested any way on her yellow-brown hair, that waved a little, was heavy, and clung close to her head.

Madame Ratignolle, more careful of her complexion, had twined a gauze veil about her head. She wore dogskin gloves, with gauntlets that protected her wrists. She was dressed in pure white, with a fluffiness of ruffles that became her. The draperies and fluttering things which she wore suited her rich, luxuriant beauty as a greater severity of line could not have done.

There were a number of bath-houses along the beach, of rough but solid construction, built with small, protecting galleries facing the water. Each house consisted of two compartments, and each family at Lebrun's possessed a compartment for itself, fitted out with all the essential para-phernalia of the bath and whatever other conveniences the owners might desire. The two women had no intention of bathing; they had just strolled down to the beach for a walk and to be alone and near the water. The Pontellier and Ratignolle compartments adjoined one another under the same roof.

Mrs. Pontellier had brought down her key through force of habit. Un-locking the door of her bath-room she went inside, and soon emerged, bringing a rug, which she spread upon the floor of the gallery, and two huge hair pillows covered with crash, which she placed against the front of the building.

The two seated themselves there in the shade of the porch, side by side, with their backs against the pillows and their feet extended. Madame Ratignolle removed her veil, wiped her face with a rather delicate hand-kerchief, and fanned herself with the fan which she always carried sus-pended somewhere about her person by a long, narrow ribbon. Edna removed her collar and opened her dress at the throat. She took the fan from Madame Ratignolle and began to fan both herself and her com-panion. It was very warm, and for a while they did nothing but exchange remarks about the heat, the sun, the glare. But there was a breeze blowing, a choppy, stiff wind that whipped the water into froth. It fluttered the skirts of the two women and kept them for a while engaged in adjusting, readjusting, tucking in, securing hair-pins and hat-pins. A few persons were sporting some distance away in the water. The beach was very still of human sound at that hour. The lady in black was reading her morning devotions on the porch of a neighboring bath-house. Two young lovers were exchanging their hearts' yearnings beneath the children's tent, which they had found unoccupied.

Edna Pontellier, casting her eyes about, had finally kept them at rest upon the sea. The day was clear and carried the gaze out as far as the blue sky went; there were a few white clouds suspended idly over the horizon. A lateen sail was visible in the direction of Cat

Island, and others to the south seemed almost motionless in the far distance.

"Of whom—of what are you thinking?" asked Adèle of her companion, whose countenance she had been watching with a little amused attention, arrested by the absorbed expression which seemed to have seized and fixed every feature into a statuesque repose.

"Nothing," returned Mrs. Pontellier, with a start, adding at once: "How stupid! But it seems to me it is the reply we make instinctively to such a question. Let me see," she went on, throwing back her head and narrowing her fine eyes till they shone like two vivid points of light. "Let me see. I was really not conscious of thinking of anything; but perhaps I can retrace my thoughts."

"Oh! never mind!" laughed Madame Ratignolle. "I am not quite so exacting. I will let you off this time. It is really too hot to think, especially to think about thinking."

"But for the fun of it," persisted Edna. "First of all, the sight of the water stretching so far away, those motionless sails against the blue sky, made a delicious picture that I just wanted to sit and look at. The hot wind beating in my face made me think—without any connection that I can trace—of a summer day in Kentucky, of a meadow that seemed as big as the ocean to the very little girl walking through the grass, which was higher than her waist. She threw out her arms as if swimming when she walked, beating the tall grass as one strikes out in the water. Oh, I see the connection now!"

"Where were you going that day in Kentucky, walking through the grass?"

"I don't remember now. I was just walking diagonally across a big field. My sun-bonnet obstructed the view. I could see only the stretch of green before me, and I felt as if I must walk on forever, without coming to the end of it. I don't remember whether I was frightened or pleased. I must have been entertained.

"Likely as not it was Sunday," she laughed; "and I was running away from prayers, from the Presbyterian service, read in a spirit of gloom by my father that chills me yet to think of."

"And have you been running away from prayers ever since, *ma chère?*" asked Madame Ratignolle, amused.

"No! oh, no!" Edna hastened to say. "I was a little unthinking child in those days, just following a misleading impulse without question. On the contrary, during one period of my life religion took a firm hold upon me; after I was twelve and until—until—why, I suppose until now, though I never thought much about it—just driven along by habit. But do you know," she broke off, turning her quick eyes upon Madame Ratignolle and leaning forward a little so as to bring her face quite close to that of her companion, "sometimes I feel this summer as if I were walking through the green meadow again; idly, aimlessly, unthinking and unguided."

Madame Ratignolle laid her hand over that of Mrs. Pontellier, which was near her. Seeing that the hand was not withdrawn, she clasped it firmly and warmly. She even stroked it a little, fondly, with the other hand, murmuring in an undertone, *"Pauvre chérie."*

The action was at first a little confusing to Edna, but she soon lent herself readily to the Creole's gentle caress. She was not accustomed to an outward and spoken expression of affection, either in herself or in others. She and her younger sister, Janet, had quarreled a good deal through force of unfortunate habit. Her older sister, Margaret, was matronly and dignified, probably from having assumed matronly and housewifely responsibilities too early in life, their mother having died when they were quite young. Margaret was not effusive; she was practical. Edna had had an occasional girl friend, but whether accidentally or not, they seemed to have been all of one type—the self-contained. She never realized that the reserve of her own character had much, perhaps everything, to do with this. Her most intimate friend at school had been one of rather exceptional intellectual gifts, who wrote fine-sounding essays, which Edna admired and strove to imitate; and with her she talked and glowed over the English classics, and sometimes held religious and political controversies.

Edna often wondered at one propensity which sometimes had inwardly disturbed her without causing any outward show or manifestation on her part. At a very early age—perhaps it was when she traversed the ocean of waving grass—she remembered that she had been passionately enamored of a dignified and sad-eyed cavalry officer who visited her father in Kentucky. She could not leave his presence when he was there, nor remove her eyes from his face, which was something like Napoleon's, with a lock of black hair falling across the forehead. But the cavalry officer melted imperceptibly out of her existence.

At another time her affections were deeply engaged by a young gentleman who visited a lady on a neighboring plantation. It was after they went to Mississippi to live. The young man was engaged to be married to the young lady, and they sometimes called upon Margaret, driving over of afternoons in a buggy. Edna was a little miss, just merging into her teens; and the realization that she herself was nothing, nothing, nothing to the engaged young man was a bitter affliction to her. But he, too, went the way of dreams.

She was a grown young woman when she was overtaken by what she supposed to be the climax of her fate. It was when the face and figure of a great tragedian began to haunt her imagination and stir her senses. The persistence of the infatuation lent it an aspect of genuineness. The hopelessness of it colored it with the lofty tones of a great passion.

The picture of the tragedian stood enframed upon her desk. Any one may possess the portrait of a tragedian without exciting suspicion or comment. (This was a sinister reflection which she cherished.) In the presence of others she expressed admiration for his exalted gifts, as she handed the photograph around and dwelt upon the fidelity of the likeness. When alone she sometimes picked it up and kissed the cold glass passionately.

Her marriage to Léonce Pontellier was purely an accident, in this respect resembling many other marriages which masquerade as the decrees of Fate. It was in the midst of her secret great passion that she met him. He fell in love, as men are in the habit of doing, and pressed his suit with an earnestness and an ardor which left nothing to be desired. He pleased her; his absolute devotion flattered her. She fancied there was a sympathy of thought and taste between them, in which fancy she was mistaken. Add to this the violent opposition of her father and her sister Margaret to her marriage with a Catholic, and we need seek no further for the motives which led her to accept Monsieur Pontellier for her husband.

The acme of bliss, which would have been a marriage with the tragedian, was not for her in this world. As the devoted wife of a man who worshiped her, she felt she would take her place with a certain dignity in the world of reality, closing the portals forever behind her upon the realm of romance and dreams.

But it was not long before the tragedian had gone to join the cavalry officer and the engaged young man and a few others; and Edna found herself face to face with the realities. She grew fond of her husband, realizing with some unaccountable satisfaction that no trace of passion or excessive and fictitious warmth colored her affection, thereby threatening its dissolution.

She was fond of her children in an uneven, impulsive way. She would sometimes gather them passionately to her heart; she would sometimes forget them. The year before they had spent part of the summer with their grandmother Pontellier in Iberville. Feeling secure regarding their happiness and welfare, she did not miss them except with an occasional intense longing. Their absence was a sort of relief, though she did not admit this, even to herself. It seemed to free her of a responsibility which she had blindly assumed and for which Fate had not fitted her.

Edna did not reveal so much as all this to Madame Ratignolle that summer day when they sat with faces turned to the sea. But a good part of it escaped her. She had put her head down on Madame Ratignolle's shoulder. She was flushed and felt intoxicated with the sound of her own voice and the unaccustomed taste of candor. It muddled her like wine, or like a first breath of freedom.

There was the sound of approaching voices. It was Robert, surrounded by a troop of children, searching for them. The two little Pontelliers were with him, and he carried Madame Ratignolle's little girl in his arms. There were other children beside, and two nurse-maids followed, looking disagreeable and resigned.

The women at once rose and began to shake out their draperies and relax their muscles. Mrs. Pontellier threw the cushions and rug into the bath-house. The children all scampered off to the awning, and they stood there in a line, gazing upon the intruding lovers, still exchanging their vows and sighs. The lovers got up, with only a silent protest, and walked slowly away somewhere else.

The children possessed themselves of the tent, and Mrs. Pontellier went over to join them.

Madame Ratignolle begged Robert to accompany her to the house; she complained of cramp in her limbs and stiffness of the joints. She leaned draggingly upon his arm as they walked.

VIII

"Do me a favor, Robert," spoke the pretty woman at his side, almost as soon as she and Robert had started on their slow, homeward way. She looked up in his face, leaning on his arm beneath the encircling shadow of the umbrella which he had lifted.

"Granted; as many as you like," he returned, glancing down into her eyes that were full of thoughtfulness and some speculation.

"I only ask for one; let Mrs. Pontellier alone."

"*Tiens!*" he exclaimed, with a sudden, boyish laugh. "*Voilà que Madame Ratignolle est jalouse!*"

"Nonsense! I'm in earnest; I mean what I say. Let Mrs. Pontellier alone."

"Why?" he asked; himself growing serious at his companion's solicitation.

"She is not one of us; she is not like us. She might make the unfortunate blunder of taking you seriously."

His face flushed with annoyance, and taking off his soft hat he began to beat it impatiently against his leg as he walked. "Why shouldn't she take me seriously?" he demanded sharply. "Am I a comedian, a clown, a jack-in-the-box? Why shouldn't she? You Creoles! I have no patience with you! Am I always to be regarded as a feature of an amusing programme? I hope Mrs. Pontellier does take me seriously. I hope she has discernment enough to find in me something besides the *blagueur*. If I thought there was any doubt—"

"Oh, enough, Robert!" she broke into his heated outburst. "You are not thinking of what you are saying. You speak with about as little reflection as we might expect from one of those children down there playing in the sand. If your attentions to any married women here were ever offered with any intention of being convincing, you would not be the gentleman we all know you to be, and you would be unfit to associate with the wives and daughters of the people who trust you."

Madame Ratignolle had spoken what she believed to be the law and the gospel. The young man shrugged his shoulders impatiently.

"Oh! well! That isn't it," slamming his hat down vehemently upon his head. "You ought to feel that such things are not flattering to say to a fellow."

"Should our whole intercourse consist of an exchange of compliments? *Ma foi!*"

"It isn't pleasant to have a woman tell you—" he went on, unheedingly, but breaking off suddenly: "Now if I were like Arobin—you remember Alcée Arobin and that story of the consul's wife at Biloxi?" And he related the story of Alcée Arobin and the consul's wife; and another about the tenor of the French Opera, who received letters which should never have been written; and still other stories, grave and gay, till Mrs. Pontellier and her possible propensity for taking young men seriously was apparently forgotten.

Madame Ratignolle, when they had regained her cottage, went in to take the hour's rest which she considered helpful. Before leaving her, Robert begged her pardon for the impatience—he called it rudeness—with which he had received her well-meant caution.

"You made one mistake, Adèle," he said, with a light smile; "there is no earthly possibility of Mrs. Pontellier ever taking me seriously. You should have warned me against taking myself seriously. Your advice might then have carried some weight and given me subject for some reflection. *Au revoir*. But you look tired," he added, solicitously. "Would you like a cup of bouillon? Shall I stir you a toddy? Let me mix you a toddy with a drop of Angostura."

She acceded to the suggestion of bouillon, which was grateful and acceptable. He went himself to the kitchen, which was a building apart from the cottages and lying to the rear of the house. And he himself brought her the golden-brown bouillon, in a dainty Sèvres cup, with a flaky cracker or two on the saucer.

She thrust a bare, white arm from the curtain which shielded her open door, and received the cup from his hands. She told him he was a *bon garçon*, and she meant it. Robert thanked her and turned away toward "the house."

The lovers were just entering the grounds of the *pension*. They were leaning toward each other as the water-oaks bent from the sea. There was not a particle of earth beneath their feet. Their heads might have been turned upside-down, so absolutely did they tread upon blue ether. The lady in black, creeping behind them, looked a trifle paler and more jaded than usual. There was no sign of Mrs. Pontellier and the children. Robert scanned the distance for any such apparition. They would doubtless remain away till the dinner hour. The young man ascended to his mother's room. It was situated at the top of the house, made up of odd angles and a queer, sloping ceiling. Two broad dormer windows looked out toward the Gulf, and as far across it as a man's eye might reach. The furnishings of the room were light, cool, and practical.

Madame Lebrun was busily engaged at the sewing-machine. A little black girl sat on the floor, and with her hands worked the treadle of the machine. The Creole woman does not take any chances which may be avoided of imperiling her health.

Robert went over and seated himself on the broad sill of one of the dormer windows. He took a book from his pocket and began energetically to read it, judging by the precision and frequency with which he turned the leaves. The sewing-machine made a resounding clatter in the room; it was of a ponderous, by-gone make. In the lulls, Robert and his mother exchanged bits of desultory conversation.

"Where is Mrs. Pontellier?"

"Down at the beach with the children."

"I promised to lend her the Goncourt. Don't forget to take it down when you go; it's there on the bookshelf over the small table." Clatter, clatter, clatter, bang! for the next five or eight minutes.

"Where is Victor going with the rockaway?"

"The rockaway? Victor?"

"Yes; down there in front. He seems to be getting ready to drive away somewhere."

"Call him." Clatter, clatter!

Robert uttered a shrill, piercing whistle which might have been heard back at the wharf.

"He won't look up."

Madame Lebrun flew to the window. She called "Victor!" She waved a handkerchief and called again. The young fellow below got into the vehicle and started the horse off at a gallop.

Madame Lebrun went back to the machine, crimson with annoyance. Victor was the younger son and brother—a *tête montée*, with a temper which invited violence and a will which no ax could break.

"Whenever you say the word I'm ready to thrash any amount of reason into him that he's able to hold."

"If your father had only lived!" Clatter, clatter, clatter, clatter, bang! It was a fixed belief with Madame Lebrun that the conduct of the universe and all things pertaining thereto would have been manifestly of a more intelligent and higher order had not Monsieur Lebrun been removed to other spheres during the early years of their married life.

"What do you hear from Montel?" Montel was a middle-aged gentleman whose vain ambition and desire for the past twenty years had been to fill the void which Monsieur Lebrun's taking off had left in the Lebrun household. Clatter, clatter, bang, clatter!

"I have a letter somewhere," looking in the machine drawer and finding the letter in the bottom of the work-basket. "He says to tell you he will be in Vera Cruz the beginning of next month"—clatter, clatter!

—"and if you still have the intention of joining him"—bang! clatter, clatter, bang!

"Why didn't you tell me so before, mother? You know I wanted—" Clatter, clatter, clatter!

"Do you see Mrs. Pontellier starting back with the children? She will be in late to luncheon again. She never starts to get ready for luncheon till the last minute." Clatter, clatter! "Where are you going?"

"Where did you say the Goncourt was?"

IX

Every light in the hall was ablaze; every lamp turned as high as it could be without smoking the chimney or threatening explosion. The lamps were fixed at intervals against the wall, encircling the whole room. Some one had gathered orange and lemon branches, and with these fashioned graceful festoons between. The dark green of the branches stood out and glistened against the white muslin curtains which draped the windows, and which puffed, floated, and flapped at the capricious will of a stiff breeze that swept up from the Gulf.

It was Saturday night a few weeks after the intimate conversation held between Robert and Madame Ratignolle on their way from the beach. An unusual number of husbands, fathers, and friends had come down to stay over Sunday; and they were being suitably entertained by their families, with the material help of Madame Lebrun. The dining tables had all been removed to one end of the hall, and the chairs ranged about in rows and in clusters. Each little family group had had its say and exchanged its domestic gossip earlier in the evening. There was now an apparent disposition to relax; to widen the circle of confidences and give a more general tone to the conversation.

Many of the children had been permitted to sit up beyond their usual bedtime. A small band of them were lying on their stomachs on the floor looking at the colored sheets of the comic papers which Mr. Pontellier had brought down. The little Pontellier boys were permitting them to do so, and making their authority felt.

Music, dancing, and a recitation or two were the entertainments furnished, or rather, offered. But there was nothing systematic about the programme, no appearance of prearrangement nor even premeditation.

At an early hour in the evening the Farival twins were prevailed upon to play the piano. They were girls of fourteen, always clad in the Virgin's colors, blue and white, having been dedicated to the Blessed Virgin at their baptism. They played a duet from "Zampa," and at the earnest solicitation of every one present followed it with the overture to "The Poet and the Peasant."

"*Allez vous-en! Sapristi!*" shrieked the parrot outside the door. He was the only being present who possessed sufficient candor to admit that he was not listening to these gracious performances for the first time that summer. Old Monsieur Farival, grandfather of the twins, grew indignant over the interruption, and insisted upon having the bird removed and consigned to regions of darkness. Victor Lebrun objected; and his decrees were as immutable as those of Fate. The parrot fortunately offered no further interruption to the entertainment, the whole venom of his nature apparently having been cherished up and hurled against the twins in that one impetuous outburst.

Later a young brother and sister gave recitations, which every one present had heard many times at winter evening entertainments in the city.

A little girl performed a skirt dance in the center of the floor. The mother played her accompaniments and at the same time watched her daughter with greedy admiration and nervous apprehension. She need have had no apprehension. The child was mistress of the situation. She had been properly dressed for the occasion in black tulle and black silk tights. Her little neck and arms were bare, and her hair, artificially crimped, stood out like fluffy black plumes over her head. Her poses were full of grace, and her little black-shod toes twinkled as they shot out and upward with a rapidity and suddenness which were bewildering.

But there was no reason why every one should not dance. Madame Ratignolle could not, so it was she who gaily consented to play for the others. She played very well, keeping excellent waltz time and infusing an expression into the strains which was indeed inspiring. She was keeping up her music on account of the children, she said; because she and her husband both considered it a means of brightening the home and making it attractive.

Almost every one danced but the twins, who could not be induced to separate during the brief period when one or the other should be whirling around the room in the arms of a man. They might have danced together, but they did not think of it.

The children were sent to bed. Some went submissively; others with shrieks and protests as they were dragged away. They had been permitted to sit up till after the ice-cream, which naturally marked the limit of human indulgence.

The ice-cream was passed around with cake—gold and silver cake arranged on platters in alternate slices; it had been made and frozen during the afternoon back of the kitchen by two black women, under the supervision of Victor. It was pronounced a great success—excellent if it had only contained a little less vanilla or a little more sugar, if it had been frozen a degree harder, and if the salt might have been kept out of portions of it. Victor was proud of his achievement, and went about recommending it and urging every one to partake of it to excess.

After Mrs. Pontellier had danced twice with her husband, once with Robert, and once with Monsieur Ratignolle, who was thin and tall and swayed like a reed in the wind when he danced, she went out on the gallery and seated herself on the low window-sill, where she commanded a view of all that went on in the hall and could look out toward the Gulf. There was a soft effulgence in the east. The moon was coming up, and its mystic shimmer was casting a million lights across the distant, restless water.

"Would you like to hear Mademoiselle Reisz play?" asked Robert, coming out on the porch where she was. Of course Edna would like to hear Mademoiselle Reisz play; but she feared it would be useless to entreat her.

"I'll ask her," he said. "I'll tell her that you want to hear her. She likes you. She will come." He turned and hurried away to one of the far cottages, where Mademoiselle Reisz was shuffling away. She was dragging a chair in and out of her room, and at intervals objecting to the crying of a baby, which a nurse in the adjoining cottage was endeavoring to put to sleep. She was a disagreeable little woman, no longer young, who had quarreled with almost every one, owing to a temper which was self-assertive and a disposition to trample upon the rights of others. Robert prevailed upon her without any too great difficulty.

She entered the hall with him during a lull in the dance. She made an awkward, imperious little bow as she went in. She was a homely woman, with a small weazened face and body and eyes that glowed. She had absolutely no taste in dress, and wore a batch of rusty black lace with a bunch of artificial violets pinned to the side of her hair.

"Ask Mrs. Pontellier what she would like to hear me play," she requested of Robert. She sat perfectly still before the piano, not touching the keys, while Robert carried her message to Edna at the window. A general air of surprise and genuine satisfaction fell upon every one as they saw the pianist enter. There was a settling down, and a prevailing air of expectancy everywhere. Edna was a trifle embarrassed at being thus signaled out for the imperious little woman's favor. She would not dare to choose, and begged that Mademoiselle Reisz would please herself in her selections.

Edna was what she herself called very fond of music. Musical strains, well rendered, had a way of evoking pictures in her mind. She sometimes liked to sit in the room of mornings when Madame Ratignolle played or practiced. One piece which that lady played Edna had entitled "Solitude." It was a short, plaintive, minor strain. The name of the piece was something else, but she called it "Solitude." When she heard it there came before her imagination the figure of a man standing beside a desolate rock on the seashore. He was naked. His attitude was one of hopeless resignation as he looked toward a distant bird winging its flight away from him.

Another piece called to her mind a dainty young woman clad in an Empire gown, taking mincing dancing steps as she came down a long avenue between tall hedges. Again, another reminded her of children at play, and still another of nothing on earth but a demure lady stroking a cat.

The very first chords which Mademoiselle Reisz struck upon the piano sent a keen tremor down Mrs. Pontellier's spinal column. It was not the first time she had heard an artist at the piano. Perhaps it was the first time she was ready, perhaps the first time her being was tempered to take an impress of the abiding truth.

She waited for the material pictures which she thought would gather and blaze before her imagination. She waited in vain. She saw no pictures of solitude, of hope, of longing, or of despair. But the very passions themselves were aroused within her soul, swaying it, lashing it, as the waves daily beat upon her splendid body. She trembled, she was choking, and the tears blinded her.

Mademoiselle had finished. She arose, and bowing her stiff, lofty bow, she went away, stopping for neither thanks nor applause. As she passed along the gallery she patted Edna upon the shoulder.

"Well, how did you like my music?" she asked. The young woman was unable to answer; she pressed the hand of the pianist convulsively.

Mademoiselle Reisz perceived her agitation and even her tears. She patted her again upon the shoulder as she said:

"You are the only one worth playing for. Those others? Bah!" and she went shuffling and sidling on down the gallery toward her room.

But she was mistaken about "those others." Her playing had aroused a fever of enthusiasm. "What passion!" "What an artist!" "I have always said no one could play Chopin like Mademoiselle Reisz!" "That last prelude! Bon Dieu! It shakes a man!"

It was growing late, and there was a general disposition to disband. But some one, perhaps it was Robert, thought of a bath at that mystic hour and under that mystic moon.

X

At all events Robert proposed it, and there was not a dissenting voice. There was not one but was ready to follow when he led the way. He did not lead the way, however, he directed the way; and he himself loitered behind with the lovers, who had betrayed a disposition to linger and hold themselves apart. He walked between them, whether with malicious or mischievous intent was not wholly clear, even to himself.

The Pontelliers and Ratignolles walked ahead; the women leaning upon the arms of their husbands. Edna could hear Robert's voice behind them, and could sometimes hear what he said. She wondered why he did not join them. It was unlike him not to. Of late he had sometimes held away from her for an entire day, redoubling his devotion upon the next and the next, as though to make up for hours that had been lost. She missed him the days when some pretext served to take him away from her, just as one misses the sun on a cloudy day without having thought much about the sun when it was shining.

The people walked in little groups toward the beach. They talked and laughed; some of them sang. There was a band playing down at Klein's hotel, and the strains reached them faintly, tempered by the distance. There were strange, rare odors abroad—a tangle of the sea smell and of weeds and damp, new-plowed earth, mingled with the heavy perfume of a field of white blossoms somewhere near. But the night sat lightly upon the sea and the land. There was no weight of darkness; there were no shadows. The white light of the moon had fallen upon the world like the mystery and the softness of sleep.

Most of them walked into the water as though into a native element. The sea was quiet now, and swelled lazily in broad billows that melted into one another and did not break except upon the beach in little foamy crests that coiled back like slow, white serpents.

Edna had attempted all summer to learn to swim. She had received instructions from both the men and women; in some instances from the children. Robert had pursued a system of lessons almost daily; and he was nearly at the point of discouragement in realizing the futility of his efforts. A certain ungovernable dread hung about her when in the water, unless there was a hand near by that might reach out and reassure her.

But that night she was like the little tottering, stumbling, clutching child, who of a sudden realizes its powers, and walks for the first time alone, boldly and with over-confidence. She could have shouted for joy. She did shout for joy, as with a sweeping stroke or two she lifted her body to the surface of the water.

A feeling of exultation overtook her, as if some power of significant import had been given her to control the working of her body and her soul. She grew daring and reckless, overestimating her strength. She wanted to swim far out, where no woman had swum before.

Her unlooked-for achievement was the subject of wonder, applause, and admiration. Each one congratulated himself that his special teachings had accomplished this desired end.

"How easy it is!" she thought. "It is nothing," she said aloud; "why did I not discover before that it was nothing. Think of the time I have lost splashing about like a baby!" She would not join the groups in their sports and bouts, but intoxicated with her newly conquered power, she swam out alone.

She turned her face seaward to gather in an impression of space and solitude, which the vast expanse of water, meeting and melting with the moonlit sky, conveyed to her excited fancy. As she swam she seemed to be reaching out for the unlimited in which to lose herself.

Once she turned and looked toward the shore, toward the people she had left there. She had not gone any great distance—that is, what would have been a great distance for an experienced swimmer. But to her un-accustomed vision the stretch of water behind her assumed the aspect of a barrier which her unaided strength would never be able to overcome.

A quick vision of death smote her soul, and for a second of time appalled and enfeebled her senses. But by an effort she rallied her staggering faculties and managed to regain the land.

She made no mention of her encounter with death and her flash of terror, except to say to her husband, "I thought I should have perished out there alone."

"You were not so very far, my dear; I was watching you," he told her.

Edna went at once to the bath-house, and she had put on her dry clothes and was ready to return home before the others had left the water. She started to walk away alone. They all called to her and shouted to her. She waved a dissenting hand, and went on, paying no further heed to their renewed cries which sought to detain her.

"Sometimes I am tempted to think that Mrs. Pontellier is capricious," said Madame Lebrun, who was amusing herself immensely and feared that Edna's abrupt departure might put an end to the pleasure.

"I know she is," assented Mr. Pontellier; "sometimes, not often."

Edna had not traversed a quarter of the distance on her way home before she was overtaken by Robert.

"Did you think I was afraid?" she asked him, without a shade of annoyance.

"No; I knew you weren't afraid."

"Then why did you come? Why didn't you stay out there with the others?"

"I never thought of it."

"Thought of what?"

"Of anything. What difference does it make?"

"I'm very tired," she uttered, complainingly.

"I know you are."

"You don't know anything about it. Why should you know? I never was so exhausted in my life. But it isn't unpleasant. A thousand emotions have swept through me to-night. I don't comprehend half of them. Don't mind what I'm saying; I am just thinking aloud. I wonder if I shall ever be stirred again as Mademoiselle Reisz's playing moved me to-night. I wonder if any night on earth will ever again be like this one. It is like a night in a dream. The people about me are like some uncanny, half-human beings. There must be spirits abroad to-night."

"There are," whispered Robert. "Didn't you know this was the twenty-eighth of August?"

"The twenty-eighth of August?"

"Yes. On the twenty-eighth of August, at the hour of midnight, and if the moon is shining—the moon must be shining—a spirit that has haunted these shores for ages rises up from the Gulf. With its own penetrating vision the spirit seeks some one mortal worthy to hold him company, worthy of being exalted for a few hours into realms of the semi-celestials. His search has always hitherto been fruitless, and he has sunk back, disheartened, into the sea. But to-night he found Mrs. Pontellier. Perhaps he will never wholly release her from the spell. Perhaps she will never again suffer a poor, unworthy earthling to walk in the shadow of her divine presence."

"Don't banter me," she said, wounded at what appeared to be his flippancy. He did not mind the entreaty, but the tone with its delicate note of pathos was like a reproach. He could not explain; he could not tell her that he had penetrated her mood and understood. He said nothing except to offer her his arm, for, by her own admission, she was exhausted. She had been walking alone with her arms hanging limp, letting her white skirts trail along the dewy path. She took his arm, but she did not lean upon it. She let her hand lie listlessly, as though her thoughts were elsewhere—somewhere in advance of her body, and she was striving to overtake them.

Robert assisted her into the hammock which swung from the post before her door out to the trunk of a tree.

"Will you stay out here and wait for Mr. Pontellier?" he asked.

"I'll stay out here. Good-night."

"Shall I get you a pillow?"

"There's one here," she said, feeling about, for they were in the shadow.

"It must be soiled; the children have been tumbling it about."

"No matter." And having discovered the pillow, she adjusted it beneath her head. She extended herself in the hammock with a deep breath of relief. She was not a supercilious or an over-dainty woman. She was not much given to reclining in the hammock, and when she did so it was with no cat-like suggestion of voluptuous ease, but with a beneficent repose which seemed to invade her whole body.

"Shall I stay with you till Mr. Pontellier comes?" asked Robert, seating himself on the outer edge of one of the steps and taking hold of the hammock rope which was fastened to the post.

"If you wish. Don't swing the hammock. Will you get my white shawl which I left on the window-sill over at the house?"

"Are you chilly?"

"No; but I shall be presently."

"Presently?" he laughed. "Do you know what time it is? How long are you going to stay out here?"

"I don't know. Will you get the shawl?"

"Of course I will," he said, rising. He went over to the house, walking along the grass. She watched his figure pass in and out of the strips of moonlight. It was past midnight. It was very quiet.

When he returned with the shawl she took it and kept it in her hand. She did not put it around her.

"Did you say I should stay till Mr. Pontellier came back?"

"I said you might if you wished to."

He seated himself again and rolled a cigarette, which he smoked in silence. Neither did Mrs. Pontellier speak. No multitude of words could have been more significant than those moments of silence, or more pregnant with the first-felt throbbings of desire.

When the voices of the bathers were heard approaching, Robert said good-night. She did not answer him. He thought she was asleep. Again she watched his figure pass in and out of the strips of moonlight as he walked away.

XI

"What are you doing out here, Edna? I thought I should find you in bed," said her husband, when he discovered her lying there. He had walked up with Madame Lebrun and left her at the house. His wife did not reply.

"Are you asleep?" he asked, bending down close to look at her.

"No." Her eyes gleamed bright and intense, with no sleepy shadows, as they looked into his.

"Do you know it is past one o'clock? Come on," and he mounted the steps and went into their room.

"Edna!" called Mr. Pontellier from within, after a few moments had gone by.

"Don't wait for me," she answered. He thrust his head through the door.

"You will take cold out there," he said, irritably. "What folly is this? Why don't you come in?"

"It isn't cold; I have my shawl."

"The mosquitoes will devour you."

"There are no mosquitoes."

She heard him moving about the room; every sound indicating impatience and irritation. Another time she would have gone in at his request. She would, through habit, have yielded to his desire; not with any sense of submission or obedience to his compelling wishes, but unthinkingly, as we walk, move, sit, stand, go through the daily treadmill of the life which has been portioned out to us.

"Edna, dear, are you not coming in soon?" he asked again, this time fondly, with a note of entreaty.

"No; I am going to stay out here."

"This is more than folly," he blurted out. "I can't permit you to stay out there all night. You must come in the house instantly."

With a writhing motion she settled herself more securely in the hammock. She perceived that her will had blazed up, stubborn and resistant. She could not at that moment have done other than denied and resisted. She wondered if her husband had ever spoken to her like that before, and if she had submitted to his command. Of course she had; she remembered that she had. But she could not realize why or how she should have yielded, feeling as she then did.

"Léonce, go to bed," she said. "I mean to stay out here. I don't wish to go in, and I don't intend to. Don't speak to me like that again; I shall not answer you."

Mr. Pontellier had prepared for bed, but he slipped on an extra garment. He opened a bottle of wine, of which he kept a small and select supply in a buffet of his own. He drank a glass of the wine and went out on the gallery and offered a glass to his wife. She did not wish any. He drew up the rocker, hoisted his slippered feet on the rail, and proceeded to smoke a cigar. He smoked two cigars; then he went inside and drank another glass of wine. Mrs. Pontellier again declined to accept a glass when it was offered to her. Mr. Pontellier once more seated himself with elevated feet, and after a reasonable interval of time smoked some more cigars.

Edna began to feel like one who awakens gradually out of a dream, a delicious, grotesque, impossible dream, to feel again the realities pressing into her soul. The physical need for sleep began to overtake her; the exuberance which had sustained and exalted her spirit left her helpless and yielding to the conditions which crowded her in.

The stillest hour of the night had come, the hour before dawn, when the world seems to hold its breath. The moon hung low, and had turned from silver to copper in the sleeping sky. The old owl no longer hooted, and the water-oaks had ceased to moan as they bent their heads.

Edna arose, cramped from lying so long and still in the hammock. She tottered up the steps, clutching feebly at the post before passing into the house.

"Are you coming in, Léonce?" she asked, turning her face toward her husband.

"Yes, dear," he answered, with a glance following a misty puff of smoke. "Just as soon as I have finished my cigar."

XII

She slept but a few hours. They were troubled and feverish hours, disturbed with dreams that were intangible, that eluded her, leaving only an impression upon her half-awakened senses of something unattainable. She was up and dressed in the cool of the early morning. The air was invigorating and steadied somewhat her faculties. However, she was not seeking refreshment or help from any source, either external or from within. She was blindly following whatever impulse moved her, as if she had placed herself in alien hands for direction, and freed her soul of responsibility.

Most of the people at that early hour were still in bed and asleep. A few, who intended to go over to the *Chênière* for mass, were moving about. The lovers, who had laid their plans the night before, were already strolling toward the wharf. The lady in black, with her Sunday prayer-book, velvet and gold-clasped, and her Sunday silver beads, was following them at no great distance. Old Monsieur Farival was up, and was more than half inclined to do anything that suggested itself. He put on his big straw hat, and taking his umbrella from the stand in the hall, followed the lady in black, never overtaking her.

The little negro girl who worked Madame Lebrun's sewing-machine was sweeping the galleries with long, absent-minded strokes of the broom. Edna sent her up into the house to awaken Robert.

"Tell him I am going to the *Chênière*. The boat is ready; tell him to hurry."

He had soon joined her. She had never sent for him before. She had never asked for him. She had never seemed to want him before. She did not appear conscious that she had done anything unusual in commanding his presence. He was apparently equally unconscious of anything extraordinary in the situation. But his face was suffused with a quiet glow when he met her.

They went together back to the kitchen to drink coffee. There was no time to wait for any nicety of service. They stood outside the window and the cook passed them their coffee and a roll, which they drank and ate from the window-sill. Edna said it tasted good. She had not thought of coffee nor of anything. He told her he had often noticed that she lacked forethought.

"Wasn't it enough to think of going to the *Chênière* and waking you up?" she laughed. "Do I have to think of everything?—as Léonce says when he's in a bad humor. I don't blame him; he'd never be in a bad humor if it weren't for me."

They took a short cut across the sands. At a distance they could see the curious procession moving toward the wharf—the lovers, shoulder to shoulder, creeping; the lady in black, gaining steadily upon them; old Monsieur Farival, losing ground inch by inch, and a young barefooted Spanish girl, with a red kerchief on her head and a basket on her arm, bringing up the rear.

Robert knew the girl, and he talked to her a little in the boat. No one present understood what they said. Her name was Mariequita. She had a round, sly, piquant face and pretty black eyes. Her hands were small, and she kept them folded over the handle of her basket. Her feet were broad and coarse. She did not strive to hide them. Edna looked at her feet, and noticed the sand and slime between her brown toes.

Beaudelet grumbled because Mariequita was there, taking up so much room. In reality he was annoyed at having old Monsieur Farival, who considered himself the better sailor of the two. But he would not quarrel with so old a man as Monsieur Farival, so he quarreled with Mariequita. The girl was deprecatory at one moment, appealing to Robert. She was saucy the next, moving her head up and down, making "eyes" at Robert and making "mouths" at Beaudelet.

The lovers were all alone. They saw nothing, they heard nothing. The lady in black was counting her beads for the third time. Old Monsieur Farival talked incessantly of what he knew about handling a boat, and of what Beaudelet did not know on the same subject.

Edna liked it all. She looked Mariequita up and down, from her ugly brown toes to her pretty black eyes, and back again.

"Why does she look at me like that?" inquired the girl of Robert.

"Maybe she thinks you are pretty. Shall I ask her?"

"No. Is she your sweetheart?"

"She's a married lady, and has two children."

"Oh! well! Francisco ran away with Sylvano's wife, who had four children. They took all his money and one of the children and stole his boat."

"Shut up!"

"Does she understand?"

"Oh, hush!"

"Are those two married over there—leaning on each other?"

"Of course not," laughed Robert.

"Of course not," echoed Mariequita, with a serious, confirmatory bob of the head.

The sun was high up and beginning to bite. The swift breeze seemed to Edna to bury the sting of it into the pores of her face and hands. Robert held his umbrella over her.

As they went cutting sidewise through the water, the sails bellied taut, with the wind filling and overflowing them. Old Monsieur Farival laughed sardonically at something as he looked at the sails, and Beaudelet swore at the old man under his breath.

Sailing across the bay to the *Chênière Caminada*, Edna felt as if she were being borne away from some anchorage which had held her fast, whose chains had been loosening—had snapped the night before when the mystic spirit was abroad, leaving her free to drift whithersoever she chose to set her sails. Robert spoke to her incessantly; he no longer noticed Mariequita. The girl had shrimps in her bamboo basket. They were covered with Spanish moss. She beat the moss down impatiently, and muttered to herself sullenly.

"Let us go to Grande Terre to-morrow?" said Robert in a low voice.

"What shall we do there?"

"Climb up the hill to the old fort and look at the little wriggling gold snakes, and watch the lizards sun themselves."

She gazed away toward Grande Terre and thought she would like to be alone there with Robert, in the sun, listening to the ocean's roar and watching the slimy lizards writhe in and out among the ruins of the old fort.

"And the next day or the next we can sail to the Bayou Brulow," he went on.

"What shall we do there?"

"Anything—cast bait for fish."

"No; we'll go back to Grande Terre. Let the fish alone."

"We'll go wherever you like," he said. "I'll have Tonie come over and help me patch and trim my boat. We shall not need Beaudelet nor any one. Are you afraid of the pirogue?"

"Oh, no."

"Then I'll take you some night in the pirogue when the moon shines. Maybe your Gulf spirit will whisper to you in which of these islands the treasures are hidden—direct you to the very spot, perhaps."

"And in a day we should be rich!" she laughed. "I'd give it all to you, the pirate gold and every bit of treasure we could dig up. I think you would know how to spend it. Pirate gold isn't a thing to be hoarded or utilized. It is something to squander and throw to the four winds, for the fun of seeing the golden specks fly."

"We'd share it, and scatter it together," he said. His face flushed.

They all went together up to the quaint little Gothic church of Our Lady of Lourdes, gleaming all brown and yellow with paint in the sun's glare.

Only Beaudelet remained behind, tinkering at his boat, and Marie-quita walked away with her basket of shrimps, casting a look of childish ill-humor and reproach at Robert from the corner of her eye.

XIII

A feeling of oppression and drowsiness overcame Edna during the service. Her head began to ache, and the lights on the altar swayed before her eyes. Another time she might have made an effort to regain her composure; but her one thought was to quit the stifling atmosphere of the church and reach the open air. She arose, climbing over Robert's feet with a muttered apology. Old Monsieur Farival, flurried, curious, stood up, but upon seeing that Robert had followed Mrs. Pontellier, he sank back into his seat. He whispered an anxious inquiry of the lady in black, who did not notice him or reply, but kept her eyes fastened upon the pages of her velvet prayer-book.

"I felt giddy and almost overcome," Edna said, lifting her hands instinctively to her head and pushing her straw hat up from her forehead.

"I couldn't have stayed through the service." They were outside in the shadow of the church. Robert was full of solicitude.

"It was folly to have thought of going in the first place, let alone staying. Come over to Madame Antoine's; you can rest there." He took her arm and led her away, looking anxiously and continuously down into her face.

How still it was, with only the voice of the sea whispering through the reeds that grew in the salt-water pools! The long line of little gray, weather-beaten houses nestled peacefully among the orange trees. It must always have been God's day on that low, drowsy island, Edna thought. They stopped, leaning over a jagged fence made of sea-drift, to ask for water. A youth, a mild-faced Acadian, was drawing water from the cistern, which was nothing more than a rusty buoy, with an opening on one side, sunk in the ground. The water which the youth handed to them in a tin pail was not cold to taste, but it was cool to her heated face, and it greatly revived and refreshed her.

Madame Antoine's cot was at the far end of the village. She welcomed them with all the native hospitality, as she would have opened her door to let the sunlight in. She was fat, and walked heavily and clumsily across the floor. She could speak no English, but when Robert made her understand that the lady who accompanied him was ill and desired to rest, she was all eagerness to make Edna feel at home and to dispose of her comfortably.

The whole place was immaculately clean, and the big, four-posted bed, snow-white, invited one to repose. It stood in a small side room which looked out across a narrow grass plot toward the shed, where there was a disabled boat lying keel upward.

Madame Antoine had not gone to mass. Her son Tonie had, but she supposed he would soon be back, and she invited Robert to be seated and wait for him. But he went and sat outside the door and smoked. Madame Antoine busied herself in the large front room preparing dinner. She was boiling mullets over a few red coals in the huge fireplace.

Edna, left alone in the little side room, loosened her clothes, removing the greater part of them. She bathed her face, her neck and arms in the basin that stood between the windows. She took off her shoes and stockings and stretched herself in the very center of the high, white bed. How luxurious it felt to rest thus in a strange, quaint bed, with its sweet country odor of laurel lingering about the sheets and mattress! She stretched her strong limbs that ached a little. She ran her fingers through her loosened hair for a while. She looked at her round arms as she held them straight up and rubbed them one after the other, observing closely, as if it were something she saw for the first time, the fine, firm quality and texture of her flesh. She clasped her hands easily above her head, and it was thus she fell asleep.

She slept lightly at first, half awake and drowsily attentive to the things about her. She could hear Madame Antoine's heavy, scraping tread as she walked back and forth on the sanded floor. Some chickens were clucking outside the windows, scratching for bits of gravel in the grass. Later she half heard the voices of Robert and Tonie talking under the shed. She did not stir. Even her eyelids rested numb and heavily over her sleepy eyes. The voices went on—Tonie's slow, Acadian drawl, Robert's quick, soft, smooth French. She understood French imperfectly unless directly addressed, and the voices were only part of the other drowsy, muffled sounds lulling her senses.

When Edna awoke it was with the conviction that she had slept long and soundly. The voices were hushed under the shed. Madame Antoine's step was no longer to be heard in the adjoining room. Even the chickens had gone elsewhere to scratch and cluck. The mosquito bar was drawn over her; the old woman had come in while she slept and let down the bar. Edna arose quietly from the bed, and looking between the curtains of the window, she saw by the slanting rays of the sun that the afternoon was far advanced. Robert was out there under the shed, reclining in the shade against the sloping keel of the overturned boat. He was reading from a book. Tonie was no longer with him. She wondered what had become of the rest of the party. She peeped out at him two or three times as she stood washing herself in the little basin between the windows.

Madame Antoine had laid some coarse, clean towels upon a chair, and had placed a box of *poudre de riz* within easy reach. Edna dabbed the powder upon her nose and cheeks as she looked at herself closely in the little distorted mirror which hung on the wall above the basin. Her eyes were bright and wide awake and her face glowed.

When she had completed her toilet she walked into the adjoining room. She was very hungry. No one was there. But there was a cloth spread upon the table that stood against the wall, and a cover was laid for one, with a crusty brown loaf and a bottle of wine beside the plate. Edna bit a piece from the brown loaf, tearing it with her strong, white teeth. She poured some of the wine into the glass and drank it down. Then she went softly out of doors, and plucking an orange from the low-hanging bough of a tree, threw it at Robert, who did not know she was awake and up.

An illumination broke over his whole face when he saw her and joined her under the orange tree.

"How many years have I slept?" she inquired. "The whole island seems changed. A new race of beings must have sprung up, leaving only you and me as past relics. How many ages ago did Madame Antoine and Tonie die? and when did our people from Grand Isle disappear from the earth?"

He familiarly adjusted a ruffle upon her shoulder.

"You have slept precisely one hundred years. I was left here to guard your slumbers; and for one hundred years I have been out under the shed reading a book. The only evil I couldn't prevent was to keep a broiled fowl from drying up."

"If it has turned to stone, still will I eat it," said Edna, moving with him into the house. "But really, what has become of Monsieur Farival and the others?"

"Gone hours ago. When they found that you were sleeping they thought it best not to awake you. Any way, I wouldn't have let them. What was I here for?"

"I wonder if Léonce will be uneasy!" she speculated, as she seated herself at table.

"Of course not; he knows you are with me," Robert replied, as he busied himself among sundry pans and covered dishes which had been left standing on the hearth.

"Where are Madame Antoine and her son?" asked Edna.

"Gone to Vespers, and to visit some friends, I believe. I am to take you back in Tonie's boat whenever you are ready to go."

He stirred the smoldering ashes till the broiled fowl began to sizzle afresh. He served her with no mean repast, dripping the coffee anew and sharing it with her. Madame Antoine had cooked little else than the mullets, but while Edna slept Robert had foraged the island. He was childishly gratified to discover her appetite, and to see the relish with which she ate the food which he had procured for her.

"Shall we go right away?" she asked, after draining her glass and brushing together the crumbs of the crusty loaf.

"The sun isn't as low as it will be in two hours," he answered.

"The sun will be gone in two hours."

"Well, let it go; who cares!"

They waited a good while under the orange trees, till Madame Antoine came back, panting, waddling, with a thousand apologies to explain her absence. Tonie did not dare to return. He was shy, and would not willingly face any woman except his mother.

It was very pleasant to stay there under the orange trees, while the sun dipped lower and lower, turning the western sky to flaming copper and gold. The shadows lengthened and crept out like stealthy, grotesque monsters across the grass.

Edna and Robert both sat upon the ground—that is, he lay upon the ground beside her, occasionally picking at the hem of her muslin gown.

Madame Antoine seated her fat body, broad and squat, upon a bench beside the door. She had been talking all the afternoon, and had wound herself up to the story-telling pitch.

And what stories she told them! But twice in her life she had left the *Chênière Caminada,* and then for the briefest span. All her years she had squatted and waddled there upon the island, gathering legends of the Baratarians and the sea. The night came on, with the moon to lighten it. Edna could hear the whispering voices of dead men and the click of muffled gold.

When she and Robert stepped into Tonie's boat, with the red lateen sail, misty spirit forms were prowling in the shadows and among the reeds, and upon the water were phantom ships, speeding to cover.

XIV

The youngest boy, Etienne, had been very naughty, Madame Ratignolle said, as she delivered him into the hands of his mother. He had been unwilling to go to bed and had made a scene; whereupon she had taken charge of him and pacified him as well as she could. Raoul had been in bed and asleep for two hours.

The youngster was in his long white nightgown, that kept tripping him up as Madame Ratignolle led him along by the hand. With the other chubby fist he rubbed his eyes, which were heavy with sleep and ill humor. Edna took him in her arms, and seating herself in the rocker, began to coddle and caress him, calling him all manner of tender names, soothing him to sleep.

It was not more than nine o'clock. No one had yet gone to bed but the children.

Léonce had been very uneasy at first, Madame Ratignolle said, and had wanted to start at once for the *Chênière*. But Monsieur Farival had assured him that his wife was only overcome with sleep and fatigue, that Tonie would bring her safely back later in the day; and he had thus been dissuaded from crossing the bay. He had gone over to Klein's, looking up some cotton broker whom he wished to see in regard to securities, exchanges, stocks, bonds, or something of the sort, Madame Ratignolle did not remember what. He said he would not remain away late. She herself was suffering from heat and oppression, she said. She carried a bottle of salts and a large fan. She would not consent to remain with Edna, for Monsieur Ratignolle was alone, and he detested above all things to be left alone.

When Etienne had fallen asleep Edna bore him into the back room, and Robert went and lifted the mosquito bar that she might lay the child comfortably in his bed. The quadroon had vanished. When they emerged from the cottage Robert bade Edna good-night.

"Do you know we have been together the whole livelong day, Robert —since early this morning?" she said at parting.

"All but the hundred years when you were sleeping. Good-night."

He pressed her hand and went away in the direction of the beach. He did not join any of the others, but walked alone toward the Gulf.

Edna stayed outside, awaiting her husband's return. She had no desire to sleep or to retire; nor did she feel like going over to sit with the Ratignolles, or to join Madame Lebrun and a group whose animated voices reached her as they sat in conversation before the house. She let her mind wander back over her stay at Grand Isle; and she tried to discover wherein this summer had been different from any and every other summer of her life. She could only realize that she herself—her present self—was in some way different from the other self. That she was seeing with different eyes and making the acquaintance of new conditions in herself that colored and changed her environment, she did not yet suspect.

She wondered why Robert had gone away and left her. It did not occur to her to think he might have grown tired of being with her the livelong day. She was not tired, and she felt that he was not. She regretted that he had gone. It was so much more natural to have him stay when he was not absolutely required to leave her.

As Edna waited for her husband she sang low a little song that Robert had sung as they crossed the bay. It began with "Ah! *Si tu savais,*" and every verse ended with "*si tu savais.*"

Robert's voice was not pretentious. It was musical and true. The voice, the notes, the whole refrain haunted her memory.

XV

When Edna entered the dining-room one evening a little late, as was her habit, an unusually animated conversation seemed to be going on. Several persons were talking at once, and Victor's voice was predominating, even over that of his mother. Edna had returned late from her bath, had dressed in some haste, and her face was flushed. Her head, set off by her dainty white gown, suggested a rich, rare blossom. She took her seat at table between old Monsieur Farival and Madame Ratignolle.

As she seated herself and was about to begin to eat her soup, which had been served when she entered the room, several persons informed her simultaneously that Robert was going to Mexico. She laid her spoon down and looked about her bewildered. He had been with her, reading to her all the morning, and had never even mentioned such a place as Mexico. She had not seen him during the afternoon; she had heard some one say he was at the house, upstairs with his mother. This she had thought nothing of, though she was surprised when he did not join her later in the afternoon, when she went down to the beach.

She looked across at him, where he sat beside Madame Lebrun, who presided. Edna's face was a blank picture of bewilderment, which she never thought of disguising. He lifted his eyebrows with the pretext of a smile as he returned her glance. He looked embarrassed and uneasy.

"When is he going?" she asked of everybody in general, as if Robert were not there to answer for himself.

"To-night!" "This very evening!" "Did you ever!" "What possesses him!" were some of the replies she gathered, uttered simultaneously in French and English.

"Impossible!" she exclaimed. "How can a person start off from Grand Isle to Mexico at a moment's notice, as if he were going over to Klein's or to the wharf or down to the beach?"

"I said all along I was going to Mexico; I've been saying so for years!"

cried Robert, in an excited and irritable tone, with the air of a man defending himself against a swarm of stinging insects.

Madame Lebrun knocked on the table with her knife handle.

"Please let Robert explain why he is going, and why he is going to-night," she called out. "Really, this table is getting to be more and more like Bedlam every day, with everybody talking at once. Sometimes—I hope God will forgive me—but positively, sometimes I wish Victor would lose the power of speech."

Victor laughed sardonically as he thanked his mother for her holy wish, of which he failed to see the benefit to anybody, except that it might afford her a more ample opportunity and license to talk herself.

Monsieur Farival thought that Victor should have been taken out in mid-ocean in his earliest youth and drowned. Victor thought there would be more logic in thus disposing of old people with an established claim for making themselves universally obnoxious. Madame Lebrun grew a trifle hysterical; Robert called his brother some sharp, hard names.

"There's nothing much to explain, mother," he said; though he explained, nevertheless—looking chiefly at Edna—that he could only meet the gentleman whom he intended to join at Vera Cruz by taking such and such a steamer, which left New Orleans on such a day; that Beaudelet was going out with his lugger-load of vegetables that night, which gave him an opportunity of reaching the city and making his vessel in time.

"But when did you make up your mind to all this?" demanded Monsieur Farival.

"This afternoon," returned Robert, with a shade of annoyance.

"At what time this afternoon?" persisted the old gentleman, with nagging determination, as if he were cross-questioning a criminal in a court of justice.

"At four o'clock this afternoon, Monsieur Farival," Robert replied, in a high voice and with a lofty air, which reminded Edna of some gentleman on the stage.

She had forced herself to eat most of her soup, and now she was picking the flaky bits of a *court bouillon* with her fork.

The lovers were profiting by the general conversation on Mexico to speak in whispers of matters which they rightly considered were interesting to no one but themselves. The lady in black had once received a pair of prayer-beads of curious workmanship from Mexico, with very special indulgence attached to them, but she had never been able to ascertain whether the indulgence extended outside the Mexican border.

Father Fochel of the Cathedral had attempted to explain it; but he had not done so to her satisfaction. And she begged that Robert would interest himself, and discover, if possible, whether she was entitled to the indulgence accompanying the remarkably curious Mexican prayer-beads.

Madame Ratignolle hoped that Robert would exercise extreme caution in dealing with the Mexicans, who, she considered, were a treacherous people, unscrupulous and revengeful. She trusted she did them no injustice in thus condemning them as a race. She had known personally but one Mexican, who made and sold excellent tamales, and whom she would have trusted implicitly, so soft-spoken was he. One day he was arrested for stabbing his wife. She never knew whether he had been hanged or not.

Victor had grown hilarious, and was attempting to tell an anecdote about a Mexican girl who served chocolate one winter in a restaurant in Dauphine Street. No one would listen to him but old Monsieur Farival, who went into convulsions over the droll story.

Edna wondered if they had all gone mad, to be talking and clamoring at that rate. She herself could think of nothing to say about Mexico or the Mexicans.

"At what time do you leave?" she asked Robert.

"At ten," he told her. "Beaudelet wants to wait for the moon."

"Are you all ready to go?"

"Quite ready. I shall only take a hand-bag, and shall pack my trunk in the city."

He turned to answer some question put to him by his mother, and Edna, having finished her black coffee, left the table.

She went directly to her room. The little cottage was close and stuffy after leaving the outer air. But she did not mind; there appeared to be a hundred different things demanding her attention indoors. She began to set the toilet-stand to rights, grumbling at the negligence of the quadroon, who was in the adjoining room putting the children to bed. She gathered together stray garments that were hanging on the backs of chairs, and put each where it belonged in closet or bureau drawer. She changed her gown for a more comfortable and commodious wrapper. She rearranged her hair, combing and brushing it with unusual energy. Then she went in and assisted the quadroon in getting the boys to bed.

They were very playful and inclined to talk—to do anything but lie quiet and go to sleep. Edna sent the quadroon away to her supper and told her she need not return. Then she sat and told the children a story.

Instead of soothing it excited them, and added to their wakefulness. She left them in heated argument, speculating about the conclusion of the tale which their mother promised to finish the following night.

The little black girl came in to say that Madame Lebrun would like to have Mrs. Pontellier go and sit with them over at the house till Mr. Robert went away. Edna returned answer that she had already undressed, that she did not feel quite well, but perhaps she would go over to the house later. She started to dress again, and got as far advanced as to remove her *peignoir*. But changing her mind once more she resumed the *peignoir*, and went outside and sat down before her door. She was over-heated and irritable, and fanned herself energetically for a while. Madame Ratignolle came down to discover what was the matter.

"All that noise and confusion at the table must have upset me," replied Edna, "and moreover, I hate shocks and surprises. The idea of Robert starting off in such a ridiculously sudden and dramatic way! As if it were a matter of life and death! Never saying a word about it all morning when he was with me."

"Yes," agreed Madame Ratignolle. "I think it was showing us all—you especially—very little consideration. It wouldn't have surprised me in any of the others; those Lebruns are all given to heroics. But I must say I should never have expected such a thing from Robert. Are you not coming down? Come on, dear; it doesn't look friendly."

"No," said Edna, a little sullenly. "I can't go to the trouble of dressing again; I don't feel like it."

"You needn't dress; you look all right; fasten a belt around your waist. Just look at me!"

"No," persisted Edna; "but you go on. Madame Lebrun might be offended if we both stayed away."

Madame Ratignolle kissed Edna good-night, and went away, being in truth rather desirous of joining in the general and animated conversation which was still in progress concerning Mexico and the Mexicans.

Somewhat later Robert came up, carrying his hand-bag.

"Aren't you feeling well?" he asked.

"Oh, well enough. Are you going right away?"

He lit a match and looked at his watch. "In twenty minutes," he said. The sudden and brief flare of the match emphasized the darkness for a while. He sat down upon a stool which the children had left out on the porch.

"Get a chair," said Edna.

"This will do," he replied. He put on his soft hat and nervously took it off again, and wiping his face with his handkerchief, complained of the heat.

"Take the fan," said Edna, offering it to him.

"Oh, no! Thank you. It does no good; you have to stop fanning some time, and feel all the more uncomfortable afterward."

"That's one of the ridiculous things which men always say. I have never known one to speak otherwise of fanning. How long will you be gone?"

"Forever, perhaps. I don't know. It depends upon a good many things."

"Well, in case it shouldn't be forever, how long will it be?"

"I don't know."

"This seems to me perfectly preposterous and uncalled for. I don't like it. I don't understand your motive for silence and mystery, never saying a word to me about it this morning." He remained silent, not offering to defend himself. He only said, after a moment:

"Don't part from me in an ill-humor. I never knew you to be out of patience with me before."

"I don't want to part in any ill-humor," she said. "But can't you understand? I've grown used to seeing you, to having you with me all the time, and your action seems unfriendly, even unkind. You don't even offer an excuse for it. Why, I was planning to be together, thinking of how pleasant it would be to see you in the city next winter."

"So was I," he blurted. "Perhaps that's the—" He stood up suddenly and held out his hand. "Good-by, my dear Mrs. Pontellier; good-by. You won't—I hope you won't completely forget me." She clung to his hand, striving to detain him.

"Write to me when you get there, won't you, Robert?" she entreated.

"I will, thank you. Good-by."

How unlike Robert! The merest acquaintance would have said something more emphatic than "I will, thank you; good-by," to such a request.

He had evidently already taken leave of the people over at the house, for he descended the steps and went to join Beaudelet, who was out there with an oar across his shoulder waiting for Robert. They walked away in the darkness. She could only hear Beaudelet's voice; Robert had apparently not even spoken a word of greeting to his companion.

Edna bit her handkerchief convulsively, striving to hold back and to hide, even from herself as she would have hidden from another, the emotion which was troubling—tearing—her. Her eyes were brimming with tears.

For the first time she recognized anew the symptoms of infatuation which she had felt incipiently as a child, as a girl in her earliest teens, and later as a young woman. The recognition did not lessen the reality, the poignancy of the revelation by any suggestion or promise of instability. The past was nothing to her; offered no lesson which she was willing to heed. The future was a mystery which she never attempted to penetrate. The present alone was significant; was hers, to torture her as it was doing then with the biting conviction that she had lost that which she had held, that she had been denied that which her impassioned, newly awakened being demanded.

XVI

"Do you miss your friend greatly?" asked Mademoiselle Reisz one morning as she came creeping up behind Edna, who had just left her cottage on her way to the beach. She spent much of her time in the water since she had acquired finally the art of swimming. As their stay at Grand Isle drew near its close, she felt that she could not give too much time to a diversion which afforded her the only real pleasurable moments that she knew. When Mademoiselle Reisz came and touched her upon the shoulder and spoke to her, the woman seemed to echo the thought which was ever in Edna's mind; or, better, the feeling which constantly possessed her.

Robert's going had some way taken the brightness, the color, the meaning out of everything. The conditions of her life were in no way changed, but her whole existence was dulled, like a faded garment which seems to be no longer worth wearing. She sought him everywhere—in others whom she induced to talk about him. She went up in the mornings to Madame Lebrun's room, braving the clatter of the old sewing-machine. She sat there and chatted at intervals as Robert had done. She gazed around the room at the pictures and photographs hanging upon the wall, and discovered in some corner an old family album, which she examined with the keenest interest, appealing to Madame Lebrun for enlightenment concerning the many figures and faces which she discovered between its pages.

There was a picture of Madame Lebrun with Robert as a baby,

seated in her lap, a round-faced infant with a fist in his mouth. The eyes alone in the baby suggested the man. And that was he also in kilts, at the age of five, wearing long curls and holding a whip in his hand. It made Edna laugh, and she laughed, too, at the portrait in his first long trousers; while another interested her, taken when he left for college, looking thin, long-faced, with eyes full of fire, ambition and great intentions. But there was no recent picture, none which suggested the Robert who had gone away five days ago, leaving a void and wilderness behind him.

"Oh, Robert stopped having his pictures taken when he had to pay for them himself! He found wiser use for his money, he says," explained Madame Lebrun. She had a letter from him, written before he left New Orleans. Edna wished to see the letter, and Madame Lebrun told her to look for it either on the table or the dresser, or perhaps it was on the mantelpiece.

The letter was on the bookshelf. It possessed the greatest interest and attraction for Edna; the envelope, its size and shape, the post-mark, the handwriting. She examined every detail of the outside before opening it. There were only a few lines, setting forth that he would leave the city that afternoon, that he had packed his trunk in good shape, that he was well, and sent her his love and begged to be affectionately remembered to all. There was no special message to Edna except a postscript saying that if Mrs. Pontellier desired to finish the book which he had been reading to her, his mother would find it in his room, among other books there on the table. Edna experienced a pang of jealousy because he had written to his mother rather than to her.

Every one seemed to take for granted that she missed him. Even her husband, when he came down the Saturday following Robert's departure, expressed regret that he had gone.

"How do you get on without him, Edna?" he asked.

"It's very dull without him," she admitted. Mr. Pontellier had seen Robert in the city, and Edna asked him a dozen questions or more. Where had they met? On Carondelet Street, in the morning. They had gone "in" and had a drink and a cigar together. What had they talked about? Chiefly about his prospects in Mexico, which Mr. Pontellier thought were promising. How did he look? How did he seem—grave, or gay, or how? Quite cheerful, and wholly taken up with the idea of his trip, which Mr. Pontellier found altogether natural in a young fellow about to seek fortune and adventure in a strange, queer country.

Edna tapped her foot impatiently, and wondered why the children persisted in playing in the sun when they might be under the trees. She went down and led them out of the sun, scolding the quadroon for not being more attentive.

It did not strike her as in the least grotesque that she should be making of Robert the object of conversation and leading her husband to speak of him. The sentiment which she entertained for Robert in no way resembled that which she felt for her husband, or had ever felt, or ever expected to feel. She had all her life long been accustomed to harbor thoughts and emotions which never voiced themselves. They had never taken the form of struggles. They belonged to her and were her own, and she entertained the conviction that she had a right to them and that they concerned no one but herself. Edna had once told Madame Ratignolle that she would never sacrifice herself for her children, or for any one. Then had followed a rather heated argument; the two women did not appear to understand each other or to be talking the same language. Edna tried to appease her friend, to explain.

"I would give up the unessential; I would give my money, I would give my life for my children; but I wouldn't give myself. I can't make it more clear; it's only something which I am beginning to comprehend, which is revealing itself to me."

"I don't know what you would call the essential, or what you mean by the unessential," said Madame Ratignolle, cheerfully; "but a woman who would give her life for her children could do no more than that— your Bible tells you so. I'm sure I couldn't do more than that."

"Oh, yes you could!" laughed Edna.

She was not surprised at Mademoiselle Reisz's question the morning that lady, following her to the beach, tapped her on the shoulder and asked if she did not greatly miss her young friend.

"Oh, good morning, Mademoiselle; is it you? Why, of course I miss Robert. Are you going down to bathe?"

"Why should I go down to bathe at the very end of the season when I haven't been in the surf all summer," replied the woman, disagreeably.

"I beg your pardon," offered Edna, in some embarrassment, for she should have remembered that Mademoiselle Reisz's avoidance of the water had furnished a theme for much pleasantry. Some among them thought it was on account of her false hair, or the dread of getting the violets wet, while others attributed it to the natural aversion for water sometimes believed to accompany the artistic temperament. Mademoiselle offered Edna some chocolates in a paper bag, which she took from her pocket, by way of showing that she bore no ill feeling. She habitually ate chocolates for their sustaining quality; they contained much nutriment in small compass, she said. They saved her from starvation, as Madame Lebrun's table was utterly impossible; and no one save so impertinent a woman as Madame Lebrun could think of offering such food to people and requiring them to pay for it.

"She must feel very lonely without her son," said Edna, desiring to change the subject. "Her favorite son, too. It must have been quite hard to let him go."

Mademoiselle laughed maliciously.

"Her favorite son! Oh, dear! Who could have been imposing such a tale upon you? Aline Lebrun lives for Victor, and for Victor alone. She has spoiled him into the worthless creature he is. She worships him and the ground he walks on. Robert is very well in a way, to give up all the money he can earn to the family, and keep the barest pittance for himself. Favorite son, indeed! I miss the poor fellow myself, my dear. I liked to see him and to hear him about the place—the only Lebrun who is worth a pinch of salt. He comes to see me often in the city. I like to play to him. That Victor! hanging would be too good for him. It's a wonder Robert hasn't beaten him to death long ago."

"I thought he had great patience with his brother," offered Edna, glad to be talking about Robert, no matter what was said.

"Oh! he thrashed him well enough a year or two ago," said Mademoiselle. "It was about a Spanish girl, whom Victor considered that he had some sort of claim upon. He met Robert one day talking to the girl, or walking with her, or bathing with her, or carrying her basket— I don't remember what;— and he became so insulting and abusive that Robert gave him a thrashing on the spot that has kept him comparatively in order for a good while. It's about time he was getting another."

"Was her name Mariequita?" asked Edna.

"Mariequita—yes, that was it; Mariequita. I had forgotten. Oh, she's a sly one, and a bad one, that Mariequita!"

Edna looked down at Mademoiselle Reisz and wondered how she could have listened to her venom so long. For some reason she felt depressed, almost unhappy. She had not intended to go into the water; but she donned her bathing suit, and left Mademoiselle alone, seated under the shade of the children's tent. The water was growing cooler as the season advanced. Edna plunged and swam about with an abandon that thrilled and invigorated her. She remained a long time in the water, half hoping that Mademoiselle Reisz would not wait for her.

But Mademoiselle waited. She was very amiable during the walk back, and raved much over Edna's appearance in her bathing suit. She talked about music. She hoped that Edna would go to see her in the city, and wrote her address with the stub of a pencil on a piece of card which she found in her pocket.

"When do you leave?" asked Edna.

"Next Monday; and you?"

"The following week," answered Edna, adding, "It has been a pleasant summer, hasn't it, Mademoiselle?"

"Well," agreed Mademoiselle Reisz, with a shrug, "rather pleasant, if it hadn't been for the mosquitoes and the Farival twins."

XVII

The Pontelliers possessed a very charming home on Esplanade Street in New Orleans. It was a large, double cottage, with a broad front veranda, whose round, fluted columns supported the sloping roof. The house was painted a dazzling white; the outside shutters, or jalousies, were green. In the yard, which was kept scrupulously neat, were flowers and plants of every description which flourishes in South Louisiana. Within doors the appointments were perfect after the conventional type. The softest carpets and rugs covered the floors; rich and tasteful draperies hung at doors and windows. There were paintings, selected with judgment and discrimination, upon the walls. The cut glass, the silver, the heavy damask which daily appeared upon the table were the envy of many women whose husbands were less generous than Mr. Pontellier.

Mr. Pontellier was very fond of walking about his house examining its various appointments and details, to see that nothing was amiss. He greatly valued his possessions, chiefly because they were his, and derived genuine pleasure from contemplating a painting, a statuette, a rare lace curtain—no matter what—after he had bought it and placed it among his household gods.

On Tuesday afternoons—Tuesday being Mrs. Pontellier's reception day—there was a constant stream of callers—women who came in carriages or in the street cars, or walked when the air was soft and distance permitted. A light-colored mulatto boy, in dress coat and bearing a diminutive silver tray for the reception of cards, admitted them. A maid, in white fluted cap, offered the callers liqueur, coffee, or chocolate, as they might desire. Mrs. Pontellier, attired in a handsome reception gown, remained in the drawing-room the entire afternoon receiving her visitors. Men sometimes called in the evening with their wives.

This had been the programme which Mrs. Pontellier had religiously followed since her marriage, six years before. Certain evenings during the week she and her husband attended the opera or sometimes the play.

Mr. Pontellier left his home in the mornings between nine and ten o'clock, and rarely returned before half-past six or seven in the evening —dinner being served at half-past seven.

He and his wife seated themselves at table one Tuesday evening, a few weeks after their return from Grand Isle. They were alone together. The boys were being put to bed; the patter of their bare, escaping feet could be heard occasionally, as well as the pursuing voice of the quadroon, lifted in mild protest and entreaty. Mrs. Pontellier did not wear her usual Tuesday reception gown; she was in ordinary house dress. Mr. Pontellier, who was observant about such things, noticed it, as he served the soup and handed it to the boy in waiting.

"Tired out, Edna? Whom did you have? Many callers?" he asked. He tasted his soup and began to season it with pepper, salt, vinegar, mustard—everything within reach.

"There were a good many," replied Edna, who was eating her soup with evident satisfaction. "I found their cards when I got home; I was out."

"Out!" exclaimed her husband, with something like genuine consternation in his voice as he laid down the vinegar cruet and looked at her through his glasses. "Why, what could have taken you out on Tuesday? What did you have to do?"

"Nothing. I simply felt like going out, and I went out."

"Well, I hope you left some suitable excuse," said her husband, somewhat appeased, as he added a dash of cayenne pepper to the soup.

"No, I left no excuse. I told Joe to say I was out, that was all."

"Why, my dear, I should think you'd understand by this time that people don't do such things; we've got to observe *les convenances* if we ever expect to get on and keep up with the procession. If you felt that you had to leave home this afternoon, you should have left some suitable explanation for your absence.

"This soup is really impossible; it's strange that woman hasn't learned yet to make a decent soup. Any free-lunch stand in town serves a better one. Was Mrs. Belthrop here?"

"Bring the tray with the cards, Joe. I don't remember who was here."

The boy retired and returned after a moment, bringing the tiny silver tray, which was covered with ladies' visiting cards. He handed it to Mrs. Pontellier.

"Give it to Mr. Pontellier," she said.

Joe offered the tray to Mr. Pontellier, and removed the soup.

Mr. Pontellier scanned the names of his wife's callers, reading some of them aloud, with comments as he read.

" 'The Misses Delasidas.' I worked a big deal in futures for their father this morning; nice girls; it's time they were getting married. 'Mrs. Belthrop.' I tell you what it is, Edna; you can't afford to snub Mrs. Belthrop. Why, Belthrop could buy and sell us ten times over. His business is worth a good, round sum to me. You'd better write her a note. 'Mrs. James Highcamp.' Hugh! the less you have to do with Mrs. Highcamp, the better. 'Madame Laforcé.' Came all the way from Carrolton, too, poor old soul. 'Miss Wiggs,' 'Mrs. Eleanor Boltons.' " He pushed the cards aside.

"Mercy!" exclaimed Edna, who had been fuming. "Why are you taking the thing so seriously and making such a fuss over it?"

"I'm not making any fuss over it. But it's just such seeming trifles that we've got to take seriously; such things count."

The fish was scorched. Mr. Pontellier would not touch it. Edna said she did not mind a little scorched taste. The roast was in some way not to his fancy, and he did not like the manner in which the vegetables were served.

"It seems to me," he said, "we spend money enough in this house to procure at least one meal a day which a man could eat and retain his self-respect."

"You used to think the cook was a treasure," returned Edna, indifferently.

"Perhaps she was when she first came; but cooks are only human. They need looking after, like any other class of persons that you employ. Suppose I didn't look after the clerks in my office, just let them run things their own way; they'd soon make a nice mess of me and my business."

"Where are you going?" asked Edna, seeing that her husband arose from table without having eaten a morsel except a taste of the highly-seasoned soup.

"I'm going to get my dinner at the club. Good night." He went into the hall, took his hat and stick from the stand, and left the house.

She was somewhat familiar with such scenes. They had often made her very unhappy. On a few previous occasions she had been completely deprived of any desire to finish her dinner. Sometimes she had gone into the kitchen to administer a tardy rebuke to the cook. Once she went to her room and studied the cookbook during an entire evening, finally writing out a menu for the week, which left her harassed with a feeling that, after all, she had accomplished no good that was worth the name.

But that evening Edna finished her dinner alone, with forced deliberation. Her face was flushed and her eyes flamed with some inward fire that lighted them. After finishing her dinner she went to her room, having instructed the boy to tell any other callers that she was indisposed.

It was a large, beautiful room, rich and picturesque in the soft, dim light which the maid had turned low. She went and stood at an open window and looked out upon the deep tangle of the garden below. All the mystery and witchery of the night seemed to have gathered there amid the perfumes and the dusky and tortuous outlines of flowers and foliage. She was seeking herself and finding herself in just such sweet, half-darkness which met her moods. But the voices were not soothing that came to her from the darkness and the sky above and the stars. They jeered and sounded mournful notes without promise, devoid even of hope. She turned back into the room and began to walk to and fro down its whole length, without stopping, without resting. She carried in her hands a thin handkerchief, which she tore into ribbons, rolled into a ball, and flung from her. Once she stopped, and taking off her wedding ring, flung it upon the carpet. When she saw it lying there, she stamped her heel upon it, striving to crush it. But her small boot heel did not make an indenture, not a mark upon the little glittering circlet.

In a sweeping passion she seized a glass vase from the table and flung it upon the tiles of the hearth. She wanted to destroy something. The crash and clatter were what she wanted to hear.

A maid, alarmed at the din of breaking glass, entered the room to discover what was the matter.

"A vase fell upon the hearth," said Edna. "Never mind; leave it till morning."

"Oh! you might get some of the glass in your feet, ma'am," insisted the young woman, picking up bits of the broken vase that were scattered upon the carpet. "And here's your ring, ma'am, under the chair."

Edna held out her hand, and taking the ring, slipped it upon her finger.

XVIII

The following morning Mr. Pontellier, upon leaving for his office, asked Edna if she would not meet him in town in order to look at some new fixtures for the library.

"I hardly think we need new fixtures, Léonce. Don't let us get anything new; you are too extravagant. I don't believe you ever think of saving or putting by."

"The way to become rich is to make money, my dear Edna, not to save it," he said. He regretted that she did not feel inclined to go with him and select new fixtures. He kissed her good-by, and told her she was not looking well and must take care of herself. She was unusually pale and very quiet.

She stood on the front veranda as he quitted the house, and absently picked a few sprays of jessamine that grew upon a trellis near by. She inhaled the odor of the blossoms and thrust them into the bosom of her white morning gown. The boys were dragging along the banquette a small "express wagon," which they had filled with blocks and sticks. The quadroon was following them with little quick steps, having assumed a fictitious animation and alacrity for the occasion. A fruit vender was crying his wares in the street.

Edna looked straight before her with a self-absorbed expression upon her face. She felt no interest in anything about her. The street, the children, the fruit vender, the flowers growing there under her eyes, were all part and parcel of an alien world which had suddenly become antagonistic.

She went back into the house. She had thought of speaking to the cook concerning her blunders of the previous night; but Mr. Pontellier had saved her that disagreeable mission, for which she was so poorly fitted. Mr. Pontellier's arguments were usually convincing with those whom he employed. He left home feeling quite sure that he and Edna would sit down that evening, and possibly a few subsequent evenings, to a dinner deserving of the name.

Edna spent an hour or two in looking over some of her old sketches. She could see their shortcomings and defects, which were glaring in her eyes. She tried to work a little, but found she was not in the humor. Finally she gathered together a few of the sketches—those which she considered the least discreditable; and she carried them with her when, a little later, she dressed and left the house. She looked handsome and distinguished in her street gown. The tan of the seashore had left her face, and her forehead was smooth, white, and polished beneath her heavy, yellow-brown hair. There were a few freckles on her face, and a small, dark mole near the under lip and one on the temple, half-hidden in her hair.

As Edna walked along the street she was thinking of Robert. She was still under the spell of her infatuation. She had tried to forget him, realizing the inutility of remembering. But the thought of him was like an obsession, ever pressing itself upon her. It was not that she dwelt upon details of their acquaintance, or recalled in any special or peculiar way his personality; it was his being, his existence, which dominated her thought, fading sometimes as if it would melt into the mist of the forgotten, reviving again with an intensity which filled her with an incomprehensible longing.

Edna was on her way to Madame Ratignolle's. Their intimacy, begun at Grand Isle, had not declined, and they had seen each other with some frequency since their return to the city. The Ratignolles lived at no great distance from Edna's home, on the corner of a side street, where Monsieur Ratignolle owned and conducted a drug store which enjoyed a steady and prosperous trade. His father had been in the business before him, and Monsieur Ratignolle stood well in the community and bore an enviable reputation for integrity and clear-headedness. His family lived in commodious apartments over the store, having an entrance on the side within the *porte cochère*. There was something which Edna thought very French, very foreign, about their whole manner of living. In the large and pleasant salon which extended across the width of the house, the Ratignolles entertained their friends once a fortnight with a *soirée musicale*, sometimes diversified by card-playing. There was a friend who played upon the 'cello. One brought his flute and another his violin, while there were some who sang and a number who performed upon the piano with various degrees of taste and agility. The Ratignolles' *soirées musicales* were widely known, and it was considered a privilege to be invited to them.

Edna found her friend engaged in assorting the clothes which had returned that morning from the laundry. She at once abandoned her occupation upon seeing Edna, who had been ushered without ceremony into her presence.

" 'Cité can do it as well as I; it is really her business," she explained to Edna, who apologized for interrupting her. And she summoned a young black woman, whom she instructed, in French, to be very careful in checking off the list which she handed her. She told her to notice particularly if a fine linen handkerchief of Monsieur Ratignolle's, which was missing last week, had been returned; and to be sure to set to one side such pieces as required mending and darning.

Then placing an arm around Edna's waist, she led her to the front of the house, to the salon, where it was cool and sweet with the odor of great roses that stood upon the hearth in jars.

Madame Ratignolle looked more beautiful than ever there at home, in a negligé which left her arms almost wholly bare and exposed the rich, melting curves of her white throat.

"Perhaps I shall be able to paint your picture some day," said Edna with a smile when they were seated. She produced the roll of sketches and started to unfold them. "I believe I ought to work again. I feel as if I wanted to be doing something. What do you think of them? Do you think it worth while to take it up again and study some more? I might study for a while with Laidpore."

She knew that Madame Ratignolle's opinion in such a matter would be next to valueless, that she herself had not alone decided, but determined; but she sought the words of praise and encouragement that would help her to put heart into her venture.

"Your talent is immense, dear!"

"Nonsense!" protested Edna, well pleased.

"Immense, I tell you," persisted Madame Ratignolle, surveying the sketches one by one, at close range, then holding them at arm's length, narrowing her eyes, and dropping her head on one side. "Surely, this Bavarian peasant is worthy of framing; and this basket of apples! never have I seen anything more lifelike. One might almost be tempted to reach out a hand and take one."

Edna could not control a feeling which bordered upon complacency at her friend's praise, even realizing, as she did, its true worth. She retained a few of the sketches, and gave all the rest to Madame Ratignolle, who appreciated the gift far beyond its value and proudly exhibited the pictures to her husband when he came up from the store a little later for his midday dinner.

Mr. Ratignolle was one of those men who are called the salt of the earth. His cheerfulness was unbounded, and it was matched by his goodness of heart, his broad charity, and common sense. He and his wife spoke English with an accent which was only discernible through its un-English emphasis and a certain carefulness and deliberation. Edna's husband spoke English with no accent whatever. The Ratignolles understood each other perfectly. If ever the fusion of two human beings into one has been accomplished on this sphere it was surely in their union.

As Edna seated herself at table with them she thought, "Better a dinner of herbs," though it did not take her long to discover that it was no dinner of herbs, but a delicious repast, simple, choice, and in every way satisfying.

Monsieur Ratignolle was delighted to see her, though he found her looking not so well as at Grand Isle, and he advised a tonic. He talked a good deal on various topics, a little politics, some city news and neighborhood gossip. He spoke with an animation and earnestness that gave an exaggerated importance to every syllable he uttered. His wife was keenly interested in everything he said, laying down her fork the better to listen, chiming in, taking the words out of his mouth.

Edna felt depressed rather than soothed after leaving them. The little glimpse of domestic harmony which had been offered her, gave her no regret, no longing. It was not a condition of life which fitted her, and she could see in it but an appalling and hopeless ennui. She was moved by a kind of commiseration for Madame Ratignolle,—a pity for that colorless existence which never uplifted its possessor beyond the region of blind contentment, in which no moment of anguish ever visited her soul, in which she would never have the taste of life's delirium. Edna vaguely wondered what she meant by "life's delirium." It had crossed her thought like some unsought, extraneous impression.

XIX

Edna could not help but think that it was very foolish, very childish, to have stamped upon her wedding ring and smashed the crystal vase upon the tiles. She was visited by no more outbursts, moving her to such futile expedients. She began to do as she liked and to feel as she liked.

She completely abandoned her Tuesdays at home, and did not return the visits of those who had called upon her. She made no ineffectual efforts to conduct her household *en bonne ménagère*, going and coming as it suited her fancy, and, so far as she was able, lending herself to any passing caprice.

Mr. Pontellier had been a rather courteous husband so long as he met a certain tacit submissiveness in his wife. But her new and unexpected line of conduct completely bewildered him. It shocked him. Then her absolute disregard for her duties as a wife angered him. When Mr. Pontellier became rude, Edna grew insolent. She had resolved never to take another step backward.

"It seems to me the utmost folly for a woman at the head of a household, and the mother of children, to spend in an atelier days which would be better employed contriving for the comfort of her family."

"I feel like painting," answered Edna. "Perhaps I shan't always feel like it."

"Then in God's name paint! but don't let the family go to the devil. There's Madame Ratignolle; because she keeps up her music, she doesn't let everything else go to chaos. And she's more of a musician than you are a painter."

"She isn't a musician, and I'm not a painter. It isn't on account of painting that I let things go."

"On account of what, then?"

"Oh! I don't know. Let me alone; you bother me."

It sometimes entered Mr. Pontellier's mind to wonder if his wife were not growing a little unbalanced mentally. He could see plainly that she was not herself. That is, he could not see that she was becoming herself and daily casting aside that fictitious self which we assume like a garment with which to appear before the world.

Her husband let her alone as she requested, and went away to his office. Edna went up to her atelier—a bright room in the top of the house. She was working with great energy and interest, without accomplishing anything, however, which satisfied her even in the smallest degree. For a time she had the whole household enrolled in the service of art. The boys posed for her. They thought it amusing at first, but the occupation soon lost its attractiveness when they discovered that it was not a game arranged especially for their entertainment. The quadroon sat for hours before Edna's palette, patient as a savage, while the house-maid took charge of the children, and the drawing-room went undusted. But the house-maid, too, served her term as model when Edna perceived that the young woman's back and shoulders were molded on classic lines, and that her hair, loosened from its confining cap, became an inspiration. While Edna worked she sometimes sang low the little air, *"Ah! si tu savais!"*

It moved her with recollections. She could hear again the ripple of the water, the flapping sail. She could see the glint of the moon upon the bay, and could feel the soft, gusty beating of the hot south wind. A subtle current of desire passed through her body, weakening her hold upon the brushes and making her eyes burn.

There were days when she was very happy without knowing why. She was happy to be alive and breathing, when her whole being seemed to be one with the sunlight, the color, the odors, the luxuriant warmth of some perfect Southern day. She liked then to wander alone into strange and unfamiliar places. She discovered many a sunny, sleepy corner, fashioned to dream in. And she found it good to dream and to be alone and unmolested.

There were days when she was unhappy, she did not know why,— when it did not seem worth while to be glad or sorry, to be alive or dead; when life appeared to her like a grotesque pandemonium and humanity like worms struggling blindly toward inevitable annihilation. She could not work on such a day, nor weave fancies to stir her pulses and warm her blood.

XX

It was during such a mood that Edna hunted up Mademoiselle Reisz. She had not forgotten the rather disagreeable impression left upon her by their last interview; but she nevertheless felt a desire to see her— above all, to listen while she played upon the piano. Quite early in the afternoon she started upon her quest for the pianist. Unfortunately she had mislaid or lost Mademoiselle Reisz's card, and looking up her address in the city directory, she found that the woman lived on Bienville Street, some distance away. The directory which fell into her hands was a year or more old, however, and upon reaching the number indicated, Edna discovered that the house was occupied by a respectable family of mulattoes who had *chambres garnies* to let. They had been living there for six months, and knew absolutely nothing of a Mademoiselle Reisz. In fact, they knew nothing of any of their neighbors; their lodgers were all

people of the highest distinction, they assured Edna. She did not linger
to discuss class distinctions with Madame Pouponne, but hastened to a
neighboring grocery store, feeling sure that Mademoiselle would have
left her address with the proprietor.

He knew Mademoiselle Reisz a good deal better than he wanted to
know her, he informed his questioner. In truth, he did not want to know
her at all, or anything concerning her—the most disagreeable and unpopular woman who ever lived in Bienville Street. He thanked heaven
she had left the neighborhood, and was equally thankful that he did not
know where she had gone.

Edna's desire to see Mademoiselle Reisz had increased tenfold since
these unlooked-for obstacles had arisen to thwart it. She was wondering
who could give her the information she sought, when it suddenly occurred
to her that Madame Lebrun would be the one most likely to do so. She
knew it was useless to ask Madame Ratignolle, who was on the most
distant terms with the musician, and preferred to know nothing concerning her. She had once been almost as emphatic in expressing herself
upon the subject as the corner grocer.

Edna knew that Madame Lebrun had returned to the city, for it was
the middle of November. And she also knew where the Lebruns lived, on
Chartres Street.

Their home from the outside looked like a prison, with iron bars before
the door and lower windows. The iron bars were a relic of the old *régime*,
and no one had ever thought of dislodging them. At the side was a high
fence enclosing the garden. A gate or door opening upon the street was
locked. Edna rang the bell at this side garden gate, and stood upon the
banquette, waiting to be admitted.

It was Victor who opened the gate for her. A black woman, wiping her
hands upon her apron, was close at his heels. Before she saw them Edna
could hear them in altercation, the woman—plainly an anomaly—claim-
ing the right to be allowed to perform her duties, one of which was to
answer the bell.

Victor was surprised and delighted to see Mrs. Pontellier, and he made
no attempt to conceal either his astonishment or his delight. He was a
dark-browed, good-looking youngster of nineteen, greatly resembling his
mother, but with ten times her impetuosity. He instructed the black
woman to go at once and inform Madame Lebrun that Mrs. Pontellier
desired to see her. The woman grumbled a refusal to do part of her duty
when she had not been permitted to do it all, and started back to her

interrupted task of weeding the garden. Whereupon Victor administered a rebuke in the form of a volley of abuse, which, owing to its rapidity and incoherence, was all but incomprehensible to Edna. Whatever it was, the rebuke was convincing, for the woman dropped her hoe and went mumbling into the house.

Edna did not wish to enter. It was very pleasant there on the side porch, where there were chairs, a wicker lounge, and a small table. She seated herself, for she was tired from her long tramp; and she began to rock gently and smooth out the folds of her silk parasol. Victor drew up his chair beside her. He at once explained that the black woman's offensive conduct was all due to imperfect training, as he was not there to take her in hand. He had only come up from the island the morning before, and expected to return next day. He stayed all winter at the island; he lived there, and kept the place in order and got things ready for the summer visitors.

But a man needed occasional relaxation, he informed Mrs. Pontellier, and every now and again he drummed up a pretext to bring him to the city. My! but he had had a time of it the evening before! He wouldn't want his mother to know, and he began to talk in a whisper. He was scintillant with recollections. Of course, he couldn't think of telling Mrs. Pontellier all about it, she being a woman and not comprehending such things. But it all began with a girl peeping and smiling at him through the shutters as he passed by. Oh! but she was a beauty! Certainly he smiled back, and went up and talked to her. Mrs. Pontellier did not know him if she supposed he was one to let an opportunity like that escape him. Despite herself, the youngster amused her. She must have betrayed in her look some degree of interest or entertainment. The boy grew more daring, and Mrs. Pontellier might have found herself, in a little while, listening to a highly colored story but for the timely appearance of Madame Lebrun.

That lady was still clad in white, according to her custom of the summer. Her eyes beamed an effusive welcome. Would not Mrs. Pontellier go inside? Would she partake of some refreshment? Why had she not been there before? How was that dear Mr. Pontellier and how were those sweet children? Had Mrs. Pontellier ever known such a warm November?

Victor went and reclined on the wicker lounge behind his mother's chair, where he commanded a view of Edna's face. He had taken her parasol from her hands while he spoke to her, and he now lifted it and twirled it above him as he lay on his back. When Madame Lebrun complained that it was *so* dull coming back to the city; that she saw *so* few people now; that even Victor, when he came up from the island for a day or two, had *so* much to occupy him and engage his time; then it was that the youth went into contortions on the lounge and winked mischievously at Edna. She somehow felt like a confederate in crime, and tried to look severe and disapproving.

There had been but two letters from Robert, with little in them, they told her. Victor said it was really not worth while to go inside for the letters, when his mother entreated him to go in search of them. He remembered the contents, which in truth he rattled off very glibly when put to the test.

One letter was written from Vera Cruz and the other from the City of Mexico. He had met Montel, who was doing everything toward his advancement. So far, the financial situation was no improvement over the one he had left in New Orleans, but of course the prospects were vastly better. He wrote of the City of Mexico, the buildings, the people and their habits, the conditions of life which he found there. He sent his love to the family. He inclosed a check to his mother, and hoped she would affectionately remember him to all his friends. That was about the substance of the two letters. Edna felt that if there had been a message for her, she would have received it. The despondent frame of mind in which she had left home began again to overtake her, and she remembered that she wished to find Mademoiselle Reisz.

Madame Lebrun knew where Mademoiselle Reisz lived. She gave Edna the address, regretting that she would not consent to stay and spend the remainder of the afternoon, and pay a visit to Mademoiselle Reisz some other day. The afternoon was already well advanced.

Victor escorted her out upon the banquette, lifted her parasol, and held it over her while he walked to the car with her. He entreated her to bear in mind that the disclosures of the afternoon were strictly confidential. She laughed and bantered him a little, remembering too late that she should have been dignified and reserved.

"How handsome Mrs. Pontellier looked!" said Madame Lebrun to her son.

"Ravishing!" he admitted. "The city atmosphere has improved her. Some way she doesn't seem like the same woman."

XXI

Some people contended that the reason Mademoiselle Reisz always chose apartments up under the roof was to discourage the approach of beggars, peddlars and callers. There were plenty of windows in her little front room. They were for the most part dingy, but as they were nearly always open it did not make so much difference. They often admitted into the room a good deal of smoke and soot; but at the same time all the light and air that there was came through them. From her windows could be seen the crescent of the river, the masts of ships and the big chimneys of the Mississippi steamers. A magnificent piano crowded the apartment. In the next room she slept, and in the third and last she harbored a gasoline stove on which she cooked her meals when disinclined to descend to the neighboring restaurant. It was there also that she ate, keeping her belongings in a rare old buffet, dingy and battered from a hundred years of use.

When Edna knocked at Mademoiselle Reisz's front room door and entered, she discovered that person standing beside the window, engaged in mending or patching an old prunella gaiter. The little musician laughed all over when she saw Edna. Her laugh consisted of a contortion of the face and all the muscles of the body. She seemed strikingly homely, standing there in the afternoon light. She still wore the shabby lace and the artificial bunch of violets on the side of her head.

"So you remembered me at last," said Mademoiselle. "I had said to myself, 'Ah, bah! she will never come.' "

"Did you want me to come?" asked Edna with a smile.

"I had not thought much about it," answered Mademoiselle. The two had seated themselves on a little bumpy sofa which stood against the wall. "I am glad, however, that you came. I have the water boiling back there, and was just about to make some coffee. You will drink a cup with me. And how is *la belle dame?* Always handsome! always healthy! always contented!" She took Edna's hand between her strong wiry fingers, holding it loosely without warmth, and executing a sort of double theme upon the back and palm.

"Yes," she went on; "I sometimes thought: 'She will never come. She promised as those women in society always do, without meaning it. She will not come.' For I really don't believe you like me, Mrs. Pontellier."

"I don't know whether I like you or not," replied Edna, gazing down at the little woman with a quizzical look.

The candor of Mrs. Pontellier's admission greatly pleased Mademoiselle Reisz. She expressed her gratification by repairing forthwith to the region of the gasoline stove and rewarding her guest with the promised cup of coffee. The coffee and the biscuit accompanying it proved very acceptable to Edna, who had declined refreshment at Madame Lebrun's and was now beginning to feel hungry. Mademoiselle set the tray which she brought in upon a small table near at hand, and seated herself once again on the lumpy sofa.

"I have had a letter from your friend," she remarked, as she poured a little cream into Edna's cup and handed it to her.

"My friend?"

"Yes, your friend Robert. He wrote to me from the City of Mexico."

"Wrote to *you?*" repeated Edna in amazement, stirring her coffee absently.

"Yes, to me. Why not? Don't stir all the warmth out of your coffee; drink it. Though the letter might as well have been sent to you; it was nothing but Mrs. Pontellier from beginning to end."

"Let me see it," requested the young woman, entreatingly.

"No; a letter concerns no one but the person who writes it and the one to whom it is written."

"Haven't you just said it concerned me from beginning to end?"

"It was written about you, not to you. 'Have you seen Mrs. Pontellier? How is she looking?' he asks. 'As Mrs. Pontellier says,' or 'as Mrs. Pontellier once said.' 'If Mrs. Pontellier should call upon you, play for her that Impromptu of Chopin's, my favorite. I heard it here a day or two ago, but not as you play it. I should like to know how it affects her,' and so on, as if he supposed we were constantly in each other's society."

"Let me see the letter."

"Oh, no."

"Have you answered it?"

"No."

"Let me see the letter."

"No, and again, no."

"Then play the Impromptu for me."

"It is growing late; what time do you have to be home?"

"Time doesn't concern me. Your question seems a little rude. Play the Impromptu."

"But you have told me nothing of yourself. What are you doing?"

"Painting!" laughed Edna. "I am becoming an artist. Think of it!"

"Ah! an artist! You have pretensions, Madame."

"Why pretensions? Do you think I could not become an artist?"

"I do not know you well enough to say. I do not know your talent or your temperament. To be an artist includes much; one must possess many gifts—absolute gifts—which have not been acquired by one's own effort. And, moreover, to succeed, the artist must possess the courageous soul."

"What do you mean by the courageous soul?"

"Courageous, *ma foi!* The brave soul. The soul that dares and defies."

"Show me the letter and play for me the Impromptu. You see that I have persistence. Does that quality count for anything in art?"

"It counts with a foolish old woman whom you have captivated," replied Mademoiselle, with her wriggling laugh.

The letter was right there at hand in the drawer of the little table upon which Edna had just placed her coffee cup. Mademoiselle opened the drawer and drew forth the letter, the topmost one. She placed it in Edna's hands, and without further comment arose and went to the piano.

Mademoiselle played a soft interlude. It was an improvisation. She sat low at the instrument, and the lines of her body settled into ungraceful curves and angles that gave it an appearance of deformity. Gradually and imperceptibly the interlude melted into the soft opening minor chords of the Chopin Impromptu.

Edna did not know when the Impromptu began or ended. She sat in the sofa corner reading Robert's letter by the fading light. Mademoiselle had glided from the Chopin into the quivering love-notes of Isolde's song, and back again to the Impromptu with its soulful and poignant longing.

The shadows deepened in the little room. The music grew strange and fantastic—turbulent, insistent, plaintive and soft with entreaty. The shadows grew deeper. The music filled the room. It floated out upon the night, over the housetops, the crescent of the river, losing itself in the silence of the upper air.

Edna was sobbing, just as she had wept one midnight at Grand Isle when strange, new voices awoke in her. She arose in some agitation to take her departure. "May I come again, Mademoiselle?" she asked at the threshold.

"Come whenever you feel like it. Be careful; the stairs and landings are dark; don't stumble."

Mademoiselle reëntered and lit a candle. Robert's letter was on the floor. She stooped and picked it up. It was crumpled and damp with tears. Mademoiselle smoothed the letter out, restored it to the envelope, and replaced it in the table drawer.

XXII

One morning on his way into town Mr. Pontellier stopped at the house of his old friend and family physician, Doctor Mandelet. The Doctor was a semi-retired physician, resting, as the saying is, upon his laurels. He bore a reputation for wisdom rather than skill—leaving the active practice of medicine to his assistants and younger contemporaries—and was much sought for in matters of consultation. A few families, united to him by bonds of friendship, he still attended when they required the services of a physician. The Pontelliers were among these.

Mr. Pontellier found the Doctor reading at the open window of his study. His house stood rather far back from the street, in the center of a delightful garden, so that it was quiet and peaceful at the old gentleman's study window. He was a great reader. He stared up disapprovingly over his eye-glasses as Mr. Pontellier entered, wondering who had the temerity to disturb him at that hour of the morning.

"Ah, Pontellier! Not sick, I hope. Come and have a seat. What news do you bring this morning?" He was quite portly, with a profusion of gray hair, and small blue eyes which age had robbed of much of their brightness but none of their penetration.

"Oh! I'm never sick, Doctor. You know that I come of tough fiber— of that old Creole race of Pontelliers that dry up and finally blow away. I came to consult—no, not precisely to consult—to talk to you about Edna. I don't know what ails her."

"Madame Pontellier not well?" marveled the Doctor. "Why, I saw her—I think it was a week ago—walking along Canal Street, the picture of health, it seemed to me."

"Yes, yes; she seems quite well," said Mr. Pontellier, leaning forward and whirling his stick between his two hands; "but she doesn't act well. She's odd, she's not like herself. I can't make her out, and I thought perhaps you'd help me."

"How does she act?" inquired the doctor.

"Well, it isn't easy to explain," said Mr. Pontellier, throwing himself back in his chair. "She lets the housekeeping go to the dickens."

"Well, well; women are not all alike, my dear Pontellier. We've got to consider—"

"I know that; I told you I couldn't explain. Her whole attitude— toward me and everybody and everything—has changed. You know I have a quick temper, but I don't want to quarrel or be rude to a woman, especially my wife; yet I'm driven to it, and feel like ten thousand devils after I've made a fool of myself. She's making it devilishly uncomfortable for me," he went on nervously. "She's got some sort of notion in her head concerning the eternal rights of women; and—you understand— we meet in the morning at the breakfast table."

The old gentleman lifted his shaggy eyebrows, protruded his thick nether lip, and tapped the arms of his chair with his cushioned finger-tips.

"What have you been doing to her, Pontellier?"

"Doing! *Parbleu!*"

"Has she," asked the Doctor, with a smile, "has she been associating of late with a circle of pseudo-intellectual women—super-spiritual superior beings? My wife has been telling me about them."

"That's the trouble," broke in Mr. Pontellier, "she hasn't been as-sociating with any one. She has abandoned her Tuesdays at home, has thrown over all her acquaintances, and goes tramping about by herself, moping in the street-cars, getting in after dark. I tell you she's peculiar. I don't like it; I feel a little worried over it."

This was a new aspect for the Doctor. "Nothing hereditary?" he asked, seriously. "Nothing peculiar about her family antecedents, is there?"

"Oh, no, indeed! She comes of sound old Presbyterian Kentucky stock. The old gentleman, her father, I have heard, used to atone for his week-day sins with his Sunday devotions. I know for a fact, that his race horses literally ran away with the prettiest bit of Kentucky farming land I ever laid eyes upon. Margaret—you know Margaret—she has all the Pres-byterianism undiluted. And the youngest is something of a vixen. By the way, she gets married in a couple of weeks from now."

"Send your wife up to the wedding," exclaimed the Doctor, foreseeing a happy solution. "Let her stay among her own people for a while; it will do her good."

"That's what I want her to do. She won't go to the marriage. She says a wedding is one of the most lamentable spectacles on earth. Nice thing for a woman to say to her husband!" exclaimed Mr. Pontellier, fuming anew at the recollection.

"Pontellier," said the Doctor, after a moment's reflection, "let your wife alone for a while. Don't bother her, and don't let her bother you. Woman, my dear friend, is a very peculiar and delicate organism—a sensitive and highly organized woman, such as I know Mrs. Pontellier to be, is especially peculiar. It would require an inspired psychologist to deal succesfully with them. And when ordinary fellows like you and me attempt to cope with their idiosyncrasies the result is bungling. Most women are moody and whimsical. This is some passing whim of your wife, due to some cause or causes which you and I needn't try to fathom. But it will pass happily over, especially if you let her alone. Send her around to see me."

"Oh! I couldn't do that; there'd be no reason for it," objected Mr. Pontellier.

"Then I'll go around and see her," said the Doctor. "I'll drop in to dinner some evening *en bon ami.*"

"Do! by all means," urged Mr. Pontellier. "What evening will you come? Say Thursday. Will you come Thursday?" he asked, rising to take his leave.

"Very well; Thursday. My wife may possibly have some engagement for me Thursday. In case she has, I shall let you know. Otherwise, you may expect me."

Mr. Pontellier turned before leaving to say:

"I am going to New York on business very soon. I have a big scheme on hand, and want to be on the field proper to pull the ropes and handle the ribbons. We'll let you in on the inside if you say so, Doctor," he laughed.

"No, I thank you, my dear sir," returned the Doctor. "I leave such ventures to you younger men with the fever of life still in your blood."

"What I wanted to say," continued Mr. Pontellier, with his hand on the knob; "I may have to be absent a good while. Would you advise me to take Edna along?"

"By all means, if she wishes to go. If not, leave her here. Don't contradict her. The mood will pass, I assure you. It may take a month, two, three months—possibly longer, but it will pass; have patience."

"Well, good-by, *à jeudi,*" said Mr. Pontellier, as he let himself out.

The Doctor would have liked during the course of conversation to ask, "Is there any man in the case?" but he knew his Creole too well to make such a blunder as that.

He did not resume his book immediately, but sat for a while meditatively looking out into the garden.

XXIII

Edna's father was in the city, and had been with them several days. She was not very warmly or deeply attached to him, but they had certain tastes in common, and when together they were companionable. His coming was in the nature of a welcome disturbance; it seemed to furnish a new direction for her emotions.

He had come to purchase a wedding gift for his daughter, Janet, and an outfit for himself in which he might make a creditable appearance at her marriage. Mr. Pontellier had selected the bridal gift, as every one immediately connected with him always deferred to his taste in such matters. And his suggestions on the question of dress—which too often assumes the nature of a problem—were of inestimable value to his father-in-law. But for the past few days the old gentleman had been upon Edna's hands, and in his society she was becoming acquainted with a new set of sensations. He had been a colonel in the Confederate army, and still maintained, with the title, the military bearing which had always accompanied it. His hair and mustache were white and silky, emphasizing the rugged bronze of his face. He was tall and thin, and wore his coats padded, which gave a fictitious breadth and depth to his shoulders and chest. Edna and her father looked very distinguished together, and excited a good deal of notice during their perambulations. Upon his arrival she began by introducing him to her atelier and making a sketch of him. He took the whole matter very seriously. If her talent had been ten-fold greater than it was, it would not have surprised him, convinced as he was that he had bequeathed to all of his daughters the germs of a masterful capability, which only depended upon their own efforts to be directed toward successful achievement.

Before her pencil he sat rigid and unflinching, as he had faced the cannon's mouth in days gone by. He resented the intrusion of the children, who gaped with wondering eyes at him, sitting so stiff up there in their mother's bright atelier. When they drew near he motioned them away with an expressive action of the foot, loath to disturb the fixed lines of his countenance, his arms, or his rigid shoulders.

Edna, anxious to entertain him, invited Mademoiselle Reisz to meet him, having promised him a treat in her piano playing; but Mademoiselle declined the invitation. So together they attended a *soirée musicale* at the Ratignolle's. Monsieur and Madame Ratignolle made much of the Colonel, installing him as the guest of honor and engaging him at once to dine with them the following Sunday, or any day which he might select. Madame coquetted with him in the most captivating and naïve manner, with eyes, gestures, and a profusion of compliments, till the Colonel's old head felt thirty years younger on his padded shoulders. Edna marveled, not comprehending. She herself was almost devoid of coquetry.

There were one or two men whom she observed at the *soirée musicale;* but she would never have felt moved to any kittenish display to attract their notice—to any feline or feminine wiles to express herself toward them. Their personality attracted her in an agreeable way. Her fancy selected them, and she was glad when a lull in the music gave them an opportunity to meet her and talk with her. Often on the street the glance of strange eyes had lingered in her memory, and sometimes had disturbed her.

Mr. Pontellier did not attend these *soirées musicales.* He considered them *bourgeois,* and found more diversion at the club. To Madame Ratignolle he said the music dispensed at her *soirées* was too "heavy," too far beyond his untrained comprehension. His excuse flattered her. But she disapproved of Mr. Pontellier's club, and she was frank enough to tell Edna so.

"It's a pity Mr. Pontellier doesn't stay home more in the evenings. I think you would be more—well, if you don't mind my saying it—more united, if he did."

"Oh! dear no!" said Edna, with a blank look in her eyes. "What should I do if he stayed home? We wouldn't have anything to say to each other."

She had not much of anything to say to her father, for that matter; but he did not antagonize her. She discovered that he interested her, though she realized that he might not interest her long; and for the first time in her life she felt as if she were thoroughly acquainted with him. He kept her busy serving him and ministering to his wants. It amused her to do so. She would not permit a servant or one of the children to do anything for him which she might do herself. Her husband noticed, and thought it was the expression of a deep filial attachment which he had never suspected.

The Colonel drank numerous "toddies" during the course of the day, which left him, however, imperturbed. He was an expert at concocting strong drinks. He had even invented some, to which he had given fantastic names, and for whose manufacture he required diverse ingredients that it devolved upon Edna to procure for him.

When Doctor Mandelet dined with the Pontelliers on Thursday he could discern in Mrs. Pontellier no trace of that morbid condition which her husband had reported to him. She was excited and in a manner radiant. She and her father had been to the race course, and their thoughts when they seated themselves at table were still occupied with the events of the afternoon, and their talk was still of the track. The Doctor had not kept pace with turf affairs. He had certain recollections of racing in what he called "the good old times" when the Lecompte stables flourished, and he drew upon this fund of memories so that he might not be left out and seem wholly devoid of the modern spirit. But he failed to impose upon the Colonel, and was even far from impressing him with this trumped-up knowledge of bygone days. Edna had staked her father on his last venture, with the most gratifying results to both of them. Besides, they had met some very charming people, according to the Colonel's impressions. Mrs. Mortimer Merriman and Mrs. James Highcamp, who were there with Alcée Arobin, had joined them and had enlivened the hours in a fashion that warmed him to think of.

Mr. Pontellier himself had no particular leaning toward horse-racing, and was even rather inclined to discourage it as a pastime, especially when he considered the fate of that blue-grass farm in Kentucky. He endeavored, in a general way, to express a particular disapproval, and only succeeded in arousing the ire and opposition of his father-in-law. A pretty dispute followed, in which Edna warmly espoused her father's cause and the Doctor remained neutral.

He observed his hostess attentively from under his shaggy brows, and noted a subtle change which had transformed her from the listless woman he had known into a being who, for the moment, seemed palpitant with the forces of life. Her speech was warm and energetic. There was no repression in her glance or gesture. She reminded him of some beautiful, sleek animal waking up in the sun.

The dinner was excellent. The claret was warm and the champagne was cold, and under their beneficent influence the threatened unpleasantness melted and vanished with the fumes of the wine.

Mr. Pontellier warmed up and grew reminiscent. He told some amusing plantation experiences, recollections of old Iberville and his youth, when he hunted 'possum in company with some friendly darky; thrashed the pecan trees, shot the grosbec, and roamed the woods and fields in mischievous idleness.

The Colonel, with little sense of humor and of the fitness of things, related a somber episode of those dark and bitter days, in which he had acted a conspicuous part and always formed a central figure. Nor was the Doctor happier in his selection, when he told the old, ever new and curious story of the waning of a woman's love, seeking strange, new channels, only to return to its legitimate source after days of fierce unrest. It was one of the many little human documents which had been unfolded to him during his long career as a physician. The story did not seem especially to impress Edna. She had one of her own to tell, of a woman who paddled away with her lover one night in a pirogue and never came back. They were lost amid the Baratarian Islands, and no one ever heard of them or found trace of them from that day to this. It was a pure invention. She said that Madame Antoine had related it to her. That, also, was an invention. Perhaps it was a dream she had had. But every glowing word seemed real to those who listened. They could feel the hot breath of the Southern night; they could hear the long sweep of the pirogue through the glistening moonlit water, the beating of birds' wings, rising startled from among the reeds in the salt-water pools; they could see the faces of the lovers, pale, close together, rapt in oblivious forgetfulness, drifting into the unknown.

The champagne was cold, and its subtle fumes played fantastic tricks with Edna's memory that night.

Outside, away from the glow of the fire and the soft lamplight, the night was chill and murky. The Doctor doubled his old-fashioned cloak across his breast as he strode home through the darkness. He knew his fellow-creatures better than most men; knew that inner life which so seldom unfolds itself to unanointed eyes. He was sorry he had accepted Pontellier's invitation. He was growing old, and beginning to need rest and an imperturbed spirit. He did not want the secrets of other lives thrust upon him.

"I hope it isn't Arobin," he muttered to himself as he walked. "I hope to heaven it isn't Alcée Arobin."

XXIV

Edna and her father had a warm, and almost violent dispute upon the subject of her refusal to attend her sister's wedding. Mr. Pontellier declined to interfere, to interpose either his influence or his authority. He was following Doctor Mandelet's advice, and letting her do as she liked. The Colonel reproached his daughter for her lack of filial kindness and respect, her want of sisterly affection and womanly consideration. His arguments were labored and unconvincing. He doubted if Janet would accept any excuse—forgetting that Edna had offered none. He doubted if Janet would ever speak to her again, and he was sure Margaret would not.

Edna was glad to be rid of her father when he finally took himself off with his wedding garments and his bridal gifts, with his padded shoulders, his Bible reading, his "toddies" and ponderous oaths.

Mr. Pontellier followed him closely. He meant to stop at the wedding on his way to New York and endeavor by every means which money and love could devise to atone somewhat for Edna's incomprehensible action.

"You are too lenient, too lenient by far, Léonce," asserted the Colonel. "Authority, coercion are what is needed. Put your foot down good and hard; the only way to manage a wife. Take my word for it."

The Colonel was perhaps unaware that he had coerced his own wife into her grave. Mr. Pontellier had a vague suspicion of it which he thought it needless to mention at that late day.

Edna was not so consciously gratified at her husband's leaving home as she had been over the departure of her father. As the day approached when he was to leave her for a comparatively long stay, she grew melting and affectionate, remembering his many acts of consideration and his repeated expressions of an ardent attachment. She was solicitous about his health and his welfare. She bustled around, looking after his clothing, thinking about heavy underwear, quite as Madame Ratignolle would have done under similar circumstances. She cried when he went away, calling him her dear, good friend, and she was quite certain she would grow lonely before very long and go to join him in New York.

But after all, a radiant peace settled upon her when she at last found herself alone. Even the children were gone. Old Madame Pontellier had come herself and carried them off to Iberville with their quadroon. The old madame did not venture to say she was afraid they would be neglected during Léonce's absence; she hardly ventured to think so. She was hungry for them—even a little fierce in her attachment. She did not want them to be wholly "children of the pavement," she always said when begging to have them for a space. She wished them to know the country, with its streams, its fields, its woods, its freedom, so delicious to the young. She wished them to taste something of the life their father had lived and known and loved when he, too, was a little child.

When Edna was at last alone, she breathed a big, genuine sigh of relief. A feeling that was unfamiliar but very delicious came over her. She walked all through the house, from one room to another, as if inspecting it for the first time. She tried the various chairs and lounges, as if she had never sat and reclined upon them before. And she perambulated around the outside of the house, investigating, looking to see if windows and shutters were secure and in order. The flowers were like new acquaintances; she approached them in a familiar spirit, and made herself at home among them. The garden walks were damp, and Edna called to the maid to bring out her rubber sandals. And there she stayed, and stooped, digging around the plants, trimming, picking dead, dry leaves. The children's little dog came out, interfering, getting in her way. She scolded him, laughed at him, played with him. The garden smelled so good and looked so pretty in the afternoon sunlight. Edna plucked all the bright flowers she could find, and went into the house with them, she and the little dog.

Even the kitchen assumed a sudden interesting character which she had never before perceived. She went in to give directions to the cook, to say that the butcher would have to bring much less meat, that they would require only half their usual quantity of bread, of milk and groceries. She told the cook that she herself would be greatly occupied during Mr. Pontellier's absence, and she begged her to take all thought and responsibility of the larder upon her own shoulders.

That night Edna dined alone. The candelabra, with a few candles in the center of the table, gave all the light she needed. Outside the circle of light in which she sat, the large dining-room looked solemn and shadowy. The cook, placed upon her mettle, served a delicious repast—a luscious tenderloin broiled *à point*. The wine tasted good; the *marron glacé* seemed to be just what she wanted. It was so pleasant, too, to dine in a comfortable *peignoir*.

She thought a little sentimentally about Léonce and the children, and wondered what they were doing. As she gave a dainty scrap or two to the doggie, she talked intimately to him about Etienne and Raoul. He was beside himself with astonishment and delight over these companionable advances, and showed his appreciation by his little quick, snappy barks and a lively agitation.

Then Edna sat in the library after dinner and read Emerson until she grew sleepy. She realized that she had neglected her reading, and determined to start anew upon a course of improving studies, now that her time was completely her own to do with as she liked.

After a refreshing bath, Edna went to bed. And as she snuggled comfortably beneath the eiderdown a sense of restfulness invaded her, such as she had not known before.

XXV

When the weather was dark and cloudy Edna could not work. She needed the sun to mellow and temper her mood to the sticking point. She had reached a stage when she seemed to be no longer feeling her way, working, when in the humor, with sureness and ease. And being devoid of ambition, and striving not toward accomplishment, she drew satisfaction from the work in itself.

On rainy or melancholy days Edna went out and sought the society of the friends she had made at Grand Isle. Or else she stayed indoors and nursed a mood with which she was becoming too familiar for her own comfort and peace of mind. It was not despair; but it seemed to her as if life were passing by, leaving its promise broken and unfulfilled. Yet there were other days when she listened, was led on and deceived by fresh promises which her youth held out to her.

She went again to the races, and again. Alcée Arobin and Mrs. Highcamp called for her one bright afternoon in Arobin's drag. Mrs. Highcamp was a worldly but unaffected, intelligent, slim, tall blonde woman in the forties, with an indifferent manner and blue eyes that stared. She had a daughter who served her as a pretext for cultivating the society of young men of fashion. Alcée Arobin was one of them. He was a familiar figure at the race course, the opera, the fashionable clubs. There was a perpetual smile in his eyes, which seldom failed to awaken a corresponding cheerfulness in any one who looked into them and listened to his good-humored voice. His manner was quiet, and at times a little insolent. He possessed a good figure, a pleasing face, not overburdened with depth of thought or feeling; and his dress was that of the conventional man of fashion.

He admired Edna extravagantly, after meeting her at the races with her father. He had met her before on other occasions, but she had seemed to him unapproachable until that day. It was at his instigation that Mrs. Highcamp called to ask her to go with them to the Jockey Club to witness the turf event of the season.

There were possibly a few track men out there who knew the race horse as well as Edna, but there was certainly none who knew it better. She sat between her two companions as one having authority to speak. She laughed at Arobin's pretensions, and deplored Mrs. Highcamp's ignorance. The race horse was a friend and intimate associate of her childhood. The atmosphere of the stables and the breath of the blue grass paddock revived in her memory and lingered in her nostrils. She did not perceive that she was talking like her father as the sleek geldings ambled in review before them. She played for very high stakes, and fortune favored her. The fever of the game flamed in her cheeks and eyes, and it got into her blood and into her brain like an intoxicant. People turned their heads to look at her, and more than one lent an attentive ear to her utterances, hoping thereby to secure the elusive but ever-desired "tip." Arobin caught the contagion of excitement which drew him to Edna like a magnet. Mrs. Highcamp remained, as usual, un-moved, with her indifferent stare and uplifted eyebrows.

Edna stayed and dined with Mrs. Highcamp upon being urged to do so. Arobin also remained and sent away his drag.

The dinner was quiet and uninteresting, save for the cheerful efforts of Arobin to enliven things. Mrs. Highcamp deplored the absence of her daughter from the races, and tried to convey to her what she had missed by going to the "Dante reading" instead of joining them. The girl held a geranium leaf up to her nose and said nothing, but looked knowing and noncommittal. Mr. Highcamp was a plain, bald-headed man, who only talked under compulsion. He was unresponsive. Mrs. Highcamp was full of delicate courtesy and consideration toward her husband. She ad-dressed most of her conversation to him at table. They sat in the library after dinner and read the evening papers together under the droplight; while the younger people went into the drawing-room near by and talked.

Miss Highcamp played some selections from Grieg upon the piano. She seemed to have apprehended all of the composer's coldness and none of his poetry. While Edna listened she could not help wondering if she had lost her taste for music.

When the time came for her to go home, Mr. Highcamp grunted a lame offer to escort her, looking down at his slippered feet with tactless concern. It was Arobin who took her home. The car ride was long, and it was late when they reached Esplanade Street. Arobin asked permission to enter for a second to light his cigarette—his match safe was empty. He filled his match safe, but did not light his cigarette until he left her, after she had expressed her willingness to go to the races with him again.

Edna was neither tired nor sleepy. She was hungry again, for the Highcamp dinner, though of excellent quality, had lacked abundance. She rummaged in the larder and brought forth a slice of Gruyère and some crackers. She opened a bottle of beer which she found in the ice-box. Edna felt extremely restless and excited. She vacantly hummed a fantastic tune as she poked at the wood embers on the hearth and munched a cracker.

She wanted something to happen—something, anything; she did not know what. She regretted that she had not made Arobin stay a half hour to talk over the horses with her. She counted the money she had won. But there was nothing else to do, so she went to bed, and tossed there for hours in a sort of monotonous agitation.

In the middle of the night she remembered that she had forgotten to write her regular letter to her husband; and she decided to do so next day and tell him about her afternoon at the Jockey Club. She lay wide awake composing a letter which was nothing like the one which she wrote next day. When the maid awoke her in the morning Edna was dreaming of Mr. Highcamp playing the piano at the entrance of a music store on Canal Street, while his wife was saying to Alcée Arobin, as they boarded an Esplanade Street car:

"What a pity that so much talent has been neglected! but I must go."

When, a few days later, Alcée Arobin again called for Edna in his drag, Mrs. Highcamp was not with him. He said they would pick her up. But as that lady had not been apprised of his intention of picking her up, she was not at home. The daughter was just leaving the house to attend the meeting of a branch Folk Lore Society, and regretted that she could not accompany them. Arobin appeared nonplused, and asked Edna if there were any one else she cared to ask.

She did not deem it worth while to go in search of any of the fashionable acquaintances from whom she had withdrawn herself. She thought of Madame Ratignolle, but knew that her fair friend did not leave the house, except to take a languid walk around the block with her husband after nightfall. Mademoiselle Reisz would have laughed at such a request from Edna. Madame Lebrun might have enjoyed the outing, but for some reason Edna did not want her. So they went alone, she and Arobin.

The afternoon was intensely interesting to her. The excitement came back upon her like a remittent fever. Her talk grew familiar and confidential. It was no labor to become intimate with Arobin. His manner invited easy confidence. The preliminary stage of becoming acquainted was one which he always endeavored to ignore when a pretty and engaging woman was concerned.

He stayed and dined with Edna. He stayed and sat beside the wood fire. They laughed and talked; and before it was time to go he was telling her how different life might have been if he had known her years before. With ingenuous frankness he spoke of what a wicked, ill-disciplined boy he had been, and impulsively drew up his cuff to exhibit upon his wrist the scar from a saber cut which he had received in a duel outside of Paris when he was nineteen. She touched his hand as she scanned the red cicatrice on the inside of his white wrist. A quick impulse that was somewhat spasmodic impelled her fingers to close in a sort of clutch upon his hand. He felt the pressure of her pointed nails in the flesh of his palm.

She arose hastily and walked toward the mantel.

"The sight of a wound or scar always agitates and sickens me," she said. "I shouldn't have looked at it."

"I beg your pardon," he entreated, following her; "it never occurred to me that it might be repulsive."

He stood close to her, and the effrontery in his eyes repelled the old, vanishing self in her, yet drew all her awakening sensuousness. He saw enough in her face to impel him to take her hand and hold it while he said his lingering good night.

"Will you go to the races again?" he asked.

"No," she said. "I've had enough of the races. I don't want to lose all the money I've won, and I've got to work when the weather is bright, instead of—"

"Yes; work; to be sure. You promised to show me your work. What morning may I come up to your atelier? To-morrow?"

"No!"

"Day after?"

"No, no."

"Oh, please don't refuse me! I know something of such things. I might help you with a stray suggestion or two."

"No. Good night. Why don't you go after you have said good night? I don't like you," she went on in a high, excited pitch, attempting to draw away her hand. She felt that her words lacked dignity and sincerity, and she knew that he felt it.

"I'm sorry you don't like me. I'm sorry I offended you. How have I offended you? What have I done? Can't you forgive me?" And he bent and pressed his lips upon her hand as if he wished never more to withdraw them.

"Mr. Arobin," she complained, "I'm greatly upset by the excitement of the afternoon; I'm not myself. My manner must have misled you in some way. I wish you to go, please." She spoke in a monotonous, dull tone. He took his hat from the table, and stood with eyes turned from her, looking into the dying fire. For a moment or two he kept an impressive silence.

"Your manner has not misled me, Mrs. Pontellier," he said finally. "My own emotions have done that. I couldn't help it. When I'm near you, how could I help it? Don't think anything of it, don't bother, please. You see, I go when you command me. If you wish me to stay away, I shall do so. If you let me come back, I—oh! you will let me come back?"

He cast one appealing glance at her, to which she made no response. Alcée Arobin's manner was so genuine that it often deceived even himself.

Edna did not care or think whether it were genuine or not. When she was alone she looked mechanically at the back of her hand which he had kissed so warmly. Then she leaned her head down on the mantelpiece. She felt somewhat like a woman who in a moment of passion is betrayed into an act of infidelity, and realizes the significance of the act without being wholly awakened from its glamour. The thought was passing vaguely through her mind, "What would he think?"

She did not mean her husband; she was thinking of Robert Lebrun. Her husband seemed to her now like a person whom she had married without love as an excuse.

She lit a candle and went up to her room. Alcée Arobin was absolutely nothing to her. Yet his presence, his manners, the warmth of his glances, and above all the touch of his lips upon her hand had acted like a narcotic upon her.

She slept a languorous sleep, interwoven with vanishing dreams.

XXVI

Alcée Arobin wrote Edna an elaborate note of apology, palpitant with sincerity. It embarrassed her; for in a cooler, quieter moment it appeared to her absurd that she should have taken his action so seriously, so dramatically. She felt sure that the significance of the whole occurrence had lain in her own self-consciousness. If she ignored his note it would give undue importance to a trivial affair. If she replied to it in a serious spirit it would still leave in his mind the impression that she had in a susceptible moment yielded to his influence. After all, it was no great matter to have one's hand kissed. She was provoked at his having written the apology. She answered in as light and bantering a spirit as she fancied it deserved, and said she would be glad to have him look in upon her at work whenever he felt the inclination and his business gave him the opportunity.

He responded at once by presenting himself at her home with all his disarming naïveté. And then there was scarcely a day which followed that she did not see him or was not reminded of him. He was prolific in pretexts. His attitude became one of good-humored subservience and tacit adoration. He was ready at all times to submit to her moods, which were as often kind as they were cold. She grew accustomed to him. They became intimate and friendly by imperceptible degrees, and then by leaps. He sometimes talked in a way that astonished her at first and brought the crimson into her face; in a way that pleased her at last, appealing to the animalism that stirred impatiently within her.

There was nothing which so quieted the turmoil of Edna's senses as a visit to Mademoiselle Reisz. It was then, in the presence of that personality which was offensive to her, that the woman, by her divine art, seemed to reach Edna's spirit and set it free.

It was misty, with heavy, lowering atmosphere, one afternoon, when Edna climbed the stairs to the pianist's apartments under the roof. Her clothes were dripping with moisture. She felt chilled and pinched as she entered the room. Mademoiselle was poking at a rusty stove that smoked a little and warmed the room indifferently. She was endeavoring to heat a pot of chocolate on the stove. The room looked cheerless and dingy to Edna as she entered. A bust of Beethoven, covered with a hood of dust, scowled at her from the mantelpiece.

"Ah! here comes the sunlight!" exclaimed Mademoiselle, rising from her knees before the stove. "Now it will be warm and bright enough; I can let the fire alone."

She closed the stove door with a bang, and approaching, assisted in removing Edna's dripping mackintosh.

"You are cold; you look miserable. The chocolate will soon be hot. But would you rather have a taste of brandy? I have scarcely touched the bottle which you brought me for my cold." A piece of red flannel was wrapped around Mademoiselle's throat; a stiff neck compelled her to hold her head on one side.

"I will take some brandy," said Edna, shivering as she removed her gloves and overshoes. She drank the liquor from the glass as a man would have done. Then flinging herself upon the uncomfortable sofa she said, "Mademoiselle, I am going to move away from my house on Esplanade Street."

"Ah!" ejaculated the musician, neither surprised nor especially interested. Nothing ever seemed to astonish her very much. She was endeavoring to adjust the bunch of violets which had become loose from its fastening in her hair. Edna drew her down upon the sofa, and taking a pin from her own hair, secured the shabby artificial flowers in their accustomed place.

"Aren't you astonished?"

"Passably. Where are you going? to New York? to Iberville? to your father in Mississippi? where?"

"Just two steps away," laughed Edna, "in a little four-room house around the corner. It looks so cozy, so inviting and restful, whenever I pass by; and it's for rent. I'm tired looking after that big house. It never seemed like mine, anyway—like home. It's too much trouble. I have to keep too many servants. I am tired bothering with them."

"That is not your true reason, *ma belle*. There is no use in telling me lies. I don't know your reason, but you have not told me the truth." Edna did not protest or endeavor to justify herself.

"The house, the money that provides for it, are not mine. Isn't that enough reason?"

"They are your husband's," returned Mademoiselle, with a shrug and a malicious elevation of the eyebrows.

"Oh! I see there is no deceiving you. Then let me tell you: It is a caprice. I have a little money of my own from my mother's estate, which my father sends me by driblets. I won a large sum this winter on the races, and I am beginning to sell my sketches. Laidpore is more and more pleased with my work; he says it grows in force and individuality. I cannot judge of that myself, but I feel that I have gained in ease and confidence. However, as I said, I have sold a good many through Laidpore. I can live in the tiny house for little or nothing, with one servant. Old Celestine, who works occasionally for me, says she will come stay with me and do my work. I know I shall like it, like the feeling of freedom and independence."

"What does your husband say?"

"I have not told him yet. I only thought of it this morning. He will think I am demented, no doubt. Perhaps you think so."

Mademoiselle shook her head slowly. "Your reason is not yet clear to me," she said.

Neither was it quite clear to Edna herself; but it unfolded itself as she sat for a while in silence. Instinct had prompted her to put away her husband's bounty in casting off her allegiance. She did not know how it would be when he returned. There would have to be an understanding, an explanation. Conditions would some way adjust themselves, she felt; but whatever came, she had resolved never again to belong to another than herself.

"I shall give a grand dinner before I leave the old house!" Edna exclaimed. "You will have to come to it, Mademoiselle. I will give you everything that you like to eat and to drink. We shall sing and laugh and be merry for once." And she uttered a sigh that came from the very depths of her being.

If Mademoiselle happened to have received a letter from Robert during the interval of Edna's visits, she would give her the letter unsolicited. And she would seat herself at the piano and play as her humor prompted her while the young woman read the letter.

The little stove was roaring; it was red-hot, and the chocolate in the tin sizzled and sputtered. Edna went forward and opened the stove door, and Mademoiselle rising, took a letter from under the bust of Beethoven and handed it to Edna.

"Another! so soon!" she exclaimed, her eyes filled with delight. "Tell me, Mademoiselle, does he know that I see his letters?"

"Never in the world! He would be angry and would never write to me again if he thought so. Does he write to you? Never a line. Does he send you a message? Never a word. It is because he loves you, poor fool, and is trying to forget you, since you are not free to listen to him or to belong to him."

"Why do you show me his letters, then?"

"Haven't you begged for them? Can I refuse you anything? Oh! you cannot deceive me," and Mademoiselle approached her beloved instrument and began to play. Edna did not at once read the letter. She sat holding it in her hand, while the music penetrated her whole being like an effulgence, warming and brightening the dark places of her soul. It prepared her for joy and exultation.

"Oh!" she exclaimed, letting the letter fall to the floor. "Why did you not tell me?" She went and grasped Mademoiselle's hands up from the keys. "Oh! unkind! malicious! Why did you not tell me?"

"That he was coming back? No great news, *ma foi*. I wonder he did not come long ago."

"But when, when?" cried Edna, impatiently. "He does not say when."

"He says 'very soon.' You know as much about it as I do; it is all in the letter."

"But why? Why is he coming? Oh, if I thought—" and she snatched the letter from the floor and turned the pages this way and that way, looking for the reason, which was left untold.

"If I were young and in love with a man," said Mademoiselle, turning on the stool and pressing her wiry hands between her knees as she looked down at Edna, who sat on the floor holding the letter, "it seems to me he would have to be some *grand esprit;* a man with lofty aims and ability to reach them; one who stood high enough to attract the notice of his fellow-men. It seems to me if I were young and in love I should never deem a man of ordinary caliber worthy of my devotion."

"Now it is you who are telling lies and seeking to deceive me, Mademoiselle; or else you have never been in love, and know nothing about it. Why," went on Edna, clasping her knees and looking up into Mademoiselle's twisted face, "do you suppose a woman knows why she loves? Does she select? Does she say to herself: 'Go to! Here is a distinguished statesman with presidential possibilities; I shall proceed to fall in love with him.' Or, 'I shall set my heart upon this musician, whose fame is on every tongue?' Or, 'This financier, who controls the world's money markets?' "

"You are purposely misunderstanding me, *ma reine*. Are you in love with Robert?"

"Yes," said Edna. It was the first time she had admitted it, and a glow overspread her face, blotching it with red spots.

"Why?" asked her companion. "Why do you love him when you ought not to?"

Edna, with a motion or two, dragged herself on her knees before Mademoiselle Reisz, who took the glowing face between her two hands.

"Why? Because his hair is brown and grows away from his temples; because he opens and shuts his eyes, and his nose is a little out of drawing; because he has two lips and a square chin, and a little finger which he can't straighten from having played baseball too energetically in his youth. Because—"

"Because you do, in short," laughed Mademoiselle. "What will you do when he comes back?" she asked.

"Do? Nothing, except feel glad and happy to be alive."

She was already glad and happy to be alive at the mere thought of his return. The murky, lowering sky, which had depressed her a few hours before, seemed bracing and invigorating as she splashed through the streets on her way home.

She stopped at a confectioner's and ordered a huge box of bonbons for the children in Iberville. She slipped a card in the box, on which she scribbled a tender message and sent an abundance of kisses.

Before dinner in the evening Edna wrote a charming letter to her husband, telling him of her intention to move for a while into the little house around the block, and to give a farewell dinner before leaving, regretting that he was not there to share it, to help her out with the menu and assist her in entertaining the guests. Her letter was brilliant and brimming with cheerfulness.

XXVII

"What is the matter with you?" asked Arobin that evening. "I never found you in such a happy mood." Edna was tired by that time, and was reclining on the lounge before the fire.

"Don't you know the weather prophet has told us we shall see the sun pretty soon?"

"Well, that ought to be reason enough," he acquiesced. "You wouldn't give me another if I sat here all night imploring you." He sat close to her on a low tabouret, and as he spoke his fingers lightly touched the hair that fell a little over her forehead. She liked the touch of his fingers through her hair, and closed her eyes sensitively.

"One of these days," she said, "I'm going to pull myself together for a while and think—try to determine what character of a woman I am; for, candidly, I don't know. By all the codes which I am acquainted with, I am a devilishly wicked specimen of the sex. But some way I can't convince myself that I am. I must think about it."

"Don't. What's the use? Why should you bother thinking about it when I can tell you what manner of woman you are." His fingers strayed occasionally down to her warm, smooth cheeks and firm chin, which was growing a little full and double.

"Oh, yes! You will tell me that I am adorable; everything that is captivating. Spare yourself the effort."

"No; I shan't tell you anything of the sort, though I shouldn't be lying if I did."

"Do you know Mademoiselle Reisz?" she asked irrelevantly.

"The pianist? I know her by sight. I've heard her play."

"She says queer things sometimes in a bantering way that you don't notice at the time and you find yourself thinking about afterward."

"For instance?"

"Well, for instance, when I left her to-day, she put her arms around me and felt my shoulder blades, to see if my wings were strong, she said. 'The bird that would soar above the level plain of tradition and prejudice must have strong wings. It is a sad spectacle to see the weaklings bruised, exhausted, fluttering back to earth.' "

"Whither would you soar?"

"I'm not thinking of any extraordinary flights. I only half comprehend her."

"I've heard she's partially demented," said Arobin.

"She seems to me wonderfully sane," Edna replied.

"I'm told she's extremely disagreeable and unpleasant. Why have you introduced her at a moment when I desired to talk of you?"

"Oh! talk of me if you like," cried Edna, clasping her hands beneath her head; "but let me think of something else while you do."

"I'm jealous of your thoughts to-night. They're making you a little kinder than usual; but some way I feel as if they were wandering, as if they were not here with me." She only looked at him and smiled. His eyes were very near. He leaned upon the lounge with an arm extended across her, while the other hand still rested upon her hair. They continued silently to look into each other's eyes. When he leaned forward and kissed her, she clasped his head, holding his lips to hers.

It was the first kiss of her life to which her nature had really responded. It was a flaming torch that kindled desire.

XXVIII

Edna cried a little that night after Arobin left her. It was only one phase of the multitudinous emotions which had assailed her. There was with her an overwhelming feeling of irresponsibility. There was the shock of the unexpected and the unaccustomed. There was her husband's reproach looking at her from the external things around her which he had provided for her external existence. There was Robert's reproach making itself felt by a quicker, fiercer, more overpowering love, which had awakened within her toward him. Above all, there was understanding. She felt as if a mist had been lifted from her eyes, enabling her to look upon and comprehend the significance of life, that monster made up of beauty and brutality. But among the conflicting sensations which assailed her, there was neither shame nor remorse. There was a dull pang of regret because it was not the kiss of love which had inflamed her, because it was not love which had held this cup of life to her lips.

XXIX

Without even waiting for an answer from her husband regarding his opinion or wishes in the matter, Edna hastened her preparations for quitting her home on Esplanade Street and moving into the little house around the block. A feverish anxiety attended her every action in that direction. There was no moment of deliberation, no interval of repose between the thought and its fulfillment. Early upon the morning following those hours passed in Arobin's society, Edna set about securing her new abode and hurrying her arrangements for occupying it. Within the precincts of her home she felt like one who has entered and lingered within the portals of some forbidden temple in which a thousand muffled voices bade her begone.

Whatever was her own in the house, everything which she had acquired aside from her husband's bounty, she caused to be transported to the other house, supplying simple and meager deficiencies from her own resources.

Arobin found her with rolled sleeves, working in company with the house-maid when he looked in during the afternoon. She was splendid and robust, and had never appeared handsomer than in the old blue gown, with a red silk handkerchief knotted at random around her head to protect her hair from the dust. She was mounted upon a high step-ladder, unhooking a picture from the wall when he entered. He had found the front door open, and had followed his ring by walking in unceremoniously.

"Come down!" he said. "Do you want to kill yourself?" She greeted him with affected carelessness, and appeared absorbed in her occupation.

If he had expected to find her languishing, reproachful, or indulging in sentimental tears, he must have been greatly surprised.

He was no doubt prepared for any emergency, ready for any one of the foregoing attitudes, just as he bent himself easily and naturally to the situation which confronted him.

"Please come down," he insisted, holding the ladder and looking up at her.

"No," she answered; "Ellen is afraid to mount the ladder. Joe is working over at the 'pigeon house'—that's the name Ellen gives it, because it's so small and looks like a pigeon house—and some one has to do this."

Arobin pulled off his coat, and expressed himself ready and willing to tempt fate in her place. Ellen brought him one of her dust-caps, and went into contortions of mirth, which she found it impossible to control, when she saw him put it on before the mirror as grotesquely as he could. Edna herself could not refrain from smiling when she fastened it at his request. So it was he who in turn mounted the ladder, unhooking pictures and curtains, and dislodging ornaments as Edna directed. When he had finished he took off his dust-cap and went out to wash his hands.

Edna was sitting on the tabouret, idly brushing the tips of a feather duster along the carpet when he came in again.

"Is there anything more you will let me do?" he asked.

"That is all," she answered. "Ellen can manage the rest." She kept the young woman occupied in the drawing-room, unwilling to be left alone with Arobin.

"What about the dinner?" he asked; "the grand event, the *coup d'état?*"

"It will be day after to-morrow. Why do you call it the *'coup d'état?'* Oh! it will be very fine; all my best of everything—crystal, silver and gold, Sèvres, flowers, music, and champagne to swim in. I'll let Léonce pay the bills. I wonder what he'll say when he sees the bills."

"And you ask me why I call it a *coup d'état?*" Arobin had put on his coat, and he stood before her and asked if his cravat was plumb. She told him it was, looking no higher than the tip of his collar.

"When do you go to the 'pigeon house?'—with all due acknowledgment to Ellen."

"Day after to-morrow, after the dinner. I shall sleep there."

"Ellen, will you very kindly get me a glass of water?" asked Arobin. "The dust in the curtains, if you will pardon me for hinting such a thing, has parched my throat to a crisp."

"While Ellen gets the water," said Edna, rising, "I will say good-by and let you go. I must get rid of this grime, and I have a million things to do and think of."

"When shall I see you?" asked Arobin, seeking to detain her, the maid having left the room.

"At the dinner, of course. You are invited."

"Not before?—not to-night or to-morrow morning or to-morrow noon or night? or the day after morning or noon? Can't you see yourself, without my telling you, what an eternity it is?"

He had followed her into the hall and to the foot of the stairway, looking up at her as she mounted with her face half turned to him.

"Not an instant sooner," she said. But she laughed and looked at him with eyes that at once gave him courage to wait and made it torture to wait.

XXX

Though Edna had spoken of the dinner as a very grand affair, it was in truth a very small affair and very select, in so much as the guests invited were few and were selected with discrimination. She had counted upon an even dozen seating themselves at her round mahogany board, forgetting for the moment that Madame Ratignolle was to the last degree *souffrante* and unpresentable, and not foreseeing that Madame Lebrun would sent a thousand regrets at the last moment. So there were only ten, after all, which made a cozy, comfortable number.

There were Mr. and Mrs. Merriman, a pretty, vivacious little woman in the thirties; her husband, a jovial fellow, something of a shallow-pate, who laughed a good deal at other people's witticisms, and had thereby made himself extremely popular. Mrs. Highcamp had accompanied them. Of course, there was Alcée Arobin; and Mademoiselle Reisz had consented to come. Edna had sent her a fresh bunch of violets with black lace trimmings for her hair. Monsieur Ratignolle brought himself and his wife's excuses. Victor Lebrun, who happened to be in the city, bent upon relaxation, had accepted with alacrity. There was a Miss Mayblunt, no longer in her teens, who looked at the world through lorgnettes and with the keenest interest. It was thought and said that she was intellectual; it was suspected of her that she wrote under a *nom de guerre*. She had come with a gentleman by the name of Gouvernail, connected with one of the daily papers, of whom nothing special could be said, except that he was observant and seemed quiet and inoffensive. Edna herself made the tenth, and at half-past eight they seated themselves at table, Arobin and Monsieur Ratignolle on either side of their hostess.

Mrs. Highcamp sat between Arobin and Victor Lebrun. Then came Mrs. Merriman, Mr. Gouvernail, Miss Mayblunt, Mr. Merriman, and Mademoiselle Reisz next to Monsieur Ratignolle.

There was something extremely gorgeous about the appearance of the table, an effect of splendor conveyed by a cover of pale yellow satin under strips of lace-work. There were wax candles in massive brass candelabra, burning softly under yellow silk shades; full, fragrant roses, yellow and red, abounded. There were silver and gold, as she had said there would be, and crystal which glittered like the gems which the women wore.

The ordinary stiff dining chairs had been discarded for the occasion and replaced by the most commodious and luxurious which could be collected throughout the house. Mademoiselle Reisz, being exceedingly diminutive, was elevated upon cushions, as small children are sometimes hoisted at table upon bulky volumes.

"Something new, Edna?" exclaimed Miss Mayblunt, with lorgnette directed toward a magnificent cluster of diamonds that sparkled, that almost sputtered, in Edna's hair, just over the center of her forehead.

"Quite new; 'brand' new, in fact; a present from my husband. It arrived this morning from New York. I may as well admit that this is my birthday, and that I am twenty-nine. In good time I expect you to drink my health. Meanwhile, I shall ask you to begin with this cocktail, composed—would you say 'composed?' " with an appeal to Miss Mayblunt—"composed by my father in honor of Sister Janet's wedding."

Before each guest stood a tiny glass that looked and sparkled like a garnet gem.

"Then, all things considered," spoke Arobin, "it might not be amiss to start out by drinking the Colonel's health in the cocktail which he composed, on the birthday of the most charming of women—the daughter whom he invented."

Mr. Merriman's laugh at this sally was such a genuine outburst and so contagious that it started the dinner with an agreeable swing that never slackened.

Miss Mayblunt begged to be allowed to keep her cocktail untouched before her, just to look at. The color was marvelous! She could compare it to nothing she had ever seen, and the garnet lights which it emitted were unspeakably rare. She pronounced the Colonel an artist, and stuck to it.

Monsieur Ratignolle was prepared to take things seriously: the *mets*, the *entre-mets*, the service, the decorations, even the people. He looked up from his pompono and inquired of Arobin if he were related to the gentleman of that name who formed one of the firm of Laitner and Arobin, lawyers. The young man admitted that Laitner was a warm personal friend, who permitted Arobin's name to decorate the firm's letterheads and to appear upon a shingle that graced Perdido Street.

"There are so many inquisitive people and institutions abounding," said Arobin, "that one is really forced as a matter of convenience these days to assume the virtue of an occupation if he has it not."

Monsieur Ratignolle stared a little, and turned to ask Mademoiselle Reisz if she considered the symphony concerts up to the standard which had been set the previous winter. Mademoiselle Reisz answered Monsieur Ratignolle in French, which Edna thought a little rude, under the circumstances, but characteristic. Mademoiselle had only disagreeable things to say of the symphony concerts, and insulting remarks to make of all the musicians of New Orleans, singly and collectively. All her interest seemed to be centered upon the delicacies placed before her.

Mr. Merriman said that Mr. Arobin's remark about inquisitive people reminded him of a man from Waco the other day at the St. Charles Hotel—but as Mr. Merriman's stories were always lame and lacking point, his wife seldom permitted him to complete them. She interrupted him to ask if he remembered the name of the author whose book she had bought the week before to send to a friend in Geneva. She was talking "books" with Mr. Gouvernail and trying to draw from him his opinion upon current literary topics. Her husband told the story of the Waco man privately to Miss Mayblunt, who pretended to be greatly amused and to think it extremely clever.

Mrs. Highcamp hung with languid but unaffected interest upon the warm and impetuous volubility of her left-hand neighbor, Victor Lebrun. Her attention was never for a moment withdrawn from him after seating herself at table; and when he turned to Mrs. Merriman, who was prettier and more vivacious than Mrs. Highcamp, she waited with easy indifference for an opportunity to reclaim his attention. There was the occasional sound of music, of mandolins, sufficiently removed to be an agreeable accompaniment rather than an interruption to the conversation. Outside the soft, monotonous splash of a fountain could be heard; the sound penetrated into the room with the heavy odor of jessamine that came through the open windows.

The golden shimmer of Edna's satin gown spread in rich folds on either side of her. There was a soft fall of lace encircling her shoulders. It was the color of her skin, without the glow, the myriad living tints that one may sometimes discover in vibrant flesh. There was something in her attitude, in her whole appearance when she leaned her head against the high-backed chair and spread her arms, which suggested the regal woman, the one who rules, who looks on, who stands alone.

But as she sat there amid her guests, she felt the old ennui overtaking her; the hopelessness which so often assailed her, which came upon her like an obsession, like something extraneous, independent of volition. It was something which announced itself; a chill breath that seemed to issue from some vast cavern wherein discords wailed. There came over her the acute longing which always summoned into her spiritual vision the presence of the beloved one, overpowering her at once with a sense of the unattainable.

The moments glided on, while a feeling of good fellowship passed around the circle like a mystic cord, holding and binding these people together with jest and laughter. Monsieur Ratignolle was the first to break the pleasant charm. At ten o'clock he excused himself. Madame Ratignolle was waiting for him at home. She was *bien souffrante*, and she was filled with vague dread, which only her husband's presence could allay.

Mademoiselle Reisz arose with Monsieur Ratignolle, who offered to escort her to the car. She had eaten well; she had tasted the good, rich wines, and they must have turned her head, for she bowed pleasantly to all as she withdrew from table. She kissed Edna upon the shoulder, and whispered: "*Bonne nuit, ma reine; soyez sage.*" She had been a little bewildered upon rising, or rather, descending from her cushions, and Monsieur Ratignolle gallantly took her arm and led her away.

Mrs. Highcamp was weaving a garland of roses, yellow and red. When she had finished the garland, she laid it lightly upon Victor's black curls. He was reclining far back in the luxurious chair, holding a glass of champagne to the light.

As if a magician's wand had touched him, the garland of roses transformed him into a vision of Oriental beauty. His cheeks were the color of crushed grapes, and his dusky eyes glowed with a languishing fire.

"*Sapristi!*" exclaimed Arobin.

But Mrs. Highcamp had one more touch to add to the picture. She took from the back of her chair a white silken scarf, with which she had covered her shoulders in the early part of the evening. She draped it across the boy in graceful folds, and in a way to conceal his black, conventional evening dress. He did not seem to mind what she did to him, only smiled, showing a faint gleam of white teeth, while he continued to gaze with narrowing eyes at the light through his glass of champagne.

"Oh! to be able to paint in color rather than in words!" exclaimed Miss Mayblunt, losing herself in a rhapsodic dream as she looked at him.

> " 'There was a graven image of Desire
>   Painted with red blood on a ground of gold.' "

murmured Gouvernail, under his breath.

The effect of the wine upon Victor was to change his accustomed volubility into silence. He seemed to have abandoned himself to a reverie, and to be seeing pleasing visions in the amber bead.

"Sing," entreated Mrs. Highcamp. "Won't you sing to us?"

"Let him alone," said Arobin.

"He's posing," offered Mr. Merriman; "let him have it out."

"I believe he's paralyzed," laughed Mrs. Merriman. And leaning over the youth's chair, she took the glass from his hand and held it to his lips. He sipped the wine slowly, and when he had drained the glass she laid it upon the table and wiped his lips with her little filmy handkerchief.

"Yes, I'll sing for you," he said, turning in his chair toward Mrs.

Highcamp. He clasped his hands behind his head, and looking up at the ceiling began to hum a little, trying his voice like a musician tuning an instrument. Then, looking at Edna, he began to sing:

> "Ah! si tu savais!"

"Stop!" she cried, "don't sing that. I don't want you to sing it," and she laid her glass so impetuously and blindly upon the table as to shatter it against a caraffe. The wine spilled over Arobin's legs and some of it trickled down upon Mrs. Highcamp's black gauze gown. Victor had lost all idea of courtesy, or else he thought his hostess was not in earnest, for he laughed and went on:

> "Ah! si tu savais
> Ce que tes yeux me disent"—

"Oh! you mustn't! you mustn't," exclaimed Edna, and pushing back her chair she got up, and going behind him placed her hand over his mouth. He kissed the soft palm that pressed upon his lips.

"No, no, I won't, Mrs. Pontellier. I didn't know you meant it," looking up at her with caressing eyes. The touch of his lips was like a pleasing sting to her hand. She lifted the garland of roses from his head and flung it across the room.

"Come, Victor; you've posed long enough. Give Mrs. Highcamp her scarf."

Mrs. Highcamp undraped the scarf from about him with her own hands. Miss Mayblunt and Mr. Gouvernail suddenly conceived the notion that it was time to say good night. And Mr. and Mrs. Merriman wondered how it could be so late.

Before parting from Victor, Mrs. Highcamp invited him to call upon her daughter, who she knew would be charmed to meet him and talk French and sing French songs with him. Victor expressed his desire and intention to call upon Miss Highcamp at the first opportunity which presented itself. He asked if Arobin were going his way. Arobin was not.

The mandolin players had long since stolen away. A profound stillness had fallen upon the broad, beautiful street. The voices of Edna's disbanding guests jarred like a discordant note upon the quiet harmony of the night.

XXXI

"Well?" questioned Arobin, who had remained with Edna after the others had departed.

"Well," she reiterated, and stood up, stretching her arms, and feeling the need to relax her muscles after having been so long seated.

"What next?" he asked.

"The servants are all gone. They left when the musicians did. I have dismissed them. The house has to be closed and locked, and I shall trot around to the pigeon house, and shall send Celestine over in the morning to straighten things up."

He looked around, and began to turn out some of the lights.

"What about upstairs?" he inquired.

"I think it is all right; but there may be a window or two unlatched. We had better look; you might take a candle and see. And bring me my wrap and hat on the foot of the bed in the middle room."

He went up with the light, and Edna began closing doors and windows. She hated to shut in the smoke and the fumes of the wine. Arobin found her cape and hat, which he brought down and helped her to put on.

When everything was secured and the lights put out, they left through the front door, Arobin locking it and taking the key, which he carried for Edna. He helped her down the steps.

"Will you have a spray of jessamine?" he asked, breaking off a few blossoms as he passed.

"No; I don't want anything."

She seemed disheartened, and had nothing to say. She took his arm, which he offered her, holding up the weight of her satin train with the other hand. She looked down, noticing the black line of his leg moving in and out so close to her against the yellow shimmer of her gown. There was the whistle of a railway train somewhere in the distance, and the midnight bells were ringing. They met no one in their short walk.

The "pigeon-house" stood behind a locked gate, and a shallow *parterre* that had been somewhat neglected. There was a small front porch, upon which a long window and the front door opened. The door opened directly into the parlor; there was no side entry. Back in the yard was a room for servants, in which old Celestine had been ensconced.

Edna had left a lamp burning low upon the table. She had succeeded in making the room look habitable and homelike. There were some books on the table and a lounge near at hand. On the floor was a fresh matting, covered with a rug or two; and on the walls hung a few tasteful pictures. But the room was filled with flowers. These were a surprise to her. Arobin had sent them, and had had Celestine distribute them during Edna's absence. Her bedroom was adjoining, and across a small passage were the dining-room and kitchen.

Edna seated herself with every appearance of discomfort.

"Are you tired?" he asked.

"Yes, and chilled, and miserable. I feel as if I had been wound up to a certain pitch—too tight—and something inside of me had snapped." She rested her head against the table upon her bare arm.

"You want to rest," he said, "and to be quiet. I'll go; I'll leave you and let you rest."

"Yes," she replied.

He stood up beside her and smoothed her hair with his soft, magnetic hand. His touch conveyed to her a certain physical comfort. She could have fallen quietly asleep there if he had continued to pass his hand over her hair. He brushed the hair upward from the nape of her neck.

"I hope you will feel better and happier in the morning," he said. "You have tried to do too much in the past few days. The dinner was the last straw; you might have dispensed with it."

"Yes," she admitted; "it was stupid."

"No, it was delightful; but it has worn you out." His hand had strayed to her beautiful shoulders, and he could feel the response of her flesh to his touch. He seated himself beside her and kissed her lightly upon the shoulder.

"I thought you were going away," she said, in an uneven voice.

"I am, after I have said good night."

"Good night," she murmured.

He did not answer, except to continue to caress her. He did not say good night until she had become supple to his gentle, seductive entreaties.

XXXII

When Mr. Pontellier learned of his wife's intention to abandon her home and take up her residence elsewhere, he immediately wrote her a letter of unqualified disapproval and remonstrance. She had given reasons which he was unwilling to acknowledge as adequate. He hoped she had not acted upon her rash impulse; and he begged her to consider first, foremost, and above all else, what people would say. He was not dreaming of scandal when he uttered this warning; that was a thing which would never have entered into his mind to consider in connection with his wife's name or his own. He was simply thinking of his financial integrity. It might get noised about that the Pontelliers had met with reverses, and were forced to conduct their *ménage* on a humbler scale than heretofore. It might do incalculable mischief to his business prospects.

But remembering Edna's whimsical turn of mind of late, and foreseeing that she had immediately acted upon her impetuous determination, he grasped the situation with his usual promptness and handled it with his well-known business tact and cleverness.

The same mail which brought to Edna his letter of disapproval carried instructions—the most minute instructions—to a well-known architect concerning the remodeling of his home, changes which he had long contemplated, and which he desired carried forward during his temporary absence.

Expert and reliable packers and movers were engaged to convey the furniture, carpets, pictures—everything movable, in short—to places of security. And in an incredibly short time the Pontellier house was turned over to the artisans. There was to be an addition—a small snuggery; there was to be frescoing, and hardwood flooring was to be put into such rooms as had not yet been subjected to this improvement.

Furthermore, in one of the daily papers appeared a brief notice to the effect that Mr. and Mrs. Pontellier were contemplating a summer sojourn abroad, and that their handsome residence on Esplanade Street was undergoing sumptuous alterations, and would not be ready for occupancy until their return. Mr. Pontellier had saved appearances!

Edna admired the skill of his maneuver, and avoided any occasion to balk his intentions. When the situation as set forth by Mr. Pontellier was accepted and taken for granted, she was apparently satisfied that it should be so.

The pigeon-house pleased her. It at once assumed the intimate character of a home, while she herself invested it with a charm which it reflected like a warm glow. There was with her a feeling of having descended in the social scale, with a corresponding sense of having risen in the spiritual. Every step which she took toward relieving herself from obligations added to her strength and expansion as an individual. She began to look with her own eyes; to see and to apprehend the deeper undercurrents of life. No longer was she content to "feed upon opinion" when her own soul had invited her.

After a little while, a few days, in fact, Edna went up and spent a week with her children in Iberville. They were delicious February days, with all the summer's promise hovering in the air.

How glad she was to see the children! She wept for very pleasure when she felt their little arms clasping her; their hard, ruddy cheeks pressed against her own glowing cheeks. She looked into their faces with hungry eyes that could not be satisfied with looking. And what stories they had to tell their mother! About the pigs, the cows, the mules! About riding to the mill behind Gluglu; fishing back in the lake with their Uncle Jasper; picking pecans with Lidie's little black brood, and hauling chips in their express wagon. It was a thousand times more fun to haul real chips for old lame Susie's real fire than to drag painted blocks along the banquette on Esplanade Street!

She went with them herself to see the pigs and the cows, to look at the darkies laying the cane, to thrash the pecan trees, and catch fish in the back lake. She lived with them a whole week long, giving them all of herself, and gathering and filling herself with their young existence. They listened, breathless, when she told them the house in Esplanade Street was crowded with workmen, hammering, nailing, sawing, and filling the place with clatter. They wanted to know where their bed was; what had been done with their rocking-horse; and where did Joe sleep, and where had Ellen gone, and the cook? But, above all, they were fired with a desire to see the little house around the block. Was there any place to play? Were there any boys next door? Raoul, with pessimistic foreboding, was convinced that there were only girls next door. Where would they sleep, and where would papa sleep? She told them the fairies would fix it all right.

The old Madame was charmed with Edna's visit, and showered all manner of delicate attentions upon her. She was delighted to know that the Esplanade Street house was in a dismantled condition. It gave her the promise and pretext to keep the children indefinitely.

It was with a wrench and a pang that Edna left her children. She carried away with her the sound of their voices and the touch of their cheeks. All along the journey homeward their presence lingered with her like the memory of a delicious song. But by the time she had regained the city the song no longer echoed in her soul. She was again alone.

XXXIII

It happened sometimes when Edna went to see Mademoiselle Reisz that the little musician was absent, giving a lesson or making some small necessary household purchase. The key was always left in a secret hiding-place in the entry, which Edna knew. If Mademoiselle happened to be away, Edna would usually enter and wait for her return.

When she knocked at Mademoiselle Reisz's door one afternoon there was no response; so unlocking the door, as usual, she entered and found the apartment deserted, as she had expected. Her day had been quite filled up, and it was for a rest, for a refuge, and to talk about Robert, that she sought out her friend.

She had worked at her canvas—a young Italian character study—all the morning, completing the work without the model; but there had been many interruptions, some incident to her modest housekeeping, and others of a social nature.

Madame Ratignolle had dragged herself over, avoiding the too public thoroughfares, she said. She complained that Edna had neglected her much of late. Besides, she was consumed with curiosity to see the little house and the manner in which it was conducted. She wanted to hear all about the dinner party; Monsieur Ratignolle had left *so* early. What had happened after he left? The champagne and grapes which Edna sent over were *too* delicious. She had so little appetite; they had refreshed and toned her stomach. Where on earth was she going to put Mr. Pontellier in that little house, and the boys? And then she made Edna promise to go to her when her hour of trial overtook her.

"At any time—any time of the day or night, dear," Edna assured her.

Before leaving Madame Ratignolle said:

"In some way you seem to me like a child, Edna. You seem to act without a certain amount of reflection which is necessary in this life. That is the reason I want to say you mustn't mind if I advise you to be a little careful while you are living here alone. Why don't you have some one come and stay with you? Wouldn't Mademoiselle Reisz come?"

"No; she wouldn't wish to come, and I shouldn't want her always with me."

"Well, the reason—you know how evil-minded the world is—some one was talking of Alcée Arobin visiting you. Of course, it wouldn't matter if

Mr. Arobin had not such a dreadful reputation. Monsieur Ratignolle was telling me that his attentions alone are considered enough to ruin a woman's name."

"Does he boast of his successes?" asked Edna, indifferently, squinting at her picture.

"No, I think not. I believe he is a decent fellow as far as that goes. But his character is so well known among the men. I shan't be able to come back and see you; it was very, very imprudent to-day."

"Mind the step!" cried Edna.

"Don't neglect me," entreated Madame Ratignolle; "and don't mind what I said about Arobin, or having some one to stay with you."

"Of course not," Edna laughed. "You may say anything you like to me." They kissed each other good-by. Madame Ratignolle had not far to go, and Edna stood on the porch a while watching her walk down the street.

Then in the afternoon Mrs. Merriman and Mrs. Highcamp had made their "party call." Edna felt that they might have dispensed with the formality. They had also come to invite her to play *vingt-et-un* one evening at Mrs. Merriman's. She was asked to go early, to dinner, and Mr. Merriman or Mr. Arobin would take her home. Edna accepted in a half-hearted way. She sometimes felt very tired of Mrs. Highcamp and Mrs. Merriman.

Late in the afternoon she sought refuge with Mademoiselle Reisz, and stayed there alone, waiting for her, feeling a kind of repose invade her with the very atmosphere of the shabby, unpretentious little room.

Edna sat at the window, which looked out over the house-tops and across the river. The window frame was filled with pots of flowers, and she sat and picked the dry leaves from a rose geranium. The day was warm, and the breeze which blew from the river was very pleasant. She removed her hat and laid it on the piano. She went on picking the leaves and digging around the plants with her hat pin. Once she thought she heard Mademoiselle Reisz approaching. But it was a young black girl, who came in, bringing a small bundle of laundry, which she deposited in the adjoining room, and went away.

Edna seated herself at the piano, and softly picked out with one hand the bars of a piece of music which lay open before her. A half-hour went by. There was the occasional sound of people going and coming in the lower hall. She was growing interested in her occupation of picking out the aria, when there was a second rap at the door. She vaguely wondered what these people did when they found Mademoiselle's door locked.

"Come in," she called, turning her face toward the door. And this time it was Robert Lebrun who presented himself. She attempted to rise; she could not have done so without betraying the agitation which mastered her at sight of him, so she fell back upon the stool, only exclaiming, "Why, Robert!"

He came and clasped her hand, seemingly without knowing what he was saying or doing.

"Mrs. Pontellier! How do you happen—oh! how well you look! Is Mademoiselle Reisz not here? I never expected to see you."

"When did you come back?" asked Edna in an unsteady voice, wiping her face with her handkerchief. She seemed ill at ease on the piano stool, and he begged her to take the chair by the window. She did so, mechanically, while he seated himself on the stool.

"I returned day before yesterday," he answered, while he leaned his arm on the keys, bringing forth a crash of discordant sound.

"Day before yesterday!" she repeated, aloud; and went on thinking to herself, "day before yesterday," in a sort of an uncomprehending way. She had pictured him seeking her at the very first hour, and he had lived under the same sky since day before yesterday; while only by accident had he stumbled upon her. Mademoiselle must have lied when she said, "Poor fool, he loves you."

"Day before yesterday," she repeated, breaking off a spray of Mademoiselle's geranium; "then if you had not met me here to-day you wouldn't—when—that is, didn't you mean to come and see me?"

"Of course, I should have gone to see you. There have been so many things—" he turned the leaves of Mademoiselle's music nervously. "I started in at once yesterday with the old firm. After all there is as much chance for me here as there was there—that is, I might find it profitable some day. The Mexicans were not very congenial."

So he had come back because the Mexicans were not congenial; because business was as profitable here as there; because of any reason, and not because he cared to be near her. She remembered the day she sat on the floor, turning the pages of his letter, seeking the reason which was left untold.

She had not noticed how he looked—only feeling his presence; but she turned deliberately and observed him. After all, he had been absent but a few months, and was not changed. His hair—the color of hers—waved back from his temples in the same way as before. His skin was not more burned than it had been at Grand Isle. She found in his eyes, when he looked at her for one silent moment, the same tender caress, with an added warmth and entreaty which had not been there before—the same glance which had penetrated to the sleeping places of her soul and awakened them.

A hundred times Edna had pictured Robert's return, and imagined their first meeting. It was usually at her home, whither he had sought her out at once. She always fancied him expressing or betraying in some way his love for her. And here, the reality was that they sat ten feet apart, she at the window, crushing geranium leaves in her hand and smelling them, he twirling around on the piano stool, saying:

"I was very much surprised to hear of Mr. Pontellier's absence; it's a wonder Mademoiselle Reisz did not tell me; and your moving—mother told me yesterday. I should think you would have gone to New York with him, or to Iberville with the children, rather than be bothered here with housekeeping. And you are going abroad, too, I hear. We shan't have you at Grand Isle next summer; it won't seem—do you see much of Mademoiselle Reisz? She often spoke of you in the few letters she wrote."

"Do you remember that you promised to write to me when you went away?" A flush overspread his whole face.

"I couldn't believe that my letters would be of any interest to you."

"That is an excuse; it isn't the truth." Edna reached for her hat on the piano. She adjusted it, sticking the hat pin through the heavy coil of hair with some deliberation.

"Are you not going to wait for Mademoiselle Reisz?" asked Robert.

"No; I have found when she is absent this long, she is liable not to come back till late." She drew on her gloves, and Robert picked up his hat.

"Won't you wait for her?" asked Edna.

"Not if you think she will not be back till late," adding, as if suddenly aware of some discourtesy in his speech, "and I should miss the pleasure of walking home with you." Edna locked the door and put the key back in its hiding-place.

They went together, picking their way across muddy streets and sidewalks encumbered with the cheap display of small tradesmen. Part of the distance they rode in the car, and after disembarking, passed the Pontellier mansion, which looked broken and half torn asunder. Robert had never known the house, and looked at it with interest.

"I never knew you in your home," he remarked.

"I am glad you did not."

"Why?" She did not answer. They went on around the corner, and it seemed as if her dreams were coming true after all, when he followed her into the little house.

"You must stay and dine with me, Robert. You see I am all alone, and it is so long since I have seen you. There is so much I want to ask you."

She took off her hat and gloves. He stood irresolute, making some excuse about his mother who expected him; he even muttered something about an engagement. She struck a match and lit the lamp on the table; it was growing dusk. When he saw her face in the lamp-light, looking pained, with all the soft lines gone out of it, he threw his hat aside and seated himself.

"Oh! you know I want to stay if you will let me!" he exclaimed. All the softness came back. She laughed, and went and put her hand on his shoulder.

"This is the first moment you have seemed like the old Robert. I'll go tell Celestine." She hurried away to tell Celestine to set an extra place. She even sent her off in search of some added delicacy which she had not thought of for herself. And she recommended great care in dripping the coffee and having the omelet done to a proper turn.

When she reëntered, Robert was turning over magazines, sketches, and things that lay upon the table in great disorder. He picked up a photograph, and exclaimed:

"Alcée Arobin! What on earth is his picture doing here?"

"I tried to make a sketch of his head one day," answered Edna, "and he thought the photograph might help me. It was at the other house. I thought it had been left there. I must have packed it up with my drawing materials."

"I should think you would give it back to him if you have finished with it."

"Oh! I have a great many such photographs. I never think of returning them. They don't amount to anything." Robert kept on looking at the picture.

"It seems to me—do you think his head worth drawing? Is he a friend of Mr. Pontellier's? You never said you knew him."

"He isn't a friend of Mr. Pontellier's; he's a friend of mine. I always knew him—that is, it is only of late that I know him pretty well. But I'd rather talk about you, and know what you have been seeing and doing and feeling out there in Mexico." Robert threw aside the picture.

"I've been seeing the waves and the white beach of Grand Isle; the quiet, grassy street of the *Chênière;* the old fort at Grande Terre. I've been working like a machine, and feeling like a lost soul. There was nothing interesting."

She leaned her head upon her hand to shade her eyes from the light.

"And what have you been seeing and doing and feeling all these days?" he asked.

"I've been seeing the waves and the white beach of Grand Isle; the quiet, grassy street of the *Chênière Caminada;* the old sunny fort at Grande Terre. I've been working with a little more comprehension than a machine, and still feeling like a lost soul. There was nothing interesting."

"Mrs. Pontellier, you are cruel," he said, with feeling, closing his eyes and resting his head back in his chair. They remained in silence till old Celestine announced dinner.

XXXIV

The dining-room was very small. Edna's round mahogany would have almost filled it. As it was there was but a step or two from the little table to the kitchen, to the mantel, the small buffet, and the side door that opened out on the narrow brick-paved yard.

A certain degree of ceremony settled upon them with the announcement of dinner. There was no return to personalities. Robert related incidents of his sojourn in Mexico, and Edna talked of events likely to interest him, which had occurred during his absence. The dinner was of ordinary quality, except for the few delicacies which she had sent out to purchase. Old Celestine, with a bandana *tignon* twisted about her head, hobbled in and out, taking a personal interest in everything; and she lingered occasionally to talk patois with Robert, whom she had known as a boy.

He went out to a neighboring cigar stand to purchase cigarette papers, and when he came back he found that Celestine had served the black coffee in the parlor.

"Perhaps I shouldn't have come back," he said. "When you are tired of me, tell me to go."

"You never tire me. You must have forgotten the hours and hours at Grand Isle in which we grew accustomed to each other and used to being together."

"I have forgotten nothing at Grand Isle," he said, not looking at her, but rolling a cigarette. His tobacco pouch, which he laid upon the table, was a fantastic embroidered silk affair, evidently the handiwork of a woman.

"You used to carry your tobacco in a rubber pouch," said Edna, picking up the pouch and examining the needlework.

"Yes; it was lost."

"Where did you buy this one? In Mexico?"

"It was given to me by a Vera Cruz girl; they are very generous," he replied, striking a match and lighting his cigarette.

"They are very handsome, I suppose, those Mexican women; very picturesque, with their black eyes and their lace scarfs."

"Some are; others are hideous. Just as you find women everywhere."

"What was she like—the one who gave you the pouch? You must have known her very well."

"She was very ordinary. She wasn't of the slightest importance. I knew her well enough."

"Did you visit at her house? Was it interesting? I should like to know and hear about the people you met, and the impressions they made on you."

"There are some people who leave impressions not so lasting as the imprint of an oar upon the water."

"Was she such a one?"

"It would be ungenerous for me to admit that she was of that order and kind." He thrust the pouch back in his pocket, as if to put away the subject with the trifle which had brought it up.

Arobin dropped in with a message from Mrs. Merriman, to say that the card party was postponed on account of the illness of one of her children.

"How do you do, Arobin?" said Robert, rising from the obscurity.

"Oh! Lebrun. To be sure! I heard yesterday you were back. How did they treat you down in Mexique?"

"Fairly well."

"But not well enough to keep you there. Stunning girls, though, in Mexico. I thought I should never get away from Vera Cruz when I was down there a couple of years ago."

"Did they embroider slippers and tobacco pouches and hat-bands and things for you?" asked Edna.

"Oh! my! no! I didn't get so deep in their regard. I fear they made more impression on me than I made on them."

"You were less fortunate than Robert, then."

"I am always less fortunate than Robert. Has he been imparting tender confidences?"

"I've been imposing myself long enough," said Robert, rising, and shaking hands with Edna. "Please convey my regards to Mr. Pontellier when you write."

He shook hands with Arobin and went away.

"Fine fellow, that Lebrun," said Arobin when Robert had gone. "I never heard you speak of him."

"I knew him last summer at Grand Isle," she replied. "Here is that photograph of yours. Don't you want it?"

"What do I want with it? Throw it away." She threw it back on the table.

"I'm not going to Mrs. Merriman's," she said. "If you see her, tell her so. But perhaps I had better write. I think I shall write now, and say that I am sorry her child is sick, and tell her not to count on me."

"It would be a good scheme," acquiesced Arobin. "I don't blame you; stupid lot!"

Edna opened the blotter, and having procured paper and pen, began to write the note. Arobin lit a cigar and read the evening paper, which he had in his pocket.

"What is the date?" she asked. He told her.

"Will you mail this for me when you go out?"

"Certainly." He read to her little bits out of the newspaper, while she straightened things on the table.

"What do you want to do?" he asked, throwing aside the paper. "Do you want to go out for a walk or a drive or anything? It would be a fine night to drive."

"No; I don't want to do anything but just be quiet. You go away and amuse yourself. Don't stay."

"I'll go away if I must; but I shan't amuse myself. You know that I only live when I am near you."

He stood up to bid her good night.

"Is that one of the things you always say to women?"

"I have said it before, but I don't think I ever came so near meaning it," he answered with a smile. There were no warm lights in her eyes; only a dreamy, absent look.

"Good night. I adore you. Sleep well," he said, and he kissed her hand and went away.

She stayed alone in a kind of reverie—a sort of stupor. Step by step she lived over every instant of the time she had been with Robert after he had entered Mademoiselle Reisz's door. She recalled his words, his looks. How few and meager they had been for her hungry heart! A vision —a transcendently seductive vision of a Mexican girl arose before her. She writhed with a jealous pang. She wondered when he would come back. He had not said he would come back. She had been with him, had heard his voice and touched his hand. But some way he had seemed nearer to her off there in Mexico.

XXXV

The morning was full of sunlight and hope. Edna could see before her no denial—only the promise of excessive joy. She lay in bed awake, with bright eyes full of speculation. "He loves you, poor fool." If she could but get that conviction firmly fixed in her mind, what mattered about the rest? She felt she had been childish and unwise the night before in giving herself over to despondency. She recapitulated the motives which no doubt explained Robert's reserve. They were not insurmountable; they would not hold if he really loved her; they could not hold against her own passion, which he must come to realize in time. She pictured him going to his business that morning. She even saw how he was dressed; how he walked down one street, and turned the corner of another; saw him bending over his desk, talking to people who entered the office, going to his lunch, and perhaps watching for her on the street. He would come to her in the afternoon or evening, sit and roll his cigarette, talk a little, and go away as he had done the night before. But how delicious it would be to have him there with her! She would have no regrets, nor seek to penetrate his reserve if he still chose to wear it.

Edna ate her breakfast only half dressed. The maid brought her a delicious printed scrawl from Raoul, expressing his love, asking her to send him some bonbons, and telling her they had found that morning ten tiny white pigs all lying in a row beside Lidie's big white pig.

A letter also came from her husband, saying he hoped to be back early in March, and then they would get ready for that journey abroad which he had promised her so long, which he felt now fully able to afford; he felt able to travel as people should, without any thought of small economies—thanks to his recent speculations in Wall Street.

Much to her surprise she received a note from Arobin, written at midnight from the club. It was to say good morning to her, to hope she had slept well, to assure her of his devotion, which he trusted she in some faintest manner returned.

All these letters were pleasing to her. She answered the children in a cheerful frame of mind, promising them bonbons, and congratulating them upon their happy find of the little pigs.

She answered her husband with friendly evasiveness,—not with any fixed design to mislead him, only because all sense of reality had gone out of her life; she had abandoned herself to Fate, and awaited the consequences with indifference.

To Arobin's note she made no reply. She put it under Celestine's stove-lid.

Edna worked several hours with much spirit. She saw no one but a picture dealer, who asked her if it were true that she was going abroad to study in Paris.

She said possibly she might, and he negotiated with her for some Parisian studies to reach him in time for the holiday trade in December.

Robert did not come that day. She was keenly disappointed. He did not come the following day, nor the next. Each morning she awoke with hope, and each night she was a prey to despondency. She was tempted to seek him out. But far from yielding to the impulse, she avoided any occasion which might throw her in his way. She did not go to Mademoiselle Reisz's nor pass by Madame Lebrun's, as she might have done if he had still been in Mexico.

When Arobin, one night, urged her to drive with him, she went—out to the lake, on the Shell Road. His horses were full of mettle, and even a little unmanageable. She liked the rapid gait at which they spun along, and the quick, sharp sound of the horses' hoofs on the hard road. They did not stop anywhere to eat or to drink. Arobin was not needlessly imprudent. But they ate and they drank when they regained Edna's little dining-room—which was comparatively early in the evening.

It was late when he left her. It was getting to be more than a passing whim with Arobin to see her and be with her. He had detected the latent sensuality, which unfolded under his delicate sense of her nature's requirements like a torpid, torrid, sensitive blossom.

There was no despondency when she fell asleep that night; nor was there hope when she awoke in the morning.

XXXVI

There was a garden out in the suburbs; a small, leafy corner, with a few green tables under the orange trees. An old cat slept all day on the stone step in the sun, and an old *mulatresse* slept her idle hours away in her chair at the open window, till some one happened to knock on one of the green tables. She had milk and cream cheese to sell, and bread and butter. There was no one who could make such excellent coffee or fry a chicken so golden brown as she.

The place was too modest to attract the attention of people of fashion, and so quiet as to have escaped the notice of those in search of pleasure and dissipation. Edna had discovered it accidentally one day when the high-board gate stood ajar. She caught sight of a little green table, blotched with the checkered sunlight that filtered through the quivering leaves overhead. Within she had found the slumbering *mulatresse*, the drowsy cat, and a glass of milk which reminded her of the milk she had tasted in Iberville.

She often stopped there during her perambulations; sometimes taking a book with her, and sitting an hour or two under the trees when she found the place deserted. Once or twice she took a quiet dinner there alone, having instructed Celestine beforehand to prepare no dinner at home. It was the last place in the city where she would have expected to meet any one she knew.

Still she was not astonished when, as she was partaking of a modest dinner late in the afternoon, looking into an open book, stroking the cat, which had made friends with her—she was not greatly astonished to see Robert come in at the tall garden gate.

"I am destined to see you only by accident," she said, shoving the cat off the chair beside her. He was surprised, ill at ease, almost embarrassed at meeting her thus so unexpectedly.

"Do you come here often?" he asked.

"I almost live here," she said.

"I used to drop in very often for a cup of Catiche's good coffee. This is the first time since I came back."

"She'll bring you a plate, and you will share my dinner. There's always enough for two—even three." Edna had intended to be indifferent and as reserved as he when she met him; she had reached the determination by a laborious train of reasoning, incident to one of her despondent moods. But her resolve melted when she saw him before her, seated there beside her in the little garden, as if a designing Providence had led him into her path.

"Why have you kept away from me, Robert?" she asked, closing the book that lay open upon the table.

"Why are you so personal, Mrs. Pontellier? Why do you force me to idiotic subterfuges?" he exclaimed with sudden warmth. "I suppose there's no use telling you I've been very busy, or that I've been sick, or that I've been to see you and not found you at home. Please let me off with any one of these excuses."

"You are the embodiment of selfishness," she said. "You save yourself something—I don't know what—but there is some selfish motive, and in sparing yourself you never consider for a moment what I think, or how I feel your neglect and indifference. I suppose this is what you would call unwomanly; but I have got into a habit of expressing myself. It doesn't matter to me, and you may think me unwomanly if you like."

"No; I only think you cruel, as I said the other day. Maybe not intentionally cruel; but you seem to be forcing me into disclosures which can result in nothing; as if you would have me bare a wound for the pleasure of looking at it, without the intention or power of healing it."

"I'm spoiling your dinner, Robert; never mind what I say. You haven't eaten a morsel."

"I only came in for a cup of coffee." His sensitive face was all disfigured with excitement.

"Isn't this a delightful place?" she remarked. "I am so glad it has never actually been discovered. It is so quiet, so sweet, here. Do you notice there is scarcely a sound to be heard? It's so out of the way; and a good walk from the car. However, I don't mind walking. I always feel so sorry for women who don't like to walk; they miss so much—so many rare little glimpses of life; and we women learn so little of life on the whole.

"Catiche's coffee is always hot. I don't know how she manages it, here in the open air. Celestine's coffee gets cold bringing it from the kitchen to the dining-room. Three lumps! How can you drink it so sweet? Take some of the cress with your chop; it's so biting and crisp. Then there's the advantage of being able to smoke with your coffee out here. Now, in the city—aren't you going to smoke?"

"After a while," he said, laying a cigar on the table.

"Who gave it to you?" she laughed.

"I bought it. I suppose I'm getting reckless; I bought a whole box." She was determined not to be personal again and make him uncomfortable.

The cat made friends with him, and climbed into his lap when he smoked his cigar. He stroked her silky fur, and talked a little about her. He looked at Edna's book, which he had read; and he told her the end, to save her the trouble of wading through it, he said.

Again he accompanied her back to her home; and it was after dusk when they reached the little "pigeon-house." She did not ask him to remain, which he was grateful for, as it permitted him to stay without the discomfort of blundering through an excuse which he had no intention of considering. He helped her to light the lamp; then she went into her room to take off her hat and to bathe her face and hands.

When she came back Robert was not examining the pictures and magazines as before; he sat off in the shadow, leaning his head back on the chair as if in a reverie. Edna lingered a moment beside the table, arranging the books there. Then she went across the room to where he sat. She bent over the arm of his chair and called his name.

"Robert," she said, "are you asleep?"

"No," he answered, looking up at her.

She leaned over and kissed him—a soft, cool, delicate kiss, whose voluptuous sting penetrated his whole being—then she moved away from him. He followed, and took her in his arms, just holding her close to him. She put her hand up to his face and pressed his cheek against her own. The action was full of love and tenderness. He sought her lips again. Then he drew her down upon the sofa beside him and held her hand in both of his.

"Now you know," he said, "now you know what I have been fighting against since last summer at Grand Isle; what drove me away and drove me back again."

"Why have you been fighting against it?" she asked. Her face glowed with soft lights.

"Why? Because you were not free; you were Léonce Pontellier's wife.

I couldn't help loving you if you were ten times his wife; but so long as I went away from you and kept away I could help telling you so." She put her free hand up to his shoulder, and then against his cheek, rubbing it softly. He kissed her again. His face was warm and flushed.

"There in Mexico I was thinking of you all the time, and longing for you."

"But not writing to me," she interrupted.

"Something put into my head that you cared for me; and I lost my senses. I forgot everything but a wild dream of your some way becoming my wife."

"Your wife!"

"Religion, loyalty, everything would give way if only you cared."

"Then you must have forgotten that I was Léonce Pontellier's wife."

"Oh! I was demented, dreaming of wild, impossible things, recalling men who had set their wives free, we have heard of such things."

"Yes, we have heard of such things."

"I came back full of vague, mad intentions. And when I got here—"

"When you got here you never came near me!" She was still caressing his cheek.

"I realized what a cur I was to dream of such a thing, even if you had been willing."

She took his face between her hands and looked into it as if she would never withdraw her eyes more. She kissed him on the forehead, the eyes, the cheeks, and the lips.

"You have been a very, very foolish boy, wasting your time dreaming of impossible things when you speak of Mr. Pontellier setting me free! I am no longer one of Mr. Pontellier's possessions to dispose of or not. I give myself where I choose. If he were to say, 'Here, Robert, take her and be happy; she is yours,' I should laugh at you both."

His face grew a little white. "What do you mean?" he asked.

There was a knock at the door. Old Celestine came in to say that Madame Ratignolle's servant had come around the back way with a message that Madame had been taken sick and begged Mrs. Pontellier to go to her immediately.

"Yes, yes," said Edna, rising; "I promised. Tell her yes—to wait for me. I'll go back with her."

"Let me walk over with you," offered Robert.

"No," she said; "I will go with the servant." She went into her room to put on her hat, and when she came in again she sat once more upon the sofa beside him. He had not stirred. She put her arms about his neck.

"Good-by, my sweet Robert. Tell me good-by." He kissed her with a degree of passion which had not before entered into his caress, and strained her to him.

"I love you," she whispered, "only you; no one but you. It was you who awoke me last summer out of a life-long, stupid dream. Oh! you have made me so unhappy with your indifference. Oh! I have suffered, suffered! Now you are here we shall love each other, my Robert. We shall be everything to each other. Nothing else in the world is of any consequence. I must go to my friend; but you will wait for me? No matter how late; you will wait for me, Robert?"

"Don't go; don't go! Oh! Edna, stay with me," he pleaded. "Why should you go? Stay with me, stay with me."

"I shall come back as soon as I can; I shall find you here." She buried her face in his neck, and said good-by again. Her seductive voice, together with his great love for her, had enthralled his senses, had deprived him of every impulse but the longing to hold her and keep her.

XXXVII

Edna looked in at the drug store. Monsieur Ratignolle was putting up a mixture himself, very carefully, dropping a red liquid into a tiny glass. He was grateful to Edna for having come; her presence would be a comfort to his wife. Madame Ratignolle's sister, who had always been with her at such trying times, had not been able to come up from the plantation, and Adèle had been inconsolable until Mrs. Pontellier so kindly promised to come to her. The nurse had been with them at night for the past week, as she lived a great distance away. And Dr. Mandelet had been coming and going all the afternoon. They were then looking for him any moment.

Edna hastened upstairs by a private stairway that led from the rear of the store to the apartments above. The children were all sleeping in a back room. Madame Ratignolle was in the salon, whither she had strayed in her suffering impatience. She sat on the sofa, clad in an ample white *peignoir*, holding a handkerchief tight in her hand with a nervous clutch. Her face was drawn and pinched, her sweet blue eyes haggard and unnatural. All her beautiful hair had been drawn back and plaited.

It lay in a long braid on the sofa pillow, coiled like a golden serpent. The nurse, a comfortable looking *Griffe* woman in white apron and cap, was urging her to return to her bedroom.

"There is no use, there is no use," she said at once to Edna. "We must get rid of Mandelet; he is getting too old and careless. He said he would be here at half-past seven; now it must be eight. See what time it is, Joséphine."

The woman was possessed of a cheerful nature, and refused to take any situation too seriously, especially a situation with which she was so familiar. She urged Madame to have courage and patience. But Madame only set her teeth hard into her under lip, and Edna saw the sweat gather in beads on her white forehead. After a moment or two she uttered a profound sigh and wiped her face with the handkerchief rolled in a ball. She appeared exhausted. The nurse gave her a fresh handkerchief, sprinkled with cologne water.

"This is too much!" she cried. "Mandelet ought to be killed! Where is Alphonse? Is it possible I am to be abandoned like this—neglected by every one?"

"Neglected, indeed!" exclaimed the nurse. Wasn't she there? And here was Mrs. Pontellier leaving, no doubt, a pleasant evening at home to devote to her? And wasn't Monsieur Ratignolle coming that very instant through the hall? And Joséphine was quite sure she had heard Doctor Mandelet's coupé. Yes, there it was, down at the door.

Adèle consented to go back to her room. She sat on the edge of a little low couch next to her bed.

Doctor Mandelet paid no attention to Madame Ratignolle's upbraidings. He was accustomed to them at such times, and was too well convinced of her loyalty to doubt it.

He was glad to see Edna, and wanted her to go with him into the salon and entertain him. But Madame Ratignolle would not consent that Edna should leave her for an instant. Between agonizing moments, she chatted a little, and said it took her mind off her sufferings.

Edna began to feel uneasy. She was seized with a vague dread. Her own like experiences seemed far away, unreal, and only half remembered. She recalled faintly an ecstasy of pain, the heavy odor of chloroform, a stupor which had deadened sensation, and an awakening to find a little new life to which she had given being, added to the great unnumbered multitude of souls that come and go.

She began to wish she had not come; her presence was not necessary.

She might have invented a pretext for staying away; she might even invent a pretext now for going. But Edna did not go. With an inward agony, with a flaming, outspoken revolt against the ways of Nature, she witnessed the scene of torture.

She was still stunned and speechless with emotion when later she leaned over her friend to kiss her and softly say good-by. Adèle, pressing her cheek, whispered in an exhausted voice: "Think of the children, Edna. Oh think of the children! Remember them!"

XXXVIII

Edna still felt dazed when she got outside in the open air. The Doctor's coupé had returned for him and stood before the *porte cochère*. She did not wish to enter the coupé, and told Doctor Mandelet she would walk; she was not afraid, and would go alone. He directed his carriage to meet him at Mrs. Pontellier's, and he started to walk home with her.

Up—away up, over the narrow street between the tall houses, the stars were blazing. The air was mild and caressing, but cool with the breath of spring and the night. They walked slowly, the Doctor with a heavy, measured tread and his hands behind him; Edna, in an absent-minded way, as she had walked one night at Grand Isle, as if her thoughts had gone ahead of her and she was striving to overtake them.

"You shouldn't have been there, Mrs. Pontellier," he said. "That was no place for you. Adèle is full of whims at such times. There were a dozen women she might have had with her, unimpressionable women. I felt that it was cruel, cruel. You shouldn't have gone."

"Oh, well!" she answered, indifferently. "I don't know that it matters after all. One has to think of the children some time or other; the sooner the better."

"When is Léonce coming back?"

"Quite soon. Some time in March."

"And you are going abroad?"

"Perhaps—no, I am not going. I'm not going to be forced into doing things. I don't want to go abroad. I want to be let alone. Nobody has any right—except children, perhaps—and even then, it seems to me— or it did seem—" She felt that her speech was voicing the incoherency of her thoughts, and stopped abruptly.

"The trouble is," sighed the Doctor, grasping her meaning intuitively, "that youth is given up to illusions. It seems to be a provision of Nature; a decoy to secure mothers for the race. And Nature takes no account of moral consequences, of arbitrary conditions which we create, and which we feel obliged to maintain at any cost."

"Yes," she said. "The years that are gone seem like dreams—if one might go on sleeping and dreaming—but to wake up and find—oh! well! perhaps it is better to wake up after all, even to suffer, rather than to remain a dupe to illusions all one's life."

"It seems to me, my dear child," said the Doctor at parting, holding her hand, "you seem to me to be in trouble. I am not going to ask for your confidence. I will only say that if ever you feel moved to give it to me, perhaps I might help you. I know I would understand, and I tell you there are not many who would—not many, my dear."

"Some way I don't feel moved to speak of things that trouble me. Don't think I am ungrateful or that I don't appreciate your sympathy. There are periods of despondency and suffering which take possession of me. But I don't want anything but my own way. That is wanting a good deal, of course, when you have to trample upon the lives, the hearts, the prejudices of others—but no matter—still, I shouldn't want to trample upon the little lives. Oh! I don't know what I'm saying, Doctor. Good night. Don't blame me for anything."

"Yes, I will blame you if you don't come and see me soon. We will talk of things you never have dreamt of talking about before. It will do us both good. I don't want you to blame yourself, whatever comes. Good night, my child."

She let herself in at the gate, but instead of entering she sat upon the step of the porch. The night was quiet and soothing. All the tearing emotion of the last few hours seemed to fall away from her like a somber, uncomfortable garment, which she had but to loosen to be rid of. She went back to that hour before Adèle had sent for her; and her senses kindled afresh in thinking of Robert's words, the pressure of his arms, and the feeling of his lips upon her own. She could picture at that moment no greater bliss on earth than possession of the beloved one. His expression of love had already given him to her in part. When she thought that he was there at hand, waiting for her, she grew numb with the intoxication of expectancy. It was so late; he would be asleep perhaps. She would awaken him with a kiss. She hoped he would be asleep that she might arouse him with her caresses.

Still, she remembered Adèle's voice whispering, "Think of the children; think of them." She meant to think of them; that determination had driven into her soul like a death wound—but not to-night. To-morrow would be time to think of everything.

Robert was not waiting for her in the little parlor. He was nowhere at hand. The house was empty. But he had scrawled on a piece of paper that lay in the lamplight:

"I love you. Good-by—because I love you."

Edna grew faint when she read the words. She went and sat on the sofa. Then she stretched herself out there, never uttering a sound. She did not sleep. She did not go to bed. The lamp sputtered and went out. She was still awake in the morning, when Celestine unlocked the kitchen door and came in to light the fire.

XXXIX

Victor, with hammer and nails and scraps of scantling, was patching a corner of one of the galleries. Mariequita sat near by, dangling her legs, watching him work, and handing him nails from the tool-box. The sun was beating down upon them. The girl had covered her head with her apron folded into a square pad. They had been talking for an hour or more. She was never tired of hearing Victor describe the dinner at Mrs. Pontellier's. He exaggerated every detail, making it appear a veritable Lucullean feast. The flowers were in tubs, he said. The champagne was quaffed from huge golden goblets. Venus rising from the foam could have presented no more entrancing a spectacle than Mrs. Pontellier, blazing with beauty and diamonds at the head of the board, while the other women were all of them youthful houris, possessed of incomparable charms.

She got it into her head that Victor was in love with Mrs. Pontellier, and he gave her evasive answers, framed so as to confirm her belief. She grew sullen and cried a little, threatening to go off and leave him to his fine ladies. There were a dozen men crazy about her at the *Chênière;* and since it was the fashion to be in love with married people, why, she could run away any time she liked to New Orleans with Célina's husband.

Célina's husband was a fool, a coward, and a pig, and to prove it to her, Victor intended to hammer his head into a jelly the next time he encountered him. This assurance was very consoling to Mariequita. She dried her eyes, and grew cheerful at the prospect.

They were still talking of the dinner and the allurements of city life when Mrs. Pontellier herself slipped around the corner of the house. The two youngsters stayed dumb with amazement before what they considered to be an apparition. But it was really she in flesh and blood, looking tired and a little travel-stained.

"I walked up from the wharf," she said, "and heard the hammering. I supposed it was you, mending the porch. It's a good thing. I was always tripping over those loose planks last summer. How dreary and deserted everythings looks!"

It took Victor some little time to comprehend that she had come in Beaudelet's lugger, that she had come alone, and for no purpose but to rest.

"There's nothing fixed up yet, you see. I'll give you my room; it's the only place."

"Any corner will do," she assured him.

"And if you can stand Philomel's cooking," he went on, "though I might try to get her mother while you are here. Do you think she would come?" turning to Mariequita.

Mariequita thought that perhaps Philomel's mother might come for a few days, and money enough.

Beholding Mrs. Pontellier make her appearance, the girl had at once suspected a lovers' rendezvous. But Victor's astonishment was so genuine, and Mrs. Pontellier's indifference so apparent, that the disturbing notion did not lodge long in her brain. She contemplated with the greatest interest this woman who gave the most sumptuous dinners in America, and who had all the men in New Orleans at her feet.

"What time will you have dinner?" asked Edna. "I'm very hungry; but don't get anything extra."

"I'll have it ready in little or no time," he said, bustling and packing away his tools. "You may go to my room to brush up and rest yourself. Mariequita will show you."

"Thank you," said Edna. "But, do you know, I have a notion to go down to the beach and take a good wash and even a little swim, before dinner?"

"The water is too cold!" they both exclaimed. "Don't think of it."

"Well, I might go down and try—dip my toes in. Why, it seems to me the sun is hot enough to have warmed the very depths of the ocean. Could you get me a couple of towels? I'd better go right away, so as to be back in time. It would be a little too chilly if I waited till this afternoon."

Mariequita ran over to Victor's room, and returned with some towels, which she gave to Edna.

"I hope you have fish for dinner," said Edna, as she started to walk away; "but don't do anything extra if you haven't."

"Run and find Philomel's mother," Victor instructed the girl. "I'll go to the kitchen and see what I can do. By Gimminy! Women have no consideration! She might have sent me word."

Edna walked on down to the beach rather mechanically, not noticing anything special except that the sun was hot. She was not dwelling upon any particular train of thought. She had done all the thinking which was necessary after Robert went away, when she lay awake upon the sofa till morning.

She had said over and over to herself: "To-day it is Arobin; to-morrow it will be some one else. It makes no difference to me, it doesn't matter about Léonce Pontellier—but Raoul and Etienne!" She understood now clearly what she had meant long ago when she said to Adèle Ratignolle that she would give up the unessential, but she would never sacrifice herself for her children.

Despondency had come upon her there in the wakeful night, and had never lifted. There was no one thing in the world that she desired. There was no human being whom she wanted near her except Robert; and she even realized that the day would come when he, too, and the thought of him would melt out of her existence, leaving her alone. The children appeared before her like antagonists who had overcome her; who had overpowered and sought to drag her into the soul's slavery for the rest of her days. But she knew a way to elude them. She was not thinking of these things when she walked down to the beach.

The water of the Gulf stretched out before her, gleaming with the million lights of the sun. The voice of the sea is seductive, never ceasing, whispering, clamoring, murmuring, inviting the soul to wander in abysses of solitude. All along the white beach, up and down, there was no living thing in sight. A bird with a broken wing was beating the air above, reeling, fluttering, circling disabled down, down to the water.

Edna had found her old bathing suit still hanging, faded, upon its accustomed peg.

She put it on, leaving her clothing in the bath-house. But when she was there beside the sea, absolutely alone, she cast the unpleasant, pricking garments from her, and for the first time in her life she stood naked in the open air, at the mercy of the sun, the breeze that beat upon her, and the waves that invited her.

How strange and awful it seemed to stand naked under the sky! how delicious! She felt like some new-born creature, opening its eyes in a familiar world that it had never known.

The foamy wavelets curled up to her white feet, and coiled like serpents about her ankles. She walked out. The water was chill, but she walked on. The water was deep, but she lifted her white body and reached out with a long, sweeping stroke. The touch of the sea is sensuous, enfolding the body in its soft, close embrace.

She went on and on. She remembered the night she swam far out, and recalled the terror that seized her at the fear of being unable to regain the shore. She did not look back now, but went on and on, thinking of the blue-grass meadow that she had traversed when a little child, believing that it had no beginning and no end.

Her arms and legs were growing tired.

She thought of Léonce and the children. They were a part of her life. But they need not have thought that they could possess her, body and soul. How Mademoiselle Reisz would have laughed, perhaps sneered, if she knew! "And you call yourself an artist! What pretensions, Madame! The artist must possess the courageous soul that dares and defies."

Exhaustion was pressing upon and overpowering her.

"Good-by—because I love you." He did not know; he did not understand. He would never understand. Perhaps Doctor Mandelet would have understood if she had seen him—but it was too late; the shore was far behind her, and her strength was gone.

She looked into the distance, and the old terror flamed up for an instant, then sank again. Edna heard her father's voice and her sister Margaret's. She heard the barking of an old dog that was chained to the sycamore tree. The spurs of the cavalry officer clanged as he walked across the porch. There was the hum of bees, and the musky odor of pinks filled the air.

APPENDIX

As explained in the Preface, this anthology presents the final version of Kate Chopin's writings, that is, the book version of the stories she included in her two collections, and the magazine or newspaper version of the stories she published only in this way. The works are arranged in order of composition within their categories. The information given below for each item is presented in the following order: page and line numbers in the present volume; the author's final title; date of composition; first magazine and/or book publication, with date; an indication of whether the original manuscript or Mrs. Chopin's own clipping of the work is extant (all such holdings except the final draft of "Charlie" are in the possession of the Missouri Historical Society); earlier titles, if any; and differences in wording between manuscript and periodical form and/or between the magazine and book versions. The earlier of any two versions is given in brackets. In three instances cancellations in the manuscript have been recorded, either to give a glimpse of the complete creative process ("Regret"), or because the canceled material is of biographical interest ("Vagabonds" and "Confidences").

Both of Kate Chopin's collections of stories appeared in more than one edition. *Bayou Folk* was published in March, 1894, by Houghton, Mifflin & Co., Boston, and reissued in 1895, 1906, and 1911. An 1895 copy at Harvard is clearly reprinted from the unchanged original plates. A copy of the 1894 edition belonging to me has served as text. *A Night in Acadie* was published in November, 1897, by Way & Williams, Chicago. Shortly thereafter Way & Williams was bought by Herbert S. Stone & Co., who—according to Sidney Kramer's *History of Stone & Kimball and Herbert S. Stone & Co.* (Chicago, 1940, p. 298)—reissued *A Night in Acadie* in 1899. No copy bearing Stone's imprint has been found, and Kramer undoubtedly referred to a reprint which is identical with the 1897 issue except that "[Second Edition]" has been added on the title page. A copy of this second edition at Harvard is evidently reprinted from the unchanged original plates. My own copy of the first edition has served as text.

While *At Fault* was never reissued, *The Awakening* was republished in 1906 by Duffield & Company, New York. A copy of the 1906 edition at the St. Louis Public Library is evidently reprinted from the unchanged original plates. This Library's copy of *At Fault* and my own copy of the first edition of *The Awakening* have served as texts.

Kate Chopin also made a number of translations, mainly of stories by Guy de Maupassant. For a complete list of her prose writings, see my book, *Kate Chopin: A Critical Biography* (Oslo and Baton Rouge, 1969).

A number of Kate Chopin's stories and poems were published in Daniel S. Rankin, *Kate Chopin and Her Creole Stories* (Philadelphia, 1932).

In addition, some of her stories appeared in my article, "Kate Chopin: An Important St. Louis Writer Reconsidered," *Missouri Historical Society Bulletin*, XIX (January, 1963), 89-114. For use in the Appendix the title has been shortened to "Kate Chopin Reconsidered."

All footnotes in the texts are Kate Chopin's own, except where otherwise indicated.

Short Stories and Sketches

37 "Emancipation. A Life Fable," undated—late 1869 or early 1870. Published in Seyersted, "Kate Chopin Reconsidered." [MS].

39 "Wiser Than a God," June, 1889. Published in the *Philadelphia Musical Journal* (Dec., 1889).

48 "A Point at Issue," Aug., 1889. Published in the St. Louis *Post-Dispatch* (Oct. 27, 1889); subtitled "A Story of Love and Reason in Which Love Triumphs"—very likely added by the editor.

59 "Miss Witherwell's Mistake," Nov., 1889. Published in *Fashion and Fancy* (St. Louis, Feb., 1891).

67 "With the Violin," Dec. 11, 1889. Published in *Spectator* (St. Louis, Dec. 6, 1890); subtitled "A Christmas Sketch"—very likely added by the editor. [clipping]. Earlier title: "The Story that Papa Konrad Told on Christmas Eve."

71 "Mrs. Mobry's Reason," Jan. 10, 1891. Published in the New Orleans *Times-Democrat* (Apr. 23, 1893) [clipping]. Earlier titles: "A Common Crime"; "A Taint in the Blood"; "The Evil that Men Do"; "Under the Apple Tree."
    Changes on the clipping:
    78/31   pipe [lute]

80 "A No-Account Creole," originally written in 1888, rewritten Jan. 24–Feb. 24, 1891. Published in *Century* (Jan., 1894) and *Bayou Folk*. Earlier titles: "Euphrasie"; "Euphrasie's Lovers."
    The following are changes made from the magazine to the book version:
    82/26   A dozen rods or more [More than a swift stone's throw]
    86/25   awaiting [waiting for]
    87/13   talk' plenty 'bout [talk' 'bout]
    89/1–2 as he . . . darkness [as he went cantering away in the darkness]
    99/23   his going [him go]

104 "For Marse Chouchoute," Mar. 14, 1891. Published in *Youth's Companion* (Aug. 20, 1891) and *Bayou Folk*. Earlier title: "Say, We Read Lectures to You."

Changes made from magazine to book version:

104/8   *et passim* Cloutierville [Centreville]
104/12 had heard the man [had listened]
104/14 the negro [the little negro]
105/16 *et passim* Verchette [Armand]
105/37–38 these, which . . . pretentious than [these, larger than]
106/5   Why . . . and stand [Suppose he should stand]
106/6–7 with the . . . dismounted [the dancers? It would not take a moment. Chouchoute dismounted]
106/24–26 Chouchoute's . . . "It take [Chouchoute's wonderful dancing. "It take]
106/27 with a fat [with fat]
106/29 I tell you! [*va!*]
107/5   Before . . . vanished [Then he vanished]
108/36–37 gate . . . courage [gate. His courage]
109/8   little . . . of yours [little black fellow of yours]

111 "The Going Away of Liza," Apr. 4, 1891. Syndicated—American Press Association (Dec., 1892) as "The Christ Light." [clipping]. Earlier title: "A Woman Comes and Goes."

Changes on the clipping:

111/10–11 stove. Presently [stove which was there. Presently]
111/15 thirty. He was [thirty; one type of the western farmer who puts his own hand to the plow. He was]
111/20 the insinuation [the gentle insinuation]
112/17 affairs [drama]
113/5   How he flung [How he got as gray as ashes an' flung]
113/21 thurselves," said Abner [thurselves." "I don't know as the Christ Light 'll hold through it, Abner." "It's held through worse, mother, if you'll try an' remember," said Abner]
113/23–24 stacked. He sat [stacked. He had also strung a blazing lantern high up above the house-top. It was an old tradition—a homely family custom of these Rydons hanging the Christ Light out on Christmas eve to swing like a star in the darkness till the stroke of mid-night. It was a beacon to the weary, the weak, the footsore, telling that the spirit of Christ dwelt within. Abner sat]
113/27–28 his voice. The two [his voice, and a look in his blue eyes that told they had been merry once. The two]

113/29 closely. Only the [closely. Not a feature in the one but finds its counterpart in the other. Only the]

113/35 station, a settin' [station, mother, a settin']

114/5 curious animals [curious pictures of them animals]

114/8 listening. Abner was [listening, often stopping in her work to look at him intently, which she could not always do, apt as he was to resent such close scrutiny when unguarded. Her thoughts easily wandered then to the time he had brought his pretty wife home; when he was happy, and when it had taken them such a little while to learn that she did not fit into their lives. Abner's mother wished sometimes that he had been more patient; for he was not always so, during those stormy scenes in which the man's love and pride were often wounded to the quick by the taunts and insults of his young and foolish wife. Now, mother Rydon knitted, listened, and mused. Abner was]

114/14–15 mother?" "Seems like [mother?" "My years ain't as good as they was once, but seems like]

114/33 had been. Whatever [had been once. Whatever]

115/5 her shoulders. When he [her shoulders. He did not belong to a class nor to a row that talks when the heart is moved; but when he]

115/7 lids, he knelt [lids, then he knelt] (Half a dozen lines have been left out because the clipping is torn in places and the lines are therefore incomplete.)

116 "The Maid of Saint Phillippe," Apr. 19, 1891. Published in *Short Stories* (New York, Nov., 1892) with this note, very likely added by the editor: "An historical incident furnishes the ground-work of this story, the heroine of which is a girl of lofty character and noble purpose. The tale describes the abandonment of Saint Phillippe in favor of the rival village of St. Louis, and shows how the latter settlement forthwith started to become a great city." [clipping]. For a further note on the story's historical background, see Seyersted, "Kate Chopin Reconsidered."

124 "A Wizard from Gettysburg," May 25, 1891. Published in *Youth's Companion* (July 7, 1892) and *Bayou Folk.*

Changes made from magazine to book version:

124/21 violently at [violently, frightened at]

126/13–14 with . . . shrug [with sagacious and disdainful shrug]

126/20 Delmandé . . . town [Delmandé with his mother drove back from town]

127/4-5 living . . . had to [living in all the hospitals of the land; toiling when he could, starving when he must]

127/25 spoken . . . pleasantly [spoken to him pleasantly as he came in]

128/11 negroes [niggers]

128/13 he dragged [he had dragged]

128/14 traversed [was traversing]

128/30-31 commanded [said]

130/7 with his [and his]

131 "A Shameful Affair," June 5 and 7, 1891. Published in the New Orleans *Times-Democrat* (Apr. 9, 1893). [clipping]

   Changes on the clipping:

   131/1 Mildred [Miss Mildred]

   133/6 finally, in [finally, fixedly, in]

   133/10-11 to . . . High [to where the river was. High]

   133/15 cool. And [cool because the river was there. And]

   136/9-10 things—" "I think [things—let him know, please, that he is at liberty to inflict any chastisement upon me that unmannerly curs deserve." "I think]

   136/10-11 ask you never to [ask you not ever to]

   136/21 wave came [wave of color came]

137 "A Rude Awakening," July 13, 1891. Published in *Youth's Companion* (Feb. 2, 1893) and *Bayou Folk*.

   Changes from magazine to book version:

   137/4 She pointed [She gesticulated]

   137/14 you think . . . sayin' [you talkin' too fas']

   138/12-15 South . . . sneaked [South. Off in the swamp beyond the bayou weird creatures of the night were crooning a lullaby. Through the small, low window before her, Lolotte could see the moss hanging heavy from great live-oak branches, making fantastic silhouettes against the eastern sky that the big, round moon was beginning to light. Lolotte's eyes grew round and big, too, as she watched the moon creep up from branch to branch. Presently the weary girl slept as profoundly as little Nonomme. After a while lazy old Sylveste looked in at her sympathetically, and seeing that she slept, hushed the two small boys. When Lolotte awoke, the cabin was dark and quiet. A little dog had sneaked]

   138/17-18 Lolotte. . . . crying [Lolotte. She started and lifted her hands. Then with a strong sense of satisfaction she bethought her that her father had a job for the morrow. With his earnings he would cheerfully buy some food proper for Nonomme. But Nonomme was crying]

138/23 dreams that night [dreams]

138/34 pole and pail [pail and pole]

138/37 anguish in her eyes [anguish]

139/19–20–22 fur my boy [fur dat boy]

139/30 her boy [the boy]

139/31 She knew [Lolotte knew]

140/2–4 boy." . . . Jacques [boy." Jacques]

140/15 upon it [upon his lips]

141/5–7 negro . . . jamb [negro man appeared in view through the dust. He stopped at the door, leaning a shoulder lazily against the jamb]

142/11–12 Sylveste . . . uneasily [Sylveste uneasily]

141/17–18 feet. . . . lurched [feet, lurched]

141/19 that was [that stood]

141/27 expected [thought]

142/8 him there [him]

143/12–13 not so . . . at once [not so much darkened that Sylveste could not at once]

143/35 Madame [Mrs.]

143/39 lead [pile]

144/22 answered [said]

145 "A Harbinger," Sept. 11, 1891. Published in *St. Louis Magazine* (apparently Nov. 1, 1891. No copies can be found of the issues of this period). [clipping]. Earlier title: "Love's Harbinger."

147 "Doctor Chevalier's Lie," Sept. 12, 1891. Published in *Vogue* (Oct. 5, 1893). [clipping].

149 "A Very Fine Fiddle," Sept. 13, 1891. Published in *Harper's Young People* (Nov. 24, 1891) and *Bayou Folk*.

151 "Boulôt and Boulotte," Sept. 20, 1891. Published in *Harper's Young People* (Dec. 8, 1891) and *Bayou Folk*.
   Change from magazine to book version:
      151/4 'Cadian [creole]

153 "Love on the Bon-Dieu," Oct. 3, 1891. Published in *Two Tales* (Boston, July 23, 1892) and *Bayou Folk*. Earlier title: "Love and Easter."
   Changes from magazine to book version:
      153/10–11 and even [and had even]
      155/35 lives there with [lives with]
      155/35 man [fellow]

158/4   greeting; it [greeting; and it]
158/17 [nor] or
158/39 lane, missy? [lane ?]
159/36 entreated [asked]
161/26 moonlight . . . in he [moonlight he]
162/31 she . . . him [she had not known him]

164 "An Embarrassing Position. Comedy in One Act," Oct. 15–22, 1891. Published in the *Mirror* (St. Louis, Dec. 19, 1895). [clipping]. Earlier titles: "A Little Comedy at Parkhams"; "An Evening at Parkhams"; "A Social Dilemma"; "An Embarrassing Situation. Drama in One Act and One Scene."

175 "Beyond the Bayou," Nov. 7, 1891. Published in *Youth's Companion* (June 15, 1893) and *Bayou Folk*.
  Changes from magazine to book version:
    175/5   woman had [woman who lived in the hut had]
    175/6   stepped. This [stepped. All was flaming red beyond there, La Folle believed. This]
    175/7   thirty-five [thirty-five years of age]
    175/8–11 La Folle . . . there had [La Folle, or the Crazy Woman, because she had been frightened literally "out of her senses" in childhood. On that far-past day, which was in the time of the Civil War, there had]
    175/12 Maître, black [Maître,—the young master,—black]
    175/13–16 mother . . . in her [mother. His pursuers were close at his heels. The horror of that spectacle had stunned Jacqueline's childish reason. And so all across the bayou seemed to her aflame with blood color, alternating with black. Alone she dwelt in her]
    175/19 But of [Of]
    175/20 fancy [imagination]
    175/21 People . . . grown [People across the bayou at Bellissime had grown]
    175/22–25 died . . . P'tit Maître [died. La Folle had not crossed the bayou. She had stood upon her side of it, wailing and lamenting. This did not astonish the people at Bellissime. They would have been amazed had she overcome her fear of everything beyond the water. P'tit Maître]
    176/1   own. She called [own. He had often been carried across the bayou as a tiny baby, that Jacqueline might be comforted by the sight of him. The child took to her from the first. Scarcely could he toddle when he began his demands to

be taken across the bayou to be fondled by La Folle. She called]

176/8   to do. For Chéri [to do. "He used to kiss me so lovingly!" La Folle said to herself in dialect. "Ah, he used to!" For Chéri]

176/10–12   cut off . . . water [cut off. But Chéri gave La Folle two of his black curls, tied with a knot of red ribbon. That was in the heat of summer, when the water]

176/13   foot, and [foot. All]

176/34   Hair. Then [hair. He let her kiss him as a special favor, and with the air of one who is getting too old to think it proper to treat him as a baby. Then]

176/35   hand [hands]

176/39   with . . . hunter [with a look of profound intention to distinguish himself as a hunter]

177/11   whence [where]

177/16   exclaimed [said]

177/33   Venez . . . secours! [*Venez donc!* Come! come! *Au secours!* Help! help! *Au secours!*"]

178/1   upon her. She clasped [upon her. But love struggled more powerfully to impel her forward. She clasped]

178/2–3   Then . . . ran [La Folle shut her eyes, ran]

178/5   She . . . quivering [She stood quivering]

178/6   the trees [the fearful trees]

178/8   Folle . . . moi [*Folle!* (O good God, pity La Folle!) *Bon Dieu, ayez pitié moi!* Good God, help me.)"]

178/11–12   world. A child [world that to her looked more crimson than flame. A child]

178/16   Quickly the cry [As quick as light, the cry]

178/21   some . . . shouted [the cry rose]

178/24–26   bloodshot . . . Some one [bloodshot. Some one]

178/29   Chéri!" This [Chéri!" The family at Bellissime rose. This]

178/36   tread. She [tread. More and more slowly she went, with clear sense and fear dead, and joy at her heart. She]

179/36–37–180/1   gone . . . down [gone. Sweet odors swooned to her from the thousand blue violets that peeped out from green, luxuriant beds. Fragrance showered down]

180/9   Then [Now]

180/10–11   soul. La Folle [soul. All the world was fair about her, and green and white and blue and silvery shinings had come again instead of that frightful fancy of interminable red! La Folle]

180/21   upon . . . beautiful [upon this new, this beautiful]

181 "After the Winter," Dec. 31, 1891. Published in the New Orleans *Times-Democrat* (Apr. 5, 1896) and *A Night in Acadie*.

Change from newspaper to book version:
187/7   it; turn it [it; to turn it]

189 "The Bênitous' Slave," Jan. 7, 1892. Published in *Harper's Young People* (Feb. 16, 1892) and *Bayou Folk*.

Changes from magazine to book version:
189/19   over [out]
190/11   this [such]
190/14   a moment's [an instant's]
190/28–29   carry; and . . . I met [carry. So Susanne does not have to miss shool nearly so often as she did. I met]

191 "A Turkey Hunt," Jan. 8, 1892. Published in *Harper's Young People* (Feb. 16, 1892) and *Bayou Folk*.

193 "Old Aunt Peggy," Jan. 8, 1892. Published in *Bayou Folk*.

194 "The Lilies," Jan. 27–28, 1892. Published in *Wide Awake* (Apr., 1893) and *A Night in Acadie*. The magazine version was titled "How the Lilies Work. ('They toil not, neither do they spin')." The motto was very likely added by the editor.

Changes from magazine to book version:
194/21   corn [crop]
194/22   the field [his field]
196/28   right [straight]
196/35   soul! what's [soul and body! what's]

199 "Ripe Figs," Feb. 26, 1892. Published in *Vogue* (Aug. 19, 1893) and *A Night in Acadie*. The magazine version was titled "Ripe Figs. (An Idyl)." The subtitle was very likely added by the editor. Earlier title: "Babette's Visit."

Changes from magazine to book version:
199/2   on the Bayou-Lafourche [on Bayou-Bœuf]
199/14   the whole long day [the whole day long]

200 "Croque-Mitaine," Feb. 27, 1892. Published in Seyersted, "Kate Chopin Reconsidered." [MS].

202 "A Little Free-Mulatto," Feb. 28, 1892. Published in Seyersted, "Kate Chopin Reconsidered." [MS].

204 "Miss McEnders," Mar. 7, 1892. Published in *Criterion* (St. Louis, Mar. 6, 1897) as "Miss McEnders. An Episode," signed "La Tour." The subtitle was very likely added by the editor. [clipping].

212 "Loka," Apr. 9–10, 1892. Published in *Youth's Companion* (Dec. 22, 1892) and *Bayou Folk*.

Changes from magazine to book version:

212/5   appeared one day at [appeared at]
212/8   But [Nevertheless]
212/9   he did . . . until [he kept her at work until]
212/18   reckoned [guessed]
213/21   She herself was [She herself, Tontine Padue, was]
214/11   consisted of [was]
214/19   was able [could]
214/23   of the many [of any of the]
214/25   for her [for Loka]
214/26   washing [wash]
215/17   shade [sun]
216/18   Run to [Run down to]
216/20   *une pareille sauvage* [one such *sauvage*]
216/24   interposed [said]
217/1   abstraction [preoccupation]
217/3   melon ['tata]
217/9   Baptiste [Padue]
217/21   "*Par exemple!* ["*Oui*, for sure;]
217/24   entreated [said]

219 "At the 'Cadian Ball," July 15–17, 1892. Published in *Two Tales*
(Boston, Oct. 22, 1892) and *Bayou Folk.*

Changes from magazine to book version:

219/5   love [have loved]
219/12–13 man's; he thought of her [man's; her]
219/16   was [had been]
220/26   visit [see]
220/30   often. Of the [often. The]
221/14   melted with tenderness [grew as tender as a kitten's]
221/16   and her nénaine [and nainaine]
221/39   top [top of them]
222/30   during [while hearing]
222/37   but . . . house [but flashed back into the house]
223/16   "nerve" after such [grit after such]
223/39   and abandon! [such *abandon!*]
224/8   in a like [in such]
224/12   fresh [a breath of]
224/16   upon a bench out in [out upon a bench in]
225/19   answered [said]
225/29   Clarisse was standing [It was Clarisse standing]
225/30   as with one [like one]
225/32   his cousin [her]

226/11 light struggling [light that was struggling]
226/37 that was [that looked]
227/15 I could n't [I would die. I couldn']

228 "A Visit to Avoyelles," Aug. 1, 1892. Published in *Vogue* (Jan. 14, 1893) and *Bayou Folk*. The magazine version of this story, together with "Désirées's Baby," was titled "Character Studies. The Father of Désirée's Baby—The Lover of Mentine." "Character Studies" was very likely added by the editor. Earlier title: "He Visits Avoyelles."
Change from magazine to book version:
228/16 Doudouce [He]

232 "Ma'ame Pélagie," Aug. 27–28, 1892. Published in the New Orleans *Times-Democrat* (Dec. 24, 1893) and *Bayou Folk*. Earlier titles: "In the Shadow of the Ruin"; "Poor Ma'ame Pélagie."
Changes from newspaper to book version:
232/1–4 When . . . walls [Thirty years ago there stood on Côte Joyeuse a stately mansion of red brick, shaped like the Pantheon, and set in the centre of a grove of majestic liveoaks. Now, only the thick walls]
232/7 stately [princely]
233/8 please [wish]
233/13 Pélagie [Sesoeur]
233/14 *et passim* Léandre [Alcibiade]
233/18 called him [had become of a nature to call him]
233/22 throbbed into [throbbed and flitted into]
233/36 was a shock [was like a shock]
234/1–2 eyes . . . seek [face, into her eyes, with that searching gaze which seeks]
234/4 And [So]
234/5–6 La Petite . . . Joyeuse [La Petite knew what awaited her at Côte Joyeuse, and she had determined upon trying to fit herself to the strange, narrow existence]
234/11 the older woman [her]
234/32 me, tante [me first in the world, tante]
234/33 continued [said]
234/33 movement, "it [movement from side to side, "it]
234/34 another life [another kind of life]
235/5–6 added . . . sin [said in a whisper, "as if it would be a sin]
235/12 took [had taken]
235/31 the woman's soft [the soft]
235/32–33 Ma'ame Pélagie [she]

337/17 right! The [right! What does it mean? Her father has
quitted home in hurried agitation. The]

237/21–22 and of brazen [and brazen]

237/35–36 his . . . Now [his cheek that has paled like alabaster!
Now]

237/36–37 are . . . show [are about her, where she stands like a
statue. So much the better. She will show]

238/4 she . . . lay [she sat, and for hours had lain]

238/26–27 brick . . . pleasant [brick. There was more of that red
brick to be seen about the place; a cabin here and there
to shelter the working people; pathways were built of it,
and the foundations of cisterns. Not a brick of the ruin had
gone to waste. Upon a corner of the handsome, pleasant]

238/30 of young [of the young]

238/32 seemed [were]

239/1 were [seemed to be]

240 "Désirée's Baby," Nov. 24, 1892. Published in *Vogue* (Jan. 14, 1893)
and *Bayou Folk*. Cf. notes for "A Visit to Avoyelles," p. 1013. When
the *Sunday Mirror* (St. Louis) reprinted the book version on Sept. 30,
1894, the editor of the *Mirror* made a few minor changes.
Changes from magazine to book version:
241/28 true [so]
241/34 lifted it [picked it up]
241/35 the baby [it]
241/36 gaze [look]
243/22 returned [said]
244/8–9 fate. Désirée [fate. After it was dealt he felt like a
remorseless murderer. Désirée]
244/13–15 afternoon . . . Désirée [afternoon. Out in the still
fields the negroes were picking cotton; and the sun was
just sinking. Désirée]
244/16 hair [head]

246 "Caline," Dec. 2, 1892. Published in *Vogue* (May 20, 1893) and
A Night in Acadie.
Changes from magazine to book version:
247/26 with [and]
248/4 week if [week or two if]

249 "The Return of Alcibiade," Dec. 5–6, 1892. Published in *St. Louis
Life* (Dec. 17, 1892) and *Bayou Folk*.
Changes from magazine to book version:
249/11 twelve [ten]

253/6   chattered . . . When [chattered like children and laughed like the birds sing. When]

253/31   Robert McFarlane [Robert McAlpin]

254/9   Mademoiselle, what [Mademoiselle—if it is not intrusive—what]

255 "In and Out of Old Natchitoches," Feb. 1–3, 1893. Published in *Two Tales* (Boston, Apr. 8, 1893) and *Bayou Folk.*

  Changes from magazine to book version:

  255/11   six months [a six-month]

  255/17   ties [rails]

  258/23   began [said]

  258/38   *autre*" [*autre que moi*"]

  260/7   kissing [offering to kiss]

  260/38   difference . . . spoke [difference, for Suzanne and Hector had spoken]

  261/13   together [altogether]

  262/29   can [can readily]

  264/8   into . . . fallen in [he had fallen into in]

  264/20   he broke in [he said]

  264/33   blurted [said]

  265/3   wait," [wait, sir."]

  265/6–9   end . . . after [end of the gallery—the part that was vine-sheltered, and where the perfume was thickest. "Hector," she said after]

  265/12   stop nor [stop what he was doing, nor]

  265/36   muscles [muscles that followed]

  266/8   return [return again]

  266/29   feeling [feelings]

268 "Mamouche," Feb. 24–25, 1893. Published in *Youth's Companion* (Apr. 19, 1894) and *A Night in Acadie.* Earlier title: "A Romantic Attachment."

  Changes from magazine to book version:

  268/6   negro [negro man]

  271/10   out [about]

  271/25   his [the]

  272/19   boy? [boy, Marsh?]

276 "Madame Célestin's Divorce," May 24–25, 1893. Published in *Bayou Folk.*

280 "An Idle Fellow," June 9, 1893. First published here. [MS].

282 "A Matter of Prejudice," June 17–18, 1893. Published in *Youth's Companion* (Sept. 25, 1895) and *A Night in Acadie.* The magazine version

was subtitled "The strange Result of disturbing Madame Carambeau"
–very likely added by the editor.

Changes from magazine to book version:
283/29 Her cheek [The cheek]
283/30 her hands [the hands]
284/4 which [that]
284/25–26 but they [but]

289 "Azélie," July 22–23, 1893. Published in *Century* (Dec., 1894) and
A Night in Acadie. Earlier titles: "Polyte's Misfortune"; "Amélite";
"Amandine."

Changes from magazine to book version:
293/37 the "key" to the [the]
295/27–28 Leave . . . Leave [Let me 'lone, I say! Let]

298 "A Lady of Bayou St. John," Aug. 24–25, 1893. Published in *Vogue*
(Sept. 21, 1893) and *Bayou Folk*.

Change from magazine to book version:
298/10 *et passim* Manna-Loulou [Manna-Lulu]

303 "La Belle Zoraïde," Sept. 21, 1893. Published in *Vogue* (Jan. 4, 1894)
and *Bayou Folk*. The magazine version was subtitled "A Tragedy of
the Old Regime"—very likely added by the editor. Earlier titles:
"Li Mouri"; "One of Man Loulou's Stories."

Changes from magazine to book version:
304/2 which [that]
305/16 Bon Dieu Seigneur [Ah, Seigneur]
305/19–20 the worst [they]
305/24 whom [that]
305/35–37 will; . . . him [will; I could not help it]
307/36 'piti.' ['mo piti.']

309 "At Chênière Caminada," Oct. 21–23, 1893. Published in the
New Orleans *Times-Democrat* (Dec. 23, 1894) and *A Night in Acadie*.
The newspaper version was titled "Tonie."

Changes from newspaper to book version:
310/11–12 *et passim* the widow . . . mother [Mme. Lebrun and
her daughter]
310/39 Madame [Madame Lebrun]
311/8 or [nor]
316/6 that could [that he craved, and that could]
316/16–18 They . . . Madame [Mademoiselle wanted to hear
the opera as often as she could, and the island was really
too dreary with everyone gone. She]
316/24 And—the [And—and the]

319 "A Gentleman of Bayou Têche," Nov. 5–7, 1893. Published in *Bayou Folk*.

325 "In Sabine," Nov. 20–22, 1893. Published in *Bayou Folk*.

333 "A Respectable Woman," Jan. 20, 1894. Published in *Vogue* (Feb. 15, 1894) and *A Night in Acadie*.
   Changes from magazine to book version:
      334/24 dressing-room [dainty dressing-room]
      334/29 thing [things]

337 "Tante Cat'rinette," Feb. 23, 1894. Published in *Atlantic Monthly* (Sept., 1894) and *A Night in Acadie*.
   Changes from magazine to book version:
      343/21 gold [gold, red]
      343/32–33 with much [with]

345 "A Dresden Lady in Dixie," Mar. 6, 1894. Published in *Catholic Home Journal* (Mar. 3, 1895) and *A Night in Acadie*. No copy of this issue of the magazine can be found.

352 "The Story of an Hour," Apr. 19, 1894. Published in *Vogue* (Dec. 6, 1894) as "The Dream of an Hour." (Reprinted in *St. Louis Life*, Jan. 5, 1895, with a few changes very likely made by the editor.) [clipping].
   Changes on the clipping:
      353/30 live for her during [live for during]
      354/8 Her fancy [How fancy]

355 "Lilacs," May 14–16, 1894. Published in the New Orleans *Times-Democrat* (Dec. 20, 1896).

366 "The Night Came Slowly," July 24, 1894. Published in *Moods* (Philadelphia, July, 1895). This story, together with "Juanita," appeared under the title "A Scrap and a Sketch." [MS (diary entry) and clipping].
   Changes from manuscript to magazine version:
      366/2 and their actions [and actions]
      366/3–4 suffer . . . talk [suffer. Is there one of them can talk]
      366/6 slowly, softly as I [slowly as I]
      366/13 shapes [outlines]
      366/13–14 Some . . . My whole [Some stole up to peep at me as little mice do. I did not care about them. My whole]
      366/17 They tell me only [They only tell me]
      366/19–20 thrills. Why do [thrills. Black night, except a brightness across the valley where lies the East, telling that the moon was coming. Only a silver glow in the sky, and the Cedar branches limned against it like an etching.—Why do]

366/21 came to-day [came here to-day]

366/23 speech . . . Shall I [speech. I hate people who teach lies. Can he tell them aught of Christ? Shall I]

Change on the clipping:

366/7 stealthily out [stealthily from out]

367 "Juanita," July 26, 1894. Published in *Moods* (Philadelphia, July, 1895). See above entry. [MS (diary entry) and clipping].

Changes from manuscript to magazine version:

367/1 *et passim* Juanita [Annie Venn]

367/2-3 *et passim* Rock Springs [Sulphur Springs]

367/3 her there three [her three]

367/4 store. She [store and Post Office. She]

367/4-5 herself. . . considering [herself; a difficult feat considering]

367/7 substantial [solid]

367/8 when I saw her [when I have seen her]

367/16 amusement [merriment]

367/20 the "Springs" ["The Cedars"]

367/23 Juanita's career [Annie's strange career]

367/24 The . . . mother [Her father had died and she and her mother]

367/26–368/1 attract [have]

367/26 hung on [hung over]

368/2 talked about [known]

368/5 these . . . attentions [these attentions]

368/6 whom [who]

368/6 in the end [after all]

368/9–10 a Texas . . . horses [a Kansas millionaire who owned a hundred black horses]

368/11–12 time. But [time. I am wholly unable to comprehend, much less explain Annie's attraction for men; perhaps Mr. Zola might; I openly confess that I cannot. But]

368/15 first became known [was first known]

368/16 cork-leg [wooden leg]

368/18–20 to a . . . The story [to an interested public; as was evinced one morning when Annie became the mother of a baby, simultaneously with the announcement that the one-legged man was its father and her husband. The story]

368/22–23 certificate. However [certificate. Some people believe the story; others have accepted it cum granis salis. But however]

368/25 affections [affection]

368/25–27 man . . . mounted [man. To no part of this domestic combination has old Mrs. Venn taken kindly save to the baby. I caught a glimpse of the curious couple when I was in Sulphur yesterday. Annie had mounted]

368/29 whither [where]

368/30 picture . . . was [picture was]

369 "Cavanelle," July 31–Aug. 6, 1894. Published in *American Jewess* (Apr., 1895) and *A Night in Acadie*. [MS].

Changes from manuscript to magazine version:

369/4 marvelously suited to [especially suited for]

369/5 was! How well [was, and how]

369/6 sold me [sold to me]

369/8 knew that Cavanelle [knew Cavanelle]

369/9–10 why he . . . rest [why he worked without rest]

369/11 of her voice that his [of that voice his]

369/14 without . . . reproach [without reproach]

369/18 satisfied . . . In a [satisfied. In a]

369/19 thank me for [thank me, madame, for]

369/20 say . . . with [say, or my name is not Léon Cavanelle, Tolville was in voice. But, madame," with]

369/21 smile of commiseration [commiserating smile]

369/23 render' as [render' like]

370/3 *soins* . . . good [*soins*; good]

370/11 step [stepping stone]

370/13 Cavanelle that [Cavanelle one day that]

370/14 meet . . . and [meet Mathilde and hear her sing; and]

370/15 her [his sister]

370/16 He . . . not [He would otherwise not]

370/18–19 The green . . . and would [The green cars, and would]

370/23 tree, . . . anything [tree, nor the knocker nor anything]

370/25 at the door [in the front door]

370/27 from the primitive *entourage* with [from the familiar entourage with]

370/28 every gesture [every one of his many gestures]

370/31 I entreat you [Je vous en prie!]

370/34 Où es . . . did not [Où es tu?" Stupid Cavanelle who did not]

370/37–38 ceremony . . . And [ceremony to my reception. And]

371/5 Hers [Here]

371/6 snap it [snap it asunder]

371/7 could hope to overcome [could overcome]

371/8 would be [would need to be]

371/11–12 offering . . . contrast [offering contrast]
371/14 limping [lame]
371/20–21 and who would [and would]
371/23 manner [way]
371/24 early morning visit [early visit]
371/26 with avidity [with wrangling and cajoling]
371/29 pouring herself a [pouring a]
371/31 and serving [but serving]
371/38 effort . . . twirling [effort I recalled them thence and became aware that Cavanelle was twirling]
372/3 The girl [Mathilde]
372/4 she touched [her fingers touched]
372/8 The feeling [It]
372/9 which [that]
372/12–13 brother had listened [brother last listened]
372/14 look . . . was [look at Cavanelle his face was]
372/16 motion [movement]
372/19–21 But it . . . what I [It certainly was an unsympathetic, stupid, hopeless voice, that never was or never could be a blessing to possess or to listen to. I cannot remember what I]
372/22 the car [the Green car]
372/26 brain [head]
372/30 that chance [that it was not my business and that chance]
372/31 wondered [marvelled]
372/32 is he . . . spell [had he been hypnotized?"]
372/33 realized [remembered]
372/34 blind, but [blind, deaf, and idiot—but]
373/2–3 death . . . for my [death in a New Orleans paper which I received regularly. There came a momentary pang of sympathy for my]
373/5 sharp . . . pain [sharp cut of the scalpel; an agonizing moment of pain]
373/10 was . . . regaling [was now doubtless regaling]
373/20 through [beneath]
373/23–24 subject . . . wound [subject. As I had rightly imagined the wound]
373/26 Mathilde's unhappy [Mathilde and her unhappy]
373/29 you living [you still living]
373/33 That [There]
374/2 which [that]

374/4   with [against]

374/7   I was . . . brutal [I restrained with difficulty a brutal]

Changes from magazine to book version:

369/16   Montreville,' an' [Montreville in the *baignoire* of the Chopin's! : an']

369/23   Mathilde, is [Mathilde, it is]

370/23   tree . . . anything [tree, nor the knocker, the number nor anything]

370/27   the entourage [the primitive *entourage*]

370/37   to our meeting [to her greeting]

371/8   would . . . be [would be]

371/33   spare [rare]

372/6   what she sang [what it was]

373/2   in a . . . paper [in the *Picayune* paper]

375   "Regret," Sept. 17, 1894. Published in *Century* (May, 1894) and
A Night in Acadie. [MS].

Changes from manuscript to magazine version (in addition, all material canceled in the manuscript is given in parentheses):

375/1   *et passim* Aurélie [Angéla]

375/9   negroes [darkies]

375/12–13   gallery . . . a small [gallery with arms akimbo, contemplating a small]

375/25   Valsin was waiting [Valsin waiting]

376/6–7   convulsive [(disconsolate) convulsive]

376/8–9   She . . . house [(Mamzelle Angéla stood contemplating) She left them on the porch of the long, low house, crowded into the narrow strip of shade;]

376/10–12   boards . . . the gallery [boards of the gallery; some chickens were scratching (near) in the grass (near the) at the foot of the steps; one had boldly mounted and was stepping solemnly and heavily and aimlessly across the gallery]

376/12   pinks [(flowers) pinks]

376/13–14   the sound . . . cotton-field [the (voices of) sound of negroes (voices) laughter coming across the fields]

376/18   with [to]

376/19   few contemplative moments [few moments]

376/23   could . . . dismissed [could have been easily dismissed]

376/24   of this nature [of such description]

376/26   give [give to them]

376/30–31   She became . . . only when [She only became acquainted with Ti Nomme's passion for flowers when]

377/4 snapped [cracked]

377/12 Mamzelle Aurélie informed [Mamzelle informed]

377/19–20 in the raisin' an' manigement [in the man'gement]

377/24 serve the [serve (her) the]

377/27–28 She got . . . basket [She reached down the sewing-basket]

377/29 the ready . . . reach [the easy and ready reach]

377/31 the laughing, the crying [the crying, the laughing]

377/32 or [nor]

377/33–34 hot, plump [hot, (fat) plump]

377/36–37 had . . . used to [had become quite accustomed to]

377/39 away [down]

378/1–2 beside the mulatto, upright [beside him upright]

378/6 Yonder [back]

378/8 in [on]

378/14 see [follow]

378/16–17 wheezing and creaking [wheezing, creaking]

378/19 She [(Mamzelle Angéla) She]

378/19 awaiting [(before) awaiting]

378/22 She gave . . . through [She gave one (swift) slow glance (across) through]

379 "The Kiss," Sept. 19, 1894. Published in *Vogue* (Jan. 17, 1895). [MS and clipping].

Changes from manuscript to magazine version:

379/5 lent [gave]

379/9 satiny . . . curled in [silky coat of the cat that lay curled up in]

379/17 rich; and she [rich—through no talent of his own, and she]

379/26 girl arise, but [girl, but]

380/4 wish [bid]

380/5–6 was extending . . . presence [was offering him one of hers: her presence]

380/13–14 in self-justification [in justification]

380/21 frankness of manner when [frankness when]

380/24 engaging but perturbed smile [engaging smile but a little perturbed]

380/31 misinterpreted [misunderstood]

380/32–33 "of course, I know ["well I know]

380/33 you, but . . . I do [you, but I do]

381/3 "Then do you really ["Oh, do you really]

381/10 "Your . . . kiss you ["Your husband has sent me over here to kiss you," he said smiling]

381/11 face . . . throat [face and neck]

381/13 tells me [says]

381/14–15 you and . . . but he [you & me," with an insolent smile, "I don't know what you've been telling him; but he]

381/26 was a little unreasonable [was rather unreasonable]

382 "Ozème's Holiday," Sept. 23–24, 1894. Published in *Century* (Aug., 1896) and *A Night in Acadie*. [MS].

Changes from manuscript to magazine version:

382/8 described. Yet he [described and yet he]

382/8–9 He worked . . . on the [He worked very faithfully for Mr. Laballière on the]

382/9–10 sort of . . . there was [sort of all-round useful, methodical way. But when the time came for his annual holiday week, there was]

382/16 negro [darky]

382/18 almost as much again for [almost again as much for]

382/21 rather long [quite long]

383/22 town for a [town the night before for a]

383/24–25 reflection. The result [reflection, and the result]

383/27 determined upon taking [determined to take]

383/29 which [that]

383/31–32 to fry . . . a cup [to wring the neck of a chicken; drip him a cup]

383/35 shallow gallery [shallow front gallery]

383/37 which from a [which at a]

383/38 bursting . . . bolls [bursting like foam from its bolls]

384/7 hand . . . in a [hand she had tied in a]

384/12 "Good . . . man! ["Good God, man!]

384/16 woman [darky]

384/19–20 had also . . . during [had been clumsily attentive during]

384/21 or a checked [or checked]

384/26–27 was'e? . . . goin' [was'e like its doin'. Who you think's]

384/35 a man . . . He [a man too; he]

384/39 o' conscience [o' sense]

385/5 he should cook [he cook]

385/9 traveling-bag . . . traveled [travelling bag for quinine which he never travelled without]

385/10–11 on a cot covered [on the bed covered]

385/13 wrangling [disputing]

385/14–15 offered . . . That [offered. That]

385/15–16 but had pursued [but pursued]

385/20 a little reflection [a moment's reflection]

385/25 sun-up, min' you [sun up in the mo'nin', mind you]

386/9 which [that]

386/11–12 fingers . . . Sandy [fingers were really as nimble as the Lord could make them in clutching the cotton from its dry shell. He had picked about fifty or more pounds by noon. Sandy]

368/18–19 criminal . . . negligence [criminal negligence]

386/20 just . . . a turn [just as there was a turn]

386/23 then [at that moment]

386/25 field, this time urging [fields; urging]

386/31 don' grumble, don' stumble [don't stumble, don't grumble]

386/39 cotton-patch [field]

387/1 succeeding [following]

387/6 softly [gently]

387/19 specs [spec]

387/22 back . . . When he [back home. As he]

387/23 into [on to]

387/28 remainder [remains]

387/32–33 "How . . . Nobody ["How come, Mista Ozème, you didn' go yonda down the coas' like you said? Nobody]

Changes from magazine to book version:

382/4 was a [was already a]

383/4 sure that there [sure there]

383/32 thought [felt]

383/34 the not unusual [the usual]

383/35 stone [sticks]

383/37 long [little]

384/3 a wood trough [a rude trough]

384/12 "Good God A'mighty, man! ["Good land, man!]

384/35 now [too]

386/24–26 loss to . . . hand [loss for Aunt Tildy and Sandy, and Ozème again took to the field, this time urging Aunt Tildy before him to do what she might with her one sound hand]

388 "A Sentimental Soul," Nov. 18–22, 1894. Published in the New Orleans *Times-Democrat* (Dec. 22, 1895) and *A Night in Acadie.*

Changes from newspaper to book version:

390/1 of [for]

390/26 a waste [a great waste]

396/6 down in [down into]

397/7 Into the [Into this]

398 "Her Letters," Nov. 29, 1894. Published in *Vogue* (Apr. 11, 18, 1895). [clipping].

> *Changes on the clipping:*
>> 401/25 daring of [daring, the magnificence of]
>> 401/30 stir in [creep into]
>> 401/38–39 letters. A half-hour [letters. He had once seen a clair-voyant hold a letter to his forehead and purport in so doing to discover its contents. He wondered for a wild moment if such a gift, for force of wishing it, might not come to him. But he was only conscious of the smooth surface of the paper, cold against his brow, like the touch of a dead woman's hand. A half-hour]

406 "Odalie Misses Mass," Jan. 28, 1895. Published in the Shreveport *Times* (July 1, 1895) and *A Night in Acadie.*

> *Change from newspaper to book version:*
>> 409/9–10 in keeping in [with keeping in]

411 "Polydore," Feb. 17, 1895. Published in *Youth's Companion* (Apr. 23, 1896) and *A Night in Acadie.* The magazine version of the story was titled: "Polydore. Two invalids, two confessions, and a penance.—A story of a stupid boy." The subtitle was very likely added by the editor.

> *Changes from magazine to book version:*
>> 411/5 individual [lad]
>> 411/17 of the [of]
>> 413/9–10 draw out de [draw de]
>> 413/19 sure it [sure that it]
>> 413/33–36 Monsieur ... interest [*the same two sentences, but in inversed order*]
>> 414/18 of a [of]

418 "Dead Men's Shoes," Feb. 21–22, 1895. Published in *Independent* (New York, Feb. 11, 1897) and *A Night in Acadie.*

> *Change from magazine to book version:*
>> 420/35 no [an']

426 "Athénaïse," Apr. 10–28, 1895. Published in *Atlantic Monthly* (Aug. and Sept., 1896) and *A Night in Acadie.* The magazine version of the story was titled "Athenaïse: A Story of Temperament." The subtitle was very likely added by the editor.

> *Changes from magazine to book version:*
>> 426/21 illuminated [illumined]
>> 426/25 with a [a]
>> 431/21 ground [grounds]

436/21 and his [and]
438/29 her to [her]
443/4 rooms [the rooms]
451/2 that [that is]
451/17–18 stunned, after . . . except [stunned, except]

455 "Two Summers and Two Souls," July 14, 1895. Published in *Vogue* (Aug. 7, 1895). Reprinted in *St. Louis Life*, Aug. 24, 1895. [clipping].

458 "The Unexpected," July 18, 1895. Published in *Vogue* (Sept. 18, 1895). Reprinted in *St. Louis Life*, Nov. 2, 1895. [clipping].
   Changes on the clipping:
   460/30 bushes [brooks]
   460/33 aslant [about]
   460/33 weedy [woody]

462 "Two Portraits," Aug. 4, 1895. Published in Rankin, *Kate Chopin and Her Creole Stories*. [MS]. Earlier titles: "The Nun, the Wife & the Wanton"; "The Nun & the Wanton."

467 "Fedora," Nov. 19, 1895. Published in *Criterion* (St. Louis, Feb. 20, 1897) as "The Falling in Love of Fedora. A Sketch," signed "La Tour." The subtitle was very likely added by the editor. [clipping].
   Change on the clipping:
   468/22–23 to touch [of touching]

470 "Vagabonds," Dec. (2?), 1895. Published in Rankin, *Kate Chopin and Her Creole Stories*. [MS].
   Cancellations on the MS (the canceled material is given in parentheses):
   471/9–10 seriously. "An' w'at [seriously. ("You know how 'tis yonder," he drawled, motioning toward the plantation. "Las' time—that l'le girl o' yo's—some the darkies tole 'er I was her cousin, an' she cry an' bellow like she want to take a fit. An' that bigges' boy o' yo's he say' I want keep clear o' that plantation, I know w'at's good fo' me." "They're a proud lot," I admitted, dismissing the subject.) "An' w'at]
   471/25–26 some o' . . . "It make [some of these days. (But unless you in a big hurry to get into the other world, you better steer clear of Chartrand's whiskey; they tell me it's reg'lar rat poison.) It make]
   472/14–15 mystery. He waited [mystery (and sin) *These two words were canceled with heavy strokes*. He waited]

473 "Madame Martel's Christmas Eve," Jan. 16–18, 1896. First published here. [MS]. Earlier title: "Madame Martel's Christmas Dream."

480 "The Recovery," Feb., 1896. Published in *Vogue* (May 21, 1896).

484 "A Night in Acadie," Mar., 1896. Published in *A Night in Acadie.*

500 "A Pair of Silk Stockings," Apr., 1896. Published in *Vogue* (Sept. 16, 1897). [clipping].

505 "Nég Créol," Apr., 1896. Published in *Atlantic Monthly* (July, 1897) and *A Night in Acadie.*

> *Changes from magazine to book version:*
> 505/16 and at [and]
> 510/31 was [were]

511 "Aunt Lympy's Interference," June, 1896. Published in *Youth's Companion* (Aug. 12, 1897). [clipping].

> *Changes on the clipping:*
> 511/8 the trees [its trees]
> 511/12–14 earth . . . of late [earth. It was pleasant at the south window, but Melitte must ply her feather-duster. She always cleaned her room thoroughly on Saturday, because of late]
> 511/19 were [was]
> 512/22 *ti tante,"* pursued [*ti tante,"*—little aunt,—pursued]
> 513/19 ramshackle [remarkable]
> 513/20 someway [somewhat]

518 "The Blind Man," July, 1896. Published in *Vogue* (May 13, 1897). [clipping].

520 "A Vocation and a Voice," Nov., 1896. Published in the *Mirror* (St. Louis, Mar. 27, 1902). [clipping].

547 "A Mental Suggestion," Dec., 1896. First published here. [MS].

557 "Suzette," Feb., 1897. Published in *Vogue* (Oct. 21, 1897). [clipping].

560 "The Locket," Mar., 1897. First published here. [MS].

566 "A Morning Walk," Apr., 1897. Published in *Criterion* (St. Louis, Apr. 17, 1897) as "An Easter Day Conversion." [clipping].

570 "An Egyptian Cigarette," Apr., 1897. Published in *Vogue* (Apr. 19, 1900). [clipping].

574 "A Family Affair," Dec. (?), 1897. Syndicated, American Press Association. Published in *Saturday Evening Post* (Sept. 9, 1899). [clipping].

586 "Elizabeth Stock's One Story," March, 1898. Published in Seyersted, "Kate Chopin Reconsidered." [MS].

> *Change on the MS:*
> 586/13 Stonelift for six [Stonelift in south west Missouri, for six]

592 "The Storm," July 19, 1898. First published here. [MS].

597 "The Godmother," Jan.–Feb. 6, 1899. Published in the *Mirror* (St. Louis, Dec. 12, 1901). Earlier title: "The Unwritten Law."

615 "A Little Country Girl," Feb. 11, 1899. First published here. [MS].

622 "A Reflection," Nov., 1899. Published in Rankin, *Kate Chopin and Her Creole Stories*. [MS]. Earlier title: "Reflections."

623 "Ti Démon," Nov., 1899. First published here. [MS].

628 "A December Day in Dixie," Jan., 1900. Published in part in Rankin, *Kate Chopin and Her Creole Stories*. [MS]. The author wrote an abbreviated version in Feb., 1900, titled "One Day in Winter." [MS]. The text printed here is that of "A December Day in Dixie," and the material given in brackets shows the changes made in the shorter version. In this one instance we thus give the *later* version in brackets.

    628/1–629/25 "The train . . . as white [The train was an hour and a half late, but I heard no complaint from any one of my fellow passengers who boarded the "Natchitoches Tap" that wintry morning, at Cypress Junction. It is true we had been fortified with a steaming hot cup of coffee at Sautier's "saloon" across the tracks; and then, there was the snow! The earth was covered with two or three inches of it; as white]

    629/26 a hundred [ten]

    629/27–28 the bayou's [the black bayou's]

    629/28 growths [growth]

    629/29 and fields [upon fields]

    629/30–31 The white, still country, and [the still country, so white and]

    630/1 "Cotton's in ["You'll see cotton in]

    630/3 "Oh! it ["It]

    630/7 "God knows. ["Goodness knows.]

    630/8 the cotton . . . forget—" [the cotton?"]

    630/9–10 Well . . . town. [Well, some friendly soul should have warned us to keep out of Natchitoches town.]

    630/11–12 said . . . hack [admonished the driver of the sepulchral old "hack" that dragged us from the station]

    630/15 breath . . . missiles [breath; missiles]

    630/17 the judges [judges]

    630/19 North-states [Northern states]

631 "The Gentleman from New Orleans," Feb. 6, 1900. First published here. [MS].

638 "Charlie," Apr., 1900. First published here. [MS]. The MS is in the possession of Mr. Robert C. Hattersley. Another MS, called "Jacques," in the possession of the Missouri Historical Society, represents an earlier draft of the first part of this story.

671 "The White Eagle," May 9, 1900. Published in *Vogue* (July 12, 1900).

674 "The Wood-Choppers," Oct. 17, 1901. Published in *Youth's Companion* (May 29, 1902). [clipping].

680 "Polly," Jan. 14, 1902. Published in *Youth's Companion* (July 3, 1902). [clipping]. Earlier title: "Polly's Opportunity."

685 "The Impossible Miss Meadows," undated—probably written in 1903. First published here. [MS].

    685/7 In "ought to have . . . ," the word "to" has been added by the present editor.

    687/26 The word "sigh" has been added by the present editor.

Essays and Comments

691 "The Western Association of Writers," June 30, 1894. Published in *Critic* (July 7, 1894). [MS].

    Changes from manuscript to magazine version:

        691/1–2 of this . . . of writers [of the Western Association of Writers]

        691/11 lovely [homely]

        691/11–12 often too [too often]

        691/20–21 standards . . . singular [standards, a sensitiveness to criticism equal to that of the Creole, and a singular]

        691/23–25 big world . . . in its [big world not wholly included in Northern Indiana and it does not lie at the Antipodes either. It is human life in its]

693 " 'Crumbling Idols.' By Hamlin Garland," undated. Published in *St. Louis Life* (Oct. 6, 1894). [clipping].

695 "The Real Edwin Booth," undated. Published in *St. Louis Life* (Oct. 13, 1894). [clipping].

697 "Emile Zola's 'Lourdes,' " undated. Published in *St. Louis Life* (Nov. 17, 1894). [clipping].

700 "Confidences," Sept., 1896. First published here. [MS]. This manuscript represents the second version of "Confidences." The first was written at the invitation of Walter Hines Page, editor of the *Atlantic Monthly*, who returned it, asking Kate Chopin to "set forth the

matter directly." "In the Confidence of a Story-Writer" represents the final version.

Cancellations in the MS (The canceled material is given in parantheses):

> 701/16–17 directly ... He did [directly, so (secretly) intimately as he (had) does to me (when I emerged from the woods). He did]
>
> 701/19 method, the manner [method (of their construction) (their spirit) the manner]
>
> 701/25–26 lacks that ... impulse [lacks that (spiritual or religious quality which gives to fiction that) dignity as well as charm—which the (religious) spiritual impulse]
>
> 701/38–702/1 cushion. She still [cushion. (Strive to cultivate the religions impulse) (But there are persons more penetrating than Madame Precieuse who think that the absence of the spiritual—the religious impulse) She still]

703 "In the Confidence of a Story-Writer," Oct., 1896. Published in *Atlantic Monthly* (Jan., 1899). Cf. above.

706 "As You Like It." This title represents a series of six undated essays, all of which were published in *Criterion* (St. Louis). [clippings]. The following are the opening lines of the individual essays and their dates of publication:

> I "I have a young friend . . ." (Feb. 13, 1897)
>
> II "It has lately been . . ." (Feb. 20, 1897)
>
> III "Several years ago . . ." (Feb. 27, 1897)
>
> IV "A while ago . . ." (Mar. 13, 1897)
>
> V "A good many of us . . ." (Mar. 20, 1897)
>
> VI "We are told . . ." (Mar. 27, 1897)
>
> A fragment of a draft for II shows these differences:
>
> 710/23–24 fabrics that enfold [fabric that enfolds]
>
> 710/24 shortly [about]
>
> 710/27–28 being is crying [being crying]

721 "On Certain Brisk, Bright Days," undated, but undoubtedly written Nov., 1899. Published in the St. Louis *Post-Dispatch* (Nov. 26, 1899). [clipping]. The title of this originally untitled essay has been supplied by the present editor.

Poems

727 "If It Might Be," undated. Published in *America* (Chicago, Jan. 10, 1889).

727 "Psyche's Lament," probably 1890. Published in Rankin, *Kate Chopin and Her Creole Stories*. [MS].

728 "The Song Everlasting," before June, 1893. This poem was printed in the "program" for the St. Louis Wednesday Club's "Reciprocity Day: An Afternoon with St. Louis Authors," Nov. 29, 1899. [MS and clipping]. Earlier titles: "Life"; "Love Everlasting." One version leaves out the last line and has "many tongued" for "thousand tongued."

728 "You and I," before June, 1893. Published in the "program" for the St. Louis Wednesday Club (cf. above). [MS and clipping]. One version has "strolled" and "stroll" instead of "walked" and "walk," and "scarce older" instead of "not older."

728 "It Matters All," before June, 1893. Published in Rankin, *Kate Chopin and Her Creole Stories*. [MS].

729 "In Dreams Throughout the Night," June 27, 1893. First published here. [MS].

729 "Good Night," undated. Published in the New Orleans *Times-Democrat* (July 22, 1894) as "Good-By." [MS].

730 "If Some Day," Aug. 16, 1895. First published here. [MS]. Earlier title: "Then Wouldst Thou Know." In one version, the fifth line reads "Should venture e'en to touch thy swarthy cheek."

730 "To Carrie B." Autumn, 1895. First published here. [MS]. Earlier titles: "To Mrs. Blackman"; "To Mrs. B—n."

731 "To Hider Schuyler—." Christmas, 1895. First published here. [MS]. One version has "choose them" instead of "choose some."

731 "To 'Billy' with a Box of Cigars," Christmas, 1895. First published here. [MS]. Earlier title: "To Billy with Cigars."

731 "To Mrs. R." Christmas, 1896. First published here. [MS]. Earlier title: "To a Lady at the Piano—Mrs. R—n."

732 "Let the Night Go," Jan. 1, 1897. First published here. [MS]. Earlier title: "The New Year." One version has "A pleasing thing" instead of "A pretty thing."

732 "There's Music Enough," May 1, 1898. Published in Rankin, *Kate Chopin and Her Creole Stories*. [MS]. Earlier title: "O, Me! O, My!" One version has "For Love is piping" instead of "With Love a-piping."

732 "An Ecstasy of Madness," July 10, 1898. Published in Rankin, *Kate Chopin and Her Creole Stories*. [MS]. Earlier title: "A Document in Madness." One version has "Too deep to tell" instead of "Too wild to tell," and "Till we find" instead of "Or we find."

733 "I Wanted God," probably late 1898. First published here. [MS]. The couplet is part of a group of poems variously called "Lines Suggested by Omar," "An Echo of the Rubaiyat," or "A Memory of the Rubaiyat."

733 "The Haunted Chamber," Feb., 1899, when the author in all likelihood had just read proofs of *The Awakening*. First published here. [MS]. It is possible that "tremulous" should read "tremendous."

734 "Life," May 10, 1899. Published in Rankin, *Kate Chopin and Her Creole Stories*. [untitled MS]. Rankin, who calls it "Life," may have taken the title from material now lost.

734 "Because," between 1895 and 1899—probably from the latter year. First published here. [MS].

735 "To the Friend of My Youth: To Kitty." Published in Rankin, *Kate Chopin and Her Creole Stories*. [untitled, undated MS]. Probably on the authority of material now lost, Rankin dated it Aug. 24, 1900, and gave it the present title.

Novels

741 *At Fault*, July 5, 1889—Apr. 20, 1890. Published for the author by Nixon-Jones Printing Co., St. Louis, Sept., 1890.

788/26 The word "news" has been added by the present editor.

881 *The Awakening*, June? 1897–Jan. 21, 1898. Published by Herbert S. Stone & Company, Chicago & New York, Apr. 22, 1899. The author's original title was "A Solitary Soul." According to a review of the book in the St. Louis *Republic* (in quoting it, Rankin gives the date as May 20, 1899, but it cannot be found in that issue), it was rumored that the publisher had furnished the new title. This cannot be verified. When Kate Chopin later added in her notebook "The Awakening" on top of "A Solitary Soul," she did not cancel the original title as was her normal practice, possibly because she would have liked to retain it as a subtitle.

938/12 The last "it" in this line has been added by the present editor.

995/4 The word "of" has been added by the present editor.